GULLIVER'S TRAVELS

GULLIVER'S TRAVELS

JONATHAN SWIFT

Trans
Atlantic
Press

This is a Transatlantic Press book

This edition published in 2012

Transatlantic Press

Sky House, Raans Road, Amersham, Bucks, HP6 6JQ, UK

Jonathan Swift asserts the moral right to be identified as the author of this work.

A catalogue record is available for this book from the British Library

ISBN 978-1-908533-09-8

Printed and bound by CPI Group (UK) Ltd, Croydon, CR0 4YY, UK

JONATHAN SWIFT

Jonathan Swift was born in Dublin in 1667. After graduating from Trinity College, for which he needed special dispensation because of disciplinary issues, he moved to England to work as secretary to politician Sir William Temple. When expected preferment didn't materialize, Swift entered the priesthood, ordained in 1694. His clerical posts included Dean of St Patrick's Cathedral in his native city, which he took up in 1713. He championed Irish causes, notably in *The Drapier's Letters* (1724), in which he targeted inequities imposed by the British overlord. Like almost all his works, it appeared under a pseodynym. His earlier satirical works include *The Battle of the Books* and *A Tale of a Tub*, aimed at "corruptions in religion and learning". But he is best known for *Gulliver's Travels* (1726), the only literary work for which he received monetary reward. That book's trenchant comments on human weaknesses and foibles prompted accusations of misanthropy. But Swift was also a great altruist, giving a significant proportion of his income to charity and bequeathing money to found a hospital in Dublin for those with mental health problems. Swift himself suffered a mental collapse in his later years, thought to have been the result of Ménières disease. He died in 1745.

GULLIVER'S TRAVELS

"I felt something alive moving on my left leg, which advancing gently forward over my breast, came almost up to my chin; when bending mine eyes downward as much as I could, I perceived it to be a human creature not six inches high…"

Ship's surgeon Lemuel Gulliver is stranded on the island of Lilliput after his boat founders. In the first of many weird and wonderful adventures he meets a diminutive people prepared to wage war over the correct way to crack an egg. The castaway also visits a land full of giants, with wasps the size of partridges; a floating island where the best brains are engaged in trying to extract sunshine from cucumbers; and a land of civilized, rational-minded horses who show up the repulsive, humanlike Yahoos in a very bad light. Both a children's fantasy classic and a scabrous satire on politicians, philosophers, scientists – indeed, humanity itself – *Gulliver's Travels* is as fresh, amusing and bitingly savage today as it was when published to wide acclaim almost three centuries ago.

‥‥•◉◉◉•‥‥

CONTENTS

PART I

A Voyage to Lilliput

CHAPTER I

The author gives some account of himself and family. His
first inducements to travel. He is shipwrecked, and swims
for his life. Gets safe on shore in the country of Lilliput; is
made a prisoner, and carried up the country.

My father had a small estate in Nottinghamshire: I was
the third of five sons. He sent me to Emanuel College
in Cambridge at fourteen years old, where I resided three
years, and applied myself close to my studies; but the charge
of maintaining me, although I had a very scanty allowance,
being too great for a narrow fortune, I was bound apprentice to
Mr. James Bates, an eminent surgeon in London, with whom
I continued four years. My father now and then sending me
small sums of money, I laid them out in learning navigation,
and other parts of the mathematics, useful to those who intend
to travel, as I always believed it would be, some time or other,
my fortune to do. When I left Mr. Bates, I went down to my
father: where, by the assistance of him and my uncle John,
and some other relations, I got forty pounds, and a promise of
thirty pounds a year to maintain me at Leyden: there I studied
physic two years and seven months, knowing it would be
useful in long voyages.

Soon after my return from Leyden, I was recommended
by my good master, Mr. Bates, to be surgeon to the Swallow,

Captain Abraham Pannel, commander; with whom I continued three years and a half, making a voyage or two into the Levant, and some other parts. When I came back I resolved to settle in London; to which Mr. Bates, my master, encouraged me, and by him I was recommended to several patients. I took part of a small house in the Old Jewry; and being advised to alter my condition, I married Mrs. Mary Burton, second daughter to Mr. Edmund Burton, hosier, in Newgate-street, with whom I received four hundred pounds for a portion.

But my good master Bates dying in two years after, and I having few friends, my business began to fail; for my conscience would not suffer me to imitate the bad practice of too many among my brethren. Having therefore consulted with my wife, and some of my acquaintance, I determined to go again to sea. I was surgeon successively in two ships, and made several voyages, for six years, to the East and West Indies, by which I got some addition to my fortune. My hours of leisure I spent in reading the best authors, ancient and modern, being always provided with a good number of books; and when I was ashore, in observing the manners and dispositions of the people, as well as learning their language; wherein I had a great facility, by the strength of my memory.

The last of these voyages not proving very fortunate, I grew weary of the sea, and intended to stay at home with my wife and family. I removed from the Old Jewry to Fetter Lane, and from thence to Wapping, hoping to get business among the sailors; but it would not turn to account. After three years expectation that things would mend, I accepted an advantageous offer from Captain William Prichard, master of the Antelope, who was making a voyage to the South Sea. We set sail from Bristol, May 4, 1699, and our voyage was at first very prosperous.

It would not be proper, for some reasons, to trouble the reader with the particulars of our adventures in those seas; let it suffice to inform him, that in our passage from thence to the East Indies, we were driven by a violent storm to the north-west of Van Diemen's Land. By an observation, we found ourselves in the latitude of 30 degrees 2 minutes south. Twelve of our crew were dead by immoderate labour and ill food; the rest were in a very weak condition. On the 5th of November, which was the beginning of summer in those parts, the weather being very hazy, the seamen spied a rock within half a cable's length of the ship; but the wind was so strong, that we were driven directly upon it, and immediately split. Six of the crew, of whom I was one, having let down the boat into the sea, made a shift to get clear of the ship and the rock. We rowed, by my computation, about three leagues, till we were able to work no longer, being already spent with labour while we were in the ship. We therefore trusted ourselves to the mercy of the waves, and in about half an hour the boat was overset by a sudden flurry from the north. What became of my companions in the boat, as well as of those who escaped on the rock, or were left in the vessel, I cannot tell; but conclude they were all lost. For my own part, I swam as fortune directed me, and was pushed forward by wind and tide. I often let my legs drop, and could feel no bottom; but when I was almost gone, and able to struggle no longer, I found myself within my depth; and by this time the storm was much abated. The declivity was so small, that I walked near a mile before I got to the shore, which I conjectured was about eight o'clock in the evening.

I then advanced forward near half a mile, but could not discover any sign of houses or inhabitants; at least I was in so weak a condition, that I did not observe them. I was extremely tired, and with that, and the heat of the weather, and about half a pint of brandy that I drank as I left the ship, I found myself much inclined to sleep. I lay down on the grass, which was very short and soft, where I slept sounder than ever I remembered to have done in my life, and, as I reckoned, about nine hours; for when I awaked, it was just day-light. I attempted to rise, but was not able to stir: for, as I happened to lie on my back, I found my arms and legs were strongly fastened on each side to the ground; and my hair, which was long and thick, tied down in the same manner. I likewise felt several slender ligatures across my body, from my arm-pits to my thighs. I could only look upwards; the sun began to grow hot, and the light offended my eyes. I heard a confused noise about me; but in the posture I lay, could see nothing except the sky. In a little time I felt something alive moving on my left leg, which advancing gently forward over my breast, came almost up to my chin; when, bending my eyes downwards as much as I could, I perceived it to be a human creature not six inches high, with a bow and arrow in his hands, and a quiver at his back. In the mean time, I felt at least forty more of the same kind (as I conjectured) following the first. I was in the utmost astonishment, and roared so loud, that they all ran back in a fright; and some of them, as I was afterwards told, were hurt with the falls they got by leaping from my sides upon the ground. However, they soon returned, and one of them, who ventured so far as to get a full sight of my face, lifting up his hands and eyes by way of admiration, cried out in a shrill but distinct voice, *Hekinah degul*: the others repeated the same words several times, but then I knew not what they meant.

I lay all this while, as the reader may believe, in great uneasiness. At length, struggling to get loose, I had the fortune to break the strings, and wrench out the pegs that fastened my left arm to the ground; for, by lifting it up to my face, I discovered the methods they had taken to bind me, and at the same time with a violent pull, which gave me excessive pain, I a little loosened the strings that tied down my hair on the left side, so that I was just able to turn my head about two inches. But the creatures ran off a second time, before I could seize them; whereupon there was a great shout in a very shrill accent, and after it ceased I heard one of them cry aloud *Tolgo phonac*;

when in an instant I felt above a hundred arrows discharged on my left hand, which, pricked me like so many needles; and besides, they shot another flight into the air, as we do bombs in Europe, whereof many, I suppose, fell on my body, (though I felt them not), and some on my face, which I immediately covered with my left hand.

When this shower of arrows was over, I fell a groaning with grief and pain; and then striving again to get loose, they discharged another volley larger than the first, and some of them attempted with spears to stick me in the sides; but by good luck I had on a buff jerkin, which they could not pierce.

I thought it the most prudent method to lie still, and my design was to continue so till night, when, my left hand being already loose, I could easily free myself: and as for the inhabitants, I had reason to believe I might be a match for the greatest army they could bring against me, if they were all of the same size with him that I saw. But fortune disposed otherwise of me.

When the people observed I was quiet, they discharged no more arrows; but, by the noise I heard, I knew their numbers increased; and about four yards from me, over against my right ear, I heard a knocking for above an hour, like that of people at work; when turning my head that way, as well as the pegs and strings would permit me, I saw a stage erected about a foot and a half from the ground, capable of holding four of the inhabitants, with two or three ladders to mount it: from whence one of them, who seemed to be a person of quality, made me a long speech, whereof I understood not one syllable.

But I should have mentioned, that before the principal person began his oration, he cried out three times, *Langro dehul san* (these words and the former were afterwards repeated and explained to me); whereupon, immediately, about fifty of the inhabitants came and cut the strings that fastened the left side of my head, which gave me the liberty of turning it to the right, and of observing the person and gesture of him that was to speak. He appeared to be of a middle age, and taller than any of the other three who attended him, whereof one was a page that held up his train, and seemed to be somewhat longer than my middle finger; the other two stood one on each side to support him. He acted every part of an orator, and I could observe many periods of threatenings, and others of promises, pity, and kindness.

I answered in a few words, but in the most submissive manner, lifting up my left hand, and both my eyes to the sun, as calling him for a witness; and being almost famished with hunger, having not eaten a morsel for some hours before I left the ship, I found the demands of nature so strong upon me, that I could not forbear showing my impatience (perhaps against the strict rules of decency) by putting my finger frequently to my mouth, to signify that I wanted food.

The *hurgo* (for so they call a great lord, as I afterwards learnt) understood me very well. He descended from the stage, and commanded that several ladders should be applied to my sides, on which above a hundred of the inhabitants mounted and walked towards my mouth, laden with baskets full of meat, which had been provided and sent thither by the king's orders, upon the first intelligence he received of me. I observed there was the flesh of several animals, but could not distinguish them by the taste. There were shoulders, legs, and loins, shaped like those of mutton, and very well dressed, but smaller than the wings of a lark. I ate them by two or three at a mouthful, and took three loaves at a time, about the bigness of musket bullets. They supplied me as fast as they could, showing a thousand marks of wonder and astonishment at my bulk and appetite.

I then made another sign, that I wanted drink. They found by my eating that a small quantity would not suffice me; and being a most ingenious people, they slung up, with great dexterity, one of their largest hogsheads, then rolled it towards my hand, and beat out the top; I drank it off at a draught, which I might well do, for it did not hold half a pint, and tasted like a small wine of Burgundy, but much more delicious. They brought me a second hogshead, which I drank in the same manner, and made signs for more; but they had none to give me.

When I had performed these wonders, they shouted for joy, and danced upon my breast, repeating several times as they did at first, *Hekinah degul*. They made me a sign that I should throw down the two hogsheads, but first warning the people below to stand out of the way, crying aloud, *Borach mevolah*; and when they saw the vessels in the air, there was a universal shout of *Hekinah degul*. I confess I was often tempted, while they were passing backwards and forwards on my body, to seize forty or fifty of the first that came in my reach, and dash them against the ground. But the remembrance of what I had felt, which probably might not be the worst they could do, and the promise of honour I made them, for so I interpreted my submissive behaviour, soon drove out these imaginations. Besides, I now considered myself as bound by the laws of hospitality, to a people who had treated me with so much expense and magnificence. However, in my thoughts I could not sufficiently wonder at the intrepidity of these diminutive mortals, who durst venture to mount and walk upon my body, while one of my hands was at liberty, without trembling at the very sight of so prodigious a creature as I must appear to them.

After some time, when they observed that I made no more demands for meat, there appeared before me a person of high rank from his imperial Majesty . His Excellency, having mounted on the small of my right leg, advanced forwards up to my face, with about a dozen of his retinue; and producing his credentials under the signet royal, which he applied close to my eyes, spoke about ten minutes without any signs of anger, but with a kind of determinate resolution, often pointing forwards, which, as I afterwards found, was towards the capital city, about half a mile distant; whither it was agreed by his Majesty in council that I must be conveyed.

I answered in few words, but to no purpose, and made a sign with my hand that was loose, putting it to the other (but over his Excellency's head for fear of hurting him or his train) and then to my own head and body, to signify that I desired my liberty.

It appeared that he understood me well enough, for he shook his head by way of disapprobation, and held his hand in a posture to show that I must be carried as a prisoner. However, he made other signs to let me understand that I should have meat and drink enough, and very good treatment. Whereupon I once more thought of attempting to break my bonds; but again, when I felt the smart of their arrows upon my face and hands, which were all in blisters, and many of the darts still sticking in them, and observing likewise that the number of my enemies increased, I gave tokens to let them know that they might do with me what they pleased. Upon this, the *hurgo* and his train withdrew, with much civility and cheerful countenances.

Soon after I heard a general shout, with frequent repetitions of the words *Peplom selan*; and I felt great numbers of people on my left side relaxing the cords to such a degree, that I was able to turn upon my right, and to ease myself with making water; which I very plentifully did, to the great astonishment of the people; who, conjecturing by my motion what I was going to do, immediately opened to the right and left on that side, to avoid the torrent, which fell with such noise and violence from me. But before this, they had daubed my face and both my hands with a sort of ointment, very pleasant to the smell, which, in a few minutes, removed all the smart of their arrows. These circumstances, added to the refreshment I had received by their victuals and drink, which were very nourishing, disposed me to sleep. I slept about eight hours, as I was afterwards assured; and it was no wonder, for the physicians, by the emperor's order, had mingled a sleepy potion in the hogsheads of wine.

It seems, that upon the first moment I was discovered sleeping on the ground, after my landing, the emperor had early notice of it by an express; and determined in council, that I should be tied in the manner I have related, (which was done in the night while I slept;) that plenty of meat and drink should be sent to me, and a machine prepared to carry me to the capital city.

This resolution perhaps may appear very bold and dangerous, and I am confident would not be imitated by any prince in Europe on the like occasion. However, in my opinion, it was extremely prudent, as well as generous: for, supposing these people had endeavoured to kill me with their spears and arrows, while I was asleep, I should certainly have awaked with the first sense of smart, which might so far have roused my rage and strength, as to have enabled me to break the strings wherewith I was tied; after which, as they were not able to make resistance, so they could expect no mercy.

These people are most excellent mathematicians, and arrived to a great perfection in mechanics, by the countenance and encouragement of the emperor, who is a renowned patron of learning. This prince has several machines fixed on wheels, for the carriage of trees and other great weights. He often builds his largest men of war, whereof some are nine feet long, in the woods where the timber grows, and has them carried on these engines three or four hundred yards to the sea.

Five hundred carpenters and engineers were immediately set at work to prepare the greatest engine they had. It was a frame of wood raised three inches from the ground, about seven feet long, and four wide, moving upon twenty-two wheels. The shout I heard was upon the arrival of this engine, which, it seems, set out in four hours after my landing. It was brought parallel to me, as I lay.

But the principal difficulty was to raise and place me in this vehicle. Eighty poles, each of one foot high, were erected for this purpose, and very strong cords, of the bigness of packthread, were fastened by hooks to many bandages, which the workmen had girt round my neck, my hands, my body, and my legs. Nine hundred of the strongest men were employed to draw up these cords, by many pulleys fastened on the poles; and thus, in less than three hours, I was raised and slung into the engine, and there tied fast. All this I was told; for, while the operation was performing, I lay in a profound sleep, by the force of that soporiferous medicine infused into my liquor. Fifteen hundred of the emperor's largest horses, each about four inches and a half high, were employed to draw me towards the metropolis, which, as I said, was half a mile distant.

About four hours after we began our journey, I awaked by a very ridiculous accident; for the carriage being stopped a while, to adjust something that was out of order, two or three of the young natives had the curiosity to see how I looked when I was asleep; they climbed up into the engine, and advancing very softly to my face, one of them, an officer in the guards, put the sharp end of his half-pike a good way up into my left nostril, which tickled my nose like a straw, and made me sneeze violently; whereupon they stole off unperceived, and it was three weeks before I knew the cause of my waking so suddenly.

We made a long march the remaining part of the day, and, rested at night with five hundred guards on each side of me, half with torches, and half with bows and arrows, ready to shoot me if I should offer to stir. The next morning at sun-rise we continued our march, and arrived within two hundred yards of the city gates about noon.

The emperor, and all his court, came out to meet us; but his great officers would by no means suffer his Majesty to endanger his person by mounting on my body.

At the place where the carriage stopped there stood an ancient temple, esteemed to be the largest in the whole kingdom; which, having been polluted some years before by an unnatural murder, was, according to the zeal of those people, looked upon as profane, and therefore had been applied to common use, and all the ornaments and furniture carried away. In this edifice it was determined I should lodge.

The great gate fronting to the north was about four feet high, and almost two feet wide, through which I could easily creep. On each side of the gate was a small window, not above six inches from the ground: into that on the left side, the king's smith conveyed fourscore and eleven chains, like those that hang to a lady's watch in Europe, and almost as large, which were locked to my left leg with six-and-thirty padlocks. Over against this temple, on the other side of the great highway, at twenty feet distance, there was a turret at least five feet high. Here the emperor ascended, with many principal lords of his court, to have an opportunity of viewing me, as I was told, for I could not see them. It was reckoned that above a hundred thousand inhabitants came out of the town upon the same errand; and, in spite of my guards, I believe there could not be fewer than ten thousand at several times, who mounted my body by the help of ladders. But a proclamation was soon issued, to forbid it upon pain of death.

When the workmen found it was impossible for me to break loose, they cut all the strings that bound me; whereupon

I rose up, with as melancholy a disposition as ever I had in my life. But the noise and astonishment of the people, at seeing me rise and walk, are not to be expressed. The chains that held my left leg were about two yards long, and gave me not only the liberty of walking backwards and forwards in a semicircle, but, being fixed within four inches of the gate, allowed me to creep in, and lie at my full length in the temple.

CHAPTER II

The emperor of Lilliput, attended by several of the nobility, comes to see the author in his confinement. The emperor's person and habit described. Learned men appointed to teach the author their language. He gains favour by his mild disposition. His pockets are searched, and his sword and pistols taken from him.

When I found myself on my feet, I looked about me, and must confess I never beheld a more entertaining prospect. The country around appeared like a continued garden, and the enclosed fields, which were generally forty feet square, resembled so many beds of flowers. These fields were intermingled with woods of half a stang, and the tallest trees, as I could judge, appeared to be seven feet high. I viewed the town on my left hand, which looked like the painted scene of a city in a theatre.

I had been for some hours extremely tired, however, so I crept into my house, and shut the door after me. But I had to come out again, and to get a little change by stepping backwards and forwards as far as my chains allowed.

I soon found that the emperor was already descended from the tower, and advancing on horseback towards me, which had like to have cost him dear; for the beast, though very well trained, yet wholly unused to such a sight, which appeared as if a mountain moved before him, reared up on its hinder feet: but that prince, who is an excellent horseman, kept his seat, till his attendants ran in, and held the bridle, while his Majesty had time to dismount. When he alighted, he surveyed me round with great admiration; but kept beyond the length of my chain. He ordered his cooks and butlers, who were already prepared, to give me victuals and drink, which they pushed forward in a sort of vehicles upon wheels, till I could reach them. I took these vehicles and soon emptied them all; twenty of them were filled with meat, and ten with liquor; each of the former afforded me two or three good mouthfuls; and I emptied the liquor of ten vessels, which was contained in earthen vials, into one vehicle, drinking it off at a draught; and so I did with the rest.

The empress, and young princes of the blood of both sexes, attended by many ladies, sat at some distance in their chairs; but upon the accident that happened to the emperor's horse, they alighted, and came near his person, which I am now going to describe. He is taller by almost the breadth of my nail, than any of his court; which alone is enough to strike an awe into the beholders. His features are strong and masculine, with an Austrian lip and arched nose, his complexion olive, his countenance erect, his body and limbs well proportioned, all his motions graceful, and his deportment majestic. He was then past his prime, being twenty-eight years and three quarters old, of which he had reigned about seven in great felicity, and generally victorious.

For the better convenience of beholding him, I lay on my side, so that my face was parallel to his, and he stood but three yards off: however, I have had him since many times in my hand, and therefore cannot be deceived in the description. His dress was very plain and simple, and the fashion of it between the Asiatic and the European; but he had on his head a light helmet of gold, adorned with jewels, and a plume on the crest.

He held his sword drawn in his hand to defend himself, if I should happen to break loose; it was almost three inches long; the hilt and scabbard were gold enriched with diamonds. His voice was shrill, but very clear and articulate; and I could distinctly hear it when I stood up.

The ladies and courtiers were all most magnificently clad; so that the spot they stood upon seemed to resemble a petticoat spread upon the ground, embroidered with figures of gold and silver.

His imperial Majesty spoke often to me, and I returned answers: but neither of us could understand a syllable.

There were several of his priests and lawyers present (as I conjectured by their habits), who were commanded to address themselves to me; and I spoke to them in as many languages as I had the least smattering of, which were High and Low Dutch, Latin, French, Spanish, Italian, and Lingua Franca, but all to no purpose.

After about two hours the court retired, and I was left with a strong guard, to prevent the impertinence, and probably the malice of the rabble, who were very impatient to crowd about me as near as they durst; and some of them had the impudence to shoot their arrows at me, as I sat on the ground by the door of my house, whereof one very narrowly missed my left eye. But the colonel ordered six of the ringleaders to be seized, and thought no punishment so proper as to deliver them bound into my hands; which some of his soldiers accordingly did, pushing them forward with the butt-ends of their pikes into my reach. I took them all in my right hand, put five of them into my coat-pocket; and as to the sixth, I made a countenance as if I would eat him alive. The poor man squalled terribly, and the colonel and his officers were in much pain, especially when they saw me take out my penknife: but I soon put them out of fear; for, looking mildly, and immediately cutting the strings he was bound with, I set him gently on the ground, and away he ran. I treated the rest in the same manner, taking them one by one out of my pocket; and I observed both the soldiers and people were highly delighted at this mark of my clemency, which was represented very much to my advantage at court.

Towards night I got with some difficulty into my house, where I lay on the ground, and continued to do so about a fortnight; during which time, the emperor gave orders to have a bed prepared for me. Six hundred beds of the common measure were brought in carriages, and worked up in my house; a hundred and fifty of their beds, sewn together, made up the breadth and length; and these were four double: which, however, kept me but very indifferently from the hardness of the floor, that was of smooth stone. By the same computation, they provided me with sheets, blankets, and coverlets, tolerable enough for one who had been so long inured to hardships.

As the news of my arrival spread through the kingdom, it brought prodigious numbers of rich, idle, and curious people to see me; so that the villages were almost emptied; and great neglect of tillage and household affairs must have ensued, if his imperial Majesty had not provided, by several proclamations and orders of state, against this inconveniency. He directed that those who had already beheld me should return home, and not presume to come within fifty yards of my house, without license from the court; whereby the secretaries of state got considerable fees.

In the mean time the emperor held frequent councils, to debate what course should be taken with me; and I was afterwards assured by a particular friend, a person of great quality, who was as much in the secret as any, that the court was under many difficulties concerning me. They apprehended my breaking loose; that my diet would be very expensive, and might cause a famine. Sometimes they determined to starve me; or at least to shoot me in the face and hands with poisoned arrows, which would soon despatch me; but again they considered, that the stench of so large a carcass might produce a plague in the metropolis, and probably spread through the whole kingdom.

In the midst of these consultations, several officers of the army went to the door of the great council-chamber, and two of them being admitted, gave an account of my behaviour to the six criminals above-mentioned; which made so favourable an impression in the breast of his Majesty and the whole board, in my behalf, that an imperial commission was issued out, obliging all the villages, nine hundred yards round the city, to deliver in every morning six beeves, forty sheep, and other victuals for my sustenance; together with a proportionable quantity of bread, and wine, and other liquors; for the due payment of which, his Majesty gave assignments upon his treasury: for this prince lives chiefly upon his own demesnes; seldom, except upon great occasions, raising any subsidies upon his subjects, who are bound to attend him in his wars at their own expense. An establishment was also made of six hundred persons to be my domestics, who had board-wages allowed for their maintenance, and tents built for them very conveniently on each side of my door.

It was likewise ordered, that three hundred tailors should make me a suit of clothes, after the fashion of the country; that six of his Majesty's greatest scholars should be employed to instruct me in their language; and lastly, that the emperor's horses, and those of the nobility and troops of guards, should be frequently exercised in my sight, to accustom themselves to me. All these orders were duly put in execution; and in about three weeks I made a great progress in learning their language; during which time the emperor frequently honoured me with his visits, and was pleased to assist my masters in teaching me.

We began already to converse together in some sort; and the first words I learnt, were to express my desire that he would please give me my liberty, which I every day repeated on my knees. His answer, as I could comprehend it, was, that this must be a work of time, not to be thought on without the advice of his council, and that first I must *lumos kelmin pesso desmar lon emposo*; that is, swear a peace with him and his kingdom. However, that I should be used with all kindness. And he advised me to acquire, by my patience and discreet behaviour, the good opinion of himself and his subjects.

He desired I would not take it ill, if he gave orders to certain proper officers to search me; for probably I might carry about me several weapons, which must needs be dangerous things, if they answered the bulk of so prodigious a person. I said His Majesty should be satisfied; for I was ready to strip myself, and turn up my pockets before him. This I delivered part in words, and part in signs. He replied, that, by the laws of the kingdom, I must be searched by two of his officers; that he knew this could not be done without my consent and assistance; and he had so good an opinion of my generosity and justice, as to trust their persons in my hands; that whatever they took from me, should be returned when I left the country, or paid for at the rate which I would set upon them.

I took up the two officers in my hands, put them first into my coat-pockets, and then into every other pocket about me, except my two fobs, and another secret pocket, which I had no mind should be searched, wherein I had some little necessaries that were of no consequence to any but myself. In one of my fobs there was a silver watch, and in the other a small quantity of gold in a purse. These gentlemen, having pen, ink, and paper, about them, made an exact inventory of every thing they saw; and when they had done, desired I would set them down, that they might deliver it to the emperor. This inventory I afterwards translated into English, and is, word for word, as follows:

Imprimis: In the right coat-pocket of the 'Great Man-Mountain' (for so I interpret the words *quinbus flestrin*,) after the strictest search, we found only one great piece of coarse-cloth, large enough to be a foot-cloth for your Majesty's chief room of state. In the left pocket we saw a huge silver chest, with a cover of the same metal, which we, the searchers, were not able to lift. We desired it should be opened, and one of us stepping into it, found himself up to the mid leg in a sort of dust, some part whereof flying up to our faces set us both a sneezing for several times together. In his right waistcoat-pocket we found a prodigious bundle of white thin substances, folded one over another, about the bigness of three men, tied with a strong cable, and marked with black figures; which we humbly conceive to be writings, every letter almost half as large as the palm of our hands. In the left there was a sort of engine, from the back of which were extended twenty long poles, resembling the pallisados before your Majesty's court: wherewith we conjecture the Man-Mountain combs his head; for we did not always trouble him with questions, because we found it a great difficulty to make him understand us. In the large pocket, on the right side of his middle cover (so I translate the word *Ranfulo*, by which they meant my breeches,) we saw a hollow pillar of iron, about the length of a man, fastened to a strong piece of timber larger than the pillar; and upon one side of the pillar, were huge pieces of iron sticking out, cut into strange figures, which we know not what to make of. In the left pocket, another engine of the same kind. In the smaller pocket on the right side, were several round flat pieces of white and red metal, of different bulk; some of the white, which seemed to be silver, were so large and heavy, that my comrade and I could hardly lift them. In the left pocket were two black pillars irregularly shaped: we could not, without difficulty, reach the top of them, as we stood at the bottom of his pocket. One of them was covered, and seemed all of a piece: but at the upper end of the other there appeared a white round substance, about twice the bigness of our heads. Within each of these was

enclosed a prodigious plate of steel; which, by our orders, we
obliged him to show us, because we apprehended they might
be dangerous engines. He took them out of their cases, and
told us, that in his own country his practice was to shave his
beard with one of these, and cut his meat with the other. There
were two pockets which we could not enter: these he called his
fobs; they were two large slits cut into the top of his middle
cover, but squeezed close by the pressure of his belly. Out
of the right fob hung a great silver chain, with a wonderful
kind of engine at the bottom. We directed him to draw out
whatever was at the end of that chain; which appeared to be a
globe, half silver, and half of some transparent metal; for, on
the transparent side, we saw certain strange figures circularly
drawn, and thought we could touch them, till we found our
fingers stopped by the lucid substance. He put this engine into
our ears, which made an incessant noise, like that of a water-
mill: and we conjecture it is either some unknown animal, or
the god that he worships; but we are more inclined to the latter
opinion, because he assured us, (if we understood him right,
for he expressed himself very imperfectly) that he seldom did
any thing without consulting it. He called it his oracle, and said,
it pointed out the time for every action of his life. From the left
fob he took out a net almost large enough for a fisherman, but
contrived to open and shut like a purse, and served him for
the same use: we found therein several massy pieces of yellow
metal, which, if they be real gold, must be of immense value.

"Having thus, in obedience to your Majesty's commands,
diligently searched all his pockets, we observed a girdle about
his waist made of the hide of some prodigious animal, from
which, on the left side, hung a sword of the length of five men;
and on the right, a bag or pouch divided into two cells, each
cell capable of holding three of your Majesty's subjects. In one
of these cells were several globes, or balls, of a most ponderous
metal, about the bigness of our heads, and requiring a strong

hand to lift them: the other cell contained a heap of certain black grains, but of no great bulk or weight, for we could hold above fifty of them in the palms of our hands.

"This is an exact inventory of what we found about the body of the Man-Mountain, who used us with great civility, and due respect to your Majesty's commission. Signed and sealed on the fourth day of the eighty-ninth moon of your Majesty's auspicious reign.

"CLEFRIN FRELOCK."

"MARSI FRELOCK."

When this inventory was read over to the emperor, he directed me, although in very gentle terms, to deliver up the several particulars. He first called for my scimitar, which I took out, scabbard and all. In the mean time he ordered three thousand of his choicest troops (who then attended him) to surround me at a distance, with their bows and arrows just ready to discharge; but I did not observe it, for mine eyes were wholly fixed upon his Majesty . He then desired me to draw my scimitar, which, although it had got some rust by the sea water, was, in most parts, exceeding bright. I did so, and immediately all the troops gave a shout between terror and surprise; for the sun shone clear, and the reflection dazzled their eyes, as I waved the scimitar to and fro in my hand. His Majesty, who is a most magnanimous prince, was less daunted than I could expect: he ordered me to return it into the scabbard, and cast it on the ground as gently as I could, about six feet from the end of my chain.

The next thing he demanded was one of the hollow iron pillars; by which he meant my pocket pistols. I drew it out, and at his desire, as well as I could, expressed to him the use of it; and charging it only with powder, which, by the closeness of my pouch, happened to escape wetting in the sea (an inconvenience against which all prudent mariners take special care to provide,) I first cautioned the emperor not to be afraid, and then I let it off in the air. The astonishment here was much greater than at the sight of my scimitar. Hundreds fell down as if they had been struck dead; and even the emperor, although he stood his ground, could not recover himself for some time. I delivered up both my pistols in the same manner as I had done my scimitar, and then my pouch of powder and bullets; begging him that the former might be kept from fire, for it would kindle with the smallest spark, and blow up his imperial palace into the air. I likewise delivered up my watch, which the emperor was very curious to see, and commanded two of his tallest yeomen of the guards to bear it on a pole upon their shoulders, as draymen in England do a barrel of ale. He was amazed at the continual noise it made, and the motion of the minute-hand, which he could easily discern; for their sight is much more acute than ours: he asked the opinions of his learned men about it, which were various and remote, as the reader may well imagine without my repeating; although indeed I could not very perfectly understand them. I then gave up my silver and copper money, my purse, with nine large pieces of gold, and some smaller ones; my knife and razor, my comb and silver snuff-box, my handkerchief and journal-book.

My scimitar, pistols, and pouch, were conveyed in carriages to his Majesty's stores; but the rest of my goods were returned me.

I had as I before observed, one private pocket, which escaped their search, wherein there was a pair of spectacles (which I sometimes use for the weakness of mine eyes,) a pocket perspective, and some other little conveniences; which, being of no consequence to the emperor, I did not think myself bound in honour to discover, and I apprehended they might be lost or spoiled if I ventured them out of my possession.

CHAPTER III

The author diverts the emperor, and his nobility of both sexes, in a very uncommon manner. The diversions of the court of Lilliput described. The author has his liberty granted him upon certain conditions.

My gentleness and good behaviour had gained so far on the emperor and his court, and indeed upon the army and people in general, that I began to conceive hopes of getting my liberty in a short time. I took all possible methods to cultivate this favourable disposition. The natives came, by degrees, to be less apprehensive of any danger from me. I would sometimes lie down, and let five or six of them dance on my hand; and at last the boys and girls would venture to come and play at hide-and-seek in my hair.

I had now made a good progress in understanding and speaking the language. The emperor had a mind one day to entertain me with several of the country shows, wherein they exceed all nations I have known, both for dexterity and magnificence. I was diverted with none so much as that of the rope-dancers, performed upon a slender white thread, extended about two feet, and twelve inches from the ground. Upon which I shall desire liberty, with the reader's patience, to enlarge a little.

This diversion is only practised by those persons who are

candidates for great employments, and high favour at court. They are trained in this art from their youth, and are not always of noble birth, or liberal education. When a great office is vacant, either by death or disgrace (which often happens,) five or six of those candidates petition the emperor to entertain his Majesty and the court with a dance on the rope; and whoever jumps the highest, without falling, succeeds in the office. Very often the chief ministers themselves are commanded to show their skill, and to convince the emperor that they have not lost their faculty. Flimnap, the treasurer, is allowed to cut a caper on the straight rope, at least an inch higher than any other lord in the whole empire. I have seen him do the summerset several times together, upon a trencher fixed on a rope which is no thicker than a common packthread in England. My friend Reldresal, principal secretary for private affairs, is, in my opinion, if I am not partial, the second after the treasurer; the rest of the great officers are much upon a par.

These diversions are often attended with fatal accidents, whereof great numbers are on record. I myself have seen two or three candidates break a limb. But the danger is much greater, when the ministers themselves are commanded to show their dexterity; for, by contending to excel themselves and their fellows, they strain so far that there is hardly one of them who has not received a fall, and some of them two or three. I was assured that, a year or two before my arrival, Flimnap would infallibly have broke his neck, if one of the king's cushions, that accidentally lay on the ground, had not weakened the force of his fall.

There is likewise another diversion, which is only shown before the emperor and empress, and first minister, upon particular occasions. The emperor lays on the table three fine silken threads of six inches long; one is blue, the other red, and the third green. These threads are proposed as prizes for those persons whom the emperor has a mind to distinguish by a peculiar mark of his favour. The ceremony is performed in his Majesty's great chamber of state, where the candidates are to undergo a trial of dexterity very different from the former, and such as I have not observed the least resemblance of in any other country of the new or old world. The emperor holds a stick in his hands, both ends parallel to the horizon, while the candidates advancing, one by one, sometimes leap over the stick, sometimes creep under it, backward and forward, several times, according as the stick is advanced or depressed. Sometimes the emperor holds one end of the stick, and his first minister the other; sometimes the minister has it entirely to himself. Whoever performs his part with most agility, and holds out the longest in leaping and creeping, is rewarded with the blue-coloured silk; the red is given to the next, and the green to the third, which they all wear girt twice round about the middle; and you see few great persons about this court who are not adorned with one of these girdles.

The horses of the army, and those of the royal stables, having been daily led before me, were no longer shy, but would come up to my very feet without starting. The riders would leap them over my hand, as I held it on the ground; and one of the emperor's huntsmen, upon a large courser, took my foot, shoe and all; which was indeed a prodigious leap.

I had the good fortune to divert the emperor one day after a very extraordinary manner. I desired he would order several sticks of two feet high, and the thickness of an ordinary cane, to be brought me; whereupon his Majesty commanded the master of his woods to give directions accordingly; and the next morning six woodmen arrived with as many carriages, drawn by eight horses to each. I took nine of these sticks, and fixing them firmly in the ground in a quadrangular figure, two feet and a half square, I took four other sticks, and tied them parallel at each corner, about two feet from the ground; then I fastened my handkerchief to the nine sticks that stood erect; and extended it on all sides, till it was tight as the top of a drum; and the four parallel sticks, rising about five inches higher than the handkerchief, served as ledges on each side. When I had finished my work, I desired the emperor to let a troop of his best horses twenty-four in number, come and exercise upon this plain.

His Majesty approved of the proposal, and I took them up, one by one, in my hands, ready mounted and armed, with the proper officers to exercise them. As soon as they got into order they divided into two parties, performed mock skirmishes, discharged blunt arrows, drew their swords, fled and pursued, attacked and retired, and in short discovered the best military discipline I ever beheld. The parallel sticks secured them and their horses from falling over the stage; and the emperor was so much delighted, that he ordered this entertainment to be repeated several days, and once was pleased to be lifted up and give the word of command; and with great difficulty persuaded even the empress herself to let me hold her in her close chair within two yards of the stage, when she was able to take a full view of the whole performance.

It was my good fortune, that no ill accident happened in these entertainments; only once a fiery horse, that belonged to one of the captains, pawing with his hoof, struck a hole in my handkerchief, and his foot slipping, he overthrew his rider and himself; but I immediately relieved them both, and covering the hole with one hand, I set down the troop with the other, in the same manner as I took them up. The horse that fell was strained in the left shoulder, but the rider got no hurt; and I repaired my handkerchief as well as I could: however, I would not trust to the strength of it any more, in such dangerous enterprises.

About two or three days before I was set at liberty, as I was entertaining the court with this kind of feat, there arrived an express to inform his Majesty, that some of his subjects, riding near the place where I was first taken up, had seen a great black substance lying on the around, very oddly shaped, extending its edges round, as wide as his Majesty's bedchamber, and rising up in the middle as high as a man; that it was no living creature, as they at first apprehended, for it lay on the grass without motion; and some of them had walked round it several times; that, by mounting upon each other's shoulders, they had got to the top, which was flat and even, and, stamping upon it, they found that it was hollow within; that they humbly conceived it might be something belonging to the Man-Mountain; and if his Majesty pleased, they would undertake to bring it with only five horses.

I presently knew what they meant, and was glad at heart to receive this intelligence. It seems, upon my first reaching the shore after our shipwreck, I was in such confusion, that before I came to the place where I went to sleep, my hat, which I had fastened with a string to my head while I was rowing, and had stuck on all the time I was swimming, fell off after I came to land; the string, as I conjecture, breaking by some accident, which I never observed, but thought my hat had been lost at sea. I entreated his imperial Majesty to give orders it might be brought to me as soon as possible, describing to him the use and the nature of it: and the next day the waggoners arrived with it, but not in a very good condition; they had bored two holes in the brim, within an inch and half of the edge, and fastened two hooks in the holes; these hooks were tied by a long cord to the harness, and thus my hat was dragged along for above half an English mile; but, the ground in that country being extremely smooth and level, it received less damage than I expected.

Two days after this adventure, the emperor, having ordered that part of his army which quarters in and about his metropolis, to be in readiness, took a fancy of diverting himself in a very singular manner. He desired I would stand like a

Colossus, with my legs as far asunder as I conveniently could. He then commanded his general (who was an old experienced leader, and a great patron of mine) to draw up the troops in close order, and march them under me; the foot by twenty-four abreast, and the horse by sixteen, with drums beating, colours flying, and pikes advanced. This body consisted of three thousand foot, and a thousand horse. His Majesty gave orders, upon pain of death, that every soldier in his march should observe the strictest order.

I had sent so many memorials and petitions for my liberty, that his Majesty at length mentioned the matter, first in the cabinet, and then in a full council; where it was opposed by none, except Skyresh Bolgolam, who was pleased, without any provocation, to be my mortal enemy. But it was carried against him by the whole board, and confirmed by the emperor. That minister was *galbet*, or admiral of the realm, very much in his master's confidence, and a person well versed in affairs, but of a morose and sour complexion. However, he was at length persuaded to comply; but prevailed that the articles and conditions upon which I should be set free, and to which I must swear, should be drawn up by himself.

These articles were brought to me by Skyresh Bolgolam in person attended by two under-secretaries, and several persons of distinction. After they were read, I was demanded to swear to the performance of them; first in the manner of my own country, and afterwards in the method prescribed by their laws; which was, to hold my right foot in my left hand, and to place the middle finger of my right hand on the crown of my head, and my thumb on the tip of my right ear. But because the reader may be curious to have some idea of the style and manner of expression peculiar to that people, as well as to know the article upon which I recovered my liberty, I have made a translation of the whole instrument, word for word, as near as I was able, which I here offer to the public.

"Golbasto Momarem Evlame Gurdilo Shefin Mully Ully Gue, most mighty Emperor of Lilliput, delight and terror of the universe, whose dominions extend five thousand *blustrugs* (about twelve miles in circumference) to the extremities of the globe; monarch of all monarchs, taller than the sons of men; whose feet press down to the centre, and whose head strikes against the sun; at whose nod the princes of the earth shake their knees; pleasant as the spring, comfortable as the summer, fruitful as autumn, dreadful as winter: his most sublime Majesty proposes to the Man-Mountain, lately arrived at our celestial dominions, the following articles, which, by a solemn oath, he shall be obliged to perform:-

"1st, The Man-Mountain shall not depart from our dominions, without our license under our great seal.

"2nd, He shall not presume to come into our metropolis, without our express order; at which time, the inhabitants shall have two hours warning to keep within doors.

"3rd, The said Man-Mountain shall confine his walks to our principal high roads, and not offer to walk, or lie down, in a meadow or field of corn.

"5th, If an express requires extraordinary despatch, the Man-Mountain shall be obliged to carry, in his pocket, the messenger and horse a six days journey, once in every moon, and return the said messenger back (if so required) safe to our imperial presence.

"6th, He shall be our ally against our enemies in the island of Blefuscu, and do his utmost to destroy their fleet, which is now preparing to invade us.

"7th, That the said Man-Mountain shall, at his times of leisure, be aiding and assisting to our workmen, in helping to raise certain great stones, towards covering the wall of the principal park, and other our royal buildings.

"8th, That the said Man-Mountain shall, in two moons' time, deliver in an exact survey of the circumference of our dominions, by a computation of his own paces round the coast.

"Lastly. That, upon his solemn oath to observe all the above articles, the said Man-Mountain shall have a daily allowance of meat and drink sufficient for the support of 1724 of our subjects, with free access to our royal person, and other marks of our favour. Given at our palace at Belfaborac, the twelfth day of the ninety-first moon of our reign.

I swore and subscribed to these articles with great cheerfulness and content, although some of them were not so honourable as I could have wished; which proceeded wholly from the malice of Skyresh Bolgolam, the high-admiral: whereupon my chains were immediately unlocked, and I was at full liberty. The emperor himself, in person, did me the honour to be by at the whole ceremony. I made my acknowledgements by prostrating myself at his Majesty's feet: but he commanded me to rise; and after many gracious expressions, which, to avoid the censure of vanity, I shall not repeat, he added, that he hoped I should prove a useful servant, and well deserve all the favours he had already conferred upon me, or might do for the future.

The reader may please to observe, that, in the last article of the recovery of my liberty, the emperor stipulates to allow me a quantity of meat and drink sufficient for the support of 1724 Lilliputians. Some time after, asking a friend at court how they came to fix on that determinate number, he told me that his Majesty's mathematicians, having taken the height of my body by the help of a quadrant, and finding it to exceed theirs in the proportion of twelve to one, they concluded from the similarity of their bodies, that mine must contain at least 1724 of theirs, and consequently would require as much food as was necessary to support that number of Lilliputians. By which the reader may conceive an idea of the ingenuity of that people, as well as the prudent and exact economy of so great a prince.

CHAPTER IV

Mildendo, the metropolis of Lilliput, described, together with the emperor's palace. A conversation between the author and a principal secretary, concerning the affairs of that empire. The author's offers to serve the emperor in his wars.

The first request I made, after I had obtained my liberty, was, that I might have license to see Mildendo, the metropolis; which the emperor easily granted me, but with a special charge to do no hurt either to the inhabitants or their houses. The people had notice, by proclamation, of my design to visit the town. The wall which encompassed it is two feet and a half high, and at least eleven inches broad, so that a coach and horses may be driven very safely round it; and it is flanked with strong towers at ten feet distance. I stepped over the great western gate, and passed very gently, and sidling, through the two principal streets, only in my short waistcoat, for fear of damaging the roofs and eaves of the houses with the skirts of my coat. I walked with the utmost circumspection, to avoid treading on any stragglers who might remain in the streets, although the orders were very strict, that all people should keep in their houses, at their own peril. The garret windows and tops of houses were so crowded with spectators, that I thought in all my travels I had not seen a more populous place. The city is an exact square, each side of the wall being five hundred feet long. The two great streets, which run across and divide it into four quarters, are five feet wide. The lanes and alleys, which I could not enter, but only view them as I passed, are from twelve to eighteen inches. The town is capable of holding five hundred thousand souls: the houses are from three to five stories: the shops and markets well provided.

The emperor's palace is in the centre of the city where the two great streets meet. It is enclosed by a wall of two feet high, and twenty feet distance from the buildings. I had his Majesty's permission to step over this wall; and, the space being so wide between that and the palace, I could easily view it on every side. The outward court is a square of forty feet, and includes two other courts: in the inmost are the royal apartments, which I was very desirous to see, but found it extremely difficult; for the great gates, from one square into another, were but eighteen inches high, and seven inches wide. Now the buildings of the outer court were at least five feet high, and it was impossible for me to stride over them without infinite damage to the pile, though the walls were strongly built of hewn stone, and four inches thick. At the same time the emperor had a great desire that I should see the magnificence of his palace; but this I was not able to do till three days after, which I spent in cutting down with my knife some of the largest trees in the royal park, about a hundred yards distant from the city. Of these trees I made two stools, each about three feet high, and strong enough to bear my weight.

The people having received notice a second time, I went again through the city to the palace with my two stools in my hands. When I came to the side of the outer court, I stood upon one stool, and took the other in my hand; this I lifted over the roof, and gently set it down on the space between the first and second court, which was eight feet wide. I then stept over the building very conveniently from one stool to the other, and drew up the first after me with a hooked stick. By this contrivance I got into the inmost court; and, lying down upon my side, I applied my face to the windows of the middle stories, which were left open on purpose, and discovered the most splendid apartments that can be imagined. There I saw the empress and the young princes, in their several lodgings, with their chief attendants about them. Her imperial Majesty was pleased to smile very graciously upon me, and gave me out of the window her hand to kiss.

But I shall not anticipate the reader with further descriptions of this kind, because I reserve them for a greater work, which is now almost ready for the press; containing a general description of this empire, from its first erection, through along series of princes; with a particular account of their wars and politics, laws, learning, and religion; their plants and animals; their peculiar manners and customs, with other matters very curious and useful; my chief design at present being only to relate such events and transactions as happened to the public or to myself during a residence of about nine months in that empire.

One morning, about a fortnight after I had obtained my liberty, Reldresal, principal secretary (as they style him) for private affairs, came to my house attended only by one servant. He ordered his coach to wait at a distance, and desired I would give him an hours audience; which I readily consented to, on account of his quality and personal merits, as well as of the many good offices he had done me during my solicitations at court. I offered to lie down that he might the more conveniently reach my ear, but he chose rather to let me hold him in my hand during our conversation.

He began with compliments on my liberty; said he might pretend to some merit in it; but, however, added, that if it had not been for the present situation of things at court, perhaps I might not have obtained it so soon.

"For," said he, "as flourishing a condition as we may appear to be in to foreigners, we labour under two mighty evils: a violent faction at home, and the danger of an invasion, by a most potent enemy, from abroad. As to the first, you are to understand, that for about seventy moons past there have been two struggling parties in this empire, under the names of *Tramecksan* and *Slamecksan*, from the high and low heels of their shoes, by which they distinguish themselves. It is alleged, indeed, that the high heels are most agreeable to our ancient constitution; but, however this be, his Majesty has determined to make use only of low heels in the administration of the government, and all offices in the gift of the crown, as you cannot but observe; and particularly that his Majesty's imperial heels are lower at least by a *drurr* than any of his court (*drurr* is a measure about the fourteenth part of an inch).

"The animosities between these two parties run so high, that they will neither eat, nor drink, nor talk with each other. We compute the *Tramecksan*, or high heels, to exceed us in number; but the power is wholly on our side. We apprehend his imperial highness, the heir to the crown, to have some tendency towards the high heels; at least we can plainly discover that one of his heels is higher than the other, which gives him a hobble in his gait.

"Now, in the midst of these intestine disquiets, we are threatened with an invasion from the island of Blefuscu, which is the other great empire of the universe, almost as large and powerful as this of his Majesty . For as to what we have heard you affirm, that there are other kingdoms and states in the world inhabited by human creatures as large as yourself, our philosophers are in much doubt, and would rather conjecture that you dropped from the moon, or one of the stars; because it is certain, that a hundred mortals of your bulk would in a short time destroy all the fruits and cattle of his Majesty's dominions: besides, our histories of six thousand moons make no mention of any other regions than the two great empires of Lilliput and Blefuscu. Which two mighty powers have, as I was going to tell you, been engaged in a most obstinate war for six-and-thirty moons past. It began upon the following occasion. It is allowed on all hands, that the primitive way of breaking eggs, before we eat them, was upon the larger end; but his present Majesty's grandfather, while he was a boy, going to eat an egg, and breaking it according to the ancient practice, happened to cut one of his fingers. Whereupon the emperor his father published an edict, commanding all his subjects, upon great penalties, to break the smaller end of their eggs. The people so highly resented this law, that our histories tell us, there have been six rebellions raised on that account; wherein one emperor lost his life, and another his crown. These civil commotions were constantly fomented by the monarchs of Blefuscu; and when they were quelled, the exiles always fled for refuge to that empire.

"It is computed that eleven thousand persons have at several times suffered death, rather than submit to break their eggs at the smaller end. Many hundred large volumes have been published upon this controversy: but the books of the Big-endians have been long forbidden, and the whole party rendered incapable by law of holding employments.

"During the course of these troubles, the emperors of Blefuscu did frequently expostulate by their ambassadors, accusing us of making a schism in religion, by offending against a fundamental doctrine of our great prophet Lustrog, in the fifty-fourth chapter of the Blundecral (which is their Alcoran). This, however, is thought to be a mere strain upon the text; for the words are these: *That all true believers break their eggs at the convenient end.* And which is the convenient end, seems, in my humble opinion to be left to every man's conscience, or at least in the power of the chief magistrate to determine.

"Now, the Big-endian exiles have found so much credit in

the emperor of Blefuscu's court, and so much private assistance and encouragement from their party here at home, that a bloody war has been carried on between the two empires for six-and-thirty moons, with various success; during which time we have lost forty capital ships, and a much a greater number of smaller vessels, together with thirty thousand of our best seamen and soldiers; and the damage received by the enemy is reckoned to be somewhat greater than ours. However, they have now equipped a numerous fleet, and are just preparing to make a descent upon us; and his imperial Majesty, placing great confidence in your valour and strength, has commanded me to lay this account of his affairs before you.

I desired the secretary to present my humble duty to the emperor; and to let him know, that I thought it would not become me, who was a foreigner, to interfere with parties; but I was ready, with the hazard of my life, to defend his person and state against all invaders.

CHAPTER V

The author, by an extraordinary stratagem, prevents an invasion. A high title of honour is conferred upon him. Ambassadors arrive from the emperor of Blefuscu, and sue for peace. The empress's apartment on fire by an accident; the author instrumental in saving the rest of the palace.

The empire of Blefuscu is an island situated to the north-east of Lilliput, from which it is parted only by a channel of eight hundred yards wide. I had not yet seen it, and upon this notice of an intended invasion, I avoided appearing on that side of the coast, for fear of being discovered, by some of the enemy's ships, who had received no intelligence of me; all intercourse between the two empires having been strictly forbidden during the war, upon pain of death, and an embargo laid by our emperor upon all vessels whatsoever.

I communicated to his Majesty a project I had formed of seizing the enemy's whole fleet; which, as our scouts assured us, lay at anchor in the harbour, ready to sail with the first fair wind. I consulted the most experienced seamen upon the depth of the channel, which they had often plumbed; who told me, that in the middle, at high-water, it was seventy *glumgluffs* deep, which is about six feet of European measure; and the rest of it fifty *glumgluffs* at most. I walked towards the north-east coast, over against Blefuscu, where, lying down behind a hillock, I took out my small perspective glass, and viewed the enemy's fleet at anchor, consisting of about fifty men of war, and a great number of transports: I then came back to my house, and gave orders (for which I had a warrant) for a great quantity of the strongest cable and bars of iron. The cable was about as thick as packthread and the bars of the length and size of a knitting-needle. I trebled the cable to make it stronger, and for the same reason I twisted three of the iron bars together, bending the extremities into a hook.

Having thus fixed fifty hooks to as many cables, I went back to the north-east coast, and putting off my coat, shoes, and stockings, walked into the sea, in my leathern jerkin, about half an hour before high water. I waded with what haste I could, and swam in the middle about thirty yards, till I felt ground. I arrived at the fleet in less than half an hour. The enemy was so frightened when they saw me, that they leaped out of their ships, and swam to shore, where there could not be fewer than thirty thousand souls. I then took my tackling, and, fastening a hook to the hole at the prow of each, I tied all the cords together at the end.

While I was thus employed, the enemy discharged several thousand arrows, many of which stuck in my hands and face, and, beside the excessive smart, gave me much disturbance in my work. My greatest apprehension was for mine eyes, which I should have infallibly lost, if I had not suddenly thought of an expedient. I kept, among other little necessaries, a pair of spectacles in a private pocket, which, as I observed before, had escaped the emperor's searchers. These I took out and fastened as strongly as I could upon my nose, and thus armed, went on boldly with my work, in spite of the enemy's arrows, many of which struck against the glasses of my spectacles, but without any other effect, further than a little to discompose them.

I had now fastened all the hooks, and, taking the knot in my hand, began to pull; but not a ship would stir, for they were all too fast held by their anchors, so that the boldest part of my enterprise remained. I therefore let go the cord, and leaving the looks fixed to the ships, I resolutely cut with my knife the cables that fastened the anchors, receiving about two hundred shots in my face and hands; then I took up the knotted end of the cables, to which my hooks were tied, and with great ease drew fifty of the enemy's largest men of war after me.

The Blefuscudians, who had not the least imagination of what I intended, were at first confounded with astonishment. They had seen me cut the cables, and thought my design was only to let the ships run adrift or fall foul on each other: but when they perceived the whole fleet moving in order, and saw me pulling at the end, they set up such a scream of grief and despair as it is almost impossible to describe or conceive. When I had got out of danger, I stopped awhile to pick out the arrows that stuck in my hands and face; and rubbed on some of the same ointment that was given me at my first arrival, as I have formerly mentioned. I then took off my spectacles, and waiting about an hour, till the tide was a little fallen, I waded through the middle with my cargo, and arrived safe at the royal port of Lilliput.

The emperor and his whole court stood on the shore, expecting the issue of this great adventure. They saw the ships move forward in a large half-moon, but could not discern me, who was up to my breast in water. When I advanced to the middle of the channel, they were yet more in pain, because I was under water to my neck. The emperor concluded me to be drowned, and that the enemy's fleet was approaching in a hostile manner: but he was soon eased of his fears; for the channel growing shallower every step I made, I came in a short time within hearing, and holding up the end of the cable, by which the fleet was fastened, I cried in a loud voice, Long live the most puissant king of Lilliput! This great prince received me at my landing with all possible encomiums, and created me a *nardac* upon the spot, which is the highest title of honour among them.

His Majesty desired I would take some other opportunity of bringing all the rest of his enemy's ships into his ports. And so unmeasureable is the ambition of princes, that he seemed to think of nothing less than reducing the whole empire of Blefuscu into a province, and governing it, by a viceroy; of destroying the Big-endian exiles, and compelling that people to break the smaller end of their eggs, by which he would remain the sole monarch of the whole world. But I endeavoured to divert him from this design, by many arguments drawn from the topics of policy as well as justice; and I plainly protested, that I would never be an instrument of bringing a free and brave people into slavery. And, when the matter was debated in council, the wisest part of the ministry were of my opinion.

This open bold declaration of mine was so opposite to the schemes and politics of his imperial Majesty, that he could never forgive me. He mentioned it in a very artful manner at council, where I was told that some of the wisest appeared, at least by their silence, to be of my opinion; but others, who were my secret enemies, could not forbear some expressions which, by a side-wind, reflected on me. And from this time began an intrigue between his Majesty and a junto of ministers, maliciously bent against me, which broke out in less than two months, and had like to have ended in my utter destruction. Of so little weight are the greatest services to princes, when put into the balance with a refusal to gratify their passions.

About three weeks after this exploit, there arrived a solemn embassy from Blefuscu, with humble offers of a peace, which was soon concluded, upon conditions very advantageous to our emperor, wherewith I shall not trouble the reader. There were six ambassadors, with a train of about five hundred persons, and their entry was very magnificent, suitable to the grandeur of their master, and the importance of their business.

When their treaty was finished, wherein I did them several good offices by the credit I now had, or at least appeared to have, at court, their excellencies, who were privately told how much I had been their friend, made me a visit in form. They began with many compliments upon my valour and generosity, invited me to that kingdom in the emperor their master's name, and desired me to show them some proofs of my prodigious strength, of which they had heard so many wonders; wherein I readily obliged them, but shall not trouble the reader with the particulars.

When I had for some time entertained their excellencies, to their infinite satisfaction and surprise, I desired they would do me the honour to present my most humble respects to the emperor their master, the renown of whose virtues had so justly filled the whole world with admiration, and whose royal person I resolved to attend, before I returned to my own country.

Accordingly, the next time I had the honour to see our emperor, I desired his general license to wait on the Blefuscudian monarch, which he was pleased to grant me, as I could perceive, in a very cold manner; but could not guess the reason, till I had a whisper from a certain person, that Flimnap and Bolgolam had represented my intercourse with those ambassadors as a mark of disaffection; from which I am sure my heart was wholly free. And this was the first time I began to conceive some imperfect idea of courts and ministers.

It is to be observed, that these ambassadors spoke to me, by an interpreter, the languages of both empires differing as much from each other as any two in Europe, and each nation priding itself upon the antiquity, beauty, and energy of their own tongue, with an avowed contempt for that of their neighbour; yet our emperor, standing upon the advantage he had got by the seizure of their fleet, obliged them to deliver their credentials, and make their speech, in the Lilliputian tongue.

And it must be confessed, that from the great intercourse of trade and commerce between both realms, from the continual reception of exiles which is mutual among them, and from the custom, in each empire, to send their young nobility and richer gentry to the other, in order to polish themselves by seeing the world, and understanding men and manners; there are few persons of distinction, or merchants, or seamen, who dwell in the maritime parts, but what can hold conversation in both tongues; as I found some weeks after, when I went to pay my respects to the emperor of Blefuscu, which, in the midst of great misfortunes, through the malice of my enemies, proved a very happy adventure to me, as I shall relate in its proper place.

The reader may remember, that when I signed those articles upon which I recovered my liberty, there were some which I disliked, upon account of their being too servile; neither could anything but an extreme necessity have forced me to submit. But being now a *nardac* of the highest rank in that empire, such offices were looked upon as below my dignity, and the emperor (to do him justice), never once mentioned them to me.

CHAPTER VI

Of the inhabitants of Lilliput; their learning, laws, and customs; the manner of educating their children. The author's way of living in that country. His vindication of a great lady.

Although I intend to leave the description of this empire to a particular treatise, yet, in the mean time, I am content to gratify the curious reader with some general ideas. As the common size of the natives is somewhat under six inches high, so there is an exact proportion in all other animals, as well as plants and trees: for instance, the tallest horses and oxen are between four and five inches in height, the sheep an inch and half, more or less: their geese about the bigness of a sparrow, and so the several gradations downwards till you come to the smallest, which to my sight, were almost invisible; but nature has adapted the eyes of the Lilliputians to all objects proper for their view: they see with great exactness, but at no great distance. And, to show the sharpness of their sight towards objects that are near, I have been much pleased with observing a cook pulling a lark, which was not so large as a common fly; and a young girl threading an invisible needle with invisible silk. Their tallest trees are about seven feet high: I mean some of those in the great royal park, the tops whereof I could but just reach with my fist clenched. The other vegetables are in the same proportion; but this I leave to the reader's imagination.

I shall say but little at present of their learning, which, for many ages, has flourished in all its branches among them: but their manner of writing is very peculiar, being neither from the left to the right, like the Europeans, nor from the right to the left, like the Arabians, nor from up to down, like the Chinese, but aslant, from one corner of the paper to the other, like ladies in England.

They bury their dead with their heads directly downward, because they hold an opinion, that in eleven thousand moons they are all to rise again; in which period the earth (which they conceive to be flat) will turn upside down, and by this means they shall, at their resurrection, be found ready standing on their feet. The learned among them confess the absurdity of this doctrine; but the practice still continues, in compliance to the vulgar.

There are some laws and customs in this empire very peculiar; and if they were not so directly contrary to those of my own dear country, I should be tempted to say a little in their justification. It is only to be wished they were as well executed. The first I shall mention, relates to informers. All crimes against the state, are punished here with the utmost severity; but, if the person accused makes his innocence plainly to appear upon his trial, the accuser is immediately put to an ignominious death; and out of his goods or lands the innocent person is quadruply recompensed for the loss of his time, for the danger he underwent, for the hardship of his imprisonment, and for all the charges he has been at in making his defence; or, if that fund be deficient, it is largely supplied by the crown. The emperor also confers on him some public mark of his favour, and proclamation is made of his innocence through the whole city.

They look upon fraud as a greater crime than theft, and therefore seldom fail to punish it with death; for they allege, that care and vigilance, with a very common understanding, may preserve a man's goods from thieves, but honesty has no defence against superior cunning; and, since it is necessary that there should be a perpetual intercourse of buying and selling, and dealing upon credit, where fraud is permitted and connived at, or has no law to punish it, the honest dealer is always undone, and the knave gets the advantage. I remember, when I was once interceding with the emperor for a criminal who had wronged his master of a great sum of money, which he had received by order and ran away with; and happening to tell his Majesty, by way of extenuation, that it was only a breach of trust, the emperor thought it monstrous in me to offer as a defence the greatest aggravation of the crime; and truly I had little to say in return, farther than the common answer, that different nations had different customs; for, I confess, I was heartily ashamed.

Although we usually call reward and punishment the two hinges upon which all government turns, yet I could never observe this maxim to be put in practice by any nation except that of Lilliput. Whoever can there bring sufficient proof, that he has strictly observed the laws of his country for seventy-three moons, has a claim to certain privileges, according to his quality or condition of life, with a proportionable sum of money out of a fund appropriated for that use: he likewise acquires the title of *snilpall*, or legal, which is added to his name, but does not descend to his posterity. And these people thought it a prodigious defect of policy among us, when I told them that our laws were enforced only by penalties, without any mention of reward. It is upon this account that the image of Justice, in their courts of judicature, is formed with six eyes, two before, as many behind, and on each side one, to signify circumspection; with a bag of gold open in her right hand, and a sword sheathed in her left, to show she is more disposed to reward than to punish.

In choosing persons for all employments, they have more regard to good morals than to great abilities; for, since government is necessary to mankind, they believe, that the common size of human understanding is fitted to some station or other; and that Providence never intended to make the management of public affairs a mystery to be comprehended only by a few persons of sublime genius, of which there seldom are three born in an age: but they suppose truth, justice, temperance, and the like, to be in every man's power; the practice of which virtues, assisted by experience and a good intention, would qualify any man for the service of his country, except where a course of study is required. But they thought the want of moral virtues was so far from being supplied by superior endowments of the mind, that employments could never be put into such dangerous hands as those of persons so qualified; and, at least, that the mistakes committed by ignorance, in a virtuous disposition, would never be of such fatal consequence to the public weal, as the practices of a man, whose inclinations led him to be corrupt, and who had great abilities to manage, to multiply, and defend his corruptions.

In like manner, the disbelief of a Divine Providence renders a man incapable of holding any public station; for, since kings avow themselves to be the deputies of Providence, the Lilliputians think nothing can be more absurd than for a prince to employ such men as disown the authority under which he acts.

In relating these and the following laws, I would only be understood to mean the original institutions, and not the most scandalous corruptions, into which these people are fallen by the degenerate nature of man. For, as to that infamous practice of acquiring great employments by dancing on the ropes, or badges of favour and distinction by leaping over sticks and creeping under them, the reader is to observe, that they were first introduced by the grandfather of the emperor now reigning, and grew to the present height by the gradual increase of party and faction.

Ingratitude is among them a capital crime, as we read it to have been in some other countries: for they reason thus; that whoever makes ill returns to his benefactor, must needs be a common enemy to the rest of mankind, from whom he has received no obligation, and therefore such a man is not fit to live.

Their notions relating to the duties of parents and children differ extremely from ours. For, since the conjunction of male and female is founded upon the great law of nature, in order to propagate and continue the species, the Lilliputians will needs have it, that men and women are joined together, like other animals, by the motives of concupiscence; and that their tenderness towards their young proceeds from the like natural principle: for which reason they will never allow that a child is under any obligation to his father for begetting him, or to his mother for bringing him into the world; which, considering the miseries of human life, was neither a benefit in itself, nor intended so by his parents, whose thoughts, in their love encounters, were otherwise employed. Upon these, and the like reasonings, their opinion is, that parents are the last of all others to be trusted with the education of their own children; and therefore they have in every town public nurseries, where all parents, except cottagers and labourers, are obliged to send their infants of both sexes to be reared and educated, when they come to the age of twenty moons, at which time they are supposed to have some rudiments of docility. These schools are of several kinds, suited to different qualities, and both sexes. They have certain professors well skilled in preparing children for such a condition of life as befits the rank of their parents, and their own capacities, as well as inclinations. I shall first say something of the male nurseries, and then of the female.

The nurseries for males of noble or eminent birth, are

provided with grave and learned professors, and their several deputies. The clothes and food of the children are plain and simple. They are bred up in the principles of honour, justice, courage, modesty, clemency, religion, and love of their country; they are always employed in some business, except in the times of eating and sleeping, which are very short, and two hours for diversions consisting of bodily exercises. They are dressed by men till four years of age, and then are obliged to dress themselves, although their quality be ever so great; and the women attendant, who are aged proportionably to ours at fifty, perform only the most menial offices. They are never suffered to converse with servants, but go together in smaller or greater numbers to take their diversions, and always in the presence of a professor, or one of his deputies; whereby they avoid those early bad impressions of folly and vice, to which our children are subject. Their parents are suffered to see them only twice a year; the visit is to last but an hour; they are allowed to kiss the child at meeting and parting; but a professor, who always stands by on those occasions, will not suffer them to whisper, or use any fondling expressions, or bring any presents of toys, sweetmeats, and the like.

The pension from each family for the education and entertainment of a child, upon failure of due payment, is levied by the emperor's officers.

The nurseries for children of ordinary gentlemen, merchants, traders, and handicrafts, are managed proportionally after the same manner; only those designed for trades are put out apprentices at eleven years old, whereas those of persons of quality continue in their exercises till fifteen, which answers to twenty-one with us: but the confinement is gradually lessened for the last three years.

In the female nurseries, the young girls of quality are educated much like the males, only they are dressed by orderly servants of their own sex; but always in the presence of a professor or deputy, till they come to dress themselves, which is at five years old. And if it be found that these nurses ever presume to entertain the girls with frightful or foolish stories, or the common follies practised by chambermaids among us, they are publicly whipped thrice about the city, imprisoned for a year, and banished for life to the most desolate part of the country. Thus the young ladies are as much ashamed of being cowards and fools as the men, and despise all personal ornaments, beyond decency and cleanliness: neither did I perceive any difference in their education made by their difference of sex, only that the exercises of the females were not altogether so robust; and that some rules were given them relating to domestic life, and a smaller compass of learning was enjoined them: for their maxim is, that among peoples of quality, a wife should be always a reasonable and agreeable companion, because she cannot always be young. When the girls are twelve years old, which among them is the marriageable age, their parents or guardians take them home, with great expressions of gratitude to the professors, and seldom without tears of the young lady and her companions.

In the nurseries of females of the meaner sort, the children are instructed in all kinds of works proper for their sex, and their several degrees: those intended for apprentices are dismissed at seven years old, the rest are kept to eleven.

The meaner families who have children at these nurseries, are obliged, besides their annual pension, which is as low as possible, to return to the steward of the nursery a small monthly share of their gettings, to be a portion for the child; and therefore all parents are limited in their expenses by the law. For the Lilliputians think nothing can be more unjust, than for people, in subservience to their own appetites, to bring children into the world, and leave the burthen of supporting them on the public. As to persons of quality, they give security to appropriate a certain sum for each child, suitable to their condition; and these funds are always managed with good husbandry and the most exact justice.

The cottagers and labourers keep their children at home, their business being only to till and cultivate the earth, and therefore their education is of little consequence to the public: but the old and diseased among them, are supported by hospitals; for begging is a trade unknown in this empire.

And here it may, perhaps, divert the curious reader, to give some account of my domestics, and my manner of living in this country, during a residence of nine months, and thirteen days. Having a head mechanically turned, and being likewise forced by necessity, I had made for myself a table and chair convenient enough, out of the largest trees in the royal park. Two hundred sempstresses were employed to make me shirts, and linen for my bed and table, all of the strongest and coarsest kind they could get; which, however, they were forced to quilt together in several folds, for the thickest was some degrees finer than lawn. Their linen is usually three inches wide, and three feet make a piece. The sempstresses took my measure as I lay on the ground, one standing at my neck, and another at my mid-leg, with a strong cord extended, that each held by the end, while a third measured the length of the cord with a rule of an inch long. Then they measured my right thumb, and desired no more; for by a mathematical computation, that twice round the thumb is once round the wrist, and so on to the neck and the waist, and by the help of my old shirt, which I displayed on the ground before them for a pattern, they fitted me exactly.

Three hundred tailors were employed in the same manner to make me clothes; but they had another contrivance for taking my measure. I kneeled down, and they raised a ladder from the ground to my neck; upon this ladder one of them mounted, and let fall a plumb-line from my collar to the floor, which just answered the length of my coat: but my waist and arms I measured myself. When my clothes were finished, which was done in my house (for the largest of theirs would not have been able to hold them), they looked like the patch-work made by the ladies in England, only that mine were all of a colour.

I had three hundred cooks to dress my victuals, in little convenient huts built about my house, where they and their families lived, and prepared me two dishes a-piece. I took up twenty waiters in my hand, and placed them on the table: a hundred more attended below on the ground, some with dishes of meat, and some with barrels of wine and other liquors slung on their shoulders; all which the waiters above drew up, as I wanted, in a very ingenious manner, by certain cords, as we draw the bucket up a well in Europe. A dish of their meat was a good mouthful, and a barrel of their liquor a reasonable draught. Their mutton yields to ours, but their beef is excellent. I have had a sirloin so large, that I have been forced to make three bites of it; but this is rare. My servants were astonished to see me eat it, bones and all, as in our country we do the leg of a lark. Their geese and turkeys I usually ate at a mouthful, and I confess they far exceed ours. Of their smaller fowl I could take up twenty or thirty at the end of my knife.

One day his imperial Majesty, being informed of my way of living, desired that himself and his royal consort, with the young princes of the blood of both sexes, might have the happiness, as he was pleased to call it, of dining with me. They came accordingly, and I placed them in chairs of state, upon my table, just over against me, with their guards about them. Flimnap, the lord high treasurer, attended there likewise with his white staff; and I observed he often looked on me with a sour countenance, which I would not seem to regard, but ate more than usual, in honour to my dear country, as well as to fill the court with admiration. I have some private reasons to believe, that this visit from his Majesty gave Flimnap an opportunity of doing me ill offices to his master. That minister had always been my secret enemy, though he outwardly caressed me more than was usual to the moroseness of his nature. He represented to the emperor the low condition of his treasury; that he was forced to take up money at a great discount; that exchequer bills would not circulate under nine per cent. below par; that I had cost his Majesty above a million and a half of sprugs (their greatest gold coin, about the bigness of a spangle) and, upon the whole, that it would be advisable in the emperor to take the first fair occasion of dismissing me.

I am here obliged to vindicate the reputation of an excellent lady, who was an innocent sufferer upon my account. The treasurer took a fancy to be jealous of his wife, from the malice of some evil tongues, who informed him that her Grace had taken a violent affection for my person; and the court scandal ran for some time, that she once came privately to my lodging. This I solemnly declare to be a most infamous falsehood, without any grounds, further than that her Grace was pleased to treat me with all innocent marks of freedom and friendship.

I own she came often to my house, but always publicly, nor ever without three more in the coach, who were usually her sister and young daughter, and some particular acquaintance; but this was common to many other ladies of the court. And I still appeal to my servants round, whether they at any time saw a coach at my door, without knowing what persons were in it. On those occasions, when a servant had given me notice, my custom was to go immediately to the door, and, after paying my respects, to take up the coach and two horses very carefully in my hands (for, if there were six horses, the postillion always unharnessed four,) and place them on a table, where I had fixed a movable rim quite round, of five inches high, to prevent accidents. And I have often had four coaches and horses at once on my table, full of company, while I sat in my chair, leaning my face towards them; and when I was engaged with one set, the coachmen would gently drive the others round my table. I have passed many an afternoon very agreeably in these conversations. But I defy the treasurer, or his two informers (I will name them, and let them make the best of it) Clustril and Drunlo, to prove that any person ever came to me incognito, except the secretary Reldresal, who was sent by express command of his imperial Majesty, as I have before related.

I should not have dwelt so long upon this particular, if it had not been a point wherein the reputation of a great lady is so nearly concerned, to say nothing of my own; though I then had the honour to be a *nardac*, which the treasurer himself is not; for all the world knows, that he is only a *glumglum*, a title inferior by one degree, as that of a marquis is to a duke in England; yet I allow he preceded me in right of his post. These false informations, which I afterwards came to the knowledge of by an accident not proper to mention, made the treasurer show his lady for some time an ill countenance, and me a worse; and although he was at last undeceived and reconciled to her, yet I lost all credit with him, and found my interest decline very fast with the emperor himself, who was, indeed, too much governed by that favourite.

CHAPTER VII

The author, being informed of a design to accuse him of high-treason, makes his escape to Blefuscu. His reception there.

Before I proceed to give an account of my leaving this kingdom, it may be proper to inform the reader of a private intrigue which had been for two months forming against me.

I had been hitherto, all my life, a stranger to courts, for which I was unqualified by the meanness of my condition. I had indeed heard and read enough of the dispositions of great princes and ministers, but never expected to have found such terrible effects of them, in so remote a country, governed, as I thought, by very different maxims from those in Europe.

When I was just preparing to pay my attendance on the emperor of Blefuscu, a considerable person at court (to whom I had been very serviceable, at a time when he lay under the highest displeasure of his imperial Majesty) came to my house very privately at night, in a close chair, and, without sending his name, desired admittance. The chairmen were dismissed; I put the chair, with his lordship in it, into my coat-pocket: and, giving orders to a trusty servant, to say I was indisposed and gone to sleep, I fastened the door of my house, placed the chair on the table, according to my usual custom, and sat down by it. After the common salutations were over, observing his lordship's countenance full of concern, and inquiring into the reason, he desired I would hear him with patience, in a matter that highly concerned my honour and my life. His speech was to the following effect, for I took notes of it as soon as he left me:

"You are to know," said he, that several committees of council have been lately called, in the most private manner, on your account; and it is but two days since his Majesty came to a full resolution.

"You are very sensible that Skyresh Bolgolam (*galbet*, or high-admiral) has been your mortal enemy, almost ever since your arrival. His original reasons I know not; but his hatred is increased since your great success against Blefuscu, by which his glory as admiral is much obscured. This lord, in conjunction with Flimnap the high-treasurer, whose enmity against you is notorious on account of his lady, Limtoc the general, Lalcon the chamberlain, and Balmuff the grand justiciary, have prepared articles of impeachment against you, for treason and other capital crimes."

This preface made me so impatient, being conscious of my own merits and innocence, that I was going to interrupt him; when he entreated me to be silent, and thus proceeded,-

Out of gratitude for the favours you have done me, I procured information of the whole proceedings, and a copy of the articles; wherein I venture my head for your service.

'*Articles of Impeachment against* QUINBUS FLESTRIN,
(*the* MAN MOUNTAIN).

"ARTICLE I

"That the said Quinbus Flestrin, having brought the imperial fleet of Blefuscu into the royal port, and being afterwards commanded by his imperial Majesty to seize all the other ships of the said empire of Blefuscu, and reduce that empire to a province, to be governed by a viceroy from hence, and to destroy and put to death, not only all the Big-endian exiles, but likewise all the people of that empire who would not immediately forsake the Big-endian heresy, he, the said Flestrin, like a false traitor against his most auspicious, serene, imperial Majesty, did petition to be excused from the said service, upon pretence of unwillingness to force the consciences, or destroy the liberties and lives of an innocent people.

"ARTICLE II

"That, whereas certain ambassadors arrived from the Court of Blefuscu, to sue for peace in his Majesty's court, he, the said Flestrin, did, like a false traitor, aid, abet, comfort, and divert, the said ambassadors, although he knew them to be servants to a prince who was lately an open enemy to his imperial Majesty, and in an open war against his said Majesty .

"ARTICLE III

"That the said Quinbus Flestrin, contrary to the duty of a faithful subject, is now preparing to make a voyage to the court and empire of Blefuscu, for which he has received only verbal license from his imperial Majesty; and, under colour of the said license, does falsely and traitorously intend to take the said voyage, and thereby to aid, comfort, and abet the emperor of Blefuscu, so lately an enemy, and in open war with his imperial Majesty aforesaid.'

"There are some other articles; but these are the most important, of which I have read you an abstract.

"In the several debates upon this impeachment, it must be confessed that his Majesty gave many marks of his great lenity; often urging the services you had done him, and endeavouring to extenuate your crimes. The treasurer and admiral insisted that you should be put to the most painful and ignominious death, by setting fire to your house at night, and the general was to attend with twenty thousand men, armed with poisoned arrows, to shoot you on the face and hands. Some of your servants were to have private orders to strew a poisonous juice on your shirts and sheets, which would soon make you tear your own flesh, and die in the utmost torture. The general came into the same opinion; so that for a long time there was a majority against you; but his Majesty resolving, if possible, to spare your life, at last brought off the chamberlain.

"Upon this incident, Reldresal, principal secretary for private affairs, who always approved himself your true friend, was commanded by the emperor to deliver his opinion, which he accordingly did; and therein justified the good thoughts you have of him. He allowed your crimes to be great, but that still there was room for mercy, the most commendable virtue in a prince, and for which his Majesty was so justly celebrated. He said, the friendship between you and him was so well known to the world, that perhaps the most honourable board might think him partial; however, in obedience to the command he had received, he would freely offer his sentiments.

"That if his Majesty, in consideration of your services, and pursuant to his own merciful disposition, would please to spare your life, and only give orders to put out both your eyes, he humbly conceived, that by this expedient justice might in some measure be satisfied, and all the world would applaud the lenity of the emperor, as well as the fair and generous proceedings of those who have the honour to be his counsellors. That the loss of your eyes would be no impediment to your bodily strength, by which you might still be useful to his Majesty; that blindness is an addition to courage, by concealing dangers from us; that the fear you had for your eyes, was the greatest difficulty in bringing over the enemy's fleet, and it would be sufficient for you to see by the eyes of the ministers, since the greatest princes do no more.

"This proposal was received with the utmost disapprobation by the whole board. Bolgolam, the admiral, could not preserve his temper, but, rising up in fury, said, he wondered how the secretary durst presume to give his opinion for preserving the life of a traitor; that the services you had performed were, by all true reasons of state, the great aggravation of your crimes; that you, who were able to extinguish the fire by discharge of urine in her Majesty's apartment (which he mentioned with horror), might, at another time, raise an inundation by the same means, to drown the whole palace; and the same strength which enabled you to bring over the enemy's fleet, might serve, upon the first discontent, to carry it back; that he had good reasons to think you were a Big-endian in your heart; and, as treason begins in the heart, before it appears in overt-acts, so he accused you as a traitor on that account, and therefore insisted you should be put to death.

"The treasurer was of the same opinion: he showed to what straits his Majesty's revenue was reduced, by the charge of maintaining you, which would soon grow insupportable; that the secretary's expedient of putting out your eyes, was so far from being a remedy against this evil, that it would probably increase it, as is manifest from the common practice of blinding some kind of fowls, after which they fed the faster, and grew sooner fat; that his sacred Majesty and the council, who are your judges, were, in their own consciences, fully convinced of your guilt, which was a sufficient argument to condemn you to death, without the formal proofs required by the strict letter of the law.

"But his imperial Majesty, fully determined against capital punishment, was graciously pleased to say, that since the council thought the loss of your eyes too easy a censure, some other way may be inflicted hereafter. And your friend the secretary, humbly desiring to be heard again, in answer to what the treasurer had objected, concerning the great charge his Majesty was at in maintaining you, said, that his Excellency, who had the sole disposal of the emperor's revenue, might easily provide against that evil, by gradually lessening your establishment; by which, for want of sufficient for you would grow weak and faint, and lose your appetite, and consequently, decay, and consume in a few months; neither would the stench of your carcass be then so dangerous, when it should become more than half diminished; and immediately upon your death five or six thousand of his Majesty's subjects might, in two or three days, cut your flesh from your bones, take it away by cart-loads, and bury it in distant parts, to prevent infection, leaving the skeleton as a monument of admiration to posterity.

"Thus, by the great friendship of the secretary, the whole affair was compromised. It was strictly enjoined, that the project of starving you by degrees should be kept a secret; but the sentence of putting out your eyes was entered on the books; none dissenting, except Bolgolam the admiral, who, being a creature of the empress, was perpetually instigated by her Majesty to insist upon your death.

"In three days your friend the secretary will be directed to come to your house, and read before you the articles of impeachment; and then to signify the great lenity and favour of his Majesty and council, whereby you are only condemned to the loss of your eyes, which his Majesty does not question you will gratefully and humbly submit to; and twenty of his Majesty's surgeons will attend, in order to see the operation well performed, by discharging very sharp-pointed arrows into the balls of your eyes, as you lie on the ground.

"I leave to your prudence what measures you will take; and to avoid suspicion, I must immediately return in as private a manner as I came.

His lordship did so; and I remained alone, under many doubts and perplexities of mind.

It was a custom introduced by this prince and his ministry

(very different, as I have been assured, from the practice of former times,) that after the court had decreed any cruel execution, either to gratify the monarch's resentment, or the malice of a favourite, the emperor always made a speech to his whole council, expressing his great lenity and tenderness, as qualities known and confessed by all the world. This speech was immediately published throughout the kingdom; nor did any thing terrify the people so much as those encomiums on his Majesty's mercy; because it was observed, that the more these praises were enlarged and insisted on, the more inhuman was the punishment, and the sufferer more innocent.

Yet, as to myself, I must confess, having never been designed for a courtier, either by my birth or education, I was so ill a judge of things, that I could not discover the lenity and favour of this sentence, but conceived it (perhaps erroneously) rather to be rigorous than gentle. I sometimes thought of standing my trial, for, although I could not deny the facts alleged in the several articles, yet I hoped they would admit of some extenuation. But having in my life perused many state-trials, which I ever observed to terminate as the judges thought fit to direct, I durst not rely on so dangerous a decision, in so critical a juncture, and against such powerful enemies.

Once I was strongly bent upon resistance, for, while I had liberty the whole strength of that empire could hardly subdue me, and I might easily with stones pelt the metropolis to pieces; but I soon rejected that project with horror, by remembering the oath I had made to the emperor, the favours I received from him, and the high title of *nardac* he conferred upon me. Neither had I so soon learned the gratitude of courtiers, to persuade myself, that his Majesty's present seventies acquitted me of all past obligations.

At last, I fixed upon a resolution, for which it is probable I may incur some censure, and not unjustly; for I confess I owe the preserving of mine eyes, and consequently my liberty, to my own great rashness and want of experience; because, if I had then known the nature of princes and ministers, which I have since observed in many other courts, and their methods of treating criminals less obnoxious than myself, I should, with great alacrity and readiness, have submitted to so easy a punishment.

But hurried on by the precipitancy of youth, and having his imperial Majesty's license to pay my attendance upon the emperor of Blefuscu, I took this opportunity, before the three days were elapsed, to send a letter to my friend the secretary, signifying my resolution of setting out that morning for Blefuscu, pursuant to the leave I had got; and, without waiting for an answer, I went to that side of the island where our fleet lay. I seized a large man of war, tied a cable to the prow, and, lifting up the anchors, I stripped myself, put my clothes (together with my coverlet, which I carried under my arm) into the vessel, and, drawing it after me, between wading and swimming arrived at the royal port of Blefuscu, where the people had long expected me: they lent me two guides to direct me to the capital city, which is of the same name. I held them in my hands, till I came within two hundred yards of the gate, and desired them to signify my arrival to one of the secretaries, and let him know, I there waited his Majesty's command. I had an answer in about an hour, that his Majesty, attended by the royal family, and great officers of the court, was coming out to receive me. I advanced a hundred yards. The emperor and his train alighted from their horses, the empress and ladies from their coaches, and I did not perceive they were in any fright or concern. I lay on the ground to kiss his Majesty's and the empress's hands. I told his Majesty, that I was come according to my promise, and with the license of the emperor my master, to have the honour of seeing so mighty a monarch, and to offer him any service in my power, consistent with my duty to my own prince; not mentioning a word of my disgrace, because I had hitherto no regular information of it, and might suppose myself wholly ignorant of any such design; neither could I reasonably conceive that the emperor would discover the secret, while I was out of his power; wherein, however, it soon appeared I was deceived.

I shall not trouble the reader with the particular account of my reception at this court, which was suitable to the generosity of so great a prince; nor of the difficulties I was in for want of a house and bed, being forced to lie on the ground, wrapped up in my coverlet.

CHAPTER VIII

The author, by a lucky accident, finds means to leave Blefuscu; and, after some difficulties, returns safe to his native country.

Three days after my arrival, walking out of curiosity to the north-east coast of the island, I observed, about half a league off in the sea, somewhat that looked like a boat overturned. I pulled off my shoes and stockings, and, wailing two or three hundred yards, I found the object to approach nearer by force of the tide; and then plainly saw it to be a real boat, which I supposed might by some tempest have been driven from a ship. Whereupon, I returned immediately towards the city, and desired his imperial Majesty to lend me twenty of the tallest vessels he had left, after the loss of his fleet, and three thousand seamen, under the command of his vice-admiral. This fleet sailed round, while I went back the shortest way to the coast, where I first discovered the boat. I found the tide had driven it still nearer. The seamen were all provided with cordage, which I had beforehand twisted to a sufficient strength. When the ships came up, I stripped myself, and waded till I came within a hundred yards off the boat, after which I was forced to swim till I got up to it. The seamen threw me the end of the cord, which I fastened to a hole in the fore-part of the boat, and the other end to a man of war.

But I found all my labour to little purpose; for, being out of my depth, I was not able to work. In this necessity I was forced to swim behind, and push the boat forward, as often as I could, with one of my hands; and the tide favouring me, I advanced so far that I could just hold up my chin and feel the ground. I rested two or three minutes, and then gave the boat another shove, and so on, till the sea was no higher than my arm-pits; and now, the most laborious part being over, I took out my other cables, which were stowed in one of the ships, and fastened them first to the boat, and then to nine of the vessels which attended me; the wind being favourable, the seamen towed, and I shoved, until we arrived within forty yards of the shore; and, waiting till the tide was out, I got dry to the boat, and by the assistance of two thousand men, with ropes and engines, I made a shift to turn it on its bottom, and found it was but little damaged.

I shall not trouble the reader with the difficulties I was under, by the help of certain paddles, which cost me ten days making, to get my boat to the royal port of Blefuscu, where a mighty concourse of people appeared upon my arrival, full of wonder at the sight of so prodigious a vessel. I told the emperor that my good fortune had thrown this boat in my way, to carry me to some place whence I might return into my native country; and begged his Majesty's orders for getting materials to fit it up, together with his license to depart; which, after some kind expostulations, he was pleased to grant.

I did very much wonder, in all this time, not to have heard of any express relating to me from our emperor to the court of Blefuscu. But I was afterward given privately to understand, that his imperial Majesty, never imagining I had the least notice of his designs, believed I was only gone to Blefuscu in performance of my promise, according to the license he had given me, which was well known at our court, and would return in a few days, when the ceremony was ended. But he was at last in pain at my long absence; and after consulting with the treasurer and the rest of that cabal, a person of quality was dispatched with the copy of the articles against me.

This envoy had instructions to represent to the monarch of Blefuscu, the great lenity of his master, who was content to punish me no farther than with the loss of mine eyes; that I had fled from justice; and if I did not return in two hours, I should be deprived of my title of *nardac*, and declared a traitor. The envoy further added, that in order to maintain the peace and amity between both empires, his master expected that his brother of Blefuscu would give orders to have me sent back to Lilliput, bound hand and foot, to be punished as a traitor.

The emperor of Blefuscu, having taken three days to consult, returned an answer consisting of many civilities and excuses. He said, that as for sending me bound, his brother knew it was impossible; that, although I had deprived him of his fleet, yet he owed great obligations to me for many good offices I had done him in making the peace. That, however, both their majesties would soon be made easy; for I had found a prodigious vessel on the shore, able to carry me on the sea, which he had given orders to fit up, with my own assistance and direction; and he hoped, in a few weeks, both empires would be freed from so insupportable an incumbrance.

With this answer the envoy returned to Lilliput; and the monarch of Blefuscu related to me all that had passed; offering me at the same time (but under the strictest confidence) his gracious protection, if I would continue in his service; wherein, although I believed him sincere, yet I resolved never more to put any confidence in princes or ministers, where I could possibly avoid it; and therefore, with all due acknowledgments for his favourable intentions, I humbly begged to be excused. I told him, that since fortune, whether good or evil, had thrown a vessel in my way, I was resolved to venture myself on the ocean, rather than be an occasion of difference between two such mighty monarchs. Neither did I find the emperor at all displeased; and I discovered, by a certain accident, that he was very glad of my resolution, and so were most of his ministers.

These considerations moved me to hasten my departure somewhat sooner than I intended; to which the court, impatient to have me gone, very readily contributed. Five hundred workmen were employed to make two sails to my boat, according to my directions, by quilting thirteen folds of their strongest linen together. I was at the pains of making ropes and cables, by twisting ten, twenty, or thirty of the thickest and strongest of theirs. A great stone that I happened to find, after a long search, by the sea-shore, served me for an anchor. I had the tallow of three hundred cows, for greasing my boat, and other uses. I was at incredible pains in cutting down some of the largest timber-trees, for oars and masts, wherein I was, however, much assisted by his Majesty's ship-carpenters, who helped me in smoothing them, after I had done the rough work.

In about a month, when all was prepared, I sent to receive his Majesty's commands, and to take my leave. The emperor and royal family came out of the palace; I lay down on my face to kiss his hand, which he very graciously gave me: so did the empress and young princes of the blood. His Majesty presented me with fifty purses of two hundred *sprugs* a-piece, together with his picture at full length, which I put immediately into one of my gloves, to keep it from being hurt. The ceremonies at my departure were too many to trouble the reader with at this time.

I stored the boat with the carcases of a hundred oxen, and three hundred sheep, with bread and drink proportionable, and as much meat ready dressed as four hundred cooks could provide. I took with me six cows and two bulls alive, with as many ewes and rams, intending to carry them into my own country, and propagate the breed. And to feed them on board,

I had a good bundle of hay, and a bag of corn. I would gladly have taken a dozen of the natives, but this was a thing the emperor would by no means permit; and, besides a diligent search into my pockets, his Majesty engaged my honour not to carry away any of his subjects, although with their own consent and desire.

Having thus prepared all things as well as I was able, I set sail on the twenty-fourth day of September 1701, at six in the morning; and when I had gone about four-leagues to the northward, the wind being at south-east, at six in the evening I descried a small island, about half a league to the north-west. I advanced forward, and cast anchor on the lee-side of the island, which seemed to be uninhabited. I then took some refreshment, and went to my rest. I slept well, and as I conjectured at least six hours, for I found the day broke in two hours after I awaked. It was a clear night. I ate my breakfast before the sun was up; and heaving anchor, the wind being favourable, I steered the same course that I had done the day before, wherein I was directed by my pocket compass. My intention was to reach, if possible, one of those islands which I had reason to believe lay to the north-east of Van Diemen's Land.

I discovered nothing all that day; but upon the next, about three in the afternoon, when I had by my computation made twenty-four leagues from Blefuscu, I descried a sail steering to the south-east; my course was due east. I hailed her, but could get no answer; yet I found I gained upon her, for the wind slackened. I made all the sail I could, and in half an hour she spied me, then hung out her ancient, and discharged a gun.

It is not easy to express the joy I was in, upon the unexpected hope of once more seeing my beloved country, and the dear pledges I left in it. The ship slackened her sails, and I came up with her between five and six in the evening, September 26th; but my heart leaped within me to see her English colours. I put my cows and sheep into my coat-pockets, and got on board with all my little cargo of provisions.

The vessel was an English merchantman, returning from Japan by the North and South seas; the captain, Mr. John Biddel, of Deptford, a very civil man, and an excellent sailor. We were now in the latitude of 30 degrees south; there were about fifty men in the ship; and here I met an old comrade of mine, one Peter Williams, who gave me a good character to the captain. This gentleman treated me with kindness, and desired I would let him know what place I came from last, and whither I was bound; which I did in a few words, but he thought I was raving, and that the dangers I underwent had disturbed my head; whereupon I took my black cattle and sheep out of my pocket, which, after great astonishment, clearly convinced him of my veracity. I then showed him the gold given me by the emperor of Blefuscu, together with his Majesty's picture at full length, and some other rarities of that country. I gave him two purses of two hundreds *sprugs* each, and promised, when we arrived in England, to make him a present of a cow and a sheep big with young.

I shall not trouble the reader with a particular account of this voyage, which was very prosperous for the most part. We arrived in the Downs on the 13th of April, 1702. I had only one misfortune, that the rats on board carried away one of my sheep; I found her bones in a hole, picked clean from the flesh. The rest of my cattle I got safe ashore, and set them a-grazing in a bowling-green at Greenwich, where the fineness of the grass made them feed very heartily, though I had always feared the contrary: neither could I possibly have preserved them in so long a voyage, if the captain had not allowed me some of his best biscuit, which, rubbed to powder, and mingled with water, was their constant food. The short time I continued in England, I made a considerable profit by showing my cattle to many persons of quality and others: and before I began my second voyage, I sold them for six hundred pounds. Since my last return I find the breed is considerably increased, especially the sheep, which I hope will prove much to the advantage of the woollen manufacture, by the fineness of the fleeces.

I stayed but two months with my wife and family, for my insatiable desire of seeing foreign countries, would suffer me to continue no longer. I left fifteen hundred pounds with my wife, and fixed her in a good house at Redriff. My remaining stock I carried with me, part in money and part in goods, in hopes to improve my fortunes. My eldest uncle John had left me an estate in land, near Epping, of about thirty pounds a-year; and I had a long lease of the Black Bull in Fetter-Lane, which yielded me as much more; so that I was not in any danger of leaving my family upon the parish. My son Johnny, named so after his uncle, was at the grammar-school, and a towardly child. My daughter Betty (who is now well married, and has children) was then at her needle-work. I took leave of my wife, and boy and girl, with tears on both sides, and went on board the Adventure, a merchant ship of three hundred tons, bound for Surat, captain John Nicholas, of Liverpool, commander. But my account of this voyage must be referred to the Second Part of my Travels.

PART II

A Voyage to
Brobdingnag

CHAPTER I

A great storm described; the long boat sent to fetch water; the author goes with it to discover the country. He is left on shore, is seized by one of the natives, and carried to a farmer's house. His reception, with several accidents that happened there. A description of the inhabitants.

Having been condemned, by nature and fortune, to active and restless life, in two months after my return, I again left my native country, and took shipping in the Downs, on the 20th day of June, 1702, in the Adventure, Captain John Nicholas, a Cornish man, commander, bound for Surat.

We had a very prosperous gale, till we arrived at the Cape of Good Hope, where we landed for fresh water; but discovering a leak, we unshipped our goods and wintered there; for the captain falling sick of an ague, we could not leave the Cape till the end of March. We then set sail, and had a good voyage till we passed the Straits of Madagascar; but having got northward of that island, and to about five degrees south latitude, the winds, which in those seas are observed to blow a constant equal gale between the north and west, from the beginning of December to the beginning of May, on the 19th of April began to blow with much greater violence, and more westerly than usual, continuing so for twenty days together: during which time, we were driven a little to the east of the Molucca

Islands, and about three degrees northward of the line, as our captain found by an observation he took the 2nd of May, at which time the wind ceased, and it was a perfect calm, whereat I was not a little rejoiced. But he, being a man well experienced in the navigation of those seas, bid us all prepare against a storm, which accordingly happened the day following: for the southern wind, called the southern monsoon, began to set in.

Finding it was likely to overblow, we took in our sprit-sail, and stood by to hand the fore-sail; but making foul weather, we looked the guns were all fast, and handed the mizen. The ship lay very broad off, so we thought it better spooning before the sea, than trying or hulling. We reefed the fore-sail and set him, and hauled aft the fore-sheet; the helm was hard a-weather. The ship wore bravely. We belayed the fore down-haul; but the sail was split, and we hauled down the yard, and got the sail into the ship, and unbound all the things clear of it.

It was a very fierce storm; the sea broke strange and dangerous. We hauled off upon the laniard of the whip-staff, and helped the man at the helm. We would not get down our topmast, but let all stand, because she scudded before the sea very well, and we knew that the top-mast being aloft, the ship was the wholesomer, and made better way through the sea, seeing we had sea-room.

When the storm was over, we set fore-sail and main-sail, and brought the ship to. Then we set the mizen, main-top-sail, and the fore-top-sail. Our course was east-north-east, the wind was at south-west. We got the starboard tacks aboard, we cast off our weather-braces and lifts; we set in the lee-braces, and hauled forward by the weather-bowlings, and hauled them tight, and belayed them, and hauled over the mizen tack to windward, and kept her full and by as near as she would lie.

During this storm, which was followed by a strong wind west-south-west, we were carried, by my computation, about five hundred leagues to the east, so that the oldest sailor on board could not tell in what part of the world we were. Our provisions held out well, our ship was staunch, and our crew all in good health; but we lay in the utmost distress for water. We thought it best to hold on the same course, rather than turn more northerly, which might have brought us to the north-west part of Great Tartary, and into the Frozen Sea.

On the 16th day of June, 1703, a boy on the top-mast discovered land. On the 17th, we came in full view of a great island, or continent (for we knew not whether;) on the south side whereof was a small neck of land jutting out into the sea, and a creek too shallow to hold a ship of above one hundred tons. We cast anchor within a league of this creek, and our captain sent a dozen of his men well armed in the long-boat, with vessels for water, if any could be found. I desired his leave to go with them, that I might see the country, and make what discoveries I could.

When we came to land we saw no river or spring, nor any sign of inhabitants. Our men therefore wandered on the shore to find out some fresh water near the sea, and I walked alone about a mile on the other side, where I observed the country all barren and rocky. I now began to be weary, and seeing nothing to entertain my curiosity, I returned gently down towards the creek; and the sea being full in my view, I saw our men already got into the boat, and rowing for life to the ship. I was going to holla after them, although it had been to little purpose, when I observed a huge creature walking after them in the sea, as fast as he could: he waded not much deeper than his knees, and took prodigious strides: but our men had the start of him half a league, and, the sea thereabouts being full of sharp-pointed rocks, the monster was not able to overtake the boat. This I was afterwards told, for I durst not stay to see the issue of the adventure; but ran as fast as I could the way I first went, and then climbed up a steep hill, which gave me some prospect of the country. I found it fully cultivated; but that which first surprised me was the length of the grass, which, in those grounds that seemed to be kept for hay, was about twenty feet high.

I fell into a high road, for so I took it to be, though it served to the inhabitants only as a foot-path through a field of barley. Here I walked on for some time, but could see little on either side, it being now near harvest, and the corn rising at least forty feet.

I was an hour walking to the end of this field, which was fenced in with a hedge of at least one hundred and twenty feet high, and the trees so lofty that I could make no computation of their altitude. There was a stile to pass from this field into the next. It had four steps, and a stone to cross over when you came to the uppermost. It was impossible for me to climb this stile, because every step was six-feet high, and the upper stone about twenty. I was endeavouring to find some gap in the hedge, when I discovered one of the inhabitants in the next field, advancing towards the stile, of the same size with him whom I saw in the sea pursuing our boat. He appeared as tall as an ordinary spire steeple, and took about ten yards at every stride, as near as I could guess. I was struck with the utmost fear and astonishment, and ran to hide myself in the corn, whence I saw him at the top of the stile looking back into the next field on the right hand, and heard him call in a voice many degrees louder than a speaking-trumpet: but the noise was so high in the air, that at first I certainly thought it was thunder.

Whereupon seven monsters, like himself, came towards him with reaping-hooks in their hands, each hook about the largeness of six scythes. These people were not so well clad as the first, whose servants or labourers they seemed to be; for, upon some words he spoke, they went to reap the corn in the field where I lay. I kept from them at as great a distance as I could, but was forced to move with extreme difficulty, for the stalks of the corn were sometimes not above a foot distant, so that I could hardly squeeze my body betwixt them.

However, I made a shift to go forward, till I came to a part of the field where the corn had been laid by the rain and wind. Here it was impossible for me to advance a step; for the stalks were so interwoven, that I could not creep through, and the beards of the fallen ears so strong and pointed, that they pierced through my clothes into my flesh. At the same time I heard the reapers not a hundred yards behind me. Being quite dispirited with toil, and wholly overcome by grief and dispair, I lay down between two ridges, and heartily wished I might there end my days. I bemoaned my desolate widow and fatherless children. I lamented my own folly and wilfulness, in attempting a second voyage, against the advice of all my friends and relations.

In this terrible agitation of mind, I could not forbear thinking of Lilliput, whose inhabitants looked upon me as the greatest prodigy that ever appeared in the world; where I was able to draw an imperial fleet in my hand, and perform those other actions, which will be recorded for ever in the chronicles of that empire, while posterity shall hardly believe them, although attested by millions. I reflected what a mortification it must prove to me, to appear as inconsiderable in this nation, as one single Lilliputian would be among us. But this I conceived was to be the least of my misfortunes; for, as human creatures are observed to be more savage and cruel in proportion to their bulk, what could I expect but to be a morsel in the mouth of the first among these enormous barbarians that should happen to seize me?

Undoubtedly philosophers are in the right, when they tell us that nothing is great or little otherwise than by comparison. It might have pleased fortune, to have let the Lilliputians find some nation, where the people were as diminutive with respect to them, as they were to me. And who knows but that even this prodigious race of mortals might be equally overmatched in some distant part of the world, whereof we have yet no discovery.

Scared and confounded as I was, I could not forbear going on with these reflections, when one of the reapers, approaching within ten yards of the ridge where I lay, made me apprehend that with the next step I should be squashed to death under his foot, or cut in two with his reaping-hook. And therefore, when he was again about to move, I screamed as loud as fear could make me: whereupon the huge creature trod short, and, looking round about under him for some time, at last espied me as I lay on the ground.

He considered awhile, with the caution of one who endeavours to lay hold on a small dangerous animal in such a manner that it shall not be able either to scratch or bite him, as I myself have sometimes done with a weasel in England.

At length he ventured to take me behind, by the middle, between his fore-finger and thumb, and brought me within three yards of his eyes, that he might behold my shape more perfectly. I guessed his meaning, and my good fortune gave me so much presence of mind, that I resolved not to struggle in the least as he held me in the air above sixty feet from the ground, although he grievously pinched my sides, for fear I should slip through his fingers. All I ventured was to raise mine eyes towards the sun, and place my hands together in a supplicating posture, and to speak some words in a humble melancholy tone, suitable to the condition I then was in: for I apprehended every moment that he would dash me against the ground, as we usually do any little hateful animal, which we have a mind to destroy. But my good star would have it, that he appeared pleased with my voice and gestures, and began to look upon me as a curiosity, much wondering to hear me pronounce articulate words, although he could not understand them.

In the meantime I was not able to forbear groaning and shedding tears, and turning my head towards my sides; letting him know, as well as I could, how cruelly I was hurt by the pressure of his thumb and finger. He seemed to apprehend my meaning; for, lifting up the lappet of his coat, he put me gently into it, and immediately ran along with me to his master, who was a substantial farmer, and the same person I had first seen in the field.

The farmer having (as I suppose by their talk) received such an account of me as his servant could give him, took a piece of a small straw, about the size of a walking-staff, and therewith lifted up the lappets of my coat; which it seems he thought to be some kind of covering that nature had given me. He blew my hairs aside to take a better view of my face. He called his hinds about him, and asked them, as I afterwards learned, whether they had ever seen in the fields any little creature that resembled me. He then placed me softly on the ground upon all fours, but I got immediately up, and walked slowly backward and forward, to let those people see I had no intent to run away.

They all sat down in a circle about me, the better to observe my motions. I pulled off my hat, and made a low bow towards the farmer. I fell on my knees, and lifted up my hands and eyes, and spoke several words as loud as I could: I took a purse of gold out of my pocket, and humbly presented it to him. He received it on the palm of his hand, then applied it close to his eye to see what it was, and afterwards turned it several times with the point of a pin (which he took out of his sleeve,) but could make nothing of it. Whereupon I made a sign that he should place his hand on the ground.

I then took the purse, and, opening it, poured all the gold into his palm. There were six Spanish pieces of four pistoles each, beside twenty or thirty smaller coins. I saw him wet the tip of his little finger upon his tongue, and take up one of my largest pieces, and then another; but he seemed to be wholly ignorant what they were. He made me a sign to put them again into my purse, and the purse again into my pocket, which, after offering it to him several times, I thought it best to do.

The farmer, by this time, was convinced I must be a rational creature. He spoke often to me; but the sound of his voice pierced my ears like that of a water-mill, yet his words were articulate enough. I answered as loud as I could in several languages, and he often laid his ear within two yards of me: but all in vain, for we were wholly unintelligible to each other. He then sent his servants to their work, and taking his handkerchief out of his pocket, he doubled and spread it on his left hand, which he placed flat on the ground with the palm upward, making me a sign to step into it, as I could easily do, for it was not above a foot in thickness. I thought it my part to obey, and, for fear of falling, laid myself at full length upon the handkerchief, with the remainder of which he lapped me up to the head for further security, and in this manner carried me home to his house. There he called his wife, and showed me to her; but she screamed and ran back, as women in England do at the sight of a toad or a spider. However, when she had a while seen my behaviour, and how well I observed the signs her husband made, she was soon reconciled, and by degrees grew extremely tender of me.

It was about twelve at noon, and a servant brought in dinner. It was only one substantial dish of meat (fit for the plain condition of a husbandman,) in a dish of about four-and-twenty feet diameter. The company were, the farmer and his wife, three children, and an old grandmother. When they were sat down, the farmer placed me at some distance from him on the table, which was thirty feet high from the floor. I was in a terrible fright, and kept as far as I could from the edge, for fear of falling. The wife minced a bit of meat, then crumbled some bread on a trencher, and placed it before me. I made her a low bow, took out my knife and fork, and fell to eat, which gave them exceeding delight. The mistress sent her maid for a small dram cup, which held about two gallons, and filled it with drink; I took up the vessel with much difficulty in both hands, and in a most respectful manner drank to her ladyship's health, expressing the words as loud as I could in English, which made the company laugh so heartily, that I was almost deafened with the noise. This liquor tasted like a small cider, and was not unpleasant.

Then the master made me a sign to come to his trencher side; but as I walked on the table, being in great surprise all the time, as the indulgent reader will easily conceive and excuse, I happened to stumble against a crust, and fell flat on my face, but received no hurt. I got up immediately, and observing the good people to be in much concern, I took my hat (which I held under my arm out of good manners,) and waving it over my head, made three huzzas, to show I had got no mischief by my fall.

But advancing forward towards my master (as I shall henceforth call him,) his youngest son, who sat next to him, an arch boy of about ten years old, took me up by the legs, and held me so high in the air, that I trembled every limb: but his father snatched me from him, and at the same time gave him such a box on the left ear, as would have felled an European troop of horse to the earth, ordering him to be taken from the table. But being afraid the boy might owe me a spite, and well remembering how mischievous all children among us naturally are to sparrows, rabbits, young kittens, and puppy dogs, I fell on my knees, and pointing to the boy, made my master to understand, as well as I could, that I desired his son might be pardoned. The father complied, and the lad took his seat again, whereupon I went to him, and kissed his hand, which my master took, and made him stroke me gently with it.

In the midst of dinner, my mistress's favourite cat leaped into her lap. I heard a noise behind me like that of a dozen stocking-weavers at work; and turning my head, I found it proceeded from the purring of that animal, who seemed to be three times larger than an ox, as I computed by the view of her head, and one of her paws, while her mistress was feeding and stroking her. The fierceness of this creature's countenance altogether discomposed me; though I stood at the farther end of the table, above fifty feet off; and although my mistress held her fast, for fear she might give a spring, and seize me in her talons.

But it happened there was no danger, for the cat took not the least notice of me when my master placed me within three yards of her. And as I have been always told, and found true by experience in my travels, that flying or discovering fear before a fierce animal, is a certain way to make it pursue or attack you, so I resolved, in this dangerous juncture, to show no manner of concern. I walked with intrepidity five or six times before the very head of the cat, and came within half a yard of her; whereupon she drew herself back, as if she were more afraid of me.

I had less apprehension concerning the dogs, whereof three or four came into the room, as it is usual in farmers' houses; one of which was a mastiff, equal in bulk to four elephants, and another a greyhound, somewhat taller than the mastiff, but not so large.

When dinner was almost done, the nurse came in with a child of a year old in her arms, who immediately spied me, and began a squall that you might have heard from London-Bridge to Chelsea, after the usual oratory of infants, to get me for a plaything. The mother, out of pure indulgence, took me up, and put me towards the child, who presently seized me by the middle, and got my head into his mouth, where I roared so loud that the urchin was frighted, and let me drop, and I should infallibly have broke my neck, if the mother had not held her apron under me. The nurse, to quiet her babe, made use of a rattle which was a kind of hollow vessel filled with great stones, and fastened by a cable to the child's waist: but all in vain; so that she was forced to apply the last remedy by giving it suck. I must confess no object ever disgusted me so much as the sight of her monstrous breast, which I cannot tell what to compare with, so as to give the curious reader an idea of its bulk, shape, and colour. It stood prominent six feet, and could not be less than sixteen in circumference. The nipple was about half the bigness of my head, and the hue both of that and the dug, so varied with spots, pimples, and freckles, that nothing could appear more nauseous: for I had a near sight of her, she sitting down, the more conveniently to give suck, and I standing on the table. This made me reflect upon the fair skins of our English ladies, who appear so beautiful to us, only because they are of our own size, and their defects not to be seen but through a magnifying glass; where we find by experiment that the smoothest and whitest skins look rough, and coarse, and ill-coloured.

I remember when I was at Lilliput, the complexion of those diminutive people appeared to me the fairest in the world; and talking upon this subject with a person of learning there, who was an intimate friend of mine, he said that my face appeared much fairer and smoother when he looked on me from the ground, than it did upon a nearer view, when I took him up in my hand, and brought him close, which he confessed was at first a very shocking sight. He said, he could discover great holes in my skin; that the stumps of my beard were ten times stronger than the bristles of a boar, and my complexion made up of several colours altogether disagreeable: although I must beg leave to say for myself, that I am as fair as most of my sex and country, and very little sunburnt by all my travels. On the other side, discoursing of the ladies in that emperor's court, he used to tell me, one had freckles; another too wide a mouth; a third too large a nose; nothing of which I was able to distinguish. I confess this reflection was obvious enough;

which, however, I could not forbear, lest the reader might think those vast creatures were actually deformed: for I must do them the justice to say, they are a comely race of people.

When dinner was done, my master went out to his labourers, and, as I could discover by his voice and gesture, gave his wife strict charge to take care of me. I was very much tired, and disposed to sleep, which my mistress perceiving, she put me on her own bed, and covered me with a clean white handkerchief, but larger and coarser than the mainsail of a man-of-war.

I slept about two hours, and dreamt I was at home with my wife and children, which aggravated my sorrows when I awaked, and found myself alone in a vast room, between two and three hundred feet wide, and above two hundred high, lying in a bed twenty yards wide. My mistress was gone about her household affairs, and had locked me in. The bed was eight yards from the floor.

While I was under these circumstances, two rats crept up the curtains, and ran smelling backwards and forwards on the bed. One of them came up almost to my face, whereupon I rose in a fright, and drew out my hanger to defend myself. These horrible animals had the boldness to attack me on both sides, and one of them held his fore-feet at my collar; but I had the good fortune to rip up his belly before he could do me any mischief. He fell down at my feet; and the other, seeing the fate of his comrade, made his escape, but not without one good wound on the back, which I gave him as he fled, and made the blood run trickling from him.

After this exploit, I walked gently to and fro on the bed, to recover my breath and loss of spirits. These creatures were of the size of a large mastiff, but infinitely more nimble and fierce; so that if I had taken off my belt before I went to sleep, I must have infallibly been torn to pieces and devoured. I measured the tail of the dead rat, and found it to be two yards long, wanting an inch; but it went against my stomach to drag the carcass off the bed, where it lay still bleeding; I observed it had yet some life, but with a strong slash across the neck, I thoroughly despatched it.

Soon after my mistress came into the room, who seeing me all bloody, ran and took me up in her hand. I pointed to the dead rat, smiling, and making other signs to show I was not hurt; whereat she was extremely rejoiced, calling the maid to take up the dead rat with a pair of tongs, and throw it out of the window. Then she set me on a table, where I showed her my hanger all bloody, and wiping it on the lappet of my coat, returned it to the scabbard.

I hope the gentle reader will excuse me for dwelling on these and the like particulars, which, however insignificant they may appear to groveling vulgar minds, yet will certainly help a philosopher to enlarge his thoughts and imagination, and apply them to the benefit of public as well as private life, which was my sole design in presenting this and other accounts of my travels to the world; wherein I have been chiefly studious of truth, without affecting any ornaments of learning or of style. But the whole scene of this voyage made so strong an impression on my mind, and is so deeply fixed in my memory, that, in committing it to paper I did not omit one material circumstance: however, upon a strict review, I blotted out several passages. Of less moment which were in my first copy, for fear of being censured as tedious and trifling, whereof travellers are often, perhaps not without justice, accused.

CHAPTER II

A description of the farmer's daughter. The author carried
to a market-town, and then to the metropolis. The
particulars of his journey.

My mistress had a daughter of nine years old, a child
of towardly parts for her age, very dexterous at her
needle, and skilful in dressing her baby. Her mother and she
contrived to fit up the baby's cradle for me against night: the
cradle was put into a small drawer of a cabinet, and the drawer
placed upon a hanging shelf for fear of the rats. This was my
bed all the time I staid with those people, though made more
convenient by degrees, as I began to learn their language and
make my wants known. This young girl was so handy, that
after I had once or twice pulled off my clothes before her, she
was able to dress and undress me, though I never gave her that
trouble when she would let me do either myself. She made me
seven shirts, and some other linen, of as fine cloth as could be
got, which indeed was coarser than sackcloth; and these she
constantly washed for me with her own hands.

She was likewise my school-mistress, to teach me the
language: when I pointed to any thing, she told me the name
of it in her own tongue, so that in a few days I was able to
call for whatever I had a mind to. She was very good-natured,
and not above forty feet high, being little for her age. She

gave me the name of Grildrig, which the family took up, and afterwards the whole kingdom. The word imports what the Latins call Nanunculus, the Italians Homunceletino, and the English Mannikin. To her I chiefly owe my preservation in that country: we never parted while I was there; I called her my Glumdalclitch, or little nurse; and should be guilty of great ingratitude, if I omitted this honourable mention of her care and affection towards me, which I heartily wish it lay in my power to requite as she deserves, instead of being the innocent, but unhappy instrument of her disgrace, as I have too much reason to fear.

It now began to be known and talked of in the neighbourhood, that my master had found a strange animal in the field, about the bigness of a *splacnuck*, but exactly shaped in every part like a human creature; which it likewise imitated in all its actions; seemed to speak in a little language of its own, had already learned several words of theirs, went erect upon two legs, was tame and gentle, would come when it was called, do whatever it was bid, had the finest limbs in the world, and a complexion fairer than a nobleman's daughter of three years old. Another farmer, who lived hard by, and was a particular friend of my master, came on a visit on purpose to inquire into the truth of this story. I was immediately produced, and placed upon a table, where I walked as I was commanded, drew my hanger, put it up again, made my reverence to my master's guest, asked him in his own language how he did, and told him he was welcome, just as my little nurse had instructed me.

This man, who was old and dim-sighted, put on his spectacles to behold me better; at which I could not forbear laughing very heartily, for his eyes appeared like the full moon shining into a chamber at two windows. Our people, who discovered the cause of my mirth, bore me company in laughing, at which the old fellow was fool enough to be angry and out of countenance. He had the character of a great miser;

and, to my misfortune, he well deserved it, by the cursed advice
he gave my master, to show me as a sight upon a market-day in
the next town, which was half an hour's riding, about two-and-
twenty miles from our house.

I guessed there was some mischief when I observed
my master and his friend whispering together, sometimes
pointing at me; and my fears made me fancy that I overheard
and understood some of their words. But the next morning
Glumdalclitch, my little nurse, told me the whole matter,
which she had cunningly picked out from her mother. The
poor girl laid me on her bosom, and fell a weeping with shame
and grief. She apprehended some mischief would happen to
me from rude vulgar folks, who might squeeze me to death,
or break one of my limbs by taking me in their hands. She had
also observed how modest I was in my nature, how nicely I
regarded my honour, and what an indignity I should conceive
it, to be exposed for money as a public spectacle, to the meanest
of the people. She said, her papa and mamma had promised
that Grildrig should be hers; but now she found they meant to
serve her as they did last year, when they pretended to give her
a lamb, and yet, as soon as it was fat, sold it to a butcher.

For my own part, I may truly affirm, that I was less concerned
than my nurse. I had a strong hope, which never left me, that
I should one day recover my liberty: and as to the ignominy of
being carried about for a monster, I considered myself to be
a perfect stranger in the country, and that such a misfortune
could never be charged upon me as a reproach, if ever I should
return to England, since the king of Great Britain himself, in
my condition, must have undergone the same distress.

My master, pursuant to the advice of his friend, carried
me in a box the next market-day to the neighbouring town,
and took along with him his little daughter, my nurse, upon
a pillion behind him. The box was close on every side, with
a little door for me to go in and out, and a few gimlet holes

to let in air. The girl had been so careful as to put the quilt of her baby's bed into it, for me to lie down on. However, I was terribly shaken and discomposed in this journey, though it was but of half an hour: for the horse went about forty feet at every step and trotted so high, that the agitation was equal to the rising and falling of a ship in a great storm, but much more frequent. Our journey was somewhat farther than from London to St. Alban's.

My master alighted at an inn which he used to frequent; and after consulting awhile with the inn-keeper, and making some necessary preparations, he hired the *grultrud*, or crier, to give notice through the town of a strange creature to be seen at the sign of the Green Eagle, not so big as a *splacnuck* (an animal in that country very finely shaped, about six feet long,) and in every part of the body resembling a human creature, could speak several words, and perform a hundred diverting tricks.

I was placed upon a table in the largest room of the inn, which might be near three hundred feet square. My little nurse stood on a low stool close to the table, to take care of me, and direct what I should do. My master, to avoid a crowd, would suffer only thirty people at a time to see me. I walked about on the table as the girl commanded; she asked me questions, as far as she knew my understanding of the language reached, and I answered them as loud as I could. I turned about several times to the company, paid my humble respects, said they were welcome, and used some other speeches I had been taught. I took up a thimble filled with liquor, which Glumdalclitch had given me for a cup, and drank their health, I drew out my hanger, and flourished with it after the manner of fencers in England. My nurse gave me a part of a straw, which I exercised as a pike, having learnt the art in my youth.

I was that day shown to twelve sets of company, and as often forced to act over again the same fopperies, till I was half dead with weariness and vexation; for those who had seen me made such wonderful reports, that the people were ready to break down the doors to come in.

My master, for his own interest, would not suffer any one to touch me except my nurse; and to prevent danger, benches were set round the table at such a distance as to put me out of every body's reach. However, an unlucky school-boy aimed a hazel nut directly at my head, which very narrowly missed me; otherwise it came with so much violence, that it would have infallibly knocked out my brains, for it was almost as large as a small pumpkin, but I had the satisfaction to see the young rogue well beaten, and turned out of the room.

My master gave public notice that he would show me again the next market-day; and in the meantime he prepared a convenient vehicle for me, which he had reason enough to do; for I was so tired with my first journey, and with entertaining company for eight hours together, that I could hardly stand upon my legs, or speak a word. It was at least three days before I recovered my strength; and that I might have no rest at home, all the neighbouring gentlemen from a hundred miles round, hearing of my fame, came to see me at my master's own house. There could not be fewer than thirty persons with their wives and children (for the country is very populous;) and my master demanded the rate of a full room whenever he showed me at home, although it were only to a single family; so that for some time I had but little ease every day of the week (except Wednesday, which is their Sabbath,) although I were not carried to the town.

My master, finding how profitable I was likely to be, resolved to carry me to the most considerable cities of the kingdom. Having therefore provided himself with all things necessary for a long journey, and settled his affairs at home, he took leave of his wife, and upon the 17th of August, 1703, about two months after my arrival, we set out for the metropolis, situate near the middle of that empire, and about three thousand miles distance from our house. My master made his daughter Glumdalclitch ride behind him. She carried me on her lap, in a box tied about her waist. The girl had lined it on all sides with the softest cloth she could get, well quilted underneath, furnished it with her baby's bed, provided me with linen and other necessaries, and made everything as convenient as she could. We had no other company but a boy of the house, who rode after us with the luggage.

My master's design was to show me in all the towns by the way, and to step out of the road for fifty or a hundred miles, to any village, or person of quality's house, where he might expect custom. We made easy journeys, of not above seven or eight score miles a-day; for Glumdalclitch, on purpose to spare me, complained she was tired with the trotting of the horse. She often took me out of my box, at my own desire, to give me air, and show me the country, but always held me fast by a leading-string.

sWe passed over five or six rivers, many degrees broader and deeper than the Nile or the Ganges: and there was hardly a rivulet so small as the Thames at London-bridge. We were ten weeks in our journey, and I was shown in eighteen large towns, besides many villages, and private families.

On the 26th day of October we arrived at the metropolis, called in their language *Lorbrulgrud*, or Pride of the Universe. My master took a lodging in the principal street of the city, not far from the royal palace, and put out bills in the usual form, containing an exact description of my person and parts. He hired a large room between three and four hundred feet wide. He provided a table sixty feet in diameter, upon which I was to act my part, and pallisadoed it round three feet from the edge, and as many high, to prevent my falling over. I was shown ten times a-day, to the wonder and satisfaction of all people. I could now speak the language tolerably well, and perfectly understood every word, that was spoken to me. Besides, I had learnt their alphabet, and could make a shift to explain a sentence here and there; for Glumdalclitch had been my instructor while we were at home, and at leisure hours during our journey. She carried a little book in her pocket, not much larger than a Sanson's Atlas; it was a common treatise for the use of young girls, giving a short account of their religion: out of this she taught me my letters, and interpreted the words.

CHAPTER III

The author sent for to court. The queen buys him of his master the farmer, and presents him to the king. He disputes with his Majesty's great scholars. An apartment at court provided for the author. He is in high favour with the queen. He stands up for the honour of his own country. His quarrels with the queen's dwarf.

The frequent labours I underwent every day, made, in a few weeks, a very considerable change in my health: the more my master got by me, the more insatiable he grew. I had quite lost my stomach, and was almost reduced to a skeleton. The farmer observed it, and concluding I must soon die, resolved to make as good a hand of me as he could.

While he was thus reasoning and resolving with himself, a *slardral*, or gentleman-usher, came from court, commanding my master to carry me immediately thither for the diversion of the queen and her ladies. Some of the latter had already been to see me, and reported strange things of my beauty, behaviour, and good sense. Her Majesty, and those who attended her, were beyond measure delighted with my demeanour. I fell on my knees, and begged the honour of kissing her imperial foot; but this gracious princess held out her little finger towards me, after I was set on the table, which I embraced in both my arms, and put the tip of it with the utmost respect to my lip.

She made me some general questions about my country and my travels, which I answered as distinctly, and in as few words as I could. She asked, whether I could be content to live at court? I bowed down to the board of the table, and humbly answered that I was my master's slave: but, if I were at my own disposal, I should be proud to devote my life to her Majesty's service. She then asked my master, whether he was willing to sell me at a good price? He, who apprehended I could not live a month, was ready enough to part with me, and demanded a thousand pieces of gold, which were ordered him on the spot, each piece being about the bigness of eight hundred moidores; but allowing for the proportion of all things between that country and Europe, and the high price of gold among them, was hardly so great a sum as a thousand guineas would be in England.

I then said to the queen, since I was now her Majesty's most humble creature and vassal, I must beg the favour, that Glumdalclitch, who had always tended me with so much care and kindness, and understood to do it so well, might be admitted into her service, and continue to be my nurse and instructor.

Her Majesty agreed to my petition, and easily got the farmer's consent, who was glad enough to have his daughter preferred at court, and the poor girl herself was not able to hide her joy. My late master withdrew, bidding me farewell, and saying he had left me in a good service; to which I replied not a word, only making him a slight bow.

The queen observed my coldness; and, when the farmer was gone out of the apartment, asked me the reason. I made bold to tell her Majesty, that I owed no other obligation to my late master, than his not dashing out the brains of a poor harmless creature, found by chance in his fields: which obligation was amply recompensed, by the gain he had made in showing me through half the kingdom, and the price he had now sold me for. That the life I had since led was laborious enough to kill an animal of ten times my strength. That my health was much impaired, by the continual drudgery of entertaining the rabble every hour of the day; and that, if my master had not thought my life in danger, her Majesty would not have got so cheap a bargain. But as I was out of all fear of being ill-treated under the protection of so great and good an empress, the ornament of nature, the darling of the world, the delight of her subjects, the phoenix of the creation, so I hoped my late master's apprehensions would appear to be groundless; for I already found my spirits revive, by the influence of her most august presence.

This was the sum of my speech, delivered with great improprieties and hesitation. The latter part was altogether framed in the style peculiar to that people, whereof I learned some phrases from Glumdalclitch, while she was carrying me to court.

The queen, giving great allowance for my defectiveness in speaking, was, however, surprised at so much wit and good sense in so diminutive an animal. She took me in her own hand, and carried me to the king, who was then retired to his cabinet. His Majesty, a prince of much gravity and austere countenance, not well observing my shape at first view, asked the queen after a cold manner how long it was since she grew fond of a *splacnuck*? for such it seems he took me to be, as I lay upon my breast in her Majesty's right hand. But this princess, who has an infinite deal of wit and humour, set me gently on my feet upon the scrutoire, and commanded me to give his Majesty an account of myself, which I did in a very few words: and Glumdalclitch who attended at the cabinet door, and could not endure I should be out of her sight, being admitted, confirmed all that had passed from my arrival at her father's house.

The king, although he be as learned a person as any in his

dominions, had been educated in the study of philosophy, and particularly mathematics; yet when he observed my shape exactly, and saw me walk erect, before I began to speak, conceived I might be a piece of clock-work (which is in that country arrived to a very great perfection) contrived by some ingenious artist. But when he heard my voice, and found what I delivered to be regular and rational, he could not conceal his astonishment.

He was by no means satisfied with the relation I gave him of the manner I came into his kingdom, but thought it a story concerted between Glumdalclitch and her father, who had taught me a set of words to make me sell at a better price. Upon this imagination, he put several other questions to me, and still received rational answers: no otherwise defective than by a foreign accent, and an imperfect knowledge in the language, with some rustic phrases which I had learned at the farmer's house, and did not suit the polite style of a court.

His Majesty sent for three great scholars, who were then in their weekly waiting, according to the custom in that country. These gentlemen, after they had a while examined my shape with much nicety, were of different opinions concerning me. They all agreed that I could not be produced according to the regular laws of nature, because I was not framed with a capacity of preserving my life, either by swiftness, or climbing of trees, or digging holes in the earth. They observed by my teeth, which they viewed with great exactness, that I was a carnivorous animal; yet most quadrupeds being an overmatch for me, and field mice, with some others, too nimble, they could not imagine how I should be able to support myself, unless I fed upon snails and other insects, which they offered, by many learned arguments, to evince that I could not possibly do. One of these virtuosi seemed to think that I might be an embryo, or abortive birth. But this opinion was rejected by the other two, who observed my limbs to be perfect and finished; and that I had lived several years, as it was manifest from my beard, the stumps whereof they plainly discovered through a magnifying glass. They would not allow me to be a dwarf, because my littleness was beyond all degrees of comparison; for the queen's favourite dwarf, the smallest ever known in that kingdom, was near thirty feet high. After much debate, they concluded unanimously, that I was only *relplum scalcath*, which is interpreted literally *lusus naturoe*; a determination exactly agreeable to the modern philosophy of Europe, whose professors, disdaining the old evasion of occult causes, whereby the followers of Aristotle endeavoured in vain to disguise their ignorance, have invented this wonderful solution of all difficulties, to the unspeakable advancement of human knowledge.

After this decisive conclusion, I entreated to be heard a word or two. I applied myself to the king, and assured his Majesty that I came from a country which abounded with several millions of both sexes, and of my own stature; where the animals, trees, and houses, were all in proportion, and where, by consequence, I might be as able to defend myself, and to find sustenance, as any of his Majesty's subjects could do here; which I took for a full answer to those gentlemen's arguments. To this they only replied with a smile of contempt, saying, that the farmer had instructed me very well in my lesson.

The king, who had a much better understanding, dismissing his learned men, sent for the farmer, who by good fortune was not yet gone out of town. Having therefore first examined him privately, and then confronted him with me and the young girl, his Majesty began to think that what we told him might possibly be true. He desired the queen to order that a particular care should be taken of me; and was of opinion that Glumdalclitch should still continue in her office of tending me, because he observed we had a great affection for each other. A convenient apartment was provided for her at court: she had a sort of governess appointed to take care of her education, a maid to dress her, and two other servants for menial offices; but the care of me was wholly appropriated to herself.

The queen commanded her own cabinet-maker to contrive a box, that might serve me for a bedchamber, after the model that Glumdalclitch and I should agree upon. This man was a most ingenious artist, and according to my direction, in three weeks finished for me a wooden chamber of sixteen feet square, and twelve high, with sash-windows, a door, and two closets, like a London bed-chamber. The board, that made the ceiling, was to be lifted up and down by two hinges, to put in a bed ready furnished by her Majesty's upholsterer, which Glumdalclitch took out every day to air, made it with her own hands, and letting it down at night, locked up the roof over me.

A nice workman, who was famous for little curiosities, undertook to make me two chairs, with backs and frames, of a substance not unlike ivory, and two tables, with a cabinet to put my things in. The room was quilted on all sides, as well as the floor and the ceiling, to prevent any accident from the carelessness of those who carried me, and to break the force of a jolt, when I went in a coach. I desired a lock for my door, to prevent rats and mice from coming in. The smith, after several attempts, made the smallest that ever was seen among them, for I have known a larger at the gate of a gentleman's house in England. I made a shift to keep the key in a pocket of my own, fearing Glumdalclitch might lose it.

The queen likewise ordered the thinnest silks that could be gotten, to make me clothes, not much thicker than an English blanket, very cumbersome till I was accustomed to them. They were after the fashion of the kingdom, partly resembling the Persian, and partly the Chinese, and are a very grave and decent habit.

The queen became so fond of my company, that she could not dine without me. I had a table placed upon the same at which her Majesty ate, just at her left elbow, and a chair to sit on. Glumdalclitch stood on a stool on the floor near my table, to assist and take care of me. I had an entire set of silver dishes and plates, and other necessaries, which, in proportion to those of the queen, were not much bigger than what I have seen in a London toy-shop for the furniture of a baby-house: these my little nurse kept in her pocket in a silver box, and gave me at meals as I wanted them, always cleaning them herself.

No person dined with the queen but the two princesses royal, the eldest sixteen years old, and the younger at that time thirteen and a month. Her Majesty used to put a bit of meat upon one of my dishes, out of which I carved for myself, and her diversion was to see me eat in miniature: for the queen (who had indeed but a weak stomach) took up, at one mouthful, as much as a dozen English farmers could eat at a meal, which to me was for some time a very nauseous sight. She would craunch the wing of a lark, bones and all, between her teeth, although it were nine times as large as that of a full-grown turkey; and put a bit of bread into her mouth as big as two twelve-penny loaves. She drank out of a golden cup, above a hogshead at a draught. Her knives were twice as long as a scythe, set straight upon the handle. The spoons, forks, and other instruments, were all in the same proportion. I remember when Glumdalclitch carried me, out of curiosity, to see some of the tables at court, where ten or a dozen of those enormous knives and forks were lifted up together, I thought I had never till then beheld so terrible a sight.

It is the custom, that every Wednesday (which, as I have observed, is their Sabbath) the king and queen, with the royal issue of both sexes, dine together in the apartment of his

Majesty, to whom I was now become a great favourite; and at these times, my little chair and table were placed at his left hand, before one of the salt-cellars. This prince took a pleasure in conversing with me, inquiring into the manners, religion, laws, government, and learning of Europe; wherein I gave him the best account I was able. His apprehension was so clear, and his judgment so exact, that he made very wise reflections and observations upon all I said.

But I confess, that, after I had been a little too copious in talking of my own beloved country, of our trade and wars by sea and land, of our schisms in religion, and parties in the state; the prejudices of his education prevailed so far, that he could not forbear taking me up in his right hand, and stroking me gently with the other, after a hearty fit of laughing, asked me, whether I was a Whig or Tory.

Then turning to his first minister, who waited behind him with a white staff, near as tall as the mainmast of the *Royal Sovereign*, he observed how contemptible a thing was human grandeur, which could be mimicked by such diminutive insects as I: and yet, says he, I dare engage these creatures have their titles and distinctions of honour; they contrive little nests and burrows, that they call houses and cities; they make a figure in dress and equipage; they love, they fight, they dispute, they cheat, they betray! And thus he continued on, while my colour came and went several times, with indignation, to hear our noble country, the mistress of arts and arms, the scourge of France, the arbitress of Europe, the seat of virtue, piety, honour, and truth, the pride and envy of the world, so contemptuously treated.

But as I was not in a condition to resent injuries, so upon mature thoughts I began to doubt whether I was injured or no. For, after having been accustomed several months to the sight and converse of this people, and observed every object upon which I cast mine eyes to be of proportionable magnitude, the horror I had at first conceived from their bulk and aspect was so far worn off, that if I had then beheld a company of English lords and ladies in their finery and birth-day clothes, acting their several parts in the most courtly manner of strutting, and bowing, and prating, to say the truth, I should have been strongly tempted to laugh as much at them as the king and his grandees did at me.

Neither, indeed, could I forbear smiling at myself, when the queen used to place me upon her hand towards a looking-glass, by which both our persons appeared before me in full view together; and there could be nothing more ridiculous than the comparison; so that I really began to imagine myself dwindled many degrees below my usual size.

Nothing angered and mortified me so much as the queen's dwarf; who being of the lowest stature that was ever in that country (for I verily think he was not full thirty feet high), became so insolent at seeing a creature so much beneath him, that he would always affect to swagger and look big as he passed by me in the queen's antechamber, while I was standing on some table talking with the lords or ladies of the court, and he seldom failed of a smart word or two upon my littleness; against which I could only revenge myself by calling him brother, challenging him to wrestle, and such repartees as are usually in the mouths of court pages.

One day, at dinner, this malicious little cub was so nettled with something I had said to him, that, raising himself upon the frame of her Majesty's chair, he took me up by the middle, as I was sitting down, not thinking any harm, and let me drop into a large silver bowl of cream, and then ran away as fast as he could. I fell over head and ears, and, if I had not been a good swimmer, it might have gone very hard with me; for Glumdalclitch in that instant happened to be at the other end of the room, and the queen was in such a fright, that she wanted presence of mind to assist me. But my little nurse ran to my relief, and took me out, after I had swallowed above a quart of cream. I was put to bed: however, I received no other damage than the loss of a suit of clothes, which was utterly spoiled.

The dwarf was soundly whipt, and as a farther punishment, forced to drink up the bowl of cream into which he had thrown me: neither was he ever restored to favour; for soon after the queen bestowed him on a lady of high quality, so that I saw him no more, to my very great satisfaction; for I could not tell to what extremities such a malicious urchin might have carried his resentment.

He had before served me a scurvy trick, which set the queen a-laughing, although at the same time she was heartily vexed, and would have immediately cashiered him, if I had not been so generous as to intercede. Her Majesty had taken a marrow-bone upon her plate, and, after knocking out the marrow, placed the bone again in the dish erect, as it stood before; the dwarf, watching his opportunity, while Glumdalclitch was gone to the side-board, mounted the stool that she stood on to take care of me at meals, took me up in both hands, and squeezing my legs together, wedged them into the marrow bone above my waist, where I stuck for some time, and made a very ridiculous figure.

I believe it was near a minute before any one knew what was become of me; for I thought it below me to cry out. But, as princes seldom get their meat hot, my legs were not scalded, only my stockings and breeches in a sad condition. The dwarf, at my entreaty, had no other punishment than a sound whipping.

I was frequently rallied by the queen upon account of my fearfulness; and she used to ask me whether the people of my country were as great cowards as myself? The occasion was this: the kingdom is much pestered with flies in summer; and these odious insects, each of them as big as a Dunstable lark, hardly gave me any rest while I sat at dinner, with their continual humming and buzzing about mine ears. They would sometimes alight upon my victuals, and leave their loathsome excrement, or spawn behind, which to me was very visible, though not to the natives of that country, whose large optics were not so acute as mine, in viewing smaller objects. Sometimes they would fix upon my nose, or forehead, where they stung me to the quick, smelling very offensively; and I could easily trace that viscous matter, which, our naturalists tell us, enables those creatures to walk with their feet upwards upon a ceiling.

I had much ado to defend myself against these detestable animals, and could not forbear starting when they came on my face. It was the common practice of the dwarf, to catch a number of these insects in his hand, as schoolboys do among us, and let them out suddenly under my nose, on purpose to frighten me, and divert the queen. My remedy was to cut them in pieces with my knife, as they flew in the air, wherein my dexterity was much admired.

I remember, one morning, when Glumdalclitch had set me in a box upon a window, as she usually did in fair days to give me air (for I durst not venture to let the box be hung on a nail out of the window, as we do with cages in England), after I had lifted up one of my sashes, and sat down at my table to eat a piece of sweet cake for my breakfast, above twenty wasps, allured by the smell, came flying into the room, humming louder than the drones of as many bagpipes.

Some of them seized my cake, and carried it piecemeal away; others flew about my head and face, confounding me with the noise, and putting me in the utmost terror of their stings. However, I had the courage to rise and draw my hanger, and attack them in the air. I dispatched four of them, but the rest got away, and I presently shut my window. These insects were as large as partridges: I took out their stings, found them an inch and a half long, and as sharp as needles. I carefully preserved them all; and having since shown them, with some other curiosities, in several parts of Europe, upon my return to England I gave three of them to Gresham College, and kept the fourth for myself.

CHAPTER IV

The country described. A proposal for correcting
modern maps. The king's palace; and some account of
the metropolis. The author's way of travelling. The chief
temple described.

I now intend to give the reader a short description of this
country, as far as I travelled in it, which was not above two
thousand miles round Lorbrulgrud, the metropolis. For the
queen, whom I always attended, never went farther when she
accompanied the king in his progresses, and there staid till
his Majesty returned from viewing his frontiers. The whole
extent of this prince's dominions reaches about six thousand
miles in length, and from three to five in breadth: whence I
cannot but conclude, that our geographers of Europe are in
a great error, by supposing nothing but sea between Japan
and California; for it was ever my opinion, that there must
be a balance of earth to counterpoise the great continent of
Tartary; and therefore they ought to correct their maps and
charts, by joining this vast tract of land to the north-west
parts of America, wherein I shall be ready to lend them my
assistance.

The kingdom is a peninsula, terminated to the north-
east by a ridge of mountains thirty miles high, which are
altogether impassable, by reason of the volcanoes upon

the tops: neither do the most learned know what sort of mortals inhabit beyond those mountains, or whether they be inhabited at all. On the three other sides, it is bounded by the ocean. There is not one seaport in the whole kingdom: and those parts of the coasts into which the rivers issue, are so full of pointed rocks, and the sea generally so rough, that there is no venturing with the smallest of their boats; so that these people are wholly excluded from any commerce with the rest of the world. But the large rivers are full of vessels, and abound with excellent fish; for they seldom get any from the sea, because the sea fish are of the same size with those in Europe, and consequently not worth catching; whereby it is manifest, that nature, in the production of plants and animals of so extraordinary a bulk, is wholly confined to this continent, of which I leave the reasons to be determined by philosophers. However, now and then they take a whale that happens to be dashed against the rocks, which the common people feed on heartily. These whales I have known so large, that a man could hardly carry one upon his shoulders; and sometimes, for curiosity, they are brought in hampers to Lorbrulgrud; I saw one of them in a dish at the king's table, which passed for a rarity, but I did not observe he was fond of it; for I think, indeed, the bigness disgusted him, although I have seen one somewhat larger in Greenland.

The country is well inhabited, for it contains fifty-one cities, near a hundred walled towns, and a great number of villages. To satisfy my curious reader, it may be sufficient to describe Lorbrulgrud. This city stands upon almost two equal parts, on each side the river that passes through. It contains above eighty thousand houses, and about six hundred thousand inhabitants. It is in length three *glomglungs* (which make about fifty-four English miles,) and two and a half in breadth; as I measured it myself in the royal map made by the king's order, which was laid on the ground on purpose for me, and extended a hundred feet: I paced the diameter and circumference several times barefoot, and, computing by the scale, measured it pretty exactly.

The king's palace is no regular edifice, but a heap of buildings, about seven miles round: the chief rooms are generally two hundred and forty feet high, and broad and long in proportion. A coach was allowed to Glumdalclitch and me, wherein her governess frequently took her out to see the town, or go among the shops; and I was always of the party, carried in my box; although the girl, at my own desire, would often take me out, and hold me in her hand, that I might more conveniently view the houses and the people, as we passed along the streets. I reckoned our coach to be about a square of Westminster-hall, but not altogether so high: however, I cannot be very exact.

One day the governess ordered our coachman to stop at several shops, where the beggars, watching their opportunity, crowded to the sides of the coach, and gave me the most horrible spectacle that ever a European eye beheld. There was a woman with a cancer in her breast, swelled to a monstrous size, full of holes, in two or three of which I could have easily crept, and covered my whole body. There was a fellow with a wen in his neck, larger than five wool-packs; and another, with a couple of wooden legs, each about twenty feet high. But the most hateful sight of all, was the lice crawling on their clothes.

Besides the large box in which I was usually carried, the queen ordered a smaller one to be made for me, of about twelve feet square, and ten high, for the convenience of travelling; because the other was somewhat too large for Glumdalclitch's lap, and cumbersome in the coach; it was made by the same artist, whom I directed in the whole contrivance. This travelling-closet was an exact square, with a window in the middle of three of the squares, and each window was latticed with iron wire on the outside, to prevent accidents in long journeys.

On the fourth side, which had no window, two strong staples were fixed, through which the person that carried me, when I had a mind to be on horseback, put a leathern belt, and buckled it about his waist. This was always the office of some grave trusty servant, in whom I could confide, whether I attended the king and queen in their progresses, or were disposed to see the gardens, or pay a visit to some great lady or minister of state in the court, when Glumdalclitch happened to be out of order; for I soon began to be known and esteemed among the greatest officers, I suppose more upon account of their majesties' favour, than any merit of my own. In journeys, when I was weary of the coach, a servant on horseback would buckle on my box, and place it upon a cushion before him; and there I had a full prospect of the country on three sides, from my three windows.

I had in this closet, a field-bed and a hammock, hung from the ceiling, two chairs and a table, neatly screwed to the floor, to prevent being tossed about by the agitation of the horse or the coach. And having been long used to sea-voyages, those motions, although sometimes very violent, did not much discompose me.

Whenever I had a mind to see the town, it was always in my travelling-closet; which Glumdalclitch held in her lap in a kind of open sedan, after the fashion of the country, borne by four men, and attended by two others in the queen's livery. The people, who had often heard of me, were very curious to crowd about the sedan, and the girl was complaisant enough to make the bearers stop, and to take me in her hand, that I might be more conveniently seen.

I was very desirous to see the chief temple, and particularly the tower belonging to it, which is reckoned the highest in the kingdom. Accordingly one day my nurse carried me thither, but I may truly say I came back disappointed; for the height is not above three thousand feet, reckoning from the ground to the highest pinnacle top; which, allowing for the difference between the size of those people and us in Europe, is no great matter for admiration, nor at all equal in proportion (if I rightly remember) to Salisbury Steeple.

But, not to detract from a nation, to which, during my life, I shall acknowledge myself extremely obliged, it must be allowed, that whatever this famous tower wants in height, is amply made up in beauty and strength: for the walls are near a hundred feet thick, built of hewn stone, whereof each is about forty feet square, and adorned on all sides with statues of gods and emperors, cut in marble, larger than the life, placed in their several niches. I measured a little finger which had fallen down from one of these statues, and lay unperceived among some rubbish, and found it exactly four feet and an inch in length. Glumdalclitch wrapped it up in her handkerchief, and carried it home in her pocket, to keep among other trinkets, of which the girl was very fond, as children at her age usually are.

The king's kitchen is indeed a noble building, vaulted at top, and about six hundred feet high. The great oven is not so wide, by ten paces, as the cupola at St. Paul's: for I measured the latter on purpose, after my return. But if I should describe the kitchen grate, the prodigious pots and kettles, the joints of meat turning on the spits, with many other particulars, perhaps I should be hardly believed; at least a severe critic would be apt to think I enlarged a little, as travellers are often suspected to do. To avoid which censure I fear I have run too much into the other extreme; and that if this treatise should happen to be translated into the language of Brobdingnag (which is the general name of that kingdom,) and transmitted thither, the king and his people would have reason to complain that I had done them an injury, by a false and diminutive representation.

His Majesty seldom keeps above six hundred horses in his stables: they are generally from fifty-four to sixty feet high. But, when he goes abroad on solemn days, he is attended, for state, by a military guard of five hundred horse, which, indeed, I thought was the most splendid sight that could be ever beheld, till I saw part of his army in battalia, whereof I shall find another occasion to speak.

CHAPTER V

Several adventurers that happened to the author. The execution of a criminal. The author shows his skill in navigation.

I should have lived happy enough in that country, if my littleness had not exposed me to several ridiculous and troublesome accidents; some of which I shall venture to relate. Glumdalclitch often carried me into the gardens of the court in my smaller box, and would sometimes take me out of it, and hold me in her hand, or set me down to walk.

I remember, before the dwarf left the queen, he followed us one day into those gardens, and my nurse having set me down, he and I being close together, near some dwarf apple trees, I must needs show my wit, by a silly allusion between him and the trees, which happens to hold in their language as it does in ours. Whereupon, the malicious rogue, watching his opportunity, when I was walking under one of them, shook it directly over my head, by which a dozen apples, each of them near as large as a Bristol barrel, came tumbling about my ears; one of them hit me on the back as I chanced to stoop, and knocked me down flat on my face; but I received no other hurt, and the dwarf was pardoned at my desire, because I had given the provocation.

Another day, Glumdalclitch left me on a smooth grass-plot

to divert myself, while she walked at some distance with her governess. In the meantime, there suddenly fell such a violent shower of hail, that I was immediately by the force of it, struck to the ground: and when I was down, the hailstones gave me such cruel bangs all over the body, as if I had been pelted with tennis-balls; however, I made a shift to creep on all fours, and shelter myself, by lying flat on my face, on the lee-side of a border of lemon-thyme, but so bruised from head to foot, that I could not go abroad in ten days. Neither is this at all to be wondered at, because nature, in that country, observing the same proportion through all her operations, a hailstone is near eighteen hundred times as large as one in Europe; which I can assert upon experience, having been so curious as to weigh and measure them.

But a more dangerous accident happened to me in the same garden, when my little nurse, believing she had put me in a secure place (which I often entreated her to do, that I might enjoy my own thoughts,) and having left my box at home, to avoid the trouble of carrying it, went to another part of the garden with her governess and some ladies of her acquaintance. While she was absent, and out of hearing, a small white spaniel that belonged to one of the chief gardeners, having got by accident into the garden, happened to range near the place where I lay: the dog, following the scent, came directly up, and taking me in his mouth, ran straight to his master wagging his tail, and set me gently on the ground. By good fortune he had been so well taught, that I was carried between his teeth without the least hurt, or even tearing my clothes.

But the poor gardener, who knew me well, and had a great kindness for me, was in a terrible fright: he gently took me up in both his hands, and asked me how I did? but I was so amazed and out of breath, that I could not speak a word. In a few minutes I came to myself, and he carried me safe to my little nurse, who, by this time, had returned to the place where she left me, and was in cruel agonies when I did not appear, nor answer when she called. She severely reprimanded the gardener on account of his dog. But the thing was hushed up, and never known at court, for the girl was afraid of the queen's anger; and truly, as to myself, I thought it would not be for my reputation, that such a story should go about.

This accident absolutely determined Glumdalclitch never to trust me abroad for the future out of her sight. I had been long afraid of this resolution, and therefore concealed from her some little unlucky adventures, that happened in those times when I was left by myself. Once a kite, hovering over the garden, made a stoop at me, and if I had not resolutely drawn my hanger, and run under a thick espalier, he would have certainly carried me away in his talons. Another time, walking to the top of a fresh mole-hill, I fell to my neck in the hole, through which that animal had cast up the earth, and coined some lie, not worth remembering, to excuse myself for spoiling my clothes. I likewise broke my right shin against the shell of a snail, which I happened to stumble over, as I was walking alone and thinking on poor England.

I cannot tell whether I were more pleased or mortified to observe, in those solitary walks, that the smaller birds did not appear to be at all afraid of me, but would hop about within a yard's distance, looking for worms and other food, with as much indifference and security as if no creature at all were near them. I remember, a thrush had the confidence to snatch out of my hand, with his bill, a of cake that Glumdalclitch had just given me for my breakfast. When I attempted to catch any of these birds, they would boldly turn against me, endeavouring to peck my fingers, which I durst not venture within their reach; and then they would hop back unconcerned, to hunt for worms or snails, as they did before.

But one day, I took a thick cudgel, and threw it with all my strength so luckily, at a linnet, that I knocked him down, and seizing him by the neck with both my hands, ran with him in triumph to my nurse. However, the bird, who had only been stunned, recovering himself gave me so many boxes with his wings, on both sides of my head and body, though I held him at arm's-length, and was out of the reach of his claws, that I was twenty times thinking to let him go. But I was soon relieved by one of our servants, who wrung off the bird's neck, and I had him next day for dinner, by the queen's command. This linnet, as near as I can remember, seemed to be somewhat larger than an English swan.

One day, a young gentleman, who was nephew to my nurse's governess, came and pressed them both to see an execution. It was of a man, who had murdered one of that gentleman's intimate acquaintance. Glumdalclitch was prevailed on to be of the company, very much against her inclination, for she was naturally tender-hearted: and, as for myself, although I abhorred such kind of spectacles, yet my curiosity tempted me to see something that I thought must be extraordinary.

The malefactor was fixed in a chair upon a scaffold erected for that purpose, and his head cut off at one blow, with a sword of about forty feet long. The veins and arteries spouted up such a prodigious quantity of blood, and so high in the air, that the great *jet d'eau* at Versailles was not equal to it for the time it lasted: and the head, when it fell on the scaffold floor, gave such a bounce as made me start, although I was at least half an English mile distant.

The queen, who often used to hear me talk of my sea-voyages, and took all occasions to divert me when I was melancholy, asked me whether I understood how to handle a sail or an oar, and whether a little exercise of rowing might not be convenient for my health? I answered, that I understood both very well: for although my proper employment had been to be surgeon or doctor to the ship, yet often, upon a pinch, I was forced to work like a common mariner. But I could not see

how this could be done in their country, where the smallest
wherry was equal to a first-rate man of war among us; and
such a boat as I could manage would never live in any of their
rivers. Her Majesty said, if I would contrive a boat, her own
joiner should make it, and she would provide a place for me
to sail in.

The fellow was an ingenious workman, and by my
instructions, in ten days, finished a pleasure-boat with all its
tackling, able conveniently to hold eight Europeans. When it
was finished, the queen was so delighted, that she ran with it in
her lap to the king, who ordered it to be put into a cistern full of
water, with me in it, by way of trial, where I could not manage
my two sculls, or little oars, for want of room. But the queen
had before contrived another project. She ordered the joiner to
make a wooden trough of three hundred feet long, fifty broad,
and eight deep; which, being well pitched, to prevent leaking,
was placed on the floor, along the wall, in an outer room of
the palace. It had a cock near the bottom to let out the water,
when it began to grow stale; and two servants could easily fill
it in half an hour.

Here I often used to row for my own diversion, as well
as that of the queen and her ladies, who thought themselves
well entertained with my skill and agility. Sometimes I would
put up my sail, and then my business was only to steer, while
the ladies gave me a gale with their fans; and, when they were
weary, some of their pages would blow my sail forward with
their breath, while I showed my art by steering starboard or
larboard as I pleased. When I had done, Glumdalclitch always
carried back my boat into her closet, and hung it on a nail to
dry.

In this exercise I once met an accident, which had like to
have cost me my life; for, one of the pages having put my boat
into the trough, the governess who attended Glumdalclitch
very officiously lifted me up, to place me in the boat: but I

happened to slip through her fingers, and should infallibly have fallen down forty feet upon the floor, if, by the luckiest chance in the world, I had not been stopped by a corking-pin that stuck in the good gentlewoman's stomacher; the head of the pin passing between my shirt and the waistband of my breeches, and thus I was held by the middle in the air, till Glumdalclitch ran to my relief.

Another time, one of the servants, whose office it was to fill my trough every third day with fresh water, was so careless as to let a huge frog (not perceiving it) slip out of his pail. The frog lay concealed till I was put into my boat, but then, seeing a resting-place, climbed up, and made it lean so much on one side, that I was forced to balance it with all my weight on the other, to prevent overturning. When the frog was got in, it hopped at once half the length of the boat, and then over my head, backward and forward, daubing my face and clothes with its odious slime. The largeness of its features made it appear the most deformed animal that can be conceived. However, I desired Glumdalclitch to let me deal with it alone. I banged it a good while with one of my sculls, and at last forced it to leap out of the boat.

But the greatest danger I ever underwent in that kingdom, was from a monkey, who belonged to one of the clerks of the kitchen. Glumdalclitch had locked me up in her closet, while she went somewhere upon business, or a visit. The weather being very warm, the closet-window was left open, as well as the windows and the door of my bigger box, in which I usually lived, because of its largeness and conveniency.

As I sat quietly meditating at my table, I heard something bounce in at the closet-window, and skip about from one side to the other: whereat, although I was much alarmed, yet I ventured to look out, but not stirring from my seat; and then I saw this frolicsome animal frisking and leaping up and down, till at last he came to my box, which he seemed to view with great pleasure and curiosity, peeping in at the door and every window. I retreated to the farther corner of my room; or box; but the monkey looking in at every side, put me in such a fright, that I wanted presence of mind to conceal myself under the bed, as I might easily have done.

After some time spent in peeping, grinning, and chattering, he at last espied me; and reaching one of his paws in at the door, as a cat does when she plays with a mouse, although I often shifted place to avoid him, he at length seized the lappet of my coat (which being made of that country silk, was very thick and strong), and dragged me out. He took me up in his right fore-foot and held me as a nurse does a child she is going to suckle, just as I have seen the same sort of creature do with a kitten in Europe; and when I offered to struggle he squeezed me so hard, that I thought it more prudent to submit. I have good reason to believe, that he took me for a young one of his own species, by his often stroking my face very gently with his other paw.

In these diversions he was interrupted by a noise at the closet door, as if somebody were opening it: whereupon he suddenly leaped up to the window at which he had come in, and thence upon the leads and gutters, walking upon three legs, and holding me in the fourth, till he clambered up to a roof that was next to ours. I heard Glumdalclitch give a shriek at the moment he was carrying me out. The poor girl was almost distracted: that quarter of the palace was all in an uproar; the servants ran for ladders; the monkey was seen by hundreds in the court, sitting upon the ridge of a building, holding me like a baby in one of his forepaws, and feeding me with the other, by cramming into my mouth some victuals he had squeezed out of the bag on one side of his chaps, and patting me when I would not eat; whereat many of the rabble below could not forbear laughing; neither do I think they justly ought to be blamed, for, without question, the sight was ridiculous enough to every body but myself. Some of the people threw up stones, hoping to drive the monkey down; but this was strictly forbidden, or else, very probably, my brains had been dashed out.

The ladders were now applied, and mounted by several men; which the monkey observing, and finding himself almost encompassed, not being able to make speed enough with his three legs, let me drop on a ridge tile, and made his escape. Here I sat for some time, five hundred yards from the ground, expecting every moment to be blown down by the wind, or to fall by my own giddiness, and come tumbling over and over from the ridge to the eaves; but an honest lad, one of my nurse's footmen, climbed up, and putting me into his breeches pocket, brought me down safe.

I was almost choked with the filthy stuff the monkey had crammed down my throat: but my dear little nurse picked it out of my mouth with a small needle, and then I fell a-vomiting, which gave me great relief. Yet I was so weak and bruised in the sides with the squeezes given me by this odious animal, that I was forced to keep my bed a fortnight. The king, queen, and all the court, sent every day to inquire after my health; and her Majesty made me several visits during my sickness. The monkey was killed, and an order made, that no such animal should be kept about the palace.

When I attended the king after my recovery, to return him thanks for his favours, he was pleased to rally me a good deal upon this adventure. He asked me, what my thoughts and speculations were, while I lay in the monkey's paw; how I liked the victuals he gave me; his manner of feeding; and whether the fresh air on the roof had sharpened my stomach. He desired to know, what I would have done upon such an occasion in my own country. I told his Majesty, that in Europe we had no monkeys, except such as were brought for curiosity from other places, and so small, that I could deal with a dozen of them together, if they presumed to attack me.

As for that monstrous animal with whom I was so lately engaged (it was indeed as large as an elephant), if my fears had suffered me to think so far as to make use of my hanger, (looking fiercely, and clapping my hand on the hilt, as I spoke) when he poked his paw into my chamber, perhaps I should have given him such a wound, as would have made him glad to withdraw it with more haste than he put it in. This I delivered in a firm tone, like a person who was jealous lest his courage should be called in question.

However, my speech produced nothing else beside a laud laughter, which all the respect due to his Majesty from those about him could not make them contain. This made me reflect, how vain an attempt it is for a man to endeavour to do himself honour among those who are out of all degree of equality or comparison with him. And yet I have seen the moral of my own behaviour very frequent in England since my return; where a little contemptible varlet, without the least title to birth, person, wit, or common-sense, shall presume to look with importance, and put himself upon a foot with the greatest persons of the kingdom.

I was every day furnishing the court with some ridiculous story: and Glumdalclitch, although she loved me to excess, yet was arch enough to inform the queen, whenever I committed any folly that she thought would be diverting to her Majesty.

The girl, who had been out of order, was carried by her governess to take the air about an hour's distance, or thirty miles from town. They alighted out of the coach near a small foot-path in a field, and Glumdalclitch setting down my travelling box, I went out of it to walk. There was a cow-dung in the path, and I must need try my activity by attempting to leap over it. I took a run, but unfortunately jumped short, and found myself just in the middle up to my knees. I waded through with some difficulty, and one of the footmen wiped me as clean as he could with his handkerchief, for I was filthily bemired;

and my nurse confined me to my box, till we returned home; where the queen was soon informed of what had passed, and the footmen spread it about the court: so that all the mirth for some days was at my expense.

CHAPTER VI

Several contrivances of the author to please the king and
queen. He shows his skill in music. The king inquires into
the state of England, which the author relates to him. The
king's observations thereon.

I used to attend the king's levee once or twice a week, and had
often seen him under the barber's hand, which indeed was
at first very terrible to behold; for the razor was almost twice
as long as an ordinary scythe. His Majesty, according to the
custom of the country, was only shaved twice a-week. I once
prevailed on the barber to give me some of the suds or lather,
out of which I picked forty or fifty of the strongest stumps of
hair. I then took a piece of fine wood, and cut it like the back
of a comb, making several holes in it at equal distances with as
small a needle as I could get from Glumdalclitch. I fixed in the
stumps so artificially, scraping and sloping them with my knife
toward the points, that I made a very tolerable comb; which
was a seasonable supply, my own being so much broken in the
teeth, that it was almost useless: neither did I know any artist
in that country so nice and exact, as would undertake to make
me another.

And this puts me in mind of an amusement, wherein I
spent many of my leisure hours. I desired the queen's woman
to save for me the combings of her Majesty's hair, whereof in

time I got a good quantity; and consulting with my friend the cabinet-maker, who had received general orders to do little jobs for me, I directed him to make two chair-frames, no larger than those I had in my box, and to bore little holes with a fine awl, round those parts where I designed the backs and seats; through these holes I wove the strongest hairs I could pick out, just after the manner of cane chairs in England.

When they were finished, I made a present of them to her Majesty; who kept them in her cabinet, and used to show them for curiosities, as indeed they were the wonder of every one that beheld them.

The queen would have me sit upon one of these chairs, but I absolutely refused to obey her, protesting I would rather die than place a dishonourable part of my body on those precious hairs, that once adorned her Majesty's head. Of these hairs (as I had always a mechanical genius) I likewise made a neat little purse, about five feet long, with her Majesty's name deciphered in gold letters, which I gave to Glumdalclitch, by the queen's consent. To say the truth, it was more for show than use, being not of strength to bear the weight of the larger coins, and therefore she kept nothing in it but some little toys that girls are fond of.

The king, who delighted in music, had frequent concerts at court, to which I was sometimes carried, and set in my box on a table to hear them: but the noise was so great that I could hardly distinguish the tunes. I am confident that all the drums and trumpets of a royal army, beating and sounding together just at your ears, could not equal it. My practice was to have my box removed from the place where the performers sat, as far as I could, then to shut the doors and windows of it, and draw the window curtains; after which I found their music not disagreeable.

I had learned in my youth to play a little upon the spinet. Glumdalclitch kept one in her chamber, and a master attended twice a-week to teach her: I called it a spinet, because it somewhat resembled that instrument, and was played upon in the same manner. A fancy came into my head, that I would entertain the king and queen with an English tune upon this instrument. But this appeared extremely difficult: for the spinet was near sixty feet long, each key being almost a foot wide, so that with my arms extended I could not reach to above five keys, and to press them down required a good smart stroke with my fist, which would be too great a labour, and to no purpose.

The method I contrived was this: I prepared two round sticks, about the bigness of common cudgels; they were thicker at one end than the other, and I covered the thicker ends with pieces of a mouse's skin, that by rapping on them I might neither damage the tops of the keys nor interrupt the sound. Before the spinet a bench was placed, about four feet below the keys, and I was put upon the bench. I ran sideling upon it, that way and this, as fast as I could, banging the proper keys with my two sticks, and made a shift to play a jig, to the great satisfaction of both their majesties; but it was the most violent exercise I ever underwent; and yet I could not strike above sixteen keys, nor consequently play the bass and treble together, as other artists do; which was a great disadvantage to my performance.

The king, who, as I before observed, was a prince of excellent understanding, would frequently order that I should be brought in my box, and set upon the table in his closet: he would then command me to bring one of my chairs out of the box, and sit down within three yards distance upon the top of the cabinet, which brought me almost to a level with his face. In this manner I had several conversations with him. I one day took the freedom to tell his Majesty, that the contempt he discovered towards Europe, and the rest of the world, did not seem answerable to those excellent qualities of mind that he was master of; that reason did not extend itself with the bulk of the body; on the contrary, we observed in our country, that the tallest persons were usually the least provided with it; that among other animals, bees and ants had the reputation of more industry, art, and sagacity, than many of the larger kinds; and that, as inconsiderable as he took me to be, I hoped I might live to do his Majesty some signal service. The king heard me with attention, and began to conceive a much better opinion of me than he had ever before. He desired I would give him as exact an account of the government of England as I possibly could; because, as fond as princes commonly are of their own customs (for so he conjectured of other monarchs, by my former discourses), he should be glad to hear of any thing that might deserve imitation.

Imagine with thyself, courteous reader, how often I then wished for the tongue of Demosthenes or Cicero, that might have enabled me to celebrate the praise of my own dear native country in a style equal to its merits and felicity.

I began my discourse by informing his Majesty, that our dominions consisted of two islands, which composed three mighty kingdoms, under one sovereign, beside our plantations in America. I dwelt long upon the fertility of our soil, and the temperature of our climate. I then spoke at large upon the constitution of an English parliament; partly made up of an illustrious body called the House of Peers; persons of the noblest blood, and of the most ancient and ample patrimonies.

I described that extraordinary care always taken of their education in arts and arms, to qualify them for being counsellors both to the king and kingdom; to have a share in the legislature; to be members of the highest court of judicature, whence there can be no appeal; and to be champions always ready for the defence of their prince and country, by their valour, conduct, and fidelity. That these were the ornament and bulwark of the kingdom, worthy followers of their most renowned ancestors, whose honour had been the reward of their virtue, from which their posterity were never once known to degenerate. To these were joined several holy persons, as part of that assembly, under the title of bishops, whose peculiar business is to take care of religion, and of those who instruct the people therein. These were searched and sought out through the whole nation, by the prince and his wisest counsellors, among such of the priesthood as were most deservedly distinguished by the sanctity of their lives, and the depth of their erudition; who were indeed the spiritual fathers of the clergy and the people.

That the other part of the parliament consisted of an assembly called the House of Commons, who were all principal gentlemen, *freely* picked and culled out by the people themselves, for their great abilities and love of their country, to represent the wisdom of the whole nation. And that these two bodies made up the most august assembly in Europe; to whom, in conjunction with the prince, the whole legislature is committed.

I then descended to the courts of justice; over which the judges, those venerable sages and interpreters of the law, presided, for determining the disputed rights and properties of men, as well as for the punishment of vice and protection of innocence. I mentioned the prudent management of our treasury; the valour and achievements of our forces, by sea and land. I computed the number of our people, by reckoning how many millions there might be of each religious sect, or political party among us. I did not omit even our sports and pastimes, or any other particular which I thought might redound to the honour of my country. And I finished all with a brief historical account of affairs and events in England for about a hundred years past.

This conversation was not ended under five audiences, each of several hours; and the king heard the whole with great attention, frequently taking notes of what I spoke, as well as memorandums of what questions he intended to ask me.

When I had put an end to these long discources, his Majesty, in a sixth audience, consulting his notes, proposed many doubts, queries, and objections, upon every article. He asked, What methods were used to cultivate the minds and bodies of our young nobility, and in what kind of business they commonly spent the first and teachable parts of their lives? What course was taken to supply that assembly, when any noble family became extinct? What qualifications were necessary in those who are to be created new lords: whether the humour of the prince, a sum of money to a court lady, or a design of strengthening a party opposite to the public interest, ever happened to be the motive in those advancements? What share of knowledge these lords had in the laws of their country, and how they came by it, so as to enable them to decide the properties of their fellow-subjects in the last resort? Whether they were always so free from avarice, partialities, or want, that a bribe, or some other sinister view, could have no place among them? Whether those holy lords I spoke of were always promoted to that rank upon account of their knowledge in religious matters, and the sanctity of their lives; had never been compliers with the times, while they were common priests; or slavish prostitute chaplains to some nobleman, whose opinions they continued servilely to follow, after they were admitted into that assembly.

He then desired to know What arts were practised in electing those whom I called commoners: whether a stranger, with a strong purse, might not influence the vulgar voters to choose him before their own landlord, or the most considerable gentleman in the neighbourhood? How it came to pass, that people were so violently bent upon getting into this assembly, which I allowed to be a great trouble and expense, often to the ruin of their families, without any salary or pension? because this appeared such an exalted strain of virtue and public spirit, that his Majesty seemed to doubt it might possibly not be always sincere: And he desired to know, Whether such zealous gentlemen could have any views of refunding themselves for the charges and trouble they were at by sacrificing the public good to the designs of a weak and vicious prince, in conjunction with a corrupted ministry. He multiplied his questions, and sifted me thoroughly upon every part of this head, proposing numberless inquiries and objections, which I think it not prudent or convenient to repeat.

Upon what I said in relation to our courts of justice, his Majesty desired to be satisfied in several points: and this I was the better able to do, having been formerly almost ruined by a long suit in chancery, which was decreed for me with costs. He asked, What time was usually spent in determining between right and wrong, and what degree of expense? Whether advocates and orators had liberty to plead in causes manifestly known to be unjust, vexatious, or oppressive? Whether party, in religion or politics, were observed to be of any weight in the scale of justice? Whether those pleading orators were persons educated in the general knowledge of equity, or only in provincial, national, and other local customs? Whether they or their judges had any part in penning those laws, which they assumed the liberty of interpreting, and glossing upon at their pleasure? Whether they had ever, at different times, pleaded for and against the same cause, and cited precedents to prove contrary opinions? Whether they were a rich or a poor corporation? Whether they received any pecuniary reward for pleading, or delivering their opinions? And particularly, whether they were ever admitted as members in the lower senate?

He fell next upon the management of our treasury; and said, he thought my memory had failed me, because I computed our taxes at about five or six millions a-year, and when I came to mention the issues, he found they sometimes amounted to more than double; for the notes he had taken were very particular in this point, because he hoped, as he told me, that the knowledge of our conduct might be useful to him, and he could not be deceived in his calculations. But, if what I told him were true, he was still at a loss how a kingdom could run out of its estate, like a private person. He asked me, who were our creditors, and where we found money to pay them. He wondered to hear me talk of such chargeable and expensive wars; that certainly we must be a quarrelsome people, or live among very bad neighbours, and that our generals must needs be richer than our kings. He asked, what business we had out of our own islands, unless upon the score of trade, or treaty, or to defend the coasts with our fleet? Above all, he was amazed to hear me talk of a mercenary standing army, in the midst of peace, and among a free people.

He said, if we were governed by our own consent, in the persons of our representatives, he could not imagine of whom we were afraid, or against whom we were to fight; and would hear my opinion, whether a private man's house might not be better defended by himself, his children, and family, than by half-a-dozen rascals, picked up at a venture in the streets for small wages, who might get a hundred times more by cutting their throats.

He laughed at my odd kind of arithmetic, as he was pleased to call it, in reckoning the numbers of our people, by a computation drawn from the several sects among us, in religion and politics. He said, he knew no reason why those, who entertain opinions prejudicial to the public, should be obliged to change, or should not be obliged to conceal them. And as it was tyranny in any government to require the first, so it was weakness not to enforce the second: for a man may be allowed to keep poisons in his closet, but not to vend them about for cordials.

He observed that among the diversions of our nobility and

gentry, I had mentioned gaming: he desired to know at what age this entertainment was usually taken up, and when it was laid down; how much of their time it employed; whether it ever went so high as to affect their fortunes; whether mean, vicious people, by their dexterity in that art, might not arrive at great riches, and sometimes keep our very nobles in dependence, as well as habituate them to vile companions, wholly take them from the improvement of their minds, and force them, by the losses they received, to learn and practise that infamous dexterity upon others.

He was perfectly astonished with the historical account gave him of our affairs during the last century; protesting it was only a heap of conspiracies, rebellions, murders, massacres, revolutions, banishments, the very worst effects that avarice, faction, hypocrisy, perfidiousness, cruelty, rage, madness, hatred, envy, lust, malice, and ambition, could produce.

His Majesty, in another audience, was at the pains to recapitulate the sum of all I had spoken; compared the questions he made with the answers I had given; then taking me into his hands, and stroking me gently, delivered himself in these words, which I shall never forget, nor the manner he spoke them in: My little friend Grildrig, you have made a most admirable panegyric upon your country; you have clearly proved, that ignorance, idleness, and vice, are the proper ingredients for qualifying a legislator; that laws are best explained, interpreted, and applied, by those whose interest and abilities lie in perverting, confounding, and eluding them. I observe among you some lines of an institution, which, in its original, might have been tolerable, but these half erased, and the rest wholly blurred and blotted by corruptions. It does not appear, from all you have said, how any one perfection is required toward the procurement of any one station among you; much less, that men are ennobled on account of their virtue; that priests are advanced for their piety or learning;

soldiers, for their conduct or valour; judges, for their integrity; senators, for the love of their country; or counsellors for their wisdom.

"As for yourself, continued the king, who have spent the greatest part of your life in travelling, I am well disposed to hope you may hitherto have escaped many vices of your country. But by what I have gathered from your own relation, and the answers I have with much pains wrung and extorted from you, I cannot but conclude the bulk of your natives to be the most pernicious race of little odious vermin that nature ever suffered to crawl upon the surface of the earth."

CHAPTER VII

The author's love of his country. He makes a proposal of much advantage to the king, which is rejected. The king's great ignorance in politics. The learning of that country very imperfect and confined. The laws, and military affairs, and parties in the state.

Nothing but an extreme love of truth could have hindered me from concealing this part of my story. It was in vain to discover my resentments, which were always turned into ridicule; and I was forced to rest with patience, while my noble and beloved country was so injuriously treated. I am as heartily sorry as any of my readers can possibly be, that such an occasion was given: but this prince happened to be so curious and inquisitive upon every particular, that it could not consist either with gratitude or good manners, to refuse giving him what satisfaction I was able.

Yet thus much I may be allowed to say in my own vindication, that I artfully eluded many of his questions, and gave to every point a more favourable turn, by many degrees, than the strictness of truth would allow. For I have always borne that laudable partiality to my own country, which Dionysius Halicarnassensis, with so much justice, recommends to an historian: I would hide the frailties and deformities of my political mother, and place her virtues and beauties in the most advantageous light. This was my sincere endeavour in those many discourses I had with that monarch, although it unfortunately failed of success.

But great allowances should be given to a king, who lives wholly secluded from the rest of the world, and must therefore be altogether unacquainted with the manners and customs that most prevail in other nations: the want of which knowledge will ever produce many prejudices, and a certain narrowness of thinking, from which we, and the politer countries of Europe, are wholly exempted. And it would be hard indeed, if so remote a prince's notions of virtue and vice were to be offered as a standard for all mankind.

To confirm what I have now said, and further to show the miserable effects of a confined education, I shall here insert a passage, which will hardly obtain belief. In hopes to ingratiate myself further into his Majesty's favour, I told him of an invention, discovered between three and four hundred years ago, to make a certain powder, into a heap of which, the smallest spark of fire falling, would kindle the whole in a moment, although it were as big as a mountain, and make it all fly up in the air together, with a noise and agitation greater than thunder.

That a proper quantity of this powder rammed into a hollow tube of brass or iron, according to its bigness, would drive a ball of iron or lead, with such violence and speed, as nothing was able to sustain its force. That the largest balls thus discharged, would not only destroy whole ranks of an army at once, but batter the strongest walls to the ground, sink down ships, with a thousand men in each, to the bottom of the sea, and when linked together by a chain, would cut through masts and rigging, divide hundreds of bodies in the middle, and lay all waste before them. That we often put this powder into large hollow balls of iron, and discharged them by an engine into some city we were besieging, which would rip up the pavements, tear the houses to pieces, burst and throw splinters on every side, dashing out the brains of all who came near. That I knew the ingredients very well, which were cheap and common; I understood the manner of compounding them, and could direct his workmen how to make those tubes, of a size proportionable to all other things in his Majesty's kingdom, and the largest need not be above a hundred feet long; twenty or thirty of which tubes, charged with the proper quantity of powder and balls, would batter down the walls of the strongest town in his dominions in a few hours, or destroy the whole metropolis, if ever it should pretend to dispute his absolute commands. This I humbly offered to his Majesty, as a small tribute of acknowledgment, in turn for so many marks that I had received, of his royal favour and protection.

The king was struck with horror at the description I had given of those terrible engines, and the proposal I had made. He was amazed, how so impotent and grovelling an insect as I (these were his expressions) could entertain such inhuman ideas, and in so familiar a manner, as to appear wholly unmoved at all the scenes of blood and desolation which I had painted as the common effects of those destructive machines; whereof, he said, some evil genius, enemy to mankind, must have been the first contriver. As for himself, he protested, that although few things delighted him so much as new discoveries in art or in nature, yet he would rather lose half his kingdom, than be privy to such a secret; which he commanded me, as I valued any life, never to mention any more.

A strange effect of narrow principles and views! that a prince possessed of every quality which procures veneration, love, and esteem; of strong parts, great wisdom, and profound learning, endowed with admirable talents, and almost adored by his subjects, should, from a nice, unnecessary scruple, whereof in Europe we can have no conception, let slip an opportunity put into his hands that would have made him absolute master of the lives, the liberties, and the fortunes of his people.

Neither do I say this, with the least intention to detract from the many virtues of that excellent king, whose character, I am sensible, will, on this account, be very much lessened in the opinion of an English reader: but I take this defect among them to have risen from their ignorance, by not having hitherto reduced politics into a science, as the more acute wits of Europe have done. For, I remember very well, in a discourse one day with the king, when I happened to say, there were several thousand books among us written upon the art of government, it gave him (directly contrary to my intention) a very mean opinion of our understandings. He professed both to abominate and despise all mystery, refinement, and intrigue, either in a prince or a minister.

He could not tell what I meant by secrets of state, where an enemy, or some rival nation, were not in the case. He confined the knowledge of governing within very narrow bounds, to common sense and reason, to justice and lenity, to the speedy determination of civil and criminal causes; with some other obvious topics, which are not worth considering. And he gave it for his opinion, that whoever could make two ears of corn, or two blades of grass, to grow upon a spot of ground where only one grew before, would deserve better of mankind, and do more essential service to his country, than the whole race of politicians put together.

The learning of this people is very defective, consisting only in morality, history, poetry, and mathematics, wherein they must be allowed to excel. But the last of these is wholly applied to what may be useful in life, to the improvement of agriculture, and all mechanical arts; so that among us, it would be little esteemed. And as to ideas, entities, abstractions, and transcendentals, I could never drive the least conception into their heads.

No law in that country must exceed in words the number of letters in their alphabet, which consists only of two and twenty. But indeed few of them extend even to that length. They are expressed in the most plain and simple terms, wherein those people are not mercurial enough to discover above one interpretation: and to write a comment upon any law, is a capital crime. As to the decision of civil causes, or proceedings against criminals, their precedents are so few, that they have little reason to boast of any extraordinary skill in either.

They have had the art of printing, as well as the Chinese, time out of mind: but their libraries are not very large; for that of the king, which is reckoned the largest, does not amount to above a thousand volumes, placed in a gallery of twelve hundred feet long, whence I had liberty to borrow what books I pleased. The queen's joiner had contrived in one of Glumdalclitch's rooms, a kind of wooden machine five-and-twenty feet high, formed like a standing ladder; the steps were each fifty feet long. It was indeed a moveable pair of stairs, the lowest end placed at ten feet distance from the wall of the chamber.

The book I had a mind to read, was put up leaning against the wall: I first mounted to the upper step of the ladder, and turning my face towards the book, began at the top of the page, and so walking to the right and left about eight or ten paces, according to the length of the lines, till I had gotten a little below the level of mine eyes, and then descending gradually till I came to the bottom: after which I mounted again, and began the other page in the same manner, and so turned over the leaf, which I could easily do with both my hands, for it was as thick and stiff as a pasteboard, and in the largest folios not above eighteen or twenty feet long.

Their style is clear, masculine, and smooth, but not florid; for they avoid nothing more than multiplying unnecessary words, or using various expressions. I have perused many of their books, especially those in history and morality. Among the rest, I was much diverted with a little old treatise, which always lay in Glumdalclitch's bed chamber, and belonged to her governess, a grave elderly gentlewoman, who dealt in writings of morality and devotion. The book treats of the weakness of human kind, and is in little esteem, except among the women and the vulgar.

However, I was curious to see what an author of that country could say upon such a subject. This writer went through all the usual topics of European moralists, showing how diminutive, contemptible, and helpless an animal was man in his own nature; how unable to defend himself from inclemencies of the air, or the fury of wild beasts: how much he was excelled by one creature in strength, by another in speed, by a third in foresight, by a fourth in industry. He added, that nature was degenerated in these latter declining ages of the world, and could now produce only small abortive births, in comparison of those in ancient times. He said it was very reasonable to think, not only that the species of men were originally much larger, but also that there must have been giants in former ages; which, as it is asserted by history and tradition, so it has been confirmed by huge bones and skulls, casually dug up in several parts of the kingdom, far exceeding the common dwindled race of men in our days.

He argued, that the very laws of nature absolutely required we should have been made, in the beginning of a size more large and robust; not so liable to destruction from every little accident, of a tile falling from a house, or a stone cast from the hand of a boy, or being drowned in a little brook. From this way of reasoning, the author drew several moral applications, useful in the conduct of life, but needless here to repeat. For my own part, I could not avoid reflecting how universally this talent was spread, of drawing lectures in morality, or indeed rather matter of discontent and repining, from the quarrels we raise with nature. And I believe, upon a strict inquiry, those quarrels might be shown as ill-grounded among us as they are among that people.

As to their military affairs, they boast that the king's army consists of a hundred and seventy-six thousand foot, and thirty-two thousand horse: if that may be called an army, which is made up of tradesmen in the several cities, and farmers in the country, whose commanders are only the nobility and gentry, without pay or reward. They are indeed perfect enough in their exercises, and under very good discipline, wherein I saw no great merit; for how should it be otherwise, where every farmer is under the command of his own landlord, and every citizen under that of the principal men in his own city, chosen after the manner of Venice, by ballot!

I have often seen the militia of Lorbrulgrud drawn out to exercise, in a great field near the city of twenty miles square. They were in all not above twenty-five thousand foot, and six thousand horse; but it was impossible for me to compute their number, considering the space of ground they took up. A cavalier, mounted on a large steed, might be about ninety feet high. I have seen this whole body of horse, upon a word of command, draw their swords at once, and brandish them in the air. Imagination can figure nothing so grand, so surprising, and so astonishing! it looked as if ten thousand flashes of lightning were darting at the same time from every quarter of the sky.

I was curious to know how this prince, to whose dominions there is no access from any other country, came to think of armies, or to teach his people the practice of military discipline. But I was soon informed, both by conversation and reading their histories; for, in the course of many ages, they have been troubled with the same disease to which the whole race of mankind is subject; the nobility often contending for power, the people for liberty, and the king for absolute dominion. All which, however happily tempered by the laws of that kingdom,

have been sometimes violated by each of the three parties, and
have more than once occasioned civil wars; the last whereof
was happily put an end to by this prince's grand-father, in a
general composition; and the militia, then settled with common
consent, has been ever since kept in the strictest duty.

CHAPTER VIII

The king and queen make a progress to the frontiers. The author attends them. The manner in which he leaves the country very particularly related. He returns to England.

I had always a strong impulse that I should some time recover my liberty, though it was impossible to conjecture by what means, or to form any project with the least hope of succeeding. The ship in which I sailed, was the first ever known to be driven within sight of that coast, and the king had given strict orders, that if at any time another appeared, it should be taken ashore, and with all its crew and passengers brought in a tumbril to Lorbrulgrud. He was strongly bent to get me a woman of my own size, by whom I might propagate the breed: but I think I should rather have died than undergone the disgrace of leaving a posterity to be kept in cages, like tame canary-birds, and perhaps, in time, sold about the kingdom, to persons of quality, for curiosities. I was indeed treated with much kindness: I was the favourite of a great king and queen, and the delight of the whole court; but it was upon such a foot as ill became the dignity of humankind. I could never forget those domestic pledges I had left behind me. I wanted to be among people, with whom I could converse upon even terms, and walk about the streets and fields without being afraid of being trod to death like a frog or a young puppy. But my deliverance came sooner than I expected, and in a manner not very common; the whole story and circumstances of which I shall faithfully relate.

I had now been two years in this country; and about the beginning of the third, Glumdalclitch and I attended the king and queen, in a progress to the south coast of the kingdom. I was carried, as usual, in my travelling-box, which as I have already described, was a very convenient closet, of twelve feet wide. And I had ordered a hammock to be fixed, by silken ropes from the four corners at the top, to break the jolts, when a servant carried me before him on horseback, as I sometimes desired; and would often sleep in my hammock, while we were upon the road. On the roof of my closet, not directly over the middle of the hammock, I ordered the joiner to cut out a hole of a foot square, to give me air in hot weather, as I slept; which hole I shut at pleasure with a board that drew backward and forward through a groove.

When we came to our journey's end, the king thought proper to pass a few days at a palace he has near Flanflasnic, a city within eighteen English miles of the seaside. Glumdalclitch and I were much fatigued: I had gotten a small cold, but the poor girl was so ill as to be confined to her chamber. I longed to see the ocean, which must be the only scene of my escape, if ever it should happen. I pretended to be worse than I really was, and desired leave to take the fresh air of the sea, with a page, whom I was very fond of, and who had sometimes been trusted with me.

I shall never forget with what unwillingness Glumdalclitch consented, nor the strict charge she gave the page to be careful of me, bursting at the same time into a flood of tears, as if she had some foreboding of what was to happen. The boy took me out in my box, about half an hours walk from the palace, towards the rocks on the sea-shore. I ordered him to set me down, and lifting up one of my sashes, cast many a wistful melancholy look towards the sea. I found myself not very well, and told the page that I had a mind to take a nap in my hammock, which I hoped would do me good. I got in, and the boy shut the window close down, to keep out the cold.

I soon fell asleep, and all I can conjecture is, while I slept, the page, thinking no danger could happen, went among the rocks to look for birds' eggs, having before observed him from my window searching about, and picking up one or two in the clefts. Be that as it will, I found myself suddenly awaked with a violent pull upon the ring, which was fastened at the top of my box for the conveniency of carriage. I felt my box raised very high in the air, and then borne forward with prodigious speed. The first jolt had like to have shaken me out of my hammock, but afterward the motion was easy enough. I called out several times, as loud as I could raise my voice, but all to no purpose. I looked towards my windows, and could see nothing but the clouds and sky.

I heard a noise just over my head, like the clapping of wings, and then began to perceive the woful condition I was in; that some eagle had got the ring of my box in his beak, with an intent to let it fall on a rock, like a tortoise in a shell, and then pick out my body, and devour it: for the sagacity and smell of this bird enables him to discover his quarry at a great distance, though better concealed than I could be within a two-inch board.

In a little time, I observed the noise and flutter of wings to increase very fast, and my box was tossed up and down, like a sign in a windy day. I heard several bangs or buffets, as I thought given to the eagle (for such I am certain it must have been that held the ring of my box in his beak), and then, all on a sudden, felt myself falling perpendicularly down, for above a minute, but with such incredible swiftness, that I almost lost my breath. My fall was stopped by a terrible squash, that sounded louder to my ears than the cataract of Niagara; after which, I was quite in the dark for another minute, and then my box began to rise so high, that I could see light from the tops of the windows. I now perceived I was fallen into the sea.

My box, by the weight of my body, the goods that were in, and the broad plates of iron fixed for strength at the four corners of the top and bottom, floated about five feet deep in water. I did then, and do now suppose, that the eagle which flew away with my box was pursued by two or three others, and forced to let me drop, while he defended himself against the rest, who hoped to share in the prey. The plates of iron fastened at the bottom of the box (for those were the strongest) preserved the balance while it fell, and hindered it from being broken on the surface of the water. Every joint of it was well grooved; and the door did not move on hinges, but up and down like a sash, which kept my closet so tight that very little water came in. I got with much difficulty out of my hammock, having first ventured to draw back the slip-board on the roof already mentioned, contrived on purpose to let in air, for want of which I found myself almost stifled.

How often did I then wish myself with my dear Glumdalclitch, from whom one single hour had so far divided me! And I may say with truth, that in the midst of my own misfortunes I could not forbear lamenting my poor nurse, the grief she would suffer for my loss, the displeasure of the queen, and the ruin of her fortune. Perhaps many travellers have not been under greater difficulties and distress than I was at this juncture, expecting every moment to see my box dashed to pieces, or at least overset by the first violent blast, or rising wave. A breach in one single pane of glass would have been immediate death: nor could any thing have preserved the windows, but the strong lattice wires placed on the outside, against accidents in travelling.

I saw the water ooze in at several crannies, although the leaks were not considerable, and I endeavoured to stop them as well as I could. I was not able to lift up the roof of my closet, which otherwise I certainly should have done, and sat on the top of it; where I might at least preserve myself some hours longer, than by being shut up (as I may call it) in the hold. Or if I escaped these dangers for a day or two, what could I expect but a miserable death of cold and hunger? I was four hours under these circumstances, expecting, and indeed wishing, every moment to be my last.

I have already told the reader that there were two strong staples fixed upon that side of my box which had no window, and into which the servant, who used to carry me on horseback, would put a leathern belt, and buckle it about his waist. Being in this disconsolate state, I heard, or at least thought I heard, some kind of grating noise on that side of my box where the staples were fixed; and soon after I began to fancy that the box was pulled or towed along the sea; for I now and then felt a sort of tugging, which made the waves rise near the tops of my windows, leaving me almost in the dark. This gave me some faint hopes of relief, although I was not able to imagine how it could be brought about.

I ventured to unscrew one of my chairs, which were always fastened to the floor; and having made a hard shift to screw it down again, directly under the slipping-board that I had lately opened, I mounted on the chair, and putting my mouth as near as I could to the hole, I called for help in a loud voice, and in all the languages I understood. I then fastened my handkerchief to a stick I usually carried, and thrusting it up the hole, waved it several times in the air, that if any boat or ship were near, the seamen might conjecture some unhappy mortal to be shut up in the box.

I found no effect from all I could do, but plainly perceived my closet to be moved along; and in the space of an hour, or better, that side of the box where the staples were, and had no windows, struck against something that was hard. I apprehended it to be a rock, and found myself tossed more than ever. I plainly heard a noise upon the cover of my closet, like that of a cable, and the grating of it as it passed through the ring. I then found myself hoisted up, by degrees, at least three feet higher than I was before. Whereupon I again thrust up my stick and handkerchief, calling for help till I was almost hoarse. In return to which, I heard a great shout repeated three times, giving me such transports of joy as are not to be conceived but by those who feel them.

I now heard a trampling over my head, and somebody calling through the hole with a loud voice, in the English tongue, If there be any body below, let them speak. I answered, I was an Englishman, drawn by ill fortune into the greatest calamity that ever any creature underwent, and begged, by all that was moving, to be delivered out of the dungeon I was in. The voice replied, I was safe, for my box was fastened to their ship; and the carpenter should immediately come and saw a hole in the cover, large enough to pull me out. I answered, that was needless, and would take up too much time; for there was no more to be done, but let one of the crew put his finger into the ring, and take the box out of the sea into the ship, and so into the captain's cabin.

Some of them, upon hearing me talk so wildly, thought I was mad: others laughed; for indeed it never came into my head, that I was now got among people of my own stature and strength. The carpenter came, and in a few minutes sawed a passage about four feet square, then let down a small ladder, upon which I mounted, and thence was taken into the ship in a very weak condition.

The sailors were all in amazement, and asked me a thousand questions, which I had no inclination to answer. I was equally confounded at the sight of so many pigmies, for such I took them to be, after having so long accustomed mine eyes to the monstrous objects I had left. But the captain, Mr. Thomas

Wilcocks, an honest worthy Shropshire man, observing I was ready to faint, took me into his cabin, gave me a cordial to comfort me, and made me turn in upon his own bed, advising me to take a little rest, of which I had great need.

Before I went to sleep, I gave him to understand that I had some valuable furniture in my box, too good to be lost: a fine hammock, a handsome field-bed, two chairs, a table, and a cabinet; that my closet was hung on all sides, or rather quilted, with silk and cotton; that if he would let one of the crew bring my closet into his cabin, I would open it there before him, and show him my goods. The captain, hearing me utter these absurdities, concluded I was raving; however (I suppose to pacify me) he promised to give order as I desired, and going upon deck, sent some of his men down into my closet, whence (as I afterwards found) they drew up all my goods, and stripped off the quilting; but the chairs, cabinet, and bedstead, being screwed to the floor, were much damaged by the ignorance of the seamen, who tore them up by force.

Then they knocked off some of the boards for the use of the ship, and when they had got all they had a mind for, let the hull drop into the sea, which by reason of many breaches made in the bottom and sides, sunk to rights. And, indeed, I was glad not to have been a spectator of the havoc they made, because I am confident it would have sensibly touched me, by bringing former passages into my mind, which I would rather have forgot.

I slept some hours, but perpetually disturbed with dreams of the place I had left, and the dangers I had escaped. However, upon waking, I found myself much recovered. It was now about eight o'clock at night, and the captain ordered supper immediately, thinking I had already fasted too long. He entertained me with great kindness, observing me not to look wildly, or talk inconsistently: and, when we were left alone, desired I would give him a relation of my travels, and by what accident I came to be set adrift, in that monstrous wooden chest.

He said that about twelve o'clock at noon, as he was looking through his glass, he spied it at a distance, and thought it was a sail, which he had a mind to make, being not much out of his course, in hopes of buying some biscuit, his own beginning to fall short. That upon coming nearer, and finding his error, he sent out his long-boat to discover what it was; that his men came back in a fright, swearing they had seen a swimming house. That he laughed at their folly, and went himself in the boat, ordering his men to take a strong cable along with them. That the weather being calm, he rowed round me several times, observed my windows and wire lattices that defended them. That he discovered two staples upon one side, which was all of boards, without any passage for light. He then commanded his men to row up to that side, and fastening a cable to one of the staples, ordered them to tow my chest, as they called it, toward the ship.

When it was there, he gave directions to fasten another cable to the ring fixed in the cover, and to raise up my chest with pulleys, which all the sailors were not able to do above two or three feet. He said, they saw my stick and handkerchief thrust out of the hole, and concluded that some unhappy man must be shut up in the cavity. I asked, whether he or the crew had seen any prodigious birds in the air, about the time he first discovered me. To which he answered, that discoursing this matter with the sailors while I was asleep, one of them said, he had observed three eagles flying towards the north, but remarked nothing of their being larger than the usual size: which I suppose must be imputed to the great height they were at; and he could not guess the reason of my question.

I then asked the captain, how far he reckoned we might be from land? He said, by the best computation he could make, we were at least a hundred leagues. I assured him, that he must be mistaken by almost half, for I had not left the country whence I came above two hours before I dropped into the sea. Whereupon he began again to think that my brain was disturbed, of which he gave me a hint, and advised me to go to bed in a cabin he had provided. I assured him, I was well refreshed with his good entertainment and company, and as much in my senses as ever I was in my life.

He then grew serious, and desired to ask me freely whether I were not troubled in my mind by the consciousness of some enormous crime, for which I was punished, at the command of some prince, by exposing me in that chest; as great criminals, in other countries, have been forced to sea in a leaky vessel, without provisions: for although he should be sorry to have taken so ill a man into his ship, yet he would engage his word to set me safe ashore, in the first port where we arrived. He added, that his suspicions were much increased by some very absurd speeches I had delivered at first to his sailors, and afterwards to himself, in relation to my closet or chest, as well as by my odd looks and behaviour while I was at supper.

I begged his patience to hear me tell my story, which I faithfully did, from the last time I left England, to the moment he first discovered me. And, as truth always forces its way into rational minds, so this honest worthy gentleman, who had some tincture of learning, and very good sense, was immediately convinced of my candour and veracity. But further to confirm all I had said, I entreated him to give order that my cabinet should be brought, of which I had the key in my pocket (for he had already informed me how the seamen disposed of my closet).

I opened it in his own presence, and showed him the small collection of rarities I made in the country from which I had been so strangely delivered. There was the comb I had contrived out of the stumps of the king's beard, and another of the same materials, but fixed into a paring of her Majesty's thumb-nail, which served for the back. There was a collection of needles and pins, from a foot to half a yard long; four wasp stings, like joiner's tacks; some combings of the queen's hair; a gold ring, which one day she made me a present of, in a most obliging manner, taking it from her little finger, and throwing it over my head like a collar. I desired the captain would please to accept this ring in return for his civilities; which he absolutely refused. I showed him a corn that I had cut off with my own hand, from a maid of honour's toe; it was about the bigness of Kentish pippin, and grown so hard, that when I returned England, I got it hollowed into a cup, and set in silver. Lastly, I desired him to see the breeches I had then on, which were made of a mouse's skin.

I could force nothing on him but a footman's tooth, which I observed him to examine with great curiosity, and found he had a fancy for it. He received it with abundance of thanks, more than such a trifle could deserve. It was drawn by an unskilful surgeon, in a mistake, from one of Glumdalclitch's men, who was afflicted with the tooth-ache, but it was as sound as any in his head. I got it cleaned, and put it into my cabinet. It was about a foot long, and four inches in diameter.

The captain was very well satisfied with this plain relation I had given him, and said, he hoped, when we returned to England, I would oblige the world by putting it on paper, and making it public. My answer was, that I thought we were already overstocked with books of travels: that nothing could now pass which was not extraordinary; wherein I doubted some authors less consulted truth, than their own vanity, or interest, or the diversion of ignorant readers; that my story could contain little beside common events, without those ornamental descriptions of strange plants, trees, birds, and other animals; or of the barbarous customs and idolatry of savage people, with which most writers abound. However, I thanked him for his good opinion, and promised to take the matter into my thoughts.

He said he wondered at one thing very much, which was, to hear me speak so loud; asking me whether the king or queen of that country were thick of hearing, I told him, it was what I had been used to for above two years past, and that I admired as much at the voices of him and his men, who seemed to me only to whisper, and yet I could hear them well enough. But, when I spoke in that country, it was like a man talking in the streets, to another looking out from the top of a steeple, unless when I was placed on a table, or held in any person's hand.

I told him I had likewise observed another thing, that, when I first got into the ship, and the sailors stood all about me, I thought they were the most little contemptible creatures I had ever beheld. For indeed, while I was in that prince's country, I could never endure to look in a glass, after mine eyes had been accustomed to such prodigious objects, because the comparison gave me so despicable a conceit of myself. The captain said, that while we were at supper, he observed me to look at every thing with a sort of wonder, and that I often seemed hardly able to contain my laughter, which he knew not well how to take, but imputed it to some disorder in my brain.

I answered it was very true; and I wondered how I could forbear, when I saw his dishes of the size of a silver three-pence, a leg of pork hardly a mouthful, a cup not so big as a nut-shell; and so I went on, describing the rest of his household-stuff and provisions, after the same manner. For, although he queen had ordered a little equipage of all things necessary for me, while I was in her service, yet my ideas were wholly taken up with what I saw on every side of me, and I winked at my own littleness, as people do at their own faults.

The captain understood my raillery very well, and merrily replied with the old English proverb, that he doubted mine eyes were bigger than my belly, for he did not observe my stomach so good, although I had fasted all day; and, continuing in his mirth, protested he would have gladly given a hundred pounds, to have seen my closet in the eagle's bill, and afterwards in its fall from so great a height into the sea; which would certainly have been a most astonishing object, worthy to have the description of it transmitted to future ages: and the comparison of Phaëton was so obvious, that he could not forbear applying it, although I did not much admire the conceit.

The captain having been at Tonquin, was, in his return to England, driven north-eastward to the latitude of 44 degrees, and longitude of 143. But meeting a trade-wind two days after I came on board him, we sailed southward a long time, and coasting New Holland, kept our course west-south-west, and then south-south-west, till we doubled the Cape of Good Hope. Our voyage was very prosperous, but I shall not trouble the reader with a journal of it. The captain called in at one or two ports, and sent in his long-boat for provisions and fresh water; but I never went out of the ship till we came into the Downs, which was on the third day of June, 1706, about nine months after my escape.

I offered to leave my goods in security for payment of my freight: but the captain protested he would not receive one farthing. We took a kind leave of each other, and I made him promise he would come to see me at my house in Redriff. I hired a horse and guide for five shillings, which I borrowed of the captain.

As I was on the road, observing the littleness of the houses, the trees, the cattle, and the people, I began to think myself in Lilliput. I was afraid of trampling on every traveller I met, and often called aloud to have them stand out of the way, so that I had like to have gotten one or two broken heads for my impertinence.

When I came to my own house, for which I was forced to inquire, one of the servants opening the door, I bent down to go in, (like a goose under a gate,) for fear of striking my head.

My wife run out to embrace me, but I stooped lower than her knees, thinking she could otherwise never be able to reach my mouth. My daughter kneeled to ask my blessing, but I could not see her till she arose, having been so long used to stand with my head and eyes erect to above sixty feet; and then I went to take her up with one hand by the waist.

I looked down upon the servants, and one or two friends who were in the house, as if they had been pigmies and I a giant. I told my wife, she had been too thrifty, for I found she had starved herself and her daughter to nothing. In short, I behaved myself so unaccountably, that they were all of the captain's opinion when he first saw me, and concluded I had lost my wits. This I mention as an instance of the great power of habit and prejudice.

In a little time, I and my family and friends came to a right understanding: but my wife protested I should never go to sea any more; although my evil destiny so ordered, that she had not power to hinder me, as the reader may know hereafter. In the mean time, I here conclude the second part of my unfortunate voyages.

PART III

A Voyage to Laputa,
Balnibarbi, Luggnagg,
Glubbdubdrib
and Japan

CHAPTER I

The author sets out on his third voyage. Is taken by pirates.
The malice of a Dutchman. His arrival at an island. He is
received into Laputa.

I had not been at home above ten days, when Captain William
Robinson, a Cornish man, commander of the *Hope Well*,
a stout ship of three hundred tons, came to my house. I had
formerly been surgeon of another ship where he was master,
and a fourth part owner, in a voyage to the Levant. He had
always treated me more like a brother, than an inferior officer;
and, hearing of my arrival, made me a visit, as I apprehended
only out of friendship, for nothing passed more than what
is usual after long absences. But repeating his visits often,
expressing his joy to find I me in good health, asking, whether
I were now settled for life? adding, that he intended a voyage
to the East Indies in two months, at last he plainly invited me,
though with some apologies, to be surgeon of the ship; that I
should have another surgeon under me, beside our two mates;
that my salary should be double to the usual pay; and that
having experienced my knowledge in sea-affairs to be at least
equal to his, he would enter into any engagement to follow my
advice, as much as if I had shared in the command.

He said so many other obliging things, and I knew him
to be so honest a man, that I could not reject this proposal;

the thirst I had of seeing the world, notwithstanding my past misfortunes, continuing as violent as ever. The only difficulty that remained, was to persuade my wife, whose consent however I at last obtained, by the prospect of advantage she proposed to her children.

We set out the 5th day of August, 1706, and arrived at Fort St. George the 11th of April, 1707. We staid there three weeks to refresh our crew, many of whom were sick. From thence we went to Tonquin, where the captain resolved to continue some time, because many of the goods he intended to buy were not ready, nor could he expect to be dispatched in several months. Therefore, in hopes to defray some of the charges he must be at, he bought a sloop, loaded it with several sorts of goods, wherewith the Tonquinese usually trade to the neighbouring islands, and putting fourteen men on board, whereof three were of the country, he appointed me master of the sloop, and gave me power to traffic, while he transacted his affairs at Tonquin.

We had not sailed above three days, when a great storm arising, we were driven five days to the north-north-east, and then to the east: after which we had fair weather, but still with a pretty strong gale from the west. Upon the tenth day we were chased by two pirates, who soon overtook us; for my sloop was so deep laden, that she sailed very slow, neither were we in a condition to defend ourselves.

We were boarded about the same time by both the pirates, who entered furiously at the head of their men; but finding us all prostrate upon our faces (for so I gave order), they pinioned us with strong ropes, and setting guard upon us, went to search the sloop.

I observed among them a Dutchman, who seemed to be of some authority, though he was not commander of either ship. He knew us by our countenances to be Englishmen, and jabbering to us in his own language, swore we should be tied back to back and thrown into the sea. I spoken Dutch tolerably well; I told him who we were, and begged him, in consideration of our being Christians and Protestants, of neighbouring countries in strict alliance, that he would move the captains to take some pity on us. This inflamed his rage; he repeated his threatenings, and turning to his companions, spoke with great vehemence in the Japanese language, as I suppose, often using the word *Christianos*.

The largest of the two pirate ships was commanded by a Japanese captain, who spoke a little Dutch, but very imperfectly. He came up to me, and after several questions, which I answered in great humility, he said, we should not die. I made the captain a very low bow, and then, turning to the Dutchman, said, I was sorry to find more mercy in a heathen, than in a brother christian. But I had soon reason to repent those foolish words: for that malicious reprobate, having often endeavoured in vain to persuade both the captains that I might be thrown into the sea (which they would not yield to, after the promise made me that I should not die), however, prevailed so far, as to have a punishment inflicted on me, worse, in all human appearance, than death itself.

My men were sent by an equal division into both the pirate ships, and my sloop new manned. As to myself, it was determined that I should be set adrift in a small canoe, with paddles and a sail, and four days' provisions; which last, the Japanese captain was so kind to double out of his own stores, and would permit no man to search me. I got down into the canoe, while the Dutchman, standing upon the deck, loaded me with all the curses and injurious terms his language could afford.

About an hour before we saw the pirates I had taken an observation, and found we were in the latitude of 46 N. and longitude of 183. When I was at some distance from the pirates, I discovered, by my pocket-glass, several islands to the south-east. I set up my sail, the wind being fair, with a design to reach the nearest of those islands, which I made a shift to do, in about three hours. It was all rocky: however I got many birds' eggs; and, striking fire, I kindled some heath and dry sea-weed, by which I roasted my eggs. I ate no other supper, being resolved to spare my provisions as much as I could. I passed the night under the shelter of a rock, strewing some heath under me, and slept pretty well.

The next day I sailed to another island, and thence to a third and fourth, sometimes using my sail, and sometimes my paddles. But, not to trouble the reader with a particular account of my distresses, let it suffice, that on the fifth day I arrived at the last island in my sight, which lay south-south-east to the former.

This island was at a greater distance than I expected, and I did not reach it in less than five hours. I encompassed it almost round, before I could find a convenient place to land in; which was a small creek, about three times the wideness of my canoe. I found the island to be all rocky, only a little intermingled with tufts of grass, and sweet-smelling herbs. I took out my small provisions and after having refreshed myself, I secured the remainder in a cave, whereof there were great numbers; I gathered plenty of eggs upon the rocks, and got a quantity of dry sea-weed, and parched grass, which I designed to kindle the next day, and roast my eggs as well as I could, for I had about me my flint, steel, match, and burning-glass.

I lay all night in the cave where I had lodged my provisions. My bed was the same dry grass and sea-weed which I intended for fuel. I slept very little, for the disquiets of my mind prevailed over my weariness, and kept me awake. I considered how impossible it was to preserve my life in so desolate a place, and how miserable my end must be: yet found myself so listless and desponding, that I had not the heart to rise; and before I could get spirits enough to creep out of my cave, the day was far advanced. I walked awhile among the rocks: the sky was perfectly clear, and the sun so hot, that I was forced to turn my face from it: when all on a sudden it became obscure, as I thought, in a manner very different from what happens by the interposition of a cloud. I turned back, and perceived a vast opaque body between me and the sun moving forwards towards the island: it seemed to be about two miles high, and hid the sun six or seven minutes; but I did not observe the air to be much colder, or the sky more darkened, than if I had stood under the shade of a mountain.

As it approached nearer over the place where I was, it appeared to be a firm substance, the bottom flat, smooth, and shining very bright, from the reflection of the sea below. I stood upon a height about two hundred yards from the shore, and saw this vast body descending almost to a parallel with me, at less than an English mile distance. I took out my pocket perspective, and could plainly discover numbers of people moving up and down the sides of it, which appeared to be sloping; but what those people where doing I was not able to distinguish.

The natural love of life gave me some inward motion of joy, and I was ready to entertain a hope that this adventure might, some way or other, help to deliver me from the desolate place and condition I was in. But at the same time the reader can hardly conceive my astonishment, to behold an island in the air, inhabited by men, who were able (as it should seem) to raise or sink, or put it into progressive motion, as they pleased. But not being at that time in a disposition to philosophise upon this phenomenon, I rather chose to observe what course the island would take, because it seemed for awhile to stand still. Yet soon after, it advanced nearer, and I could see the sides of it encompassed with several gradations of galleries, and stairs, at certain intervals, to descend from one to the other.

In the lowest gallery, I beheld some people fishing with

long angling rods, and others looking on. I waved my cap (for my hat was long since worn out) and my handkerchief toward the island; and upon its nearer approach, I called and shouted with the utmost strength of my voice; and then looking circumspectly, I beheld a crowd gather to that side which was most in my view. I found by their pointing towards me and to each other, that they plainly discovered me, although they made no return to my shouting. But I could see four or five men running in great haste, up the stairs, to the top of the island, who then disappeared. I happened rightly to conjecture, that these were sent for orders to some person in authority upon this occasion.

The number of people increased, and, in less than half all hour, the island was moved and raised in such a manner, that the lowest gallery appeared in a parallel of less then a hundred yards distance from the height where I stood. I then put myself in the most supplicating posture, and spoke in the humblest accent, but received no answer. Those who stood nearest over against me, seemed to be persons of distinction, as I supposed by their habit. They conferred earnestly with each other, looking often upon me. At length one of them called out in a clear, polite, smooth dialect, not unlike in sound to the Italian: and therefore I returned an answer in that language, hoping at least that the cadence might be more agreeable to his ears. Although neither of us understood the other, yet my meaning was easily known, for the people saw the distress I was in.

They made signs for me to come down from the rock, and go towards the shore, which I accordingly did; and the flying island being raised to a convenient height, the verge directly over me, a chain was let down from the lowest gallery, with a seat fastened to the bottom, to which I fixed myself, and was drawn up by pulleys.

CHAPTER II

The humours and dispositions of the Laputians described.
An account of their learning. Of the king and his court.
The author's reception there. The inhabitants subject to
fear and disquietudes. An account of the women.

At my alighting, I was surrounded with a crowd of people,
but those who stood nearest seemed to be of better
quality. They beheld me with all the marks and circumstances
of wonder; neither indeed was I much in their debt, having
never till then seen a race of mortals so singular in their shapes,
habits, and countenances. Their heads were all reclined, either
to the right, or the left; one of their eyes turned inward, and
the other directly up to the zenith. Their outward garments
were adorned with the figures of suns, moons, and stars;
interwoven with those of fiddles, flutes, harps, trumpets,
guitars, harpsichords, and many other instruments of music,
unknown to us in Europe. I observed, here and there, many in
the habit of servants, with a blown bladder, fastened like a flail
to the end of a stick, which they carried in their hands. In each
bladder was a small quantity of dried peas, or little pebbles,
as I was afterwards informed. With these bladders, they now
and then flapped the mouths and ears of those who stood near
them, of which practice I could not then conceive the meaning.
It seems the minds of these people are so taken up with intense

speculations, that they neither can speak, nor attend to the discourses of others, without being roused by some external taction upon the organs of speech and hearing; for which reason, those persons who are able to afford it always keep a flapper (the original is *climenole*) in their family, as one of their domestics; nor ever walk abroad, or make visits, without him. And the business of this officer is, when two, three, or more persons are in company, gently to strike with his bladder the mouth of him who is to speak, and the right ear of him or them to whom the speaker addresses himself. This flapper is likewise employed diligently to attend his master in his walks, and upon occasion to give him a soft flap on his eyes; because he is always so wrapped up in cogitation, that he is in manifest danger of falling down every precipice, and bouncing his head against every post; and in the streets, of justling others, or being justled himself into the kennel.

It was necessary to give the reader this information, without which he would be at the same loss with me to understand the proceedings of these people, as they conducted me up the stairs to the top of the island, and from thence to the royal palace. While we were ascending, they forgot several times what they were about, and left me to myself, till their memories were again roused by their flappers; for they appeared altogether unmoved by the sight of my foreign habit and countenance, and by the shouts of the vulgar, whose thoughts and minds were more disengaged.

At last we entered the palace, and proceeded into the chamber of presence, where I saw the king seated on his throne, attended on each side by persons of prime quality. Before the throne, was a large table filled with globes and spheres, and mathematical instruments of all kinds. His Majesty took not the least notice of us, although our entrance was not without sufficient noise, by the concourse of all persons belonging to the court. But he was then deep in a problem; and we attended at least an hour, before he could solve it.

There stood by him, on each side, a young page with flaps in their hands, and when they saw he was at leisure, one of them gently struck his mouth, and the other his right ear; at which he startled like one awaked on the sudden, and looking towards me and the company I was in, recollected the occasion of our coming, whereof he had been informed before. He spoke some words, whereupon immediately a young man with a flap came up to my side, and flapped me gently on the right ear; but I made signs, as well as I could, that I had no occasion for such an instrument; which, as I afterwards found, gave his Majesty, and the whole court, a very mean opinion of my understanding.

The king, as far as I could conjecture, asked me several questions, and I addressed myself to him in all the languages I had. When it was found I could neither understand nor be understood, I was conducted by his order to an apartment in his palace (this prince being distinguished above all his predecessors for his hospitality to strangers), where two servants were appointed to attend me. My dinner was brought, and four persons of quality, whom I remembered to have seen very near the king's person, did me the honour to dine with me.

We had two courses, of three dishes each. In the first course, there was a shoulder of mutton cut into an equilateral triangle, a piece of beef into a rhomboides, and a pudding into a cycloid. The second course was two ducks trussed up in the form of fiddles; sausages and puddings resembling flutes and hautboys, and a breast of veal in the shape of a harp. The servants cut our bread into cones, cylinders, parallelograms, and several other mathematical figures.

While we were at dinner, I made bold to ask the names of several things in their language, and those noble persons, by the assistance of their flappers, delighted to give me answers, hoping to raise my admiration of their great abilities if I could be brought to converse with them. I was soon able to call for bread and drink, or whatever else I wanted.

After dinner my company withdrew, and a person was sent to me by the king's order, attended by a flapper. He brought with him pen, ink, and paper, and three or four books, giving me to understand by signs, that he was sent to teach me the language. We sat together four hours, in which time I wrote down a great number of words in columns, with the translations over against them; I likewise made a shift to learn several short sentences; for my tutor would order one of my servants to fetch something, to turn about, to make a bow, to sit, or to stand, or walk, and the like. Then I took down the sentence in writing.

He showed me also, in one of his books, the figures of the sun, moon, and stars, the zodiac, the tropics, and polar circles, together with the denominations of many plains and solids. He gave me the names and descriptions of all the musical instruments, and the general terms of art in playing on each of them. After he had left me, I placed all my words, with their interpretations, in alphabetical order. And thus, in a few days, by the help of a very faithful memory, I got some insight into their language.

The word, which I interpret the flying or floating island, is in the original, *Laputa*, whereof I could never learn the true etymology. *Lap*, in the old obsolete language, signifies high; and *untuh*, a governor; from which they say, by corruption, was derived *Laputa*, from *Lapuntuh*. But I do not approve of this derivation, which seems to be a little strained. I ventured to offer to the learned among them a conjecture of my own, that Laputa was *quasi lap outed*; *lap*, signifying properly, the dancing of the sunbeams in the sea, and *outed*, a wing; which, however, I shall not obtrude, but submit to the judicious reader.

Those to whom the king had entrusted me, observing how

ill I was clad, ordered a tailor to come next morning, and take measure for a suit of clothes. This operator did his office after a different manner from those of his trade in Europe. He first took my altitude by a quadrant, and then, with a rule and compasses, described the dimensions and outlines of my whole body, all which he entered upon paper; and in six days brought my clothes very ill made, and quite out of shape, by happening to mistake a figure in the calculation. But my comfort was, that I observed such accidents very frequent, and little regarded.

During my confinement for want of clothes, and by an indisposition that held me some days longer, I much enlarged my dictionary; and when I went next to court, was able to understand many things the king spoke, and to return him some kind of answers. His Majesty had given orders, that the island should move north-east and by east, to the vertical point over Lagado, the metropolis of the whole kingdom below, upon the firm earth. It was about ninety leagues distant, and our voyage lasted four days and a half. I was not in the least sensible of the progressive motion made in the air by the island.

On the second morning, about eleven o'clock, the king himself in person, attended by his nobility, courtiers, and officers, having prepared all their musical instruments, played on them for three hours without intermission, so that I was quite stunned with the noise; neither could I possibly guess the meaning, till my tutor informed me. He said that, the people of their island had their ears adapted to hear the music of the spheres, which always played at certain periods, and the court was now prepared to bear their part, in whatever instrument they most excelled.

In our journey towards Lagado, the capital city, his Majesty ordered that the island should stop over certain towns and villages, from whence he might receive the petitions of his subjects. And to this purpose, several packthreads were let down, with small weights at the bottom. On these packthreads the people strung their petitions, which mounted up directly, like the scraps of paper fastened by school boys at the end of the string that holds their kite. Sometimes we received wine and victuals from below, which were drawn up by pulleys.

The knowledge I had in mathematics, gave me great assistance in acquiring their phraseology, which depended much upon that science, and music; and in the latter I was not unskilled. Their ideas are perpetually conversant in lines and figures. If they would, for example, praise the beauty of a woman, or any other animal, they describe it by rhombs, circles, parallelograms, ellipses, and other geometrical terms, or by words of art drawn from music, needless here to repeat. I observed in the king's kitchen all sorts of mathematical and musical instruments, after the figures of which they cut up the joints that were served to his Majesty's table.

Their houses are very ill built, the walls bevil, without one right angle in any apartment; and this defect arises from the contempt they bear to practical geometry, which they despise as vulgar and mechanic; those instructions they give being too refined for the intellects of their workmen, which occasions perpetual mistakes. And although they are dexterous enough upon a piece of paper, in the management of the rule, the pencil, and the divider, yet in the common actions and behaviour of life, I have not seen a more clumsy, awkward, and unhandy people, nor so slow and perplexed in their conceptions upon all other subjects, except those of mathematics and music. They are very bad reasoners, and vehemently given to opposition, unless when they happen to be of the right opinion, which is seldom their case. Imagination, fancy, and invention, they are wholly strangers to, nor have any words in their language, by which those ideas can be expressed; the whole compass of their thoughts and mind being shut up within the two forementioned sciences.

Most of them, and especially those who deal in the

astronomical part, have great faith in judicial astrology, although they are ashamed to own it publicly. But what I chiefly admired, and thought altogether unaccountable, was the strong disposition I observed in them towards news and politics, perpetually inquiring into public affairs, giving their judgments in matters of state, and passionately disputing every inch of a party opinion.

I have indeed observed the same disposition among most of the mathematicians I have known in Europe, although I could never discover the least analogy between the two sciences; unless those people suppose, that because the smallest circle has as many degrees as the largest, therefore the regulation and management of the world require no more abilities than the handling and turning of a globe; but I rather take this quality to spring from a very common infirmity of human nature, inclining us to be most curious and conceited in matters where we have least concern, and for which we are least adapted by study or nature.

These people are under continual disquietudes, never enjoying a minutes peace of mind; and their disturbances proceed from causes which very little affect the rest of mortals. Their apprehensions arise from several changes they dread in the celestial bodies: for instance, that the earth, by the continual approaches of the sun towards it, must, in course of time, be absorbed, or swallowed up; that the face of the sun, will, by degrees, be encrusted with its own effluvia, and give no more light to the world; that the earth very narrowly escaped a brush from the tail of the last comet, which would have infallibly reduced it to ashes; and that the next, which they have calculated for one-and-thirty years hence, will probably destroy us.

If in its perihelion, it should approach within a certain degree of the sun (as by their calculations they have reason to dread) it will receive a degree of heat ten thousand times more intense than that of red hot glowing iron, and in its absence from the sun, carry a blazing tail ten hundred thousand and fourteen miles long, through which, if the earth should pass at the distance of one hundred thousand miles from the nucleus, or main body of the comet, it must in its passage be set on fire, and reduced to ashes: that the sun, daily spending its rays without any nutriment to supply them, will at last be wholly consumed and annihilated; which must be attended with the destruction of this earth, and of all the planets that receive their light from it.

They are so perpetually alarmed with the apprehensions of these, and the like impending dangers, that they can neither sleep quietly in their beds, nor have any relish for the common pleasures and amusements of life. When they meet an acquaintance in the morning, the first question is about the sun's health, how he looked at his setting and rising, and what hopes they have to avoid the stroke of the approaching comet. This conversation they are apt to run into with the same temper that boys discover in delighting to hear terrible stories of spirits and hobgoblins, which they greedily listen to, and dare not go to bed for fear.

The women of the island have abundance of vivacity: they, contemn their husbands, and are exceedingly fond of strangers, whereof there is always a considerable number from the continent below, attending at court, either upon affairs of the several towns and corporations, or their own particular occasions, but are much despised, because they want the same endowments. Among these the ladies choose their gallants: but the vexation is, that they act with too much ease and security; for the husband is always so rapt in speculation, that the mistress and lover may proceed to the greatest familiarities before his face, if he be but provided with paper and implements, and without his flapper at his side.

The wives and daughters lament their confinement to the

island, although I think it the most delicious spot of ground in the world; and although they live here in the greatest plenty and magnificence, and are allowed to do whatever they please, they long to see the world, and take the diversions of the metropolis, which they are not allowed to do without a particular license from the king; and this is not easy to be obtained, because the people of quality have found, by frequent experience, how hard it is to persuade their women to return from below.

This may perhaps pass with the reader rather for an European or English story, than for one of a country so remote. But he may please to consider, that the caprices of womankind are not limited by any climate or nation, and that they are much more uniform, than can be easily imagined.

In about a month's time, I had made a tolerable proficiency in their language, and was able to answer most of the king's questions, when I had the honour to attend him. His Majesty discovered not the least curiosity to inquire into the laws, government, history, religion, or manners of the countries where I had been; but confined his questions to the state of mathematics, and received the account I gave him with great contempt and indifference, though often roused by his flapper on each side.

CHAPTER III

A phenomenon solved by modern philosophy and astronomy. The Laputians' great improvements in the latter. The king's method of suppressing insurrections.

I desired leave of this prince to see the curiosities of the island, which he was graciously pleased to grant, and ordered my tutor to attend me. I chiefly wanted to know, to what cause, in art or in nature, it owed its several motions, whereof I will now give a philosophical account to the reader.

The flying or floating island is exactly circular, its diameter 7837 yards, or about four miles and a half, and consequently contains ten thousand acres. It is three hundred yards thick. The bottom, or under surface, which appears to those who view it below, is one even regular plate of adamant, shooting up to the height of about two hundred yards. Above it lie the several minerals in their usual order, and over all is a coat of rich mould, ten or twelve feet deep.

The declivity of the upper surface, from the circumference to the centre, is the natural cause why all the dews and rains, which fall upon the island, are conveyed in small rivulets toward the middle, where they are emptied into four large basins, each of about half a mile in circuit, and two hundred yards distant from the centre. From these basins the water is continually exhaled by the sun in the daytime, which effectually prevents their overflowing. Besides, as it is in the power of the monarch to raise the island above the region of clouds and vapours, he can prevent the falling of dews and rain whenever he pleases. For the highest clouds cannot rise above two miles, as naturalists agree, at least they were never known to do so in that country.

At the centre of the island there is a chasm about fifty yards in diameter, whence the astronomers descend into a large dome, which is therefore called *flandona gagnole*, or the astronomer's cave, situated at the depth of a hundred yards beneath the upper surface of the adamant. In this cave are twenty lamps continually burning, which, from the reflection of the adamant, cast a strong light into every part. The place is stored with great variety of sextants, quadrants, telescopes, astrolabes, and other astronomical instruments.

But the greatest curiosity, upon which the fate of the island depends, is a loadstone of a prodigious size, in shape resembling a weaver's shuttle. It is in length six yards, and in the thickest part at least three yards over. This magnet is sustained by a very strong axle of adamant passing through its middle, upon which it plays, and is poised so exactly that the weakest hand can turn it. It is hooped round with a hollow cylinder of adamant, four feet yards in diameter, placed horizontally, and supported by eight adamantine feet, each six yards high. In the middle of the concave side, there is a groove twelve inches deep, in which the extremities of the axle are lodged, and turned round as there is occasion.

The stone cannot be removed from its place by any force, because the hoop and its feet are one continued piece with that body of adamant which constitutes the bottom of the island.

By means of this loadstone, the island is made to rise and fall, and move from one place to another. For, with respect to that part of the earth over which the monarch presides, the stone is endued at one of its sides with an attractive power, and at the other with a repulsive. Upon placing the magnet erect, with its attracting end towards the earth, the island descends; but when the repelling extremity points downwards, the island mounts directly upwards. When the position of the stone is oblique, the motion of the island is so too: for in this magnet, the forces always act in lines parallel to its direction.

By this oblique motion, the island is conveyed to different parts of the monarch's dominions. To explain the manner of its progress, let $A B$ represent a line drawn across the dominions of Balnibarbi, let the line $c d$ represent the loadstone, of which let d be the repelling end, and c the attracting end, the island being over C: let the stone be placed in position $c d$, with its repelling end downwards; then the island will be driven upwards obliquely towards D. When it is arrived at D, let the stone be turned upon its axle, till its attracting end points towards E, and then the island will be carried obliquely towards E; where, if the stone be again turned upon its axle till it stands in the position EF, with its repelling point downwards, the island will rise obliquely towards F, where, by directing the attracting end towards G, the island may be carried to G, and from G to H, by turning the stone, so as to make its repelling extremity to point directly downward.

Thus, by changing the situation of the stone, as often as there is occasion, the island is made to rise and fall by turns in an oblique direction, and by those alternate risings and fallings (the obliquity being not considerable) is conveyed from one part of the dominions to the other.

But it must be observed, that this island cannot move beyond the extent of the dominions below, nor can it rise above the height of four miles. For which the astronomers (who have written large systems concerning the stone) assign the following reason: that the magnetic virtue does not extend beyond the distance of four miles, and that the mineral, which acts upon the stone in the bowels of the earth, and in the sea about six leagues distant from the shore, is not diffused through the whole globe, but terminated with the limits of the king's dominions; and it was easy, from the great advantage of such a superior situation, for a prince to bring under his obedience whatever country lay within the attraction of that magnet.

When the stone is put parallel to the plane of the horizon, the island stands still; for in that case the extremities of it, being at equal distance from the earth, act with equal force, the one in drawing downwards, the other in pushing upwards, and consequently no motion can ensue.

This loadstone is under the care of certain astronomers, who, from time to time, give it such positions as the monarch directs. They spend the greatest part of their lives in observing the celestial bodies, which they do by the assistance of glasses, far excelling ours in goodness. For, although their largest telescopes do not exceed three feet, they magnify much more than those of a hundred with us, and show the stars with greater clearness. This advantage has enabled them to extend their discoveries much further than our astronomers in Europe; for they have made a catalogue of ten thousand fixed stars, whereas the largest of ours do not contain above one third part of that number. They have likewise discovered two lesser stars, or satellites, which revolve about Mars; whereof the innermost is distant from the centre of the primary planet exactly three of his diameters, and the outermost, five; the former revolves in the space of ten hours, and the latter in twenty-one and a half; so that the squares of their periodical times are very near in the same proportion with the cubes of their distance from the centre of Mars; which evidently shows them to be governed by the same law of gravitation that influences the other heavenly bodies.

They have observed ninety-three different comets, and settled their periods with great exactness. If this be true (and they affirm it with great confidence) it is much to be wished, that their observations were made public, whereby the theory of comets, which at present is very lame and defective, might be brought to the same perfection with other arts of astronomy.

The king would be the most absolute prince in the universe, if he could but prevail on a ministry to join with him; but these having their estates below on the continent, and considering that the office of a favourite has a very uncertain tenure, would never consent to the enslaving of their country.

If any town should engage in rebellion or mutiny, fall into violent factions, or refuse to pay the usual tribute, the king has two methods of reducing them to obedience. The first and the mildest course is, by keeping the island hovering over such a town, and the lands about it, whereby he can deprive them of the benefit of the sun and the rain, and consequently afflict the inhabitants with dearth and diseases: and if the crime deserve it, they are at the same time pelted from above with great stones, against which they have no defence but by creeping into cellars or caves, while the roofs of their houses are beaten to pieces.

But if they still continue obstinate, or offer to raise insurrections, he proceeds to the last remedy, by letting the island drop directly upon their heads, which makes a universal destruction both of houses and men. However, this is an extremity to which the prince is seldom driven, neither indeed is he willing to put it in execution; nor dare his ministers advise him to an action, which, as it would render them odious to the people, so it would be a great damage to their own estates, which all lie below; for the island is the king's demesne.

But there is still indeed a more weighty reason, why the kings of this country have been always averse from executing so terrible an action, unless upon the utmost necessity. For, if the town intended to be destroyed should have in it any tall rocks, as it generally falls out in the larger cities, a situation probably chosen at first with a view to prevent such a catastrophe; or if it abound in high spires, or pillars of stone, a sudden fall might endanger the bottom or under surface of the island, which, although it consist, as I have said, of one entire adamant, two hundred yards thick, might happen to crack by too great a shock, or burst by approaching too near the fires from the houses below, as the backs, both of iron and stone, will often do in our chimneys.

Of all this the people are well apprised, and understand how far to carry their obstinacy, where their liberty or property is concerned. And the king, when he is highest provoked, and most determined to press a city to rubbish, orders the island to descend with great gentleness, out of a pretence of tenderness to his people, but, indeed, for fear of breaking the adamantine bottom; in which case, it is the opinion of all their philosophers, that the loadstone could no longer hold it up, and the whole mass would fall to the ground.

By a fundamental law of this realm, neither the king, nor either of his two eldest sons, are permitted to leave the island; nor the queen, till she is past child-bearing.

CHAPTER IV

The author leaves Laputa; is conveyed to Balnibarbi; arrives at the metropolis. A description of the metropolis, and the country adjoining. The author hospitably received by a great lord. His conversation with that lord.

Although I cannot say that I was ill treated in this island, yet I must confess I thought myself too much neglected, not without some degree of contempt; for neither prince nor people appeared to be curious in any part of knowledge, except mathematics and music, wherein I was far their inferior, and upon that account very little regarded.

On the other side, after having seen all the curiosities of the island, I was very desirous to leave it, being heartily weary of those people. They were indeed excellent in two sciences for which I have great esteem, and wherein I am not unversed; but, at the same time, so abstracted and involved in speculation, that I never met with such disagreeable companions. I conversed only with women, tradesmen, flappers, and court-pages, during two months of my abode there; by which, at last, I rendered myself extremely contemptible; yet these were the only people from whom I could ever receive a reasonable answer.

I had obtained, by hard study, a good degree of knowledge in their language: I was weary of being confined to an island where I received so little countenance, and resolved to leave it with the first opportunity.

There was a great lord at court, nearly related to the king, and for that reason alone used with respect. He was universally reckoned the most ignorant and stupid person among them. He had performed many eminent services for the crown, had great natural and acquired parts, adorned with integrity and honour; but so ill an ear for music, that his detractors reported, he had been often known to beat time in the wrong place; neither could his tutors, without extreme difficulty, teach him to demonstrate the most easy proposition in the mathematics.

He was pleased to show me many marks of favour, often did me the honour of a visit, desired to be informed in the affairs of Europe, the laws and customs, the manners and learning of the several countries where I had travelled. He listened to me with great attention, and made very wise observations on all I spoke. He had two flappers attending him for state, but never made use of them, except at court and in visits of ceremony, and would always command them to withdraw, when we were alone together.

I entreated this illustrious person, to intercede in my behalf with his Majesty, for leave to depart; which he accordingly did, as he was pleased to tell me, with regret: for indeed he had made me several offers very advantageous, which, however, I refused, with expressions of the highest acknowledgment.

On the 16th of February I took leave of his Majesty and the court. The king made me a present to the value of about two hundred pounds English, and my protector, his kinsman, as much more, together with a letter of recommendation to a friend of his in Lagado, the metropolis. The island being then hovering over a mountain about two miles from it, I was let down from the lowest gallery, in the same manner as I had been taken up.

The continent, as far as it is subject to the monarch of the flying island, passes under the general name of *Balnibarbi*; and the metropolis, as I said before, is called *Lagado*. I felt some little satisfaction in finding myself on firm ground. I walked to the city without any concern, being clad like one of the natives, and sufficiently instructed to converse with them. I soon found out the person's house to whom I was recommended, presented my letter from his friend the grandee in the island, and was received with much kindness. This great lord, whose name was Munodi, ordered me an apartment in his own house, where I continued during my stay, and was entertained in a most hospitable manner.

The next morning after my arrival, he took me in his chariot to see the town, which is about half the bigness of London; but the houses very strangely built, and most of them out of repair. The people in the streets walked fast, looked wild, their eyes fixed, and were generally in rags. We passed through one of the town gates, and went about three miles into the country, where I saw many labourers working with several sorts of tools in the ground, but was not able to conjecture what they were about: neither did observe any expectation either of corn or grass, although the soil appeared to be excellent. I could not forbear admiring at these odd appearances, both in town and country; and I made bold to desire my conductor, that he would be pleased to explain to me, what could be meant by so many busy heads, hands, and faces, both in the streets and the fields, because I did not discover any good effects they produced; but, on the contrary, I never knew a soil so unhappily cultivated, houses so ill contrived and so ruinous, or a people whose countenances and habit expressed so much misery and want.

This lord Munodi was a person of the first rank, and had been some years governor of Lagado; but, by a cabal of ministers, was discharged for insufficiency. However, the king treated him with tenderness, as a well-meaning man, but of a low contemptible understanding.

When I gave that free censure of the country and its inhabitants, he made no further answer than by telling me, that I had not been long enough among them to form a judgment; and that the different nations of the world had different customs; with other common topics to the same purpose. But, when we returned to his palace, he asked me how I liked the building, what absurdities I observed, and what quarrel I had with the dress or looks of his domestics? This he might safely do; because every thing about him was magnificent, regular, and polite. I answered, that his Excellency's prudence, quality, and fortune, had exempted him from those defects, which folly and beggary had produced in others. He said, if I would go with him to his country-house, about twenty miles distant, where his estate lay, there would be more leisure for this kind of conversation. I told his Excellency that I was entirely at his disposal; and accordingly we set out next morning.

During our journey he made me observe the several methods used by farmers in managing their lands, which to me were wholly unaccountable; for, except in some very few places, I could not discover one ear of corn or blade of grass. But, in three hours travelling, the scene was wholly altered; we came into a most beautiful country; farmers' houses, at small distances, neatly built; the fields enclosed, containing vineyards, corn-grounds, and meadows. Neither do I remember to have seen a more delightful prospect. His Excellency observed my countenance to clear up; he told me, with a sigh, that there his estate began, and would continue the same, till we should come to his house: that his countrymen ridiculed and despised him, for managing his affairs no better, and for setting so ill an example to the kingdom; which, however, was followed by very few, such as were old, and wilful, and weak like himself.

We came at length to the house, which was indeed a noble structure, built according to the best rules of ancient architecture. The fountains, gardens, walks, avenues, and groves, were all disposed with exact judgment and taste. I gave due praises to every thing I saw, whereof his Excellency took not the least notice till after supper; when, there being no third companion, he told me with a very melancholy air that he doubted he must throw down his houses in town and country, to rebuild them after the present mode; destroy all his plantations, and cast others into such a form as modern usage required, and give the same directions to all his tenants, unless he would submit to incur the censure of pride, singularity, affectation, ignorance, caprice, and perhaps increase his Majesty's displeasure; that the admiration I appeared to be under would cease or diminish, when he had informed me of some particulars which, probably, I never heard of at court, the people there being too much taken up in their own speculations, to have regard to what passed here below.

The sum of his discourse was to this effect: That about forty years ago, certain persons went up to Laputa, either upon business or diversion, and, after five months continuance, came back with a very little smattering in mathematics, but full of volatile spirits acquired in that airy region: that these persons, upon their return, began to dislike the management of every thing below, and fell into schemes of putting all arts, sciences, languages, and mechanics, upon a new foot. To this end, they procured a royal patent for erecting an academy of projectors in Lagado; and the humour prevailed so strongly among the people, that there is not a town of any consequence in the kingdom without such an academy. In these colleges the professors contrive new rules and methods of agriculture and building, and new instruments, and tools for all trades and manufactures; whereby, as they undertake, one man shall do the work of ten; a palace may be built in a week, of materials so durable as to last for ever without repairing. All the fruits of the earth shall come to maturity at whatever season we think fit to choose, and increase a hundred fold more than they do at present; with innumerable other happy proposals.

The only inconvenience is, that none of these projects are yet brought to perfection; and in the mean time, the whole country lies miserably waste, the houses in ruins, and the people without food or clothes. By all which, instead of being discouraged, they are fifty times more violently bent upon prosecuting their schemes, driven equally on by hope and despair: that as for himself, being not of an enterprising spirit, he was content to go on in the old forms, to live in the houses his ancestors had built, and act as they did, in every part of life, without innovation: that some few other persons of quality and gentry had done the same, but were looked on with an eye of contempt and ill-will, as enemies to art, ignorant, and ill common-wealth's men, preferring their own ease and sloth before the general improvement of their country.

His lordship added that he would not, by any further particulars, prevent the pleasure I should certainly take in viewing the grand academy, whither he was resolved I should go. He only desired me to observe a ruined building, upon the side of a mountain about three miles distant, of which he gave me this account: That he had a very convenient mill within half a mile of his house, turned by a current from a large river, and sufficient for his own family, as well as a great number of his tenants.

About seven years ago, a club of those projectors came to him with proposals to destroy this mill, and build another on the side of that mountain, on the long ridge whereof a long canal must be cut, for a repository of water, to be conveyed up by pipes and engines to supply the mill, because the wind and air upon a height agitated the water, and thereby made it fitter for motion, and because the water, descending down a declivity, would turn the mill with half the current of a river whose course is more upon a level. He said, that being then not very well with the court, and pressed by many of his friends, he complied with the proposal; and after employing a hundred men for two years, the work miscarried, the projectors went off, laying the blame entirely upon him, railing at him ever since, and putting others upon the same experiment, with equal assurance of success, as well as equal disappointment.

In a few days we came back to town; and his Excellency, considering the bad character he had in the academy, would not go with me himself, but recommended me to a friend of his, to bear me company thither. My lord was pleased to represent me as a great admirer of projects, and a person of much curiosity and easy belief; which, indeed, was not without truth; for I had myself been a sort of projector in my younger days.

CHAPTER V

The author permitted to see the grand academy of Lagado.
The academy largely described. The arts wherein the
professors employ themselves.

This academy is not an entire single building, but a
continuation of several houses on both sides of a street,
which growing waste, was purchased and applied to that use.

I was received very kindly by the warden, and went for
many days to the academy. Every room has in it one or more
projectors; and I believe I could not be in fewer than five
hundred rooms.

The first man I saw was of a meagre aspect, with sooty hands
and face, his hair and beard long, ragged, and singed in several
places. His clothes, shirt, and skin, were all of the same colour.
He has been eight years upon a project for extracting sunbeams
out of cucumbers, which were to be put in phials hermetically
sealed, and let out to warm the air in raw inclement summers.
He told me, he did not doubt, that, in eight years more, he
should be able to supply the governor's gardens with sunshine,
at a reasonable rate: but he complained that his stock was low,
and entreated me to give him something as an encouragement
to ingenuity, especially since this had been a very dear season
for cucumbers. I made him a small present, for my lord had
furnished me with money on purpose, because he knew their

practice of begging from all who go to see them.

I saw another at work to calcine ice into gunpowder; who likewise showed me a treatise he had written concerning the malleability of fire, which he intended to publish.

There was a most ingenious architect, who had contrived a new method for building houses, by beginning at the roof, and working downward to the foundation; which he justified to me, by the like practice of those two prudent insects, the bee and the spider.

There was a man born blind, who had several apprentices in his own condition: their employment was to mix colours for painters, which their master taught them to distinguish by feeling and smelling. It was indeed my misfortune to find them at that time not very perfect in their lessons, and the professor himself happened to be generally mistaken. This artist is much encouraged and esteemed by the whole fraternity.

In another apartment I was highly pleased with a projector who had found a device of ploughing the ground with hogs, to save the charges of ploughs, cattle, and labour. The method is this: in an acre of ground you bury, at six inches distance and eight deep, a quantity of acorns, dates, chestnuts, and other mast or vegetables, whereof these animals are fondest; then you drive six hundred or more of them into the field, where, in a few days, they will root up the whole ground in search of their food, and make it fit for sowing, at the same time manuring it with their dung: it is true, upon experiment, they found the charge and trouble very great, and they had little or no crop. However it is not doubted, that this invention may be capable of great improvement.

I went into another room, where the walls and ceiling were all hung round with cobwebs, except a narrow passage for the artist to go in and out. At my entrance, he called aloud to me, not to disturb his webs. He lamented the fatal mistake the world had been so long in, of using silkworms, while we had such plenty of domestic insects who infinitely excelled the former, because they understood how to weave, as well as spin. And he proposed further, that by employing spiders, the charge of dyeing silks should be wholly saved; whereof I was fully convinced, when he showed me a vast number of flies most beautifully coloured, wherewith he fed his spiders, assuring us that the webs would take a tincture from them; and as he had them of all hues, he hoped to fit everybody's fancy, as soon as he could find proper food for the flies, of certain gums, oils, and other glutinous matter, to give a strength and consistence to the threads.

There was an astronomer, who had undertaken to place a sun-dial upon the great weathercock on the town-house, by adjusting the annual and diurnal motions of the earth and sun, so as to answer and coincide with all accidental turnings of the wind.

I visited many other apartments, but shall not trouble my reader with all the curiosities I observed, being studious of brevity.

I had hitherto seen only one side of the academy, the other being appropriated to the advancers of speculative learning, of whom I shall say something, when I have mentioned one illustrious person more, who is called among them the universal artist. He told us he had been thirty years employing his thoughts for the improvement of human life. He had two large rooms full of wonderful curiosities, and fifty men at work. Some were condensing air into a dry tangible substance, by extracting the nitre, and letting the aqueous or fluid particles percolate; others softening marble, for pillows and pin-cushions; others petrifying the hoofs of a living horse, to preserve them from foundering.

The artist himself was at that time busy upon two great designs; the first, to sow land with chaff, wherein he affirmed the true seminal virtue to be contained, as he demonstrated by several experiments, which I was not skilful enough to comprehend. The other was, by a certain composition of gums, minerals, and vegetables, outwardly applied, to prevent the growth of wool upon two young lambs; and he hoped, in a reasonable time to propagate the breed of naked sheep, all over the kingdom.

We crossed a walk to the other part of the academy, where, as I have already said, the projectors in speculative learning resided.

The first professor I saw, was in a very large room, with forty pupils about him. After salutation, observing me to look earnestly upon a frame, which took up the greatest part of both the length and breadth of the room, he said, Perhaps I might wonder to see him employed in a project for improving speculative knowledge, by practical and mechanical operations. But the world would soon be sensible of its usefulness; and he flattered himself, that a more noble, exalted thought never sprang in any other man's head. Every one knew how laborious the usual method is of attaining to arts and sciences; whereas, by his contrivance, the most ignorant person, at a reasonable charge, and with a little bodily labour, might write books in philosophy, poetry, politics, laws, mathematics, and theology, without the least assistance from genius or study.

He then led me to the frame, about the sides, whereof all his pupils stood in ranks. It was twenty feet square, placed in the middle of the room. The superfices was composed of several bits of wood, about the bigness of a die, but some larger than others. They were all linked together by slender wires. These bits of wood were covered, on every square, with paper pasted on them; and on these papers were written all the words of their language, in their several moods, tenses, and declensions; but without any order. The professor then desired me to observe; for he was going to set his engine at work. The pupils, at his command, took each of them hold of an iron handle, whereof there were forty fixed round the edges of the frame; and giving them a sudden turn, the whole disposition of the words was entirely changed.

He then commanded six-and-thirty of the lads, to read the several lines softly, as they appeared upon the frame; and where they found three or four words together that might make part of a sentence, they dictated to the four remaining boys, who were scribes. This work was repeated three or four times, and at every turn, the engine was so contrived, that the words shifted into new places, as the square bits of wood moved upside down.

Six hours a day the young students were employed in this labour; and the professor showed me several volumes in large folio, already collected, of broken sentences, which he intended to piece together, and out of those rich materials, to give the world a complete body of all arts and sciences; which, however, might be still improved, and much expedited, if the public would raise a fund for making and employing five hundred such frames in Lagado, and oblige the managers to contribute in common their several collections.

He assured me that this invention had employed all his thoughts from his youth; that he had emptied the whole vocabulary into his frame, and made the strictest computation of the general proportion there is in books between the numbers of particles, nouns, and verbs, and other parts of speech.

I made my humblest acknowledgment to this illustrious person, for his great communicativeness; and promised, if ever I had the good fortune to return to my native country, that I would do him justice, as the sole inventor of this wonderful machine; the form and contrivance of which I desired leave to delineate on paper, as in the figure here annexed. I told him, although it were the custom of our learned in Europe to steal inventions from each other, who had thereby at least this advantage, that it became a controversy which was the right owner; yet I would take such caution, that he should have the honour entire, without a rival.

We next went to the school of languages, where three professors sat in consultation upon improving that of their own country.

The first project was, to shorten discourse, by cutting polysyllables into one, and leaving out verbs and participles, because, in reality, all things imaginable are but nouns.

The other project was, a scheme for entirely abolishing all words whatsoever; and this was urged as a great advantage in point of health, as well as brevity. For it is plain, that every word we speak is, in some degree, a diminution of our lunge by corrosion, and, consequently, contributes to the shortening of our lives. An expedient was therefore offered, that since words are only names for things, it would be more convenient for all men to carry about them such things as were necessary to express a particular business they are to discourse on. And this invention would certainly have taken place, to the great ease as well as health of the subject, if the women, in conjunction with the vulgar and illiterate, had not threatened to raise a rebellion unless they might be allowed the liberty to speak with their tongues, after the manner of their forefathers; such constant irreconcilable enemies to science are the common people.

However, many of the most learned and wise adhere to the new scheme of expressing themselves by things; which has only this inconvenience attending it, that if a man's business be very great, and of various kinds, he must be obliged, in proportion, to carry a greater bundle of things upon his back, unless he can afford one or two strong servants to attend him. I have often beheld two of those sages almost sinking under the weight of their packs, like pedlars among us, who, when they met in the street, would lay down their loads, open their sacks, and hold conversation for an hour together; then put up their implements, help each other to resume their burdens, and take their leave.

But for short conversations, a man may carry implements in his pockets, and under his arms, enough to supply him; and in his house, he cannot be at a loss. Therefore the room where company meet who practise this art, is full of all things, ready at hand, requisite to furnish matter for this kind of artificial converse.

Another great advantage proposed by this invention was, that it would serve as a universal language, to be understood in all civilised nations, whose goods and utensils are generally of the same kind, or nearly resembling, so that their uses might easily be comprehended. And thus ambassadors would be qualified to treat with foreign princes, or ministers of state, to whose tongues they were utter strangers.

I was at the mathematical school, where the master taught his pupils after a method scarce imaginable to us in Europe. The proposition, and demonstration, were fairly written on a thin wafer, with ink composed of a cephalic tincture. This, the student was to swallow upon a fasting stomach, and for three days following, eat nothing but bread and water. As the wafer digested, the tincture mounted to his brain, bearing the proposition along with it. But the success has not hitherto been answerable, partly by some error in the *quantum* or composition, and partly by the perverseness of lads, to whom this bolus is so nauseous, that they generally steal aside, and discharge it upwards, before it can operate; neither have they been yet persuaded to use so long an abstinence, as the prescription requires.

CHAPTER VI

A further account of the academy. The author proposes
some improvements, which are honourably received.

In the school of political projectors, I was but ill entertained;
the professors appearing, in my judgment, wholly out
of their senses, which is a scene that never fails to make me
melancholy. These unhappy people were proposing schemes
for persuading monarchs to choose favourites upon the score
of their wisdom, capacity, and virtue; of teaching ministers to
consult the public good; of rewarding merit, great abilities,
eminent services; of instructing princes to know their true
interest, by placing it on the same foundation with that of
their people; of choosing for employments persons qualified
to exercise them, with many other wild, impossible chimeras,
that never entered before into the heart of man to conceive;
and confirmed in me the old observation, that there is nothing
so extravagant and irrational, which some philosophers have
not maintained for truth.

But, however, I shall so far do justice to this part of the
Academy, as to acknowledge that all of them were not so
visionary. There was a most ingenious doctor, who seemed
to be perfectly versed in the whole nature and system of
government. This illustrious person had very usefully
employed his studies, in finding out effectual remedies for all

diseases and corruptions to which the several kinds of public administration are subject, by the vices or infirmities of those who govern, as well as by the licentiousness of those who are to obey.

For instance: whereas all writers and reasoners have agreed, that there is a strict universal resemblance between the natural and the political body; can there be any thing more evident, than that the health of both must be preserved, and the diseases cured, by the same prescriptions? It is allowed, that senates and great councils are often troubled with redundant, ebullient, and other peccant humours; with many diseases of the head, and more of the heart; with strong convulsions, with grievous contractions of the nerves and sinews in both hands, but especially the right; with spleen, flatus, vertigos, and deliriums; with scrofulous tumours, full of fetid purulent matter; with sour frothy ructations: with canine appetites, and crudeness of digestion, besides many others, needless to mention.

This doctor therefore proposed, that upon the meeting of the senate, certain physicians should attend it the three first days of their sitting, and at the close of each day's debate feel the pulses of every senator; after which, having maturely considered and consulted upon the nature of the several maladies, and the methods of cure, they should on the fourth day return to the senate house, attended by their apothecaries stored with proper medicines; and before the members sat, administer to each of them lenitives, aperitives, abstersives, corrosives, restringents, palliatives, laxatives, cephalalgics, icterics, apophlegmatics, acoustics, as their several cases required; and, according as these medicines should operate, repeat, alter, or omit them, at the next meeting.

This project could not be of any great expense to the public; and might in my poor opinion, be of much use for the despatch of business, in those countries where senates have any share in the legislative power; beget unanimity, shorten debates, open a few mouths which are now closed, and close many more which are now open; curb the petulancy of the young, and correct the positiveness of the old; rouse the stupid, and damp the pert.

Again: because it is a general complaint, that the favourites of princes are troubled with short and weak memories; the same doctor proposed, that whoever attended a first minister, after having told his business, with the utmost brevity and in the plainest words, should, at his departure, give the said minister a tweak by the nose, or a kick in the belly, or tread on his corns, or lug him thrice by both ears, or run a pin into his breech; or pinch his arm black and blue, to prevent forgetfulness; and at every levee day, repeat the same operation, till the business were done, or absolutely refused.

He likewise directed, that every senator in the great council of a nation, after he had delivered his opinion, and argued in the defence of it, should be obliged to give his vote directly contrary; because if that were done, the result would infallibly terminate in the good of the public.

When parties in a state are violent, he offered a wonderful contrivance to reconcile them. The method is this: You take a hundred leaders of each party; you dispose them into couples of such whose heads are nearest of a size; then let two nice operators saw off the occiput of each couple at the same time, in such a manner that the brain may be equally divided. Let the occiputs, thus cut off, be interchanged, applying each to the head of his opposite party-man. It seems indeed to be a work that requires some exactness, but the professor assured us, that if it were dexterously performed, the cure would be infallible.

For he argued thus: that the two half brains being left to debate the matter between themselves within the space of one skull, would soon come to a good understanding, and produce that moderation, as well as regularity of thinking, so much to be wished for in the heads of those, who imagine they come into the world only to watch and govern its motion: and as to the difference of brains, in quantity or quality, among those who are directors in faction, the doctor assured us, from his own knowledge, that it was a perfect trifle.

I heard a very warm debate between two professors, about the most commodious and effectual ways and means of raising money, without grieving the subject. The first affirmed, the justest method would be, to lay a certain tax upon vices and folly; and the sum fixed upon every man to be rated, after the fairest manner, by a jury of his neighbours. The second was of an opinion directly contrary; to tax those qualities of body and mind, for which men chiefly value themselves; the rate to be more or less, according to the degrees of excelling; the decision whereof should be left entirely to their own breast.

The highest tax was upon men who are the greatest favourites of the other sex, and the assessments, according to the number and nature of the favours they have received; for which, they are allowed to be their own vouchers. Wit, valour, and politeness, were likewise proposed to be largely taxed, and collected in the same manner, by every person's giving his own word for the quantum of what he possessed. But as to honour, justice, wisdom, and learning, they should not be taxed at all; because they are qualifications of so singular a kind, that no man will either allow them in his neighbour or value them in himself.

The women were proposed to be taxed according to their beauty and skill in dressing, wherein they had the same privilege with the men, to be determined by their own judgment. But constancy, chastity, good sense, and good nature, were not rated, because they would not bear the charge of collecting.

To keep senators in the interest of the crown, it was proposed that the members should raffle for employment; every man first taking an oath, and giving security, that he would vote for the court, whether he won or not; after which, the losers had, in their turn, the liberty of raffling upon the next vacancy. Thus, hope and expectation would be kept alive; none would complain of broken promises, but impute their disappointments wholly to fortune, whose shoulders are broader and stronger than those of a ministry.

Another professor showed me a large paper of instructions for discovering plots and conspiracies against the government. He advised great statesmen to examine into the diet of all suspected persons; their times of eating; upon which side they lay in bed; with which hand they wipe their posteriors; take a strict view of their excrements, and, from the colour, the odour, the taste, the consistence, the crudeness or maturity of digestion, form a judgment of their thoughts and designs; because men are never so serious, thoughtful, and intent, as when they are at stool, which he found by frequent experiment; for, in such conjunctures, when he used, merely as a trial, to consider which was the best way of murdering the king, his ordure would have a tincture of green; but quite different, when he thought only of raising an insurrection, or burning the metropolis.

The whole discourse was written with great acuteness, containing many observations, both curious and useful for politicians; but, as I conceived, not altogether complete. This I ventured to tell the author, and offered, if he pleased, to supply him with some additions. He received my proposition with more compliance than is usual among writers, especially those of the projecting species, professing he would be glad to receive further information.

I told him, that in the kingdom of Tribnia,[3] by the natives called Langdon, where I had sojourned some time in my travels, the bulk of the people consist in a manner wholly of discoverers, witnesses, informers, accusers, prosecutors, evidences, swearers, together with their several subservient and subaltern instruments, all under the colours, the conduct, and the pay of ministers of state, and their deputies. The plots, in that kingdom, are usually the workmanship of those persons who desire to raise their own characters of profound politicians; to restore new vigour to a crazy administration; to stifle or divert general discontents; to fill their coffers with forfeitures; and raise, or sink the opinion of public credit, as either shall best answer their private advantage.

It is first agreed and settled among them, what suspected persons shall be accused of a plot; then, effectual care is taken to secure all their letters and papers, and put the owners in chains. These papers are delivered to a set of artists, very dexterous in finding out the mysterious meanings of words, syllables, and letters: for instance, they can discover a close stool, to signify a privy council; a flock of geese, a senate; a lame dog, an invader; the plague, a standing army; a buzzard, a prime minister; the gout, a high priest; a gibbet, a secretary of state; a chamber pot, a committee of grandees; a sieve, a court lady; a broom, a revolution; a mouse-trap, an employment; a bottomless pit, a treasury; a sink, a court; a cap and bells, a favourite; a broken reed, a court of justice; an empty tun, a general; a running sore, the administration.[5]

Where this method fails, they have two others more effectual, which the learned among them call acrostics and anagrams. First, they can decipher all initial letters into political meanings. Thus *N*, shall signify a plot; *B*, a regiment of horse; *L*, a fleet at sea; or, secondly, by transposing the letters of the alphabet in any suspected paper, they can lay open the deepest designs of a discontented party. So, for example, if I should say, in a letter to a friend, 'Our brother Tom has just got the piles,' a skilful decipherer would discover, that the same letters which compose that sentence, may be analysed into the following words: Resist, a plot is brought home, the tour. And this is the anagrammatic method.

The professor made me great acknowledgments for

communicating these observations, and promised to make honourable mention of me in his treatise.

I saw nothing in this country that could invite me to a longer continuance, and began to think of returning home to England.

CHAPTER VII

The author leaves Lagado: arrives at Maldonada. No ship
ready. He takes a short voyage to Glubbdubdrib. His
reception by the governor.

The continent, of which this kingdom is apart, extends
itself, as I have reason to believe, eastward, to that
unknown tract of America westward of California; and north,
to the Pacific Ocean, which is not above a hundred and fifty
miles from Lagado; where there is a good port, and much
commerce with the great island of Luggnagg, situated to the
north-west about 29 degrees north latitude, and 140 longitude.
This island of Luggnagg stands south-eastward of Japan, about
a hundred leagues distant. There is a strict alliance between
the Japanese emperor and the king of Luggnagg; which affords
frequent opportunities of sailing from one island to the other.
I determined therefore to direct my course this way, in order to
my return to Europe. I hired two mules, with a guide, to show
me the way, and carry my small baggage. I took leave of my
noble protector, who had shown me so much favour, and made
me a generous present at my departure.

My journey was without any accident or adventure worth
relating. When I arrived at the port of Maldonada (for so it is
called) there was no ship in the harbour bound for Luggnagg,
nor likely to be in some time. The town is about as large as

Portsmouth. I soon fell into some acquaintance, and was very hospitably received. A gentleman of distinction said to me, that since the ships bound for Luggnagg could not be ready in less than a month, it might be no disagreeable amusement for me to take a trip to the little island of Glubbdubdrib, about five leagues off to the south-west. He offered himself and a friend to accompany me, and that I should be provided with a small convenient bark for the voyage.

Glubbdubdrib, as nearly as I can interpret the word, signifies the island of sorcerers or magicians. It is about one third as large as the Isle of Wight, and extremely fruitful: it is governed by the head of a certain tribe, who are all magicians. This tribe marries only among each other, and the eldest in succession is prince or governor. He has a noble palace, and a park of about three thousand acres, surrounded by a wall of hewn stone twenty feet high. In this park are several small enclosures for cattle, corn, and gardening.

The governor and his family are served and attended by domestics of a kind somewhat unusual. By his skill in necromancy he has a power of calling whom he pleases from the dead, and commanding their service for twenty-four hours, but no longer; nor can he call the same persons up again in less than three months, except upon very extraordinary occasions.

When we arrived at the island, which was about eleven in the morning, one of the gentlemen who accompanied me went to the governor, and desired admittance for a stranger, who came on purpose to have the honour of attending on his highness. This was immediately granted, and we all three entered the gate of the palace between two rows of guards, armed and dressed after a very antic manner, and with something in their countenances that made my flesh creep with a horror I cannot express. We passed through several apartments, between servants of the same sort, ranked on each side as before, till we came to the chamber of presence; where, after three profound obeisances, and a few general questions, we were permitted to sit on three stools, near the lowest step of his highness's throne.

He understood the language of Balnibarbi, although it was different from that of this island. He desired me to give him some account of my travels; and, to let me see that I should be treated without ceremony, he dismissed all his attendants with a turn of his finger; at which, to my great astonishment, they vanished in an instant, like visions in a dream when we awake on a sudden. I could not recover myself in some time, till the governor assured me, that I should receive no hurt: and observing my two companions to be under no concern, who had been often entertained in the same manner, I began to take courage, and related to his highness a short history of my several adventures; yet not without some hesitation, and frequently looking behind me to the place where I had seen those domestic spectres.

I had the honour to dine with the governor, where a new set of ghosts served up the meat, and waited at table. I now observed myself to be less terrified than I had been in the morning. I stayed till sunset, but humbly desired his highness to excuse me for not accepting his invitation of lodging in the palace. My two friends and I lay at a private house in the town adjoining, which is the capital of this little island; and the next morning we returned to pay our duty to the governor, as he was pleased to command us.

After this manner we continued in the island for ten days, most part of every day with the governor, and at night in our lodging. I soon grew so familiarized to the sight of spirits, that after the third or fourth time they gave me no emotion at all: or, if I had any apprehensions left, my curiosity prevailed over them. For his highness the governor ordered me to call up whatever persons I would choose to name, and in whatever numbers, among all the dead from the beginning of the world to the present time, and command them to answer any questions I should think fit to ask; with this condition, that my questions must be confined within the compass of the times they lived in. And one thing I might depend upon, that they would certainly tell me the truth, for lying was a talent of no use in the lower world.

I made my humble acknowledgments to his highness for so great a favour. We were in a chamber, from whence there was a fair prospect into the park. And because my first inclination was to be entertained with scenes of pomp and magnificence, I desired to see Alexander the Great at the head of his army, just after the battle of Arbela: which, upon a motion of the governor's finger, immediately appeared in a large field, under the window where we stood. Alexander was called up into the room: it was with great difficulty that I understood his Greek, and had but little of my own. He assured me upon his honour that he was not poisoned, but died of a bad fever by excessive drinking.

Next, I saw Hannibal passing the Alps, who told me he had not a drop of vinegar in his camp.

I saw Caesar and Pompey at the head of their troops, just ready to engage. I saw the former, in his last great triumph. I desired that the senate of Rome might appear before me, in one large chamber, and an assembly of somewhat a later age in counterview, in another. The first seemed to be an assembly of heroes and demigods; the other, a knot of pedlars, pick-pockets, highwayman, and bullies.

The governor, at my request, gave the sign for Caesar and Brutus to advance towards us. I was struck with a profound veneration at the sight of Brutus, and could easily discover the most consummate virtue, the greatest intrepidity and firmness of mind, the truest love of his country, and general benevolence for mankind, in every lineament of his countenance. I observed, with much pleasure, that these two persons were in good intelligence with each other; and Caesar freely confessed to me, that the greatest actions of his own life were not equal, by many degrees, to the glory of taking it away. I had the honour to have much conversation with Brutus, and was told that his ancestor Junius, Socrates, Epaminondas, Cato the younger, Sir Thomas More, and himself were perpetually together: a sextum-virate, to which all the ages of the world cannot add a seventh.

It would be tedious to trouble the reader with relating what vast numbers of illustrious persons were called up to gratify that insatiable desire I had to see the world in every period of antiquity placed before me. I chiefly fed mine eyes with beholding the destroyers of tyrants and usurpers, and the restorers of liberty to oppressed and injured nations. But it is impossible to express the satisfaction I received in my own mind, after such a manner as to make it a suitable entertainment to the reader.

CHAPTER VIII

A further account of Glubbdubdrib. Ancient and modern history corrected.

Having a desire to see those ancients who were most renowned for wit and learning, I set apart one day on purpose. I proposed that Homer and Aristotle might appear at the head of all their commentators; but these were so numerous, that some hundreds were forced to attend in the court, and outward rooms of the palace. I knew, and could distinguish those two heroes, at first sight, not only from the crowd, but from each other. Homer was the taller and comelier person of the two, walked very erect for one of his age, and his eyes were the most quick and piercing I ever beheld. Aristotle stooped much, and made use of a staff. His visage was meagre, his hair lank and thin, and his voice hollow.

I soon discovered that both of them were perfect strangers to the rest of the company, and had never seen or heard of them before; and I had a whisper from a ghost who shall be nameless, that these commentators always kept in the most distant quarters from their principals, in the lower world, through a consciousness of shame and guilt, because they had so horribly misrepresented the meaning of those authors to posterity.

I introduced Didymus and Eustathius to Homer, and

prevailed on him to treat them better than perhaps they deserved, for he soon found they wanted a genius to enter into the spirit of a poet. But Aristotle was out of all patience with the account I gave him of Scotus and Ramus, as I presented them to him; and he asked them, whether the rest of the tribe were as great dunces as themselves.

I then desired the governor to call up Descartes and Gassendi, with whom I prevailed to explain their systems to Aristotle. This great philosopher freely acknowledged his own mistakes in natural philosophy, because he proceeded in many things upon conjecture, as all men must do; and he found that Gassendi, who had made the doctrine of Epicurus as palatable as he could, and the vortices of Descartes, were equally to be exploded. He predicted the same fate to *attraction*, whereof the present learned are such zealous asserters. He said, that new systems of nature were but new fashions, which would vary in every age; and even those, who pretend to demonstrate them from mathematical principles, would flourish but a short period of time, and be out of vogue when that was determined.

I spent five days in conversing with many others of the ancient learned. I saw most of the first Roman emperors. I prevailed on the governor to call up Heliogabalus's cooks to dress us a dinner, but they could not show us much of their skill, for want of materials. A helot of Agesilaus made us a dish of Spartan broth, but I was not able to get down a second spoonful.

The two gentlemen, who conducted me to the island, were pressed by their private affairs to return in three days, which I employed in seeing some of the modern dead, who had made the greatest figure, for two or three hundred years past, in our own and other countries of Europe; and having been always a great admirer of old illustrious families, I desired the governor would call up a dozen or two of kings, with their ancestors in order for eight or nine generations. But my disappointment was grievous and unexpected. For, instead of a long train with royal diadems, I saw in one family two fiddlers, three spruce courtiers, and an Italian prelate. In another, a barber, an abbot, and two cardinals. I have too great a veneration for crowned heads, to dwell any longer on so nice a subject. But as to counts, marquises, dukes, earls, and the like, I was not so scrupulous.

And I confess, it was not without some pleasure, that I found myself able to trace the particular features, by which certain families are distinguished, up to their originals. I could plainly discover whence one family derives a long chin; why a second has abounded with knaves for two generations, and fools for two more; why a third happened to be crack-brained, and a fourth to be sharpers; whence it came, what Polydore Virgil says of a certain great house, *Nec vir fortis, nec foemina casta*; how cruelty, falsehood, and cowardice, grew to be characteristics by which certain families are distinguished as much as by their coats of arms.

I was chiefly disgusted with modern history. For having strictly examined all the persons of greatest name in the courts of princes, for a hundred years past, I found how the world had been misled by prostitute writers, to ascribe the greatest exploits in war, to cowards; the wisest counsel, to fools; sincerity, to flatterers; Roman virtue, to betrayers of their country; piety, to atheists; chastity, to sodomites; truth, to informers: how many innocent and excellent persons had been condemned to death or banishment by the practising of great ministers upon the corruption of judges, and the malice of factions: how many villains had been exalted to the highest places of trust, power, dignity, and profit: how great a share in the motions and events of courts, councils, and senates might be challenged by bawds, whores, pimps, parasites, and buffoons. How low an opinion I had of human wisdom and integrity, when I was truly informed of the springs and motives of great enterprises and revolutions in the world, and of the contemptible accidents to which they owed their success.

Here I discovered the roguery and ignorance of those who pretend to write anecdotes, or secret history; who send so many kings to their graves with a cup of poison; will repeat the discourse between a prince and chief minister, where no witness was by; unlock the thoughts and cabinets of ambassadors and secretaries of state; and have the perpetual misfortune to be mistaken.

Here I discovered the true causes of many great events that have surprised the world; how a whore can govern the back-stairs, the back-stairs a council, and the council a senate. A general confessed, in my presence, that he got a victory purely by the force of cowardice and ill conduct; and an admiral, that, for want of proper intelligence, he beat the enemy, to whom he intended to betray the fleet. Three kings protested to me, that in their whole reigns they never did once prefer any person of merit, unless by mistake, or treachery of some minister in whom they confided; neither would they do it if they were to live again: and they showed, with great strength of reason, that the royal throne could not be supported without corruption, because that positive, confident, restiff temper, which virtue infused into a man, was a perpetual clog to public business.

I had the curiosity to inquire in a particular manner, by what methods great numbers had procured to themselves high titles of honour, and prodigious estates; and I confined my inquiry to a very modern period: however, without grating upon present times, because I would be sure to give no offence even to foreigners (for I hope the reader need not be told, that I do not in the least intend my own country, in what I say upon this occasion,) a great number of persons concerned were called up; and, upon a very slight examination, discovered such a scene of infamy, that I cannot reflect upon it without some seriousness.

Perjury, oppression, subornation, fraud, pandarism, and the like infirmities, were among the most excusable arts they had to mention; and for these I gave, as it was reasonable, great allowance. But when some confessed they owed their greatness and wealth to sodomy, or incest; others, to the prostituting of their own wives and daughters; others, to the betraying of their country or their prince; some, to poisoning; more to the perverting of justice, in order to destroy the innocent, I hope I may be pardoned, if these discoveries inclined me a little to abate of that profound veneration, which I am naturally apt to pay to persons of high rank, who ought to be treated with the utmost respect due to their sublime dignity, by us their inferiors.

I had often read of some great services done to princes and states, and desired to see the persons by whom those services were performed. Upon inquiry I was told, that their names were to be found on no record, except a few of them, whom history has represented as the vilest of rogues and traitors. As to the rest, I had never once heard of them. They all appeared with dejected looks, and in the meanest habit; most of them telling me, they died in poverty and disgrace, and the rest on a scaffold or a gibbet.

Among others, there was one person, whose case appeared a little singular. He had a youth about eighteen years old standing by his side. He told me, he had for many years been commander of a ship; and in the sea fight at Actium had the good fortune to break through the enemy's great line of battle, sink three of their capital ships, and take a fourth, which was the sole cause of Antony's flight, and of the victory that ensued; that the youth standing by him, his only son, was killed in the action.

He added, that upon the confidence of some merit, the war being at an end, he went to Rome, and solicited at the court of Augustus to be preferred to a greater ship, whose commander had been killed; but, without any regard to his pretensions, it was given to a boy who had never seen the sea, the son of Libertina, who waited on one of the emperor's mistresses. Returning back to his own vessel, he was charged with neglect of duty, and the ship given to a favourite page of Publicola, the vice-admiral; whereupon he retired to a poor farm at a great distance from Rome, and there ended his life. I was so curious to know the truth of this story, that I desired Agrippa might be called, who was admiral in that fight. He appeared, and confirmed the whole account: but with much more advantage to the captain, whose modesty had extenuated or concealed a great part of his merit.

I was surprised to find corruption grown so high and so quick in that empire, by the force of luxury so lately introduced; which made me less wonder at many parallel cases in other countries, where vices of all kinds have reigned so much longer, and where the whole praise, as well as pillage, has been engrossed by the chief commander, who perhaps had the least title to either.

As every person called up made exactly the same appearance he had done in the world, it gave me melancholy reflections to observe how much the race of human kind was degenerated among us within these hundred years past.

I descended so low, as to desire some English yeoman of the old stamp might be summoned to appear; once so famous for the simplicity of their manners, diet, and dress; for justice in their dealings; for their true spirit of liberty; for their valour, and love of their country. Neither could I be wholly unmoved, after comparing the living with the dead, when I considered how all these pure native virtues were prostituted for a piece of money by their grand-children; who, in selling their votes and managing at elections, have acquired every vice and corruption that can possibly be learned in a court.

CHAPTER IX

The author returns to Maldonada. Sails to the kingdom
of Luggnagg. The author confined. He is sent for to court.
The manner of his admittance. The king's great lenity to
his subjects.

The day of our departure being come, I took leave of his
highness, the Governor of Glubbdubdrib, and returned
with my two companions to Maldonada, where, after a
fortnight's waiting, a ship was ready to sail for Luggnagg. The
two gentlemen, and some others, were so generous and kind
as to furnish me with provisions, and see me on board. I was
a month in this voyage. We had one violent storm, and were
under a necessity of steering westward to get into the trade
wind, which holds for above sixty leagues. On the 21st of April,
1708, we sailed into the river of Clumegnig, which is a seaport
town, at the south-east point of Luggnagg. We cast anchor
within a league of the town, and made a signal for a pilot. Two
of them came on board in less than half an hour, by whom we
were guided between certain shoals and rocks, which are very
dangerous in the passage, to a large basin, where a fleet may
ride in safety within a cable's length of the town-wall.

Some of our sailors, whether out of treachery or
inadvertence, had informed the pilots that I was a stranger,
and great traveller; whereof these gave notice to a custom-

house officer, by whom I was examined very strictly upon my landing. This officer spoke to me in the language of Balnibarbi, which, by the force of much commerce, is generally understood in that town, especially by seamen and those employed in the customs. I gave him a short account of some particulars, and made my story as plausible and consistent as I could; but I thought it necessary to disguise my country, and call myself a Hollander; because my intentions were for Japan, and I knew the Dutch were the only Europeans permitted to enter into that kingdom.

I therefore told the officer, that having been shipwrecked on the coast of Balnibarbi, and cast on a rock, I was received up into Laputa, or the flying island (of which he had often heard), and was now endeavouring to get to Japan, whence I might find a convenience of returning to my own country. The officer said, I must be confined till he could receive orders from court, for which he would write immediately, and hoped to receive an answer in a fortnight. I was carried to a convenient lodging with a sentry placed at the door; however, I had the liberty of a large garden, and was treated with humanity enough, being maintained all the time at the king's charge. I was invited by several persons, chiefly out of curiosity, because it was reported that I came from countries very remote, of which they had never heard.

I hired a young man, who came in the same ship, to be an interpreter; he was a native of Luggnagg, but had lived some years at Maldonada, and was a perfect master of both languages. By his assistance, I was able to hold a conversation with those who came to visit me; but this consisted only of their questions, and my answers.

The despatch came from court about the time we expected. It contained a warrant for conducting me and my retinue to Traldragdubh, Trildrogdrib for it is pronounced both ways as near as I can remember, by a party of ten horse. All my retinue was that poor lad for an interpreter, whom I persuaded into my service, and, at my humble request, we had each of us a mule to ride on. A messenger was despatched half a day's journey before us, to give the king notice of my approach, and to desire, that his Majesty would please to appoint a day and hour, when it would by his gracious pleasure that I might have the honour to lick the dust before his footstool.

This is the court style, and I found it to be more than matter of form: for, upon my admittance two days after my arrival, I was commanded to crawl upon my belly, and lick the floor as I advanced; but, on account of my being a stranger, care was taken to have it made so clean, that the dust was not offensive. However, this was a peculiar grace, not allowed to any but persons of the highest rank, when they desire an admittance. Nay, sometimes the floor is strewed with dust on purpose, when the person to be admitted happens to have powerful enemies at court; and I have seen a great lord with his mouth so crammed, that when he had crept to the proper distance from the throne; he was not able to speak a word. Neither is there any remedy; because it is capital for those, who receive an audience to spit or wipe their mouths in his Majesty's presence.

There is indeed another custom, which I cannot altogether approve of: when the king has a mind to put any of his nobles to death in a gentle indulgent manner, he commands the floor to be strewed with a certain brown powder of a deadly composition, which being licked up, infallibly kills him in twenty-four hours. But in justice to this prince's great clemency, and the care he has of his subjects' lives (wherein it were much to be wished that the Monarchs of Europe would imitate him), it must be mentioned for his honour, that strict orders are given to have the infected parts of the floor well washed after every such execution, which, if his domestics neglect, they are in danger of incurring his royal displeasure.

I myself heard him give directions, that one of his pages

should be whipped, whose turn it was to give notice about washing the floor after an execution, but maliciously had omitted it; by which neglect a young lord of great hopes, coming to an audience, was unfortunately poisoned, although the king at that time had no design against his life. But this good prince was so gracious as to forgive the poor page his whipping, upon promise that he would do so no more, without special orders.

To return from this digression. When I had crept within four yards of the throne, I raised myself gently upon my knees, and then striking my forehead seven times against the ground, I pronounced the following words, as they had been taught me the night before, *Ickpling gloffthrobb squut serumm blhiop mlashnalt zwin tnodbalkuffh slhiophad gurdlubh asht.* This is the compliment, established by the laws of the land, for all persons admitted to the king's presence. It may be rendered into English thus: May your celestial Majesty outlive the sun, eleven moons and a half.

To this the king returned some answer, which, although I could not understand, yet I replied as I had been directed: *Fluft drin yalerick dwuldom prastrad mirpush,* which properly signifies, My tongue is in the mouth of my friend; and by this expression was meant, that I desired leave to bring my interpreter; whereupon the young man already mentioned was accordingly introduced, by whose intervention I answered as many questions as his Majesty could put in above an hour. I spoke in the Balnibarbian tongue, and my interpreter delivered my meaning in that of Luggnagg.

The king was much delighted with my company, and ordered his *bliffmarklub,* or high-chamberlain, to appoint a lodging in the court for me and my interpreter; with a daily allowance for my table, and a large purse of gold for my common expenses.

I staid three months in this country, out of perfect obedience to his Majesty; who was pleased highly to favour me, and made me very honourable offers. But I thought it more consistent with prudence and justice to pass the remainder of my days with my wife and family.

CHAPTER X

The Luggnaggians commended. A particular description
of the Struldbrugs, with many conversations between the
author and some eminent persons upon that subject.

The Luggnaggians are a polite and generous people; and
although they are not without some share of that pride
which is peculiar to all Eastern countries, yet they show
themselves courteous to strangers, especially such who
are countenanced by the court. I had many acquaintance,
and among persons of the best fashion; and being always
attended by my interpreter, the conversation we had was not
disagreeable.

One day, in much good company, I was asked by a person
of quality, whether I had seen any of their struldbrugs, or
immortals? I said, I had not; and desired he would explain to
me what he meant by such an appellation, applied to a mortal
creature. He told me that sometimes, though very rarely,
a child happened to be born in a family, with a red circular
spot in the forehead, directly over the left eyebrow, which
was an infallible mark that it should never die. The spot, as he
described it, was about the compass of a silver threepence, but
in the course of time grew larger, and changed its colour; for
at twelve years old it became green, so continued till five and
twenty, then turned to a deep blue: at five and forty it grew coal

black, and as large as an English shilling; but never admitted any further alteration.

He said, these births were so rare, that he did not believe there could be above eleven hundred struldbrugs, of both sexes, in the whole kingdom; of which he computed about fifty in the metropolis, and, among the rest, a young girl born; about three years ago: that these productions were not peculiar to any family, but a mere effect of chance; and the children of the struldbrugs themselves were equally mortal with the rest of the people.

I freely own myself to have been struck with inexpressible delight, upon hearing this account: and the person who gave it me happening to understand the Balnibarbian language, which I spoke very well, I could not forbear breaking out into expressions, perhaps a little too extravagant. I cried out, as in a rapture, Happy nation, where every child hath at least a chance for being immortal! Happy people, who enjoy so many living examples of ancient virtue, and have masters ready to instruct them in the wisdom of all former ages! but happiest, beyond all comparison, are those excellent struldbrugs, who, being born exempt from that universal calamity of human nature, have their minds free and disengaged, without the weight and depression of spirits caused by the continual apprehensions of death!

I discovered my admiration that I had not observed any of these illustrious persons at court; the black spot on the forehead being so remarkable a distinction, that I could not have easily overlooked it: and it was impossible that his Majesty, a most judicious prince, should not provide himself with a good number of such wise and able counsellors. Yet perhaps the virtue of those reverend sages was too strict for the corrupt and libertine manners of a court: and we often find by experience, that young men are too opinionated and volatile to be guided by the sober dictates of their seniors.

However, since the king was pleased to allow me access to his royal person, I was resolved, upon the very first occasion, to deliver my opinion to him on this matter freely and at large, by the help of my interpreter; and whether he would please to take my advice or not, yet in one thing I was determined, that his Majesty having frequently offered me an establishment in this country, I would, with great thankfulness, accept the favour, and pass my life here in the conversation of those superior beings the struldbrugs, if they would please to admit me.

The gentleman to whom I addressed my discourse, because (as I have already observed) he spoke the language of Balnibarbi, said to me, with a sort of a smile which usually arises from pity to the ignorant, that he was glad of any occasion to keep me among them, and desired my permission to explain to the company what I had spoke. He did so, and they talked together for some time in their own language, whereof I understood not a syllable, neither could I observe by their countenances, what impression my discourse had made on them. After a short silence, the same person told me, that his friends and mine (so he thought fit to express himself) were very much pleased with the judicious remarks I had made on the great happiness and advantages of immortal life, and they were desirous to know, in a particular manner, what scheme of living I should have formed to myself, if it had fallen to my lot to have been born a *struldbrug*.

I answered, it was easy to be eloquent on so copious and delightful a subject, especially to me, who had been often apt to amuse myself with visions of what I should do, if I were a king, a general, or a great lord: and upon this very case, I had frequently run over the whole system how I should employ myself, and pass the time, if I were sure to live for ever.

That, if it had been my good fortune to come into the world a *struldbrug*, as soon as I could discover my own happiness, by understanding the difference between life and death, I would first resolve, by all arts and methods, whatsoever, to procure myself riches. In the pursuit of which, by thrift and management, I might reasonably expect, in about two hundred years, to be the wealthiest man in the kingdom. In the second place, I would, from my earliest youth, apply myself to the study of arts and sciences, by which I should arrive in time to excel all others in learning. Lastly, I would carefully record every action and event of consequence, that happened in the public, impartially draw the characters of the several successions of princes and great ministers of state, with my own observations on every point. I would exactly set down the several changes in customs, language, fashions of dress, diet, and diversions. By all which acquirements, I should be a living treasure of knowledge and wisdom, and certainly become the oracle of the nation.

I would never marry after threescore, but live in a hospitable manner, yet still on the saving side. I would entertain myself in forming and directing the minds of hopeful young men, by convincing them, from my own remembrance, experience, and observation, fortified by numerous examples, of the usefulness of virtue in public and private life. But my choice and constant companions should be a set of my own immortal brotherhood; among whom, I would elect a dozen from the most ancient, down to my own contemporaries.

Where any of these wanted fortunes, I would provide them with convenient lodges round my own estate, and have some of them always at my table; only mingling a few of the most valuable among you mortals, whom length of time would harden me to lose with little or no reluctance, and treat your posterity after the same manner; just as a man diverts himself with the annual succession of pinks and tulips in his garden, without regretting the loss of those which withered the preceding year.

These struldbrugs and I would mutually communicate our observations and memorials, through the course of time; remark the several gradations by which corruption steals into the world, and oppose it in every step, by giving perpetual warning and instruction to mankind; which, added to the strong influence of our own example, would probably prevent that continual degeneracy of human nature so justly complained of in all ages.

Add to this, the pleasure of seeing the various revolutions of states and empires; the changes in the lower and upper world; ancient cities in ruins, and obscure villages become the seats of kings; famous rivers lessening into shallow brooks; the ocean leaving one coast dry, and overwhelming another; the discovery of many countries yet unknown; barbarity overrunning the politest nations, and the most barbarous become civilized. I should then see the discovery of the longitude, the perpetual motion, the universal medicine, and many other great inventions, brought to the utmost perfection.

What wonderful discoveries should we make in astronomy, by outliving and confirming our own predictions; by observing the progress and return of comets, with the changes of motion in the sun, moon, and stars.

I enlarged upon many other topics, which the natural desire of endless life, and sublunary happiness, could easily furnish me with. When I had ended, and the sum of my discourse had been interpreted, as before, to the rest of the company, there was a good deal of talk among them in the language of the country, not without some laughter at my expense. At last, the same gentleman who had been my interpreter, said, he was desired by the rest to set me right in a few mistakes, which I had fallen into through the common imbecility of human nature, and upon that allowance was less answerable for them.

This breed of struldbrugs was peculiar to their country, for there were no such people either in Balnibarbi or Japan, where he had the honour to be ambassador from his Majesty, and found the natives in both those kingdoms very hard to believe that the fact was possible: and it appeared from my astonishment when he first mentioned the matter to me, that I received it as a thing wholly new, and scarcely to be credited. That in the two kingdoms above mentioned, where, during his residence, he had conversed very much, he observed long life to be the universal desire and wish of mankind. That whoever had one foot in the grave was sure to hold back the other as strongly as he could. That the oldest had still hopes of living one day longer, and looked on death as the greatest evil, from which nature always prompted him to retreat. Only in this island of Luggnagg the appetite for living was not so eager, from the continual example of the struldbrugs before their eyes.

That the system of living contrived by me, was unreasonable and unjust; because it supposed a perpetuity of youth, health, and vigour, which no man could be so foolish to hope, however extravagant he may be in his wishes. That the question therefore was not, whether a man would choose to be always in the prime of youth, attended with prosperity and health; but how he would pass a perpetual life under all the usual disadvantages which old age brings along with it. For although few men will avow their desires of being immortal, upon such hard conditions, yet in the two kingdoms before mentioned, of Balnibarbi and Japan, he observed that every man desired to put off death some time longer, let it approach ever so late: and he rarely heard of any man who died willingly, except he were incited by the extremity of grief or torture. And he appealed to me, whether in those countries I had travelled, as well as my own, I had not observed the same general disposition.

After this preface, he gave me a particular account of the struldbrugs among them. He said, they commonly acted like mortals till about thirty years old; after which, by degrees, they grew melancholy and dejected, increasing in both till they came to fourscore. This he learned from their own confession: for otherwise, there not being above two or three of that species born in an age, they were too few to form a general observation by. When they came to fourscore years, which is reckoned the extremity of living in this country, they had not only all the follies and infirmities of other old men, but many more which arose from the dreadful prospect of never dying. They were not only opinionative, peevish, covetous, morose, vain, talkative, but incapable of friendship, and dead to all natural affection, which never descended below their grandchildren. Envy and impotent desires are their prevailing passions. But those objects against which their envy seems principally directed, are the vices of the younger sort and the deaths of the old. By reflecting on the former, they find themselves cut off from all possibility of pleasure; and whenever they see a funeral, they lament and repine that others have gone to a harbour of rest to which they themselves never can hope to arrive.

They have no remembrance of anything but what they learned and observed in their youth and middle-age, and even that is very imperfect; and for the truth or particulars of any fact, it is safer to depend on common tradition, than upon their best recollections. The least miserable among them appear to be those who turn to dotage, and entirely lose their memories; these meet with more pity and assistance, because they want many bad qualities which abound in others.

If a struldbrug happen to marry one of his own kind, the marriage is dissolved of course, by the courtesy of the kingdom, as soon as the younger of the two comes to be fourscore; for the law thinks it a reasonable indulgence, that those who are condemned, without any fault of their own, to a perpetual continuance in the world, should not have their misery doubled by the load of a wife.

As soon as they have completed the term of eighty years,

they are looked on as dead in law; their heirs immediately succeed to their estates; only a small pittance is reserved for their support; and the poor ones are maintained at the public charge. After that period, they are held incapable of any employment of trust or profit; they cannot purchase lands, or take leases; neither are they allowed to be witnesses in any cause, either civil or criminal, not even for the decision of meers and bounds.

At ninety, they lose their teeth and hair; they have at that age no distinction of taste, but eat and drink whatever they can get, without relish or appetite. The diseases they were subject to still continue, without increasing or diminishing. In talking, they forget the common appellation of things, and the names of persons, even of those who are their nearest friends and relations. For the same reason, they never can amuse themselves with reading, because their memory will not serve to carry them from the beginning of a sentence to the end; and by this defect, they are deprived of the only entertainment whereof they might otherwise be capable.

The language of this country being always upon the flux, the struldbrugs of one age do not understand those of another; neither are they able, after two hundred years, to hold any conversation (farther than by a few general words) with their neighbours the mortals; and thus they lie under the disadvantage of living like foreigners in their own country.

This was the account given me of the struldbrugs, as near as I can remember. I afterwards saw five or six of different ages, the youngest not above two hundred years old, who were brought to me at several times by some of my friends; but although they were told, that I was a great traveller, and had seen all the world, they had not the least curiosity to ask me a question; only desired I would give them *slumskudask*, or a token of remembrance; which is a modest way of begging, to avoid the law, that strictly forbids it, because they are provided for by the public, although indeed with a very scanty allowance.

They are despised and hated by all sorts of people. When one of them is born, it is reckoned ominous, and their birth is recorded very particularly so that you may know their age by consulting the register, which, however, has not been kept above a thousand years past, or at least has been destroyed by time or public disturbances. But the usual way of computing how old they are, is by asking them what kings or great persons they can remember, and then consulting history; for infallibly the last prince in their mind did not begin his reign after they were fourscore years old.

They were the most mortifying sight I ever beheld; and the women more horrible than the men. Besides the usual deformities in extreme old age, they acquired an additional ghastliness, in proportion to their number of years, which is not to be described; and among half a dozen, I soon distinguished which was the eldest, although there was not above a century or two between them.

The reader will easily believe, that from what I had hear and seen, my keen appetite for perpetuity of life was much abated. I grew heartily ashamed of the pleasing visions I had formed; and thought no tyrant could invent a death into which I would not run with pleasure, from such a life. The king heard of all that had passed between me and my friends upon this occasion, and rallied me very pleasantly; wishing I could send a couple of struldbrugs to my own country, to arm our people against the fear of death; but this, it seems, is forbidden by the fundamental laws of the kingdom, or else I should have been well content with the trouble and expense of transporting them.

I could not but agree, that the laws of this kingdom relative to the struldbrugs were founded upon the strongest reasons, and such as any other country would be under the necessity of enacting, in the like circumstances. Otherwise, as avarice is the necessary consequence of old age, those immortals would in time become proprietors of the whole nation, and engross the civil power, which, for want of abilities to manage, must end in the ruin of the public.

CHAPTER XI

The author leaves Luggnagg, and sails to Japan. From thence he returns in a Dutch ship to Amsterdam, and from Amsterdam to England.

I thought this account of the struldbrugs might be some entertainment to the reader, because it seems to be a little out of the common way; at least I do not remember to have met the like in any book of travels that has come to my hands: and if I am deceived, my excuse must be, that it is necessary for travellers who describe the same country, very often to agree in dwelling on the same particulars, without deserving the censure of having borrowed or transcribed from those who wrote before them.

There is indeed a perpetual commerce between this kingdom and the great empire of Japan; and it is very probable, that the Japanese authors may have given some account of the struldbrugs; but my stay in Japan was so short, and I was so entirely a stranger to the language, that I was not qualified to make any inquiries. But I hope the Dutch, upon this notice, will be curious and able enough to supply my defects.

His Majesty having often pressed me to accept some employment in his court, and finding me absolutely determined to return to my native country, was pleased to give me his license to depart; and honoured me with a letter of recommendation, under his own hand, to the Emperor of Japan. He likewise presented me with four hundred and forty-four large pieces of gold (this nation delighting in even numbers), and a red diamond, which I sold in England for eleven hundred pounds.

On the 6th of May, 1709, I took a solemn leave of his Majesty, and all my friends. This prince was so gracious as to order a guard to conduct me to Glanguenstald, which is a royal port to the south-west part of the island. In six days I found a vessel ready to carry me to Japan, and spent fifteen days in the voyage. We landed at a small port-town called Xamoschi, situated on the south-east part of Japan; the town lies on the western point, where there is a narrow strait leading northward into along arm of the sea, upon the north-west part of which, Yedo, the metropolis, stands.

At landing, I showed the custom-house officers my letter from the king of Luggnagg to his imperial Majesty . They knew the seal perfectly well; it was as broad as the palm of my hand. The impression was, A king lifting up a lame beggar from the earth. The magistrates of the town, hearing of my letter, received me as a public minister. They provided me with carriages and servants, and bore my charges to Yedo; where I was admitted to an audience, and delivered my letter, which was opened with great ceremony, and explained to the Emperor by an interpreter, who then gave me notice, by his Majesty's order, that I should signify my request, and, whatever it were, it should be granted, for the sake of his royal brother of Luggnagg.

This interpreter was a person employed to transact affairs with the Hollanders. He soon conjectured, by my countenance, that I was a European, and therefore repeated his Majesty's commands in Low Dutch, which he spoke perfectly well. I answered, as I had before determined, that I was a Dutch merchant, shipwrecked in a very remote country, whence I had travelled by sea and land to Luggnagg, and then took shipping for Japan; where I knew my countrymen often traded, and with some of these I hoped to get an opportunity of returning into Europe: I therefore most humbly entreated his royal favour, to give order that I should be conducted in safety to Nangasac. To this I added another petition, that for the sake of my patron the king of Luggnagg, his Majesty would condescend to excuse my performing the ceremony imposed on my countrymen, of trampling upon the crucifix: because I had been thrown into his kingdom by my misfortunes, without any intention of trading.

When this latter petition was interpreted to the Emperor, he seemed a little surprised; and said, he believed I was the first of my countrymen who ever made any scruple in this point; and that he began to doubt, whether I was a real Hollander, or not; but rather suspected I must be a Christian. However, for the reasons I had offered, but chiefly to gratify the king of Luggnagg by an uncommon mark of his favour, he would comply with the singularity of my humour; but the affair must be managed with dexterity, and his officers should be commanded to let me pass, as it were by forgetfulness. For he assured me, that if the secret should be discovered by my countrymen the Dutch, they would cut my throat in the voyage. I returned my thanks, by the interpreter, for so unusual a favour; and some troops being at that time on their march to Nangasac, the commanding officer had orders to convey me safe thither, with particular instructions about the business of the crucifix.

On the 9th day of June, 1709, I arrived at Nangasac, after a very long and troublesome journey. I soon fell into the company of some Dutch sailors belonging to the Amboyna, of Amsterdam, a stout ship of 450 tons. I had lived long in Holland, pursuing my studies at Leyden, and I spoke Dutch well. The seamen soon knew whence I came last: they were curious to inquire into my voyages and course of life. I made up a story as short and probable as I could, but concealed the greatest part. I knew many persons in Holland. I was able to invent names for my parents, whom I pretended to be obscure people in the province of Gelderland. I would have given the captain (one Theodorus Vangrult) what he pleased to ask for my voyage to Holland; but understanding I was a surgeon, he was contented to take half the usual rate, on condition that I would serve him in the way of my calling.

Before we took shipping, I was often asked by some of the crew, whether I had performed the ceremony above mentioned? I evaded the question by general answers; that I had satisfied the Emperor and court in all particulars. However, a malicious rogue of a skipper went to an officer, and pointing to me, told him, I had not yet trampled on the crucifix; but the other, who had received instructions to let me pass, gave the rascal twenty strokes on the shoulders with a bamboo; after which I was no more troubled with such questions.

Nothing happened worth mentioning in this voyage. We sailed with a fair wind to the Cape of Good Hope, where we staid only to take in fresh water. On the 10th of April, 1710, we arrived safe at Amsterdam, having lost only three men by sickness in the voyage, and a fourth, who fell from the foremast into the sea, not far from the coast of Guinea. From Amsterdam I soon after set sail for England, in a small vessel belonging to that city.

On the 16th of April we put in at the Downs. I landed next morning, and saw once more my native country, after an absence of five years and six months complete. I went straight to Redriff, where I arrived the same day at two in the afternoon, and found my wife and family in good health.

PART IV

———•••◦◦((◦◦•••———

A Voyage to
the Country of the
Houyhnhnms

CHAPTER I

The author sets out as captain of a ship. His men conspire
against him, confine him a long time to his cabin, and set
him on shore in an unknown land. He travels up into the
country. The Yahoos, a strange sort of animal, described.
The author meets two Houyhnhnms.

I continued at home with my wife and children about five
months, in a very happy condition, if I could have learned
the lesson of knowing when I was well. I left my poor wife big
with child, and accepted an advantageous offer made me to be
captain of the Adventurer, a stout merchantman of 350 tons:
for I understood navigation well, and being grown weary of a
surgeon's employment at sea, which, however, I could exercise
upon occasion, I took a skilful young man of that calling, one
Robert Purefoy, into my ship.

We set sail from Portsmouth upon the 7th day of
September, 1710; on the 14th we met with Captain Pocock, of
Bristol, at Teneriffe, who was going to the bay of Campechy to
cut logwood. On the 16th, he was parted from us by a storm;
I heard since my return, that his ship foundered, and none
escaped but one cabin boy. He was an honest man, and a good
sailor, but a little too positive in his own opinions, which was
the cause of his destruction, as it has been with several others;
for if he had followed my advice, he might have been safe at

home with his family at this time, as well as myself.

I had several men who died in my ship of calentures, so that I was forced to get recruits out of Barbadoes and the Leeward Islands, where I touched, by the direction of the merchants who employed me; which I had soon too much cause to repent: for I found afterwards, that most of them had been buccaneers. I had fifty hands onboard; and my orders were, that I should trade with the Indians in the South-Sea, and make what discoveries I could. These rogues, whom I had picked up, debauched my other men, and they all formed a conspiracy to seize the ship, and secure me; which they did one morning, rushing into my cabin, and binding me hand and foot, threatening to throw me overboard, if I offered to stir. I told them, I was their prisoner, and would submit. This they made me swear to do, and then they unbound me, only fastening one of my legs with a chain, near my bed, and placed a sentry at my door with his piece charged, who was commanded to shoot me dead if I attempted my liberty.

They sent me own victuals and drink, and took the government of the ship to themselves. Their design was to turn pirates and, plunder the Spaniards, which they could not do till they got more men. But first they resolved to sell the goods the ship, and then go to Madagascar for recruits, several among them having died since my confinement. They sailed many weeks, and traded with the Indians; but I knew not what course they took, being kept a close prisoner in my cabin, and expecting nothing less than to be murdered, as they often threatened me.

Upon the 9th day of May, 1711, one James Welch came down to my cabin, and said, he had orders from the captain to set me ashore. I expostulated with him, but in vain; neither would he so much as tell me who their new captain was. They forced me into the long-boat, letting me put on my best suit of clothes, which were as good as new, and take a small bundle of

linen, but no arms, except my hanger; and they were so civil as
not to search my pockets, into which I conveyed what money I
had, with some other little necessaries.

They rowed about a league, and then set me down on a
strand. I desired them to tell me what country it was. They
all swore, they knew no more than myself; but said, that the
captain (as they called him) was resolved, after they had sold
the lading, to get rid of me in the first place where they could
discover land. They pushed off immediately, advising me to
make haste for fear of being overtaken by the tide, and so bade
me farewell.

In this desolate condition I advanced forward, and soon got
upon firm ground, where I sat down on a bank to rest myself,
and consider what I had best do. When I was a little refreshed,
I went up into the country, resolving to deliver myself to the
first savages I should meet, and purchase my life from them
by some bracelets, glass rings, and other toys, which sailors
usually provide themselves with in those voyages, and whereof
I had some about me. The land was divided by long rows of
trees, not regularly planted, but naturally growing; there was
great plenty of grass, and several fields of oats.

I walked very circumspectly, for fear of being surprised, or
suddenly shot with an arrow from behind, or on either side. I
fell into a beaten road, where I saw many tracts of human feet,
and some of cows, but most of horses. At last I beheld several
animals in a field, and one or two of the same kind sitting in
trees. Their shape was very singular and deformed, which a
little discomposed me, so that I lay down behind a thicket to
observe them better. Some of them coming forward near the
place where I lay, gave me an opportunity of distinctly marking
their form.

Their heads and breasts were covered with a thick hair,
some frizzled, and others lank; they had beards like goats,
and a long ridge of hair down their backs, and the fore parts

of their legs and feet; but the rest of their bodies was bare, so that I might see their skins, which were of a brown buff colour. They had no tails, nor any hair at all on their buttocks, except about the anus, which, I presume, nature had placed there to defend them as they sat on the ground, for this posture they used, as well as lying down, and often stood on their hind feet. They climbed high trees as nimbly as a squirrel, for they had strong extended claws before and behind, terminating in sharp points, and hooked. They would often spring, and bound, and leap, with prodigious agility. The females were not so large as the males; they had long lank hair on their heads, but none on their faces, nor any thing more than a sort of down on the rest of their bodies, except about the anus and pudenda. The dugs hung between their fore feet, and often reached almost to the ground as they walked. The hair of both sexes was of several colours, brown, red, black, and yellow. Upon the whole, I never beheld, in all my travels, so disagreeable an animal, or one against which I naturally conceived so strong an antipathy. So that, thinking I had seen enough, full of contempt and aversion, I got up, and pursued the beaten road, hoping it might direct me to the cabin of some Indian.

I had not got far, when I met one of these creatures full in my way, and coming up directly to me. The ugly monster, when he saw me, distorted several ways, every feature of his visage, and stared, as at an object he had never seen before; then approaching nearer, lifted up his fore-paw, whether out of curiosity or mischief I could not tell; but I drew my hanger, and gave him a good blow with the flat side of it, for I durst not strike with the edge, fearing the inhabitants might be provoked against me, if they should come to know that I had killed or maimed any of their cattle. When the beast felt the smart, he drew back, and roared so loud, that a herd of at least forty came flocking about me from the next field, howling and making odious faces; but I ran to the body of a tree, and leaning my back against it, kept them off by waving my hanger.

In the midst of this distress, I observed them all to run away on a sudden as fast as they could; at which I ventured to leave the tree and pursue the road, wondering what it was that could put them into this fright. But looking on my left hand, I saw a horse walking softly in the field; which my persecutors having sooner discovered, was the cause of their flight. The horse started a little, when he came near me, but soon recovering himself, looked full in my face with manifest tokens of wonder; he viewed my hands and feet, walking round me several times. I would have pursued my journey, but he placed himself directly in the way, yet looking with a very mild aspect, never offering the least violence.

We stood gazing at each other for some time; at last I took the boldness to reach my hand towards his neck with a design to stroke it, using the common style and whistle of jockeys, when they are going to handle a strange horse. But this animal seemed to receive my civilities with disdain, shook his head, and bent his brows, softly raising up his right fore-foot to remove my hand. Then he neighed three or four times, but in so different a cadence, that I almost began to think he was speaking to himself, in some language of his own.

While he and I were thus employed, another horse came up; who applying himself to the first in a very formal manner, they gently struck each other's right hoof before, neighing several times by turns, and varying the sound, which seemed to be almost articulate. They went some paces off, as if it were to confer together, walking side by side, backward and forward, like persons deliberating upon some affair of weight, but often turning their eyes towards me, as it were to watch that I might not escape. I was amazed to see such actions and behaviour in brute beasts; and concluded with myself, that if the inhabitants of this country were endued with a proportionable degree of reason, they must needs be the wisest people upon earth.

This thought gave me so much comfort, that I resolved to go forward, until I could discover some house or village, or meet with any of the natives, leaving the two horses to discourse together as they pleased. But the first, who was a dapple gray, observing me to steal off, neighed after me in so expressive a tone, that I fancied myself to understand what he meant; whereupon I turned back, and came near to him to expect his farther commands: but concealing my fear as much as I could, for I began to be in some pain how this adventure might terminate; and the reader will easily believe I did not much like my present situation.

The two horses came up close to me, looking with great earnestness upon my face and hands. The gray steed rubbed my hat all round with his right fore-hoof, and discomposed it so much that I was forced to adjust it better by taking it off and settling it again; whereat, both he and his companion (who was a brown bay) appeared to be much surprised: the latter felt the lappet of my coat, and finding it to hang loose about me, they both looked with new signs of wonder. He stroked my right hand, seeming to admire the softness and colour; but he squeezed it so hard between his hoof and his pastern, that I was forced to roar; after which they both touched me with all possible tenderness. They were under great perplexity about my shoes and stockings, which they felt very often, neighing to each other, and using various gestures, not unlike those of a philosopher, when he would attempt to solve some new and difficult phenomenon.

Upon the whole, the behaviour of these animals was so orderly and rational, so acute and judicious, that I at last concluded they must needs be magicians, who had thus metamorphosed themselves upon some design, and seeing a stranger in the way, resolved to divert themselves with him;

or, perhaps, were really amazed at the sight of a man so very different in habit, feature, and complexion, from those who might probably live in so remote a climate.

Upon the strength of this reasoning, I ventured to address them in the following manner: Gentlemen, if you be conjurers, as I have good cause to believe, you can understand my language; therefore I make bold to let your worships know that I am a poor distressed Englishman, driven by his misfortunes upon your coast; and I entreat one of you to let me ride upon his back, as if he were a real horse, to some house or village where I can be relieved. In return of which favour, I will make you a present of this knife and bracelet (taking them out of my pocket).

The two creatures stood silent while I spoke, seeming to listen with great attention, and when I had ended, they neighed frequently towards each other, as if they were engaged in serious conversation. I plainly observed that their language expressed the passions very well, and the words might, with little pains, be resolved into an alphabet more easily than the Chinese.

I could frequently distinguish the word Yahoo, which was repeated by each of them several times: and although it was impossible for me to conjecture what it meant, yet while the two horses were busy in conversation, I endeavoured to practise this word upon my tongue; and as soon as they were silent, I boldly pronounced Yahoo in a loud voice, imitating at the same time, as near as I could, the neighing of a horse; at which they were both visibly surprised; and the gray repeated the same word twice, as if he meant to teach me the right accent; wherein I spoke after him as well as I could, and found myself perceivably to improve every time, though very far from any degree of perfection. Then the bay tried me with a second word, much harder to be pronounced; but reducing it to the English orthography, may be spelt thus, Houyhnhnm.

I did not succeed in this so well as in the former; but after two or three farther trials, I had better fortune; and they both appeared amazed at my capacity.

After some further discourse, which I then conjectured might relate to me, the two friends took their leaves, with the same compliment of striking each other's hoof; and the gray made me signs that I should walk before him; wherein I thought it prudent to comply, till I could find a better director. When I offered to slacken my pace, he would cry *Hhuun Hhuun*: I guessed his meaning, and gave him to understand, as well as I could, that I was weary, and not able to walk faster; upon which he would stand awhile to let me rest.

CHAPTER II

The author conducted by a Houyhnhnm to his house. The house described. The author's reception. The food of the Houyhnhnms. The author in distress for want of meat. Is at last relieved. His manner of feeding in this country.

Having travelled about three miles, we came to a long kind of building, made of timber stuck in the ground, and wattled across; the roof was low and covered with straw. I now began to be a little comforted; and took out some toys, which travellers usually carry for presents to the savage Indians of America, and other parts, in hopes the people of the house would be thereby encouraged to receive me kindly. The horse made me a sign to go in first; it was a large room with a smooth clay floor, and a rack and manger, extending the whole length on one side.

There were three nags and two mares, not eating, but some of them sitting down upon their hams, which I very much wondered at; but wondered more to see the rest employed in domestic business; these seemed but ordinary cattle. However, this confirmed my first opinion, that a people who could so far civilise brute animals, must needs excel in wisdom all the nations of the world. The gray came in just after, and thereby prevented any ill treatment which the others might have given me. He neighed to them several times in a style of authority, and received answers.

Beyond this room there were three others, reaching the length of the house, to which you passed through three doors, opposite to each other, in the manner of a vista. We went through the second room towards the third. Here the gray walked in first, beckoning me to attend: I waited in the second room, and got ready my presents for the master and mistress of the house; they were two knives, three bracelets of false pearls, a small looking-glass, and a bead necklace. The horse neighed three or four times, and I waited to hear some answers in a human voice, but I heard no other returns than in the same dialect, only one or two a little shriller than his. I began to think that this house must belong to some person of great note among them, because there appeared so much ceremony before I could gain admittance.

But that a man of quality should be served all by horses, was beyond my comprehension. I feared my brain was disturbed by my sufferings and misfortunes. I roused myself, and looked about me in the room where I was left alone: this was furnished like the first, only after a more elegant manner. I rubbed my eyes often, but the same objects still occurred. I pinched my arms and sides to awake myself, hoping I might be in a dream. I then absolutely concluded, that all these appearances could be nothing else but necromancy and magic. But I had no time to pursue these reflections; for the gray horse came to the door, and made me a sign to follow him into the third room where I saw a very comely mare, together with a colt and foal, sitting on their haunches upon mats of straw, not unartfully made, and perfectly neat and clean.

The mare soon after my entrance rose from her mat, and coming up close, after having nicely observed my hands and face, gave me a most contemptuous look; and turning to the horse, I heard the word Yahoo often repeated betwixt them; the meaning of which word I could not then comprehend, although it was the first I had learned to pronounce. But I was soon better informed, to my everlasting mortification; for the horse, beckoning to me with his head, and repeating the *Hhuun, Hhuun,* as he did upon the road, which I understood was to attend him, led me out into a kind of court, where was another building, at some distance from the house.

Here we entered, and I saw three of those detestable creatures, which I first met after my landing, feeding upon roots, and the flesh of some animals, which I afterwards found to be that of asses and dogs, and now and then a cow, dead by accident or disease. They were all tied by the neck with strong withes fastened to a beam; they held their food between the claws of their fore feet, and tore it with their teeth.

The master horse ordered a sorrel nag, one of his servants, to untie the largest of these animals, and take him into the yard. The beast and I were brought close together, and by our countenances diligently compared both by master and servant, who thereupon repeated several times the word Yahoo. My horror and astonishment are not to be described, when I observed in this abominable animal, a perfect human figure: the face of it indeed was flat and broad, the nose depressed, the lips large, and the mouth wide; but these differences are common to all savage nations, where the lineaments of the countenance are distorted, by the natives suffering their infants to lie grovelling on the earth, or by carrying them on their backs, nuzzling with their face against the mothers' shoulders. The fore-feet of the Yahoo differed from my hands in nothing else but the length of the nails, the coarseness and brownness of the palms, and the hairiness on the backs. There was the same resemblance between our feet, with the same differences; which I knew very well, though the horses did not, because of my shoes and stockings; the same in every part of our bodies except as to hairiness and colour, which I have already described.

The great difficulty that seemed to stick with the two horses, was to see the rest of my body so very different from that of a Yahoo, for which I was obliged to my clothes, whereof they had no conception. The sorrel nag offered me a root, which he held (after their manner, as we shall describe in its proper place) between his hoof and pastern; I took it in my hand, and, having smelt it, returned it to him again as civilly as I could. He brought out of the Yahoos' kennel a piece of ass's flesh; but it smelt so offensively that I turned from it with loathing: he then threw it to the Yahoo, by whom it was greedily devoured. He afterwards showed me a wisp of hay, and a fetlock full of oats; but I shook my head, to signify that neither of these were food for me.

Indeed I now apprehended that I must absolutely starve, if I did not get to some of my own species; for as to those filthy Yahoos, although there were few greater lovers of mankind at that time than myself, yet I confess I never saw any sensitive being so detestable on all accounts; and the more I came near them the more hateful they grew, while I stayed in that country. This the master horse observed by my behaviour, and therefore sent the Yahoo back to his kennel. He then put his fore-hoof to his mouth, at which I was much surprised, although he did it with ease, and with a motion that appeared perfectly natural, and made other signs, to know what I would eat; but I could not return him such an answer as he was able to apprehend; and if he had understood me, I did not see how it was possible to contrive any way for finding myself nourishment.

While we were thus engaged, I observed a cow passing by, whereupon I pointed to her, and expressed a desire to go and milk her. This had its effect; for he led me back into the house, and ordered a mare-servant to open a room, where a good store of milk lay in earthen and wooden vessels, after a very orderly and cleanly manner. She gave me a large bowlful, of which I drank very heartily, and found myself well refreshed.

About noon, I saw coming towards the house a kind of
vehicle drawn like a sledge by four Yahoos. There was in it an
old steed, who seemed to be of quality; he alighted with his
hind-feet forward, having by accident got a hurt in his left fore-
foot. He came to dine with our horse, who received him with
great civility. They dined in the best room, and had oats boiled
in milk for the second course, which the old horse ate warm,
but the rest cold. Their mangers were placed circular in the
middle of the room, and divided into several partitions, round
which they sat on their haunches, upon bosses of straw.

In the middle was a large rack, with angles answering to
every partition of the manger; so that each horse and mare
ate their own hay, and their own mash of oats and milk, with
much decency and regularity. The behaviour of the young colt
and foal appeared very modest, and that of the master and
mistress extremely cheerful and complaisant to their guest. The
gray ordered me to stand by him; and much discourse passed
between him and his friend concerning me, as I found by the
stranger's often looking on me, and the frequent repetition of
the word Yahoo.

I happened to wear my gloves, which the master gray
observing, seemed perplexed, discovering signs of wonder
what I had done to my fore-feet. He put his hoof three or four
times to them, as if he would signify, that I should reduce them
to their former shape, which I presently did, pulling off both
my gloves, and putting them into my pocket. This occasioned
farther talk; and I saw the company was pleased with my
behaviour, whereof I soon found the good effects. I was
ordered to speak the few words I understood; and while they
were at dinner, the master taught me the names for oats, milk,
fire, water, and some others, which I could readily pronounce
after him, having from my youth a great facility in learning
languages.

When dinner was done, the master horse took me aside,

and by signs and words made me understand the concern he was in that I had nothing to eat. Oats in their tongue are called *hlunnh*. This word I pronounced two or three times; for although I had refused them at first, yet, upon second thoughts, I considered that I could contrive to make of them a kind of bread, which might be sufficient, with milk, to keep me alive, till I could make my escape to some other country, and to creatures of my own species. The horse immediately ordered a white mare servant of his family to bring me a good quantity of oats in a sort of wooden tray. These I heated before the fire, as well as I could, and rubbed them till the husks came off, which I made a shift to winnow from the grain. I ground and beat them between two stones; then took water, and made them into a paste or cake, which I toasted at the fire and eat warm with milk. It was at first a very insipid diet, though common enough in many parts of Europe, but grew tolerable by time; and having been often reduced to hard fare in my life, this was not the first experiment I had made how easily nature is satisfied.

And I cannot but observe, that I never had one hours sickness while I stayed in this island. It is true, I sometimes made a shift to catch a rabbit, or bird, by springs made of Yahoo's hairs; and I often gathered wholesome herbs, which I boiled, and ate as salads with my bread; and now and then, for a rarity, I made a little butter, and drank the whey. I was at first at a great loss for salt, but custom soon reconciled me to the want of it; and I am confident that the frequent use of salt among us is an effect of luxury, and was first introduced only as a provocative to drink, except where it is necessary for preserving flesh in long voyages, or in places remote from great markets; for we observe no animal to be fond of it but man, and as to myself, when I left this country, it was a great while before I could endure the taste of it in anything that I ate.

This is enough to say upon the subject of my diet,

wherewith other travellers fill their books, as if the readers were personally concerned whether we fare well or ill. However, it was necessary to mention this matter, lest the world should think it impossible that I could find sustenance for three years in such a country, and among such inhabitants.

When it grew towards evening, the master horse ordered a place for me to lodge in; it was but six yards from the house and separated from the stable of the Yahoos. Here I got some straw, and covering myself with my own clothes, slept very sound. But I was in a short time better accommodated, as the reader shall know hereafter, when I come to treat more particularly about my way of living.

CHAPTER III

The author studies to learn the language. The Houyhnhnm, his master, assists in teaching him. The language described. Several Houyhnhnms of quality come out of curiosity to see the author. He gives his master a short account of his voyage.

My principal endeavour was to learn the language, which my master (for so I shall henceforth call him), and his children, and every servant of his house, were desirous to teach me; for they looked upon it as a prodigy, that a brute animal should discover such marks of a rational creature. I pointed to every thing, and inquired the name of it, which I wrote down in my journal-book when I was alone, and corrected my bad accent by desiring those of the family to pronounce it often. In this employment, a sorrel nag, one of the under-servants, was very ready to assist me.

In speaking, they pronounced through the nose and throat, and their language approaches nearest to the High-Dutch, or German, of any I know in Europe; but is much more graceful and significant. The emperor Charles V. made almost the same observation, when he said that if he were to speak to his horse, it should be in High-Dutch.

The curiosity and impatience of my master were so great, that he spent many hours of his leisure to instruct me. He was

convinced (as he afterwards told me) that I must be a Yahoo;
but my teachableness, civility, and cleanliness, astonished him;
which were qualities altogether opposite to those animals. He
was most perplexed about my clothes, reasoning sometimes
with himself, whether they were a part of my body: for I never
pulled them off till the family were asleep, and got them on
before they waked in the morning. My master was eager to
learn whence I came; how I acquired those appearances of
reason, which I discovered in all my actions; and to know my
story from my own mouth, which he hoped he should soon do
by the great proficiency I made in learning and pronouncing
their words and sentences. To help my memory, I formed all
I learned into the English alphabet, and writ the words down,
with the translations. This last, after some time, I ventured to
do in my master's presence. It cost me much trouble to explain
to him what I was doing; for the inhabitants have not the least
idea of books or literature.

In about ten weeks time, I was able to understand most
of his questions; and in three months, could give him some
tolerable answers. He was extremely curious to know from
what part of the country I came, and how I was taught to
imitate a rational creature; because the Yahoos (whom he
saw I exactly resembled in my head, hands, and face, that
were only visible), with some appearance of cunning, and the
strongest disposition to mischief, were observed to be the most
unteachable of all brutes.

I answered that I came over the sea, from a far place, with
many others of my own kind, in a great hollow vessel made of
the bodies of trees: that my companions forced me to land on
this coast, and then left me to shift for myself. It was with some
difficulty, and by the help of many signs, that I brought him to
understand me. He replied, that I must needs be mistaken, or
that I said the thing which was not; for they have no word in
their language to express lying or falsehood. He knew it was

impossible that there could be a country beyond the sea, or that a parcel of brutes could move a wooden vessel whither they pleased upon water. He was sure no Houyhnhnm alive could make such a vessel, nor would trust Yahoos to manage it.

The word Houyhnhnm, in their tongue, signifies a horse, and, in its etymology, the perfection of nature. I told my master, that I was at a loss for expression, but would improve as fast as I could; and hoped, in a short time, I should be able to tell him wonders. He was pleased to direct his own mare, his colt, and foal, and the servants of the family, to take all opportunities of instructing me; and every day, for two or three hours, he was at the same pains himself. Several horses and mares of quality in the neighbourhood came often to our house, upon the report spread of a wonderful Yahoo, that could speak like a Houyhnhnm, and seemed, in his words and actions, to discover some glimmerings of reason. These delighted to converse with me: they put many questions, and received such answers as I was able to return. By all these advantages I made so great a progress, that, in five months from my arrival I understood whatever was spoken, and could express myself tolerably well.

The Houyhnhnms, who came to visit my master out of a design of seeing and talking with me, could hardly believe me to be a right Yahoo, because my body had a different covering from others of my kind. They were astonished to observe me without the usual hair or skin, except on my head, face, and hands; but I discovered that secret to my master upon an accident which happened about a fortnight before.

I have already told the reader, that every night, when the family were gone to bed, it was my custom to strip, and cover myself with my clothes. It happened, one morning early, that my master sent for me by the sorrel nag, who was his valet. When he came I was fast asleep, my clothes fallen off on one side, and my shirt above my waist. I awaked at the noise he made, and observed him to deliver his message in some disorder; after which he went to my master, and in a great fright gave him a very confused account of what he had seen. This I presently discovered, for, going as soon as I was dressed to pay my attendance upon his honour, he asked me the meaning of what his servant had reported: that I was not the same thing when I slept, as I appeared to be at other times.

I had hitherto concealed the secret of my dress, in order to distinguish myself, as much as possible, from that cursed race of Yahoos; but now I found it in vain to do so any longer. Besides, I considered that my clothes and shoes would soon wear out, which already were in a declining condition, and must be supplied by some contrivance from the hides of Yahoos, or other brutes; whereby the whole secret would be known. I therefore told my master, that in the country whence I came, those of my kind always covered their bodies with the hairs of certain animals prepared by art, as well for decency as to avoid the inclemencies of air, both hot and cold; of which, as to my own person, I would give him immediate conviction, if he pleased to command me. Whereupon I first unbuttoned my coat, and pulled it off. I did the same with my waistcoat. I drew off my shoes, stockings, and breeches.

My master observed the whole performance with great signs of curiosity and admiration. He took up all my clothes in his pastern, one piece after another, and examined them diligently; he then stroked my body very gently, and looked round me several times; after which, he said, it was plain I must be a perfect Yahoo; but that I differed very much from the rest of my species in the softness, whiteness, and smoothness of my skin; my want of hair in several parts of my body; the shape and shortness of my claws behind and before; and my affectation of walking continually on my two hinder feet. He desired to see no more; and gave me leave to put on my clothes again, for I was shuddering with cold.

I expressed my uneasiness at his giving me so often the appellation of Yahoo, an odious animal, for which I had so utter a hatred and contempt: I begged he would forbear applying that word to me, and make the same order in his family and among his friends whom he suffered to see me. I requested likewise, that the secret of my having a false covering to my body, might be known to none but himself, at least as long as my present clothing should last; for as to what the sorrel nag, his valet, had observed, his honour might command him to conceal it.

All this my master very graciously consented to; and thus the secret was kept till my clothes began to wear out, which I was forced to supply by several contrivances that shall hereafter be mentioned. In the meantime, he desired I would go on with my utmost diligence to learn their language, because he was more astonished at my capacity for speech and reason, than at the figure of my body, whether it were covered or not; adding, that he waited with some impatience to hear the wonders which I promised to tell him.

From thenceforward he doubled the pains he had been at to instruct me: he brought me into all company, and made them treat me with civility; because, as he told them, privately, this would put me into good humour, and make me more diverting.

Every day, when I waited on him, beside the trouble he was at in teaching, he would ask me several questions concerning myself, which I answered as well as I could, and by these means he had already received some general ideas, though very imperfect. It would be tedious to relate the several steps by which I advanced to a more regular conversation; but the first account I gave of myself in any order and length was to this purpose:

That I came from a very far country, as I already had attempted to tell him, with about fifty more of my own species;

that we travelled upon the seas in a great hollow vessel made of wood, and larger than his Honour's house. I described the ship to him in the best terms I could, and explained, by the help of my handkerchief displayed, how it was driven forward by the wind. That upon a quarrel among us, I was set on shore on this coast, where I walked forward, without knowing whither, till he delivered me from the persecution of those execrable Yahoos.

He asked me, who made the ship, and how it was possible that the Houyhnhnms of my country would leave it to the management of brutes? My answer was, that I durst proceed no further in my relation, unless he would give me his word and honour that he would not be offended, and then I would tell him the wonders I had so often promised. He agreed; and I went on by assuring him, that the ship was made by creatures like myself; who, in all the countries I had travelled, as well as in my own, were the only governing rational animals; and that upon my arrival hither, I was as much astonished to see the Houyhnhnms act like rational beings, as he, or his friends, could be, in finding some marks of reason in a creature he was pleased to call a Yahoo; to which I owned my resemblance in every part, but could not account for their degenerate and brutal nature.

I said farther, that if good fortune ever restored me to my native country, to relate my travels hither, as I resolved to do, everybody would believe, that I said the thing that was not, that I invented the story out of my own head; and (with all possible respect to himself, his family, and friends, and under his promise of not being offended) our countrymen would hardly think it probable that a Houyhnhnm should be the presiding creature of a nation, and a Yahoo the brute.

CHAPTER IV

The Houyhnhnm's notion of truth and falsehood. The author's discourse disapproved by his master. The author gives a more particular account of himself, and the accidents of his voyage.

My master heard me with great appearances of uneasiness in his countenance; because doubting, or not believing, are so little known in this country, that the inhabitants cannot tell how to behave themselves under such circumstances. And I remember, in frequent discourses with my master concerning the nature of manhood in other parts of the world, having occasion to talk of lying and false representation, it was with much difficulty that he comprehended what I meant, although he had otherwise a most acute judgment.

For he argued thus: that the use of speech was to make us understand one another, and to receive information of facts; now, if any one said the thing which was not, these ends were defeated, because I cannot properly be said to understand him; and I am so far from receiving information, that he leaves me worse than in ignorance; for I am led to believe a thing black, when it is white, and short, when it is long. And these were all the notions he had concerning that faculty of lying, so perfectly well understood, and so universally practised, among human creatures.

To return from this digression. When I asserted that the Yahoos were the only governing animals in my country, which my master said was altogether past his conception, he desired to know, whether we had Houyhnhnms among us, and what was their employment? I told him, we had great numbers; that in summer they grazed in the fields, and in winter were kept in houses with hay and oats, where Yahoo servants were employed to rub their skins smooth, comb their manes, pick their feet, serve them with food, and make their beds.

I understand you well, said my master: it is now very plain, from all you have spoken, that whatever share of reason the Yahoos pretend to, the Houyhnhnms are your masters; I heartily wish our Yahoos would be so tractable.

I begged his Honour would please to excuse me from proceeding any further, because I was very certain that the account he expected from me would be highly displeasing. But he insisted in commanding me to let him know the best and the worst. I told him he should be obeyed.

I owned that the Houyhnhnms among us, whom we called horses, were the most generous and comely animals we had; that they excelled in strength and swiftness; and when they belonged to persons of quality, were employed in travelling, racing, or drawing chariots; they were treated with much kindness and care, till they fell into diseases, or became foundered in the feet; but then they were sold, and used to all kind of drudgery till they died; after which their skins were stripped, and sold for what they were worth, and their bodies left to be devoured by dogs and birds of prey. But the common race of horses had not so good fortune, being kept by farmers and carriers, and other mean people, who put them to greater labour, and fed them worse. I described, as well as I could, our way of riding; the shape and use of a bridle, a saddle, a spur, and a whip; of harness and wheels. I added, that we fastened plates of a certain hard substance, called iron, at the bottom of their feet, to preserve their hoofs from being broken by the stony ways, on which we often travelled.

My master, after some expressions of great indignation, wondered how we dared to venture upon a Houyhnhnm's back; for he was sure, that the weakest servant in his house would be able to shake off the strongest Yahoo; or by lying down and rolling on his back, squeeze the brute to death. I answered that our horses were trained up, from three or four years old, to the several uses we intended them for; that if any of them proved intolerably vicious, they were employed for carriages; that they were severely beaten, while they were young, for any mischievous tricks; that the males, designed for the common use of riding or draught, were generally castrated about two years after their birth, to take down their spirits, and make them more tame and gentle; that they were indeed sensible of rewards and punishments; but his honour would please to consider, that they had not the least tincture of reason, any more than the Yahoos in this country.

It put me to the pains of many circumlocutions, to give my master a right idea of what I spoke; for their language does not abound in variety of words, because their wants and passions are fewer than among us. But it is impossible to express his noble resentment at our savage treatment of the Houyhnhnm race; particularly after I had explained the manner and use of castrating horses among us, to hinder them from propagating their kind, and to render them more servile. He said, if it were possible there could be any country where Yahoos alone were endued with reason, they certainly must be the governing animal; because reason in time will always prevail against brutal strength. But, considering the frame of our bodies, and especially of mine, he thought no creature of equal bulk was so ill-contrived for employing that reason in the common offices of life; whereupon he desired to know whether those among whom I lived resembled me, or the Yahoos of his country.

I assured him, that I was as well shaped as most of my age; but the younger, and the females, were much more soft and tender, and the skins of the latter generally as white as milk.

He said, I differed indeed from other Yahoos, being much more cleanly, and not altogether so deformed; but, in point of real advantage, he thought I differed for the worse: that my nails were of no use either to my fore or hinder feet; as to my fore feet, he could not properly call them by that name, for he never observed me to walk upon them; that they were too soft to bear the ground; that I generally went with them uncovered; neither was the covering I sometimes wore on them of the same shape, or so strong as that on my feet behind: that I could not walk with any security, for if either of my hinder feet slipped, I must inevitably fail.

He then began to find fault with other parts of my body: the flatness of my face, the prominence of my nose, mine eyes placed directly in front, so that I could not look on either side without turning my head: that I was not able to feed myself, without lifting one of my fore-feet to my mouth: and therefore nature had placed those joints to answer that necessity. He knew not what could be the use of those several clefts and divisions in my feet behind; that these were too soft to bear the hardness and sharpness of stones, without a covering made from the skin of some other brute; that my whole body wanted a fence against heat and cold, which I was forced to put on and off every day, with tediousness and trouble.

Lastly, that he observed every animal in this country naturally to abhor the Yahoos, whom the weaker avoided, and the stronger drove from them. So that, supposing us to have the gift of reason, he could not see how it were possible to cure that natural antipathy, which every creature discovered against us; nor consequently how we could tame and render them serviceable. However, he would, as he said, debate the matter no farther, because he was more desirous to know my own story, the country where I was born, and the several actions and events of my life, before I came hither.

I assured him how extremely desirous I was that he should be satisfied on every point; but I doubted much, whether it would be possible for me to explain myself on several subjects, whereof his honour could have no conception; because I saw nothing in his country to which I could resemble them; that, however, I would do my best, and strive to express myself by similitudes, humbly desiring his assistance when I wanted proper words; which he was pleased to promise me.

I said my birth was of honest parents, in an island called England; which was remote from his country, as many days' journey as the strongest of his honour's servants could travel in the annual course of the sun; that I was bred a surgeon, whose trade it is to cure wounds and hurts in the body, gotten by accident or violence; that my country was governed by a female man, whom we called queen; that I left it to get riches, whereby I might maintain myself and family, when I should return; that, in my last voyage, I was commander of the ship, and had about fifty Yahoos under me, many of which died at sea, and I was forced to supply them by others picked out from several nations; that our ship was twice in danger of being sunk, the first time by a great storm, and the second by striking against a rock.

Here my master interposed, by asking me, how I could persuade strangers, out of different countries, to venture with me, after the losses I had sustained, and the hazards I had run? I said, they were fellows of desperate fortunes, forced to fly from the places of their birth on account of their poverty or their crimes. Some were undone by lawsuits; others spent all they had in drinking, whoring, and gaming; others fled for treason; many for murder, theft, poisoning, robbery, perjury, forgery, coining false money, for committing rapes, or sodomy; for flying from their colours, or deserting to the enemy; and most of them had broken prison; none of these durst return to their native countries, for fear of being hanged, or of starving in a jail; and therefore they were under the necessity of seeking a livelihood in other places.

During this discourse, my master was pleased to interrupt me several times. I had made use of many circumlocutions in describing to him the nature of the several crimes for which most of our crew had been forced to fly their country. This labour took up several days' conversation, before he was able to comprehend me. He was wholly at a loss to know what could be the use or necessity of practising those vices. To clear up which, I endeavoured to give some ideas of the desire of power and riches; of the terrible effects of lust, intemperance, malice, and envy.

All this I was forced to define and describe by putting cases and making suppositions. After which, like one whose imagination was struck with something never seen or heard of before, he would lift up his eyes with amazement and indignation. Power, government, war, law, punishment, and a thousand other things, had no terms wherein that language could express them, which made the difficulty almost insuperable, to give my master any conception of what I meant. But being of an excellent understanding, much improved by contemplation and converse, he at last arrived at a competent knowledge of what human nature, in our parts of the world, is capable to perform, and desired I would give him some particular account of that land which we call Europe, but especially of my own country.

CHAPTER V

The author at his master's command, informs him of the state of England. The causes of war among the princes of Europe. The author begins to explain the English constitution.

The reader may please to observe, that the following extract of many conversations I had with my master, contains a summary of the most material points which were discoursed at several times for above two years; his honour often desiring fuller satisfaction, as I farther improved in the Houyhnhnm tongue. I laid before him, as well as I could, the whole state of Europe; I discoursed of trade and manufactures, of arts and sciences; and the answers I gave to all the questions he made, as they arose upon several subjects, were a fund of conversation not to be exhausted.

But I shall here only set down the substance of what passed between us concerning my own country, reducing it in order as well as I can, without any regard to time or other circumstances, while I strictly adhere to truth. My only concern is, that I shall hardly be able to do justice to my master's arguments and expressions, which must needs suffer by my want of capacity, as well as by a translation into our barbarous English.

In obedience, therefore, to his honour's commands, I related to him the Revolution under the Prince of Orange;

the long war with France, entered into by the said prince, and renewed by his successor, the present queen, wherein the greatest powers of Christendom were engaged, and which still continued: I computed, at his request, that about a million of Yahoos might have been killed in the whole progress of it; and perhaps a hundred or more cities taken, and five times as many ships burnt or sunk.

He asked me, what were the usual causes or motives that made one country go to war with another.

I answered they were innumerable; but I should only mention a few of the chief. Sometimes the ambition of princes, who never think they have land or people enough to govern; sometimes the corruption of ministers, who engage their master in a war, in order to stifle or divert the clamour of the subjects against their evil administration. Difference in opinions has cost many millions of lives: for instance, whether flesh be bread, or bread be flesh; whether the juice of a certain berry be blood or wine; whether whistling be a vice or a virtue; whether it be better to kiss a post, or throw it into the fire; what is the best colour for a coat, whether black, white, red, or gray; and whether it should be long or short, narrow or wide, dirty or clean; with many more. Neither are any wars so furious and bloody, or of so long a continuance, as those occasioned by difference in opinion, especially if it be in things indifferent.

Sometimes the quarrel between two princes is to decide which of them shall dispossess a third of his dominions, where neither of them pretend to any right. Sometimes one prince quarrels with another for fear the other should quarrel with him. Sometimes a war is entered upon, because the enemy is too strong; and sometimes, because he is too weak. Sometimes our neighbours want the things which we have, or have the things which we want, and we both fight, till they take ours, or give us theirs. It is a very justifiable cause of a war, to invade a country after the people have been wasted by famine, destroyed by pestilence, or embroiled by factions among themselves.

It is justifiable to enter into war against our nearest ally, when one of his towns lies convenient for us, or a territory of land, that would render our dominions round and complete.

If a prince sends forces into a nation, where the people are poor and ignorant, he may lawfully put half of them to death, and make slaves of the rest, in order to civilize and reduce them from their barbarous way of living. It is a very kingly, honourable, and frequent practice, when one prince desires the assistance of another, to secure him against an invasion, that the assistant, when he has driven out the invader, should seize on the dominions himself, and kill, imprison, or banish, the prince he came to relieve.

Alliance by blood, or marriage, is a frequent cause of war between princes; and the nearer the kindred is, the greater their disposition to quarrel; poor nations are hungry, and rich nations are proud; and pride and hunger will ever be at variance.

For these reasons, the trade of a soldier is held the most honourable of all others; because a soldier is a Yahoo hired to kill, in cold blood, as many of his own species, who have never offended him, as possibly he can.

There is likewise a kind of beggarly princes in Europe, not able to make war by themselves, who hire out their troops to richer nations, for so much a day to each man; of which they keep three-fourths to themselves, and it is the best part of their maintenance: such are those in many northern parts of Europe.

What you have told me, said my master, upon the subject of war, does indeed discover most admirably the effects of that reason you pretend to: however, it is happy that the shame is greater than the danger; and that nature has left you utterly incapable of doing much mischief.

For your mouths lying flat with your faces, you can hardly

bite each other to any purpose, unless by consent. Then as to the claws upon your feet before and behind, they are so short and tender, that one of our Yahoos would drive a dozen of yours before him. And therefore, in recounting the numbers of those who have been killed in battle, I cannot but think you have said the thing which is not.

I could not forbear shaking my head, and smiling a little at his ignorance. And being no stranger to the art of war, I gave him a description of cannons, culverins, muskets, carabines, pistols, bullets, powder, swords, bayonets, battles, sieges, retreats, attacks, undermines, countermines, bombardments, sea fights, ships sunk with a thousand men, twenty thousand killed on each side, dying groans, limbs flying in the air, smoke, noise, confusion, trampling to death under horses' feet, flight, pursuit, victory; fields strewed with carcases, left for food to dogs and wolves and birds of prey; plundering, stripping, ravishing, burning, and destroying. And to set forth the valour of my own dear countrymen, I assured him, that I had seen them blow up a hundred enemies at once in a siege, and as many in a ship, and beheld the dead bodies drop down in pieces from the clouds, to the great diversion of the spectators.

I was going on to more particulars, when my master commanded me silence. He said, whoever understood the nature of Yahoos, might easily believe it possible for so vile an animal to be capable of every action I had named, if their strength and cunning equalled their malice. But as my discourse had increased his abhorrence of the whole species, so he found it gave him a disturbance in his mind to which he was wholly a stranger before.

He thought his ears, being used to such abominable words, might, by degrees, admit them with less detestation: that although he hated the Yahoos of this country, yet he no more blamed them for their odious qualities, than he did a *gnnayh* (a bird of prey) for its cruelty, or a sharp stone for cutting his hoof. But when a creature pretending to reason could be capable of such enormities, he dreaded lest the corruption of that faculty might be worse than brutality itself. He seemed therefore confident, that, instead of reason we were only possessed of some quality fitted to increase our natural vices; as the reflection from a troubled stream returns the image of an ill shapen body, not only larger but more distorted.

He added, that he had heard too much upon the subject of war, both in this and some former discourses. There was another point, which a little perplexed him at present. I had informed him, that some of our crew left their country on account of being ruined by law; that I had already explained the meaning of the word; but he was at a loss how it should come to pass, that the law, which was intended for every man's preservation, should be any man's ruin. Therefore he desired to be further satisfied what I meant by law, and the dispensers thereof, according to the present practice in my own country; because he thought nature and reason were sufficient guides for a reasonable animal, as we pretended to be, in showing us what he ought to do, and what to avoid.

I assured his Honour, that the law was a science in which I had not much conversed, further than by employing advocates, in vain, upon some injustices that had been done me: however, I would give him all the satisfaction I was able.

I said there was a society of men among us, bred up from their youth in the art of proving, by words multiplied for the purpose, that white is black, and black is white, according as they are paid. To this society all the rest of the people are slaves. For example, if my neighbour has a mind to my cow, he has a lawyer to prove that he ought to have my cow from me. I must then hire another to defend my right, it being against all rules of law that any man should be allowed to speak for himself. Now, in this case, I, who am the right owner, lie under two great disadvantages: first, my lawyer, being practised almost from his cradle in defending falsehood, is quite out of his element when he would be an advocate for justice, which is an unnatural office he always attempts with great awkwardness, if not with ill-will.

The second disadvantage is, that my lawyer must proceed with great caution, or else he will be reprimanded by the judges, and abhorred by his brethren, as one that would lessen the practice of the law. And therefore I have but two methods to preserve my cow. The first is, to gain over my adversary's lawyer with a double fee, who will then betray his client by insinuating that he hath justice on his side. The second way is for my lawyer to make my cause appear as unjust as he can, by allowing the cow to belong to my adversary: and this, if it be skilfully done, will certainly bespeak the favour of the bench.

Now your Honour is to know, that these judges are persons appointed to decide all controversies of property, as well as for the trial of criminals, and picked out from the most dexterous lawyers, who are grown old or lazy; and having been biassed all their lives against truth and equity, lie under such a fatal necessity of favouring fraud, perjury, and oppression, that I have known some of them refuse a large bribe from the side where justice lay, rather than injure the faculty, by doing any thing unbecoming their nature or their office.

"It is a maxim among these lawyers that whatever has been done before, may legally be done again: and therefore they take special care to record all the decisions formerly made against common justice, and the general reason of mankind. These, under the name of precedents, they produce as authorities to justify the most iniquitous opinions; and the judges never fail of directing accordingly.

"In pleading, they studiously avoid entering into the merits of the cause; but are loud, violent, and tedious, in dwelling upon all circumstances which are not to the purpose. For instance, in the case already mentioned; they never desire to know what claim or title my adversary has to my cow; but whether the said cow were red or black; her horns long or short; whether the field I graze her in be round or square; whether she was milked at home or abroad; what diseases she is subject to, and the like; after which they consult precedents, adjourn the cause from time to time, and in ten, twenty, or thirty years, come to an issue.

"It is likewise to be observed, that this society has a peculiar cant and jargon of their own, that no other mortal can understand, and wherein all their laws are written, which they take special care to multiply; whereby they have wholly confounded the very essence of truth and falsehood, of right and wrong; so that it will take thirty years to decide, whether the field left me by my ancestors for six generations belongs to me, or to a stranger three hundred miles off.

"In the trial of persons accused for crimes against the state, the method is much more short and commendable: the judge first sends to sound the disposition of those in power, after which he can easily hang or save a criminal, strictly preserving all due forms of law.

Here my master interposing, said, it was a pity, that creatures endowed with such prodigious abilities of mind, as these lawyers, by the description I gave of them, must certainly be, were not rather encouraged to be instructors of others in wisdom and knowledge. In answer to which I assured his honour, that in all points out of their own trade, they were usually the most ignorant and stupid generation among us, the most despicable in common conversation, avowed enemies to all knowledge and learning, and equally disposed to pervert the general reason of mankind in every other subject of discourse as in that of their own profession.

CHAPTER VI

A continuation of the state of England under Queen Anne.
The character of a first minister of state in European courts.

My master was yet wholly at a loss to understand what motives could incite this race of lawyers to perplex, disquiet, and weary themselves, and engage in a confederacy of injustice, merely for the sake of injuring their fellow-animals; neither could he comprehend what I meant in saying, they did it for hire. Whereupon I was at much pains to describe to him the use of money, the materials it was made of, and the value of the metals; that when a Yahoo had got a great store of this precious substance, he was able to purchase whatever he had a mind to; the finest clothing, the noblest houses, great tracts of land, the most costly meats and drinks, and have his choice of the most beautiful females.

Therefore since money alone was able to perform all these feats, our Yahoos thought they could never have enough of it to spend, or to save, as they found themselves inclined, from their natural bent either to profusion or avarice; that the rich man enjoyed the fruit of the poor man's labour, and the latter were a thousand to one in proportion to the former; that the bulk of our people were forced to live miserably, by labouring every day for small wages, to make a few live plentifully.

I enlarged myself much on these, and many other

particulars to the same purpose; but his honour was still to seek; for he went upon a supposition, that all animals had a title to their share in the productions of the earth, and especially those who presided over the rest. Therefore he desired I would let him know, what these costly meats were, and how any of us happened to want them? Whereupon I enumerated as many sorts as came into my head, with the various methods of dressing them, which could not be done without sending vessels by sea to every part of the world, as well for liquors to drink as for sauces and innumerable other conveniences. I assured him that this whole globe of earth must be at least three times gone round before one of our better female Yahoos could get her breakfast, or a cup to put it in.

He said that must needs be a miserable country which cannot furnish food for its own inhabitants. But what he chiefly wondered at was, how such vast tracts of ground as I described should be wholly without fresh water, and the people put to the necessity of sending over the sea for drink. I replied that England (the dear place of my nativity) was computed to produce three times the quantity of food more than its inhabitants are able to consume, as well as liquors extracted from grain, or pressed out of the fruit of certain trees, which made excellent drink, and the same proportion in every other convenience of life. But, in order to feed the luxury and intemperance of the males, and the vanity of the females, we sent away the greatest part of our necessary things to other countries, whence, in return, we brought the materials of diseases, folly, and vice, to spend among ourselves. Hence it follows of necessity, that vast numbers of our people are compelled to seek their livelihood by begging, robbing, stealing, cheating, pimping, flattering, suborning, forswearing, forging, gaming, lying, fawning, hectoring, voting, scribbling, stargazing, poisoning, whoring, canting, libelling, freethinking, and the like occupations: every one of which terms I was at much pains to make him understand.

That wine was not imported among us from foreign countries to supply the want of water or other drinks, but because it was a sort of liquid which made us merry by putting us out of our senses, diverted all melancholy thoughts, begat wild extravagant imaginations in the brain, raised our hopes and banished our fears, suspended every office of reason for a time, and deprived us of the use of our limbs, till we fell into a profound sleep; although it must be confessed, that we always awaked sick and dispirited; and that the use of this liquor filled us with diseases which made our lives uncomfortable and short.

But beside all this, the bulk of our people supported themselves by furnishing the necessities or conveniences of life to the rich and to each other. For instance, when I am at home, and dressed as I ought to be, I carry on my body the workmanship of a hundred tradesmen; the building and furniture of my house employ as many more, and five times the number to adorn my wife.

I was going on to tell him of another sort of people, who get their livelihood by attending the sick, having, upon some occasions, informed his honour that many of my crew had died of diseases. But here it was with the utmost difficulty that I brought him to apprehend what I meant. He could easily conceive, that a Houyhnhnm, grew weak and heavy a few days before his death, or by some accident might hurt a limb; but that nature, who works all things to perfection, should suffer any pains to breed in our bodies, he thought impossible, and desired to know the reason of so unaccountable an evil.

I told him we fed on a thousand things which operated contrary to each other; that we ate when we were not hungry, and drank without the provocation of thirst; that we sat whole nights drinking strong liquors, without eating a bit, which disposed us to sloth, inflamed our bodies, and precipitated or prevented digestion; that prostitute female Yahoos acquired a certain malady, which bred rottenness in the bones of those who fell into their embraces; that this, and many other diseases, were propagated from father to son; so that great numbers came into the world with complicated maladies upon them; that it would be endless to give him a catalogue of all diseases incident to human bodies, for they would not be fewer than five or six hundred, spread over every limb and joint in short, every part, external and intestine, having diseases appropriated to itself. To remedy which, there was a sort of people bred up among us in the profession, or pretence, of curing the sick. And because I had some skill in the faculty, I would, in gratitude to his honour, let him know the whole mystery and method by which they proceed.

Their fundamental is, that all diseases arise from repletion; whence they conclude, that a great evacuation of the body is necessary, either through the natural passage or upwards at the mouth. Their next business is from herbs, minerals, gums, oils, shells, salts, juices, sea-weed, excrements, barks of trees, serpents, toads, frogs, spiders, dead men's flesh and bones, birds, beasts, and fishes, to form a composition, for smell and taste, the most abominable, nauseous, and detestable, they can possibly contrive, which the stomach immediately rejects with loathing, and this they call a vomit; or else, from the same store-house, with some other poisonous additions, they command us to take in at the orifice above or below (just as the physician then happens to be disposed) a medicine equally annoying and disgustful to the bowels; which, relaxing the belly, drives down all before it; and this they call a purge.

But besides real diseases, we are subject to many that are only imaginary, for which the physicians have invented imaginary cures; these have their several names, and so have the drugs that are proper for them; and with these our female Yahoos are always infested.

One great Excellency in this tribe, is their skill at prognostics, wherein they seldom fail; their predictions in real diseases, when they rise to any degree of malignity, generally portending death, which is always in their power, when recovery is not: and therefore, upon any unexpected signs of amendment, after they have pronounced their sentence, rather than be accused as false prophets, they know how to approve their sagacity to the world, by a seasonable dose.

They are likewise of special use to husbands and wives who are grown weary of their mates; to eldest sons, to great ministers of state, and often to princes.

I had formerly, upon occasion, discoursed with my master upon the nature of government in general, and particularly of our own excellent constitution, deservedly the wonder and envy of the whole world. But having here accidentally mentioned a minister of state, he commanded me, some time after, to inform him, what species of Yahoo I particularly meant by that appellation.

I told him that a first or chief minister of state, who was the person I intended to describe, was the creature wholly exempt from joy and grief, love and hatred, pity and anger; at least, makes use of no other passions, but a violent desire of wealth, power, and titles; that he applies his words to all uses, except to the indication of his mind; that he never tells a truth but with an intent that you should take it for a lie; nor a lie, but with a design that you should take it for a truth; that those he speaks worst of behind their backs are in the surest way of preferment; and whenever he begins to praise you to others, or to yourself, you are from that day forlorn. The worst mark you can receive is a promise, especially when it is confirmed with an oath; after which, every wise man retires, and gives over all hopes.

There are three methods, by which a man may rise to be chief minister. The first is, by knowing how, with prudence, to dispose of a wife, a daughter, or a sister; the second, by betraying or undermining his predecessor; and the third is, by a furious zeal, in public assemblies, against the corruption's of the court. But a wise prince would rather choose to employ those who practise the last of these methods; because such zealots prove always the most obsequious and subservient to the will and passions of their master.

That these ministers, having all employments at their disposal, preserve themselves in power, by bribing the majority of a senate or great council; and at last, by an expedient, called an act of indemnity (whereof I described the nature to him), they secure themselves from after-reckonings, and retire from the public laden with the spoils of the nation.

The palace of a chief minister is a seminary to breed up others in his own trade: the pages, lackeys, and porters, by imitating their master, become ministers of state in their several districts, and learn to excel in the three principal ingredients, of insolence, lying, and bribery. Accordingly, they have a subaltern court paid to them by persons of the best rank; and sometimes by the force of dexterity and impudence, arrive, through several gradations, to be successors to their lord.

One day, in discourse, my master, having heard me mention the nobility of my country, was pleased to make me a compliment which I could not pretend to deserve: that he was sure I must have been born of some noble family, because I far exceeded in shape, colour, and cleanliness, all the Yahoos of his nation, although I seemed to fail in strength and agility, which must be imputed to my different way of living from those other brutes; and besides I was not only endowed with the faculty of speech, but likewise with some rudiments of reason, to a degree that, with all his acquaintance, I passed for a prodigy.

He made me observe that among the Houyhnhnms, the white, the sorrel, and the iron-gray, were not so exactly shaped as the bay, the dapple-gray, and the black; nor born with equal talents of mind, or a capacity to improve them; and therefore continued always in the condition of servants, without ever aspiring to match out of their own race, which in that country would be reckoned monstrous and unnatural.

I made his Honour my most humble acknowledgments for the good opinion he was pleased to conceive of me, but assured him at the same time, that my birth was of the lower sort, having been born of plain honest parents, who were just able to give me a tolerable education; that nobility, among us, was altogether a different thing from the idea he had of it; that our young noblemen are bred from their childhood in idleness and luxury; that, as soon as years will permit, they consume their vigour, and contract odious diseases among lewd females; and when their fortunes are almost ruined, they marry some woman of mean birth, disagreeable person, and unsound constitution (merely for the sake of money), whom they hate and despise. That the productions of such marriages are generally scrofulous, rickety, or deformed children; by which means the family seldom continues above three generations, unless the wife takes care to provide a healthy father, among her neighbours or domestics, in order to improve and continue the breed. That a weak diseased body, a meagre countenance, and sallow complexion, are the true marks of noble blood; and a healthy robust appearance is so disgraceful in a man of quality, that the world concludes his real father to have been a groom or a coachman. The imperfections of his mind run parallel with those of his body, being a composition of spleen, dullness, ignorance, caprice, sensuality, and pride.

Without the consent of this illustrious body, no law can be enacted, repealed, or altered: and these nobles have likewise the decision of all our possessions, without appeal.

CHAPTER VII

The author's great love of his native country. His master's observations upon the constitution and administration of England, as described by the author, with parallel cases and comparisons. His master's observations upon human nature.

The reader may be disposed to wonder how I could prevail on myself to give so free a representation of my own species, among a race of mortals who are already too apt to conceive the vilest opinion of humankind, from that entire congruity between me and their Yahoos. But I must freely confess, that the many virtues of those excellent quadrupeds, placed in opposite view to human corruptions, had so far opened my eyes and enlarged my understanding, that I began to view the actions and passions of man in a very different light, and to think the honour of my own kind not worth managing; which, besides, it was impossible for me to do, before a person of so acute a judgment as my master, who daily convinced me of a thousand faults in myself, whereof I had not the least perception before, and which, with us, would never be numbered even among human infirmities. I had likewise learned, from his example, an utter detestation of all falsehood or disguise; and truth appeared so amiable to me, that I determined upon sacrificing every thing to it.

Let me deal so candidly with the reader as to confess that there was yet a much stronger motive for the freedom I took in my representation of things. I had not yet been a year in this country before I contracted such a love and veneration for the inhabitants, that I entered on a firm resolution never to return to humankind, but to pass the rest of my life among these admirable Houyhnhnms, in the contemplation and practice of every virtue, where I could have no example or incitement to vice. But it was decreed by fortune, my perpetual enemy, that so great a felicity should not fall to my share. However, it is now some comfort to reflect, that in what I said of my countrymen, I extenuated their faults as much as I durst before so strict an examiner; and upon every article gave as favourable a turn as the matter would bear. For, indeed, who is there alive that will not be swayed by his bias and partiality to the place of his birth?

I have related the substance of several conversations I had with my master during the greatest part of the time I had the honour to be in his service; but have, indeed, for brevity sake, omitted much more than is here set down.

When I had answered all his questions, and his curiosity seemed to be fully satisfied, he sent for me one morning early, and commanded me to sit down at some distance (an honour which he had never before conferred upon me). He said, he had been very seriously considering my whole story, as far as it related both to myself and my country; that he looked upon us as a sort of animals, to whose share, by what accident he could not conjecture, some small pittance of reason had fallen, whereof we made no other use, than by its assistance, to aggravate our natural corruptions, and to acquire new ones, which nature had not given us; that we disarmed ourselves of the few abilities she had bestowed; had been very successful in multiplying our original wants, and seemed to spend our whole lives in vain endeavours to supply them by our own inventions.

That, as to myself, it was manifest I had neither the strength nor agility of a common Yahoo; that I walked infirmly on my hinder feet; had found out a contrivance to make my claws of no use or defence, and to remove the hair from my chin, which was intended as a shelter from the sun and the weather: lastly, that I could neither run with speed, nor climb trees like my brethren (as he called them) the Yahoos in his country.

That our institutions of government and law were plainly owing to our gross defects in reason, and by consequence in virtue; because reason alone is sufficient to govern a rational creature; which was, therefore, a character we had no pretence to challenge, even from the account I had given of my own people; although he manifestly perceived, that, in order to favour them, I had concealed many particulars, and often said the thing which was not.

He was the more confirmed in this opinion, because, he observed, that as I agreed in every feature of my body with other Yahoos, except where it was to my real disadvantage in point of strength, speed, and activity, the shortness of my claws, and some other particulars where nature had no part; so from the representation I had given him of our lives, our manners, and our actions, he found as near a resemblance in the disposition of our minds.

He said the Yahoos were known to hate one another, more than they did any different species of animals; and the reason usually assigned was, the odiousness of their own shapes, which all could see in the rest, but not in themselves. He had therefore begun to think it not unwise in us to cover our bodies, and by that invention conceal many of our deformities from each other, which would else be hardly supportable. But he now found he had been mistaken, and that the dissensions of those brutes in his country were owing to the same cause with ours, as I had described them. "For if" said he, "you throw among five Yahoos as much food as would be sufficient for fifty, they will, instead of eating peaceably, fall together by the ears, each single one impatient to have all to itself;" and therefore a servant was usually employed to stand by while they were feeding abroad, and those kept at home were tied at a distance from each other: that if a cow died of age or accident, before a Houyhnhnm could secure it for his own Yahoos, those in the neighbourhood would come in herds to seize it, and then would ensue such a battle as I had described, with terrible wounds made by their claws on both sides, although they seldom were able to kill one another, for want of such convenient instruments of death as we had invented. At other times, the like battles have been fought between the Yahoos of several neighbourhoods, without any visible cause; those of one district watching all opportunities to surprise the next, before they are prepared. But if they find their project has miscarried, they return home, and, for want of enemies, engage in what I call a civil war among themselves.

That in some fields of his country there are certain shining stones of several colours, whereof the Yahoos are violently fond: and when part of these stones is fixed in the earth, as it sometimes happens, they will dig with their claws for whole days to get them out; then carry them away, and hide them by heaps in their kennels; but still looking round with great caution, for fear their comrades should find out their treasure.

My master said, he could never discover the reason of this unnatural appetite, or how these stones could be of any use to a Yahoo; but now he believed it might proceed from the same principle of avarice which I had ascribed to mankind. That he had once, by way of experiment, privately removed a heap of these stones from the place where one of his Yahoos had buried it; whereupon the sordid animal, missing his treasure, by his loud lamenting brought the whole herd to the place, there miserably howled, then fell to biting and tearing the rest, began to pine away, would neither eat, nor sleep, nor work, till he ordered a servant privately to convey the stones into the same hole, and hide them as before; which, when his Yahoo had found, he presently recovered his spirits and good humour, but took good care to remove them to a better hiding place, and has ever since been a very serviceable brute.

My master further assured me, which I also observed myself, that in the fields where the shining stones abound, the fiercest and most frequent battles are fought, occasioned by perpetual inroads of the neighbouring Yahoos.

He said it was common, when two Yahoos discovered such a stone in a field, and were contending which of them should be the proprietor, a third would take the advantage, and carry it away from them both; which my master would needs contend to have some kind of resemblance with our suits at law; wherein I thought it for our credit not to undeceive him; since the decision he mentioned was much more equitable than many decrees among us; because the plaintiff and defendant there lost nothing beside the stone they contended for: whereas our courts of equity would never have dismissed the cause, while either of them had any thing left.

My master, continuing his discourse, said, there was nothing that rendered the Yahoos more odious, than their undistinguishing appetite to devour every thing that came in their way, whether herbs, roots, berries, the corrupted flesh of animals, or all mingled together: and it was peculiar in their temper, that they were fonder of what they could get by rapine or stealth, at a greater distance, than much better food provided for them at home. If their prey held out, they would eat till they were ready to burst; after which, nature had pointed out to them a certain root that gave them a general evacuation.

There was also another kind of root, very juicy, but somewhat rare and difficult to be found, which the Yahoos sought for with much eagerness, and would suck it with great delight; it produced in them the same effects that wine has upon us. It would make them sometimes hug, and sometimes tear one another; they would howl, and grin, and chatter, and reel, and tumble, and then fall asleep in the mud.

I did, indeed observe that the Yahoos were the only animals in this country subject to any diseases; which, however, were much fewer than horses have among us, and contracted, not by any ill-treatment they meet with, but by the nastiness and greediness of that sordid brute. Neither has their language any more than a general appellation for those maladies, which is borrowed from the name of the beast, and called *hnea*-Yahoo, or Yahoo's evil.

As to learning, government, arts, manufactures, and the like, my master confessed, he could find little or no resemblance between the Yahoos of that country and those in ours; for he only meant to observe what parity there was in our natures.

He had heard, indeed, some curious Houyhnhnm*s* observe, that in most herds there was a sort of ruling Yahoo (as among us there is generally some leading or principal stag in a park), who was always more deformed in body, and mischievous in disposition, than any of the rest; that this leader had usually a favourite as like himself as he could get. This favourite is hated by the whole herd, and therefore, to protect himself, keeps always near the person of his leader. He usually continues in office till a worse can be found; but the very moment he is discarded, his successor, at the head of all theYahoos in that district, young and old, male and female, come in a body, and discharge their excrements upon him from head to foot. But how far this might be applicable to our courts, and favourites, and ministers of state, my master said I could best determine.

I durst make no return to this malicious insinuation, which debased human understanding below the sagacity of a common hound, who has judgment enough to distinguish and follow the cry of the ablest dog in the pack, without being ever mistaken.

Another thing he wondered at in the Yahoos, was their strange disposition to nastiness and dirt; whereas there appears to be a natural love of cleanliness in all other animals. As to the two former accusations, I was glad to let them pass without any reply, because I had not a word to offer upon them in defence of my species, which otherwise I certainly had done from my own inclinations. But I could have easily vindicated humankind from the imputation of singularity upon the last article, if there had been any swine in that country (as unluckily for me there were not), which, although it may be a sweeter quadruped than a Yahoo, cannot, I humbly conceive, in justice, pretend to more cleanliness; and so his honour himself must have owned, if he had seen their filthy way of feeding, and their custom of wallowing and sleeping in the mud.

My master likewise mentioned another quality which his servants had discovered in several Yahoos, and to him was wholly unaccountable. He said, a fancy would sometimes take a Yahoo to retire into a corner, to lie down, and howl, and groan, and spurn away all that came near him, although he were young and fat, wanted neither food nor water, nor did the servant imagine what could possibly ail him. And the only remedy they found was, to set him to hard work, after which he would infallibly come to himself. To this I was silent out of partiality to my own kind; yet here I could plainly discover the true seeds of spleen, which only seizes on the lazy, the luxurious, and the rich; who, if they were forced to undergo the same regimen, I would undertake for the cure.

CHAPTER VIII

The author relates several particulars of the Yahoos. The great virtues of the Houyhnhnms. The education and exercise of their youth. Their general assembly.

As I ought to have understood human nature much better than I supposed it possible for my master to do, so it was easy to apply the character he gave of the Yahoos to myself and my countrymen; and I believed I could yet make further discoveries, from my own observation. I therefore often begged his honour to let me go among the herds of Yahoos in the neighbourhood; to which he always very graciously consented, being perfectly convinced that the hatred I bore these brutes would never suffer me to be corrupted by them; and his honour ordered one of his servants, a strong sorrel nag, very honest and good-natured, to be my guard; without whose protection I durst not undertake such adventures. For I have already told the reader how much I was pestered by these odious animals, upon my first arrival; and I afterwards failed very narrowly, three or four times, of falling into their clutches, when I happened to stray at any distance without my hanger. And I have reason to believe they had some imagination that I was of their own species, which I often assisted myself by stripping up my sleeves, and showing my naked arms and breasts in their sight, when my protector was with me. At which times they would approach as near as they durst, and imitate my actions after the manner of monkeys, but ever with great signs of hatred; as a tame jackdaw with cap and stockings is always persecuted by the wild ones, when he happens to be got among them.

They are prodigiously nimble from their infancy. However, I once caught a young male of three years old, and endeavoured, by all marks of tenderness, to make it quiet; but the little imp fell a squalling, and scratching, and biting with such violence, that I was forced to let it go; and it was high time, for a whole troop of old ones came about us at the noise, but finding the cub was safe (for away it ran), and my sorrel nag being by, they durst not venture near us. I observed the young animal's flesh to smell very rank, and the stink was somewhat between a weasel and a fox, but much more disagreeable.

By what I could discover, the Yahoos appear to be the most unteachable of all animals: their capacity never reaching higher than to draw or carry burdens. Yet I am of opinion, this defect arises chiefly from a perverse, restive disposition; for they are cunning, malicious, treacherous, and revengeful. They are strong and hardy, but of a cowardly spirit, and, by consequence, insolent, abject, and cruel. It is observed, that the red haired of both sexes are more libidinous and mischievous than the rest, whom yet they much exceed in strength and activity.

The Houyhnhnms keep the Yahoos for present use in huts not far from the house; but the rest are sent abroad to certain fields, where they dig up roots, eat several kinds of herbs, and search about for carrion, or sometimes catch weasels and *luhimuhs* (a sort of wild rat), which they greedily devour. Nature has taught them to dig deep holes with their nails on the side of a rising ground, wherein they lie by themselves; only the kennels of the females are larger, sufficient to hold two or three cubs.

They swim from their infancy like frogs, and are able to

continue long under water, where they often take fish, which the females carry home to their young.

Having lived three years in this country, the reader, I suppose, will expect that I should, like other travellers, give him some account of the manners and customs of its inhabitants, which it was indeed my principal study to learn.

As these noble Houyhnhnms are endowed by nature with a general disposition to all virtues, and have no conceptions or ideas of what is evil in a rational creature, so their grand maxim is, to cultivate reason, and to be wholly governed by it. Neither is reason among them a point problematical, as with us, where men can argue with plausibility on both sides of the question, but strikes you with immediate conviction; as it must needs do, where it is not mingled, obscured, or discoloured, by passion and interest.

I remember it was with extreme difficulty that I could bring my master to understand the meaning of the word opinion, or how a point could be disputable; because reason taught us to affirm or deny only where we are certain; and beyond our knowledge we cannot do either. So that controversies, wranglings, disputes, and positiveness, in false or dubious propositions, are evils unknown among the Houyhnhnms.

In the like manner, when I used to explain to him our several systems of natural philosophy, he would laugh, that a creature pretending to reason, should value itself upon the knowledge of other people's conjectures, and in things where that knowledge, if it were certain, could be of no use. Wherein he agreed entirely with the sentiments of Socrates, as Plato delivers them; which I mention as the highest honour I can do that prince of philosophers. I have often since reflected, what destruction such doctrine would make in the libraries of Europe; and how many paths of fame would be then shut up in the learned world.

Friendship and benevolence are the two principal virtues

among the Houyhnhnms; and these not confined to particular objects, but universal to the whole race; for a stranger from the remotest part is equally treated with the nearest neighbour, and wherever he goes, looks upon himself as at home. They preserve decency and civility in the highest degrees, but are altogether ignorant of ceremony. They have no fondness for their colts or foals, but the care they take in educating them proceeds entirely from the dictates of reason. And I observed my master to show the same affection to his neighbour's issue, that he had for his own. They will have it that nature teaches them to love the whole species, and it is reason only that makes a distinction of persons, where there is a superior degree of virtue.

In their marriages, they are exactly careful to choose such colours as will not make any disagreeable mixture in the breed. Strength is chiefly valued in the male, and comeliness in the female; not upon the account of love, but to preserve the race from degenerating; for where a female happens to excel in strength, a consort is chosen, with regard to comeliness.

Courtship, love, presents, jointures, settlements have no place in their thoughts, or terms whereby to express them in their language. The young couple meet, and are joined, merely because it is the determination of their parents and friends; it is what they see done every day, and they look upon it as one of the necessary actions of a reasonable being. But the violation of marriage, or any other unchastity, was never heard of; and the married pair pass their lives with the same friendship and mutual benevolence, that they bear to all others of the same species who come in their way, without jealousy, fondness, quarrelling, or discontent.

In educating the youth of both sexes, their method is admirable, and highly deserves our imitation. These are not suffered to taste a grain of oats, except upon certain days, till eighteen years old; nor milk, but very rarely; and in summer they graze two hours in the morning, and as many in the evening, which their parents likewise observe; but the servants are not allowed above half that time, and a great part of their grass is brought home, which they eat at the most convenient hours, when they can be best spared from work.

Temperance, industry, exercise, and cleanliness, are the lessons equally enjoined to the young ones of both sexes: and my master thought it monstrous in us, to give the females a different kind of education from the males, except in some articles of domestic management; whereby, as he truly observed, one half of our natives were good for nothing but bringing children into the world; and to trust the care of our children to such useless animals, he said, was yet a greater instance of brutality.

But the Houyhnhnms train up their youth to strength, speed, and hardiness, by exercising them in running races up and down steep hills, and over hard stony grounds; and when they are all in a sweat, they are ordered to leap over head and ears into a pond or river. Four times a year the youth of a certain district meet to show their proficiency in running and leaping, and other feats of strength and agility; where the victor is rewarded with a song in his or her praise. On this festival, the servants drive a herd of Yahoos into the field, laden with hay, and oats, and milk, for a repast to the Houyhnhnms; after which, these brutes are immediately driven back again, for fear of being noisome to the assembly.

Every fourth year, at the vernal equinox, there is a representative council of the whole nation, which meets in a plain about twenty miles from our house, and continues about five or six days. Here they inquire into the state and condition of the several districts; whether they abound or be deficient in hay or oats, or cows, or Yahoos.

And wherever there is any want (which is but seldom) it is immediately supplied by unanimous consent and contribution.

Here likewise the regulation of children is settled: as for instance, if a Houyhnhnm has two males, he changes one of them with another that has two females; and when a child has been lost by any casualty, where the mother is past breeding, it is determined what family in the district shall breed another to supply the loss.

CHAPTER IX

A grand debate at the general assembly of the
Houyhnhnms, and how it was determined. The learning
of the Houyhnhnms. Their buildings. Their manner of
burials. The defectiveness of their language.

One of these grand assemblies was held in my time, about
three months before my departure, whither my master
went as the representative of our district. In this council was
resumed their old debate, and indeed the only debate that
ever happened in their country; whereof my master, after his
return, give me a very particular account.

The question to be debated was, whether the Yahoos
should be exterminated from the face of the earth? One of
the members for the affirmative offered several arguments of
great strength and weight, alleging, that as the Yahoos were
the most filthy, noisome, and deformed animals which nature
ever produced, so they were the most restive and indocible,
mischievous and malicious; they would privately suck the
teats of the Houyhnhnms' cows, kill and devour their cats,
trample down their oats and grass, if they were not continually
watched, and commit a thousand other extravagancies.

He took notice of a general tradition, that Yahoos had not
been always in their country; but that many ages ago, two of
these brutes appeared together upon a mountain; whether

produced by the heat of the sun upon corrupted mud and slime, or from the ooze and froth of the sea, was never known; that these Yahoos engendered, and their brood, in a short time, grew so numerous as to overrun and infest the whole nation; that the Houyhnhnms, to get rid of this evil, made a general hunting, and at last enclosed the whole herd; and destroying the elder, every Houyhnhnm kept two young ones in a kennel, and brought them to such a degree of tameness, as an animal, so savage by nature, can be capable of acquiring, using them for draught and carriage.

That there seemed to be much truth in this tradition, and that those creatures could not be *yinhniamshy* (or aborigines of the land), because of the violent hatred the Houyhnhnms, as well as all other animals, bore them, which, although their evil disposition sufficiently deserved, could never have arrived at so high a degree if they had been aborigines, or else they would have long since been rooted out; that the inhabitants, taking a fancy to use the service of the Yahoos, had, very imprudently, neglected to cultivate the breed of asses, which are a comely animal, easily kept, more tame and orderly, without any offensive smell, strong enough for labour, although they yield to the other in agility of body, and if their braying be no agreeable sound, it is far preferable to the horrible howlings of the Yahoos.

Several others declared their sentiments to the same purpose, when my master proposed an expedient to the assembly, whereof he had indeed borrowed the hint from me. He approved of the tradition mentioned by the honourable member who spoke before, and affirmed, that the two Yahoos said to be seen first among them, had been driven thither over the sea; that coming to land, and being forsaken by their companions, they retired to the mountains, and degenerating by degrees, became in process of time much more savage than those of their own species in the country whence these two originals came. The reason of this assertion was, that he had now in his possession a certain wonderful Yahoo (meaning myself) which most of them had heard of, and many of them had seen.

He then related to them how he first found me; that my body was all covered with an artificial composure of the skins and hairs of other animals; that I spoke in a language of my own, and had thoroughly learned theirs; that I had related to him the accidents which brought me thither; that when he saw me without my covering, I was an exact Yahoo in every part, only of a whiter colour, less hairy, and with shorter claws. He added, how I had endeavoured to persuade him, that in my own and other countries, the Yahoos acted as the governing, rational animal, and held the Houyhnhnms in servitude; that he observed in me all the qualities of a Yahoo, only a little more civilized by some tincture of reason, which, however, was in a degree as far inferior to the Houyhnhnm race, as the Yahoos of their country were to me.

This was all my master thought fit to tell me, at that time, of what passed in the grand council. But he was pleased to conceal one particular, which related personally to myself, whereof I soon felt the unhappy effect, as the reader will know in its proper place, and whence I date all the succeeding misfortunes of my life.

The Houyhnhnms have no letters, and consequently their knowledge is all traditional. But there happening few events of any moment among a people so well united, naturally disposed to every virtue, wholly governed by reason, and cut off from all commerce with other nations, the historical part is easily preserved without burdening their memories.

I have already observed that they are subject to no diseases, and therefore can have no need of physicians. However, they have excellent medicines, composed of herbs, to cure accidental bruises and cuts in the pastern or frog of the foot, by sharp stones, as well as other maims and hurts in the several parts of the body.

They calculate the year by the revolution of the sun and moon, but use no subdivisions into weeks. They are well enough acquainted with the motions of those two luminaries, and understand the nature of eclipses; and this is the utmost progress of their astronomy.

In poetry, they must be allowed to excel all other mortals; wherein the justness of their similes, and the minuteness as well as exactness of their descriptions, are indeed inimitable. Their verses abound very much in both of these, and usually contain either some exalted notions of friendship and benevolence or the praises of those who were victors in races and other bodily exercises.

Their buildings, although very rude and simple, are not inconvenient, but well contrived to defend them from all injuries of cold and heat. They have a kind of tree, which at forty years old loosens in the root, and falls with the first storm: it grows very straight, and being pointed like stakes with a sharp stone (for the Houyhnhnms know not the use of iron), they stick them erect in the ground, about ten inches asunder, and then weave in oat straw, or sometimes wattles, between them. The roof is made after the same manner, and so are the doors.

The Houyhnhnms use the hollow part, between the pastern and the hoof of their fore-foot, as we do our hands, and this with greater dexterity than I could at first imagine. I have seen a white mare of our family thread a needle (which I lent her on purpose) with that joint. They milk their cows, reap their oats, and do all the work which requires hands, in the same manner.

They have a kind of hard flints, which, by grinding against other stones, they form into instruments, that serve instead of wedges, axes, and hammers. With tools made of these flints, they likewise cut their hay, and reap their oats, which there grow naturally in several fields; the Yahoos draw home the sheaves in carriages, and the servants tread them in certain covered huts to get out the grain, which is kept in stores. They make a rude kind of earthen and wooden vessels, and bake the former in the sun.

If they can avoid casualties, they die only of old age, and are buried in the obscurest places that can be found, their friends and relations expressing neither joy nor grief at their departure; nor does the dying person discover the least regret that he is leaving the world, any more than if he were upon returning home from a visit to one of his neighbours.

I remember my master having once made an appointment with a friend and his family to come to his house, upon some affair of importance: on the day fixed, the mistress and her two children came very late; she made two excuses, first for her husband, who, as she said, happened that very morning to *Ihnuwnh*. The word is strongly expressive in their language, but not easily rendered into English; it signifies, to retire to his first mother. Her excuse for not coming sooner, was, that her husband dying late in the morning, she was a good while consulting her servants about a convenient place where his body should be laid; and I observed, she behaved herself at our house as cheerfully as the rest. She died about three months after.

They live generally to seventy, or seventy-five years, very seldom to fourscore. Some weeks before their death, they feel a gradual decay; but without pain. During this time they are much visited by their friends, because they cannot go abroad with their usual ease and satisfaction. However, about ten days before their death, which they seldom fail in computing, they return the visits that have been made them by those who are nearest in the neighbourhood, being carried in a convenient sledge drawn byYahoos; which vehicle they use, not only upon this occasion, but when they grow old, upon long journeys, or when they are lamed by any accident: and therefore when the dying Houyhnhnms return those visits, they take a solemn leave of their friends, as if they were going to some remote part of the country, where they designed to pass the rest of their lives.

I know not whether it may be worth observing, that the Houyhnhnms have no word in their language to express any thing that is evil, except what they borrow from the deformities or ill qualities of the Yahoos. Thus they denote the folly of a servant, an omission of a child, a stone that cuts their feet, a continuance of foul or unseasonable weather, and the like, by adding to each the epithet of Yahoo. For instance, *Hhnm Yahoo*; *Whnaholm Yahoo*, *Ynlhmndwihlma Yahoo*, and an ill-contrived house *Ynholmhnmrohlnw Yahoo*.

I could, with great pleasure, enlarge further upon the manners and virtues of this excellent people; but intending in a short time to publish a volume by itself, expressly upon that subject, I refer the reader thither; and, in the mean time, proceed to relate my own sad catastrophe.

CHAPTER X

The author's economy, and happy life, among the Houyhnhnms. His great improvement in virtue by conversing with them. Their conversations. The author has notice given him by his master, that he must depart from the country. He falls into a swoon for grief; but submits. He contrives and finishes a canoe by the help of a fellow-servant, and puts to sea at a venture.

I had settled my little economy to my own heart's content. My master had ordered a room to be made for me, after their manner, about six yards from the house: the sides and floors of which I plastered with clay, and covered with rush-mats of my own contriving. I had beaten hemp, which there grows wild, and made of it a sort of ticking; this I filled with the feathers of several birds I had taken with springes made of Yahoos' hairs, and were excellent food. I had worked two chairs with my knife, the sorrel nag helping me in the grosser and more laborious part.

When my clothes were worn to rags, I made myself others with the skins of rabbits, and of a certain beautiful animal, about the same size, called *Nnuhnoh*, the skin of which is covered with a fine down. Of these I also made very tolerable stockings. I soled my shoes with wood, which I cut from a tree, and fitted to the upper-leather; and when this was worn out,

I supplied it with the skins of Yahoos dried in the sun. I often got honey out of hollow trees, which I mingled with water, or ate with my bread.

No man could more verify the truth of these two maxims, That nature is very easily satisfied; and, That necessity is the mother of invention.

I enjoyed perfect health of body, and tranquillity of mind; I did not feel the treachery or inconstancy of a friend, nor the injuries of a secret or open enemy. I had no occasion of bribing, flattering, or pimping, to procure the favour of any great man, or of his minion; I wanted no fence against fraud or oppression: here was neither physician to destroy my body, nor lawyer to ruin my fortune; no informer to watch my words and actions, or forge accusations against me for hire: here were no gibers, censurers, backbiters, pickpockets, highwaymen, housebreakers, attorneys, bawds, buffoons, gamesters, politicians, wits, splenetics, tedious talkers, controvertists, ravishers, murderers, robbers, virtuosos; no leaders, or followers, of party and faction; no encouragers to vice, by seducement or examples; no dungeon, axes, gibbets, whipping-posts, or pillories; no cheating shopkeepers or mechanics; no pride, vanity, or affectation; no fops, bullies, drunkards, strolling whores, or poxes; no ranting, lewd, expensive wives; no stupid, proud pedants; no importunate, overbearing, quarrelsome, noisy, roaring, empty, conceited, swearing companions; no scoundrels raised from the dust upon the merit of their vices, or nobility thrown into it on account of their virtues; no lords, fiddlers, judges, or dancing-masters.

I had the favour of being admitted to several Houyhnhnms, who came to visit or dine with my master; where his honour graciously suffered me to wait in the room, and listen to their discourse. Both he and his company would often descend to ask me questions, and receive my answers. I had also sometimes the honour of attending my master in his visits to others. I never presumed to speak, except in answer to a question; and then I did it with inward regret, because it was a loss of so much time for improving myself; but I was infinitely delighted with the station of an humble auditor in such conversations, where nothing passed but what was useful, expressed in the fewest and most significant words; where, as I have already said, the greatest decency was observed, without the least degree of ceremony; where no person spoke without being pleased himself, and pleasing his companions; where there was no interruption, tediousness, heat, or difference of sentiments.

They have a notion, that when people are met together, a short silence does much improve conversation: this I found to be true; for during those little intermissions of talk, new ideas would arise in their minds, which very much enlivened the discourse. Their subjects are, generally on friendship and benevolence, on order and economy; sometimes upon the visible operations of nature, or ancient traditions; upon the bounds and limits of virtue; upon the unerring rules of reason, or upon some determinations to be taken at the next great assembly: and often upon the various excellences of poetry.

I may add, without vanity, that my presence often gave them sufficient matter for discourse, because it afforded my master an occasion of letting his friends into the history of me and my country, upon which they were all pleased to descant, in a manner not very advantageous to humankind: and for that reason I shall not repeat what they said; only I may be allowed to observe, that his honour, to my great admiration, appeared to understand the nature of Yahoos much better than myself. He went through all our vices and follies, and discovered many, which I had never mentioned to him, by only supposing what qualities a Yahoo of their country, with a small proportion of reason, might be capable of exerting; and concluded, with too much probability, how vile, as well as miserable, such a creature must be.

I freely confess, that all the little knowledge I have of any value, was acquired by the lectures I received from my master, and from hearing the discourses of him and his friends; to which I should be prouder to listen, than to dictate to the greatest and wisest assembly in Europe. I admired the strength, comeliness, and speed of the inhabitants; and such a constellation of virtues, in such amiable persons, produced in me the highest veneration. At first, indeed, I did not feel that natural awe, which the Yahoos and all other animals bear toward them; but it grew upon me by decrees, much sooner than I imagined, and was mingled with a respectful love and gratitude, that they would condescend to distinguish me from the rest of my species.

When I thought of my family, my friends, my countrymen, or the human race in general, I considered them, as they really were, Yahoos in shape and disposition, perhaps a little more civilized, and qualified with the gift of speech; but making no other use of reason, than to improve and multiply those vices whereof their brethren in this country had only the share that nature allotted them. When I happened to behold the reflection of my own form in a lake or fountain, I turned away my face in horror and detestation of myself, and could better endure the sight of a common Yahoo than of my own person.

By conversing with the Houyhnhnms, and looking upon them with delight, I fell to imitate their gait and gesture, which is now grown into a habit; and my friends often tell me, in a blunt way, that I trot like a horse; which, however, I take for a great compliment. Neither shall I disown, that in speaking I am apt to fall into the voice and manner of the Houyhnhnms, and hear myself ridiculed on that account, without the least mortification.

In the midst of all this happiness, and when I looked upon myself to be fully settled for life, my master sent for me one morning a little earlier than his usual hour. I observed by his countenance that he was in some perplexity, and at a loss how to begin what he had to speak.

After a short silence, he told me, he did not know how I would take what he was going to say: that in the last general assembly, when the affair of the Yahoos was entered upon, the representatives had taken offence at his keeping a Yahoo (meaning myself) in his family, more like a Houyhnhnm than a brute animal; that he was known frequently to converse with me, as if he could receive some advantage or pleasure in my company; that such a practice was not agreeable to reason or nature, or a thing ever heard of before among them.

The assembly did therefore exhort him either to employ me like the rest of my species, or command me to swim back to the place whence I came: that the first of these expedients was utterly rejected by all the Houyhnhnms who had ever seen me at his house or their own; for they alleged, that because I had some rudiments of reason, added to the natural pravity of those animals, it was to be feared I might be able to seduce them into the woody and mountainous parts of the country, and bring them in troops by night to destroy the Houyhnhnms' cattle, as being naturally of the ravenous kind, and averse from labour.

My master added, that he was daily pressed by the Houyhnhnms of the neighbourhood to have the assembly's exhortation executed, which he could not put off much longer. He doubted it would be impossible for me to swim to another country; and therefore wished I would contrive some sort of vehicle, resembling those I had described to him, that might carry me on the sea; in which work I should have the assistance of his own servants, as well as those of his neighbours. He concluded, that for his own part, he could have been content to keep me in his service as long as I lived; because he found I had cured myself of some bad habits and dispositions, by endeavouring, as far as my inferior nature was capable, to imitate the Houyhnhnms.

I should here observe to the reader, that a decree of the general assembly in this country is expressed by the word *Hnhloayn*, which signifies an exhortation, as near as I can render it; for they have no conception how a rational creature can be compelled, but only advised, or exhorted; because no person can disobey reason, without giving up his claim to be a rational creature.

I was struck with the utmost grief and despair at my master's discourse; and being unable to support the agonies I was under, I fell into a swoon at his feet. When I came to myself, he told me that he concluded I had been dead; (for these people are subject to no such imbecilities of nature).

I answered in a faint voice, that death would have been too great a happiness; that although I could not blame the assembly's exhortation, or the urgency of his friends; yet, in my weak and corrupt judgment, I thought it might consist with reason to have been less rigorous; that I could not swim a league, and probably the nearest land to theirs might be distant above a hundred: that many materials, necessary for making a small vessel to carry me off, were wholly wanting in this country; which, however, I would attempt, in obedience and gratitude to his honour, although I concluded the thing to be impossible, and therefore looked on myself as already devoted to destruction.

That the certain prospect of an unnatural death was the least of my evils; for, supposing I should escape with life by some strange adventure, how could I think with temper of passing my days among Yahoos, and relapsing into my old corruptions, for want of examples to lead and keep me within the paths of virtue? that I knew too well upon what solid reasons all the determinations of the wise Houyhnhnms were founded, not to be shaken by arguments of mine, a miserable

Yahoo; and therefore, after presenting him with my humble
thanks for the offer of his servants' assistance in making a
vessel, and desiring a reasonable time for so difficult a work,
I told him I would endeavour to preserve a wretched being;
and if ever I returned to England, was not without hopes of
being useful to my own species, by celebrating the praises of
the renowned Houyhnhnms, and proposing their virtues to
the imitation of mankind.

My master, in a few words, made me a very gracious
reply; allowed me the space of two months to finish my boat;
and ordered the sorrel nag, my fellow-servant (for so, at this
distance, I may presume to call him), to follow my instruction;
because I told my master, that his help would be sufficient, and
I knew he had a tenderness for me.

In his company, my first business was to go to that part of
the coast where my rebellious crew had ordered me to be set
on shore. I got upon a height, and looking on every side into
the sea; fancied I saw a small island toward the north-east. I
took out my pocket glass, and could then clearly distinguish
it above five leagues off, as I computed; but it appeared to the
sorrel nag to be only a blue cloud: for as he had no conception
of any country beside his own, so he could not be as expert
in distinguishing remote objects at sea, as we who so much
converse in that element.

After I had discovered this island, I considered no further;
but resolved it should if possible, be the first place of my
banishment, leaving the consequence to fortune.

I returned home, and consulting with the sorrel nag, we
went into a copse at some distance, where I with my knife,
and he with a sharp flint, fastened very artificially after their
manner, to a wooden handle, cut down several oak wattles,
about the thickness of a walking-staff, and some larger pieces.
But I shall not trouble the reader with a particular description
of my own mechanics; let it suffice to say, that in six weeks

time with the help of the sorrel nag, who performed the parts that required most labour, I finished a sort of Indian canoe, but much larger, covering it with the skins of Yahoos, well stitched together with hempen threads of my own making.

My sail was likewise composed of the skins of the same animal; but I made use of the youngest I could get, the older being too tough and thick; and I likewise provided myself with four paddles. I laid in a stock of boiled flesh, of rabbits and fowls, and took with me two vessels, one filled with milk and the other with water.

I tried my canoe in a large pond, near my master's house, and then corrected in it what was amiss; stopping all the chinks with Yahoos' tallow, till I found it staunch, and able to bear me and my freight; and, when it was as complete as I could possibly make it, I had it drawn on a carriage very gently by Yahoos to the sea-side, under the conduct of the sorrel nag and another servant.

When all was ready, and the day came for my departure, I took leave of my master and lady and the whole family, my eyes flowing with tears, and my heart quite sunk with grief. But his honour, out of curiosity, and, perhaps, (if I may speak without vanity,) partly out of kindness, was determined to see me in my canoe, and got several of his neighbouring friends to accompany him.

I was forced to wait above an hour for the tide; and then observing the wind very fortunately bearing toward the island to which I intended to steer my course, I took a second leave of my master: but as I was going to prostrate myself to kiss his hoof, he did me the honour to raise it gently to my mouth. I am not ignorant how much I have been censured for mentioning this last particular. Detractors are pleased to think it improbable, that so illustrious a person should descend to give so great a mark of distinction to a creature so inferior as I. Neither have I forgotten how apt some travellers are to boast of extraordinary favours they have received. But, if these censurers were better acquainted with the noble and courteous disposition of the Houyhnhnms, they would soon change their opinion.

I paid my respects to the rest of the Houyhnhnms in his honour's company; then getting into my canoe, I pushed off from shore.

CHAPTER XI

The author's dangerous voyage. He arrives at New Holland, hoping to settle there. Is wounded with an arrow by one of the natives. Is seized and carried by force into a Portuguese ship. The great civilities of the captain. The author arrives at England.

I began this desperate voyage on February 15, 1714–15, at nine o'clock in the morning. The wind was very favourable; however, I made use at first only of my paddles; but considering I should soon be weary, and that the wind might chop about, I ventured to set up my little sail; and thus, with the help of the tide, I went at the rate of a league and a half an hour, as near as I could guess. My master and his friends continued on the shore till I was almost out of sight; and I often heard the sorrel nag (who always loved me) crying out, *Hnuy illa nyha, majah Yahoo*, Take care of thyself, gentle Yahoo.

My design was, if possible, to discover some small island uninhabited, yet sufficient, by my labour, to furnish me with the necessaries of life, which I would have thought a greater happiness, than to be first minister in the politest court of Europe; so horrible was the idea I conceived of returning to live in the society, and under the government of Yahoos. For in such a solitude as I desired, I could at least enjoy my own thoughts, and reflect with delight on the virtues of those inimitable

Houyhnhnms, without an opportunity of degenerating into the vices and corruptions of my own species.

The reader may remember what I related, when my crew conspired against me, and confined me to my cabin; how I continued there several weeks without knowing what course we took; and when I was put ashore in the long-boat, how the sailors told me, with oaths, whether true or false, that they knew not in what part of the world we were. However, I did then believe us to be about 10 degrees southward of the Cape of Good Hope, or about 45 degrees southern latitude, as I gathered from some general words I overheard among them, being I supposed to the south-east in their intended voyage to Madagascar. And although this were little better than conjecture, yet I resolved to steer my course eastward, hoping to reach the south-west coast of New Holland, and perhaps some such island as I desired lying westward of it.

The wind was full west, and by six in the evening I computed I had gone eastward at least eighteen leagues; when I spied a very small island about half a league off, which I soon reached. It was nothing but a rock, with one creek naturally arched by the force of tempests. Here I put in my canoe, and climbing a part of the rock, I could plainly discover land to the east, extending from south to north.

I lay all night in my canoe; and repeating my voyage early in the morning, I arrived in seven hours to the south-east point of New Holland. This confirmed me in the opinion I have long entertained, that the maps and charts place this country at least three degrees more to the east than it really is; which thought I communicated many years ago to my worthy friend, Mr. Herman Moll, and gave him my reasons for it, although he has rather chosen to follow other authors.

I saw no inhabitants in the place where I landed, and being unarmed, I was afraid of venturing far into the country. I found some shellfish on the shore, and ate them raw, not daring to kindle a fire, for fear of being discovered by the natives. I continued three days feeding on oysters and limpets, to save my own provisions; and I fortunately found a brook of excellent water, which gave me great relief.

On the fourth day, venturing out early a little too far, I saw twenty or thirty natives upon a height not above five hundred yards from me. They were stark naked, men, women, and children, round a fire, as I could discover by the smoke. One of them spied me, and gave notice to the rest; five of them advanced toward me, leaving the women and children at the fire. I made what haste I could to the shore, and, getting into my canoe, shoved off: the savages, observing me retreat, ran after me: and before I could get far enough into the sea, discharged an arrow which wounded me deeply on the inside of my left knee: I shall carry the mark to my grave. I apprehended the arrow might be poisoned, and paddling out of the reach of their darts (being a calm day), I made a shift to suck the wound, and dress it as well as I could.

I was at a loss what to do, for I durst not return to the same landing-place, but stood to the north, and was forced to paddle, for the wind, though very gentle, was against me, blowing north-west. As I was looking about for a secure landing-place, I saw a sail to the north-north-east, which appearing every minute more visible, I was in some doubt whether I should wait for them or not; but at last my detestation of the Yahoo race prevailed: and turning my canoe, I sailed and paddled together to the south, and got into the same creek whence I set out in the morning, choosing rather to trust myself among these barbarians, than live with European Yahoos. I drew up my canoe as close as I could to the shore, and hid myself behind a stone by the little brook, which, as I have already said, was excellent water.

The ship came within half a league of this creek, and sent her long boat with vessels to take in fresh water (for the place, it seems, was very well known); but I did not observe it, till the boat was almost on shore; and it was too late to seek another hiding-place. The seamen at their landing observed my canoe, and rummaging it all over, easily conjectured that the owner could not be far off. Four of them, well armed, searched every cranny and lurking-hole, till at last they found me flat on my face behind the stone. They gazed awhile in admiration at my strange uncouth dress; my coat made of skins, my wooden-soled shoes, and my furred stockings; whence, however, they concluded, I was not a native of the place, who all go naked.

One of the seamen, in Portuguese, bid me rise, and asked who I was. I understood that language very well, and getting upon my feet, said, I was a poor Yahoo banished from the Houyhnhnms, and desired they would please to let me depart. They admired to hear me answer them in their own tongue, and saw by my complexion I must be a European; but were at a loss to know what I meant by Yahoos and Houyhnhnms; and at the same time fell a-laughing at my strange tone in speaking, which resembled the neighing of a horse. I trembled all the while betwixt fear and hatred. I again desired leave to depart, and was gently moving to my canoe; but they laid hold of me, desiring to know, what country I was of? whence I came? with many other questions. I told them I was born in England, whence I came about five years ago, and then their country and ours were at peace. I therefore hoped they would not treat me as an enemy, since I meant them no harm, but was a poor Yahoo seeking some desolate place where to pass the remainder of his unfortunate life.

When they began to talk, I thought I never heard or saw any thing more unnatural; for it appeared to me as monstrous as if a dog or a cow should speak in England, or aYahoo in Houyhnhnmland.

The honest Portuguese were equally amazed at my strange dress, and the odd manner of delivering my words, which, however, they understood very well. They spoke to me with great humanity, and said, they were sure the captain would carry me gratis to Lisbon, whence I might return to my own country; that two of the seamen would go back to the ship, inform the captain of what they had seen, and receive his orders; in the mean time, unless I would give my solemn oath not to fly, they would secure me by force. I thought it best to comply with their proposal. They were very curious to know my story, but I gave them very little satisfaction, and they all conjectured that my misfortunes had impaired my reason. In two hours the boat, which went laden with vessels of water, returned, with the captain's command to fetch me on board. I fell on my knees to preserve my liberty; but all was in vain; and the men, having tied me with cords, heaved me into the boat, whence I was taken into the ship, and thence into the captain's cabin.

His name was Pedro de Mendez; he was a very courteous and generous person. He entreated me to give some account of myself, and desired to know what I would eat or drink; said, I should be used as well as himself; and spoke so many obliging things, that I wondered to find such civilities from a Yahoo. However, I remained silent and sullen; I was ready to faint at the very smell of him and his men.

At last I desired something to eat out of my own canoe; but he ordered me a chicken, and some excellent wine, and then directed that I should be put to bed in a very clean cabin. I would not undress myself, but lay on the bed-clothes, and in half an hour stole out, when I thought the crew was at dinner, and getting to the side of the ship, was going to leap into the sea, and swim for my life, rather than continue among Yahoos. But one of the seamen prevented me, and having informed the captain, I was chained to my cabin.

After dinner, Don Pedro came to me, and desired to know my reason for so desperate an attempt; assured me, he only meant to do me all the service he was able; and spoke so very movingly, that at last I descended to treat him like an animal which had some little portion of reason.

I gave him a very short relation of my voyage; of the conspiracy against me by my own men; of the country where they set me on shore, and of my five years residence there. All which he looked upon as if it were a dream or a vision; whereat I took great offence; for I had quite forgot the faculty of lying, so peculiar to Yahoos, in all countries where they preside, and, consequently, their disposition of suspecting truth in others of their own species.

I asked him, whether it were the custom in his country to say the thing which was not? I assured him, I had almost forgot what he meant by falsehood, and if I had lived a thousand years in Houyhnhnmland, I should never have heard a lie from the meanest servant; that I was altogether indifferent whether he believed me or not; but, however, in return for his favours, I would give so much allowance to the corruption of his nature, as to answer any objection he would please to make, and then he might easily discover the truth.

The captain, a wise man, after many endeavours to catch me tripping in some part of my story, at last began to have a better opinion of my veracity. But he added, that since I professed so inviolable an attachment to truth, I must give him my word and honour to bear him company in this voyage, without attempting any thing against my life; or else he would continue me a prisoner till we arrived at Lisbon. I gave him the promise he required; but at the same time protested, that I would suffer the greatest hardships, rather than return to live among Yahoos.

Our voyage passed without any considerable accident. In gratitude to the captain, I sometimes sat with him, at his earnest request, and strove to conceal my antipathy against human kind, although it often broke out; which he suffered to pass without observation. But the greatest part of the day I confined myself to my cabin, to avoid seeing any of the crew.

The captain had often entreated me to strip myself of my savage dress, and offered to lend me the best suit of clothes he had. This I would not be prevailed on to accept, abhorring to cover myself with any thing that had been on the back of a Yahoo. I only desired he would lend me two clean shirts, which, having been washed since he wore them, I believed would not so much defile me. These I changed every second day, and washed them myself.

We arrived at Lisbon, Nov. 5, 1715. At our landing, the captain forced me to cover myself with his cloak, to prevent the rabble from crowding about me. I was conveyed to his own house; and at my earnest request he led me up to the highest room backwards. I conjured him to conceal from all persons what I had told him of the Houyhnhnms; because the least hint of such a story would not only draw numbers of people to see me, but probably put me in danger of being imprisoned, or burnt by the Inquisition.

The captain persuaded me to accept a suit of clothes newly made; but I would not suffer the tailor to take my measure; however, Don Pedro being almost of my size, they fitted me well enough. He accoutred me with other necessaries, all new, which I aired for twenty-four hours before I would use them.

The captain had no wife, nor above three servants, none of which were suffered to attend at meals; and his whole deportment was so obliging, added to very good human understanding, that I really began to tolerate his company. He gained so far upon me, that I ventured to look out of the back window. By degrees I was brought into another room, whence I peeped into the street, but drew my head back in a fright. In a week's time he seduced me down to the door. I found my terror gradually lessened, but my hatred and contempt seemed to increase. I was at last bold enough to walk the street in his company, but kept my nose well stopped with rue, or sometimes with tobacco.

In ten days, Don Pedro, to whom I had given some account of my domestic affairs, put it upon me, as a matter of honour and conscience, that I ought to return to my native country, and live at home with my wife and children. He told me, there was an English ship in the port just ready to sail, and he would furnish me with all things necessary. It would be tedious to repeat his arguments, and my contradictions. He said it was altogether impossible to find such a solitary island as I desired to live in; but I might command in my own house, and pass my time in a manner as recluse as I pleased.

I complied at last, finding I could not do better. I left Lisbon the 24th day of November, in an English merchantman, but who was the master I never inquired. Don Pedro accompanied me to the ship, and lent me twenty pounds. He took kind leave of me, and embraced me at parting, which I bore as well as I could. During this last voyage I had no commerce with the master or any of his men; but, pretending I was sick, kept close in my cabin. On the fifth of December, 1715, we cast anchor in the Downs, about nine in the morning, and at three in the afternoon I got safe to my house at Rotherhith.

My wife and family received me with great surprise and joy, because they concluded me certainly dead; but I must freely confess the sight of them filled me only with hatred, disgust, and contempt; and the more, by reflecting on the near alliance I had to them. For although, since my unfortunate exile from the Houyhnhnm country, I had compelled myself to tolerate the sight of Yahoos, and to converse with Don Pedro de Mendez, yet my memory and imagination were perpetually filled with the virtues and ideas of those exalted Houyhnhnms.

As soon as I entered the house, my wife took me in her arms, and kissed me; at which, having not been used to the touch of that odious animal for so many years, I fell into a swoon for almost an hour. At the time I am writing, it is five years since my last return to England. During the first year, I could not endure my wife or children in my presence; the very smell of them was intolerable; much less could I suffer them to eat in the same room. To this hour they dare not presume to touch my bread, or drink out of the same cup, neither was I ever able to let one of them take me by the hand. The first money I laid out was to buy two young stone-horses, which I keep in a good stable; and next to them, the groom is my greatest favourite, for I feel my spirits revived by the smell he contracts in the stable. My horses understand me tolerably well; I converse with them at least four hours every day. They are strangers to bridle or saddle; they live in great amity with me and friendship to each other.

CHAPTER XII

The author's veracity. His design in publishing this work.
His censure of those travellers who swerve from the truth.
The author clears himself from any sinister ends in writing.
An objection answered. The method of planting colonies.
His native country commended. The right of the crown to
those countries described by the author is justified. The
difficulty of conquering them. The author takes his last
leave of the reader; proposes his manner of living for the
future; gives good advice, and concludeth.

Thus, gentle reader, I have given thee a faithful history of
my travels for sixteen years and above seven months:
wherein I have not been so studious of ornament as of truth. I
could, perhaps, like others, have astonished thee with strange
improbable tales; but I rather chose to relate plain matter of
fact, in the simplest manner and style; because my principal
design was to inform, and not to amuse thee.

It is easy for us who travel into remote countries, which
are seldom visited by Englishmen or other Europeans, to
form descriptions of wonderful animals both at sea and land.
Whereas a traveller's chief aim should be to make men wiser
and better, and to improve their minds by the bad, as well
as good, example of what they deliver concerning foreign
places.

I could heartily wish a law was enacted, that every traveller, before he were permitted to publish his voyages, should be obliged to make oath before the Lord High Chancellor, that all he intended to print was absolutely true to the best of his knowledge; for then the world would no longer be deceived, as it usually is, while some writers, to make their works pass the better upon the public, impose the grossest falsities on the unwary reader.

I have perused several books of travels with great delight in my younger days; but having since gone over most parts of the globe, and been able to contradict many fabulous accounts from my own observation, it has given me a great disgust against this part of reading, and some indignation to see the credulity of mankind so impudently abused. Therefore, since my acquaintance were pleased to think my poor endeavours might not be unacceptable to my country, I imposed on myself, as a maxim never to be swerved from, that I would strictly adhere to truth; neither indeed can I be ever under the least temptation to vary from it, while I retain in my mind the lectures and example of my noble master and the other illustrious Houyhnhnms of whom I had so long the honour to be an humble hearer.

—*Nec si miserum Fortuna Sinonem*
Finxit, vanum etiam, mendacemque improba finget.

I know very well, how little reputation is to be got by writings which require neither genius nor learning, nor indeed any other talent, except a good memory, or an exact journal.

I know likewise, that writers of travels, like dictionary-makers, are sunk into oblivion by the weight and bulk of those who come last, and therefore lie uppermost. And it is highly probable, that such travellers, who shall hereafter visit the countries described in this work of mine, may, by detecting my errors (if there be any), and adding many new discoveries of their own, justle me out of vogue, and stand in my place, making the world forget that ever I was an author. This indeed would be too great a mortification, if I wrote for fame: but as my sole intention was the public good, I cannot be altogether disappointed. For who can read of the virtues I have mentioned in the glorious Houyhnhnms, without being ashamed of his own vices, when he considers himself as the reasoning, governing animal of his country?

I shall say nothing of those remote nations where Yahoos preside; among which the least corrupted are the Brobdingnagians, whose wise maxims in morality and government it would be our happiness to observe.

But I forbear descanting further, and rather leave the judicious reader to his own remarks and application.

I am not a little pleased that this work of mine can possibly meet with no censurers: for what objections can be made against a writer, who relates only plain facts, that happened in such distant countries, where we have not the least interest, with respect either to trade or negotiations?

I have carefully avoided every fault with which common writers of travels are often too justly charged. Besides, I meddle not the least with any party, but write without passion, prejudice, or ill-will against any man, or number of men, whatsoever. I write for the noblest end, to inform and instruct mankind; over whom I may, without breach of modesty, pretend to some superiority, from the advantages I received by conversing so long among the most accomplished Houyhnhnms. I write without any view to profit or praise. I never suffer a word to pass that may look like reflection, or possibly give the least offence, even to those who are most ready to take it. So that I hope I may with justice pronounce myself an author perfectly blameless; against whom the tribes of Answerers, Considerers, Observers, Reflectors, Detectors,

Remarkers, will never be able to find matter for exercising their talents.

I confess, it was whispered to me, that I was bound in duty, as a subject of England, to have given in a memorial to a secretary of state at my first coming over; because, whatever lands are discovered by a subject belong to the crown. But I doubt whether our conquests in the countries I treat of would be as easy as those of Ferdinando Cortez over the naked Americans. The Lilliputians, I think, are hardly worth the charge of a fleet and army to reduce them; and I question whether it might be prudent or safe to attempt the Brobdingnagians; or whether an English army would be much at their ease with the Flying Island over their heads.

The Houyhnhnms indeed appear not to be so well prepared for war, a science to which they are perfect strangers, and especially against missive weapons. However, supposing myself to be a minister of state, I could never give my advice for invading them. Their prudence, unanimity, unacquaintedness with fear, and their love of their country, would amply supply all defects in the military art. Imagine twenty thousand of them breaking into the midst of an European army, confounding the ranks, overturning the carriages, battering the warriors' faces into mummy by terrible yerks from their hinder hoofs; for they would well deserve the character given to Augustus: *Recalcitrat undique tutus.*

But, instead of proposals for conquering that magnanimous nation, I rather wish they were in a capacity, or disposition, to send a sufficient number of their inhabitants for civilizing Europe, by teaching us the first principles of honour, justice, truth, temperance, public spirit, fortitude, chastity, friendship, benevolence, and fidelity. The names of all which virtues are still retained among us in most languages, and are to be met with in modern, as well as ancient authors; which I am able to assert from my own small reading.

But I had another reason, which made me less forward to enlarge his Majesty's dominions by my discoveries. To say the truth, I had conceived a few scruples with relation to the distributive justice of princes upon those occasions. For instance, a crew of pirates are driven by a storm they know not whither; at length a boy discovers land from the topmast; they go on shore to rob and plunder, they see a harmless people, are entertained with kindness; they give the country a new name; they take formal possession of it for their king; they set up a rotten plank, or a stone, for a memorial; they murder two or three dozen of the natives, bring away a couple more, by force, for a sample; return home, and get their pardon.

Here commences a new dominion acquired with a title by divine right. Ships are sent with the first opportunity; the natives driven out or destroyed; their princes tortured to discover their gold; a free license given to all acts of inhumanity and lust, the earth reeking with the blood of its inhabitants: and this execrable crew of butchers, employed in so pious an expedition, is a modern colony, sent to convert and civilize an idolatrous and barbarous people.

But this description, I confess, does by no means affect the British nation, who may be an example to the whole world for their wisdom, care, and justice in planting colonies; their liberal endowments for the advancement of religion and learning; their choice of devout and able pastors to propagate Christianity; their caution in stocking their provinces with people of sober lives and conversations from this the mother kingdom; their strict regard to the distribution of justice, in supplying the civil administration through all their colonies with officers of the greatest abilities, utter strangers to corruption; and, to crown all, by sending the most vigilant and virtuous governors, who have no other views than the happiness of the people over whom they preside, and the honour of the king their master.

But as those countries which I have described do not appear to have any desire of being conquered and enslaved, murdered or driven out by colonies, nor abound either in gold, silver, sugar, or tobacco, I did humbly conceive, they were by no means proper objects of our zeal, our valour, or our interest.

However, if those whom it more concerns think fit to be of another opinion, I am ready to depose, when I shall be lawfully called, that no European did ever visit those countries before me. I mean, if the inhabitants ought to be believed, unless a dispute may arise concerning the two Yahoos, said to have been seen many years ago upon a mountain in Houyhnhnmland.

But, as to the formality of taking possession in my sovereign's name, it never came once into my thoughts; and if it had, yet, as my affairs then stood, I should perhaps, in point of prudence and self-preservation, have put it off to a better opportunity.

Having thus answered the only objection that can ever be raised against me as a traveller, I here take a final leave of all my courteous readers, and return to enjoy my own speculations in my little garden at Redriff; to apply those excellent lessons of virtue which I learned among the Houyhnhnms; to instruct the Yahoos of my own family, is far as I shall find them docible animals; to behold my figure often in a glass, and thus, if possible, habituate myself by time to tolerate the sight of a human creature; to lament the brutality to Houyhnhnms in my own country, but always treat their persons with respect, for the sake of my noble master, his family, his friends, and the whole Houyhnhnm race, whom these of ours have the honour to resemble in all their lineaments, however their intellectuals came to degenerate.

I began last week to permit my wife to sit at dinner with me, at the farthest end of a long table; and to answer (but with the utmost brevity) the few questions I asked her. Yet, the smell of a Yahoo continuing very offensive, I always keep my nose well stopped with rue, lavender, or tobacco leaves. And, although it be hard for a man late in life to remove old habits, I am not altogether out of hopes, in some time, to suffer a neighbour Yahoo in my company, without the apprehensions I am yet under of his teeth or his claws.

My reconcilement to the Yahoo kind in general might not be so difficult, if they would be content with those vices and follies only which nature has entitled them to. I am not in the least provoked at the sight of a lawyer, a pickpocket, a colonel, a fool, a lord, a gamester, a politician, a whoremonger, a physician, an evidence, a suborner, an attorney, a traitor, or the like; this is all according to the due course of things: but when I behold a lump of deformity and diseases, both in body and mind, smitten with pride, it immediately breaks all the measures of my patience; neither shall I be ever able to comprehend how such an animal, and such a vice, could tally together.

The wise and virtuous Houyhnhnms, who abound in all excellences that can adorn a rational creature, have no name for this vice in their language, which has no terms to express any thing that is evil, except those whereby they describe the detestable qualities of their Yahoos, among which they were not able to distinguish this of pride, for want of thoroughly understanding human nature, as it shows itself in other countries where that animal presides. But I, who had more experience, could plainly observe some rudiments of it among the wild Yahoos.

But the Houyhnhnms, who live under the government of reason, are no more proud of the good qualities they possess, than I should be for not wanting a leg or an arm; which no man in his wits would boast of, although he must be miserable without them. I dwell the longer upon this subject from the desire I have to make the society of an English Yahoo by any means not insupportable; and therefore I here entreat those who have any tincture of this absurd vice, that they will not presume to come in my sight.

The Jungle Book

The Jungle Book

Rudyard Kipling

Trans
Atlantic
Press

This is a Transatlantic Press book

This edition published in 2012

Transatlantic Press

Sky House, Raans Road, Amersham, Bucks, HP6 6JQ, UK

Rudyard Kipling asserts the moral right to be identified as the author of this work.

Cover image copyright GettyImages

Author biography copyright Transatlantic Press

A catalogue record is available for this book from the British Library

ISBN 978-1-908533-76-0

Printed and bound by CPI Group (UK) Ltd, Croydon, CR0 4YY

RUDYARD KIPLING

Rudyard Kipling was born on 30 December 1865 in Bombay, where his father, John Lockwood Kipling, taught at the city's School of Art. His mother, Alice, was sister-in-law to artist Edward Burne-Jones, while one of her nephews, Stanley Baldwin, went on to become British prime minister. The family moved to Lahore, where John Kipling took up an appointment as museum curator, but at the age of five Rudyard was sent to England to be educated, an unhappy experience he fictionalised in *Baa Baa Black Sheep* (1888). He later studied at United Services College in Westward Ho!, Devonshire, which provided further grist to the artistic mill, *Stalky and Co* (1899) becoming a much loved story of school life. On completing his education Kipling returned to Lahore to take up a journalist's post at the Civil and Military Gazette. He began to publish poems and stories, and made his mark in 1886 with the collection *Departmental Ditties*. He followed that with *Plain Tales from the Hills* and *Soldiers Three* in a fertile period that also produced *Wee Willie Winkie*. Returning to England in 1889, he met American writer-publisher Wolcott Balestier, with whom he collaborated on *The Naulakha* (1892). That same year he published *Barrack-Room Ballads* to great acclaim. He also married Balestier's sister, Caroline, and for a time the couple resided in Vermont, her family home. His two *Jungle Books* (1894 and 1895) date from this period, and he also worked on *Captains Courageous*. The latter was published in 1897, by which time the Kiplings had returned to England. The *Just So Stories* (1902) were written in the wake of a tragedy, the death of a daughter. In *Kim* (1901), regarded as his finest full-length work, he created a memorable picture of India. A staunch champion of Empire, Kipling spoke of 'the white man's burden', alienating many with his political views. For some his patriotic fervour spilled over into jingoism; to others he was an astute observer and chronicler of the age in which he lived. His literary achievements brought him the Nobel Prize in 1907, the first English writer to be thus honoured. *Rewards and Fairies* appeared in 1910, a collection including the oft-quoted poem *If*. The family suffered further tragedy when son John was lost in World War One. Kipling, who became a member of the Imperial War Graves Commission, chose the words inscribed at the cemeteries for the fallen: 'Their Names Liveth For Evermore'. His later work includes *Debits and Credits* (1926) and *Limits and Renewals* (1932). He died in January 1936, aged 70.

THE JUNGLE BOOK

'Shere Khan does us great honour,' said Father Wolf,
but his eyes were very angry. 'What does Shere Khan want?'
'My quarry. A man's cub went this way,' said Shere Khan.

A naked baby, barely able to walk, becomes separated from its parents during an attack by the ferocious tiger Shere Khan. Adopted by a wolf pack and named Mowgli, the child is raised in the ways of the jungle. Baloo the bear and Bagheera the black panther help to educate the 'man cub', but to other animals, such as the lawless, treacherous Monkey-People, he is a prized target. Shere Khan, meanwhile, is biding his time. He turns the wolf pack against Mowgli, hoping he will finally have his prey…

As well as relating Mowgli's strange and exciting adventures, *The Jungle Book* tales introduce a wealth of other memorable characters, including Toomai, the young elephant-handler, and heroic mongoose Rikki-Tikki-Tavi.

CONTENTS

MOWGLI'S BROTHERS

Now Chil the Kite brings home the night
 That Mang the Bat sets free—
The herds are shut in byre and hut
 For loosed till dawn are we.
This is the hour of pride and power,
 Talon and tush and claw.
Oh, hear the call!—Good hunting all
 That keep the Jungle Law!

Night-Song in the Jungle

It was seven o'clock of a very warm evening in the Seeonee hills when Father Wolf woke up from his day's rest, scratched himself, yawned, and spread out his paws one after the other to get rid of the sleepy feeling in their tips. Mother Wolf lay with her big gray nose dropped across her four tumbling, squealing cubs, and the moon shone into the mouth of the cave where they all lived. "Augrh!" said Father Wolf "it is time to hunt again"; and he was going to spring down hill when a little shadow with a bushy tail crossed the threshold and whined: "Good luck go with you, O Chief of the Wolves; and good luck and strong white teeth go with noble children that they may never forget the hungry in this world."

It was the jackal—Tabaqui, the Dish-licker—and the wolves of India despise Tabaqui because he runs about making mischief, and telling tales, and eating rags and pieces of leather from the village rubbish-heaps. But they are afraid of him too, because Tabaqui, more than anyone else in the Jungle, is apt to go mad, and then he forgets that he was ever afraid of anyone, and runs through the forest biting everything in his way. Even the tiger runs and hides when little Tabaqui goes mad, for madness is the most disgraceful thing that can overtake a wild creature. We call it hydrophobia, but they call it *dewanee*—the madness—and run.

"Enter, then, and look," said Father Wolf stiffly; "but there is no food here."

"For a wolf, no," said Tabaqui, "but for so mean a person as myself a dry bone is a good feast. Who are we, the *Gidur-log* [the jackal people], to pick and choose?" He scuttled to the back of the cave, where he found the bone of a buck with some meat on it, and sat cracking the end merrily.

"All thanks for this good meal," he said, licking his lips. "How beautiful are the noble children! How large are their eyes! And so young too! Indeed, indeed, I might have remembered that the children of Kings are men from the beginning."

Now, Tabaqui knew as well as anyone else that there is nothing so unlucky as to compliment children to their faces; and it pleased him to see Mother and Father Wolf look uncomfortable.

Tabaqui sat still, rejoicing in the mischief that he had made, and then he said spitefully:

"Shere Khan, the Big One, has shifted his hunting grounds. He will hunt among these hills for the next moon, so he has told me."

Shere Khan was the tiger who lived near the Waingunga River, twenty miles away.

"He has no right!" Father Wolf began angrily—"By the Law of the Jungle he has no right to change his quarters without due warning. He will frighten every head of game within ten miles, and I—I have to kill for two, these days."

"His mother did not call him Lungri [the Lame One] for nothing," said Mother Wolf quietly. "He has been lame in one foot from his birth. That is why he has only killed cattle. Now the villagers of the Waingunga are angry with him, and he has come here to make *our* villagers angry. They will scour the Jungle for him when he is far away, and we and our children must run when the grass is set alight. Indeed, we are very grateful to Shere Khan!"

"Shall I tell him of your gratitude?" said Tabaqui.

"Out!" snapped Father Wolf. "Out and hunt with thy master. Thou hast done harm enough for one night."

"I go," said Tabaqui quietly. "Ye can hear Shere Khan below in the thickets. I might have saved myself the message."

Father Wolf listened, and below in the valley that ran down to a little river he heard the dry, angry, snarly, singsong whine of a tiger who has caught nothing and does not care if all the Jungle knows it.

"The fool!" said Father Wolf. "To begin a night's work with that noise! Does he think that our buck are like his fat Waingunga bullocks?"

"H'sh. It is neither bullock nor buck he hunts to-night," said Mother Wolf. "It is Man." The whine had changed to a sort of humming purr that seemed to come from every quarter of the compass. It was the noise that bewilders woodcutters and gypsies sleeping in the open, and makes them run sometimes into the very mouth of the tiger.

"Man!" said Father Wolf, showing all his white teeth. "Faugh! Are there not enough beetles and frogs in the tanks that he must eat Man, and on our ground too!"

The Law of the Jungle, which never orders anything without a reason, forbids every beast to eat Man except when he is killing to show his children how to kill, and then he must hunt outside the hunting grounds of his pack or tribe. The real reason for this is that man-killing means, sooner or later, the arrival of white men on elephants, with guns, and hundreds of brown men with gongs and rockets and torches.

Then everybody in the Jungle suffers. The reason the beasts give among themselves is that Man is the weakest and most defenseless of all living things, and it is unsportsmanlike to touch him. They say too—and it is true—that man-eaters become mangy, and lose their teeth.

The purr grew louder, and ended in the full-throated "Aaarh!" of the tiger's charge.

Then there was a howl—an untigerish howl—from Shere Khan. "He has missed," said Mother Wolf. "What is it?"

Father Wolf ran out a few paces and heard Shere Khan muttering and mumbling savagely as he tumbled about in the scrub.

"The fool has had no more sense than to jump at a woodcutter's campfire, and has burned his feet," said Father Wolf with a grunt. "Tabaqui is with him."

"Something is coming uphill," said Mother Wolf, twitching one ear. "Get ready."

The bushes rustled a little in the thicket, and Father Wolf dropped with his haunches under him, ready for his leap. Then, if you had been watching, you would have seen the most wonderful thing in the world—the wolf checked in mid-spring. He made his bound before he saw what it was he was jumping at, and then he tried to stop himself. The result was that he shot up straight into the air for four or five feet, landing almost where he left ground.

"Man!" he snapped. "A man's cub. Look!"

Directly in front of him, holding on by a low branch, stood a naked brown baby who could just walk—as soft and as dimpled a little atom as ever came to a wolf's cave at night. He looked up into Father Wolf's face, and laughed.

"Is that a man's cub?" said Mother Wolf. "I have never seen one. Bring it here."

A wolf accustomed to moving his own cubs can, if necessary, mouth an egg without breaking it, and though

Father Wolf's jaws closed right on the child's back not a tooth even scratched the skin as he laid it down among the cubs.

"How little! How naked, and—how bold!" said Mother Wolf softly. The baby was pushing his way between the cubs to get close to the warm hide. "*Ahai!* He is taking his meal with the others. And so this is a man's cub. Now, was there ever a wolf that could boast of a man's cub among her children?"

"I have heard now and again of such a thing, but never in our Pack or in my time," said Father Wolf. "He is altogether without hair, and I could kill him with a touch of my foot. But see, he looks up and is not afraid."

The moonlight was blocked out of the mouth of the cave, for Shere Khan's great square head and shoulders were thrust into the entrance. Tabaqui, behind him, was squeaking: "My lord, my lord, it went in here!"

"Shere Khan does us great honor," said Father Wolf, but his eyes were very angry. "What does Shere Khan need?"

"My quarry. A man's cub went this way," said Shere Khan. "Its parents have run off. Give it to me."

Shere Khan had jumped at a woodcutter's camp-fire, as Father Wolf had said, and was furious from the pain of his burned feet. But Father Wolf knew that the mouth of the cave was too narrow for a tiger to come in by. Even where he was, Shere Khan's shoulders and forepaws were cramped for want of room, as a man's would be if he tried to fight in a barrel.

"The Wolves are a free people," said Father Wolf. "They take orders from the Head of the Pack, and not from any striped cattle-killer. The man's cub is ours—to kill if we choose."

"Ye choose and ye do not choose! What talk is this of choosing? By the bull that I killed, am I to stand nosing into your dog's den for my fair dues? It is I, Shere Khan, who speak!"

The tiger's roar filled the cave with thunder. Mother Wolf shook herself clear of the cubs and sprang forward, her eyes, like two green moons in the darkness, facing the blazing eyes of Shere Khan.

"And it is I, Raksha [The Demon], who answers. The man's cub is mine, Lungri—mine to me! He shall not be killed. He shall live to run with the Pack and to hunt with the Pack; and in the end, look you, hunter of little naked cubs—frog-eater—fish-killer—he shall hunt *thee*! Now get hence, or by the Sambhur that I killed (*I* eat no starved cattle), back thou goest to thy mother, burned beast of the Jungle, lamer than ever thou camest into the world! Go!"

Father Wolf looked on amazed. He had almost forgotten the days when he won Mother Wolf in fair fight from five other wolves, when she ran in the Pack and was not called The Demon for compliment's sake. Shere Khan might have faced Father Wolf, but he could not stand up against Mother Wolf, for he knew that where he was she had all the advantage of the ground, and would fight to the death. So he backed out of the cave mouth growling, and when he was clear he shouted:

"Each dog barks in his own yard! We will see what the Pack will say to this fostering of man-cubs. The cub is mine, and to my teeth he will come in the end, O bush-tailed thieves!"

Mother Wolf threw herself down panting among the cubs, and Father Wolf said to her gravely:

"Shere Khan speaks this much truth. The cub must be shown to the Pack. Wilt thou still keep him, Mother?"

"Keep him!" she gasped. "He came naked, by night, alone and very hungry; yet he was not afraid! Look, he has pushed one of my babes to one side already. And that lame butcher would have killed him and would have run off to the Waingunga while the villagers here hunted through all our lairs in revenge! Keep him? Assuredly I will keep him. Lie still, little frog. O thou Mowgli—for Mowgli the Frog I will call thee—the time will come when thou wilt hunt Shere Khan as he has hunted thee."

"But what will our Pack say?" said Father Wolf.

The Law of the Jungle lays down very clearly that any wolf may, when he marries, withdraw from the Pack he belongs to; but as soon as his cubs are old enough to stand on their feet he must bring them to the Pack Council, which is generally held once a month at full moon, in order that the other wolves may identify them. After that inspection the cubs are free to run where they please, and until they have killed their first buck no excuse is accepted if a grown wolf of the Pack kills one of them. The punishment is death where the murderer can be found; and if you think for a minute you will see that this must be so.

Father Wolf waited till his cubs could run a little, and then on the night of the Pack Meeting took them and Mowgli and Mother Wolf to the Council Rock—a hilltop covered with stones and boulders where a hundred wolves could hide. Akela, the great gray Lone Wolf, who led all the Pack by strength and cunning, lay out at full length on his rock, and below him sat forty or more wolves of every size and color, from badger-colored veterans who could handle a buck alone to young black three-year-olds who thought they could. The Lone Wolf had led them for a year now. He had fallen twice into a wolf trap in his youth, and once he had been beaten and left for dead; so he knew the manners and customs of men. There was very little talking at the Rock. The cubs tumbled over each other in the center of the circle where their mothers and fathers sat, and now and again a senior wolf would go quietly up to a cub, look at him carefully, and return to his place on noiseless feet. Sometimes a mother would push her cub far out into the moonlight to be sure that he had not been overlooked. Akela from his rock would cry: "Ye know the Law—ye know the Law. Look well, O Wolves!" And the anxious mothers would take up the call: "Look—look well, O Wolves!"

At last—and Mother Wolf's neck bristles lifted as the time came—Father Wolf pushed "Mowgli the Frog," as they called him, into the center, where he sat laughing and playing with some pebbles that glistened in the moonlight.

Akela never raised his head from his paws, but went on with the monotonous cry: "Look well!" A muffled roar came up from behind the rocks—the voice of Shere Khan crying: "The cub is mine. Give him to me. What have the Free People to do with a man's cub?" Akela never even twitched his ears. All he said was: "Look well, O Wolves! What have the Free People to do with the orders of any save the Free People? Look well!"

There was a chorus of deep growls, and a young wolf in his fourth year flung back Shere Khan's question to Akela: "What have the Free People to do with a man's cub?" Now, the Law of the Jungle lays down that if there is any dispute as to the right of a cub to be accepted by the Pack, he must be spoken for by at least two members of the Pack who are not his father and mother.

"Who speaks for this cub?" said Akela. "Among the Free People who speaks?" There was no answer and Mother Wolf got ready for what she knew would be her last fight, if things came to fighting.

Then the only other creature who is allowed at the Pack Council—Baloo, the sleepy brown bear who teaches the wolf cubs the Law of the Jungle: old Baloo, who can come and go where he pleases because he eats only nuts and roots and honey—rose upon his hind quarters and grunted.

"The man's cub—the man's cub?" he said. "*I* speak for the man's cub. There is no harm in a man's cub. I have no gift of words, but I speak the truth. Let him run with the Pack, and be entered with the others. I myself will teach him."

"We need yet another," said Akela. "Baloo has spoken, and he is our teacher for the young cubs. Who speaks besides Baloo?"

A black shadow dropped down into the circle. It was Bagheera the Black Panther, inky black all over, but with the panther markings showing up in certain lights like the pattern of watered silk. Everybody knew Bagheera, and nobody cared to cross his path; for he was as cunning as Tabaqui, as bold as the wild buffalo, and as reckless as the wounded elephant. But he had a voice as soft as wild honey dripping from a tree, and a skin softer than down.

"O Akela, and ye the Free People," he purred, "I have no right in your assembly, but the Law of the Jungle says that if there is a doubt which is not a killing matter in regard to a new cub, the life of that cub may be bought at a price. And the Law does not say who may or may not pay that price. Am I right?"

"Good! Good!" said the young wolves, who are always hungry. "Listen to Bagheera. The cub can be bought for a price. It is the Law."

"Knowing that I have no right to speak here, I ask your leave."

"Speak then," cried twenty voices.

"To kill a naked cub is shame. Besides, he may make better sport for you when he is grown. Baloo has spoken in his behalf. Now to Baloo's word I will add one bull, and a fat one, newly killed, not half a mile from here, if ye will accept the man's cub according to the Law. Is it difficult?"

There was a clamor of scores of voices, saying: "What matter? He will die in the winter rains. He will scorch in the sun. What harm can a naked frog do us? Let him run with the Pack. Where is the bull, Bagheera? Let him be accepted." And then came Akela's deep bay, crying: "Look well—look well, O Wolves!"

Mowgli was still deeply interested in the pebbles, and he did not notice when the wolves came and looked at him one by one. At last they all went down the hill for the dead bull, and only Akela, Bagheera, Baloo, and Mowgli's own wolves were left. Shere Khan roared still in the night, for he was very angry that Mowgli had not been handed over to him.

"Ay, roar well," said Bagheera, under his whiskers, "for the time will come when this naked thing will make thee roar to another tune, or I know nothing of man."

"It was well done," said Akela. "Men and their cubs are very wise. He may be a help in time."

"Truly, a help in time of need; for none can hope to lead the Pack forever," said Bagheera.

Akela said nothing. He was thinking of the time that comes to every leader of every pack when his strength goes from him and he gets feebler and feebler, till at last he is killed by the wolves and a new leader comes up—to be killed in his turn.

"Take him away," he said to Father Wolf, "and train him as befits one of the Free People."

And that is how Mowgli was entered into the Seeonee Wolf Pack for the price of a bull and on Baloo's good word.

Now you must be content to skip ten or eleven whole years, and only guess at all the wonderful life that Mowgli led among the wolves, because if it were written out it would fill ever so many books. He grew up with the cubs, though they, of course, were grown wolves almost before he was a child. And Father Wolf taught him his business, and the meaning of things in the Jungle, till every rustle in the grass, every breath of the warm night air, every note of the owls above his head, every scratch of a bat's claws as it roosted for a while in a tree, and every splash of every little fish jumping in a pool meant just as much to him as the work of his office means to a business man. When he was not learning he sat out in the sun and slept, and ate and went to sleep again. When he felt dirty or hot he swam in the forest pools; and when he wanted honey (Baloo told him that honey and nuts were just as pleasant to eat as raw meat) he climbed up for it, and that Bagheera showed him how to do. Bagheera would lie out on a branch and call, "Come along, Little Brother," and at first Mowgli would cling like the sloth, but afterward he would fling himself through the branches almost as boldly as the gray ape. He took his place at the Council Rock, too, when the Pack met, and there he discovered that if he stared hard at any wolf, the wolf would be forced to drop his eyes, and so he used to stare for fun. At other times he would pick the long thorns out of the pads of his friends, for wolves suffer terribly from thorns and burs in their coats. He would go down the hillside into the cultivated lands by night, and look very curiously at the villagers in their huts, but he had a mistrust of men because Bagheera showed him a square box with a drop gate so cunningly hidden in the Jungle that he nearly walked into it, and told him that it was a trap. He loved better than anything else to go with Bagheera into the dark warm heart of the forest, to sleep all through the drowsy day, and at night see how Bagheera did his killing. Bagheera killed right and left as he felt hungry, and so did Mowgli—with one exception. As soon as he was old enough to understand things, Bagheera told him that he must never touch cattle because he had been bought into the Pack at the price of a bull's life. "All the Jungle is thine," said Bagheera, "and thou canst kill everything that thou art strong enough to kill; but for the sake of the bull that bought thee thou must never kill or eat any cattle young or old. That is the Law of the Jungle." Mowgli obeyed faithfully.

And he grew and grew strong as a boy must grow who does not know that he is learning any lessons, and who has nothing in the world to think of except things to eat.

Mother Wolf told him once or twice that Shere Khan was not a creature to be trusted, and that some day he must kill Shere Khan; but though a young wolf would have remembered that advice every hour, Mowgli forgot it because he was only a boy—though he would have called himself a wolf if he had been able to speak in any human tongue.

Shere Khan was always crossing his path in the Jungle,

for as Akela grew older and feebler the lame tiger had come to be great friends with the younger wolves of the Pack, who followed him for scraps, a thing Akela would never have allowed if he had dared to push his authority to the proper bounds. Then Shere Khan would flatter them and wonder that such fine young hunters were content to be led by a dying wolf and a man's cub. "They tell me," Shere Khan would say, "that at Council ye dare not look him between the eyes"; and the young wolves would growl and bristle.

Bagheera, who had eyes and ears everywhere, knew something of this, and once or twice he told Mowgli in so many words that Shere Khan would kill him some day; and Mowgli would laugh and answer: "I have the Pack and I have thee; and Baloo, though he is so lazy, might strike a blow or two for my sake. Why should I be afraid?"

It was one very warm day that a new notion came to Bagheera—born of something that he had heard. Perhaps Ikki the Porcupine had told him; but he said to Mowgli when they were deep in the Jungle, as the boy lay with his head on Bagheera's beautiful black skin: "Little Brother, how often have I told thee that Shere Khan is thy enemy?"

"As many times as there are nuts on that palm," said Mowgli, who, naturally, could not count. "What of it? I am sleepy, Bagheera, and Shere Khan is all long tail and loud talk—like Mao, the Peacock."

"But this is no time for sleeping. Baloo knows it; I know it; the Pack know it; and even the foolish, foolish deer know. Tabaqui has told thee too."

"Ho! ho!" said Mowgli. "Tabaqui came to me not long ago with some rude talk that I was a naked man's cub and not fit to dig pig-nuts. But I caught Tabaqui by the tail and swung him twice against a palm-tree to teach him better manners."

"That was foolishness, for though Tabaqui is a mischief-maker, he would have told thee of something that concerned thee closely. Open those eyes, Little Brother. Shere Khan dare not kill thee in the Jungle. But remember, Akela is very old, and soon the day comes when he cannot kill his buck, and then he will be leader no more. Many of the wolves that looked thee over when thou wast brought to the Council first are old too, and the young wolves believe, as Shere Khan has taught them, that a man-cub has no place with the Pack. In a little time thou wilt be a man."

"And what is a man that he should not run with his brothers?" said Mowgli. "I was born in the Jungle. I have obeyed the Law of the Jungle, and there is no wolf of ours from whose paws I have not pulled a thorn. Surely they are my brothers!"

Bagheera stretched himself at full length and half shut his eyes. "Little Brother," said he, "feel under my jaw."

Mowgli put up his strong brown hand, and just under Bagheera's silky chin, where the giant rolling muscles were all hid by the glossy hair, he came upon a little bald spot.

"There is no one in the Jungle that knows that *I*, Bagheera, carry that mark—the mark of the collar; and yet, Little Brother, I was born among men, and it was among men that my mother died—in the cages of the King's Palace at Oodeypore. It was because of this that I paid the price for thee at the Council when thou wast a little naked cub. Yes, I too was born among men. I had never seen the Jungle. They fed me behind bars from an iron pan till one night I felt that I was Bagheera—the Panther—and no man's plaything, and I broke the silly lock with one blow of my paw and came away. And because I had learned the ways of men, I became more terrible in the Jungle than Shere Khan. Is it not so?"

"Yes," said Mowgli, "all the Jungle fear Bagheera—all except Mowgli."

"Oh, *thou* art a man's cub," said the Black Panther very tenderly; "and even as I returned to my Jungle, so thou must go back to men at last—to the men who are thy brothers—if thou art not killed in the Council."

"But why—but why should any wish to kill me?" said Mowgli.

"Look at me," said Bagheera. And Mowgli looked at him steadily between the eyes. The big panther turned his head away in half a minute.

"*That* is why," he said, shifting his paw on the leaves. "Not even I can look thee between the eyes, and I was born among men, and I love thee, Little Brother. The others they hate thee because their eyes cannot meet thine; because thou art wise; because thou hast pulled out thorns from their feet—because thou art a man."

"I did not know these things," said Mowgli sullenly, and he frowned under his heavy black eyebrows.

"What is the Law of the Jungle? Strike first and then give tongue. By thy very carelessness they know that thou art a man. But be wise. It is in my heart that when Akela misses his next kill—and at each hunt it costs him more to pin the buck— the Pack will turn against him and against thee. They will hold a Jungle Council at the Rock, and then—and then—I have it!" said Bagheera, leaping up. "Go thou down quickly to the men's huts in the valley, and take some of the Red Flower which they grow there, so that when the time comes thou mayest have even a stronger friend than I or Baloo or those of the Pack that love thee. Get the Red Flower."

By Red Flower Bagheera meant fire, only no creature in the Jungle will call fire by its proper name. Every beast lives in deadly fear of it, and invents a hundred ways of describing it.

"The Red Flower?" said Mowgli. "That grows outside their huts in the twilight. I will get some."

"There speaks the man's cub," said Bagheera proudly. "Remember that it grows in little pots. Get one swiftly, and keep it by thee for time of need."

"Good!" said Mowgli. "I go. But art thou sure, O my Bagheera"—he slipped his arm around the splendid neck and looked deep into the big eyes—"art thou sure that all this is Shere Khan's doing?"

"By the Broken Lock that freed me, I am sure, Little Brother."

"Then, by the Bull that bought me, I will pay Shere Khan full tale for this, and it may be a little over," said Mowgli, and he bounded away.

"That is a man. That is all a man," said Bagheera to himself, lying down again. "Oh, Shere Khan, never was a blacker hunting than that frog-hunt of thine ten years ago!"

Mowgli was far and far through the forest, running hard, and his heart was hot in him. He came to the cave as the evening mist rose, and drew breath, and looked down the valley. The cubs were out, but Mother Wolf, at the back of the cave, knew by his breathing that something was troubling her frog.

"What is it, Son?" she said.

"Some bat's chatter of Shere Khan," he called back. "I hunt among the plowed fields tonight," and he plunged downward through the bushes, to the stream at the bottom of the valley. There he checked, for he heard the yell of the Pack hunting, heard the bellow of a hunted sambhur, and the snort as the buck turned at bay. Then there were wicked, bitter howls from the young wolves: "Akela! Akela! Let the Lone Wolf show his strength. Room for the leader of the Pack! Spring, Akela!"

The Lone Wolf must have sprung and missed his hold, for Mowgli heard the snap of his teeth and then a yelp as the sambhur knocked him over with his forefoot.

He did not wait for anything more, but dashed on; and the yells grew fainter behind him as he ran into the croplands where the villagers lived.

"Bagheera spoke truth," he panted, as he nestled down in some cattle fodder by the window of a hut. "To-morrow is one day both for Akela and for me."

Then he pressed his face close to the window and watched the fire on the hearth. He saw the husbandman's wife get up and feed it in the night with black lumps; and when the morning came and the mists were all white and cold, he saw the man's child pick up a wicker pot plastered inside with earth, fill it with lumps of red-hot charcoal, put it under his blanket, and go out to tend the cows in the byre.

"Is that all?" said Mowgli. "If a cub can do it, there is nothing to fear"; so he strode round the corner and met the boy, took the pot from his hand, and disappeared into the mist while the boy howled with fear.

"They are very like me," said Mowgli, blowing into the pot as he had seen the woman do. "This thing will die if I do not give it things to eat"; and he dropped twigs and dried bark on the red stuff. Halfway up the hill he met Bagheera with the morning dew shining like moonstones on his coat.

"Akela has missed," said the Panther. "They would have killed him last night, but they needed thee also. They were looking for thee on the hill."

"I was among the plowed lands. I am ready. See!" Mowgli held up the fire-pot.

"Good! Now, I have seen men thrust a dry branch into that stuff, and presently the Red Flower blossomed at the end of it. Art thou not afraid?"

"No. Why should I fear? I remember now—if it is not a dream—how, before I was a Wolf, I lay beside the Red Flower, and it was warm and pleasant."

All that day Mowgli sat in the cave tending his fire pot and dipping dry branches into it to see how they looked. He found a branch that satisfied him, and in the evening when Tabaqui came to the cave and told him rudely enough that he was wanted at the Council Rock, he laughed till Tabaqui ran away. Then Mowgli went to the Council, still laughing.

Akela the Lone Wolf lay by the side of his rock as a sign that the leadership of the Pack was open, and Shere Khan with his following of scrap-fed wolves walked to and fro openly being flattered. Bagheera lay close to Mowgli, and the fire pot was between Mowgli's knees. When they were all gathered together, Shere Khan began to speak—a thing he would never have dared to do when Akela was in his prime.

"He has no right," whispered Bagheera. "Say so. He is a dog's son. He will be frightened."

Mowgli sprang to his feet. "Free People," he cried, "does Shere Khan lead the Pack? What has a tiger to do with our leadership?"

"Seeing that the leadership is yet open, and being asked to speak—" Shere Khan began.

"By whom?" said Mowgli. "Are we *all* jackals, to fawn on this cattle butcher? The leadership of the Pack is with the Pack alone."

There were yells of "Silence, thou man's cub!" "Let him speak. He has kept our Law"; and at last the seniors of the Pack thundered: "Let the Dead Wolf speak." When a leader of the Pack has missed his kill, he is called the Dead Wolf as long as he lives, which is not long as a rule.

Akela raised his old head wearily:

"Free People, and ye too, jackals of Shere Khan, for many seasons I have led ye to and from the kill, and in all that time not one has been trapped or maimed. Now I have missed my kill. Ye know how that plot was made. Ye know how ye brought me up to an untried buck to make my weakness known. It was cleverly done. Your right is to kill me here on the Council Rock, now. Therefore, I ask, who comes to make an end of the Lone Wolf? For it is my right, by the Law of the Jungle, that ye come one by one."

There was a long hush, for no single wolf cared to fight Akela to the death. Then Shere Khan roared: "Bah! What have we to do with this toothless fool? He is doomed to die! It is the man-cub who has lived too long. Free People, he was my meat from the first. Give him to me. I am weary of this man-wolf folly. He has troubled the Jungle for ten seasons. Give me the man-cub, or I will hunt here always, and not give you one bone. He is a man, a man's child, and from the marrow of my bones I hate him!"

Then more than half the Pack yelled: "A man! A man! What has a man to do with us? Let him go to his own place."

"And turn all the people of the villages against us?" clamored Shere Khan. "No, give him to me. He is a man, and none of us can look him between the eyes."

Akela lifted his head again and said, "He has eaten our food. He has slept with us. He has driven game for us. He has broken no word of the Law of the Jungle."

"Also, I paid for him with a bull when he was accepted. The worth of a bull is little, but Bagheera's honor is something that he will perhaps fight for," said Bagheera in his gentlest voice.

"A bull paid ten years ago!" the Pack snarled. "What do we care for bones ten years old?"

"Or for a pledge?" said Bagheera, his white teeth bared under his lip. "Well are ye called the Free People!"

"No man's cub can run with the people of the Jungle," howled Shere Khan. "Give him to me!"

"He is our brother in all but blood," Akela went on, "and ye would kill him here! In truth, I have lived too long. Some of ye are eaters of cattle, and of others I have heard that, under Shere Khan's teaching, ye go by dark night and snatch children from the villager's doorstep. Therefore I know ye to be cowards, and it is to cowards I speak. It is certain that I must die, and my life is of no worth, or I would offer that in the man-cub's place. But for the sake of the Honor of the Pack—a little matter that by being without a leader ye have forgotten—I promise that if ye let the man-cub go to his own place, I will not, when my time comes to die, bare one tooth against ye. I will die without fighting. That will at least save the Pack three lives. More I cannot do; but if ye will, I can save ye the shame that comes of killing a brother against whom there is no fault—a brother spoken for and bought into the Pack according to the Law of the Jungle."

"He is a man—a man—a man!" snarled the Pack. And most of the wolves began to gather round Shere Khan, whose tail was beginning to switch.

"Now the business is in thy hands," said Bagheera to Mowgli. "*We* can do no more except fight."

Mowgli stood upright—the fire pot in his hands. Then he stretched out his arms, and yawned in the face of the Council; but he was furious with rage and sorrow, for, wolflike, the wolves had never told him how they hated him. "Listen you!" he cried. "There is no need for this dog's jabber. Ye have told me so often tonight that I am a man (and indeed I would have been a wolf with you to my life's end), that I feel your words are true. So I do not call ye my brothers any more, but *sag* [dogs], as a man should. What ye will do, and what ye will not do, is not yours to say. That matter is with *me*; and that we may see the matter more plainly, I, the man, have brought here a little of the Red Flower which ye, dogs, fear."

He flung the fire pot on the ground, and some of the red coals lit a tuft of dried moss that flared up, as all the Council drew back in terror before the leaping flames.

Mowgli thrust his dead branch into the fire till the twigs lit and crackled, and whirled it above his head among the cowering wolves.

"Thou art the master," said Bagheera in an undertone. "Save Akela from the death. He was ever thy friend."

Akela, the grim old wolf who had never asked for mercy in his life, gave one piteous look at Mowgli as the boy stood all naked, his long black hair tossing over his shoulders in the light of the blazing branch that made the shadows jump and quiver.

"Good!" said Mowgli, staring round slowly. "I see that ye are dogs. I go from you to my own people—if they be my own people. The Jungle is shut to me, and I must forget your talk and your companionship. But I will be more merciful than ye are. Because I was all but your brother in blood, I promise that when I am a man among men I will not betray ye to men as ye have betrayed me." He kicked the fire with his foot, and the sparks flew up. "There shall be no war between any of us in the Pack. But here is a debt to pay before I go." He strode forward to where Shere Khan sat blinking stupidly at the flames, and caught him by the tuft on his chin. Bagheera followed in case of accidents. "Up, dog!" Mowgli cried. "Up, when a man speaks, or I will set that coat ablaze!"

Shere Khan's ears lay flat back on his head, and he shut his eyes, for the blazing branch was very near.

"This cattle-killer said he would kill me in the Council because he had not killed me when I was a cub. Thus and thus, then, do we beat dogs when we are men. Stir a whisker, Lungri, and I ram the Red Flower down thy gullet!" He beat Shere Khan over the head with the branch, and the tiger whimpered and whined in an agony of fear.

"Pah! Singed jungle-cat—go now! But remember when next I come to the Council Rock, as a man should come, it will be with Shere Khan's hide on my head. For the rest, Akela goes free to live as he pleases. Ye will *not* kill him, because that is not my will. Nor do I think that ye will sit here any longer, lolling out your tongues as though ye were somebodies, instead of dogs whom I drive out—thus! Go!" The fire was burning furiously at the end of the branch, and Mowgli struck right and left round the circle, and the wolves ran howling with the sparks burning their fur. At last there were only Akela, Bagheera, and perhaps ten wolves that had taken Mowgli's part. Then something began to hurt Mowgli inside him, as he had never been hurt in his life before, and he caught his breath and sobbed, and the tears ran down his face.

"What is it? What is it?" he said. "I do not wish to leave the Jungle, and I do not know what this is. Am I dying, Bagheera?"

"No, Little Brother. Those are only tears such as men use," said Bagheera. "Now I know thou art a man, and a man's cub no longer. The Jungle is shut indeed to thee henceforward. Let them fall, Mowgli. They are only tears." So Mowgli sat and cried as though his heart would break; and he had never cried in all his life before.

"Now," he said, "I will go to men. But first I must say farewell to my mother." And he went to the cave where she lived with Father Wolf, and he cried on her coat, while the four cubs howled miserably.

"Ye will not forget me?" said Mowgli.

"Never while we can follow a trail," said the cubs. "Come to the foot of the hill when thou art a man, and we will talk to thee; and we will come into the croplands to play with thee by night."

"Come soon!" said Father Wolf. "Oh, wise little frog, come again soon; for we be old, thy mother and I."

"Come soon," said Mother Wolf, "little naked son of mine. For, listen, child of man, I loved thee more than ever I loved my cubs."

"I will surely come," said Mowgli. "And when I come it will be to lay out Shere Khan's hide upon the Council Rock. Do not forget me! Tell them in the Jungle never to forget me!"

The dawn was beginning to break when Mowgli went down the hillside alone, to meet those mysterious things that are called men.

HUNTING-SONG OF THE SEEONEE PACK

As the dawn was breaking the Sambhur belled
  Once, twice and again!
And a doe leaped up, and a doe leaped up
From the pond in the wood where the wild deer sup.
This I, scouting alone, beheld,
  Once, twice and again!

As the dawn was breaking the Sambhur belled
  Once, twice and again!
And a wolf stole back, and a wolf stole back
To carry the word to the waiting pack,
And we sought and we found and we bayed on his track
  Once, twice and again!

As the dawn was breaking the Wolf Pack yelled
  Once, twice and again!
Feet in the Jungle that leave no mark!
Eyes that can see in the dark—the dark!
Tongue—give tongue to it! Hark! O hark!
  Once, twice and again!

KAA'S HUNTING

His spots are the joy of the Leopard: his horns are the
    Buffalo's pride.
Be clean, for the strength of the hunter is known by the
    gloss of his hide.
If ye find that the Bullock can toss you, or the heavy-browed
    Sambhur can gore;
Ye need not stop work to inform us: we knew it ten seasons
    before.
Oppress not the cubs of the stranger, but hail them as Sister
    and Brother,
For though they are little and fubsy, it may be the Bear is
    their mother.
"There is none like to me!" says the Cub in the pride of his
    earliest kill;
But the Jungle is large and the Cub he is small. Let him
    think and be still.

Maxims of Baloo

All that is told here happened some time before Mowgli
was turned out of the Seeonee Wolf Pack, or revenged
himself on Shere Khan the tiger. It was in the days when Baloo
was teaching him the Law of the Jungle. The big, serious, old
brown bear was delighted to have so quick a pupil, for the
young wolves will only learn as much of the Law of the Jungle
as applies to their own pack and tribe, and run away as soon as
they can repeat the Hunting Verse: "Feet that make no noise;
eyes that can see in the dark; ears that can hear the winds in

their lairs, and sharp white teeth, all these things are the marks of our brothers except Tabaqui the Jackal and the Hyaena whom we hate." But Mowgli, as a man-cub, had to learn a great deal more than this. Sometimes Bagheera the Black Panther would come lounging through the Jungle to see how his pet was getting on, and would purr with his head against a tree while Mowgli recited the day's lesson to Baloo. The boy could climb almost as well as he could swim, and swim almost as well as he could run. So Baloo, the Teacher of the Law, taught him the Wood and Water Laws: how to tell a rotten branch from a sound one; how to speak politely to the wild bees when he came upon a hive of them fifty feet above ground; what to say to Mang the Bat when he disturbed him in the branches at midday; and how to warn the water-snakes in the pools before he splashed down among them. None of the Jungle-People like being disturbed, and all are very ready to fly at an intruder. Then, too, Mowgli was taught the Strangers' Hunting Call, which must be repeated aloud till it is answered, whenever one of the Jungle-People hunts outside his own grounds. It means, translated: "Give me leave to hunt here because I am hungry; and the answer is, "Hunt then for food, but not for pleasure."

All this will show you how much Mowgli had to learn by heart, and he grew very tired of saying the same thing over a hundred times. But, as Baloo said to Bagheera, one day when Mowgli had been cuffed and run off in a temper, "A Man-cub is a Man-cub, and he must learn *all* the Law of the Jungle."

"But think how small he is," said the Black Panther, who would have spoiled Mowgli if he had had his own way. "How can his little head carry all thy long talk?"

"Is there anything in the Jungle too little to be killed? No. That is why I teach him these things, and that is why I hit him, very softly, when he forgets."

"Softly! What dost thou know of softness, old Iron-feet?" Bagheera grunted. "His face is all bruised today by thy—

softness. Ugh."

"Better he should be bruised from head to foot by me who love him than that he should come to harm through ignorance," Baloo answered very earnestly. "I am now teaching him the Master-words of the Jungle that shall protect him with the birds and the Snake-People, and all that hunt on four feet, except his own pack. He can now claim protection, if he will only remember the words, from all in the Jungle. Is not that worth a little beating?"

"Well, look to it then that thou dost not kill the Man-cub. He is no tree trunk to sharpen thy blunt claws upon. But what are those Master-Words? I am more likely to give help than to ask it"—Bagheera stretched out one paw and admired the steel-blue, ripping-chisel talons at the end of it—"still I should like to know."

"I will call Mowgli and he shall say them—if he will. Come, Little Brother!"

"My head is ringing like a bee tree," said a sullen little voice over their heads, and Mowgli slid down a tree trunk very angry and indignant, adding as he reached the ground: "I come for Bagheera and not for thee, fat old Baloo!"

"That is all one to me," said Baloo, though he was hurt and grieved. "Tell Bagheera, then, the Master-words of the Jungle that I have taught thee this day."

"Master-Words for which people?" said Mowgli, delighted to show off. "The Jungle has many tongues. *I* know them all."

"A little thou knowest, but not much. See, O Bagheera, they never thank their teacher. Not one small wolfling has ever come back to thank old Baloo for his teachings. Say the word for the Hunting-People, then—great scholar."

"We be of one blood, ye and I," said Mowgli, giving the words the Bear accent which all the Hunting-People use.

"Good. Now for the birds."

Mowgli repeated, with the Kite's whistle at the end of the

sentence.

"Now for the Snake-People," said Bagheera.

The answer was a perfectly indescribable hiss, and Mowgli kicked up his feet behind, clapped his hands together to applaud himself, and jumped on to Bagheera's back, where he sat sideways, drumming with his heels on the glossy skin and making the worst faces he could think of at Baloo.

"There—there! That was worth a little bruise," said the brown bear tenderly. "Some day thou wilt remember me." Then he turned aside to tell Bagheera how he had begged the Master-Words from Hathi the Wild Elephant, who knows all about these things, and how Hathi had taken Mowgli down to a pool to get the Snake Word from a water-snake, because Baloo could not pronounce it, and how Mowgli was now reasonably safe against all accidents in the Jungle, because neither snake, bird, nor beast would hurt him.

"No one then is to be feared," Baloo wound up, patting his big furry stomach with pride.

"Except his own tribe," said Bagheera, under his breath; and then aloud to Mowgli, "Have a care for my ribs, Little Brother! What is all this dancing up and down?"

Mowgli had been trying to make himself heard by pulling at Bagheera's shoulder fur and kicking hard. When the two listened to him he was shouting at the top of his voice, "And so I shall have a tribe of my own, and lead them through the branches all day long."

"What is this new folly, little dreamer of dreams?" said Bagheera.

"Yes, and throw branches and dirt at old Baloo," Mowgli went on. "They have promised me this. Ah!"

"*Whoof!*" Baloo's big paw scooped Mowgli off Bagheera's back, and as the boy lay between the big fore-paws he could see the Bear was angry.

"Mowgli," said Baloo, "thou hast been talking with the

Bandar-log—the Monkey-People."

Mowgli looked at Bagheera to see if the Panther was angry too, and Bagheera's eyes were as hard as jade stones.

"Thou hast been with the Monkey-People—the gray apes—the people without a law—the eaters of everything. That is great shame."

"When Baloo hurt my head," said Mowgli (he was still on his back), "I went away, and the gray apes came down from the trees and had pity on me. No one else cared." He snuffled a little.

"The pity of the Monkey-People!" Baloo snorted. "The stillness of the mountain stream! The cool of the summer sun! And then, Man-cub?"

"And then, and then, they gave me nuts and pleasant things to eat, and they—they carried me in their arms up to the top of the trees and said I was their blood brother except that I had no tail, and should be their leader some day."

"They have no leader," said Bagheera. "They lie. They have always lied."

"They were very kind and bade me come again. Why have I never been taken among the Monkey-People? They stand on their feet as I do. They do not hit me with their hard paws. They play all day. Let me get up! Bad Baloo, let me up! I will play with them again."

"Listen, Man-cub," said the Bear, and his voice rumbled like thunder on a hot night. "I have taught thee all the Law of the Jungle for all the peoples of the Jungle—except the Monkey-Folk who live in the trees. They have no Law. They are outcasts. They have no speech of their own, but use the stolen words which they overhear when they listen, and peep, and wait up above in the branches. Their way is not our way. They are without leaders. They have no remembrance. They boast and chatter and pretend that they are a great people about to do great affairs in the Jungle, but the falling of a nut turns their minds to laughter and all is forgotten. We of the Jungle have no dealings with them. We do not drink where the monkeys drink; we do not go where the monkeys go; we do not hunt where they hunt; we do not die where they die. Hast thou ever heard me speak of the *Bandar-log* till today?"

"No," said Mowgli in a whisper, for the forest was very still now Baloo had finished.

"The Jungle-People put them out of their mouths and out of their minds. They are very many, evil, dirty, shameless, and they desire, if they have any fixed desire, to be noticed by the Jungle-People. But we do *not* notice them even when they throw nuts and filth on our heads."

He had hardly spoken when a shower of nuts and twigs spattered down through the branches; and they could hear coughings and howlings and angry jumpings high up in the air among the thin branches.

"The Monkey-People are forbidden," said Baloo, "forbidden to the Jungle-People. Remember."

"Forbidden," said Bagheera, "but I still think Baloo should have warned thee against them."

"I—I? How was I to guess he would play with such dirt. The Monkey-People! Faugh!"

A fresh shower came down on their heads and the two trotted away, taking Mowgli with them. What Baloo had said about the monkeys was perfectly true. They belonged to the tree-tops, and as beasts very seldom look up, there was no occasion for the monkeys and the Jungle-People to cross each other's path. But whenever they found a sick wolf, or a wounded tiger, or bear, the monkeys would torment him, and would throw sticks and nuts at any beast for fun and in the hope of being noticed. Then they would howl and shriek senseless songs, and invite the Jungle-People to climb up their trees and fight them, or would start furious battles over nothing among themselves, and leave the dead monkeys where the Jungle-

People could see them. They were always just going to have a leader, and laws and customs of their own, but they never did, because their memories would not hold over from day to day, and so they compromised things by making up a saying, "What the *Bandar-log* think now the Jungle will think later," and that comforted them a great deal. None of the beasts could reach them, but on the other hand none of the beasts would notice them, and that was why they were so pleased when Mowgli came to play with them, and they heard how angry Baloo was.

They never meant to do any more—the *Bandar-log* never mean anything at all; but one of them invented what seemed to him a brilliant idea, and he told all the others that Mowgli would be a useful person to keep in the tribe, because he could weave sticks together for protection from the wind; so, if they caught him, they could make him teach them. Of course Mowgli, as a woodcutter's child, inherited all sorts of instincts, and used to make little huts of fallen branches without thinking how he came to do it and the Monkey-People, watching in the trees, considered his play most wonderful. This time, they said, they were really going to have a leader and become the wisest people in the Jungle—so wise that everyone else would notice and envy them. Therefore they followed Baloo and Bagheera and Mowgli through the Jungle very quietly till it was time for the midday nap, and Mowgli, who was very much ashamed of himself, slept between the Panther and the Bear, resolving to have no more to do with the Monkey-People.

The next thing he remembered was feeling hands on his legs and arms—hard, strong, little hands—and then a swash of branches in his face, and then he was staring down through the swaying boughs as Baloo woke the Jungle with his deep cries and Bagheera bounded up the trunk with every tooth bared. The *Bandar-log* howled with triumph and scuffled away to the upper branches where Bagheera dared not follow, shouting: "He has noticed us! Bagheera has noticed us. All the

Jungle-People admire us for our skill and our cunning." Then they began their flight; and the flight of the Monkey-People through tree-land is one of the things nobody can describe. They have their regular roads and crossroads, up hills and down hills, all laid out from fifty to seventy or a hundred feet above ground, and by these they can travel even at night if necessary. Two of the strongest monkeys caught Mowgli under the arms and swung off with him through the treetops, twenty feet at a bound. Had they been alone they could have gone twice as fast, but the boy's weight held them back. Sick and giddy as Mowgli was he could not help enjoying the wild rush, though the glimpses of earth far down below frightened him, and the terrible check and jerk at the end of the swing over nothing but empty air brought his heart between his teeth. His escort would rush him up a tree till he felt the thinnest topmost branches crackle and bend under them, and then with a cough and a whoop would fling themselves into the air outward and downward, and bring up, hanging by their hands or their feet to the lower limbs of the next tree. Sometimes he could see for miles and miles across the still green Jungle, as a man on the top of a mast can see for miles across the sea, and then the branches and leaves would lash him across the face, and he and his two guards would be almost down to earth again. So, bounding and crashing and whooping and yelling, the whole tribe of *Bandar-log* swept along the tree-roads with Mowgli their prisoner.

For a time he was afraid of being dropped: then he grew angry but knew better than to struggle, and then he began to think. The first thing was to send back word to Baloo and Baghcera, for, at the pace the monkeys were going, he knew his friends would be left far behind. It was useless to look down, for he could only see the topsides of the branches, so he stared upward and saw, far away in the blue, Chil the Kite balancing and wheeling as he kept watch over the Jungle waiting for things to die. Chil saw that the monkeys were carrying something, and dropped a few hundred yards to find out whether their load was good to eat. He whistled with surprise when he saw Mowgli being dragged up to a treetop and heard him give the Kite call for—"We be of one blood, thou and I." The waves of the branches closed over the boy, but Chil balanced away to the next tree in time to see the little brown face come up again. "Mark my trail!" Mowgli shouted. "Tell Baloo of the Seeonee Pack and Bagheera of the Council Rock."

"In whose name, Brother?" Chil had never seen Mowgli before, though of course he had heard of him.

"Mowgli, the Frog. Man-cub they call me! Mark my trail!"

The last words were shrieked as he was being swung through the air, but Chil nodded and rose up till he looked no bigger than a speck of dust, and there he hung, watching with his telescope eyes the swaying of the treetops as Mowgli's escort whirled along.

"They never go far," he said with a chuckle. "They never do what they set out to do. Always pecking at new things are the *Bandar-log*. This time, if I have any eye-sight, they have pecked down trouble for themselves, for Baloo is no fledgling and Bagheera can, as I know, kill more than goats."

So he rocked on his wings, his feet gathered up under him, and waited.

Meantime, Baloo and Bagheera were furious with rage and grief. Bagheera climbed as he had never climbed before, but the thin branches broke beneath his weight, and he slipped down, his claws full of bark.

"Why didst thou not warn the Man-cub?" he roared to poor Baloo, who had set off at a clumsy trot in the hope of overtaking the monkeys. "What was the use of half slaying him with blows if thou didst not warn him?"

"Haste! O haste! We—we may catch them yet!" Baloo panted.

"At that speed! It would not tire a wounded cow. Teacher of the Law—cub-beater—a mile of that rolling to and fro would burst thee open. Sit still and think! Make a plan. This is no time for chasing. They may drop him if we follow too close."

"*Arrula! Whoo!* They may have dropped him already, being tired of carrying him. Who can trust the *Bandar-log*? Put dead bats on my head! Give me black bones to eat! Roll me into the hives of the wild bees that I may be stung to death, and bury me with the *Hyena*, for I am most miserable of bears! *Arulala! Wahooa!* O Mowgli, Mowgli! Why did I not warn thee against the Monkey-Folk instead of breaking thy head? Now perhaps I may have knocked the day's lesson out of his mind, and he will be alone in the Jungle without the Master-Words."

Baloo clasped his paws over his ears and rolled to and fro moaning.

"At least he gave me all the Words correctly a little time ago," said Bagheera impatiently. "Baloo, thou hast neither memory nor respect. What would the Jungle think if I, the Black Panther, curled myself up like Ikki the Porcupine, and howled?"

"What do I care what the Jungle thinks? He may be dead by now."

"Unless and until they drop him from the branches in sport, or kill him out of idleness, I have no fear for the Man-cub. He is wise and well taught, and above all he has the eyes that make the Jungle-People afraid. But (and it is a great evil) he is in the power of the *Bandar-log*, and they, because they live in trees, have no fear of any of our people." Bagheera licked one forepaw thoughtfully.

"Fool that I am! Oh, fat, brown, root-digging fool that I am," said Baloo, uncoiling himself with a jerk, "it is true what Hathi the Wild Elephant says: `*To each his own fear*'; and they, the *Bandar-log*, fear Kaa the Rock Snake. He can climb as well as they can. He steals the young monkeys in the night. The whisper of his name makes their wicked tails cold. Let us go to Kaa."

"What will he do for us? He is not of our tribe, being footless—and with most evil eyes," said Bagheera.

"He is very old and very cunning. Above all, he is always hungry," said Baloo hopefully. "Promise him many goats."

"He sleeps for a full month after he has once eaten. He may be asleep now, and even were he awake what if he would rather kill his own goats?" Bagheera, who did not know much about Kaa, was naturally suspicious.

"Then in that case, thou and I together, old hunter, might make him see reason." Here Baloo rubbed his faded brown shoulder against the Panther, and they went off to look for Kaa the Rock Python.

They found him stretched out on a warm ledge in the afternoon sun, admiring his beautiful new coat, for he had been in retirement for the last ten days changing his skin, and now he was very splendid—darting his big blunt-nosed head along the ground, and twisting the thirty feet of his body into fantastic knots and curves, and licking his lips as he thought of his dinner to come.

"He has not eaten," said Baloo, with a grunt of relief, as soon as he saw the beautifully mottled brown and yellow jacket. "Be careful, Bagheera! He is always a little blind after he has changed his skin, and very quick to strike."

Kaa was not a poison-snake—in fact he rather despised the poison-snakes as cowards—but his strength lay in his hug, and when he had once lapped his huge coils round anybody there was no more to be said. "Good hunting!" cried Baloo, sitting up on his haunches. Like all snakes of his breed Kaa was rather deaf, and did not hear the call at first. Then he curled up ready for any accident, his head lowered.

"Good hunting for us all," he answered. "Oho, Baloo, what dost thou do here? Good hunting, Bagheera. One of us at least needs food. Is there any news of game afoot? A doe now, or even a young buck? I am as empty as a dried well."

"We are hunting," said Baloo carelessly. He knew that you must not hurry Kaa. He is too big.

"Give me permission to come with you," said Kaa. "A blow more or less is nothing to thee, Bagheera or Baloo, but I—I have to wait and wait for days in a wood-path and climb half a night on the mere chance of a young ape. Psshaw! The branches are not what they were when I was young. Rotten twigs and dry boughs are they all."

"Maybe thy great weight has something to do with the matter," said Baloo.

"I am a fair length—a fair length," said Kaa with a little pride. "But for all that, it is the fault of this new-grown timber. I came very near to falling on my last hunt—very near indeed—and the noise of my slipping, for my tail was not tight wrapped around the tree, waked the *Bandar-log*, and they called me most evil names."

"Footless, yellow earth-worm," said Bagheera under his whiskers, as though he were trying to remember something.

"Sssss! Have they ever called me *that*?" said Kaa.

"Something of that kind it was that they shouted to us last moon, but we never noticed them. They will say anything—even that thou hast lost all thy teeth, and wilt not face anything bigger than a kid, because (they are indeed shameless, these *Bandar-log*)—because thou art afraid of the he-goat's horns," Bagheera went on sweetly.

Now a snake, especially a wary old python like Kaa, very seldom shows that he is angry, but Baloo and Bagheera could see the big swallowing muscles on either side of Kaa's throat ripple and bulge.

"The *Bandar-log* have shifted their grounds," he said quietly. "When I came up into the sun today I heard them whooping among the tree-tops."

"It—it is the *Bandar-log* that we follow now," said Baloo, but the words stuck in his throat, for that was the first time in his memory that one of the Jungle-People had owned to being interested in the doings of the monkeys.

"Beyond doubt then it is no small thing that takes two such hunters—leaders in their own Jungle I am certain—on the trail of the *Bandar-log*," Kaa replied courteously, as he swelled with curiosity.

"Indeed," Baloo began, "I am no more than the old and sometimes very foolish Teacher of the Law to the Seeonee wolf-cubs, and Bagheera here—"

"Is Bagheera," said the Black Panther, and his jaws shut with a snap, for he did not believe in being humble. "The trouble is this, Kaa. Those nut-stealers and pickers of palm leaves have stolen away our Man-cub of whom thou hast perhaps heard."

"I heard some news from Ikki (his quills make him presumptuous) of a man-thing that was entered into a wolf pack, but I did not believe. Ikki is full of stories half heard and very badly told."

"But it is true. He is such a Man-cub as never was," said Baloo. "The best and wisest and boldest of Man-cubs—my own pupil, who shall make the name of Baloo famous through all the Jungles; and besides, I—we—love him, Kaa."

"Ts! Ts!" said Kaa, weaving his head to and fro. "I also have known what love is. There are tales I could tell that—"

"That need a clear night when we are all well fed to praise properly," said Bagheera quickly. "Our Man-cub is in the hands of the *Bandar-log* now, and we know that of all the Jungle-People they fear Kaa alone."

"They fear me alone. They have good reason," said Kaa. "Chattering, foolish, vain—vain, foolish, and chattering, are the monkeys. But a man-thing in their hands is in no good luck. They grow tired of the nuts they pick, and throw them down. They carry a branch half a day, meaning to do great things with it, and then they snap it in two. That man-thing is not to be envied. They called me also—'yellow fish' was it not?"

"Worm—worm—earth-worm," said Bagheera, "as well as other things which I cannot now say for shame."

"We must remind them to speak well of their master. Aaa-ssp! We must help their wandering memories. Now, whither went they with the cub?"

"The Jungle alone knows. Toward the sunset, I believe," said Baloo. "We had thought that thou wouldst know, Kaa."

"I? How? I take them when they come in my way, but I do not hunt the *Bandar-log*, or frogs—or green scum on a water-hole, for that matter."

"Up, Up! Up, Up! Hillo! Illo! Illo, look up, Baloo of the Seeonee Wolf Pack!"

Baloo looked up to see where the voice came from, and there was Chil the Kite, sweeping down with the sun shining on the upturned flanges of his wings. It was near Chil's bedtime, but he had ranged all over the Jungle looking for the Bear and had missed him in the thick foliage.

"What is it?" said Baloo.

"I have seen Mowgli among the *Bandar-log*. He bade me tell you. I watched. The *Bandar-log* have taken him beyond the river to the monkey city—to the Cold Lairs. They may stay there for a night, or ten nights, or an hour. I have told the bats to watch through the dark time. That is my message. Good hunting, all you below!"

"Full gorge and a deep sleep to you, Chil," cried Bagheera. "I will remember thee in my next kill, and put aside the head for thee alone, O best of kites!"

"It is nothing. It is nothing. The boy held the Master-Word. I could have done no less," and Chil circled up again to his roost.

"He has not forgotten to use his tongue," said Baloo with

a chuckle of pride. "To think of one so young remembering the Master-Word for the birds too while he was being pulled across trees!"

"It was most firmly driven into him," said Bagheera. "But I am proud of him, and now we must go to the Cold Lairs."

They all knew where that place was, but few of the Jungle People ever went there, because what they called the Cold Lairs was an old deserted city, lost and buried in the Jungle, and beasts seldom use a place that men have once used. The wild boar will, but the hunting tribes do not. Besides, the monkeys lived there as much as they could be said to live anywhere, and no self-respecting animal would come within eyeshot of it except in times of drought, when the half-ruined tanks and reservoirs held a little water.

"It is half a night's journey—at full speed," said Bagheera, and Baloo looked very serious. "I will go as fast as I can," he said anxiously.

"We dare not wait for thee. Follow, Baloo. We must go on the quick-foot—Kaa and I."

"Feet or no feet, I can keep abreast of all thy four," said Kaa shortly. Baloo made one effort to hurry, but had to sit down panting, and so they left him to come on later, while Bagheera hurried forward, at the quick panther-canter. Kaa said nothing, but, strive as Bagheera might, the huge Rock-python held level with him. When they came to a hill stream, Bagheera gained, because he bounded across while Kaa swam, his head and two feet of his neck clearing the water, but on level ground Kaa made up the distance.

"By the Broken Lock that freed me," said Bagheera, when twilight had fallen, "thou art no slow goer!"

"I am hungry," said Kaa. "Besides, they called me speckled frog."

"Worm—earth-worm, and yellow to boot."

"All one. Let us go on," and Kaa seemed to pour himself

along the ground, finding the shortest road with his steady eyes, and keeping to it.

In the Cold Lairs the Monkey-People were not thinking of Mowgli's friends at all. They had brought the boy to the Lost City, and were very much pleased with themselves for the time. Mowgli had never seen an Indian city before, and though this was almost a heap of ruins it seemed very wonderful and splendid. Some king had built it long ago on a little hill. You could still trace the stone causeways that led up to the ruined gates where the last splinters of wood hung to the worn, rusted hinges. Trees had grown into and out of the walls; the battlements were tumbled down and decayed, and wild creepers hung out of the windows of the towers on the walls in bushy hanging clumps.

A great roofless palace crowned the hill, and the marble of the courtyards and the fountains was split, and stained with red and green, and the very cobblestones in the courtyard where the king's elephants used to live had been thrust up and apart by grasses and young trees. From the palace you could see the rows and rows of roofless houses that made up the city looking like empty honeycombs filled with blackness; the shapeless block of stone that had been an idol in the square where four roads met; the pits and dimples at street corners where the public wells once stood, and the shattered domes of temples with wild figs sprouting on their sides. The monkeys called the place their city, and pretended to despise the Jungle-People because they lived in the forest. And yet they never knew what the buildings were made for nor how to use them. They would sit in circles on the hall of the king's council chamber, and scratch for fleas and pretend to be men; or they would run in and out of the roofless houses and collect pieces of plaster and old bricks in a corner, and forget where they had hidden them, and fight and cry in scuffling crowds, and then break off to play up and down the terraces of the king's garden, where they would shake the rose trees and the oranges in sport to see the fruit and flowers fall. They explored all the passages and dark tunnels in the palace and the hundreds of little dark rooms, but they never remembered what they had seen and what they had not; and so drifted about in ones and twos or crowds telling each other that they were doing as men did. They drank at the tanks and made the water all muddy, and then they fought over it, and then they would all rush together in mobs and shout: "There is no one in the Jungle so wise and good and clever and strong and gentle as the *Bandar-log*." Then all would begin again till they grew tired of the city and went back to the tree-tops, hoping the Jungle-People would notice them.

Mowgli, who had been trained under the Law of the Jungle, did not like or understand this kind of life. The monkeys dragged him into the Cold Lairs late in the afternoon, and instead of going to sleep, as Mowgli would have done after a long journey, they joined hands and danced about and sang their foolish songs. One of the monkeys made a speech and told his companions that Mowgli's capture marked a new thing in the history of the *Bandar-log*, for Mowgli was going to show them how to weave sticks and canes together as a protection against rain and cold. Mowgli picked up some creepers and began to work them in and out, and the monkeys tried to imitate; but in a very few minutes they lost interest and began to pull their friends' tails or jump up and down on all fours, coughing.

"I wish to eat," said Mowgli. "I am a stranger in this part of the Jungle. Bring me food, or give me leave to hunt here."

Twenty or thirty monkeys bounded away to bring him nuts and wild pawpaws. But they fell to fighting on the road, and it was too much trouble to go back with what was left of the fruit. Mowgli was sore and angry as well as hungry, and he roamed through the empty city giving the Strangers' Hunting Call from time to time, but no one answered him, and Mowgli felt that he had reached a very bad place indeed. "All that Baloo has said about the *Bandar-log* is true," he thought to himself. "They have no Law, no Hunting Call, and no leaders—nothing but foolish words and little picking thievish hands. So if I am starved or killed here, it will be all my own fault. But I must try to return to my own Jungle. Baloo will surely beat me, but that is better than chasing silly rose leaves with the *Bandar-log*."

No sooner had he walked to the city wall than the monkeys pulled him back, telling him that he did not know how happy he was, and pinching him to make him grateful. He set his teeth and said nothing, but went with the shouting monkeys to a terrace above the red sandstone reservoirs that were half-full of rain water. There was a ruined summer-house of white marble in the center of the terrace, built for queens dead a hundred years ago. The domed roof had half fallen in and blocked up the underground passage from the palace by which the queens used to enter. But the walls were made of screens of marble tracery—beautiful milk-white fretwork, set with agates and cornelians and jasper and lapis lazuli, and as the moon came up behind the hill it shone through the open work, casting shadows on the ground like black velvet embroidery. Sore, sleepy, and hungry as he was, Mowgli could not help laughing when the *Bandar-log* began, twenty at a time, to tell him how great and wise and strong and gentle they were, and how foolish he was to wish to leave them. "We are great. We are free. We are wonderful. We are the most wonderful people in all the Jungle! We all say so, and so it must be true," they shouted. "Now as you are a new listener and can carry our words back to the Jungle-People so that they may notice us in future, we will tell you all about our most excellent selves." Mowgli made no objection, and the monkeys gathered by hundreds and hundreds on the terrace to listen to their own speakers singing the praises of the *Bandar-log*, and whenever a speaker stopped for want of breath they would all shout together: "This is true;

we all say so." Mowgli nodded and blinked, and said "Yes" when they asked him a question, and his head spun with the noise. "Tabaqui the Jackal must have bitten all these people," he said to himself, "and now they have madness. Certainly this is *dewanee*, the madness. Do they never go to sleep? Now there is a cloud coming to cover that moon. If it were only a big enough cloud I might try to run away in the darkness. But I am tired."

That same cloud was being watched by two good friends in the ruined ditch below the city wall, for Bagheera and Kaa, knowing well how dangerous the Monkey-People were in large numbers, did not wish to run any risks. The monkeys never fight unless they are a hundred to one, and few in the Jungle care for those odds.

"I will go to the west wall," Kaa whispered, "and come down swiftly with the slope of the ground in my favor. They will not throw themselves upon *my* back in their hundreds, but—"

"I know it," said Bagheera. "Would that Baloo were here, but we must do what we can. When that cloud covers the moon I shall go to the terrace. They hold some sort of council there over the boy."

"Good hunting," said Kaa grimly, and glided away to the west wall. That happened to be the least ruined of any, and the big snake was delayed awhile before he could find a way up the stones. The cloud hid the moon, and as Mowgli wondered what would come next he heard Bagheera's light feet on the terrace. The Black Panther had raced up the slope almost without a sound and was striking—he knew better than to waste time in biting—right and left among the monkeys, who were seated round Mowgli in circles fifty and sixty deep. There was a howl of fright and rage, and then as Bagheera tripped on the rolling kicking bodies beneath him, a monkey shouted: "There is only one here! Kill him! Kill." A scuffling mass of monkeys, biting, scratching, tearing, and pulling, closed over Bagheera, while five or six laid hold of Mowgli, dragged him up the wall of the summerhouse and pushed him through the hole of the broken dome. A man-trained boy would have been badly bruised, for the fall was a good fifteen feet, but Mowgli fell as Baloo had taught him to fall, and landed on his feet.

"Stay there," shouted the monkeys, "till we have killed thy friends, and later we will play with thee—if the Poison-People leave thee alive."

"We be of one blood, ye and I," said Mowgli, quickly giving the Snake's Call. He could hear rustling and hissing in the rubbish all round him and gave the call a second time, to make sure.

"Even ssso! Down hoods all!" said half a dozen low voices (every ruin in India becomes sooner or later a dwelling place of snakes, and the old summerhouse was alive with cobras). "Stand still, Little Brother, for thy feet may do us harm."

Mowgli stood as quietly as he could, peering through the open-work and listening to the furious din of the fight round the Black Panther—the yells and chatterings and scufflings, and Bagheera's deep, hoarse cough as he backed and bucked and twisted and plunged under the heaps of his enemies. For the first time since he was born, Bagheera was fighting for his life.

"Baloo must be at hand; Bagheera would not have come alone," Mowgli thought; and then he called aloud: "To the tank, Bagheera. Roll to the water tanks. Roll and plunge! Get to the water!"

Bagheera heard, and the cry that told him Mowgli was safe gave him new courage. He worked his way desperately, inch by inch, straight for the reservoirs, halting in silence. Then from the ruined wall nearest the Jungle rose up the rumbling war-shout of Baloo. The old Bear had done his best, but he could not come before. "Bagheera," he shouted, "I am here. I climb! I haste! *Ahuwora!* The stones slip under my feet! Wait my coming, O most infamous *Bandar-log!*" He panted up the terrace only to disappear to the head in a wave of monkeys, but he threw himself squarely on his haunches, and, spreading out his forepaws, hugged as many as he could hold, and then began to hit with a regular *bat-bat-bat*, like the flipping strokes of a paddle wheel. A crash and a splash told Mowgli that Bagheera had fought his way to the tank where the monkeys could not follow. The Panther lay gasping for breath, his head just out of the water, while the monkeys stood three deep on the red steps, dancing up and down with rage, ready to spring upon him from all sides if he came out to help Baloo. It was then that Bagheera lifted up his dripping chin, and in despair gave the Snake's Call for protection—"We be of one blood, ye and I"—for he believed that Kaa had turned tail at the last minute. Even Baloo, half smothered under the monkeys on the edge of the terrace, could not help chuckling as he heard the Black Panther asking for help.

Kaa had only just worked his way over the west wall, landing with a wrench that dislodged a coping stone into the ditch. He had no intention of losing any advantage of the ground, and coiled and uncoiled himself once or twice, to be sure that every foot of his long body was in working order. All that while the fight with Baloo went on, and the monkeys yelled in the tank round Bagheera, and Mang the Bat, flying to and fro, carried the news of the great battle over the Jungle, till even Hathi the Wild Elephant trumpeted, and, far away, scattered bands of the Monkey-Folk woke and came leaping along the tree-roads to help their comrades in the Cold Lairs, and the noise of the fight roused all the day birds for miles round. Then Kaa came straight, quickly, and anxious to kill. The fighting strength of a python is in the driving blow of his head backed by all the strength and weight of his body. If you can imagine a lance, or a battering ram, or a hammer weighing nearly half a ton driven by a cool, quiet mind living in the handle of it, you can roughly

imagine what Kaa was like when he fought. A python four or
five feet long can knock a man down if he hits him fairly in
the chest, and Kaa was thirty feet long, as you know. His first
stroke was delivered into the heart of the crowd round Baloo—
was sent home with shut mouth in silence, and there was no
need of a second. The monkeys scattered with cries of—"Kaa!
It is Kaa! Run! Run!"

Generations of monkeys had been scared into good
behavior by the stories their elders told them of Kaa, the night
thief, who could slip along the branches as quietly as moss
grows, and steal away the strongest monkey that ever lived; of
old Kaa, who could make himself look so like a dead branch
or a rotten stump that the wisest were deceived, till the branch
caught them. Kaa was everything that the monkeys feared in
the Jungle, for none of them knew the limits of his power, none
of them could look him in the face, and none had ever come
alive out of his hug. And so they ran, stammering with terror,
to the walls and the roofs of the houses, and Baloo drew a deep
breath of relief. His fur was much thicker than Bagheera's, but
he had suffered sorely in the fight. Then Kaa opened his mouth
for the first time and spoke one long hissing word, and the far-
away monkeys, hurrying to the defense of the Cold Lairs, stayed
where they were, cowering, till the loaded branches bent and
crackled under them. The monkeys on the walls and the empty
houses stopped their cries, and in the stillness that fell upon
the city Mowgli heard Bagheera shaking his wet sides as he
came up from the tank. Then the clamor broke out again. The
monkeys leaped higher up the walls. They clung around the
necks of the big stone idols and shrieked as they skipped along
the battlements, while Mowgli, dancing in the summerhouse,
put his eye to the screenwork and hooted owl-fashion between
his front teeth, to show his derision and contempt.

"Get the Man-cub out of that trap; I can do no more,"
Bagheera gasped. "Let us take the Man-cub and go. They may

THE JUNGLE BOOK   55

attack again."

"They will not move till I order them. Stay you sssso!" Kaa hissed, and the city was silent once more. "I could not come before, Brother, but I *think* I heard thee call"—this was to Bagheera.

"I—I may have cried out in the battle," Bagheera answered. "Baloo, art thou hurt?"

"I am not sure that they did not pull me into a hundred little bearlings," said Baloo gravely, shaking one leg after the other. "Wow! I am sore. Kaa, we owe thee, I think, our lives—Bagheera and I."

"No matter. Where is the Manling?"

"Here, in a trap. I cannot climb out," cried Mowgli. The curve of the broken dome was above his head.

"Take him away. He dances like Mao the Peacock. He will crush our young," said the cobras inside.

"Hah!" said Kaa with a chuckle, "he has friends everywhere, this Manling. Stand back, Manling. And hide you, O Poison-People. I break down the wall."

Kaa looked carefully till he found a discolored crack in the marble tracery showing a weak spot, made two or three light taps with his head to get the distance, and then lifting up six feet of his body clear of the ground, sent home half a dozen full-power smashing blows, nose-first. The screen-work broke and fell away in a cloud of dust and rubbish, and Mowgli leaped through the opening and flung himself between Baloo and Bagheera—an arm around each big neck.

"Art thou hurt?" said Baloo, hugging him softly.

"I am sore, hungry, and not a little bruised; but, oh, they have handled ye grievously, my Brothers! Ye bleed."

"Others also," said Bagheera, licking his lips and looking at the monkey-dead on the terrace and round the tank.

"It is nothing, it is nothing, if thou art safe, oh, my pride of all little frogs!" whimpered Baloo.

"Of that we shall judge later," said Bagheera, in a dry voice that Mowgli did not at all like. "But here is Kaa to whom we owe the battle and thou owest thy life. Thank him according to our customs, Mowgli."

Mowgli turned and saw the great Python's head swaying a foot above his own.

"So this is the Manling," said Kaa. "Very soft is his skin, and he is not unlike the *Bandar-log*. Have a care, Manling, that I do not mistake thee for a monkey some twilight when I have newly changed my coat."

"We be one blood, thou and I," Mowgli answered. "I take my life from thee tonight. My kill shall be thy kill if ever thou art hungry, O Kaa."

"All thanks, Little Brother," said Kaa, though his eyes twinkled. "And what may so bold a hunter kill? I ask that I may follow when next he goes abroad."

"I kill nothing—I am too little—but I drive goats toward such as can use them. When thou art empty come to me and see if I speak the truth. I have some skill in these—he held out his hands—and if ever thou art in a trap, I may pay the debt which I owe to thee, to Bagheera, and to Baloo, here. Good hunting to ye all, my masters."

"Well said," growled Baloo, for Mowgli had returned thanks very prettily. The Python dropped his head lightly for a minute on Mowgli's shoulder. "A brave heart and a courteous tongue," said he. "They shall carry thee far through the Jungle, Manling. But now go hence quickly with thy friends. Go and sleep, for the moon sets, and what follows it is not well that thou shouldst see."

The moon was sinking behind the hills and the lines of trembling monkeys huddled together on the walls and battlements looked like ragged shaky fringes of things. Baloo went down to the tank for a drink and Bagheera began to put his fur in order, as Kaa glided out into the center of the terrace and brought his jaws together with a ringing snap that drew all the monkeys' eyes upon him.

"The moon sets," he said. "Is there yet light enough to see?"

From the walls came a moan like the wind in the tree-tops: "We see, O Kaa."

"Good. Begins now the Dance—the Dance of the Hunger of Kaa. Sit still and watch."

He turned twice or thrice in a big circle, weaving his head from right to left. Then he began making loops and figures of eight with his body, and soft, oozy triangles that melted into squares and five-sided figures, and coiled mounds, never resting, never hurrying, and never stopping his low humming song. It grew darker and darker, till at last the dragging, shifting coils disappeared, but they could hear the rustle of the scales.

Baloo and Bagheera stood still as stone, growling in their throats, their neck hair bristling, and Mowgli watched and wondered.

"*Bandar-log,*" said the voice of Kaa at last, "can ye stir foot or hand without my order? Speak!"

"Without thy order we cannot stir foot or hand, O Kaa!"

"Good! Come all one pace nearer to me."

The lines of the monkeys swayed forward helplessly, and Baloo and Bagheera took one stiff step forward with them.

"Nearer!" hissed Kaa, and they all moved again.

Mowgli laid his hands on Baloo and Bagheera to get them away, and the two great beasts started as though they had been waked from a dream.

"Keep thy hand on my shoulder," Bagheera whispered. "Keep it there, or I must go back—must go back to Kaa. *Aah!*"

"It is only old Kaa making circles on the dust," said Mowgli; "let us go"; and the three slipped off through a gap in the walls to the Jungle.

"*Whoof!*" said Baloo, when he stood under the still trees again. "Never more will I make an ally of Kaa," and he shook himself all over.

"He knows more than we," said Bagheera, trembling. "In a little time, had I stayed, I should have walked down his throat."

"Many will walk by that road before the moon rises again," said Baloo. "He will have good hunting—after his own fashion."

"But what was the meaning of it all?" said Mowgli, who did not know anything of a python's powers of fascination. "I saw no more than a big snake making foolish circles till the dark came. And his nose was all sore. Ho! Ho!"

"Mowgli," said Bagheera angrily, "his nose was sore on *thy* account, as my ears and sides and paws, and Baloo's neck and shoulders are bitten on *thy* account. Neither Baloo nor Bagheera will be able to hunt with pleasure for many days."

"It is nothing," said Baloo; "we have the Man-cub again."

"True, but he has cost us heavily in time which might have been spent in good hunting, in wounds, in hair—I am half plucked along my back—and last of all, in honor. For, remember, Mowgli, I, who am the Black Panther, was forced to call upon Kaa for protection, and Baloo and I were both made stupid as little birds by the Hunger-Dance. All this, Man-cub, came of thy playing with the *Bandar-log*."

"True, it is true," said Mowgli sorrowfully. "I am an evil Man-cub, and my stomach is sad in me."

"*Mf!* What says the Law of the Jungle, Baloo?"

Baloo did not wish to bring Mowgli into any more trouble, but he could not tamper with the Law, so he mumbled: "Sorrow never stays punishment. But remember, Bagheera, he is very little."

"I will remember. But he has done mischief, and blows must be dealt now. Mowgli, hast thou anything to say?"

"Nothing. I did wrong. Baloo and thou are wounded. It is just."

Bagheera gave him half a dozen love-taps; from a panther's point of view (they would hardly have waked one of his own cubs), but for a seven-year-old boy they amounted to as severe a beating as you could wish to avoid. When it was all over Mowgli sneezed, and picked himself up without a word.

"Now," said Bagheera, "jump on my back, Little Brother, and we will go home."

One of the beauties of Jungle Law is that punishment settles all scores. There is no nagging afterward.

Mowgli laid his head down on Bagheera's back and slept so deeply that he never waked when he was put down by Mother Wolf's side in the home-cave.

ROAD-SONG OF THE
BANDAR-LOG

Here we go in a flung festoon,
Half-way up to the jealous moon!
Don't you envy our pranceful bands?
Don't you wish you had extra hands?
Wouldn't you like if your tails were—so—
Curved in the shape of a Cupid's bow?
  Now you're angry, but—never mind,
  Brother, thy tail hangs down behind!

Here we sit in a branchy row,
Thinking of beautiful things we know;
Dreaming of deeds that we mean to do,
All complete, in a minute or two—
Something noble and grand and good,
Won by merely wishing we could.
  We've forgotten, but—never mind,
  Brother, thy tail hangs down behind!

All the talk we ever have heard
Uttered by bat or beast or bird—
Hide or fin or scale or feather—
Jabber it quickly and all together!
Excellent! Wonderful! Once again!
Now we are talking just like men!
  Let's pretend we are ... never mind,
  Brother, thy tail hangs down behind!
  This is the way of the Monkey-kind.

4

*Then join our leaping lines that scumfish through the
pines,
That rocket by where, light and high, the wild grape
swings.
By the rubbish in our wake, and the noble noise we
make,
Be sure, be sure, we're going to do some splendid
    things!*

"TIGER! TIGER!"

What of the hunting, hunter bold?
  Brother, the watch was long and cold.
What of the quarry ye went to kill?
  Brother, he crops in the Jungle still.
Where is the power that made your pride?
  Brother, it ebbs from my flank and side.
Where is the haste that ye hurry by?
  Brother, I go to my lair—to die!

Now we must go back to the first tale. When Mowgli left the wolf's cave after the fight with the Pack at the Council Rock, he went down to the plowed lands where the villagers lived, but he would not stop there because it was too near to the Jungle, and he knew that he had made at least one bad enemy at the Council. So he hurried on, keeping to the rough road that ran down the valley, and followed it at a steady jog-trot for nearly twenty miles, till he came to a country that he did not know. The valley opened out into a great plain dotted over with rocks and cut up by ravines. At one end stood a little village, and at the other the thick Jungle came down in a sweep to the grazing-grounds, and stopped there as though it had been cut off with a hoe. All over the plain, cattle and buffaloes were grazing, and when the little boys in charge of the herds saw Mowgli they shouted and ran away, and the yellow pariah dogs that hang about every Indian village barked. Mowgli walked on, for he was feeling hungry, and when he came to the village gate he saw the big thorn-bush that was drawn up before the gate at twilight, pushed to one side.

"Umph!" he said, for he had come across more than one such barricade in his night rambles after things to eat. "So men are afraid of the People of the Jungle here also." He sat down by the gate, and when a man came out he stood up, opened his mouth, and pointed down it to show that he wanted food. The man stared, and ran back up the one street of the village shouting for the priest, who was a big, fat man dressed in white, with a red and yellow mark on his forehead. The priest came to the gate, and with him at least a hundred people, who stared and talked and shouted and pointed at Mowgli.

"They have no manners, these Men Folk," said Mowgli to himself. "Only the gray ape would behave as they do." So he threw back his long hair and frowned at the crowd.

"What is there to be afraid of?" said the priest. "Look at the marks on his arms and legs. They are the bites of wolves. He is but a wolf-child run away from the Jungle."

Of course, in playing together, the cubs had often nipped Mowgli harder than they intended, and there were white scars all over his arms and legs. But he would have been the last person in the world to call these bites, for he knew what real biting meant.

"Arre! Arre!" said two or three women together. "To be bitten by wolves, poor child! He is a handsome boy. He has eyes like red fire. By my honor, Messua, he is not unlike thy boy that was taken by the tiger."

"Let me look," said a woman with heavy copper rings on her wrists and ankles, and she peered at Mowgli under the palm of her hand. "Indeed he is not. He is thinner, but he has the very look of my boy."

The priest was a clever man, and he knew that Messua was wife to the richest villager in the place. So he looked up at the sky for a minute and said solemnly: "What the Jungle has taken the Jungle has restored. Take the boy into thy house, my sister, and forget not to honor the priest who sees so far into the lives of men."

"By the Bull that bought me," said Mowgli to himself, "but all this talking is like another looking-over by the Pack! Well, if I am a man, a man I must become."

The crowd parted as the woman beckoned Mowgli to her hut, where there was a red lacquered bedstead, a great earthen grain chest with funny raised patterns on it, half a dozen copper cooking pots, an image of a Hindu god in a little alcove, and on the wall a real looking glass, such as they sell at the country fairs.

She gave him a long drink of milk and some bread, and then she laid her hand on his head and looked into his eyes; for she thought perhaps that he might be her real son come back from the Jungle where the tiger had taken him. So she said, "Nathoo, O Nathoo!" Mowgli did not show that he knew the name. "Dost thou not remember the day when I gave thee thy new shoes?" She touched his foot, and it was almost as hard as horn. "No," she said sorrowfully, "those feet have never worn shoes, but thou art very like my Nathoo, and thou shalt be my son."

Mowgli was uneasy, because he had never been under a roof before. But as he looked at the thatch, he saw that he could tear it out any time if he wanted to get away, and that the window had no fastenings. "What is the good of a man," he said to himself at last, "if he does not understand man's talk? Now I am as silly and dumb as a man would be with us in the Jungle. I must speak their talk."

It was not for fun that he had learned while he was with the wolves to imitate the challenge of bucks in the Jungle and the grunt of the little wild pig. So, as soon as Messua pronounced a word Mowgli would imitate it almost perfectly, and before dark he had learned the names of many things in the hut.

There was a difficulty at bedtime, because Mowgli would

not sleep under anything that looked so like a panther trap as that hut, and when they shut the door he went through the window. "Give him his will," said Messua's husband. "Remember he can never till now have slept on a bed. If he is indeed sent in the place of our son he will not run away."

So Mowgli stretched himself in some long, clean grass at the edge of the field, but before he had closed his eyes a soft gray nose poked him under the chin.

"Phew!" said Gray Brother (he was the eldest of Mother Wolf's cubs). "This is a poor reward for following thee twenty miles. Thou smellest of wood smoke and cattle—altogether like a man already. Wake, Little Brother; I bring news."

"Are all well in the Jungle?" said Mowgli, hugging him.

"All except the wolves that were burned with the Red Flower. Now, listen. Shere Khan has gone away to hunt far off till his coat grows again, for he is badly singed. When he returns he swears that he will lay thy bones in the Waingunga."

"There are two words to that. I also have made a little promise. But news is always good. I am tired to-night—very tired with new things, Gray Brother—but bring me the news always."

"Thou wilt not forget that thou art a wolf? Men will not make thee forget?" said Gray Brother anxiously.

"Never. I will always remember that I love thee and all in our cave. But also I will always remember that I have been cast out of the Pack."

"And that thou mayest be cast out of another pack. Men are only men, Little Brother, and their talk is like the talk of frogs in a pond. When I come down here again, I will wait for thee in the bamboos at the edge of the grazing-ground."

For three months after that night Mowgli hardly ever left the village gate, he was so busy learning the ways and customs of men. First he had to wear a cloth round him, which annoyed him horribly; and then he had to learn about money, which he did not in the least understand, and about plowing, of which he did not see the use. Then the little children in the village made him very angry. Luckily, the Law of the Jungle had taught him to keep his temper, for in the Jungle life and food depend on keeping your temper; but when they made fun of him because he would not play games or fly kites, or because he mispronounced some word, only the knowledge that it was unsportsmanlike to kill little naked cubs kept him from picking them up and breaking them in two.

He did not know his own strength in the least. In the Jungle he knew he was weak compared with the beasts, but in the village people said that he was as strong as a bull.

And Mowgli had not the faintest idea of the difference that caste makes between man and man. When the potter's donkey slipped in the clay pit, Mowgli hauled it out by the tail, and helped to stack the pots for their journey to the market at Khanhiwara. That was very shocking, too, for the potter is a low-caste man, and his donkey is worse. When the priest scolded him, Mowgli threatened to put him on the donkey too, and the priest told Messua's husband that Mowgli had better be set to work as soon as possible; and the village head-man told Mowgli that he would have to go out with the buffaloes next day, and herd them while they grazed. No one was more pleased than Mowgli; and that night, because he had been appointed a servant of the village, as it were, he went off to a circle that met every evening on a masonry platform under a great fig-tree. It was the village club, and the head-man and the watchman and the barber, who knew all the gossip of the village, and old Buldeo, the village hunter, who had a Tower musket, met and smoked. The monkeys sat and talked in the upper branches, and there was a hole under the platform where a cobra lived, and he had his little platter of milk every night because he was sacred; and the old men sat around the tree and talked, and pulled at the big hookahs (the water-pipes) till

far into the night. They told wonderful tales of gods and men
and ghosts; and Buldeo told even more wonderful ones of the
ways of beasts in the Jungle, till the eyes of the children sitting
outside the circle bulged out of their heads. Most of the tales
were about animals, for the Jungle was always at their door.
The deer and the wild pig grubbed up their crops, and now
and again the tiger carried off a man at twilight, within sight
of the village gates.

Mowgli, who naturally knew something about what they
were talking of, had to cover his face not to show that he was
laughing, while Buldeo, the Tower musket across his knees,
climbed on from one wonderful story to another, and Mowgli's
shoulders shook.

Buldeo was explaining how the tiger that had carried away
Messua's son was a ghost-tiger, and his body was inhabited by
the ghost of a wicked, old money-lender, who had died some
years ago. "And I know that this is true," he said, "because
Purun Dass always limped from the blow that he got in a riot
when his account books were burned, and the tiger that I
speak of, he limps, too, for the tracks of his pads are unequal."

"True, true, that must be the truth," said the gray-beards,
nodding together.

"Are all these tales such cobwebs and moon talk?" said
Mowgli. "That tiger limps because he was born lame, as
everyone knows. To talk of the soul of a money-lender in a
beast that never had the courage of a jackal is child's talk."

Buldeo was speechless with surprise for a moment, and the
head-man stared.

"Oho! It is the Jungle brat, is it?" said Buldeo. "If thou art so
wise, better bring his hide to Khanhiwara, for the Government
has set a hundred rupees on his life. Better still, talk not when
thy elders speak."

Mowgli rose to go. "All the evening I have lain here
listening," he called back over his shoulder, "and, except once

or twice, Buldeo has not said one word of truth concerning the Jungle, which is at his very doors. How, then, shall I believe the tales of ghosts and gods and goblins which he says he has seen?"

"It is full time that boy went to herding," said the head-man, while Buldeo puffed and snorted at Mowgli's impertinence.

The custom of most Indian villages is for a few boys to take the cattle and buffaloes out to graze in the early morning, and bring them back at night. The very cattle that would trample a white man to death allow themselves to be banged and bullied and shouted at by children that hardly come up to their noses. So long as the boys keep with the herds they are safe, for not even the tiger will charge a mob of cattle. But if they straggle to pick flowers or hunt lizards, they are sometimes carried off. Mowgli went through the village street in the dawn, sitting on the back of Rama, the great herd bull; and the slaty-blue buffaloes, with their long, backward-sweeping horns and savage eyes, rose out their byres, one by one, and followed him, and Mowgli made it very clear to the children with him that he was the master. He beat the buffaloes with a long, polished bamboo, and told Kamya, one of the boys, to graze the cattle by themselves, while he went on with the buffaloes, and to be very careful not to stray away from the herd.

An Indian grazing ground is all rocks and scrub and tussocks and little ravines, among which the herds scatter and disappear. The buffaloes generally keep to the pools and muddy places, where they lie wallowing or basking in the warm mud for hours. Mowgli drove them on to the edge of the plain where the Waingunga came out of the Jungle; then he dropped from Rama's neck, trotted off to a bamboo clump, and found Gray Brother. "Ah," said Gray Brother, "I have waited here very many days. What is the meaning of this cattle-herding work?"

"It is an order," said Mowgli. "I am a village herd for a while. What news of Shere Khan?"

"He has come back to this country, and has waited here a long time for thee. Now he has gone off again, for the game is scarce. But he means to kill thee."

"Very good," said Mowgli. "So long as he is away do thou or one of the four brothers sit on that rock, so that I can see thee as I come out of the village. When he comes back wait for me in the ravine by the *dhâk* tree in the center of the plain. We need not walk into Shere Khan's mouth."

Then Mowgli picked out a shady place, and lay down and slept while the buffaloes grazed round him. Herding in India is one of the laziest things in the world. The cattle move and crunch, and lie down, and move on again, and they do not even low. They only grunt, and the buffaloes very seldom say anything, but get down into the muddy pools one after another, and work their way into the mud till only their noses and staring china-blue eyes show above the surface, and then they lie like logs. The sun makes the rocks dance in the heat, and the herd children hear one kite (never any more) whistling almost out of sight overhead, and they know that if they died, or a cow died, that kite would sweep down, and the next kite miles away would see him drop and follow, and the next, and the next, and almost before they were dead there would be a score of hungry kites come out of nowhere. Then they sleep and wake and sleep again, and weave little baskets of dried grass and put grasshoppers in them; or catch two praying mantises and make them fight; or string a necklace of red and black Jungle nuts; or watch a lizard basking on a rock, or a snake hunting a frog near the wallows. Then they sing long, long songs with odd native quavers at the end of them, and the day seems longer than most people's whole lives, and perhaps they make a mud castle with mud figures of men and horses and buffaloes, and put reeds into the men's hands, and pretend that they are kings and the figures are their armies, or that they are gods to be worshipped. Then evening comes and the children call, and the buffaloes lumber up out of the sticky mud with noises like gunshots going off one after the other, and they all string across the gray plain back to the twinkling village lights.

Day after day Mowgli would lead the buffaloes out to their wallows, and day after day he would see Gray Brother's back a mile and a half away across the plain (so he knew that Shere Khan had not come back), and day after day he would lie on the grass listening to the noises round him, and dreaming of old days in the Jungle. If Shere Khan had made a false step with his lame paw up in the Jungles by the Waingunga, Mowgli would have heard him in those long, still mornings.

At last a day came when he did not see Gray Brother at the signal place, and he laughed and headed the buffaloes for the ravine by the *dhâk* tree, which was all covered with golden-red flowers. There sat Gray Brother, every bristle on his back lifted.

"He has hidden for a month to throw thee off thy guard. He crossed the ranges last night with Tabaqui, hot-foot on thy trail," said the Wolf, panting.

Mowgli frowned. "I am not afraid of Shere Khan, but Tabaqui is very cunning."

"Have no fear," said Gray Brother, licking his lips a little. "I met Tabaqui in the dawn. Now he is telling all his wisdom to the kites, but he told *me* everything before I broke his back. Shere Khan's plan is to wait for thee at the village gate this evening—for thee and for no one else. He is lying up now, in the big dry ravine of the Waingunga."

"Has he eaten today, or does he hunt empty?" said Mowgli, for the answer meant life and death to him.

"He killed at dawn—a pig—and he has drunk too. Remember, Shere Khan could never fast, even for the sake of revenge."

"Oh! Fool, fool! What a cub's cub it is! Eaten and drunk too, and he thinks that I shall wait till he has slept! Now, where does he lie up? If there were but ten of us we might pull him down as he lies. These buffaloes will not charge unless they wind him, and I cannot speak their language. Can we get behind his track so that they may smell it?"

"He swam far down the Waingunga to cut that off," said Gray Brother.

"Tabaqui told him that, I know. He would never have thought of it alone." Mowgli stood with his finger in his mouth, thinking. "The big ravine of the Waingunga. That opens out on the plain not half a mile from here. I can take the herd round through the Jungle to the head of the ravine and then sweep down—but he would slink out at the foot. We must block that end. Gray Brother, canst thou cut the herd in two for me?"

"Not I, perhaps—but I have brought a wise helper." Gray Brother trotted off and dropped into a hole. Then there lifted up a huge gray head that Mowgli knew well, and the hot air was filled with the most desolate cry of all the Jungle—the hunting howl of a wolf at midday.

"Akela! Akela!" said Mowgli, clapping his hands. "I might have known that thou wouldst not forget me. We have a big work in hand. Cut the herd in two, Akela. Keep the cows and calves together, and the bulls and the plow buffaloes by themselves."

The two wolves ran, ladies'-chain fashion, in and out of the herd, which snorted and threw up its head, and separated into two clumps. In one, the cow-buffaloes stood with their calves in the center, and glared and pawed, ready, if a wolf would only stay still, to charge down and trample the life out of him. In the other, the bulls and the young bulls snorted and stamped, but though they looked more imposing they were much less dangerous, for they had no calves to protect. No six men could have divided the herd so neatly.

"What orders!" panted Akela. "They are trying to join again."

Mowgli slipped on to Rama's back. "Drive the bulls away to the left, Akela. Gray Brother, when we are gone, hold the cows together, and drive them into the foot of the ravine."

"How far?" said Gray Brother, panting and snapping.

"Till the sides are higher than Shere Khan can jump," shouted Mowgli. "Keep them there till we come down." The bulls swept off as Akela bayed, and Gray Brother stopped in front of the cows. They charged down on him, and he ran just before them to the foot of the ravine, as Akela drove the bulls far to the left.

"Well done! Another charge and they are fairly started. Careful, now—careful, Akela. A snap too much and the bulls will charge. *Hujah!* This is wilder work than driving black-buck. Didst thou think these creatures could move so swiftly?" Mowgli called.

"I have—have hunted these too in my time," gasped Akela in the dust. "Shall I turn them into the Jungle?"

"Ay! Turn. Swiftly turn them! Rama is mad with rage. Oh, if I could only tell him what I need of him to-day."

The bulls were turned, to the right this time, and crashed into the standing thicket. The other herd-children, watching with the cattle half a mile away, hurried to the village as fast as their legs could carry them, crying that the buffaloes had gone mad and run away.

But Mowgli's plan was simple enough. All he wanted to do was to make a big circle uphill and get at the head of the ravine, and then take the bulls down it and catch Shere Khan between the bulls and the cows; for he knew that after a meal and a full drink Shere Khan would not be in any condition to fight or to clamber up the sides of the ravine. He was soothing the buffaloes now by voice, and Akela had dropped far to the rear, only whimpering once or twice to hurry the rear-guard. It was a long, long circle, for they did not wish to get too near the ravine and give Shere Khan warning. At last Mowgli rounded up the bewildered herd at the head of the ravine on a grassy patch that sloped steeply down to the ravine itself. From that height you could see across the tops of the trees down to the plain below; but what Mowgli looked at was the sides of the ravine, and he saw with a great deal of satisfaction that they ran nearly straight up and down, while the vines and creepers that hung over them would give no foothold to a tiger who wanted to get out.

"Let them breathe, Akela," he said, holding up his hand. "They have not winded him yet. Let them breathe. I must tell Shere Khan who comes. We have him in the trap."

He put his hands to his mouth and shouted down the ravine—it was almost like shouting down a tunnel—and the echoes jumped from rock to rock.

After a long time there came back the drawling, sleepy snarl of a full-fed tiger just wakened.

"Who calls?" said Shere Khan, and a splendid peacock fluttered up out of the ravine screeching.

"I, Mowgli. Cattle thief, it is time to come to the Council Rock! Down—hurry them down, Akela! Down, Rama, down!"

The herd paused for an instant at the edge of the slope, but Akela gave tongue in the full hunting-yell, and they pitched over one after the other, just as steamers shoot rapids, the sand and stones spurting up round them. Once started, there was no chance of stopping, and before they were fairly in the bed of the ravine Rama winded Shere Khan and bellowed.

"Ha! Ha!" said Mowgli, on his back. "Now thou knowest!" and the torrent of black horns, foaming muzzles, and staring eyes whirled down the ravine just as boulders go down in floodtime; the weaker buffaloes being shouldered out to the sides of the ravine where they tore through the creepers. They knew what the business was before them—the terrible charge of the buffalo herd against which no tiger can hope to stand. Shere Khan heard the thunder of their hoofs, picked himself up, and lumbered down the ravine, looking from side to side for some way of escape, but the walls of the ravine were straight and he had to hold on, heavy with his dinner and his drink, willing to do anything rather than fight. The herd splashed through the pool he had just left, bellowing till the narrow cut rang. Mowgli heard an answering bellow from the foot of the ravine, saw Shere Khan turn (the tiger knew if the worst came to the worst it was better to meet the bulls than the cows with their calves), and then Rama tripped, stumbled, and went on again over something soft, and, with the bulls at his heels, crashed full into the other herd, while the weaker buffaloes were lifted clean off their feet by the shock of the meeting. That charge carried both herds out into the plain, goring and stamping and snorting. Mowgli watched his time, and slipped off Rama's neck, laying about him right and left with his stick.

"Quick, Akela! Break them up. Scatter them, or they will be fighting one another. Drive them away, Akela. *Hai*, Rama! *Hai, hai, hai!* my children. Softly now, softly! It is all over."

Akela and Gray Brother ran to and fro nipping the buffaloes' legs, and though the herd wheeled once to charge up the ravine again, Mowgli managed to turn Rama, and the others followed him to the wallows.

Shere Khan needed no more trampling. He was dead, and the kites were coming for him already.

"Brothers, that was a dog's death," said Mowgli, feeling for the knife he always carried in a sheath round his neck now that he lived with men. "But he would never have shown fight. His hide will look well on the Council Rock. We must get to work swiftly."

A boy trained among men would never have dreamed of skinning a ten-foot tiger alone, but Mowgli knew better than anyone else how an animal's skin is fitted on, and how it can be taken off. But it was hard work, and Mowgli slashed and tore and grunted for an hour, while the wolves lolled out their tongues, or came forward and tugged as he ordered them.

Presently a hand fell on his shoulder, and looking up he saw Buldeo with the Tower musket. The children had told the village about the buffalo stampede, and Buldeo went out angrily, only too anxious to correct Mowgli for not taking better care of the herd. The wolves dropped out of sight as soon as they saw the man coming.

"What is this folly?" said Buldeo angrily. "To think that thou canst skin a tiger! Where did the buffaloes kill him? It is the Lame Tiger too, and there is a hundred rupees on his head. Well, well, we will overlook thy letting the herd run off, and perhaps I will give thee one of the rupees of the reward when I have taken the skin to Khanhiwara." He fumbled in his waist cloth for flint and steel, and stooped down to singe Shere Khan's whiskers. Most native hunters always singe a tiger's whiskers to prevent his ghost from haunting them.

"Hum!" said Mowgli, half to himself as he ripped back the skin of a forepaw. "So thou wilt take the hide to Khanhiwara for the reward, and perhaps give me one rupee? Now it is in my mind that I need the skin for my own use. Heh! Old man, take away that fire!"

"What talk is this to the chief hunter of the village? Thy luck and the stupidity of thy buffaloes have helped thee to this kill. The tiger has just fed, or he would have gone twenty miles by this time. Thou canst not even skin him properly, little beggar brat, and forsooth I, Buldeo, must be told not to singe his whiskers. Mowgli, I will not give thee one anna of the reward, but only a very big beating. Leave the carcass!"

"By the Bull that bought me," said Mowgli, who was trying to get at the shoulder, "must I stay babbling to an old ape all noon? Here, Akela, this man plagues me."

Buldeo, who was still stooping over Shere Khan's head, found himself sprawling on the grass, with a gray wolf standing over him, while Mowgli went on skinning as though he were alone in all India.

"Ye-es," he said, between his teeth. "Thou art altogether right, Buldeo. Thou wilt never give me one anna of the reward. There is an old war between this lame tiger and myself—a very old war, and—I have won."

To do Buldeo justice, if he had been ten years younger he would have taken his chance with Akela had he met the wolf in the woods, but a wolf who obeyed the orders of this boy who had private wars with man-eating tigers was not a common animal. It was sorcery, magic of the worst kind, thought Buldeo, and he wondered whether the amulet round his neck would protect him. He lay as still as still, expecting every minute to see Mowgli turn into a tiger too.

"Maharaj! Great King," he said at last in a husky whisper.

"Yes," said Mowgli, without turning his head, chuckling a little.

"I am an old man. I did not know that thou wast anything more than a herd-boy. May I rise up and go away, or will thy servant tear me to pieces?"

"Go, and peace go with thee. Only, another time do not meddle with my game. Let him go, Akela."

Buldeo hobbled away to the village as fast as he could, looking back over his shoulder in case Mowgli should change into something terrible. When he got to the village he told a tale of magic and enchantment and sorcery that made the priest look very grave.

Mowgli went on with his work, but it was nearly twilight before he and the wolves had drawn the great gay skin clear of the body.

"Now we must hide this and take the buffaloes home! Help me to herd them, Akela."

The herd rounded up in the misty twilight, and when they got near the village Mowgli saw lights, and heard the conches and bells in the temple blowing and banging. Half the village seemed to be waiting for him by the gate. "That is because I have killed Shere Khan," he said to himself. But a shower of stones whistled about his ears, and the villagers shouted: "Sorcerer! Wolf's brat! Jungle demon! Go away! Get hence quickly or the priest will turn thee into a wolf again. Shoot, Buldeo, shoot!"

The old Tower musket went off with a bang, and a young buffalo bellowed in pain.

"More sorcery!" shouted the villagers. "He can turn bullets. Buldeo, that was *thy* buffalo."

"Now what is this?" said Mowgli, bewildered, as the stones flew thicker.

"They are not unlike the Pack, these brothers of thine," said Akela, sitting down composedly. "It is in my head that, if bullets mean anything, they would cast thee out."

"Wolf! Wolf's cub! Go away!" shouted the priest, waving a sprig of the sacred *tulsi* plant.

"Again? Last time it was because I was a man. This time it is because I am a wolf. Let us go, Akela."

A woman—it was Messua—ran across to the herd, and cried: "Oh, my son, my son! They say thou art a sorcerer who can turn himself into a beast at will. I do not believe, but go away or they will kill thee. Buldeo says thou art a wizard, but I know thou hast avenged Nathoo's death."

"Come back, Messua!" shouted the crowd. "Come back, or we will stone thee."

Mowgli laughed a little short ugly laugh, for a stone had hit him in the mouth. "Run back, Messua. This is one of the foolish tales they tell under the big tree at dusk. I have at least paid for thy son's life. Farewell; and run quickly, for I shall send the herd in more swiftly than their brickbats. I am no wizard, Messua. Farewell!"

"Now, once more, Akela," he cried. "Bring the herd in."

The buffaloes were anxious enough to get to the village. They hardly needed Akela's yell, but charged through the gate like a whirlwind, scattering the crowd right and left.

"Keep count!" shouted Mowgli scornfully. "It may be that I have stolen one of them. Keep count, for I will do your herding no more. Fare you well, children of men, and thank Messua that I do not come in with my wolves and hunt you up and down your street."

He turned on his heel and walked away with the Lone Wolf, and as he looked up at the stars he felt happy. "No more sleeping in traps for me, Akela. Let us get Shere Khan's skin and go away. No, we will not hurt the village, for Messua was kind to me."

When the moon rose over the plain, making it look all milky, the horrified villagers saw Mowgli, with two wolves at his heels and a bundle on his head, trotting across at the steady wolf's trot that eats up the long miles like fire. Then they banged the temple bells and blew the conches louder than ever; and Messua cried, and Buldeo embroidered the story of his adventures in the Jungle, till he ended by saying that Akela stood up on his hind legs and talked like a man.

The moon was just going down when Mowgli and the two wolves came to the hill of the Council Rock, and they stopped at Mother Wolf's cave.

"They have cast me out from the Man-Pack, Mother," shouted Mowgli, "but I come with the hide of Shere Khan to keep my word." Mother Wolf walked stiffly from the cave with the cubs behind her, and her eyes glowed as she saw the skin.

"I told him on that day, when he crammed his head and shoulders into this cave, hunting for thy life, Little Frog—I told him that the hunter would be the hunted. It is well done."

"Little Brother, it is well done," said a deep voice in the thicket. "We were lonely in the Jungle without thee," and Bagheera came running to Mowgli's bare feet. They clambered up the Council Rock together, and Mowgli spread the skin out on the flat stone where Akela used to sit, and pegged it down with four slivers of bamboo, and Akela lay down upon it, and called the old call to the Council, "Look—look well, O Wolves," exactly as he had called when Mowgli was first brought there.

Ever since Akela had been deposed, the Pack had been without a leader, hunting and fighting at their own pleasure. But they answered the call from habit; and some of them were lame from the traps they had fallen into, and some limped from shot wounds, and some were mangy from eating bad food, and many were missing. But they came to the Council Rock, all that were left of them, and saw Shere Khan's striped hide on the rock, and the huge claws dangling at the end of the empty dangling feet. It was then that Mowgli made up a song that came up into his throat all by itself, and he shouted it aloud, leaping up and down on the rattling skin, and beating time with his heels till he had no more breath left, while Gray Brother and Akela howled between the verses.

"Look well, O Wolves. Have I kept my word?" said Mowgli. And the wolves bayed "Yes," and one tattered wolf howled:

"Lead us again, O Akela. Lead us again, O Man-cub, for we be sick of this lawlessness, and we would be the Free People once more."

"Nay," purred Bagheera, "that may not be. When ye are full-fed, the madness may come upon you again. Not for nothing are ye called the Free People. Ye fought for freedom, and it is yours. Eat it, O Wolves."

"Man-Pack and Wolf-Pack have cast me out," said Mowgli. "Now I will hunt alone in the Jungle."

"And we will hunt with thee," said the four cubs.

So Mowgli went away and hunted with the four cubs in the Jungle from that day on. But he was not always alone, because, years afterward, he became a man and married.

But that is a story for grown-ups.

MOWGLI'S SONG

That he sang at the Council Rock when he danced
on Shere Khan's hide

The Song of Mowgli—I, Mowgli, am singing. Let the Jungle
    listen to the things I have done.

Shere Khan said he would kill—would kill! At the gates in the
    twilight he would kill Mowgli, the Frog!

He ate and he drank. Drink deep, Shere Khan, for when wilt
    thou drink again? Sleep and dream of the kill.

I am alone on the grazing-grounds. Gray Brother, come to me!
    Come to me, Lone Wolf, for there is big game afoot!

Bring up the great bull buffaloes, the blue-skinned herd bulls
    with the angry eyes. Drive them to and fro as I order.

Sleepest thou still, Shere Khan? Wake, oh, wake! Here come I,
    and the bulls are behind.

Rama, the King of the Buffaloes, stamped with his foot. Waters
    of the Waingunga, whither went Shere Khan?

He is not Ikki to dig holes, nor Mao, the Peacock, that he
    should fly. He is not Mang the Bat, to hang in the branches.
    Little bamboos that creak together, tell me where he ran.

Ow! He is there. *Ahoo!* He is there. Under the feet of Rama
    lies the Lame One! Up, Shere Khan! Up and kill!
    Here is meat; break the necks of the bulls!

Hsh! He is asleep. We will not wake him, for his strength is very
    great. The kites have come down to see it. The black ants
    have come up to know it. There is a great assembly in his
    honor.

Alala! I have no cloth to wrap me. The kites will see that I am
    naked. I am ashamed to meet all these people.

Lend me thy coat, Shere Khan. Lend me thy gay striped coat
    that I may go to the Council Rock.

By the Bull that bought me I made a promise—a little promise.
    Only thy coat is lacking before I keep my word.

With the knife—with the knife that men use—with the knife of
    the hunter, the man, I will stoop down for my gift.

Waters of the Waingunga, bear witness that Shere Khan gives
    me his coat for the love that he bears me. Pull, Gray Brother!
    Pull, Akela! Heavy is the hide of Shere Khan.

The Man Pack are angry. They throw stones and talk child's
    talk. My mouth is bleeding. Let me run away.

Through the night, through the hot night, run swiftly with me,
    my brothers. We will leave the lights of the village and go
    to the low moon.

Waters of the Waingunga, the Man-Pack have cast me out. I
    did them no harm, but they were afraid of me. Why?

Wolf-Pack, ye have cast me out too. The Jungle is shut to me
    and the village gates are shut. Why?

As Mang flies between the beasts and birds, so fly I between
    the village and the Jungle. Why?

I dance on the hide of Shere Khan, but my heart is very heavy.
    My mouth is cut and wounded with the stones from the
    village, but my heart is very light, because I have come back
    to the Jungle. Why?

These two things fight together in me as the snakes fight in the
    spring.

The water comes out of my eyes; yet I laugh while it falls.
    Why?

I am two Mowglis, but the hide of Shere Khan is under my
    feet.

All the Jungle knows that I have killed Shere Khan. Look—
    look well, O Wolves!

Ahae! My heart is heavy with the things that I do not
    understand.

THE WHITE SEAL

Oh! hush thee, my baby, the night is behind us,
  And black are the waters that sparkled so green.
The moon, o'er the combers, looks downward to find us
  At rest in the hollows that rustle between.
Where billow meets billow, then soft be thy pillow;
  Ah, weary wee flipperling, curl at thy ease!
The storm shall not wake thee, nor shark overtake thee,
  Asleep in the arms of the slow-swinging seas!

Seal Lullaby

All these things happened several years ago at a place called Novastoshnah, or North East Point, on the Island of St. Paul, away and away in the Bering Sea. Limmershin, the Winter Wren, told me the tale when he was blown on to the rigging of a steamer going to Japan, and I took him down into my cabin and warmed and fed him for a couple of days till he was fit to fly back to St. Paul's again. Limmershin is a very quaint little bird, but he knows how to tell the truth.

Nobody comes to Novastoshnah except on business, and the only people who have regular business there are the seals. They come in the summer months by hundreds and hundreds of thousands out of the cold gray sea; for Novastoshnah Beach has the finest accommodation for seals of any place in all the world.

Sea Catch knew that, and every spring would swim from whatever place he happened to be in—would swim like a torpedo-boat straight for Novastoshnah and spend a month fighting with his companions for a good place on the rocks, as close to the sea as possible. Sea Catch was fifteen years old, a huge gray fur seal with almost a mane on his shoulders, and long, wicked dog teeth. When he heaved himself up on his front flippers he stood more than four feet clear of the ground, and his weight, if anyone had been bold enough to weigh him, was nearly seven hundred pounds. He was scarred all over with the marks of savage fights, but he was always ready for just one fight more. He would put his head on one side, as though he were afraid to look his enemy in the face; then he would shoot it out like lightning, and when the big teeth were firmly fixed on the other seal's neck, the other seal might get away if he could, but Sea Catch would not help him.

Yet Sea Catch never chased a beaten seal, for that was against the Rules of the Beach. He only wanted room by the sea for his nursery. But as there were forty or fifty thousand other seals hunting for the same thing each spring, the whistling, bellowing, roaring, and blowing on the beach were something frightful.

From a little hill called Hutchinson's Hill, you could look over three and a half miles of ground covered with fighting seals; and the surf was dotted all over with the heads of seals hurrying to land and begin their share of the fighting. They fought in the breakers, they fought in the sand, and they fought on the smooth-worn basalt rocks of the nurseries, for they were just as stupid and unaccommodating as men. Their wives never came to the island until late in May or early in June, for they did not care to be torn to pieces; and the young two-, three-, and four-year-old seals who had not begun housekeeping went inland about half a mile through the ranks of the fighters and played about on the sand dunes in droves and legions, and rubbed off every single green thing that grew. They were called the holluschickie—the bachelors—and there were perhaps two or three hundred thousand of them at Novastoshnah alone.

Sea Catch had just finished his forty-fifth fight one spring when Matkah, his soft, sleek, gentle-eyed wife, came up out of the sea, and he caught her by the scruff of the neck and dumped her down on his reservation, saying gruffly: "Late as usual. Where *have you* been?"

It was not the fashion for Sea Catch to eat anything during the four months he stayed on the beaches, and so his temper was generally bad. Matkah knew better than to answer back. She looked round and cooed: "How thoughtful of you. You've taken the old place again."

"I should think I had," said Sea Catch. "Look at me!"

He was scratched and bleeding in twenty places; one eye was almost out, and his sides were torn to ribbons.

"Oh, you men, you men!" Matkah said, fanning herself with her hind flipper. "Why can't you be sensible and settle your places quietly? You look as though you had been fighting with the Killer Whale."

"I haven't been doing anything *but* fight since the middle of May. The beach is disgracefully crowded this season. I've met at least a hundred seals from Lukannon Beach, house hunting. Why can't people stay where they belong?"

"I've often thought we should be much happier if we hauled out at Otter Island instead of this crowded place," said Matkah.

"Bah! Only the holluschickie go to Otter Island. If we went there they would say we were afraid. We must preserve appearances, my dear."

Sea Catch sunk his head proudly between his fat shoulders and pretended to go to sleep for a few minutes, but all the time he was keeping a sharp lookout for a fight. Now that all the seals and their wives were on the land, you could hear their clamor miles out to sea above the loudest gales. At the lowest counting there were over a million seals on the beach—old seals, mother seals, tiny babies, and holluschickie, fighting, scuffling, bleating, crawling, and playing together—going down to the sea and coming up from it in gangs and regiments, lying over every foot of ground as far as the eye could reach, and skirmishing about in brigades through the fog. It is nearly always foggy at Novastoshnah, except when the sun comes out and makes everything look all pearly and rainbow-colored for a little while.

Kotick, Matkah's baby, was born in the middle of that confusion, and he was all head and shoulders, with pale, watery blue eyes, as tiny seals must be, but there was something about his coat that made his mother look at him very closely.

"Sea Catch," she said, at last, "our baby's going to be white!"

"Empty clam-shells and dry seaweed!" snorted Sea Catch. "There never has been such a thing in the world as a white seal."

"I can't help that," said Matkah; "there's going to be now." And she sang the low, crooning seal song that all the mother seals sing to their babies:

> You mustn't swim till you're six weeks old,
>   Or your head will be sunk by your heels;
> And summer gales and Killer Whales
>   Are bad for baby seals.
>
> Are bad for baby seals, dear rat,
>   As bad as bad can be;
> But splash and grow strong,
> And you can't be wrong.
>   Child of the Open Sea!

Of course the little fellow did not understand the words at first. He paddled and scrambled about by his mother's side, and learned to scuffle out of the way when his father was fighting with another seal, and the two rolled and roared up and down the slippery rocks. Matkah used to go to sea to get things to eat, and the baby was fed only once in two days, but then he ate all he could and throve upon it.

The first thing he did was to crawl inland, and there he met tens of thousands of babies of his own age, and they played together like puppies, went to sleep on the clean sand, and played again. The old people in the nurseries took no notice of them, and the holluschickie kept to their own grounds, and the babies had a beautiful playtime.

When Matkah came back from her deep-sea fishing she would go straight to their playground and call as a sheep calls for a lamb, and wait until she heard Kotick bleat. Then she would take the straightest of straight lines in his direction, striking out with her fore flippers and knocking the youngsters head over heels right and left. There were always a few hundred mothers hunting for their children through the playgrounds, and the babies were kept lively. But, as Matkah told Kotick, "So long as you don't lie in muddy water and get mange, or rub the hard sand into a cut or scratch, and so long as you never go swimming when there is a heavy sea, nothing will hurt you here."

Little seals can no more swim than little children, but they are unhappy till they learn. The first time that Kotick went down to the sea a wave carried him out beyond his depth, and his big head sank and his little hind flippers flew up exactly as his mother had told him in the song, and if the next wave had not thrown him back again he would have drowned.

After that, he learned to lie in a beach-pool and let the wash of the waves just cover him and lift him up while he paddled, but he always kept his eye open for big waves that might hurt. He was two weeks learning to use his flippers; and all that while he floundered in and out of the water, and coughed and grunted and crawled up the beach and took catnaps on the sand, and went back again, until at last he found that he truly belonged to the water.

Then you can imagine the times that he had with his companions, ducking under the rollers; or coming in on top of a comber and landing with a swash and a splutter as the big wave went whirling far up the beach; or standing up on his tail and scratching his head as the old people did; or playing "I'm the King of the Castle" on slippery, weedy rocks that just stuck out of the wash. Now and then he would see a thin fin, like a big shark's fin, drifting along close to shore, and he knew that that was the Killer Whale, the Grampus, who eats young seals when he can get them; and Kotick would head for the beach like an arrow, and the fin would jig off slowly, as if it were looking for nothing at all.

Late in October the seals began to leave St. Paul's for the deep sea, by families and tribes, and there was no more fighting over the nurseries, and the holluschickie played anywhere they liked. "Next year," said Matkah to Kotick, "you will be a holluschickie; but this year you must learn how to catch fish."

They set out together across the Pacific, and Matkah showed Kotick how to sleep on his back with his flippers tucked down by his side and his little nose just out of the water. No cradle is so comfortable as the long, rocking swell of the Pacific. When Kotick felt his skin tingle all over, Matkah told him he was learning the "feel of the water," and that tingly, prickly feelings meant bad weather coming, and he must swim hard and get away.

"In a little time," she said, "you'll know where to swim to, but just now we'll follow Sea Pig, the Porpoise, for he is very wise." A school of porpoises were ducking and tearing through the water, and little Kotick followed them as fast as he could. "How do you know where to go to?" he panted. The leader of the school rolled his white eye and ducked under. "My tail tingles, youngster," he said. "That means there's a gale behind me. Come along! When you're south of the Sticky Water [he meant the Equator] and your tail tingles, that means there's a gale in front of you and you must head north. Come along! The water feels bad here."

This was one of very many things that Kotick learned, and he was always learning. Matkah taught him to follow the cod and the halibut along the under-sea banks and wrench the rockling out of his hole among the weeds; how to skirt the wrecks lying a hundred fathoms below water and dart like a rifle bullet in at one porthole and out at another as the fishes ran; how to dance on the top of the waves when the lightning was racing all over the sky, and wave his flipper politely to the stumpy-tailed Albatross and the Man-of-war Hawk as they went down the wind; how to jump three or four feet clear of the water like a dolphin, flippers close to the side and tail curved; to leave the flying fish alone because they are all bony; to take the shoulder-piece out of a cod at full speed ten fathoms deep, and never to stop and look at a boat or a ship, but particularly a row-boat. At the end of six months what Kotick did not know about deep-sea fishing was not worth the knowing. And all that time he never set flipper on dry ground.

One day, however, as he was lying half asleep in the warm water somewhere off the Island of Juan Fernandez, he felt faint and lazy all over, just as human people do when the spring is in their legs, and he remembered the good firm beaches of Novastoshnah seven thousand miles away, the games his companions played, the smell of the seaweed, the seal roar, and the fighting. That very minute he turned north, swimming steadily, and as he went on he met scores of his mates, all bound for the same place, and they said: "Greeting, Kotick! This year we are all holluschickie, and we can dance the Fire-dance in the breakers off Lukannon and play on the new grass. But where did you get that coat?"

Kotick's fur was almost pure white now, and though he felt very proud of it, he only said, "Swim quickly! My bones are aching for the land." And so they all came to the beaches where they had been born, and heard the old seals, their fathers, fighting in the rolling mist.

That night Kotick danced the Fire-dance with the yearling seals. The sea is full of fire on summer nights all the way down from Novastoshnah to Lukannon, and each seal leaves a wake like burning oil behind him and a flaming flash when he jumps, and the waves break in great phosphorescent streaks and swirls. Then they went inland to the holluschickie grounds and rolled up and down in the new wild wheat and told stories of what they had done while they had been at sea. They talked about the Pacific as boys would talk about a wood that they had been nutting in, and if anyone had understood them he could have gone away and made such a chart of that ocean as never was. The three- and four-year-old holluschickie romped down from Hutchinson's Hill crying: "Out of the way, youngsters! The sea is deep and you don't know all that's in it yet. Wait till you've rounded the Horn. Hi, you yearling, where did you get that white coat?"

"I didn't get it," said Kotick; "it grew." And just as he was going to roll the speaker over, a couple of black-haired men with flat red faces came from behind a sand dune, and Kotick, who had never seen a man before, coughed and lowered his head. The holluschickie just bundled off a few yards and sat staring stupidly. The men were no less than Kerick Booterin, the chief of the seal-hunters on the island, and Patalamon, his son. They came from the little village not half a mile from the sea nurseries, and they were deciding what seals they would drive up to the killing pens—for the seals were driven just like sheep—to be turned into seal-skin jackets later on.

"Ho!" said Patalamon. "Look! There's a white seal!"

Kerick Booterin turned nearly white under his oil and smoke, for he was an Aleut, and Aleuts are not clean people. Then he began to mutter a prayer. "Don't touch him,

Patalamon. There has never been a white seal since—since I was born. Perhaps it is old Zaharrof's ghost. He was lost last year in the big gale."

"I'm not going near him," said Patalamon. "He's unlucky. Do you really think he is old Zaharrof come back? I owe him for some gulls' eggs."

"Don't look at him," said Kerick. "Head off that drove of four-year-olds. The men ought to skin two hundred to-day, but it's the beginning of the season and they are new to the work. A hundred will do. Quick!"

Patalamon rattled a pair of seal's shoulder bones in front of a herd of holluschickie and they stopped dead, puffing and blowing. Then he stepped near and the seals began to move, and Kerick headed them inland, and they never tried to get back to their companions. Hundreds and hundreds of thousands of seals watched them being driven, but they went on playing just the same. Kotick was the only one who asked questions, and none of his companions could tell him anything, except that the men always drove seals in that way for six weeks or two months of every year.

"I am going to follow," he said, and his eyes nearly popped out of his head as he shuffled along in the wake of the herd.

"The white seal is coming after us," cried Patalamon. "That's the first time a seal has ever come to the killing-grounds alone."

"Hsh! Don't look behind you," said Kerick. "It is Zaharrof's ghost! I must speak to the priest about this."

The distance to the killing-grounds was only half a mile, but it took an hour to cover, because if the seals went too fast Kerick knew that they would get heated and then their fur would come off in patches when they were skinned. So they went on very slowly, past Sea Lion's Neck, past Webster House, till they came to the Salt House just beyond the sight of the seals on the beach. Kotick followed, panting and wondering. He thought that he was at the world's end, but the roar of the seal-nurseries behind him sounded as loud as the roar of a train in a tunnel. Then Kerick sat down on the moss and pulled out a heavy pewter watch and let the drove cool off for thirty minutes, and Kotick could hear the fog-dew dripping off the brim of his cap. Then ten or twelve men, each with an iron-bound club three or four feet long, came up, and Kerick pointed out one or two of the drove that were bitten by their companions or too hot, and the men kicked those aside with their heavy boots made of the skin of a walrus's throat, and then Kerick said, "Let go!" and then the men clubbed the seals on the head as fast as they could.

Ten minutes later little Kotick did not recognize his friends any more, for their skins were ripped off from the nose to the hind flippers, whipped off and thrown down on the ground in a pile.

That was enough for Kotick. He turned and galloped (a seal can gallop very swiftly for a short time) back to the sea; his little new mustache bristling with horror. At Sea-Lion's Neck, where the great sea-lions sit on the edge of the surf, he flung himself flipper-overhead into the cool water and rocked there, gasping miserably. "What's here?" said a sea-lion gruffly, for as a rule the sea-lions keep themselves to themselves.

"*Scoochnie! Ochen scoochnie!*" ("I'm lonesome, very lonesome!") said Kotick. "They're killing all the holluschickie on *all* the beaches!"

The sea-lion turned his head inshore. "Nonsense!" he said. "Your friends are making as much noise as ever. You must have seen old Kerick polishing off a drove. He's done that for thirty years."

"It's horrible," said Kotick, backing water as a wave went over him, and steadying himself with a screw stroke of his flippers that brought him all standing within three inches of a jagged edge of rock.

"Well done for a yearling!" said the sea-lion, who could

appreciate good swimming. "I suppose it *is* rather awful from your way of looking at it, but if you seals will come here year after year, of course the men get to know of it, and unless you can find an island where no men ever come you will always be driven."

"Isn't there any such island?" began Kotick.

"I've followed the *poltoos* [the halibut] for twenty years, and I can't say I've found it yet. But look here—you seem to have a fondness for talking to your betters—suppose you go to Walrus Islet and talk to Sea Vitch. He may know something. Don't flounce off like that. It's a six-mile swim, and if I were you I should haul out and take a nap first, little one."

Kotick thought that that was good advice, so he swam round to his own beach, hauled out, and slept for half an hour, twitching all over, as seals will. Then he headed straight for Walrus Islet, a little low sheet of rocky island almost due northeast from Novastoshnah, all ledges and rock and gulls' nests, where the walrus herded by themselves.

He landed close to old Sea Vitch—the big, ugly, bloated, pimpled, fat-necked, long-tusked walrus of the North Pacific, who has no manners except when he is asleep—as he was then, with his hind flippers half in and half out of the surf.

"Wake up!" barked Kotick, for the gulls were making a great noise.

"Hah! Ho! Hmph! What's that?" said Sea Vitch, and he struck the next walrus a blow with his tusks and waked him up, and the next struck the next, and so on till they were all awake and staring in every direction but the right one.

"Hi! It's me," said Kotick, bobbing in the surf and looking like a little white slug.

"Well! May I be—skinned!" said Sea Vitch, and they all looked at Kotick as you can fancy a club full of drowsy old gentlemen would look at a little boy. Kotick did not care to hear any more about skinning just then; he had seen enough of it. So he called out: "Isn't there any place for seals to go where men don't ever come?"

"Go and find out," said Sea Vitch, shutting his eyes. "Run away. We're busy here."

Kotick made his dolphin-jump in the air and shouted as loud as he could: "Clam-eater! Clam-eater!" He knew that Sea Vitch never caught a fish in his life but always rooted for clams and seaweed; though he pretended to be a very terrible person. Naturally the Chickies and the Gooverooskies and the Epatkas, the Burgomaster Gulls and the Kittiwakes and the Puffins, who are always looking for a chance to be rude, took up the cry, and—so Limmershin told me—for nearly five minutes you could not have heard a gun fired on Walrus Islet. All the population was yelling and screaming "Clam-eater! *Stareek* [old man]!" while Sea Vitch rolled from side to side grunting and coughing.

"*Now* will you tell?" said Kotick, all out of breath.

"Go and ask Sea Cow," said Sea Vitch. "If he is living still, he'll be able to tell you."

"How shall I know Sea Cow when I meet him?" said Kotick, sheering off.

"He's the only thing in the sea uglier than Sea Vitch," screamed a Burgomaster Gull, wheeling under Sea Vitch's nose. "Uglier, and with worse manners! *Stareek!*"

Kotick swam back to Novastoshnah, leaving the gulls to scream. There he found that no one sympathized with him in his little attempt to discover a quiet place for the seals. They told him that men had always driven the holluschickie—it was part of the day's work—and that if he did not like to see ugly things he should not have gone to the killing grounds. But none of the other seals had seen the killing, and that made the difference between him and his friends. Besides, Kotick was a white seal.

"What you must do," said old Sea Catch, after he had heard

his son's adventures, "is to grow up and be a big seal like your father, and have a nursery on the beach, and then they will leave you alone. In another five years you ought to be able to fight for yourself." Even gentle Matkah, his mother, said: "You will never be able to stop the killing. Go and play in the sea, Kotick." And Kotick went off and danced the Fire-dance with a very heavy little heart.

That autumn he left the beach as soon as he could, and set off alone because of a notion in his bullet-head. He was going to find Sea Cow, if there was such a person in the sea, and he was going to find a quiet island with good firm beaches for seals to live on, where men could not get at them. So he explored and explored by himself from the North to the South Pacific, swimming as much as three hundred miles in a day and a night. He met with more adventures than can be told, and narrowly escaped being caught by the Basking Shark, and the Spotted Shark, and the Hammerhead, and he met all the untrustworthy ruffians that loaf up and down the seas, and the heavy polite fish, and the scarlet spotted scallops that are moored in one place for hundreds of years, and grow very proud of it; but he never met Sea Cow, and he never found an island that he could fancy.

If the beach was good and hard, with a slope behind it for seals to play on, there was always the smoke of a whaler on the horizon, boiling down blubber, and Kotick knew what *that* meant. Or else he could see that seals had once visited the island and been killed off, and Kotick knew that where men had come once they would come again.

He picked up with an old stumpy-tailed albatross, who told him that Kerguelen Island was the very place for peace and quiet, and when Kotick went down there he was all but smashed to pieces against some wicked black cliffs in a heavy sleet-storm with lightning and thunder. Yet as he pulled out against the gale he could see that even there had once been a seal-nursery. And it was so in all the other islands that he visited.

Limmershin gave a long list of them, for he said that Kotick spent five seasons exploring, with a four months' rest each year at Novastoshnah, when the holluschickie used to make fun of him and his imaginary islands. He went to the Gallapagos, a horrid dry place on the Equator, where he was nearly baked to death; he went to the Georgia Islands, the Orkneys, Emerald Island, Little Nightingale Island, Gough's Island, Bouvet's Island, the Crossets, and even to a little speck of an island south of the Cape of Good Hope. But everywhere the People of the Sea told him the same things. Seals had come to those islands once upon a time, but men had killed them all off. Even when he swam thousands of miles out of the Pacific and got to a place called Cape Corrientes (that was when he was coming back from Gough's Island), he found a few hundred mangy seals on a rock and they told him that men came there too.

That nearly broke his heart, and he headed round the Horn back to his own beaches; and on his way north he hauled out on an island full of green trees, where he found an old, old seal who was dying, and Kotick caught fish for him and told him all his sorrows. "Now," said Kotick, "I am going back to Novastoshnah, and if I am driven to the killing-pens with the holluschickie I shall not care."

The old seal said, "Try once more. I am the last of the Lost Rookery of Masafuera, and in the days when men killed us by the hundred thousand there was a story on the beaches that some day a white seal would come out of the North and lead the seal people to a quiet place. I am old, and I shall never live to see that day, but others will. Try once more."

And Kotick curled up his mustache (it was a beauty) and said, "I am the only white seal that has ever been born on the beaches, and I am the only seal, black or white, who ever thought of looking for new islands."

This cheered him immensely; and when he came back to Novastoshnah that summer, Matkah, his mother, begged him to marry and settle down, for he was no longer a holluschick but a full-grown sea-catch, with a curly white mane on his shoulders, as heavy, as big, and as fierce as his father. "Give me another season," he said. "Remember, mother, it is always the seventh wave that goes farthest up the beach."

Curiously enough, there was another seal who thought that she would put off marrying till the next year, and Kotick danced the Fire-dance with her all down Lukannon Beach the night before he set off on his last exploration.

This time he went westward, because he had fallen on the trail of a great shoal of halibut, and he needed at least one hundred pounds of fish a day to keep him in good condition. He chased them till he was tired, and then he curled himself up and went to sleep on the hollows of the ground swell that sets in to Copper Island. He knew the coast perfectly well, so about midnight, when he felt himself gently bumped on a weed-bed, he said, "Hm, tide's running strong tonight," and turning over under water opened his eyes slowly and stretched. Then he jumped like a cat, for he saw huge things nosing about in the shoal water and browsing on the heavy fringes of the weeds.

"By the Great Combers of Magellan!" he said, beneath his mustache. "Who in the Deep Sea are these people?"

They were like no walrus, sea-lion, seal, bear, whale, shark, fish, squid, or scallop that Kotick had ever seen before. They were between twenty and thirty feet long, and they had no hind flippers, but a shovel-like tail that looked as if it had been whittled out of wet leather. Their heads were the most foolish-looking things you ever saw, and they balanced on the ends of their tails in deep water when they weren't grazing, bowing solemnly to each other and waving their front flippers as a fat man waves his arm.

"Ahem!" said Kotick. "Good sport, gentlemen?" The big

things answered by bowing and waving their flippers like the Frog-Footman. When they began feeding again Kotick saw that their upper lip was split into two pieces that they could twitch apart about a foot and bring together again with a whole bushel of seaweed between the splits. They tucked the stuff into their mouths and chumped solemnly.

"Messy style of feeding, that," said Kotick. They bowed again, and Kotick began to lose his temper. "Very good," he said. "If you do happen to have an extra joint in your front flipper you needn't show off so. I see you bow gracefully, but I should like to know your names." The split lips moved and twitched; and the glassy green eyes stared, but they did not speak.

"Well!" said Kotick. "You're the only people I've ever met uglier than Sea Vitch—and with worse manners."

Then he remembered in a flash what the Burgomaster gull had screamed to him when he was a little yearling at Walrus Islet, and he tumbled backward in the water, for he knew that he had found Sea Cow at last.

The sea cows went on schlooping and grazing and chumping in the weed, and Kotick asked them questions in every language that he had picked up in his travels; and the Sea People talk nearly as many languages as human beings. But the sea cows did not answer because Sea Cow cannot talk. He has only six bones in his neck where he ought to have seven, and they say under the sea that that prevents him from speaking even to his companions. But, as you know, he has an extra joint in his foreflipper, and by waving it up and down and about he makes what answers to a sort of clumsy telegraphic code.

By daylight Kotick's mane was standing on end and his temper was gone where the dead crabs go. Then the Sea Cow began to travel northward very slowly, stopping to hold absurd bowing councils from time to time, and Kotick followed them, saying to himself, "People who are such idiots as these are would have been killed long ago if they hadn't found out some safe island. And what is good enough for the Sea Cow is good enough for the Sea Catch. All the same, I wish they'd hurry."

It was weary work for Kotick. The herd never went more than forty or fifty miles a day, and stopped to feed at night, and kept close to the shore all the time; while Kotick swam round them, and over them, and under them, but he could not hurry them up one-half mile. As they went farther north they held a bowing council every few hours, and Kotick nearly bit off his mustache with impatience till he saw that they were following up a warm current of water, and then he respected them more.

One night they sank through the shiny water—sank like stones—and for the first time since he had known them began to swim quickly. Kotick followed, and the pace astonished him, for he never dreamed that Sea Cow was anything of a swimmer. They headed for a cliff by the shore—a cliff that ran down into deep water, and plunged into a dark hole at the foot of it, twenty fathoms under the sea. It was a long, long swim, and Kotick badly wanted fresh air before he was out of the dark tunnel they led him through.

"My wig!" he said, when he rose, gasping and puffing, into open water at the farther end. "It was a long dive, but it was worth it."

The sea cows had separated and were browsing lazily along the edges of the finest beaches that Kotick had ever seen. There were long stretches of smooth-worn rock running for miles, exactly fitted to make seal-nurseries, and there were play-grounds of hard sand sloping inland behind them, and there were rollers for seals to dance in, and long grass to roll in, and sand dunes to climb up and down, and, best of all, Kotick knew by the feel of the water, which never deceives a true sea catch, that no men had ever come there.

The first thing he did was to assure himself that the fishing was good, and then he swam along the beaches and counted up the delightful low sandy islands half hidden in the beautiful rolling fog. Away to the northward, out to sea, ran a line of bars and shoals and rocks that would never let a ship come within six miles of the beach, and between the islands and the mainland was a stretch of deep water that ran up to the perpendicular cliffs, and somewhere below the cliffs was the mouth of the tunnel.

"It's Novastoshnah over again, but ten times better," said Kotick. "Sea Cow must be wiser than I thought. Men can't come down the cliffs, even if there were any men; and the shoals to seaward would knock a ship to splinters. If any place in the sea is safe, this is it."

He began to think of the seal he had left behind him, but though he was in a hurry to go back to Novastoshnah, he thoroughly explored the new country, so that he would be able to answer all questions.

Then he dived and made sure of the mouth of the tunnel, and raced through to the southward. No one but a sea cow or a seal would have dreamed of there being such a place, and when he looked back at the cliffs even Kotick could hardly believe that he had been under them.

He was six days going home, though he was not swimming slowly; and when he hauled out just above Sea-Lion's Neck the first person he met was the seal who had been waiting for him, and she saw by the look in his eyes that he had found his island at last.

But the holluschickie and Sea Catch, his father, and all the other seals laughed at him when he told them what he had discovered, and a young seal about his own age said, "This is all very well, Kotick, but you can't come from no one knows where and order us off like this. Remember we've been fighting for our nurseries, and that's a thing you never did. You preferred prowling about in the sea."

The other seals laughed at this, and the young seal began

twisting his head from side to side. He had just married that year, and was making a great fuss about it.

"I've no nursery to fight for," said Kotick. "I only want to show you all a place where you will be safe. What's the use of fighting?"

"Oh, if you're trying to back out, of course I've no more to say," said the young seal with an ugly chuckle.

"Will you come with me if I win?" said Kotick. And a green light came into his eye, for he was very angry at having to fight at all.

"Very good," said the young seal carelessly. "*If* you win, I'll come."

He had no time to change his mind, for Kotick's head was out and his teeth sunk in the blubber of the young seal's neck. Then he threw himself back on his haunches and hauled his enemy down the beach, shook him, and knocked him over. Then Kotick roared to the seals: "I've done my best for you these five seasons past. I've found you the island where you'll be safe, but unless your heads are dragged off your silly necks you won't believe. I'm going to teach you now. Look out for yourselves!"

Limmershin told me that never in his life—and Limmershin sees ten thousand big seals fighting every year—never in all his little life did he see anything like Kotick's charge into the nurseries. He flung himself at the biggest sea-catch he could find, caught him by the throat, choked him and bumped him and banged him till he grunted for mercy, and then threw him aside and attacked the next. You see, Kotick had never fasted for four months as the big seals did every year, and his deep-sea swimming trips kept him in perfect condition, and, best of all, he had never fought before. His curly white mane stood up with rage, and his eyes flamed, and his big dog teeth glistened, and he was splendid to look at.

Old Sea Catch, his father, saw him tearing past, hauling the grizzled old seals about as though they had been halibut, and upsetting the young bachelors in all directions; and Sea Catch gave a roar and shouted: "He may be a fool, but he is the best fighter on the beaches! Don't tackle your father, my son! He's with you!"

Kotick roared in answer, and old Sea Catch waddled in with his mustache on end, blowing like a locomotive, while Matkah and the seal that was going to marry Kotick cowered down and admired their men-folk. It was a gorgeous fight, for the two fought as long as there was a seal that dared lift up his head, and when there were none they paraded grandly up and down the beach side by side, bellowing.

At night, just as the Northern Lights were winking and flashing through the fog, Kotick climbed a bare rock and looked down on the scattered nurseries and the torn and bleeding seals. "Now," he said, "I've taught you your lesson."

"My wig!" said old Sea Catch, boosting himself up stiffly, for he was fearfully mauled. "The Killer Whale himself could not have cut them up worse. Son, I'm proud of you, and what's more, I'll come with you to your island—if there is such a place."

"Hear you, fat pigs of the sea. Who comes with me to the Sea Cow's tunnel? Answer, or I shall teach you again," roared Kotick.

There was a murmur like the ripple of the tide all up and down the beaches. "We will come," said thousands of tired voices. "We will follow Kotick, the White Seal."

Then Kotick dropped his head between his shoulders and shut his eyes proudly. He was not a white seal any more, but red from head to tail. All the same he would have scorned to look at or touch one of his wounds.

A week later he and his army (nearly ten thousand holluschickie and old seals) went away north to the Sea Cow's tunnel, Kotick leading them, and the seals that stayed at

Novastoshnah called them idiots. But next spring, when they all met off the fishing banks of the Pacific, Kotick's seals told such tales of the new beaches beyond Sea Cow's tunnel that more and more seals left Novastoshnah.

Of course it was not all done at once, for the seals are not very clever, and they need a long time to turn things over in their minds, but year after year more seals went away from Novastoshnah, and Lukannon, and the other nurseries, to the quiet, sheltered beaches where Kotick sits all the summer through, getting bigger and fatter and stronger each year, while the holluschickie play around him, in that sea where no man comes.

LUKANNON

(This is the great deep-sea song that all the St. Paul seals sing
when they are heading back to their beaches in the summer.
It is a sort of very sad seal National Anthem.)

I met my mates in the morning (and, oh, but I am old!)
Where roaring on the ledges the summer ground-swell rolled;
I heard them lift the chorus that drowned the breakers' song—
The Beaches of Lukannon—two million voices strong!

The song of pleasant stations beside the salt lagoons,
The song of blowing squadrons that shuffled down the dunes,
The song of midnight dances that churned the sea to flame—
The Beaches of Lukannon—before the sealers came!

I met my mates in the morning (I'll never meet them more!);
They came and went in legions that darkened all the shore.
And through the foam-flecked offing as far as voice could
reach
We hailed the landing-parties and we sang them up the beach.

The Beaches of Lukannon—the winter wheat so tall—
The dripping, crinkled lichens, and the sea-fog drenching all!
The platforms of our playground, all shining smooth and worn!
The Beaches of Lukannon—the home where we were born!

I met my mates in the morning, a broken, scattered band.
Men shoot us in the water and club us on the land;
Men drive us to the Salt House like silly sheep and tame,
And still we sing Lukannon—before the sealers came.

Wheel down, wheel down to southward; oh, Gooverooska, go!
And tell the Deep-Sea Viceroys the story of our woe;
Ere, empty as the shark's egg the tempest flings ashore,
The Beaches of Lukannon shall know their sons no more!

"RIKKI-TIKKI-TAVI"

At the hole where he went in
Red-Eye called to Wrinkle-Skin.
Hear what little Red-Eye saith:
"Nag, come up and dance with death!"

Eye to eye and head to head,
   (Keep the measure, Nag.)
This shall end when one is dead;
   (At thy pleasure, Nag.)
Turn for turn and twist for twist—
   (Run and hide thee, Nag.)
Hah! The hooded Death has missed!
   (Woe betide thee, Nag!)

This is the story of the great war that Rikki-tikki-tavi fought single-handed, through the bathrooms of the big bungalow in Segowlee cantonment. Darzee, the tailor-bird, helped him, and Chuchundra, the musk-rat, who never comes out into the middle of the floor, but always creeps round by the wall, gave him advice, but Rikki-tikki did the real fighting.

He was a mongoose, rather like a little cat in his fur and his tail, but quite like a weasel in his head and his habits. His eyes and the end of his restless nose were pink. He could scratch himself anywhere he pleased with any leg, front or back, that he chose to use. He could fluff up his tail till it looked like a bottle-brush, and his war cry as he scuttled through the long grass was: "*Rikk-tikk-tikki-tikki-tchk!*"

One day, a high summer flood washed him out of the burrow where he lived with his father and mother, and carried him, kicking and clucking, down a roadside ditch. He found a little wisp of grass floating there, and clung to it till he lost his senses. When he revived, he was lying in the hot sun on the middle of a garden path, very draggled indeed, and a small boy was saying: "Here's a dead mongoose. Let's have a funeral."

"No," said his mother, "let's take him in and dry him. Perhaps he isn't really dead."

They took him into the house, and a big man picked him up between his finger and thumb and said he was not dead but half choked. So they wrapped him in cotton wool, and warmed him over a little fire, and he opened his eyes and sneezed.

"Now," said the big man (he was an Englishman who had just moved into the bungalow); "don't frighten him, and we'll see what he'll do."

It is the hardest thing in the world to frighten a mongoose, because he is eaten up from nose to tail with curiosity. The motto of all the mongoose family is "Run and find out," and Rikki-tikki was a true mongoose. He looked at the cotton-wool, decided that it was not good to eat, ran all round the table, sat up and put his fur in order, scratched himself, and jumped on the small boy's shoulder.

"Don't be frightened, Teddy," said his father. "That's his way of making friends."

"Ouch! He's tickling under my chin," said Teddy.

Rikki-tikki looked down between the boy's collar and neck, snuffed at his ear, and climbed down to the floor, where he sat rubbing his nose.

"Good gracious," said Teddy's mother, "and that's a wild creature! I suppose he's so tame because we've been kind to him."

"All mongooses are like that," said her husband. "If Teddy doesn't pick him up by the tail, or try to put him in a cage, he'll run in and out of the house all day long. Let's give him something to eat."

They gave him a little piece of raw meat. Rikki-tikki liked it immensely, and when it was finished he went out into the veranda and sat in the sunshine and fluffed up his fur to make it dry to the roots. Then he felt better.

"There are more things to find out about in this house," he said to himself, "than all my family could find out in all their lives. I shall certainly stay and find out."

He spent all that day roaming over the house. He nearly drowned himself in the bath-tubs, put his nose into the ink on a writing table, and burned it on the end of the big man's cigar, for he climbed up in the big man's lap to see how writing was done. At nightfall he ran into Teddy's nursery to watch how kerosene lamps were lighted, and when Teddy went to bed Rikki-tikki climbed up too; but he was a restless companion, because he had to get up and attend to every noise all through the night, and find out what made it. Teddy's mother and father came in, the last thing, to look at their boy, and Rikki-tikki was awake on the pillow. "I don't like that," said Teddy's mother; "he may bite the child." "He'll do no such thing," said the father. "Teddy's safer with that little beast than if he had a bloodhound to watch him. If a snake came into the nursery now—"

But Teddy's mother wouldn't think of anything so awful.

Early in the morning Rikki-tikki came to early breakfast in the veranda riding on Teddy's shoulder, and they gave him banana and some boiled egg. He sat on all their laps one after the other, because every well-brought-up mongoose always hopes to be a house mongoose some day and have rooms to run about in; and Rikki-tikki's mother (she used to live in the general's house at Segowlee) had carefully told Rikki what to do if ever he came across white men.

Then Rikki-tikki went out into the garden to see what was

to be seen. It was a large garden, only half cultivated, with bushes, as big as summer-houses, of Marshal Niel roses, lime and orange trees, clumps of bamboos, and thickets of high grass. Rikki-tikki licked his lips. "This is a splendid hunting-ground," he said, and his tail grew bottle-brushy at the thought of it, and he scuttled up and down the garden, snuffing here and there till he heard very sorrowful voices in a thorn-bush.

It was Darzee, the Tailorbird, and his wife. They had made a beautiful nest by pulling two big leaves together and stitching them up the edges with fibers, and had filled the hollow with cotton and downy fluff. The nest swayed to and fro, as they sat on the rim and cried.

"What is the matter?" asked Rikki-tikki.

"We are very miserable," said Darzee. "One of our babies fell out of the nest yesterday and Nag ate him."

"H'm!" said Rikki-tikki, "that is very sad—but I am a stranger here. Who is Nag?"

Darzee and his wife only cowered down in the nest without answering, for from the thick grass at the foot of the bush there came a low hiss—a horrid cold sound that made Rikki-tikki jump back two clear feet. Then inch by inch out of the grass rose up the head and spread hood of Nag, the big black cobra, and he was five feet long from tongue to tail. When he had lifted one-third of himself clear of the ground, he stayed balancing to and fro exactly as a dandelion tuft balances in the wind, and he looked at Rikki-tikki with the wicked snake's eyes that never change their expression, whatever the snake may be thinking of.

"Who is Nag?" said he. "*I* am Nag. The great God Brahm put his mark upon all our people, when the first cobra spread his hood to keep the sun off Brahm as he slept. Look, and be afraid!"

He spread out his hood more than ever, and Rikki-tikki saw the spectacle-mark on the back of it that looks exactly like the eye part of a hook-and-eye fastening. He was afraid for the minute, but it is impossible for a mongoose to stay frightened for any length of time, and though Rikki-tikki had never met a live cobra before, his mother had fed him on dead ones, and he knew that all a grown mongoose's business in life was to fight and eat snakes. Nag knew that too and, at the bottom of his cold heart, he was afraid.

"Well," said Rikki-tikki, and his tail began to fluff up again, "marks or no marks, do you think it is right for you to eat fledglings out of a nest?"

Nag was thinking to himself, and watching the least little movement in the grass behind Rikki-tikki. He knew that mongooses in the garden meant death sooner or later for him and his family, but he wanted to get Rikki-tikki off his guard. So he dropped his head a little, and put it on one side.

"Let us talk," he said. "You eat eggs. Why should not I eat birds?"

"Behind you! Look behind you!" sang Darzee.

Rikki-tikki knew better than to waste time in staring. He jumped up in the air as high as he could go, and just under him whizzed by the head of Nagaina, Nag's wicked wife. She had crept up behind him as he was talking, to make an end of him. He heard her savage hiss as the stroke missed. He came down almost across her back, and if he had been an old mongoose he would have known that then was the time to break her back with one bite; but he was afraid of the terrible lashing return stroke of the cobra. He bit, indeed, but did not bite long enough, and he jumped clear of the whisking tail, leaving Nagaina torn and angry.

"Wicked, wicked Darzee!" said Nag, lashing up as high as he could reach toward the nest in the thorn-bush. But Darzee had built it out of reach of snakes, and it only swayed to and fro.

Rikki-tikki felt his eyes growing red and hot (when a

mongoose's eyes grow red, he is angry), and he sat back on his tail and hind legs like a little kangaroo, and looked all round him, and chattered with rage. But Nag and Nagaina had disappeared into the grass. When a snake misses its stroke, it never says anything or gives any sign of what it means to do next. Rikki-tikki did not care to follow them, for he did not feel sure that he could manage two snakes at once. So he trotted off to the gravel path near the house, and sat down to think. It was a serious matter for him.

If you read the old books of natural history, you will find they say that when the mongoose fights the snake and happens to get bitten, he runs off and eats some herb that cures him. That is not true. The victory is only a matter of quickness of eye and quickness of foot—snake's blow against mongoose's jump—and as no eye can follow the motion of a snake's head when it strikes, this makes things much more wonderful than any magic herb. Rikki-tikki knew he was a young mongoose, and it made him all the more pleased to think that he had managed to escape a blow from behind. It gave him confidence in himself, and when Teddy came running down the path, Rikki-tikki was ready to be petted.

But just as Teddy was stooping, something wriggled a little in the dust, and a tiny voice said: "Be careful. I am Death!" It was Karait, the dusty brown snakeling that lies for choice on the dusty earth; and his bite is as dangerous as the cobra's. But he is so small that nobody thinks of him, and so he does the more harm to people.

Rikki-tikki's eyes grew red again, and he danced up to Karait with the peculiar rocking, swaying motion that he had inherited from his family. It looks very funny, but it is so perfectly balanced a gait that you can fly off from it at any angle you please, and in dealing with snakes this is an advantage. If Rikki-tikki had only known, he was doing a much more dangerous thing than fighting Nag, for Karait is so small, and can turn so quickly, that unless Rikki bit him close to the back of the head, he would get the return stroke in his eye or his lip. But Rikki did not know. His eyes were all red, and he rocked back and forth, looking for a good place to hold. Karait struck out. Rikki jumped sideways and tried to run in, but the wicked little dusty gray head lashed within a fraction of his shoulder, and he had to jump over the body, and the head followed his heels close.

Teddy shouted to the house: "Oh, look here! Our mongoose is killing a snake." And Rikki-tikki heard a scream from Teddy's mother. His father ran out with a stick, but by the time he came up, Karait had lunged out once too far, and Rikki-tikki had sprung, jumped on the snake's back, dropped his head far between his forelegs, bitten as high up the back as he could get hold, and rolled away. That bite paralyzed Karait, and Rikki-tikki was just going to eat him up from the tail, after the custom of his family at dinner, when he remembered that a full meal makes a slow mongoose, and if he wanted all his strength and quickness ready, he must keep himself thin.

He went away for a dust-bath under the castor-oil bushes, while Teddy's father beat the dead Karait. "What is the use of that?" thought Rikki-tikki. "I have settled it all;" and then Teddy's mother picked him up from the dust and hugged him, crying that he had saved Teddy from death, and Teddy's father said that he was a providence, and Teddy looked on with big scared eyes. Rikki-tikki was rather amused at all the fuss, which, of course, he did not understand. Teddy's mother might just as well have petted Teddy for playing in the dust. Rikki was thoroughly enjoying himself.

That night at dinner, walking to and fro among the wine-glasses on the table, he might have stuffed himself three times over with nice things. But he remembered Nag and Nagaina, and though it was very pleasant to be patted and petted by Teddy's mother, and to sit on Teddy's shoulder, his eyes would get red from time to time, and he would go off into his long war cry of "*Rikk-tikk-tikki-tikki-tchk!*"

Teddy carried him off to bed, and insisted on Rikki-tikki sleeping under his chin. Rikki-tikki was too well bred to bite or scratch, but as soon as Teddy was asleep he went off for his nightly walk round the house, and in the dark he ran up against Chuchundra, the musk-rat, creeping around by the wall. Chuchundra is a broken-hearted little beast. He whimpers and cheeps all the night, trying to make up his mind to run into the middle of the room, but he never gets there.

"Don't kill me," said Chuchundra, almost weeping. "Rikki-tikki, don't kill me!"

"Do you think a snake-killer kills muskrats?" said Rikki-tikki scornfully.

"Those who kill snakes get killed by snakes," said Chuchundra, more sorrowfully than ever. "And how am I to be sure that Nag won't mistake me for you some dark night?"

"There's not the least danger," said Rikki-tikki; "but Nag is in the garden, and I know you don't go there."

"My cousin Chua, the rat, told me—" said Chuchundra, and then he stopped.

"Told you what?"

"H'sh! Nag is everywhere, Rikki-tikki. You should have talked to Chua in the garden."

"I didn't—so you must tell me. Quick, Chuchundra, or I'll bite you!"

Chuchundra sat down and cried till the tears rolled off his whiskers. "I am a very poor man," he sobbed. "I never had spirit enough to run out into the middle of the room. H'sh! I mustn't tell you anything. Can't you *hear*, Rikki-tikki?"

Rikki-tikki listened. The house was as still as still, but he thought he could just catch the faintest *scratch-scratch* in the world—a noise as faint as that of a wasp walking on a window-pane—the dry scratch of a snake's scales on brick-work.

"That's Nag or Nagaina," he said to himself, "and he is crawling into the bath-room sluice. You're right, Chuchundra; I should have talked to Chua."

He stole off to Teddy's bath-room, but there was nothing there, and then to Teddy's mother's bathroom. At the bottom of the smooth plaster wall there was a brick pulled out to make a sluice for the bath water, and as Rikki-tikki stole in by the masonry curb where the bath is put, he heard Nag and Nagaina whispering together outside in the moonlight.

"When the house is emptied of people," said Nagaina to her husband, "*he* will have to go away, and then the garden will be our own again. Go in quietly, and remember that the big man who killed Karait is the first one to bite. Then come out and tell me, and we will hunt for Rikki-tikki together."

"But are you sure that there is anything to be gained by killing the people?" said Nag.

"Everything. When there were no people in the bungalow, did we have any mongoose in the garden? So long as the bungalow is empty, we are king and queen of the garden; and remember that as soon as our eggs in the melon bed hatch (as they may tomorrow), our children will need room and quiet."

"I had not thought of that," said Nag. "I will go, but there is no need that we should hunt for Rikki-tikki afterward. I will kill the big man and his wife, and the child if I can, and come away quietly. Then the bungalow will be empty, and Rikki-tikki will go."

Rikki-tikki tingled all over with rage and hatred at this, and then Nag's head came through the sluice, and his five feet of cold body followed it. Angry as he was, Rikki-tikki was very frightened as he saw the size of the big cobra. Nag coiled himself up, raised his head, and looked into the bathroom in the dark, and Rikki could see his eyes glitter.

"Now, if I kill him here, Nagaina will know; and if I fight him on the open floor, the odds are in his favor. What am I to do?" said Rikki-tikki-tavi.

Nag waved to and fro, and then Rikki-tikki heard him drinking from the biggest water-jar that was used to fill the bath. "That is good," said the snake. "Now, when Karait was killed, the big man had a stick. He may have that stick still, but when he comes in to bathe in the morning he will not have a stick. I shall wait here till he comes. Nagaina—do you hear me?—I shall wait here in the cool till daytime."

There was no answer from outside, so Rikki-tikki knew Nagaina had gone away. Nag coiled himself down, coil by coil, round the bulge at the bottom of the water jar, and Rikki-tikki stayed still as death. After an hour he began to move, muscle by muscle, toward the jar. Nag was asleep, and Rikki-tikki looked at his big back, wondering which would be the best place for a good hold. "If I don't break his back at the first jump," said Rikki, "he can still fight. And if he fights—oh, Rikki!" He looked at the thickness of the neck below the hood, but that was too much for him; and a bite near the tail would only make Nag savage.

"It must be the head'" he said at last; "the head above the hood; and, when I am once there, I must not let go."

Then he jumped. The head was lying a little clear of the water jar, under the curve of it; and, as his teeth met, Rikki braced his back against the bulge of the red earthenware to hold down the head. This gave him just one second's purchase, and he made the most of it. Then he was battered to and fro as a rat is shaken by a dog—to and fro on the floor, up and down, and around in great circles, but his eyes were red and he held on as the body cart-whipped over the floor, upsetting the tin dipper and the soap-dish and the flesh-brush, and banged against the tin side of the bath. As he held he closed his jaws tighter and tighter, for he made sure he would be banged to death, and, for the honor of his family, he preferred to be found with his teeth locked. He was dizzy, aching, and felt shaken to pieces when something went off like a thunderclap just behind him. A hot wind knocked him senseless and red fire singed his fur. The big man had been wakened by the noise, and had fired both barrels of a shotgun into Nag just behind the hood.

Rikki-tikki held on with his eyes shut, for now he was quite sure he was dead. But the head did not move, and the big man picked him up and said, "It's the mongoose again, Alice. The little chap has saved *our* lives now."

Then Teddy's mother came in with a very white face, and saw what was left of Nag, and Rikki-tikki dragged himself to Teddy's bedroom and spent half the rest of the night shaking himself tenderly to find out whether he really was broken into forty pieces, as he fancied.

When morning came he was very stiff, but well pleased with his doings. "Now I have Nagaina to settle with, and she will be worse than five Nags, and there's no knowing when the eggs she spoke of will hatch. Goodness! I must go and see Darzee," he said.

Without waiting for breakfast, Rikki-tikki ran to the thornbush where Darzee was singing a song of triumph at the top of his voice. The news of Nag's death was all over the garden, for the sweeper had thrown the body on the rubbish-heap.

"Oh, you stupid tuft of feathers!" said Rikki-tikki angrily. "Is this the time to sing?"

"Nag is dead—is dead—is dead!" sang Darzee. "The valiant Rikki-tikki caught him by the head and held fast. The big man brought the bang-stick, and Nag fell in two pieces! He will never eat my babies again."

"All that's true enough. But where's Nagaina?" said Rikki-tikki, looking carefully round him.

"Nagaina came to the bathroom sluice and called for Nag," Darzee went on; "and Nag came out on the end of a stick—the sweeper picked him up on the end of a stick and threw him upon the rubbish heap. Let us sing about the great, the red-eyed Rikki-tikki!" And Darzee filled his throat and sang.

"If I could get up to your nest, I'd roll your babies out!" said Rikki-tikki. "You don't know when to do the right thing at the right time. You're safe enough in your nest there, but it's war for me down here. Stop singing a minute, Darzee."

"For the great, the beautiful Rikki-tikki's sake I will stop," said Darzee. "What is it, O Killer of the terrible Nag?"

"Where is Nagaina, for the third time?"

"On the rubbish heap by the stables, mourning for Nag. Great is Rikki-tikki with the white teeth."

"Bother my white teeth! Have you ever heard where she keeps her eggs?"

"In the melon-bed, on the end nearest the wall, where the sun strikes nearly all day. She hid them there weeks ago."

"And you never thought it worth while to tell me? The end nearest the wall, you said?"

"Rikki-tikki, you are not going to eat her eggs?"

"Not eat exactly; no. Darzee, if you have a grain of sense you will fly off to the stables and pretend that your wing is broken, and let Nagaina chase you away to this bush. I must get to the melon-bed, and if I went there now she'd see me."

Darzee was a feather-brained little fellow who could never hold more than one idea at a time in his head. And just because he knew that Nagaina's children were born in eggs like his own, he didn't think at first that it was fair to kill them. But his wife was a sensible bird, and she knew that cobra's eggs meant young cobras later on. So she flew off from the nest, and left Darzee to keep the babies warm, and continue his song about the death of Nag. Darzee was very like a man in some ways.

She fluttered in front of Nagaina by the rubbish heap and cried out, "Oh, my wing is broken! The boy in the house threw a stone at me and broke it." Then she fluttered more desperately than ever.

Nagaina lifted up her head and hissed, "You warned Rikki-tikki when I would have killed him. Indeed and truly, you've chosen a bad place to be lame in." And she moved toward Darzee's wife, slipping along over the dust.

"The boy broke it with a stone!" shrieked Darzee's wife.

"Well! It may be some consolation to you when you're dead to know that I shall settle accounts with the boy. My husband lies on the rubbish heap this morning, but before night the boy in the house will lie very still. What is the use of running away? I am sure to catch you. Little fool, look at me!"

Darzee's wife knew better than to do *that*, for a bird who looks at a snake's eyes gets so frightened that she cannot move. Darzee's wife fluttered on, piping sorrowfully, and never leaving the ground, and Nagaina quickened her pace.

Rikki-tikki heard them going up the path from the stables, and he raced for the end of the melon-patch near the wall. There, in the warm litter above the melons, very cunningly hidden, he found twenty-five eggs, about the size of a bantam's eggs, but with whitish skin instead of shell.

"I was not a day too soon," he said, for he could see the baby cobras curled up inside the skin, and he knew that the minute they were hatched they could each kill a man or a mongoose. He bit off the tops of the eggs as fast as he could, taking care to crush the young cobras, and turned over the litter from time to time to see whether he had missed any. At last there were only three eggs left, and Rikki-tikki began to chuckle to himself, when he heard Darzee's wife screaming:

"Rikki-tikki, I led Nagaina toward the house, and she has gone into the veranda, and—oh, come quickly—she means killing!"

Rikki-tikki smashed two eggs, and tumbled backward down the melon-bed with the third egg in his mouth, and scuttled to the veranda as hard as he could put foot to the ground. Teddy and his mother and father were there at early breakfast, but

Rikki-tikki saw that they were not eating anything. They sat stone-still, and their faces were white. Nagaina was coiled up on the matting by Teddy's chair, within easy striking distance of Teddy's bare leg, and she was swaying to and fro, singing a song of triumph.

"Son of the big man that killed Nag," she hissed, "stay still. I am not ready yet. Wait a little. Keep very still, all you three! If you move I strike, and if you do not move I strike. Oh, foolish people, who killed my Nag!"

Teddy's eyes were fixed on his father, and all his father could do was to whisper, "Sit still, Teddy. You mustn't move. Teddy, keep still."

Then Rikki-tikki came up and cried, "Turn round, Nagaina. Turn and fight!"

"All in good time," said she, without moving her eyes. "I will settle my account with *you* presently. Look at your friends, Rikki-tikki. They are still and white. They are afraid. They dare not move, and if you come a step nearer I strike."

"Look at your eggs," said Rikki-tikki, "in the melon-bed near the wall. Go and look, Nagaina!"

The big snake turned half around, and saw the egg on the veranda. "Ah-h! Give it to me," she said.

Rikki-tikki put his paws one on each side of the egg, and his eyes were blood-red. "What price for a snake's egg? For a young cobra? For a young king cobra? For the last—the very last of the brood? The ants are eating all the others down by the melon-bed."

Nagaina spun clear round, forgetting everything for the sake of the one egg; and Rikki-tikki saw Teddy's father shoot out a big hand, catch Teddy by the shoulder, and drag him across the little table with the tea-cups, safe and out of reach of Nagaina.

"Tricked! Tricked! Tricked! *Rikk-tck-tck!*" chuckled Rikki-tikki. "The boy is safe, and it was I—I—I that caught Nag by the hood last night in the bathroom." Then he began to jump up and down, all four feet together, his head close to the floor. "He threw me to and fro, but he could not shake me off. He was dead before the big man blew him in two. I did it! *Rikki-tikki-tck-tck!* Come then, Nagaina. Come and fight with me. You shall not be a widow long."

Nagaina saw that she had lost her chance of killing Teddy, and the egg lay between Rikki-tikki's paws. "Give me the egg, Rikki-tikki. Give me the last of my eggs, and I will go away and never come back," she said, lowering her hood.

"Yes, you will go away, and you will never come back. For you will go to the rubbish heap with Nag. Fight, widow! The big man has gone for his gun! Fight!"

Rikki-tikki was bounding all round Nagaina, keeping just out of reach of her stroke, his little eyes like hot coals. Nagaina gathered herself together and flung out at him. Rikki-tikki jumped up and backward. Again and again and again she struck, and each time her head came with a whack on the matting of the veranda and she gathered herself together like a watch-spring. Then Rikki-tikki danced in a circle to get behind her, and Nagaina spun round to keep her head to his head, so that the rustle of her tail on the matting sounded like dry leaves blown along by the wind.

He had forgotten the egg. It still lay on the veranda, and Nagaina came nearer and nearer to it, till at last, while Rikki-tikki was drawing breath, she caught it in her mouth, turned to the veranda steps, and flew like an arrow down the path, with Rikki-tikki behind her. When the cobra runs for her life, she goes like a whip-lash flicked across a horse's neck.

Rikki-tikki knew that he must catch her, or all the trouble would begin again. She headed straight for the long grass by the thorn-bush, and as he was running Rikki-tikki heard Darzee still singing his foolish little song of triumph. But Darzee's wife was wiser. She flew off her nest as Nagaina came along, and flapped her wings about Nagaina's head. If Darzee had helped they might have turned her, but Nagaina only lowered her hood and went on. Still, the instant's delay brought Rikki-tikki up to her, and as she plunged into the rat-hole where she and Nag used to live, his little white teeth were clenched on her tail, and he went down with her—and very few mongooses, however wise and old they may be, care to follow a cobra into its hole. It was dark in the hole; and Rikki-tikki never knew when it might open out and give Nagaina room to turn and strike at him. He held on savagely, and stuck out his feet to act as brakes on the dark slope of the hot, moist earth.

Then the grass by the mouth of the hole stopped waving, and Darzee said, "It is all over with Rikki-tikki! We must sing his death-song. Valiant Rikki-tikki is dead! For Nagaina will surely kill him underground."

So he sang a very mournful song that he made up on the spur of the minute, and just as he got to the most touching part, the grass quivered again, and Rikki-tikki, covered with dirt, dragged himself out of the hole leg by leg, licking his whiskers. Darzee stopped with a little shout. Rikki-tikki shook some of the dust out of his fur and sneezed. "It is all over," he said. "The widow will never come out again." And the red ants that live between the grass stems heard him, and began to troop down one after another to see if he had spoken the truth.

Rikki-tikki curled himself up in the grass and slept where he was—slept and slept till it was late in the afternoon, for he had done a hard day's work.

"Now," he said, when he awoke, "I will go back to the house. Tell the Coppersmith, Darzee, and he will tell the garden that Nagaina is dead."

The Coppersmith is a bird who makes a noise exactly like the beating of a little hammer on a copper pot; and the reason he is always making it is because he is the town crier to every Indian garden, and tells all the news to everybody who

THE JUNGLE BOOK   121

cares to listen. As Rikki-tikki went up the path, he heard his "attention" notes like a tiny dinner gong, and then the steady "*Ding-dong-tock!* Nag is dead—*dong!* Nagaina is dead! *Ding-dong-tock!*" That set all the birds in the garden singing, and the frogs croaking, for Nag and Nagaina used to eat frogs as well as little birds.

When Rikki got to the house, Teddy and Teddy's mother (she looked very white still, for she had been fainting) and Teddy's father came out and almost cried over him; and that night he ate all that was given him till he could eat no more, and went to bed on Teddy's shoulder, where Teddy's mother saw him when she came to look late at night.

"He saved our lives and Teddy's life," she said to her husband. "Just think, he saved all our lives."

Rikki-tikki woke up with a jump, for the mongooses are light sleepers.

"Oh, it's you," said he. "What are you bothering for? All the cobras are dead. And if they weren't, I'm here."

Rikki-tikki had a right to be proud of himself. But he did not grow too proud, and he kept that garden as a mongoose should keep it, with tooth and jump and spring and bite, till never a cobra dared show its head inside the walls.

DARZEE'S CHANT
(Sung in honor of Rikki-tikki-tavi)

Singer and tailor am I—
    Doubled the joys that I know—
Proud of my lilt to the sky,
    Proud of the house that I sew—
Over and under, so weave I my music—so weave I the
    house that I sew.

Sing to your fledglings again,
    Mother, oh lift up your head!
Evil that plagued us is slain,
    Death in the garden lies dead.
Terror that hid in the roses is impotent—flung on the
    dung-hill and dead!

Who has delivered us, who?
    Tell me his nest and his name.
Rikki, the valiant, the true,
    Tikki, with eyeballs of flame,
Rikk-tikki-tikki, the ivory-fanged, the hunter with
    eyeballs of flame!

Give him the Thanks of the Birds,
    Bowing with tail feathers spread!
Praise him with nightingale words—
    Nay, I will praise him instead.
Hear! I will sing you the praise of the bottle-tailed
    Rikki, with eyeballs of red!

*(Here Rikki-tikki interrupted, and the rest of the song
is lost.)*

TOOMAI
OF THE ELEPHANTS

I will remember what I was, I am sick of rope and chain—
  I will remember my old strength and all my forest affairs.
I will not sell my back to man for a bundle of sugar-cane,
  I will go out to my own kind, and the wood-folk in their lairs.

I will go out until the day, until the morning break,
  Out to the wind's untainted kiss, the water's clean caress:
I will forget my ankle-ring and snap my picket stake.
  I will revisit my lost loves, and playmates masterless!

Kala Nag, which means Black Snake, had served the Indian
Government in every way that an elephant could serve
it for forty-seven years, and as he was fully twenty years old
when he was caught, that makes him nearly seventy—a ripe
age for an elephant. He remembered pushing, with a big
leather pad on his forehead, at a gun stuck in deep mud, and
that was before the Afghan War of 1842, and he had not then
come to his full strength. His mother Radha Pyari—Radha the
darling—who had been caught in the same drive with Kala
Nag, told him, before his little-milk tusks had dropped out,
that elephants who were afraid always got hurt. Kala Nag knew
that that advice was good, for the first time that he saw a shell
burst he backed, screaming, into a stand of piled rifles, and the
bayonets pricked him in all his softest places. So, before he was
twenty-five, he gave up being afraid, and so he was the best-
loved and the best-looked-after elephant in the service of the

Government of India. He had carried tents, twelve hundred pounds' weight of tents, on the march in Upper India. He had been hoisted into a ship at the end of a steam crane and taken for days across the water, and made to carry a mortar on his back in a strange and rocky country very far from India, and had seen the Emperor Theodore lying dead in Magdala, and had come back again in the steamer entitled, so the soldiers said, to the Abyssinian War medal. He had seen his fellow elephants die of cold and epilepsy and starvation and sunstroke up at a place called Ali Musjid, ten years later; and afterward he had been sent down thousands of miles south to haul and pile big balks of teak in the timberyards at Moulmein. There he had half killed an insubordinate young elephant who was shirking his fair share of work.

After that he was taken off timber-hauling, and employed, with a few score other elephants who were trained to the business, in helping to catch wild elephants among the Garo hills. Elephants are very strictly preserved by the Indian Government. There is one whole department which does nothing else but hunt them, and catch them, and break them in, and send them up and down the country as they are needed for work.

Kala Nag stood ten fair feet at the shoulders, and his tusks had been cut off short at five feet, and bound round the ends, to prevent them splitting, with bands of copper; but he could do more with those stumps than any untrained elephant could do with the real sharpened ones.

When, after weeks and weeks of cautious driving of scattered elephants across the hills, the forty or fifty wild monsters were driven into the last stockade, and the big drop gate, made of tree trunks lashed together, jarred down behind them, Kala Nag, at the word of command, would go into that flaring, trumpeting pandemonium (generally at night, when the flicker of the torches made it difficult to judge distances), and, picking out the biggest and wildest tusker of the mob, would hammer him and hustle him into quiet while the men on the backs of the other elephants roped and tied the smaller ones.

There was nothing in the way of fighting that Kala Nag, the old wise Black Snake, did not know, for he had stood up more than once in his time to the charge of the wounded tiger, and, curling up his soft trunk to be out of harm's way, had knocked the springing brute sideways in mid-air with a quick sickle cut of his head, that he had invented all by himself; had knocked him over, and kneeled upon him with his huge knees till the life went out with a gasp and a howl, and there was only a fluffy striped thing on the ground for Kala Nag to pull by the tail.

"Yes," said Big Toomai, his driver, the son of Black Toomai who had taken him to Abyssinia, and grandson of Toomai of the Elephants who had seen him caught, "there is nothing that the Black Snake fears except me. He has seen three generations of us feed him and groom him, and he will live to see four."

"He is afraid of *me* also," said Little Toomai, standing up to his full height of four feet, with only one rag upon him. He was ten years old, the eldest son of Big Toomai, and, according to custom, he would take his father's place on Kala Nag's neck when he grew up, and would handle the heavy iron ankus, the elephant goad, that had been worn smooth by his father, and his grandfather, and his great-grandfather.

He knew what he was talking of; for he had been born under Kala Nag's shadow, had played with the end of his trunk before he could walk, had taken him down to water as soon as he could walk, and Kala Nag would no more have dreamed of disobeying his shrill little orders than he would have dreamed of killing him on that day when Big Toomai carried the little brown baby under Kala Nag's tusks, and told him to salute his master that was to be.

"Yes," said Little Toomai, "he is afraid of *me*," and he took long strides up to Kala Nag, called him a fat old pig, and made him lift up his feet one after the other.

"Wah!" said Little Toomai, "thou art a big elephant," and he wagged his fluffy head, quoting his father. "The Government may pay for elephants, but they belong to us mahouts. When thou art old, Kala Nag, there will come some rich rajah, and he will buy thee from the Government, on account of thy size and thy manners, and then thou wilt have nothing to do but to carry gold earrings in thy ears, and a gold howdah on thy back, and a red cloth covered with gold on thy sides, and walk at the head of the processions of the King. Then I shall sit on thy neck, O Kala Nag, with a silver ankus, and men will run before us with golden sticks, crying, 'Room for the King's elephant!' That will be good, Kala Nag, but not so good as this hunting in the Jungles."

"Umph!" said Big Toomai. "Thou art a boy, and as wild as a buffalo-calf. This running up and down among the hills is not the best Government service. I am getting old, and I do not love wild elephants. Give me brick elephant lines, one stall to each elephant, and big stumps to tie them to safely, and flat, broad roads to exercise upon, instead of this come-and-go camping. Aha, the Cawnpore barracks were good. There was a bazaar close by, and only three hours' work a day."

Little Toomai remembered the Cawnpore elephant-lines and said nothing. He very much preferred the camp life, and hated those broad, flat roads, with the daily grubbing for grass in the forage reserve, and the long hours when there was nothing to do except to watch Kala Nag fidgeting in his pickets.

What Little Toomai liked was to scramble up bridle-paths that only an elephant could take; the dip into the valley below; the glimpses of the wild elephants browsing miles away; the rush of the frightened pig and peacock under Kala Nag's feet; the blinding warm rains, when all the hills and valleys smoked; the beautiful misty mornings when nobody knew where they would camp that night; the steady, cautious drive of the wild elephants, and the mad rush and blaze and hullabaloo of the last night's drive, when the elephants poured into the stockade like boulders in a landslide, found that they could not get out, and flung themselves at the heavy posts only to be driven back by yells and flaring torches and volleys of blank cartridge.

Even a little boy could be of use there, and Toomai was as useful as three boys. He would get his torch and wave it, and yell with the best. But the really good time came when the driving out began, and the Keddah—that is, the stockade—looked like a picture of the end of the world, and men had to make signs to one another, because they could not hear themselves speak. Then Little Toomai would climb up to the top of one of the quivering stockade posts, his sun-bleached brown hair flying loose all over his shoulders, and he looking like a goblin in the torch-light. And as soon as there was a lull you could hear his high-pitched yells of encouragement to Kala Nag, above the trumpeting and crashing, and snapping of ropes, and groans of the tethered elephants. "*Maîl, maîl, Kala Nag!* (Go on, go on, Black Snake!) *Dant do!* (Give him the tusk!) *Somalo! Somalo!* (Careful, careful!) *Maro! Mar!* (Hit him, hit him!) Mind the post! *Arre! Arre! Hai! Yai! Kya-a-ah!*" he would shout, and the big fight between Kala Nag and the wild elephant would sway to and fro across the Keddah, and the old elephant catchers would wipe the sweat out of their eyes, and find time to nod to Little Toomai wriggling with joy on the top of the posts.

He did more than wriggle. One night he slid down from the post and slipped in between the elephants and threw up the loose end of a rope, which had dropped, to a driver who was trying to get a purchase on the leg of a kicking young calf (calves always give more trouble than full-grown animals). Kala Nag saw him, caught him in his trunk, and handed him up to Big Toomai, who slapped him then and there, and put him back on the post.

Next morning he gave him a scolding and said: "Are not good brick elephant lines and a little tent carrying enough, that thou must needs go elephant catching on thy own account, little worthless? Now those foolish hunters, whose pay is less than my pay, have spoken to Petersen Sahib of the matter." Little Toomai was frightened. He did not know much of white men, but Petersen Sahib was the greatest white man in the world to him. He was the head of all the Keddah operations— the man who caught all the elephants for the Government of India, and who knew more about the ways of elephants than any living man.

"What—what will happen?" said Little Toomai.

"Happen! The worst that can happen. Petersen Sahib is a madman. Else why should he go hunting these wild devils? He may even require thee to be an elephant-catcher, to sleep anywhere in these fever-filled Jungles, and at last to be trampled to death in the Keddah. It is well that this nonsense ends safely. Next week the catching is over, and we of the plains are sent back to our stations. Then we will march on smooth roads, and forget all this hunting. But, son, I am angry that thou shouldst meddle in the business that belongs to these dirty Assamese jungle-folk. Kala Nag will obey none but me, so I must go with him into the Keddah; but he is only a fighting elephant, and he does not help to rope them. So I sit at my ease, as befits a mahout—not a mere hunter—a mahout, I say, and a man who gets a pension at the end of his service. Is the family of Toomai of the Elephants to be trodden underfoot in the dirt of a Keddah? Bad one! Wicked one! Worthless son! Go and wash Kala Nag and attend to his ears, and see that there are no thorns in his feet; or else Petersen Sahib will surely catch thee and make thee a wild hunter—a follower of elephant's foot tracks, a jungle-bear. Bah! Shame! Go!"

Little Toomai went off without saying a word, but he told Kala Nag all his grievances while he was examining his feet. "No matter," said Little Toomai, turning up the fringe of Kala Nag's huge right ear. "They have said my name to Petersen Sahib, and perhaps—and perhaps—and perhaps—who knows? Hai! That is a big thorn that I have pulled out!"

The next few days were spent in getting the elephants together, in walking the newly caught wild elephants up and down between a couple of tame ones to prevent them giving too much trouble on the downward march to the plains, and in taking stock of the blankets and ropes and things that had been worn out or lost in the forest.

Petersen Sahib came in on his clever she-elephant Pudmini; he had been paying off other camps among the hills, for the season was coming to an end, and there was a native clerk sitting at a table under a tree, to pay the drivers their wages. As each man was paid he went back to his elephant, and joined the line that stood ready to start. The catchers, and hunters, and beaters, the men of the regular Keddah, who stayed in the Jungle year in and year out, sat on the backs of the elephants that belonged to Petersen Sahib's permanent force, or leaned against the trees with their guns across their arms, and made fun of the drivers who were going away, and laughed when the newly caught elephants broke the line and ran about.

Big Toomai went up to the clerk with Little Toomai behind him, and Machua Appa, the head-tracker, said in an undertone to a friend of his, "There goes one piece of good elephant-stuff at least. 'Tis a pity to send that young jungle-cock to molt in the plains."

Now Petersen Sahib had ears all over him, as a man must have who listens to the most silent of all living things—the wild elephant. He turned where he was lying all along on Pudmini's back and said, "What is that? I did not know of a man among the plains-drivers who had wit enough to rope even a dead elephant."

"This is not a man, but a boy. He went into the Keddah at

the last drive, and threw Barmao there the rope, when we were trying to get that young calf with the blotch on his shoulder away from his mother."

Machua Appa pointed at Little Toomai, and Petersen Sahib looked, and Little Toomai bowed to the earth.

"He throw a rope? He is smaller than a picket-pin. Little one, what is thy name?" said Petersen Sahib.

Little Toomai was too frightened to speak, but Kala Nag was behind him, and Toomai made a sign with his hand, and the elephant caught him up in his trunk and held him level with Pudmini's forehead, in front of the great Petersen Sahib. Then Little Toomai covered his face with his hands, for he was only a child, and except where elephants were concerned, he was just as bashful as a child could be.

"Oho!" said Petersen Sahib, smiling underneath his mustache, "and why didst thou teach thy elephant *that* trick? Was it to help thee steal green corn from the roofs of the houses when the ears are put out to dry?"

"Not green corn, Protector of the Poor—melons," said Little Toomai, and all the men sitting about broke into a roar of laughter. Most of them had taught their elephants that trick when they were boys. Little Toomai was hanging eight feet up in the air, and he wished very much that he were eight feet underground.

"He is Toomai, my son, Sahib," said Big Toomai, scowling. "He is a very bad boy, and he will end in a jail, Sahib."

"Of that I have my doubts," said Petersen Sahib. "A boy who can face a full Keddah at his age does not end in jails. See, little one, here are four annas to spend in sweetmeats because thou hast a little head under that great thatch of hair. In time thou mayest become a hunter too." Big Toomai scowled more than ever. "Remember, though, that Keddahs are not good for children to play in," Petersen Sahib went on.

"Must I never go there, Sahib?" asked Little Toomai with

a big gasp.

"Yes." Petersen Sahib smiled again. "When thou hast seen the elephants dance. That is the proper time. Come to me when thou hast seen the elephants dance, and then I will let thee go into all the Keddahs."

There was another roar of laughter, for that is an old joke among elephant-catchers, and it means just never. There are great cleared flat places hidden away in the forests that are called elephants' ball-rooms, but even these are only found by accident, and no man has ever seen the elephants dance. When a driver boasts of his skill and bravery the other drivers say, "And when didst *thou* see the elephants dance?"

Kala Nag put Little Toomai down, and he bowed to the earth again and went away with his father, and gave the silver four-anna piece to his mother, who was nursing his baby brother, and they all were put up on Kala Nag's back, and the line of grunting, squealing elephants rolled down the hill path to the plains. It was a very lively march on account of the new elephants, who gave trouble at every ford, and needed coaxing or beating every other minute.

Big Toomai prodded Kala Nag spitefully, for he was very angry, but Little Toomai was too happy to speak. Petersen Sahib had noticed him, and given him money, so he felt as a private soldier would feel if he had been called out of the ranks and praised by his commander-in-chief.

"What did Petersen Sahib mean by the elephant-dance?" he said, at last, softly to his mother.

Big Toomai heard him and grunted. "That thou shouldst never be one of these hill-buffaloes of trackers. *That* was what he meant. Oh, you in front, what is blocking the way?"

An Assamese driver, two or three elephants ahead, turned round angrily, crying: "Bring up Kala Nag, and knock this youngster of mine into good behavior. Why should Petersen Sahib have chosen *me* to go down with you donkeys of the rice fields? Lay your beast alongside, Toomai, and let him prod with his tusks. By all the Gods of the Hills, these new elephants are possessed, or else they can smell their companions in the Jungle."

Kala Nag hit the new elephant in the ribs and knocked the wind out of him, as Big Toomai said, "We have swept the hills of wild elephants at the last catch. It is only your carelessness in driving. Must I keep order along the whole line?"

"Hear him!" said the other driver. "*We* have swept the hills! Ho! Ho! You are very wise, you plains-people. Anyone but a mud-head who never saw the Jungle would know that *they* know that the drives are ended for the season. Therefore all the wild elephants to-night will—but why should I waste wisdom on a river-turtle?"

"What will they do?" Little Toomai called out.

"*Ohé*, little one. Art thou there? Well, I will tell thee, for thou hast a cool head. They will dance, and it behooves thy father, who has swept *all* the hills of *all* the elephants, to double-chain his pickets to-night."

"What talk is this?" said Big Toomai. "For forty years, father and son, we have tended elephants, and we have never heard such moonshine about dances."

"Yes; but a plains-man who lives in a hut knows only the four walls of his hut. Well, leave thy elephants unshackled tonight and see what comes. As for their dancing, I have seen the place where— How many windings has the Dihang River? Here is another ford, and we must swim the calves. Stop still, you behind there."

And in this way, talking and wrangling and splashing through the rivers, they made their first march to a sort of receiving camp for the new elephants. But they lost their tempers long before they got there.

Then the elephants were chained by their hind legs to their big stumps of pickets, and extra ropes were fitted to the new elephants, and the fodder was piled before them, and the hill drivers went back to Petersen Sahib through the afternoon light, telling the plains-drivers to be extra careful that night, and laughing when the plains-drivers asked the reason.

Little Toomai attended to Kala Nag's supper, and as evening fell, wandered through the camp, unspeakably happy, in search of a tom-tom. When an Indian child's heart is full, he does not run about and make a noise in an irregular fashion. He sits down to a sort of revel all by himself. And Little Toomai had been spoken to by Petersen Sahib! If he had not found what he wanted, I believe he would have been ill. But the sweetmeat seller in the camp lent him a little tom-tom—a drum beaten with the flat of the hand—and he sat down, cross-legged, before Kala Nag as the stars began to come out, the tom-tom in his lap, and he thumped and he thumped and he thumped, and the more he thought of the great honor that had been done to him, the more he thumped, all alone among the elephant fodder. There was no tune and no words, but the thumping made him happy.

The new elephants strained at their ropes, and squealed and trumpeted from time to time, and he could hear his mother in the camp hut putting his small brother to sleep with an old, old song about the great God Shiv, who once told all the animals what they should eat. It is a very soothing lullaby, and the first verse says:

> Shiv, who poured the harvest and made the winds to blow,
> Sitting at the doorways of a day of long ago,
> Gave to each his portion, food and toil and fate,
> From the King upon the *guddee* to the Beggar at the gate.
>   All things made he—Shiva the Preserver.
> Mahadeo! Mahadeo! He made all—
> Thorn for the camel, fodder for the kine,
> And mother's heart for sleepy head, O little son of mine!

Little Toomai came in with a joyous *tunk-a-tunk* at the end of each verse, till he felt sleepy and stretched himself on the fodder at Kala Nag's side.

At last the elephants began to lie down one after another as is their custom, till only Kala Nag at the right of the line was left standing up; and he rocked slowly from side to side, his ears put forward to listen to the night wind as it blew very slowly across the hills. The air was full of all the night noises that, taken together, make one big silence—the click of one bamboo stem against the other, the rustle of something alive in the undergrowth, the scratch and squawk of a half-waked bird (birds are awake in the night much more often than we imagine), and the fall of water ever so far away. Little Toomai slept for some time, and when he waked it was brilliant moonlight, and Kala Nag was still standing up with his ears cocked. Little Toomai turned, rustling in the fodder, and watched the curve of his big back against half the stars in heaven, and while he watched he heard, so far away that it sounded no more than a pinhole of noise pricked through the stillness, the "hoot-toot" of a wild elephant.

All the elephants in the lines jumped up as if they had been shot, and their grunts at last waked the sleeping mahouts, and they came out and drove in the picket pegs with big mallets, and tightened this rope and knotted that till all was quiet. One new elephant had nearly grubbed up his picket, and Big Toomai took off Kala Nag's leg-chain and shackled that elephant fore-foot to hind-foot, but slipped a loop of grass string round Kala Nag's leg, and told him to remember that he was tied fast. He knew that he and his father and his grandfather had done the very same thing hundreds of times before. Kala Nag did not answer to the order by gurgling, as he usually did. He stood still, looking out across the moonlight, his head a little raised and his ears spread like fans, up to the great folds of the Garo hills.

"Look to him if he grows restless in the night," said Big Toomai to Little Toomai, and he went into the hut and slept. Little Toomai was just going to sleep, too, when he heard the coir string snap with a little "tang," and Kala Nag rolled out of his pickets as slowly and as silently as a cloud rolls out of the mouth of a valley. Little Toomai pattered after him, barefooted, down the road in the moonlight, calling under his breath, "Kala Nag! Kala Nag! Take me with you, O Kala Nag!" The elephant turned, without a sound, took three strides back to the boy in the moonlight, put down his trunk, swung him up to his neck, and almost before Little Toomai had settled his knees, slipped into the forest.

There was one blast of furious trumpeting from the lines, and then the silence shut down on everything, and Kala Nag began to move. Sometimes a tuft of high grass washed along his sides as a wave washes along the sides of a ship, and sometimes a cluster of wild-pepper vines would scrape along his back, or a bamboo would creak where his shoulder touched it; but between those times he moved absolutely without any sound, drifting through the thick Garo forest as though it had been smoke. He was going uphill, but though Little Toomai watched the stars in the rifts of the trees, he could not tell in what direction.

Then Kala Nag reached the crest of the ascent and stopped for a minute, and Little Toomai could see the tops of the trees lying all speckled and furry under the moonlight for miles and miles, and the blue-white mist over the river in the hollow. Toomai leaned forward and looked, and he felt that the forest was awake below him—awake and alive and crowded. A big brown fruit-eating bat brushed past his ear; a porcupine's quills rattled in the thicket; and in the darkness between the tree-stems he heard a hog-bear digging hard in the moist warm earth, and snuffing as it digged.

Then the branches closed over his head again, and Kala

Nag began to go down into the valley—not quietly this time, but as a runaway gun goes down a steep bank—in one rush. The huge limbs moved as steadily as pistons, eight feet to each stride, and the wrinkled skin of the elbow points rustled. The undergrowth on either side of him ripped with a noise like torn canvas, and the saplings that he heaved away right and left with his shoulders sprang back again and banged him on the flank, and great trails of creepers, all matted together, hung from his tusks as he threw his head from side to side and plowed out his pathway. Then Little Toomai laid himself down close to the great neck lest a swinging bough should sweep him to the ground, and he wished that he were back in the lines again.

The grass began to get squashy, and Kala Nag's feet sucked and squelched as he put them down, and the night mist at the bottom of the valley chilled Little Toomai. There was a splash and a trample, and the rush of running water, and Kala Nag strode through the bed of a river, feeling his way at each step. Above the noise of the water, as it swirled round the elephant's legs, Little Toomai could hear more splashing and some trumpeting both upstream and down—great grunts and angry snortings, and all the mist about him seemed to be full of rolling, wavy shadows.

"*Ai!*" he said, half aloud, his teeth chattering. "The elephant-folk are out tonight. It *is* the dance, then!"

Kala Nag swashed out of the water, blew his trunk clear, and began another climb. But this time he was not alone, and he had not to make his path. That was made already, six feet wide, in front of him, where the bent Jungle-grass was trying to recover itself and stand up. Many elephants must have gone that way only a few minutes before. Little Toomai looked back, and behind him a great wild tusker with his little pig's eyes glowing like hot coals was just lifting himself out of the misty river. Then the trees closed up again, and they went on and up, with trumpetings and crashings, and the sound of breaking branches on every side of them.

At last Kala Nag stood still between two tree-trunks at the very top of the hill. They were part of a circle of trees that grew round an irregular space of some three or four acres, and in all that space, as Little Toomai could see, the ground had been trampled down as hard as a brick floor. Some trees grew in the center of the clearing, but their bark was rubbed away, and the white wood beneath showed all shiny and polished in the patches of moonlight. There were creepers hanging from the upper branches, and the bells of the flowers of the creepers, great waxy white things like convolvuluses, hung down fast asleep. But within the limits of the clearing there was not a single blade of green—nothing but the trampled earth.

The moonlight showed it all iron gray, except where some elephants stood upon it, and their shadows were inky black. Little Toomai looked, holding his breath, with his eyes starting out of his head, and as he looked, more and more and more elephants swung out into the open from between the tree trunks. Little Toomai could only count up to ten, and he counted again and again on his fingers till he lost count of the tens, and his head began to swim. Outside the clearing he could hear them crashing in the undergrowth as they worked their way up the hillside, but as soon as they were within the circle of the tree trunks they moved like ghosts.

There were white-tusked wild males, with fallen leaves and nuts and twigs lying in the wrinkles of their necks and the folds of their ears; fat, slow-footed she-elephants, with restless, little pinky black calves only three or four feet high running under their stomachs; young elephants with their tusks just beginning to show, and very proud of them; lanky, scraggy old-maid elephants, with their hollow anxious faces, and trunks like rough bark; savage old bull elephants, scarred from shoulder to flank with great weals and cuts of bygone fights, and the caked dirt of their solitary mud baths dropping from their shoulders; and there was one with a broken tusk and the marks of the full-stroke, the terrible drawing scrape, of a tiger's claws on his side.

They were standing head to head, or walking to and fro across the ground in couples, or rocking and swaying all by themselves—scores and scores of elephants.

Toomai knew that so long as he lay still on Kala Nag's neck nothing would happen to him, for even in the rush and scramble of a Keddah drive a wild elephant does not reach up with his trunk and drag a man off the neck of a tame elephant. And these elephants were not thinking of men that night. Once they started and put their ears forward when they heard the chinking of a leg iron in the forest, but it was Pudmini, Petersen Sahib's pet elephant, her chain snapped short off, grunting, snuffling up the hillside. She must have broken her pickets and come straight from Petersen Sahib's camp; and Little Toomai saw another elephant, one that he did not know, with deep rope galls on his back and breast. He, too, must have run away from some camp in the hills about.

At last there was no sound of any more elephants moving in the forest, and Kala Nag rolled out from his station between the trees and went into the middle of the crowd, clucking and gurgling, and all the elephants began to talk in their own tongue, and to move about.

Still lying down, Little Toomai looked down upon scores and scores of broad backs, and wagging ears, and tossing trunks, and little rolling eyes. He heard the click of tusks as they crossed other tusks by accident, and the dry rustle of trunks twined together, and the chafing of enormous sides and shoulders in the crowd, and the incessant flick and *hissh* of the great tails. Then a cloud came over the moon, and he sat in black darkness. But the quiet, steady hustling and pushing and gurgling went on just the same. He knew that there were elephants all round Kala Nag, and that there was no chance of backing him out of the assembly; so he set his teeth and shivered. In a Keddah at least there was torchlight and shouting, but here he was all alone in the dark, and once a trunk came up and touched him on the knee.

Then an elephant trumpeted, and they all took it up for five or ten terrible seconds. The dew from the trees above spattered down like rain on the unseen backs, and a dull booming noise began, not very loud at first, and Little Toomai could not tell what it was. But it grew and grew, and Kala Nag lifted up one forefoot and then the other, and brought them down on the ground—one-two, one-two, as steadily as trip-hammers. The elephants were stamping all together now, and it sounded like a war drum beaten at the mouth of a cave. The dew fell from the trees till there was no more left to fall, and the booming went on, and the ground rocked and shivered, and Little Toomai put his hands up to his ears to shut out the sound. But it was all one gigantic jar that ran through him—this stamp of hundreds of heavy feet on the raw earth. Once or twice he could feel Kala Nag and all the others surge forward a few strides, and the thumping would change to the crushing sound of juicy green things being bruised, but in a minute or two the boom of feet on hard earth began again. A tree was creaking and groaning somewhere near him. He put out his arm and felt the bark, but Kala Nag moved forward, still tramping, and he could not tell where he was in the clearing. There was no sound from the elephants, except once, when two or three little calves squeaked together. Then he heard a thump and a shuffle, and the booming went on. It must have lasted fully two hours, and Little Toomai ached in every nerve, but he knew by the smell of the night air that the dawn was coming.

The morning broke in one sheet of pale yellow behind the green hills, and the booming stopped with the first ray, as though the light had been an order. Before Little Toomai had got the ringing out of his head, before even he had shifted his position, there was not an elephant in sight except Kala Nag, Pudmini, and the elephant with the rope-galls, and there was neither sign nor rustle nor whisper down the hillsides to show where the others had gone.

Little Toomai stared again and again. The clearing, as he remembered it, had grown in the night. More trees stood in the middle of it, but the undergrowth and the Jungle grass at the sides had been rolled back. Little Toomai stared once more. Now he understood the trampling. The elephants had stamped out more room—had stamped the thick grass and juicy cane to trash, the trash into slivers, the slivers into tiny fibers, and the fibers into hard earth.

"Wah!" said Little Toomai, and his eyes were very heavy. "Kala Nag, my lord, let us keep by Pudmini and go to Petersen Sahib's camp, or I shall drop from thy neck."

The third elephant watched the two go away, snorted, wheeled round, and took his own path. He may have belonged to some little native king's establishment, fifty or sixty or a hundred miles away.

Two hours later, as Petersen Sahib was eating early breakfast, his elephants, who had been double-chained that night, began to trumpet, and Pudmini, mired to the shoulders, with Kala Nag, very footsore, shambled into the camp.

Little Toomai's face was gray and pinched, and his hair was full of leaves and drenched with dew, but he tried to salute Petersen Sahib, and cried faintly: "The dance—the elephant dance! I have seen it, and—I die!" As Kala Nag sat down, he slid off his neck in a dead faint.

But, since native children have no nerves worth speaking of, in two hours he was lying very contentedly in Petersen Sahib's hammock with Petersen Sahib's shooting-coat under his head, and a glass of warm milk, a little brandy, with a dash of quinine, inside of him; and while the old hairy, scarred hunters of the Jungles sat three-deep before him, looking at him as though he were a spirit, he told his tale in short words, as a child will, and wound up with:

"Now, if I lie in one word, send men to see, and they will find that the elephant-folk have trampled down more room in their dance-room, and they will find ten and ten, and many times ten, tracks leading to that dance-room. They made more room with their feet. I have seen it. Kala Nag took me, and I saw. Also Kala Nag is very leg-weary!"

Little Toomai lay back and slept all through the long afternoon and into the twilight, and while he slept Petersen Sahib and Machua Appa followed the track of the two elephants for fifteen miles across the hills. Petersen Sahib had spent eighteen years in catching elephants, and he had only once before found such a dance-place. Machua Appa had no need to look twice at the clearing to see what had been done there, or to scratch with his toe in the packed, rammed earth.

"The child speaks truth," said he. "All this was done last night, and I have counted seventy tracks crossing the river. See, Sahib, where Pudmini's leg-iron cut the bark of that tree! Yes; she was there too."

They looked at one another and up and down, and they wondered. For the ways of elephants are beyond the wit of any man, black or white, to fathom.

"Forty years and five," said Machua Appa, "have I followed my lord, the elephant, but never have I heard that any child of man had seen what this child has seen. By all the Gods of the Hills, it is—what can we say?" and he shook his head.

When they got back to camp it was time for the evening meal. Petersen Sahib ate alone in his tent, but he gave orders that the camp should have two sheep and some fowls, as well as a double ration of flour and rice and salt, for he knew that there would be a feast.

Big Toomai had come up hotfoot from the camp in the plains to search for his son and his elephant, and now that he had found them he looked at them as though he were afraid of them both. And there was a feast by the blazing campfires in front of the lines of picketed elephants, and Little Toomai was the hero of it all. And the big brown elephant catchers, the trackers and drivers and ropers, and the men who know all the secrets of breaking the wildest elephants, passed him from one to the other, and they marked his forehead with blood from the breast of a newly killed jungle-cock, to show that he was a forester, initiated and free of all the Jungles.

And at last, when the flames died down, and the red light of the logs made the elephants look as though they had been dipped in blood too, Machua Appa, the head of all the drivers of all the Keddahs—Machua Appa, Petersen Sahib's other self, who had never seen a made road in forty years: Machua Appa, who was so great that he had no other name than Machua Appa—leaped to his feet, with Little Toomai held high in the air above his head, and shouted: "Listen, my brothers. Listen, too, you my lords in the lines there, for I, Machua Appa, am speaking! This little one shall no more be called Little Toomai, but Toomai of the Elephants, as his great-grandfather was called before him. What never man has seen he has seen through the long night, and the favor of the elephant-folk and of the Gods of the Jungles is with him. He shall become a great tracker. He shall become greater than I, even I—Machua Appa! He shall follow the new trail, and the stale trail, and the mixed trail, with a clear eye! He shall take no harm in the Keddah when he runs under their bellies to rope the wild tuskers; and if he slips before the feet of the charging bull-elephant, the bull-elephant shall know who he is and shall not crush him. *Aihai!* my lords in the chains,"—he whirled up the line of pickets— "here is the little one that has seen your dances in your hidden places—the sight that never man saw! Give him honor, my lords! *Salaam karo*, my children. Make your salute to Toomai of the Elephants! Gunga Pershad, ahaa! Hira Guj, Birchi Guj,

Kuttar Guj, ahaa! Pudmini—thou hast seen him at the dance, and thou too, Kala Nag, my pearl among elephants!—ahaa! Together! To Toomai of the Elephants. *Barrao!*"

And at that last wild yell the whole line flung up their trunks till the tips touched their foreheads, and broke out into the full salute—the crashing trumpet-peal that only the Viceroy of India hears—the Salaamut of the Keddah.

But it was all for the sake of Little Toomai, who had seen what never man had seen before—the dance of the elephants at night and alone in the heart of the Garo hills!

SHIV

AND THE GRASSHOPPER

(The song that Toomai's Mother sang to the Baby)

Shiv, who poured the harvest and made the winds to blow,
Sitting at the doorways of a day of long ago,
Gave to each his portion, food and toil and fate,
From the King upon the *guddee* to the Beggar at the gate.
All things made he—Shiva the Preserver.
Mahadeo! Mahadeo! He made all—
Thorn for the camel, fodder for the kine,
And mother's heart for sleepy head, O little son of mine!

Wheat he gave to rich folk, millet to the poor,
Broken scraps for holy men that beg from door to door;
Battle to the tiger, carrion to the kite,
And rags and bones to wicked wolves without the wall at night.
Naught he found too lofty, none he saw too low—
Parbati beside him watched them come and go;
Thought to cheat her husband, turning Shiv to jest—
Stole the little grasshopper and hid it in her breast.
So she tricked him, Shiva the Preserver.
Mahadeo! Mahadeo! turn and see.
Tall are the camels, heavy are the kine,
But this was Least of Little Things, O little son of mine!

When the dole was ended, laughingly she said,
'Master, of a million mouths, is not one unfed?'
Laughing, Shiv made answer, "All have had their part,
Even he, the little one, hidden next thy heart."

From her breast she plucked it, Parbati the thief,
Saw the Least of Little Things gnawed a new-grown leaf!
Saw and feared and wondered, making prayer to Shiv,
Who hath surely given meat to all that live.

All things made he—Shiva the Preserver.
Mahadeo! Mahadeo! He made all—
Thorn for the camel, fodder for the kine,
And mother's heart for sleepy head, O little son of mine!

HER MAJESTY'S SERVANTS

You can work it out by Fractions or by simple Rule of Three,
But the way of Tweedle-dum is not the way of Tweedle-dee.
You can twist it, you can turn it, you can plait it till you drop,
But the way of Pilly Winky's not the way of Winkie Pop!

It had been raining heavily for one whole month—raining
on a camp of thirty thousand men and thousands of
camels, elephants, horses, bullocks, and mules all gathered
together at a place called Rawalpindi, to be reviewed by the
Viceroy of India. He was receiving a visit from the Amir of
Afghanistan—a wild king of a very wild country and the
Amir had brought with him for a bodyguard eight hundred
men and horses who had never seen a camp or a locomotive
before in their lives—savage men and savage horses from
somewhere at the back of Central Asia. Every night a mob
of these horses would be sure to break their heel ropes and
stampede up and down the camp through the mud in the
dark, or the camels would break loose and run about and fall
over the ropes of the tents, and you can imagine how pleasant
that was for men trying to go to sleep. My tent lay far away
from the camel lines, and I thought it was safe. But one night
a man popped his head in and shouted, "Get out, quick!
They're coming! My tent's gone!"

I knew who "they" were, so I put on my boots and
waterproof and scuttled out into the slush. Little Vixen, my
fox-terrier, went out through the other side; and then there
was a roaring and a grunting and bubbling, and I saw the tent

cave in, as the pole snapped, and begin to dance about like a mad ghost. A camel had blundered into it, and wet and angry as I was, I could not help laughing. Then I ran on, because I did not know how many camels might have got loose, and before long I was out of sight of the camp, plowing my way through the mud.

At last I fell over the tail-end of a gun, and by that knew I was somewhere near the Artillery lines where the cannon were stacked at night. As I did not want to plowter about any more in the drizzle and the dark, I put my waterproof over the muzzle of one gun, and made a sort of wigwam with two or three rammers that I found, and lay along the tail of another gun, wondering where Vixen had got to, and where I might be.

Just as I was getting ready to go to sleep I heard a jingle of harness and a grunt, and a mule passed me shaking his wet ears. He belonged to a screw-gun battery, for I could hear the rattle of the straps and rings and chains and things on his saddle pad. The screw-guns are tiny little cannon made in two pieces, that are screwed together when the time comes to use them. They are taken up mountains, anywhere that a mule can find a road, and they are very useful for fighting in rocky country.

Behind the mule there was a camel, with his big soft feet squelching and slipping in the mud, and his neck bobbing to and fro like a strayed hen's. Luckily, I knew enough of beast language—not wild-beast language, but camp-beast language, of course—from the natives to know what he was saying.

He must have been the one that flopped into my tent, for he called to the mule, "What shall I do? Where shall I go? I have fought with a white thing that waved, and it took a stick and hit me on the neck." (That was my broken tent pole, and I was very glad to know it.) "Shall we run on?"

"Oh, it was you," said the mule, "you and your friends, that have been disturbing the camp? All right. You'll be beaten for this in the morning. But I may as well give you something on account now."

I heard the harness jingle as the mule backed and caught the camel two kicks in the ribs that rang like a drum. "Another time," he said, "you'll know better than to run through a mule battery at night, shouting 'Thieves and fire!' Sit down, and keep your silly neck quiet."

The camel doubled up camel-fashion, like a two-foot rule, and sat down whimpering. There was a regular beat of hoofs in the darkness, and a big troop-horse cantered up as steadily as though he were on parade, jumped a gun tail, and landed close to the mule.

"It's disgraceful," he said, blowing out his nostrils. "Those camels have racketed through our lines again—the third time this week. How's a horse to keep his condition if he isn't allowed to sleep. Who's here?"

"I'm the breech-piece mule of number two gun of the First Screw Battery," said the mule, "and the other's one of your friends. He's waked me up too. Who are you?"

"Number Fifteen, E troop, Ninth Lancers—Dick Cunliffe's horse. Stand over a little, there."

"Oh, beg your pardon," said the mule. "It's too dark to see much. Aren't these camels too sickening for anything? I walked out of my lines to get a little peace and quiet here."

"My lords," said the camel humbly, "we dreamed bad dreams in the night, and we were very much afraid. I am only a baggage camel of the 39th Native Infantry, and I am not as brave as you are, my lords."

"Then why didn't you stay and carry baggage for the 39th Native Infantry, instead of running all round the camp?" said the mule.

"They were such very bad dreams," said the camel. "I am sorry. Listen! What is that? Shall we run on again?"

"Sit down," said the mule, "or you'll snap your long stick-legs between the guns." He cocked one ear and listened. "Bullocks!" he said. "Gun-bullocks. On my word, you and your friends have waked the camp very thoroughly. It takes a good deal of prodding to put up a gun-bullock."

I heard a chain dragging along the ground, and a yoke of the great sulky white bullocks that drag the heavy siege guns when the elephants won't go any nearer to the firing, came shouldering along together. And almost stepping on the chain was another battery mule, calling wildly for "Billy."

"That's one of our recruits," said the old mule to the troop-horse. "He's calling for me. Here, youngster, stop squealing. The dark never hurt anybody yet."

The gun-bullocks lay down together and began chewing the cud, but the young mule huddled close to Billy.

"Things!" he said. "Fearful and horrible things, Billy! They came into our lines while we were asleep. D'you think they'll kill us?"

"I've a very great mind to give you a number-one kicking," said Billy. "The idea of a fourteen-hand mule with your training disgracing the battery before this gentleman!"

"Gently, gently!" said the troop-horse. "Remember they are always like this to begin with. The first time I ever saw a man (it was in Australia when I was a three-year-old) I ran for half a day, and if I'd seen a camel, I should have been running still."

Nearly all our horses for the English cavalry are brought to India from Australia, and are broken in by the troopers themselves.

"True enough," said Billy. "Stop shaking, youngster. The first time they put the full harness with all its chains on my back I stood on my forelegs and kicked every bit of it off. I hadn't learned the real science of kicking then, but the battery said they had never seen anything like it."

"But this wasn't harness or anything that jingled," said the young mule. "You know I don't mind that now, Billy. It was Things like trees, and they fell up and down the lines and bubbled; and my head-rope broke, and I couldn't find my driver, and I couldn't find you, Billy, so I ran off with—with these gentlemen."

"H'm!" said Billy. "As soon as I heard the camels were loose I came away on my own account. When a battery—a screw-gun mule calls gun-bullocks gentlemen, he must be very badly shaken up. Who are you fellows on the ground there?"

The gun-bullocks rolled their cuds, and answered both together: "The seventh yoke of the first gun of the Big Gun Battery. We were asleep when the camels came, but when we were trampled on we got up and walked away. It is better to lie quiet in the mud than to be disturbed on good bedding. We told your friend here that there was nothing to be afraid of, but he knew so much that he thought otherwise. Wah!"

They went on chewing.

"That comes of being afraid," said Billy. "You get laughed at by gun-bullocks. I hope you like it, young un."

The young mule's teeth snapped, and I heard him say something about not being afraid of any beefy old bullock in the world. But the bullocks only clicked their horns together and went on chewing.

"Now, don't be angry *after* you've been afraid. That's the worst kind of cowardice," said the troop-horse. "Anybody can be forgiven for being scared in the night, *I* think, if they see things they don't understand. We've broken out of our pickets, again and again, four hundred and fifty of us, just because a new recruit got to telling tales of whip-snakes at home in Australia till we were scared to death of the loose ends of our head-ropes."

"That's all very well in camp," said Billy. "I'm not above stampeding myself, for the fun of the thing, when I haven't been out for a day or two. But what do you do on active service?"

"Oh, that's quite another set of new shoes," said the troop-horse. "Dick Cunliffe's on my back then, and drives his knees into me, and all I have to do is to watch where I am putting my feet, and to keep my hind legs well under me, and be bridle-wise."

"What's bridle-wise?" said the young mule.

"By the Blue Gums of the Back Blocks," snorted the troop-horse, "do you mean to say that you aren't taught to be bridle-wise in your business? How can you do anything, unless you can spin round at once when the rein is pressed on your neck? It means life or death to your man, and of course that's life and death to you. Get round with your hind legs under you the instant you feel the rein on your neck. If you haven't room to swing round, rear up a little and come round on your hind legs. That's being bridle-wise."

"We aren't taught that way," said Billy the mule stiffly. "We're taught to obey the man at our head: step off when he says so, and step in when he says so. I suppose it comes to the same thing. Now, with all this fine fancy business and rearing, which must be very bad for your hocks, what do you *do*?"

"That depends," said the troop-horse. "Generally I have to go in among a lot of yelling, hairy men with knives—long shiny knives, worse than the farrier's knives—and I have to take care that Dick's boot is just touching the next man's boot without crushing it. I can see Dick's lance to the right of my right eye, and I know I'm safe. I shouldn't care to be the man or horse that stood up to Dick and me when we're in a hurry."

"Don't the knives hurt?" said the young mule.

"Well, I got one cut across the chest once, but that wasn't Dick's fault—"

"A lot I should have cared whose fault it was, if it hurt!" said the young mule.

"You must," said the troop-horse. "If you don't trust your

man, you may as well run away at once. That's what some of
our horses do, and I don't blame them. As I was saying, it wasn't
Dick's fault. The man was lying on the ground, and I stretched
myself not to tread on him, and he slashed up at me. Next time
I have to go over a man lying down I shall step on him—hard."

"H'm!" said Billy. "It sounds very foolish. Knives are dirty
things at any time. The proper thing to do is to climb up a
mountain with a well-balanced saddle, hang on by all four feet
and your ears too, and creep and crawl and wriggle along, till
you come out hundreds of feet above anyone else on a ledge
where there's just room enough for your hoofs. Then you stand
still and keep quiet—never ask a man to hold your head, young
un—keep quiet while the guns are being put together, and then
you watch the little poppy shells drop down into the tree-tops
ever so far below."

"Don't you ever trip?" said the troop-horse.

"They say that when a mule trips you can split a hen's ear,"
said Billy. "Now and again *per-haps* a badly packed saddle will
upset a mule, but it's very seldom. I wish I could show you our
business. It's beautiful. Why, it took me three years to find out
what the men were driving at. The science of the thing is never
to show up against the sky line, because, if you do, you may
get fired at. Remember that, young un. Always keep hidden
as much as possible, even if you have to go a mile out of your
way. I lead the battery when it comes to that sort of climbing."

"Fired at without the chance of running into the people
who are firing!" said the troop-horse, thinking hard. "I couldn't
stand that. I should want to charge—with Dick."

"Oh, no, you wouldn't. You know that as soon as the guns
are in position *they'll* do all the charging. That's scientific and
neat; but knives—pah!"

The baggage-camel had been bobbing his head to and fro
for some time past, anxious to get a word in edgewise. Then I
heard him say, as he cleared his throat, nervously:

"I—I—I have fought a little, but not in that climbing way or that running way."

"No. Now you mention it," said Billy, "you don't look as though you were made for climbing or running—much. Well, how was it, old Hay-bales?"

"The proper way," said the camel. "We all sat down—"

"Oh, my crupper and breastplate!" said the troop-horse under his breath. "Sat down!"

"We sat down—a hundred of us," the camel went on, "in a big square, and the men piled our packs and saddles, outside the square, and they fired over our backs, the men did, on all sides of the square."

"What sort of men? Any men that came along?" said the troop-horse. "They teach us in riding school to lie down and let our masters fire across us, but Dick Cunliffe is the only man I'd trust to do that. It tickles my girths, and, besides, I can't see with my head on the ground."

"What does it matter who fires across you?" said the camel. "There are plenty of men and plenty of other camels close by, and a great many clouds of smoke. I am not frightened then. I sit still and wait."

"And yet," said Billy, "you dream bad dreams and upset the camp at night. Well, well! Before I'd lie down, not to speak of sitting down, and let a man fire across me, my heels and his head would have something to say to each other. Did you ever hear anything so awful as that?"

There was a long silence, and then one of the gun-bullocks lifted up his big head and said, "This is very foolish indeed. There is only one way of fighting."

"Oh, go on," said Billy. "*Please* don't mind me. I suppose you fellows fight standing on your tails?"

"Only one way," said the two together. (They must have been twins.) "This is that way. To put all twenty yoke of us to the big gun as soon as Two Tails trumpets." ("Two Tails" is camp slang for the elephant.)

"What does Two Tails trumpet for?" said the young mule.

"To show that he is not going any nearer to the smoke on the other side. Two Tails is a great coward. Then we tug the big gun all together—*Heya—Hullah! Heeyah! Hullah!* We do not climb like cats nor run like calves. We go across the level plain, twenty yoke of us, till we are unyoked again, and we graze while the big guns talk across the plain to some town with mud walls, and pieces of the wall fall out, and the dust goes up as though many cattle were coming home."

"Oh! And you choose that time for grazing?" said the young mule.

"That time or any other. Eating is always good. We eat till we are yoked up again and tug the gun back to where Two Tails is waiting for it. Sometimes there are big guns in the city that speak back, and some of us are killed, and then there is all the more grazing for those that are left. This is Fate. None the less, Two Tails is a great coward. That is the proper way to fight. We are brothers from Hapur. Our father was a sacred bull of Shiva. We have spoken."

"Well, I've certainly learned something tonight," said the troop-horse. "Do you gentlemen of the screw-gun battery feel inclined to eat when you are being fired at with big guns, and Two Tails is behind you?"

"About as much as we feel inclined to sit down and let men sprawl all over us, or run into people with knives. I never heard such stuff. A mountain ledge, a well-balanced load, a driver you can trust to let you pick your own way, and I'm your mule. But—the other things—no!" said Billy, with a stamp of his foot.

"Of course," said the troop-horse, "everyone is not made in the same way, and I can quite see that your family, on your father's side, would fail to understand a great many things."

"Never you mind my family on my father's side," said Billy angrily, for every mule hates to be reminded that his father was a donkey. "My father was a Southern gentleman, and he could pull down and bite and kick into rags every horse he came across. Remember that, you big brown Brumby!"

Brumby means wild horse without any breeding. Imagine the feelings of Sunol if a car-horse called her a "skate," and you can imagine how the Australian horse felt. I saw the white of his eye glitter in the dark.

"See here, you son of an imported Malaga jackass," he said between his teeth, "I'd have you know that I'm related on my mother's side to Carbine, winner of the Melbourne Cup, and where I come from we aren't accustomed to being ridden over roughshod by any parrot-mouthed, pig-headed mule in a pop-gun pea-shooter battery. Are you ready?"

"On your hind legs!" squealed Billy. They both reared up facing each other, and I was expecting a furious fight, when a gurgly, rumbly voice, called out of the darkness to the right: "Children, what are you fighting about there? Be quiet."

Both beasts dropped down with a snort of disgust, for neither horse nor mule can bear to listen to an elephant's voice.

"It's Two Tails!" said the troop-horse. "I can't stand him. A tail at each end isn't fair!"

"My feelings exactly," said Billy, crowding into the troop-horse for company. "We're very alike in some things."

"I suppose we've inherited them from our mothers," said the troop-horse. "It's not worth quarreling about. Hi! Two Tails, are you tied up?"

"Yes," said Two Tails, with a laugh all up his trunk. "I'm picketed for the night. I've heard what you fellows have been saying. But don't be afraid. I'm not coming over."

The bullocks and the camel said, half aloud, "Afraid of Two Tails—what nonsense!" And the bullocks went on, "We are sorry that you heard, but it is true. Two Tails, why are you afraid of the guns when they fire?"

"Well," said Two Tails, rubbing one hind leg against the

other, exactly like a little boy saying a poem, "I don't quite know whether you'd understand."

"We don't, but we have to pull the guns," said the bullocks.

"I know it, and I know you are a good deal braver than you think you are. But it's different with me. My battery captain called me a Pachydermatous Anachronism the other day."

"That's another way of fighting, I suppose?" said Billy, who was recovering his spirits.

"*You* don't know what that means, of course, but I do. It means betwixt and between, and that is just where I am. I can see inside my head what will happen when a shell bursts, and you bullocks can't."

"I can," said the troop-horse. "At least a little bit. I try not to think about it."

"I can see more than you, and I *do* think about it. I know there's a great deal of me to take care of, and I know that nobody knows how to cure me when I'm sick. All they can do is to stop my driver's pay till I get well, and I can't trust my driver."

"Ah!" said the troop-horse. "That explains it. I can trust Dick."

"You could put a whole regiment of Dicks on my back without making me feel any better. I know just enough to be uncomfortable, and not enough to go on in spite of it."

"We do not understand," said the bullocks.

"I know you don't. I'm not talking to you. You don't know what blood is."

"We do," said the bullocks. "It is red stuff that soaks into the ground and smells."

The troop-horse gave a kick and a bound and a snort.

"Don't talk of it," he said. "I can smell it now, just thinking of it. It makes me want to run—when I haven't Dick on my back."

"But it is not here," said the camel and the bullocks. "Why

are you so stupid?"

"It's vile stuff," said Billy. "I don't want to run, but I don't want to talk about it."

"There you are!" said Two Tails, waving his tail to explain.

"Surely. Yes, we have been here all night," said the bullocks.

Two Tails stamped his foot till the iron ring on it jingled. "Oh, I'm not talking to *you*. You can't see inside your heads."

"No. We see out of our four eyes," said the bullocks. "We see straight in front of us."

"If I could do that and nothing else, you wouldn't be needed to pull the big guns at all. If I was like my captain—he can see things inside his head before the firing begins, and he shakes all over, but he knows too much to run away—if I was like him I could pull the guns. But if I were as wise as all that I should never be here. I should be a king in the forest, as I used to be, sleeping half the day and bathing when I liked. I haven't had a good bath for a month."

"That's all very fine," said Billy. "But giving a thing a long name doesn't make it any better."

"H'sh!" said the troop-horse. "I think I understand what Two Tails means."

"You'll understand better in a minute," said Two Tails angrily. "Now you just explain to me why you don't like *this*!"

He began trumpeting furiously at the top of his trumpet.

"Stop that!" said Billy and the troop-horse together, and I could hear them stamp and shiver. An elephant's trumpeting is always nasty, especially on a dark night.

"I shan't stop," said Two Tails. "Won't you explain that, please? *Hhrrmph! Rrrt! Rrrmph! Rrrhha!*" Then he stopped suddenly, and I heard a little whimper in the dark, and knew that Vixen had found me at last. She knew as well as I did that if there is one thing in the world the elephant is more afraid of than another it is a little barking dog. So she stopped to bully Two Tails in his pickets, and yapped round his big feet. Two

Tails shuffled and squeaked. "Go away, little dog!" he said. "Don't snuff at my ankles, or I'll kick at you. Good little dog— nice little doggie, then! Go home, you yelping little beast! Oh, why doesn't someone take her away? She'll bite me in a minute."

"Seems to me," said Billy to the troop-horse, "that our friend Two Tails is afraid of most things. Now, if I had a full meal for every dog I've kicked across the parade-ground I should be as fat as Two Tails nearly."

I whistled, and Vixen ran up to me, muddy all over, and licked my nose, and told me a long tale about hunting for me all through the camp. I never let her know that I understood beast talk, or she would have taken all sorts of liberties. So I buttoned her into the breast of my overcoat, and Two Tails shuffled and stamped and growled to himself.

"Extraordinary! Most extraordinary!" he said. "It runs in our family. Now, where has that nasty little beast gone to?"

I heard him feeling about with his trunk.

"We all seem to be affected in various ways," he went on, blowing his nose. "Now, you gentlemen were alarmed, I believe, when I trumpeted."

"Not alarmed, exactly," said the troop-horse, "but it made me feel as though I had hornets where my saddle ought to be. Don't begin again."

"I'm frightened of a little dog, and the camel here is frightened by bad dreams in the night."

"It is very lucky for us that we haven't all got to fight in the same way," said the troop-horse.

"What I want to know," said the young mule, who had been quiet for a long time—"what I want to know is, why we have to fight at all."

"Because we're told to," said the troop-horse, with a snort of contempt.

"Orders," said Billy the mule, and his teeth snapped.

"*Hukm hai!*" (It is an order!), said the camel with a gurgle, and Two Tails and the bullocks repeated, "*Hukm hai!*"

"Yes, but who gives the orders?" said the recruit-mule.

"The man who walks at your head—Or sits on your back— Or holds the nose rope—Or twists your tail," said Billy and the troop-horse and the camel and the bullocks one after the other.

"But who gives them the orders?"

"Now you want to know too much, young un," said Billy, "and that is one way of getting kicked. All you have to do is to obey the man at your head and ask no questions."

"He's quite right," said Two Tails. "I can't always obey, because I'm betwixt and between. But Billy's right. Obey the man next to you who gives the order, or you'll stop all the battery, besides getting a thrashing."

The gun-bullocks got up to go. "Morning is coming," they said. "We will go back to our lines. It is true that we only see out of our eyes, and we are not very clever. But still, we are the only people to-night who have not been afraid. Good-night, you brave people."

Nobody answered, and the troop-horse said, to change the conversation, "Where's that little dog? A dog means a man somewhere about."

"Here I am," yapped Vixen, "under the gun-tail with my man. You big, blundering beast of a camel you, you upset our tent. My man's very angry."

"Phew!" said the bullocks. "He must be white!"

"Of course he is," said Vixen. "Do you suppose I'm looked after by a black bullock-driver?"

"*Huah! Ouach! Ugh!*" said the bullocks. "Let us get away quickly."

They plunged forward in the mud, and managed somehow to run their yoke on the pole of an ammunition wagon, where it jammed.

"Now you *have* done it," said Billy calmly. "Don't struggle. You're hung up till daylight. What on earth's the matter?"

The bullocks went off into the long hissing snorts that Indian cattle give, and pushed and crowded and slued and stamped and slipped and nearly fell down in the mud, grunting savagely.

"You'll break your necks in a minute," said the troop-horse. "What's the matter with white men? I live with 'em."

"They—eat—us! Pull!" said the near bullock. The yoke snapped with a twang, and they lumbered off together.

I never knew before what made Indian cattle so scared of Englishmen. We eat beef—a thing that no cattle-driver touches—and of course the cattle do not like it.

"May I be flogged with my own pad-chains! Who'd have thought of two big lumps like those losing their heads?" said Billy.

"Never mind. I'm going to look at this man. Most of the white men, I know, have things in their pockets," said the troop-horse.

"I'll leave you, then. I can't say I'm over-fond of 'em myself. Besides, white men who haven't a place to sleep in are more than likely to be thieves, and I've a good deal of Government property on my back. Come along, young un, and we'll go back to our lines. Good-night, Australia! See you on parade to-morrow, I suppose. Good-night, old Hay-bales!—try to control your feelings, won't you? Good-night, Two Tails! If you pass us on the ground tomorrow, don't trumpet. It spoils our formation."

Billy the mule stumped off with the swaggering limp of an old campaigner, as the troop-horse's head came nuzzling into my breast, and I gave him biscuits; while Vixen, who is a most conceited little dog, told him fibs about the scores of horses that she and I kept.

"I'm coming to the parade to-morrow in my dog-cart," she said. "Where will you be?"

"On the left hand of the second squadron. I set the time for

THE JUNGLE BOOK   161

all my troop, little lady," he said politely. "Now I must go back
to Dick. My tail's all muddy, and he'll have two hours' hard
work dressing me for parade."

The big parade of all the thirty thousand men was held
that afternoon, and Vixen and I had a good place close to the
Viceroy and the Amir of Afghanistan, with high, big black hat
of astrakhan wool and the great diamond star in the center.
The first part of the review was all sunshine, and the regiments
went by in wave upon wave of legs all moving together, and
guns all in a line, till our eyes grew dizzy. Then the cavalry
came up, to the beautiful cavalry canter of "Bonnie Dundee,"
and Vixen cocked her ear where she sat on the dog-cart. The
second squadron of the Lancers shot by, and there was the
troop-horse, with his tail like spun silk, his head pulled into
his breast, one ear forward and one back, setting the time for
all his squadron, his legs going as smoothly as waltz music.
Then the big guns came by, and I saw Two Tails and two other
elephants harnessed in line to a forty-pounder siege-gun, while
twenty yoke of oxen walked behind. The seventh pair had a
new yoke, and they looked rather stiff and tired. Last came
the screw-guns, and Billy the mule carried himself as though
he commanded all the troops, and his harness was oiled and
polished till it winked. I gave a cheer all by myself for Billy the
mule, but he never looked right or left.

The rain began to fall again, and for a while it was too
misty to see what the troops were doing. They had made a
big half circle across the plain, and were spreading out into
a line. That line grew and grew and grew till it was three-
quarters of a mile long from wing to wing—one solid wall
of men, horses, and guns. Then it came on straight toward
the Viceroy and the Amir, and as it got nearer the ground
began to shake, like the deck of a steamer when the engines
are going fast.

Unless you have been there you cannot imagine what a

frightening effect this steady come-down of troops has on the spectators, even when they know it is only a review. I looked at the Amir. Up till then he had not shown the shadow of a sign of astonishment or anything else. But now his eyes began to get bigger and bigger, and he picked up the reins on his horse's neck and looked behind him. For a minute it seemed as though he were going to draw his sword and slash his way out through the English men and women in the carriages at the back. Then the advance stopped dead, the ground stood still, the whole line saluted, and thirty bands began to play all together. That was the end of the review, and the regiments went off to their camps in the rain, and an infantry band struck up:

> The animals went in two by two,
> Hurrah!
> The animals went in two by two,
> The elephant and the battery mul',
> and they all got into the Ark
> For to get out of the rain!

Then I heard an old grizzled, long-haired Central Asian chief, who had come down with the Amir, asking questions of a native officer.

"Now," said he, "in what manner was this wonderful thing done?"

And the officer answered, "An order was given, and they obeyed."

"But are the beasts as wise as the men?" said the chief.

"They obey, as the men do. Mule, horse, elephant, or bullock, he obeys his driver, and the driver his sergeant, and the sergeant his lieutenant, and the lieutenant his captain, and the captain his major, and the major his colonel, and the colonel his brigadier commanding three regiments, and the brigadier the general, who obeys the Viceroy, who is the servant of the Empress. Thus it is done."

"Would it were so in Afghanistan!" said the chief, "for there we obey only our own wills."

"And for that reason," said the native officer, twirling his mustache, "your Amir whom you do not obey must come here and take orders from our Viceroy."

PARADE SONG OF THE CAMP ANIMALS

•

Elephants of the Gun-Teams

We lent to Alexander the strength of Hercules,
The wisdom of our foreheads, the cunning of our knees;
We bowed our necks to service: they ne'er were loosed again—
Make way there—way for the ten-foot teams
    Of the Forty-Pounder train!

Gun-Bullocks

Those heroes in their harnesses avoid a cannon-ball,
And what they know of powder upsets them one and all;
Then we come into action and tug the guns again—
Make way there—way for the twenty yoke
    Of the Forty-Pounder train!

Cavalry Horses

By the brand on my withers, the finest of tunes
Is played by the Lancers, Hussars, and Dragoons,
And it's sweeter than "Stables" or "Water" to me,
The Cavalry Canter of "Bonnie Dundee"!

Then feed us and break us and handle and groom,
And give us good riders and plenty of room,
And launch us in column of squadron and see
The way of the war-horse to "Bonnie Dundee"!

Screw-Gun Mules

As me and my companions
    were scrambling up a hill,
The path was lost in rolling stones, but
...... we went forward still;
For we can wriggle and climb, my lads,
    and turn up everywhere,
And it's our delight on a mountain
.......height, with a leg or two to spare!
Good luck to every sergeant, then, that
    lets us pick our road!
Bad luck to all the driver-men that
    cannot pack a load!
For we can wriggle and climb, my lads,
    and turn up everywhere,
  And, it's our delight on a mountain
    height, with a leg or two to spare!

Commissariat Camels

We haven't a camelty tune of our own
To help us trollop along,
But every neck is a hair trombone
(*Rtt-ta-ta-ta!* is a hair trombone!)
And this our marching-song:
Can't! Don't! Shan't! Won't!
Pass it along the line!
Somebody's pack has slid from his back,
'Wish it were only mine!
Somebody's load has tipped off in the road—
Cheer for a halt and a row!
Urrr! Yarrh! Grr! Arrh!
Somebody's catching it now!

All The Beasts Together

Children of the Camp are we,
Serving each in his degree;
Children of the yoke and goad,
Pack and harness, pad and load.
See our line across the plain,
Like a heel-rope bent again,
Reaching, writhing, rolling far,
Sweeping all away to war!
While the men that walk beside,
Dusty, silent, heavy-eyed,
Cannot tell why we or they
March and suffer day by day.

> *Children of the Camp are we,*
> *Serving each in his degree;*
> *Children of the yoke and goad,*
> *Pack and harness, pad and load!*

The Strange Case of
Dr Jekyll
and Mr Hyde

The Strange Case of
Dr Jekyll
and Mr Hyde

Robert Louis Stevenson

Trans
Atlantic
Press

This is a Transatlantic Press book
This edition published in 2012

Transatlantic Press
Sky House, Raans Road, Amersham, Bucks, HP6 6JQ, UK

Cover image © GettyImages
Author biography © Transatlantic Press

A catalogue record is available for this book from the British Library

ISBN 978-1-908533-16-6

Printed and bound by CPI Group (UK) Ltd, Croydon, CR0 4YY, UK

ROBERT LOUIS STEVENSON

Robert Louis Stevenson was born in Edinburgh in 1850, the son of an engineer who specialised in the field of lighthouse construction. He flirted briefly with the idea of following in his father's footsteps, embarking on an engineering degree in his hometown university. But he had neither the constitution – he was dogged by ill health throughout his life – nor the inclination to pursue that course and instead became a law student. His roving spirit and desire to write put the brakes on a legal career before it started. Having got into print in magazines and periodicals, Stevenson published *An Inland Voyage* (1878) and *Travels with a Donkey in the Cévennes* (1879), accounts of his travels through France and Belgium. *Treasure Island* (1883) brought him fame, and his later novels, such as *Kidnapped* (1886), its sequel *Catriona* (1893) and *The Master of Ballantrae* (1889) established his reputation in the historical adventure genre. He provided thrills of a different kind with *The Strange Case of Dr. Jekyll and Mr. Hyde*, which ranks among the best in the Gothic literature tradition. In 1888 he set sail for the South Seas with his family, settling in Samoa, where he spent his final years. He became a great advocate for the islanders, who in turn had great affection for the man they called "Tusitala" – "Teller of Tales". Stevenson died from a cerebral haemorrhage in 1894, leaving an unfinished novel, *Weir of Hermiston*, which was published posthumously.

THE STRANGE CASE OF DR JEKYLL AND MR HYDE

"…my virtue slumbered; my evil, kept awake by ambition, was alert and swift to seize the occasion; and the thing that was projected was Edward Hyde."

Dr Henry Jekyll is convinced that inside him instincts for good vie with darker impulses. Interested in separating these competing forces within, he develops a potion that brings his evil side to the fore: the hideous Mr. Hyde, who engages in wanton violence unencumbered by moral restraint. At first Jekyll remains in command of the situation, but the transformations spin out of control and his malevolent alter ego threatens to get the upper hand. What began as a fascinating scientific experiment becomes a battle to prevent unfettered evil from wreaking untold havoc.

Stevenson uses multiple narratives to weave a gripping supernatural tale with an unpalatable core conceit: that base instincts lurk within us, dormant, suppressed, waiting to be triggered.

The Strange Case of
Dr Jekyll
and Mr Hyde

CONTENTS

CHAPTER 1
Story of the door

MR. UTTERSON the lawyer was a man of a rugged countenance, that was never lighted by a smile; cold, scanty and embarrassed in discourse; backward in sentiment; lean, long, dusty, dreary, and yet somehow lovable. At friendly meetings, and when the wine was to his taste, something eminently human beaconed from his eye; something indeed which never found its way into his talk, but which spoke not only in these silent symbols of the after-dinner face, but more often and loudly in the acts of his life. He was austere with himself; drank gin when he was alone, to mortify a taste for vintages; and though he enjoyed the theatre, had not crossed the doors of one for twenty years. But he had an approved tolerance for others; sometimes wondering, almost with envy, at the high pressure of spirits involved in their misdeeds; and in any extremity inclined to help rather than to reprove. "I incline to Cain's heresy," he used to say quaintly: "I let my brother go to the devil in his own way." In this character, it was frequently his fortune to be the last reputable acquaintance and the last good influence in the lives of down-going men. And to such as these, so long as they came about his chambers, he never marked a shade of change in his demeanour.

No doubt the feat was easy to Mr. Utterson; for he was undemonstrative at the best, and even his friendship seemed to be founded in a similar catholicity of good-nature. It is the mark of a modest man to accept his friendly circle ready-made from the hands of opportunity; and that was the lawyer's way.

His friends were those of his own blood or those whom he had known the longest; his affections, like ivy, were the growth of time, they implied no aptness in the object. Hence, no doubt, the bond that united him to Mr. Richard Enfield, his distant kinsman, the well-known man about town. It was a nut to crack for many, what these two could see in each other, or what subject they could find in common. It was reported by those who encountered them in their Sunday walks, that they said nothing, looked singularly dull, and would hail with obvious relief the appearance of a friend. For all that, the two men put the greatest store by these excursions, counted them the chief jewel of each week, and not only set aside occasions of pleasure, but even resisted the calls of business, that they might enjoy them uninterrupted.

It chanced on one of these rambles that their way led them down a by-street in a busy quarter of London. The street was small and what is called quiet, but it drove a thriving trade on the week-days. The inhabitants were all doing well, it seemed, and all emulously hoping to do better still, and laying out the surplus of their gains in coquetry; so that the shop fronts stood along that thoroughfare with an air of invitation, like rows of smiling saleswomen. Even on Sunday, when it veiled its more florid charms and lay comparatively empty of passage, the street shone out in contrast to its dingy neighbourhood, like a fire in a forest; and with its freshly painted shutters, well-polished brasses, and general cleanliness and gaiety of note, instantly caught and pleased the eye of the passenger.

Two doors from one corner, on the left hand going east, the line was broken by the entry of a court; and just at that point, a certain sinister block of building thrust forward its gable on the street. It was two stories high; showed no window, nothing but a door on the lower story and a blind forehead of discoloured wall on the upper; and bore in every feature, the marks of prolonged and sordid negligence. The door, which was equipped with neither bell nor knocker, was blistered and distained. Tramps slouched into the recess and struck matches on the panels; children kept shop upon the steps; the schoolboy had tried his knife on the mouldings; and for close on a generation, no one had appeared to drive away these random visitors or to repair their ravages.

Mr. Enfield and the lawyer were on the other side of the by-street; but when they came abreast of the entry, the former lifted up his cane and pointed.

"Did you ever remark that door?" he asked; and when his companion had replied in the affirmative, "It is connected in my mind," added he, "with a very odd story."

"Indeed!" said Mr. Utterson, with a slight change of voice, "and what was that?"

"Well, it was this way," returned Mr. Enfield: "I was coming home from some place at the end of the world, about three o'clock of a black winter morning, and my way lay through a part of town where there was literally nothing to be seen but lamps. Street after street, and all the folks asleep - street after street, all lighted up as if for a procession and all as empty as a church - till at last I got into that state of mind when a man listens and listens and begins to long for the sight of a policeman. All at once, I saw two figures: one a little man who was stumping along eastward at a good walk, and the other a girl of maybe eight or ten who was running as hard as she was able down a cross street. Well, sir, the two ran into one another naturally enough at the corner; and then came the horrible part of the thing; for the man trampled calmly over the child's body and left her screaming on the ground. It sounds nothing to hear, but it was hellish to see. It wasn't like a man; it was like some damned Juggernaut. I gave a view-halloa, took to my heels, collared my gentleman, and brought him back to where there was already quite a group about the screaming child. He was perfectly cool and made no resistance, but gave me one

look, so ugly that it brought out the sweat on me like running.
The people who had turned out were the girl's own family; and
pretty soon, the doctor, for whom she had been sent, put in
his appearance. Well, the child was not much the worse, more
frightened, according to the Sawbones; and there you might
have supposed would be an end to it. But there was one curious
circumstance. I had taken a loathing to my gentleman at first
sight. So had the child's family, which was only natural. But
the doctor's case was what struck me. He was the usual cut-
and-dry apothecary, of no particular age and colour, with a
strong Edinburgh accent, and about as emotional as a bagpipe.
Well, sir, he was like the rest of us; every time he looked at
my prisoner, I saw that Sawbones turn sick and white with the
desire to kill him. I knew what was in his mind, just as he knew
what was in mine; and killing being out of the question, we did
the next best. We told the man we could and would make such
a scandal out of this, as should make his name stink from one
end of London to the other. If he had any friends or any credit,
we undertook that he should lose them. And all the time, as
we were pitching it in red hot, we were keeping the women off
him as best we could, for they were as wild as harpies. I never
saw a circle of such hateful faces; and there was the man in the
middle, with a kind of black, sneering coolness - frightened
too, I could see that - but carrying it off, sir, really like Satan.
'If you choose to make capital out of this accident,' said he,
'I am naturally helpless. No gentleman but wishes to avoid a
scene,' says he. 'Name your figure.' Well, we screwed him up to
a hundred pounds for the child's family; he would have clearly
liked to stick out; but there was something about the lot of us
that meant mischief, and at last he struck. The next thing was
to get the money; and where do you think he carried us but to
that place with the door? - whipped out a key, went in, and
presently came back with the matter of ten pounds in gold and
a cheque for the balance on Coutts's, drawn payable to bearer

and signed with a name that I can't mention, though it's one of the points of my story, but it was a name at least very well known and often printed. The figure was stiff; but the signature was good for more than that, if it was only genuine. I took the liberty of pointing out to my gentleman that the whole business looked apocryphal, and that a man does not, in real life, walk into a cellar door at four in the morning and come out of it with another man's cheque for close upon a hundred pounds. But he was quite easy and sneering. 'Set your mind at rest,' says he; 'I will stay with you till the banks open and cash the cheque myself.' So we all set off, the doctor, and the child's father, and our friend and myself, and passed the rest of the night in my chambers; and next day, when we had breakfasted, went in a body to the bank. I gave in the check myself, and said I had every reason to believe it was a forgery. Not a bit of it. The cheque was genuine."

"Tut-tut," said Mr. Utterson.

"I see you feel as I do," said Mr. Enfield. "Yes, it's a bad story. For my man was a fellow that nobody could have to do with, a really damnable man; and the person that drew the cheque is the very pink of the proprieties, celebrated too, and (what makes it worse) one of your fellows who do what they call good. Black-mail, I suppose; an honest man paying through the nose for some of the capers of his youth. Black-Mail House is what I call that place with the door, in consequence. Though even that, you know, is far from explaining all," he added, and with the words fell into a vein of musing.

From this he was recalled by Mr. Utterson asking rather suddenly: "And you don't know if the drawer of the cheque lives there?"

"A likely place, isn't it?" returned Mr. Enfield. "But I happen to have noticed his address; he lives in some square or other."

"And you never asked about the - place with the door?" said Mr. Utterson.

"No, sir: I had a delicacy," was the reply. "I feel very strongly about putting questions; it partakes too much of the style of the day of judgment. You start a question, and it's like starting a stone. You sit quietly on the top of a hill; and away the stone goes, starting others; and presently some bland old bird (the last you would have thought of) is knocked on the head in his own back-garden and the family have to change their name. No, sir, I make it a rule of mine: the more it looks like Queer Street, the less I ask."

"A very good rule, too," said the lawyer.

"But I have studied the place for myself," continued Mr. Enfield. "It seems scarcely a house. There is no other door, and nobody goes in or out of that one but, once in a great while, the gentleman of my adventure. There are three windows looking on the court on the first floor; none below; the windows are always shut but they're clean. And then there is a chimney which is generally smoking; so somebody must live there. And yet it's not so sure; for the buildings are so packed together about that court, that it's hard to say where one ends and another begins."

The pair walked on again for a while in silence; and then - "Enfield," said Mr. Utterson, "that's a good rule of yours."

"Yes, I think it is," returned Enfield.

"But for all that," continued the lawyer, "there's one point I want to ask: I want to ask the name of that man who walked over the child."

"Well," said Mr. Enfield, "I can't see what harm it would do. It was a man of the name of Hyde."

"Hm," said Mr. Utterson. "What sort of a man is he to see?"

"He is not easy to describe. There is something wrong with his appearance; something displeasing, something downright detestable. I never saw a man I so disliked, and yet I scarce know why. He must be deformed somewhere; he gives a strong feeling of deformity, although I couldn't specify the point. He's an extraordinary-looking man, and yet I really can name nothing out of the way. No, sir; I can make no hand of it; I can't describe him. And it's not want of memory; for I declare I can see him this moment."

Mr. Utterson again walked some way in silence and obviously under a weight of consideration. "You are sure he used a key?" he inquired at last.

"My dear sir..." began Enfield, surprised out of himself.

"Yes, I know," said Utterson; "I know it must seem strange. The fact is, if I do not ask you the name of the other party, it is because I know it already. You see, Richard, your tale has gone home. If you have been inexact in any point, you had better correct it."

"I think you might have warned me," returned the other, with a touch of sullenness. "But I have been pedantically exact, as you call it. The fellow had a key; and what's more, he has it still. I saw him use it, not a week ago."

Mr. Utterson sighed deeply but said never a word; and the young man presently resumed. "Here is another lesson to say nothing," said he. "I am ashamed of my long tongue. Let us make a bargain never to refer to this again."

"With all my heart," said the lawyer. "I shake hands on that, Richard."

CHAPTER 2
Search for Mr. Hyde

THAT evening Mr. Utterson came home to his bachelor
house in sombre spirits and sat down to dinner without
relish. It was his custom of a Sunday, when this meal was
over, to sit close by the fire, a volume of some dry divinity
on his reading-desk, until the clock of the neighbouring
church rang out the hour of twelve, when he would go soberly
and gratefully to bed. On this night, however, as soon as the
cloth was taken away, he took up a candle and went into his
business-room. There he opened his safe, took from the most
private part of it a document endorsed on the envelope as Dr.
Jekyll's Will, and sat down with a clouded brow to study its
contents. The will was holograph, for Mr. Utterson, though he
took charge of it now that it was made, had refused to lend the
least assistance in the making of it; it provided not only that,
in case of the decease of Henry Jekyll, M.D., D.C.L., L.L.D.,
F.R.S., etc., all his possessions were to pass into the hands of
his "friend and benefactor Edward Hyde," but that in case of
Dr. Jekyll's "disappearance or unexplained absence for any
period exceeding three calendar months," the said Edward
Hyde should step into the said Henry Jekyll's shoes without
further delay and free from any burthen or obligation, beyond
the payment of a few small sums to the members of the
doctor's household. This document had long been the lawyer's
eyesore. It offended him both as a lawyer and as a lover of
the sane and customary sides of life, to whom the fanciful
was the immodest. And hitherto it was his ignorance of Mr.

Hyde that had swelled his indignation; now, by a sudden turn, it was his knowledge. It was already bad enough when the name was but a name of which he could learn no more. It was worse when it began to be clothed upon with detestable attributes; and out of the shifting, insubstantial mists that had so long baffled his eye, there leaped up the sudden, definite presentment of a fiend.

"I thought it was madness," he said, as he replaced the obnoxious paper in the safe, "and now I begin to fear it is disgrace."

With that he blew out his candle, put on a great-coat, and set forth in the direction of Cavendish Square, that citadel of medicine, where his friend, the great Dr. Lanyon, had his house and received his crowding patients. "If any one knows, it will be Lanyon," he had thought.

The solemn butler knew and welcomed him; he was subjected to no stage of delay, but ushered direct from the door to the dining-room where Dr. Lanyon sat alone over his wine. This was a hearty, healthy, dapper, red-faced gentleman, with a shock of hair prematurely white, and a boisterous and decided manner. At sight of Mr. Utterson, he sprang up from his chair and welcomed him with both hands. The geniality, as was the way of the man, was somewhat theatrical to the eye; but it reposed on genuine feeling. For these two were old friends, old mates both at school and college, both thorough respecters of themselves and of each other, and, what does not always follow, men who thoroughly enjoyed each other's company.

After a little rambling talk, the lawyer led up to the subject which so disagreeably pre-occupied his mind.

"I suppose, Lanyon," said he "you and I must be the two oldest friends that Henry Jekyll has?"

"I wish the friends were younger," chuckled Dr. Lanyon. "But I suppose we are. And what of that? I see little of him now."

"Indeed?" said Utterson. "I thought you had a bond of common interest."

"We had," was the reply. "But it is more than ten years since Henry Jekyll became too fanciful for me. He began to go wrong, wrong in mind; and though of course I continue to take an interest in him for old sake's sake, as they say, I see and I have seen devilish little of the man. Such unscientific balderdash," added the doctor, flushing suddenly purple, "would have estranged Damon and Pythias."

This little spirit of temper was somewhat of a relief to Mr. Utterson. "They have only differed on some point of science," he thought; and being a man of no scientific passions (except in the matter of conveyancing), he even added: "It is nothing worse than that!" He gave his friend a few seconds to recover his composure, and then approached the question he had come to put. "Did you ever come across a *protégé* of his - one Hyde?" he asked.

"Hyde?" repeated Lanyon. "No. Never heard of him. Since my time."

That was the amount of information that the lawyer carried back with him to the great, dark bed on which he tossed to and fro, until the small hours of the morning began to grow large. It was a night of little ease to his toiling mind, toiling in mere darkness and besieged by questions.

Six o'clock struck on the bells of the church that was so conveniently near to Mr. Utterson's dwelling, and still he was digging at the problem. Hitherto it had touched him on the intellectual side alone; but now his imagination also was engaged, or rather enslaved; and as he lay and tossed in the gross darkness of the night and the curtained room, Mr. Enfield's tale went by before his mind in a scroll of lighted pictures. He would be aware of the great field of lamps of a nocturnal city; then of the figure of a man walking swiftly; then of a child running from the doctor's; and then these met, and that human

Juggernaut trod the child down and passed on regardless of her screams. Or else he would see a room in a rich house, where his friend lay asleep, dreaming and smiling at his dreams; and then the door of that room would be opened, the curtains of the bed plucked apart, the sleeper recalled, and lo! there would stand by his side a figure to whom power was given, and even at that dead hour, he must rise and do its bidding. The figure in these two phases haunted the lawyer all night; and if at any time he dozed over, it was but to see it glide more stealthily through sleeping houses, or move the more swiftly and still the more swiftly, even to dizziness, through wider labyrinths of lamplighted city, and at every street-corner crush a child and leave her screaming. And still the figure had no face by which he might know it; even in his dreams, it had no face, or one that baffled him and melted before his eyes; and thus it was that there sprang up and grew apace in the lawyer's mind a singularly strong, almost an inordinate, curiosity to behold the features of the real Mr. Hyde. If he could but once set eyes on him, he thought the mystery would lighten and perhaps roll altogether away, as was the habit of mysterious things when well examined. He might see a reason for his friend's strange preference or bondage (call it which you please) and even for the startling clause of the will. At least it would be a face worth seeing: the face of a man who was without bowels of mercy: a face which had but to show itself to raise up, in the mind of the unimpressionable Enfield, a spirit of enduring hatred.

From that time forward, Mr. Utterson began to haunt the door in the by-street of shops. In the morning before office hours, at noon when business was plenty, and time scarce, at night under the face of the fogged city moon, by all lights and at all hours of solitude or concourse, the lawyer was to be found on his chosen post.

"If he be Mr. Hyde," he had thought, "I shall be Mr. Seek."

And at last his patience was rewarded. It was a fine dry

night; frost in the air; the streets as clean as a ballroom floor; the lamps, unshaken, by any wind, drawing a regular pattern of light and shadow. By ten o'clock, when the shops were closed, the by-street was very solitary and, in spite of the low growl of London from all round, very silent. Small sounds carried far; domestic sounds out of the houses were clearly audible on either side of the roadway; and the rumour of the approach of any passenger preceded him by a long time. Mr. Utterson had been some minutes at his post, when he was aware of an odd, light footstep drawing near. In the course of his nightly patrols, he had long grown accustomed to the quaint effect with which the footfalls of a single person, while he is still a great way off, suddenly spring out distinct from the vast hum and clatter of the city. Yet his attention had never before been so sharply and decisively arrested; and it was with a strong, superstitious prevision of success that he withdrew into the entry of the court.

The steps drew swiftly nearer, and swelled out suddenly louder as they turned the end of the street. The lawyer, looking forth from the entry, could soon see what manner of man he had to deal with. He was small and very plainly dressed, and the look of him, even at that distance, went somehow strongly against the watcher's inclination. But he made straight for the door, crossing the roadway to save time; and as he came, he drew a key from his pocket like one approaching home.

Mr. Utterson stepped out and touched him on the shoulder as he passed. "Mr. Hyde, I think?"

Mr. Hyde shrank back with a hissing intake of the breath. But his fear was only momentary; and though he did not look the lawyer in the face, he answered coolly enough: "That is my name. What do you want?"

"I see you are going in," returned the lawyer. "I am an old friend of Dr. Jekyll's - Mr. Utterson of Gaunt Street - you must have heard my name; and meeting you so conveniently, I thought you might admit me."

"You will not find Dr. Jekyll; he is from home," replied Mr. Hyde, blowing in the key. And then suddenly, but still without looking up, "How did you know me?" he asked.

"On your side," said Mr. Utterson, "will you do me a favour?"

"With pleasure," replied the other. "What shall it be?"

"Will you let me see your face?" asked the lawyer.

Mr. Hyde appeared to hesitate, and then, as if upon some sudden reflection, fronted about with an air of defiance; and the pair stared at each other pretty fixedly for a few seconds. "Now I shall know you again," said Mr. Utterson. "It may be useful."

"Yes," returned Mr. Hyde, "it is as well we have, met; and *à propos*, you should have my address." And he gave a number of a street in Soho.

"Good God!" thought Mr. Utterson, "can he, too, have been thinking of the will?" But he kept his feelings to himself and only grunted in acknowledgment of the address.

"And now," said the other, "how did you know me?"

"By description," was the reply.

"Whose description?"

"We have common friends," said Mr. Utterson.

"Common friends?" echoed Mr. Hyde, a little hoarsely. "Who are they?"

"Jekyll, for instance," said the lawyer.

"He never told you," cried Mr. Hyde, with a flush of anger. "I did not think you would have lied."

"Come," said Mr. Utterson, "that is not fitting language."

The other snarled aloud into a savage laugh; and the next moment, with extraordinary quickness, he had unlocked the door and disappeared into the house.

The lawyer stood awhile when Mr. Hyde had left him, the picture of disquietude. Then he began slowly to mount the street, pausing every step or two and putting his hand to his brow like a man in mental perplexity. The problem he was thus debating as he walked, was one of a class that is rarely solved. Mr. Hyde was pale and dwarfish, he gave an impression of deformity without any nameable malformation, he had a displeasing smile, he had borne himself to the lawyer with a sort of murderous mixture of timidity and boldness, and he spoke with a husky, whispering and somewhat broken voice; all these were points against him, but not all of these together could explain the hitherto unknown disgust, loathing, and fear with which Mr. Utterson regarded him. "There must be something else," said the perplexed gentleman. "There is something more, if I could find a name for it. God bless me, the man seems hardly human! Something troglodytic, shall we say? or can it be the old story of Dr. Fell? or is it the mere radiance of a foul soul that thus transpires through, and transfigures, its clay continent? The last, I think; for, O my poor old Harry Jekyll, if ever I read Satan's signature upon a face, it is on that of your new friend."

Round the corner from the by-street, there was a square of ancient, handsome houses, now for the most part decayed from their high estate and let in flats and chambers to all sorts and conditions of men: map-engravers, architects, shady lawyers, and the agents of obscure enterprises. One house, however, second from the corner, was still occupied entire; and at the door of this, which wore a great air of wealth and comfort, though it was now plunged in darkness except for the fan-light, Mr. Utterson stopped and knocked. A well-dressed, elderly servant opened the door.

"Is Dr. Jekyll at home, Poole?" asked the lawyer.

"I will see, Mr. Utterson," said Poole, admitting the visitor, as he spoke, into a large, low-roofed, comfortable hall, paved with flags, warmed (after the fashion of a country house) by a bright, open fire, and furnished with costly cabinets of oak.

"Will you wait here by the fire, sir? or shall I give you a light in the dining room?"

"Here, thank you," said the lawyer, and he drew near and leaned on the tall fender. This hall, in which he was now left alone, was a pet fancy of his friend the doctor's; and Utterson himself was wont to speak of it as the pleasantest room in London. But to-night there was a shudder in his blood; the face of Hyde sat heavy on his memory; he felt (what was rare with him) a nausea and distaste of life; and in the gloom of his spirits, he seemed to read a menace in the flickering of the firelight on the polished cabinets and the uneasy starting of the shadow on the roof. He was ashamed of his relief, when Poole presently returned to announce that Dr. Jekyll was gone out.

"I saw Mr. Hyde go in by the old dissecting-room door, Poole," he said. "Is that right, when Dr. Jekyll is from home?"

"Quite right, Mr. Utterson, sir," replied the servant. "Mr. Hyde has a key."

"Your master seems to repose a great deal of trust in that young man, Poole," resumed the other musingly.

"Yes, sir, he do indeed," said Poole. "We have all orders to obey him."

"I do not think I ever met Mr. Hyde?" asked Utterson.

"O, dear no, sir. He never dines here," replied the butler. "Indeed we see very little of him on this side of the house; he mostly comes and goes by the laboratory."

"Well, good-night, Poole."

"Good-night, Mr. Utterson."

And the lawyer set out homeward with a very heavy heart. "Poor Harry Jekyll," he thought, "my mind misgives me he is in deep waters! He was wild when he was young; a long while ago to be sure; but in the law of God, there is no statute of limitations. Ay, it must be that; the ghost of some old sin, the cancer of some concealed disgrace: punishment coming, *pede claudo*, years after memory has forgotten and self-love condoned the fault." And the lawyer, scared by the thought, brooded a while on his own past, groping in all the corners of memory, lest by chance some Jack-in-the-Box of an old iniquity should leap to light there. His past was fairly blameless; few men could read the rolls of their life with less apprehension; yet he was humbled to the dust by the many ill things he had done, and raised up again into a sober and fearful gratitude by the many that he had come so near to doing, yet avoided. And then by a return on his former subject, he conceived a spark of hope. "This Master Hyde, if he were studied," thought he, "must have secrets of his own; black secrets, by the look of him; secrets compared to which poor Jekyll's worst would be like sunshine. Things cannot continue as they are. It turns me cold to think of this creature stealing like a thief to Harry's bedside; poor Harry, what a wakening! And the danger of it; for if this Hyde suspects the existence of the will, he may grow impatient to inherit. Ah, I must put my shoulder to the wheel - if Jekyll will but let me," he added, "if Jekyll will only let me." For once more he saw before his mind's eye, as clear as a transparency, the strange clauses of the will.

CHAPTER 3

Dr. Jekyll was quite at ease

A FORTNIGHT later, by excellent good fortune, the doctor gave one of his pleasant dinners to some five or six old cronies, all intelligent, reputable men and all judges of good wine; and Mr. Utterson so contrived that he remained behind after the others had departed. This was no new arrangement, but a thing that had befallen many scores of times. Where Utterson was liked, he was liked well. Hosts loved to detain the dry lawyer, when the light-hearted and the loose-tongued had already their foot on the threshold; they liked to sit a while in his unobtrusive company, practising for solitude, sobering their minds in the man's rich silence after the expense and strain of gaiety. To this rule, Dr. Jekyll was no exception; and as he now sat on the opposite side of the fire - a large, well-made, smooth-faced man of fifty, with something of a slyish cast perhaps, but every mark of capacity and kindness - you could see by his looks that he cherished for Mr. Utterson a sincere and warm affection.

"I have been wanting to speak to you, Jekyll," began the latter. "You know that will of yours?"

A close observer might have gathered that the topic was distasteful; but the doctor carried it off gaily. "My poor Utterson," said he, "you are unfortunate in such a client. I never saw a man so distressed as you were by my will; unless it were that hide-bound pedant, Lanyon, at what he called my scientific heresies. Oh, I know he's a good fellow - you needn't frown - an excellent fellow, and I always mean to see more of him; but a hide-bound pedant for all that; an ignorant, blatant pedant. I was never more disappointed in any man than Lanyon."

"You know I never approved of it," pursued Utterson, ruthlessly disregarding the fresh topic.

"My will? Yes, certainly, I know that," said the doctor, a trifle sharply. "You have told me so."

"Well, I tell you so again," continued the lawyer. "I have been learning something of young Hyde."

The large handsome face of Dr. Jekyll grew pale to the very lips, and there came a blackness about his eyes. "I do not care to hear more," said he. "This is a matter I thought we had agreed to drop."

"What I heard was abominable," said Utterson.

"It can make no change. You do not understand my position," returned the doctor, with a certain incoherency of manner. "I am painfully situated, Utterson; my position is a very strange - a very strange one. It is one of those affairs that cannot be mended by talking."

"Jekyll," said Utterson, "you know me: I am a man to be trusted. Make a clean breast of this in confidence; and I make no doubt I can get you out of it."

"My good Utterson," said the doctor, "this is very good of you, this is downright good of you, and I cannot find words to thank you in. I believe you fully; I would trust you before any man alive, ay, before myself, if I could make the choice; but indeed it isn't what you fancy; it is not so bad as that; and just to put your good heart at rest, I will tell you one thing: the moment I choose, I can be rid of Mr. Hyde. I give you my hand upon that; and I thank you again and again; and I will just add one little word, Utterson, that I'm sure you'll take in good part: this is a private matter, and I beg of you to let it sleep."

Utterson reflected a little, looking in the fire.

"I have no doubt you are perfectly right," he said at last, getting to his feet.

"Well, but since we have touched upon this business, and for the last time I hope," continued the doctor, "there is one point I should like you to understand. I have really a very great interest in poor Hyde. I know you have seen him; he told me so; and I fear he was rude. But, I do sincerely take a great, a very great interest in that young man; and if I am taken away, Utterson, I wish you to promise me that you will bear with him and get his rights for him. I think you would, if you knew all; and it would be a weight off my mind if you would promise."

"I can't pretend that I shall ever like him," said the lawyer.

"I don't ask that," pleaded Jekyll, laying his hand upon the other's arm; "I only ask for justice; I only ask you to help him for my sake, when I am no longer here."

Utterson heaved an irrepressible sigh. "Well," said he, "I promise."

CHAPTER 4
The Carew murder case

NEARLY a year later, in the month of October, 18 —, London was startled by a crime of singular ferocity and rendered all the more notable by the high position of the victim. The details were few and startling. A maid servant living alone in a house not far from the river, had gone up-stairs to bed about eleven. Although a fog rolled over the city in the small hours, the early part of the night was cloudless, and the lane, which the maid's window overlooked, was brilliantly lit by the full moon. It seems she was romantically given, for she sat down upon her box, which stood immediately under the window, and fell into a dream of musing. Never (she used to say, with streaming tears, when she narrated that experience), never had she felt more at peace with all men or thought more kindly of the world. And as she so sat she became aware of an aged and beautiful gentleman with white hair, drawing near along the lane; and advancing to meet him, another and very small gentleman, to whom at first she paid less attention. When they had come within speech (which was just under the maid's eyes) the older man bowed and accosted the other with a very pretty manner of politeness. It did not seem as if the subject of his address were of great importance; indeed, from his pointing, it sometimes appeared as if he were only inquiring his way; but the moon shone on his face as he spoke, and the girl was pleased to watch it, it seemed to breathe such an innocent and old-world kindness of disposition, yet with something high too, as of a well-founded self-content. Presently her eye wandered to the other, and she was surprised to recognise in him a certain Mr. Hyde, who had once visited her master and for whom she had conceived a dislike. He had in his hand a heavy cane, with which he was trifling; but he answered never a word, and seemed to listen with an ill-contained impatience. And then all of a sudden he broke out in a great flame of anger, stamping with his foot, brandishing the cane, and carrying on (as the maid described it) like a madman. The old gentleman took a step back, with the air of one very much surprised and a trifle hurt; and at that Mr. Hyde broke out of all bounds and clubbed him to the earth. And next moment, with ape-like fury, he was trampling his victim under foot and hailing down a storm of blows, under which the bones were audibly shattered and the body jumped upon the roadway. At the horror of these sights and sounds, the maid fainted.

It was two o'clock when she came to herself and called for the police. The murderer was gone long ago; but there lay his victim in the middle of the lane, incredibly mangled. The stick with which the deed had been done, although it was of some rare and very tough and heavy wood, had broken in the middle under the stress of this insensate cruelty; and one splintered half had rolled in the neighbouring gutter - the other, without doubt, had been carried away by the murderer. A purse and a gold watch were found upon the victim: but no cards or papers, except a sealed and stamped envelope, which he had been probably carrying to the post, and which bore the name and address of Mr. Utterson.

This was brought to the lawyer the next morning, before he was out of bed; and he had no sooner seen it, and been told the circumstances, than he shot out a solemn lip. "I shall say nothing till I have seen the body," said he; "this may be very serious. Have the kindness to wait while I dress." And with the same grave countenance he hurried through his breakfast and drove to the police station, whither the body had been carried.

As soon as he came into the cell, he nodded.

"Yes," said he, "I recognise him. I am sorry to say that this is Sir Danvers Carew."

"Good God, sir," exclaimed the officer, "is it possible?" And the next moment his eye lighted up with professional ambition. "This will make a deal of noise," he said. "And perhaps you can help us to the man." And he briefly narrated what the maid had seen, and showed the broken stick.

Mr. Utterson had already quailed at the name of Hyde; but when the stick was laid before him, he could doubt no longer; broken and battered as it was, he recognised it for one that he had himself presented many years before to Henry Jekyll.

"Is this Mr. Hyde a person of small stature?" he inquired.

"Particularly small and particularly wicked-looking, is what the maid calls him," said the officer.

Mr. Utterson reflected; and then, raising his head, "If you will come with me in my cab," he said, "I think I can take you to his house."

It was by this time about nine in the morning, and the first fog of the season. A great chocolate-coloured pall lowered over heaven, but the wind was continually charging and routing these embattled vapours; so that as the cab crawled from street to street, Mr. Utterson beheld a marvellous number of degrees and hues of twilight; for here it would be dark like the back-end of evening; and there would be a glow of a rich, lurid brown, like the light of some strange conflagration; and here, for a moment, the fog would be quite broken up, and a haggard shaft of daylight would glance in between the swirling wreaths. The dismal quarter of Soho seen under these changing glimpses, with its muddy ways, and slatternly passengers, and its lamps, which had never been extinguished or had been kindled afresh to combat this mournful re-invasion of darkness, seemed, in the lawyer's eyes, like a district of some city in a nightmare. The thoughts of his mind, besides, were of the gloomiest dye;

and when he glanced at the companion of his drive, he was conscious of some touch of that terror of the law and the law's officers, which may at times assail the most honest.

As the cab drew up before the address indicated, the fog lifted a little and showed him a dingy street, a gin palace, a low French eating-house, a shop for the retail of penny numbers and twopenny salads, many ragged children huddled in the doorways, and many women of different nationalities passing out, key in hand, to have a morning glass; and the next moment the fog settled down again upon that part, as brown as umber, and cut him off from his blackguardly surroundings. This was the home of Henry Jekyll's favourite; of a man who was heir to a quarter of a million sterling.

An ivory-faced and silvery-haired old woman opened the door. She had an evil face, smoothed by hypocrisy; but her manners were excellent. Yes, she said, this was Mr. Hyde's, but he was not at home; he had been in that night very late, but had gone away again in less than an hour; there was nothing strange in that; his habits were very irregular, and he was often absent; for instance, it was nearly two months since she had seen him till yesterday.

"Very well, then, we wish to see his rooms," said the lawyer; and when the woman began to declare it was impossible, "I had better tell you who this person is," he added. "This is Inspector Newcomen of Scotland Yard."

A flash of odious joy appeared upon the woman's face. "Ah!" said she, "he is in trouble! What has he done?"

Mr. Utterson and the inspector exchanged glances. "He don't seem a very popular character," observed the latter. "And now, my good woman, just let me and this gentleman have a look about us."

In the whole extent of the house, which but for the old woman remained otherwise empty, Mr. Hyde had only used a couple of rooms; but these were furnished with luxury and good taste. A closet was filled with wine; the plate was of silver, the napery elegant; a good picture hung upon the walls, a gift (as Utterson supposed) from Henry Jekyll, who was much of a connoisseur; and the carpets were of many plies and agreeable in colour. At this moment, however, the rooms bore every mark of having been recently and hurriedly ransacked; clothes lay about the floor, with their pockets inside out; lock-fast drawers stood open; and on the hearth there lay a pile of grey ashes, as though many papers had been burned. From these embers the inspector disinterred the butt-end of a green cheque-book, which had resisted the action of the fire; the other half of the stick was found behind the door; and as this clinched his suspicions, the officer declared himself delighted. A visit to the bank, where several thousand pounds were found to be lying to the murderer's credit, completed his gratification.

"You may depend upon it, sir," he told Mr. Utterson: "I have him in my hand. He must have lost his head, or he never would have left the stick or, above all, burned the cheque-book. Why, money's life to the man. We have nothing to do but wait for him at the bank, and get out the handbills."

This last, however, was not so easy of accomplishment; for Mr. Hyde had numbered few familiars - even the master of the servant-maid had only seen him twice; his family could nowhere be traced; he had never been photographed; and the few who could describe him differed widely, as common observers will. Only on one point, were they agreed; and that was the haunting sense of unexpressed deformity with which the fugitive impressed his beholders.

CHAPTER 5

Incident of the letter

IT was late in the afternoon, when Mr. Utterson found his way to Dr. Jekyll's door, where he was at once admitted by Poole, and carried down by the kitchen offices and across a yard which had once been a garden, to the building which was indifferently known as the laboratory or the dissecting-rooms. The doctor had bought the house from the heirs of a celebrated surgeon; and his own tastes being rather chemical than anatomical, had changed the destination of the block at the bottom of the garden. It was the first time that the lawyer had been received in that part of his friend's quarters; and he eyed the dingy, windowless structure with curiosity, and gazed round with a distasteful sense of strangeness as he crossed the theatre, once crowded with eager students and now lying gaunt and silent, the tables laden with chemical apparatus, the floor strewn with crates and littered with packing straw, and the light falling dimly through the foggy cupola. At the further end, a flight of stairs mounted to a door covered with red baize; and through this, Mr. Utterson was at last received into the doctor's cabinet. It was a large room, fitted round with glass presses, furnished, among other things, with a cheval-glass and a business table, and looking out upon the court by three dusty windows barred with iron. A fire burned in the grate; a lamp was set lighted on the chimney shelf, for even in the houses the fog began to lie thickly; and there, close up to the warmth, sat Dr. Jekyll, looking deadly sick. He did not rise to meet his visitor, but held out a cold hand and bade him welcome in a changed voice.

"And now," said Mr. Utterson, as soon as Poole had left them, "you have heard the news?"

The doctor shuddered. "They were crying it in the square," he said. "I heard them in my dining-room."

"One word," said the lawyer. "Carew was my client, but so are you, and I want to know what I am doing. You have not been mad enough to hide this fellow?"

"Utterson, I swear to God," cried the doctor, "I swear to God I will never set eyes on him again. I bind my honour to you that I am done with him in this world. It is all at an end. And indeed he does not want my help; you do not know him as I do; he is safe, he is quite safe; mark my words, he will never more be heard of."

The lawyer listened gloomily; he did not like his friend's feverish manner. "You seem pretty sure of him," said he; "and for your sake, I hope you may be right. If it came to a trial, your name might appear."

"I am quite sure of him," replied Jekyll; "I have grounds for certainty that I cannot share with any one. But there is one thing on which you may advise me. I have - I have received a letter; and I am at a loss whether I should show it to the police. I should like to leave it in your hands, Utterson; you would judge wisely, I am sure; I have so great a trust in you."

"You fear, I suppose, that it might lead to his detection?" asked the lawyer.

"No," said the other. "I cannot say that I care what becomes of Hyde; I am quite done with him. I was thinking of my own character, which this hateful business has rather exposed."

Utterson ruminated a while; he was surprised at his friend's selfishness, and yet relieved by it. "Well," said he, at last, "let me see the letter."

The letter was written in an odd, upright hand and

signed "Edward Hyde": and it signified, briefly enough, that the writer's benefactor, Dr. Jekyll, whom he had long so unworthily repaid for a thousand generosities, need labour under no alarm for his safety, as he had means of escape on which he placed a sure dependence. The lawyer liked this letter well enough; it put a better colour on the intimacy than he had looked for; and he blamed himself for some of his past suspicions.

"Have you the envelope?" he asked.

"I burned it," replied Jekyll, "before I thought what I was about. But it bore no postmark. The note was handed in."

"Shall I keep this and sleep upon it?" asked Utterson.

"I wish you to judge for me entirely," was the reply. "I have lost confidence in myself."

"Well, I shall consider," returned the lawyer. "And now one word more: it was Hyde who dictated the terms in your will about that disappearance?"

The doctor seemed seized with a qualm of faintness: he shut his mouth tight and nodded.

"I knew it," said Utterson. "He meant to murder you. You have had a fine escape."

"I have had what is far more to the purpose," returned the doctor solemnly: "I have had a lesson - O God, Utterson, what a lesson I have had!" And he covered his face for a moment with his hands.

On his way out, the lawyer stopped and had a word or two with Poole. "By the by," said he, "there was a letter handed in today: what was the messenger like?" But Poole was positive nothing had come except by post; "and only circulars by that," he added.

This news sent off the visitor with his fears renewed. Plainly the letter had come by the laboratory door; possibly, indeed, it had been written in the cabinet; and if that were so, it must be differently judged, and handled with the more caution. The newsboys, as he went, were crying themselves hoarse along the footways: "Special edition. Shocking murder of an M. P." That was the funeral oration of one friend and client; and he could not help a certain apprehension lest the good name of another should be sucked down in the eddy of the scandal. It was, at least, a ticklish decision that he had to make; and self-reliant as he was by habit, he began to cherish a longing for advice. It was not to be had directly; but perhaps, he thought, it might be fished for.

Presently after, he sat on one side of his own hearth, with Mr. Guest, his head clerk, upon the other, and midway between, at a nicely calculated distance from the fire, a bottle of a particular old wine that had long dwelt unsunned in the foundations of his house. The fog still slept on the wing above the drowned city, where the lamps glimmered like carbuncles; and through the muffle and smother of these fallen clouds, the procession of the town's life was still rolling in through the great arteries with a sound as of a mighty wind. But the room was gay with firelight. In the bottle the acids were long ago resolved; the imperial dye had softened with time, As the colour grows richer in stained windows; and the glow of hot autumn afternoons on hillside vineyards was ready to be set free and to disperse the fogs of London. Insensibly the lawyer melted. There was no man from whom he kept fewer secrets than Mr. Guest; and he was not always sure that he kept as many as he meant. Guest had often been on business to the doctor's; he knew Poole; he could scarce have failed to hear of Mr. Hyde's familiarity about the house; he might draw conclusions: was it not as well, then, that he should see a letter which put that mystery to rights? and above all since Guest, being a great student and critic of handwriting, would consider the step natural and obliging? The clerk, besides, was a man of counsel; he would scarce read so strange a document without dropping a remark; and by that remark Mr. Utterson might shape his future course.

"This is a sad business about Sir Danvers," he said.

"Yes, sir, indeed. It has elicited a great deal of public feeling," returned Guest. "The man, of course, was mad."

"I should like to hear your views on that," replied Utterson. "I have a document here in his handwriting; it is between ourselves, for I scarce know what to do about it; it is an ugly business at the best. But there it is; quite in your way a murderer's autograph."

Guest's eyes brightened, and he sat down at once and studied it with passion. "No, sir," he said: "not mad; but it is an odd hand."

"And by all accounts a very odd writer," added the lawyer.

Just then the servant entered with a note.

"Is that from Dr. Jekyll, sir?" inquired the clerk. "I thought I knew the writing. Anything private, Mr. Utterson?"

"Only an invitation to dinner. Why? Do you want to see it?"

"One moment. I thank you, sir"; and the clerk laid the two sheets of paper alongside and sedulously compared their contents. "Thank you, sir," he said at last, returning both; "it's a very interesting autograph."

There was a pause, during which Mr. Utterson struggled with himself. "Why did you compare them, Guest?" he inquired suddenly.

"Well, sir," returned the clerk, "there's a rather singular resemblance; the two hands are in many points identical: only differently sloped."

"Rather quaint," said Utterson.

"It is, as you say, rather quaint," returned Guest.

"I wouldn't speak of this note, you know," said the master.

"No, sir," said the clerk. "I understand."

But no sooner was Mr. Utterson alone that night than he locked the note into his safe, where it reposed from that time forward. "What!" he thought. "Henry Jekyll forge for a murderer!" And his blood ran cold in his veins.

CHAPTER 6

Remarkable incident
of Dr Lanyon

TIME ran on; thousands of pounds were offered in reward, for the death of Sir Danvers was resented as a public injury; but Mr. Hyde had disappeared out of the ken of the police as though he had never existed. Much of his past was unearthed, indeed, and all disreputable: tales came out of the man's cruelty, at once so callous and violent; of his vile life, of his strange associates, of the hatred that seemed to have surrounded his career; but of his present whereabouts, not a whisper. From the time he had left the house in Soho on the morning of the murder, he was simply blotted out; and gradually, as time drew on, Mr. Utterson began to recover from the hotness of his alarm, and to grow more at quiet with himself. The death of Sir Danvers was, to his way of thinking, more than paid for by the disappearance of Mr. Hyde. Now that that evil influence had been withdrawn, a new life began for Dr. Jekyll. He came out of his seclusion, renewed relations with his friends, became once more their familiar guest and entertainer; and whilst he had always been, known for charities, he was now no less distinguished for religion. He was busy, he was much in the open air, he did good; his face seemed to open and brighten, as if with an inward consciousness of service; and for more than two months, the doctor was at peace.

On the 8th of January Utterson had dined at the doctor's with a small party; Lanyon had been there; and the face of the host had looked from one to the other as in the old days when the trio were inseparable friends. On the 12th, and again on the 14th, the door was shut against the lawyer. "The doctor was confined to the house," Poole said, "and saw no one." On the 15th, he tried again, and was again refused; and having now been used for the last two months to see his friend almost daily, he found this return of solitude to weigh upon his spirits. The fifth night he had in Guest to dine with him; and the sixth he betook himself to Dr. Lanyon's.

There at least he was not denied admittance; but when he came in, he was shocked at the change which had taken place in the doctor's appearance. He had his death-warrant written legibly upon his face. The rosy man had grown pale; his flesh had fallen away; he was visibly balder and older; and yet it was not so much, these tokens of a swift physical decay that arrested the lawyer's notice, as a look in the eye and quality of manner that seemed to testify to some deep-seated terror of the mind. It was unlikely that the doctor should fear death; and yet that was what Utterson was tempted to suspect. "Yes," he thought; "he is a doctor, he must know his own state and that his days are counted; and the knowledge is more than he can bear." And yet when Utterson remarked on his ill-looks, it was with an air of greatness that Lanyon declared himself a doomed man.

"I have had a shock," he said, "and I shall never recover. It is a question of weeks. Well, life has been pleasant; I liked it; yes, sir, I used to like it. I sometimes think if we knew all, we should be more glad to get away."

"Jekyll is ill, too," observed Utterson. "Have you seen him?"

But Lanyon's face changed, and he held up a trembling hand. "I wish to see or hear no more of Dr. Jekyll," he said in a loud, unsteady voice. "I am quite done with that person; and I beg that you will spare me any allusion to one whom I regard as dead."

"Tut-tut," said Mr. Utterson; and then after a considerable pause, "Can't I do anything?" he inquired. "We are three very old friends, Lanyon; we shall not live to make others."

"Nothing can be done," returned Lanyon; "ask himself."

"He will not see me," said the lawyer.

"I am not surprised at that," was the reply. "Some day, Utterson, after I am dead, you may perhaps come to learn the right and wrong of this. I cannot tell you. And in the meantime, if you can sit and talk with me of other things, for God's sake, stay and do so; but if you cannot keep clear of this accursed topic, then, in God's name, go, for I cannot bear it."

As soon as he got home, Utterson sat down and wrote to Jekyll, complaining of his exclusion from the house, and asking the cause of this unhappy break with Lanyon; and the next day brought him a long answer, often very pathetically worded, and sometimes darkly mysterious in drift. The quarrel with Lanyon was incurable. "I do not blame our old friend," Jekyll wrote, "but I share his view that we must never meet. I mean from henceforth to lead a life of extreme seclusion; you must not be surprised, nor must you doubt my friendship, if my door is often shut even to you. You must suffer me to go my own dark way. I have brought on myself a punishment and a danger that I cannot name. If I am the chief of sinners, I am the chief of sufferers also. I could not think that this earth contained a place for sufferings and terrors so unmanning; and you can do but one thing, Utterson, to lighten this destiny, and that is to respect my silence." Utterson was amazed; the dark influence of Hyde had been withdrawn, the doctor had returned to his old tasks and amities; a week ago, the prospect had smiled with every promise of a cheerful and an honoured age; and now in a moment, friendship, and peace of mind, and the whole tenor of his life were wrecked. So great and unprepared a change pointed to madness; but in view of Lanyon's manner and words, there must lie for it some deeper ground.

A week afterwards Dr. Lanyon took to his bed, and in something less than a fortnight he was dead. The night after the funeral, at which he had been sadly affected, Utterson locked the door of his business room, and sitting there by the light of a melancholy candle, drew out and set before him an envelope addressed by the hand and sealed with the seal of his dead friend. "Private: for the hands of G. J. Utterson alone, and in case of his predecease *to be destroyed unread,*" so it was emphatically superscribed; and the lawyer dreaded to behold the contents. "I have buried one friend to-day," he thought: "what if this should cost me another?" And then he condemned the fear as a disloyalty, and broke the seal. Within there was another enclosure, likewise sealed, and marked upon the cover as "not to be opened till the death or disappearance of Dr. Henry Jekyll." Utterson could not trust his eyes. Yes, it was disappearance; here again, as in the mad will which he had long ago restored to its author, here again were the idea of a disappearance and the name of Henry Jekyll bracketed. But in the will, that idea had sprung from the sinister suggestion of the man Hyde; it was set there with a purpose all too plain and horrible. Written by the hand of Lanyon, what should it mean? A great curiosity came on the trustee, to disregard the prohibition and dive at once to the bottom of these mysteries; but professional honour and faith to his dead friend were stringent obligations; and the packet slept in the inmost corner of his private safe.

It is one thing to mortify curiosity, another to conquer it; and it may be doubted if, from that day forth, Utterson desired the society of his surviving friend with the same eagerness. He thought of him kindly; but his thoughts were disquieted and fearful. He went to call indeed; but he was perhaps relieved to be denied admittance; perhaps, in his heart, he preferred to speak with Poole upon the doorstep and surrounded by the air and sounds of the open city, rather than to be admitted into that house of voluntary bondage, and to sit and speak with its inscrutable recluse. Poole had, indeed, no very pleasant news to communicate. The doctor, it appeared, now more than ever confined himself to the cabinet over the laboratory, where he would sometimes even sleep; he was out of spirits, he had grown very silent, he did not read; it seemed as if he had something on his mind. Utterson became so used to the unvarying character of these reports, that he fell off little by little in the frequency of his visits.

CHAPTER 7

Incident at the window

IT chanced on Sunday, when Mr. Utterson was on his usual walk with Mr. Enfield, that their way lay once again through the by-street; and that when they came in front of the door, both stopped to gaze on it.

"Well," said Enfield, "that story's at an end at least. We shall never see more of Mr. Hyde."

"I hope not," said Utterson. "Did I ever tell you that I once saw him, and shared your feeling of repulsion?"

"It was impossible to do the one without the other," returned Enfield. "And by the way, what an ass you must have thought me, not to know that this was a back way to Dr. Jekyll's! It was partly your own fault that I found it out, even when I did."

"So you found it out, did you?" said Utterson. "But if that be so, we may step into the court and take a look at the windows. To tell you the truth, I am uneasy about poor Jekyll; and even outside, I feel as if the presence of a friend might do him good."

The court was very cool and a little damp, and full of premature twilight, although the sky, high up overhead, was still bright with sunset. The middle one of the three windows was half-way open; and sitting close beside it, taking the air with an infinite sadness of mien, like some disconsolate prisoner, Utterson saw Dr. Jekyll.

"What! Jekyll! Jekyll!" he cried. "I trust you are better."

"I am very low, Utterson," replied the doctor, drearily, "very low. It will not last long, thank God."

"You stay too much indoors," said the lawyer. "You should be out, whipping up the circulation like Mr. Enfield and me. (This is my cousin - Mr. Enfield - Dr. Jekyll.) Come, now; get your hat and take a quick turn with us."

"You are very good," sighed the other. "I should like to very much; but no, no, no, it is quite impossible; I dare not. But indeed, Utterson, I am very glad to see you; this is really a great pleasure; I would ask you and Mr. Enfield up, but the place is really not fit."

"Why then," said the lawyer, good-naturedly, "the best thing we can do is to stay down here and speak with you from where we are."

"That is just what I was about to venture to propose," returned the doctor with a smile. But the words were hardly uttered, before the smile was struck out of his face and succeeded by an expression of such abject terror and despair, as froze the very blood of the two gentlemen below. They saw it but for a glimpse, for the window was instantly thrust down; but that glimpse had been sufficient, and they turned and left the court without a word. In silence, too, they traversed the by-street; and it was not until they had come into a neighbouring thoroughfare, where even upon a Sunday there were still some stirrings of life, that Mr. Utterson at last turned and looked at his companion. They were both pale; and there was an answering horror in their eyes.

"God forgive us, God forgive us," said Mr. Utterson.

But Mr. Enfield only nodded his head very seriously and walked on once more in silence.

CHAPTER 8
The last night

MR. UTTERSON was sitting by his fireside one evening after dinner, when he was surprised to receive a visit from Poole.

"Bless me, Poole, what brings you here?" he cried; and then taking a second look at him, "What ails you?" he added; "is the doctor ill?"

"Mr. Utterson," said the man, "there is something wrong."

"Take a seat, and here is a glass of wine for you," said the lawyer. "Now, take your time, and tell me plainly what you want."

"You know the doctor's ways, sir," replied Poole, "and how he shuts himself up. Well, he's shut up again in the cabinet; and I don't like it, sir - I wish I may die if I like it. Mr. Utterson, sir, I'm afraid."

"Now, my good man," said the lawyer, "be explicit. What are you afraid of?"

"I've been afraid for about a week," returned Poole, doggedly disregarding the question, "and I can bear it no more."

The man's appearance amply bore out his words; his manner was altered for the worse; and except for the moment when he had first announced his terror, he had not once looked the lawyer in the face. Even now, he sat with the glass of wine untasted on his knee, and his eyes directed to a corner of the floor. "I can bear it no more," he repeated.

"Come," said the lawyer, "I see you have some good reason, Poole; I see there is something seriously amiss. Try to tell me what it is."

"I think there's been foul play," said Poole, hoarsely.

"Foul play!" cried the lawyer, a good deal frightened and rather inclined to be irritated in consequence. "What foul play? What does the man mean?"

"I daren't say, sir," was the answer; "but will you come along with me and see for yourself?"

Mr. Utterson's only answer was to rise and get his hat and great-coat; but he observed with wonder the greatness of the relief that appeared upon the butler's face, and perhaps with no less, that the wine was still untasted when he set it down to follow.

It was a wild, cold, seasonable night of March, with a pale moon, lying on her back as though the wind had tilted her, and a flying wrack of the most diaphanous and lawny texture. The wind made talking difficult, and flecked the blood into the face. It seemed to have swept the streets unusually bare of passengers, besides; for Mr. Utterson thought he had never seen that part of London so deserted. He could have wished it otherwise; never in his life had he been conscious of so sharp a wish to see and touch his fellow-creatures; for struggle as he might, there was borne in upon his mind a crushing anticipation of calamity. The square, when they got there, was all full of wind and dust, and the thin trees in the garden were lashing themselves along the railing. Poole, who had kept all the way a pace or two ahead, now pulled up in the middle of the pavement, and in spite of the biting weather, took off his hat and mopped his brow with a red pocket-handkerchief. But for all the hurry of his coming, these were not the dews of exertion that he wiped away, but the moisture of some strangling anguish; for his face was white and his voice, when he spoke, harsh and broken.

"Well, sir," he said, "here we are, and God grant there be nothing wrong."

"Amen, Poole," said the lawyer.

Thereupon the servant knocked in a very guarded manner; the door was opened on the chain; and a voice asked from within, "Is that you, Poole?"

"It's all right," said Poole. "Open the door."

The hall, when they entered it, was brightly lighted up; the fire was built high; and about the hearth the whole of the servants, men and women, stood huddled together like a flock of sheep. At the sight of Mr. Utterson, the housemaid broke into hysterical whimpering; and the cook, crying out, "Bless God! it's Mr. Utterson," ran forward as if to take him in her arms.

"What, what? Are you all here?" said the lawyer peevishly. "Very irregular, very unseemly; your master would be far from pleased."

"They're all afraid," said Poole.

Blank silence followed, no one protesting; only the maid lifted up her voice and now wept loudly.

"Hold your tongue!" Poole said to her, with a ferocity of accent that testified to his own jangled nerves; and indeed, when the girl had so suddenly raised the note of her lamentation, they had all started and turned toward the inner door with faces of dreadful expectation. "And now," continued the butler, addressing the knife-boy, "reach me a candle, and we'll get this through hands at once." And then he begged Mr. Utterson to follow him, and led the way to the back-garden.

"Now, sir," said he, "you come as gently as you can. I want you to hear, and I don't want you to be heard. And see here, sir, if by any chance he was to ask you in, don't go."

Mr. Utterson's nerves, at this unlooked-for termination, gave a jerk that nearly threw him from his balance; but he re-collected his courage and followed the butler into the laboratory building and through the surgical theatre, with its lumber of crates and bottles, to the foot of the stair. Here Poole motioned him to stand on one side and listen; while he himself, setting down the candle and making a great and obvious call on his resolution, mounted the steps and knocked with a somewhat uncertain hand on the red baize of the cabinet door.

"Mr. Utterson, sir, asking to see you," he called; and even as he did so, once more violently signed to the lawyer to give ear.

A voice answered from within: "Tell him I cannot see any one," it said complainingly.

"Thank you, sir," said Poole, with a note of something like triumph in his voice; and taking up his candle, he led Mr. Utterson back across the yard and into the great kitchen, where the fire was out and the beetles were leaping on the floor.

"Sir," he said, looking Mr. Utterson in the eyes, "was that my master's voice?"

"It seems much changed," replied the lawyer, very pale, but giving look for look.

"Changed? Well, yes, I think so," said the butler. "Have I been twenty years in this man's house, to be deceived about his voice? No, sir; master's made away with; he was made, away with eight days ago, when we heard him cry out upon the name of God; and *who's* in there instead of him, and *why* it stays there, is a thing that cries to Heaven, Mr. Utterson!"

"This is a very strange tale, Poole; this is rather a wild tale, my man," said Mr. Utterson, biting his finger. "Suppose it were as you suppose, supposing Dr. Jekyll to have been - well, murdered, what could induce the murderer to stay? That won't hold water; it doesn't commend itself to reason."

"Well, Mr. Utterson, you are a hard man to satisfy, but I'll do it yet," said Poole. "All this last week (you must know) him, or it, or whatever it is that lives in that cabinet, has been crying night and day for some sort of medicine and cannot get it to his mind. It was sometimes his way - the master's, that is - to write his orders on a sheet of paper and throw it on the stair. We've had nothing else this week back; nothing but papers, and a closed door, and the very meals left there to be smuggled in when nobody was looking. Well, sir, every day, ay, and twice and thrice in the same day, there have been orders and complaints, and I have been sent flying to all the wholesale chemists in town. Every time I brought the stuff back, there would be another paper telling me to return it, because it was not pure, and another order to a different firm. This drug is wanted bitter bad, sir, whatever for."

"Have you any of these papers?" asked Mr. Utterson.

Poole felt in his pocket and handed out a crumpled note, which the lawyer, bending nearer to the candle, carefully examined. Its contents ran thus: "Dr. Jekyll presents his compliments to Messrs. Maw. He assures them that their last sample is impure and quite useless for his present purpose. In the year 18 —, Dr. J. purchased a somewhat large quantity from Messrs. M. He now begs them to search with the most sedulous care, and should any of the same quality be left, to forward it to him at once. Expense is no consideration. The importance of this to Dr. J. can hardly be exaggerated." So far the letter had run composedly enough, but here with a sudden splutter of the pen, the writer's emotion had broken loose. "For God's sake," he had added, "find me some of the old."

"This is a strange note," said Mr. Utterson; and then sharply, "How do you come to have it open?"

"The man at Maw's was main angry, sir, and he threw it back to me like so much dirt," returned Poole.

"This is unquestionably the doctor's hand, do you know?" resumed the lawyer.

"I thought it looked like it," said the servant rather sulkily; and then, with another voice, "But what matters hand-of-write?" he said. "I've seen him!"

"Seen him?" repeated Mr. Utterson. "Well?"

"That's it!" said Poole. "It was this way. I came suddenly into the theatre from the garden. It seems he had slipped out to look for this drug or whatever it is; for the cabinet door was open, and there he was at the far end of the room digging among the crates. He looked up when I came in, gave a kind of cry, and whipped up-stairs into the cabinet. It was but for one minute that I saw him, but the hair stood upon my head like quills. Sir, if that was my master, why had he a mask upon his face? If it was my master, why did he cry out like a rat, and run from me? I have served him long enough. And then…" The man paused and passed his hand over his face.

"These are all very strange circumstances," said Mr. Utterson, "but I think I begin to see daylight. Your master, Poole, is plainly seized with one of those maladies that both torture and deform the sufferer; hence, for aught I know, the alteration of his voice; hence the mask and the avoidance of his friends; hence his eagerness to find this drug, by means of which the poor soul retains some hope of ultimate recovery - God grant that he be not deceived! There is my explanation; it is sad enough, Poole, ay, and appalling to consider; but it is plain and natural, hangs well together, and delivers us from all exorbitant alarms."

"Sir," said the butler, turning to a sort of mottled pallor, "that thing was not my master, and there's the truth. My master" – here he looked round him and began to whisper - "is a tall, fine build of a man, and this was more of a dwarf." Utterson attempted to protest. "O, sir," cried Poole, "do you think I do not know my master after twenty years? Do you think I do not know where his head comes to in the cabinet door, where I saw him every morning of my life? No, Sir, that thing in the mask was never Dr. Jekyll - God knows what it was, but it was never Dr. Jekyll; and it is the belief of my heart that there was murder done."

"Poole," replied the lawyer, "if you say that, it will become my duty to make certain. Much as I desire to spare your master's feelings, much as I am puzzled by this note which seems to prove him to be still alive, I shall consider it my duty to break in that door."

"Ah Mr. Utterson, that's talking!" cried the butler.

"And now comes the second question," resumed Utterson: "Who is going to do it?"

"Why, you and me," was the undaunted reply.

"That's very well said," returned the lawyer; "and whatever comes of it, I shall make it my business to see you are no loser."

"There is an axe in the theatre," continued Poole; "and you might take the kitchen poker for yourself."

The lawyer took that rude but weighty instrument into his hand, and balanced it. "Do you know, Poole," he said, looking up, "that you and I are about to place ourselves in a position of some peril?"

"You may say so, sir, indeed," returned the butler.

"It is well, then, that we should be frank," said the other. "We both think more than we have said; let us make a clean breast. This masked figure that you saw, did you recognise it?"

"Well, sir, it went so quick, and the creature was so doubled up, that I could hardly swear to that," was the answer. "But if you mean, was it Mr. Hyde? - why, yes, I think it was! You see, it was much of the same bigness; and it had the same quick, light way with it; and then who else could have got in by the laboratory door? You have not forgot, sir that at the time of the murder he had still the key with him? But that's not all. I don't know, Mr. Utterson, if ever you met this Mr. Hyde?"

"Yes," said the lawyer, "I once spoke with him."

"Then you must know as well as the rest of us that there was something queer about that gentleman - something that gave a man a turn - I don't know rightly how to say it, sir, beyond this: that you felt it in your marrow kind of cold and thin."

"I own I felt something of what you describe," said Mr. Utterson.

"Quite so, sir," returned Poole. "Well, when that masked thing like a monkey jumped from among the chemicals and whipped into the cabinet, it went down my spine like ice. Oh, I know it's not evidence, Mr. Utterson. I'm book-learned enough for that; but a man has his feelings, and I give you my Bible-word it was Mr. Hyde!"

"Ay, ay," said the lawyer. "My fears incline to the same point. Evil, I fear, founded - evil was sure to come - of that connection. Ay, truly, I believe you; I believe poor Harry is killed; and I believe his murderer (for what purpose, God alone can tell) is still lurking in his victim's room. Well, let our name be vengeance. Call Bradshaw."

The footman came at the summons, very white and nervous.

"Pull yourself together, Bradshaw," said the lawyer. "This suspense, I know, is telling upon all of you; but it is now our intention to make an end of it. Poole, here, and I are going to force our way into the cabinet. If all is well, my shoulders are broad enough to bear the blame. Meanwhile, lest anything should really be amiss, or any malefactor seek to escape by the back, you and the boy must go round the corner with a pair of good sticks and take your post at the laboratory door. We give you ten minutes to get to your stations."

As Bradshaw left, the lawyer looked at his watch. "And now, Poole, let us get to ours," he said; and taking the poker under his arm, led the way into the yard. The scud had banked over the moon, and it was now quite dark. The wind, which only broke in puffs and draughts into that deep well of building, tossed the light of the candle to and fro about their steps, until they came into the shelter of the theatre, where they sat down silently to wait. London hummed solemnly all around; but nearer at hand, the stillness was only broken by the sounds of a footfall moving to and fro along the cabinet floor.

"So it will walk all day, sir," whispered Poole; "ay, and the better part of the night. Only when a new sample comes from the chemist, there's a bit of a break. Ah, it's an ill conscience that's such an enemy to rest! Ah, sir, there's blood foully shed in every step of it! But hark again, a little closer - put your heart in your ears, Mr. Utterson, and tell me, is that the doctor's foot?"

The steps fell lightly and oddly, with a certain swing, for all they went so slowly; it was different indeed from the heavy creaking tread of Henry Jekyll. Utterson sighed. "Is there never anything else?" he asked.

Poole nodded. "Once," he said. "Once I heard it weeping!"

"Weeping? how that?" said the lawyer, conscious of a sudden chill of horror.

"Weeping like a woman or a lost soul," said the butler. "I came away with that upon my heart, that I could have wept too."

But now the ten minutes drew to an end. Poole disinterred the axe from under a stack of packing straw; the candle was set upon the nearest table to light them to the attack; and they drew near with bated breath to where that patient foot was still going up and down, up and down, in the quiet of the night.

"Jekyll," cried Utterson, with a loud voice, "I demand to see you." He paused a moment, but there came no reply. "I give you fair warning, our suspicions are aroused, and I must and shall see you," he resumed; "if not by fair means, then by foul! if not of your consent, then by brute force!"

"Utterson," said the voice, "for God's sake, have mercy!"

"Ah, that's not Jekyll's voice - it's Hyde's!" cried Utterson. "Down with the door, Poole!"

Poole swung the axe over his shoulder; the blow shook the building, and the red baize door leaped against the lock and hinges. A dismal screech, as of mere animal terror, rang from the cabinet. Up went the axe again, and again the panels crashed and the frame bounded; four times the blow fell; but the wood was tough and the fittings were of excellent workmanship; and it was not until the fifth, that the lock burst in sunder and the wreck of the door fell inwards on the carpet.

The besiegers, appalled by their own riot and the stillness that had succeeded, stood back a little and peered in. There lay the cabinet before their eyes in the quiet lamplight, a good fire glowing and chattering on the hearth, the kettle singing its thin strain, a drawer or two open, papers neatly set forth on the business-table, and nearer the fire, the things laid out for tea: the quietest room, you would have said, and, but for the glazed presses full of chemicals, the most commonplace that night in London.

Right in the midst there lay the body of a man sorely contorted and still twitching. They drew near on tiptoe, turned it on its back and beheld the face of Edward Hyde. He was dressed in clothes far too large for him, clothes of the doctor's bigness; the cords of his face still moved with a semblance of life, but life was quite gone; and by the crushed phial in the hand and the strong smell of kernels that hung upon the air, Utterson knew that he was looking on the body of a self-destroyer.

"We have come too late," he said sternly, "whether to save or punish. Hyde is gone to his account; and it only remains for us to find the body of your master."

The far greater proportion of the building was occupied by the theatre, which filled almost the whole ground story and was lighted from above, and by the cabinet, which formed an upper story at one end and looked upon the court. A corridor joined the theatre to the door on the by-street; and with this the cabinet communicated separately by a second flight of stairs. There were besides a few dark closets and a spacious cellar. All these they now thoroughly examined. Each closet needed but a glance, for all were empty, and all, by the dust that fell from their doors, had stood long unopened. The cellar, indeed, was filled with crazy lumber, mostly dating from the times of the surgeon who was Jekyll's predecessor; but even as they opened the door they were advertised of the uselessness of further search, by the fall of a perfect mat of cobweb which had for years sealed up the entrance. Nowhere was there any trace of Henry Jekyll, dead or alive.

Poole stamped on the flags of the corridor. "He must be buried here," he said, hearkening to the sound.

"Or he may have fled," said Utterson, and he turned to examine the door in the by-street. It was locked; and lying near by on the flags, they found the key, already stained with rust.

"This does not look like use," observed the lawyer.

"Use!" echoed Poole. "Do you not see, sir, it is broken? much as if a man had stamped on it."

"Ah" continued Utterson, "and the fractures, too, are rusty." The two men looked at each other with a scare. "This is beyond me, Poole," said the lawyer. "Let us go back to the cabinet."

They mounted the stair in silence, and still with an occasional awe-struck glance at the dead body, proceeded more thoroughly to examine the contents of the cabinet. At one table, there were traces of chemical work, various measured heaps of some white salt being laid on glass saucers, as though for an experiment in which the unhappy man had been prevented.

"That is the same drug that I was always bringing him," said Poole; and even as he spoke, the kettle with a startling noise boiled over.

This brought them to the fireside, where the easy-chair was drawn cosily up, and the tea-things stood ready to the sitter's elbow, the very sugar in the cup. There were several books on a shelf; one lay beside the tea-things open, and Utterson was amazed to find it a copy of a pious work, for which Jekyll had several times expressed a great esteem, annotated, in his own hand, with startling blasphemies.

Next, in the course of their review of the chamber, the searchers came to the cheval glass, into whose depths they looked with an involuntary horror. But it was so turned as to show them nothing but the rosy glow playing on the roof, the fire sparkling in a hundred repetitions along the glazed front of the presses, and their own pale and fearful countenances stooping to look in.

"This glass have seen some strange things, sir," whispered Poole.

"And surely none stranger than itself," echoed the lawyer in the same tones. "For what did Jekyll" - he caught himself up at the word with a start, and then conquering the weakness - "what could Jekyll want with it?" he said.

"You may say that!" said Poole. Next they turned to the business-table. On the desk among the neat array of papers, a large envelope was uppermost, and bore, in the doctor's hand, the name of Mr. Utterson. The lawyer unsealed it, and several enclosures fell to the floor. The first was a will, drawn in the same eccentric terms as the one which he had returned six months before, to serve as a testament in case of death and as a deed of gift in case of disappearance; but, in place of the name of Edward Hyde, the lawyer, with indescribable amazement, read the name of Gabriel John Utterson. He looked at Poole, and then back at the paper, and last of all at the dead malefactor stretched upon the carpet.

"My head goes round," he said. "He has been all these days in possession; he had no cause to like me; he must have raged to see himself displaced; and he has not destroyed this document."

He caught up the next paper; it was a brief note in the doctor's hand and dated at the top. "Oh Poole!" the lawyer cried, "he was alive and here this day. He cannot have been disposed of in so short a space, he must be still alive, he must have fled! And then, why fled? and how? and in that case, can we venture to declare this suicide? Oh, we must be careful. I foresee that we may yet involve your master in some dire catastrophe."

"Why don't you read it, sir?" asked Poole.

"Because I fear," replied the lawyer solemnly. "God grant I have no cause for it!" And with that he brought the paper to his eyes and read as follows:-

"MY DEAR UTTERSON, - When this shall fall into your hands, I shall have disappeared, under what circumstances I have not the penetration to foresee, but my instinct and all the circumstances of my nameless situation tell me that the end is sure and must be early. Go then, and first read the narrative which Lanyon warned me he was to place in your hands; and if you care to hear more, turn to the confession of

"Your unworthy and unhappy friend,
"HENRY JEKYLL."

"There was a third enclosure?" asked Utterson.

"Here, sir," said Poole, and gave into his hands a considerable packet sealed in several places.

The lawyer put it in his pocket. "I would say nothing of this paper. If your master has fled or is dead, we may at least save his credit. It is now ten; I must go home and read these documents in quiet; but I shall be back before midnight, when we shall send for the police."

They went out, locking the door of the theatre behind them; and Utterson, once more leaving the servants gathered about the fire in the hall, trudged back to his office to read the two narratives in which this mystery was now to be explained.

CHAPTER 9

Dr. Lanyon's Narrative

ON the ninth of January, now four days ago, I received by the evening delivery a registered envelope, addressed in the hand of my colleague and old school-companion, Henry Jekyll. I was a good deal surprised by this; for we were by no means in the habit of correspondence; I had seen the man, dined with him, indeed, the night before; and I could imagine nothing in our intercourse that should justify formality of registration. The contents increased my wonder; for this is how the letter ran:-

"10th December, 18 —

"DEAR LANYON, - You are one of my oldest friends; and although we may have differed at times on scientific questions, I cannot remember, at least on my side, any break in our affection. There was never a day when, if you had said to me, 'Jekyll, my life, my honour, my reason, depend upon you,' I would not have sacrificed my left hand to help you. Lanyon, my life, my honour my reason, are all at your mercy; if you fail me to-night I am lost. You might suppose, after this preface, that I am going to ask you for something dishonourable to grant. Judge for yourself.

"I want you to postpone all other engagements for to-night - ay, even if you were summoned to the bedside of an emperor; to take a cab, unless your carriage should be actually at the door; and with this letter in your hand for consultation, to drive straight to my house. Poole, my butler, has his orders; you will find, him waiting your arrival with a locksmith. The door of my cabinet is then to be forced: and you are to go in alone; to open the glazed press (letter E) on the left hand, breaking the lock if it be shut; and to draw out, *with all its contents as they stand*, the fourth drawer from the top or (which is the same thing) the third from the bottom. In my extreme distress of wind, I have a morbid fear of misdirecting you; but even if I am in error, you may know the right drawer by its contents: some powders, a phial and a paper book. This drawer I beg of you to carry back with you to Cavendish Square exactly as it stands.

"That is the first part of the service: now for the second. You should be back, if you set out at once on the receipt of this, long before midnight; but I will leave you that amount of margin, not only in the fear of one of those obstacles that can neither be prevented nor foreseen, but because an hour when your servants are in bed is to be preferred for what will then remain to do. At midnight, then, I have to ask you to be alone in your consulting-room, to admit with your own hand into the house a man who will present himself in my name, and to place in his hands the drawer that you will have brought with you from my cabinet. Then you will have played your part and earned my gratitude completely. Five minutes afterwards, if you insist upon an explanation, you will have understood that these arrangements are of capital importance; and that by the neglect of one of them, fantastic as they must appear, you might have charged your conscience with my death or the shipwreck of my reason.

"Confident as I am that you will not trifle with this appeal, my heart sinks and my hand trembles at the bare thought of such a possibility. Think of me at this hour, in a strange place, labouring under a blackness of distress that no fancy can exaggerate, and yet well aware that, if you will but punctually serve me, my troubles will roll away like a story that is told. Serve me, my dear Lanyon, and save

"Your friend,
"H. J.

"P. S. - I had already sealed this up when a fresh terror struck upon my soul. It is possible that the postoffice may fail me, and this letter not come into your hands until to-morrow morning. In that case, dear Lanyon, do my errand when it shall be most convenient for you in the course of the day; and once more expect my messenger at midnight. It may then already be too late; and if that night passes without event, you will know that you have seen the last of Henry Jekyll."

Upon the reading of this letter, I made sure my colleague was insane; but till that was proved beyond the possibility of doubt, I felt bound to do as he requested. The less I understood of this farrago, the less I was in a position to judge of its importance; and an appeal so worded could not be set aside without a grave responsibility. I rose accordingly from table, got into a hansom, and drove straight to Jekyll's house. The butler was awaiting my arrival; he had received by the same post as mine a registered letter of instruction, and had sent at once for a locksmith and a carpenter. The tradesmen came while we were yet speaking; and we moved in a body to old Dr. Denman's surgical theatre, from which (as you are doubtless aware) Jekyll's private cabinet is most conveniently entered. The door was very strong, the lock excellent; the carpenter avowed he would have great trouble and have to do much damage, if force were to be used; and the locksmith was near despair. But this last was a handy fellow, and after two hours' work, the door stood open. The press marked E was unlocked; and I took out the drawer, had it filled up with straw and tied in a sheet, and returned with it to Cavendish Square.

Here I proceeded to examine its contents. The powders were neatly enough made up, but not with the nicety of the dispensing chemist; so that it was plain they were of Jekyll's private manufacture; and when I opened one of the wrappers I found what seemed to me a simple crystalline salt of a white colour. The phial, to which I next turned my attention, might have been about half-full of a blood-red liquor, which was highly pungent to the sense of smell and seemed to me to contain phosphorus and some volatile ether. At the other ingredients I could make no guess. The book was an ordinary version-book and contained little but a series of dates. These covered a period of many years, but I observed that the entries ceased nearly a year ago and quite abruptly. Here and there a brief remark was appended to a date, usually no more than a single word: "double" occurring perhaps six times in a total of several hundred entries; and once very early in the list and followed by several marks of exclamation, "total failure!!!" All this, though it whetted my curiosity, told me little that was definite. Here were a phial of some tincture, a paper of some salt, and the record of a series of experiments that had led (like too many of Jekyll's investigations) to no end of practical usefulness. How could the presence of these articles in my house affect either the honour, the sanity, or the life of my flighty colleague? If his messenger could go to one place, why could he not go to another? And even granting some impediment, why was this gentleman to be received by me in secret? The more I reflected the more convinced I grew that I was dealing with a case of cerebral disease: and though I dismissed my servants to bed, I loaded an old revolver, that I might be found in some posture of self-defence.

Twelve o'clock had scarce rung out over London, ere the knocker sounded very gently on the door. I went myself at the summons, and found a small man crouching against the pillars of the portico.

"Are you come from Dr. Jekyll?" I asked.

He told me "yes" by a constrained gesture; and when I had bidden him enter, he did not obey me without a searching backward glance into the darkness of the square. There was a policeman not far off, advancing with his bull's eye open; and at the sight, I thought my visitor started and made greater haste.

These particulars struck me, I confess, disagreeably; and as I followed him into the bright light of the consulting-room, I kept my hand ready on my weapon. Here, at last, I had a chance of clearly seeing him. I had never set eyes on him before, so much was certain. He was small, as I have said; I was struck besides with the shocking expression of his face, with his remarkable combination of great muscular activity and great apparent debility of constitution, and - last but not least - with the odd, subjective disturbance caused by his neighbourhood. This bore some resemblance to incipient rigour, and was accompanied by a marked sinking of the pulse. At the time, I set it down to some idiosyncratic, personal distaste, and merely wondered at the acuteness of the symptoms; but I have since had reason to believe the cause to lie much deeper in the nature of man, and to turn on some nobler hinge than the principle of hatred.

This person (who had thus, from the first moment of his entrance, struck in me what I can only describe as a disgustful curiosity) was dressed in a fashion that would have made an ordinary person laughable; his clothes, that is to say, although they were of rich and sober fabric, were enormously too large for him in every measurement - the trousers hanging on his legs and rolled up to keep them from the ground, the waist of the coat below his haunches, and the collar sprawling wide upon his shoulders. Strange to relate, this ludicrous accoutrement was far from moving me to laughter. Rather, as there was something abnormal and misbegotten in the very essence of the creature that now faced me - something seizing, surprising, and revolting - this fresh disparity seemed but to fit in with and to reinforce it; so that to my interest in the man's nature and character, there was added a curiosity as to his origin, his life, his fortune and status in the world.

These observations, though they have taken so great a space to be set down in, were yet the work of a few seconds. My visitor was, indeed, on fire with sombre excitement.

"Have you got it?" he cried. "Have you got it?" And so lively was his impatience that he even laid his hand upon my arm and sought to shake me.

I put him back, conscious at his touch of a certain icy pang along my blood. "Come, sir," said I. "You forget that I have not yet the pleasure of your acquaintance. Be seated, if you please." And I showed him an example, and sat down myself in my customary seat and with as fair an imitation of my ordinary manner to a patient, as the lateness of the hour, the nature of my pre-occupations, and the horror I had of my visitor, would suffer me to muster.

"I beg your pardon, Dr. Lanyon," he replied civilly enough. "What you say is very well founded; and my impatience has shown its heels to my politeness. I come here at the instance of your colleague, Dr. Henry Jekyll, on a piece of business of some moment; and I understood…" He paused and put his hand to his throat, and I could see, in spite of his collected manner, that he was wrestling against the approaches of the hysteria - "I understood, a drawer…"

But here I took pity on my visitor's suspense, and some perhaps on my own growing curiosity.

"There it is, sir," said I, pointing to the drawer, where it lay on the floor behind a table and still covered with the sheet.

He sprang to it, and then paused, and laid his hand upon his heart: I could hear his teeth grate with the convulsive action of his jaws; and his face was so ghastly to see that I grew alarmed both for his life and reason.

"Compose yourself," said I.

He turned a dreadful smile to me, and as if with the decision of despair, plucked away the sheet. At sight of the contents, he uttered one loud sob of such immense relief that I sat petrified. And the next moment, in a voice that was already fairly well under control, "Have you a graduated glass?" he asked.

I rose from my place with something of an effort and gave him what he asked.

He thanked me with a smiling nod, measured out a few minims of the red tincture and added one of the powders. The mixture, which was at first of a reddish hue, began, in proportion as the crystals melted, to brighten in colour, to effervesce audibly, and to throw off small fumes of vapour. Suddenly and at the same moment, the ebullition ceased and the compound changed to a dark purple, which faded again more slowly to a watery green. My visitor, who had watched these metamorphoses with a keen eye, smiled, set down the glass upon the table, and then turned and looked upon me with an air of scrutiny.

"And now," said he, "to settle what remains. Will you be wise? will you be guided? will you suffer me to take this glass in my hand and to go forth from your house without further parley? or has the greed of curiosity too much command of you? Think before you answer, for it shall be done as you decide. As you decide, you shall be left as you were before, and neither richer nor wiser, unless the sense of service rendered to a man in mortal distress may be counted as a kind of riches of the soul. Or, if you shall so prefer to choose, a new province of knowledge and new avenues to fame and power shall be laid open to you, here, in this room, upon the instant; and your sight shall be blasted by a prodigy to stagger the unbelief of Satan."

"Sir," said I, affecting a coolness that I was far from truly possessing, "you speak enigmas, and you will perhaps not wonder that I hear you with no very strong impression of belief. But I have gone too far in the way of inexplicable services to pause before I see the end."

"It is well," replied my visitor. "Lanyon, you remember your vows: what follows is under the seal of our profession. And now, you who have so long been bound to the most narrow and material views, you who have denied the virtue of transcendental medicine, you who have derided your superiors - behold!"

He put the glass to his lips and drank at one gulp. A cry followed; he reeled, staggered, clutched at the table and held on, staring with injected eyes, gasping with open mouth; and as I looked there came, I thought, a change - he seemed to swell - his face became suddenly black and the features seemed to melt and alter - and the next moment, I had sprung to my feet and leaped back against the wall, my arm raised to shield me from that prodigy, my mind submerged in terror.

"O God!" I screamed, and "O God!" again and again; for there before my eyes - pale and shaken, and half-fainting, and groping before him with his hands, like a man restored from death - there stood Henry Jekyll!

What he told me in the next hour, I cannot bring my mind to set on paper. I saw what I saw, I heard what I heard, and my soul sickened at it; and yet now when that sight has faded from my eyes, I ask myself if I believe it, and I cannot answer. My life is shaken to its roots; sleep has left me; the deadliest terror sits by me at all hours of the day and night; I feel that my days are numbered, and that I must die; and yet I shall die incredulous. As for the moral turpitude that man unveiled to me, even with tears of penitence, I cannot, even in memory, dwell on it without a start of horror. I will say but one thing, Utterson, and that (if you can bring your mind to credit it) will be more than enough. The creature who crept into my house that night was, on Jekyll's own confession, known by the name of Hyde and hunted for in every corner of the land as the murderer of Carew.

Hastie Lanyon

CHAPTER 10

Henry Jekyll's full statement of the case

I WAS born in the year 18 — to a large fortune, endowed besides with excellent parts, inclined by nature to industry, fond of the respect of the wise and good among my fellow-men, and thus, as might have been supposed, with every guarantee of an honourable and distinguished future. And indeed the worst of my faults was a certain impatient gaiety of disposition, such as has made the happiness of many, but such as I found it hard to reconcile with my imperious desire to carry my head high, and wear a more than commonly grave countenance before the public. Hence it came about that I concealed my pleasures; and that when I reached years of reflection, and began to look round me and take stock of my progress and position in the world, I stood already committed to a profound duplicity of life. Many a man would have even blazoned such irregularities as I was guilty of; but from the high views that I had set before me, I regarded and hid them with an almost morbid sense of shame. It was thus rather the exacting nature of my aspirations than any particular degradation in my faults, that made me what I was and, with even a deeper trench than in the majority of men, severed in me those provinces of good and ill which divide and compound man's dual nature. In this case, I was driven to reflect deeply and inveterately on that hard law of life, which lies at the root of religion and is one of the most plentiful springs of distress. Though so profound a double-dealer, I was in no sense a hypocrite; both sides of me were in dead earnest; I was no more myself when I laid aside restraint and plunged in shame, than when I laboured, in the eye of day, at the furtherance of knowledge or the relief of sorrow and suffering. And it chanced that the direction of my scientific studies, which led wholly toward the mystic and the transcendental, re-acted and shed a strong light on this consciousness of the perennial war among my members. With every day, and from both sides of my intelligence, the moral and the intellectual, I thus drew steadily nearer to that truth, by whose partial discovery I have been doomed to such a dreadful shipwreck: that man is not truly one, but truly two. I say two, because the state of my own knowledge does not pass beyond that point. Others will follow, others will outstrip me on the same lines; and I hazard the guess that man will be ultimately known for a mere polity of multifarious, incongruous, and independent denizens. I, for my part, from the nature of my life, advanced infallibly in one direction and in one direction only. It was on the moral side, and in my own person, that I learned to recognise the thorough and primitive duality of man; I saw that, of the two natures that contended in the field of my consciousness, even if I could rightly be said to be either, it was only because I was radically both; and from an early date, even before the course of my scientific discoveries had begun to suggest the most naked possibility of such a miracle, I had learned to dwell with pleasure, as a beloved day-dream, on the thought of the separation of these elements. If each, I told myself, could but be housed in separate identities, life would be relieved of all that was unbearable; the unjust delivered from the aspirations might go his way, and remorse of his more upright twin; and the just could walk steadfastly and securely on his upward path, doing the good things in which he found his pleasure, and no longer exposed to disgrace and penitence by the hands of this extraneous evil. It was the curse of mankind that these incongruous fagots were thus bound together that in the agonised womb of consciousness, these polar twins should be continuously struggling. How, then, were they dissociated?

I was so far in my reflections when, as I have said, a side-light began to shine upon the subject from the laboratory table. I began to perceive more deeply than it has ever yet been stated, the trembling immateriality, the mist-like transience of this seemingly so solid body in which we walk attired. Certain agents I found to have the power to shake and to pluck back that fleshly vestment, even as a wind might toss the curtains of a pavilion. For two good reasons, I will not enter deeply into this scientific branch of my confession. First, because I have been made to learn that the doom and burthen of our life is bound for ever on man's shoulders, and when the attempt is made to cast it off, it but returns upon us with more unfamiliar and more awful pressure. Second, because, as my narrative will make, alas! too evident, my discoveries were incomplete. Enough, then, that I not only recognised my natural body for the mere aura and effulgence of certain of the powers that made up my spirit, but managed to compound a drug by which these powers should be dethroned from their supremacy, and a second form and countenance substituted, none the less natural to me because they were the expression, and bore the stamp, of lower elements in my soul.

I hesitated long before I put this theory to the test of practice. I knew well that I risked death; for any drug that so potently controlled and shook the very fortress of identity, might by the least scruple of an overdose or at the least inopportunity in the moment of exhibition, utterly blot out that immaterial tabernacle which I looked to it to change. But the temptation of a discovery so singular and profound, at last overcame the suggestions of alarm. I had long since prepared my tincture; I purchased at once, from a firm of wholesale chemists, a large quantity of a particular salt which I knew, from my experiments, to be the last ingredient required; and late one accursed night, I compounded the elements, watched them boil and smoke together in the glass, and when the ebullition had subsided, with a strong glow of courage, drank off the potion.

The most racking pangs succeeded: a grinding in the bones, deadly nausea, and a horror of the spirit that cannot be exceeded at the hour of birth or death. Then these agonies began swiftly to subside, and I came to myself as if out of a great sickness. There was something strange in my sensations, something indescribably new and, from its very novelty, incredibly sweet. I felt younger, lighter, happier in body; within I was conscious of a heady recklessness, a current of disordered sensual images running like a mill-race in my fancy, a solution of the bonds of obligation, an unknown but not an innocent freedom of the soul. I knew myself, at the first breath of this new life, to be more wicked, tenfold more wicked, sold a slave to my original evil; and the thought, in that moment, braced and delighted me like wine. I stretched out my hands, exulting in the freshness of these sensations; and in the act, I was suddenly aware that I had lost in stature.

There was no mirror, at that date, in my room; that which stands beside me as I write, was brought there later on and for the very purpose of these transformations. The night, however, was far gone into the morning - the morning, black as it was, was nearly ripe for the conception of the day - the inmates of my house were locked in the most rigorous hours of slumber; and I determined, flushed as I was with hope and triumph, to venture in my new shape as far as to my bedroom. I crossed the yard, wherein the constellations looked down upon me, I could have thought, with wonder, the first creature of that sort that their unsleeping vigilance had yet disclosed to them; I stole through the corridors, a stranger in my own house; and coming to my room, I saw for the first time the appearance of Edward Hyde.

I must here speak by theory alone, saying not that which I know, but that which I suppose to be most probable. The evil side of my nature, to which I had now transferred the stamping efficacy, was less robust and less developed than the good which I had just deposed. Again, in the course of my life, which had been, after all, nine-tenths a life of effort, virtue, and control, it had been much less exercised and much less exhausted. And hence, as I think, it came about that Edward Hyde was so much smaller, slighter, and younger than Henry Jekyll. Even as good shone upon the countenance of the one, evil was written broadly and plainly on the face of the other. Evil besides (which I must still believe to be the lethal side of man) had left on that body an imprint of deformity and decay. And yet when I looked upon that ugly idol in the glass, I was conscious of no repugnance, rather of a leap of welcome. This, too, was myself. It seemed natural and human. In my eyes it bore a livelier image of the spirit, it seemed more express and single, than the imperfect and divided countenance I had been hitherto accustomed to call mine. And in so far I was doubtless right. I have observed that when I wore the semblance of Edward Hyde, none could come near to me at first without a visible misgiving of the flesh. This, as I take it, was because all human beings, as we meet them, are commingled out of good and evil: and Edward Hyde, alone in the ranks of mankind, was pure evil.

I lingered but a moment at the mirror: the second and conclusive experiment had yet to be attempted; it yet remained to be seen if I had lost my identity beyond redemption and must flee before daylight from a house that was no longer mine; and hurrying back to my cabinet, I once more prepared and drank the cup, once more suffered the pangs of dissolution, and came to myself once more with the character, the stature, and the face of Henry Jekyll.

That night I had come to the fatal cross-roads. Had

I approached my discovery in a more noble spirit, had I risked the experiment while under the empire of generous or pious aspirations, all must have been otherwise, and from these agonies of death and birth, I had come forth an angel instead of a fiend. The drug had no discriminating action; it was neither diabolical nor divine; it but shook the doors of the prison-house of my disposition; and like the captives of Philippi, that which stood within ran forth. At that time my virtue slumbered; my evil, kept awake by ambition, was alert and swift to seize the occasion; and the thing that was projected was Edward Hyde. Hence, although I had now two characters as well as two appearances, one was wholly evil, and the other was still the old Henry Jekyll, that incongruous compound of whose reformation and improvement I had already learned to despair. The movement was thus wholly toward the worse.

Even at that time, I had not yet conquered my aversion to the dryness of a life of study. I would still be merrily disposed at times; and as my pleasures were (to say the least) undignified, and I was not only well known and highly considered, but growing toward the elderly man, this incoherency of my life was daily growing more unwelcome. It was on this side that my new power tempted me until I fell in slavery. I had but to drink the cup, to doff at once the body of the noted professor, and to assume, like a thick cloak, that of Edward Hyde. I smiled at the notion; it seemed to me at the time to be humorous; and I made my preparations with the most studious care. I took and furnished that house in Soho, to which Hyde was tracked by the police; and engaged as housekeeper a creature whom I well knew to be silent and unscrupulous. On the other side, I announced to my servants that a Mr. Hyde (whom I described) was to have full liberty and power about my house in the square; and to parry mishaps, I even called and made myself a familiar object, in my second character. I next drew up that will to which you so much objected; so that if anything befell me in the person of Dr. Jekyll, I could enter on that of Edward Hyde without pecuniary loss. And thus fortified, as I supposed, on every side, I began to profit by the strange immunities of my position.

Men have before hired bravos to transact their crimes, while their own person and reputation sat under shelter. I was the first that ever did so for his pleasures. I was the first that could thus plod in the public eye with a load of genial respectability, and in a moment, like a schoolboy, strip off these lendings and spring headlong into the sea of liberty. But for me, in my impenetrable mantle, the safety was complete. Think of it - I did not even exist! Let me but escape into my laboratory door, give me but a second or two to mix and swallow the draught that I had always standing ready; and whatever he had done, Edward Hyde would pass away like the stain of breath upon a mirror; and there in his stead, quietly at home, trimming the midnight lamp in his study, a man who could afford to laugh at suspicion, would be Henry Jekyll.

The pleasures which I made haste to seek in my disguise were, as I have said, undignified; I would scarce use a harder term. But in the hands of Edward Hyde, they soon began to turn toward the monstrous. When I would come back from these excursions, I was often plunged into a kind of wonder at my vicarious depravity. This familiar that I called out of my own soul, and sent forth alone to do his good pleasure, was a being inherently malign and villainous; his every act and thought centred on self; drinking pleasure with bestial avidity from any degree of torture to another; relentless like a man of stone. Henry Jekyll stood at times aghast before the acts of Edward Hyde; but the situation was apart from ordinary laws, and insidiously relaxed the grasp of conscience. It was Hyde, after all, and Hyde alone, that was guilty. Jekyll was no worse; he woke again to his good qualities seemingly unimpaired; he would even make haste, where it was possible, to undo the evil done by Hyde. And thus his conscience slumbered.

Into the details of the infamy at which I thus connived (for even now I can scarce grant that I committed it) I have no design of entering; I mean but to point out the warnings and the successive steps with which my chastisement approached. I met with one accident which, as it brought on no consequence, I shall no more than mention. An act of cruelty to a child aroused against me the anger of a passer-by, whom I recognised the other day in the person of your kinsman; the doctor and the child's family joined him; there were moments when I feared for my life; and at last, in order to pacify their too just resentment, Edward Hyde had to bring them to the door, and pay them in a cheque drawn in the name of Henry Jekyll. But this danger was easily eliminated from the future, by opening an account at another bank in the name of Edward Hyde himself; and when, by sloping my own hand backward, I had supplied my double with a signature, I thought I sat beyond the reach of fate.

Some two months before the murder of Sir Danvers, I had been out for one of my adventures, had returned at a late hour, and woke the next day in bed with somewhat odd sensations. It was in vain I looked about me; in vain I saw the decent furniture and tall proportions of my room in the square; in vain that I recognised the pattern of the bed-curtains and the design of the mahogany frame; something still kept insisting that I was not where I was, that I had not wakened where I seemed to be, but in the little room in Soho where I was accustomed to sleep in the body of Edward Hyde. I smiled to myself, and, in my psychological way began lazily to inquire into the elements of this illusion, occasionally, even as I did so, dropping back into a comfortable morning doze. I was still so engaged when, in one of my more wakeful moments, my eyes fell upon my hand. Now the hand of Henry Jekyll (as you have often remarked) was professional in shape and size: it was large, firm, white, and comely. But the hand which I now saw, clearly enough, in the yellow light of a mid-London morning, lying half shut on the bed-clothes, was lean, corded, knuckly, of a dusky pallor and thickly shaded with a swart growth of hair. It was the hand of Edward Hyde.

I must have stared upon it for near half a minute, sunk as I was in the mere stupidity of wonder, before terror woke up in my breast as sudden and startling as the crash of cymbals; and bounding from my bed, I rushed to the mirror. At the sight that met my eyes, my blood was changed into something exquisitely thin and icy. Yes, I had gone to bed Henry Jekyll, I had awakened Edward Hyde. How was this to be explained? I asked myself, and then, with another bound of terror - how was it to be remedied? It was well on in the morning; the servants were up; all my drugs were in the cabinet - a long journey down two pairs of stairs, through the back passage, across the open court and through the anatomical theatre, from where I was then standing horror-struck. It might indeed be possible to cover my face; but of what use was that, when I was unable to conceal the alteration in my stature? And then with an overpowering sweetness of relief, it came back upon my mind that the servants were already used to the coming and going of my second self. I had soon dressed, as well as I was able, in clothes of my own size: had soon passed through the house, where Bradshaw stared and drew back at seeing Mr. Hyde at such an hour and in such a strange array; and ten minutes later, Dr. Jekyll had returned to his own shape and was sitting down, with a darkened brow, to make a feint of breakfasting.

Small indeed was my appetite. This inexplicable incident, this reversal of my previous experience, seemed, like the Babylonian finger on the wall, to be spelling out the letters of my judgment; and I began to reflect more seriously than ever before on the issues and possibilities of my double existence. That part of me which I had the power of projecting, had lately been much exercised and nourished; it had seemed to me of late as though the body of Edward Hyde had grown in stature, as though (when I wore that form) I were conscious of a more generous tide of blood; and I began to spy a danger that, if this were much prolonged, the balance of my nature might be permanently overthrown, the power of voluntary change be forfeited, and the character of Edward Hyde become irrevocably mine. The power of the drug had not been always equally displayed. Once, very early in my career, it had totally failed me; since then I had been obliged on more than one occasion to double, and once, with infinite risk of death, to treble the amount; and these rare uncertainties had cast hitherto the sole shadow on my contentment. Now, however, and in the light of that morning's accident, I was led to remark that whereas, in the beginning, the difficulty had been to throw off the body of Jekyll, it had of late gradually but decidedly transferred itself to the other side. All things therefore seemed to point to this: that I was slowly losing hold of my original and better self, and becoming slowly incorporated with my second and worse.

Between these two, I now felt I had to choose. My two natures had memory in common, but all other faculties were most unequally shared between them. Jekyll (who was composite) now with the most sensitive apprehensions, now with a greedy gusto, projected and shared in the pleasures and adventures of Hyde; but Hyde was indifferent to Jekyll, or but remembered him as the mountain bandit remembers the cavern in which he conceals himself from pursuit. Jekyll had more than a father's interest; Hyde had more than a son's indifference. To cast in my lot with Jekyll, was to die to those appetites which I had long secretly indulged and had of late begun to pamper. To cast it in with Hyde, was to die to a thousand interests and aspirations, and to become, at a blow and for ever, despised and friendless. The bargain might appear unequal; but there was still another consideration in the scales; for while Jekyll would suffer smartingly in the fires of abstinence, Hyde would be not even conscious of all that he had lost. Strange as my circumstances were, the terms of this debate are as old and commonplace as man; much the same inducements and alarms cast the die for any tempted and trembling sinner; and it fell out with me, as it falls with so vast a majority of my fellows, that I chose the better part and was found wanting in the strength to keep to it.

Yes, I preferred the elderly and discontented doctor, surrounded by friends and cherishing honest hopes; and bade a resolute farewell to the liberty, the comparative youth, the light step, leaping impulses and secret pleasures, that I had enjoyed in the disguise of Hyde. I made this choice perhaps with some unconscious reservation, for I neither gave up the house in Soho, nor destroyed the clothes of Edward Hyde, which still lay ready in my cabinet. For two months, however, I was true to my determination; for two months I led a life of such severity as I had never before attained to, and enjoyed the compensations of an approving conscience. But time began at last to obliterate the freshness of my alarm; the praises of conscience began to grow into a thing of course; I began to be tortured with throes and longings, as of Hyde struggling after freedom; and at last, in an hour of moral weakness, I once again compounded and swallowed the transforming draught.

I do not suppose that, when a drunkard reasons with himself upon his vice, he is once out of five hundred times affected by the dangers that he runs through his brutish, physical insensibility; neither had I, long as I had considered my position, made enough allowance for the complete moral insensibility and insensate readiness to evil, which were the leading characters of Edward Hyde. Yet it was by these that I was punished. My devil had been long caged, he came out roaring. I was conscious, even when I took the draught, of a more unbridled, a more furious propensity to ill. It must have been this, I suppose, that stirred in my soul that tempest of impatience with which I listened to the civilities of my unhappy victim; I declare, at least, before God, no man morally sane could have been guilty of that crime upon so pitiful a provocation; and that I struck in no more reasonable spirit than that in which a sick child may break a plaything. But I had voluntarily stripped myself of all those balancing instincts by which even the worst of us continues to walk with some degree of steadiness among temptations; and in my case, to be tempted, however slightly, was to fall.

Instantly the spirit of hell awoke in me and raged. With a transport of glee, I mauled the unresisting body, tasting delight from every blow; and it was not till weariness had begun to succeed, that I was suddenly, in the top fit of my delirium, struck through the heart by a cold thrill of terror. A mist dispersed; I saw my life to be forfeit; and fled from the scene of these excesses, at once glorying and trembling, my lust of evil gratified and stimulated, my love of life screwed to the topmost peg. I ran to the house in Soho, and (to make assurance doubly sure) destroyed my papers; thence I set out through the lamplit streets, in the same divided ecstasy of mind, gloating on my crime, light-headedly devising others in the future, and yet still hastening and still hearkening in my wake for the steps of the avenger. Hyde had a song upon his lips as he compounded the draught, and as he drank it, pledged the dead man. The pangs of transformation had not done tearing him, before Henry Jekyll, with streaming tears of gratitude and remorse, had fallen upon his knees and lifted his clasped hands to God. The veil of self-indulgence was rent from head to foot, I saw my life as a whole: I followed it up from the days of childhood, when I had walked with my father's hand, and through the self-denying toils of my professional life, to arrive again and again, with the same sense of unreality, at the damned horrors of the evening. I could have screamed aloud; I sought with tears and prayers to smother down the crowd of hideous images and sounds with which my memory swarmed against me; and still, between the petitions, the ugly face of my iniquity stared into my soul. As the acuteness of this remorse began to die away, it was succeeded by a sense of joy. The problem of my conduct was solved. Hyde was thenceforth impossible; whether I would or not, I was now confined to the better part of my existence; and oh, how I rejoiced to think it! with what willing humility, I embraced anew the restrictions of natural life! with what sincere renunciation, I locked the door by which I had so often gone and come, and ground the key under my heel!

The next day came the news that the murder had been overlooked, that the guilt of Hyde was patent to the world, and that the victim was a man high in public estimation. It was not only a crime, it had been a tragic folly. I think I was glad to know it; I think I was glad to have my better impulses thus buttressed and guarded by the terrors of the scaffold. Jekyll was now my city of refuge; let but Hyde peep out an instant, and the hands of all men would be raised to take and slay him.

I resolved in my future conduct to redeem the past; and I can say with honesty that my resolve was fruitful of some good. You know yourself how earnestly in the last months of last year, I laboured to relieve suffering; you know that much was done for others, and that the days passed quietly, almost happily for myself. Nor can I truly say that I wearied of this beneficent and innocent life; I think instead that I daily enjoyed it more completely; but I was still cursed with my duality of purpose; and as the first edge of my penitence wore off, the lower side of me, so long indulged, so recently chained down, began to growl for licence. Not that I dreamed of resuscitating Hyde; the bare idea of that would startle me to frenzy: no, it was in my own person, that I was once more tempted to trifle with my conscience; and it was as an ordinary secret sinner, that I at last fell before the assaults of temptation.

There comes an end to all things; the most capacious measure is filled at last; and this brief condescension to evil finally destroyed the balance of my soul. And yet I was not alarmed; the fall seemed natural, like a return to the old days before I had made discovery. It was a fine, clear, January day, wet under foot where the frost had melted, but cloudless overhead; and the Regent's Park was full of winter chirrupings and sweet with spring odours. I sat in the sun on a bench; the animal within me licking the chops of memory; the spiritual side a little drowsed, promising subsequent penitence, but not yet moved to begin. After all, I reflected, I was like my neighbours; and then I smiled, comparing myself with other men, comparing my active goodwill with the lazy cruelty of their neglect. And at the very moment of that vain-glorious thought, a qualm came over me, a horrid nausea and the most deadly shuddering. These passed away, and left me faint; and then as in its turn the faintness subsided, I began to be aware of a change in the temper of my thoughts, a greater boldness, a contempt of danger, a solution of the bonds of obligation. I looked down; my clothes hung formlessly on my shrunken limbs; the hand that lay on my knee was corded and hairy. I was once more Edward Hyde. A moment before I had been safe of all men's respect, wealthy, beloved - the cloth laying for me in the dining-room at home; and now I was the common quarry of mankind, hunted, houseless, a known murderer, thrall to the gallows.

My reason wavered, but it did not fail me utterly. I have more than once observed that, in my second character, my faculties seemed sharpened to a point and my spirits more tensely elastic; thus it came about that, where Jekyll perhaps might have succumbed, Hyde rose to the importance of the moment. My drugs were in one of the presses of my cabinet; how was I to reach them? That was the problem that (crushing my temples in my hands) I set myself to solve. The laboratory door I had closed. If I sought to enter by the house, my own servants would consign me to the gallows. I saw I must employ another hand, and thought of Lanyon. How was he to be reached? how persuaded? Supposing that I escaped capture in the streets, how was I to make my way into his presence? and how should I, an unknown and displeasing visitor, prevail on the famous physician to rifle the study of his colleague, Dr. Jekyll? Then I remembered that of my original character, one part remained to me: I could write my own hand; and once I had conceived that kindling spark, the way that I must follow became lighted up from end to end.

Thereupon, I arranged my clothes as best I could, and summoning a passing hansom, drove to an hotel in Portland Street, the name of which I chanced to remember. At my appearance (which was indeed comical enough, however tragic a fate these garments covered) the driver could not conceal his mirth. I gnashed my teeth upon him with a gust of devilish fury; and the smile withered from his face - happily for him - yet more happily for myself, for in another instant I had certainly dragged him from his perch. At the inn, as I entered, I looked about me with so black a countenance as made the attendants tremble; not a look did they exchange in my presence; but obsequiously took my orders, led me to a private room, and brought me wherewithal to write. Hyde in danger of his life was a creature new to me; shaken with inordinate anger, strung to the pitch of murder, lusting to inflict pain. Yet the creature was astute; mastered his fury with a great effort of the will; composed his two important letters, one to Lanyon and one to Poole; and that he might receive actual evidence of their being posted, sent them out with directions that they should be registered.

Thenceforward, he sat all day over the fire in the private room, gnawing his nails; there he dined, sitting alone with his fears, the waiter visibly quailing before his eye; and thence, when the night was fully come, he set forth in the corner of a closed cab, and was driven to and fro about the streets of the city. He, I say - I cannot say, I. That child of Hell had nothing human; nothing lived in him but fear and hatred. And when at last, thinking the driver had begun to grow suspicious, he discharged the cab and ventured on foot, attired in his misfitting clothes, an object marked out for observation, into the midst of the nocturnal passengers, these two base passions raged within him like a tempest. He walked fast, hunted by his fears, chattering to himself, skulking through the less-frequented thoroughfares, counting the minutes that still divided him from midnight. Once a woman spoke to him, offering, I think, a box of lights. He smote her in the face, and she fled.

When I came to myself at Lanyon's, the horror of my old friend perhaps affected me somewhat: I do not know; it was at least but a drop in the sea to the abhorrence with which I looked back upon these hours. A change had come over me. It was no longer the fear of the gallows, it was the horror of being Hyde that racked me. I received Lanyon's condemnation partly in a dream; it was partly in a dream that I came home to my own house and got into bed. I slept after the prostration of the day, with a stringent and profound slumber which not even the nightmares that wrung me could avail to break. I awoke in the morning shaken, weakened, but refreshed. I still hated and feared the thought of the brute that slept within me, and I had not of course forgotten the appalling dangers of the day before; but I was once more at home, in my own house and close to my drugs; and gratitude for my escape shone so strong in my soul that it almost rivalled the brightness of hope.

I was stepping leisurely across the court after breakfast, drinking the chill of the air with pleasure, when I was seized again with those indescribable sensations that heralded the change; and I had but the time to gain the shelter of my cabinet, before I was once again raging and freezing with the passions of Hyde. It took on this occasion a double dose to recall me to myself; and alas! Six hours after, as I sat looking sadly in the fire, the pangs returned, and the drug had to be re-administered. In short, from that day forth it seemed only by a great effort as of gymnastics, and only under the immediate stimulation of the drug, that I was able to wear the countenance of Jekyll. At all hours of the day and night, I would be taken with the premonitory shudder; above all, if I slept, or even dozed for a moment in my chair, it was always as Hyde that I awakened. Under the strain of this continually-impending doom and by the sleeplessness to which I now condemned myself, ay, even beyond what I had thought possible to man, I became, in my own person, a creature eaten up and emptied by fever, languidly weak both in body and mind, and solely occupied by one thought: the horror of my other self. But when I slept, or when the virtue of the medicine wore off, I would leap almost without transition (for the pangs of transformation grew daily less marked) into the possession of a fancy brimming with images of terror, a soul boiling with causeless hatreds, and a body that seemed not strong enough to contain the raging energies of life. The powers of Hyde seemed to have grown with the sickliness of Jekyll. And certainly the hate that now divided them was equal on each side. With Jekyll, it was a thing of vital instinct. He had now seen the full deformity of that creature that shared with him some of the phenomena of consciousness, and was co-heir with him to death: and beyond these links of community, which in themselves made the most poignant part of his distress, he thought of Hyde, for all his energy of life, as of something not only hellish but inorganic. This was the shocking thing; that the slime of the pit seemed to utter cries and voices; that the amorphous dust gesticulated and sinned; that what was dead, and had no shape, should usurp the offices of life. And this again, that that insurgent horror was knit to him closer than a wife, closer than an eye; lay caged in his flesh, where he heard it mutter and felt it struggle to be born; and at every hour of weakness, and in the confidence of slumber, prevailed against him and deposed him out of life. The hatred of Hyde for Jekyll, was of a different order. His terror of the gallows drove him continually to commit temporary suicide, and return to his subordinate station of a part instead of a person; but he loathed the necessity, he loathed the despondency into which Jekyll was now fallen, and he resented the dislike with which he was himself regarded. Hence the ape-like tricks that he would play me, scrawling in my own hand blasphemies on the pages of my books, burning the letters and destroying the portrait of my father; and indeed, had it not been for his fear of death, he would long ago have ruined himself in order to involve me in the ruin. But his love of life is wonderful; I go further: I, who sicken and freeze at the mere thought of him, when I recall the abjection and passion of this attachment, and when I know how he fears my power to cut him off by suicide, I find it in my heart to pity him.

It is useless, and the time awfully fails me, to prolong this description; no one has ever suffered such torments, let that suffice; and yet even to these, habit brought - no, not alleviation - but a certain callousness of soul, a certain acquiescence of despair; and my punishment might have gone on for years, but for the last calamity which has now fallen, and which has finally severed me from my own face and nature. My provision of the salt, which had never been renewed since the date of the first experiment, began to run low. I sent out for a fresh supply, and mixed the draught; the ebullition followed, and the first change of colour, not the second; I drank it and it was without efficiency. You will learn from Poole how I have had London ransacked; it was in vain; and I am now persuaded that my first supply was impure, and that it was that unknown impurity which lent efficacy to the draught.

About a week has passed, and I am now finishing this

statement under the influence of the last of the old powders. This, then, is the last time, short of a miracle, that Henry Jekyll can think his own thoughts or see his own face (now how sadly altered!) in the glass. Nor must I delay too long to bring my writing to an end; for if my narrative has hitherto escaped destruction, it has been by a combination of great prudence and great good luck. Should the throes of change take me in the act of writing it, Hyde will tear it in pieces; but if some time shall have elapsed after I have laid it by, his wonderful selfishness and Circumscription to the moment will probably save it once again from the action of his ape-like spite. And indeed the doom that is closing on us both, has already changed and crushed him. Half an hour from now, when I shall again and for ever re-indue that hated personality, I know how I shall sit shuddering and weeping in my chair, or continue, with the most strained and fear-struck ecstasy of listening, to pace up and down this room (my last earthly refuge) and give ear to every sound of menace. Will Hyde die upon the scaffold? or will he find courage to release himself at the last moment? God knows; I am careless; this is my true hour of death, and what is to follow concerns another than myself. Here then, as I lay down the pen and proceed to seal up my confession, I bring the life of that unhappy Henry Jekyll to an end.

Kidnapped

Kidnapped

Robert Louis Stevenson

This is a Transatlantic Press book
This edition published in 2012

Transatlantic Press
Sky House, Raans Road, Amersham, Bucks, HP6 6JQ, UK

ISBN 978-1-908533-79-1

Printed and bound by CPI Group (UK) Ltd, Croydon, CR0 4YY

ROBERT LOUIS STEVENSON

Robert Louis Stevenson was born in Edinburgh in 1850, the son of an engineer who specialised in the field of lighthouse construction. He flirted briefly with the idea of following in his father's footsteps, embarking on an engineering degree in his hometown university. But he had neither the constitution – he was dogged by ill health throughout his life – nor the inclination to pursue that course and instead became a law student. His roving spirit and desire to write put the brakes on a legal career before it started. Having got into print in magazines and periodicals, Stevenson published *An Inland Voyage* (1878) and *Travels with a Donkey in the Cévennes* (1879), accounts of his travels through France and Belgium. *Treasure Island* (1883) brought him fame, and his later novels, such as *Kidnapped* (1886), its sequel *Catriona* (1893) and *The Master of Ballantrae* (1889) established his reputation in the historical adventure genre. He provided thrills of a different kind with *The Strange Case of Dr Jekyll and Mr Hyde*, which ranks among the best in the Gothic literature tradition. In 1888 he set sail for the South Seas with his family, settling in Samoa, where he spent his final years. He became a great advocate for the islanders, who in turn had great affection for the man they called 'Tusitala' – 'Teller of Tales'. Stevenson died from a cerebral haemorrhage in 1894, leaving an unfinished novel, *Weir of Hermiston,* which was published posthumously.

KIDNAPPED

"The woman's face lit up with a malignant anger.
'That is the house of Shaws!' she cried.
'Blood built it; blood stopped the building of it;
blood shall bring it down.' "

With the death of his father, David Balfour is left orphaned and impoverished. He receives a strange inheritance: a sealed letter to be delivered to one Ebenezer Balfour – an uncle he never knew he had. At the cold, forbidding house where the miserly Ebenezer lives, David is given a frosty reception. He soon suspects that his father may have been the elder brother, and that Ebenezer is a usurper. Those suspicions gain credence when he narrowly avoids a death-trap laid by his uncle, and are confirmed when he is duped aboard a ship bound for the Carolinas. A collision off the Hebrides brings David an ally in the shape of Alan Breck, who is rescued from the stricken vessel. Breck is a fiery, romantic, Jacobite Highlander, while David is from the Lowlands, rooted in the rationalist, pro-Hanoverian, Whig tradition, but the two forge an unlikely bond in the fight for freedom and justice.

CONTENTS

DEDICATION

MY DEAR CHARLES BAXTER,

If you ever read this tale, you will likely ask yourself more questions than I should care to answer: as for instance how the Appin murder has come to fall in the year 1751, how the Torran rocks have crept so near to Earraid, or why the printed trial is silent as to all that touches David Balfour. These are nuts beyond my ability to crack. But if you tried me on the point of Alan's guilt or innocence, I think I could defend the reading of the text. To this day you will find the tradition of Appin clear in Alan's favour. If you inquire, you may even hear that the descendants of "the other man" who fired the shot are in the country to this day. But that other man's name, inquire as you please, you shall not hear; for the Highlander values a secret for itself and for the congenial exercise of keeping it I might go on for long to justify one point and own another indefensible; it is more honest to confess at once how little I am touched by the desire of accuracy. This is no furniture for the scholar's library, but a book for the winter evening school-room when the tasks are over and the hour for bed draws near; and honest Alan, who was a grim old fire-eater in his day has in this new avatar no more desperate purpose than to steal some young gentleman's attention from his Ovid, carry him awhile into the Highlands and the last century, and pack him to bed with some engaging images to mingle with his dreams.

As for you, my dear Charles, I do not even ask you to like this tale. But perhaps when he is older, your son will; he may then be pleased to find his father's name on the fly-leaf; and in the meanwhile it pleases me to set it there, in memory of many days that were happy and some (now perhaps as pleasant to remember) that were sad. If it is strange for me to look back from a distance both in time and space on these bygone adventures of our youth, it must be stranger for you who tread the same streets—who may to-morrow open the door of the old Speculative, where we begin to rank with Scott and Robert Emmet and the beloved and inglorious Macbean—or may pass the corner of the close where that great society, the L. J. R., held its meetings and drank its beer, sitting in the seats of Burns and his companions. I think I see you, moving there by plain daylight, beholding with your natural eyes those places that have now become for your companion a part of the scenery of dreams. How, in the intervals of present business, the past must echo in your memory! Let it not echo often without some kind thoughts of your friend,

R.L.S.

SKERRYVORE,
   BOURNEMOUTH.

CHAPTER I

I SET OFF UPON MY JOURNEY TO THE HOUSE OF SHAWS

I will begin the story of my adventures with a certain morning early in the month of June, the year of grace 1751, when I took the key for the last time out of the door of my father's house. The sun began to shine upon the summit of the hills as I went down the road; and by the time I had come as far as the manse, the blackbirds were whistling in the garden lilacs, and the mist that hung around the valley in the time of the dawn was beginning to arise and die away.

Mr. Campbell, the minister of Essendean, was waiting for me by the garden gate, good man! He asked me if I had breakfasted; and hearing that I lacked for nothing, he took my hand in both of his and clapped it kindly under his arm.

"Well, Davie, lad," said he, "I will go with you as far as the ford, to set you on the way."

And we began to walk forward in silence.

"Are ye sorry to leave Essendean?" said he, after awhile.

"Why, sir," said I, "if I knew where I was going, or what was likely to become of me, I would tell you candidly. Essendean is a good place indeed, and I have been very happy there; but then I have never been anywhere else. My father and mother, since they are both dead, I shall be no nearer to in Essendean than in the Kingdom of Hungary, and, to speak truth, if I thought I had a chance to better myself where I was going I would go with a good will."

"Ay?" said Mr. Campbell. "Very well, Davie. Then it behoves me to tell your fortune; or so far as I may. When your mother was gone, and your father (the worthy, Christian man) began to sicken for his end, he gave me in charge a certain letter, which he said was your inheritance. 'So soon,' says he, 'as I am gone, and the house is redd up and the gear disposed of' (all which, Davie, hath been done), 'give my boy this letter into his hand, and start him off to the house of Shaws, not far from Cramond. That is the place I came from,' he said, 'and it's where it befits that my boy should return. He is a steady lad,' your father said, 'and a canny goer; and I doubt not he will come safe, and be well lived where he goes.'"

"The house of Shaws!" I cried. "What had my poor father to do with the house of Shaws?"

"Nay," said Mr. Campbell, "who can tell that for a surety? But the name of that family, Davie, boy, is the name you bear—Balfours of Shaws: an ancient, honest, reputable house, peradventure in these latter days decayed. Your father, too, was a man of learning as befitted his position; no man more plausibly conducted school; nor had he the manner or the speech of a common dominie; but (as ye will yourself remember) I took aye a pleasure to have him to the manse to meet the gentry; and those of my own house, Campbell of Kilrennet, Campbell of Dunswire, Campbell of Minch, and others, all well-kenned gentlemen, had pleasure in his society. Lastly, to put all the elements of this affair before you, here is the testamentary letter itself, superscrived by the own hand of our departed brother."

He gave me the letter, which was addressed in these words: "To the hands of Ebenezer Balfour, Esquire, of Shaws, in his house of Shaws, these will be delivered by my son, David Balfour." My heart was beating hard at this great prospect now suddenly opening before a lad of seventeen years of age, the son of a poor country dominie in the Forest of Ettrick.

"Mr. Campbell," I stammered, "and if you were in my shoes, would you go?"

"Of a surety," said the minister, "that would I, and without pause. A pretty lad like you should get to Cramond (which is near in by Edinburgh) in two days of walk. If the worst came to the worst, and your high relations (as I cannot but suppose them to be somewhat of your blood) should put you to the door, ye can but walk the two days back again and risp at the manse door. But I would rather hope that ye shall be well received, as your poor father forecast for you, and for anything that I ken come to be a great man in time. And here, Davie, laddie," he resumed, "it lies near upon my conscience to improve this parting, and set you on the right guard against the dangers of the world."

Here he cast about for a comfortable seat, lighted on a big boulder under a birch by the trackside, sate down upon it with a very long, serious upper lip, and the sun now shining in upon us between two peaks, put his pocket-handkerchief over his cocked hat to shelter him. There, then, with uplifted forefinger, he first put me on my guard against a considerable number of heresies, to which I had no temptation, and urged upon me to be instant in my prayers and reading of the Bible. That done, he drew a picture of the great house that I was bound to, and how I should conduct myself with its inhabitants.

"Be soople, Davie, in things immaterial," said he. "Bear ye this in mind, that, though gentle born, ye have had a country rearing. Dinnae shame us, Davie, dinnae shame us! In yon great, muckle house, with all these domestics, upper and under, show yourself as nice, as circumspect, as quick at the conception, and as slow of speech as any. As for the laird—remember he's the laird; I say no more: honour to whom honour. It's a pleasure to obey a laird; or should be, to the young."

"Well, sir," said I, "it may be; and I'll promise you I'll try to make it so."

"Why, very well said," replied Mr. Campbell, heartily. "And now to come to the material, or (to make a quibble) to the immaterial. I have here a little packet which contains four things." He tugged it, as he spoke, and with some great difficulty, from the skirt pocket of his coat. "Of these four things, the first is your legal due: the little pickle money for your father's books and plenishing, which I have bought (as I have explained from the first) in the design of re-selling at a profit to the incoming dominie. The other three are gifties that Mrs. Campbell and myself would be blithe of your acceptance. The first, which is round, will likely please ye best at the first off-go; but, O Davie, laddie, it's but a drop of water in the sea; it'll help you but a step, and vanish like the morning. The second, which is flat and square and written upon, will stand by you through life, like a good staff for the road, and a good pillow to your head in sickness. And as for the last, which is cubical, that'll see you, it's my prayerful wish, into a better land."

With that he got upon his feet, took off his hat, and prayed a little while aloud, and in affecting terms, for a young man setting out into the world; then suddenly took me in his arms and embraced me very hard; then held me at arm's length, looking at me with his face all working with sorrow; and then whipped about, and crying good-bye to me, set off backward by the way that we had come at a sort of jogging run. It might have been laughable to another; but I was in no mind to laugh. I watched him as long as he was in sight; and he never stopped hurrying, nor once looked back. Then it came in upon my mind that this was all his sorrow at my departure; and my conscience smote me hard and fast, because I, for my part, was overjoyed to get away out of that quiet country-side, and go to a great, busy house, among rich and respected gentlefolk of my own name and blood.

"Davie, Davie," I thought, "was ever seen such black

ingratitude? Can you forget old favours and old friends at the mere whistle of a name? Fie, fie; think shame."

And I sat down on the boulder the good man had just left, and opened the parcel to see the nature of my gifts. That which he had called cubical, I had never had much doubt of; sure enough it was a little Bible, to carry in a plaid-neuk. That which he had called round, I found to be a shilling piece; and the third, which was to help me so wonderfully both in health and sickness all the days of my life, was a little piece of coarse yellow paper, written upon thus in red ink:

"TO MAKE LILLY OF THE VALLEY WATER.—Take the flowers of lilly of the valley and distil them in sack, and drink a spoonful or two as there is occasion. It restores speech to those that have the dumb palsey. It is good against the Gout; it comforts the heart and strengthens the memory; and the flowers, put into a Glasse, close stopt, and set into ane hill of ants for a month, then take it out, and you will find a liquor which comes from the flowers, which keep in a vial; it is good, ill or well, and whether man or woman."

And then, in the minister's own hand, was added:

"Likewise for sprains, rub it in; and for the cholic, a great spoonful in the hour."

To be sure, I laughed over this; but it was rather tremulous laughter; and I was glad to get my bundle on my staff's end and set out over the ford and up the hill upon the farther side; till, just as I came on the green drove-road running wide through the heather, I took my last look of Kirk Essendean, the trees about the manse, and the big rowans in the kirkyard where my father and my mother lay.

CHAPTER II

I COME TO MY JOURNEY'S END

On the forenoon of the second day, coming to the top of a hill, I saw all the country fall away before me down to the sea; and in the midst of this descent, on a long ridge, the city of Edinburgh smoking like a kiln. There was a flag upon the castle, and ships moving or lying anchored in the firth; both of which, for as far away as they were, I could distinguish clearly; and both brought my country heart into my mouth.

Presently after, I came by a house where a shepherd lived, and got a rough direction for the neighbourhood of Cramond; and so, from one to another, worked my way to the westward of the capital by Colinton, till I came out upon the Glasgow road. And there, to my great pleasure and wonder, I beheld a regiment marching to the fifes, every foot in time; an old red-faced general on a grey horse at the one end, and at the other the company of Grenadiers, with their Pope's-hats. The pride of life seemed to mount into my brain at the sight of the red coats and the hearing of that merry music.

A little farther on, and I was told I was in Cramond parish, and began to substitute in my inquiries the name of the house of Shaws. It was a word that seemed to surprise those of whom I sought my way. At first I thought the plainness of my appearance, in my country habit, and that all dusty from the road, consorted ill with the greatness of the place to which I was bound. But after two, or maybe three, had given me the same look and the same answer, I began to take it in my head there was something strange about the Shaws itself.

The better to set this fear at rest, I changed the form of my inquiries; and spying an honest fellow coming along a lane on the shaft of his cart, I asked him if he had ever heard tell of a house they called the house of Shaws.

He stopped his cart and looked at me, like the others.

"Ay" said he. "What for?"

"It's a great house?" I asked.

"Doubtless," says he. "The house is a big, muckle house."

"Ay," said I, "but the folk that are in it?"

"Folk?" cried he. "Are ye daft? There's nae folk there—to call folk."

"What?" say I; "not Mr. Ebenezer?"

"Ou, ay" says the man; "there's the laird, to be sure, if it's him you're wanting. What'll like be your business, mannie?"

"I was led to think that I would get a situation," I said, looking as modest as I could.

"What?" cries the carter, in so sharp a note that his very horse started; and then, "Well, mannie," he added, "it's nane of my affairs; but ye seem a decent-spoken lad; and if ye'll take a word from me, ye'll keep clear of the Shaws."

The next person I came across was a dapper little man in a beautiful white wig, whom I saw to be a barber on his rounds; and knowing well that barbers were great gossips, I asked him plainly what sort of a man was Mr. Balfour of the Shaws.

"Hoot, hoot, hoot," said the barber, "nae kind of a man, nae kind of a man at all;" and began to ask me very shrewdly what my business was; but I was more than a match for him at that, and he went on to his next customer no wiser than he came.

I cannot well describe the blow this dealt to my illusions. The more indistinct the accusations were, the less I liked them, for they left the wider field to fancy. What kind of a great house was this, that all the parish should start and stare to be asked the way to it? or what sort of a gentleman, that his ill-fame should be thus current on the wayside? If an hour's walking would have brought me back to Essendean, had left my adventure then and there, and returned to Mr. Campbell's. But when I had come so far a way already, mere shame would not suffer me to desist till I had put the matter to the touch of proof; I was bound, out of mere self-respect, to carry it through; and little as I liked the sound of what I heard, and slow as I began to travel, I still kept asking my way and still kept advancing.

It was drawing on to sundown when I met a stout, dark, sour-looking woman coming trudging down a hill; and she, when I had put my usual question, turned sharp about, accompanied me back to the summit she had just left, and pointed to a great bulk of building standing very bare upon a green in the bottom of the next valley. The country was pleasant round about, running in low hills, pleasantly watered and wooded, and the crops, to my eyes, wonderfully good; but the house itself appeared to be a kind of ruin; no road led up to it; no smoke arose from any of the chimneys; nor was there any semblance of a garden. My heart sank. "That!" I cried.

The woman's face lit up with a malignant anger. "That is the house of Shaws!" she cried. "Blood built it; blood stopped the building of it; blood shall bring it down. See here!" she cried again—"I spit upon the ground, and crack my thumb at it! Black be its fall! If ye see the laird, tell him what ye hear; tell him this makes the twelve hunner and nineteen time that Jennet Clouston has called down the curse on him and his house, byre and stable, man, guest, and master, wife, miss, or bairn—black, black be their fall!"

And the woman, whose voice had risen to a kind of eldritch sing-song, turned with a skip, and was gone. I stood where she left me, with my hair on end. In those days folk still believed in witches and trembled at a curse; and this one, falling so pat, like a wayside omen, to arrest me ere I carried out my purpose, took the pith out of my legs.

I sat me down and stared at the house of Shaws. The more I looked, the pleasanter that country-side appeared; being all set with hawthorn bushes full of flowers; the fields dotted with sheep; a fine flight of rooks in the sky; and every sign of a kind soil and climate; and yet the barrack in the midst of it went sore against my fancy.

Country folk went by from the fields as I sat there on the side of the ditch, but I lacked the spirit to give them a good-e'en. At last the sun went down, and then, right up against the yellow sky, I saw a scroll of smoke go mounting, not much thicker, as it seemed to me, than the smoke of a candle; but still there it was, and meant a fire, and warmth, and cookery, and some living inhabitant that must have lit it; and this comforted my heart.

So I set forward by a little faint track in the grass that led in my direction. It was very faint indeed to be the only way to a place of habitation; yet I saw no other. Presently it brought me to stone uprights, with an unroofed lodge beside them, and coats of arms upon the top. A main entrance it was plainly meant to be, but never finished; instead of gates of wrought iron, a pair of hurdles were tied across with a straw rope; and as there were no park walls, nor any sign of avenue, the track that I was following passed on the right hand of the pillars, and went wandering on toward the house.

The nearer I got to that, the drearier it appeared. It seemed like the one wing of a house that had never been finished. What should have been the inner end stood open on the upper floors, and showed against the sky with steps and stairs of uncompleted masonry. Many of the windows were unglazed, and bats flew in and out like doves out of a dove-cote.

The night had begun to fall as I got close; and in three of the lower windows, which were very high up and narrow, and well barred, the changing light of a little fire began to glimmer.

Was this the palace I had been coming to? Was it within

these walls that I was to seek new friends and begin great fortunes? Why, in my father's house on Essen-Waterside, the fire and the bright lights would show a mile away, and the door open to a beggar's knock!

I came forward cautiously, and giving ear as I came, heard some one rattling with dishes, and a little dry, eager cough that came in fits; but there was no sound of speech, and not a dog barked.

The door, as well as I could see it in the dim light, was a great piece of wood all studded with nails; and I lifted my hand with a faint heart under my jacket, and knocked once. Then I stood and waited. The house had fallen into a dead silence; a whole minute passed away, and nothing stirred but the bats overhead. I knocked again, and hearkened again. By this time my ears had grown so accustomed to the quiet, that I could hear the ticking of the clock inside as it slowly counted out the seconds; but whoever was in that house kept deadly still, and must have held his breath.

I was in two minds whether to run away; but anger got the upper hand, and I began instead to rain kicks and buffets on the door, and to shout out aloud for Mr. Balfour. I was in full career, when I heard the cough right overhead, and jumping back and looking up, beheld a man's head in a tall nightcap, and the bell mouth of a blunderbuss, at one of the first-storey windows.

"It's loaded," said a voice.

"I have come here with a letter," I said, "to Mr. Ebenezer Balfour of Shaws. Is he here?"

"From whom is it?" asked the man with the blunderbuss.

"That is neither here nor there," said I, for I was growing very wroth.

"Well," was the reply, "ye can put it down upon the doorstep, and be off with ye."

"I will do no such thing," I cried. "I will deliver it into

Mr. Balfour's hands, as it was meant I should. It is a letter of introduction."

"A what?" cried the voice, sharply.

I repeated what I had said.

"Who are ye, yourself?" was the next question, after a considerable pause.

"I am not ashamed of my name," said I. "They call me David Balfour."

At that, I made sure the man started, for I heard the blunderbuss rattle on the window-sill; and it was after quite a long pause, and with a curious change of voice, that the next question followed:

"Is your father dead?"

I was so much surprised at this, that I could find no voice to answer, but stood staring.

"Ay" the man resumed, "he'll be dead, no doubt; and that'll be what brings ye chapping to my door." Another pause, and then defiantly, "Well, man," he said, "I'll let ye in;" and he disappeared from the window.

CHAPTER III

I MAKE ACQUAINTANCE OF
MY UNCLE

Presently there came a great rattling of chains and bolts, and the door was cautiously opened and shut to again behind me as soon as I had passed.

"Go into the kitchen and touch naething," said the voice; and while the person of the house set himself to replacing the defences of the door, I groped my way forward and entered the kitchen.

The fire had burned up fairly bright, and showed me the barest room I think I ever put my eyes on. Half-a-dozen dishes stood upon the shelves; the table was laid for supper with a bowl of porridge, a horn spoon, and a cup of small beer. Besides what I have named, there was not another thing in that great, stone-vaulted, empty chamber but lockfast chests arranged along the wall and a corner cupboard with a padlock.

As soon as the last chain was up, the man rejoined me. He was a mean, stooping, narrow-shouldered, clay-faced creature; and his age might have been anything between fifty and seventy. His nightcap was of flannel, and so was the nightgown that he wore, instead of coat and waistcoat, over his ragged shirt. He was long unshaved; but what most distressed and even daunted me, he would neither take his eyes away from me nor look me fairly in the face. What he was, whether by trade or birth, was more than I could fathom; but he seemed most like an old, unprofitable serving-man, who should have been left in charge of that big house upon board wages.

"Are ye sharp-set?" he asked, glancing at about the level of my knee. "Ye can eat that drop parritch?"

I said I feared it was his own supper.

"O," said he, "I can do fine wanting it. I'll take the ale, though, for it slockens (moistens) my cough." He drank the cup about half out, still keeping an eye upon me as he drank; and then suddenly held out his hand. "Let's see the letter," said he.

I told him the letter was for Mr. Balfour; not for him.

"And who do ye think I am?" says he. "Give me Alexander's letter."

"You know my father's name?"

"It would be strange if I didnae," he returned, "for he was my born brother; and little as ye seem to like either me or my house, or my good parritch, I'm your born uncle, Davie, my man, and you my born nephew. So give us the letter, and sit down and fill your kyte."

If I had been some years younger, what with shame, weariness, and disappointment, I believe I had burst into tears. As it was, I could find no words, neither black nor white, but handed him the letter, and sat down to the porridge with as little appetite for meat as ever a young man had.

Meanwhile, my uncle, stooping over the fire, turned the letter over and over in his hands.

"Do ye ken what's in it?" he asked, suddenly.

"You see for yourself, sir," said I, "that the seal has not been broken."

"Ay," said he, "but what brought you here?"

"To give the letter," said I.

"No," says he, cunningly, "but ye'll have had some hopes, nae doubt?"

"I confess, sir," said I, "when I was told that I had kinsfolk well-to-do, I did indeed indulge the hope that they might help me in my life. But I am no beggar; I look for no favours at your hands, and I want none that are not freely given. For as poor as I appear, I have friends of my own that will be blithe to help me."

"Hoot-toot!" said Uncle Ebenezer, "dinnae fly up in the snuff at me. We'll agree fine yet. And, Davie, my man, if you're done with that bit parritch, I could just take a sup of it myself. Ay," he continued, as soon as he had ousted me from the stool and spoon, "they're fine, halesome food—they're grand food, parritch." He murmured a little grace to himself and fell to. "Your father was very fond of his meat, I mind; he was a hearty, if not a great eater; but as for me, I could never do mair than pyke at food." He took a pull at the small beer, which probably reminded him of hospitable duties, for his next speech ran thus: "If ye're dry ye'll find water behind the door."

To this I returned no answer, standing stiffly on my two feet, and looking down upon my uncle with a mighty angry heart. He, on his part, continued to eat like a man under some pressure of time, and to throw out little darting glances now at my shoes and now at my home-spun stockings. Once only, when he had ventured to look a little higher, our eyes met; and no thief taken with a hand in a man's pocket could have shown more lively signals of distress. This set me in a muse, whether his timidity arose from too long a disuse of any human company; and whether perhaps, upon a little trial, it might pass off, and my uncle change into an altogether different man. From this I was awakened by his sharp voice.

"Your father's been long dead?" he asked.

"Three weeks, sir," said I.

"He was a secret man, Alexander—a secret, silent man," he continued. "He never said muckle when he was young. He'll never have spoken muckle of me?"

"I never knew, sir, till you told it me yourself, that he had any brother."

"Dear me, dear me!" said Ebenezer. "Nor yet of Shaws, I dare say?"

"Not so much as the name, sir," said I.

"To think o' that!" said he. "A strange nature of a man!" For all that, he seemed singularly satisfied, but whether with himself, or me, or with this conduct of my father's, was more than I could read. Certainly, however, he seemed to be outgrowing that distaste, or ill-will, that he had conceived at first against my person; for presently he jumped up, came across the room behind me, and hit me a smack upon the shoulder. "We'll agree fine yet!" he cried. "I'm just as glad I let you in. And now come awa' to your bed."

To my surprise, he lit no lamp or candle, but set forth into the dark passage, groped his way, breathing deeply, up a flight of steps, and paused before a door, which he unlocked. I was close upon his heels, having stumbled after him as best I might; and then he bade me go in, for that was my chamber. I did as he bid, but paused after a few steps, and begged a light to go to bed with.

"Hoot-toot!" said Uncle Ebenezer, "there's a fine moon."

"Neither moon nor star, sir, and pit-mirk," said I. "I cannae see the bed."

"Hoot-toot, hoot-toot!" said he. "Lights in a house is a thing I dinnae agree with. I'm unco feared of fires. Good-night to ye, Davie, my man." And before I had time to add a further protest, he pulled the door to, and I heard him lock me in from the outside.

I did not know whether to laugh or cry. The room was as cold as a well, and the bed, when I had found my way to it, as damp as a peat-hag; but by good fortune I had caught up my bundle and my plaid, and rolling myself in the latter, I lay down upon the floor under lee of the big bedstead, and fell speedily asleep.

With the first peep of day I opened my eyes, to find myself

in a great chamber, hung with stamped leather, furnished with fine embroidered furniture, and lit by three fair windows. Ten years ago, or perhaps twenty, it must have been as pleasant a room to lie down or to awake in as a man could wish; but damp, dirt, disuse, and the mice and spiders had done their worst since then. Many of the window-panes, besides, were broken; and indeed this was so common a feature in that house, that I believe my uncle must at some time have stood a siege from his indignant neighbours—perhaps with Jennet Clouston at their head.

Meanwhile the sun was shining outside; and being very cold in that miserable room, I knocked and shouted till my gaoler came and let me out. He carried me to the back of the house, where was a draw-well, and told me to "wash my face there, if I wanted;" and when that was done, I made the best of my own way back to the kitchen, where he had lit the fire and was making the porridge. The table was laid with two bowls and two horn spoons, but the same single measure of small beer. Perhaps my eye rested on this particular with some surprise, and perhaps my uncle observed it; for he spoke up as if in answer to my thought, asking me if I would like to drink ale—for so he called it.

I told him such was my habit, but not to put himself about.

"Na, na," said he; "I'll deny you nothing in reason."

He fetched another cup from the shelf; and then, to my great surprise, instead of drawing more beer, he poured an accurate half from one cup to the other. There was a kind of nobleness in this that took my breath away; if my uncle was certainly a miser, he was one of that thorough breed that goes near to make the vice respectable.

When we had made an end of our meal, my uncle Ebenezer unlocked a drawer, and drew out of it a clay pipe and a lump of tobacco, from which he cut one fill before he locked it up again. Then he sat down in the sun at one of the windows and silently smoked. From time to time his eyes came coasting round to me, and he shot out one of his questions. Once it was, "And your mother?" and when I had told him that she, too, was dead, "Ay, she was a bonnie lassie!" Then, after another long pause, "Whae were these friends o' yours?"

I told him they were different gentlemen of the name of Campbell; though, indeed, there was only one, and that the minister, that had ever taken the least note of me; but I began to think my uncle made too light of my position, and finding myself all alone with him, I did not wish him to suppose me helpless.

He seemed to turn this over in his mind; and then, "Davie, my man," said he, "ye've come to the right bit when ye came to your uncle Ebenezer. I've a great notion of the family, and I mean to do the right by you; but while I'm taking a bit think to mysel' of what's the best thing to put you to—whether the law, or the meenistry, or maybe the army, whilk is what boys are fondest of—I wouldnae like the Balfours to be humbled before a wheen Hieland Campbells, and I'll ask you to keep your tongue within your teeth. Nae letters; nae messages; no kind of word to onybody; or else—there's my door."

"Uncle Ebenezer," said I, "I've no manner of reason to suppose you mean anything but well by me. For all that, I would have you to know that I have a pride of my own. It was by no will of mine that I came seeking you; and if you show me your door again, I'll take you at the word."

He seemed grievously put out. "Hoots-toots," said he, "ca' cannie, man—ca' cannie! Bide a day or two. I'm nae warlock, to find a fortune for you in the bottom of a parritch bowl; but just you give me a day or two, and say naething to naebody, and as sure as sure, I'll do the right by you."

"Very well," said I, "enough said. If you want to help me, there's no doubt but I'll be glad of it, and none but I'll be grateful."

It seemed to me (too soon, I dare say) that I was getting the upper hand of my uncle; and I began next to say that I must have the bed and bedclothes aired and put to sun-dry; for nothing would make me sleep in such a pickle.

"Is this my house or yours?" said he, in his keen voice, and then all of a sudden broke off. "Na, na," said he, "I didnae mean that. What's mine is yours, Davie, my man, and what's yours is mine. Blood's thicker than water; and there's naebody but you and me that ought the name." And then on he rambled about the family, and its ancient greatness, and his father that began to enlarge the house, and himself that stopped the building as a sinful waste; and this put it in my head to give him Jennet Clouston's message.

"The limmer!" he cried. "Twelve hunner and fifteen—that's every day since I had the limmer rowpit! Dod, David, I'll have her roasted on red peats before I'm by with it! A witch—a proclaimed witch! I'll aff and see the session clerk."

And with that he opened a chest, and got out a very old and well-preserved blue coat and waistcoat, and a good enough beaver hat, both without lace. These he threw on any way, and taking a staff from the cupboard, locked all up again, and was for setting out, when a thought arrested him.

"I cannae leave you by yoursel' in the house," said he. "I'll have to lock you out."

The blood came to my face. "If you lock me out," I said, "it'll be the last you'll see of me in friendship."

He turned very pale, and sucked his mouth in.

"This is no the way" he said, looking wickedly at a corner of the floor—"this is no the way to win my favour, David."

"Sir," says I, "with a proper reverence for your age and our common blood, I do not value your favour at a boddle's purchase. I was brought up to have a good conceit of myself; and if you were all the uncle, and all the family, I had in the world ten times over, I wouldn't buy your liking at such prices."

Uncle Ebenezer went and looked out of the window for awhile. I could see him all trembling and twitching, like a man with palsy. But when he turned round, he had a smile upon his face.

"Well, well," said he, "we must bear and forbear. I'll no go; that's all that's to be said of it."

"Uncle Ebenezer," I said, "I can make nothing out of this. You use me like a thief; you hate to have me in this house; you let me see it, every word and every minute: it's not possible that you can like me; and as for me, I've spoken to you as I never thought to speak to any man. Why do you seek to keep me, then? Let me gang back—let me gang back to the friends I have, and that like me!"

"Na, na; na, na," he said, very earnestly. "I like you fine; we'll agree fine yet; and for the honour of the house I couldnae let you leave the way ye came. Bide here quiet, there's a good lad; just you bide here quiet a bittie, and ye'll find that we agree."

"Well, sir," said I, after I had thought the matter out in silence, "I'll stay awhile. It's more just I should be helped by my own blood than strangers; and if we don't agree, I'll do my best it shall be through no fault of mine."

CHAPTER IV

I RUN A GREAT DANGER IN THE
HOUSE OF SHAWS

For a day that was begun so ill, the day passed fairly well. We had the porridge cold again at noon, and hot porridge at night; porridge and small beer was my uncle's diet. He spoke but little, and that in the same way as before, shooting a question at me after a long silence; and when I sought to lead him to talk about my future, slipped out of it again. In a room next door to the kitchen, where he suffered me to go, I found a great number of books, both Latin and English, in which I took great pleasure all the afternoon. Indeed, the time passed so lightly in this good company, that I began to be almost reconciled to my residence at Shaws; and nothing but the sight of my uncle, and his eyes playing hide and seek with mine, revived the force of my distrust.

One thing I discovered, which put me in some doubt. This was an entry on the fly-leaf of a chap-book (one of Patrick Walker's) plainly written by my father's hand and thus conceived: "To my brother Ebenezer on his fifth birthday" Now, what puzzled me was this: That, as my father was of course the younger brother, he must either have made some strange error, or he must have written, before he was yet five, an excellent, clear manly hand of writing.

I tried to get this out of my head; but though I took down many interesting authors, old and new, history, poetry, and story-book, this notion of my father's hand of writing stuck to me; and when at length I went back into the kitchen, and sat down once more to porridge and small beer, the first thing I said to Uncle Ebenezer was to ask him if my father had not been very quick at his book.

"Alexander? No him!" was the reply. "I was far quicker mysel'; I was a clever chappie when I was young. Why, I could read as soon as he could."

This puzzled me yet more; and a thought coming into my head, I asked if he and my father had been twins.

He jumped upon his stool, and the horn spoon fell out of his hand upon the floor. "What gars ye ask that?" he said, and he caught me by the breast of the jacket, and looked this time straight into my eyes: his own were little and light, and bright like a bird's, blinking and winking strangely.

"What do you mean?" I asked, very calmly, for I was far stronger than he, and not easily frightened. "Take your hand from my jacket. This is no way to behave."

My uncle seemed to make a great effort upon himself. "Dod man, David," he said, "ye should-nae speak to me about your father. That's where the mistake is." He sat awhile and shook, blinking in his plate: "He was all the brother that ever I had," he added, but with no heart in his voice; and then he caught up his spoon and fell to supper again, but still shaking.

Now this last passage, this laying of hands upon my person and sudden profession of love for my dead father, went so clean beyond my comprehension that it put me into both fear and hope. On the one hand, I began to think my uncle was perhaps insane and might be dangerous; on the other, there came up into my mind (quite unbidden by me and even discouraged) a story like some ballad I had heard folk singing, of a poor lad that was a rightful heir and a wicked kinsman that tried to keep him from his own. For why should my uncle play a part with a relative that came, almost a beggar, to his door, unless in his heart he had some cause to fear him?

With this notion, all unacknowledged, but nevertheless getting firmly settled in my head, I now began to imitate his covert looks; so that we sat at table like a cat and a mouse, each stealthily observing the other. Not another word had he to say to me, black or white, but was busy turning something secretly over in his mind; and the longer we sat and the more I looked at him, the more certain I became that the something was unfriendly to myself.

When he had cleared the platter, he got out a single pipeful of tobacco, just as in the morning, turned round a stool into the chimney corner, and sat awhile smoking, with his back to me.

"Davie," he said, at length, "I've been thinking;" then he paused, and said it again. "There's a wee bit siller that I half promised ye before ye were born," he continued; "promised it to your father. O, naething legal, ye understand; just gentlemen daffing at their wine. Well, I keepit that bit money separate—it was a great expense, but a promise is a promise—and it has grown by now to be a matter of just precisely—just exactly"—and here he paused and stumbled—"of just exactly forty pounds!" This last he rapped out with a sidelong glance over his shoulder; and the next moment added, almost with a scream, "Scots!"

The pound Scots being the same thing as an English shilling, the difference made by this second thought was considerable; I could see, besides, that the whole story was a lie, invented with some end which it puzzled me to guess; and I made no attempt to conceal the tone of raillery in which I answered—

"O, think again, sir! Pounds sterling, I believe!"

"That's what I said," returned my uncle: "pounds sterling! And if you'll step out-by to the door a minute, just to see what kind of a night it is, I'll get it out to ye and call ye in again."

I did his will, smiling to myself in my contempt that he should think I was so easily to be deceived. It was a dark night, with a few stars low down; and as I stood just outside the door, I heard a hollow moaning of wind far off among the hills. I said to myself there was something thundery and changeful in the weather, and little knew of what a vast importance that should prove to me before the evening passed.

When I was called in again, my uncle counted out into my hand seven and thirty golden guinea pieces; the rest was in his hand, in small gold and silver; but his heart failed him there, and he crammed the change into his pocket.

"There," said he, "that'll show you! I'm a queer man, and strange wi' strangers; but my word is my bond, and there's the proof of it."

Now, my uncle seemed so miserly that I was struck dumb by this sudden generosity, and could find no words in which to thank him.

"No a word!" said he. "Nae thanks; I want nae thanks. I do my duty. I'm no saying that everybody would have done it; but for my part (though I'm a careful body, too) it's a pleasure to me to do the right by my brother's son; and it's a pleasure to me to think that now we'll agree as such near friends should."

I spoke him in return as handsomely as I was able; but all the while I was wondering what would come next, and why he had parted with his precious guineas; for as to the reason he had given, a baby would have refused it.

Presently he looked towards me sideways.

"And see here," says he, "tit for tat."

I told him I was ready to prove my gratitude in any reasonable degree, and then waited, looking for some monstrous demand. And yet, when at last he plucked up courage to speak, it was only to tell me (very properly, as I thought) that he was growing old and a little broken, and that he would expect me to help him with the house and the bit garden.

I answered, and expressed my readiness to serve.

"Well," he said, "let's begin." He pulled out of his pocket a rusty key. "There," says he, "there's the key of the stair-tower at the far end of the house. Ye can only win into it from the outside, for that part of the house is no finished. Gang ye in there, and up the stairs, and bring me down the chest that's at the top. There's papers in't," he added.

"Can I have a light, sir?" said I.

"Na," said he, very cunningly. "Nae lights in my house."

"Very well, sir," said I. "Are the stairs good?"

"They're grand," said he; and then, as I was going, "Keep to the wall," he added; "there's nae bannisters. But the stairs are grand underfoot."

Out I went into the night. The wind was still moaning in the distance, though never a breath of it came near the house of Shaws. It had fallen blacker than ever; and I was glad to feel along the wall, till I came the length of the stairtower door at the far end of the unfinished wing. I had got the key into the keyhole and had just turned it, when all upon a sudden, without sound of wind or thunder, the whole sky lighted up with wild fire and went black again. I had to put my hand over my eyes to get back to the colour of the darkness; and indeed I was already half blinded when I stepped into the tower.

It was so dark inside, it seemed a body could scarce breathe; but I pushed out with foot and hand, and presently struck the wall with the one, and the lowermost round of the stair with the other. The wall, by the touch, was of fine hewn stone; the steps too, though somewhat steep and narrow, were of polished masonwork, and regular and solid underfoot. Minding my uncle's word about the bannisters, I kept close to the tower side, and felt my way in the pitch darkness with a beating heart.

The house of Shaws stood some five full storeys high, not counting lofts. Well, as I advanced, it seemed to me the stair grew airier and a thought more lightsome; and I was wondering what might be the cause of this change, when a second blink of the summer lightning came and went. If I did not cry out, it was because fear had me by the throat; and if I did not fall, it was more by Heaven's mercy than my own strength. It was not only that the flash shone in on every side through breaches in the wall, so that I seemed to be clambering aloft upon an open scaffold, but the same passing brightness showed me the steps were of unequal length, and that one of my feet rested that moment within two inches of the well.

This was the grand stair! I thought; and with the thought, a gust of a kind of angry courage came into my heart. My uncle had sent me here, certainly to run great risks, perhaps to die. I swore I would settle that "perhaps," if I should break my neck for it; got me down upon my hands and knees; and as slowly as a snail, feeling before me every inch, and testing the solidity of every stone, I continued to ascend the stair. The darkness, by contrast with the flash, appeared to have redoubled; nor was that all, for my ears were now troubled and my mind confounded by a great stir of bats in the top part of the tower, and the foul beasts, flying downwards, sometimes beat about my face and body.

The tower, I should have said, was square; and in every corner the step was made of a great stone of a different shape to join the flights. Well, I had come close to one of these turns, when, feeling forward as usual, my hand slipped upon an edge and found nothing but emptiness beyond it. The stair had been carried no higher; to set a stranger mounting it in the darkness was to send him straight to his death; and (although, thanks to the lightning and my own precautions, I was safe enough) the mere thought of the peril in which I might have stood, and the dreadful height I might have fallen from, brought out the sweat upon my body and relaxed my joints.

But I knew what I wanted now, and turned and groped my way down again, with a wonderful anger in my heart. About half-way down, the wind sprang up in a clap and shook the tower, and died again; the rain followed; and before I had reached the ground level it fell in buckets. I put out my head into the storm, and looked along towards the kitchen. The door, which I had shut behind me when I left, now stood open, and shed a little glimmer of light; and I thought I could see a figure standing in the rain, quite still, like a man hearkening. And then there came a blinding flash, which showed me my uncle plainly, just where I had fancied him to stand; and hard upon the heels of it, a great tow-row of thunder.

Now, whether my uncle thought the crash to be the sound of my fall, or whether he heard in it God's voice denouncing murder, I will leave you to guess. Certain it is, at least, that he was seized on by a kind of panic fear, and that he ran into the house and left the door open behind him. I followed as softly as I could, and, coming unheard into the kitchen, stood and watched him.

He had found time to open the corner cupboard and bring out a great case bottle of aqua vitae, and now sat with his back towards me at the table. Ever and again he would be seized with a fit of deadly shuddering and groan aloud, and carrying the bottle to his lips, drink down the raw spirits by the mouthful.

I stepped forward, came close behind him where he sat, and suddenly clapping my two hands down upon his shoulders— "Ah!" cried I.

My uncle gave a kind of broken cry like a sheep's bleat, flung up his arms, and tumbled to the floor like a dead man. I was somewhat shocked at this; but I had myself to look to first of all, and did not hesitate to let him lie as he had fallen. The keys were hanging in the cupboard; and it was my design to furnish myself with arms before my uncle should come again to his senses and the power of devising evil. In the cupboard were a few bottles, some apparently of medicine; a great many bills and other papers, which I should willingly enough have rummaged, had I had the time; and a few necessaries that were nothing to my purpose. Thence I turned to the chests. The first was full of meal; the second of moneybags and papers tied into sheaves; in the third, with many other things (and these for the most part clothes) I found a rusty, ugly-looking Highland dirk without the scabbard. This, then, I concealed inside my waistcoat, and turned to my uncle.

He lay as he had fallen, all huddled, with one knee up and one arm sprawling abroad; his face had a strange colour of blue, and he seemed to have ceased breathing. Fear came on me that he was dead; then I got water and dashed it in his face; and with that he seemed to come a little to himself, working his mouth and fluttering his eyelids. At last he looked up and saw me, and there came into his eyes a terror that was not of this world.

"Come, come," said I; "sit up."

"Are ye alive?" he sobbed. "O man, are ye alive?"

"That am I," said I. "Small thanks to you!"

He had begun to seek for his breath with deep sighs. "The blue phial," said he—"in the aumry—the blue phial." His breath came slower still.

I ran to the cupboard, and, sure enough, found there a blue phial of medicine, with the dose written on it on a paper, and this I administered to him with what speed I might.

"It's the trouble," said he, reviving a little; "I have a trouble, Davie. It's the heart."

I set him on a chair and looked at him. It is true I felt some pity for a man that looked so sick, but I was full besides of righteous anger; and I numbered over before him the points on which I wanted explanation: why he lied to me at every word; why he feared that I should leave him; why he disliked it to be hinted that he and my father were twins—"Is that because it is true?" I asked; why he had given me money to which I was convinced I had no claim; and, last of all, why he had tried to kill me. He heard me all through in silence; and then, in a broken voice, begged me to let him go to bed.

"I'll tell ye the morn," he said; "as sure as death I will."

And so weak was he that I could do nothing but consent. I locked him into his room, however, and pocketed the key, and then returning to the kitchen, made up such a blaze as had not shone there for many a long year, and wrapping myself in my plaid, lay down upon the chests and fell asleep.

CHAPTER V

I GO TO THE QUEEN'S FERRY

Much rain fell in the night; and the next morning there blew a bitter wintry wind out of the north-west, driving scattered clouds. For all that, and before the sun began to peep or the last of the stars had vanished, I made my way to the side of the burn, and had a plunge in a deep whirling pool. All aglow from my bath, I sat down once more beside the fire, which I replenished, and began gravely to consider my position.

There was now no doubt about my uncle's enmity; there was no doubt I carried my life in my hand, and he would leave no stone unturned that he might compass my destruction. But I was young and spirited, and like most lads that have been country-bred, I had a great opinion of my shrewdness. I had come to his door no better than a beggar and little more than a child; he had met me with treachery and violence; it would be a fine consummation to take the upper hand, and drive him like a herd of sheep.

I sat there nursing my knee and smiling at the fire; and I saw myself in fancy smell out his secrets one after another, and grow to be that man's king and ruler. The warlock of Essendean, they say, had made a mirror in which men could read the future; it must have been of other stuff than burning coal; for in all the shapes and pictures that I sat and gazed at, there was never a ship, never a seaman with a hairy cap, never a big bludgeon for my silly head, or the least sign of all those tribulations that were ripe to fall on me.

Presently, all swollen with conceit, I went up-stairs and gave my prisoner his liberty. He gave me good-morning civilly; and I gave the same to him, smiling down upon him, from the heights of my sufficiency. Soon we were set to breakfast, as it might have been the day before.

"Well, sir," said I, with a jeering tone, "have you nothing more to say to me?" And then, as he made no articulate reply, "It will be time, I think, to understand each other," I continued. "You took me for a country Johnnie Raw, with no more mother-wit or courage than a porridge-stick. I took you for a good man, or no worse than others at the least. It seems we were both wrong. What cause you have to fear me, to cheat me, and to attempt my life—"

He murmured something about a jest, and that he liked a bit of fun; and then, seeing me smile, changed his tone, and assured me he would make all clear as soon as we had breakfasted. I saw by his face that he had no lie ready for me, though he was hard at work preparing one; and I think I was about to tell him so, when we were interrupted by a knocking at the door.

Bidding my uncle sit where he was, I went to open it, and found on the doorstep a half-grown boy in sea-clothes. He had no sooner seen me than he began to dance some steps of the sea-hornpipe (which I had never before heard of far less seen), snapping his fingers in the air and footing it right cleverly. For all that, he was blue with the cold; and there was something in his face, a look between tears and laughter, that was highly pathetic and consisted ill with this gaiety of manner.

"What cheer, mate?" says he, with a cracked voice.

I asked him soberly to name his pleasure.

"O, pleasure!" says he; and then began to sing:

"For it's my delight, of a shiny night,
In the season of the year."

"Well," said I, "if you have no business at all, I will even be so unmannerly as to shut you out."

"Stay, brother!" he cried. "Have you no fun about you? or do you want to get me thrashed? I've brought a letter from old Heasyoasy to Mr. Belflower." He showed me a letter as he spoke. "And I say, mate," he added, "I'm mortal hungry."

"Well," said I, "come into the house, and you shall have a bite if I go empty for it."

With that I brought him in and set him down to my own place, where he fell-to greedily on the remains of breakfast, winking to me between whiles, and making many faces, which I think the poor soul considered manly. Meanwhile, my uncle had read the letter and sat thinking; then, suddenly, he got to his feet with a great air of liveliness, and pulled me apart into the farthest corner of the room.

"Read that," said he, and put the letter in my hand.

Here it is, lying before me as I write:

> "The Hawes Inn, at the Queen's Ferry.
>
> "Sir,—I lie here with my hawser up and down, and send my cabin-boy to informe. If you have any further commands for over-seas, to-day will be the last occasion, as the wind will serve us well out of the firth. I will not seek to deny that I have had crosses with your doer, Mr. Rankeillor; of which, if not speedily redd up, you may looke to see some losses follow. I have drawn a bill upon you, as per margin, and am, sir, your most obedt., humble servant,
>
> Elias Hoseason.

"You see, Davie," resumed my uncle, as soon as he saw that I had done, "I have a venture with this man Hoseason, the captain of a trading brig, the *Covenant*, of Dysart. Now, if you and me was to walk over with yon lad, I could see the captain at the Hawes, or maybe on board the *Covenant* if there was papers to be signed; and so far from a loss of time, we can jog on to the lawyer, Mr. Rankeillor's. After a' that's come and gone, ye would be swier to believe me upon my naked word; but ye'll believe Rankeillor. He's factor to half the gentry in these parts; an auld man, forby: highly respeckit, and he kenned your father."

I stood awhile and thought. I was going to some place of shipping, which was doubtless populous, and where my uncle durst attempt no violence, and, indeed, even the society of the cabin-boy so far protected me. Once there, I believed I could force on the visit to the lawyer, even if my uncle were now insincere in proposing it; and, perhaps, in the bottom of my heart, I wished a nearer view of the sea and ships. You are to remember I had lived all my life in the inland hills, and just two days before had my first sight of the firth lying like a blue floor, and the sailed ships moving on the face of it, no bigger than toys. One thing with another, I made up my mind.

"Very well," says I, "let us go to the Ferry."

My uncle got into his hat and coat, and buckled an old rusty cutlass on; and then we trod the fire out, locked the door, and set forth upon our walk.

The wind, being in that cold quarter the north-west, blew nearly in our faces as we went. It was the month of June; the grass was all white with daisies, and the trees with blossom; but, to judge by our blue nails and aching wrists, the time might have been winter and the whiteness a December frost.

Uncle Ebenezer trudged in the ditch, jogging from side to side like an old ploughman coming home from work. He never said a word the whole way; and I was thrown for talk on the cabin-boy. He told me his name was Ransome, and that he had followed the sea since he was nine, but could not say how old he was, as he had lost his reckoning. He showed me tattoo marks, baring his breast in the teeth of the wind and in spite of my remonstrances, for I thought it was enough to kill him;

he swore horribly whenever he remembered, but more like a silly schoolboy than a man; and boasted of many wild and bad things that he had done: stealthy thefts, false accusations, ay, and even murder; but all with such a dearth of likelihood in the details, and such a weak and crazy swagger in the delivery, as disposed me rather to pity than to believe him.

I asked him of the brig (which he declared was the finest ship that sailed) and of Captain Hoseason, in whose praises he was equally loud. Heasyoasy (for so he still named the skipper) was a man, by his account, that minded for nothing either in heaven or earth; one that, as people said, would "crack on all sail into the day of judgment;" rough, fierce, unscrupulous, and brutal; and all this my poor cabin-boy had taught himself to admire as something seamanlike and manly. He would only admit one flaw in his idol. "He ain't no seaman," he admitted. "That's Mr. Shuan that navigates the brig; he's the finest seaman in the trade, only for drink; and I tell you I believe it! Why, look'ere;" and turning down his stocking he showed me a great, raw, red wound that made my blood run cold. "He done that— Mr. Shuan done it," he said, with an air of pride.

"What!" I cried, "do you take such savage usage at his hands? Why, you are no slave, to be so handled!"

"No," said the poor moon-calf, changing his tune at once, "and so he'll find. See'ere;" and he showed me a great case-knife, which he told me was stolen. "O," says he, "let me see him, try; I dare him to; I'll do for him! O, he ain't the first!" And he confirmed it with a poor, silly, ugly oath.

I have never felt such pity for any one in this wide world as I felt for that half-witted creature, and it began to come over me that the brig *Covenant* (for all her pious name) was little better than a hell upon the seas.

"Have you no friends?" said I.

He said he had a father in some English seaport, I forget which. "He was a fine man, too," he said, "but he's dead."

"In Heaven's name," cried I, "can you find no reputable life on shore?"

"O, no," says he, winking and looking very sly, "they would put me to a trade. I know a trick worth two of that, I do!"

I asked him what trade could be so dreadful as the one he followed, where he ran the continual peril of his life, not alone from wind and sea, but by the horrid cruelty of those who were his masters. He said it was very true; and then began to praise the life, and tell what a pleasure it was to get on shore with money in his pocket, and spend it like a man, and buy apples, and swagger, and surprise what he called stick-in-the-mud boys. "And then it's not all as bad as that," says he; "there's worse off than me: there's the twenty-pounders. O, laws! you should see them taking on. Why, I've seen a man as old as you, I dessay"—(to him I seemed old)—"ah, and he had a beard, too—well, and as soon as we cleared out of the river, and he had the drug out of his head—my! how he cried and carried on! I made a fine fool of him, I tell you! And then there's little uns, too: oh, little by me! I tell you, I keep them in order. When we carry little uns, I have a rope's end of my own to wollop'em." And so he ran on, until it came in on me what he meant by twenty-pounders were those unhappy criminals who were sent over-seas to slavery in North America, or the still more unhappy innocents who were kidnapped or trepanned (as the word went) for private interest or vengeance.

Just then we came to the top of the hill, and looked down on the Ferry and the Hope. The Firth of Forth (as is very well known) narrows at this point to the width of a good-sized river, which makes a convenient ferry going north, and turns the upper reach into a landlocked haven for all manner of ships. Right in the midst of the narrows lies an islet with some ruins; on the south shore they have built a pier for the service of the Ferry; and at the end of the pier, on the other side of the road, and backed against a pretty garden of holly-trees and hawthorns, I could see the building which they called the Hawes Inn.

The town of Queensferry lies farther west, and the neighbourhood of the inn looked pretty lonely at that time of day, for the boat had just gone north with passengers. A skiff, however, lay beside the pier, with some seamen sleeping on the thwarts; this, as Ransome told me, was the brig's boat waiting for the captain; and about half a mile off, and all alone in the anchorage, he showed me the Covenant herself. There was a sea-going bustle on board; yards were swinging into place; and as the wind blew from that quarter, I could hear the song of the sailors as they pulled upon the ropes. After all I had listened to upon the way, I looked at that ship with an extreme abhorrence; and from the bottom of my heart I pitied all poor souls that were condemned to sail in her.

We had all three pulled up on the brow of the hill; and now I marched across the road and addressed my uncle. "I think it right to tell you, sir." says I, "there's nothing that will bring me on board that *Covenant*."

He seemed to waken from a dream. "Eh?" he said. "What's that?"

I told him over again.

"Well, well," he said, "we'll have to please ye, I suppose. But what are we standing here for? It's perishing cold; and if I'm no mistaken, they're busking the *Covenant* for sea."

CHAPTER VI

WHAT BEFELL AT THE QUEEN'S FERRY

As soon as we came to the inn, Ransome led us up the stair to a small room, with a bed in it, and heated like an oven by a great fire of coal. At a table hard by the chimney, a tall, dark, sober-looking man sat writing. In spite of the heat of the room, he wore a thick sea-jacket, buttoned to the neck, and a tall hairy cap drawn down over his ears; yet I never saw any man, not even a judge upon the bench, look cooler, or more studious and self-possessed, than this ship-captain.

He got to his feet at once, and coming forward, offered his large hand to Ebenezer. "I am proud to see you, Mr. Balfour," said he, in a fine deep voice, "and glad that ye are here in time. The wind's fair, and the tide upon the turn; we'll see the old coal-bucket burning on the Isle of May before to-night."

"Captain Hoseason," returned my uncle, "you keep your room unco hot."

"It's a habit I have, Mr. Balfour," said the skipper. "I'm a cold-rife man by my nature; I have a cold blood, sir. There's neither fur, nor flannel—no, sir, nor hot rum, will warm up what they call the temperature. Sir, it's the same with most men that have been carbonadoed, as they call it, in the tropic seas."

"Well, well, captain," replied my uncle, "we must all be the way we're made."

But it chanced that this fancy of the captain's had a great share in my misfortunes. For though I had promised myself not to let my kinsman out of sight, I was both so impatient for a nearer look of the sea, and so sickened by the closeness of the room, that when he told me to "run down-stairs and play myself awhile," I was fool enough to take him at his word.

Away I went, therefore, leaving the two men sitting down to a bottle and a great mass of papers; and crossing the road in front of the inn, walked down upon the beach. With the wind in that quarter, only little wavelets, not much bigger than I had seen upon a lake, beat upon the shore. But the weeds were new to me—some green, some brown and long, and some with little bladders that crackled between my fingers. Even so far up the firth, the smell of the sea-water was exceedingly salt and stirring; the *Covenant*, besides, was beginning to shake out her sails, which hung upon the yards in clusters; and the spirit of all that I beheld put me in thoughts of far voyages and foreign places.

I looked, too, at the seamen with the skiff—big brown fellows, some in shirts, some with jackets, some with coloured handkerchiefs about their throats, one with a brace of pistols stuck into his pockets, two or three with knotty bludgeons, and all with their case-knives. I passed the time of day with one that looked less desperate than his fellows, and asked him of the sailing of the brig. He said they would get under way as soon as the ebb set, and expressed his gladness to be out of a port where there were no taverns and fiddlers; but all with such horrifying oaths, that I made haste to get away from him.

This threw me back on Ransome, who seemed the least wicked of that gang, and who soon came out of the inn and ran to me, crying for a bowl of punch. I told him I would give him no such thing, for neither he nor I was of an age for such indulgences. "But a glass of ale you may have, and welcome," said I. He mopped and mowed at me, and called me names; but he was glad to get the ale, for all that; and presently we were set down at a table in the front room of the inn, and both eating and drinking with a good appetite.

Here it occurred to me that, as the landlord was a man of that county, I might do well to make a friend of him. I offered him a share, as was much the custom in those days; but he was far too great a man to sit with such poor customers as Ransome and myself, and he was leaving the room, when I called him back to ask if he knew Mr. Rankeillor.

"Hoot, ay," says he, "and a very honest man. And, O, by-the-by," says he, "was it you that came in with Ebenezer?" And when I had told him yes, "Ye'll be no friend of his?" he asked, meaning, in the Scottish way, that I would be no relative.

I told him no, none.

"I thought not," said he, "and yet ye have a kind of gliff of Mr. Alexander."

I said it seemed that Ebenezer was ill-seen in the country.

"Nae doubt," said the landlord. "He's a wicked auld man, and there's many would like to see him girning in the tow. Jennet Clouston and mony mair that he has harried out of house and hame. And yet he was ance a fine young fellow, too. But that was before the sough gaed abroad about Mr. Alexander, that was like the death of him.

"And what was it?" I asked.

"Ou, just that he had killed him," said the landlord. "Did ye never hear that?"

"And what would he kill him for?" said I.

"And what for, but just to get the place," said he.

"The place?" said I. "The Shaws?"

"Nae other place that I ken," said he.

"Ay, man?" said I. "Is that so? Was my—was Alexander the eldest son?"

"'Deed was he," said the landlord. "What else would he have killed him for?"

And with that he went away, as he had been impatient to do from the beginning.

Of course, I had guessed it a long while ago; but it is one

thing to guess, another to know; and I sat stunned with my good fortune, and could scarce grow to believe that the same poor lad who had trudged in the dust from Ettrick Forest not two days ago, was now one of the rich of the earth, and had a house and broad lands, and might mount his horse tomorrow. All these pleasant things, and a thousand others, crowded into my mind, as I sat staring before me out of the inn window, and paying no heed to what I saw; only I remember that my eye lighted on Captain Hoseason down on the pier among his seamen, and speaking with some authority. And presently he came marching back towards the house, with no mark of a sailor's clumsiness, but carrying his fine, tall figure with a manly bearing, and still with the same sober, grave expression on his face. I wondered if it was possible that Ransome's stories could be true, and half disbelieved them; they fitted so ill with the man's looks. But indeed, he was neither so good as I supposed him, nor quite so bad as Ransome did; for, in fact, he was two men, and left the better one behind as soon as he set foot on board his vessel.

The next thing, I heard my uncle calling me, and found the pair in the road together. It was the captain who addressed me, and that with an air (very flattering to a young lad) of grave equality.

"Sir," said he, "Mr. Balfour tells me great things of you; and for my own part, I like your looks. I wish I was for longer here, that we might make the better friends; but we'll make the most of what we have. Ye shall come on board my brig for half an hour, till the ebb sets, and drink a bowl with me."

Now, I longed to see the inside of a ship more than words can tell; but I was not going to put myself in jeopardy, and I told him my uncle and I had an appointment with a lawyer.

"Ay, ay," said he, "he passed me word of that. But, ye see, the boat'll set ye ashore at the town pier, and that's but a penny stonecast from Rankeillor's house." And here he suddenly leaned down and whispered in my ear: "Take care of the old tod; he means mischief. Come aboard till I can get a word with ye." And then, passing his arm through mine, he continued aloud, as he set off towards his boat: "But, come, what can I bring ye from the Carolinas? Any friend of Mr. Balfour's can command. A roll of tobacco? Indian feather-work? a skin of a wild beast? a stone pipe? the mocking-bird that mews for all the world like a cat? the cardinal bird that is as red as blood?— take your pick and say your pleasure."

By this time we were at the boat-side, and he was handing me in. I did not dream of hanging back; I thought (the poor fool!) that I had found a good friend and helper, and I was rejoiced to see the ship. As soon as we were all set in our places, the boat was thrust off from the pier and began to move over the waters: and what with my pleasure in this new movement and my surprise at our low position, and the appearance of the shores, and the growing bigness of the brig as we drew near to it, I could hardly understand what the captain said, and must have answered him at random.

As soon as we were alongside (where I sat fairly gaping at the ship's height, the strong humming of the tide against its sides, and the pleasant cries of the seamen at their work) Hoseason, declaring that he and I must be the first aboard, ordered a tackle to be sent down from the main-yard. In this I was whipped into the air and set down again on the deck, where the captain stood ready waiting for me, and instantly slipped back his arm under mine. There I stood some while, a little dizzy with the unsteadiness of all around me, perhaps a little afraid, and yet vastly pleased with these strange sights; the captain meanwhile pointing out the strangest, and telling me their names and uses.

"But where is my uncle?" said I suddenly.

"Ay," said Hoseason, with a sudden grimness, "that's the point."

I felt I was lost. With all my strength, I plucked myself clear of him and ran to the bulwarks. Sure enough, there was the boat pulling for the town, with my uncle sitting in the stern. I gave a piercing cry—"Help, help! Murder!"—so that both sides of the anchorage rang with it, and my uncle turned round where he was sitting, and showed me a face full of cruelty and terror.

It was the last I saw. Already strong hands had been plucking me back from the ship's side; and now a thunderbolt seemed to strike me; I saw a great flash of fire, and fell senseless.

CHAPTER VII

I GO TO SEA IN THE BRIG
COVENANT OF DYSART

I came to myself in darkness, in great pain, bound hand and foot, and deafened by many unfamiliar noises. There sounded in my ears a roaring of water as of a huge mill-dam, the thrashing of heavy sprays, the thundering of the sails, and the shrill cries of seamen. The whole world now heaved giddily up, and now rushed giddily downward; and so sick and hurt was I in body, and my mind so much confounded, that it took me a long while, chasing my thoughts up and down, and ever stunned again by a fresh stab of pain, to realise that I must be lying somewhere bound in the belly of that unlucky ship, and that the wind must have strengthened to a gale. With the clear perception of my plight, there fell upon me a blackness of despair, a horror of remorse at my own folly, and a passion of anger at my uncle, that once more bereft me of my senses.

When I returned again to life, the same uproar, the same confused and violent movements, shook and deafened me; and presently, to my other pains and distresses, there was added the sickness of an unused landsman on the sea. In that time of my adventurous youth, I suffered many hardships; but none that was so crushing to my mind and body, or lit by so few hopes, as these first hours aboard the brig.

I heard a gun fire, and supposed the storm had proved too strong for us, and we were firing signals of distress. The thought of deliverance, even by death in the deep sea, was welcome to me. Yet it was no such matter; but (as I was afterwards told) a common habit of the captain's, which I here set down to show that even the worst man may have his kindlier side. We were then passing, it appeared, within some miles of Dysart, where the brig was built, and where old Mrs. Hoseason, the captain's mother, had come some years before to live; and whether outward or inward bound, the *Covenant* was never suffered to go by that place by day, without a gun fired and colours shown.

I had no measure of time; day and night were alike in that ill-smelling cavern of the ship's bowels where, I lay; and the misery of my situation drew out the hours to double. How long, therefore, I lay waiting to hear the ship split upon some rock, or to feel her reel head foremost into the depths of the sea, I have not the means of computation. But sleep at length stole from me the consciousness of sorrow.

I was awakened by the light of a hand-lantern shining in my face. A small man of about thirty, with green eyes and a tangle of fair hair, stood looking down at me.

"Well," said he, "how goes it?"

I answered by a sob; and my visitor then felt my pulse and temples, and set himself to wash and dress the wound upon my scalp.

"Ay," said he, "a sore dunt. What, man? Cheer up! The world's no done; you've made a bad start of it but you'll make a better. Have you had any meat?"

I said I could not look at it: and thereupon he gave me some brandy and water in a tin pannikin, and left me once more to myself.

The next time he came to see me, I was lying betwixt sleep and waking, my eyes wide open in the darkness, the sickness quite departed, but succeeded by a horrid giddiness and swimming that was almost worse to bear. I ached, besides, in every limb, and the cords that bound me seemed to be of fire. The smell of the hole in which I lay seemed to have become a

part of me; and during the long interval since his last visit I had
suffered tortures of fear, now from the scurrying of the ship's
rats, that sometimes pattered on my very face, and now from
the dismal imaginings that haunt the bed of fever.

The glimmer of the lantern, as a trap opened, shone in
like the heaven's sunlight; and though it only showed me the
strong, dark beams of the ship that was my prison, I could
have cried aloud for gladness. The man with the green eyes
was the first to descend the ladder, and I noticed that he came
somewhat unsteadily. He was followed by the captain. Neither
said a word; but the first set to and examined me, and dressed
my wound as before, while Hoseason looked me in my face
with an odd, black look.

"Now, sir, you see for yourself," said the first: "a high fever,
no appetite, no light, no meat: you see for yourself what that
means."

"I am no conjurer, Mr. Riach," said the captain.

"Give me leave, sir" said Riach; "you've a good head upon
your shoulders, and a good Scotch tongue to ask with; but I
will leave you no manner of excuse; I want that boy taken out
of this hole and put in the forecastle."

"What ye may want, sir, is a matter of concern to nobody
but yoursel'," returned the captain; "but I can tell ye that which
is to be. Here he is; here he shall bide."

"Admitting that you have been paid in a proportion," said
the other, "I will crave leave humbly to say that I have not. Paid
I am, and none too much, to be the second officer of this old
tub, and you ken very well if I do my best to earn it. But I was
paid for nothing more."

"If ye could hold back your hand from the tin-pan, Mr.
Riach, I would have no complaint to make of ye," returned
the skipper; "and instead of asking riddles, I make bold to say
that ye would keep your breath to cool your porridge. We'll be
required on deck," he added, in a sharper note, and set one foot

upon the ladder.

But Mr. Riach caught him by the sleeve.

"Admitting that you have been paid to do a murder—" he began.

Hoseason turned upon him with a flash.

"What's that?" he cried. "What kind of talk is that?"

"It seems it is the talk that you can understand," said Mr. Riach, looking him steadily in the face.

"Mr. Riach, I have sailed with ye three cruises," replied the captain. "In all that time, sir, ye should have learned to know me: I'm a stiff man, and a dour man; but for what ye say the now—fie, fie!—it comes from a bad heart and a black conscience. If ye say the lad will die—"

"Ay, will he!" said Mr. Riach.

"Well, sir, is not that enough?" said Hoseason. "Flit him where ye please!"

Thereupon the captain ascended the ladder; and I, who had lain silent throughout this strange conversation, beheld Mr. Riach turn after him and bow as low as to his knees in what was plainly a spirit of derision. Even in my then state of sickness, I perceived two things: that the mate was touched with liquor, as the captain hinted, and that (drunk or sober) he was like to prove a valuable friend.

Five minutes afterwards my bonds were cut, I was hoisted on a man's back, carried up to the forecastle, and laid in a bunk on some sea-blankets; where the first thing that I did was to lose my senses.

It was a blessed thing indeed to open my eyes again upon the daylight, and to find myself in the society of men. The forecastle was a roomy place enough, set all about with berths, in which the men of the watch below were seated smoking, or lying down asleep. The day being calm and the wind fair, the scuttle was open, and not only the good daylight, but from time to time (as the ship rolled) a dusty beam of sunlight shone in, and dazzled and delighted me. I had no sooner moved, moreover, than one of the men brought me a drink of something healing which Mr. Riach had prepared, and bade me lie still and I should soon be well again. There were no bones broken, he explained: "A clour on the head was naething. Man," said he, "it was me that gave it ye!"

Here I lay for the space of many days a close prisoner, and not only got my health again, but came to know my companions. They were a rough lot indeed, as sailors mostly are: being men rooted out of all the kindly parts of life, and condemned to toss together on the rough seas, with masters no less cruel. There were some among them that had sailed with the pirates and seen things it would be a shame even to speak of; some were men that had run from the king's ships, and went with a halter round their necks, of which they made no secret; and all, as the saying goes, were "at a word and a blow" with their best friends. Yet I had not been many days shut up with them before I began to be ashamed of my first judgment, when I had drawn away from them at the Ferry pier, as though they had been unclean beasts. No class of man is altogether bad, but each has its own faults and virtues; and these shipmates of mine were no exception to the rule. Rough they were, sure enough; and bad, I suppose; but they had many virtues. They were kind when it occurred to them, simple even beyond the simplicity of a country lad like me, and had some glimmerings of honesty.

There was one man, of maybe forty, that would sit on my berthside for hours and tell me of his wife and child. He was a fisher that had lost his boat, and thus been driven to the deep-sea voyaging. Well, it is years ago now: but I have never forgotten him. His wife (who was "young by him," as he often told me) waited in vain to see her man return; he would never again make the fire for her in the morning, nor yet keep the bairn when she was sick. Indeed, many of these poor fellows (as the event proved) were upon their last cruise; the deep seas and cannibal fish received them; and it is a thankless business to speak ill of the dead.

Among other good deeds that they did, they returned my money, which had been shared among them; and though it was about a third short, I was very glad to get it, and hoped great good from it in the land I was going to. The ship was bound for the Carolinas; and you must not suppose that I was going to that place merely as an exile. The trade was even then much depressed; since that, and with the rebellion of the colonies and the formation of the United States, it has, of course, come to an end; but in those days of my youth, white men were still sold into slavery on the plantations, and that was the destiny to which my wicked uncle had condemned me.

The cabin-boy Ransome (from whom I had first heard of these atrocities) came in at times from the round-house, where he berthed and served, now nursing a bruised limb in silent agony, now raving against the cruelty of Mr. Shuan. It made my heart bleed; but the men had a great respect for the chief mate, who was, as they said, "the only seaman of the whole jing-bang, and none such a bad man when he was sober." Indeed, I found there was a strange peculiarity about our two mates: that Mr. Riach was sullen, unkind, and harsh when he was sober, and Mr. Shuan would not hurt a fly except when he was drinking. I asked about the captain; but I was told drink made no difference upon that man of iron.

I did my best in the small time allowed me to make some thing like a man, or rather I should say something like a boy, of the poor creature, Ransome. But his mind was scarce truly human. He could remember nothing of the time before he came to sea; only that his father had made clocks, and had a starling in the parlour, which could whistle "The North Countrie;" all else had been blotted out in these years of hardship and cruelties. He had a strange notion of the dry land, picked up from sailor's stories: that it was a place where lads were put to some kind of slavery called a trade, and where apprentices were continually lashed and clapped into foul prisons. In a town, he thought every second person a decoy, and every third house a place in which seamen would be drugged and murdered. To be sure, I would tell him how kindly I had myself been used upon that dry land he was so much afraid of, and how well fed and carefully taught both by my friends and my parents: and if he had been recently hurt, he would weep bitterly and swear to run away; but if he was in his usual crackbrain humour, or (still more) if he had had a glass of spirits in the roundhouse, he would deride the notion.

It was Mr. Riach (Heaven forgive him!) who gave the boy drink; and it was, doubtless, kindly meant; but besides that it was ruin to his health, it was the pitifullest thing in life to see this unhappy, unfriended creature staggering, and dancing, and talking he knew not what. Some of the men laughed, but not all; others would grow as black as thunder (thinking, perhaps, of their own childhood or their own children) and bid him stop that nonsense, and think what he was doing. As for me, I felt ashamed to look at him, and the poor child still comes about me in my dreams.

All this time, you should know, the *Covenant* was meeting continual head-winds and tumbling up and down against head-seas, so that the scuttle was almost constantly shut, and the forecastle lighted only by a swinging lantern on a beam. There was constant labour for all hands; the sails had to be made and shortened every hour; the strain told on the men's temper; there was a growl of quarrelling all day, long from berth to berth; and as I was never allowed to set my foot on deck, you can picture to yourselves how weary of my life I grew to be, and how impatient for a change.

And a change I was to get, as you shall hear; but I must first tell of a conversation I had with Mr. Riach, which put a little heart in me to bear my troubles. Getting him in a favourable stage of drink (for indeed he never looked near me when he was sober), I pledged him to secrecy, and told him my whole story.

He declared it was like a ballad; that he would do his best to help me; that I should have paper, pen, and ink, and write one line to Mr. Campbell and another to Mr. Rankeillor; and that if I had told the truth, ten to one he would be able (with their help) to pull me through and set me in my rights.

"And in the meantime," says he, "keep your heart up. You're not the only one, I'll tell you that. There's many a man hoeing tobacco over-seas that should be mounting his horse at his own door at home; many and many! And life is all a variorum, at the best. Look at me: I'm a laird's son and more than half a doctor, and here I am, man-Jack to Hoseason!"

I thought it would be civil to ask him for his story.

He whistled loud.

"Never had one," said he. "I like fun, that's all." And he skipped out of the forecastle.

CHAPTER VIII

THE ROUND-HOUSE

One night, about eleven o'clock, a man of Mr. Riach's watch (which was on deck) came below for his jacket; and instantly there began to go a whisper about the forecastle that "Shuan had done for him at last." There was no need of a name; we all knew who was meant; but we had scarce time to get the idea rightly in our heads, far less to speak of it, when the scuttle was again flung open, and Captain Hoseason came down the ladder. He looked sharply round the bunks in the tossing light of the lantern; and then, walking straight up to me, he addressed me, to my surprise, in tones of kindness.

"My man," said he, "we want ye to serve in the round-house. You and Ransome are to change berths. Run away aft with ye."

Even as he spoke, two seamen appeared in the scuttle, carrying Ransome in their arms; and the ship at that moment giving a great sheer into the sea, and the lantern swinging, the light fell direct on the boy's face. It was as white as wax, and had a look upon it like a dreadful smile. The blood in me ran cold, and I drew in my breath as if I had been struck.

"Run away aft; run away aft with ye!" cried Hoseason.

And at that I brushed by the sailors and the boy (who neither spoke nor moved), and ran up the ladder on deck.

The brig was sheering swiftly and giddily through a long, cresting swell. She was on the starboard tack, and on the left hand, under the arched foot of the foresail, I could see the sunset still quite bright. This, at such an hour of the night, surprised me greatly; but I was too ignorant to draw the true conclusion—that we were going north-about round Scotland, and were now on the high sea between the Orkney and Shetland Islands, having avoided the dangerous currents of the Pentland Firth. For my part, who had been so long shut in the dark and knew nothing of head-winds, I thought we might be half-way or more across the Atlantic. And indeed (beyond that I wondered a little at the lateness of the sunset light) I gave no heed to it, and pushed on across the decks, running between the seas, catching at ropes, and only saved from going overboard by one of the hands on deck, who had been always kind to me.

The round-house, for which I was bound, and where I was now to sleep and serve, stood some six feet above the decks, and considering the size of the brig, was of good dimensions. Inside were a fixed table and bench, and two berths, one for the captain and the other for the two mates, turn and turn about. It was all fitted with lockers from top to bottom, so as to stow away the officers' belongings and a part of the ship's stores; there was a second store-room underneath, which you entered by a hatchway in the middle of the deck; indeed, all the best of the meat and drink and the whole of the powder were collected in this place; and all the firearms, except the two pieces of brass ordnance, were set in a rack in the aftermost wall of the round-house. The most of the cutlasses were in another place.

A small window with a shutter on each side, and a skylight in the roof, gave it light by, day; and after dark there was a lamp always burning. It was burning when I entered, not brightly, but enough to show Mr. Shuan sitting at the table, with the brandy bottle and a tin pannikin in front of him. He was a tall man, strongly made and very black; and he stared before him on the table like one stupid.

He took no notice of my coming in; nor did he move when the captain followed and leant on the berth beside me, looking darkly at the mate. I stood in great fear of Hoseason, and had my reasons for it; but something told me I need not be afraid of him just then; and I whispered in his ear: "How is he?" He shook his head like one that does not know and does not wish to think, and his face was very stern.

Presently Mr. Riach came in. He gave the captain a glance that meant the boy was dead as plain as speaking, and took his place like the rest of us; so that we all three stood without a word, staring down at Mr. Shuan, and Mr. Shuan (on his side) sat without a word, looking hard upon the table.

All of a sudden he put out his hand to take the bottle; and at that Mr. Riach started forward and caught it away from him, rather by surprise than violence, crying out, with an oath, that there had been too much of this work altogether, and that a judgment would fall upon the ship. And as he spoke (the weather sliding-doors standing open) he tossed the bottle into the sea.

Mr. Shuan was on his feet in a trice; he still looked dazed, but he meant murder, ay, and would have done it, for the second time that night, had not the captain stepped in between him and his victim.

"Sit down!" roars the captain. "Ye sot and swine, do ye know what ye've done? Ye've murdered the boy!"

Mr. Shuan seemed to understand; for he sat down again, and put up his hand to his brow.

"Well," he said, "he brought me a dirty pannikin!"

At that word, the captain and I and Mr. Riach all looked at each other for a second with a kind of frightened look; and then Hoseason walked up to his chief officer, took him by the shoulder, led him across to his bunk, and bade him lie down and go to sleep, as you might speak to a bad child. The murderer cried a little, but he took off his sea-boots and obeyed.

"Ah!" cried Mr. Riach, with a dreadful voice, "ye should have interfered long syne. It's too late now."

"Mr. Riach," said the captain, "this night's work must never be kennt in Dysart. The boy went overboard, sir; that's what the story is; and I would give five pounds out of my pocket it was true!" He turned to the table. "What made ye throw the good bottle away?" he added. "There was nae sense in that, sir. Here, David, draw me another. They're in the bottom locker;" and he tossed me a key. "Ye'll need a glass yourself, sir," he added to Riach. "Yon was an ugly thing to see."

So the pair sat down and hob-a-nobbed; and while they did so, the murderer, who had been lying and whimpering in his berth, raised himself upon his elbow and looked at them and at me.

That was the first night of my new duties; and in the course of the next day I had got well into the run of them. I had to serve at the meals, which the captain took at regular hours, sitting down with the officer who was off duty; all the day through I would be running with a dram to one or other of my three masters; and at night I slept on a blanket thrown on the deck boards at the aftermost end of the round-house, and right in the draught of the two doors. It was a hard and a cold bed; nor was I suffered to sleep without interruption; for some one would be always coming in from deck to get a dram, and when a fresh watch was to be set, two and sometimes all three would sit down and brew a bowl together. How they kept their health, I know not, any more than how I kept my own.

And yet in other ways it was an easy service. There was no cloth to lay; the meals were either of oatmeal porridge or salt junk, except twice a week, when there was duff: and though I was clumsy enough and (not being firm on my sealegs) sometimes fell with what I was bringing them, both Mr. Riach and the captain were singularly patient. I could not but fancy they were making up lee-way with their consciences, and that they would scarce have been so good with me if they had not been worse with Ransome.

As for Mr. Shuan, the drink or his crime, or the two together, had certainly troubled his mind. I cannot say I ever saw him in his proper wits. He never grew used to my being there, stared at me continually (sometimes, I could have thought, with terror), and more than once drew back from my hand when I was serving him. I was pretty sure from the first that he had no clear mind of what he had done, and on my second day in the round-house I had the proof of it. We were alone, and he had been staring at me a long time, when all at once, up he got, as pale as death, and came close up to me, to my great terror. But I had no cause to be afraid of him.

"You were not here before?" he asked.

"No, sir," said I."

"There was another boy?" he asked again; and when I had answered him, "Ah!" says he, "I thought that," and went and sat down, without another word, except to call for brandy.

You may think it strange, but for all the horror I had, I was still sorry for him. He was a married man, with a wife in Leith; but whether or no he had a family, I have now forgotten; I hope not.

Altogether it was no very hard life for the time it lasted, which (as you are to hear) was not long. I was as well fed as the best of them; even their pickles, which were the great dainty, I was allowed my share of; and had I liked I might have been drunk from morning to night, like Mr. Shuan. I had company, too, and good company of its sort. Mr. Riach, who had been to the college, spoke to me like a friend when he was not sulking, and told me many curious things, and some that were informing; and even the captain, though he kept me at the stick's end the most part of the time, would sometimes unbuckle a bit, and tell me of the fine countries he had visited.

The shadow of poor Ransome, to be sure, lay on all four of us, and on me and Mr. Shuan in particular, most heavily. And then I had another trouble of my own. Here I was, doing

dirty work for three men that I looked down upon, and one
of whom, at least, should have hung upon a gallows; that was
for the present; and as for the future, I could only see myself
slaving alongside of negroes in the tobacco fields. Mr. Riach,
perhaps from caution, would never suffer me to say another
word about my story; the captain, whom I tried to approach,
rebuffed me like a dog and would not hear a word; and as the
days came and went, my heart sank lower and lower, till I was
even glad of the work which kept me from thinking.

CHAPTER IX

THE MAN WITH THE BELT OF GOLD

More than a week went by, in which the ill-luck that had hitherto pursued the *Covenant* upon this voyage grew yet more strongly marked. Some days she made a little way; others, she was driven actually back. At last we were beaten so far to the south that we tossed and tacked to and fro the whole of the ninth day, within sight of Cape Wrath and the wild, rocky coast on either hand of it. There followed on that a council of the officers, and some decision which I did not rightly understand, seeing only the result: that we had made a fair wind of a foul one and were running south.

The tenth afternoon there was a falling swell and a thick, wet, white fog that hid one end of the brig from the other. All afternoon, when I went on deck, I saw men and officers listening hard over the bulwarks—"for breakers," they said; and though I did not so much as understand the word, I felt danger in the air, and was excited.

Maybe about ten at night, I was serving Mr. Riach and the captain at their supper, when the ship struck something with a great sound, and we heard voices singing out. My two masters leaped to their feet.

"She's struck!" said Mr. Riach.

"No, sir," said the captain. "We've only run a boat down."

And they hurried out.

The captain was in the right of it. We had run down a boat in the fog, and she had parted in the midst and gone to the bottom with all her crew but one. This man (as I heard afterwards) had been sitting in the stern as a passenger, while the rest were on the benches rowing. At the moment of the blow, the stern had been thrown into the air, and the man (having his hands free, and for all he was encumbered with a frieze overcoat that came below his knees) had leaped up and caught hold of the brig's bowsprit. It showed he had luck and much agility and unusual strength, that he should have thus saved himself from such a pass. And yet, when the captain brought him into the round-house, and I set eyes on him for the first time, he looked as cool as I did.

He was smallish in stature, but well set and as nimble as a goat; his face was of a good open expression, but sunburnt very dark, and heavily freckled and pitted with the small-pox; his eyes were unusually light and had a kind of dancing madness in them, that was both engaging and alarming; and when he took off his great-coat, he laid a pair of fine silver-mounted pistols on the table, and I saw that he was belted with a great sword. His manners, besides, were elegant, and he pledged the captain handsomely. Altogether I thought of him, at the first sight, that here was a man I would rather call my friend than my enemy.

The captain, too, was taking his observations, but rather of the man's clothes than his person. And to be sure, as soon as he had taken off the great-coat, he showed forth mighty fine for the round-house of a merchant brig: having a hat with feathers, a red waistcoat, breeches of black plush, and a blue coat with silver buttons and handsome silver lace; costly clothes, though somewhat spoiled with the fog and being slept in.

"I'm vexed, sir, about the boat," says the captain.

"There are some pretty men gone to the bottom," said the stranger, "that I would rather see on the dry land again than half a score of boats."

"Friends of yours?" said Hoseason.

"You have none such friends in your country," was the reply. "They would have died for me like dogs."

"Well, sir," said the captain, still watching him, "there are more men in the world than boats to put them in."

"And that's true, too," cried the other, "and ye seem to be a gentleman of great penetration."

"I have been in France, sir," says the captain, so that it was plain he meant more by the words than showed upon the face of them.

"Well, sir," says the other, "and so has many a pretty man, for the matter of that."

"No doubt, sir" says the captain, "and fine coats."

"Oho!" says the stranger, "is that how the wind sets?" And he laid his hand quickly on his pistols.

"Don't be hasty," said the captain. "Don't do a mischief before ye see the need of it. Ye've a French soldier's coat upon your back and a Scotch tongue in your head, to be sure; but so has many an honest fellow in these days, and I dare say none the worse of it."

"So?" said the gentleman in the fine coat: "are ye of the honest party?" (meaning, Was he a Jacobite? for each side, in these sort of civil broils, takes the name of honesty for its own).

"Why, sir," replied the captain, "I am a true-blue Protestant, and I thank God for it." (It was the first word of any religion I had ever heard from him, but I learnt afterwards he was a great church-goer while on shore.) "But, for all that," says he, "I can be sorry to see another man with his back to the wall."

"Can ye so, indeed?" asked the Jacobite. "Well, sir, to be quite plain with ye, I am one of those honest gentlemen that were in trouble about the years forty-five and six; and (to be still quite plain with ye) if I got into the hands of any of the red-coated gentry, it's like it would go hard with me. Now, sir, I was for France; and there was a French ship cruising here to pick me up; but she gave us the go-by in the fog—as I wish from the heart that ye had done yoursel'! And the best that I can say is this: If ye can set me ashore where I was going, I have that upon me will reward you highly for your trouble."

"In France?" says the captain. "No, sir; that I cannot do. But where ye come from—we might talk of that."

And then, unhappily, he observed me standing in my corner, and packed me off to the galley to get supper for the gentleman. I lost no time, I promise you; and when I came back into the round-house, I found the gentleman had taken a money-belt from about his waist, and poured out a guinea or two upon the table. The captain was looking at the guineas, and then at the belt, and then at the gentleman's face; and I thought he seemed excited.

"Half of it," he cried, "and I'm your man!"

The other swept back the guineas into the belt, and put it on again under his waistcoat. "I have told ye sir" said he, "that not one doit of it belongs to me. It belongs to my chieftain," and here he touched his hat, "and while I would be but a silly messenger to grudge some of it that the rest might come safe, I should show myself a hound indeed if I bought my own carcase any too dear. Thirty guineas on the sea-side, or sixty if ye set me on the Linnhe Loch. Take it, if ye will; if not, ye can do your worst."

"Ay," said Hoseason. "And if I give ye over to the soldiers?"

"Ye would make a fool's bargain," said the other. "My chief, let me tell you, sir, is forfeited, like every honest man in Scotland. His estate is in the hands of the man they call King George; and it is his officers that collect the rents, or try to collect them. But for the honour of Scotland, the poor tenant bodies take a thought upon their chief lying in exile; and this money is a part of that very rent for which King George is looking. Now, sir, ye seem to me to be a man that understands things: bring this money within the reach of Government, and how much of it'll come to you?"

"Little enough, to be sure," said Hoseason; and then, "if they, knew" he added, drily. "But I think, if I was to try, that I could hold my tongue about it."

"Ah, but I'll begowk ye there!" cried the gentleman. "Play me false, and I'll play you cunning. If a hand is laid upon me, they shall ken what money it is."

"Well," returned the captain, "what must be must. Sixty guineas, and done. Here's my hand upon it."

"And here's mine," said the other.

And thereupon the captain went out (rather hurriedly, I thought), and left me alone in the round-house with the stranger.

At that period (so soon after the forty-five) there were many exiled gentlemen coming back at the peril of their lives, either to see their friends or to collect a little money; and as for the Highland chiefs that had been forfeited, it was a common matter of talk how their tenants would stint themselves to send them money, and their clansmen outface the soldiery to get it in, and run the gauntlet of our great navy to carry it across. All this I had, of course, heard tell of; and now I had a man under my eyes whose life was forfeit on all these counts and upon one more, for he was not only a rebel and a smuggler of rents, but had taken service with King Louis of France. And as if all this were not enough, he had a belt full of golden guineas round his loins. Whatever my opinions, I could not look on such a man without a lively interest.

"And so you're a Jacobite?" said I, as I set meat before him.

"Ay," said he, beginning to eat. "And you, by your long face, should be a Whig?"

"Betwixt and between," said I, not to annoy him; for indeed I was as good a Whig as Mr. Campbell could make me.

"And that's naething," said he. "But I'm saying, Mr. Betwixt-and-Between," he added, "this bottle of yours is dry; and it's hard if I'm to pay sixty guineas and be grudged a dram upon the back of it."

"I'll go and ask for the key," said I, and stepped on deck.

The fog was as close as ever, but the swell almost down. They had laid the brig to, not knowing precisely where they were, and the wind (what little there was of it) not serving well for their true course. Some of the hands were still hearkening for breakers; but the captain and the two officers were in the waist with their heads together. It struck me (I don't know why) that they were after no good; and the first word I heard, as I drew softly near, more than confirmed me.

It was Mr. Riach, crying out as if upon a sudden thought: "Couldn't we wile him out of the round-house?"

"He's better where he is," returned Hoseason; "he hasn't room to use his sword."

"Well, that's true," said Riach; "but he's hard to come at."

"Hut!" said Hoseason. "We can get the man in talk, one upon each side, and pin him by the two arms; or if that'll not hold, sir, we can make a run by both the doors and get him under hand before he has the time to draw."

At this hearing, I was seized with both fear and anger at these treacherous, greedy, bloody men that I sailed with. My first mind was to run away; my second was bolder.

"Captain," said I, "the gentleman is seeking a dram, and the bottle's out. Will you give me the key?"

They all started and turned about.

"Why, here's our chance to get the firearms!" Riach cried; and then to me: "Hark ye, David," he said, "do ye ken where the pistols are?"

"Ay, ay," put in Hoseason. "David kens; David's a good lad. Ye see, David my man, yon wild Hielandman is a danger to the ship, besides being a rank foe to King George, God bless him!"

I had never been so be-Davided since I came on board: but I said Yes, as if all I heard were quite natural.

"The trouble is," resumed the captain, "that all our firelocks, great and little, are in the round-house under this man's nose; likewise the powder. Now, if I, or one of the officers, was to go in and take them, he would fall to thinking. But a lad like you, David, might snap up a horn and a pistol or two without remark. And if ye can do it cleverly, I'll bear it in mind when it'll be good for you to have friends; and that's when we come to Carolina."

Here Mr. Riach whispered him a little.

"Very right, sir," said the captain; and then to myself: "And see here, David, yon man has a beltful of gold, and I give you my word that you shall have your fingers in it."

I told him I would do as he wished, though indeed I had scarce breath to speak with; and upon that he gave me the key of the spirit locker, and I began to go slowly back to the round-house. What was I to do? They were dogs and thieves; they had stolen me from my own country; they had killed poor Ransome; and was I to hold the candle to another murder? But then, upon the other hand, there was the fear of death very plain before me; for what could a boy and a man, if they were as brave as lions, against a whole ship's company?

I was still arguing it back and forth, and getting no great clearness, when I came into the round-house and saw the Jacobite eating his supper under the lamp; and at that my mind was made up all in a moment. I have no credit by it; it was by no choice of mine, but as if by compulsion, that I walked right up to the table and put my hand on his shoulder.

"Do ye want to be killed?" said I. He sprang to his feet, and looked a question at me as clear as if he had spoken.

"O!" cried I, "they're all murderers here; it's a ship full of them! They've murdered a boy already. Now it's you."

"Ay, ay" said he; "but they have n't got me yet." And then looking at me curiously, "Will ye stand with me?"

"That will I!" said I. "I am no thief, nor yet murderer. I'll stand by you."

"Why, then," said he, "what's your name?"

"David Balfour," said I; and then, thinking that a man with so fine a coat must like fine people, I added for the first time, "of Shaws."

It never occurred to him to doubt me, for a Highlander is used to see great gentlefolk in great poverty; but as he had no estate of his own, my words nettled a very childish vanity he had.

"My name is Stewart," he said, drawing himself up. "Alan Breck, they call me. A king's name is good enough for me, though I bear it plain and have the name of no farm-midden to clap to the hind-end of it."

And having administered this rebuke, as though it were something of a chief importance, he turned to examine our defences.

The round-house was built very strong, to support the breaching of the seas. Of its five apertures, only the skylight and the two doors were large enough for the passage of a man. The doors, besides, could be drawn close: they were of stout oak, and ran in grooves, and were fitted with hooks to keep them either shut or open, as the need arose. The one that was already shut I secured in this fashion; but when I was proceeding to slide to the other, Alan stopped me.

"David," said he—"for I cannae bring to mind the name of your landed estate, and so will make so bold as to call you David—that door, being open, is the best part of my defences."

"It would be yet better shut," says I.

"Not so, David," says he. "Ye see, I have but one face; but so long as that door is open and my face to it, the best part of my enemies will be in front of me, where I would aye wish to find them."

Then he gave me from the rack a cutlass (of which there were a few besides the firearms), choosing it with great care, shaking his head and saying he had never in all his life seen poorer weapons; and next he set me down to the table with a powder-horn, a bag of bullets and all the pistols, which he bade me charge.

"And that will be better work, let me tell you," said he, "for a gentleman of decent birth, than scraping plates and raxingdrams to a wheen tarry sailors."

Thereupon he stood up in the midst with his face to the door, and drawing his great sword, made trial of the room he had to wield it in.

"I must stick to the point," he said, shaking his head; "and that's a pity, too. It doesn't set my genius, which is all for the upper guard. And, now" said he, "do you keep on charging the pistols, and give heed to me."

I told him I would listen closely. My chest was tight, my mouth dry, the light dark to my eyes; the thought of the numbers that were soon to leap in upon us kept my heart in a flutter: and the sea, which I heard washing round the brig, and where I thought my dead body would be cast ere morning, ran in my mind strangely.

"First of all," said he, "how many are against us?"

I reckoned them up; and such was the hurry of my mind, I had to cast the numbers twice. "Fifteen," said I.

Alan whistled. "Well," said he, "that can't be cured. And now follow me. It is my part to keep this door, where I look for the main battle. In that, ye have no hand. And mind and dinnae fire to this side unless they get me down; for I would rather have ten foes in front of me than one friend like you cracking pistols at my back."

I told him, indeed I was no great shot.

"And that's very bravely said," he cried, in a great admiration of my candour. "There's many a pretty gentleman that wouldnae dare to say it."

"But then, sir" said I, "there is the door behind you" which they may perhaps break in."

"Ay," said he, "and that is a part of your work. No sooner the pistols charged, than ye must climb up into yon bed where ye're handy at the window; and if they lift hand, against the door, ye're to shoot. But that's not all. Let's make a bit of a soldier of ye, David. What else have ye to guard?"

"There's the skylight," said I. "But indeed, Mr. Stewart, I would need to have eyes upon both sides to keep the two of them; for when my face is at the one, my back is to the other."

"And that's very true," said Alan. "But have ye no ears to your head?"

"To be sure!" cried I. "I must hear the bursting of the glass!"

"Ye have some rudiments of sense," said Alan, grimly.

CHAPTER X

THE SIEGE OF THE ROUND-HOUSE

But now our time of truce was come to an end. Those on deck had waited for my coming till they grew impatient; and scarce had Alan spoken, when the captain showed face in the open door.

"Stand!" cried Alan, and pointed his sword at him. The captain stood, indeed; but he neither winced nor drew back a foot.

"A naked sword?" says he. "This is a strange return for hospitality."

"Do ye see me?" said Alan. "I am come of kings; I bear a king's name. My badge is the oak. Do ye see my sword? It has slashed the heads off mair Whigamores than you have toes upon your feet. Call up your vermin to your back, sir, and fall on! The sooner the clash begins, the sooner ye'll taste this steel throughout your vitals."

The captain said nothing to Alan, but he looked over at me with an ugly look. "David," said he, "I'll mind this;" and the sound of his voice went through me with a jar.

Next moment he was gone.

"And now," said Alan, "let your hand keep your head, for the grip is coming."

Alan drew a dirk, which he held in his left hand in case they should run in under his sword. I, on my part, clambered up into the berth with an armful of pistols and something of a heavy heart, and set open the window where I was to watch. It was a small part of the deck that I could overlook, but enough for our purpose. The sea had gone down, and the wind was steady and kept the sails quiet; so that there was a great stillness in the ship, in which I made sure I heard the sound of muttering voices. A little after, and there came a clash of steel upon the deck, by which I knew they were dealing out the cutlasses and one had been let fall; and after that, silence again.

I do not know if I was what you call afraid; but my heart beat like a bird's, both quick and little; and there was a dimness came before my eyes which I continually rubbed away, and which continually returned. As for hope, I had none; but only a darkness of despair and a sort of anger against all the world that made me long to sell my life as dear as I was able. I tried to pray, I remember, but that same hurry of my mind, like a man running, would not suffer me to think upon the words; and my chief wish was to have the thing begin and be done with it.

It came all of a sudden when it did, with a rush of feet and a roar, and then a shout from Alan, and a sound of blows and some one crying out as if hurt. I looked back over my shoulder, and saw Mr. Shuan in the doorway, crossing blades with Alan.

"That's him that killed the boy!" I cried.

"Look to your window!" said Alan; and as I turned back to my place, I saw him pass his sword through the mate's body.

It was none too soon for me to look to my own part; for my head was scarce back at the window, before five men, carrying a spare yard for a battering-ram, ran past me and took post to drive the door in. I had never fired with a pistol in my life, and not often with a gun; far less against a fellow-creature. But it was now or never; and just as they swang the yard, I cried out: "Take that!" and shot into their midst.

I must have hit one of them, for he sang out and gave back a step, and the rest stopped as if a little disconcerted. Before they had time to recover, I sent another ball over their heads; and at my third shot (which went as wide as the second) the whole party threw down the yard and ran for it.

Then I looked round again into the deck-house. The whole place was full of the smoke of my own firing, just as my ears seemed to be burst with the noise of the shots. But there was Alan, standing as before; only now his sword was running blood to the hilt, and himself so swelled with triumph and fallen into so fine an attitude, that he looked to be invincible. Right before him on the floor was Mr. Shuan, on his hands and knees; the blood was pouring from his mouth, and he was sinking slowly lower, with a terrible, white face; and just as I looked, some of those from behind caught hold of him by the heels and dragged him bodily out of the round-house. I believe he died as they were doing it.

"There's one of your Whigs for ye!" cried Alan; and then turning to me, he asked if I had done much execution.

I told him I had winged one, and thought it was the captain.

"And I've settled two," says he. "No, there's not enough blood let; they'll be back again. To your watch, David. This was but a dram before meat."

I settled back to my place, re-charging the three pistols I had fired, and keeping watch with both eye and ear.

Our enemies were disputing not far off upon the deck, and that so loudly that I could hear a word or two above the washing of the seas.

"It was Shuan bauchled it," I heard one say.

And another answered him with a "Wheesht, man! He's paid the piper."

After that the voices fell again into the same muttering as before. Only now, one person spoke most of the time, as though laying down a plan, and first one and then another answered him briefly, like men taking orders. By this, I made sure they were coming on again, and told Alan.

"It's what we have to pray for," said he. "Unless we can give them a good distaste of us, and done with it, there'll be nae sleep for either you or me. But this time, mind, they'll be in earnest."

By this, my pistols were ready, and there was nothing to do but listen and wait. While the brush lasted, I had not the time to think if I was frighted; but now, when all was still again, my mind ran upon nothing else. The thought of the sharp swords and the cold steel was strong in me; and presently, when I began to hear stealthy steps and a brushing of men's clothes against the round-house wall, and knew they were taking their places in the dark, I could have found it in my mind to cry out aloud.

All this was upon Alan's side; and I had begun to think my share of the fight was at an end, when I heard some one drop softly on the roof above me.

Then there came a single call on the sea-pipe, and that was the signal. A knot of them made one rush of it, cutlass in hand, against the door; and at the same moment, the glass of the skylight was dashed in a thousand pieces, and a man leaped through and landed on the floor. Before he got his feet, I had clapped a pistol to his back, and might have shot him, too; only at the touch of him (and him alive) my whole flesh misgave me, and I could no more pull the trigger than I could have flown.

He had dropped his cutlass as he jumped, and when he felt the pistol, whipped straight round and laid hold of me, roaring out an oath; and at that either my courage came again, or I grew so much afraid as came to the same thing; for I gave a shriek and shot him in the midst of the body. He gave the most horrible, ugly groan and fell to the floor. The foot of a second fellow, whose legs were dangling through the skylight, struck me at the same time upon the head; and at that I snatched another pistol and shot this one through the thigh, so that he slipped through and tumbled in a lump on his companion's body. There was no talk of missing, any more than there was time to aim; I clapped the muzzle to the very place and fired.

I might have stood and stared at them for long, but I heard Alan shout as if for help, and that brought me to my senses.

He had kept the door so long; but one of the seamen, while he was engaged with others, had run in under his guard and caught him about the body. Alan was dirking him with his left hand, but the fellow clung like a leech. Another had broken in and had his cutlass raised. The door was thronged with their faces. I thought we were lost, and catching up my cutlass, fell on them in flank.

But I had not time to be of help. The wrestler dropped at last; and Alan, leaping back to get his distance, ran upon the others like a bull, roaring as he went. They broke before him like water, turning, and running, and falling one against another in their haste. The sword in his hands flashed like quicksilver into the huddle of our fleeing enemies; and at every flash there came the scream of a man hurt. I was still thinking we were lost, when lo! they were all gone, and Alan was driving them along the deck as a sheep-dog chases sheep.

Yet he was no sooner out than he was back again, being as cautious as he was brave; and meanwhile the seamen continued running and crying out as if he was still behind them; and we heard them tumble one upon another into the forecastle, and clap-to the hatch upon the top.

The round-house was like a shambles; three were dead inside, another lay in his death agony across the threshold; and there were Alan and I victorious and unhurt.

He came up to me with open arms. "Come to my arms!" he cried, and embraced and kissed me hard upon both cheek. "David," said he, "I love you like a brother. And O, man," he cried in a kind of ecstasy, "am I no a bonny fighter?"

Thereupon he turned to the four enemies, passed his sword clean through each of them, and tumbled them out of doors one after the other. As he did so, he kept humming and singing and whistling to himself, like a man trying to recall an air; only what HE was trying was to make one. All the while, the flush was in his face, and his eyes were as bright as a five-year-old child's with a new toy. And presently he sat down upon the table, sword in hand; the air that he was making all the time began to run a little clearer, and then clearer still; and then out he burst with a great voice into a Gaelic song.

I have translated it here, not in verse (of which I have no skill) but at least in the king's English. He sang it often afterwards, and the thing became popular; so that I have, heard it, and had it explained to me, many's the time.

This is the song of the sword of Alan:
The smith made it,
The fire set it;
Now it shines in the hand of Alan Breck.

Their eyes were many and bright,
Swift were they to behold,
Many the hands they guided:
The sword was alone.

The dun deer troop over the hill,
They are many, the hill is one:
The dun deer vanish,
The hill remains.

Come to me from the hills of heather,
Come from the isles of the sea.
O far-beholding eagles,
Here is your meat.

Now this song which he made (both words and music) in the hour of our victory, is something less than just to me, who stood beside him in the tussle. Mr. Shuan and five more were either killed outright or thoroughly disabled; but of these, two fell by my hand, the two that came by the skylight. Four more were hurt, and of that number, one (and he not the least important) got his hurt from me. So that, altogether, I did my fair share both of the killing and the wounding, and might have claimed a place in Alan's verses. But poets have to think upon their rhymes; and in good prose talk, Alan always did me more than justice.

In the meanwhile, I was innocent of any wrong being done me. For not only I knew no word of the Gaelic; but what with the long suspense of the waiting, and the scurry and strain of our two spirts of fighting, and more than all, the horror I had of some of my own share in it, the thing was no sooner over than I was glad to stagger to a seat. There was that tightness on my chest that I could hardly breathe; the thought of the two men I had shot sat upon me like a nightmare; and all upon a sudden, and before I had a guess of what was coming, I began to sob and cry like any child.

Alan clapped my shoulder, and said I was a brave lad and wanted nothing but a sleep.

"I'll take the first watch," said he. "Ye've done well by me, David, first and last; and I wouldn't lose you for all Appin—no, nor for Breadalbane."

So I made up my bed on the floor; and he took the first spell, pistol in hand and sword on knee, three hours by the captain's watch upon the wall. Then he roused me up, and I took my turn of three hours; before the end of which it was broad day, and a very quiet morning, with a smooth, rolling sea that tossed the ship and made the blood run to and fro on the round-house floor, and a heavy rain that drummed upon the roof. All my watch there was nothing stirring; and by the banging of the helm, I knew they had even no one at the tiller. Indeed (as I learned afterwards) there were so many of them hurt or dead, and the rest in so ill a temper, that Mr. Riach and the captain had to take turn and turn like Alan and me, or the brig might have gone ashore and nobody the wiser. It was a mercy the night had fallen so still, for the wind had gone down as soon as the rain began. Even as it was, I judged by the wailing of a great number of gulls that went crying and fishing round the ship, that she must have drifted pretty near the coast or one of the islands of the Hebrides; and at last, looking out of the door of the round-house, I saw the great stone hills of Skye on the right hand, and, a little more astern, the strange isle of Rum.

CHAPTER XI

THE CAPTAIN KNUCKLES UNDER

Alan and I sat down to breakfast about six of the clock. The floor was covered with broken glass and in a horrid mess of blood, which took away my hunger. In all other ways we were in a situation not only agreeable but merry; having ousted the officers from their own cabin, and having at command all the drink in the ship—both wine and spirits—and all the dainty part of what was eatable, such as the pickles and the fine sort of bread. This, of itself, was enough to set us in good humour, but the richest part of it was this, that the two thirstiest men that ever came out of Scotland (Mr. Shuan being dead) were now shut in the fore-part of the ship and condemned to what they hated most—cold water.

"And depend upon it," Alan said, "we shall hear more of them ere long. Ye may keep a man from the fighting, but never from his bottle."

We made good company for each other. Alan, indeed, expressed himself most lovingly; and taking a knife from the table, cut me off one of the silver buttons from his coat.

"I had them," says he, "from my father, Duncan Stewart; and now give ye one of them to be a keepsake for last night's work. And wherever ye go and show that button, the friends of Alan Breck will come around you."

He said this as if he had been Charlemagne, and commanded armies; and indeed, much as I admired his courage, I was always in danger of smiling at his vanity: in danger, I say, for had I not kept my countenance, I would be afraid to think what a quarrel might have followed.

As soon as we were through with our meal he rummaged in the captain's locker till he found a clothes-brush; and then taking off his coat, began to visit his suit and brush away the stains, with such care and labour as I supposed to have been only usual with women. To be sure, he had no other; and, besides (as he said), it belonged to a king and so behoved to be royally looked after.

For all that, when I saw what care he took to pluck out the threads where the button had been cut away, I put a higher value on his gift.

He was still so engaged when we were hailed by Mr. Riach from the deck, asking for a parley; and I, climbing through the skylight and sitting on the edge of it, pistol in hand and with a bold front, though inwardly in fear of broken glass, hailed him back again and bade him speak out. He came to the edge of the round-house, and stood on a coil of rope, so that his chin was on a level with the roof; and we looked at each other awhile in silence. Mr. Riach, as I do not think he had been very forward in the battle, so he had got off with nothing worse than a blow upon the cheek: but he looked out of heart and very weary, having been all night afoot, either standing watch or doctoring the wounded.

"This is a bad job," said he at last, shaking his head.

"It was none of our choosing," said I.

"The captain," says he, "would like to speak with your friend. They might speak at the window."

"And how do we know what treachery he means?" cried I.

"He means none, David," returned Mr. Riach, "and if he did, I'll tell ye the honest truth, we couldnae get the men to follow."

"Is that so?" said I.

"I'll tell ye more than that," said he. "It's not only the men;

it's me. I'm frich'ened, Davie." And he smiled across at me.
"No," he continued, "what we want is to be shut of him."

Thereupon I consulted with Alan, and the parley was
agreed to and parole given upon either side; but this was not
the whole of Mr. Riach's business, and he now begged me for
a dram with such instancy and such reminders of his former
kindness, that at last I handed him a pannikin with about a
gill of brandy. He drank a part, and then carried the rest down
upon the deck, to share it (I suppose) with his superior.

A little after, the captain came (as was agreed) to one of the
windows, and stood there in the rain, with his arm in a sling,
and looking stern and pale, and so old that my heart smote me
for having fired upon him.

Alan at once held a pistol in his face.

"Put that thing up!" said the captain. "Have I not passed my
word, sir? or do ye seek to affront me?"

"Captain," says Alan, "I doubt your word is a breakable.
Last night ye haggled and argle-bargled like an apple-wife; and
then passed me your word, and gave me your hand to back it;
and ye ken very well what was the upshot. Be damned to your
word!" says he.

"Well, well, sir," said the captain, "ye'll get little good by
swearing." (And truly that was a fault of which the captain was
quite free.) "But we have other things to speak," he continued,
bitterly. "Ye've made a sore hash of my brig; I haven't hands
enough left to work her; and my first officer (whom I could ill
spare) has got your sword throughout his vitals, and passed
without speech. There is nothing left me, sir, but to put back
into the port of Glasgow after hands; and there (by your leave)
ye will find them that are better able to talk to you."

"Ay?" said Alan; "and faith, I'll have a talk with them
mysel'! Unless there's naebody speaks English in that town, I
have a bonny tale for them. Fifteen tarry sailors upon the one
side, and a man and a halfling boy upon the other! O, man, it's

peetiful!"

Hoseason flushed red.

"No," continued Alan, "that'll no do. Ye'll just have to set me ashore as we agreed."

"Ay," said Hoseason, "but my first officer is dead—ye ken best how. There's none of the rest of us acquaint with this coast, sir; and it's one very dangerous to ships."

"I give ye your choice," says Alan. "Set me on dry ground in Appin, or Ardgour, or in Morven, or Arisaig, or Morar; or, in brief, where ye please, within thirty miles of my own country; except in a country of the Campbells. That's a broad target. If ye miss that, ye must be as feckless at the sailoring as I have found ye at the fighting. Why, my poor country people in their bit cobles pass from island to island in all weathers, ay, and by night too, for the matter of that."

"A coble's not a ship, sir," said the captain. "It has nae draught of water."

"Well, then, to Glasgow if ye list!" says Alan. "We'll have the laugh of ye at the least."

"My mind runs little upon laughing," said the captain. "But all this will cost money, sir."

"Well, sir" says Alan, "I am nae weathercock. Thirty guineas, if ye land me on the sea-side; and sixty, if ye put me in the Linnhe Loch."

"But see, sir, where we lie, we are but a few hours' sail from Ardnamurchan," said Hoseason. "Give me sixty, and I'll set ye there."

"And I'm to wear my brogues and run jeopardy of the red-coats to please you?" cries Alan. "No, sir; if ye want sixty guineas earn them, and set me in my own country."

"It's to risk the brig, sir," said the captain, "and your own lives along with her."

"Take it or want it," says Alan.

"Could ye pilot us at all?" asked the captain, who was

frowning to himself.

"Well, it's doubtful," said Alan. "I'm more of a fighting man (as ye have seen for yoursel') than a sailor-man. But I have been often enough picked up and set down upon this coast, and should ken something of the lie of it."

The captain shook his head, still frowning.

"If I had lost less money on this unchancy cruise," says he, "I would see you in a rope's end before I risked my brig, sir. But be it as ye will. As soon as I get a slant of wind (and there's some coming, or I'm the more mistaken) I'll put it in hand. But there's one thing more. We may meet in with a king's ship and she may lay us aboard, sir, with no blame of mine: they keep the cruisers thick upon this coast, ye ken who for. Now, sir, if that was to befall, ye might leave the money."

"Captain," says Alan, "if ye see a pennant, it shall be your part to run away. And now, as I hear you're a little short of brandy in the fore-part, I'll offer ye a change: a bottle of brandy against two buckets of water."

That was the last clause of the treaty, and was duly executed on both sides; so that Alan and I could at last wash out the round-house and be quit of the memorials of those whom we had slain, and the captain and Mr. Riach could be happy again in their own way, the name of which was drink.

CHAPTER XII

I HEAR OF THE RED FOX

Before we had done cleaning out the round-house, a breeze sprang up from a little to the east of north. This blew off the rain and brought out the sun.

And here I must explain; and the reader would do well to look at a map. On the day when the fog fell and we ran down Alan's boat, we had been running through the Little Minch. At dawn after the battle, we lay becalmed to the east of the Isle of Canna or between that and Isle Eriska in the chain of the Long Island. Now to get from there to the Linnhe Loch, the straight course was through the narrows of the Sound of Mull. But the captain had no chart; he was afraid to trust his brig so deep among the islands; and the wind serving well, he preferred to go by west of Tiree and come up under the southern coast of the great Isle of Mull.

All day the breeze held in the same point, and rather freshened than died down; and towards afternoon, a swell began to set in from round the outer Hebrides. Our course, to go round about the inner isles, was to the west of south, so that at first we had this swell upon our beam, and were much rolled about. But after nightfall, when we had turned the end of Tiree and began to head more to the east, the sea came right astern.

Meanwhile, the early part of the day, before the swell came up, was very pleasant; sailing, as we were, in a bright sunshine and with many mountainous islands upon different sides. Alan and I sat in the round-house with the doors open on each side (the wind being straight astern), and smoked a pipe or two of the captain's fine tobacco. It was at this time we heard each other's stories, which was the more important to me, as I gained some knowledge of that wild Highland country on which I was so soon to land. In those days, so close on the back of the great rebellion, it was needful a man should know what he was doing when he went upon the heather.

It was I that showed the example, telling him all my misfortune; which he heard with great good-nature. Only, when I came to mention that good friend of mine, Mr. Campbell the minister, Alan fired up and cried out that he hated all that were of that name.

"Why," said I, "he is a man you should be proud to give your hand to."

"I know nothing I would help a Campbell to," says he, "unless it was a leaden bullet. I would hunt all of that name like blackcocks. If I lay dying, I would crawl upon my knees to my chamber window for a shot at one."

"Why, Alan," I cried, "what ails ye at the Campbells?"

"Well," says he, "ye ken very well that I am an Appin Stewart, and the Campbells have long harried and wasted those of my name; ay, and got lands of us by treachery—but never with the sword," he cried loudly, and with the word brought down his fist upon the table. But I paid the less attention to this, for I knew it was usually said by those who have the underhand. "There's more than that," he continued, "and all in the same story: lying words, lying papers, tricks fit for a peddler, and the show of what's legal over all, to make a man the more angry."

"You that are so wasteful of your buttons," said I, "I can hardly think you would be a good judge of business."

"Ah!" says he, falling again to smiling, "I got my wastefulness from the same man I got the buttons from; and that was my poor father, Duncan Stewart, grace be to him! He was the prettiest man of his kindred; and the best swordsman in the Hielands, David, and that is the same as to say, in all the world, I should ken, for it was him that taught me. He was in the Black Watch, when first it was mustered; and, like other gentlemen privates, had a gillie at his back to carry his firelock for him on the march. Well, the King, it appears, was wishful to see Hieland swordsmanship; and my father and three more were chosen out and sent to London town, to let him see it at the best. So they were had into the palace and showed the whole art of the sword for two hours at a stretch, before King George and Queen Carline, and the Butcher Cumberland, and many more of whom I havenae mind. And when they were through, the King (for all he was a rank usurper) spoke them fair and gave each man three guineas in his hand. Now, as they were going out of the palace, they had a porter's lodge to go, by; and it came in on my father, as he was perhaps the first private Hieland gentleman that had ever gone by that door, it was right he should give the poor porter a proper notion of their quality. So he gives the King's three guineas into the man's hand, as if it was his common custom; the three others that came behind him did the same; and there they were on the street, never a penny the better for their pains. Some say it was one, that was the first to fee the King's porter; and some say it was another; but the truth of it is, that it was Duncan Stewart, as I am willing to prove with either sword or pistol. And that was the father that I had, God rest him!"

"I think he was not the man to leave you rich," said I.

"And that's true," said Alan. "He left me my breeks to cover me, and little besides. And that was how I came to enlist, which was a black spot upon my character at the best of times, and would still be a sore job for me if I fell among the red-coats."

"What," cried I, "were you in the English army?"

"That was I," said Alan. "But I deserted to the right side at Preston Pans—and that's some comfort."

I could scarcely share this view: holding desertion under

arms for an unpardonable fault in honour. But for all I was so young, I was wiser than say my thought. "Dear, dear," says I, "the punishment is death."

"Ay" said he, "if they got hands on me, it would be a short shrift and a lang tow for Alan! But I have the King of France's commission in my pocket, which would aye be some protection."

"I misdoubt it much," said I.

"I have doubts mysel," said Alan drily.

"And, good heaven, man," cried I, "you that are a condemned rebel, and a deserter, and a man of the French King's—what tempts ye back into this country? It's a braving of Providence."

"Tut!" says Alan, "I have been back every year since forty-six!"

"And what brings ye, man?" cried I.

"Well, ye see, I weary for my friends and country," said he. "France is a braw place, nae doubt; but I weary for the heather and the deer. And then I have bit things that I attend to. Whiles I pick up a few lads to serve the King of France: recruits, ye see; and that's aye a little money. But the heart of the matter is the business of my chief, Ardshiel."

"I thought they called your chief Appin," said I.

"Ay, but Ardshiel is the captain of the clan," said he, which scarcely cleared my mind. "Ye see, David, he that was all his life so great a man, and come of the blood and bearing the name of kings, is now brought down to live in a French town like a poor and private person. He that had four hundred swords at his whistle, I have seen, with these eyes of mine, buying butter in the market-place, and taking it home in a kale-leaf. This is not only a pain but a disgrace to us of his family and clan. There are the bairns forby, the children and the hope of Appin, that must be learned their letters and how to hold a sword, in that far country. Now, the tenants of Appin have to pay a rent to King George; but their hearts are staunch, they are true to their chief; and what with love and a bit of pressure, and maybe a threat or two, the poor folk scrape up a second rent for Ardshiel. Well, David, I'm the hand that carries it." And he struck the belt about his body, so that the guineas rang.

"Do they pay both?" cried I.

"Ay, David, both," says he.

"What! two rents?" I repeated.

"Ay, David," said he. "I told a different tale to yon captain man; but this is the truth of it. And it's wonderful to me how little pressure is needed. But that's the handiwork of my good kinsman and my father's friend, James of the Glens: James Stewart, that is: Ardshiel's half-brother. He it is that gets the money in, and does the management."

This was the first time I heard the name of that James Stewart, who was afterwards so famous at the time of his hanging. But I took little heed at the moment, for all my mind was occupied with the generosity of these poor Highlanders.

"I call it noble," I cried. "I'm a Whig, or little better; but I call it noble."

"Ay" said he, "ye're a Whig, but ye're a gentleman; and that's what does it. Now, if ye were one of the cursed race of Campbell, ye would gnash your teeth to hear tell of it. If ye were the Red Fox..." And at that name, his teeth shut together, and he ceased speaking. I have seen many a grim face, but never a grimmer than Alan's when he had named the Red Fox.

"And who is the Red Fox?" I asked, daunted, but still curious.

"Who is he?" cried Alan. "Well, and I'll tell you that. When the men of the clans were broken at Culloden, and the good cause went down, and the horses rode over the fetlocks in the best blood of the north, Ardshiel had to flee like a poor deer upon the mountains—he and his lady and his bairns. A sair job we had of it before we got him shipped; and while he still lay in the heather, the English rogues, that couldnae come at his life, were striking at his rights. They stripped him of his powers; they stripped him of his lands; they plucked the weapons from the hands of his clansmen, that had borne arms for thirty centuries; ay, and the very clothes off their backs—so that it's now a sin to wear a tartan plaid, and a man may be cast into a gaol if he has but a kilt about his legs. One thing they couldnae kill. That was the love the clansmen bore their chief. These guineas are the proof of it. And now, in there steps a man, a Campbell, red-headed Colin of Glenure—"

"Is that him you call the Red Fox?" said I.

"Will ye bring me his brush?" cries Alan, fiercely. "Ay, that's the man. In he steps, and gets papers from King George, to be so-called King's factor on the lands of Appin. And at first he sings small, and is hail-fellow-well-met with Sheamus—that's James of the Glens, my chieftain's agent. But by-and-by, that came to his ears that I have just told you; how the poor commons of Appin, the farmers and the crofters and the boumen, were wringing their very plaids to get a second rent, and send it over-seas for Ardshiel and his poor bairns. What was it ye called it, when I told ye?"

"I called it noble, Alan," said I.

"And you little better than a common Whig!" cries Alan. "But when it came to Colin Roy, the black Campbell blood in him ran wild. He sat gnashing his teeth at the wine table. What! should a Stewart get a bite of bread, and him not be able to prevent it? Ah! Red Fox, if ever I hold you at a gun's end, the Lord have pity upon ye!" (Alan stopped to swallow down his anger.) "Well, David, what does he do? He declares all the farms to let. And, thinks he, in his black heart, 'I'll soon get other tenants that'll overbid these Stewarts, and Maccolls, and Macrobs' (for these are all names in my clan, David); 'and then,' thinks he, 'Ardshiel will have to hold his bonnet on a French roadside.'"

"Well," said I, "what followed?"

Alan laid down his pipe, which he had long since suffered to go out, and set his two hands upon his knees.

"Ay," said he, "ye'll never guess that! For these same Stewarts, and Maccolls, and Macrobs (that had two rents to pay, one to King George by stark force, and one to Ardshiel by natural kindness) offered him a better price than any Campbell in all broad Scotland; and far he sent seeking them—as far as to the sides of Clyde and the cross of Edinburgh—seeking, and fleeching, and begging them to come, where there was a Stewart to be starved and a red-headed hound of a Campbell to be pleasured!"

"Well, Alan," said I, "that is a strange story, and a fine one, too. And Whig as I may be, I am glad the man was beaten."

"Him beaten?" echoed Alan. "It's little ye ken of Campbells, and less of the Red Fox. Him beaten? No: nor will be, till his blood's on the hillside! But if the day comes, David man, that I can find time and leisure for a bit of hunting, there grows not enough heather in all Scotland to hide him from my vengeance!"

"Man Alan," said I, "ye are neither very wise nor very Christian to blow off so many words of anger. They will do the man ye call the Fox no harm, and yourself no good. Tell me your tale plainly out. What did he next?"

"And that's a good observe, David," said Alan. "Troth and indeed, they will do him no harm; the more's the pity! And barring that about Christianity (of which my opinion is quite otherwise, or I would be nae Christian), I am much of your mind."

"Opinion here or opinion there," said I, "it's a kent thing that Christianity forbids revenge."

"Ay" said he, "it's well seen it was a Campbell taught ye! It would be a convenient world for them and their sort, if there was no such a thing as a lad and a gun behind a heather bush! But that's nothing to the point. This is what he did."

"Ay" said I, "come to that."

"Well, David," said he, "since he couldnae be rid of the loyal commons by fair means, he swore he would be rid of them by foul. Ardshiel was to starve: that was the thing he aimed at. And since them that fed him in his exile wouldnae be bought out—right or wrong, he would drive them out. Therefore he sent for lawyers, and papers, and red-coats to stand at his back. And the kindly folk of that country must all pack and tramp, every father's son out of his father's house, and out of the place where he was bred and fed, and played when he was a callant. And who are to succeed them? Bare-leggit beggars! King George is to whistle for his rents; he maun dow with less; he can spread his butter thinner: what cares Red Colin? If he can hurt Ardshiel, he has his wish; if he can pluck the meat from my chieftain's table, and the bit toys out of his children's hands, he will gang hame singing to Glenure!"

"Let me have a word," said I. "Be sure, if they take less rents, be sure Government has a finger in the pie. It's not this Campbell's fault, man—it's his orders. And if ye killed this Colin, what better would ye be? There would be another factor in his shoes, as fast as spur can drive."

"Ye're a good lad in a fight," said Alan; "but, man! ye have Whig blood in ye!"

He spoke kindly enough, but there was so much anger under his contempt that I thought it was wise to change the conversation. I expressed my wonder how, with the Highlands covered with troops, and guarded like a city in a siege, a man in his situation could come and go without arrest.

"It's easier than ye would think," said Alan. "A bare hillside (ye see) is like all one road; if there's a sentry at one place, ye just go by another. And then the heather's a great help. And everywhere there are friends' houses and friends' byres and haystacks. And besides, when folk talk of a country covered with troops, it's but a kind of a byword at the best. A soldier covers nae mair of it than his boot-soles. I have fished a water with a sentry on the other side of the brae, and killed a fine trout; and I have sat in a heather bush within six feet of another, and learned a real bonny tune from his whistling. This was it," said he, and whistled me the air.

"And then, besides," he continued, "it's no sae bad now as it was in forty-six. The Hielands are what they call pacified. Small wonder, with never a gun or a sword left from Cantyre to Cape Wrath, but what tenty folk have hidden in their thatch! But what I would like to ken, David, is just how long? Not long, ye would think, with men like Ardshiel in exile and men like the Red Fox sitting birling the wine and oppressing the poor at home. But it's a kittle thing to decide what folk'll bear, and what they will not. Or why would Red Colin be riding his horse all over my poor country of Appin, and never a pretty lad to put a bullet in him?"

And with this Alan fell into a muse, and for a long time sate very sad and silent.

I will add the rest of what I have to say about my friend, that he was skilled in all kinds of music, but principally pipe-music; was a well-considered poet in his own tongue; had read several books both in French and English; was a dead shot, a good angler, and an excellent fencer with the small sword as well as with his own particular weapon. For his faults, they were on his face, and I now knew them all. But the worst of them, his childish propensity to take offence and to pick quarrels, he greatly laid aside in my case, out of regard for the battle of the round-house. But whether it was because I had done well myself, or because I had been a witness of his own much greater prowess, is more than I can tell. For though he had a great taste for courage in other men, yet he admired it most in Alan Breck.

CHAPTER XIII

THE LOSS OF THE BRIG

It was already late at night, and as dark as it ever would be at that season of the year (and that is to say, it was still pretty bright), when Hoseason clapped his head into the round-house door.

"Here," said he, "come out and see if ye can pilot."

"Is this one of your tricks?" asked Alan.

"Do I look like tricks?" cries the captain. "I have other things to think of—my brig's in danger!"

By the concerned look of his face, and, above all, by the sharp tones in which he spoke of his brig, it was plain to both of us he was in deadly earnest; and so Alan and I, with no great fear of treachery, stepped on deck.

The sky was clear; it blew hard, and was bitter cold; a great deal of daylight lingered; and the moon, which was nearly full, shone brightly. The brig was close hauled, so as to round the southwest corner of the Island of Mull, the hills of which (and Ben More above them all, with a wisp of mist upon the top of it) lay full upon the lar-board bow. Though it was no good point of sailing for the *Covenant*, she tore through the seas at a great rate, pitching and straining, and pursued by the westerly swell.

Altogether it was no such ill night to keep the seas in; and I had begun to wonder what it was that sat so heavily upon the captain, when the brig rising suddenly on the top of a high swell, he pointed and cried to us to look. Away on the lee bow, a thing like a fountain rose out of the moonlit sea, and immediately after we heard a low sound of roaring.

"What do ye call that?" asked the captain, gloomily.

"The sea breaking on a reef," said Alan. "And now ye ken where it is; and what better would ye have?"

"Ay," said Hoseason, "if it was the only one."

And sure enough, just as he spoke there came a second fountain farther to the south.

"There!" said Hoseason. "Ye see for yourself. If I had kent of these reefs, if I had had a chart, or if Shuan had been spared, it's not sixty guineas, no, nor six hundred, would have made me risk my brig in sic a stoneyard! But you, sir, that was to pilot us, have ye never a word?"

"I'm thinking," said Alan, "these'll be what they call the Torran Rocks."

"Are there many of them?" says the captain.

"Truly, sir, I am nae pilot," said Alan; "but it sticks in my mind there are ten miles of them."

Mr. Riach and the captain looked at each other.

"There's a way through them, I suppose?" said the captain.

"Doubtless," said Alan, "but where? But it somehow runs in my mind once more that it is clearer under the land."

"So?" said Hoseason. "We'll have to haul our wind then, Mr. Riach; we'll have to come as near in about the end of Mull as we can take her, sir; and even then we'll have the land to kep the wind off us, and that stoneyard on our lee. Well, we're in for it now, and may as well crack on."

With that he gave an order to the steersman, and sent Riach to the foretop. There were only five men on deck, counting the officers; these being all that were fit (or, at least, both fit and willing) for their work. So, as I say, it fell to Mr. Riach to go aloft, and he sat there looking out and hailing the deck with news of all he saw.

"The sea to the south is thick," he cried; and then, after a while, "it does seem clearer in by the land."

"Well, sir," said Hoseason to Alan, "we'll try your way of it. But I think I might as well trust to a blind fiddler. Pray God you're right."

"Pray God I am!" says Alan to me. "But where did I hear it? Well, well, it will be as it must."

As we got nearer to the turn of the land the reefs began to be sown here and there on our very path; and Mr. Riach sometimes cried down to us to change the course. Sometimes, indeed, none too soon; for one reef was so close on the brig's weather board that when a sea burst upon it the lighter sprays fell upon her deck and wetted us like rain.

The brightness of the night showed us these perils as clearly as by day, which was, perhaps, the more alarming. It showed me, too, the face of the captain as he stood by the steersman, now on one foot, now on the other, and sometimes blowing in his hands, but still listening and looking and as steady as steel. Neither he nor Mr. Riach had shown well in the fighting; but I saw they were brave in their own trade, and admired them all the more because I found Alan very white.

"Ochone, David," says he, "this is no the kind of death I fancy!"

"What, Alan!" I cried, "you're not afraid?"

"No," said he, wetting his lips, "but you'll allow, yourself, it's a cold ending."

By this time, now and then sheering to one side or the other to avoid a reef, but still hugging the wind and the land, we had got round Iona and begun to come alongside Mull. The tide at the tail of the land ran very strong, and threw the brig about. Two hands were put to the helm, and Hoseason himself would sometimes lend a help; and it was strange to see three strong men throw their weight upon the tiller, and it (like a living thing) struggle against and drive them back. This would have been the greater danger had not the sea been for some while free of obstacles. Mr. Riach, besides, announced from the top that he saw clear water ahead.

"Ye were right," said Hoseason to Alan. "Ye have saved the brig, sir. I'll mind that when we come to clear accounts." And I believe he not only meant what he said, but would have done it; so high a place did the *Covenant* hold in his affections.

But this is matter only for conjecture, things having gone otherwise than he forecast.

"Keep her away a point," sings out Mr. Riach. "Reef to windward!"

And just at the same time the tide caught the brig, and threw the wind out of her sails. She came round into the wind like a top, and the next moment struck the reef with such a dunch as threw us all flat upon the deck, and came near to shake Mr. Riach from his place upon the mast.

I was on my feet in a minute. The reef on which we had struck was close in under the southwest end of Mull, off a little isle they call Earraid, which lay low and black upon the larboard. Sometimes the swell broke clean over us; sometimes it only ground the poor brig upon the reef, so that we could hear her beat herself to pieces; and what with the great noise of the sails, and the singing of the wind, and the flying of the spray in the moonlight, and the sense of danger, I think my head must have been partly turned, for I could scarcely understand the things I saw.

Presently I observed Mr. Riach and the seamen busy round the skiff, and, still in the same blank, ran over to assist them; and as soon as I set my hand to work, my mind came clear again. It was no very easy task, for the skiff lay amidships and was full of hamper, and the breaking of the heavier seas continually forced us to give over and hold on; but we all wrought like horses while we could.

Meanwhile such of the wounded as could move came clambering out of the fore-scuttle and began to help; while the rest that lay helpless in their bunks harrowed me with screaming and begging to be saved.

The captain took no part. It seemed he was struck stupid. He stood holding by the shrouds, talking to himself and groaning out aloud whenever the ship hammered on the rock. His brig was like wife and child to him; he had looked on, day by day, at the mishandling of poor Ransome; but when it came to the brig, he seemed to suffer along with her.

All time of our working at the boat, I remember only one other thing: that I asked Alan, looking across at the shore, what country it was; and he answered, it was the worst possible for him, for it was a land of the Campbells.

We had one of the wounded men told off to keep a watch upon the seas and cry us warning. Well, we had the boat about ready to be launched, when this man sang out pretty shrill: "For God's sake, hold on!" We knew by his tone that it was something more than ordinary; and sure enough, there followed a sea so huge that it lifted the brig right up and canted her over on her beam. Whether the cry came too late, or my hold was too weak, I know not; but at the sudden tilting of the ship I was cast clean over the bulwarks into the sea.

I went down, and drank my fill, and then came up, and got a blink of the moon, and then down again. They say a man sinks a third time for good. I cannot be made like other folk, then; for I would not like to write how often I went down, or how often I came up again. All the while, I was being hurled along, and beaten upon and choked, and then swallowed whole; and the thing was so distracting to my wits, that I was neither sorry nor afraid.

Presently, I found I was holding to a spar, which helped me somewhat. And then all of a sudden I was in quiet water, and began to come to myself.

It was the spare yard I had got hold of, and I was amazed to see how far I had travelled from the brig. I hailed her, indeed;

but it was plain she was already out of cry. She was still holding together; but whether or not they had yet launched the boat, I was too far off and too low down to see.

While I was hailing the brig, I spied a tract of water lying between us where no great waves came, but which yet boiled white all over and bristled in the moon with rings and bubbles. Sometimes the whole tract swung to one side, like the tail of a live serpent; sometimes, for a glimpse, it would all disappear and then boil up again. What it was I had no guess, which for the time increased my fear of it; but I now know it must have been the roost or tide race, which had carried me away so fast and tumbled me about so cruelly, and at last, as if tired of that play, had flung out me and the spare yard upon its landward margin.

I now lay quite becalmed, and began to feel that a man can die of cold as well as of drowning. The shores of Earraid were close in; I could see in the moonlight the dots of heather and the sparkling of the mica in the rocks.

"Well," thought I to myself, "if I cannot get as far as that, it's strange!"

I had no skill of swimming, Essen Water being small in our neighbourhood; but when I laid hold upon the yard with both arms, and kicked out with both feet, I soon begun to find that I was moving. Hard work it was, and mortally slow; but in about an hour of kicking and splashing, I had got well in between the points of a sandy bay surrounded by low hills.

The sea was here quite quiet; there was no sound of any surf; the moon shone clear; and I thought in my heart I had never seen a place so desert and desolate. But it was dry land; and when at last it grew so shallow that I could leave the yard and wade ashore upon my feet, I cannot tell if I was more tired or more grateful. Both, at least, I was: tired as I never was before that night; and grateful to God as I trust I have been often, though never with more cause.

CHAPTER XIV

THE ISLET

With my stepping ashore I began the most unhappy part of my adventures. It was half-past twelve in the morning, and though the wind was broken by the land, it was a cold night. I dared not sit down (for I thought I should have frozen), but took off my shoes and walked to and fro upon the sand, bare-foot, and beating my breast with infinite weariness. There was no sound of man or cattle; not a cock crew, though it was about the hour of their first waking; only the surf broke outside in the distance, which put me in mind of my perils and those of my friend. To walk by the sea at that hour of the morning, and in a place so desert-like and lonesome, struck me with a kind of fear.

As soon as the day began to break I put on my shoes and climbed a hill—the ruggedest scramble I ever undertook—falling, the whole way, between big blocks of granite, or leaping from one to another. When I got to the top the dawn was come. There was no sign of the brig, which must have lifted from the reef and sunk. The boat, too, was nowhere to be seen. There was never a sail upon the ocean; and in what I could see of the land was neither house nor man.

I was afraid to think what had befallen my shipmates, and afraid to look longer at so empty a scene. What with my wet clothes and weariness, and my belly that now began to ache with hunger, I had enough to trouble me without that. So I set off eastward along the south coast, hoping to find a house where I might warm myself, and perhaps get news of those I had lost. And at the worst, I considered the sun would soon rise and dry my clothes.

After a little, my way was stopped by a creek or inlet of the sea, which seemed to run pretty deep into the land; and as I had no means to get across, I must needs change my direction to go about the end of it. It was still the roughest kind of walking; indeed the whole, not only of Earraid, but of the neighbouring part of Mull (which they call the Ross) is nothing but a jumble of granite rocks with heather in among. At first the creek kept narrowing as I had looked to see; but presently to my surprise it began to widen out again. At this I scratched my head, but had still no notion of the truth: until at last I came to a rising ground, and it burst upon me all in a moment that I was cast upon a little barren isle, and cut off on every side by the salt seas.

Instead of the sun rising to dry me, it came on to rain, with a thick mist; so that my case was lamentable.

I stood in the rain, and shivered, and wondered what to do, till it occurred to me that perhaps the creek was fordable. Back I went to the narrowest point and waded in. But not three yards from shore, I plumped in head over ears; and if ever I was heard of more, it was rather by God's grace than my own prudence. I was no wetter (for that could hardly be), but I was all the colder for this mishap; and having lost another hope was the more unhappy.

And now, all at once, the yard came in my head. What had carried me through the roost would surely serve me to cross this little quiet creek in safety. With that I set off, undaunted, across the top of the isle, to fetch and carry it back. It was a weary tramp in all ways, and if hope had not buoyed me up, I must have cast myself down and given up. Whether with the sea salt, or because I was growing fevered, I was distressed with thirst, and had to stop, as I went, and drink the peaty water out of the hags.

I came to the bay at last, more dead than alive; and at the first glance, I thought the yard was something farther out than when I left it. In I went, for the third time, into the sea. The sand was smooth and firm, and shelved gradually down, so that I could wade out till the water was almost to my neck and the little waves splashed into my face. But at that depth my feet began to leave me, and I durst venture in no farther. As for the yard, I saw it bobbing very quietly some twenty feet beyond.

I had borne up well until this last disappointment; but at that I came ashore, and flung myself down upon the sands and wept.

The time I spent upon the island is still so horrible a thought to me, that I must pass it lightly over. In all the books I have read of people cast away, they had either their pockets full of tools, or a chest of things would be thrown upon the beach along with them, as if on purpose. My case was very different. I had nothing in my pockets but money and Alan's silver button; and being inland bred, I was as much short of knowledge as of means.

I knew indeed that shell-fish were counted good to eat; and among the rocks of the isle I found a great plenty of limpets, which at first I could scarcely strike from their places, not knowing quickness to be needful. There were, besides, some of the little shells that we call buckies; I think periwinkle is the English name. Of these two I made my whole diet, devouring them cold and raw as I found them; and so hungry was I, that at first they seemed to me delicious.

Perhaps they were out of season, or perhaps there was something wrong in the sea about my island. But at least I had no sooner eaten my first meal than I was seized with giddiness and retching, and lay for a long time no better than dead. A second trial of the same food (indeed I had no other) did better with me, and revived my strength. But as long as

I was on the island, I never knew what to expect when I had eaten; sometimes all was well, and sometimes I was thrown into a miserable sickness; nor could I ever distinguish what particular fish it was that hurt me.

All day it streamed rain; the island ran like a sop, there was no dry spot to be found; and when I lay down that night, between two boulders that made a kind of roof, my feet were in a bog.

The second day I crossed the island to all sides. There was no one part of it better than another; it was all desolate and rocky; nothing living on it but game birds which I lacked the means to kill, and the gulls which haunted the outlying rocks in a prodigious number. But the creek, or strait, that cut off the isle from the main-land of the Ross, opened out on the north into a bay, and the bay again opened into the Sound of Iona; and it was the neighbourhood of this place that I chose to be my home; though if I had thought upon the very name of home in such a spot, I must have burst out weeping.

I had good reasons for my choice. There was in this part of the isle a little hut of a house like a pig's hut, where fishers used to sleep when they came there upon their business; but the turf roof of it had fallen entirely in; so that the hut was of no use to me, and gave me less shelter than my rocks. What was more important, the shell-fish on which I lived grew there in great plenty; when the tide was out I could gather a peck at a time: and this was doubtless a convenience. But the other reason went deeper. I had become in no way used to the horrid solitude of the isle, but still looked round me on all sides (like a man that was hunted), between fear and hope that I might see some human creature coming. Now, from a little up the hillside over the bay, I could catch a sight of the great, ancient church and the roofs of the people's houses in Iona. And on the other hand, over the low country of the Ross, I saw smoke go up, morning and evening, as if from a homestead in a hollow of the land.

I used to watch this smoke, when I was wet and cold, and had my head half turned with loneliness; and think of the fireside and the company, till my heart burned. It was the same with the roofs of Iona. Altogether, this sight I had of men's homes and comfortable lives, although it put a point on my own sufferings, yet it kept hope alive, and helped me to eat my raw shell-fish (which had soon grown to be a disgust), and saved me from the sense of horror I had whenever I was quite alone with dead rocks, and fowls, and the rain, and the cold sea.

I say it kept hope alive; and indeed it seemed impossible that I should be left to die on the shores of my own country, and within view of a church-tower and the smoke of men's houses. But the second day passed; and though as long as the light lasted I kept a bright look-out for boats on the Sound or men passing on the Ross, no help came near me. It still rained, and I turned in to sleep, as wet as ever, and with a cruel sore throat, but a little comforted, perhaps, by having said good-night to my next neighbours, the people of Iona.

Charles the Second declared a man could stay outdoors more days in the year in the climate of England than in any other. This was very like a king, with a palace at his back and changes of dry clothes. But he must have had better luck on his flight from Worcester than I had on that miserable isle. It was the height of the summer; yet it rained for more than twenty-four hours, and did not clear until the afternoon of the third day.

This was the day of incidents. In the morning I saw a red deer, a buck with a fine spread of antlers, standing in the rain on the top of the island; but he had scarce seen me rise from under my rock, before he trotted off upon the other side. I supposed he must have swum the strait; though what should bring any creature to Earraid, was more than I could fancy.

A little after, as I was jumping about after my limpets, I was startled by a guinea-piece, which fell upon a rock in front of me and glanced off into the sea. When the sailors gave me my money again, they kept back not only about a third of the whole sum, but my father's leather purse; so that from that day out, I carried my gold loose in a pocket with a button. I now saw there must be a hole, and clapped my hand to the place in a great hurry. But this was to lock the stable door after the steed was stolen. I had left the shore at Queensferry with near on fifty pounds; now I found no more than two guinea-pieces and a silver shilling.

It is true I picked up a third guinea a little after, where it lay shining on a piece of turf. That made a fortune of three pounds and four shillings, English money, for a lad, the rightful heir of an estate, and now starving on an isle at the extreme end of the wild Highlands.

This state of my affairs dashed me still further; and, indeed my plight on that third morning was truly pitiful. My clothes were beginning to rot; my stockings in particular were quite worn through, so that my shanks went naked; my hands had grown quite soft with the continual soaking; my throat was very sore, my strength had much abated, and my heart so turned against the horrid stuff I was condemned to eat, that the very sight of it came near to sicken me.

And yet the worst was not yet come.

There is a pretty high rock on the northwest of Earraid, which (because it had a flat top and overlooked the Sound) I was much in the habit of frequenting; not that ever I stayed in one place, save when asleep, my misery giving me no rest. Indeed, I wore myself down with continual and aimless goings and comings in the rain.

As soon, however, as the sun came out, I lay down on the top of that rock to dry myself. The comfort of the sunshine is a thing I cannot tell. It set me thinking hopefully of my deliverance, of which I had begun to despair; and I scanned the sea and the Ross with a fresh interest. On the south of my rock, a part of the island jutted out and hid the open ocean, so that a boat could thus come quite near me upon that side, and I be none the wiser.

Well, all of a sudden, a coble with a brown sail and a pair of fishers aboard of it, came flying round that corner of the isle, bound for Iona. I shouted out, and then fell on my knees on the rock and reached up my hands and prayed to them. They were near enough to hear—I could even see the colour of their hair; and there was no doubt but they observed me, for they cried out in the Gaelic tongue, and laughed. But the boat never turned aside, and flew on, right before my eyes, for Iona.

I could not believe such wickedness, and ran along the shore from rock to rock, crying on them piteously even after they were out of reach of my voice, I still cried and waved to them; and when they were quite gone, I thought my heart would have burst. All the time of my troubles I wept only twice. Once, when I could not reach the yard, and now, the second time, when these fishers turned a deaf ear to my cries. But this time I wept and roared like a wicked child, tearing up the turf with my nails, and grinding my face in the earth. If a wish would kill men, those two fishers would never have seen morning, and I should likely have died upon my island.

When I was a little over my anger, I must eat again, but with such loathing of the mess as I could now scarce control. Sure enough, I should have done as well to fast, for my fishes poisoned me again. I had all my first pains; my throat was so sore I could scarce swallow; I had a fit of strong shuddering, which clucked my teeth together; and there came on me that dreadful sense of illness, which we have no name for either in Scotch or English. I thought I should have died, and made my peace with God, forgiving all men, even my uncle and the fishers; and as soon as I had thus made up my mind to the worst, clearness came upon me; I observed the night was falling dry; my clothes were dried a good deal; truly, I was in a better case than ever before, since I had landed on the isle; and so I got to sleep at last, with a thought of gratitude.

The next day (which was the fourth of this horrible life of mine) I found my bodily strength run very low. But the sun shone, the air was sweet, and what I managed to eat of the shell-fish agreed well with me and revived my courage.

I was scarce back on my rock (where I went always the first thing after I had eaten) before I observed a boat coming down the Sound, and with her head, as I thought, in my direction.

I began at once to hope and fear exceedingly; for I thought these men might have thought better of their cruelty and be coming back to my assistance. But another disappointment, such as yesterday's, was more than I could bear. I turned my back, accordingly, upon the sea, and did not look again till I had counted many hundreds. The boat was still heading for the island. The next time I counted the full thousand, as slowly as I could, my heart beating so as to hurt me. And then it was out of all question. She was coming straight to Earraid!

I could no longer hold myself back, but ran to the seaside and out, from one rock to another, as far as I could go. It is a marvel I was not drowned; for when I was brought to a stand at last, my legs shook under me, and my mouth was so dry, I must wet it with the sea-water before I was able to shout.

All this time the boat was coming on; and now I was able to perceive it was the same boat and the same two men as yesterday. This I knew by their hair, which the one had of a bright yellow and the other black. But now there was a third man along with them, who looked to be of a better class.

As soon as they were come within easy speech, they let down their sail and lay quiet. In spite of my supplications, they drew no nearer in, and what frightened me most of all, the new man tee-hee'd with laughter as he talked and looked at me.

Then he stood up in the boat and addressed me a long while, speaking fast and with many wavings of his hand. I told him I had no Gaelic; and at this he became very angry, and I began to suspect he thought he was talking English. Listening very close, I caught the word "whateffer" several times; but all the rest was Gaelic and might have been Greek and Hebrew for me.

"Whatever," said I, to show him I had caught a word.

"Yes, yes—yes, yes," says he, and then he looked at the other men, as much as to say, "I told you I spoke English," and began again as hard as ever in the Gaelic.

This time I picked out another word, "tide." Then I had a flash of hope. I remembered he was always waving his hand towards the mainland of the Ross.

"Do you mean when the tide is out—?" I cried, and could not finish.

"Yes, yes," said he. "Tide."

At that I turned tail upon their boat (where my adviser had once more begun to tee-hee with laughter), leaped back the way I had come, from one stone to another, and set off running across the isle as I had never run before. In about half an hour I came out upon the shores of the creek; and, sure enough, it was shrunk into a little trickle of water, through which I dashed, not above my knees, and landed with a shout on the main island.

A sea-bred boy would not have stayed a day on Earraid; which is only what they call a tidal islet, and except in the bottom of the neaps, can be entered and left twice in every twenty-four hours, either dry-shod, or at the most by wading. Even I, who had the tide going out and in before me in the bay, and even watched for the ebbs, the better to get my shellfish— even I (I say) if I had sat down to think, instead of raging at my fate, must have soon guessed the secret, and got free. It was no wonder the fishers had not understood me. The wonder was rather that they had ever guessed my pitiful illusion, and taken the trouble to come back. I had starved with cold and hunger on that island for close upon one hundred hours. But for the fishers, I might have left my bones there, in pure folly. And even as it was, I had paid for it pretty dear, not only in past sufferings, but in my present case; being clothed like a beggarman, scarce able to walk, and in great pain of my sore throat.

I have seen wicked men and fools, a great many of both; and I believe they both get paid in the end; but the fools first.

CHAPTER XV

THE LAD WITH THE SILVER BUTTON:
THROUGH THE ISLE OF MULL

The Ross of Mull, which I had now got upon, was rugged and trackless, like the isle I had just left; being all bog, and brier, and big stone. There may be roads for them that know that country well; but for my part I had no better guide than my own nose, and no other landmark than Ben More.

I aimed as well as I could for the smoke I had seen so often from the island; and with all my great weariness and the difficulty of the way came upon the house in the bottom of a little hollow about five or six at night. It was low and longish, roofed with turf and built of unmortared stones; and on a mound in front of it, an old gentleman sat smoking his pipe in the sun.

With what little English he had, he gave me to understand that my shipmates had got safe ashore, and had broken bread in that very house on the day after.

"Was there one," I asked, "dressed like a gentleman?"

He said they all wore rough great-coats; but to be sure, the first of them, the one that came alone, wore breeches and stockings, while the rest had sailors' trousers.

"Ah," said I, "and he would have a feathered hat?"

He told me, no, that he was bareheaded like myself.

At first I thought Alan might have lost his hat; and then the rain came in my mind, and I judged it more likely he had it out of harm's way under his great-coat. This set me smiling, partly because my friend was safe, partly to think of his vanity in dress.

And then the old gentleman clapped his hand to his brow, and cried out that I must be the lad with the silver button.

"Why, yes!" said I, in some wonder.

"Well, then," said the old gentleman, "I have a word for you, that you are to follow your friend to his country, by Torosay."

He then asked me how I had fared, and I told him my tale. A south-country man would certainly have laughed; but this old gentleman (I call him so because of his manners, for his clothes were dropping off his back) heard me all through with nothing but gravity and pity. When I had done, he took me by the hand, led me into his hut (it was no better) and presented me before his wife, as if she had been the Queen and I a duke.

The good woman set oat-bread before me and a cold grouse, patting my shoulder and smiling to me all the time, for she had no English; and the old gentleman (not to be behind) brewed me a strong punch out of their country spirit. All the while I was eating, and after that when I was drinking the punch, I could scarce come to believe in my good fortune; and the house, though it was thick with the peat-smoke and as full of holes as a colander, seemed like a palace.

The punch threw me in a strong sweat and a deep slumber; the good people let me lie; and it was near noon of the next day before I took the road, my throat already easier and my spirits quite restored by good fare and good news. The old gentleman, although I pressed him hard, would take no money, and gave me an old bonnet for my head; though I am free to own I was no sooner out of view of the house than I very jealously washed this gift of his in a wayside fountain.

Thought I to myself: "If these are the wild Highlanders, I could wish my own folk wilder."

I not only started late, but I must have wandered nearly half the time. True, I met plenty of people, grubbing in little miserable fields that would not keep a cat, or herding little kine about the bigness of asses. The Highland dress being forbidden by law since the rebellion, and the people condemned to the Lowland habit, which they much disliked, it was strange to see the variety of their array. Some went bare, only for a hanging cloak or great-coat, and carried their trousers on their backs like a useless burthen: some had made an imitation of the tartan with little parti-coloured stripes patched together like an old wife's quilt; others, again, still wore the Highland philabeg, but by putting a few stitches between the legs transformed it into a pair of trousers like a Dutchman's. All those makeshifts were condemned and punished, for the law was harshly applied, in hopes to break up the clan spirit; but in that out-of-the-way, sea-bound isle, there were few to make remarks and fewer to tell tales.

They seemed in great poverty; which was no doubt natural, now that rapine was put down, and the chiefs kept no longer an open house; and the roads (even such a wandering, country by—track as the one I followed) were infested with beggars. And here again I marked a difference from my own part of the country. For our Lowland beggars—even the gownsmen themselves, who beg by patent—had a louting, flattering way with them, and if you gave them a plaek and asked change, would very civilly return you a boddle. But these Highland beggars stood on their dignity, asked alms only to buy snuff (by their account) and would give no change.

To be sure, this was no concern of mine, except in so far as it entertained me by the way. What was much more to the purpose, few had any English, and these few (unless they were of the brotherhood of beggars) not very anxious to place it at my service. I knew Torosay to be my destination, and repeated the name to them and pointed; but instead of simply pointing in reply, they would give me a screed of the Gaelic that set me foolish; so it was small wonder if I went out of my road as often as I stayed in it.

At last, about eight at night, and already very weary, I came to a lone house, where I asked admittance, and was refused, until I bethought me of the power of money in so poor a country, and held up one of my guineas in my finger and thumb. Thereupon, the man of the house, who had hitherto pretended to have no English, and driven me from his door by signals, suddenly began to speak as clearly as was needful, and agreed for five shillings to give me a night's lodging and guide me the next day to Torosay.

I slept uneasily that night, fearing I should be robbed; but I might have spared myself the pain; for my host was no robber, only miserably poor and a great cheat. He was not alone in his poverty; for the next morning, we must go five miles about to the house of what he called a rich man to have one of my guineas changed. This was perhaps a rich man for Mull; he would have scarce been thought so in the south; for it took all he had—the whole house was turned upside down, and a neighbour brought under contribution, before he could scrape together twenty shillings in silver. The odd shilling he kept for himself, protesting he could ill afford to have so great a sum of money lying "locked up." For all that he was very courteous and well spoken, made us both sit down with his family to dinner, and brewed punch in a fine china bowl, over which my rascal guide grew so merry that he refused to start.

I was for getting angry, and appealed to the rich man (Hector Maclean was his name), who had been a witness to our bargain and to my payment of the five shillings. But Maclean had taken his share of the punch, and vowed that no gentleman should leave his table after the bowl was brewed; so there was nothing for it but to sit and hear Jacobite toasts and Gaelic songs, till all were tipsy and staggered off to the bed or the barn for their night's rest.

Next day (the fourth of my travels) we were up before five

upon the clock; but my rascal guide got to the bottle at once, and it was three hours before I had him clear of the house, and then (as you shall hear) only for a worse disappointment.

As long as we went down a heathery valley that lay before Mr. Maclean's house, all went well; only my guide looked constantly over his shoulder, and when I asked him the cause, only grinned at me. No sooner, however, had we crossed the back of a hill, and got out of sight of the house windows, than he told me Torosay lay right in front, and that a hill-top (which he pointed out) was my best landmark.

"I care very little for that," said I, "since you are going with me."

The impudent cheat answered me in the Gaelic that he had no English.

"My fine fellow," I said, "I know very well your English comes and goes. Tell me what will bring it back? Is it more money you wish?"

"Five shillings mair," said he, "and hersel' will bring ye there."

I reflected awhile and then offered him two, which he accepted greedily, and insisted on having in his hands at once "for luck," as he said, but I think it was rather for my misfortune.

The two shillings carried him not quite as many miles; at the end of which distance, he sat down upon the wayside and took off his brogues from his feet, like a man about to rest.

I was now red-hot. "Ha!" said I, "have you no more English?"

He said impudently, "No."

At that I boiled over, and lifted my hand to strike him; and he, drawing a knife from his rags, squatted back and grinned at me like a wildcat. At that, forgetting everything but my anger, I ran in upon him, put aside his knife with my left, and struck him in the mouth with the right. I was a strong lad and very angry, and he but a little man; and he went down before me heavily. By good luck, his knife flew out of his hand as he fell.

I picked up both that and his brogues, wished him a good morning, and set off upon my way, leaving him barefoot and disarmed. I chuckled to myself as I went, being sure I was done with that rogue, for a variety of reasons. First, he knew he could have no more of my money; next, the brogues were worth in that country only a few pence; and, lastly, the knife, which was really a dagger, it was against the law for him to carry.

In about half an hour of walk, I overtook a great, ragged man, moving pretty fast but feeling before him with a staff. He was quite blind, and told me he was a catechist, which should have put me at my ease. But his face went against me; it seemed dark and dangerous and secret; and presently, as we began to go on alongside, I saw the steel butt of a pistol sticking from under the flap of his coat-pocket. To carry such a thing meant a fine of fifteen pounds sterling upon a first offence, and transportation to the colonies upon a second. Nor could I quite see why a religious teacher should go armed, or what a blind man could be doing with a pistol.

I told him about my guide, for I was proud of what I had done, and my vanity for once got the heels of my prudence. At the mention of the five shillings he cried out so loud that I made up my mind I should say nothing of the other two, and was glad he could not see my blushes.

"Was it too much?" I asked, a little faltering.

"Too much!" cries he. "Why, I will guide you to Torosay myself for a dram of brandy. And give you the great pleasure of my company (me that is a man of some learning) in the bargain."

I said I did not see how a blind man could be a guide; but at that he laughed aloud, and said his stick was eyes enough for an eagle.

"In the Isle of Mull, at least," says he, "where I know every stone and heather-bush by mark of head. See, now," he said, striking right and left, as if to make sure, "down there a burn is running; and at the head of it there stands a bit of a small hill with a stone cocked upon the top of that; and it's hard at the foot of the hill, that the way runs by to Torosay; and the way here, being for droves, is plainly trodden, and will show grassy through the heather."

I had to own he was right in every feature, and told my wonder.

"Ha!" says he, "that's nothing. Would ye believe me now, that before the Act came out, and when there were weepons in this country, I could shoot? Ay, could I!" cries he, and then with a leer: "If ye had such a thing as a pistol here to try with, I would show ye how it's done."

I told him I had nothing of the sort, and gave him a wider berth. If he had known, his pistol stuck at that time quite plainly out of his pocket, and I could see the sun twinkle on the steel of the butt. But by the better luck for me, he knew nothing, thought all was covered, and lied on in the dark.

He then began to question me cunningly, where I came from, whether I was rich, whether I could change a five-shilling piece for him (which he declared he had that moment in his sporran), and all the time he kept edging up to me and I avoiding him. We were now upon a sort of green cattle-track which crossed the hills towards Torosay, and we kept changing sides upon that like ancers in a reel. I had so plainly the upper-hand that my spirits rose, and indeed I took a pleasure in this game of blindman's buff; but the catechist grew angrier and angrier, and at last began to swear in Gaelic and to strike for my legs with his staff.

Then I told him that, sure enough, I had a pistol in my pocket as well as he, and if he did not strike across the hill due south I would even blow his brains out.

He became at once very polite, and after trying to soften me for some time, but quite in vain, he cursed me once more in Gaelic and took himself off. I watched him striding along, through bog and brier, tapping with his stick, until he turned the end of a hill and disappeared in the next hollow. Then I struck on again for Torosay, much better pleased to be alone than to travel with that man of learning. This was an unlucky day; and these two, of whom I had just rid myself, one after the other, were the two worst men I met with in the Highlands.

At Torosay, on the Sound of Mull and looking over to the mainland of Morven, there was an inn with an innkeeper, who was a Maclean, it appeared, of a very high family; for to keep an inn is thought even more genteel in the Highlands than it is with us, perhaps as partaking of hospitality, or perhaps because the trade is idle and drunken. He spoke good English, and finding me to be something of a scholar, tried me first in French, where he easily beat me, and then in the Latin, in which I don't know which of us did best. This pleasant rivalry put us at once upon friendly terms; and I sat up and drank punch with him (or to be more correct, sat up and watched him drink it), until he was so tipsy that he wept upon my shoulder.

I tried him, as if by accident, with a sight of Alan's button; but it was plain he had never seen or heard of it. Indeed, he bore some grudge against the family and friends of Ardshiel, and before he was drunk he read me a lampoon, in very good Latin, but with a very ill meaning, which he had made in elegiac verses upon a person of that house.

When I told him of my catechist, he shook his head, and said I was lucky to have got clear off. "That is a very dangerous man," he said; "Duncan Mackiegh is his name; he can shoot by the ear at several yards, and has been often accused of highway robberies, and once of murder."

"The cream of it is," says I, "that he called himself a catechist."

"And why should he not?" says he, "when that is what he is. It was Maclean of Duart gave it to him because he was blind.

But perhaps it was a peety," says my host, "for he is always on the road, going from one place to another to hear the young folk say their religion; and, doubtless, that is a great temptation to the poor man."

At last, when my landlord could drink no more, he showed me to a bed, and I lay down in very good spirits; having travelled the greater part of that big and crooked Island of Mull, from Earraid to Torosay, fifty miles as the crow flies, and (with my wanderings) much nearer a hundred, in four days and with little fatigue. Indeed I was by far in better heart and health of body at the end of that long tramp than I had been at the beginning.

CHAPTER XVI

THE LAD WITH THE SILVER BUTTON:
ACROSS MORVEN

There is a regular ferry from Torosay to Kinlochaline on the mainland. Both shores of the Sound are in the country of the strong clan of the Macleans, and the people that passed the ferry with me were almost all of that clan. The skipper of the boat, on the other hand, was called Neil Roy Macrob; and since Macrob was one of the names of Alan's clansmen, and Alan himself had sent me to that ferry, I was eager to come to private speech of Neil Roy.

In the crowded boat this was of course impossible, and the passage was a very slow affair. There was no wind, and as the boat was wretchedly equipped, we could pull but two oars on one side, and one on the other. The men gave way, however, with a good will, the passengers taking spells to help them, and the whole company giving the time in Gaelic boat-songs. And what with the songs, and the sea-air, and the good-nature and spirit of all concerned, and the bright weather, the passage was a pretty thing to have seen.

But there was one melancholy part. In the mouth of Loch Aline we found a great sea-going ship at anchor; and this I supposed at first to be one of the King's cruisers which were kept along that coast, both summer and winter, to prevent communication with the French. As we got a little nearer, it became plain she was a ship of merchandise; and what still more puzzled me, not only her decks, but the sea-beach also, were quite black with people, and skiffs were continually plying to and fro between them. Yet nearer, and there began to come to our ears a great sound of mourning, the people on board and those on the shore crying and lamenting one to another so as to pierce the heart.

Then I understood this was an emigrant ship bound for the American colonies.

We put the ferry-boat alongside, and the exiles leaned over the bulwarks, weeping and reaching out their hands to my fellow-passengers, among whom they counted some near friends. How long this might have gone on I do not know, for they seemed to have no sense of time: but at last the captain of the ship, who seemed near beside himself (and no great wonder) in the midst of this crying and confusion, came to the side and begged us to depart.

Thereupon Neil sheered off; and the chief singer in our boat struck into a melancholy air, which was presently taken up both by the emigrants and their friends upon the beach, so that it sounded from all sides like a lament for the dying. I saw the tears run down the cheeks of the men and women in the boat, even as they bent at the oars; and the circumstances and the music of the song (which is one called "Lochaber no more") were highly affecting even to myself.

At Kinlochaline I got Neil Roy upon one side on the beach, and said I made sure he was one of Appin's men.

"And what for no?" said he.

"I am seeking somebody," said I; "and it comes in my mind that you will have news of him. Alan Breck Stewart is his name." And very foolishly, instead of showing him the button, I sought to pass a shilling in his hand.

At this he drew back. "I am very much affronted," he said; "and this is not the way that one shentleman should behave to another at all. The man you ask for is in France; but if he was in my sporran," says he, "and your belly full of shillings, I would not hurt a hair upon his body."

I saw I had gone the wrong way to work, and without wasting time upon apologies, showed him the button lying in the hollow of my palm.

"Aweel, aweel," said Neil; "and I think ye might have begun with that end of the stick, whatever! But if ye are the lad with the silver button, all is well, and I have the word to see that ye come safe. But if ye will pardon me to speak plainly," says he, "there is a name that you should never take into your mouth, and that is the name of Alan Breck; and there is a thing that ye would never do, and that is to offer your dirty money to a Hieland shentleman."

It was not very easy to apologise; for I could scarce tell him (what was the truth) that I had never dreamed he would set up to be a gentleman until he told me so. Neil on his part had no wish to prolong his dealings with me, only to fulfil his orders and be done with it; and he made haste to give me my route. This was to lie the night in Kinlochaline in the public inn; to cross Morven the next day to Ardgour, and lie the night in the house of one John of the Claymore, who was warned that I might come; the third day, to be set across one loch at Corran and another at Balachulish, and then ask my way to the house of James of the Glens, at Aucharn in Duror of Appin. There was a good deal of ferrying, as you hear; the sea in all this part running deep into the mountains and winding about their roots. It makes the country strong to hold and difficult to travel, but full of prodigious wild and dreadful prospects.

I had some other advice from Neil: to speak with no one by the way, to avoid Whigs, Campbells, and the "red-soldiers;" to leave the road and lie in a bush if I saw any of the latter coming, "for it was never chancy to meet in with them;" and in brief, to conduct myself like a robber or a Jacobite agent, as perhaps Neil thought me.

The inn at Kinlochaline was the most beggarly vile place

that ever pigs were styed in, full of smoke, vermin, and silent Highlanders. I was not only discontented with my lodging, but with myself for my mismanagement of Neil, and thought I could hardly be worse off. But very wrongly, as I was soon to see; for I had not been half an hour at the inn (standing in the door most of the time, to ease my eyes from the peat smoke) when a thunderstorm came close by, the springs broke in a little hill on which the inn stood, and one end of the house became a running water. Places of public entertainment were bad enough all over Scotland in those days; yet it was a wonder to myself, when I had to go from the fireside to the bed in which I slept, wading over the shoes.

Early in my next day's journey I overtook a little, stout, solemn man, walking very slowly with his toes turned out, sometimes reading in a book and sometimes marking the place with his finger, and dressed decently and plainly in something of a clerical style.

This I found to be another catechist, but of a different order from the blind man of Mull: being indeed one of those sent out by the Edinburgh Society for Propagating Christian Knowledge, to evangelise the more savage places of the Highlands. His name was Henderland; he spoke with the broad south-country tongue, which I was beginning to weary for the sound of; and besides common countryship, we soon found we had a more particular bond of interest. For my good friend, the minister of Essendean, had translated into the Gaelic in his by-time a number of hymns and pious books which Henderland used in his work, and held in great esteem. Indeed, it was one of these he was carrying and reading when we met.

We fell in company at once, our ways lying together as far as to Kingairloch. As we went, he stopped and spoke with all the wayfarers and workers that we met or passed; and though of course I could not tell what they discoursed about, yet I judged Mr. Henderland must be well liked in the countryside, for I observed many of them to bring out their mulls and share a pinch of snuff with him.

I told him as far in my affairs as I judged wise; as far, that is, as they were none of Alan's; and gave Balachulish as the place I was travelling to, to meet a friend; for I thought Aucharn, or even Duror, would be too particular, and might put him on the scent.

On his part, he told me much of his work and the people he worked among, the hiding priests and Jacobites, the Disarming Act, the dress, and many other curiosities of the time and place. He seemed moderate; blaming Parliament in several points, and especially because they had framed the Act more severely against those who wore the dress than against those who carried weapons.

This moderation put it in my mind to question him of the Red Fox and the Appin tenants; questions which, I thought, would seem natural enough in the mouth of one travelling to that country.

He said it was a bad business. "It's wonderful," said he, "where the tenants find the money, for their life is mere starvation. (Ye don't carry such a thing as snuff, do ye, Mr. Balfour? No. Well, I'm better wanting it.) But these tenants (as I was saying) are doubtless partly driven to it. James Stewart in Duror (that's him they call James of the Glens) is half-brother to Ardshiel, the captain of the clan; and he is a man much looked up to, and drives very hard. And then there's one they call Alan Breck—"

"Ah!" I cried, "what of him?"

"What of the wind that bloweth where it listeth?" said Henderland. "He's here and awa; here to-day and gone to-morrow: a fair heather-cat. He might be glowering at the two of us out of yon whin-bush, and I wouldnae wonder! Ye'll no carry such a thing as snuff, will ye?"

I told him no, and that he had asked the same thing more

than once.

"It's highly possible," said he, sighing. "But it seems strange ye shouldnae carry it. However, as I was saying, this Alan Breck is a bold, desperate customer, and well kent to be James's right hand. His life is forfeit already; he would boggle at naething; and maybe, if a tenant-body was to hang back he would get a dirk in his wame."

"You make a poor story of it all, Mr. Henderland," said I. "If it is all fear upon both sides, I care to hear no more of it."

"Na," said Mr. Henderland, "but there's love too, and self-denial that should put the like of you and me to shame. There's something fine about it; no perhaps Christian, but humanly fine. Even Alan Breck, by all that I hear, is a child to be respected. There's many a lying sneck-draw sits close in kirk in our own part of the country, and stands well in the world's eye, and maybe is a far worse man, Mr. Balfour, than yon misguided shedder of man's blood. Ay, ay, we might take a lesson by them.—Ye'll perhaps think I've been too long in the Hielands?" he added, smiling to me.

I told him not at all; that I had seen much to admire among the Highlanders; and if he came to that, Mr. Campbell himself was a Highlander.

"Ay," said he, "that's true. It's a fine blood."

"And what is the King's agent about?" I asked.

"Colin Campbell?" says Henderland. "Putting his head in a bees' byke!"

"He is to turn the tenants out by force, I hear?" said I.

"Yes," says he, "but the business has gone back and forth, as folk say. First, James of the Glens rode to Edinburgh, and got some lawyer (a Stewart, nae doubt—they all hing together like bats in a steeple) and had the proceedings stayed. And then Colin Campbell cam' in again, and had the upper-hand before the Barons of Exchequer. And now they tell me the first of the tenants are to flit to-morrow. It's to begin at Duror under James's very windows, which doesnae seem wise by my humble way of it."

"Do you think they'll fight?" I asked.

"Well," says Henderland, "they're disarmed—or supposed to be—for there's still a good deal of cold iron lying by in quiet places. And then Colin Campbell has the sogers coming. But for all that, if I was his lady wife, I wouldnae be well pleased till I got him home again. They're queer customers, the Appin Stewarts."

I asked if they were worse than their neighbours.

"No they," said he. "And that's the worst part of it. For if Colin Roy can get his business done in Appin, he has it all to begin again in the next country, which they call Mamore, and which is one of the countries of the Camerons. He's King's Factor upon both, and from both he has to drive out the tenants; and indeed, Mr. Balfour (to be open with ye), it's my belief that if he escapes the one lot, he'll get his death by the other."

So we continued talking and walking the great part of the day; until at last, Mr. Henderland after expressing his delight in my company, and satisfaction at meeting with a friend of Mr. Campbell's ("whom," says he, "I will make bold to call that sweet singer of our covenanted Zion"), proposed that I should make a short stage, and lie the night in his house a little beyond Kingairloch. To say truth, I was overjoyed; for I had no great desire for John of the Claymore, and since my double misadventure, first with the guide and next with the gentleman skipper, I stood in some fear of any Highland stranger. Accordingly we shook hands upon the bargain, and came in the afternoon to a small house, standing alone by the shore of the Linnhe Loch. The sun was already gone from the desert mountains of Ardgour upon the hither side, but shone on those of Appin on the farther; the loch lay as still as a lake, only the gulls were crying round the sides of it; and the whole place seemed solemn and uncouth.

We had no sooner come to the door of Mr. Henderland's dwelling, than to my great surprise (for I was now used to the politeness of Highlanders) he burst rudely past me, dashed into the room, caught up a jar and a small horn-spoon, and began ladling snuff into his nose in most excessive quantities. Then he had a hearty fit of sneezing, and looked round upon me with a rather silly smile.

"It's a vow I took," says he. "I took a vow upon me that I wouldnae carry it. Doubtless it's a great privation; but when I think upon the martyrs, not only to the Scottish Covenant but to other points of Christianity, I think shame to mind it."

As soon as we had eaten (and porridge and whey was the best of the good man's diet) he took a grave face and said he had a duty to perform by Mr. Campbell, and that was to inquire into my state of mind towards God. I was inclined to smile at him since the business of the snuff; but he had not spoken long before he brought the tears into my eyes. There are two things that men should never weary of, goodness and humility; we get none too much of them in this rough world among cold, proud people; but Mr. Henderland had their very speech upon his tongue. And though I was a good deal puffed up with my adventures and with having come off, as the saying is, with flying colours; yet he soon had me on my knees beside a simple, poor old man, and both proud and glad to be there.

Before we went to bed he offered me sixpence to help me on my way, out of a scanty store he kept in the turf wall of his house; at which excess of goodness I knew not what to do. But at last he was so earnest with me that I thought it the more mannerly part to let him have his way, and so left him poorer than myself.

CHAPTER XVII

THE DEATH OF THE RED FOX

The next day Mr. Henderland found for me a man who had a boat of his own and was to cross the Linnhe Loch that afternoon into Appin, fishing. Him he prevailed on to take me, for he was one of his flock; and in this way I saved a long day's travel and the price of the two public ferries I must otherwise have passed.

It was near noon before we set out; a dark day with clouds, and the sun shining upon little patches. The sea was here very deep and still, and had scarce a wave upon it; so that I must put the water to my lips before I could believe it to be truly salt. The mountains on either side were high, rough and barren, very black and gloomy in the shadow of the clouds, but all silver-laced with little watercourses where the sun shone upon them. It seemed a hard country, this of Appin, for people to care as much about as Alan did.

There was but one thing to mention. A little after we had started, the sun shone upon a little moving clump of scarlet close in along the water-side to the north. It was much of the same red as soldiers' coats; every now and then, too, there came little sparks and lightnings, as though the sun had struck upon bright steel.

I asked my boatman what it should be, and he answered he supposed it was some of the red soldiers coming from Fort William into Appin, against the poor tenantry of the country. Well, it was a sad sight to me; and whether it was because of my thoughts of Alan, or from something prophetic in my bosom, although this was but the second time I had seen King George's troops, I had no good will to them.

At last we came so near the point of land at the entering in of Loch Leven that I begged to be set on shore. My boatman (who was an honest fellow and mindful of his promise to the catechist) would fain have carried me on to Balachulish; but as this was to take me farther from my secret destination, I insisted, and was set on shore at last under the wood of Lettermore (or Lettervore, for I have heard it both ways) in Alan's country of Appin.

This was a wood of birches, growing on a steep, craggy side of a mountain that overhung the loch. It had many openings and ferny howes; and a road or bridle track ran north and south through the midst of it, by the edge of which, where was a spring, I sat down to eat some oat-bread of Mr. Henderland's and think upon my situation.

Here I was not only troubled by a cloud of stinging midges, but far more by the doubts of my mind. What I ought to do, why I was going to join myself with an outlaw and a would-be murderer like Alan, whether I should not be acting more like a man of sense to tramp back to the south country direct, by my own guidance and at my own charges, and what Mr. Campbell or even Mr. Henderland would think of me if they should ever learn my folly and presumption: these were the doubts that now began to come in on me stronger than ever.

As I was so sitting and thinking, a sound of men and horses came to me through the wood; and presently after, at a turning of the road, I saw four travellers come into view. The way was in this part so rough and narrow that they came single and led their horses by the reins. The first was a great, red-headed gentleman, of an imperious and flushed face, who carried his hat in his hand and fanned himself, for he was in a breathing heat. The second, by his decent black garb and white wig, I correctly took to be a lawyer. The third was a servant, and wore some part of his clothes in tartan, which showed that his master was of a Highland family, and either an outlaw or else in singular good odour with the Government, since the wearing of tartan was against the Act. If I had been better versed in these things, I would have known the tartan to be of the Argyle (or Campbell) colours. This servant had a good-sized portmanteau strapped on his horse, and a net of lemons (to brew punch with) hanging at the saddle-bow; as was often enough the custom with luxurious travellers in that part of the country.

As for the fourth, who brought up the tail, I had seen his like before, and knew him at once to be a sheriff's officer.

I had no sooner seen these people coming than I made up my mind (for no reason that I can tell) to go through with my adventure; and when the first came alongside of me, I rose up from the bracken and asked him the way to Aucharn.

He stopped and looked at me, as I thought, a little oddly; and then, turning to the lawyer, "Mungo," said he, "there's many a man would think this more of a warning than two pyats. Here am I on my road to Duror on the job ye ken; and here is a young lad starts up out of the bracken, and speers if I am on the way to Aucharn."

"Glenure," said the other, "this is an ill subject for jesting."

These two had now drawn close up and were gazing at me, while the two followers had halted about a stone-cast in the rear.

"And what seek ye in Aucharn?" said Colin Roy Campbell of Glenure, him they called the Red Fox; for he it was that I had stopped.

"The man that lives there," said I.

"James of the Glens," says Glenure, musingly; and then to the lawyer: "Is he gathering his people, think ye?"

"Anyway," says the lawyer, "we shall do better to bide where we are, and let the soldiers rally us."

"If you are concerned for me," said I, "I am neither of his people nor yours, but an honest subject of King George, owing no man and fearing no man."

"Why, very well said," replies the Factor. "But if I may make so bold as ask, what does this honest man so far from his country? and why does he come seeking the brother of Ardshiel? I have power here, I must tell you. I am King's Factor upon several of these estates, and have twelve files of soldiers at my back."

"I have heard a waif word in the country," said I, a little nettled, "that you were a hard man to drive."

He still kept looking at me, as if in doubt.

"Well," said he, at last, "your tongue is bold; but I am no unfriend to plainness. If ye had asked me the way to the door of James Stewart on any other day but this, I would have set ye right and bidden ye God speed. But to-day—eh, Mungo?" And he turned again to look at the lawyer.

But just as he turned there came the shot of a firelock from higher up the hill; and with the very sound of it Glenure fell upon the road.

"O, I am dead!" he cried, several times over.

The lawyer had caught him up and held him in his arms, the servant standing over and clasping his hands. And now the wounded man looked from one to another with scared eyes, and there was a change in his voice, that went to the heart.

"Take care of yourselves," says he. "I am dead."

He tried to open his clothes as if to look for the wound, but his fingers slipped on the buttons. With that he gave a great sigh, his head rolled on his shoulder, and he passed away.

The lawyer said never a word, but his face was as sharp as a pen and as white as the dead man's; the servant broke out into a great noise of crying and weeping, like a child; and I, on my side, stood staring at them in a kind of horror. The sheriff's officer had run back at the first sound of the shot, to hasten the coming of the soldiers.

At last the lawyer laid down the dead man in his blood upon the road, and got to his own feet with a kind of stagger.

I believe it was his movement that brought me to my senses; for he had no sooner done so than I began to scramble up the hill, crying out, "The murderer! the murderer!"

So little a time had elapsed, that when I got to the top of the first steepness, and could see some part of the open mountain, the murderer was still moving away at no great distance. He was a big man, in a black coat, with metal buttons, and carried a long fowling-piece.

"Here!" I cried. "I see him!"

At that the murderer gave a little, quick look over his shoulder, and began to run. The next moment he was lost in a fringe of birches; then he came out again on the upper side, where I could see him climbing like a jackanapes, for that part was again very steep; and then he dipped behind a shoulder, and I saw him no more.

All this time I had been running on my side, and had got a good way up, when a voice cried upon me to stand.

I was at the edge of the upper wood, and so now, when I halted and looked back, I saw all the open part of the hill below me.

The lawyer and the sheriff's officer were standing just above the road, crying and waving on me to come back; and on their left, the red-coats, musket in hand, were beginning to struggle singly out of the lower wood.

"Why should I come back?" I cried. "Come you on!"

"Ten pounds if ye take that lad!" cried the lawyer. "He's an accomplice. He was posted here to hold us in talk."

At that word (which I could hear quite plainly, though it was to the soldiers and not to me that he was crying it) my heart came in my mouth with quite a new kind of terror. Indeed, it is one thing to stand the danger of your life, and quite another to run the peril of both life and character. The thing, besides, had come so suddenly, like thunder out of a clear sky, that I was all amazed and helpless.

The soldiers began to spread, some of them to run, and others to put up their pieces and cover me; and still I stood.

"Jock in here among the trees," said a voice close by.

Indeed, I scarce knew what I was doing, but I obeyed; and as I did so, I heard the firelocks bang and the balls whistle in the birches.

Just inside the shelter of the trees I found Alan Breck standing, with a fishing-rod. He gave me no salutation; indeed it was no time for civilities; only "Come!" says he, and set off running along the side of the mountain towards Balaehulish; and I, like a sheep, to follow him.

Now we ran among the birches; now stooping behind low humps upon the mountain-side; now crawling on all fours among the heather. The pace was deadly: my heart seemed bursting against my ribs; and I had neither time to think nor breath to speak with. Only I remember seeing with wonder, that Alan every now and then would straighten himself to his full height and look back; and every time he did so, there came a great far-away cheering and crying of the soldiers.

Quarter of an hour later, Alan stopped, clapped down flat in the heather, and turned to me.

"Now," said he, "it's earnest. Do as I do, for your life."

And at the same speed, but now with infinitely more precaution, we traced back again across the mountain-side by the same way that we had come, only perhaps higher; till at last Alan threw himself down in the upper wood of Lettermore, where I had found him at the first, and lay, with his face in the bracken, panting like a dog.

My own sides so ached, my head so swam, my tongue so hung out of my mouth with heat and dryness, that I lay beside him like one dead.

CHAPTER XVIII

I TALK WITH ALAN
IN THE WOOD OF LETTERMORE

Alan was the first to come round. He rose, went to the border of the wood, peered out a little, and then returned and sat down.

"Well," said he, "yon was a hot burst, David."

I said nothing, nor so much as lifted my face. I had seen murder done, and a great, ruddy, jovial gentleman struck out of life in a moment; the pity of that sight was still sore within me, and yet that was but a part of my concern. Here was murder done upon the man Alan hated; here was Alan skulking in the trees and running from the troops; and whether his was the hand that fired or only the head that ordered, signified but little. By my way of it, my only friend in that wild country was blood-guilty in the first degree; I held him in horror; I could not look upon his face; I would have rather lain alone in the rain on my cold isle, than in that warm wood beside a murderer.

"Are ye still wearied?" he asked again.

"No," said I, still with my face in the bracken; "no, I am not wearied now, and I can speak. You and me must twine," I said. "I liked you very well, Alan, but your ways are not mine, and they're not God's: and the short and the long of it is just that we must twine."

"I will hardly twine from ye, David, without some kind of reason for the same," said Alan, mighty gravely. "If ye ken anything against my reputation, it's the least thing that ye should do, for old acquaintance' sake, to let me hear the name of it; and if ye have only taken a distaste to my society, it will be proper for me to judge if I'm insulted."

"Alan," said I, "what is the sense of this? Ye ken very well yon Campbell-man lies in his blood upon the road."

He was silent for a little; then says he, "Did ever ye hear tell of the story of the Man and the Good People?"—by which he meant the fairies.

"No," said I, "nor do I want to hear it."

"With your permission, Mr. Balfour, I will tell it you, whatever," says Alan. "The man, ye should ken, was cast upon a rock in the sea, where it appears the Good People were in use to come and rest as they went through to Ireland. The name of this rock is called the Skerryvore, and it's not far from where we suffered ship-wreck. Well, it seems the man cried so sore, if he could just see his little bairn before he died! that at last the king of the Good People took peety upon him, and sent one flying that brought back the bairn in a poke and laid it down beside the man where he lay sleeping. So when the man woke, there was a poke beside him and something into the inside of it that moved. Well, it seems he was one of these gentry that think aye the worst of things; and for greater security, he stuck his dirk throughout that poke before he opened it, and there was his bairn dead. I am thinking to myself, Mr. Balfour, that you and the man are very much alike."

"Do you mean you had no hand in it?" cried I, sitting up.

"I will tell you first of all, Mr. Balfour of Shaws, as one friend to another," said Alan, "that if I were going to kill a gentleman, it would not be in my own country, to bring trouble on my clan; and I would not go wanting sword and gun, and with a long fishing-rod upon my back."

"Well," said I, "that's true!"

"And now," continued Alan, taking out his dirk and laying

his hand upon it in a certain manner, "I swear upon the Holy Iron I had neither art nor part, act nor thought in it."

"I thank God for that!" cried I, and offered him my hand.

He did not appear to see it.

"And here is a great deal of work about a Campbell!" said he. "They are not so scarce, that I ken!"

"At least," said I, "you cannot justly blame me, for you know very well what you told me in the brig. But the temptation and the act are different, I thank God again for that. We may all be tempted; but to take a life in cold blood, Alan!" And I could say no more for the moment. "And do you know who did it?" I added. "Do you know that man in the black coat?"

"I have nae clear mind about his coat," said Alan cunningly, "but it sticks in my head that it was blue."

"Blue or black, did ye know him?" said I.

"I couldnae just conscientiously swear to him," says Alan. "He gaed very close by me, to be sure, but it's a strange thing that I should just have been tying my brogues."

"Can you swear that you don't know him, Alan?" I cried, half angered, half in a mind to laugh at his evasions.

"Not yet," says he; "but I've a grand memory for forgetting, David."

"And yet there was one thing I saw clearly," said I; "and that was, that you exposed yourself and me to draw the soldiers."

"It's very likely," said Alan; "and so would any gentleman. You and me were innocent of that transaction."

"The better reason, since we were falsely suspected, that we should get clear," I cried. "The innocent should surely come before the guilty."

"Why, David," said he, "the innocent have aye a chance to get assoiled in court; but for the lad that shot the bullet, I think the best place for him will be the heather. Them that havenae dipped their hands in any little difficulty, should be very mindful of the case of them that have. And that is the good Christianity. For if it was the other way round about, and the lad whom I couldnae just clearly see had been in our shoes, and we in his (as might very well have been), I think we would be a good deal obliged to him oursel's if he would draw the soldiers."

When it came to this, I gave Alan up. But he looked so innocent all the time, and was in such clear good faith in what he said, and so ready to sacrifice himself for what he deemed his duty, that my mouth was closed. Mr. Henderland's words came back to me: that we ourselves might take a lesson by these wild Highlanders. Well, here I had taken mine. Alan's morals were all tail-first; but he was ready to give his life for them, such as they were.

"Alan," said I, "I'll not say it's the good Christianity as I understand it, but it's good enough. And here I offer ye my hand for the second time."

Whereupon he gave me both of his, saying surely I had cast a spell upon him, for he could forgive me anything. Then he grew very grave, and said we had not much time to throw away, but must both flee that country: he, because he was a deserter, and the whole of Appin would now be searched like a chamber, and every one obliged to give a good account of himself; and I, because I was certainly involved in the murder.

"O!" says I, willing to give him a little lesson, "I have no fear of the justice of my country."

"As if this was your country!" said he. "Or as if ye would be tried here, in a country of Stewarts!"

"It's all Scotland," said I.

"Man, I whiles wonder at ye," said Alan. "This is a Campbell that's been killed. Well, it'll be tried in Inverara, the Campbells' head place; with fifteen Campbells in the jury-box and the biggest Campbell of all (and that's the Duke) sitting cocking on the bench. Justice, David? The same justice, by all the world, as Glenure found awhile ago at the roadside."

This frightened me a little, I confess, and would have frightened me more if I had known how nearly exact were Alan's predictions; indeed it was but in one point that he exaggerated, there being but eleven Campbells on the jury; though as the other four were equally in the Duke's dependence, it mattered less than might appear. Still, I cried out that he was unjust to the Duke of Argyle, who (for all he was a Whig) was yet a wise and honest nobleman.

"Hoot!" said Alan, "the man's a Whig, nae doubt; but I would never deny he was a good chieftain to his clan. And what would the clan think if there was a Campbell shot, and naebody hanged, and their own chief the Justice General? But I have often observed," says Alan, "that you Low-country bodies have no clear idea of what's right and wrong."

At this I did at last laugh out aloud, when to my surprise, Alan joined in, and laughed as merrily as myself.

"Na, na," said he, "we're in the Hielands, David; and when I tell ye to run, take my word and run. Nae doubt it's a hard thing to skulk and starve in the Heather, but it's harder yet to lie shackled in a red-coat prison."

I asked him whither we should flee; and as he told me "to the Lowlands," I was a little better inclined to go with him; for, indeed, I was growing impatient to get back and have the upper-hand of my uncle. Besides, Alan made so sure there would be no question of justice in the matter, that I began to be afraid he might be right. Of all deaths, I would truly like least to die by the gallows; and the picture of that uncanny instrument came into my head with extraordinary clearness (as I had once seen it engraved at the top of a pedlar's ballad) and took away my appetite for courts of justice.

"I'll chance it, Alan," said I. "I'll go with you."

"But mind you," said Alan, "it's no small thing. Ye maun lie bare and hard, and brook many an empty belly. Your bed shall be the moorcock's, and your life shall be like the hunted deer's, and ye shall sleep with your hand upon your weapons. Ay, man, ye shall taigle many a weary foot, or we get clear! I tell ye this at the start, for it's a life that I ken well. But if ye ask what other chance ye have, I answer: Nane. Either take to the heather with me, or else hang."

"And that's a choice very easily made," said I; and we shook hands upon it.

"And now let's take another keek at the red-coats," says Alan, and he led me to the north-eastern fringe of the wood.

Looking out between the trees, we could see a great side of mountain, running down exceeding steep into the waters of the loch. It was a rough part, all hanging stone, and heather, and big scrogs of birchwood; and away at the far end towards Balachulish, little wee red soldiers were dipping up and down over hill and howe, and growing smaller every minute. There was no cheering now, for I think they had other uses for what breath was left them; but they still stuck to the trail, and doubtless thought that we were close in front of them.

Alan watched them, smiling to himself.

"Ay," said he, "they'll be gey weary before they've got to the end of that employ! And so you and me, David, can sit down and eat a bite, and breathe a bit longer, and take a dram from my bottle. Then we'll strike for Aucharn, the house of my kinsman, James of the Glens, where I must get my clothes, and my arms, and money to carry us along; and then, David, we'll cry, 'Forth, Fortune!' and take a cast among the heather."

So we sat again and ate and drank, in a place whence we could see the sun going down into a field of great, wild, and houseless mountains, such as I was now condemned to wander in with my companion. Partly as we so sat, and partly afterwards, on the way to Aucharn, each of us narrated his adventures; and I shall here set down so much of Alan's as seems either curious or needful.

It appears he ran to the bulwarks as soon as the wave was

passed; saw me, and lost me, and saw me again, as I tumbled in the roost; and at last had one glimpse of me clinging on the yard. It was this that put him in some hope I would maybe get to land after all, and made him leave those clues and messages which had brought me (for my sins) to that unlucky country of Appin.

In the meanwhile, those still on the brig had got the skiff launched, and one or two were on board of her already, when there came a second wave greater than the first, and heaved the brig out of her place, and would certainly have sent her to the bottom, had she not struck and caught on some projection of the reef. When she had struck first, it had been bows-on, so that the stern had hitherto been lowest. But now her stern was thrown in the air, and the bows plunged under the sea; and with that, the water began to pour into the fore-scuttle like the pouring of a mill-dam.

It took the colour out of Alan's face, even to tell what followed. For there were still two men lying impotent in their bunks; and these, seeing the water pour in and thinking the ship had foundered, began to cry out aloud, and that with such harrowing cries that all who were on deck tumbled one after another into the skiff and fell to their oars. They were not two hundred yards away, when there came a third great sea; and at that the brig lifted clean over the reef; her canvas filled for a moment, and she seemed to sail in chase of them, but settling all the while; and presently she drew down and down, as if a hand was drawing her; and the sea closed over the Covenant of Dysart.

Never a word they spoke as they pulled ashore, being stunned with the horror of that screaming; but they had scarce set foot upon the beach when Hoseason woke up, as if out of a muse, and bade them lay hands upon Alan. They hung back indeed, having little taste for the employment; but Hoseason was like a fiend, crying that Alan was alone, that he had a great sum about him, that he had been the means of losing the brig and drowning all their comrades, and that here was both revenge and wealth upon a single cast. It was seven against one; in that part of the shore there was no rock that Alan could set his back to; and the sailors began to spread out and come behind him.

"And then," said Alan, "the little man with the red head—I havenae mind of the name that he is called."

"Riach," said I.

"Ay" said Alan, "Riach! Well, it was him that took up the clubs for me, asked the men if they werenae feared of a judgment, and, says he 'Dod, I'll put my back to the Hielandman's mysel'.' That's none such an entirely bad little man, yon little man with the red head," said Alan. "He has some spunks of decency."

"Well," said I, "he was kind to me in his way."

"And so he was to Alan," said he; "and by my troth, I found his way a very good one! But ye see, David, the loss of the ship and the cries of these poor lads sat very ill upon the man; and I'm thinking that would be the cause of it."

"Well, I would think so," says I; "for he was as keen as any of the rest at the beginning. But how did Hoseason take it?"

"It sticks in my mind that he would take it very ill," says Alan. "But the little man cried to me to run, and indeed I thought it was a good observe, and ran. The last that I saw they were all in a knot upon the beach, like folk that were not agreeing very well together."

"What do you mean by that?" said I.

"Well, the fists were going," said Alan; "and I saw one man go down like a pair of breeks. But I thought it would be better no to wait. Ye see there's a strip of Campbells in that end of Mull, which is no good company for a gentleman like me. If it hadnae been for that I would have waited and looked for ye mysel', let alone giving a hand to the little man." (It was droll how Alan dwelt on Mr. Riach's stature, for, to say the truth, the one was not much smaller than the other.) "So," says he, continuing, "I set my best foot forward, and whenever I met in with any one I cried out there was a wreck ashore. Man, they didnae stop to fash with me! Ye should have seen them linking for the beach! And when they got there they found they had had the pleasure of a run, which is aye good for a Campbell. I'm thinking it was a judgment on the clan that the brig went down in the lump and didnae break. But it was a very unlucky thing for you, that same; for if any wreck had come ashore they would have hunted high and low, and would soon have found ye."

CHAPTER XIX

THE HOUSE OF FEAR

Night fell as we were walking, and the clouds, which had broken up in the afternoon, settled in and thickened, so that it fell, for the season of the year, extremely dark. The way we went was over rough mountainsides; and though Alan pushed on with an assured manner, I could by no means see how he directed himself.

At last, about half-past ten of the clock, we came to the top of a brae, and saw lights below us. It seemed a house door stood open and let out a beam of fire and candle-light; and all round the house and steading five or six persons were moving hurriedly about, each carrying a lighted brand.

"James must have tint his wits," said Alan. "If this was the soldiers instead of you and me, he would be in a bonny mess. But I dare say he'll have a sentry on the road, and he would ken well enough no soldiers would find the way that we came."

Hereupon he whistled three times, in a particular manner. It was strange to see how, at the first sound of it, all the moving torches came to a stand, as if the bearers were affrighted; and how, at the third, the bustle began again as before.

Having thus set folks' minds at rest, we came down the brae, and were met at the yard gate (for this place was like a well-doing farm) by a tall, handsome man of more than fifty, who cried out to Alan in the Gaelic.

"James Stewart," said Alan, "I will ask ye to speak in Scotch, for here is a young gentleman with me that has nane of the other. This is him," he added, putting his arm through mine, "a young gentleman of the Lowlands, and a laird in his country too, but I am thinking it will be the better for his health if we give his name the go-by."

James of the Glens turned to me for a moment, and greeted me courteously enough; the next he had turned to Alan.

"This has been a dreadful accident," he cried. "It will bring trouble on the country." And he wrung his hands.

"Hoots!" said Alan, "ye must take the sour with the sweet, man. Colin Roy is dead, and be thankful for that!"

"Ay" said James, "and by my troth, I wish he was alive again! It's all very fine to blow and boast beforehand; but now it's done, Alan; and who's to bear the wyte of it? The accident fell out in Appin—mind ye that, Alan; it's Appin that must pay; and I am a man that has a family."

While this was going on I looked about me at the servants. Some were on ladders, digging in the thatch of the house or the farm buildings, from which they brought out guns, swords, and different weapons of war; others carried them away; and by the sound of mattock blows from somewhere farther down the brae, I suppose they buried them. Though they were all so busy, there prevailed no kind of order in their efforts; men struggled together for the same gun and ran into each other with their burning torches; and James was continually turning about from his talk with Alan, to cry out orders which were apparently never understood. The faces in the torchlight were like those of people overborne with hurry and panic; and though none spoke above his breath, their speech sounded both anxious and angry.

It was about this time that a lassie came out of the house carrying a pack or bundle; and it has often made me smile to think how Alan's instinct awoke at the mere sight of it.

"What's that the lassie has?" he asked.

"We're just setting the house in order, Alan," said James,

in his frightened and somewhat fawning way. "They'll search Appin with candles, and we must have all things straight. We're digging the bit guns and swords into the moss, ye see; and these, I am thinking, will be your ain French clothes. We'll be to bury them, I believe."

"Bury my French clothes!" cried Alan. "Troth, no!" And he laid hold upon the packet and retired into the barn to shift himself, recommending me in the meanwhile to his kinsman.

James carried me accordingly into the kitchen, and sat down with me at table, smiling and talking at first in a very hospitable manner. But presently the gloom returned upon him; he sat frowning and biting his fingers; only remembered me from time to time; and then gave me but a word or two and a poor smile, and back into his private terrors. His wife sat by the fire and wept, with her face in her hands; his eldest son was crouched upon the floor, running over a great mass of papers and now and again setting one alight and burning it to the bitter end; all the while a servant lass with a red face was rummaging about the room, in a blind hurry of fear, and whimpering as she went; and every now and again one of the men would thrust in his face from the yard, and cry for orders.

At last James could keep his seat no longer, and begged my permission to be so unmannerly as walk about. "I am but poor company altogether, sir," says he, "but I can think of nothing but this dreadful accident, and the trouble it is like to bring upon quite innocent persons."

A little after he observed his son burning a paper which he thought should have been kept; and at that his excitement burst out so that it was painful to witness. He struck the lad repeatedly.

"Are you gone gyte?" he cried. "Do you wish to hang your father?" and forgetful of my presence, carried on at him a long time together in the Gaelic, the young man answering nothing; only the wife, at the name of hanging, throwing her apron over her face and sobbing out louder than before.

This was all wretched for a stranger like myself to hear and
see; and I was right glad when Alan returned, looking like
himself in his fine French clothes, though (to be sure) they
were now grown almost too battered and withered to deserve
the name of fine. I was then taken out in my turn by another
of the sons, and given that change of clothing of which I had
stood so long in need, and a pair of Highland brogues made
of deer-leather, rather strange at first, but after a little practice
very easy to the feet.

By the time I came back Alan must have told his story; for
it seemed understood that I was to fly with him, and they were
all busy upon our equipment. They gave us each a sword and
pistols, though I professed my inability to use the former; and
with these, and some ammunition, a bag of oatmeal, an iron
pan, and a bottle of right French brandy, we were ready for the
heather. Money, indeed, was lacking. I had about two guineas
left; Alan's belt having been despatched by another hand, that
trusty messenger had no more than seventeen-pence to his
whole fortune; and as for James, it appears he had brought
himself so low with journeys to Edinburgh and legal expenses
on behalf of the tenants, that he could only scrape together
three-and-five-pence-halfpenny, the most of it in coppers.

"This'll no do," said Alan.

"Ye must find a safe bit somewhere near by," said James,
"and get word sent to me. Ye see, ye'll have to get this business
prettily off, Alan. This is no time to be stayed for a guinea or
two. They're sure to get wind of ye, sure to seek ye, and by my
way of it, sure to lay on ye the wyte of this day's accident. If
it falls on you, it falls on me that am your near kinsman and
harboured ye while ye were in the country. And if it comes
on me—" he paused, and bit his fingers, with a white face. "It
would be a painful thing for our friends if I was to hang," said
he.

"It would be an ill day for Appin," says Alan.

"It's a day that sticks in my throat," said James. "O man, man, man—man Alan! you and me have spoken like two fools!" he cried, striking his hand upon the wall so that the house rang again.

"Well, and that's true, too," said Alan; "and my friend from the Lowlands here" (nodding at me) "gave me a good word upon that head, if I would only have listened to him."

"But see here," said James, returning to his former manner, "if they lay me by the heels, Alan, it's then that you'll be needing the money. For with all that I have said and that you have said, it will look very black against the two of us; do ye mark that? Well, follow me out, and ye'll, I'll see that I'll have to get a paper out against ye mysel'; have to offer a reward for ye; ay, will I! It's a sore thing to do between such near friends; but if I get the dirdum of this dreadful accident, I'll have to fend for myself, man. Do ye see that?"

He spoke with a pleading earnestness, taking Alan by the breast of the coat.

"Ay" said Alan, "I see that."

"And ye'll have to be clear of the country, Alan—ay, and clear of Scotland—you and your friend from the Lowlands, too. For I'll have to paper your friend from the Lowlands. Ye see that, Alan—say that ye see that!"

I thought Alan flushed a bit. "This is unco hard on me that brought him here, James," said he, throwing his head back. "It's like making me a traitor!"

"Now, Alan, man!" cried James. "Look things in the face! He'll be papered anyway; Mungo Campbell'll be sure to paper him; what matters if I paper him too? And then, Alan, I am a man that has a family." And then, after a little pause on both sides, "And, Alan, it'll be a jury of Campbells," said he.

"There's one thing," said Alan, musingly, "that naebody kens his name."

"Nor yet they shallnae, Alan! There's my hand on that," cried James, for all the world as if he had really known my name and was foregoing some advantage. "But just the habit he was in, and what he looked like, and his age, and the like? I couldnae well do less."

"I wonder at your father's son," cried Alan, sternly. "Would ye sell the lad with a gift? Would ye change his clothes and then betray him?"

"No, no, Alan," said James. "No, no: the habit he took off—the habit Mungo saw him in." But I thought he seemed crestfallen; indeed, he was clutching at every straw, and all the time, I dare say, saw the faces of his hereditary foes on the bench, and in the jury-box, and the gallows in the background.

"Well, sir" says Alan, turning to me, "what say ye to, that? Ye are here under the safeguard of my honour; and it's my part to see nothing done but what shall please you."

"I have but one word to say," said I; "for to all this dispute I am a perfect stranger. But the plain common-sense is to set the blame where it belongs, and that is on the man who fired the shot. Paper him, as ye call it, set the hunt on him; and let honest, innocent folk show their faces in safety." But at this both Alan and James cried out in horror; bidding me hold my tongue, for that was not to be thought of; and asking me what the Camerons would think? (which confirmed me, it must have been a Cameron from Mamore that did the act) and if I did not see that the lad might be caught? "Ye havenae surely thought of that?" said they, with such innocent earnestness, that my hands dropped at my side and I despaired of argument.

"Very well, then," said I, "paper me, if you please, paper Alan, paper King George! We're all three innocent, and that seems to be what's wanted. But at least, sir," said I to James, recovering from my little fit of annoyance, "I am Alan's friend, and if I can be helpful to friends of his, I will not stumble at the risk."

I thought it best to put a fair face on my consent, for I saw Alan troubled; and, besides (thinks I to myself), as soon as my back is turned, they will paper me, as they call it, whether I consent or not. But in this I saw I was wrong; for I had no sooner said the words, than Mrs. Stewart leaped out of her chair, came running over to us, and wept first upon my neck and then on Alan's, blessing God for our goodness to her family.

"As for you, Alan, it was no more than your bounden duty," she said. "But for this lad that has come here and seen us at our worst, and seen the goodman fleeching like a suitor, him that by rights should give his commands like any king—as for you, my lad," she says, "my heart is wae not to have your name, but I have your face; and as long as my heart beats under my bosom, I will keep it, and think of it, and bless it." And with that she kissed me, and burst once more into such sobbing, that I stood abashed.

"Hoot, hoot," said Alan, looking mighty silly. "The day comes unco soon in this month of July; and to-morrow there'll be a fine to-do in Appin, a fine riding of dragoons, and crying of 'Cruachan!' and running of red-coats; and it behoves you and me to the sooner be gone."

Thereupon we said farewell, and set out again, bending somewhat eastwards, in a fine mild dark night, and over much the same broken country as before.

CHAPTER XX

THE FLIGHT IN THE HEATHER:
THE ROCKS

Sometimes we walked, sometimes ran; and as it drew on to morning, walked ever the less and ran the more. Though, upon its face, that country appeared to be a desert, yet there were huts and houses of the people, of which we must have passed more than twenty, hidden in quiet places of the hills. When we came to one of these, Alan would leave me in the way, and go himself and rap upon the side of the house and speak awhile at the window with some sleeper awakened. This was to pass the news; which, in that country, was so much of a duty that Alan must pause to attend to it even while fleeing for his life; and so well attended to by others, that in more than half of the houses where we called they had heard already of the murder. In the others, as well as I could make out (standing back at a distance and hearing a strange tongue), the news was received with more of consternation than surprise.

For all our hurry, day began to come in while we were still far from any shelter. It found us in a prodigious valley, strewn with rocks and where ran a foaming river. Wild mountains stood around it; there grew there neither grass nor trees; and I have sometimes thought since then, that it may have been the valley called Glencoe, where the massacre was in the time of King William. But for the details of our itinerary, I am all to seek; our way lying now by short cuts, now by great detours; our pace being so hurried, our time of journeying usually by night; and the names of such places as I asked and heard being in the Gaelic tongue and the more easily forgotten.

The first peep of morning, then, showed us this horrible place, and I could see Alan knit his brow.

"This is no fit place for you and me," he said. "This is a place they're bound to watch."

And with that he ran harder than ever down to the water-side, in a part where the river was split in two among three rocks. It went through with a horrid thundering that made my belly quake; and there hung over the lynn a little mist of spray. Alan looked neither to the right nor to the left, but jumped clean upon the middle rock and fell there on his hands and knees to check himself, for that rock was small and he might have pitched over on the far side. I had scarce time to measure the distance or to understand the peril before I had followed him, and he had caught and stopped me.

So there we stood, side by side upon a small rock slippery with spray, a far broader leap in front of us, and the river dinning upon all sides. When I saw where I was, there came on me a deadly sickness of fear, and I put my hand over my eyes. Alan took me and shook me; I saw he was speaking, but the roaring of the falls and the trouble of my mind prevented me from hearing; only I saw his face was red with anger, and that he stamped upon the rock. The same look showed me the water raging by, and the mist hanging in the air: and with that I covered my eyes again and shuddered.

The next minute Alan had set the brandy bottle to my lips, and forced me to drink about a gill, which sent the blood into my head again. Then, putting his hands to his mouth, and his mouth to my ear, he shouted, "Hang or drown!" and turning his back upon me, leaped over the farther branch of the stream, and landed safe. I was now alone upon the rock, which gave me the more room; the brandy was singing in my ears; I had this good example fresh before me, and just wit enough to see that if I did not leap at once, I should never leap at all. I bent low on my knees and flung myself forth, with that kind of anger of despair that has sometimes stood me in stead of courage. Sure enough, it was but my hands that reached the full length; these slipped, caught again, slipped again; and I was sliddering back into the lynn, when Alan seized me, first by the hair, then by the collar, and with a great strain dragged me into safety.

Never a word he said, but set off running again for his life, and I must stagger to my feet and run after him. I had been weary before, but now I was sick and bruised, and partly drunken with the brandy; I kept stumbling as I ran, I had a stitch that came near to overmaster me; and when at last Alan paused under a great rock that stood there among a number of others, it was none too soon for David Balfour.

A great rock I have said; but by rights it was two rocks leaning together at the top, both some twenty feet high, and at the first sight inaccessible. Even Alan (though you may say he had as good as four hands) failed twice in an attempt to climb them; and it was only at the third trial, and then by standing on my shoulders and leaping up with such force as I thought must have broken my collar-bone, that he secured a lodgment. Once there, he let down his leathern girdle; and with the aid of that and a pair of shallow footholds in the rock, I scrambled up beside him.

Then I saw why we had come there; for the two rocks, being both somewhat hollow on the top and sloping one to the other, made a kind of dish or saucer, where as many as three or four men might have lain hidden.

All this while Alan had not said a word, and had run and climbed with such a savage, silent frenzy of hurry, that I knew that he was in mortal fear of some miscarriage. Even now we were on the rock he said nothing, nor so much as relaxed the frowning look upon his face; but clapped flat down, and keeping only one eye above the edge of our place of shelter scouted all round the compass. The dawn had come quite, clear; we could see the stony sides of the valley, and its bottom, which was bestrewed with rocks, and the river, which went from one side to another, and made white falls; but nowhere the smoke of a house, nor any living creature but some eagles screaming round a cliff.

Then at last Alan smiled.

"Ay" said he, "now we have a chance;" and then looking at me with some amusement. "Ye're no very gleg at the jumping," said he.

At this I suppose I coloured with mortification, for he added at once, "Hoots! small blame to ye! To be feared of a thing and yet to do it, is what makes the prettiest kind of a man. And then there was water there, and water's a thing that dauntons even me. No, no," said Alan, "it's no you that's to blame, it's me."

I asked him why.

"Why," said he, "I have proved myself a gomeral this night. For first of all I take a wrong road, and that in my own country of Appin; so that the day has caught us where we should never have been; and thanks to that, we lie here in some danger and mair discomfort. And next (which is the worst of the two, for a man that has been so much among the heather as myself) I have come wanting a water-bottle, and here we lie for a long summer's day with naething but neat spirit. Ye may think that a small matter; but before it comes night, David, ye'll give me news of it."

I was anxious to redeem my character, and offered, if he would pour out the brandy, to run down and fill the bottle at the river.

"I wouldnae waste the good spirit either," says he. "It's been a good friend to you this night; or in my poor opinion, ye would still be cocking on yon stone. And what's mair," says he, "ye may have observed (you that's a man of so much penetration) that Alan Breck Stewart was perhaps walking quicker than his ordinar.'"

"You!" I cried, "you were running fit to burst."

"Was I so?" said he. "Well, then, ye may depend upon it, there was nae time to be lost. And now here is enough said; gang you to your sleep, lad, and I'll watch."

Accordingly, I lay down to sleep; a little peaty earth had drifted in between the top of the two rocks, and some bracken grew there, to be a bed to me; the last thing I heard was still the crying of the eagles.

I dare say it would be nine in the morning when I was roughly awakened, and found Alan's hand pressed upon my mouth.

"Wheesht!" he whispered. "Ye were snoring."

"Well," said I, surprised at his anxious and dark face, "and why not?"

He peered over the edge of the rock, and signed to me to do the like.

It was now high day, cloudless, and very hot. The valley was as clear as in a picture. About half a mile up the water was a camp of red-coats; a big fire blazed in their midst, at which some were cooking; and near by, on the top of a rock about as high as ours, there stood a sentry, with the sun sparkling on his arms. All the way down along the river-side were posted other sentries; here near together, there widelier scattered; some planted like the first, on places of command, some on the ground level and marching and counter-marching, so as to meet half-way. Higher up the glen, where the ground was more open, the chain of posts was continued by horse-soldiers, whom we could see in the distance riding to and fro. Lower down, the infantry continued; but as the stream was suddenly swelled by the confluence of a considerable burn, they were more widely set, and only watched the fords and stepping-stones.

I took but one look at them, and ducked again into my place. It was strange indeed to see this valley, which had lain so solitary in the hour of dawn, bristling with arms and dotted with the red coats and breeches.

"Ye see," said Alan, "this was what I was afraid of, Davie: that they would watch the burn-side. They began to come in about two hours ago, and, man! but ye're a grand hand at the sleeping! We're in a narrow place. If they get up the sides of the hill, they could easy spy us with a glass; but if they'll only keep in the foot of the valley, we'll do yet. The posts are thinner down the water; and, come night, we'll try our hand at getting by them."

"And what are we to do till night?" I asked.

"Lie here," says he, "and birstle."

That one good Scotch word, "birstle," was indeed the most of the story of the day that we had now to pass. You are to remember that we lay on the bare top of a rock, like scones upon a girdle; the sun beat upon us cruelly; the rock grew so heated, a man could scarce endure the touch of it; and the little patch of earth and fern, which kept cooler, was only large enough for one at a time. We took turn about to lie on the naked rock, which was indeed like the position of that saint that was martyred on a gridiron; and it ran in my mind how strange it was, that in the same climate and at only a few days' distance, I should have suffered so cruelly, first from cold upon my island and now from heat upon this rock.

All the while we had no water, only raw brandy for a drink, which was worse than nothing; but we kept the bottle as cool as we could, burying it in the earth, and got some relief by bathing our breasts and temples.

The soldiers kept stirring all day in the bottom of the valley, now changing guard, now in patrolling parties hunting among the rocks. These lay round in so great a number, that to look for men among them was like looking for a needle in a bottle of hay; and being so hopeless a task, it was gone about with the less care. Yet we could see the soldiers pike their bayonets among the heather, which sent a cold thrill into my vitals; and they would sometimes hang about our rock, so that we scarce dared to breathe.

It was in this way that I first heard the right English speech; one fellow as he went by actually clapping his hand upon the sunny face of the rock on which we lay, and plucking it off again with an oath. "I tell you it's 'ot," says he; and I was amazed at the clipping tones and the odd sing-song in which he spoke, and no less at that strange trick of dropping out the letter "h." To be sure, I had heard Ransome; but he had taken his ways from all sorts of people, and spoke so imperfectly at the best, that I set down the most of it to childishness. My surprise was all the greater to hear that manner of speaking in the mouth of a grown man; and indeed I have never grown used to it; nor yet altogether with the English grammar, as perhaps a very critical eye might here and there spy out even in these memoirs.

The tediousness and pain of these hours upon the rock grew only the greater as the day went on; the rock getting still the hotter and the sun fiercer. There were giddiness, and sickness, and sharp pangs like rheumatism, to be supported. I minded then, and have often minded since, on the lines in our Scotch psalm:—

> "The moon by night thee shall not smite,
> Nor yet the sun by day;"

and indeed it was only by God's blessing that we were neither of us sun-smitten.

At last, about two, it was beyond men's bearing, and there was now temptation to resist, as well as pain to thole. For the sun being now got a little into the west, there came a patch of shade on the east side of our rock, which was the side sheltered from the soldiers.

"As well one death as another," said Alan, and slipped over the edge and dropped on the ground on the shadowy side.

I followed him at once, and instantly fell all my length, so weak was I and so giddy with that long exposure. Here, then, we lay for an hour or two, aching from head to foot, as weak as water, and lying quite naked to the eye of any soldier who should have strolled that way. None came, however, all passing by on the other side; so that our rock continued to be our shield even in this new position.

Presently we began again to get a little strength; and as the soldiers were now lying closer along the river-side, Alan proposed that we should try a start. I was by this time afraid of but one thing in the world; and that was to be set back upon the rock; anything else was welcome to me; so we got ourselves at once in marching order, and began to slip from rock to rock one after the other, now crawling flat on our bellies in the shade, now making a run for it, heart in mouth.

The soldiers, having searched this side of the valley after a fashion, and being perhaps somewhat sleepy with the sultriness of the afternoon, had now laid by much of their vigilance, and stood dozing at their posts or only kept a look-out along the banks of the river; so that in this way, keeping down the valley and at the same time towards the mountains, we drew steadily away from their neighbourhood. But the business was the most wearing I had ever taken part in. A man had need of a hundred eyes in every part of him, to keep concealed in that uneven country and within cry of so many and scattered sentries. When we must pass an open place, quickness was not all, but a swift judgment not only of the lie of the whole country, but of the solidity of every stone on which we must set foot; for the afternoon was now fallen so breathless that the rolling of a pebble sounded abroad like a pistol shot, and would start the echo calling among the hills and cliffs.

By sundown we had made some distance, even by our slow rate of progress, though to be sure the sentry on the rock was still plainly in our view. But now we came on something that put all fears out of season; and that was a deep rushing burn, that tore down, in that part, to join the glen river. At the sight of this we cast ourselves on the ground and plunged head and shoulders in the water; and I cannot tell which was the more pleasant, the great shock as the cool stream went over us, or the greed with which we drank of it.

We lay there (for the banks hid us), drank again and again, bathed our chests, let our wrists trail in the running water till they ached with the chill; and at last, being wonderfully renewed, we got out the meal-bag and made drammach in the iron pan. This, though it is but cold water mingled with oatmeal, yet makes a good enough dish for a hungry man; and where there are no means of making fire, or (as in our case) good reason for not making one, it is the chief stand-by of those who have taken to the heather.

As soon as the shadow of the night had fallen, we set forth again, at first with the same caution, but presently with more boldness, standing our full height and stepping out at a good pace of walking. The way was very intricate, lying up the steep sides of mountains and along the brows of cliffs; clouds had come in with the sunset, and the night was dark and cool; so that I walked without much fatigue, but in continual fear of falling and rolling down the mountains, and with no guess at our direction.

The moon rose at last and found us still on the road; it was in its last quarter, and was long beset with clouds; but after awhile shone out and showed me many dark heads of mountains, and was reflected far underneath us on the narrow arm of a sea-loch.

At this sight we both paused: I struck with wonder to find myself so high and walking (as it seemed to me) upon clouds;

Alan to make sure of his direction.

Seemingly he was well pleased, and he must certainly have judged us out of ear-shot of all our enemies; for throughout the rest of our night-march he beguiled the way with whistling of many tunes, warlike, merry, plaintive; reel tunes that made the foot go faster; tunes of my own south country that made me fain to be home from my adventures; and all these, on the great, dark, desert mountains, making company upon the way.

CHAPTER XXI

THE FLIGHT IN THE HEATHER:
THE HEUGH OF CORRYNAKIEGH

Early as day comes in the beginning of July, it was still dark when we reached our destination, a cleft in the head of a great mountain, with a water running through the midst, and upon the one hand a shallow cave in a rock. Birches grew there in a thin, pretty wood, which a little farther on was changed into a wood of pines. The burn was full of trout; the wood of cushat-doves; on the open side of the mountain beyond, whaups would be always whistling, and cuckoos were plentiful. From the mouth of the cleft we looked down upon a part of Mamore, and on the sea-loch that divides that country from Appin; and this from so great a height as made it my continual wonder and pleasure to sit and behold them.

The name of the cleft was the Heugh of Corrynakiegh; and although from its height and being so near upon the sea, it was often beset with clouds, yet it was on the whole a pleasant place, and the five days we lived in it went happily.

We slept in the cave, making our bed of heather bushes which we cut for that purpose, and covering ourselves with Alan's great-coat. There was a low concealed place, in a turning of the glen, where we were so bold as to make fire: so that we could warm ourselves when the clouds set in, and cook hot porridge, and grill the little trouts that we caught with our hands under the stones and overhanging banks of the burn. This was indeed our chief pleasure and business; and not only to save our meal against worse times, but with a rivalry that much amused us, we spent a great part of our days at the water-side, stripped to the waist and groping about or (as they say) guddling for these fish. The largest we got might have been a quarter of a pound; but they were of good flesh and flavour, and when broiled upon the coals, lacked only a little salt to be delicious.

In any by-time Alan must teach me to use my sword, for my ignorance had much distressed him; and I think besides, as I had sometimes the upper-hand of him in the fishing, he was not sorry to turn to an exercise where he had so much the upper-hand of me. He made it somewhat more of a pain than need have been, for he stormed at me all through the lessons in a very violent manner of scolding, and would push me so close that I made sure he must run me through the body. I was often tempted to turn tail, but held my ground for all that, and got some profit of my lessons; if it was but to stand on guard with an assured countenance, which is often all that is required. So, though I could never in the least please my master, I was not altogether displeased with myself.

In the meanwhile, you are not to suppose that we neglected our chief business, which was to get away.

"It will be many a long day," Alan said to me on our first morning, "before the red-coats think upon seeking Corrynakiegh; so now we must get word sent to James, and he must find the siller for us."

"And how shall we send that word?" says I. "We are here in a desert place, which yet we dare not leave; and unless ye get the fowls of the air to be your messengers, I see not what we shall be able to do."

"Ay?" said Alan. "Ye're a man of small contrivance, David."

Thereupon he fell in a muse, looking in the embers of the fire; and presently, getting a piece of wood, he fashioned it in a cross, the four ends of which he blackened on the coals. Then he looked at me a little shyly.

"Could ye lend me my button?" says he. "It seems a strange thing to ask a gift again, but I own I am laith to cut another."

I gave him the button; whereupon he strung it on a strip of his great-coat which he had used to bind the cross; and tying in a little sprig of birch and another of fir, he looked upon his work with satisfaction.

"Now," said he, "there is a little clachan" (what is called a hamlet in the English) "not very far from Corrynakiegh, and it has the name of Koalisnacoan. There there are living many friends of mine whom I could trust with my life, and some that I am no just so sure of. Ye see, David, there will be money set upon our heads; James himsel' is to set money on them; and as for the Campbells, they would never spare siller where there was a Stewart to be hurt. If it was otherwise, I would go down to Koalisnacoan whatever, and trust my life into these people's hands as lightly as I would trust another with my glove."

"But being so?" said I.

"Being so," said he, "I would as lief they didnae see me. There's bad folk everywhere, and what's far worse, weak ones. So when it comes dark again, I will steal down into that clachan, and set this that I have been making in the window of a good friend of mine, John Breck Maccoll, a bouman of Appin's."

"With all my heart," says I; "and if he finds it, what is he to think?"

"Well," says Alan, "I wish he was a man of more penetration, for by my troth I am afraid he will make little enough of it! But this is what I have in my mind. This cross is something in the nature of the crosstarrie, or fiery cross, which is the signal of gathering in our clans; yet he will know well enough the clan is not to rise, for there it is standing in his window, and no word with it. So he will say to himsel', *The clan is not to rise, but there is something.* Then he will see my button, and that was Duncan Stewart's. And then he will say to himself, *The son of Duncan is in the heather, and has need of me."*

"Well," said I, "it may be. But even supposing so, there is a good deal of heather between here and the Forth."

"And that is a very true word," says Alan. "But then John Breck will see the sprig of birch and the sprig of pine; and he will say to himsel' (if he is a man of any penetration at all, which I misdoubt), *Alan will be lying in a wood which is both of pines and birches.* Then he will think to himself, *That is not so very rife hereabout*; and then he will come and give us a look up in Corrynakiegh. And if he does not, David, the devil may fly away with him, for what I care; for he will no be worth the salt to his porridge."

"Eh, man," said I, drolling with him a little, "you're very ingenious! But would it not be simpler for you to write him a few words in black and white?"

"And that is an excellent observe, Mr. Balfour of Shaws," says Alan, drolling with me; "and it would certainly be much simpler for me to write to him, but it would be a sore job for John Breck to read it. He would have to go to the school for two-three years; and it's possible we might be wearied waiting on him."

So that night Alan carried down his fiery cross and set it in the bouman's window. He was troubled when he came back; for the dogs had barked and the folk run out from their houses; and he thought he had heard a clatter of arms and seen a red-coat come to one of the doors. On all accounts we lay the next day in the borders of the wood and kept a close look-out, so that if it was John Breck that came we might be ready to guide him, and if it was the red-coats we should have time to get away.

About noon a man was to be spied, straggling up the open side of the mountain in the sun, and looking round him as he came, from under his hand. No sooner had Alan seen him than he whistled; the man turned and came a little towards us: then Alan would give another "peep!" and the man would come still nearer; and so by the sound of whistling, he was guided to the spot where we lay.

He was a ragged, wild, bearded man, about forty, grossly disfigured with the small pox, and looked both dull and savage. Although his English was very bad and broken, yet Alan (according to his very handsome use, whenever I was by) would suffer him to speak no Gaelic. Perhaps the strange language made him appear more backward than he really was; but I thought he had little good-will to serve us, and what he had was the child of terror.

Alan would have had him carry a message to James; but the bouman would hear of no message. "She was forget it," he said in his screaming voice; and would either have a letter or wash his hands of us.

I thought Alan would be gravelled at that, for we lacked the means of writing in that desert. But he was a man of more resources than I knew; searched the wood until he found the quill of a cushat-dove, which he shaped into a pen; made himself a kind of ink with gunpowder from his horn and water from the running stream; and tearing a corner from his French military commission (which he carried in his pocket, like a talisman to keep him from the gallows), he sat down and wrote as follows:

"DEAR KINSMAN,—Please send the money by the bearer to the place he kens of.

"Your affectionate cousin,
"A. S."

This he intrusted to the bouman, who promised to make what manner of speed he best could, and carried it off with him down the hill.

He was three full days gone, but about five in the evening of the third, we heard a whistling in the wood, which Alan answered; and presently the bouman came up the water-side, looking for us, right and left. He seemed less sulky than before, and indeed he was no doubt well pleased to have got to the end of such a dangerous commission.

He gave us the news of the country; that it was alive with red-coats; that arms were being found, and poor folk brought in trouble daily; and that James and some of his servants were already clapped in prison at Fort William, under strong suspicion of complicity. It seemed it was noised on all sides that Alan Breck had fired the shot; and there was a bill issued for both him and me, with one hundred pounds reward.

This was all as bad as could be; and the little note the bouman had carried us from Mrs. Stewart was of a miserable sadness. In it she besought Alan not to let himself be captured, assuring him, if he fell in the hands of the troops, both he and James were no better than dead men. The money she had sent was all that she could beg or borrow, and she prayed heaven we could be doing with it. Lastly, she said, she enclosed us one of the bills in which we were described.

This we looked upon with great curiosity and not a little fear, partly as a man may look in a mirror, partly as he might look into the barrel of an enemy's gun to judge if it be truly aimed. Alan was advertised as "a small, pock-marked, active man of thirty-five or thereby, dressed in a feathered hat, a French side-coat of blue with silver buttons, and lace a great deal tarnished, a red waistcoat and breeches of black, shag;" and I as "a tall strong lad of about eighteen, wearing an old blue coat, very ragged, an old Highland bonnet, a long homespun waistcoat, blue breeches; his legs bare, low-country shoes, wanting the toes; speaks like a Lowlander, and has no beard."

Alan was well enough pleased to see his finery so fully remembered and set down; only when he came to the word tarnish, he looked upon his lace like one a little mortified. As for myself, I thought I cut a miserable figure in the bill; and yet was well enough pleased too, for since I had changed these rags, the description had ceased to be a danger and become a source of safety.

"Alan," said I, "you should change your clothes."

"Na, troth!" said Alan, "I have nae others. A fine sight I would be, if I went back to France in a bonnet!"

This put a second reflection in my mind: that if I were to separate from Alan and his tell-tale clothes I should be safe against arrest, and might go openly about my business. Nor was this all; for suppose I was arrested when I was alone, there was little against me; but suppose I was taken in company with the reputed murderer, my case would begin to be grave. For generosity's sake I dare not speak my mind upon this head; but I thought of it none the less.

I thought of it all the more, too, when the bouman brought out a green purse with four guineas in gold, and the best part of another in small change. True, it was more than I had. But then Alan, with less than five guineas, had to get as far as France; I, with my less than two, not beyond Queensferry; so that taking things in their proportion, Alan's society was not only a peril to my life, but a burden on my purse.

But there was no thought of the sort in the honest head of my companion. He believed he was serving, helping, and protecting me. And what could I do but hold my peace, and chafe, and take my chance of it?

"It's little enough," said Alan, putting the purse in his pocket, "but it'll do my business. And now, John Breck, if ye will hand me over my button, this gentleman and me will be for taking the road."

But the bouman, after feeling about in a hairy purse that hung in front of him in the Highland manner (though he wore otherwise the Lowland habit, with sea-trousers), began to roll his eyes strangely, and at last said, "Her nainsel will loss it," meaning he thought he had lost it.

"What!" cried Alan, "you will lose my button, that was my father's before me? Now I will tell you what is in my mind, John Breck: it is in my mind this is the worst day's work that ever ye did since ye was born."

And as Alan spoke, he set his hands on his knees and looked at the bouman with a smiling mouth, and that dancing light in his eyes that meant mischief to his enemies.

Perhaps the bouman was honest enough; perhaps he had meant to cheat and then, finding himself alone with two of us in a desert place, cast back to honesty as being safer; at least, and all at once, he seemed to find that button and handed it to Alan.

"Well, and it is a good thing for the honour of the Maccolls," said Alan, and then to me, "Here is my button back again, and I thank you for parting with it, which is of a piece with all your friendships to me." Then he took the warmest parting of the bouman. "For," says he, "ye have done very well by me, and set your neck at a venture, and I will always give you the name of a good man."

Lastly, the bouman took himself off by one way; and Alan I (getting our chattels together) struck into another to resume our flight.

CHAPTER XXII

THE FLIGHT IN THE HEATHER:
THE MOOR

Some seven hours' incessant, hard travelling brought us early in the morning to the end of a range of mountains. In front of us there lay a piece of low, broken, desert land, which we must now cross. The sun was not long up, and shone straight in our eyes; a little, thin mist went up from the face of the moorland like a smoke; so that (as Alan said) there might have been twenty squadron of dragoons there and we none the wiser.

We sat down, therefore, in a howe of the hill-side till the mist should have risen, and made ourselves a dish of drammach, and held a council of war.

"David," said Alan, "this is the kittle bit. Shall we lie here till it comes night, or shall we risk it, and stave on ahead?"

"Well," said I, "I am tired indeed, but I could walk as far again, if that was all."

"Ay, but it isnae," said Alan, "nor yet the half. This is how we stand: Appin's fair death to us. To the south it's all Campbells, and no to be thought of. To the north; well, there's no muckle to be gained by going north; neither for you, that wants to get to Queensferry, nor yet for me, that wants to get to France. Well, then, we'll can strike east."

"East be it!" says I, quite cheerily; but I was thinking in to myself: "O, man, if you would only take one point of the compass and let me take any other, it would be the best for both of us."

"Well, then, east, ye see, we have the muirs," said Alan. "Once there, David, it's mere pitch-and-toss. Out on yon bald, naked, flat place, where can a body turn to? Let the red-coats come over a hill, they can spy you miles away; and the sorrow's in their horses' heels, they would soon ride you down. It's no good place, David; and I'm free to say, it's worse by daylight than by dark."

"Alan," said I, "hear my way of it. Appin's death for us; we have none too much money, nor yet meal; the longer they seek, the nearer they may guess where we are; it's all a risk; and I give my word to go ahead until we drop."

Alan was delighted. "There are whiles," said he, "when ye are altogether too canny and Whiggish to be company for a gentleman like me; but there come other whiles when ye show yoursel' a mettle spark; and it's then, David, that I love ye like a brother."

The mist rose and died away, and showed us that country lying as waste as the sea; only the moorfowl and the pewees crying upon it, and far over to the east, a herd of deer, moving like dots. Much of it was red with heather; much of the rest broken up with bogs and hags and peaty pools; some had been burnt black in a heath fire; and in another place there was quite a forest of dead firs, standing like skeletons. A wearier-looking desert man never saw; but at least it was clear of troops, which was our point.

We went down accordingly into the waste, and began to make our toilsome and devious travel towards the eastern verge. There were the tops of mountains all round (you are to remember) from whence we might be spied at any moment; so it behoved us to keep in the hollow parts of the moor, and when these turned aside from our direction to move upon its naked face with infinite care. Sometimes, for half an hour together, we must crawl from one heather bush to another, as hunters do when they are hard upon the deer. It was a clear day again, with a blazing sun; the water in the brandy bottle was soon gone; and altogether, if I had guessed what it would be to crawl half the time upon my belly and to walk much of the rest stooping nearly to the knees, I should certainly have held back from such a killing enterprise.

Toiling and resting and toiling again, we wore away the morning; and about noon lay down in a thick bush of heather to sleep. Alan took the first watch; and it seemed to me I had scarce closed my eyes before I was shaken up to take the second. We had no clock to go by; and Alan stuck a sprig of heath in the ground to serve instead; so that as soon as the shadow of the bush should fall so far to the east, I might know to rouse him. But I was by this time so weary that I could have slept twelve hours at a stretch; I had the taste of sleep in my throat; my joints slept even when my mind was waking; the hot smell of the heather, and the drone of the wild bees, were like possets to me; and every now and again I would give a jump and find I had been dozing.

The last time I woke I seemed to come back from farther away, and thought the sun had taken a great start in the heavens. I looked at the sprig of heath, and at that I could have cried aloud: for I saw I had betrayed my trust. My head was nearly turned with fear and shame; and at what I saw, when I looked out around me on the moor, my heart was like dying in my body. For sure enough, a body of horse-soldiers had come down during my sleep, and were drawing near to us from the south-east, spread out in the shape of a fan and riding their horses to and fro in the deep parts of the heather.

When I waked Alan, he glanced first at the soldiers, then at the mark and the position of the sun, and knitted his brows with a sudden, quick look, both ugly and anxious, which was all the reproach I had of him.

"What are we to do now?" I asked.

"We'll have to play at being hares," said he. "Do ye see yon mountain?" pointing to one on the north-eastern sky.

"Ay," said I.

"Well, then," says he, "let us strike for that. Its name is Ben Alder. it is a wild, desert mountain full of hills and hollows, and if we can win to it before the morn, we may do yet."

"But, Alan," cried I, "that will take us across the very coming of the soldiers!"

"I ken that fine," said he; "but if we are driven back on Appin, we are two dead men. So now, David man, be brisk!"

With that he began to run forward on his hands and knees with an incredible quickness, as though it were his natural way of going. All the time, too, he kept winding in and out in the lower parts of the moorland where we were the best concealed. Some of these had been burned or at least scathed with fire; and there rose in our faces (which were close to the ground) a blinding, choking dust as fine as smoke. The water was long out; and this posture of running on the hands and knees brings an overmastering weakness and weariness, so that the joints ache and the wrists faint under your weight.

Now and then, indeed, where was a big bush of heather, we lay awhile, and panted, and putting aside the leaves, looked back at the dragoons. They had not spied us, for they held straight on; a half-troop, I think, covering about two miles of ground, and beating it mighty thoroughly as they went. I had awakened just in time; a little later, and we must have fled in front of them, instead of escaping on one side. Even as it was, the least misfortune might betray us; and now and again, when a grouse rose out of the heather with a clap of wings, we lay as still as the dead and were afraid to breathe.

The aching and faintness of my body, the labouring of my heart, the soreness of my hands, and the smarting of my throat and eyes in the continual smoke of dust and ashes, had soon grown to be so unbearable that I would gladly have given up.

Nothing but the fear of Alan lent me enough of a false kind of courage to continue. As for himself (and you are to bear in mind that he was cumbered with a great-coat) he had first turned crimson, but as time went on the redness began to be mingled with patches of white; his breath cried and whistled as it came; and his voice, when he whispered his observations in my ear during our halts, sounded like nothing human. Yet he seemed in no way dashed in spirits, nor did he at all abate in his activity, so that I was driven, to marvel at the man's endurance.

At length, in the first gloaming of the night, we heard a trumpet sound, and looking back from among the heather, saw the troop beginning to collect. A little after, they had built a fire and camped for the night, about the middle of the waste.

At this I begged and besought that we might lie down and sleep.

"There shall be no sleep the night!" said Alan. "From now on, these weary dragoons of yours will keep the crown of the muirland, and none will get out of Appin but winged fowls. We got through in the nick of time, and shall we jeopard what we've gained? Na, na, when the day comes, it shall find you and me in a fast place on Ben Alder."

"Alan," I said, "it's not the want of will: it's the strength that I want. If I could, I would; but as sure as I'm alive I cannot."

"Very well, then," said Alan. "I'll carry ye."

I looked to see if he were jesting; but no, the little man was in dead earnest; and the sight of so much resolution shamed me.

"Lead away!" said I. "I'll follow."

He gave me one look as much as to say, "Well done, David!" and off he set again at his top speed.

It grew cooler and even a little darker (but not much) with the coming of the night. The sky was cloudless; it was still early in July, and pretty far north; in the darkest part of that night, you would have needed pretty good eyes to read, but for all

that, I have often seen it darker in a winter mid-day. Heavy
dew fell and drenched the moor like rain; and this refreshed
me for a while. When we stopped to breathe, and I had time
to see all about me, the clearness and sweetness of the night,
the shapes of the hills like things asleep, and the fire dwindling
away behind us, like a bright spot in the midst of the moor,
anger would come upon me in a clap that I must still drag
myself in agony and eat the dust like a worm.

By what I have read in books, I think few that have held a
pen were ever really wearied, or they would write of it more
strongly. I had no care of my life, neither past nor future, and
I scarce remembered there was such a lad as David Balfour. I
did not think of myself, but just of each fresh step which I was
sure would be my last, with despair—and of Alan, who was the
cause of it, with hatred. Alan was in the right trade as a soldier;
this is the officer's part to make men continue to do things,
they know not wherefore, and when, if the choice was offered,
they would lie down where they were and be killed. And I dare
say I would have made a good enough private; for in these last
hours it never occurred to me that I had any choice but just to
obey as long as I was able, and die obeying.

Day began to come in, after years, I thought; and by that
time we were past the greatest danger, and could walk upon our
feet like men, instead of crawling like brutes. But, dear heart
have mercy! what a pair we must have made, going double like
old grandfathers, stumbling like babes, and as white as dead
folk. Never a word passed between us; each set his mouth and
kept his eyes in front of him, and lifted up his foot and set it
down again, like people lifting weights at a country play; all the
while, with the moorfowl crying "peep!" in the heather, and
the light coming slowly clearer in the east.

I say Alan did as I did. Not that ever I looked at him, for I
had enough ado to keep my feet; but because it is plain he must
have been as stupid with weariness as myself, and looked as

little where we were going, or we should not have walked into an ambush like blind men.

It fell in this way. We were going down a heathery brae, Alan leading and I following a pace or two behind, like a fiddler and his wife; when upon a sudden the heather gave a rustle, three or four ragged men leaped out, and the next moment we were lying on our backs, each with a dirk at his throat.

I don't think I cared; the pain of this rough handling was quite swallowed up by the pains of which I was already full; and I was too glad to have stopped walking to mind about a dirk. I lay looking up in the face of the man that held me; and I mind his face was black with the sun, and his eyes very light, but I was not afraid of him. I heard Alan and another whispering in the Gaelic; and what they said was all one to me.

Then the dirks were put up, our weapons were taken away, and we were set face to face, sitting in the heather.

"They are Cluny's men," said Alan. "We couldnae have fallen better. We're just to bide here with these, which are his out-sentries, till they can get word to the chief of my arrival."

Now Cluny Macpherson, the chief of the clan Vourich, had been one of the leaders of the great rebellion six years before; there was a price on his life; and I had supposed him long ago in France, with the rest of the heads of that desperate party. Even tired as I was, the surprise of what I heard half wakened me.

"What," I cried, "is Cluny still here?"

"Ay, is he so!" said Alan. "Still in his own country and kept by his own clan. King George can do no more."

I think I would have asked farther, but Alan gave me the put-off. "I am rather wearied," he said, "and I would like fine to get a sleep." And without more words, he rolled on his face in a deep heather bush, and seemed to sleep at once.

There was no such thing possible for me. You have heard grasshoppers whirring in the grass in the summer time? Well,

I had no sooner closed my eyes, than my body, and above all my head, belly, and wrists, seemed to be filled with whirring grasshoppers; and I must open my eyes again at once, and tumble and toss, and sit up and lie down; and look at the sky which dazzled me, or at Cluny's wild and dirty sentries, peering out over the top of the brae and chattering to each other in the Gaelic.

That was all the rest I had, until the messenger returned; when, as it appeared that Cluny would be glad to receive us, we must get once more upon our feet and set forward. Alan was in excellent good spirits, much refreshed by his sleep, very hungry, and looking pleasantly forward to a dram and a dish of hot collops, of which, it seems, the messenger had brought him word. For my part, it made me sick to hear of eating. I had been dead-heavy before, and now I felt a kind of dreadful lightness, which would not suffer me to walk. I drifted like a gossamer; the ground seemed to me a cloud, the hills a feather-weight, the air to have a current, like a running burn, which carried me to and fro. With all that, a sort of horror of despair sat on my mind, so that I could have wept at my own helplessness.

I saw Alan knitting his brows at me, and supposed it was in anger; and that gave me a pang of light-headed fear, like what a child may have. I remember, too, that I was smiling, and could not stop smiling, hard as I tried; for I thought it was out of place at such a time. But my good companion had nothing in his mind but kindness; and the next moment, two of the gillies had me by the arms, and I began to be carried forward with great swiftness (or so it appeared to me, although I dare say it was slowly enough in truth), through a labyrinth of dreary glens and hollows and into the heart of that dismal mountain of Ben Alder.

CHAPTER XXIII

CLUNY'S CAGE

We came at last to the foot of an exceeding steep wood, which scrambled up a craggy hillside, and was crowned by a naked precipice.

"It's here," said one of the guides, and we struck up hill.

The trees clung upon the slope, like sailors on the shrouds of a ship, and their trunks were like the rounds of a ladder, by which we mounted.

Quite at the top, and just before the rocky face of the cliff sprang above the foliage, we found that strange house which was known in the country as "Cluny's Cage." The trunks of several trees had been wattled across, the intervals strengthened with stakes, and the ground behind this barricade levelled up with earth to make the floor. A tree, which grew out from the hillside, was the living centre-beam of the roof. The walls were of wattle and covered with moss. The whole house had something of an egg shape; and it half hung, half stood in that steep, hillside thicket, like a wasp's nest in a green hawthorn.

Within, it was large enough to shelter five or six persons with some comfort. A projection of the cliff had been cunningly employed to be the fireplace; and the smoke rising against the face of the rock, and being not dissimilar in colour, readily escaped notice from below.

This was but one of Cluny's hiding-places; he had caves, besides, and underground chambers in several parts of his country; and following the reports of his scouts, he moved from one to another as the soldiers drew near or moved away. By this manner of living, and thanks to the affection of his clan, he had not only stayed all this time in safety, while so many others had fled or been taken and slain: but stayed four or five years longer, and only went to France at last by the express command of his master. There he soon died; and it is strange to reflect that he may have regretted his Cage upon Ben Alder.

When we came to the door he was seated by his rock chimney, watching a gillie about some cookery. He was mighty plainly habited, with a knitted nightcap drawn over his ears, and smoked a foul cutty pipe. For all that he had the manners of a king, and it was quite a sight to see him rise out of his place to welcome us.

"Well, Mr. Stewart, come awa', sir!" said he, "and bring in your friend that as yet I dinna ken the name of."

"And how is yourself, Cluny?" said Alan. "I hope ye do brawly, sir. And I am proud to see ye, and to present to ye my friend the Laird of Shaws, Mr. David Balfour."

Alan never referred to my estate without a touch of a sneer, when we were alone; but with strangers, he rang the words out like a herald.

"Step in by, the both of ye, gentlemen," says Cluny. "I make ye welcome to my house, which is a queer, rude place for certain, but one where I have entertained a royal personage, Mr. Stewart—ye doubtless ken the personage I have in my eye. We'll take a dram for luck, and as soon as this handless man of mine has the collops ready, we'll dine and take a hand at the cartes as gentlemen should. My life is a bit driegh," says he, pouring out the brandy; "I see little company, and sit and twirl my thumbs, and mind upon a great day that is gone by, and weary for another great day that we all hope will be upon the road. And so here's a toast to ye: The Restoration!"

Thereupon we all touched glasses and drank. I am sure I wished no ill to King George; and if he had been there himself in proper person, it's like he would have done as I did. No sooner had I taken out the drain than I felt hugely better, and could look on and listen, still a little mistily perhaps, but no longer with the same groundless horror and distress of mind.

It was certainly a strange place, and we had a strange host. In his long hiding, Cluny had grown to have all manner of precise habits, like those of an old maid. He had a particular place, where no one else must sit; the Cage was arranged in a particular way, which none must disturb; cookery was one of his chief fancies, and even while he was greeting us in, he kept an eye to the collops.

It appears, he sometimes visited or received visits from his wife and one or two of his nearest friends, under the cover of night; but for the more part lived quite alone, and communicated only with his sentinels and the gillies that waited on him in the Cage. The first thing in the morning, one of them, who was a barber, came and shaved him, and gave him the news of the country, of which he was immoderately greedy. There was no end to his questions; he put them as earnestly as a child; and at some of the answers, laughed out of all bounds of reason, and would break out again laughing at the mere memory, hours after the barber was gone.

To be sure, there might have been a purpose in his questions; for though he was thus sequestered, and like the other landed gentlemen of Scotland, stripped by the late Act of Parliament of legal powers, he still exercised a patriarchal justice in his clan. Disputes were brought to him in his hiding-hole to be decided; and the men of his country, who would have snapped their fingers at the Court of Session, laid aside revenge and paid down money at the bare word of this forfeited and hunted outlaw. When he was angered, which was often enough, he gave his commands and breathed threats of punishment like any, king; and his gillies trembled and crouched away from him like children before a hasty father. With each of them, as he entered, he ceremoniously shook hands, both parties touching their bonnets at the same time in a military manner. Altogether, I had a fair chance to see some of the inner workings of a Highland clan; and this with a proscribed, fugitive chief; his country conquered; the troops riding upon all sides in quest of him, sometimes within a mile of where he lay; and when the least of the ragged fellows whom he rated and threatened, could have made a fortune by betraying him.

On that first day, as soon as the collops were ready, Cluny gave them with his own hand a squeeze of a lemon (for he was well supplied with luxuries) and bade us draw in to our meal.

"They," said he, meaning the collops, "are such as I gave his Royal Highness in this very house; bating the lemon juice, for at that time we were glad to get the meat and never fashed for kitchen. Indeed, there were mair dragoons than lemons in my country in the year forty-six."

I do not know if the collops were truly very good, but my heart rose against the sight of them, and I could eat but little. All the while Cluny entertained us with stories of Prince Charlie's stay in the Cage, giving us the very words of the speakers, and rising from his place to show us where they stood. By these, I gathered the Prince was a gracious, spirited boy, like the son of a race of polite kings, but not so wise as Solomon. I gathered, too, that while he was in the Cage, he was often drunk; so the fault that has since, by all accounts, made such a wreck of him, had even then begun to show itself.

We were no sooner done eating than Cluny brought out an old, thumbed, greasy pack of cards, such as you may find in a mean inn; and his eyes brightened in his face as he proposed that we should fall to playing.

Now this was one of the things I had been brought up to eschew like disgrace; it being held by my father neither the part of a Christian nor yet of a gentleman to set his own livelihood and fish for that of others, on the cast of painted pasteboard.

To be sure, I might have pleaded my fatigue, which was excuse enough; but I thought it behoved that I should bear a testimony. I must have got very red in the face, but I spoke steadily, and told them I had no call to be a judge of others, but for my own part, it was a matter in which I had no clearness.

Cluny stopped mingling the cards. "What in deil's name is this?" says he. "What kind of Whiggish, canting talk is this, for the house of Cluny Macpherson?"

"I will put my hand in the fire for Mr. Balfour," says Alan. "He is an honest and a mettle gentleman, and I would have ye bear in mind who says it. I bear a king's name," says he, cocking his hat; "and I and any that I call friend are company for the best. But the gentleman is tired, and should sleep; if he has no mind to the cartes, it will never hinder you and me. And I'm fit and willing, sir, to play ye any game that ye can name."

"Sir," says Cluny, "in this poor house of mine I would have you to ken that any gentleman may follow his pleasure. If your friend would like to stand on his head, he is welcome. And if either he, or you, or any other man, is not preceesely satisfied, I will be proud to step outside with him."

I had no will that these two friends should cut their throats for my sake.

"Sir," said I, "I am very wearied, as Alan says; and what's more, as you are a man that likely has sons of your own, I may tell you it was a promise to my father."

"Say nae mair, say nae mair," said Cluny, and pointed me to a bed of heather in a corner of the Cage. For all that he was displeased enough, looked at me askance, and grumbled when he looked. And indeed it must be owned that both my scruples and the words in which I declared them, smacked somewhat of the Covenanter, and were little in their place among wild Highland Jacobites.

What with the brandy and the venison, a strange heaviness had come over me; and I had scarce lain down upon the bed before I fell into a kind of trance, in which I continued almost the whole time of our stay in the Cage. Sometimes I was broad awake and understood what passed; sometimes I only heard voices, or men snoring, like the voice of a silly river; and the plaids upon the wall dwindled down and swelled out again, like firelight shadows on the roof. I must sometimes have spoken or cried out, for I remember I was now and then amazed at being answered; yet I was conscious of no particular nightmare, only of a general, black, abiding horror—a horror of the place I was in, and the bed I lay in, and the plaids on the wall, and the voices, and the fire, and myself.

The barber-gillie, who was a doctor too, was called in to prescribe for me; but as he spoke in the Gaelic, I understood not a word of his opinion, and was too sick even to ask for a translation. I knew well enough I was ill, and that was all I cared about.

I paid little heed while I lay in this poor pass. But Alan and Cluny were most of the time at the cards, and I am clear that Alan must have begun by winning; for I remember sitting up, and seeing them hard at it, and a great glittering pile of as much as sixty or a hundred guineas on the table. It looked strange enough, to see all this wealth in a nest upon a cliff-side, wattled about growing trees. And even then, I thought it seemed deep water for Alan to be riding, who had no better battle-horse than a green purse and a matter of five pounds.

The luck, it seems, changed on the second day. About noon I was wakened as usual for dinner, and as usual refused to eat, and was given a dram with some bitter infusion which the barber had prescribed. The sun was shining in at the open door of the Cage, and this dazzled and offended me. Cluny sat at the table, biting the pack of cards. Alan had stooped over the bed, and had his face close to my eyes; to which, troubled as they were with the fever, it seemed of the most shocking bigness.

He asked me for a loan of my money.

"What for?" said I.

"O, just for a loan," said he.

"But why?" I repeated. "I don't see."

"Hut, David!" said Alan, "ye wouldnae grudge me a loan?"

I would, though, if I had had my senses! But all I thought of then was to get his face away, and I handed him my money.

On the morning of the third day, when we had been forty-eight hours in the Cage, I awoke with a great relief of spirits, very weak and weary indeed, but seeing things of the right size and with their honest, everyday appearance. I had a mind to eat, moreover, rose from bed of my own movement, and as soon as we had breakfasted, stepped to the entry of the Cage and sat down outside in the top of the wood. It was a grey day with a cool, mild air: and I sat in a dream all morning, only disturbed by the passing by of Cluny's scouts and servants coming with provisions and reports; for as the coast was at that time clear, you might almost say he held court openly.

When I returned, he and Alan had laid the cards aside, and were questioning a gillie; and the chief turned about and spoke to me in the Gaelic.

"I have no Gaelic, sir," said I.

Now since the card question, everything I said or did had the power of annoying Cluny. "Your name has more sense than yourself, then," said he angrily, "for it's good Gaelic. But the point is this. My scout reports all clear in the south, and the question is, have ye the strength to go?"

I saw cards on the table, but no gold; only a heap of little written papers, and these all on Cluny's side. Alan, besides, had an odd look, like a man not very well content; and I began to have a strong misgiving.

"I do not know if I am as well as I should be," said I, looking at Alan; "but the little money we have has a long way to carry us."

Alan took his under-lip into his mouth, and looked upon the ground.

"David," says he at last, "I've lost it; there's the naked truth."

"My money too?" said I.

"Your money too," says Alan, with a groan. "Ye shouldnae have given it me. I'm daft when I get to the cartes."

"Hoot-toot! hoot-toot!" said Cluny. "It was all daffing; it's all nonsense. Of course you'll have your money back again, and the double of it, if ye'll make so free with me. It would be a singular thing for me to keep it. It's not to be supposed that I would be any hindrance to gentlemen in your situation; that would be a singular thing!" cries he, and began to pull gold out of his pocket with a mighty red face.

Alan said nothing, only looked on the ground.

"Will you step to the door with me, sir?" said I.

Cluny said he would be very glad, and followed me readily enough, but he looked flustered and put out.

"And now, sir," says I, "I must first acknowledge your generosity."

"Nonsensical nonsense!" cries Cluny. "Where's the generosity? This is just a most unfortunate affair; but what would ye have me do—boxed up in this bee-skep of a cage of mine—but just set my friends to the cartes, when I can get them? And if they lose, of course, it's not to be supposed—" And here he came to a pause.

"Yes," said I, "if they lose, you give them back their money; and if they win, they carry away yours in their pouches! I have said before that I grant your generosity; but to me, sir, it's a very painful thing to be placed in this position."

There was a little silence, in which Cluny seemed always as if he was about to speak, but said nothing. All the time he grew redder and redder in the face.

"I am a young man," said I, "and I ask your advice. Advise me as you would your son. My friend fairly lost his money, after having fairly gained a far greater sum of yours; can I accept it back again? Would that be the right part for me to play? Whatever I do, you can see for yourself it must be hard upon a man of any pride."

"It's rather hard on me, too, Mr. Balfour," said Cluny, "and ye give me very much the look of a man that has entrapped poor people to their hurt. I wouldnae have my friends come to any house of mine to accept affronts; no," he cried, with a sudden heat of anger, "nor yet to give them!"

"And so you see, sir," said I, "there is something to be said upon my side; and this gambling is a very poor employ for gentlefolks. But I am still waiting your opinion."

I am sure if ever Cluny hated any man it was David Balfour. He looked me all over with a warlike eye, and I saw the challenge at his lips. But either my youth disarmed him, or perhaps his own sense of justice. Certainly it was a mortifying matter for all concerned, and not least Cluny; the more credit that he took it as he did.

"Mr. Balfour," said he, "I think you are too nice and covenanting, but for all that you have the spirit of a very pretty gentleman. Upon my honest word, ye may take this money— it's what I would tell my son—and here's my hand along with it!"

CHAPTER XXIV

THE FLIGHT IN THE HEATHER:
THE QUARREL

Alan and I were put across Loch Errocht under cloud of night, and went down its eastern shore to another hiding-place near the head of Loch Rannoch, whither we were led by one of the gillies from the Cage. This fellow carried all our luggage and Alan's great-coat in the bargain, trotting along under the burthen, far less than the half of which used to weigh me to the ground, like a stout hill pony with a feather; yet he was a man that, in plain contest, I could have broken on my knee.

Doubtless it was a great relief to walk disencumbered; and perhaps without that relief, and the consequent sense of liberty and lightness, I could not have walked at all. I was but new risen from a bed of sickness; and there was nothing in the state of our affairs to hearten me for much exertion; travelling, as we did, over the most dismal deserts in Scotland, under a cloudy heaven, and with divided hearts among the travellers.

For long, we said nothing; marching alongside or one behind the other, each with a set countenance: I, angry and proud, and drawing what strength I had from these two violent and sinful feelings; Alan angry and ashamed, ashamed that he had lost my money, angry that I should take it so ill.

The thought of a separation ran always the stronger in my mind; and the more I approved of it, the more ashamed I grew of my approval. It would be a fine, handsome, generous thing, indeed, for Alan to turn round and say to me: "Go, I am in the most danger, and my company only increases yours." But for me to turn to the friend who certainly loved me, and say to him: "You are in great danger, I am in but little; your friendship is a burden; go, take your risks and bear your hardships alone—" no, that was impossible; and even to think of it privily to myself, made my cheeks to burn.

And yet Alan had behaved like a child, and (what is worse) a treacherous child. Wheedling my money from me while I lay half-conscious was scarce better than theft; and yet here he was trudging by my side, without a penny to his name, and by what I could see, quite blithe to sponge upon the money he had driven me to beg. True, I was ready to share it with him; but it made me rage to see him count upon my readiness.

These were the two things uppermost in my mind; and I could open my mouth upon neither without black ungenerosity. So I did the next worst, and said nothing, nor so much as looked once at my companion, save with the tail of my eye.

At last, upon the other side of Loch Errocht, going over a smooth, rushy place, where the walking was easy, he could bear it no longer, and came close to me.

"David," says he, "this is no way for two friends to take a small accident. I have to say that I'm sorry; and so that's said. And now if you have anything, ye'd better say it."

"O," says I, "I have nothing."

He seemed disconcerted; at which I was meanly pleased.

"No," said he, with rather a trembling voice, "but when I say I was to blame?"

"Why, of course, ye were to blame," said I, coolly; "and you will bear me out that I have never reproached you."

"Never," says he; "but ye ken very well that ye've done worse. Are we to part? Ye said so once before. Are ye to say it again? There's hills and heather enough between here and the two seas, David; and I will own I'm no very keen to stay where I'm no wanted."

This pierced me like a sword, and seemed to lay bare my private disloyalty.

"Alan Breck!" I cried; and then: "Do you think I am one to turn my back on you in your chief need? You dursn't say it to my face. My whole conduct's there to give the lie to it. It's true, I fell asleep upon the muir; but that was from weariness, and you do wrong to cast it up to me—"

"Which is what I never did," said Alan.

"But aside from that," I continued, "what have I done that you should even me to dogs by such a supposition? I never yet failed a friend, and it's not likely I'll begin with you. There are things between us that I can never forget, even if you can."

"I will only say this to ye, David," said Alan, very quietly, "that I have long been owing ye my life, and now I owe ye money. Ye should try to make that burden light for me."

This ought to have touched me, and in a manner it did, but the wrong manner. I felt I was behaving, badly; and was now not only angry with Alan, but angry with myself in the bargain; and it made me the more cruel.

"You asked me to speak," said I. "Well, then, I will. You own yourself that you have done me a disservice; I have had to swallow an affront: I have never reproached you, I never named the thing till you did. And now you blame me," cried I, "because I cannae laugh and sing as if I was glad to be affronted. The next thing will be that I'm to go down upon my knees and thank you for it! Ye should think more of others, Alan Breck. If ye thought more of others, ye would perhaps speak less about yourself; and when a friend that likes you very well has passed over an offence without a word, you would be blithe to let it lie, instead of making it a stick to break his back with. By your own way of it, it was you that was to blame; then it shouldnae be you to seek the quarrel."

"Aweel," said Alan, "say nae mair."

And we fell back into our former silence; and came to our journey's end, and supped, and lay down to sleep, without another word.

The gillie put us across Loch Rannoch in the dusk of the next day, and gave us his opinion as to our best route. This was to get us up at once into the tops of the mountains: to go round by a circuit, turning the heads of Glen Lyon, Glen Lochay, and Glen Dochart, and come down upon the lowlands by Kippen and the upper waters of the Forth. Alan was little pleased with a route which led us through the country of his blood-foes, the Glenorchy Campbells. He objected that by turning to the east, we should come almost at once among the Athole Stewarts, a race of his own name and lineage, although following a different chief, and come besides by a far easier and swifter way to the place whither we were bound. But the gillie, who was indeed the chief man of Cluny's scouts, had good reasons to give him on all hands, naming the force of troops in every district, and alleging finally (as well as I could understand) that we should nowhere be so little troubled as in a country of the Campbells.

Alan gave way at last, but with only half a heart. "It's one of the dowiest countries in Scotland," said he. "There's naething there that I ken, but heath, and crows, and Campbells. But I see that ye're a man of some penetration; and be it as ye please!"

We set forth accordingly by this itinerary; and for the best part of three nights travelled on eerie mountains and among the well-heads of wild rivers; often buried in mist, almost continually blown and rained upon, and not once cheered by any glimpse of sunshine. By day, we lay and slept in the drenching heather; by night, incessantly clambered upon break-neck hills and among rude crags. We often wandered; we were often so involved in fog, that we must lie quiet till it lightened. A fire was never to be thought of. Our only food was drammach and a portion of cold meat that we had carried from the Cage; and as for drink, Heaven knows we had no want of water.

This was a dreadful time, rendered the more dreadful by the gloom of the weather and the country. I was never warm; my teeth chattered in my head; I was troubled with a very sore throat, such as I had on the isle; I had a painful stitch in my side, which never left me; and when I slept in my wet bed, with the rain beating above and the mud oozing below me, it was to live over again in fancy the worst part of my adventures—to see the tower of Shaws lit by lightning, Ransome carried below on the men's backs, Shuan dying on the round-house floor, or Colin Campbell grasping at the bosom of his coat. From such broken slumbers, I would be aroused in the gloaming, to sit up in the same puddle where I had slept, and sup cold drammach; the rain driving sharp in my face or running down my back in icy trickles; the mist enfolding us like as in a gloomy chamber—or, perhaps, if the wind blew, falling suddenly apart and showing us the gulf of some dark valley where the streams were crying aloud.

The sound of an infinite number of rivers came up from all round. In this steady rain the springs of the mountain were broken up; every glen gushed water like a cistern; every stream was in high spate, and had filled and overflowed its channel. During our night tramps, it was solemn to hear the voice of them below in the valleys, now booming like thunder, now with an angry cry. I could well understand the story of the Water Kelpie, that demon of the streams, who is fabled to keep wailing and roaring at the ford until the coming of the doomed traveller. Alan I saw believed it, or half believed it; and when the cry of the river rose more than usually sharp, I was little surprised (though, of course, I would still be shocked) to see him cross himself in the manner of the Catholics.

During all these horrid wanderings we had no familiarity,

scarcely even that of speech. The truth is that I was sickening for my grave, which is my best excuse. But besides that I was of an unforgiving disposition from my birth, slow to take offence, slower to forget it, and now incensed both against my companion and myself. For the best part of two days he was unweariedly kind; silent, indeed, but always ready to help, and always hoping (as I could very well see) that my displeasure would blow by. For the same length of time I stayed in myself, nursing my anger, roughly refusing his services, and passing him over with my eyes as if he had been a bush or a stone.

The second night, or rather the peep of the third day, found us upon a very open hill, so that we could not follow our usual plan and lie down immediately to eat and sleep. Before we had reached a place of shelter, the grey had come pretty clear, for though it still rained, the clouds ran higher; and Alan, looking in my face, showed some marks of concern.

"Ye had better let me take your pack," said he, for perhaps the ninth time since we had parted from the scout beside Loch Rannoch.

"I do very well, I thank you," said I, as cold as ice.

Alan flushed darkly. "I'll not offer it again," he said. "I'm not a patient man, David."

"I never said you were," said I, which was exactly the rude, silly speech of a boy of ten.

Alan made no answer at the time, but his conduct answered for him. Henceforth, it is to be thought, he quite forgave himself for the affair at Cluny's; cocked his hat again, walked jauntily, whistled airs, and looked at me upon one side with a provoking smile.

The third night we were to pass through the western end of the country of Balquhidder. It came clear and cold, with a touch in the air like frost, and a northerly wind that blew the clouds away and made the stars bright. The streams were full, of course, and still made a great noise among the hills; but I observed that Alan thought no more upon the Kelpie, and was in high good spirits. As for me, the change of weather came too late; I had lain in the mire so long that (as the Bible has it) my very clothes "abhorred me." I was dead weary, deadly sick and full of pains and shiverings; the chill of the wind went through me, and the sound of it confused my ears. In this poor state I had to bear from my companion something in the nature of a persecution. He spoke a good deal, and never without a taunt. "Whig" was the best name he had to give me. "Here," he would say, "here's a dub for ye to jump, my Whiggie! I ken you're a fine jumper!" And so on; all the time with a gibing voice and face.

I knew it was my own doing, and no one else's; but I was too miserable to repent. I felt I could drag myself but little farther; pretty soon, I must lie down and die on these wet mountains like a sheep or a fox, and my bones must whiten there like the bones of a beast. My head was light perhaps; but I began to love the prospect, I began to glory in the thought of such a death, alone in the desert, with the wild eagles besieging my last moments. Alan would repent then, I thought; he would remember, when I was dead, how much he owed me, and the remembrance would be torture. So I went like a sick, silly, and bad-hearted schoolboy, feeding my anger against a fellow-man, when I would have been better on my knees, crying on God for mercy. And at each of Alan's taunts, I hugged myself. "Ah!" thinks I to myself, "I have a better taunt in readiness; when I lie down and die, you will feel it like a buffet in your face; ah, what a revenge! ah, how you will regret your ingratitude and cruelty!"

All the while, I was growing worse and worse. Once I had fallen, my leg simply doubling under me, and this had struck Alan for the moment; but I was afoot so briskly, and set off again with such a natural manner, that he soon forgot the incident. Flushes of heat went over me, and then spasms of shuddering. The stitch in my side was hardly bearable. At last I began to feel that I could trail myself no farther: and with that, there came on me all at once the wish to have it out with Alan, let my anger blaze, and be done with my life in a more sudden manner. He had just called me "Whig." I stopped.

"Mr. Stewart," said I, in a voice that quivered like a fiddle-string, "you are older than I am, and should know your manners. Do you think it either very wise or very witty to cast my politics in my teeth? I thought, where folk differed, it was the part of gentlemen to differ civilly; and if I did not, I may tell you I could find a better taunt than some of yours."

Alan had stopped opposite to me, his hat cocked, his hands in his breeches pockets, his head a little on one side. He listened, smiling evilly, as I could see by the starlight; and when I had done he began to whistle a Jacobite air. It was the air made in mockery of General Cope's defeat at Preston Pans:

> "Hey, Johnnie Cope, are ye waukin' yet?
> And are your drums a-beatin' yet?"

And it came in my mind that Alan, on the day of that battle, had been engaged upon the royal side.

"Why do ye take that air, Mr. Stewart?" said I. "Is that to remind me you have been beaten on both sides?"

The air stopped on Alan's lips. "David!" said he.

"But it's time these manners ceased," I continued; "and I mean you shall henceforth speak civilly of my King and my good friends the Campbells."

"I am a Stewart—" began Alan.

"O!" says I, "I ken ye bear a king's name. But you are to remember, since I have been in the Highlands, I have seen a good many of those that bear it; and the best I can say of them is this, that they would be none the worse of washing."

"Do you know that you insult me?" said Alan, very low.

"I am sorry for that," said I, "for I am not done; and if you distaste the sermon, I doubt the pirliecue will please you as little. You have been chased in the field by the grown men of my party; it seems a poor kind of pleasure to out-face a boy. Both the Campbells and the Whigs have beaten you; you have run before them like a hare. It behoves you to speak of them as of your betters."

Alan stood quite still, the tails of his great-coat clapping behind him in the wind.

"This is a pity" he said at last. "There are things said that cannot be passed over."

"I never asked you to," said I. "I am as ready as yourself."

"Ready?" said he.

"Ready," I repeated. "I am no blower and boaster like some that I could name. Come on!" And drawing my sword, I fell on guard as Alan himself had taught me.

"David!" he cried. "Are ye daft? I cannae draw upon ye, David. It's fair murder."

"That was your look-out when you insulted me," said I.

"It's the truth!" cried Alan, and he stood for a moment, wringing his mouth in his hand like a man in sore perplexity. "It's the bare truth," he said, and drew his sword. But before I could touch his blade with mine, he had thrown it from him and fallen to the ground. "Na, na," he kept saying, "na, na—I cannae, I cannae."

At this the last of my anger oozed all out of me; and I found myself only sick, and sorry, and blank, and wondering at myself. I would have given the world to take back what I had said; but a word once spoken, who can recapture it? I minded me of all Alan's kindness and courage in the past, how he had helped and cheered and borne with me in our evil days; and then recalled my own insults, and saw that I had lost for ever that doughty friend. At the same time, the sickness that hung upon me seemed to redouble, and the pang in my side was like a sword for sharpness. I thought I must have swooned where I stood.

This it was that gave me a thought. No apology could blot out what I had said; it was needless to think of one, none could cover the offence; but where an apology was vain, a mere cry for help might bring Alan back to my side. I put my pride away from me. "Alan!" I said; "if ye cannae help me, I must just die here."

He started up sitting, and looked at me.

"It's true," said I. "I'm by with it. O, let me get into the bield of a house—I'll can die there easier." I had no need to pretend; whether I chose or not, I spoke in a weeping voice that would have melted a heart of stone.

"Can ye walk?" asked Alan.

"No," said I, "not without help. This last hour my legs have been fainting under me; I've a stitch in my side like a red-hot iron; I cannae breathe right. If I die, ye'll can forgive me, Alan? In my heart, I liked ye fine—even when I was the angriest."

"Wheesht, wheesht!" cried Alan. "Dinna say that! David man, ye ken—" He shut his mouth upon a sob. "Let me get my arm about ye," he continued; "that's the way! Now lean upon me hard. Gude kens where there's a house! We're in Balwhidder, too; there should be no want of houses, no, nor friends' houses here. Do ye gang easier so, Davie?"

"Ay" said I, "I can be doing this way;" and I pressed his arm with my hand.

Again he came near sobbing. "Davie," said he, "I'm no a right man at all; I have neither sense nor kindness; I could nae remember ye were just a bairn, I couldnae see ye were dying on your feet; Davie, ye'll have to try and forgive me."

"O man, let's say no more about it!" said I. "We're neither one of us to mend the other—that's the truth! We must just bear and forbear, man Alan. O, but my stitch is sore! Is there nae house?"

"I'll find a house to ye, David," he said, stoutly. "We'll follow down the burn, where there's bound to be houses. My poor man, will ye no be better on my back?"

"O, Alan," says I, "and me a good twelve inches taller?"

"Ye're no such a thing," cried Alan, with a start. "There may be a trifling matter of an inch or two; I'm no saying I'm just exactly what ye would call a tall man, whatever; and I dare say," he added, his voice tailing off in a laughable manner, "now when I come to think of it, I dare say ye'll be just about right. Ay, it'll be a foot, or near hand; or may be even mair!"

It was sweet and laughable to hear Alan eat his words up in the fear of some fresh quarrel. I could have laughed, had not my stitch caught me so hard; but if I had laughed, I think I must have wept too.

"Alan," cried I, "what makes ye so good to me? What makes ye care for such a thankless fellow?"

"'Deed, and I don't, know" said Alan. "For just precisely what I thought I liked about ye, was that ye never quarrelled:— and now I like ye better!"

CHAPTER XXV

IN BALQUHIDDER

At the door of the first house we came to, Alan knocked, which was of no very safe enterprise in such a part of the Highlands as the Braes of Balquhidder. No great clan held rule there; it was filled and disputed by small septs, and broken remnants, and what they call "chiefless folk," driven into the wild country about the springs of Forth and Teith by the advance of the Campbells. Here were Stewarts and Maclarens, which came to the same thing, for the Maclarens followed Alan's chief in war, and made but one clan with Appin. Here, too, were many of that old, proscribed, nameless, red-handed clan of the Macgregors. They had always been ill-considered, and now worse than ever, having credit with no side or party in the whole country of Scotland. Their chief, Macgregor of Macgregor, was in exile; the more immediate leader of that part of them about Balquhidder, James More, Rob Roy's eldest son, lay waiting his trial in Edinburgh Castle; they were in ill-blood with Highlander and Lowlander, with the Grahames, the Maclarens, and the Stewarts; and Alan, who took up the quarrel of any friend, however distant, was extremely wishful to avoid them.

Chance served us very well; for it was a household of Maclarens that we found, where Alan was not only welcome for his name's sake but known by reputation. Here then I was got to bed without delay, and a doctor fetched, who found me in a sorry plight. But whether because he was a very good doctor, or I a very young, strong man, I lay bedridden for no more than a week, and before a month I was able to take the road again with a good heart.

All this time Alan would not leave me though I often pressed him, and indeed his foolhardiness in staying was a common subject of outcry with the two or three friends that were let into the secret. He hid by day in a hole of the braes under a little wood; and at night, when the coast was clear, would come into the house to visit me. I need not say if I was pleased to see him; Mrs. Maclaren, our hostess, thought nothing good enough for such a guest; and as Duncan Dhu (which was the name of our host) had a pair of pipes in his house, and was much of a lover of music, this time of my recovery was quite a festival, and we commonly turned night into day.

The soldiers let us be; although once a party of two companies and some dragoons went by in the bottom of the valley, where I could see them through the window as I lay in bed. What was much more astonishing, no magistrate came near me, and there was no question put of whence I came or whither I was going; and in that time of excitement, I was as free of all inquiry as though I had lain in a desert. Yet my presence was known before I left to all the people in Balquhidder and the adjacent parts; many coming about the house on visits and these (after the custom of the country) spreading the news among their neighbours. The bills, too, had now been printed. There was one pinned near the foot of my bed, where I could read my own not very flattering portrait and, in larger characters, the amount of the blood money that had been set upon my life. Duncan Dhu and the rest that knew that I had come there in Alan's company, could have entertained no doubt of who I was; and many others must have had their guess. For though I had changed my clothes, I could not change my age or person; and Lowland boys of eighteen were not so rife in these parts of the world, and above all about that time, that they could fail to put one thing with another, and connect me with the bill. So it was, at least. Other folk keep a secret among two or three near friends, and somehow it leaks out; but among these clansmen, it is told to a whole countryside, and they will keep it for a century.

There was but one thing happened worth narrating; and that is the visit I had of Robin Oig, one of the sons of the notorious Rob Roy. He was sought upon all sides on a charge of carrying a young woman from Balfron and marrying her (as was alleged) by force; yet he stepped about Balquhidder like a gentleman in his own walled policy. It was he who had shot James Maclaren at the plough stilts, a quarrel never satisfied; yet he walked into the house of his blood enemies as a rider might into a public inn.

Duncan had time to pass me word of who it was; and we looked at one another in concern. You should understand, it was then close upon the time of Alan's coming; the two were little likely to agree; and yet if we sent word or sought to make a signal, it was sure to arouse suspicion in a man under so dark a cloud as the Macgregor.

He came in with a great show of civility, but like a man among inferiors; took off his bonnet to Mrs. Maclaren, but clapped it on his head again to speak to Duncan; and leaving thus set himself (as he would have thought) in a proper light, came to my bedside and bowed.

"I am given to know, sir," says he, "that your name is Balfour."

"They call me David Balfour," said I, "at your service."

"I would give ye my name in return, sir," he replied, "but it's one somewhat blown upon of late days; and it'll perhaps suffice if I tell ye that I am own brother to James More Drummond or Macgregor, of whom ye will scarce have failed to hear."

"No, sir," said I, a little alarmed; "nor yet of your father, Macgregor-Campbell." And I sat up and bowed in bed; for

I thought best to compliment him, in case he was proud of having had an outlaw to his father.

He bowed in return. "But what I am come to say, sir," he went on, "is this. In the year '45, my brother raised a part of the 'Gregara' and marched six companies to strike a stroke for the good side; and the surgeon that marched with our clan and cured my brother's leg when it was broken in the brush at Preston Pans, was a gentleman of the same name precisely as yourself. He was brother to Balfour of Baith; and if you are in any reasonable degree of nearness one of that gentleman's kin, I have come to put myself and my people at your command."

You are to remember that I knew no more of my descent than any cadger's dog; my uncle, to be sure, had prated of some of our high connections, but nothing to the present purpose; and there was nothing left me but that bitter disgrace of owning that I could not tell.

Robin told me shortly he was sorry he had put himself about, turned his back upon me without a sign of salutation, and as he went towards the door, I could hear him telling Duncan that I was "only some kinless loon that didn't know his own father." Angry as I was at these words, and ashamed of my own ignorance, I could scarce keep from smiling that a man who was under the lash of the law (and was indeed hanged some three years later) should be so nice as to the descent of his acquaintances.

Just in the door, he met Alan coming in; and the two drew back and looked at each other like strange dogs. They were neither of them big men, but they seemed fairly to swell out with pride. Each wore a sword, and by a movement of his haunch, thrust clear the hilt of it, so that it might be the more readily grasped and the blade drawn.

"Mr. Stewart, I am thinking," says Robin.

"Troth, Mr. Macgregor, it's not a name to be ashamed of," answered Alan.

"I did not know ye were in my country, sir," says Robin.

"It sticks in my mind that I am in the country of my friends the Maclarens," says Alan.

"That's a kittle point," returned the other. "There may be two words to say to that. But I think I will have heard that you are a man of your sword?"

"Unless ye were born deaf, Mr. Macgregor, ye will have heard a good deal more than that," says Alan. "I am not the only man that can draw steel in Appin; and when my kinsman and captain, Ardshiel, had a talk with a gentleman of your name, not so many years back, I could never hear that the Macgregor had the best of it."

"Do ye mean my father, sir?" says Robin.

"Well, I wouldnae wonder," said Alan. "The gentleman I have in my mind had the ill-taste to clap Campbell to his name."

"My father was an old man," returned Robin.

"The match was unequal. You and me would make a better pair, sir."

"I was thinking that," said Alan.

I was half out of bed, and Duncan had been hanging at the elbow of these fighting cocks, ready to intervene upon the least occasion. But when that word was uttered, it was a case of now or never; and Duncan, with something of a white face to be sure, thrust himself between.

"Gentlemen," said he, "I will have been thinking of a very different matter, whateffer. Here are my pipes, and here are you two gentlemen who are baith acclaimed pipers. It's an auld dispute which one of ye's the best. Here will be a braw chance to settle it."

"Why, sir," said Alan, still addressing Robin, from whom indeed he had not so much as shifted his eyes, nor yet Robin from him, "why, sir," says Alan, "I think I will have heard some sough of the sort. Have ye music, as folk say? Are ye a bit of a piper?"

"I can pipe like a Macrimmon!" cries Robin.

"And that is a very bold word," quoth Alan.

"I have made bolder words good before now," returned Robin, "and that against better adversaries."

"It is easy to try that," says Alan.

Duncan Dhu made haste to bring out the pair of pipes that was his principal possession, and to set before his guests a mutton-ham and a bottle of that drink which they call Athole brose, and which is made of old whiskey, strained honey and sweet cream, slowly beaten together in the right order and proportion. The two enemies were still on the very breach of a quarrel; but down they sat, one upon each side of the peat fire, with a mighty show of politeness. Maclaren pressed them to taste his mutton-ham and "the wife's brose," reminding them the wife was out of Athole and had a name far and wide for her skill in that confection. But Robin put aside these hospitalities as bad for the breath.

"I would have ye to remark, sir," said Alan, "that I havenae broken bread for near upon ten hours, which will be worse for the breath than any brose in Scotland."

"I will take no advantages, Mr. Stewart," replied Robin. "Eat and drink; I'll follow you."

Each ate a small portion of the ham and drank a glass of the brose to Mrs. Maclaren; and then after a great number of civilities, Robin took the pipes and played a little spring in a very ranting manner.

"Ay, ye can, blow" said Alan; and taking the instrument from his rival, he first played the same spring in a manner identical with Robin's; and then wandered into variations, which, as he went on, he decorated with a perfect flight of grace-notes, such as pipers love, and call the "warblers."

I had been pleased with Robin's playing, Alan's ravished me.

"That's no very bad, Mr. Stewart," said the rival, "but ye show a poor device in your warblers."

"Me!" cried Alan, the blood starting to his face. "I give ye the lie."

"Do ye own yourself beaten at the pipes, then," said Robin, "that ye seek to change them for the sword?"

"And that's very well said, Mr. Macgregor," returned Alan; "and in the meantime" (laying a strong accent on the word) "I take back the lie. I appeal to Duncan."

"Indeed, ye need appeal to naebody," said Robin. "Ye're a far better judge than any Maclaren in Balquhidder: for it's a God's truth that you're a very creditable piper for a Stewart. Hand me the pipes." Alan did as he asked; and Robin proceeded to imitate and correct some part of Alan's variations, which it seemed that he remembered perfectly.

"Ay, ye have music," said Alan, gloomily.

"And now be the judge yourself, Mr. Stewart," said Robin; and taking up the variations from the beginning, he worked them throughout to so new a purpose, with such ingenuity and sentiment, and with so odd a fancy and so quick a knack in the grace-notes, that I was amazed to hear him.

As for Alan, his face grew dark and hot, and he sat and gnawed his fingers, like a man under some deep affront. "Enough!" he cried. "Ye can blow the pipes—make the most of that." And he made as if to rise.

But Robin only held out his hand as if to ask for silence, and struck into the slow measure of a pibroch. It was a fine piece of music in itself, and nobly played; but it seems, besides, it was a piece peculiar to the Appin Stewarts and a chief favourite with Alan. The first notes were scarce out, before there came a change in his face; when the time quickened, he seemed to grow restless in his seat; and long before that piece was at an end, the last signs of his anger died from him, and he had no thought but for the music.

"Robin Oig," he said, when it was done, "ye are a great piper. I am not fit to blow in the same kingdom with ye. Body of me! ye have mair music in your sporran than I have in my head! And though it still sticks in my mind that I could maybe show ye another of it with the cold steel, I warn ye beforehand—it'll no be fair! It would go against my heart to haggle a man that can blow the pipes as you can!"

Thereupon that quarrel was made up; all night long the brose was going and the pipes changing hands; and the day had come pretty bright, and the three men were none the better for what they had been taking, before Robin as much as thought upon the road.

CHAPTER XXVI

END OF THE FLIGHT:
WE PASS THE FORTH

The month, as I have said, was not yet out, but it was already far through August, and beautiful warm weather, with every sign of an early and great harvest, when I was pronounced able for my journey. Our money was now run to so low an ebb that we must think first of all on speed; for if we came not soon to Mr. Rankeillor's, or if when we came there he should fail to help me, we must surely starve. In Alan's view, besides, the hunt must have now greatly slackened; and the line of the Forth and even Stirling Bridge, which is the main pass over that river, would be watched with little interest.

"It's a chief principle in military affairs," said he, "to go where ye are least expected. Forth is our trouble; ye ken the saying, 'Forth bridles the wild Hielandman.' Well, if we seek to creep round about the head of that river and come down by Kippen or Balfron, it's just precisely there that they'll be looking to lay hands on us. But if we stave on straight to the auld Brig of Stirling, I'll lay my sword they let us pass unchallenged."

The first night, accordingly, we pushed to the house of a Maclaren in Strathire, a friend of Duncan's, where we slept the twenty-first of the month, and whence we set forth again about the fall of night to make another easy stage. The twenty-second we lay in a heather bush on the hillside in Uam Var, within view of a herd of deer, the happiest ten hours of sleep in a fine, breathing sunshine and on bone-dry ground, that I have ever tasted. That night we struck Allan Water, and followed it down; and coming to the edge of the hills saw the whole Carse of Stirling underfoot, as flat as a pancake, with the town and castle on a hill in the midst of it, and the moon shining on the Links of Forth.

"Now," said Alan, "I kenna if ye care, but ye're in your own land again. We passed the Hieland Line in the first hour; and now if we could but pass yon crooked water, we might cast our bonnets in the air."

In Allan Water, near by where it falls into the Forth, we found a little sandy islet, overgrown with burdock, butterbur and the like low plants, that would just cover us if we lay flat. Here it was we made our camp, within plain view of Stirling Castle, whence we could hear the drums beat as some part of the garrison paraded. Shearers worked all day in a field on one side of the river, and we could hear the stones going on the hooks and the voices and even the words of the men talking. It behoved to lie close and keep silent. But the sand of the little isle was sun-warm, the green plants gave us shelter for our heads, we had food and drink in plenty; and to crown all, we were within sight of safety.

As soon as the shearers quit their work and the dusk began to fall, we waded ashore and struck for the Bridge of Stirling, keeping to the fields and under the field fences.

The bridge is close under the castle hill, an old, high, narrow bridge with pinnacles along the parapet; and you may conceive with how much interest I looked upon it, not only as a place famous in history, but as the very doors of salvation to Alan and myself. The moon was not yet up when we came there; a few lights shone along the front of the fortress, and lower down a few lighted windows in the town; but it was all mighty still, and there seemed to be no guard upon the passage.

I was for pushing straight across; but Alan was more wary.

"It looks unco' quiet," said he; "but for all that we'll lie down here cannily behind a dyke, and make sure."

So we lay for about a quarter of an hour, whiles whispering, whiles lying still and hearing nothing earthly but the washing of the water on the piers. At last there came by an old, hobbling woman with a crutch stick; who first stopped a little, close to where we lay, and bemoaned herself and the long way she had travelled; and then set forth again up the steep spring of the bridge. The woman was so little, and the night still so dark, that we soon lost sight of her; only heard the sound of her steps, and her stick, and a cough that she had by fits, draw slowly farther away.

"She's bound to be across now," I whispered.

"Na," said Alan, "her foot still sounds boss upon the bridge."

And just then—"Who goes?" cried a voice, and we heard the butt of a musket rattle on the stones. I must suppose the sentry had been sleeping, so that had we tried, we might have passed unseen; but he was awake now, and the chance forfeited.

"This'll never do," said Alan. "This'll never, never do for us, David."

And without another word, he began to crawl away through the fields; and a little after, being well out of eye-shot, got to his feet again, and struck along a road that led to the eastward. I could not conceive what he was doing; and indeed I was so sharply cut by the disappointment, that I was little likely to be pleased with anything. A moment back and I had seen myself knocking at Mr. Rankeillor's door to claim my inheritance, like a hero in a ballad; and here was I back again, a wandering, hunted blackguard, on the wrong side of Forth.

"Well?" said I.

"Well," said Alan, "what would ye have? They're none such fools as I took them for. We have still the Forth to pass, Davie—

weary fall the rains that fed and the hillsides that guided it!"

"And why go east?" said I.

"Ou, just upon the chance!" said he. "If we cannae pass the river, we'll have to see what we can do for the firth."

"There are fords upon the river, and none upon the firth," said I.

"To be sure there are fords, and a bridge forbye," quoth Alan; "and of what service, when they are watched?"

"Well," said I, "but a river can be swum."

"By them that have the skill of it," returned he; "but I have yet to hear that either you or me is much of a hand at that exercise; and for my own part, I swim like a stone."

"I'm not up to you in talking back, Alan," I said; "but I can see we're making bad worse. If it's hard to pass a river, it stands to reason it must be worse to pass a sea."

"But there's such a thing as a boat," says Alan, "or I'm the more deceived."

"Ay, and such a thing as money," says I. "But for us that have neither one nor other, they might just as well not have been invented."

"Ye think so?" said Alan.

"I do that," said I.

"David," says he, "ye're a man of small invention and less faith. But let me set my wits upon the hone, and if I cannae beg, borrow, nor yet steal a boat, I'll make one!"

"I think I see ye!" said I. "And what's more than all that: if ye pass a bridge, it can tell no tales; but if we pass the firth, there's the boat on the wrong side—somebody must have brought it— the country-side will all be in a bizz—-"

"Man!" cried Alan, "if I make a boat, I'll make a body to take it back again! So deave me with no more of your nonsense, but walk (for that's what you've got to do)—and let Alan think for ye."

All night, then, we walked through the north side of the

Carse under the high line of the Ochil mountains; and by Alloa and Clackmannan and Culross, all of which we avoided: and about ten in the morning, mighty hungry and tired, came to the little clachan of Limekilns. This is a place that sits near in by the water-side, and looks across the Hope to the town of the Queensferry. Smoke went up from both of these, and from other villages and farms upon all hands. The fields were being reaped; two ships lay anchored, and boats were coming and going on the Hope. It was altogether a right pleasant sight to me; and I could not take my fill of gazing at these comfortable, green, cultivated hills and the busy people both of the field and sea.

For all that, there was Mr. Rankeillor's house on the south shore, where I had no doubt wealth awaited me; and here was I upon the north, clad in poor enough attire of an outlandish fashion, with three silver shillings left to me of all my fortune, a price set upon my head, and an outlawed man for my sole company.

"O, Alan!" said I, "to think of it! Over there, there's all that heart could want waiting me; and the birds go over, and the boats go over—all that please can go, but just me only! O, man, but it's a heart-break!"

In Limekilns we entered a small change-house, which we only knew to be a public by the wand over the door, and bought some bread and cheese from a good-looking lass that was the servant. This we carried with us in a bundle, meaning to sit and eat it in a bush of wood on the sea-shore, that we saw some third part of a mile in front. As we went, I kept looking across the water and sighing to myself; and though I took no heed of it, Alan had fallen into a muse. At last he stopped in the way.

"Did ye take heed of the lass we bought this of?" says he, tapping on the bread and cheese.

"To be sure," said I, "and a bonny lass she was."

"Ye thought that?" cries he. "Man, David, that's good news."

"In the name of all that's wonderful, why so?" says I. "What good can that do?"

"Well," said Alan, with one of his droll looks, "I was rather in hopes it would maybe get us that boat."

"If it were the other way about, it would be liker it," said I.

"That's all that you ken, ye see," said Alan. "I don't want the lass to fall in love with ye, I want her to be sorry for ye, David; to which end there is no manner of need that she should take you for a beauty. Let me see" (looking me curiously over). "I wish ye were a wee thing paler; but apart from that ye'll do fine for my purpose—ye have a fine, hang-dog, rag-and-tatter, clappermaclaw kind of a look to ye, as if ye had stolen the coat from a potato-bogle. Come; right about, and back to the change-house for that boat of ours."

I followed him, laughing.

"David Balfour," said he, "ye're a very funny gentleman by your way of it, and this is a very funny employ for ye, no doubt. For all that, if ye have any affection for my neck (to say nothing of your own) ye will perhaps be kind enough to take this matter responsibly. I am going to do a bit of play-acting, the bottom ground of which is just exactly as serious as the gallows for the pair of us. So bear it, if ye please, in mind, and conduct yourself according."

"Well, well," said I, "have it as you will."

As we got near the clachan, he made me take his arm and hang upon it like one almost helpless with weariness; and by the time he pushed open the change-house door, he seemed to be half carrying me. The maid appeared surprised (as well she might be) at our speedy return; but Alan had no words to spare for her in explanation, helped me to a chair, called for a tass of brandy with which he fed me in little sips, and then breaking up the bread and cheese helped me to eat it like a nursery-lass; the whole with that grave, concerned, affectionate countenance, that might have imposed upon a judge. It was small wonder if the maid were taken with the picture we presented, of a poor, sick, overwrought lad and his most tender comrade. She drew quite near, and stood leaning with her back on the next table.

"What's like wrong with him?" said she at last.

Alan turned upon her, to my great wonder, with a kind of fury. "Wrong?" cries he. "He's walked more hundreds of miles than he has hairs upon his chin, and slept oftener in wet heather than dry sheets. Wrong, quo' she! Wrong enough, I would think! Wrong, indeed!" and he kept grumbling to himself as he fed me, like a man ill-pleased.

"He's young for the like of that," said the maid.

"Ower young," said Alan, with his back to her.

"He would be better riding," says she.

"And where could I get a horse to him?" cried Alan, turning on her with the same appearance of fury. "Would ye have me steal?"

I thought this roughness would have sent her off in dudgeon, as indeed it closed her mouth for the time. But my companion knew very well what he was doing; and for as simple as he was in some things of life, had a great fund of roguishness in such affairs as these.

"Ye neednae tell me," she said at last—"ye're gentry."

"Well," said Alan, softened a little (I believe against his will) by this artless comment, "and suppose we were? Did ever you hear that gentrice put money in folk's pockets?"

She sighed at this, as if she were herself some disinherited great lady. "No," says she, "that's true indeed."

I was all this while chafing at the part I played, and sitting tongue-tied between shame and merriment; but somehow at this I could hold in no longer, and bade Alan let me be, for I was better already. My voice stuck in my throat, for I ever hated to take part in lies; but my very embarrassment helped on the plot, for the lass no doubt set down my husky voice to sickness and fatigue.

"Has he nae friends?" said she, in a tearful voice.

"That has he so!" cried Alan, "if we could but win to them!—friends and rich friends, beds to lie in, food to eat, doctors to see to him—and here he must tramp in the dubs and sleep in the heather like a beggarman."

"And why that?" says the lass.

"My dear," said Alan, "I cannae very safely say; but I'll tell ye what I'll do instead," says he, "I'll whistle ye a bit tune." And with that he leaned pretty far over the table, and in a mere breath of a whistle, but with a wonderful pretty sentiment, gave her a few bars of "Charlie is my darling."

"Wheesht," says she, and looked over her shoulder to the door.

"That's it," said Alan.

"And him so young!" cries the lass.

"He's old enough to—" and Alan struck his forefinger on the back part of his neck, meaning that I was old enough to lose my head.

"It would be a black shame," she cried, flushing high.

"It's what will be, though," said Alan, "unless we manage the better."

At this the lass turned and ran out of that part of the house, leaving us alone together. Alan in high good humour at the furthering of his schemes, and I in bitter dudgeon at being called a Jacobite and treated like a child.

"Alan," I cried, "I can stand no more of this."

"Ye'll have to sit it then, Davie," said he. "For if ye upset the pot now, ye may scrape your own life out of the fire, but Alan Breck is a dead man."

This was so true that I could only groan; and even my groan served Alan's purpose, for it was overheard by the lass as she came flying in again with a dish of white puddings and a bottle of strong ale.

"Poor lamb!" says she, and had no sooner set the meat before us, than she touched me on the shoulder with a little friendly touch, as much as to bid me cheer up. Then she told us to fall to, and there would be no more to pay; for the inn was her own, or at least her father's, and he was gone for the day to Pittencrieff. We waited for no second bidding, for bread and cheese is but cold comfort and the puddings smelt excellently well; and while we sat and ate, she took up that same place by the next table, looking on, and thinking, and frowning to herself, and drawing the string of her apron through her hand.

"I'm thinking ye have rather a long tongue," she said at last to Alan.

"Ay" said Alan; "but ye see I ken the folk I speak to."

"I would never betray ye," said she, "if ye mean that."

"No," said he, "ye're not that kind. But I'll tell ye what ye would do, ye would help."

"I couldnae," said she, shaking her head. "Na, I couldnae."

"No," said he, "but if ye could?"

She answered him nothing.

"Look here, my lass," said Alan, "there are boats in the Kingdom of Fife, for I saw two (no less) upon the beach, as I came in by your town's end. Now if we could have the use of a boat to pass under cloud of night into Lothian, and some secret, decent kind of a man to bring that boat back again and keep his counsel, there would be two souls saved— mine to all likelihood—his to a dead surety. If we lack that boat, we have but three shillings left in this wide world; and where to go, and how to do, and what other place there is for us except the chains of a gibbet—I give you my naked word, I kenna! Shall we go wanting, lassie? Are ye to lie in your warm bed and think upon us, when the wind gowls in the chimney and the rain tirls on the roof? Are ye to eat your meat by the cheeks of a red fire, and think upon this poor sick lad of mine, biting his finger ends on a blae muir for cauld and hunger? Sick or sound, he must aye be moving; with the death grapple at his throat he must aye be trailing in the rain on the lang roads; and when he gants his last on a rickle of cauld stanes, there will be nae friends near him but only me and God."

At this appeal, I could see the lass was in great trouble of mind, being tempted to help us, and yet in some fear she might be helping malefactors; and so now I determined to step in myself and to allay her scruples with a portion of the truth.

"Did ever you, hear" said I, "of Mr. Rankeillor of the Ferry?"

"Rankeillor the writer?" said she. "I daur say that!"

"Well," said I, "it's to his door that I am bound, so you may judge by that if I am an ill-doer; and I will tell you more, that though I am indeed, by a dreadful error, in some peril of my life, King George has no truer friend in all Scotland than myself."

Her face cleared up mightily at this, although Alan's darkened.

"That's more than I would ask," said she. "Mr. Rankeillor is a kennt man." And she bade us finish our meat, get clear of the clachan as soon as might be, and lie close in the bit wood on the sea-beach. "And ye can trust me," says she, "I'll find some means to put you over."

At this we waited for no more, but shook hands with her upon the bargain, made short work of the puddings, and set forth again from Limekilns as far as to the wood. It was a small piece of perhaps a score of elders and hawthorns and a few young ashes, not thick enough to veil us from passersby upon the road or beach. Here we must lie, however, making the best of the brave warm weather and the good hopes we now had of a deliverance, and planing more particularly what remained for us to do.

We had but one trouble all day; when a strolling piper came and sat in the same wood with us; a red-nosed, bleareyed, drunken dog, with a great bottle of whisky in his pocket, and a long story of wrongs that had been done him by all sorts of persons, from the Lord President of the Court of Session, who had denied him justice, down to the Bailies of Inverkeithing who had given him more of it than he desired. It was impossible but he should conceive some suspicion of two men lying all day concealed in a thicket and having no business to allege. As long as he stayed there he kept us in hot water with prying questions; and after he was gone, as he was a man not very likely to hold his tongue, we were in the greater impatience to be gone ourselves.

The day came to an end with the same brightness; the night fell quiet and clear; lights came out in houses and hamlets and then, one after another, began to be put out; but it was past eleven, and we were long since strangely tortured with anxieties, before we heard the grinding of oars upon the rowing-pins. At that, we looked out and saw the lass herself coming rowing to us in a boat. She had trusted no one with our affairs, not even her sweetheart, if she had one; but as soon as her father was asleep, had left the house by a window, stolen a neighbour's boat, and come to our assistance single-handed.

I was abashed how to find expression for my thanks; but she was no less abashed at the thought of hearing them; begged us to lose no time and to hold our peace, saying (very properly) that the heart of our matter was in haste and silence; and so, what with one thing and another, she had set us on the Lothian shore not far from Carriden, had shaken hands with us, and was out again at sea and rowing for Limekilns, before there was one word said either of her service or our gratitude.

Even after she was gone, we had nothing to say, as indeed nothing was enough for such a kindness. Only Alan stood a great while upon the shore shaking his head.

"It is a very fine lass," he said at last. "David, it is a very fine lass." And a matter of an hour later, as we were lying in a den on the sea-shore and I had been already dozing, he broke out again in commendations of her character. For my part, I could say nothing, she was so simple a creature that my heart smote me both with remorse and fear: remorse because we had traded upon her ignorance; and fear lest we should have anyway involved her in the dangers of our situation.

CHAPTER XXVII

I COME TO MR. RANKEILLOR

The next day it was agreed that Alan should fend for himself till sunset; but as soon as it began to grow dark, he should lie in the fields by the roadside near to Newhalls, and stir for naught until he heard me whistling. At first I proposed I should give him for a signal the "Bonnie House of Airlie," which was a favourite of mine; but he objected that as the piece was very commonly known, any ploughman might whistle it by accident; and taught me instead a little fragment of a Highland air, which has run in my head from that day to this, and will likely run in my head when I lie dying. Every time it comes to me, it takes me off to that last day of my uncertainty, with Alan sitting up in the bottom of the den, whistling and beating the measure with a finger, and the grey of the dawn coming on his face.

I was in the long street of Queensferry before the sun was up. It was a fairly built burgh, the houses of good stone, many slated; the town-hall not so fine, I thought, as that of Peebles, nor yet the street so noble; but take it altogether, it put me to shame for my foul tatters.

As the morning went on, and the fires began to be kindled, and the windows to open, and the people to appear out of the houses, my concern and despondency grew ever the blacker. I saw now that I had no grounds to stand upon; and no clear proof of my rights, nor so much as of my own identity. If it was all a bubble, I was indeed sorely cheated and left in a sore pass.

Even if things were as I conceived, it would in all likelihood take time to establish my contentions; and what time had I to spare with less than three shillings in my pocket, and a condemned, hunted man upon my hands to ship out of the country? Truly, if my hope broke with me, it might come to the gallows yet for both of us. And as I continued to walk up and down, and saw people looking askance at me upon the street or out of windows, and nudging or speaking one to another with smiles, I began to take a fresh apprehension: that it might be no easy matter even to come to speech of the lawyer, far less to convince him of my story.

For the life of me I could not muster up the courage to address any of these reputable burghers; I thought shame even to speak with them in such a pickle of rags and dirt; and if I had asked for the house of such a man as Mr. Rankeillor, I suppose they would have burst out laughing in my face. So I went up and down, and through the street, and down to the harbour-side, like a dog that has lost its master, with a strange gnawing in my inwards, and every now and then a movement of despair. It grew to be high day at last, perhaps nine in the forenoon; and I was worn with these wanderings, and chanced to have stopped in front of a very good house on the landward side, a house with beautiful, clear glass windows, flowering knots upon the sills, the walls new-harled and a chase-dog sitting yawning on the step like one that was at home. Well, I was even envying this dumb brute, when the door fell open and there issued forth a shrewd, ruddy, kindly, consequential man in a well-powdered wig and spectacles. I was in such a plight that no one set eyes on me once, but he looked at me again; and this gentleman, as it proved, was so much struck with my poor appearance that he came straight up to me and asked me what I did.

I told him I was come to the Queensferry on business, and taking heart of grace, asked him to direct me to the house of

Mr. Rankeillor.

"Why," said he, "that is his house that I have just come out of; and for a rather singular chance, I am that very man."

"Then, sir," said I, "I have to beg the favour of an interview."

"I do not know your name," said he, "nor yet your face."

"My name is David Balfour," said I.

"David Balfour?" he repeated, in rather a high tone, like one surprised. "And where have you come from, Mr. David Balfour?" he asked, looking me pretty drily in the face.

"I have come from a great many strange places, sir," said I; "but I think it would be as well to tell you where and how in a more private manner."

He seemed to muse awhile, holding his lip in his hand, and looking now at me and now upon the causeway of the street.

"Yes," says he, "that will be the best, no doubt." And he led me back with him into his house, cried out to some one whom I could not see that he would be engaged all morning, and brought me into a little dusty chamber full of books and documents. Here he sate down, and bade me be seated; though I thought he looked a little ruefully from his clean chair to my muddy rags. "And now," says he, "if you have any business, pray be brief and come swiftly to the point. *Nec gemino bellum Trojanum orditur ab ovo*—do you understand that?" says he, with a keen look.

"I will even do as Horace says, sir," I answered, smiling, "and carry you in *medias res*." He nodded as if he was well pleased, and indeed his scrap of Latin had been set to test me. For all that, and though I was somewhat encouraged, the blood came in my face when I added: "I have reason to believe myself some rights on the estate of Shaws."

He got a paper book out of a drawer and set it before him open. "Well?" said he.

But I had shot my bolt and sat speechless.

"Come, come, Mr. Balfour," said he, "you must continue.

Where were you born?"

"In Essendean, sir," said I, "the year 1733, the 12th of March."

He seemed to follow this statement in his paper book; but what that meant I knew not. "Your father and mother?" said he.

"My father was Alexander Balfour, schoolmaster of that place," said I, "and my mother Grace Pitarrow; I think her people were from Angus."

"Have you any papers proving your identity?" asked Mr. Rankeillor.

"No, sir," said I, "but they are in the hands of Mr. Campbell, the minister, and could be readily produced. Mr. Campbell, too, would give me his word; and for that matter, I do not think my uncle would deny me."

"Meaning Mr. Ebenezer Balfour?" says he.

"The same," said I.

"Whom you have seen?" he asked.

"By whom I was received into his own house," I answered.

"Did you ever meet a man of the name of Hoseason?" asked Mr. Rankeillor.

"I did so, sir, for my sins," said I; "for it was by his means and the procurement of my uncle, that I was kidnapped within sight of this town, carried to sea, suffered shipwreck and a hundred other hardships, and stand before you to-day in this poor accoutrement."

"You say you were shipwrecked," said Rankeillor; "where was that?"

"Off the south end of the Isle of Mull," said I. "The name of the isle on which I was cast up is the Island Earraid."

"Ah!" says he, smiling, "you are deeper than me in the geography. But so far, I may tell you, this agrees pretty exactly with other informations that I hold. But you say you were kidnapped; in what sense?"

"In the plain meaning of the word, sir," said I. "I was on my way to your house, when I was trepanned on board the brig, cruelly struck down, thrown below, and knew no more of anything till we were far at sea. I was destined for the plantations; a fate that, in God's providence, I have escaped."

"The brig was lost on June the 27th," says he, looking in his book, "and we are now at August the 24th. Here is a considerable hiatus, Mr. Balfour, of near upon two months. It has already caused a vast amount of trouble to your friends; and I own I shall not be very well contented until it is set right."

"Indeed, sir," said I, "these months are very easily filled up; but yet before I told my story, I would be glad to know that I was talking to a friend."

"This is to argue in a circle," said the lawyer. "I cannot be convinced till I have heard you. I cannot be your friend till I am properly informed. If you were more trustful, it would better befit your time of life. And you know, Mr. Balfour, we have a proverb in the country that evil-doers are aye evil-dreaders."

"You are not to forget, sir," said I, "that I have already suffered by my trustfulness; and was shipped off to be a slave by the very man that (if I rightly understand) is your employer?"

All this while I had been gaining ground with Mr. Rankeillor, and in proportion as I gained ground, gaining confidence. But at this sally, which I made with something of a smile myself, he fairly laughed aloud.

"No, no," said he, "it is not so bad as that. *Fui, non sum*. I was indeed your uncle's man of business; but while you (*imberbis juvenis custode remoto*) were gallivanting in the west, a good deal of water has run under the bridges; and if your ears did not sing, it was not for lack of being talked about. On the very day of your sea disaster, Mr. Campbell stalked into my office, demanding you from all the winds. I had never heard of your existence; but I had known your father; and from matters in my competence (to be touched upon hereafter) I was disposed to fear the worst. Mr. Ebenezer admitted having seen you; declared (what seemed improbable) that he had given you considerable sums; and that you had started for the continent of Europe, intending to fulfil your education, which was probable and praiseworthy. Interrogated how you had come to send no word to Mr. Campbell, he deponed that you had expressed a great desire to break with your past life. Further interrogated where you now were, protested ignorance, but believed you were in Leyden. That is a close sum of his replies. I am not exactly sure that any one believed him," continued Mr. Rankeillor with a smile; "and in particular he so much disrelished me expressions of mine that (in a word) he showed me to the door. We were then at a full stand; for whatever shrewd suspicions we might entertain, we had no shadow of probation. In the very article, comes Captain Hoseason with the story of your drowning; whereupon all fell through; with no consequences but concern to Mr. Campbell, injury to my pocket, and another blot upon your uncle's character, which could very ill afford it. And now, Mr. Balfour," said he, "you understand the whole process of these matters, and can judge for yourself to what extent I may be trusted."

Indeed he was more pedantic than I can represent him, and placed more scraps of Latin in his speech; but it was all uttered with a fine geniality of eye and manner which went far to conquer my distrust. Moreover, I could see he now treated me as if I was myself beyond a doubt; so that first point of my identity seemed fully granted.

"Sir," said I, "if I tell you my story, I must commit a friend's life to your discretion. Pass me your word it shall be sacred; and for what touches myself, I will ask no better guarantee than just your face."

He passed me his word very seriously. "But," said he, "these are rather alarming prolocutions; and if there are in your story any little jostles to the law, I would beg you to bear in mind that

I am a lawyer, and pass lightly."

Thereupon I told him my story from the first, he listening with his spectacles thrust up and his eyes closed, so that I sometimes feared he was asleep. But no such matter! he heard every word (as I found afterward) with such quickness of hearing and precision of memory as often surprised me. Even strange outlandish Gaelic names, heard for that time only, he remembered and would remind me of, years after. Yet when I called Alan Breck in full, we had an odd scene. The name of Alan had of course rung through Scotland, with the news of the Appin murder and the offer of the reward; and it had no sooner escaped me than the lawyer moved in his seat and opened his eyes.

"I would name no unnecessary names, Mr. Balfour," said he; "above all of Highlanders, many of whom are obnoxious to the law."

"Well, it might have been better not," said I, "but since I have let it slip, I may as well continue."

"Not at all," said Mr. Rankeillor. "I am somewhat dull of hearing, as you may have remarked; and I am far from sure I caught the name exactly. We will call your friend, if you please, Mr. Thomson—that there may be no reflections. And in future, I would take some such way with any Highlander that you may have to mention—dead or alive."

By this, I saw he must have heard the name all too clearly, and had already guessed I might be coming to the murder. If he chose to play this part of ignorance, it was no matter of mine; so I smiled, said it was no very Highland-sounding name, and consented. Through all the rest of my story Alan was Mr. Thomson; which amused me the more, as it was a piece of policy after his own heart. James Stewart, in like manner, was mentioned under the style of Mr. Thomson's kinsman; Colin Campbell passed as a Mr. Glen; and to Cluny, when I came to that part of my tale, I gave the name of "Mr.

Jameson, a Highland chief." It was truly the most open farce, and I wondered that the lawyer should care to keep it up; but, after all, it was quite in the taste of that age, when there were two parties in the state, and quiet persons, with no very high opinions of their own, sought out every cranny to avoid offence to either.

"Well, well," said the lawyer, when I had quite done, "this is a great epic, a great Odyssey of yours. You must tell it, sir, in a sound Latinity when your scholarship is riper; or in English if you please, though for my part I prefer the stronger tongue. You have rolled much; quae regio in terris—what parish in Scotland (to make a homely translation) has not been filled with your wanderings? You have shown, besides, a singular aptitude for getting into false positions; and, yes, upon the whole, for behaving well in them. This Mr. Thomson seems to me a gentleman of some choice qualities, though perhaps a trifle bloody-minded. It would please me none the worse, if (with all his merits) he were soused in the North Sea, for the man, Mr. David, is a sore embarrassment. But you are doubtless quite right to adhere to him; indubitably, he adhered to you. It comes—we may say—he was your true companion; nor less paribus curis vestigia figit, for I dare say you would both take an orra thought upon the gallows. Well, well, these days are fortunately, by; and I think (speaking humanly) that you are near the end of your troubles."

As he thus moralised on my adventures, he looked upon me with so much humour and benignity that I could scarce contain my satisfaction. I had been so long wandering with lawless people, and making my bed upon the hills and under the bare sky, that to sit once more in a clean, covered house, and to talk amicably with a gentleman in broadcloth, seemed mighty elevations. Even as I thought so, my eye fell on my unseemly tatters, and I was once more plunged in confusion. But the lawyer saw and understood me. He rose, called over the stair to lay another plate, for Mr. Balfour would stay to dinner, and led me into a bedroom in the upper part of the house. Here he set before me water and soap, and a comb; and laid out some clothes that belonged to his son; and here, with another apposite tag, he left me to my toilet.

CHAPTER XXVIII

I GO IN QUEST OF MY INHERITANCE

I made what change I could in my appearance; and blithe was I to look in the glass and find the beggarman a thing of the past, and David Balfour come to life again. And yet I was ashamed of the change too, and, above all, of the borrowed clothes. When I had done, Mr. Rankeillor caught me on the stair, made me his compliments, and had me again into the cabinet.

"Sit ye down, Mr. David," said he, "and now that you are looking a little more like yourself, let me see if I can find you any news. You will be wondering, no doubt, about your father and your uncle? To be sure it is a singular tale; and the explanation is one that I blush to have to offer you. For," says he, really with embarrassment, "the matter hinges on a love affair."

"Truly," said I, "I cannot very well join that notion with my uncle."

"But your uncle, Mr. David, was not always old," replied the lawyer, "and what may perhaps surprise you more, not always ugly. He had a fine, gallant air; people stood in their doors to look after him, as he went by upon a mettle horse. I have seen it with these eyes, and I ingenuously confess, not altogether without envy; for I was a plain lad myself and a plain man's son; and in those days it was a case of *Odi te, qui bellus es, Sabelle.*"

"It sounds like a dream," said I.

"Ay, ay," said the lawyer, "that is how it is with youth and age. Nor was that all, but he had a spirit of his own that seemed to promise great things in the future. In 1715, what must he do but run away to join the rebels? It was your father that pursued him, found him in a ditch, and brought him back *multum gementem*; to the mirth of the whole country. However, *majora canamus*—the two lads fell in love, and that with the same lady. Mr. Ebenezer, who was the admired and the beloved, and the spoiled one, made, no doubt, mighty certain of the victory; and when he found he had deceived himself, screamed like a peacock. The whole country heard of it; now he lay sick at home, with his silly family standing round the bed in tears; now he rode from public-house to public-house, and shouted his sorrows into the lug of Tom, Dick, and Harry. Your father, Mr. David, was a kind gentleman; but he was weak, dolefully weak; took all this folly with a long countenance; and one day—by your leave!—resigned the lady. She was no such fool, however; it's from her you must inherit your excellent good sense; and she refused to be bandied from one to another. Both got upon their knees to her; and the upshot of the matter for that while was that she showed both of them the door. That was in August; dear me! the same year I came from college. The scene must have been highly farcical."

I thought myself it was a silly business, but I could not forget my father had a hand in it. "Surely, sir, it had some note of tragedy," said I.

"Why, no, sir, not at all," returned the lawyer. "For tragedy implies some ponderable matter in dispute, some *dignus vindice nodus*; and this piece of work was all about the petulance of a young ass that had been spoiled, and wanted nothing so much as to be tied up and soundly belted. However, that was not your father's view; and the end of it was, that from concession to concession on your father's part, and from one height to another of squalling, sentimental selfishness upon your uncle's, they came at last to drive a sort of bargain, from whose ill results you have recently been smarting. The one man took the lady, the other the estate. Now, Mr. David, they talk a great deal of charity and generosity; but in this disputable state of life, I often think the happiest consequences seem to flow when a gentleman consults his lawyer, and takes all the law allows him. Anyhow, this piece of Quixotry on your father's part, as it was unjust in itself, has brought forth a monstrous family of injustices. Your father and mother lived and died poor folk; you were poorly reared; and in the meanwhile, what a time it has been for the tenants on the estate of Shaws! And I might add (if it was a matter I cared much about) what a time for Mr. Ebenezer!"

"And yet that is certainly the strangest part of all," said I, "that a man's nature should thus change."

"True," said Mr. Rankeillor. "And yet I imagine it was natural enough. He could not think that he had played a handsome part. Those who knew the story gave him the cold shoulder; those who knew it not, seeing one brother disappear, and the other succeed in the estate, raised a cry of murder; so that upon all sides he found himself evited. Money was all he got by his bargain; well, he came to think the more of money. He was selfish when he was young, he is selfish now that he is old; and the latter end of all these pretty manners and fine feelings you have seen for yourself."

"Well, sir," said I, "and in all this, what is my position?"

"The estate is yours beyond a doubt," replied the lawyer. "It matters nothing what your father signed, you are the heir of entail. But your uncle is a man to fight the indefensible; and it would be likely your identity that he would call in question. A lawsuit is always expensive, and a family lawsuit always scandalous; besides which, if any of your doings with your friend Mr. Thomson were to come out, we might find that we had burned our fingers. The kidnapping, to be sure, would be a court card upon our side, if we could only prove it. But it may be difficult to prove; and my advice (upon the whole) is to make a very easy bargain with your uncle, perhaps even leaving him at Shaws where he has taken root for a quarter of a century, and contenting yourself in the meanwhile with a fair provision."

I told him I was very willing to be easy, and that to carry family concerns before the public was a step from which I was naturally much averse. In the meantime (thinking to myself) I began to see the outlines of that scheme on which we afterwards acted.

"The great affair," I asked, "is to bring home to him the kidnapping?"

"Surely," said Mr. Rankeillor, "and if possible, out of court. For mark you here, Mr. David: we could no doubt find some men of the Covenant who would swear to your reclusion; but once they were in the box, we could no longer check their testimony, and some word of your friend Mr. Thomson must certainly crop out. Which (from what you have let fall) I cannot think to be desirable."

"Well, sir," said I, "here is my way of it." And I opened my plot to him.

"But this would seem to involve my meeting the man Thomson?" says he, when I had done.

"I think so, indeed, sir," said I.

"Dear doctor!" cries he, rubbing his brow. "Dear doctor! No, Mr. David, I am afraid your scheme is inadmissible. I say nothing against your friend, Mr. Thomson: I know nothing against him; and if I did—mark this, Mr. David!—it would be my duty to lay hands on him. Now I put it to you: is it wise to meet? He may have matters to his charge. He may not have told you all. His name may not be even Thomson!" cries the lawyer, twinkling; "for some of these fellows will pick up names by the roadside as another would gather haws."

"You must be the judge, sir," said I.

But it was clear my plan had taken hold upon his fancy, for he kept musing to himself till we were called to dinner and the company of Mrs. Rankeillor; and that lady had scarce left us again to ourselves and a bottle of wine, ere he was back harping on my proposal. When and where was I to meet my friend Mr. Thomson; was I sure of Mr. T.'s discretion; supposing we could catch the old fox tripping, would I consent to such and such a term of an agreement—these and the like questions he kept asking at long intervals, while he thoughtfully rolled his wine upon his tongue. When I had answered all of them, seemingly to his contentment, he fell into a still deeper muse, even the claret being now forgotten. Then he got a sheet of paper and a pencil, and set to work writing and weighing every word; and at last touched a bell and had his clerk into the chamber.

"Torrance," said he, "I must have this written out fair against to-night; and when it is done, you will be so kind as put on your hat and be ready to come along with this gentleman and me, for you will probably be wanted as a witness."

"What, sir," cried I, as soon as the clerk was gone, "are you to venture it?"

"Why, so it would appear," says he, filling his glass. "But let us speak no more of business. The very sight of Torrance brings in my head a little droll matter of some years ago, when I had made a tryst with the poor oaf at the cross of Edinburgh. Each had gone his proper errand; and when it came four o'clock, Torrance had been taking a glass and did not know his master, and I, who had forgot my spectacles, was so blind without them, that I give you my word I did not know my own clerk." And thereupon he laughed heartily.

I said it was an odd chance, and smiled out of politeness; but what held me all the afternoon in wonder, he kept returning and dwelling on this story, and telling it again with fresh details and laughter; so that I began at last to be quite put out of countenance and feel ashamed for my friend's folly.

Towards the time I had appointed with Alan, we set out from the house, Mr. Rankeillor and I arm in arm, and Torrance following behind with the deed in his pocket and a covered basket in his hand. All through the town, the lawyer was bowing right and left, and continually being button-holed by gentlemen on matters of burgh or private business; and I could see he was one greatly looked up to in the county. At last we were clear of the houses, and began to go along the side of the haven and towards the Hawes Inn and the Ferry pier, the scene of my misfortune. I could not look upon the place without emotion, recalling how many that had been there with me that day were now no more: Ransome taken, I could hope, from the evil to come; Shuan passed where I dared not follow him; and the poor souls that had gone down with the brig in her last plunge. All these, and the brig herself, I had outlived; and come through these hardships and fearful perils without scath. My only thought should have been of gratitude; and yet I could not behold the place without sorrow for others and a chill of recollected fear.

I was so thinking when, upon a sudden, Mr. Rankeillor cried out, clapped his hand to his pockets, and began to laugh.

"Why," he cries, "if this be not a farcical adventure! After all that I said, I have forgot my glasses!"

At that, of course, I understood the purpose of his anecdote, and knew that if he had left his spectacles at home, it had been done on purpose, so that he might have the benefit of Alan's help without the awkwardness of recognising him. And indeed it was well thought upon; for now (suppose things to go the very worst) how could Rankeillor swear to my friend's identity, or how be made to bear damaging evidence against myself? For all that, he had been a long while of finding out his want, and had spoken to and recognised a good few persons as we came through the town; and I had little doubt myself that he saw reasonably well.

As soon as we were past the Hawes (where I recognised the landlord smoking his pipe in the door, and was amazed to see him look no older) Mr. Rankeillor changed the order of march, walking behind with Torrance and sending me forward in the manner of a scout. I went up the hill, whistling from time to time my Gaelic air; and at length I had the pleasure to hear it answered and to see Alan rise from behind a bush. He was somewhat dashed in spirits, having passed a long day alone skulking in the county, and made but a poor meal in an alehouse near Dundas. But at the mere sight of my clothes, he began to brighten up; and as soon as I had told him in what a forward state our matters were and the part I looked to him to play in what remained, he sprang into a new man.

"And that is a very good notion of yours," says he; "and I dare to say that you could lay your hands upon no better man to put it through than Alan Breck. It is not a thing (mark ye) that any one could do, but takes a gentleman of penetration. But it sticks in my head your lawyer-man will be somewhat wearying to see me," says Alan.

Accordingly I cried and waved on Mr. Rankeillor, who came up alone and was presented to my friend, Mr. Thomson.

"Mr. Thomson, I am pleased to meet you," said he. "But I have forgotten my glasses; and our friend, Mr. David here" (clapping me on the shoulder), "will tell you that I am little better than blind, and that you must not be surprised if I pass you by to-morrow."

This he said, thinking that Alan would be pleased; but the Highlandman's vanity was ready to startle at a less matter than that.

"Why, sir," says he, stiffly, "I would say it mattered the less as we are met here for a particular end, to see justice done to Mr. Balfour; and by what I can see, not very likely to have much else in common. But I accept your apology, which was a very proper one to make."

"And that is more than I could look for, Mr. Thomson," said Rankeillor, heartily. "And now as you and I are the chief actors in this enterprise, I think we should come into a nice agreement; to which end, I propose that you should lend me your arm, for (what with the dusk and the want of my glasses) I am not very clear as to the path; and as for you, Mr. David, you will find Torrance a pleasant kind of body to speak with. Only let me remind you, it's quite needless he should hear more of your adventures or those of—ahem—Mr. Thomson."

Accordingly these two went on ahead in very close talk, and Torrance and I brought up the rear.

Night was quite come when we came in view of the house of Shaws. Ten had been gone some time; it was dark and mild, with a pleasant, rustling wind in the south-west that covered the sound of our approach; and as we drew near we saw no glimmer of light in any portion of the building. It seemed my uncle was already in bed, which was indeed the best thing for our arrangements. We made our last whispered consultations some fifty yards away; and then the lawyer and Torrance and I crept quietly up and crouched down beside the corner of the house; and as soon as we were in our places, Alan strode to the door without concealment and began to knock.

CHAPTER XXIX

I COME INTO MY KINGDOM

For some time Alan volleyed upon the door, and his knocking only roused the echoes of the house and neighbourhood. At last, however, I could hear the noise of a window gently thrust up, and knew that my uncle had come to his observatory. By what light there was, he would see Alan standing, like a dark shadow, on the steps; the three witnesses were hidden quite out of his view; so that there was nothing to alarm an honest man in his own house. For all that, he studied his visitor awhile in silence, and when he spoke his voice had a quaver of misgiving.

"What's this?" says he. "This is nae kind of time of night for decent folk; and I hae nae trokings wi' night-hawks. What brings ye here? I have a blunderbush."

"Is that yoursel', Mr. Balfour?" returned Alan, stepping back and looking up into the darkness. "Have a care of that blunderbuss; they're nasty things to burst."

"What brings ye here? and whae are ye?" says my uncle, angrily.

"I have no manner of inclination to rowt out my name to the country-side," said Alan; "but what brings me here is another story, being more of your affair than mine; and if ye're sure it's what ye would like, I'll set it to a tune and sing it to you."

"And what is't?" asked my uncle.

"David," says Alan.

"What was that?" cried my uncle, in a mighty changed voice.

"Shall I give ye the rest of the name, then?" said Alan.

There was a pause; and then, "I'm thinking I'll better let ye in," says my uncle, doubtfully.

"I dare say that," said Alan; "but the point is, Would I go? Now I will tell you what I am thinking. I am thinking that it is here upon this doorstep that we must confer upon this business; and it shall be here or nowhere at all whatever; for I would have you to understand that I am as stiffnecked as yoursel', and a gentleman of better family."

This change of note disconcerted Ebenezer; he was a little while digesting it, and then says he, "Weel, weel, what must be must," and shut the window. But it took him a long time to get down-stairs, and a still longer to undo the fastenings, repenting (I dare say) and taken with fresh claps of fear at every second step and every bolt and bar. At last, however, we heard the creak of the hinges, and it seems my uncle slipped gingerly out and (seeing that Alan had stepped back a pace or two) sate him down on the top doorstep with the blunderbuss ready in his hands.

"And, now" says he, "mind I have my blunderbush, and if ye take a step nearer ye're as good as deid."

"And a very civil speech," says Alan, "to be sure."

"Na," says my uncle, "but this is no a very chanty kind of a proceeding, and I'm bound to be prepared. And now that we understand each other, ye'll can name your business."

"Why," says Alan, "you that are a man of so much understanding, will doubtless have perceived that I am a Hieland gentleman. My name has nae business in my story; but the county of my friends is no very far from the Isle of Mull, of which ye will have heard. It seems there was a ship lost in those parts; and the next day a gentleman of my family was seeking wreck-wood for his fire along the sands, when he came upon a lad that was half drowned. Well, he brought him to; and he and some other gentleman took and clapped him in an auld, ruined castle, where from that day to this he has been a great expense to my friends. My friends are a wee wild-like, and not so particular about the law as some that I could name; and finding that the lad owned some decent folk, and was your born nephew, Mr. Balfour, they asked me to give ye a bit call and confer upon the matter. And I may tell ye at the off-go, unless we can agree upon some terms, ye are little likely to set eyes upon him. For my friends," added Alan, simply, "are no very well off."

My uncle cleared his throat. "I'm no very caring," says he. "He wasnae a good lad at the best of it, and I've nae call to interfere."

"Ay, ay," said Alan, "I see what ye would be at: pretending ye don't care, to make the ransom smaller."

"Na," said my uncle, "it's the mere truth. I take nae manner of interest in the lad, and I'll pay nae ransome, and ye can make a kirk and a mill of him for what I care."

"Hoot, sir," says Alan. "Blood's thicker than water, in the deil's name! Ye cannae desert your brother's son for the fair shame of it; and if ye did, and it came to be kennt, ye wouldnae be very popular in your country-side, or I'm the more deceived."

"I'm no just very popular the way it is," returned Ebenezer; "and I dinnae see how it would come to be kennt. No by me, onyway; nor yet by you or your friends. So that's idle talk, my buckie," says he.

"Then it'll have to be David that tells it," said Alan.

"How that?" says my uncle, sharply.

"Ou, just this, way" says Alan. "My friends would doubtless keep your nephew as long as there was any likelihood of siller to be made of it, but if there was nane, I am clearly of opinion they would let him gang where he pleased, and be damned to him!"

"Ay, but I'm no very caring about that either," said my uncle. "I wouldnae be muckle made up with that."

"I was thinking that," said Alan.

"And what for why?" asked Ebenezer.

"Why, Mr. Balfour," replied Alan, "by all that I could hear, there were two ways of it: either ye liked David and would pay to get him back; or else ye had very good reasons for not wanting him, and would pay for us to keep him. It seems it's not the first; well then, it's the second; and blythe am I to ken it, for it should be a pretty penny in my pocket and the pockets of my friends."

"I dinnae follow ye there," said my uncle.

"No?" said Alan. "Well, see here: you dinnae want the lad back; well, what do ye want done with him, and how much will ye pay?"

My uncle made no answer, but shifted uneasily on his seat.

"Come, sir," cried Alan. "I would have you to ken that I am a gentleman; I bear a king's name; I am nae rider to kick my shanks at your hall door. Either give me an answer in civility, and that out of hand; or by the top of Glencoe, I will ram three feet of iron through your vitals."

"Eh, man," cried my uncle, scrambling to his feet, "give me a meenit! What's like wrong with ye? I'm just a plain man and nae dancing master; and I'm tryin to be as ceevil as it's morally possible. As for that wild talk, it's fair disrepitable. Vitals, says you! And where would I be with my blunderbush?" he snarled.

"Powder and your auld hands are but as the snail to the swallow against the bright steel in the hands of Alan," said the other. "Before your jottering finger could find the trigger, the hilt would dirl on your breast-bane."

"Eh, man, whae's denying it?" said my uncle. "Pit it as ye please, hae't your ain way; I'll do naething to cross ye. Just tell me what like ye'll be wanting, and ye'll see that we'll can agree fine."

"Troth, sir," said Alan, "I ask for nothing but plain dealing.

In two words: do ye want the lad killed or kept?"

"O, sirs!" cried Ebenezer. "O, sirs, me! that's no kind of language!"

"Killed or kept!" repeated Alan.

"O, keepit, keepit!" wailed my uncle. "We'll have nae bloodshed, if you please."

"Well," says Alan, "as ye please; that'll be the dearer."

"The dearer?" cries Ebenezer. "Would ye fyle your hands wi' crime?"

"Hoot!" said Alan, "they're baith crime, whatever! And the killing's easier, and quicker, and surer. Keeping the lad'll be a fashious job, a fashious, kittle business."

"I'll have him keepit, though," returned my uncle. "I never had naething to do with onything morally wrong; and I'm no gaun to begin to pleasure a wild Hielandman."

"Ye're unco scrupulous," sneered Alan.

"I'm a man o' principle," said Ebenezer, simply; "and if I have to pay for it, I'll have to pay for it. And besides," says he, "ye forget the lad's my brother's son."

"Well, well," said Alan, "and now about the price. It's no very easy for me to set a name upon it; I would first have to ken some small matters. I would have to ken, for instance, what ye gave Hoseason at the first off-go?"

"Hoseason!" cries my uncle, struck aback. "What for?"

"For kidnapping David," says Alan.

"It's a lee, it's a black lee!" cried my uncle. "He was never kidnapped. He leed in his throat that tauld ye that. Kidnapped? He never was!"

"That's no fault of mine nor yet of yours," said Alan; "nor yet of Hoseason's, if he's a man that can be trusted."

"What do ye mean?" cried Ebenezer. "Did Hoseason tell ye?"

"Why, ye donnered auld runt, how else would I ken?" cried Alan. "Hoseason and me are partners; we gang shares; so ye can see for yoursel' what good ye can do leeing. And I must plainly say ye drove a fool's bargain when ye let a man like the sailor-man so far forward in your private matters. But that's past praying for; and ye must lie on your bed the way ye made it. And the point in hand is just this: what did ye pay him?"

"Has he tauld ye himsel'?" asked my uncle.

"That's my concern," said Alan.

"Weel," said my uncle, "I dinnae care what he said, he leed, and the solemn God's truth is this, that I gave him twenty pound. But I'll be perfec'ly honest with ye: forby that, he was to have the selling of the lad in Caroliny, whilk would be as muckle mair, but no from my pocket, ye see."

"Thank you, Mr. Thomson. That will do excellently well," said the lawyer, stepping forward; and then mighty civilly, "Good-evening, Mr. Balfour," said he.

And, "Good-evening, Uncle Ebenezer," said I.

And, "It's a braw nicht, Mr. Balfour" added Torrance.

Never a word said my uncle, neither black nor white; but just sat where he was on the top door-step and stared upon us like a man turned to stone. Alan filched away his blunderbuss; and the lawyer, taking him by the arm, plucked him up from the doorstep, led him into the kitchen, whither we all followed, and set him down in a chair beside the hearth, where the fire was out and only a rush-light burning.

There we all looked upon him for a while, exulting greatly in our success, but yet with a sort of pity for the man's shame.

"Come, come, Mr. Ebenezer," said the lawyer, "you must not be down-hearted, for I promise you we shall make easy terms. In the meanwhile give us the cellar key, and Torrance shall draw us a bottle of your father's wine in honour of the event." Then, turning to me and taking me by the hand, "Mr. David," says he, "I wish you all joy in your good fortune, which I believe to be deserved." And then to Alan, with a spice of drollery, "Mr. Thomson, I pay you my compliment; it was most artfully conducted; but in one point you somewhat outran my comprehension. Do I understand your name to be James? or Charles? or is it George, perhaps?"

"And why should it be any of the three, sir?" quoth Alan, drawing himself up, like one who smelt an offence.

"Only, sir, that you mentioned a king's name," replied Rankeillor; "and as there has never yet been a King Thomson, or his fame at least has never come my way, I judged you must refer to that you had in baptism."

This was just the stab that Alan would feel keenest, and I am free to confess he took it very ill. Not a word would he answer, but stepped off to the far end of the kitchen, and sat down and sulked; and it was not till I stepped after him, and gave him my hand, and thanked him by title as the chief spring of my success, that he began to smile a bit, and was at last prevailed upon to join our party.

By that time we had the fire lighted, and a bottle of wine uncorked; a good supper came out of the basket, to which Torrance and I and Alan set ourselves down; while the lawyer and my uncle passed into the next chamber to consult. They stayed there closeted about an hour; at the end of which period they had come to a good understanding, and my uncle and I set our hands to the agreement in a formal manner. By the terms of this, my uncle bound himself to satisfy Rankeillor as to his intromissions, and to pay me two clear thirds of the yearly income of Shaws.

So the beggar in the ballad had come home; and when I lay down that night on the kitchen chests, I was a man of means and had a name in the country. Alan and Torrance and Rankeillor slept and snored on their hard beds; but for me who had lain out under heaven and upon dirt and stones, so many days and nights, and often with an empty belly, and in fear of death, this good change in my case unmanned me more than any of the former evil ones; and I lay till dawn, looking at the fire on the roof and planning the future.

CHAPTER XXX

GOOD-BYE

So far as I was concerned myself, I had come to port; but I had still Alan, to whom I was so much beholden, on my hands; and I felt besides a heavy charge in the matter of the murder and James of the Glens. On both these heads I unbosomed to Rankeillor the next morning, walking to and fro about six of the clock before the house of Shaws, and with nothing in view but the fields and woods that had been my ancestors' and were now mine. Even as I spoke on these grave subjects, my eye would take a glad bit of a run over the prospect, and my heart jump with pride.

About my clear duty to my friend, the lawyer had no doubt. I must help him out of the county at whatever risk; but in the case of James, he was of a different mind.

"Mr. Thomson," says he, "is one thing, Mr. Thomson's kinsman quite another. I know little of the facts, but I gather that a great noble (whom we will call, if you like, the D. of A.) has some concern and is even supposed to feel some animosity in the matter. The D. of A. is doubtless an excellent nobleman; but, Mr. David, *timeo qui nocuere deos*. If you interfere to balk his vengeance, you should remember there is one way to shut your testimony out; and that is to put you in the dock. There, you would be in the same pickle as Mr. Thomson's kinsman. You will object that you are innocent; well, but so is he. And to be tried for your life before a Highland jury, on a Highland quarrel and with a Highland Judge upon the bench, would be a brief transition to the gallows."

Now I had made all these reasonings before and found no very good reply to them; so I put on all the simplicity I could. "In that case, sir," said I, "I would just have to be hanged— would I not?"

"My dear boy," cries he, "go in God's name, and do what you think is right. It is a poor thought that at my time of life I should be advising you to choose the safe and shameful; and I take it back with an apology. Go and do your duty; and be hanged, if you must, like a gentleman. There are worse things in the world than to be hanged."

"Not many, sir," said I, smiling.

"Why, yes, sir," he cried, "very many. And it would be ten times better for your uncle (to go no farther afield) if he were dangling decently upon a gibbet."

Thereupon he turned into the house (still in a great fervour of mind, so that I saw I had pleased him heartily) and there he wrote me two letters, making his comments on them as he wrote.

"This," says he, "is to my bankers, the British Linen Company, placing a credit to your name. Consult Mr. Thomson, he will know of ways; and you, with this credit, can supply the means. I trust you will be a good husband of your money; but in the affair of a friend like Mr. Thompson, I would be even prodigal. Then for his kinsman, there is no better way than that you should seek the Advocate, tell him your tale, and offer testimony; whether he may take it or not, is quite another matter, and will turn on the D. of A. Now, that you may reach the Lord Advocate well recommended, I give you here a letter to a namesake of your own, the learned Mr. Balfour of Pilrig, a man whom I esteem. It will look better that you should be presented by one of your own name; and the laird of Pilrig is much looked up to in the Faculty and stands well with Lord Advocate Grant. I would not trouble him, if I were you, with any particulars; and (do you know?) I think it would be needless to refer to Mr. Thomson. Form yourself upon the laird, he is a good model; when you deal with the Advocate, be discreet; and in all these matters, may the Lord guide you, Mr. David!"

Thereupon he took his farewell, and set out with Torrance for the Ferry, while Alan and I turned our faces for the city of Edinburgh. As we went by the footpath and beside the gateposts and the unfinished lodge, we kept looking back at the house of my fathers. It stood there, bare and great and smokeless, like a place not lived in; only in one of the top windows, there was the peak of a nightcap bobbing up and down and back and forward, like the head of a rabbit from a burrow. I had little welcome when I came, and less kindness while I stayed; but at least I was watched as I went away.

Alan and I went slowly forward upon our way, having little heart either to walk or speak. The same thought was uppermost in both, that we were near the time of our parting; and remembrance of all the bygone days sate upon us sorely. We talked indeed of what should be done; and it was resolved that Alan should keep to the county, biding now here, now there, but coming once in the day to a particular place where I might be able to communicate with him, either in my own person or by messenger. In the meanwhile, I was to seek out a lawyer, who was an Appin Stewart, and a man therefore to be wholly trusted; and it should be his part to find a ship and to arrange for Alan's safe embarkation. No sooner was this business done, than the words seemed to leave us; and though I would seek to jest with Alan under the name of Mr. Thomson, and he with me on my new clothes and my estate, you could feel very well that we were nearer tears than laughter.

We came the by-way over the hill of Corstorphine; and when we got near to the place called Rest-and-be-Thankful, and looked down on Corstorphine bogs and over to the city and the castle on the hill, we both stopped, for we both knew without a word said that we had come to where our ways parted. Here he repeated to me once again what had been agreed upon between us: the address of the lawyer, the daily hour at which Alan might be found, and the signals that were to be made by any that came seeking him. Then I gave what money I had (a guinea or two of Rankeillor's) so that he should not starve in the meanwhile; and then we stood a space, and looked over at Edinburgh in silence.

"Well, good-bye," said Alan, and held out his left hand.

"Good-bye," said I, and gave the hand a little grasp, and went off down hill.

Neither one of us looked the other in the face, nor so long as he was in my view did I take one back glance at the friend I was leaving. But as I went on my way to the city, I felt so lost and lonesome, that I could have found it in my heart to sit down by the dyke, and cry and weep like any baby.

It was coming near noon when I passed in by the West Kirk and the Grassmarket into the streets of the capital. The huge height of the buildings, running up to ten and fifteen storeys, the narrow arched entries that continually vomited passengers, the wares of the merchants in their windows, the hubbub and endless stir, the foul smells and the fine clothes, and a hundred other particulars too small to mention, struck me into a kind of stupor of surprise, so that I let the crowd carry me to and fro; and yet all the time what I was thinking of was Alan at Rest-and-be-Thankful; and all the time (although you would think I would not choose but be delighted with these braws and novelties) there was a cold gnawing in my inside like a remorse for something wrong.

The hand of Providence brought me in my drifting to the very doors of the British Linen Company's bank.

The Adventures of
Tom Sawyer

The Adventures of
Tom Sawyer

Mark Twain

Trans
Atlantic
Press

This is a Transatlantic Press book
This edition published in 2012

Transatlantic Press
Sky House, Raans Road, Amersham, Bucks, HP6 6JQ

Mark Twain asserts the moral right to be identified as the author of this work.

Cover image copyright GettyImages
Author biography copyright Transatlantic Press

A catalogue record is available for this book from the British Library

ISBN 978-1-908533-13-5

Printed and bound by CPI Group (UK) Ltd, Croydon, CR0 4YY

MARK TWAIN

Mark Twain was the pseudonym adopted by Samuel Langhorne Clemens. Steamboat pilot was one of Clemens's many occupations before he made his name as a writer, hence he would have been familiar with the cry "mark twain," signaling a river depth of two fathoms. He was born in Florida, Missouri, on November 30, 1835, the family moving to Hannibal when he was four years old in pursuit of one of his father's numerous abortive business ventures. Following his father's death in 1847, Clemens left school and worked as a printer, later moving into journalism. His talent as a humorist gained recognition, notably with the publication of *The Celebrated Jumping Frog of Calaveras County and Other Sketches* (1867) and *The Innocents Abroad* (1869). In *Roughing It* (1872) he described his time out West, which included a spell as a gold miner. He turned to fiction with *The Gilded Age* (1873), a satire on post-Civil War America for which he collaborated with newspaperman Charles Dudley Warner. *The Adventures of Tom Sawyer* appeared in 1876, its celebrated sequel, *The Adventures of Huckleberry Finn* eight years later. His output in between these landmark publications includes his famous medieval tale of switched identities, *The Prince and the Pauper* (1881). Later works in what was a prolific career include *A Connecticut Yankee in King Arthur's Court* (1889) and *Pudd'nhead Wilson* (1894). Hugely popular on the lecture circuit, Clemens had all but abandoned that pursuit by the 1890s, but financial problems forced him to take on worldwide speaking engagements. His later years were also touched by tragedy. Having lost a son in infancy, he outlived two of his daughters and his wife, Olivia Langdon, an industrialist's daughter he had married in 1870. Mark Twain died at his Redding, Connecticut, home on April 21, 1910, aged 74.

THE ADVENTURES OF TOM SAWYER

Impish, resourceful Tom Sawyer spends his time trying to stay one step ahead of his Aunt Polly, playing hookey from school and persuading other boys to carry out punishments meant for him. Becky Thatcher is the object of Tom's affections, but when it comes to midnight escapades in a graveyard, local waif Huckleberry Finn is the ideal confederate. There, while testing out a theory for curing warts, the duo witness a dastardly crime that offers Tom the chance to be an unlikely hero...

Mark Twain mined the rich seam of his own youth for the characters, locations, and events that light up this landmark in American fiction. Loved by children of all ages down the years, *The Adventures of Tom Sawyer* also succeeded brilliantly in meeting the author's aim "to pleasantly remind adults of what they once were themselves."

PREFACE

Most of the adventures recorded in this book really occurred; one or two were experiences of my own, the rest those of boys who were schoolmates of mine. Huck Finn is drawn from life; Tom Sawyer also, but not from an individual—he is a combination of the characteristics of three boys whom I knew, and therefore belongs to the composite order of architecture.

The odd superstitions touched upon were all prevalent among children and slaves in the West at the period of this story—that is to say, thirty or forty years ago.

Although my book is intended mainly for the entertainment of boys and girls, I hope it will not be shunned by men and women on that account, for part of my plan has been to try to pleasantly remind adults of what they once were themselves, and of how they felt and thought and talked, and what queer enterprises they sometimes engaged in.

The Author
Hartford, 1876

CHAPTER 1

Y-o-u-u Tom-Aunt Polly Decides Upon her Duty
—Tom Practices Music—The Challenge—A Private Entrance

"TOM!"

No answer.

"Tom!"

No answer.

"What's gone with that boy, I wonder? You TOM!"

No answer.

The old lady pulled her spectacles down and looked over them about the room; then she put them up and looked out under them. She seldom or never looked *through* them for so small a thing as a boy; they were her state pair, the pride of her heart, and were built for "style," not service—she could have seen through a pair of stove-lids just as well. She looked perplexed for a moment, and then said, not fiercely, but still loud enough for the furniture to hear:

"Well, I lay if I get hold of you I'll—"

She did not finish, for by this time she was bending down and punching under the bed with the broom, and so she needed breath to punctuate the punches with. She resurrected nothing but the cat.

"I never did see the beat of that boy!"

She went to the open door and stood in it and looked out among the tomato vines and "jimpson" weeds that constituted the garden. No Tom. So she lifted up her voice at an angle calculated for distance and shouted:

"Y-o-u-u *Tom*!"

There was a slight noise behind her and she turned just in time to seize a small boy by the slack of his roundabout and arrest his flight.

"There! I might 'a' thought of that closet. What you been doing in there?"

"Nothing."

"Nothing! Look at your hands. And look at your mouth. What *is* that truck?"

"*I* don't know, aunt."

"Well, *I* know. It's jam—that's what it is. Forty times I've said if you didn't let that jam alone I'd skin you. Hand me that switch."

The switch hovered in the air—the peril was desperate—

"My! Look behind you, aunt!"

The old lady whirled round, and snatched her skirts out of danger. The lad fled on the instant, scrambled up the high board-fence, and disappeared over it.

His aunt Polly stood surprised a moment, and then broke into a gentle laugh.

"Hang the boy, can't I never learn anything? Ain't he played me tricks enough like that for me to be looking out for him by this time? But old fools is the biggest fools there is. Can't learn an old dog new tricks, as the saying is. But my goodness, he never plays them alike, two days, and how is a body to know what's coming? He 'pears to know just how long he can torment me before I get my dander up, and he knows if he can make out to put me off for a minute or make me laugh, it's all down again and I can't hit him a lick. I ain't doing my duty by that boy, and that's the Lord's truth, goodness knows. Spare the rod and spile the child, as the Good Book says. I'm a laying up sin and suffering for us both, *I* know. He's full of the Old Scratch, but laws-a-me! he's my own dead sister's boy, poor thing, and I ain't got the heart to lash him, somehow.

Every time I let him off, my conscience does hurt me so, and every time I hit him my old heart most breaks. Well-a-well, man that is born of woman is of few days and full of trouble, as the Scripture says, and I reckon it's so. He'll play hookey this evening, * and [* Southwestern for "afternoon"] I'll just be obleeged to make him work, tomorrow, to punish him. It's mighty hard to make him work Saturdays, when all the boys is having holiday, but he hates work more than he hates anything else, and I've *got* to do some of my duty by him, or I'll be the ruination of the child."

Tom did play hookey, and he had a very good time. He got back home barely in season to help Jim, the small colored boy, saw next-day's wood and split the kindlings before supper—at least he was there in time to tell his adventures to Jim while Jim did three-fourths of the work. Tom's younger brother (or rather half-brother) Sid was already through with his part of the work (picking up chips), for he was a quiet boy, and had no adventurous, trouble-some ways.

While Tom was eating his supper, and stealing sugar as opportunity offered, Aunt Polly asked him questions that were full of guile, and very deep—for she wanted to trap him into damaging revealments. Like many other simple-hearted souls, it was her pet vanity to believe she was endowed with a talent for dark and mysterious diplomacy, and she loved to contemplate her most transparent devices as marvels of low cunning. Said she:

"Tom, it was middling warm in school, warn't it?"

"Yes'm."

"Powerful warm, warn't it?"

"Yes'm."

"Didn't you want to go in a-swimming, Tom?"

A bit of a scare shot through Tom—a touch of uncomfortable suspicion. He searched Aunt Polly's face, but it told him nothing. So he said:

"No'm—well, not very much."

The old lady reached out her hand and felt Tom's shirt, and said:

"But you ain't too warm now, though." And it flattered her to reflect that she had discovered that the shirt was dry without anybody knowing that that was what she had in her mind. But in spite of her, Tom knew where the wind lay, now. So he forestalled what might be the next move:

"Some of us pumped on our heads—mine's damp yet. See?"

Aunt Polly was vexed to think she had overlooked that bit of circumstantial evidence, and missed a trick. Then she had a new inspiration:

"Tom, you didn't have to undo your shirt collar where I sewed it, to pump on your head, did you? Unbutton your jacket!"

The trouble vanished out of Tom's face. He opened his jacket. His shirt collar was securely sewed.

"Bother! Well, go 'long with you. I'd made sure you'd played hookey and been a-swimming. But I forgive ye, Tom. I reckon you're a kind of a singed cat, as the saying is—better'n you look. *this* time."

She was half sorry her sagacity had miscarried, and half glad that Tom had stumbled into obedient conduct for once.

But Sidney said:

"Well, now, if I didn't think you sewed his collar with white thread, but it's black."

"Why, I did sew it with white! Tom!"

But Tom did not wait for the rest. As he went out at the door he said:

"Siddy, I'll lick you for that."

In a safe place Tom examined two large needles which were thrust into the lapels of his jacket, and had thread bound about them—one needle carried white thread and the other black. He said:

"She'd never noticed if it hadn't been for Sid. Confound it! sometimes she sews it with white, and sometimes she sews it with black. I wish to gee-miny she'd stick to one or t'other—I can't keep the run of 'em. But I bet you I'll lam Sid for that. I'll learn him!"

He was not the Model Boy of the village. He knew the model boy very well though—and loathed him.

Within two minutes, or even less, he had forgotten all his troubles. Not because his troubles were one whit less heavy and bitter to him than a man's are to a man, but because a new and powerful interest bore them down and drove them out of his mind for the time—just as men's misfortunes are forgotten in the excitement of new enterprises. This new interest was a valued novelty in whistling, which he had just acquired from a negro, and he was suffering to practise it un-disturbed. It consisted in a peculiar bird-like turn, a sort of liquid warble, produced by touching the tongue to the roof of the mouth at short intervals in the midst of the music—the reader probably remembers how to do it, if he has ever been a boy. Diligence and attention soon gave him the knack of it, and he strode down the street with his mouth full of harmony and his soul full of gratitude. He felt much as an astronomer feels who has discovered a new planet—no doubt, as far as strong, deep, unalloyed pleasure is concerned, the advantage was with the boy, not the astronomer.

The summer evenings were long. It was not dark, yet. Presently Tom checked his whistle. A stranger was before him—a boy a shade larger than himself. A new-comer of any age or either sex was an im-pressive curiosity in the poor little shabby village of St. Petersburg. This boy was well dressed, too—well dressed on a week-day. This was simply as-tounding. His cap was a dainty thing, his close-buttoned blue cloth roundabout was new and natty, and so were his pantaloons. He had shoes on—and it was only Friday. He even wore a necktie, a bright bit of ribbon. He had a citified air about him that ate into Tom's vitals. The more Tom stared at the splendid marvel, the higher he turned up his nose at his finery and the shabbier and shabbier his own outfit seemed to him to grow. Neither boy spoke. If one moved, the other moved—but only sidewise, in a circle; they kept face to face and eye to eye all the time. Finally Tom said:

"I can lick you!"

"I'd like to see you try it."

"Well, I can do it."

"No you can't, either."

"Yes I can."

"No you can't."

"I can."

"You can't."

"Can!"

"Can't!"

An uncomfortable pause. Then Tom said:

"What's your name?"

"'Tisn't any of your business, maybe."

"Well I 'low I'll *make* it my business."

"Well why don't you?"

"If you say much, I will."

"Much—much—*much*. There now."

"Oh, you think you're mighty smart, *don't* you? I could lick you with one hand tied behind me, if I wanted to."

"Well why don't you *do* it? You *say* you can do it."

"Well I *will*, if you fool with me."

"Oh yes—I've seen whole families in the same fix."

"Smarty! You think you're *some*, now, *don't* you? Oh, what a hat!"

"You can lump that hat if you don't like it. I dare you to knock it off—and anybody that'll take a dare will suck eggs."

"You're a liar!"

"You're another."

"You're a fighting liar and dasn't take it up."

"Aw—take a walk!"

"Say—if you give me much more of your sass I'll take and bounce a rock off'n your head."

"Oh, of *course* you will."

"Well I *will*."

"Well why don't you *do* it then? What do you keep *saying* you will for? Why don't you *do* it? It's because you're afraid."

"I *ain't* afraid."

"You are."

"I ain't."

"You are."

Another pause, and more eying and sidling around each other. Presently they were shoulder to shoulder. Tom said:

"Get away from here!"

"Go away yourself!"

"I won't."

"*I* won't either."

So they stood, each with a foot placed at an angle as a brace, and both shoving with might and main, and glowering at each other with hate. But neither could get an advantage. After struggling till both were hot and flushed, each relaxed his strain with watchful caution, and Tom said:

"You're a coward and a pup. I'll tell my big brother on you, and he can thrash you with his little finger, and I'll make him do it, too."

"What do I care for your big brother? I've got a brother that's bigger than he is—and what's more, he can throw him over that fence, too." (Both brothers were imaginary.)

"That's a lie."

"*Your* saying so don't make it so."

Tom drew a line in the dust with his big toe, and said:

"I dare you to step over that, and I'll lick you till you can't stand up. Anybody that'll take a dare will steal sheep."

The new boy stepped over promptly, and said:

"Now you said you'd do it, now let's see you do it."

"Don't you crowd me now; you better look out."

"Well, you *said* you'd do it—why don't you do it?"

"By jingo! for two cents I *will* do it."

The new boy took two broad coppers out of his pocket and held them out with derision. Tom struck them to the ground. In an instant both boys were rolling and tumbling in the dirt, gripped together like cats; and for the space of a minute they tugged and tore at each other's hair and clothes, punched and scratched each other's nose, and covered themselves with dust and glory. Presently the confusion took form, and through the fog of battle Tom appeared, seated astride the new boy, and pounding him with his fists. "Holler 'nuff!" said he.

The boy only struggled to free himself. He was crying—mainly from rage.

"Holler 'nuff!"—and the pounding went on.

At last the stranger got out a smothered "'Nuff!" and Tom let him up and said:

"Now that'll learn you. Better look out who you're fooling with next time."

The new boy went off brushing the dust from his clothes, sobbing, snuffling, and occasionally looking back and shaking his head and threatening what he would do to Tom the "next time he caught him out." To which Tom responded with jeers, and started off in high feather, and as soon as his back was turned the new boy snatched up a stone, threw it and hit him between the shoulders and then turned tail and ran like an antelope. Tom chased the traitor home, and thus found out where he lived. He then held a position at the gate for some time, daring the enemy to come outside, but the enemy only made faces at him through the window and declined. At last the enemy's mother appeared, and called Tom a bad, vicious, vulgar child, and ordered him away. So he went away; but he said he "'lowed" to "lay" for that boy.

He got home pretty late that night, and when he climbed cautiously in at the window, he uncovered an ambuscade, in the person of his aunt; and when she saw the state his clothes were in her resolution to turn his Saturday holiday into captivity at hard labor became adamantine in its firmness.

CHAPTER 2

Strong Temptations—Strategic Movements
—The Innocents Beguiled

SATURDAY morning was come, and all the summer world was bright and fresh, and brimming with life. There was a song in every heart; and if the heart was young the music issued at the lips. There was cheer in every face and a spring in every step. The locust-trees were in bloom and the fragrance of the blossoms filled the air. Cardiff Hill, beyond the village and above it, was green with vegetation and it lay just far enough away to seem a Delectable Land, dreamy, reposeful, and inviting.

Tom appeared on the sidewalk with a bucket of whitewash and a long-handled brush. He surveyed the fence, and all gladness left him and a deep melancholy settled down upon his spirit. Thirty yards of board fence nine feet high. Life to him seemed hollow, and existence but a burden. Sighing, he dipped his brush and passed it along the topmost plank; repeated the operation; did it again; compared the insignificant whitewashed streak with the far-reaching continent of unwhitewashed fence, and sat down on a tree-box discouraged. Jim came skipping out at the gate with a tin pail, and singing Buffalo Gals. Bringing water from the town pump had always been hateful work in Tom's eyes, before, but now it did not strike him so. He remembered that there was company at the pump. White, mulatto, and negro boys and girls were always there waiting their turns, resting, trading playthings, quarrelling, fighting, skylarking. And he remembered that although the pump was only a hundred and fifty yards off, Jim never got back with a bucket of water under an hour—and even then somebody generally had to go after him. Tom said:

"Say, Jim, I'll fetch the water if you'll whitewash some."

Jim shook his head and said:

"Can't, Mars Tom. Ole missis, she tole me I got to go an' git dis water an' not stop foolin' roun' wid anybody. She say she spec' Mars Tom gwine to ax me to whitewash, an' so she tole me go 'long an' 'tend to my own business—she 'lowed *she'd* 'tend to de whitewashin'."

"Oh, never you mind what she said, Jim. That's the way she always talks. Gimme the bucket—I won't be gone only a a minute. *She* won't ever know."

"Oh, I dasn't, Mars Tom. Ole missis she'd take an' tar de head off'n me. 'Deed she would."

"*She!* She never licks anybody—whacks 'em over the head with her thimble—and who cares for that, I'd like to know. She talks awful, but talk don't hurt—anyways it don't if she don't cry. Jim, I'll give you a marvel. I'll give you a white alley!"

Jim began to waver.

"White alley, Jim! And it's a bully taw."

"My! Dat's a mighty gay marvel, I tell you! But Mars Tom I's powerful 'fraid ole missis—"

"And besides, if you will I'll show you my sore toe."

Jim was only human—this attraction was too much for him. He put down his pail, took the white alley, and bent over the toe with absorbing interest while the bandage was being unwound. In another moment he was flying down the street with his pail and a tingling rear, Tom was whitewashing with vigor, and Aunt Polly was retiring from the field with a slipper in her hand and triumph in her eye.

But Tom's energy did not last. He began to think of the fun he had planned for this day, and his sorrows multiplied.

Soon the free boys would come tripping along on all sorts of delicious expeditions, and they would make a world of fun of him for having to work—the very thought of it burnt him like fire. He got out his worldly wealth and examined it—bits of toys, marbles, and trash; enough to buy an exchange of WORK, maybe, but not half enough to buy so much as half an hour of pure freedom. So he returned his straitened means to his pocket, and gave up the idea of trying to buy the boys. At this dark and hopeless moment an inspiration burst upon him! Nothing less than a great, magnificent inspiration.

He took up his brush and went tranquilly to work. Ben Rogers hove in sight presently—the very boy, of all boys, whose ridicule he had been dreading. Ben's gait was the hop-skip-and-jump—proof enough that his heart was light and his anticipations high. He was eating an apple, and giving a long, melodious whoop, at intervals, followed by a deep-toned ding-dong-dong, ding-dong-dong, for he was personating a steamboat. As he drew near, he slackened speed, took the middle of the street, leaned far over to starboard and rounded to ponderously and with laborious pomp and circumstance—for he was personating the Big Missouri, and considered himself to be drawing nine feet of water. He was boat and captain and engine-bells combined, so he had to imagine himself standing on his own hurricane-deck giving the orders and executing them:

"Stop her, sir! Ting-a-ling-ling!" The headway ran almost out, and he drew up slowly toward the sidewalk.

"Ship up to back! Ting-a-ling-ling!" His arms straightened and stiffened down his sides.

"Set her back on the stabboard! Ting-a-ling-ling! Chow! ch-chow-wow! Chow!" His right hand, mean-time, describing stately circles—for it was representing a forty-foot wheel.

"Let her go back on the labboard! Ting-a-ling-ling! Chow-ch-chow-chow!" The left hand began to describe circles.

"Stop the stabboard! Ting-a-ling-ling! Stop the labboard! Come ahead on the stabboard! Stop her! Let your outside turn over slow! Ting-a-ling- ling! Chow-ow-ow! Get out that head-line! *Lively* now! Come—out with your spring-line—what're you about there! Take a turn round that stump with the bight of it! Stand by that stage, now—let her go! Done with the engines, sir! Ting-a-ling-ling! *sh't! sh't! sh't* (trying the gauge-cocks).

Tom went on whitewashing—paid no attention to the steamboat. Ben stared a moment and then said: "*Hi-yi! You're* up a stump, ain't you!"

No answer. Tom surveyed his last touch with the eye of an artist, then he gave his brush another gentle sweep and surveyed the result, as before. Ben ranged up alongside of him. Tom's mouth watered for the apple, but he stuck to his work. Ben said:

"Hello, old chap, you got to work, hey?"

Tom wheeled suddenly and said:

"Why, it's you, Ben! I warn't noticing."

"Say—I'm going in a-swimming, I am. Don't you wish you could? But of course you'd druther *work*—wouldn't you? Course you would!"

Tom contemplated the boy a bit and said:

"What do you call work?"

"Why, ain't *that* work?"

Tom resumed his whitewashing, and answered carelessly:

"Well, maybe it is, and maybe it ain't. All I know, is, it suits Tom Sawyer."

"Oh come, now, you don't mean to let on that you *like* it?"

The brush continued to move.

"Like it? Well, I don't see why I oughtn't to like it. Does a boy get a chance to whitewash a fence every day?"

That put the thing in a new light. Ben stopped nibbling his apple. Tom swept his brush daintily back and forth—stepped back to note the effect—added a touch here and there—

criticised the effect again—Ben watching every move and getting more and more interested, more and more absorbed. Presently he said:

"Say, Tom, let *me* whitewash a little."

Tom considered, was about to consent; but he altered his mind:

"No—no—I reckon it wouldn't hardly do, Ben. You see, Aunt Polly's awful particular about this fence—right here on the street, you know—but if it was the back fence I wouldn't mind and *she* wouldn't. Yes, she's awful particular about this fence; it's got to be done very careful; I reckon there ain't one boy in a thousand, maybe two thousand, that can do it the way it's got to be done."

"No—is that so? Oh come, now—lemme just try. Only just a little—I'd let *you*, if you was me, Tom."

"Ben, I'd like to, honest injun; but Aunt Polly—well, Jim wanted to do it, but she wouldn't let him; Sid wanted to do it, and she wouldn't let Sid. Now don't you see how I'm fixed? If you was to tackle this fence and anything was to happen to it—"

"Oh, shucks, I'll be just as careful. Now lemme try. Say—I'll give you the core of my apple."

"Well, here—No, Ben, now don't. I'm afeard—"

"I'll give you *all* of it!"

Tom gave up the brush with reluctance in his face, but alacrity in his heart. And while the late steamer Big Missouri worked and sweated in the sun, the retired artist sat on a barrel in the shade close by, dangled his legs, munched his apple, and planned the slaughter of more innocents. There was no lack of material; boys happened along every little while; they came to jeer, but remained to whitewash. By the time Ben was fagged out, Tom had traded the next chance to Billy Fisher for a kite, in good repair; and when he played out, Johnny Miller bought in for a dead rat and a string to swing it with—and so on, and so on, hour after hour. And when the middle of the afternoon came, from being a poor poverty-stricken boy in the morning, Tom was literally rolling in wealth. He had besides the things before mentioned, twelve marbles, part of a jews-harp, a piece of blue bottle-glass to look through, a spool cannon, a key that wouldn't unlock anything, a fragment of chalk, a glass stopper of a decanter, a tin soldier, a couple of tadpoles, six fire-crackers, a kitten with only one eye, a brass door-knob, a dog-collar—but no dog—the handle of a knife, four pieces of orange-peel, and a dilapidated old window sash.

He had had a nice, good, idle time all the while—plenty of company—and the fence had three coats of whitewash on it! If he hadn't run out of whitewash he would have bankrupted every boy in the village.

Tom said to himself that it was not such a hollow world, after all. He had discovered a great law of human action, without knowing it—namely, that in order to make a man or a boy covet a thing, it is only necessary to make the thing difficult to attain. If he had been a great and wise philosopher, like the writer of this book, he would now have comprehended that Work consists of whatever a body is *obliged* to do, and that Play consists of whatever a body is not obliged to do. And this would help him to understand why constructing artificial flowers or performing on a tread-mill is work, while rolling ten-pins or climbing Mont Blanc is only amusement. There are wealthy gentlemen in England who drive four-horse passenger-coaches twenty or thirty miles on a daily line, in the summer, because the privilege costs them considerable money; but if they were offered wages for the service, that would turn it into work and then they would resign.

The boy mused awhile over the substantial change which had taken place in his worldly circumstances, and then wended toward headquarters to report.

CHAPTER 3

Tom as a General—Triumph and Reward
—Dismal Felicity—Commission and Omission

TOM presented himself before Aunt Polly, who was sitting by an open window in a pleasant rearward apartment, which was bedroom, breakfast-room, dining-room, and library, combined. The balmy summer air, the restful quiet, the odor of the flowers, and the drowsing murmur of the bees had had their effect, and she was nodding over her knitting—for she had no company but the cat, and it was asleep in her lap. Her spectacles were propped up on her gray head for safety. She had thought that of course Tom had deserted long ago, and she wondered at seeing him place himself in her power again in this intrepid way. He said: "Mayn't I go and play now, aunt?"

"What, a'ready? How much have you done?"

"It's all done, aunt."

"Tom, don't lie to me—I can't bear it."

"I ain't, aunt; it *is* all done."

Aunt Polly placed small trust in such evidence. She went out to see for herself; and she would have been content to find twenty per cent. of Tom's statement true. When she found the entire fence white-washed, and not only whitewashed but elaborately coated and recoated, and even a streak added to the ground, her astonishment was almost unspeakable. She said:

"Well, I never! There's no getting round it, you *can* work when you're a mind to, Tom." And then she diluted the compliment by adding, "But it's powerful seldom you're a mind to, I'm bound to say. Well, go 'long and play; but mind you get back some time in a week, or I'll tan you."

She was so overcome by the splendor of his achievement that she took him into the closet and selected a choice apple and delivered it to him, along with an improving lecture upon the added value and flavor a treat took to itself when it came without sin through virtuous effort. And while she closed with a happy Scriptural flourish, he "hooked" a doughnut.

Then he skipped out, and saw Sid just starting up the outside stairway that led to the back rooms on the second floor. Clods were handy and the air was full of them in a twinkling. They raged around Sid like a hail-storm; and before Aunt Polly could collect her surprised faculties and sally to the rescue, six or seven clods had taken personal effect, and Tom was over the fence and gone. There was a gate, but as a general thing he was too crowded for time to make use of it. His soul was at peace, now that he had settled with Sid for calling attention to his black thread and getting him into trouble.

Tom skirted the block, and came round into a muddy alley that led by the back of his aunt's cow-stable. He presently got safely beyond the reach of capture and punishment, and hastened toward the public square of the village, where two "military" companies of boys had met for conflict, according to previous appointment. Tom was General of one of these armies, Joe Harper (a bosom friend) General of the other. These two great commanders did not condescend to fight in person—that being better suited to the still smaller fry—but sat together on an eminence and conducted the field operations by orders delivered through aides-de-camp. Tom's army won a great victory, after a long and hard-fought battle. Then the dead were counted, prisoners exchanged, the terms of the next disagreement agreed upon, and the day for the necessary battle appointed; after which the armies fell into line and marched away, and Tom turned homeward alone.

As he was passing by the house where Jeff Thatcher lived, he saw a new girl in the garden—a lovely little blue-eyed creature with yellow hair plaited into two long-tails, white summer frock and embroidered pan-talettes. The fresh-crowned hero fell without firing a shot. A certain Amy Lawrence vanished out of his heart and left not even a memory of herself behind. He had thought he loved her to distraction; he had regarded his passion as adoration; and behold it was only a poor little evanescent partiality. He had been months winning her; she had confessed hardly a week ago; he had been the happiest and the proudest boy in the world only seven short days, and here in one instant of time she had gone out of his heart like a casual stranger whose visit is done.

He worshipped this new angel with furtive eye, till he saw that she had discovered him; then he pretended he did not know she was present, and began to "show off" in all sorts of absurd boyish ways, in order to win her admiration. He kept up this grotesque foolishness for some time; but by-and-by, while he was in the midst of some dangerous gymnastic performances, he glanced aside and saw that the little girl was wending her way toward the house. Tom came up to the fence and leaned on it, grieving, and hoping she would tarry yet awhile longer. She halted a moment on the steps and then moved toward the door. Tom heaved a great sigh as she put her foot on the threshold. But his face lit up, right away, for she tossed a pansy over the fence a moment before she disappeared.

The boy ran around and stopped within a foot or two of the flower, and then shaded his eyes with his hand and began to look down street as if he had discovered something of interest going on in that direction. Presently he picked up a straw and began trying to balance it on his nose, with his head tilted far back; and as he moved from side to side, in his efforts, he edged nearer and nearer toward the pansy; finally his bare foot rested upon it, his pliant toes closed upon it, and he hopped away with the treasure and disappeared round the corner. But only for a minute—only while he could button the flower inside his jacket, next his heart—or next his stomach, possibly, for he was not much posted in anatomy, and not hypercritical, anyway.

He returned, now, and hung about the fence till nightfall, "showing off," as before; but the girl never exhibited herself again, though Tom comforted himself a little with the hope that she had been near some window, meantime, and been aware of his attentions. Finally he strode home reluctantly, with his poor head full of visions.

All through supper his spirits were so high that his aunt wondered "what had got into the child." He took a good scolding about clodding Sid, and did not seem to mind it in the least. He tried to steal sugar under his aunt's very nose, and got his knuckles rapped for it. He said:

"Aunt, you don't whack Sid when he takes it."

"Well, Sid don't torment a body the way you do. You'd be always into that sugar if I warn't watching you."

Presently she stepped into the kitchen, and Sid, happy in his immunity, reached for the sugar-bowl—a sort of glorying over Tom which was wellnigh unbearable. But Sid's fingers slipped and the bowl dropped and broke. Tom was in ecstasies. In such ecstasies that he even controlled his tongue and was silent. He said to himself that he would not speak a word, even when his aunt came in, but would sit perfectly still till she asked who did the mischief; and then he would tell, and there would be nothing so good in the world as to see that pet model "catch it." He was so brimful of exultation that he could hardly hold himself when the old lady came back and stood above the wreck discharging lightnings of wrath from over her spectacles. He said to himself, "Now it's coming!" And the next instant he was sprawling on the floor! The potent palm was uplifted to strike again when Tom cried out:

"Hold on, now, what 'er you belting *me* for?—Sid broke it!"

Aunt Polly paused, perplexed, and Tom looked for healing pity. But when she got her tongue again, she only said:

"Umf! Well, you didn't get a lick amiss, I reckon. You been into some other audacious mischief when I wasn't around, like enough."

Then her conscience reproached her, and she yearned to say something kind and loving; but she judged that this would be construed into a confession that she had been in the wrong, and discipline forbade that. So she kept silence, and went about her affairs with a troubled heart. Tom sulked in a corner and exalted his woes. He knew that in her heart his aunt was on her knees to him, and he was morosely gratified by the consciousness of it. He would hang out no signals, he would take notice of none. He knew that a yearning glance fell upon him, now and then, through a film of tears, but he refused recognition of it. He pictured himself lying sick unto death and his aunt bending over him beseeching one little forgiving word, but he would turn his face to the wall, and die with that word unsaid. Ah, how would she feel then? And he pictured himself brought home from the river, dead, with his curls all wet, and his sore heart at rest. How she would throw herself upon him, and how her tears would fall like rain, and her lips pray God to give her back her boy and she would never, never abuse him any more! But he would lie there cold and white and make no sign—a poor little sufferer, whose griefs were at an end. He so worked upon his feelings with the pathos of these dreams, that he had to keep swallowing, he was so like to choke; and his eyes swam in a blur of water, which overflowed when he winked, and ran down and trickled from the end of his nose. And such a luxury to him was this petting of his sorrows, that he could not bear to have any worldly cheeriness or any grating delight intrude upon it; it was too sacred for such contact; and so, presently, when his cousin Mary danced in, all alive with the joy of seeing home again after an age-long visit of one week to the country, he got up and moved in clouds and darkness out at one door as she brought song and sunshine in at the other.

He wandered far from the accustomed haunts of boys, and sought desolate places that were in harmony with his spirit. A log raft in the river invited him, and he seated himself on its outer edge and contemplated the dreary vastness of the stream, wishing, the while, that he could only be drowned, all at once and unconsciously, without undergoing the uncomfortable routine devised by nature. Then he thought of his flower. He got it out, rumpled and wilted, and it mightily increased his dismal felicity. He wondered if *she* would pity him if she knew? Would she cry, and wish that she had a right to put her arms around his neck and comfort him? Or would she turn coldly away like all the hollow world? This picture brought such an agony of pleasurable suffering that he worked it over and over again in his mind and set it up in new and varied lights, till he wore it threadbare. At last he rose up sighing and departed in the darkness.

About half-past nine or ten o'clock he came along the deserted street to where the Adored Unknown lived; he paused a moment; no sound fell upon his listening ear; a candle was casting a dull glow upon the curtain of a second-story window. Was the sacred presence there? He climbed the fence, threaded his stealthy way through the plants, till he stood under that window; he looked up at it long, and with emotion; then he laid him down on the ground under it, disposing himself upon his back, with his hands clasped upon his breast and holding his poor wilted flower. And thus he would die—out in the cold world, with no shelter over his homeless head, no friendly hand to wipe the death-damps from his brow, no loving face to bend pityingly over him when the great agony came. And thus *she* would see him when she looked out upon the glad morning, and oh! would she drop one little tear upon his poor, lifeless form, would she heave one little sigh to see a bright young life so rudely blighted, so untimely cut down?

The window went up, a maid-servant's discordant voice profaned the holy calm, and a deluge of water drenched the prone martyr's remains!

The strangling hero sprang up with a relieving snort. There was a whiz as of a missile in the air, mingled with the murmur of a curse, a sound as of shivering glass followed, and a small, vague form went over the fence and shot away in the gloom.

Not long after, as Tom, all undressed for bed, was surveying his drenched garments by the light of a tallow dip, Sid woke up; but if he had any dim idea of making any "references to allusions," he thought better of it and held his peace, for there was danger in Tom's eye.

Tom turned in without the added vexation of prayers, and Sid made mental note of the omission.

CHAPTER 4

Mental Acrobatics—Attending Sunday—School
—The Superintendent—"Showing off"—Tom Lionized

THE sun rose upon a tranquil world, and beamed down upon the peaceful village like a benediction. Breakfast over, Aunt Polly had family worship: it began with a prayer built from the ground up of solid courses of Scriptural quotations, welded together with a thin mortar of originality; and from the summit of this she delivered a grim chapter of the Mosaic Law, as from Sinai.

Then Tom girded up his loins, so to speak, and went to work to "get his verses." Sid had learned his lesson days before. Tom bent all his energies to the memorizing of five verses, and he chose part of the Sermon on the Mount, because he could find no verses that were shorter. At the end of half an hour Tom had a vague general idea of his lesson, but no more, for his mind was traversing the whole field of human thought, and his hands were busy with distracting recreations. Mary took his book to hear him recite, and he tried to find his way through the fog:

"Blessed are the—a—a—"

"Poor"—

"Yes—poor; blessed are the poor—a—a—"

"In spirit—"

"In spirit; blessed are the poor in spirit, for they—they—"

"*Theirs*—"

"For *theirs*. Blessed are the poor in spirit, for theirs is the

kingdom of heaven. Blessed are they that mourn, for they—
they—"

"Sh—"

"For they—a—"

"S, H, A—"

"For they S, H—Oh, I don't know what it is!"

"*Shall!*"

"Oh, *shall*! for they shall—for they shall—a—a—shall
mourn—a—a—blessed are they that shall—they that—a—
they that shall mourn, for they shall—a—shall *what*? Why
don't you tell me, Mary?—what do you want to be so mean
for?"

"Oh, Tom, you poor thick-headed thing, I'm not teasing
you. I wouldn't do that. You must go and learn it again. Don't
you be discouraged, Tom, you'll manage it—and if you do, I'll
give you something ever so nice. There, now, that's a good boy."

"All right! What is it, Mary, tell me what it is."

"Never you mind, Tom. You know if I say it's nice, it is nice."

"You bet you that's so, Mary. All right, I'll tackle it again."

And he did "tackle it again"—and under the double
pressure of curiosity and prospective gain he did it with such
spirit that he accomplished a shining success. Mary gave him a
brand-new "Barlow" knife worth twelve and a half cents; and
the convulsion of delight that swept his system shook him to
his foundations. True, the knife would not cut anything, but
it was a "sure-enough" Barlow, and there was inconceivable
grandeur in that—though where the Western boys ever got
the idea that such a weapon could possibly be counterfeited
to its injury is an imposing mystery and will always remain so,
perhaps. Tom contrived to scarify the cupboard with it, and
was arranging to begin on the bureau, when he was called off
to dress for Sunday-school.

Mary gave him a tin basin of water and a piece of soap, and
he went outside the door and set the basin on a little bench

there; then he dipped the soap in the water and laid it down; turned up his sleeves; poured out the water on the ground, gently, and then entered the kitchen and began to wipe his face diligently on the towel behind the door. But Mary removed the towel and said:

"Now ain't you ashamed, Tom. You mustn't be so bad. Water won't hurt you."

Tom was a trifle disconcerted. The basin was refilled, and this time he stood over it a little while, gathering resolution; took in a big breath and began. When he entered the kitchen presently, with both eyes shut and groping for the towel with his hands, an honorable testimony of suds and water was dripping from his face. But when he emerged from the towel, he was not yet satisfactory, for the clean territory stopped short at his chin and his jaws, like a mask; below and beyond this line there was a dark expanse of unirrigated soil that spread downward in front and backward around his neck. Mary took him in hand, and when she was done with him he was a man and a brother, without distinction of color, and his saturated hair was neatly brushed, and its short curls wrought into a dainty and symmetrical general effect. (He privately smoothed out the curls, with labor and difficulty, and plastered his hair close down to his head; for he held curls to be effeminate, and his own filled his life with bitterness.) Then Mary got out a suit of his clothing that had been used only on Sundays during two years—they were simply called his "other clothes"—and so by that we know the size of his wardrobe. The girl "put him to rights" after he had dressed himself; she buttoned his neat roundabout up to his chin, turned his vast shirt collar down over his shoulders, brushed him off and crowned him with his speckled straw hat. He now looked exceedingly improved and uncomfortable. He was fully as uncomfortable as he looked; for there was a restraint about whole clothes and cleanliness that galled him. He hoped that Mary would forget his shoes, but the hope was blighted; she coated them thoroughly with tallow, as was the custom, and brought them out. He lost his temper and said he was always being made to do everything he didn't want to do. But Mary said, persuasively:

"Please, Tom—there's a good boy."

So he got into the shoes snarling. Mary was soon ready, and the three children set out for Sunday-school—a place that Tom hated with his whole heart; but Sid and Mary were fond of it.

Sabbath-school hours were from nine to half-past ten; and then church service. Two of the children always remained for the sermon voluntarily, and the other always remained too— for stronger reasons. The church's high-backed, uncushioned pews would seat about three hundred persons; the edifice was but a small, plain affair, with a sort of pine board tree-box on top of it for a steeple. At the door Tom dropped back a step and accosted a Sunday-dressed comrade:

"Say, Billy, got a yaller ticket?"

"Yes."

"What'll you take for her?"

"What'll you give?"

"Piece of lickrish and a fish-hook."

"Less see 'em."

Tom exhibited. They were satisfactory, and the property changed hands. Then Tom traded a couple of white alleys for three red tickets, and some small trifle or other for a couple of blue ones. He waylaid other boys as they came, and went on buying tickets of various colors ten or fifteen minutes longer. He entered the church, now, with a swarm of clean and noisy boys and girls, proceeded to his seat and started a quarrel with the first boy that came handy. The teacher, a grave, elderly man, interfered; then turned his back a moment and Tom pulled a boy's hair in the next bench, and was absorbed in his book when the boy turned around; stuck a pin in another boy, presently, in order to hear him say "Ouch!" and got a new reprimand from his teacher. Tom's whole class were of a pattern—restless, noisy, and troublesome. When they came to recite their lessons, not one of them knew his verses perfectly, but had to be prompted all along. However, they worried through, and each got his reward—in small blue tickets, each with a passage of Scripture on it; each blue ticket was pay for two verses of the recitation. Ten blue tickets equalled a red one, and could be exchanged for it; ten red tickets equalled a yellow one; for ten yellow tickets the superintendent gave a very plainly bound Bible (worth forty cents in those easy times) to the pupil. How many of my readers would have the industry and application to memorize two thousand verses, even for a Doré Bible? And yet Mary had acquired two Bibles in this way—it was the patient work of two years—and a boy of German parentage had won four or five. He once recited three thousand verses without stopping; but the strain upon his mental faculties was too great, and he was little better than an idiot from that day forth—a grievous misfortune for the school, for on great occasions, before company, the superintendent (as Tom expressed it) had always made this boy come out and "spread himself." Only the older pupils managed to keep their tickets and stick to their tedious work long enough to get a Bible, and so the delivery of one of these prizes was a rare and noteworthy circumstance; the successful pupil was so great and conspicuous for that day that on the spot every scholar's heart was fired with a fresh ambition that often lasted a couple of weeks. It is possible that Tom's mental stomach had never really hungered for one of those prizes, but unquestionably his entire being had for many a day longed for the glory and the *éclat* that came with it.

In due course the superintendent stood up in front of the pulpit, with a closed hymn-book in his hand and his forefinger inserted between its leaves, and commanded attention. When a Sunday-school superintendent makes his customary little speech, a hymn-book in the hand is as necessary as is the inevitable sheet of music in the hand of a singer who stands forward on the platform and sings a solo at a concert—though why, is a mystery: for neither the hymn-book nor the sheet of music is ever referred to by the sufferer. This superintendent was a slim creature of thirty-five, with a sandy goatee and short sandy hair; he wore a stiff standing-collar whose upper edge almost reached his ears and whose sharp points curved forward abreast the corners of his mouth—a fence that compelled a straight lookout ahead, and a turning of the whole body when a side view was required; his chin was propped on a spreading cravat which was as broad and as long as a bank-note, and had fringed ends; his boot toes were turned sharply up, in the fashion of the day, like sleigh-runners—an effect patiently and laboriously produced by the young men by sitting with their toes pressed against a wall for hours together. Mr. Walters was very earnest of mien, and very sincere and honest at heart; and he held sacred things and places in such reverence, and so separated them from worldly matters, that unconsciously to himself his Sunday-school voice had acquired a peculiar intonation which was wholly absent on week-days. He began after this fashion:

"Now, children, I want you all to sit up just as straight and pretty as you can and give me all your attention for a minute or two. There—that is it. That is the way good little boys and girls should do. I see one little girl who is looking out of the window—I am afraid she thinks I am out there somewhere— perhaps up in one of the trees making a speech to the little birds. [Applausive titter.] I want to tell you how good it makes me feel to see so many bright, clean little faces assembled in a place like this, learning to do right and be good." And so forth and so on. It is not necessary to set down the rest of the oration. It was of a pattern which does not vary, and so it is familiar to us all.

The latter third of the speech was marred by the resumption

of fights and other recreations among certain of the bad boys, and by fidgetings and whisperings that extended far and wide, washing even to the bases of isolated and incorruptible rocks like Sid and Mary. But now every sound ceased suddenly, with the subsidence of Mr. Walters' voice, and the conclusion of the speech was received with a burst of silent gratitude.

A good part of the whispering had been occasioned by an event which was more or less rare—the entrance of visitors: lawyer Thatcher, accompanied by a very feeble and aged man; a fine, portly, middle-aged gentleman with iron-gray hair; and a dignified lady who was doubtless the latter's wife. The lady was leading a child. Tom had been restless and full of chafings and repinings; conscience-smitten, too—he could not meet Amy Lawrence's eye, he could not brook her loving gaze. But when he saw this small newcomer his soul was all ablaze with bliss in a moment. The next moment he was "showing off" with all his might—cuffing boys, pulling hair, making faces—in a word, using every art that seemed likely to fascinate a girl and win her applause. His exaltation had but one alloy—the memory of his humiliation in this angel's garden—and that record in sand was fast washing out, under the waves of happiness that were sweeping over it now.

The visitors were given the highest seat of honor, and as soon as Mr. Walters' speech was finished, he introduced them to the school. The middle-aged man turned out to be a prodigious personage—no less a one than the county judge— altogether the most august creation these children had ever looked upon—and they wondered what kind of material he was made of—and they half wanted to hear him roar, and were half afraid he might, too. He was from Constantinople, twelve miles away—so he had travelled, and seen the world—these very eyes had looked upon the county court-house—which was said to have a tin roof. The awe which these reflections inspired was attested by the impressive silence and the ranks of staring eyes. This was the great Judge Thatcher, brother of their own lawyer. Jeff Thatcher immediately went forward, to be familiar with the great man and be envied by the school. It would have been music to his soul to hear the whisperings:

"Look at him, Jim! He's a going up there. Say—look! he's a going to shake hands with him—he *is* shaking hands with him! By jings, don't you wish you was Jeff?"

Mr. Walters fell to "showing off," with all sorts of official bustlings and activities, giving orders, delivering judgments, discharging directions here, there, everywhere that he could find a target. The librarian "showed off"—running hither and thither with his arms full of books and making a deal of the splutter and fuss that insect authority delights in. The young lady teachers "showed off"—bending sweetly over pupils that were lately being boxed, lifting pretty warning fingers at bad little boys and patting good ones lovingly. The young gentlemen teachers "showed off" with small scoldings and other little displays of authority and fine attention to discipline—and most of the teachers, of both sexes, found business up at the library, by the pulpit; and it was business that frequently had to be done over again two or three times (with much seeming vexation). The little girls "showed off" in various ways, and the little boys "showed off" with such diligence that the air was thick with paper wads and the murmur of scufflings. And above it all the great man sat and beamed a majestic judicial smile upon all the house, and warmed himself in the sun of his own grandeur—for he was "showing off," too.

There was only one thing wanting to make Mr. Walters' ecstasy complete, and that was a chance to deliver a Bible-prize and exhibit a prodigy. Several pupils had a few yellow tickets, but none had enough—he had been around among the star pupils inquiring. He would have given worlds, now, to have that German lad back again with a sound mind.

And now at this moment, when hope was dead, Tom Sawyer

came forward with nine yellow tickets, nine red tickets, and ten blue ones, and demanded a Bible. This was a thunderbolt out of a clear sky. Walters was not expecting an application from this source for the next ten years. But there was no getting around it—here were the certified checks, and they were good for their face. Tom was therefore elevated to a place with the Judge and the other elect, and the great news was announced from headquarters. It was the most stunning surprise of the decade, and so profound was the sensation that it lifted the new hero up to the judicial one's altitude, and the school had two marvels to gaze upon in place of one. The boys were all eaten up with envy—but those that suffered the bitterest pangs were those who perceived too late that they themselves had contributed to this hated splendor by trading tickets to Tom for the wealth he had amassed in selling whitewashing privileges. These despised themselves, as being the dupes of a wily fraud, a guileful snake in the grass.

The prize was delivered to Tom with as much effusion as the superintendent could pump up under the circumstances; but it lacked somewhat of the true gush, for the poor fellow's instinct taught him that there was a mystery here that could not well bear the light, perhaps; it was simply preposterous that *this* boy had warehoused two thousand sheaves of Scriptural wisdom on his premises—a dozen would strain his capacity, without a doubt.

Amy Lawrence was proud and glad, and she tried to make Tom see it in her face—but he wouldn't look. She wondered; then she was just a grain troubled; next a dim suspicion came and went—came again; she watched; a furtive glance told her worlds—and then her heart broke, and she was jealous, and angry, and the tears came and she hated everybody. Tom most of all (she thought).

Tom was introduced to the Judge; but his tongue was tied, his breath would hardly come, his heart quaked—partly because of the awful greatness of the man, but mainly because he was *her* parent. He would have liked to fall down and worship him, if it were in the dark. The Judge put his hand on Tom's head and called him a fine little man, and asked him what his name was. The boy stammered, gasped, and got it out:

"Tom."

"Oh, no, not Tom—it is—"

"Thomas."

"Ah, that's it. I thought there was more to it, maybe. That's very well. But you've another one I daresay, and you'll tell it to me, won't you?"

"Tell the gentleman your other name, Thomas," said Walters, "and say sir. You mustn't forget your manners."

"Thomas Sawyer—sir."

"That's it! That's a good boy. Fine boy. Fine, manly little fellow. Two thousand verses is a great many—very, very great many. And you never can be sorry for the trouble you took to learn them; for knowledge is worth more than anything there is in the world; it's what makes great men and good men; you'll be a great man and a good man yourself, some day, Thomas, and then you'll look back and say, It's all owing to the precious Sunday-school privileges of my boyhood—it's all owing to my dear teachers that taught me to learn—it's all owing to the good superintendent, who encouraged me, and watched over me, and gave me a beautiful Bible—a splendid elegant Bible— to keep and have it all for my own, always—it's all owing to right bringing up! That is what you will say, Thomas—and you wouldn't take any money for those two thousand verses—no indeed you wouldn't. And now you wouldn't mind telling me and this lady some of the things you've learned—no, I know you wouldn't—for we are proud of little boys that learn. Now, no doubt you know the names of all the twelve disciples. Won't you tell us the names of the first two that were appointed?"

Tom was tugging at a button-hole and looking sheepish.

He blushed, now, and his eyes fell. Mr. Walters' heart sank within him. He said to himself, it is not possible that the boy can answer the simplest question—why *did* the Judge ask him? Yet he felt obliged to speak up and say:

"Answer the gentleman, Thomas—don't be afraid."

Tom still hung fire.

"Now I know you'll tell *me*," said the lady. "The names of the first two disciples were—"

"*David and Goliath!*"

Let us draw the curtain of charity over the rest of the scene.

CHAPTER 5

A Useful Minister—In Church—The Climax

ABOUT half-past ten the cracked bell of the small church began to ring, and presently the people began to gather for the morning sermon. The Sunday-school children distributed themselves about the house and occupied pews with their parents, so as to be under supervision. Aunt Polly came, and Tom and Sid and Mary sat with her—Tom being placed next the aisle, in order that he might be as far away from the open window and the seductive outside summer scenes as possible. The crowd filed up the aisles: the aged and needy postmaster, who had seen better days; the mayor and his wife—for they had a mayor there, among other unnecessaries; the justice of the peace; the widow Douglass, fair, smart, and forty, a generous, good-hearted soul and well-to-do, her hill mansion the only palace in the town, and the most hospitable and much the most lavish in the matter of festivities that St. Petersburg could boast; the bent and venerable Major and Mrs. Ward; lawyer Riverson, the new notable from a distance; next the belle of the village, followed by a troop of lawn-clad and ribbon-decked young heart-breakers; then all the young clerks in town in a body—for they had stood in the vestibule sucking their cane-heads, a circling wall of oiled and simpering admirers, till the last girl had run their gantlet; and last of all came the Model Boy, Willie Mufferson, taking as heedful care of his mother as if she were cut glass. He always brought his mother to church, and was the pride of all the matrons. The boys all hated him, he was so good. And besides, he had been "thrown up to them" so much. His white handkerchief was hanging out of his pocket behind, as usual on Sundays—accidentally. Tom had no handkerchief, and he looked upon boys who had as snobs.

The congregation being fully assembled, now, the bell rang once more, to warn laggards and stragglers, and then a solemn hush fell upon the church which was only broken by the tittering and whispering of the choir in the gallery. The choir always tittered and whispered all through service. There was once a church choir that was not ill-bred, but I have forgotten where it was, now. It was a great many years ago, and I can scarcely remember anything about it, but I think it was in some foreign country.

The minister gave out the hymn, and read it through with a relish, in a peculiar style which was much admired in that part of the country. His voice began on a medium key and climbed steadily up till it reached a certain point, where it bore with strong emphasis upon the topmost word and then plunged down as if from a spring-board:

Shall I be car-ri-ed toe the skies, on flow'ry *beds*

of ease,

Whilst others fight to win the prize, and sail thro' *blood-*

y seas?

He was regarded as a wonderful reader. At church "sociables" he was always called upon to read poetry; and when he was through, the ladies would lift up their hands and let them fall helplessly in their laps, and "wall" their eyes, and shake their heads, as much as to say, "Words cannot express it; it is too beautiful, *too* beautiful for this mortal earth."

After the hymn had been sung, the Rev. Mr. Sprague turned himself into a bulletin-board, and read off "notices" of meetings and societies and things till it seemed that the list would stretch out to the crack of doom—a queer custom which is still kept up in America, even in cities, away here in this age of abundant newspapers. Often, the less there is to justify a traditional custom, the harder it is to get rid of it.

And now the minister prayed. A good, generous prayer it was, and went into details: it pleaded for the church, and the little children of the church; for the other churches of the village; for the village itself; for the county; for the State; for the State officers; for the United States; for the churches of the United States; for Congress; for the President; for the officers of the Government; for poor sailors, tossed by stormy seas; for the oppressed millions groaning under the heel of European monarchies and Oriental despotisms; for such as have the light and the good tidings, and yet have not eyes to see nor ears to hear withal; for the heathen in the far islands of the sea; and closed with a supplication that the words he was about to speak might find grace and favor, and be as seed sown in fertile ground, yielding in time a grateful harvest of good. Amen.

There was a rustling of dresses, and the standing congregation sat down. The boy whose history this book relates did not enjoy the prayer, he only endured it—if he even did that much. He was restive all through it; he kept tally of the details of the prayer, unconsciously—for he was not listening, but he knew the ground of old, and the clergyman's regular route over it—and when a little trifle of new matter was interlarded, his ear detected it and his whole nature resented it; he considered additions unfair, and scoundrelly. In the midst of the prayer a fly had lit on the back of the pew in front of him and tortured his spirit by calmly rubbing its hands together, embracing its head with its arms, and polishing it so vigorously that it seemed to almost part company with the body, and the slender thread of a neck was exposed to view; scraping its wings with its hind legs and smoothing them to its body as if they had been coat-tails; going through its whole toilet as tranquilly as if it knew it was perfectly safe. As indeed it was; for as sorely as Tom's hands itched to grab for it they did not dare—he believed his soul would be instantly destroyed if he did such a thing while the prayer was going on. But with the closing sentence his hand began to curve and steal forward; and the instant the "Amen" was out the fly was a prisoner of war. His aunt detected the act and made him let it go.

The minister gave out his text and droned along monotonously through an argument that was so prosy that many a head by and by began to nod—and yet it was an argument that dealt in limitless fire and brimstone and thinned the predestined elect down to a company so small as to be hardly worth the saving. Tom counted the pages of the sermon; after church he always knew how many pages there had been, but he seldom knew anything else about the discourse. However, this time he was really interested for a little while. The minister made a grand and moving picture of the assembling together of the world's hosts at the millennium when the lion and the lamb should lie down together and a little child should lead them. But the pathos, the lesson, the moral of the great spectacle were lost upon the boy; he only thought of the conspicuousness of the principal character before the on-looking nations; his face lit with the thought, and he said to himself that he wished he could be that child, if it was a tame lion.

Now he lapsed into suffering again, as the dry argument was resumed. Presently he bethought him of a treasure he had and got it out. It was a large black beetle with formidable jaws—a "pinchbug," he called it. It was in a percussion-cap box. The first thing the beetle did was to take him by the finger. A natural fillip followed, the beetle went floundering into the aisle and lit on its back, and the hurt finger went into the boy's mouth. The beetle lay there working its helpless legs, unable to turn over. Tom eyed it, and longed for it; but it was safe out of his reach. Other people uninterested in the sermon found relief in the beetle, and they eyed it too. Presently a vagrant poodle dog came idling along, sad at heart, lazy with the summer softness and the quiet, weary of captivity, sighing for change. He spied the beetle; the drooping tail lifted and wagged. He surveyed the prize; walked around it; smelt at it from a safe distance; walked around it again; grew bolder, and took a closer smell; then lifted his lip and made a gingerly snatch at it, just missing it; made another, and another; began to enjoy the diversion; subsided to his stomach with the beetle between his paws, and continued his experiments; grew weary at last, and then indifferent and absent-minded. His head nodded, and little by little his chin descended and touched the enemy, who seized it. There was a sharp yelp, a flirt of the poodle's head, and the beetle fell a couple of yards away, and lit on its back once more. The neighboring spectators shook with a gentle inward joy, several faces went behind fans and hand-kerchiefs, and Tom was entirely happy. The dog looked foolish, and probably felt so; but there was resentment in his heart, too, and a craving for revenge. So he went to the beetle and began a wary attack on it again; jumping at it from every point of a circle, lighting with his fore-paws within an inch of the creature, making even closer snatches at it with his teeth, and jerking his head till his ears flapped again. But he grew tired once more, after a while; tried to amuse himself with a fly but found no relief; followed an ant around, with his nose close to the floor, and quickly wearied of that; yawned, sighed, forgot the beetle entirely, and sat down on it. Then there was a wild yelp of agony and the poodle went sailing up the aisle; the yelps continued, and so did the dog; he crossed the house in front of the altar; he flew down the other aisle; he crossed before the doors; he clamored up the home-stretch; his anguish grew with his progress, till presently he was but a woolly comet moving in its orbit with the gleam and the speed of light. At last the frantic sufferer sheered from its course, and sprang into its master's lap; he flung it out of the window, and the voice of distress quickly thinned away and died in the distance.

By this time the whole church was red-faced and suffocating with suppressed laughter, and the sermon had come to a dead standstill. The discourse was resumed presently, but it went lame and halting, all possibility of impressiveness being at an end; for even the gravest sentiments were constantly being received with a smothered burst of unholy mirth, under cover of some remote pew-back, as if the poor parson had said a rarely facetious thing. It was a genuine relief to the whole congregation when the ordeal was over and the benediction pronounced.

Tom Sawyer went home quite cheerful, thinking to himself that there was some satisfaction about divine service when there was a bit of variety in it. He had but one marring thought; he was willing that the dog should play with his pinchbug, but he did not think it was upright in him to carry it off.

CHAPTER 6

Self-Examination—Dentistry—The Midnight Charm
—Witches and Devils—Cautious Approaches—Happy Hours

MONDAY morning found Tom Sawyer miserable. Monday morning always found him so—because it began another week's slow suffering in school. He generally began that day with wishing he had had no intervening holiday, it made the going into captivity and fetters again so much more odious.

Tom lay thinking. Presently it occurred to him that he wished he was sick; then he could stay home from school. Here was a vague possibility. He canvassed his system. No ailment was found, and he investigated again. This time he thought he could detect colicky symptoms, and he began to encourage them with considerable hope. But they soon grew feeble, and presently died wholly away. He reflected further. Suddenly he discovered something. One of his upper front teeth was loose. This was lucky; he was about to begin to groan, as a "starter," as he called it, when it occurred to him that if he came into court with that argument, his aunt would pull it out, and that would hurt. So he thought he would hold the tooth in reserve for the present, and seek further. Nothing offered for some little time, and then he remembered hearing the doctor tell about a certain thing that laid up a patient for two or three weeks and threatened to make him lose a finger. So the boy eagerly drew his sore toe from under the sheet and held it up for inspection. But now he did not know the necessary symptoms. However, it seemed well worth while to chance it, so he fell to groaning with considerable spirit.

But Sid slept on unconscious.

Tom groaned louder, and fancied that he began to feel pain in the toe.

No result from Sid.

Tom was panting with his exertions by this time. He took a rest and then swelled himself up and fetched a succession of admirable groans.

Sid snored on.

Tom was aggravated. He said, "Sid, Sid!" and shook him. This course worked well, and Tom began to groan again. Sid yawned, stretched, then brought himself up on his elbow with a snort, and began to stare at Tom. Tom went on groaning. Sid said:

"Tom! Say, Tom!"

No response.

"Here, Tom! *Tom!* What is the matter, Tom?" And he shook him and looked in his face anxiously.

Tom moaned out:

"Oh, don't, Sid. Don't joggle me."

"Why, what's the matter, Tom? I must call auntie."

"No—never mind. It'll be over by and by, maybe. Don't call anybody."

"But I must! *Don't* groan so, Tom, it's awful. How long you been this way?"

"Hours. Ouch! Oh, don't stir so, Sid, you'll kill me."

"Tom, why didn't you wake me sooner? Oh, Tom, *don'y*! It makes my flesh crawl to hear you. Tom, what is the matter?"

"I forgive you everything, Sid. [Groan.] Everything you've ever done to me. When I'm gone—"

"Oh, Tom, you ain't dying, are you? Don't, Tom—oh, don't. Maybe—"

"I forgive everybody, Sid. [Groan.] Tell 'em so, Sid. And Sid, you give my window-sash and my cat with one eye to that new girl that's come to town, and tell her—"

But Sid had snatched his clothes and gone. Tom was suffering in reality, now, so handsomely was his imagination working, and so his groans had gathered quite a genuine tone.

Sid flew downstairs and said:

"Oh, Aunt Polly, come! Tom's dying!"

"Dying!"

"Yes'm. Don't wait—come quick!"

"Rubbage! I don't believe it!"

But she fled upstairs, nevertheless, with Sid and Mary at her heels. And her face grew white, too, and her lip trembled. When she reached the bedside she gasped out:

"You, Tom! Tom, what's the matter with you?"

"Oh, auntie, I'm—"

"What's the matter with you—what *is* the matter with you, child?"

"Oh, auntie, my sore toe's mortified!"

The old lady sank down into a chair and laughed a little, then cried a little, then did both together. This restored her and she said:

"Tom, what a turn you did give me. Now you shut up that nonsense and climb out of this."

The groans ceased and the pain vanished from the toe. The boy felt a little foolish, and he said:

"Aunt Polly, it *seemed* mortified, and it hurt so I never minded my tooth at all."

"Your tooth, indeed! What's the matter with your tooth?"

"One of them's loose, and it aches perfectly awful."

"There, there, now, don't begin that groaning again. Open your mouth. Well—your tooth *is* loose, but you're not going to die about that. Mary, get me a silk thread, and a chunk of fire out of the kitchen."

Tom said:

"Oh, please, auntie, don't pull it out. It don't hurt any more. I wish I may never stir if it does. Please don't, auntie. *I* don't want to stay home from school."

"Oh, you don't, don't you? So all this row was because you thought you'd get to stay home from school and go a-fishing? Tom, Tom, I love you so, and you seem to try every way you can to break my old heart with your outrageousness." By this time the dental instruments were ready. The old lady made one end of the silk thread fast to Tom's tooth with a loop and tied the other to the bedpost. Then she seized the chunk of fire and suddenly thrust it almost into the boy's face. The tooth hung dangling by the bedpost, now.

But all trials bring their compensations. As Tom wended to school after breakfast, he was the envy of every boy he met because the gap in his upper row of teeth enabled him to expectorate in a new and admirable way. He gathered quite a following of lads interested in the exhibition; and one that had cut his finger and had been a centre of fascination and homage up to this time, now found himself suddenly without an adherent, and shorn of his glory. His heart was heavy, and he said with a disdain which he did not feel that it wasn't anything to spit like Tom Sawyer; but another boy said, "Sour grapes!" and he wandered away a dismantled hero.

Shortly Tom came upon the juvenile pariah of the village, Huckleberry Finn, son of the town drunkard. Huckleberry was cordially hated and dreaded by all the mothers of the town, because he was idle and lawless and vulgar and bad—and because all their children admired him so, and delighted in his forbidden society, and wished they dared to be like him. Tom was like the rest of the respectable boys, in that he envied Huckleberry his gaudy outcast condition, and was under strict orders not to play with him. So he played with him every time he got a chance. Huckleberry was always dressed in the cast-off clothes of full-grown men, and they were in perennial bloom and fluttering with rags. His hat was a vast ruin with a wide crescent lopped out of its brim; his coat, when he wore one, hung nearly to his heels and had the rearward buttons far down the back; but one suspender supported his trousers; the seat of the trousers bagged low and contained nothing, the fringed legs dragged in the dirt when not rolled up.

Huckleberry came and went, at his own free will. He slept on doorsteps in fine weather and in empty hogsheads in wet; he did not have to go to school or to church, or call any being master or obey anybody; he could go fishing or swimming when and where he chose, and stay as long as it suited him; nobody forbade him to fight; he could sit up as late as he pleased; he was always the first boy that went barefoot in the spring and the last to resume leather in the fall; he never had to wash, nor put on clean clothes; he could swear wonderfully. In a word, everything that goes to make life precious that boy had. So thought every harassed, hampered, respectable boy in St. Petersburg.

Tom hailed the romantic outcast:

"Hello, Huckleberry!"

"Hello yourself, and see how you like it."

"What's that you got?"

"Dead cat."

"Lemme see him, Huck. My, he's pretty stiff. Where'd you get him?"

"Bought him off'n a boy."

"What did you give?"

"I give a blue ticket and a bladder that I got at the slaughter-house."

"Where'd you get the blue ticket?"

"Bought it off'n Ben Rogers two weeks ago for a hoop-stick."

"Say—what is dead cats good for, Huck?"

"Good for? Cure warts with."

"No! Is that so? I know something that's better."

"I bet you don't. What is it?"

"Why, spunk-water."

"Spunk-water! I wouldn't give a dern for spunk-water."

"You wouldn't, wouldn't you? D'you ever try it?"

"No, I hain't. But Bob Tanner did."

"Who told you so!"

"Why, he told Jeff Thatcher, and Jeff told Johnny Baker, and Johnny told Jim Hollis, and Jim told Ben Rogers, and Ben told a nigger, and the nigger told me. There now!"

"Well, what of it? They'll all lie. Leastways all but the nigger. I don't know *him*. But I never see a nigger that *wouldn't* lie. Shucks! Now you tell me how Bob Tanner done it, Huck."

"Why, he took and dipped his hand in a rotten stump where the rain-water was."

"In the daytime?"

"Certainly."

"With his face to the stump?"

"Yes. Least I reckon so."

"Did he *say* anything?"

"I don't reckon he did. I don't know."

"Aha! Talk about trying to cure warts with spunk-water such a blame fool way as that! Why, that ain't a-going to do any good. You got to go all by yourself, to the middle of the woods, where you know there's a spunk- water stump, and just as it's midnight you back up against the stump and jam your hand in and say:

'Barley-corn, barley-corn, injun-meal shorts,
Spunk-water, spunk-water, swaller these warts,'

and then walk away quick, eleven steps, with your eyes shut, and then turn around three times and walk home without speaking to anybody. Because if you speak the charm's busted."

"Well, that sounds like a good way; but that ain't the way Bob Tanner done."

"No, sir, you can bet he didn't, becuz he's the wartiest boy in this town; and he wouldn't have a wart on him if he'd knowed how to work spunk-water. I've took off thousands of warts off of my hands that way, Huck. I play with frogs so much that I've always got considerable many warts. Sometimes I take 'em off with a bean."

"Yes, bean's good. I've done that."

"Have you? What's your way?"

"You take and split the bean, and cut the wart so as to get some blood, and then you put the blood on one piece of the bean and take and dig a hole and bury it 'bout midnight at the crossroads in the dark of the moon, and then you burn up the rest of the bean. You see that piece that's got the blood on it will keep drawing and drawing, trying to fetch the other piece to it, and so that helps the blood to draw the wart, and pretty soon off she comes."

"Yes, that's it, Huck—that's it; though when you're burying it if you say 'Down bean; off wart; come no more to bother me!' it's better. That's the way Joe Harper does, and he's been nearly to Coonville and most everywheres. But say—how do you cure 'em with dead cats?"

"Why, you take your cat and go and get in the grave-yard 'long about midnight when somebody that was wicked has been buried; and when it's midnight a devil will come, or maybe two or three, but you can't see 'em, you can only hear something like the wind, or maybe hear 'em talk; and when they're taking that feller away, you heave your cat after 'em and say, 'Devil follow corpse, cat follow devil, warts follow cat, I'm done with ye!' That'll fetch *any*wart."

"Sounds right. D'you ever try it, Huck?"

"No, but old Mother Hopkins told me."

"Well, I reckon it's so, then. Becuz they say she's a witch."

"Say! Why, Tom, I *know* she is. She witched pap. Pap says so his own self. He come along one day, and he see she was a-witching him, so he took up a rock, and if she hadn't dodged, he'd a got her. Well, that very night he rolled off 'n a shed wher' he was a layin drunk, and broke his arm."

"Why, that's awful. How did he know she was a-witching him?"

"Lord, pap can tell, easy. Pap says when they keep looking at you right stiddy, they're a-witching you. Specially if they mumble. Becuz when they mumble they're saying the Lord's Prayer backards."

"Say, Hucky, when you going to try the cat?"

"To-night. I reckon they'll come after old Hoss Williams to-night."

"But they buried him Saturday. Didn't they get him Saturday night?"

"Why, how you talk! How could their charms work till midnight?—and *then* it's Sunday. Devils don't slosh around much of a Sunday, I don't reckon."

"I never thought of that. That's so. Lemme go with you?"

"Of course—if you ain't afeard."

"Afeard! 'Tain't likely. Will you meow?"

"Yes—and you meow back, if you get a chance. Last time, you kep' me a-meowing around till old Hays went to throwing rocks at me and says 'Dern that cat!' and so I hove a brick through his window—but don't you tell."

"I won't. I couldn't meow that night, becuz auntie was watching me, but I'll meow this time. Say—what's that?"

"Nothing but a tick."

"Where'd you get him?"

"Out in the woods."

"What'll you take for him?"

"I don't know. I don't want to sell him."

"All right. It's a mighty small tick, anyway."

"Oh, anybody can run a tick down that don't belong to them. I'm satisfied with it. It's a good enough tick for me."

"Sho, there's ticks a plenty. I could have a thousand of 'em if I wanted to."

"Well, why don't you? Becuz you know mighty well you can't. This is a pretty early tick, I reckon. It's the first one I've seen this year."

"Say, Huck—I'll give you my tooth for him."

"Less see it."

Tom got out a bit of paper and carefully unrolled it. Huckleberry viewed it wistfully. The temptation was very strong. At last he said:

"Is it genuwyne?"

Tom lifted his lip and showed the vacancy.

"Well, all right," said Huckleberry, "it's a trade."

Tom enclosed the tick in the percussion-cap box that had lately been the pinchbug's prison, and the boys separated, each feeling wealthier than before.

When Tom reached the little isolated frame school-house, he strode in briskly, with the manner of one who had come with all honest speed. He hung his hat on a peg and flung himself into his seat with business-like alacrity. The master, throned on high in his great splint-bottom arm-chair, was dozing, lulled by the drowsy hum of study. The interruption roused him.

"Thomas Sawyer!"

Tom knew that when his name was pronounced in full, it meant trouble.

"Sir!"

"Come up here. Now, sir, why are you late again, as usual?"

Tom was about to take refuge in a lie, when he saw two long tails of yellow hair hanging down a back that he recognized by the electric sympathy of love; and by that form was *the only vacant place* on the girls' side of the school-house. He instantly said:

"*I stopped to talk with Huckleberry Finn!*"

The master's pulse stood still, and he stared helplessly. The buzz of study ceased. The pupils wondered if this foolhardy boy had lost his mind. The master said:

"You—you did what?"

"Stopped to talk with Huckleberry Finn."

There was no mistaking the words.

"Thomas Sawyer, this is the most astounding confession I have ever listened to. No mere ferule will answer for this offence. Take off your jacket."

The master's arm performed until it was tired and the stock of switches notably diminished. Then the order followed:

"Now, sir, go and sit with the *girls*! And let this be a warning to you."

The titter that rippled around the room appeared to abash the boy, but in reality that result was caused rather more by his worshipful awe of his unknown idol and the dread pleasure that lay in his high good fortune. He sat down upon the end of the pine bench and the girl hitched herself away from him with a toss of her head. Nudges and winks and whispers traversed the room, but Tom sat still, with his arms upon the long, low desk before him, and seemed to study his book.

By and by attention ceased from him, and the accustomed school murmur rose upon the dull air once more. Presently the boy began to steal furtive glances at the girl. She observed it, "made a mouth" at him and gave him the back of her head for the space of a minute. When she cautiously faced around again, a peach lay before her. She thrust it away. Tom gently put it back. She thrust it away again, but with less animosity. Tom patiently returned it to its place. Then she let it remain. Tom scrawled on his slate, "Please take it—I got more." The girl glanced at the words, but made no sign. Now the boy began to draw something on the slate, hiding his work with his left hand. For a time the girl refused to notice; but her human curiosity presently began to manifest itself by hardly perceptible signs. The boy worked on, apparently unconscious. The girl made a sort of non-committal attempt to see, but the boy did not betray that he was aware of it. At last she gave in and hesitatingly whispered:

"Let me see it."

Tom partly uncovered a dismal caricature of a house with two gable ends to it and a corkscrew of smoke issuing from the chimney. Then the girl's interest began to fasten itself upon the work and she forgot everything else. When it was finished, she gazed a moment, then whispered:

"It's nice—make a man."

The artist erected a man in the front yard, that resembled a derrick. He could have stepped over the house; but the girl was not hypercritical; she was satisfied with the monster, and whispered:

"It's a beautiful man—now make me coming along."

Tom drew an hour-glass with a full moon and straw limbs to it and armed the spreading fingers with a portentous fan. The girl said:

"It's ever so nice—I wish I could draw."

"It's easy," whispered Tom, "I'll learn you."

"Oh, will you? When?"

"At noon. Do you go home to dinner?"

"I'll stay if you will."

"Good—that's a whack. What's your name?"

"Becky Thatcher. What's yours? Oh, I know. It's Thomas Sawyer."

"That's the name they lick me by. I'm Tom when I'm good. You call me Tom, will you?"

"Yes."

Now Tom began to scrawl something on the slate, hiding the words from the girl. But she was not backward this time. She begged to see. Tom said:

"Oh, it ain't anything."

"Yes it is."

"No it ain't. You don't want to see."

"Yes I do, indeed I do. Please let me."

"You'll tell."

"No I won't—deed and deed and double deed won't."

"You won't tell anybody at all? Ever, as long as you live?"

"No, I won't ever tell *any*body. Now let me."

"Oh, YOU don't want to see!"

"Now that you treat me so, I *will* see." And she put her small hand upon his and a little scuffle ensued, Tom pretending to resist in earnest but letting his hand slip by degrees till these words were revealed: "*I love you.*"

"Oh, you bad thing!" And she hit his hand a smart rap, but reddened and looked pleased, nevertheless.

Just at this juncture the boy felt a slow, fateful grip closing on his ear, and a steady lifting impulse. In that wise he was borne across the house and deposited in his own seat, under a peppering fire of giggles from the whole school. Then the master stood over him during a few awful moments, and finally moved away to his throne without saying a word. But although Tom's ear tingled, his heart was jubilant.

As the school quieted down Tom made an honest effort to study, but the turmoil within him was too great. In turn he took his place in the reading class and made a botch of it; then in the geography class and turned lakes into mountains, mountains into rivers, and rivers into continents, till chaos was come again; then in the spelling class, and got "turned down," by a succession of mere baby words, till he brought up at the foot and yielded up the pewter medal which he had worn with ostentation for months.

CHAPTER 7

A Treaty Entered Into—Early Lessons—A Mistake Made

THE harder Tom tried to fasten his mind on his book, the more his ideas wandered. So at last, with a sigh and a yawn, he gave it up. It seemed to him that the noon recess would never come. The air was utterly dead. There was not a breath stirring. It was the sleepiest of sleepy days. The drowsing murmur of the five and twenty studying scholars soothed the soul like the spell that is in the murmur of bees. Away off in the flaming sunshine, Cardiff Hill lifted its soft green sides through a shimmering veil of heat, tinted with the purple of distance; a few birds floated on lazy wing high in the air; no other living thing was visible but some cows, and they were asleep. Tom's heart ached to be free, or else to have something of interest to do to pass the dreary time. His hand wandered into his pocket and his face lit up with a glow of gratitude that was prayer, though he did not know it. Then furtively the percussion-cap box came out. He released the tick and put him on the long flat desk. The creature probably glowed with a gratitude that amounted to prayer, too, at this moment, but it was premature: for when he started thankfully to travel off, Tom turned him aside with a pin and made him take a new direction.

Tom's bosom friend sat next him, suffering just as Tom had been, and now he was deeply and gratefully interested in this entertainment in an instant. This bosom friend was Joe Harper. The two boys were sworn friends all the week, and embattled enemies on Saturdays. Joe took a pin out of his lapel and began to assist in exercising the prisoner. The sport grew in interest momently. Soon Tom said that they were interfering with each other, and neither getting the fullest benefit of the tick. So he put Joe's slate on the desk and drew a line down the middle of it from top to bottom.

"Now," said he, "as long as he is on your side you can stir him up and I'll let him alone; but if you let him get away and get on my side, you're to leave him alone as long as I can keep him from crossing over."

"All right, go ahead; start him up."

The tick escaped from Tom, presently, and crossed the equator. Joe harassed him awhile, and then he got away and crossed back again. This change of base occurred often. While one boy was worrying the tick with absorbing interest, the other would look on with interest as strong, the two heads bowed together over the slate, and the two souls dead to all things else. At last luck seemed to settle and abide with Joe. The tick tried this, that, and the other course, and got as excited and as anxious as the boys themselves, but time and again just as he would have victory in his very grasp, so to speak, and Tom's fingers would be twitching to begin, Joe's pin would deftly head him off, and keep possession. At last Tom could stand it no longer. The temptation was too strong. So he reached out and lent a hand with his pin. Joe was angry in a moment. Said he:

"Tom, you let him alone."

"I only just want to stir him up a little, Joe."

"No, sir, it ain't fair; you just let him alone."

"Blame it, I ain't going to stir him much."

"Let him alone, I tell you."

"I won't!"

"You shall—he's on my side of the line."

"Look here, Joe Harper, whose is that tick?"

"I don't care whose tick he is—he's on my side of the line, and you sha'n't touch him."

"Well, I'll just bet I will, though. He's my tick and I'll do what I blame please with him, or die!"

A tremendous whack came down on Tom's shoulders, and its duplicate on Joe's; and for the space of two minutes the dust continued to fly from the two jackets and the whole school to enjoy it. The boys had been too absorbed to notice the hush that had stolen upon the school awhile before when the master came tiptoeing down the room and stood over them. He had contemplated a good part of the performance before he contributed his bit of variety to it.

When school broke up at noon, Tom flew to Becky Thatcher, and whispered in her ear:

"Put on your bonnet and let on you're going home; and when you get to the corner, give the rest of 'em the slip, and turn down through the lane and come back. I'll go the other way and come it over 'em the same way."

So the one went off with one group of scholars, and the other with another. In a little while the two met at the bottom of the lane, and when they reached the school they had it all to themselves. Then they sat together, with a slate before them, and Tom gave Becky the pencil and held her hand in his, guiding it, and so created another surprising house. When the interest in art began to wane, the two fell to talking. Tom was swimming in bliss. He said:

"Do you love rats?"

"No! I hate them!"

"Well, I do, too—*live* ones. But I mean dead ones, to swing round your head with a string."

"No, I don't care for rats much, anyway. What I like is chewing-gum."

"Oh, I should say so! I wish I had some now."

"Do you? I've got some. I'll let you chew it awhile, but you must give it back to me."

That was agreeable, so they chewed it turn about, and

dangled their legs against the bench in excess of contentment.

"Was you ever at a circus?" said Tom.

"Yes, and my pa's going to take me again some time, if I'm good."

"I been to the circus three or four times—lots of times. Church ain't shucks to a circus. There's things going on at a circus all the time. I'm going to be a clown in a circus when I grow up."

"Oh, are you! That will be nice. They're so lovely, all spotted up."

"Yes, that's so. And they get slathers of money—most a dollar a day, Ben Rogers says. Say, Becky, was you ever engaged?"

"What's that?"

"Why, engaged to be married."

"No."

"Would you like to?"

"I reckon so. I don't know. What is it like?"

"Like? Why it ain't like anything. You only just tell a boy you won't ever have anybody but him, ever ever ever, and then you kiss and that's all. Anybody can do it."

"Kiss? What do you kiss for?"

"Why, that, you know, is to—well, they always do that."

"Everybody?"

"Why, yes, everybody that's in love with each other. Do you remember what I wrote on the slate?"

"Ye—yes."

"What was it?"

"I sha'n't tell you."

"Shall I tell *you*?"

"Ye—yes—but some other time."

"No, now."

"No, not now—to-morrow."

"Oh, no, *now*. Please, Becky—I'll whisper it, I'll whisper it ever so easy."

Becky hesitating, Tom took silence for consent, and passed his arm about her waist and whispered the tale ever so softly, with his mouth close to her ear. And then he added:

"Now you whisper it to me—just the same."

She resisted, for a while, and then said:

"You turn your face away so you can't see, and then I will. But you mustn't ever tell anybody—*will* you, Tom? Now you won't, *will* you?"

"No, indeed, indeed I won't. Now, Becky."

He turned his face away. She bent timidly around till her breath stirred his curls and whispered, "I—love—you!"

Then she sprang away and ran around and around the desks and benches, with Tom after her, and took refuge in a corner at last, with her little white apron to her face. Tom clasped her about her neck and pleaded:

"Now, Becky, it's all done—all over but the kiss. Don't you be afraid of that—it ain't anything at all. Please, Becky." And he tugged at her apron and the hands.

By and by she gave up, and let her hands drop; her face, all glowing with the struggle, came up and submitted. Tom kissed the red lips and said:

"Now it's all done, Becky. And always after this, you know, you ain't ever to love anybody but me, and you ain't ever to marry anybody but me, ever never and forever. Will you?"

"No, I'll never love anybody but you, Tom, and I'll never marry anybody but you—and you ain't to ever marry anybody but me, either."

"Certainly. Of course. That's *part* of it. And always coming to school or when we're going home, you're to walk with me, when there ain't anybody looking—and you choose me and I choose you at parties, because that's the way you do when you're engaged."

"It's so nice. I never heard of it before."

"Oh, it's ever so gay! Why, me and Amy Lawrence—"

The big eyes told Tom his blunder and he stopped, confused.

"Oh, Tom! Then I ain't the first you've ever been engaged to!"

The child began to cry. Tom said:

"Oh, don't cry, Becky, I don't care for her any more."

"Yes, you do, Tom—you know you do."

Tom tried to put his arm about her neck, but she pushed him away and turned her face to the wall, and went on crying. Tom tried again, with soothing words in his mouth, and was repulsed again. Then his pride was up, and he strode away and went outside. He stood about, restless and uneasy, for a while, glancing at the door, every now and then, hoping she would repent and come to find him. But she did not. Then he began to feel badly and fear that he was in the wrong. It was a hard struggle with him to make new advances, now, but he nerved himself to it and entered. She was still standing back there in the corner, sobbing, with her face to the wall. Tom's heart smote him. He went to her and stood a moment, not knowing exactly how to proceed. Then he said hesitatingly:

"Becky, I—I don't care for anybody but you."

No reply—but sobs.

"Becky"—pleadingly. "Becky, won't you say something?"

More sobs.

Tom got out his chiefest jewel, a brass knob from the top of an andiron, and passed it around her so that she could see it, and said:

"Please, Becky, won't you take it?"

She struck it to the floor. Then Tom marched out of the house and over the hills and far away, to return to school no more that day. Presently Becky began to suspect. She ran to the door; he was not in sight; she flew around to the play-yard; he was not there. Then she called:

"Tom! Come back, Tom!"

She listened intently, but there was no answer. She had no companions but silence and loneliness. So she sat down to cry again and upbraid herself; and by this time the scholars began to gather again, and she had to hide her griefs and still her broken heart and take up the cross of a long, dreary, aching afternoon, with none among the strangers about her to exchange sorrows with.

CHAPTER 8

Tom Decides on his Course—Old Scenes Re-enacted

TOM dodged hither and thither through lanes until he was well out of the track of returning scholars, and then fell into a moody jog. He crossed a small "branch" two or three times, because of a prevailing juvenile superstition that to cross water baffled pursuit. Half an hour later he was disappearing behind the Douglas mansion on the summit of Cardiff Hill, and the school-house was hardly distinguishable away off in the valley behind him. He entered a dense wood, picked his pathless way to the centre of it, and sat down on a mossy spot under a spreading oak. There was not even a zephyr stirring; the dead noonday heat had even stilled the songs of the birds; nature lay in a trance that was broken by no sound but the occasional far-off hammering of a wood-pecker, and this seemed to render the pervading silence and sense of loneliness the more profound. The boy's soul was steeped in melancholy; his feelings were in happy accord with his surroundings. He sat long with his elbows on his knees and his chin in his hands, meditating. It seemed to him that life was but a trouble, at best, and he more than half envied Jimmy Hodges, so lately released; it must be very peaceful, he thought, to lie and slumber and dream forever and ever, with the wind whispering through the trees and caressing the grass and the flowers over the grave, and nothing to bother and grieve about, ever any more. If he only had a clean Sunday-school record he could be willing to go, and be done with it all. Now as to this girl. What had he done? Nothing. He had meant the best in the world, and been treated like a dog—like a very dog. She would be sorry some day—maybe when it was too late. Ah, if he could only die *temporarily*!

But the elastic heart of youth cannot be compressed into one constrained shape long at a time. Tom presently began to drift insensibly back into the concerns of this life again. What if he turned his back, now, and disappeared mysteriously? What if he went away—ever so far away, into unknown countries beyond the seas—and never came back any more! How would she feel then! The idea of being a clown recurred to him now, only to fill him with disgust. For frivolity and jokes and spotted tights were an offense, when they intruded themselves upon a spirit that was exalted into the vague august realm of the romantic. No, he would be a soldier, and return after long years, all war-worn and illustrious. No—better still, he would join the Indians, and hunt buffaloes and go on the warpath in the mountain ranges and the trackless great plains of the Far West, and away in the future come back a great chief, bristling with feathers, hideous with paint, and prance into Sunday-school, some drowsy summer morning, with a blood-curdling war-whoop, and sear the eyeballs of all his companions with unappeasable envy. But no, there was something gaudier even than this. He would be a pirate! That was it! *Now* his future lay plain before him, and glowing with unimaginable splendor. How his name would fill the world, and make people shudder! How gloriously he would go plowing the dancing seas, in his long, low, black-hulled racer, the Spirit of the Storm, with his grisly flag flying at the fore! And at the zenith of his fame, how he would suddenly appear at the old village and stalk into church, brown and weather-beaten, in his black velvet doublet and trunks, his great jack-boots, his crimson sash, his belt bristling with horse-pistols, his crime-rusted cutlass at his side, his slouch hat with waving plumes, his black flag unfurled, with the skull and crossbones on it, and hear with swelling ecstasy the whisperings, "It's Tom Sawyer the Pirate!—the Black Avenger of the Spanish Main!"

Yes, it was settled; his career was determined. He would run away from home and enter upon it. He would start the very next morning. Therefore he must now begin to get ready. He would collect his resources together. He went to a rotten log near at hand and began to dig under one end of it with his Barlow knife. He soon struck wood that sounded hollow. He put his hand there and uttered this incantation impressively:

"What hasn't come here, *come*! What's here, *stay* here!"

Then he scraped away the dirt, and exposed a pine shingle. He took it up and disclosed a shapely little treasure-house whose bottom and sides were of shingles. In it lay a marble. Tom's astonishment was bound-less! He scratched his head with a perplexed air, and said:

"Well, that beats anything!"

Then he tossed the marble away pettishly, and stood cogitating. The truth was, that a superstition of his had failed, here, which he and all his comrades had always looked upon as infallible. If you buried a marble with certain necessary incantations, and left it alone a fortnight, and then opened the place with the incantation he had just used, you would find that all the marbles you had ever lost had gathered themselves together there, meantime, no matter how widely they had been separated. But now, this thing had actually and unquestionably failed. Tom's whole structure of faith was shaken to its foundations. He had many a time heard of this thing succeeding but never of its failing before. It did not occur to him that he had tried it several times before, himself, but could never find the hiding-places afterward. He puzzled over the matter some time, and finally decided that some witch had interfered and broken the charm. He thought he would satisfy himself on that point; so he searched around till he found a small sandy spot with a little funnel-shaped depression in it. He laid himself down and put his mouth close to this depression and called—

Doodle-bug, doodle-bug, tell me what I want to know!
Doodle-bug, doodle-bug, tell me what I want to know!

The sand began to work, and presently a small black bug appeared for a second and then darted under again in a fright.

"He dasn't tell! So it *was* a witch that done it. I just knowed it."

He well knew the futility of trying to contend against witches, so he gave up discouraged. But it occurred to him that he might as well have the marble he had just thrown away, and therefore he went and made a patient search for it. But he could not find it. Now he went back to his treasure-house and carefully placed himself just as he had been standing when he tossed the marble away; then he took another marble from his pocket and tossed it in the same way, saying:

"Brother, go find your brother!"

He watched where it stopped, and went there and looked. But it must have fallen short or gone too far; so he tried twice more. The last repetition was successful. The two marbles lay within a foot of each other.

Just here the blast of a toy tin trumpet came faintly down the green aisles of the forest. Tom flung off his jacket and trousers, turned a suspender into a belt, raked away some brush behind the rotten log, disclosing a rude bow and arrow, a lath sword and a tin trumpet, and in a moment had seized these things and bounded away, barelegged, with fluttering shirt. He presently halted under a great elm, blew an answering blast, and then began to tiptoe and look warily out, this way and that. He said cautiously—to an imaginary company:

"Hold, my merry men! Keep hid till I blow."

Now appeared Joe Harper, as airily clad and elaborately armed as Tom. Tom called:

"Hold! Who comes here into Sherwood Forest without my pass?"

"Guy of Guisborne wants no man's pass. Who art thou that—that—"

"Dares to hold such language," said Tom, prompting—for they talked "by the book," from memory.

"Who art thou that dares to hold such language?"

"I, indeed! I am Robin Hood, as thy caitiff carcase soon shall know."

"Then art thou indeed that famous outlaw? Right gladly will I dispute with thee the passes of the merry wood. Have at thee!"

They took their lath swords, dumped their other traps on the ground, struck a fencing attitude, foot to foot, and began a grave, careful combat, "two up and two down." Presently Tom said:

"Now, if you've got the hang, go it lively!"

So they "went it lively," panting and perspiring with the work. By and by Tom shouted:

"Fall! fall! Why don't you fall?"

"I sha'n't! Why don't you fall yourself? You're getting the worst of it."

"Why, that ain't anything. *I* can't fall; that ain't the way it is in the book. The book says, 'Then with one back-handed stroke he slew poor Guy of Guisborne.' You're to turn around and let me hit you in the back."

There was no getting around the authorities, so Joe turned, received the whack and fell.

"Now," said Joe, getting up, "you got to let me kill *you*. That's fair."

"Why, I can't do that, it ain't in the book."

"Well, it's blamed mean—that's all."

"Well, say, Joe, you can be Friar Tuck or Much the miller's son, and lam me with a quarter-staff; or I'll be the Sheriff of Nottingham and you be Robin Hood a little while and kill me."

This was satisfactory, and so these adventures were carried out. Then Tom became Robin Hood again, and was allowed by the treacherous nun to bleed his strength away through his neglected wound. And at last Joe, representing a whole tribe of weeping outlaws, dragged him sadly forth, gave his bow into his feeble hands, and Tom said, "Where this arrow falls, there bury poor Robin Hood under the greenwood tree." Then he shot the arrow and fell back and would have died, but he lit on a nettle and sprang up too gaily for a corpse.

The boys dressed themselves, hid their accoutrements, and went off grieving that there were no outlaws any more, and wondering what modern civilization could claim to have done to compensate for their loss. They said they would rather be outlaws a year in Sherwood Forest than President of the United States forever.

CHAPTER 9

A Solemn Situation—Grave Subjects Introduced
—Injun Joe Explains

A T half-past nine, that night, Tom and Sid were sent to bed, as usual. They said their prayers, and Sid was soon asleep. Tom lay awake and waited, in restless impatience. When it seemed to him that it must be nearly daylight, he heard the clock strike ten! This was despair. He would have tossed and fidgeted, as his nerves demanded, but he was afraid he might wake Sid. So he lay still, and stared up into the dark. Everything was dismally still. By and by, out of the stillness, little, scarcely perceptible noises began to emphasize themselves. The ticking of the clock began to bring itself into notice. Old beams began to crack mysteriously. The stairs creaked faintly. Evidently spirits were abroad. A measured, muffled snore issued from Aunt Polly's chamber. And now the tiresome chirping of a cricket that no human ingenuity could locate, began. Next the ghastly ticking of a death-watch in the wall at the bed's head made Tom shudder—it meant that somebody's days were numbered. Then the howl of a far-off dog rose on the night air, and was answered by a fainter howl from a remoter distance. Tom was in an agony. At last he was satisfied that time had ceased and eternity begun; he began to doze, in spite of himself; the clock chimed eleven, but he did not hear it. And then there came, mingling with his half-formed dreams, a most melancholy caterwauling. The raising of a neighboring window disturbed him. A cry of "Scat! you devil!" and the crash of an empty bottle against the back of his aunt's woodshed brought him wide awake, and a single minute later he was dressed and out of the window and creeping along the roof of the "ell" on all fours. He "meow'd" with caution once or twice, as he went; then jumped to the roof of the woodshed and thence to the ground. Huckleberry Finn was there, with his dead cat. The boys moved off and disappeared in the gloom. At the end of half an hour they were wading through the tall grass of the graveyard.

It was a graveyard of the old-fashioned Western kind. It was on a hill, about a mile and a half from the village. It had a crazy board fence around it, which leaned inward in places, and outward the rest of the time, but stood upright nowhere. Grass and weeds grew rank over the whole cemetery. All the old graves were sunken in, there was not a tombstone on the place; round-topped, worm-eaten boards staggered over the graves, leaning for support and finding none. "Sacred to the memory of" So-and-So had been painted on them once, but it could no longer have been read, on the most of them, now, even if there had been light.

A faint wind moaned through the trees, and Tom feared it might be the spirits of the dead, complaining at being disturbed. The boys talked little, and only under their breath, for the time and the place and the pervading solemnity and silence oppressed their spirits. They found the sharp new heap they were seeking, and ensconced themselves within the protection of three great elms that grew in a bunch within a few feet of the grave.

Then they waited in silence for what seemed a long time. The hooting of a distant owl was all the sound that troubled the dead stillness. Tom's reflections grew oppressive. He must force some talk. So he said in a whisper:

"Hucky, do you believe the dead people like it for us to be here?"

Huckleberry whispered:

"I wisht I knowed. It's awful solemn like, a*in't* it?"

"I bet it is."

There was a considerable pause, while the boys canvassed this matter inwardly. Then Tom whispered:

"Say, Hucky—do you reckon Hoss Williams hears us talking?"

"O' course he does. Least his sperrit does."

Tom, after a pause:

"I wish I'd said *Mister* Williams. But I never meant any harm. Everybody calls him Hoss."

"A body can't be too partic'lar how they talk 'bout these-yer dead people, Tom."

This was a damper, and conversation died again.

Presently Tom seized his comrade's arm and said:

"*Sh!*"

"What is it, Tom?" And the two clung together with beating hearts.

"*Sh!* There 'tis again! Didn't you hear it?"

"I—"

"There! Now you hear it."

"Lord, Tom, they're coming! They're coming, sure. What'll we do?"

"I dono. Think they'll see us?"

"Oh, Tom, they can see in the dark, same as cats. I wisht I hadn't come."

"Oh, don't be afeard. I don't believe they'll bother us. We ain't doing any harm. If we keep perfectly still, maybe they won't notice us at all."

"I'll try to, Tom, but, Lord, I'm all of a shiver."

"Listen!"

The boys bent their heads together and scarcely breathed. A muffled sound of voices floated up from the far end of the graveyard.

"Look! See there!" whispered Tom. "What is it?"

"It's devil-fire. Oh, Tom, this is awful."

Some vague figures approached through the gloom, swinging an old-fashioned tin lantern that freckled the ground with innumerable little spangles of light. Presently Huckleberry whispered with a shudder:

"It's the devils sure enough. Three of 'em! Lordy, Tom, we're goners! Can you pray?"

"I'll try, but don't you be afeard. They ain't going to hurt us. 'Now I lay me down to sleep, I—'"

"*Sh!*"

"What is it, Huck?"

"They're *humans*! One of 'em is, anyway. One of 'em's old Muff Potter's voice."

"No—'tain't so, is it?"

"I bet I know it. Don't you stir nor budge. *He* ain't sharp enough to notice us. Drunk, the same as usual, likely—blamed old rip!"

"All right, I'll keep still. Now they're stuck. Can't find it. Here they come again. Now they're hot. Cold again. Hot again. Red hot! They're p'inted right, this time. Say, Huck, I know another o' them voices; it's Injun Joe."

"That's so—that murderin' half-breed! I'd druther they was devils a dern sight. What kin they be up to?"

The whisper died wholly out, now, for the three men had reached the grave and stood within a few feet of the boys' hiding-place.

"Here it is," said the third voice; and the owner of it held the lantern up and revealed the face of young Doctor Robinson.

Potter and Injun Joe were carrying a handbarrow with a rope and a couple of shovels on it. They cast down their load and began to open the grave. The doctor put the lantern at the head of the grave and came and sat down with his back against one of the elm trees. He was so close the boys could have touched him.

"Hurry, men!" he said, in a low voice; "the moon might come out at any moment."

They growled a response and went on digging. For some time there was no noise but the grating sound of the spades discharging their freight of mould and gravel. It was very monotonous. Finally a spade struck upon the coffin with a dull woody accent, and within another minute or two the men had hoisted it out on the ground. They pried off the lid with their shovels, got out the body and dumped it rudely on the ground. The moon drifted from behind the clouds and exposed the pallid face. The barrow was got ready and the corpse placed on it, covered with a blanket, and bound to its place with the rope. Potter took out a large spring-knife and cut off the dangling end of the rope and then said:

"Now the cussed thing's ready, Sawbones, and you'll just out with another five, or here she stays."

"That's the talk!" said Injun Joe.

"Look here, what does this mean?" said the doctor. "You required your pay in advance, and I've paid you."

"Yes, and you done more than that," said Injun Joe, approaching the doctor, who was now standing. "Five years ago you drove me away from your father's kitchen one night, when I come to ask for something to eat, and you said I warn't there for any good; and when I swore I'd get even with you if it took a hundred years, your father had me jailed for a vagrant. Did you think I'd forget? The Injun blood ain't in me for nothing. And now I've *got* you, and you got to *settle*, you know!"

He was threatening the doctor, with his fist in his face, by this time. The doctor struck out suddenly and stretched the ruffian on the ground. Potter dropped his knife, and exclaimed:

"Here, now, don't you hit my pard!" and the next moment he had grappled with the doctor and the two were struggling with might and main, trampling the grass and tearing the ground with their heels. Injun Joe sprang to his feet, his eyes flaming with passion, snatched up Potter's knife, and went creeping, catlike and stooping, round and round about the combatants, seeking an opportunity. All at once the doctor flung himself free, seized the heavy headboard of Williams' grave and felled Potter to the earth with it—and in the same instant the half-breed saw his chance and drove the knife to the hilt in the young man's breast. He reeled and fell partly upon Potter, flooding him with his blood, and in the same moment the clouds blotted out the dreadful spectacle and the two frightened boys went speeding away in the dark.

Presently, when the moon emerged again, Injun Joe was standing over the two forms, contemplating them. The doctor murmured inarticulately, gave a long gasp or two and was still. The half-breed muttered:

"*That* score is settled—damn you."

Then he robbed the body. After which he put the fatal knife in Potter's open right hand, and sat down on the dismantled coffin. Three—four—five minutes passed, and then Potter began to stir and moan. His hand closed upon the knife; he raised it, glanced at it, and let it fall, with a shudder. Then he sat up, pushing the body from him, and gazed at it, and then around him, confusedly. His eyes met Joe's.

"Lord, how is this, Joe?" he said.

"It's a dirty business," said Joe, without moving.

"What did you do it for?"

"I! I never done it!"

"Look here! That kind of talk won't wash."

Potter trembled and grew white.

"I thought I'd got sober. I'd no business to drink to-night. But it's in my head yet—worse'n when we started here. I'm all in a muddle; can't recollect anything of it, hardly. Tell me, Joe—*honest*, now, old feller—did I do it? Joe, I never meant to—'pon my soul and honor, I never meant to, Joe. Tell me how it was, Joe. Oh, it's awful—and him so young and promising."

"Why, you two was scuffling, and he fetched you one with the headboard and you fell flat; and then up you come, all reeling and staggering like, and snatched the knife and jammed it into him, just as he fetched you another awful clip—and here you've laid, as dead as a wedge til now."

"Oh, I didn't know what I was a-doing. I wish I may die this minute if I did. It was all on account of the whiskey and the excitement, I reckon. I never used a weepon in my life before, Joe. I've fought, but never with weepons. They'll all say that. Joe, don't tell! Say you won't tell, Joe—that's a good feller. I always liked you, Joe, and stood up for you, too. Don't you remember? You *won't* tell, *will* you, Joe?" And the poor creature dropped on his knees before the stolid murderer, and clasped his appealing hands.

"No, you've always been fair and square with me, Muff Potter, and I won't go back on you. There, now, that's as fair as a man can say."

"Oh, Joe, you're an angel. I'll bless you for this the longest day I live." And Potter began to cry.

"Come, now, that's enough of that. This ain't any time for blubbering. You be off yonder way and I'll go this. Move, now, and don't leave any tracks behind you."

Potter started on a trot that quickly increased to a run. The half-breed stood looking after him. He muttered:

"If he's as much stunned with the lick and fuddled with the rum as he had the look of being, he won't think of the knife till he's gone so far he'll be afraid to come back after it to such a place by himself—chicken-heart!"

Two or three minutes later the murdered man, the blanketed corpse, the lidless coffin, and the open grave were under no inspection but the moon's. The stillness was complete again, too.

CHAPTER X

The Solemn Oath—Terror Brings Repentance
—Mental Punishment

THE two boys flew on and on, toward the village, speechless with horror. They glanced backward over their shoulders from time to time, apprehensively, as if they feared they might be followed. Every stump that started up in their path seemed a man and an enemy, and made them catch their breath; and as they sped by some outlying cottages that lay near the village, the barking of the aroused watch-dogs seemed to give wings to their feet.

"If we can only get to the old tannery before we break down!" whispered Tom, in short catches between breaths. "I can't stand it much longer."

Huckleberry's hard pantings were his only reply, and the boys fixed their eyes on the goal of their hopes and bent to their work to win it. They gained steadily on it, and at last, breast to breast, they burst through the open door and fell grateful and exhausted in the sheltering shadows beyond. By and by their pulses slowed down, and Tom whispered:

"Huckleberry, what do you reckon'll come of this?"

"If Doctor Robinson dies, I reckon hanging'll come of it."

"Do you though?"

"Why, I *know* it, Tom."

Tom thought a while, then he said:

"Who'll tell? We?"

"What are you talking about? S'pose something happened

and Injun Joe *didn't* hang? Why, he'd kill us some time or other, just as dead sure as we're a laying here."

"That's just what I was thinking to myself, Huck."

"If anybody tells, let Muff Potter do it, if he's fool enough. He's generally drunk enough."

Tom said nothing—went on thinking. Presently he whispered:

"Huck, Muff Potter don't *know* it. How can he tell?"

"What's the reason he don't know it?"

"Because he'd just got that whack when Injun Joe done it. D'you reckon he could see anything? D'you reckon he knowed anything?"

"By hokey, that's so, Tom!"

"And besides, look-a-here—maybe that whack done for *him*!"

"No, 'taint likely, Tom. He had liquor in him; I could see that; and besides, he always has. Well, when pap's full, you might take and belt him over the head with a church and you couldn't phase him. He says so, his own self. So it's the same with Muff Potter, of course. But if a man was dead sober, I reckon maybe that whack might fetch him; I dono."

After another reflective silence, Tom said:

"Hucky, you sure you can keep mum?"

"Tom, we *got* to keep mum. *You* know that. That Injun devil wouldn't make any more of drownding us than a couple of cats, if we was to squeak 'bout this and they didn't hang him. Now, look-a-here, Tom, less take and swear to one another—that's what we got to do—swear to keep mum."

"I'm agreed. It's the best thing. Would you just hold hands and swear that we—"

"Oh no, that wouldn't do for this. That's good enough for little rubbishy common things—specially with gals, cuz *they* go back on you anyway, and blab if they get in a huff—but there orter be writing 'bout a big thing like this. And blood."

Tom's whole being applauded this idea. It was deep, and dark, and awful; the hour, the circumstances, the surroundings, were in keeping with it. He picked up a clean pine shingle that lay in the moon-light, took a little fragment of "red keel" out of his pocket, got the moon on his work, and painfully scrawled these lines, emphasizing each slow down-stroke by clamping his tongue between his teeth, and letting up the pressure on the up-strokes:

Huck Finn and Tom Sawyer swears they will keep mum about This and They wish They may Drop down dead in Their Tracks if They ever Tell and Rot.

Huckleberry was filled with admiration of Tom's facility in writing, and the sublimity of his language. He at once took a pin from his lapel and was going to prick his flesh, but Tom said:

"Hold on! Don't do that. A pin's brass. It might have verdigrease on it."

"What's verdigrease?"

"It's p'ison. That's what it is. You just swaller some of it once—you'll see."

So Tom unwound the thread from one of his needles, and each boy pricked the ball of his thumb and squeezed out a drop of blood. In time, after many squeezes, Tom managed to sign his initials, using the ball of his little finger for a pen. Then he showed Huckleberry how to make an H and an F, and the oath was complete. They buried the shingle close to the wall, with some dismal ceremonies and incantations, and the fetters that bound their tongues were considered to be locked and the key thrown away.

A figure crept stealthily through a break in the other end of the ruined building, now, but they did not notice it.

"Tom," whispered Huckleberry, "does this keep us from

ever telling—*always*?"

"Of course it does. It don't make any difference *what* happens, we got to keep mum. We'd drop down dead—don't *you* know that?"

"Yes, I reckon that's so."

They continued to whisper for some little time. Presently a dog set up a long, lugubrious howl just outside—within ten feet of them. The boys clasped each other suddenly, in an agony of fright.

"Which of us does he mean?" gasped Huckleberry.

"I dono—peep through the crack. Quick!"

"No, *you*, Tom!"

"I can't—I can't *do* it, Huck!"

"Please, Tom. There 'tis again!"

"Oh, lordy, I'm thankful!" whispered Tom. "I know his voice. It's Bull Harbison." *

[* If Mr. Harbison owned a slave named Bull, Tom would have spoken of him as "Harbison's Bull," but a son or a dog of that name was "Bull Harbison."]

"Oh, that's good—I tell you, Tom, I was most scared to death; I'd a bet anything it was a *stray* dog."

The dog howled again. The boys' hearts sank once more.

"Oh, my! that ain't no Bull Harbison!" whispered Huckleberry. "*Do*, Tom!"

Tom, quaking with fear, yielded, and put his eye to the crack. His whisper was hardly audible when he said:

"Oh, Huck, *It's a stray dog*!"

"Quick, Tom, quick! Who does he mean?"

"Huck, he must mean us both—we're right together."

"Oh, Tom, I reckon we're goners. I reckon there ain't no mistake 'bout where *I'll* go to. I been so wicked."

"Dad fetch it! This comes of playing hookey and doing everything a feller's told *not* to do. I might a been good, like Sid, if I'd a tried—but no, I wouldn't, of course. But if ever I get off this time, I lay I'll just *waller* in Sunday-schools!" And Tom began to snuffle a little.

"*You* bad!" and Huckleberry began to snuffle too. "Consound it, Tom Sawyer, you're just old pie, 'long-side o' what I am. Oh, *lordy*, lordy, lordy, I wisht I only had half your chance."

Tom choked off and whispered:

"Look, Hucky, look! He's got his *back* to us!"

Hucky looked, with joy in his heart.

"Well, he has, by jingoes! Did he before?"

"Yes, he did. But I, like a fool, never thought. Oh, this is bully, you know. *Now* who can he mean?"

The howling stopped. Tom pricked up his ears.

"Sh! What's that?" he whispered.

"Sounds like—like hogs grunting. No—it's somebody snoring, Tom."

"That *is* it! Where 'bouts is it, Huck?"

"I bleeve it's down at 'tother end. Sounds so, anyway. Pap used to sleep there, sometimes, 'long with the hogs, but laws bless you, he just lifts things when *he* snores. Besides, I reckon he ain't ever coming back to this town any more."

The spirit of adventure rose in the boys' souls once more.

"Hucky, do you das't to go if I lead?"

"I don't like to, much. Tom, s'pose it's Injun Joe!"

Tom quailed. But presently the temptation rose up strong again and the boys agreed to try, with the understanding that they would take to their heels if the snoring stopped. So they went tiptoeing stealthily down, the one behind the other. When they had got to within five steps of the snorer, Tom stepped on a stick, and it broke with a sharp snap. The man moaned, writhed a little, and his face came into the moonlight. It was Muff Potter. The boys' hearts had stood still, and their hopes too, when the man moved, but their fears passed away now. They tip-toed out, through the broken weather-boarding, and stopped at a little distance to exchange a parting word. That long, lugubrious howl rose on the night air again! They turned and saw the strange dog standing within a few feet of where Potter was lying, and *facing* Potter, with his nose pointing heavenward.

"Oh, geeminy, it's *him*!" exclaimed both boys, in a breath.

"Say, Tom—they say a stray dog come howling around Johnny Miller's house, 'bout midnight, as much as two weeks ago; and a whippoorwill come in and lit on the banisters and sung, the very same evening; and there ain't anybody dead there yet."

"Well, I know that. And suppose there ain't. Didn't Gracie Miller fall in the kitchen fire and burn herself terrible the very next Saturday?"

"Yes, but she ain't *dead*. And what's more, she's getting better, too."

"All right, you wait and see. She's a goner, just as dead sure as Muff Potter's a goner. That's what the niggers say, and they know all about these kind of things, Huck."

Then they separated, cogitating. When Tom crept in at his bedroom window the night was almost spent. He undressed with excessive caution, and fell asleep congratulating himself that nobody knew of his escapade. He was not aware that the gently-snoring Sid was awake, and had been so for an hour.

When Tom awoke, Sid was dressed and gone. There was a late look in the light, a late sense in the atmosphere. He was startled. Why had he not been called—persecuted till he was up, as usual? The thought filled him with bodings. Within five minutes he was dressed and down-stairs, feeling sore and drowsy. The family were still at table, but they had finished breakfast. There was no voice of rebuke; but there were averted eyes; there was a silence and an air of solemnity that struck a chill to the culprit's heart. He sat down and tried to seem gay, but it was up-hill work; it roused no smile, no response, and he lapsed into silence and let his heart sink down to the depths.

After breakfast his aunt took him aside, and Tom almost brightened in the hope that he was going to be flogged; but it was not so. His aunt wept over him and asked him how he could go and break her old heart so; and finally told him to go on, and ruin himself and bring her gray hairs with sorrow to the grave, for it was no use for her to try any more. This was worse than a thousand whippings, and Tom's heart was sorer now than his body. He cried, he pleaded for forgiveness, promised to reform over and over again, and then received his dismissal, feeling that he had won but an imperfect forgiveness and established but a feeble confidence.

He left the presence too miserable to even feel revengeful toward Sid; and so the latter's prompt retreat through the back gate was unnecessary. He moped to school gloomy and sad, and took his flogging, along with Joe Harper, for playing hookey the day before, with the air of one whose heart was busy with heavier woes and wholly dead to trifles. Then he betook himself to his seat, rested his elbows on his desk and his jaws in his hands, and stared at the wall with the stony stare of suffering that has reached the limit and can no further go. His elbow was pressing against some hard substance. After a long time he slowly and sadly changed his position, and took up this object with a sigh. It was in a paper. He unrolled it. A long, lingering, colossal sigh followed, and his heart broke. It was his brass andiron knob!

This final feather broke the camel's back.

CHAPTER 11

Muff Potter Comes Himself—Tom's Conscience at Work

CLOSE upon the hour of noon the whole village was suddenly electrified with the ghastly news. No need of the as yet un-dreamed-of telegraph; the tale flew from man to man, from group to group, from house to house, with little less than telegraphic speed. Of course the schoolmaster gave holiday for that afternoon; the town would have thought strangely of him if he had not.

A gory knife had been found close to the murdered man, and it had been recognized by somebody as belonging to Muff Potter—so the story ran. And it was said that a belated citizen had come upon Potter washing himself in the "branch" about one or two o'clock in the morning, and that Potter had at once sneaked off—suspicious circumstances, especially the washing which was not a habit with Potter. It was also said that the town had been ransacked for this "murderer" (the public are not slow in the matter of sifting evidence and arriving at a verdict), but that he could not be found. Horsemen had departed down all the roads in every direction, and the Sheriff "was confident" that he would be captured before night.

All the town was drifting toward the graveyard. Tom's heartbreak vanished and he joined the procession, not because he would not a thousand times rather go anywhere else, but because an awful, unaccountable fascination drew him on. Arrived at the dreadful place, he wormed his small body through the crowd and saw the dismal spectacle. It seemed to him an age since he was there before. Somebody pinched his arm. He turned, and his eyes met Huckleberry's. Then both looked elsewhere at once, and wondered if anybody had noticed anything in their mutual glance. But everybody was talking, and intent upon the grisly spectacle before them.

"Poor fellow!" "Poor young fellow!" "This ought to be a lesson to grave robbers!" "Muff Potter'll hang for this if they catch him!" This was the drift of remark; and the minister said, "It was a judgment; His hand is here."

Now Tom shivered from head to heel; for his eye fell upon the stolid face of Injun Joe. At this moment the crowd began to sway and struggle, and voices shouted, "It's him! it's him! he's coming himself!"

"Who? Who?" from twenty voices.

"Muff Potter!"

"Hallo, he's stopped!—Look out, he's turning! Don't let him get away!"

People in the branches of the trees over Tom's head said he wasn't trying to get away—he only looked doubtful and perplexed.

"Infernal impudence!" said a bystander; "wanted to come and take a quiet look at his work, I reckon—didn't expect any company."

The crowd fell apart, now, and the Sheriff came through, ostentatiously leading Potter by the arm. The poor fellow's face was haggard, and his eyes showed the fear that was upon him. When he stood before the murdered man, he shook as with a palsy, and he put his face in his hands and burst into tears.

"I didn't do it, friends," he sobbed; "'pon my word and honor I never done it."

"Who's accused you?" shouted a voice.

This shot seemed to carry home. Potter lifted his face and looked around him with a pathetic hopelessness in his eyes. He saw Injun Joe, and exclaimed:

"Oh, Injun Joe, you promised me you'd never—"

"Is that your knife?" and it was thrust before him by the Sheriff.

Potter would have fallen if they had not caught him and eased him to the ground. Then he said:

"Something told me 't if I didn't come back and get—" He shuddered; then waved his nerveless hand with a vanquished gesture and said, "Tell 'em, Joe, tell 'em—it ain't any use any more."

Then Huckleberry and Tom stood dumb and staring, and heard the stony-hearted liar reel off his serene statement, they expecting every moment that the clear sky would deliver God's lightnings upon his head, and wondering to see how long the stroke was delayed. And when he had finished and still stood alive and whole, their wavering impulse to break their oath and save the poor betrayed prisoner's life faded and vanished away, for plainly this miscreant had sold himself to Satan and it would be fatal to meddle with the property of such a power as that.

"Why didn't you leave? What did you want to come here for?" somebody said.

"I couldn't help it—I couldn't help it," Potter moaned. "I wanted to run away, but I couldn't seem to come anywhere but here." And he fell to sobbing again.

Injun Joe repeated his statement, just as calmly, a few minutes afterward on the inquest, under oath; and the boys, seeing that the lightnings were still withheld, were confirmed in their belief that Joe had sold himself to the devil. He was now become, to them, the most balefully interesting object they had ever looked upon, and they could not take their fascinated eyes from his face.

They inwardly resolved to watch him nights, when opportunity should offer, in the hope of getting a glimpse of his dread master.

Injun Joe helped to raise the body of the murdered man and put it in a wagon for removal; and it was whispered through the shuddering crowd that the wound bled a little! The boys thought that this happy circumstance would turn suspicion in the right direction; but they were disappointed, for more than one villager remarked:

"It was within three feet of Muff Potter when it done it."

Tom's fearful secret and gnawing conscience disturbed his sleep for as much as a week after this; and at breakfast one morning Sid said:

"Tom, you pitch around and talk in your sleep so much that you keep me awake half the time."

Tom blanched and dropped his eyes.

"It's a bad sign," said Aunt Polly, gravely. "What you got on your mind, Tom?"

"Nothing. Nothing 't I know of." But the boy's hand shook so that he spilled his coffee.

"And you do talk such stuff," Sid said. "Last night you said, 'It's blood, it's blood, that's what it is!' You said that over and over. And you said, 'Don't torment me so—I'll tell!' Tell *what*? What is it you'll tell?"

Everything was swimming before Tom. There is no telling what might have happened, now, but luckily the concern passed out of Aunt Polly's face and she came to Tom's relief without knowing it. She said:

"Sho! It's that dreadful murder. I dream about it most every night myself. Sometimes I dream it's me that done it."

Mary said she had been affected much the same way. Sid seemed satisfied. Tom got out of the presence as quick as he plausibly could, and after that he complained of toothache for a week, and tied up his jaws every night. He never knew that Sid lay nightly watching, and frequently slipped the bandage free and then leaned on his elbow listening a good while at a time, and afterward slipped the bandage back to its place again.

Tom's distress of mind wore off gradually and the toothache grew irksome and was discarded. If Sid really managed to make anything out of Tom's disjointed mutterings, he kept it to himself.

It seemed to Tom that his schoolmates never would get done holding inquests on dead cats, and thus keeping his trouble present to his mind. Sid noticed that Tom never was coroner at one of these inquiries, though it had been his habit to take the lead in all new enterprises; he noticed, too, that Tom never acted as a witness—and that was strange; and Sid did not overlook the fact that Tom even showed a marked aversion to these inquests, and always avoided them when he could. Sid marvelled, but said nothing. However, even inquests went out of vogue at last, and ceased to torture Tom's conscience.

Every day or two, during this time of sorrow, Tom watched his opportunity and went to the little grated jail-window and smuggled such small comforts through to the "murderer" as he could get hold of. The jail was a trifling little brick den that stood in a marsh at the edge of the village, and no guards were afforded for it; indeed, it was seldom occupied. These offerings greatly helped to ease Tom's conscience.

The villagers had a strong desire to tar-and-feather Injun Joe and ride him on a rail, for body-snatching, but so formidable was his character that nobody could be found who was willing to take the lead in the matter, so it was dropped. He had been careful to begin both of his inquest-statements with the fight, without confessing the grave-robbery that preceded it; therefore it was deemed wisest not to try the case in the courts at present.

CHAPTER 12

Tom Shows his Generosity—Aunt Polly Weakens

ONE of the reasons why Tom's mind had drifted away from its secret troubles was, that it had found a new and weighty matter to interest itself about. Becky Thatcher had stopped coming to school. Tom had struggled with his pride a few days, and tried to "whistle her down the wind," but failed. He began to find himself hanging around her father's house, nights, and feeling very miserable. She was ill. What if she should die! There was distraction in the thought. He no longer took an interest in war, nor even in piracy. The charm of life was gone; there was nothing but dreariness left. He put his hoop away, and his bat; there was no joy in them any more. His aunt was concerned. She began to try all manner of remedies on him. She was one of those people who are infatuated with patent medicines and all new-fangled methods of producing health or mending it. She was an inveterate experimenter in these things. When something fresh in this line came out she was in a fever, right away, to try it; not on herself, for she was never ailing, but on anybody else that came handy. She was a subscriber for all the "Health" periodicals and phrenological frauds; and the solemn ignorance they were inflated with was breath to her nostrils. All the "rot" they contained about ventilation, and how to go to bed, and how to get up, and what to eat, and what to drink, and how much exercise to take, and what frame of mind to keep one's self in, and what sort of clothing to wear, was all gospel to her, and she never observed that her health-journals of the current month customarily upset everything they had recommended the month before. She was as simple-hearted and honest as the day was long, and so she was an easy victim. She gathered together her quack periodicals and her quack medicines, and thus armed with death, went about on her pale horse, metaphorically speaking, with "hell following after." But she never suspected that she was not an angel of healing and the balm of Gilead in disguise, to the suffering neighbors.

The water treatment was new, now, and Tom's low condition was a windfall to her. She had him out at daylight every morning, stood him up in the wood-shed and drowned him with a deluge of cold water; then she scrubbed him down with a towel like a file, and so brought him to; then she rolled him up in a wet sheet and put him away under blankets till she sweated his soul clean and "the yellow stains of it came through his pores"—as Tom said.

Yet notwithstanding all this, the boy grew more and more melancholy and pale and dejected. She added hot baths, sitz baths, shower baths, and plunges. The boy remained as dismal as a hearse. She began to assist the water with a slim oatmeal diet and blister-plasters. She calculated his capacity as she would a jug's, and filled him up every day with quack cure-alls.

Tom had become indifferent to persecution by this time. This phase filled the old lady's heart with consternation. This indifference must be broken up at any cost. Now she heard of Pain-killer for the first time. She ordered a lot at once. She tasted it and was filled with gratitude. It was simply fire in a liquid form. She dropped the water treatment and everything else, and pinned her faith to Pain-killer. She gave Tom a teaspoonful and watched with the deepest anxiety for the result. Her troubles were instantly at rest, her soul at peace again; for the "indifference" was broken up. The boy could not have shown a wilder, heartier interest, if she had built a fire under him.

Tom felt that it was time to wake up; this sort of life might be romantic enough, in his blighted condition, but it was getting to have too little sentiment and too much distracting variety about it. So he thought over various plans for relief, and finally hit upon that of professing to be fond of Pain-killer. He asked for it so often that he became a nuisance, and his aunt ended by telling him to help himself and quit bothering her. If it had been Sid, she would have had no misgivings to alloy her delight; but since it was Tom, she watched the bottle clandestinely. She found that the medicine did really diminish, but it did not occur to her that the boy was mending the health of a crack in the sitting-room floor with it.

One day Tom was in the act of dosing the crack when his aunt's yellow cat came along, purring, eyeing the teaspoon avariciously, and begging for a taste. Tom said:

"Don't ask for it unless you want it, Peter."

But Peter signified that he did want it.

"You better make sure."

Peter was sure.

"Now you've asked for it, and I'll give it to you, because there ain't anything mean about me; but if you find you don't like it, you mustn't blame anybody but your own self."

Peter was agreeable. So Tom pried his mouth open and poured down the Pain-killer. Peter sprang a couple of yards in the air, and then delivered a war-whoop and set off round and round the room, banging against furniture, upsetting flower-pots, and making general havoc. Next he rose on his hind feet and pranced around, in a frenzy of enjoyment, with his head over his shoulder and his voice proclaiming his unappeasable happiness. Then he went tearing around the house again spreading chaos and destruction in his path. Aunt Polly entered in time to see him throw a few double summersets, deliver a final mighty hurrah, and sail through the open window, carrying the rest of the flower-pots with him. The old lady stood petrified with astonishment, peering over her glasses; Tom lay on the floor expiring with laughter.

"Tom, what on earth ails that cat?"

"*I* don't know, aunt," gasped the boy.

"Why, I never see anything like it. What *did* make him act so?"

"Deed I don't know, Aunt Polly; cats always act so when they're having a good time."

"They do, do they?" There was something in the tone that made Tom apprehensive.

"Yes'm. That is, I believe they do."

"You *do*?"

"Yes'm."

The old lady was bending down, Tom watching, with interest emphasized by anxiety. Too late he divined her "drift." The handle of the telltale tea-spoon was visible under the bed-valance. Aunt Polly took it, held it up. Tom winced, and dropped his eyes. Aunt Polly raised him by the usual handle— his ear—and cracked his head soundly with her thimble.

"Now, sir, what did you want to treat that poor dumb beast so, for?"

"I done it out of pity for him—because he hadn't any aunt."

"Hadn't any aunt!—you numskull. What has that got to do with it?"

"Heaps. Because if he'd had one she'd a burnt him out herself! She'd a roasted his bowels out of him 'thout any more feeling than if he was a human!"

Aunt Polly felt a sudden pang of remorse. This was putting the thing in a new light; what was cruelty to a cat *might* be cruelty to a boy, too. She began to soften; she felt sorry. Her eyes watered a little, and she put her hand on Tom's head and said gently:

"I was meaning for the best, Tom. And, Tom, it *did* do you good."

Tom looked up in her face with just a perceptible twinkle peeping through his gravity.

"I know you was meaning for the best, aunty, and so was I with Peter. It done *him* good, too. I never see him get around so since—"

"Oh, go 'long with you, Tom, before you aggravate me again. And you try and see if you can't be a good boy, for once, and you needn't take any more medicine."

Tom reached school ahead of time. It was noticed that this strange thing had been occurring every day latterly. And now, as usual of late, he hung about the gate of the schoolyard instead of playing with his comrades. He was sick, he said, and he looked it. He tried to seem to be looking everywhere but whither he really was looking—down the road. Presently Jeff Thatcher hove in sight, and Tom's face lighted; he gazed a moment, and then turned sorrowfully away. When Jeff arrived, Tom accosted him; and "led up" warily to opportunities for remark about Becky, but the giddy lad never could see the bait. Tom watched and watched, hoping whenever a frisking frock came in sight, and hating the owner of it as soon as he saw she was not the right one. At last frocks ceased to appear, and he dropped hopelessly into the dumps; he entered the empty schoolhouse and sat down to suffer. Then one more frock passed in at the gate, and Tom's heart gave a great bound. The next instant he was out, and "going on" like an Indian; yelling, laughing, chasing boys, jumping over the fence at risk of life and limb, throwing handsprings, standing on his head—doing all the heroic things he could conceive of, and keeping a furtive eye out, all the while, to see if Becky Thatcher was noticing. But she seemed to be unconscious of it all; she never looked. Could it be possible that she was not aware that he was there? He carried his exploits to her immediate vicinity; came war-whooping around, snatched a boy's cap, hurled it to the roof of the schoolhouse, broke through a group of boys, tumbling them in every direction, and fell sprawling, himself, under Becky's nose, almost upsetting her—and she turned, with her nose in the air, and he heard her say: "Mf! some people think they're mighty smart—always showing off!"

Tom's cheeks burned. He gathered himself up and sneaked off, crushed and crestfallen.

CHAPTER 13

The Young Pirates—Going to the Rendezvous
—The Camp—Fire Talk

TOM'S mind was made up now. He was gloomy and desperate. He was a forsaken, friendless boy, he said; nobody loved him; when they found out what they had driven him to, perhaps they would be sorry; he had tried to do right and get along, but they would not let him; since nothing would do them but to be rid of him, let it be so; and let them blame HIM for the consequences—why shouldn't they? What right had the friendless to complain? Yes, they had forced him to it at last: he would lead a life of crime. There was no choice.

By this time he was far down Meadow Lane, and the bell for school to "take up" tinkled faintly upon his ear. He sobbed, now, to think he should never, never hear that old familiar sound any more—it was very hard, but it was forced on him; since he was driven out into the cold world, he must submit—but he forgave them. Then the sobs came thick and fast.

Just at this point he met his soul's sworn comrade, Joe Harper—hard-eyed, and with evidently a great and dismal purpose in his heart. Plainly here were "two souls with but a single thought." Tom, wiping his eyes with his sleeve, began to blubber out something about a resolution to escape from hard usage and lack of sympathy at home by roaming abroad into the great world never to return; and ended by hoping that Joe would not forget him.

But it transpired that this was a request which Joe had just been going to make of Tom, and had come to hunt him up for that purpose. His mother had whipped him for drinking some cream which he had never tasted and knew nothing about; it was plain that she was tired of him and wished him to go; if she felt that way, there was nothing for him to do but succumb; he hoped she would be happy, and never regret having driven her poor boy out into the unfeeling world to suffer and die.

As the two boys walked sorrowing along, they made a new compact to stand by each other and be brothers and never separate till death relieved them of their troubles. Then they began to lay their plans. Joe was for being a hermit, and living on crusts in a remote cave, and dying, some time, of cold and want and grief; but after listening to Tom, he conceded that there were some conspicuous advantages about a life of crime, and so he consented to be a pirate.

Three miles below St. Petersburg, at a point where the Mississippi River was a trifle over a mile wide, there was a long, narrow, wooded island, with a shallow bar at the head of it, and this offered well as a rendezvous. It was not inhabited; it lay far over toward the further shore, abreast a dense and almost wholly unpeopled forest. So Jackson's Island was chosen. Who were to be the subjects of their piracies was a matter that did not occur to them. Then they hunted up Huckleberry Finn, and he joined them promptly, for all careers were one to him; he was indifferent. They presently separated to meet at a lonely spot on the river-bank two miles above the village at the favorite hour—which was midnight. There was a small log raft there which they meant to capture. Each would bring hooks and lines, and such provision as he could steal in the most dark and mysterious way—as became outlaws. And before the afternoon was done, they had all managed to enjoy the sweet glory of spreading the fact that pretty soon the town would "hear something." All who got this vague hint were cautioned to "be mum and wait."

About midnight Tom arrived with a boiled ham and a few trifles, and stopped in a dense undergrowth on a small bluff overlooking the meeting-place. It was starlight, and very still. The mighty river lay like an ocean at rest. Tom listened a moment, but no sound disturbed the quiet. Then he gave a low, distinct whistle. It was answered from under the bluff. Tom whistled twice more; these signals were answered in the same way. Then a guarded voice said:

"Who goes there?"

"Tom Sawyer, the Black Avenger of the Spanish Main. Name your names."

"Huck Finn the Red-Handed, and Joe Harper the Terror of the Seas." Tom had furnished these titles, from his favorite literature.

"'Tis well. Give the countersign."

Two hoarse whispers delivered the same awful word simultaneously to the brooding night:

"*Blood!*"

Then Tom tumbled his ham over the bluff and let himself down after it, tearing both skin and clothes to some extent in the effort. There was an easy, comfortable path along the shore under the bluff, but it lacked the advantages of difficulty and danger so valued by a pirate.

The Terror of the Seas had brought a side of bacon, and had about worn himself out with getting it there. Finn the Red-Handed had stolen a skillet and a quantity of half-cured leaf tobacco, and had also brought a few corn-cobs to make pipes with. But none of the pirates smoked or "chewed" but himself. The Black Avenger of the Spanish Main said it would never do to start without some fire. That was a wise thought; matches were hardly known there in that day. They saw a fire smouldering upon a great raft a hundred yards above, and they went stealthily thither and helped themselves to a chunk. They made an imposing adventure of it, saying, "Hist!" every now and then, and suddenly halting with finger on lip; moving with hands on imaginary dagger-hilts; and giving orders in dismal whispers that if "the foe" stirred, to "let him have it to the hilt," because "dead men tell no tales." They knew well enough that the raftsmen were all down at the village laying in stores or having a spree, but still that was no excuse for their conducting this thing in an unpiratical way.

They shoved off, presently, Tom in command, Huck at the after oar and Joe at the forward. Tom stood amidships, gloomy-browed, and with folded arms, and gave his orders in a low, stern whisper:

"Luff, and bring her to the wind!"

"Aye-aye, sir!"

"Steady, steady-y-y-y!"

"Steady it is, sir!"

"Let her go off a point!"

"Point it is, sir!"

As the boys steadily and monotonously drove the raft toward mid-stream it was no doubt understood that these orders were given only for "style," and were not intended to mean anything in particular.

"What sail's she carrying?"

"Courses, tops'ls, and flying-jib, sir."

"Send the r'yals up! Lay out aloft, there, half a dozen of ye—foretopmaststuns'l! Lively, now!"

"Aye-aye, sir!"

"Shake out that maintogalans'l! Sheets and braces! *Now* my hearties!"

"Aye-aye, sir!"

"Hellum-a-lee—hard a port! Stand by to meet her when she comes! Port, port! *Now*, men! With a will! Stead-y-y-y!"

"Steady it is, sir!"

The raft drew beyond the middle of the river; the boys pointed her head right, and then lay on their oars. The river was not high, so there was not more than a two or three mile current. Hardly a word was said during the next three-quarters of an hour. Now the raft was passing before the distant town. Two or three glimmering lights showed where it lay, peacefully sleeping, beyond the vague vast sweep of star-gemmed water, unconscious of the tremendous event that was happening. The Black Avenger stood still with folded arms, "looking his last" upon the scene of his former joys and his later sufferings, and wishing "she" could see him now, abroad on the wild sea, facing peril and death with dauntless heart, going to his doom with a grim smile on his lips. It was but a small strain on his imagination to remove Jackson's Island beyond eye-shot of the village, and so he "looked his last" with a broken and satisfied heart. The other pirates were looking their last, too; and they all looked so long that they came near letting the current drift them out of the range of the island. But they discovered the danger in time, and made shift to avert it. About two o'clock in the morning the raft grounded on the bar two hundred yards above the head of the island, and they waded back and forth until they had landed their freight. Part of the little raft's belongings consisted of an old sail, and this they spread over a nook in the bushes for a tent to shelter their provisions; but they themselves would sleep in the open air in good weather, as became outlaws.

They built a fire against the side of a great log twenty or thirty steps within the sombre depths of the forest, and then cooked some bacon in the frying-pan for supper, and used up half of the corn "pone" stock they had brought. It seemed glorious sport to be feasting in that wild, free way in the virgin forest of an unexplored and uninhabited island, far from the haunts of men, and they said they never would return to civilization. The climbing fire lit up their faces and threw its ruddy glare upon the pillared tree-trunks of their forest temple, and upon the varnished foliage and festooning vines.

When the last crisp slice of bacon was gone, and the last allowance of corn pone devoured, the boys stretched themselves out on the grass, filled with contentment. They could have found a cooler place, but they would not deny themselves such a romantic feature as the roasting campfire.

"*Ain't* it gay?" said Joe.

"It's *nuts!*" said Tom. "What would the boys say if they could see us?"

"Say? Well, they'd just die to be here—hey, Hucky!"

"I reckon so," said Huckleberry; "anyways, I'm suited. I don't want nothing better'n this. I don't ever get enough to eat, gen'ally—and here they can't come and pick at a feller and bullyrag him so."

"It's just the life for me," said Tom. "You don't have to get up, mornings, and you don't have to go to school, and wash, and all that blame foolishness. You see a pirate don't have to do *anything*, Joe, when he's ashore, but a hermit *he* has to be praying considerable, and then he don't have any fun, anyway, all by himself that way."

"Oh yes, that's so," said Joe, "but I hadn't thought much about it, you know. I'd a good deal rather be a pirate, now that I've tried it."

"You see," said Tom, "people don't go much on hermits, nowadays, like they used to in old times, but a pirate's always respected. And a hermit's got to sleep on the hardest place he can find, and put sackcloth and ashes on his head, and stand out in the rain, and—"

"What does he put sackcloth and ashes on his head for?" inquired Huck.

"I dono. But they've *got* to do it. Hermits always do. You'd have to do that if you was a hermit."

"Dern'd if I would," said Huck.

"Well, what would you do?"

"I dono. But I wouldn't do that."

"Why, Huck, you'd *have* to. How'd you get around it?"

"Why, I just wouldn't stand it. I'd run away."

"Run away! Well, you *would* be a nice old slouch of a hermit. You'd be a disgrace."

The Red-Handed made no response, being better employed. He had finished gouging out a cob, and now he fitted a weed stem to it, loaded it with tobacco, and was pressing a coal to the charge and blowing a cloud of fragrant smoke—he was in the full bloom of luxurious contentment. The other pirates envied him this majestic vice, and secretly resolved to acquire it shortly. Presently Huck said:

"What does pirates have to do?"

Tom said:

"Oh, they have just a bully time—take ships and burn them, and get the money and bury it in awful places in their island where there's ghosts and things to watch it, and kill everybody in the ships—make 'em walk a plank."

"And they carry the women to the island," said Joe; "they don't kill the women."

"No," assented Tom, "they don't kill the women—they're too noble. And the women's always beautiful, too.

"And don't they wear the bulliest clothes! Oh no! All gold and silver and di'monds," said Joe, with enthusiasm.

"Who?" said Huck.

"Why, the pirates."

Huck scanned his own clothing forlornly.

"I reckon I ain't dressed fitten for a pirate," said he, with a regretful pathos in his voice; "but I ain't got none but these."

But the other boys told him the fine clothes would come fast enough, after they should have begun their adventures. They made him understand that his poor rags would do to begin with, though it was customary for wealthy pirates to start with a proper wardrobe.

Gradually their talk died out and drowsiness began to steal

upon the eyelids of the little waifs. The pipe dropped from the fingers of the Red-Handed, and he slept the sleep of the conscience-free and the weary. The Terror of the Seas and the Black Avenger of the Spanish Main had more difficulty in getting to sleep. They said their prayers inwardly, and lying down, since there was nobody there with authority to make them kneel and recite aloud; in truth, they had a mind not to say them at all, but they were afraid to proceed to such lengths as that, lest they might call down a sudden and special thunderbolt from heaven. Then at once they reached and hovered upon the imminent verge of sleep—but an intruder came, now, that would not "down." It was conscience. They began to feel a vague fear that they had been doing wrong to run away; and next they thought of the stolen meat, and then the real torture came. They tried to argue it away by reminding conscience that they had purloined sweetmeats and apples scores of times; but conscience was not to be appeased by such thin plausibilities; it seemed to them, in the end, that there was no getting around the stubborn fact that taking sweetmeats was only "hooking," while taking bacon and hams and such valuables was plain simple stealing—and there was a command against that in the Bible. So they inwardly resolved that so long as they remained in the business, their piracies should not again be sullied with the crime of stealing. Then conscience granted a truce, and these curiously inconsistent pirates fell peacefully to sleep.

CHAPTER 14

Camp-Life—A Sensation—Tom Steals Away from Camp

WHEN Tom awoke in the morning, he wondered where he was. He sat up and rubbed his eyes and looked around. Then he comprehended. It was the cool gray dawn, and there was a delicious sense of repose and peace in the deep pervading calm and silence of the woods. Not a leaf stirred; not a sound obtruded upon great Nature's meditation. Beaded dewdrops stood upon the leaves and grasses. A white layer of ashes covered the fire, and a thin blue breath of smoke rose straight into the air. Joe and Huck still slept.

Now, far away in the woods a bird called; another answered; presently the hammering of a woodpecker was heard. Gradually the cool dim gray of the morning whitened, and as gradually sounds multiplied and life manifested itself. The marvel of Nature shaking off sleep and going to work unfolded itself to the musing boy. A little green worm came crawling over a dewy leaf, lifting two-thirds of his body into the air from time to time and "sniffing around," then proceeding again—for he was measuring, Tom said; and when the worm approached him, of its own accord, he sat as still as a stone, with his hopes rising and falling, by turns, as the creature still came toward him or seemed inclined to go elsewhere; and when at last it considered a painful moment with its curved body in the air and then came decisively down upon Tom's leg and began a journey over him, his whole heart was glad—for that meant that he was going to have a new suit of clothes—without the shadow of a doubt a gaudy piratical uniform. Now a procession of ants appeared, from nowhere in particular, and went about their labors; one struggled manfully by with a dead spider five times as big as itself in its arms, and lugged it straight up a tree-trunk. A brown spotted lady-bug climbed the dizzy height of a grass blade, and Tom bent down close to it and said:

> Lady-bug, lady-bug, fly away home,
> Your house is on fire, your children's alone;

and she took wing and went off to see about it—which did not surprise the boy, for he knew of old that this insect was credulous about conflagrations, and he had practised upon its simplicity more than once. A tumblebug came next, heaving sturdily at its ball, and Tom touched the creature, to see it shut its legs against its body and pretend to be dead. The birds were fairly rioting by this time. A catbird, the Northern mocker, lit in a tree over Tom's head, and trilled out her imitations of her neighbors in a rapture of enjoyment; then a shrill jay swept down, a flash of blue flame, and stopped on a twig almost within the boy's reach, cocked his head to one side and eyed the strangers with a consuming curiosity; a gray squirrel and a big fellow of the "fox" kind came skurrying along, sitting up at intervals to inspect and chatter at the boys, for the wild things had probably never seen a human being before and scarcely knew whether to be afraid or not. All Nature was wide awake and stirring, now; long lances of sunlight pierced down through the dense foliage far and near, and a few butterflies came fluttering upon the scene.

Tom stirred up the other pirates and they all clattered away with a shout, and in a minute or two were stripped and chasing after and tumbling over each other in the shallow limpid water of the white sandbar. They felt no longing for the little village sleeping in the distance beyond the majestic waste of water. A vagrant current or a slight rise in the river had carried off their raft, but this only gratified them, since its going was something like burning the bridge between them and civilization.

They came back to camp wonderfully refreshed, glad-hearted, and ravenous; and they soon had the camp-fire blazing up again. Huck found a spring of clear cold water close by, and the boys made cups of broad oak or hickory leaves, and felt that water, sweetened with such a wildwood charm as that, would be a good enough substitute for coffee. While Joe was slicing bacon for breakfast, Tom and Huck asked him to hold on a minute; they stepped to a promising nook in the river-bank and threw in their lines; almost immediately they had reward. Joe had not had time to get impatient before they were back again with some handsome bass, a couple of sun-perch and a small catfish—provisions enough for quite a family. They fried the fish with the bacon, and were astonished; for no fish had ever seemed so delicious before. They did not know that the quicker a fresh-water fish is on the fire after he is caught the better he is; and they reflected little upon what a sauce open-air sleeping, open-air exercise, bathing, and a large ingredient of hunger make, too.

They lay around in the shade, after breakfast, while Huck had a smoke, and then went off through the woods on an exploring expedition. They tramped gayly along, over decaying logs, through tangled underbrush, among solemn monarchs of the forest, hung from their crowns to the ground with a drooping regalia of grape-vines. Now and then they came upon snug nooks carpeted with grass and jeweled with flowers.

They found plenty of things to be delighted with, but nothing to be astonished at. They discovered that the island was about three miles long and a quarter of a mile wide, and that the shore it lay closest to was only separated from it by a narrow channel hardly two hundred yards wide. They took a swim about every hour, so it was close upon the middle of the afternoon when they got back to camp. They were too hungry to stop to fish, but they fared sumptuously upon cold ham, and then threw themselves down in the shade to talk. But the talk soon began to drag, and then died. The stillness, the solemnity that brooded in the woods, and the sense of loneliness, began to tell upon the spirits of the boys. They fell to thinking. A sort of undefined longing crept upon them. This took dim shape, presently—it was budding homesickness. Even Finn the Red-Handed was dreaming of his doorsteps and empty hogsheads. But they were all ashamed of their weakness, and none was brave enough to speak his thought.

For some time, now, the boys had been dully conscious of a peculiar sound in the distance, just as one sometimes is of the ticking of a clock which he takes no distinct note of. But now this mysterious sound became more pronounced, and forced a recognition. The boys started, glanced at each other, and then each assumed a listening attitude. There was a long silence, profound and unbroken; then a deep, sullen boom came floating down out of the distance.

"What is it!" exclaimed Joe, under his breath.

"I wonder," said Tom in a whisper.

"'Tain't thunder," said Huckleberry, in an awed tone, "becuz thunder—"

"Hark!" said Tom. "Listen—don't talk."

They waited a time that seemed an age, and then the same muffled boom troubled the solemn hush.

"Let's go and see."

They sprang to their feet and hurried to the shore toward the town. They parted the bushes on the bank and peered out over the water. The little steam ferry-boat was about a mile below the village, drifting with the current. Her broad deck seemed crowded with people. There were a great many skiffs rowing about or floating with the stream in the neighborhood of the ferryboat, but the boys could not determine what the men in them were doing. Presently a great jet of white smoke burst from the ferryboat's side, and as it expanded and rose in a lazy cloud, that same dull throb of sound was borne to the listeners again. "I know now!" exclaimed Tom; "somebody's drownded!"

"That's it!" said Huck; "they done that last summer, when Bill Turner got drownded; they shoot a cannon over the water, and that makes him come up to the top. Yes, and they take loaves of bread and put quicksilver in 'em and set 'em afloat, and wherever there's anybody that's drownded, they'll float right there and stop."

"Yes, I've heard about that," said Joe. "I wonder what makes the bread do that."

"Oh, it ain't the bread, so much," said Tom; "I reckon it's mostly what they *say* over it before they start it out."

"But they don't say anything over it," said Huck. "I've seen 'em and they don't."

"Well, that's funny," said Tom. "But maybe they say it to themselves. Of *course* they do. Anybody might know that."

The other boys agreed that there was reason in what Tom said, because an ignorant lump of bread, uninstructed by an incantation, could not be expected to act very intelligently when set upon an errand of such gravity.

"By jings, I wish I was over there, now," said Joe.

"I do too" said Huck "I'd give heaps to know who it is."

The boys still listened and watched. Presently a revealing thought flashed through Tom's mind, and he exclaimed:

"Boys, I know who's drownded—it's us!"

They felt like heroes in an instant. Here was a gorgeous triumph; they were missed; they were mourned; hearts were breaking on their account; tears were being shed; accusing memories of unkindness to these poor lost lads were rising up, and unavailing regrets and remorse were being indulged; and best of all, the departed were the talk of the whole town, and the envy of all the boys, as far as this dazzling notoriety was concerned. This was fine. It was worth while to be a pirate, after all.

As twilight drew on, the ferryboat went back to her accustomed business and the skiffs disappeared. The pirates returned to camp. They were jubilant with vanity over their new grandeur and the illustrious trouble they were making. They caught fish, cooked supper and ate it, and then fell to guessing at what the village was thinking and saying about them; and the pictures they drew of the public distress on their account were gratifying to look upon—from their point of view. But when the shadows of night closed them in, they gradually ceased to talk, and sat gazing into the fire, with their minds evidently wandering elsewhere. The excitement was gone, now, and Tom and Joe could not keep back thoughts of certain persons at home who were not enjoying this fine frolic as much as they were. Misgivings came; they grew troubled and unhappy; a sigh or two escaped, unawares. By and by Joe timidly ventured upon a roundabout "feeler" as to how the others might look upon a return to civilization—not right now, but—

Tom withered him with derision! Huck, being uncommitted as yet, joined in with Tom, and the waverer quickly "explained," and was glad to get out of the scrape with as little taint of chicken-hearted home-sickness clinging to his garments as he could. Mutiny was effectually laid to rest for the moment.

As the night deepened, Huck began to nod, and presently to snore. Joe followed next. Tom lay upon his elbow motionless, for some time, watching the two intently. At last he got up cautiously, on his knees, and went searching among the grass and the flickering reflections flung by the campfire. He picked up and inspected several large semi-cylinders of the thin white bark of a sycamore, and finally chose two which seemed to suit him. Then he knelt by the fire and painfully wrote something upon each of these with his "red keel"; one he rolled up and put in his jacket pocket, and the other he put in Joe's hat and removed it to a little distance from the owner. And he also put into the hat certain schoolboy treasures of almost inestimable value—among them a lump of chalk, an India-rubber ball, three fishhooks, and one of that kind of marbles known as a "sure 'nough crystal." Then he tiptoed his way cautiously among the trees till he felt that he was out of hearing, and straightway broke into a keen run in the direction of the sandbar.

CHAPTER 15

Tom Reconnoiters—Learns the Situation—Reports at Camp

A FEW minutes later Tom was in the shoal water of the
bar, wading toward the Illinois shore. Before the depth
reached his middle he was halfway over; the current would
permit no more wading, now, so he struck out confidently
to swim the remaining hundred yards. He swam quartering
upstream, but still was swept downward rather faster than
he had expected. However, he reached the shore finally, and
drifted along till he found a low place and drew himself out. He
put his hand on his jacket pocket, found his piece of bark safe,
and then struck through the woods, following the shore, with
streaming garments. Shortly before ten o'clock he came out
into an open place opposite the village, and saw the ferryboat
lying in the shadow of the trees and the high bank. Everything
was quiet under the blinking stars. He crept down the bank,
watching with all his eyes, slipped into the water, swam three
or four strokes and climbed into the skiff that did "yawl" duty
at the boat's stern. He laid himself down under the thwarts and
waited, panting.

Presently the cracked bell tapped and a voice gave the order
to "cast off." A minute or two later the skiff's head was standing
high up, against the boat's swell, and the voyage was begun.
Tom felt happy in his success, for he knew it was the boat's
last trip for the night. At the end of a long twelve or fifteen
minutes the wheels stopped, and Tom slipped overboard and
swam ashore in the dusk, landing fifty yards downstream, out

of danger of possible stragglers.

He flew along unfrequented alleys, and shortly found himself at his aunt's back fence. He climbed over, approached the "ell," and looked in at the sitting-room window, for a light was burning there. There sat Aunt Polly, Sid, Mary, and Joe Harper's mother, grouped together, talking. They were by the bed, and the bed was between them and the door. Tom went to the door and began to softly lift the latch; then he pressed gently and the door yielded a crack; he continued pushing cautiously, and quaking every time it creaked, till he judged he might squeeze through on his knees; so he put his head through and began, warily.

"What makes the candle blow so?" said Aunt Polly. Tom hurried up. "Why, that door's open, I believe. Why, of course it is. No end of strange things now. Go 'long and shut it, Sid."

Tom disappeared under the bed just in time. He lay and "breathed" himself for a time, and then crept to where he could almost touch his aunt's foot.

"But as I was saying," said Aunt Polly, "he warn't *bad*, so to say—only misch*ee*vous. Only just giddy, and harum-scarum, you know. He warn't any more responsible than a colt. *He* never meant any harm, and he was the best-hearted boy that ever was"—and she began to cry.

"It was just so with my Joe—always full of his devilment, and up to every kind of mischief, but he was just as unselfish and kind as he could be—and laws bless me, to think I went and whipped him for taking that cream, never once recollecting that I throwed it out myself because it was sour, and I never to see him again in this world, never, never, never, poor abused boy!" And Mrs. Harper sobbed as if her heart would break.

"I hope Tom's better off where he is," said Sid, "but if he'd been better in some ways—"

"*Sid!*" Tom felt the glare of the old lady's eye, though he could not see it. "Not a word against my Tom, now that he's gone! God'll take care of *him*—never you trouble *your*self, sir! Oh, Mrs. Harper, I don't know how to give him up! I don't know how to give him up! He was such a comfort to me, although he tormented my old heart out of me, 'most."

"The Lord giveth and the Lord hath taken away—Blessed be the name of the Lord! But it's *so* hard—Oh, it's so hard! Only last Saturday my Joe busted a firecracker right under my nose and I knocked him sprawling. Little did I know then, how soon—Oh, if it was to do over again I'd hug him and bless him for it."

"Yes, yes, yes, I know just how you feel, Mrs. Harper, I know just exactly how you feel. No longer ago than yesterday noon, my Tom took and filled the cat full of Pain-killer, and I did think the cretur would tear the house down. And God forgive me, I cracked Tom's head with my thimble, poor boy, poor dead boy. But he's out of all his troubles now. And the last words I ever heard him say was to reproach—"

But this memory was too much for the old lady, and she broke entirely down. Tom was snuffling, now, himself—and more in pity of himself than anybody else. He could hear Mary crying, and putting in a kindly word for him from time to time. He began to have a nobler opinion of himself than ever before. Still, he was sufficiently touched by his aunt's grief to long to rush out from under the bed and overwhelm her with joy— and the theatrical gorgeousness of the thing appealed strongly to his nature, too, but he resisted and lay still.

He went on listening, and gathered by odds and ends that it was conjectured at first that the boys had got drowned while taking a swim; then the small raft had been missed; next, certain boys said the missing lads had promised that the village should "hear something" soon; the wise-heads had "put this and that together" and decided that the lads had gone off on that raft and would turn up at the next town below, presently; but toward noon the raft had been found, lodged against the

Missouri shore some five or six miles below the village—
and then hope perished; they must be drowned, else hunger
would have driven them home by nightfall if not sooner. It
was believed that the search for the bodies had been a fruitless
effort merely because the drowning must have occurred in
mid-channel, since the boys, being good swimmers, would
otherwise have escaped to shore. This was Wednesday night.
If the bodies continued missing until Sunday, all hope would
be given over, and the funerals would be preached on that
morning. Tom shuddered.

Mrs. Harper gave a sobbing goodnight and turned to go.
Then with a mutual impulse the two bereaved women flung
themselves into each other's arms and had a good, consoling
cry, and then parted. Aunt Polly was tender far beyond her
wont, in her goodnight to Sid and Mary. Sid snuffled a bit and
Mary went off crying with all her heart.

Aunt Polly knelt down and prayed for Tom so touchingly,
so appealingly, and with such measureless love in her words
and her old trembling voice, that he was weltering in tears
again, long before she was through.

He had to keep still long after she went to bed, for she
kept making broken-hearted ejaculations from time to time,
tossing unrestfully, and turning over. But at last she was still,
only moaning a little in her sleep. Now the boy stole out, rose
gradually by the bedside, shaded the candle-light with his
hand, and stood regarding her. His heart was full of pity for
her. He took out his sycamore scroll and placed it by the candle.
But something occurred to him, and he lingered considering.
His face lighted with a happy solution of his thought; he put
the bark hastily in his pocket. Then he bent over and kissed the
faded lips, and straightway made his stealthy exit, latching the
door behind him.

He threaded his way back to the ferry landing, found
nobody at large there, and walked boldly on board the boat, for

he knew she was tenantless except that there was a watchman, who always turned in and slept like a graven image. He untied the skiff at the stern, slipped into it, and was soon rowing cautiously upstream. When he had pulled a mile above the village, he started quartering across and bent himself stoutly to his work. He hit the landing on the other side neatly, for this was a familiar bit of work to him. He was moved to capture the skiff, arguing that it might be considered a ship and therefore legitimate prey for a pirate, but he knew a thorough search would be made for it and that might end in revelations. So he stepped ashore and entered the woods.

He sat down and took a long rest, torturing himself meanwhile to keep awake, and then started warily down the home-stretch. The night was far spent. It was broad daylight before he found himself fairly abreast the island bar. He rested again until the sun was well up and gilding the great river with its splendor, and then he plunged into the stream. A little later he paused, dripping, upon the threshold of the camp, and heard Joe say:

"No, Tom's true-blue, Huck, and he'll come back. He won't desert. He knows that would be a disgrace to a pirate, and Tom's too proud for that sort of thing. He's up to something or other. Now I wonder what?"

"Well, the things is ours, anyway, ain't they?"

"Pretty near, but not yet, Huck. The writing says they are if he ain't back here to breakfast."

"Which he is!" exclaimed Tom, with fine dramatic effect, stepping grandly into camp.

A sumptuous breakfast of bacon and fish was shortly provided, and as the boys set to work upon it, Tom recounted (and adorned) his adventures. They were a vain and boastful company of heroes when the tale was done. Then Tom hid himself away in a shady nook to sleep till noon, and the other pirates got ready to fish and explore.

CHAPTER 16

A Day's Amusements—Tom Reveals a Secret—The Pirates
take a Lesson —A Night Surprise—An Indian War

AFTER dinner all the gang turned out to hunt for turtle
eggs on the bar. They went about poking sticks into the
sand, and when they found a soft place they went down on
their knees and dug with their hands. Sometimes they would
take fifty or sixty eggs out of one hole. They were perfectly
round white things a trifle smaller than an English walnut.
They had a famous fried-egg feast that night, and another on
Friday morning.

After breakfast they went whooping and prancing out on
the bar, and chased each other round and round, shedding
clothes as they went, until they were naked, and then continued
the frolic far away up the shoal water of the bar, against the stiff
current, which latter tripped their legs from under them from
time to time and greatly increased the fun. And now and then
they stooped in a group and splashed water in each other's
faces with their palms, gradually approaching each other,
with averted faces to avoid the strangling sprays, and finally
gripping and struggling till the best man ducked his neighbor,
and then they all went under in a tangle of white legs and arms
and came up blowing, sputtering, laughing, and gasping for
breath at one and the same time.

When they were well exhausted, they would run out and
sprawl on the dry, hot sand, and lie there and cover themselves
up with it, and by and by break for the water again and go

through the original performance once more. Finally it occurred to them that their naked skin represented flesh-colored "tights" very fairly; so they drew a ring in the sand and had a circus—with three clowns in it, for none would yield this proudest post to his neighbor.

Next they got their marbles and played "knucks" and "ringtaw" and "keeps" till that amusement grew stale. Then Joe and Huck had another swim, but Tom would not venture, because he found that in kicking off his trousers he had kicked his string of rattlesnake rattles off his ankle, and he wondered how he had escaped cramp so long without the protection of this mysterious charm. He did not venture again until he had found it, and by that time the other boys were tired and ready to rest. They gradually wandered apart, dropped into the "dumps," and fell to gazing longingly across the wide river to where the village lay drowsing in the sun. Tom found himself writing *Becky* in the sand with his big toe; he scratched it out, and was angry with himself for his weakness. But he wrote it again, nevertheless; he could not help it. He erased it once more and then took himself out of temptation by driving the other boys together and joining them.

But Joe's spirits had gone down almost beyond resurrection. He was so homesick that he could hardly endure the misery of it. The tears lay very near the surface. Huck was melancholy, too. Tom was downhearted, but tried hard not to show it. He had a secret which he was not ready to tell, yet, but if this mutinous depression was not broken up soon, he would have to bring it out. He said, with a great show of cheerfulness:

"I bet there's been pirates on this island before, boys. We'll explore it again. They've hid treasures here somewhere. How'd you feel to light on a rotten chest full of gold and silver—hey?"

But it roused only faint enthusiasm, which faded out, with no reply. Tom tried one or two other seductions; but they failed, too. It was discouraging work. Joe sat poking up the sand with a stick and looking very gloomy. Finally he said:

"Oh, boys, let's give it up. I want to go home. It's so lonesome."

"Oh no, Joe, you'll feel better by and by," said Tom. "Just think of the fishing that's here."

"I don't care for fishing. I want to go home."

"But, Joe, there ain't such another swimming-place anywhere."

"Swimming's no good. I don't seem to care for it, somehow, when there ain't anybody to say I sha'n't go in. I mean to go home."

"Oh, shucks! Baby! You want to see your mother, I reckon."

"Yes, I *do* want to see my mother—and you would, too, if you had one. I ain't any more baby than you are." And Joe snuffled a little.

"Well, we'll let the crybaby go home to his mother, *won't* we, Huck? Poor thing—does it want to see its mother? And so it shall. *You* like it here, *don't* you, Huck? We'll stay, won't we?"

Huck said, "Y-e-s"—without any heart in it.

"I'll never speak to you again as long as I live," said Joe, rising. "There now!" And he moved moodily away and began to dress himself.

"Who cares!" said Tom. "Nobody wants you to. Go 'long home and get laughed at. Oh, you're a nice pirate. Huck and me ain't crybabies. We'll stay, won't we, Huck? Let him go if he wants to. I reckon we can get along without him, per'aps."

But Tom was uneasy, nevertheless, and was alarmed to see Joe go sullenly on with his dressing. And then it was discomforting to see Huck eying Joe's preparations so wistfully, and keeping up such an ominous silence. Presently, without a parting word, Joe began to wade off toward the Illinois shore. Tom's heart began to sink. He glanced at Huck. Huck could not bear the look, and dropped his eyes. Then he said:

"I want to go, too, Tom. It was getting so lonesome anyway,

and now it'll be worse. Let's us go, too, Tom."

"I won't! You can all go, if you want to. I mean to stay."

"Tom, I better go."

"Well, go 'long—who's hendering you."

Huck began to pick up his scattered clothes. He said:

"Tom, I wisht you'd come, too. Now you think it over. We'll wait for you when we get to shore."

"Well, you'll wait a blame long time, that's all."

Huck started sorrowfully away, and Tom stood looking after him, with a strong desire tugging at his heart to yield his pride and go along too. He hoped the boys would stop, but they still waded slowly on. It suddenly dawned on Tom that it was become very lonely and still. He made one final struggle with his pride, and then darted after his comrades, yelling:

"Wait! Wait! I want to tell you something!"

They presently stopped and turned around. When he got to where they were, he began unfolding his secret, and they listened moodily till at last they saw the "point" he was driving at, and then they set up a warwhoop of applause and said it was "splendid!" and said if he had told them at first, they wouldn't have started away. He made a plausible excuse; but his real reason had been the fear that not even the secret would keep them with him any very great length of time, and so he had meant to hold it in reserve as a last seduction.

The lads came gayly back and went at their sports again with a will, chattering all the time about Tom's stupendous plan and admiring the genius of it. After a dainty egg and fish dinner, Tom said he wanted to learn to smoke, now. Joe caught at the idea and said he would like to try, too. So Huck made pipes and filled them. These novices had never smoked anything before but cigars made of grapevine, and they "bit" the tongue, and were not considered manly anyway.

Now they stretched themselves out on their elbows and began to puff, charily, and with slender confidence. The smoke had an unpleasant taste, and they gagged a little, but Tom said:

"Why, it's just as easy! If I'd a knowed *this* was all, I'd a learnt long ago."

"So would I," said Joe. "It's just nothing."

"Why, many a time I've looked at people smoking, and thought well I wish I could do that; but I never thought I could," said Tom.

"That's just the way with me, hain't it, Huck? You've heard me talk just that way—haven't you, Huck? I'll leave it to Huck if I haven't."

"Yes—heaps of times," said Huck.

"Well, I have too," said Tom; "oh, hundreds of times. Once down by the slaughter-house. Don't you remember, Huck? Bob Tanner was there, and Johnny Miller, and Jeff Thatcher, when I said it. Don't you remember, Huck, 'bout me saying that?"

"Yes, that's so," said Huck. "That was the day after I lost a white alley. No, 'twas the day before."

"There—I told you so," said Tom. "Huck recollects it."

"I bleeve I could smoke this pipe all day," said Joe. "*I* don't feel sick."

"Neither do I," said Tom. "I could smoke it all day. But I bet you Jeff Thatcher couldn't."

"Jeff Thatcher! Why, he'd keel over just with two draws. Just let him try it once. *He'd* see!"

"I bet he would. And Johnny Miller—I wish could see Johnny Miller tackle it once."

"Oh, don't *I*!" said Joe. "Why, I bet you Johnny Miller couldn't any more do this than nothing. Just one little snifter would fetch *him*."

"'Deed it would, Joe. Say—I wish the boys could see us now."

"So do I."

"Say—boys, don't say anything about it, and some time when they're around, I'll come up to you and say, 'Joe, got a pipe? I want a smoke.' And you'll say, kind of careless like, as if it warn't anything, you'll say, 'Yes, I got my *old* pipe, and another one, but my tobacker ain't very good.' And I'll say, 'Oh, that's all right, if it's *strong* enough.' And then you'll out with the pipes, and we'll light up just as ca'm, and then just see 'em look!"

"By jings, that'll be gay, Tom! I wish it was *now*!"

"So do I! And when we tell 'em we learned when we was off pirating, won't they wish they'd been along?"

"Oh, I reckon not! I'll just *bet* they will!"

So the talk ran on. But presently it began to flag a trifle, and grow disjointed. The silences widened; the expectoration marvellously increased. Every pore inside the boys' cheeks became a spouting fountain; they could scarcely bail out the cellars under their tongues fast enough to prevent an inundation; little overflowings down their throats occurred in spite of all they could do, and sudden retchings followed every time. Both boys were looking very pale and miserable, now. Joe's pipe dropped from his nerveless fingers. Tom's followed. Both fountains were going furiously and both pumps bailing with might and main. Joe said feebly:

"I've lost my knife. I reckon I better go and find it."

Tom said, with quivering lips and halting utterance:

"I'll help you. You go over that way and I'll hunt around by the spring. No, you needn't come, Huck—we can find it."

So Huck sat down again, and waited an hour. Then he found it lonesome, and went to find his comrades. They were wide apart in the woods, both very pale, both fast asleep. But something informed him that if they had had any trouble they had got rid of it.

They were not talkative at supper that night. They had a humble look, and when Huck prepared his pipe after the meal and was going to prepare theirs, they said no, they were not feeling very well—something they ate at dinner had disagreed with them.

About midnight Joe awoke, and called the boys. There was a brooding oppressiveness in the air that seemed to bode something. The boys huddled themselves together and sought the friendly companionship of the fire, though the dull dead heat of the breathless atmosphere was stifling. They sat still, intent and waiting. The solemn hush continued. Beyond the light of the fire everything was swallowed up in the blackness of darkness. Presently there came a quivering glow that vaguely revealed the foliage for a moment and then vanished. By and by another came, a little stronger. Then another. Then a faint moan came sighing through the branches of the forest and the boys felt a fleeting breath upon their cheeks, and shuddered with the fancy that the Spirit of the Night had gone by. There was a pause. Now a weird flash turned night into day and showed every little grassblade, separate and distinct, that grew about their feet. And it showed three white, startled faces, too. A deep peal of thunder went rolling and tumbling down the heavens and lost itself in sullen rumblings in the distance. A sweep of chilly air passed by, rustling all the leaves and snowing the flaky ashes broadcast about the fire. Another fierce glare lit up the forest and an instant crash followed that seemed to rend the treetops right over the boys' heads. They clung together in terror, in the thick gloom that followed. A few big raindrops fell pattering upon the leaves.

"Quick! boys, go for the tent!" exclaimed Tom.

They sprang away, stumbling over roots and among vines in the dark, no two plunging in the same direction. A furious blast roared through the trees, making everything sing as it went. One blinding flash after another came, and peal on peal of deafening thunder. And now a drenching rain poured down and the rising hurricane drove it in sheets along the ground. The boys cried out to each other, but the roaring wind and the booming thunderblasts drowned their voices utterly. However, one by one they straggled in at last and took shelter under the tent, cold, scared, and streaming with water; but to have company in misery seemed something to be grateful for. They could not talk, the old sail flapped so furiously, even if the other noises would have allowed them. The tempest rose higher and higher, and presently the sail tore loose from its fastenings and went winging away on the blast. The boys seized each others' hands and fled, with many tumblings and bruises, to the shelter of a great oak that stood upon the riverbank. Now the battle was at its highest. Under the ceaseless conflagration of lightning that flamed in the skies, everything below stood out in cleancut and shadowless distinctness: the bending trees, the billowy river, white with foam, the driving spray of spumeflakes, the dim outlines of the high bluffs on the other side, glimpsed through the drifting cloudrack and the slanting veil of rain. Every little while some giant tree yielded the fight and fell crashing through the younger growth; and the unflagging thunderpeals came now in ear-splitting explosive bursts, keen and sharp, and unspeakably appalling. The storm culminated in one matchless effort that seemed likely to tear the island to pieces, burn it up, drown it to the treetops, blow it away, and deafen every creature in it, all at one and the same moment. It was a wild night for homeless young heads to be out in.

But at last the battle was done, and the forces retired with weaker and weaker threatenings and grumblings, and peace resumed her sway. The boys went back to camp, a good deal awed; but they found there was still something to be thankful for, because the great sycamore, the shelter of their beds, was a ruin, now, blasted by the lightnings, and they were not under it when the catastrophe happened.

Everything in camp was drenched, the campfire as well; for they were but heedless lads, like their generation, and had made no provision against rain. Here was matter for dismay, for they were soaked through and chilled. They were eloquent in their distress; but they presently discovered that the fire had eaten so far up under the great log it had been built against (where it curved upward and separated itself from the ground), that a handbreadth or so of it had escaped wetting; so they patiently wrought until, with shreds and bark gathered from the under sides of sheltered logs, they coaxed the fire to burn again. Then they piled on great dead boughs till they had a roaring furnace, and were gladhearted once more. They dried their boiled ham and had a feast, and after that they sat by the fire and expanded and glorified their midnight adventure until morning, for there was not a dry spot to sleep on, anywhere around.

As the sun began to steal in upon the boys, drowsiness came over them, and they went out on the sandbar and lay down to sleep. They got scorched out by and by, and drearily set about getting breakfast. After the meal they felt rusty, and stiff-jointed, and a little homesick once more. Tom saw the signs, and fell to cheering up the pirates as well as he could. But they cared nothing for marbles, or circus, or swimming, or anything. He reminded them of the imposing secret, and raised a ray of cheer. While it lasted, he got them interested in a new device. This was to knock off being pirates, for a while, and be Indians for a change. They were attracted by this idea; so it was not long before they were stripped, and striped from head to heel with black mud, like so many zebras—all of them chiefs, of course—and then they went tearing through the woods to attack an English settlement.

By and by they separated into three hostile tribes, and darted upon each other from ambush with dreadful warwhoops, and killed and scalped each other by thousands. It was a gory day. Consequently it was an extremely satisfactory one.

They assembled in camp toward suppertime, hungry and happy; but now a difficulty arose—hostile Indians could not break the bread of hospitality together without first making peace, and this was a simple impossibility without smoking a pipe of peace. There was no other process that ever they had heard of. Two of the savages almost wished they had remained pirates. However, there was no other way; so with such show of cheerfulness as they could muster they called for the pipe and took their whiff as it passed, in due form.

And behold, they were glad they had gone into savagery, for they had gained something; they found that they could now smoke a little without having to go and hunt for a lost knife; they did not get sick enough to be seriously uncomfortable. They were not likely to fool away this high promise for lack of effort. No, they practised cautiously, after supper, with right fair success, and so they spent a jubilant evening. They were prouder and happier in their new acquirement than they would have been in the scalping and skinning of the Six Nations. We will leave them to smoke and chatter and brag, since we have no further use for them at present.

CHAPTER 17

Memories of the Lost Heroes—The Point in Tom's Secret

BUT there was no hilarity in the little town that same tranquil Saturday afternoon. The Harpers, and Aunt Polly's family, were being put into mourning, with great grief and many tears. An unusual quiet possessed the village, although it was ordinarily quiet enough, in all conscience. The villagers conducted their concerns with an absent air, and talked little; but they sighed often. The Saturday holiday seemed a burden to the children. They had no heart in their sports, and gradually gave them up.

In the afternoon Becky Thatcher found herself moping about the deserted schoolhouse yard, and feeling very melancholy. But she found nothing there to comfort her. She soliloquized:

"Oh, if I only had a brass andiron-knob again! But I haven't got anything now to remember him by." And she choked back a little sob.

Presently she stopped, and said to herself:

"It was right here. Oh, if it was to do over again, I wouldn't say that—I wouldn't say it for the whole world. But he's gone now; I'll never, never, never see him any more."

This thought broke her down, and she wandered away, with tears rolling down her cheeks. Then quite a group of boys and girls—playmates of Tom's and Joe's—came by, and stood looking over the paling fence and talking in reverent tones of how Tom did so-and-so the last time they saw him, and how Joe said this and that small trifle (pregnant with awful prophecy, as they could easily see now!)—and each speaker pointed out the exact spot where the lost lads stood at the time, and then added something like "and I was a-standing just so—just as I am now, and as if you was him—I was as close as that—and he smiled, just this way—and then something seemed to go all over me, like—awful, you know—and I never thought what it meant, of course, but I can see now!"

Then there was a dispute about who saw the dead boys last in life, and many claimed that dismal distinction, and offered evidences, more or less tampered with by the witness; and when it was ultimately decided who *did* see the departed last, and exchanged the last words with them, the lucky parties took upon themselves a sort of sacred importance, and were gaped at and envied by all the rest. One poor chap, who had no other grandeur to offer, said with tolerably manifest pride in the remembrance:

"Well, Tom Sawyer he licked me once."

But that bid for glory was a failure. Most of the boys could say that, and so that cheapened the distinction too much. The group loitered away, still recalling memories of the lost heroes, in awed voices.

When the Sunday-school hour was finished, the next morning, the bell began to toll, instead of ringing in the usual way. It was a very still Sabbath, and the mournful sound seemed in keeping with the musing hush that lay upon nature. The villagers began to gather, loitering a moment in the vestibule to converse in whispers about the sad event. But there was no whispering in the house; only the funereal rustling of dresses as the women gathered to their seats disturbed the silence there. None could remember when the little church had been so full before. There was finally a waiting pause, an expectant dumbness, and then Aunt Polly entered, followed by Sid and Mary, and they by the Harper family, all in deep black, and the whole congregation, the old minister as well, rose reverently and stood until the mourners were seated in the front pew. There was another communing silence, broken at intervals by muffled sobs, and then the minister spread his hands abroad and prayed. A moving hymn was sung, and the text followed: "I am the Resurrection and the Life."

As the service proceeded, the clergyman drew such pictures of the graces, the winning ways, and the rare promise of the lost lads that every soul there, thinking he recognized these pictures, felt a pang in remembering that he had persistently blinded himself to them always before, and had as persistently seen only faults and flaws in the poor boys. The minister related many a touching incident in the lives of the departed, too, which illustrated their sweet, generous natures, and the people could easily see, now, how noble and beautiful those episodes were, and remembered with grief that at the time they occurred they had seemed rank rascalities, well deserving of the cowhide. The congregation became more and more moved, as the pathetic tale went on, till at last the whole company broke down and joined the weeping mourners in a chorus of anguished sobs, the preacher himself giving way to his feelings, and crying in the pulpit.

There was a rustle in the gallery, which nobody noticed; a moment later the church door creaked; the minister raised his streaming eyes above his handkerchief, and stood transfixed! First one and then another pair of eyes followed the minister's, and then almost with one impulse the congregation rose and stared while the three dead boys came marching up the aisle, Tom in the lead, Joe next, and Huck, a ruin of drooping rags, sneaking sheepishly in the rear! They had been hid in the unused gallery listening to their own funeral sermon!

Aunt Polly, Mary, and the Harpers threw themselves upon their restored ones, smothered them with kisses and poured out thanksgivings, while poor Huck stood abashed and uncomfortable, not knowing exactly what to do or where to hide from so many unwelcoming eyes. He wavered, and started to slink away, but Tom seized him and said:

"Aunt Polly, it ain't fair. Somebody's got to be glad to see Huck."

"And so they shall. I'm glad to see him, poor motherless thing!" And the loving attentions Aunt Polly lavished upon him were the one thing capable of making him more uncomfortable than he was before.

Suddenly the minister shouted at the top of his voice: "Praise God from whom all blessings flow—sing!—and put your hearts in it!"

And they did. Old Hundred swelled up with a triumphant burst, and while it shook the rafters Tom Sawyer the Pirate looked around upon the envying juveniles about him and confessed in his heart that this was the proudest moment of his life.

As the "sold" congregation trooped out they said they would almost be willing to be made ridiculous again to hear Old Hundred sung like that once more.

Tom got more cuffs and kisses that day—according to Aunt Polly's varying moods—than he had earned before in a year; and he hardly knew which expressed the most gratefulness to God and affection for himself.

CHAPTER 18

Tom's Feelings Investigated—Wonderful Dream—Becky
Thatcher Overshadowed—Tom Becomes Jealous
—Black Revenge

THAT was Tom's great secret—the scheme to return home
with his brother pirates and attend their own funerals.
They had paddled over to the Missouri shore on a log, at
dusk on Saturday, landing five or six miles below the village;
they had slept in the woods at the edge of the town till nearly
daylight, and had then crept through back lanes and alleys and
finished their sleep in the gallery of the church among a chaos
of invalided benches.

At breakfast, Monday morning, Aunt Polly and Mary were
very loving to Tom, and very attentive to his wants. There was
an unusual amount of talk. In the course of it Aunt Polly said:

"Well, I don't say it wasn't a fine joke, Tom, to keep
everybody suffering 'most a week so you boys had a good time,
but it is a pity you could be so hard-hearted as to let *me* suffer
so. If you could come over on a log to go to your funeral, you
could have come over and give me a hint some way that you
warn't *dead*, but only run off."

"Yes, you could have done that, Tom," said Mary; "and I
believe you would if you had thought of it."

"Would you, Tom?" said Aunt Polly, her face lighting
wistfully. "Say, now, would you, if you'd thought of it?"

"I—well, I don't know. 'Twould 'a' spoiled everything."

"Tom, I hoped you loved me that much," said Aunt Polly,

with a grieved tone that discomforted the boy. "It would have been something if you'd cared enough to *think* of it, even if you didn't *do* it."

"Now, auntie, that ain't any harm," pleaded Mary; "it's only Tom's giddy way—he is always in such a rush that he never thinks of anything."

"More's the pity. Sid would have thought. And Sid would have come and *done* it, too. Tom, you'll look back, some day, when it's too late, and wish you'd cared a little more for me when it would have cost you so little."

"Now, auntie, you know I do care for you," said Tom.

"I'd know it better if you acted more like it."

"I wish now I'd thought," said Tom, with a repentant tone; "but I dreamt about you, anyway. That's something, ain't it?"

"It ain't much—a cat does that much—but it's better than nothing. What did you dream?"

"Why, Wednesday night I dreamt that you was sitting over there by the bed, and Sid was sitting by the woodbox, and Mary next to him."

"Well, so we did. So we always do. I'm glad your dreams could take even that much trouble about us."

"And I dreamt that Joe Harper's mother was here."

"Why, she *was* here! Did you dream any more?"

"Oh, lots. But it's so dim, now."

"Well, *try* to recollect—can't you?"

"Somehow it seems to me that the wind—the wind blowed the—the—"

"Try harder, Tom! The wind did blow something. Come!"

Tom pressed his fingers on his forehead an anxious minute, and then said:

"I've got it now! I've got it now! It blowed the candle!"

"Mercy on us! Go *on*, Tom—go on!"

"And it seems to me that you said, 'Why, I believe that that door—'"

"Go *on*, Tom!"

"Just let me study a moment—just a moment. Oh, yes—you said you believed the door was open."

"As I'm sitting here, I did! Didn't I, Mary! Go on!"

"And then—and then—well I won't be certain, but it seems like as if you made Sid go and—and—"

"Well? Well? What did I make him do, Tom? What did I make him do?"

"You made him—you—Oh, you made him shut it."

"Well, for the land's sake! I never heard the beat of that in all my days! Don't tell *me* there ain't anything in dreams, any more. Sereny Harper shall know of this before I'm an hour older. I'd like to see her get around *this* with her rubbage 'bout superstition. Go on, Tom!"

"Oh, it's all getting just as bright as day, now. Next you said I warn't *bad*, only mischeevous and harum-scarum, and not any more responsible than—than—I think it was a colt, or something."

"And so it was! Well, goodness gracious! Go on, Tom!"

"And then you began to cry."

"So I did. So I did. Not the first time, neither. And then—"

"Then Mrs. Harper she began to cry, and said Joe was just the same, and she wished she hadn't whipped him for taking cream when she'd throwed it out her own self—"

"Tom! The sperrit was upon you! You was a prophesying—that's what you was doing! Land alive, go on, Tom!"

"Then Sid he said—he said—"

"I don't think I said anything," said Sid.

"Yes you did, Sid," said Mary.

"Shut your heads and let Tom go on! What did he say, Tom?"

"He said—I *think* he said he hoped I was better off where I was gone to, but if I'd been better sometimes—"

"*There*, d'you hear that! It was his very words!"

"And you shut him up sharp."

"I lay I did! There must 'a' been an angel there. There *was* an angel there, somewheres!"

"And Mrs. Harper told about Joe scaring her with a firecracker, and you told about Peter and the Pain-killer—"

"Just as true as I live!"

"And then there was a whole lot of talk 'bout dragging the river for us, and 'bout having the funeral Sunday, and then you and old Miss Harper hugged and cried, and she went."

"It happened just so! It happened just so, as sure as I'm a-sitting in these very tracks. Tom, you couldn't told it more like if you'd 'a' seen it! And *then* what? Go on, Tom!"

"Then I thought you prayed for me—and I could see you and hear every word you said. And you went to bed, and I was so sorry that I took and wrote on a piece of sycamore bark, '*We ain't dead—we are only off being pirates*,' and put it on the table by the candle; and then you looked so good, laying there asleep, that I thought I went and leaned over and kissed you on the lips."

"Did you, Tom, *did* you! I just forgive you everything for that!" And she seized the boy in a crushing embrace that made him feel like the guiltiest of villains.

"It was very kind, even though it was only a—dream," Sid soliloquized just audibly.

"Shut up, Sid! A body does just the same in a dream as he'd do if he was awake. Here's a big Milum apple I've been saving for you, Tom, if you was ever found again—now go 'long to school. I'm thankful to the good God and Father of us all I've got you back, that's long-suffering and merciful to them that believe on Him and keep His word, though goodness knows I'm unworthy of it, but if only the worthy ones got His blessings and had His hand to help them over the rough places, there's few enough would smile here or ever enter into His rest when the long night comes. Go 'long Sid, Mary, Tom—take yourselves off—you've hendered me long enough."

The children left for school, and the old lady to call on Mrs. Harper and vanquish her realism with Tom's marvellous dream. Sid had better judgment than to utter the thought that was in his mind as he left the house. It was this: "Pretty thin— as long a dream as that, without any mistakes in it!"

What a hero Tom was become, now! He did not go skipping and prancing, but moved with a dignified swagger as became a pirate who felt that the public eye was on him. And indeed it was; he tried not to seem to see the looks or hear the remarks as he passed along, but they were food and drink to him. Smaller boys than himself flocked at his heels, as proud to be seen with him, and tolerated by him, as if he had been the drummer at the head of a procession or the elephant leading a menagerie into town. Boys of his own size pretended not to know he had been away at all; but they were consuming with envy, nevertheless. They would have given anything to have that swarthy sun-tanned skin of his, and his glittering notoriety; and Tom would not have parted with either for a circus. At school the children made so much of him and of Joe, and delivered such eloquent admiration from their eyes, that the two heroes were not long in becoming insufferably "stuck-up." They began to tell their adventures to hungry listeners—but they only began; it was not a thing likely to have an end, with imaginations like theirs to furnish material. And finally, when they got out their pipes and went serenely puffing around, the very summit of glory was reached.

Tom decided that he could be independent of Becky Thatcher now. Glory was sufficient. He would live for glory. Now that he was distinguished, maybe she would be wanting to "make up." Well, let her—she should see that he could be as indifferent as some other people. Presently she arrived. Tom pretended not to see her. He moved away and joined a group of boys and girls and began to talk. Soon he observed that she was tripping gayly back and forth with flushed face and dancing eyes, pretending to be busy chasing schoolmates, and screaming with laughter when she made a capture; but he noticed that she always made her captures in his vicinity, and that she seemed to cast a conscious eye in his direction at such times, too. It gratified all the vicious vanity that was in him; and so, instead of winning him, it only "set him up" the more and made him the more diligent to avoid betraying that he knew she was about. Presently she gave over skylarking, and moved irresolutely about, sighing once or twice and glancing furtively and wistfully toward Tom. Then she observed that now Tom was talking more particularly to Amy Lawrence than to any one else. She felt a sharp pang and grew disturbed and uneasy at once. She tried to go away, but her feet were treacherous, and carried her to the group instead. She said to a girl almost at Tom's elbow—with sham vivacity:

"Why, Mary Austin! you bad girl, why didn't you come to Sunday-school?"

"I did come—didn't you see me?"

"Why, no! Did you? Where did you sit?"

"I was in Miss Peters' class, where I always go. I saw *you*"

"Did you? Why, it's funny I didn't see you. I wanted to tell you about the picnic."

"Oh, that's jolly. Who's going to give it?"

"My ma's going to let me have one."

"Oh, goody; I hope she'll let *me* come."

"Well, she will. The picnic's for me. She'll let anybody come that I want, and I want you."

"That's ever so nice. When is it going to be?"

"By and by. Maybe about vacation."

"Oh, won't it be fun! You going to have all the girls and boys?"

"Yes, every one that's friends to me—or wants to be"; and she glanced ever so furtively at Tom, but he talked right along to Amy Lawrence about the terrible storm on the island, and how the lightning tore the great sycamore tree "all to flinders" while he was "standing within three feet of it."

"Oh, may I come?" said Grace Miller.

"Yes."

"And me?" said Sally Rogers.

"Yes."

"And me, too?" said Susy Harper. "And Joe?"

"Yes."

And so on, with clapping of joyful hands till all the group had begged for invitations but Tom and Amy. Then Tom turned coolly away, still talking, and took Amy with him. Becky's lips trembled and the tears came to her eyes; she hid these signs with a forced gayety and went on chattering, but the life had gone out of the picnic, now, and out of everything else; she got away as soon as she could and hid herself and had what her sex call "a good cry." Then she sat moody, with wounded pride, till the bell rang. She roused up, now, with a vindictive cast in her eye, and gave her plaited tails a shake and said she knew what *she'd* do.

At recess Tom continued his flirtation with Amy with jubilant self-satisfaction. And he kept drifting about to find Becky and lacerate her with the performance. At last he spied her, but there was a sudden falling of his mercury. She was sitting cosily on a little bench behind the schoolhouse looking at a picture-book with Alfred Temple—and so absorbed were they, and their heads so close together over the book, that they did not seem to be conscious of anything in the world besides. Jealousy ran red-hot through Tom's veins. He began to hate himself for throwing away the chance Becky had offered for a reconciliation. He called himself a fool, and all the hard names he could think of. He wanted to cry with vexation. Amy chatted happily along, as they walked, for her heart was singing, but Tom's tongue had lost its function. He did not hear

THE ADVENTURES OF TOM SAWYER 139

what Amy was saying, and whenever she paused expectantly he could only stammer an awkward assent, which was as often misplaced as otherwise. He kept drifting to the rear of the schoolhouse, again and again, to sear his eyeballs with the hateful spectacle there. He could not help it. And it maddened him to see, as he thought he saw, that Becky Thatcher never once suspected that he was even in the land of the living. But she did see, nevertheless; and she knew she was winning her fight, too, and was glad to see him suffer as she had suffered.

Amy's happy prattle became intolerable. Tom hinted at things he had to attend to; things that must be done; and time was fleeting. But in vain—the girl chirped on. Tom thought, "Oh, hang her, ain't I ever going to get rid of her?" At last he must be attending to those things—and she said artlessly that she would be "around" when school let out. And he hastened away, hating her for it.

"Any other boy!" Tom thought, grating his teeth. "Any boy in the whole town but that Saint Louis smarty that thinks he dresses so fine and is aristocracy! Oh, all right, I licked you the first day you ever saw this town, mister, and I'll lick you again! You just wait till I catch you out! I'll just take and—"

And he went through the motions of thrashing an imaginary boy—pummelling the air, and kicking and gouging. "Oh, you do, do you? You holler 'nough, do you? Now, then, let that learn you!" And so the imaginary flogging was finished to his satisfaction.

Tom fled home at noon. His conscience could not endure any more of Amy's grateful happiness, and his jealousy could bear no more of the other distress. Becky resumed her picture inspections with Alfred, but as the minutes dragged along and no Tom came to suffer, her triumph began to cloud and she lost interest; gravity and absentmindedness followed, and then melancholy; two or three times she pricked up her ear at a footstep, but it was a false hope; no Tom came. At last she grew entirely miserable and wished she hadn't carried it so far. When poor Alfred, seeing that he was losing her, he did not know how, kept exclaiming: "Oh, here's a jolly one! look at this!" she lost patience at last, and said, "Oh, don't bother me! I don't care for them!" and burst into tears, and got up and walked away.

Alfred dropped alongside and was going to try to comfort her, but she said:

"Go away and leave me alone, can't you! I hate you!"

So the boy halted, wondering what he could have done— for she had said she would look at pictures all through the nooning—and she walked on, crying. Then Alfred went musing into the deserted schoolhouse. He was humiliated and angry. He easily guessed his way to the truth—the girl had simply made a convenience of him to vent her spite upon Tom Sawyer. He was far from hating Tom the less when this thought occurred to him. He wished there was some way to get that boy into trouble without much risk to himself. Tom's spelling-book fell under his eye. Here was his opportunity. He gratefully opened to the lesson for the afternoon and poured ink upon the page.

Becky, glancing in at a window behind him at the moment, saw the act, and moved on, without discovering herself. She started homeward, now, intending to find Tom and tell him; Tom would be thankful and their troubles would be healed. Before she was half way home, however, she had changed her mind. The thought of Tom's treatment of her when she was talking about her picnic came scorching back and filled her with shame. She resolved to let him get whipped on the damaged spelling-book's account, and to hate him forever, into the bargain.

CHAPTER 19

Tom Tells the Truth

TOM arrived at home in a dreary mood, and the first thing his aunt said to him showed him that he had brought his sorrows to an unpromising market:

"Tom, I've a notion to skin you alive!"

"Auntie, what have I done?"

"Well, you've done enough. Here I go over to Sereny Harper, like an old softy, expecting I'm going to make her believe all that rubbage about that dream, when lo and behold you she'd found out from Joe that you was over here and heard all the talk we had that night. Tom, I don't know what is to become of a boy that will act like that. It makes me feel so bad to think you could let me go to Sereny Harper and make such a fool of myself and never say a word."

This was a new aspect of the thing. His smartness of the morning had seemed to Tom a good joke before, and very ingenious. It merely looked mean and shabby now. He hung his head and could not think of anything to say for a moment. Then he said:

"Auntie, I wish I hadn't done it—but I didn't think."

"Oh, child, you never think. You never think of anything but your own selfishness. You could think to come all the way over here from Jackson's Island in the night to laugh at our troubles, and you could think to fool me with a lie about a dream; but you couldn't ever think to pity us and save us from sorrow."

"Auntie, I know now it was mean, but I didn't mean to be mean. I didn't, honest. And besides, I didn't come over here to laugh at you that night."

"What did you come for, then?"

"It was to tell you not to be uneasy about us, because we hadn't got drownded."

"Tom, Tom, I would be the thankfullest soul in this world if I could believe you ever had as good a thought as that, but you know you never did—and I know it, Tom."

"Indeed and 'deed I did, auntie—I wish I may never stir if I didn't."

"Oh, Tom, don't lie—don't do it. It only makes things a hundred times worse."

"It ain't a lie, auntie; it's the truth. I wanted to keep you from grieving—that was all that made me come."

"I'd give the whole world to believe that—it would cover up a power of sins, Tom. I'd 'most be glad you'd run off and acted so bad. But it ain't reasonable; because, why didn't you tell me, child?"

"Why, you see, when you got to talking about the funeral, I just got all full of the idea of our coming and hiding in the church, and I couldn't somehow bear to spoil it. So I just put the bark back in my pocket and kept mum."

"What bark?"

"The bark I had wrote on to tell you we'd gone pirating. I wish, now, you'd waked up when I kissed you—I do, honest."

The hard lines in his aunt's face relaxed and a sudden tenderness dawned in her eyes.

"*Did* you kiss me, Tom?"

"Why, yes, I did."

"Are you sure you did, Tom?"

"Why, yes, I did, auntie—certain sure."

"What did you kiss me for, Tom?"

"Because I loved you so, and you laid there moaning and I

was so sorry."

The words sounded like truth. The old lady could not hide a tremor in her voice when she said:

"Kiss me again, Tom!—and be off with you to school, now, and don't bother me any more."

The moment he was gone, she ran to a closet and got out the ruin of a jacket which Tom had gone pirating in. Then she stopped, with it in her hand, and said to herself:

"No, I don't dare. Poor boy, I reckon he's lied about it—but it's a blessed, blessed lie, there's such a comfort come from it. I hope the Lord—I *know* the Lord will forgive him, because it was such good-heartedness in him to tell it. But I don't want to find out it's a lie. I won't look."

She put the jacket away, and stood by musing a minute. Twice she put out her hand to take the garment again, and twice she refrained. Once more she ventured, and this time she fortified herself with the thought: "It's a good lie—it's a good lie—I won't let it grieve me." So she sought the jacket pocket. A moment later she was reading Tom's piece of bark through flowing tears and saying: "I could forgive the boy, now, if he'd committed a million sins.

CHAPTER 20

Becky in a Dilemma
—Tom's Nobility Asserts Itself

THERE was something about Aunt Polly's manner, when she kissed Tom, that swept away his low spirits and made him lighthearted and happy again. He started to school and had the luck of coming upon Becky Thatcher at the head of Meadow Lane. His mood always determined his manner. Without a moment's hesitation he ran to her and said:

"I acted mighty mean today, Becky, and I'm so sorry. I won't ever, ever do that way again, as long as ever I live—please make up, won't you?"

The girl stopped and looked him scornfully in the face:

"I'll thank you to keep yourself *to* yourself, Mr. Thomas Sawyer. I'll never speak to you again."

She tossed her head and passed on. Tom was so stunned that he had not even presence of mind enough to say "Who cares, Miss Smarty?" until the right time to say it had gone by. So he said nothing. But he was in a fine rage, nevertheless. He moped into the schoolyard wishing she were a boy, and imagining how he would trounce her if she were. He presently encountered her and delivered a stinging remark as he passed. She hurled one in return, and the angry breach was complete. It seemed to Becky, in her hot resentment, that she could hardly wait for school to "take in," she was so impatient to see Tom flogged for the injured spelling-book. If she had had any lingering notion of exposing Alfred Temple,

Tom's offensive fling had driven it entirely away.

Poor girl, she did not know how fast she was nearing trouble herself. The master, Mr. Dobbins, had reached middle age with an unsatisfied ambition. The darling of his desires was, to be a doctor, but poverty had decreed that he should be nothing higher than a village schoolmaster. Every day he took a mysterious book out of his desk and absorbed himself in it at times when no classes were reciting. He kept that book under lock and key. There was not an urchin in school but was perishing to have a glimpse of it, but the chance never came. Every boy and girl had a theory about the nature of that book; but no two theories were alike, and there was no way of getting at the facts in the case. Now, as Becky was passing by the desk, which stood near the door, she noticed that the key was in the lock! It was a precious moment. She glanced around; found herself alone, and the next instant she had the book in her hands. The titlepage—Professor Somebody's *Anatomy*—carried no information to her mind; so she began to turn the leaves. She came at once upon a handsomely engraved and colored frontispiece—a human figure, stark naked. At that moment a shadow fell on the page and Tom Sawyer stepped in at the door and caught a glimpse of the picture. Becky snatched at the book to close it, and had the hard luck to tear the pictured page half down the middle. She thrust the volume into the desk, turned the key, and burst out crying with shame and vexation.

"Tom Sawyer, you are just as mean as you can be, to sneak up on a person and look at what they're looking at."

"How could I know you was looking at anything?"

"You ought to be ashamed of yourself, Tom Sawyer; you know you're going to tell on me, and oh, what shall I do, what shall I do! I'll be whipped, and I never was whipped in school."

Then she stamped her little foot and said:

"*Be* so mean if you want to! I know something that's going

to happen. You just wait and you'll see! Hateful, hateful, hateful!"—and she flung out of the house with a new explosion of crying.

Tom stood still, rather flustered by this onslaught. Presently he said to himself:

"What a curious kind of a fool a girl is! Never been licked in school! Shucks! What's a licking! That's just like a girl— they're so thin-skinned and chicken-hearted. Well, of course I ain't going to tell old Dobbins on this little fool, because there's other ways of getting even on her, that ain't so mean; but what of it? Old Dobbins will ask who it was tore his book. Nobody'll answer. Then he'll do just the way he always does—ask first one and then t'other, and when he comes to the right girl he'll know it, without any telling. Girls' faces always tell on them. They ain't got any backbone. She'll get licked. Well, it's a kind of a tight place for Becky Thatcher, because there ain't any way out of it." Tom conned the thing a moment longer, and then added: "All right, though; she'd like to see me in just such a fix—let her sweat it out!"

Tom joined the mob of skylarking scholars outside. In a few moments the master arrived and school "took in." Tom did not feel a strong interest in his studies. Every time he stole a glance at the girls' side of the room Becky's face troubled him. Considering all things, he did not want to pity her, and yet it was all he could do to help it. He could get up no exultation that was really worthy the name. Presently the spelling-book discovery was made, and Tom's mind was entirely full of his own matters for a while after that. Becky roused up from her lethargy of distress and showed good interest in the proceedings. She did not expect that Tom could get out of his trouble by denying that he spilt the ink on the book himself; and she was right. The denial only seemed to make the thing worse for Tom. Becky supposed she would be glad of that, and she tried to believe she was glad of it, but she found she was not certain. When the worst came to the worst, she had an impulse to get up and tell on Alfred Temple, but she made an effort and forced herself to keep still—because, said she to herself, "he'll tell about me tearing the picture sure. I wouldn't say a word, not to save his life!"

Tom took his whipping and went back to his seat not at all broken-hearted, for he thought it was possible that he had unknowingly upset the ink on the spelling-book himself, in some skylarking bout—he had denied it for form's sake and because it was custom, and had stuck to the denial from principle.

A whole hour drifted by, the master sat nodding in his throne, the air was drowsy with the hum of study. By and by, Mr. Dobbins straightened himself up, yawned, then unlocked his desk, and reached for his book, but seemed undecided whether to take it out or leave it. Most of the pupils glanced up languidly, but there were two among them that watched his movements with intent eyes. Mr. Dobbins fingered his book absently for a while, then took it out and settled himself in his chair to read! Tom shot a glance at Becky. He had seen a hunted and helpless rabbit look as she did, with a gun levelled at its head. Instantly he forgot his quarrel with her. Quick—something must be done! done in a flash, too! But the very imminence of the emergency paralyzed his invention. Good!—he had an inspiration! He would run and snatch the book, spring through the door and fly. But his resolution shook for one little instant, and the chance was lost—the master opened the volume. If Tom only had the wasted opportunity back again! Too late. There was no help for Becky now, he said. The next moment the master faced the school. Every eye sank under his gaze. There was that in it which smote even the innocent with fear. There was silence while one might count ten—the master was gathering his wrath. Then he spoke: "Who tore this book?"

There was not a sound. One could have heard a pin drop.

The stillness continued; the master searched face after face for signs of guilt.

"Benjamin Rogers, did you tear this book?"

A denial. Another pause.

"Joseph Harper, did you?"

Another denial. Tom's uneasiness grew more and more intense under the slow torture of these proceedings. The master scanned the ranks of boys—considered a while, then turned to the girls:

"Amy Lawrence?"

A shake of the head.

"Gracie Miller?"

The same sign.

"Susan Harper, did you do this?"

Another negative. The next girl was Becky Thatcher. Tom was trembling from head to foot with excitement and a sense of the hopelessness of the situation.

"Rebecca Thatcher" [Tom glanced at her face—it was white with terror]—"did you tear—no, look me in the face" [her hands rose in appeal]—"did you tear this book?"

A thought shot like lightning through Tom's brain. He sprang to his feet and shouted—"*I* done it!"

The school stared in perplexity at this incredible folly. Tom stood a moment, to gather his dismembered faculties; and when he stepped forward to go to his punishment the surprise, the gratitude, the adoration that shone upon him out of poor Becky's eyes seemed pay enough for a hundred floggings. Inspired by the splendor of his own act, he took without an outcry the most merciless flaying that even Mr. Dobbins had ever administered; and also received with indifference the added cruelty of a command to remain two hours after school should be dismissed—for he knew who would wait for him outside till his captivity was done, and not count the tedious time as loss, either.

Tom went to bed that night planning vengeance against Alfred Temple; for with shame and repentance Becky had told him all, not forgetting her own treachery; but even the longing for vengeance had to give way, soon, to pleasanter musings, and he fell asleep at last with Becky's latest words lingering dreamily in his ear—

"Tom, how *could* you be so noble!"

CHAPTER 21

Youthful Eloquence—
Compositions by the Young Ladies—A Lengthy Vision
—The Boy's Vengeance Satisfied

VACATION was approaching. The schoolmaster, always severe, grew severer and more exacting than ever, for he wanted the school to make a good showing on "Examination" day. His rod and his ferule were seldom idle now—at least among the smaller pupils. Only the biggest boys, and young ladies of eighteen and twenty, escaped lashing. Mr. Dobbins' lashings were very vigorous ones, too; for although he carried, under his wig, a perfectly bald and shiny head, he had only reached middle age, and there was no sign of feebleness in his muscle. As the great day approached, all the tyranny that was in him came to the surface; he seemed to take a vindictive pleasure in punishing the least shortcomings. The consequence was, that the smaller boys spent their days in terror and suffering and their nights in plotting revenge. They threw away no opportunity to do the master a mischief. But he kept ahead all the time. The retribution that followed every vengeful success was so sweeping and majestic that the boys always retired from the field badly worsted. At last they conspired together and hit upon a plan that promised a dazzling victory. They swore in the signpainter's boy, told him the scheme, and asked his help. He had his own reasons for being delighted, for the master boarded in his father's family and had given the boy ample cause to hate him. The master's wife would go on a visit to the country in a few days, and there would be nothing to interfere with the plan; the master always prepared himself for great occasions by getting pretty well fuddled, and the signpainter's boy said that when the dominie had reached the proper condition on Examination Evening he would "manage the thing" while he napped in his chair; then he would have him awakened at the right time and hurried away to school.

In the fulness of time the interesting occasion arrived. At eight in the evening the schoolhouse was brilliantly lighted, and adorned with wreaths and festoons of foliage and flowers. The master sat throned in his great chair upon a raised platform, with his blackboard behind him. He was looking tolerably mellow. Three rows of benches on each side and six rows in front of him were occupied by the dignitaries of the town and by the parents of the pupils. To his left, back of the rows of citizens, was a spacious temporary platform upon which were seated the scholars who were to take part in the exercises of the evening; rows of small boys, washed and dressed to an intolerable state of discomfort; rows of gawky big boys; snowbanks of girls and young ladies clad in lawn and muslin and conspicuously conscious of their bare arms, their grandmothers' ancient trinkets, their bits of pink and blue ribbon and the flowers in their hair. All the rest of the house was filled with non-participating scholars.

The exercises began. A very little boy stood up and sheepishly recited, "You'd scarce expect one of my age to speak in public on the stage," etc.—accompanying himself with the painfully exact and spasmodic gestures which a machine might have used—supposing the machine to be a trifle out of order. But he got through safely, though cruelly scared, and got a fine round of applause when he made his manufactured bow and retired.

A little shamefaced girl lisped, "Mary had a little lamb," etc., performed a compassion-inspiring curtsy, got her meed of applause, and sat down flushed and happy.

Tom Sawyer stepped forward with conceited confidence and soared into the unquenchable and indestructible "Give me liberty or give me death" speech, with fine fury and frantic gesticulation, and broke down in the middle of it. A ghastly stage-fright seized him, his legs quaked under him and he was like to choke. True, he had the manifest sympathy of the house but he had the house's silence, too, which was even worse than its sympathy. The master frowned, and this completed the disaster. Tom struggled awhile and then retired, utterly defeated. There was a weak attempt at applause, but it died early.

"The Boy Stood on the Burning Deck" followed; also "The Assyrian Came Down," and other declamatory gems. Then there were reading exercises, and a spelling fight. The meagre Latin class recited with honor. The prime feature of the evening was in order, now—original "compositions" by the young ladies. Each in her turn stepped forward to the edge of the platform, cleared her throat, held up her manuscript (tied with dainty ribbon), and proceeded to read, with labored attention to "expression" and punctuation. The themes were the same that had been illuminated upon similar occasions by their mothers before them, their grandmothers, and doubtless all their ancestors in the female line clear back to the Crusades. "Friendship" was one; "Memories of Other Days"; "Religion in History"; "Dream Land"; "The Advantages of Culture"; "Forms of Political Government Compared and Contrasted"; "Melancholy"; "Filial Love"; "Heart Longings," etc., etc.

A prevalent feature in these compositions was a nursed and petted melancholy; another was a wasteful and opulent gush of "fine language"; another was a tendency to lug in by the ears particularly prized words and phrases until they were worn entirely out; and a peculiarity that conspicuously marked and marred them was the inveterate and intolerable sermon that wagged its crippled tail at the end of each and every one of them. No matter what the subject might be, a brainracking effort was made to squirm it into some aspect or other that the moral and religious mind could contemplate with edification. The glaring insincerity of these sermons was not sufficient to compass the banishment of the fashion from the schools, and it is not sufficient today; it never will be sufficient while the world stands, perhaps. There is no school in all our land where the young ladies do not feel obliged to close their compositions with a sermon; and you will find that the sermon of the most frivolous and the least religious girl in the school is always the longest and the most relentlessly pious. But enough of this. Homely truth is unpalatable.

Let us return to the "Examination." The first composition that was read was one entitled "Is this, then, Life?" Perhaps the reader can endure an extract from it:

"In the common walks of life, with what delightful emotions does the youthful mind look forward to some anticipated scene of festivity! Imagination is busy sketching rose-tinted pictures of joy. In fancy, the voluptuous votary of fashion sees herself amid the festive throng, 'the observed of all observers.' Her graceful form, arrayed in snowy robes, is whirling through the mazes of the joyous dance; her eye is brightest, her step is lightest in the gay assembly.

"In such delicious fancies time quickly glides by, and the welcome hour arrives for her entrance into the Elysian world, of which she has had such bright dreams. How fairy-like does everything appear to her enchanted vision! Each new scene is more charming than the last. But after a while she finds that beneath this goodly exterior, all is vanity, the flattery which once charmed her soul, now grates harshly upon her ear; the ballroom has lost its charms; and with wasted health and imbittered heart, she turns away with the conviction that earthly pleasures cannot satisfy the longings of the soul!"

And so forth and so on. There was a buzz of gratification froêm time to time during the reading, accompanied by whispered ejaculations of "How sweet!" "How eloquent!" "So true!" etc., and after the thing had closed with a peculiarly afflicting sermon the applause was enthusiastic.

Then arose a slim, melancholy girl, whose face had the "interesting" paleness that comes of pills and indigestion, and read a "poem." Two stanzas of it will do:

A MISSOURI MAIDEN'S FAREWELL TO ALABAMA

Alabama, goodbye! I love thee well!
But yet for a while do I leave thee now!
Sad, yes, sad thoughts of thee my heart doth swell,
And burning recollections throng my brow!
For I have wandered through thy flowery woods;
Have roamed and read near Tallapoosa's stream;
Have listened to Tallassee's warring floods,
And wooed on Coosa's side Aurora's beam.

"Yet shame I not to bear an o'erfull heart,
Nor blush to turn behind my tearful eyes;
'Tis from no stranger land I now must part,
'Tis to no strangers left I yield these sighs.
Welcome and home were mine within this State,
Whose vales I leave—whose spires fade fast from me
And cold must be mine eyes, and heart, and tête,
When, dear Alabama! they turn cold on thee!

There were very few there who knew what "*tête*" meant, but the poem was very satisfactory, nevertheless.

Next appeared a dark-complexioned, black-eyed, black-haired young lady, who paused an impressive moment, assumed a tragic expression, and began to read in a measured, solemn tone:

A vision

"Dark and tempestuous was night. Around the throne on high not a single star quivered; but the deep intonations of the heavy thunder constantly vibrated upon the ear; whilst the terrific lightning revelled in angry mood through the cloudy chambers of heaven, seeming to scorn the power exerted over its terror by the illustrious Franklin! Even the boisterous winds unanimously came forth from their mystic homes, and blustered about as if to enhance by their aid the wildness of the scene. At such a time, so dark,so dreary, for human sympathy my very spirit sighed; but instead thereof,

> *My dearest friend, my counsellor, my comforter and guide—*
> *My joy in grief, my second bliss in joy,' came to my side.*

She moved like one of those bright beings pictured in the sunny walks of fancy's Eden by the romantic and young, a queen of beauty unadorned save by her own transcendent loveliness. So soft was her step, it failed to make even a sound, and but for the magical thrill imparted by her genial touch, as other unobtrusive beauties, she would have glided away unperceived—unsought. A strange sadness rested upon her features, like icy tears upon the robe of December, as she pointed to the contending elements without, and bade me contemplate the two beings presented."

This nightmare occupied some ten pages of manuscript and wound up with a sermon so destructive of all hope to non-Presbyterians that it took the first prize. This composition was considered to be the very finest effort of the evening. The mayor of the village, in delivering the prize to the author of it, made a warm speech in which he said that it was by far the most "eloquent" thing he had ever listened to, and that Daniel Webster himself might well be proud of it.

It may be remarked, in passing, that the number of compositions in which the word "beauteous" was over-fondled, and human experience referred to as "life's page," was up to the usual average.

Now the master, mellow almost to the verge of geniality, put his chair aside, turned his back to the audience, and began to draw a map of America on the blackboard, to exercise the geography class upon. But he made a sad business of it with his unsteady hand, and a smothered titter rippled over the house. He knew what the matter was, and set himself to right it. He sponged out lines and remade them; but he only distorted them more than ever, and the tittering was more pronounced. He threw his entire attention upon his work, now, as if determined not to be put down by the mirth. He felt that all eyes were fastened upon him; he imagined he was succeeding, and yet the tittering continued; it even manifestly increased. And well it might. There was a garret above, pierced with a scuttle over his head; and down through this scuttle came a cat, suspended around the haunches by a string; she had a rag tied about her head and jaws to keep her from mewing; as she slowly descended she curved upward and clawed at the string, she swung downward and clawed at the intangible air. The tittering rose higher and higher—the cat was within six inches of the absorbed teacher's head—down, down, a little lower, and she grabbed his wig with her desperate claws, clung to it, and was snatched up into the garret in an instant with her trophy still in her possession! And how the light did blaze abroad from the master's bald pate—for the signpainter's boy had *gilded* it!

That broke up the meeting. The boys were avenged. Vacation had come.

Note:—The pretended "compositions" quoted in this chapter are taken without alteration from a volume entitled

Prose and Poetry, by a Western Lady—but they are exactly and precisely after the schoolgirl pattern, and hence are much happier than any mere imitations could be.

CHAPTER 22

Tom's Confidence Betrayed—Expects Signal Punishment

TOM joined the new order of Cadets of Temperance, being attracted by the showy character of their "regalia." He promised to abstain from smoking, chewing, and profanity as long as he remained a member. Now he found out a new thing—namely, that to promise not to do a thing is the surest way in the world to make a body want to go and do that very thing. Tom soon found himself tormented with a desire to drink and swear; the desire grew to be so intense that nothing but the hope of a chance to display himself in his red sash kept him from withdrawing from the order. Fourth of July was coming; but he soon gave that up—gave it up before he had worn his shackles over forty-eight hours—and fixed his hopes upon old Judge Frazer, justice of the peace, who was apparently on his deathbed and would have a big public funeral, since he was so high an official. During three days Tom was deeply concerned about the Judge's condition and hungry for news of it. Sometimes his hopes ran high—so high that he would venture to get out his regalia and practise before the looking-glass. But the Judge had a most discouraging way of fluctuating. At last he was pronounced upon the mend—and then convalescent. Tom was disgusted; and felt a sense of injury, too. He handed in his resignation at once—and that night the Judge suffered a relapse and died. Tom resolved that he would never trust a man like that again.

The funeral was a fine thing. The Cadets paraded in a style

calculated to kill the late member with envy. Tom was a free boy again, however—there was something in that. He could drink and swear, now—but found to his surprise that he did not want to. The simple fact that he could, took the desire away, and the charm of it.

Tom presently wondered to find that his coveted vacation was beginning to hang a little heavily on his hands.

He attempted a diary—but nothing happened during three days, and so he abandoned it.

The first of all the negro minstrel shows came to town, and made a sensation. Tom and Joe Harper got up a band of performers and were happy for two days.

Even the Glorious Fourth was in some sense a failure, for it rained hard, there was no procession in consequence, and the greatest man in the world (as Tom supposed), Mr. Benton, an actual United States Senator, proved an overwhelming disappointment—for he was not twenty-five feet high, nor even anywhere in the neighborhood of it.

A circus came. The boys played circus for three days afterward in tents made of rag carpeting—admission, three pins for boys, two for girls—and then circusing was abandoned.

A phrenologist and a mesmerizer came—and went again and left the village duller and drearier than ever.

There were some boys-and-girls' parties, but they were so few and so delightful that they only made the aching voids between ache the harder.

Becky Thatcher was gone to her Constantinople home to stay with her parents during vacation—so there was no bright side to life anywhere.

The dreadful secret of the murder was a chronic misery. It was a very cancer for permanency and pain.

Then came the measles.

During two long weeks Tom lay a prisoner, dead to the world and its happenings. He was very ill, he was interested in nothing. When he got upon his feet at last and moved feebly downtown, a melancholy change had come over everything and every creature. There had been a "revival," and everybody had "got religion," not only the adults, but even the boys and girls. Tom went about, hoping against hope for the sight of one blessed sinful face, but disappointment crossed him everywhere. He found Joe Harper studying a Testament, and turned sadly away from the depressing spectacle. He sought Ben Rogers, and found him visiting the poor with a basket of tracts. He hunted up Jim Hollis, who called his attention to the precious blessing of his late measles as a warning. Every boy he encountered added another ton to his depression; and when, in desperation, he flew for refuge at last to the bosom of Huckleberry Finn and was received with a Scriptural quotation, his heart broke and he crept home and to bed realizing that he alone of all the town was lost, forever and forever.

And that night there came on a terrific storm, with driving rain, awful claps of thunder and blinding sheets of lightning. He covered his head with the bedclothes and waited in a horror of suspense for his doom; for he had not the shadow of a doubt that all this hubbub was about him. He believed he had taxed the forbearance of the powers above to the extremity of endurance and that this was the result. It might have seemed to him a waste of pomp and ammunition to kill a bug with a battery of artillery, but there seemed nothing incongruous about the getting up such an expensive thunderstorm as this to knock the turf from under an insect like himself.

By and by the tempest spent itself and died without accomplishing its object. The boy's first impulse was to be grateful, and reform. His second was to wait—for there might not be any more storms.

The next day the doctors were back; Tom had relapsed. The three weeks he spent on his back this time seemed an entire age. When he got abroad at last he was hardly grateful that he had been spared, remembering how lonely was his estate, how companionless and forlorn he was. He drifted listlessly down the street and found Jim Hollis acting as judge in a juvenile court that was trying a cat for murder, in the presence of her victim, a bird. He found Joe Harper and Huck Finn up an alley eating a stolen melon. Poor lads! they—like Tom—had suffered a relapse.

CHAPTER 23

Old Muff's Friends—
Muff Potter in Court —Muff Potter Saved

A T last the sleepy atmosphere was stirred—and vigorously: the murder trial came on in the court. It became the absorbing topic of village talk immediately. Tom could not get away from it. Every reference to the murder sent a shudder to his heart, for his troubled conscience and fears almost persuaded him that these remarks were put forth in his hearing as "feelers"; he did not see how he could be suspected of knowing anything about the murder, but still he could not be comfortable in the midst of this gossip. It kept him in a cold shiver all the time. He took Huck to a lonely place to have a talk with him. It would be some relief to unseal his tongue for a little while; to divide his burden of distress with another sufferer. Moreover, he wanted to assure himself that Huck had remained discreet.

"Huck, have you ever told anybody about—that?"

"'Bout what?"

"You know what."

"Oh—'course I haven't."

"Never a word?"

"Never a solitary word, so help me. What makes you ask?"

"Well, I was afeard."

"Why, Tom Sawyer, we wouldn't be alive two days if that got found out. *You* know that."

Tom felt more comfortable. After a pause:

"Huck, they couldn't anybody get you to tell, could they?"

"Get me to tell? Why, if I wanted that halfbreed devil to drownd me they could get me to tell. They ain't no different way."

"Well, that's all right, then. I reckon we're safe as long as we keep mum. But let's swear again, anyway. It's more surer."

"I'm agreed."

So they swore again with dread solemnities.

"What is the talk around, Huck? I've heard a power of it."

"Talk? Well, it's just Muff Potter, Muff Potter, Muff Potter all the time. It keeps me in a sweat, constant, so's I want to hide som'ers."

"That's just the same way they go on round me. I reckon he's a goner. Don't you feel sorry for him, sometimes?"

"Most always—most always. He ain't no account; but then he hain't ever done anything to hurt anybody. Just fishes a little, to get money to get drunk on—and loafs around considerable; but lord, we all do that—leastways most of us—preachers and such like. But he's kind of good—he give me half a fish, once, when there warn't enough for two; and lots of times he's kind of stood by me when I was out of luck."

"Well, he's mended kites for me, Huck, and knitted hooks on to my line. I wish we could get him out of there."

"My! we couldn't get him out, Tom. And besides, 'twouldn't do any good; they'd ketch him again."

"Yes—so they would. But I hate to hear 'em abuse him so like the dickens when he never done—that."

"I do too, Tom. Lord, I hear 'em say he's the bloodiest looking villain in this country, and they wonder he wasn't ever hung before."

"Yes, they talk like that, all the time. I've heard 'em say that if he was to get free they'd lynch him."

"And they'd do it, too."

The boys had a long talk, but it brought them little comfort.

As the twilight drew on, they found themselves hanging about the neighborhood of the little isolated jail, perhaps with an undefined hope that something would happen that might clear away their difficulties. But nothing happened; there seemed to be no angels or fairies interested in this luckless captive.

The boys did as they had often done before—went to the cell grating and gave Potter some tobacco and matches. He was on the ground floor and there were no guards.

His gratitude for their gifts had always smote their consciences before—it cut deeper than ever, this time. They felt cowardly and treacherous to the last degree when Potter said:

"You've been mighty good to me, boys—better'n anybody else in this town. And I don't forget it, I don't. Often I says to myself, says I, 'I used to mend all the boys' kites and things, and show 'em where the good fishin' places was, and befriend 'em what I could, and now they've all forgot old Muff when he's in trouble; but Tom don't, and Huck don't—*they* don't forget him, says I, 'and I don't forget them.' Well, boys, I done an awful thing—drunk and crazy at the time—that's the only way I account for it—and now I got to swing for it, and it's right. Right, and *best*, too, I reckon—hope so, anyway. Well, we won't talk about that. I don't want to make *you* feel bad; you've befriended me. But what I want to say, is, don't *you* ever get drunk—then you won't ever get here. Stand a litter furder west—so—that's it; it's a prime comfort to see faces that's friendly when a body's in such a muck of trouble, and there don't none come here but yourn. Good friendly faces—good friendly faces. Git up on one another's backs and let me touch 'em. That's it. Shake hands—yourn'll come through the bars, but mine's too big. Little hands, and weak—but they've helped Muff Potter a power, and they'd help him more if they could."

Tom went home miserable, and his dreams that night were full of horrors. The next day and the day after, he hung about the courtroom, drawn by an almost irresistible impulse to go in, but forcing himself to stay out. Huck was having the same experience. They studiously avoided each other. Each wandered away, from time to time, but the same dismal fascination always brought them back presently. Tom kept his ears open when idlers sauntered out of the courtroom, but invariably heard distressing news—the toils were closing more and more relentlessly around poor Potter. At the end of the second day the village talk was to the effect that Injun Joe's evidence stood firm and unshaken, and that there was not the slightest question as to what the jury's verdict would be.

Tom was out late, that night, and came to bed through the window. He was in a tremendous state of excitement. It was hours before he got to sleep. All the village flocked to the courthouse the next morning, for this was to be the great day. Both sexes were about equally represented in the packed audience. After a long wait the jury filed in and took their places; shortly afterward, Potter, pale and haggard, timid and hopeless, was brought in, with chains upon him, and seated where all the curious eyes could stare at him; no less conspicuous was Injun Joe, stolid as ever. There was another pause, and then the judge arrived and the sheriff proclaimed the opening of the court. The usual whisperings among the lawyers and gathering together of papers followed. These details and accompanying delays worked up an atmosphere of preparation that was as impressive as it was fascinating.

Now a witness was called who testified that he found Muff Potter washing in the brook, at an early hour of the morning that the murder was discovered, and that he immediately sneaked away. After some further questioning, counsel for the prosecution said:

"Take the witness."

The prisoner raised his eyes for a moment, but dropped them again when his own counsel said:

"I have no questions to ask him."

The next witness proved the finding of the knife near the corpse. Counsel for the prosecution said:

"Take the witness."

"I have no questions to ask him," Potter's lawyer replied.

A third witness swore he had often seen the knife in Potter's possession.

"Take the witness."

Counsel for Potter declined to question him. The faces of the audience began to betray annoyance. Did this attorney mean to throw away his client's life without an effort?

Several witnesses deposed concerning Potter's guilty behavior when brought to the scene of the murder. They were allowed to leave the stand without being cross-questioned.

Every detail of the damaging circumstances that occurred in the graveyard upon that morning which all present remembered so well was brought out by credible witnesses, but none of them were cross-examined by Potter's lawyer. The perplexity and dissatisfaction of the house expressed itself in murmurs and provoked a reproof from the bench. Counsel for the prosecution now said:

"By the oaths of citizens whose simple word is above suspicion, we have fastened this awful crime, beyond all possibility of question, upon the unhappy prisoner at the bar. We rest our case here."

A groan escaped from poor Potter, and he put his face in his hands and rocked his body softly to and fro, while a painful silence reigned in the courtroom. Many men were moved, and many women's compassion testified itself in tears. Counsel for the defence rose and said:

"Your honor, in our remarks at the opening of this trial, we foreshadowed our purpose to prove that our client did this fearful deed while under the influence of a blind and irresponsible delirium produced by drink. We have changed our mind. We shall not offer that plea." [Then to the clerk:] "Call Thomas Sawyer!"

A puzzled amazement awoke in every face in the house, not even excepting Potter's. Every eye fastened itself with wondering interest upon Tom as he rose and took his place upon the stand. The boy looked wild enough, for he was badly scared. The oath was administered.

"Thomas Sawyer, where were you on the seventeenth of June, about the hour of midnight?"

Tom glanced at Injun Joe's iron face and his tongue failed him. The audience listened breathless, but the words refused to come. After a few moments, however, the boy got a little of his strength back, and managed to put enough of it into his voice to make part of the house hear:

"In the graveyard!"

"A little bit louder, please. Don't be afraid. You were—"

"In the graveyard."

A contemptuous smile flitted across Injun Joe's face.

"Were you anywhere near Horse Williams' grave?"

"Yes, sir."

"Speak up—just a trifle louder. How near were you?"

"Near as I am to you."

"Were you hidden, or not?"

"I was hid."

"Where?"

"Behind the elms that's on the edge of the grave."

Injun Joe gave a barely perceptible start.

"Any one with you?"

"Yes, sir. I went there with—"

"Wait—wait a moment. Never mind mentioning your companion's name. We will produce him at the proper time. Did you carry anything there with you."

Tom hesitated and looked confused.

"Speak out, my boy—don't be diffident. The truth is always

respectable. What did you take there?"

"Only a—a—dead cat."

There was a ripple of mirth, which the court checked.

"We will produce the skeleton of that cat. Now, my boy, tell us everything that occurred—tell it in your own way—don't skip anything, and don't be afraid."

Tom began—hesitatingly at first, but as he warmed to his subject his words flowed more and more easily; in a little while every sound ceased but his own voice; every eye fixed itself upon him; with parted lips and bated breath the audience hung upon his words, taking no note of time, rapt in the ghastly fascinations of the tale. The strain upon pent emotion reached its climax when the boy said:

"—and as the doctor fetched the board around and Muff Potter fell, Injun Joe jumped with the knife and—"

Crash! Quick as lightning the half-breed sprang for a window, tore his way through all opposers, and was gone!

CHAPTER 24

Tom as the Village Hero—
Days of Splendor and Nights of Horror—Pursuit of Injun Joe

TOM was a glittering hero once more—the pet of the old, the envy of the young. His name even went into immortal print, for the village paper magnified him. There were some that believed he would be President, yet, if he escaped hanging.

As usual, the fickle, unreasoning world took Muff Potter to its bosom and fondled him as lavishly as it had abused him before. But that sort of conduct is to the world's credit; therefore it is not well to find fault with it.

Tom's days were days of splendor and exultation to him, but his nights were seasons of horror. Injun Joe infested all his dreams, and always with doom in his eye. Hardly any temptation could persuade the boy to stir abroad after nightfall. Poor Huck was in the same state of wretchedness and terror, for Tom had told the whole story to the lawyer the night before the great day of the trial, and Huck was sore afraid that his share in the business might leak out, yet, notwithstanding Injun Joe's flight had saved him the suffering of testifying in court. The poor fellow had got the attorney to promise secrecy, but what of that? Since Tom's harassed conscience had managed to drive him to the lawyer's house by night and wring a dread tale from lips that had been sealed with the dismalest and most formidable of oaths, Huck's confidence in the human race was wellnigh obliterated.

Daily Muff Potter's gratitude made Tom glad he had

spoken; but nightly he wished he had sealed up his tongue.

Half the time Tom was afraid Injun Joe would never be captured; the other half he was afraid he would be. He felt sure he never could draw a safe breath again until that man was dead and he had seen the corpse.

Rewards had been offered, the country had been scoured, but no Injun Joe was found. One of those omniscient and aweinspiring marvels, a detective, came up from St. Louis, moused around, shook his head, looked wise, and made that sort of astounding success which members of that craft usually achieve. That is to say, he "found a clew." But you can't hang a "clew" for murder, and so after that detective had got through and gone home, Tom felt just as insecure as he was before.

The slow days drifted on, and each left behind it a slightly lightened weight of apprehension.

CHAPTER 25

About Kings and Diamonds—
Search for the Treasure —Dead People and Ghosts

THERE comes a time in every rightly-constructed boy's life when he has a raging desire to go somewhere and dig for hidden treasure. This desire suddenly came upon Tom one day. He sallied out to find Joe Harper, but failed of success. Next he sought Ben Rogers; he had gone fishing. Presently he stumbled upon Huck Finn the Red-Handed. Huck would answer. Tom took him to a private place and opened the matter to him confidentially. Huck was willing. Huck was always willing to take a hand in any enterprise that offered entertainment and required no capital, for he had a troublesome superabundance of that sort of time which is *not* money.

"Where'll we dig?" said Huck.

"Oh, most anywhere."

"Why, is it hid all around?"

"No, indeed it ain't. It's hid in mighty particular places, Huck—sometimes on islands, sometimes in rotten chests under the end of a limb of an old dead tree, just where the shadow falls at midnight; but mostly under the floor in ha'nted houses."

"Who hides it?"

"Why, robbers, of course—who'd you reckon? Sunday-school sup'rintendents?"

"I don't know. If 'twas mine I wouldn't hide it; I'd spend it and have a good time."

"So would I. But robbers don't do that way. They always hide it and leave it there."

"Don't they come after it any more?"

"No, they think they will, but they generally forget the marks, or else they die. Anyway, it lays there a long time and gets rusty; and by and by somebody finds an old yellow paper that tells how to find the marks—a paper that's got to be ciphered over about a week because it's mostly signs and hy'roglyphics."

"Hyro—which?"

"Hy'roglyphics—pictures and things, you know, that don't seem to mean anything."

"Have you got one of them papers, Tom?"

"No."

"Well then, how you going to find the marks?"

"I don't want any marks. They always bury it under a ha'nted house or on an island, or under a dead tree that's got one limb sticking out. Well, we've tried Jackson's Island a little, and we can try it again some time; and there's the old ha'nted house up the Still-House branch, and there's lots of dead-limb trees—dead loads of 'em."

"Is it under all of them?"

"How you talk! No!"

"Then how you going to know which one to go for?"

"Go for all of 'em!"

"Why, Tom, it'll take all summer."

"Well, what of that? Suppose you find a brass pot with a hundred dollars in it, all rusty and gray, or rotten chest full of di'monds. How's that?"

Huck's eyes glowed.

"That's bully. Plenty bully enough for me. Just you gimme the hundred dollars and I don't want no di'monds."

"All right. But I bet you I ain't going to throw off on di'monds. Some of 'em's worth twenty dollars apiece—there ain't any, hardly, but's worth six bits or a dollar."

"No! Is that so?"

"Cert'nly—anybody'll tell you so. Hain't you ever seen one, Huck?"

"Not as I remember."

"Oh, kings have slathers of them."

"Well, I don' know no kings, Tom."

"I reckon you don't. But if you was to go to Europe you'd see a raft of 'em hopping around."

"Do they hop?"

"Hop?—your granny! No!"

"Well, what did you say they did, for?"

"Shucks, I only meant you'd *see* 'em—not hopping, of course—what do they want to hop for?—but I mean you'd just see 'em—scattered around, you know, in a kind of a general way. Like that old humpbacked Richard."

"Richard? What's his other name?"

"He didn't have any other name. Kings don't have any but a given name."

"No?"

"But they don't."

"Well, if they like it, Tom, all right; but I don't want to be a king and have only just a given name, like a nigger. But say—where you going to dig first?"

"Well, I don't know. S'pose we tackle that old dead-limb tree on the hill t'other side of Still-House branch?"

"I'm agreed."

So they got a crippled pick and a shovel, and set out on their three-mile tramp. They arrived hot and panting, and threw themselves down in the shade of a neighboring elm to rest and have a smoke.

"I like this," said Tom.

"So do I."

"Say, Huck, if we find a treasure here, what you going to do with your share?"

"Well, I'll have pie and a glass of soda every day, and I'll go to every circus that comes along. I bet I'll have a gay time."

"Well, ain't you going to save any of it?"

"Save it? What for?"

"Why, so as to have something to live on, by and by."

"Oh, that ain't any use. Pap would come back to thish-yer town some day and get his claws on it if I didn't hurry up, and I tell you he'd clean it out pretty quick. What you going to do with yourn, Tom?"

"I'm going to buy a new drum, and a sure'nough sword, and a red necktie and a bull pup, and get married."

"Married!"

"That's it."

"Tom, you—why, you ain't in your right mind."

"Wait—you'll see."

"Well, that's the foolishest thing you could do. Look at pap and my mother. Fight! Why, they used to fight all the time. I remember, mighty well."

"That ain't anything. The girl I'm going to marry won't fight."

"Tom, I reckon they're all alike. They'll all comb a body. Now you better think 'bout this awhile. I tell you you better. What's the name of the gal?"

"It ain't a gal at all—it's a girl."

"It's all the same, I reckon; some says gal, some says girl—both's right, like enough. Anyway, what's her name, Tom?"

"I'll tell you some time—not now."

"All right—that'll do. Only if you get married I'll be more lonesomer than ever."

"No you won't. You'll come and live with me. Now stir out of this and we'll go to digging."

They worked and sweated for half an hour. No result. They toiled another halfhour. Still no result. Huck said:

"Do they always bury it as deep as this?"

"Sometimes—not always. Not generally. I reckon we haven't got the right place."

So they chose a new spot and began again. The labor dragged a little, but still they made progress. They pegged away in silence for some time. Finally Huck leaned on his shovel, swabbed the beaded drops from his brow with his sleeve, and said:

"Where you going to dig next, after we get this one?"

"I reckon maybe we'll tackle the old tree that's over yonder on Cardiff Hill back of the widow's."

"I reckon that'll be a good one. But won't the widow take it away from us, Tom? It's on her land."

"*She* take it away! Maybe she'd like to try it once. Whoever finds one of these hid treasures, it belongs to him. It don't make any difference whose land it's on."

That was satisfactory. The work went on. By and by Huck said:

"Blame it, we must be in the wrong place again. What do you think?"

"It *is* mighty curious, Huck. I don't understand it. Sometimes witches interfere. I reckon maybe that's what's the trouble now."

"Shucks! Witches ain't got no power in the daytime."

"Well, that's so. I didn't think of that. Oh, *I* know what the matter is! What a blamed lot of fools we are! You got to find out where the shadow of the limb falls at midnight, and that's where you dig!"

"Then consound it, we've fooled away all this work for nothing. Now hang it all, we got to come back in the night. It's an awful long way. Can you get out?"

"I bet I will. We've got to do it tonight, too, because if somebody sees these holes they'll know in a minute what's here and they'll go for it."

"Well, I'll come around and maow tonight."

"All right. Let's hide the tools in the bushes."

The boys were there that night, about the appointed time. They sat in the shadow waiting. It was a lonely place, and an hour made solemn by old traditions. Spirits whispered in the rustling leaves, ghosts lurked in the murky nooks, the deep baying of a hound floated up out of the distance, an owl answered with his sepulchral note. The boys were subdued by these solemnities, and talked little. By and by they judged that twelve had come; they marked where the shadow fell, and began to dig. Their hopes commenced to rise. Their interest grew stronger, and their industry kept pace with it. The hole deepened and still deepened, but every time their hearts jumped to hear the pick strike upon something, they only suffered a new disappointment. It was only a stone or a chunk. At last Tom said:

"It ain't any use, Huck, we're wrong again."

"Well, but we *can't* be wrong. We spotted the shadder to a dot."

"I know it, but then there's another thing."

"What's that?".

"Why, we only guessed at the time. Like enough it was too late or too early."

Huck dropped his shovel.

"That's it," said he. "That's the very trouble. We got to give this one up. We can't ever tell the right time, and besides this kind of thing's too awful, here this time of night with witches and ghosts a-fluttering around so. I feel as if something's behind me all the time; and I'm afeard to turn around, becuz maybe there's others in front a-waiting for a chance. I been creeping all over, ever since I got here."

"Well, I've been pretty much so, too, Huck. They most always put in a dead man when they bury a treasure under a tree, to look out for it."

"Lordy!"

"Yes, they do. I've always heard that."

"Tom, I don't like to fool around much where there's dead people. A body's bound to get into trouble with 'em, sure."

"I don't like to stir 'em up, either. S'pose this one here was to stick his skull out and say something!"

"Don't Tom! It's awful."

"Well, it just is. Huck, I don't feel comfortable a bit."

"Say, Tom, let's give this place up, and try somewheres else."

"All right, I reckon we better."

"What'll it be?"

Tom considered awhile; and then said:

"The ha'nted house. That's it!"

"Blame it, I don't like ha'nted houses, Tom. Why, they're a dern sight worse'n dead people. Dead people might talk, maybe, but they don't come sliding around in a shroud, when you ain't noticing, and peep over your shoulder all of a sudden and grit their teeth, the way a ghost does. I couldn't stand such a thing as that, Tom—nobody could."

"Yes, but, Huck, ghosts don't travel around only at night. They won't hender us from digging there in the daytime."

"Well, that's so. But you know mighty well people don't go about that ha'nted house in the day nor the night."

"Well, that's mostly because they don't like to go where a man's been murdered, anyway—but nothing's ever been seen around that house except in the night—just some blue lights slipping by the windows—no regular ghosts."

"Well, where you see one of them blue lights flickering around, Tom, you can bet there's a ghost mighty close behind it. It stands to reason. Becuz *you* know that they don't anybody but ghosts use 'em."

"Yes, that's so. But anyway they don't come around in the daytime, so what's the use of our being afeard?"

"Well, all right. We'll tackle the ha'nted house if you say

so—but I reckon it's taking chances."

They had started down the hill by this time. There in the middle of the moonlit valley below them stood the "ha'nted" house, utterly isolated, its fences gone long ago, rank weeds smothering the very doorsteps, the chimney crumbled to ruin, the window-sashes vacant, a corner of the roof caved in. The boys gazed awhile, half expecting to see a blue light flit past a window; then talking in a low tone, as befitted the time and the circumstances, they struck far off to the right, to give the haunted house a wide berth, and took their way homeward through the woods that adorned the rearward side of Cardiff Hill.

CHAPTER 26

The Haunted House—Sleepy Ghosts —
A Box of Gold—Bitter Luck

ABOUT noon the next day the boys arrived at the dead tree; they had come for their tools. Tom was impatient to go to the haunted house; Huck was measurably so, also—but suddenly said:

"Lookyhere, Tom, do you know what day it is?"

Tom mentally ran over the days of the week, and then quickly lifted his eyes with a startled look in them—

"My! I never once thought of it, Huck!"

"Well, I didn't neither, but all at once it popped onto me that it was Friday."

"Blame it, a body can't be too careful, Huck. We might 'a' got into an awful scrape, tackling such a thing on a Friday."

"*Might!* Better say we *would*! There's some lucky days, maybe, but Friday ain't."

"Any fool knows that. I don't reckon *you* was the first that found it out, Huck."

"Well, I never said I was, did I? And Friday ain't all, neither. I had a rotten bad dream last night—dreamt about rats."

"No! Sure sign of trouble. Did they fight?"

"No."

"Well, that's good, Huck. When they don't fight it's only a sign that there's trouble around, you know. All we got to do is to look mighty sharp and keep out of it. We'll drop this thing for today, and play. Do you know Robin Hood, Huck?"

"No. Who's Robin Hood?"

"Why, he was one of the greatest men that was ever in England—and the best. He was a robber."

"Cracky, I wisht I was. Who did he rob?"

"Only sheriffs and bishops and rich people and kings, and such like. But he never bothered the poor. He loved 'em. He always divided up with 'em perfectly square."

"Well, he must 'a' been a brick."

"I bet you he was, Huck. Oh, he was the noblest man that ever was. They ain't any such men now, I can tell you. He could lick any man in England, with one hand tied behind him; and he could take his yew bow and plug a ten-cent piece every time, a mile and a half."

"What's a *yew* bow?"

"I don't know. It's some kind of a bow, of course. And if he hit that dime only on the edge he would set down and cry— and curse. But we'll play Robin Hood—it's nobby fun. I'll learn you."

"I'm agreed."

So they played Robin Hood all the afternoon, now and then casting a yearning eye down upon the haunted house and passing a remark about the morrow's prospects and possibilities there. As the sun began to sink into the west they took their way homeward athwart the long shadows of the trees and soon were buried from sight in the forests of Cardiff Hill.

On Saturday, shortly after noon, the boys were at the dead tree again. They had a smoke and a chat in the shade, and then dug a little in their last hole, not with great hope, but merely because Tom said there were so many cases where people had given up a treasure after getting down within six inches of it, and then somebody else had come along and turned it up with a single thrust of a shovel. The thing failed this time, however, so the boys shouldered their tools and went away feeling that they had not trifled with fortune, but had fulfilled all the requirements that belong to the business of treasure-hunting.

When they reached the haunted house there was something so weird and grisly about the dead silence that reigned there under the baking sun, and something so depressing about the loneliness and desolation of the place, that they were afraid, for a moment, to venture in. Then they crept to the door and took a trembling peep. They saw a weedgrown, floorless room, unplastered, an ancient fireplace, vacant windows, a ruinous staircase; and here, there, and everywhere hung ragged and abandoned cobwebs. They presently entered, softly, with quickened pulses, talking in whispers, ears alert to catch the slightest sound, and muscles tense and ready for instant retreat.

In a little while familiarity modified their fears and they gave the place a critical and interested examination, rather admiring their own boldness, and wondering at it, too. Next they wanted to look upstairs. This was something like cutting off retreat, but they got to daring each other, and of course there could be but one result—they threw their tools into a corner and made the ascent. Up there were the same signs of decay. In one corner they found a closet that promised mystery, but the promise was a fraud—there was nothing in it. Their courage was up now and well in hand. They were about to go down and begin work when—

"*Sh!*" said Tom.

"What is it?" whispered Huck, blanching with fright.

"*Sh!*... There!... Hear it?"

"Yes!... Oh, my! Let's run!"

"Keep still! Don't you budge! They're coming right toward the door."

The boys stretched themselves upon the floor with their eyes to knotholes in the planking, and lay waiting, in a misery of fear.

"They've stopped.... No—coming.... Here they are. Don't

whisper another word, Huck. My goodness, I wish I was out of this!"

Two men entered. Each boy said to himself: "There's the old deaf and dumb Spaniard that's been about town once or twice lately—never saw t'other man before."

"T'other" was a ragged, unkempt creature, with nothing very pleasant in his face. The Spaniard was wrapped in a *serapé*; he had bushy white whiskers; long white hair flowed from under his sombrero, and he wore green goggles. When they came in, "t'other" was talking in a low voice; they sat down on the ground, facing the door, with their backs to the wall, and the speaker continued his remarks. His manner became less guarded and his words more distinct as he proceeded:

"No," said he, "I've thought it all over, and I don't like it. It's dangerous."

"Dangerous!" grunted the "deaf and dumb" Spaniard—to the vast surprise of the boys. "Milksop!"

This voice made the boys gasp and quake. It was Injun Joe's! There was silence for some time. Then Joe said:

"What's any more dangerous than that job up yonder—but nothing's come of it."

"That's different. Away up the river so, and not another house about. 'Twon't ever be known that we tried, anyway, long as we didn't succeed."

"Well, what's more dangerous than coming here in the daytime!—anybody would suspicion us that saw us."

"I know that. But there warn't any other place as handy after that fool of a job. I want to quit this shanty. I wanted to yesterday, only it warn't any use trying to stir out of here, with those infernal boys playing over there on the hill right in full view."

"Those infernal boys" quaked again under the inspiration of this remark, and thought how lucky it was that they had remembered it was Friday and concluded to wait a day. They wished in their hearts they had waited a year.

The two men got out some food and made a luncheon. After a long and thoughtful silence, Injun Joe said:

"Look here, lad—you go back up the river where you belong. Wait there till you hear from me. I'll take the chances on dropping into this town just once more, for a look. We'll do that 'dangerous' job after I've spied around a little and think things look well for it. Then for Texas! We'll leg it together!"

This was satisfactory. Both men presently fell to yawning, and Injun Joe said:

"I'm dead for sleep! It's your turn to watch."

He curled down in the weeds and soon began to snore. His comrade stirred him once or twice and he became quiet. Presently the watcher began to nod; his head drooped lower and lower, both men began to snore now.

The boys drew a long, grateful breath. Tom whispered:

"Now's our chance—come!"

Huck said:

"I can't—I'd die if they was to wake."

Tom urged—Huck held back. At last Tom rose slowly and softly, and started alone. But the first step he made wrung such a hideous creak from the crazy floor that he sank down almost dead with fright. He never made a second attempt. The boys lay there counting the dragging moments till it seemed to them that time must be done and eternity growing gray; and then they were grateful to note that at last the sun was setting.

Now one snore ceased. Injun Joe sat up, stared around— smiled grimly upon his comrade, whose head was drooping upon his knees—stirred him up with his foot and said:

"Here! *You're* a watchman, ain't you! All right, though— nothing's happened."

"My! have I been asleep?"

"Oh, partly, partly. Nearly time for us to be moving, pard. What'll we do with what little swag we've got left?"

"I don't know—leave it here as we've always done, I reckon. No use to take it away till we start south. Six hundred and fifty in silver's something to carry."

"Well—all right—it won't matter to come here once more."

"No—but I'd say come in the night as we used to do—it's better."

"Yes: but look here; it may be a good while before I get the right chance at that job; accidents might happen; 'tain't in such a very good place; we'll just regularly bury it—and bury it deep."

"Good idea," said the comrade, who walked across the room, knelt down, raised one of the rearward hearth-stones and took out a bag that jingled pleasantly. He subtracted from it twenty or thirty dollars for himself and as much for Injun Joe, and passed the bag to the latter, who was on his knees in the corner, now, digging with his bowie-knife.

The boys forgot all their fears, all their miseries in an instant. With gloating eyes they watched every movement. Luck!—the splendor of it was beyond all imagination! Six hundred dollars was money enough to make half a dozen boys rich! Here was treasure-hunting under the happiest auspices—there would not be any bothersome uncertainty as to where to dig. They nudged each other every moment—eloquent nudges and easily understood, for they simply meant—"Oh, but ain't you glad *now* we're here!"

Joe's knife struck upon something.

"Hello!" said he.

"What is it?" said his comrade.

"Half-rotten plank—no, it's a box, I believe. Here—bear a hand and we'll see what it's here for. Never mind, I've broke a hole."

He reached his hand in and drew it out—

"Man, it's money!"

The two men examined the handful of coins. They were

gold. The boys above were as excited as themselves, and as delighted.

Joe's comrade said:

"We'll make quick work of this. There's an old rusty pick over amongst the weeds in the corner the other side of the fireplace—I saw it a minute ago."

He ran and brought the boys' pick and shovel. Injun Joe took the pick, looked it over critically, shook his head, muttered something to himself, and then began to use it. The box was soon unearthed. It was not very large; it was iron bound and had been very strong before the slow years had injured it. The men contemplated the treasure awhile in blissful silence.

"Pard, there's thousands of dollars here," said Injun Joe.

"'Twas always said that Murrel's gang used to be around here one summer," the stranger observed.

"I know it," said Injun Joe; "and this looks like it, I should say."

"Now you won't need to do that job."

The halfbreed frowned. Said he:

"You don't know me. Least you don't know all about that thing. 'Tain't robbery altogether—it's *revenge*!" and a wicked light flamed in his eyes. "I'll need your help in it. When it's finished—then Texas. Go home to your Nance and your kids, and stand by till you hear from me."

"Well—if you say so; what'll we do with this—bury it again?"

"Yes. [Ravishing delight overhead.] NO! by the great Sachem, no! [Profound distress overhead.] I'd nearly forgot. That pick had fresh earth on it! [The boys were sick with terror in a moment.] What business has a pick and a shovel here? What business with fresh earth on them? Who brought them here—and where are they gone? Have you heard anybody?— seen anybody? What! bury it again and leave them to come and see the ground disturbed? Not exactly—not exactly. We'll take it to my den."

"Why, of course! Might have thought of that before. You mean Number One?"

"No—Number Two—under the cross. The other place is bad—too common."

"All right. It's nearly dark enough to start."

Injun Joe got up and went about from window to window cautiously peeping out. Presently he said:

"Who could have brought those tools here? Do you reckon they can be upstairs?"

The boys' breath forsook them. Injun Joe put his hand on his knife, halted a moment, undecided, and then turned toward the stairway. The boys thought of the closet, but their strength was gone. The steps came creaking up the stairs—the intolerable distress of the situation woke the stricken resolution of the lads—they were about to spring for the closet, when there was a crash of rotten timbers and Injun Joe landed on the ground amid the debris of the ruined stairway. He gathered himself up cursing, and his comrade said:

"Now what's the use of all that? If it's anybody, and they're up there, let them *stay* there—who cares? If they want to jump down, now, and get into trouble, who objects? It will be dark in fifteen minutes—and then let them follow us if they want to. I'm willing. In my opinion, whoever hove those things in here caught a sight of us and took us for ghosts or devils or something. I'll bet they're running yet."

Joe grumbled awhile; then he agreed with his friend that what daylight was left ought to be economized in getting things ready for leaving. Shortly afterward they slipped out of the house in the deepening twilight, and moved toward the river with their precious box.

Tom and Huck rose up, weak but vastly relieved, and stared after them through the chinks between the logs of the house. Follow? Not they. They were content to reach ground again without broken necks, and take the townward track over the hill. They did not talk much. They were too much absorbed in hating themselves—hating the ill luck that made them take the spade and the pick there. But for that, Injun Joe never would have suspected. He would have hidden the silver with the gold to wait there till his "revenge" was satisfied, and then he would have had the misfortune to find that money turn up missing. Bitter, bitter luck that the tools were ever brought there!

They resolved to keep a lookout for that Spaniard when he should come to town spying out for chances to do his revengeful job, and follow him to "Number Two," wherever that might be. Then a ghastly thought occurred to Tom.

"Revenge? What if he means *us*, Huck!"

"Oh, don't!" said Huck, nearly fainting.

They talked it all over, and as they entered town they agreed to believe that he might possibly mean somebody else—at least that he might at least mean nobody but Tom, since only Tom had testified.

Very, very small comfort it was to Tom to be alone in danger! Company would be a palpable improvement, he thought.

CHAPTER 27

Doubts to be Settled—The Young Detectives

THE adventure of the day mightily tormented Tom's dreams that night. Four times he had his hands on that rich treasure and four times it wasted to nothingness in his fingers as sleep forsook him and wakefulness brought back the hard reality of his misfortune. As he lay in the early morning recalling the incidents of his great adventure, he noticed that they seemed curiously subdued and far away—somewhat as if they had happened in another world, or in a time long gone by. Then it occurred to him that the great adventure itself must be a dream! There was one very strong argument in favor of this idea—namely, that the quantity of coin he had seen was too vast to be real. He had never seen as much as fifty dollars in one mass before, and he was like all boys of his age and station in life, in that he imagined that all references to "hundreds" and "thousands" were mere fanciful forms of speech, and that no such sums really existed in the world. He never had supposed for a moment that so large a sum as a hundred dollars was to be found in actual money in any one's possession. If his notions of hidden treasure had been analyzed, they would have been found to consist of a handful of real dimes and a bushel of vague, splendid, ungraspable dollars.

But the incidents of his adventure grew sensibly sharper and clearer under the attrition of thinking them over, and so he presently found himself leaning to the impression that the thing might not have been a dream, after all. This uncertainty must be swept away. He would snatch a hurried breakfast and go and find Huck. Huck was sitting on the gunwale of a flatboat, listlessly dangling his feet in the water and looking very melancholy. Tom concluded to let Huck lead up to the subject. If he did not do it, then the adventure would be proved to have been only a dream.

"Hello, Huck!"

"Hello, yourself."

Silence, for a minute.

"Tom, if we'd 'a' left the blame tools at the dead tree, we'd 'a' got the money. Oh, ain't it awful!"

"'Tain't a dream, then, 'tain't a dream! Somehow I most wish it was. Dog'd if I don't, Huck."

"What ain't a dream?"

"Oh, that thing yesterday. I been half thinking it was."

"Dream! If them stairs hadn't broke down you'd 'a' seen how much dream it was! I've had dreams enough all night— with that patch-eyed Spanish devil going for me all through 'em—rot him!"

"No, not rot him. *Find* him! Track the money!"

"Tom, we'll never find him. A feller don't have only one chance for such a pile—and that one's lost. I'd feel mighty shaky if I was to see him, anyway."

"Well, so'd I; but I'd like to see him, anyway—and track him out—to his Number Two."

"Number Two—yes, that's it. I been thinking 'bout that. But I can't make nothing out of it. What do you reckon it is?"

"I dono. It's too deep. Say, Huck—maybe it's the number of a house!"

"Goody!... No, Tom, that ain't it. If it is, it ain't in this one-horse town. They ain't no numbers here."

"Well, that's so. Lemme think a minute. Here—it's the number of a room—in a tavern, you know!"

"Oh, that's the trick! They ain't only two taverns. We can

find out quick."

"You stay here, Huck, till I come."

Tom was off at once. He did not care to have Huck's company in public places. He was gone half an hour. He found that in the best tavern, No. 2 had long been occupied by a young lawyer, and was still so occupied. In the less ostentatious house, No. 2 was a mystery. The tavern-keeper's young son said it was kept locked all the time, and he never saw anybody go into it or come out of it except at night; he did not know any particular reason for this state of things; had had some little curiosity, but it was rather feeble; had made the most of the mystery by entertaining himself with the idea that that room was "ha'nted"; had noticed that there was a light in there the night before.

"That's what I've found out, Huck. I reckon that's the very No. 2 we're after."

"I reckon it is, Tom. Now what you going to do?"

"Lemme think."

Tom thought a long time. Then he said:

"I'll tell you. The back door of that No. 2 is the door that comes out into that little close alley between the tavern and the old rattle trap of a brick store. Now you get hold of all the doorkeys you can find, and I'll nip all of auntie's, and the first dark night we'll go there and try 'em. And mind you, keep a lookout for Injun Joe, because he said he was going to drop into town and spy around once more for a chance to get his revenge. If you see him, you just follow him; and if he don't go to that No. 2, that ain't the place."

"Lordy, I don't want to foller him by myself!"

"Why, it'll be night, sure. He mightn't ever see you—and if he did, maybe he'd never think anything."

"Well, if it's pretty dark I reckon I'll track him. I dono—I dono. I'll try."

"You bet I'll follow him, if it's dark, Huck. Why, he might 'a' found out he couldn't get his revenge, and be going right after that money."

"It's so, Tom, it's so. I'll foller him; I will, by jingoes!"

"Now you're *talking*! Don't you ever weaken, Huck, and I won't."

CHAPTER 28

An Attempt at No. Two—Huck Mounts Guard

THAT night Tom and Huck were ready for their adventure. They hung about the neighborhood of the tavern until after nine, one watching the alley at a distance and the other the tavern door. Nobody entered the alley or left it; nobody resembling the Spaniard entered or left the tavern door. The night promised to be a fair one; so Tom went home with the understanding that if a considerable degree of darkness came on, Huck was to come and "maow," whereupon he would slip out and try the keys. But the night remained clear, and Huck closed his watch and retired to bed in an empty sugar hogshead about twelve.

Tuesday the boys had the same ill luck. Also Wednesday. But Thursday night promised better. Tom slipped out in good season with his aunt's old tin lantern, and a large towel to blindfold it with. He hid the lantern in Huck's sugar hogshead and the watch began. An hour before midnight the tavern closed up and its lights (the only ones thereabouts) were put out. No Spaniard had been seen. Nobody had entered or left the alley. Everything was auspicious. The blackness of darkness reigned, the perfect stillness was interrupted only by occasional mutterings of distant thunder.

Tom got his lantern, lit it in the hogshead, wrapped it closely in the towel, and the two adventurers crept in the gloom toward the tavern. Huck stood sentry and Tom felt his way into the alley. Then there was a season of waiting anxiety that weighed upon Huck's spirits like a mountain. He began to wish he could see a flash from the lantern—it would frighten him, but it would at least tell him that Tom was alive yet. It seemed hours since Tom had disappeared. Surely he must have fainted; maybe he was dead; maybe his heart had burst under terror and excitement. In his uneasiness Huck found himself drawing closer and closer to the alley; fearing all sorts of dreadful things, and momentarily expecting some catastrophe to happen that would take away his breath. There was not much to take away, for he seemed only able to inhale it by thimblefuls, and his heart would soon wear itself out, the way it was beating. Suddenly there was a flash of light and Tom came tearing by him: "Run!" said he; "run, for your life!"

He needn't have repeated it; once was enough; Huck was making thirty or forty miles an hour before the repetition was uttered. The boys never stopped till they reached the shed of a deserted slaughter-house at the lower end of the village. Just as they got within its shelter the storm burst and the rain poured down. As soon as Tom got his breath he said:

"Huck, it was awful! I tried two of the keys, just as soft as I could; but they seemed to make such a power of racket that I couldn't hardly get my breath I was so scared. They wouldn't turn in the lock, either. Well, without noticing what I was doing, I took hold of the knob, and open comes the door! It warn't locked! I hopped in, and shook off the towel, and, *great Caesar's ghost*!"

"What!—what'd you see, Tom?"

"Huck, I most stepped onto Injun Joe's hand!"

"No!"

"Yes! He was lying there, sound asleep on the floor, with his old patch on his eye and his arms spread out."

"Lordy, what did you do? Did he wake up?"

"No, never budged. Drunk, I reckon. I just grabbed that towel and started!"

"I'd never 'a' thought of the towel, I bet!"

"Well, I would. My aunt would make me mighty sick if I lost it."

"Say, Tom, did you see that box?"

"Huck, I didn't wait to look around. I didn't see the box, I didn't see the cross. I didn't see anything but a bottle and a tin cup on the floor by Injun Joe; yes, I saw two barrels and lots more bottles in the room. Don't you see, now, what's the matter with that ha'nted room?"

"How?"

"Why, it's ha'nted with whiskey! Maybe *all* the Temperance Taverns have got a ha'nted room, hey, Huck?"

"Well, I reckon maybe that's so. Who'd 'a' thought such a thing? But say, Tom, now's a mighty good time to get that box, if Injun Joe's drunk."

"It is, that! You try it!"

Huck shuddered.

"Well, no—I reckon not."

"And I reckon not, Huck. Only one bottle alongside of Injun Joe ain't enough. If there'd been three, he'd be drunk enough and I'd do it."

There was a long pause for reflection, and then Tom said:

"Lookyhere, Huck, less not try that thing any more till we know Injun Joe's not in there. It's too scary. Now, if we watch every night, we'll be dead sure to see him go out, some time or other, and then we'll snatch that box quicker'n lightning."

"Well, I'm agreed. I'll watch the whole night long, and I'll do it every night, too, if you'll do the other part of the job."

"All right, I will. All you got to do is to trot up Hooper Street a block and maow—and if I'm asleep, you throw some gravel at the window and that'll fetch me."

"Agreed, and good as wheat!"

"Now, Huck, the storm's over, and I'll go home. It'll begin to be daylight in a couple of hours. You go back and watch that long, will you?"

"I said I would, Tom, and I will. I'll ha'nt that tavern every night for a year! I'll sleep all day and I'll stand watch all night."

"That's all right. Now, where you going to sleep?"

"In Ben Rogers' hayloft. He lets me, and so does his pap's nigger man, Uncle Jake. I tote water for Uncle Jake whenever he wants me to, and any time I ask him he gives me a little something to eat if he can spare it. That's a mighty good nigger, Tom. He likes me, becuz I don't ever act as if I was above him. Sometime I've set right down and eat *with* him. But you needn't tell that. A body's got to do things when he's awful hungry he wouldn't want to do as a steady thing."

"Well, if I don't want you in the daytime, I'll let you sleep. I won't come bothering around. Any time you see something's up, in the night, just skip right around and meow."

CHAPTER 29

The Picnic—Huck on Injun Joe's Track —
The "Revenge" Job—Aid for the Widow

THE first thing Tom heard on Friday morning was a glad piece of news—Judge Thatcher's family had come back to town the night before. Both Injun Joe and the treasure sunk into secondary importance for a moment, and Becky took the chief place in the boy's interest. He saw her and they had an exhausting good time playing "hispy" and "gully-keeper" with a crowd of their schoolmates. The day was completed and crowned in a peculiarly satisfactory way: Becky teased her mother to appoint the next day for the long-promised and long-delayed picnic, and she consented. The child's delight was boundless; and Tom's not more moderate. The invitations were sent out before sunset, and straightway the young folks of the village were thrown into a fever of preparation and pleasurable anticipation. Tom's excitement enabled him to keep awake until a pretty late hour, and he had good hopes of hearing Huck's "maow," and of having his treasure to astonish Becky and the picnickers with, next day; but he was disappointed. No signal came that night.

Morning came, eventually, and by ten or eleven o'clock a giddy and rollicking company were gathered at Judge Thatcher's, and everything was ready for a start. It was not the custom for elderly people to mar the picnics with their presence. The children were considered safe enough under the wings of a few young ladies of eighteen and a few young gentlemen of twenty-three or thereabouts. The old steam ferry-boat was chartered for the occasion; presently the gay throng filed up the main street laden with provision-baskets. Sid was sick and had to miss the fun; Mary remained at home to entertain him. The last thing Mrs. Thatcher said to Becky, was:

"You'll not get back till late. Perhaps you'd better stay all night with some of the girls that live near the ferry-landing, child."

"Then I'll stay with Susy Harper, mamma."

"Very well. And mind and behave yourself and don't be any trouble."

Presently, as they tripped along, Tom said to Becky:

"Say—I'll tell you what we'll do. 'Stead of going to Joe Harper's we'll climb right up the hill and stop at the Widow Douglas'. She'll have ice-cream! She has it most every day— dead loads of it. And she'll be awful glad to have us."

"Oh, that will be fun!"

Then Becky reflected a moment and said:

"But what will mamma say?"

"How'll she ever know?"

The girl turned the idea over in her mind, and said reluctantly:

"I reckon it's wrong—but—"

"But shucks! Your mother won't know, and so what's the harm? All she wants is that you'll be safe; and I bet you she'd 'a' said go there if she'd 'a' thought of it. I know she would!"

The Widow Douglas' splendid hospitality was a tempting bait. It and Tom's persuasions presently carried the day. So it was decided to say nothing anybody about the night's programme. Presently it occurred to Tom that maybe Huck might come this very night and give the signal. The thought took a deal of the spirit out of his anticipations. Still he could not bear to give up the fun at Widow Douglas'. And why should he give it up, he reasoned—the signal did not come the night before, so why should it be any more likely to come tonight? The sure fun of the evening outweighed the uncertain treasure; and, boy-like, he determined to yield to the stronger inclination and not allow himself to think of the box of money another time that day.

Three miles below town the ferryboat stopped at the mouth of a woody hollow and tied up. The crowd swarmed ashore and soon the forest distances and craggy heights echoed far and near with shoutings and laughter. All the different ways of getting hot and tired were gone through with, and by-and-by the rovers straggled back to camp fortified with responsible appetites, and then the destruction of the good things began. After the feast there was a refreshing season of rest and chat in the shade of spreading oaks. By-and-by somebody shouted:

"Who's ready for the cave?"

Everybody was. Bundles of candles were procured, and straightway there was a general scamper up the hill. The mouth of the cave was up the hillside—an opening shaped like a letter A. Its massive oaken door stood unbarred. Within was a small chamber, chilly as an icehouse, and walled by Nature with solid limestone that was dewy with a cold sweat. It was romantic and mysterious to stand here in the deep gloom and look out upon the green valley shining in the sun. But the impressiveness of the situation quickly wore off, and the romping began again. The moment a candle was lighted there was a general rush upon the owner of it; a struggle and a gallant defence followed, but the candle was soon knocked down or blown out, and then there was a glad clamor of laughter and a new chase. But all things have an end. By-and-by the procession went filing down the steep descent of the main avenue, the flickering rank of lights dimly revealing the lofty walls of rock almost to their point of junction sixty feet overhead. This main avenue was not more than eight or ten feet wide. Every few steps other lofty and still narrower crevices branched from it on either hand—for McDougal's cave was but a vast labyrinth of crooked aisles that ran into each other and out again and led nowhere. It was said that one might wander days and nights together through its intricate tangle of rifts and chasms, and never find the end of the cave; and that he might go down, and down, and still down, into the earth, and it was just the same—labyrinth under labyrinth, and no end to any of them. No man "knew" the cave. That was an impossible thing. Most of the young men knew a portion of it, and it was not customary to venture much beyond this known portion. Tom Sawyer knew as much of the cave as any one.

The procession moved along the main avenue some three-quarters of a mile, and then groups and couples began to slip aside into branch avenues, fly along the dismal corridors, and take each other by surprise at points where the corridors joined again. Parties were able to elude each other for the space of half an hour without going beyond the "known" ground.

By-and-by, one group after another came straggling back to the mouth of the cave, panting, hilarious, smeared from head to foot with tallow drippings, daubed with clay, and entirely delighted with the success of the day. Then they were astonished to find that they had been taking no note of time and that night was about at hand. The clanging bell had been calling for half an hour. However, this sort of close to the day's adventures was romantic and therefore satisfactory. When the ferryboat with her wild freight pushed into the stream, nobody cared sixpence for the wasted time but the captain of the craft.

Huck was already upon his watch when the ferryboat's lights went glinting past the wharf. He heard no noise on board, for the young people were as subdued and still as people usually are who are nearly tired to death. He wondered what boat it was, and why she did not stop at the wharf—and then he dropped her out of his mind and put his attention upon his business. The night was growing cloudy and dark. Ten o'clock came, and the noise of vehicles ceased, scattered lights began to wink out, all straggling foot-passengers disappeared, the village betook itself to its slumbers and left the small watcher alone with the silence and the ghosts. Eleven o'clock came, and the tavern lights were put out; darkness everywhere, now. Huck waited what seemed a weary long time, but nothing happened. His faith was weakening. Was there any use? Was there really any use? Why not give it up and turn in?

A noise fell upon his ear. He was all attention in an instant. The alley door closed softly. He sprang to the corner of the brick store. The next moment two men brushed by him, and one seemed to have something under his arm. It must be that box! So they were going to remove the treasure. Why call Tom now? It would be absurd—the men would get away with the box and never be found again. No, he would stick to their wake and follow them; he would trust to the darkness for security from discovery. So communing with himself, Huck stepped out and glided along behind the men, cat-like, with bare feet, allowing them to keep just far enough ahead not to be invisible.

They moved up the river street three blocks, then turned to the left up a crossstreet. They went straight ahead, then, until they came to the path that led up Cardiff Hill; this they took. They passed by the old Welshman's house, halfway up the hill, without hesitating, and still climbed upward. Good, thought Huck, they will bury it in the old quarry. But they never stopped at the quarry. They passed on, up the summit. They plunged into the narrow path between the tall sumach bushes, and were at once hidden in the gloom. Huck closed up and shortened his distance, now, for they would never be able to see him. He trotted along awhile; then slackened his pace, fearing he was gaining too fast; moved on a piece, then stopped altogether; listened; no sound; none, save that he seemed to hear the beating of his own heart. The hooting of an owl came over the hill—ominous sound! But no footsteps. Heavens, was everything lost! He was about to spring with winged feet, when a man cleared his throat not four feet from him! Huck's heart shot into his throat, but he swallowed it again; and then he stood there shaking as if a dozen agues had taken charge of him at once, and so weak that he thought he must surely fall to the ground. He knew where he was. He knew he was within five steps of the stile leading into Widow Douglas' grounds. Very well, he thought, let them bury it there; it won't be hard to find.

Now there was a voice—a very low voice—Injun Joe's:

"Damn her, maybe she's got company—there's lights, late as it is."

"I can't see any."

This was that stranger's voice—the stranger of the haunted house. A deadly chill went to Huck's heart—this, then, was the "revenge" job! His thought was, to fly. Then he remembered that the Widow Douglas had been kind to him more than once, and maybe these men were going to murder her. He wished he dared venture to warn her; but he knew he didn't dare—they might come and catch him. He thought all this and more in the moment that elapsed between the stranger's remark and Injun Joe's next—which was—

"Because the bush is in your way. Now—this way—now you see, don't you?"

"Yes. Well, there *is* company there, I reckon. Better give it up."

"Give it up, and I just leaving this country forever! Give it up and maybe never have another chance. I tell you again, as I've told you before, I don't care for her swag—you may have it. But her husband was rough on me—many times he was rough on me—and mainly he was the justice of the peace that jugged me for a vagrant. And that ain't all. It ain't a millionth part of it! He had me *horsewhipped*!—horsewhipped in front of the jail, like a nigger!—with all the town looking on! HORSEWHIPPED!—do you understand? He took advantage of me and died. But I'll take it out of *er*."

"Oh, don't kill her! Don't do that!"

"Kill? Who said anything about killing? I would kill *him* if he was here; but not her. When you want to get revenge on a woman you don't kill her—bosh! you go for her looks. You slit her nostrils—you notch her ears like a sow!"

"By God, that's—"

"Keep your opinion to yourself! It will be safest for you. I'll tie her to the bed. If she bleeds to death, is that my fault? I'll not cry, if she does. My friend, you'll help me in this thing—for MY sake—that's why you're here—I mightn't be able alone. If you flinch, I'll kill you. Do you understand that? And if I have to kill you, I'll kill her—and then I reckon nobody'll ever know much about who done this business."

"Well, if it's got to be done, let's get at it. The quicker the better—I'm all in a shiver."

"Do it *now*? And company there? Look here—I'll get suspicious of you, first thing you know. No—we'll wait till the lights are out—there's no hurry."

Huck felt that a silence was going to ensue—a thing still more awful than any amount of murderous talk; so he held his breath and stepped gingerly back; planted his foot carefully and firmly, after balancing, one-legged, in a precarious way and almost toppling over, first on one side and then on the other. He took another step back, with the same elaboration and the same risks; then another and another, and—a twig snapped under his foot! His breath stopped and he listened. There was no sound—the stillness was perfect. His gratitude was measureless. Now he turned in his tracks, between the walls of sumach bushes—turned himself as carefully as if he were a ship—and then stepped quickly but cautiously along. When he emerged at the quarry he felt secure, and so he picked up his nimble heels and flew. Down, down he sped, till he reached the Welshman's. He banged at the door, and presently the heads of the old man and his two stalwart sons were thrust from windows.

"What's the row there? Who's banging? What do you want?"

"Let me in—quick! I'll tell everything."

"Why, who are you?"

"Huckleberry Finn—quick, let me in!"

"Huckleberry Finn, indeed! It ain't a name to open many doors, I judge! But let him in, lads, and let's see what's the trouble."

"Please don't ever tell I told you," were Huck's first words when he got in. "Please don't—I'd be killed, sure—but the widow's been good friends to me sometimes, and I want to tell—I *will* tell if you'll promise you won't ever say it was me."

"By George, he *has* got something to tell, or he wouldn't act so!" exclaimed the old man; "out with it and nobody here'll ever tell, lad."

Three minutes later the old man and his sons, well armed, were up the hill, and just entering the sumach path on tiptoe, their weapons in their hands. Huck accompanied them no further. He hid behind a great bowlder and fell to listening. There was a lagging, anxious silence, and then all of a sudden there was an explosion of firearms and a cry.

Huck waited for no particulars. He sprang away and sped down the hill as fast as his legs could carry him.

CHAPTER 30

The Welchman Reports—Huck Under Fire—
The Story Circulated —A New Sensation—
Hope Giving Way to Despair

A S the earliest suspicion of dawn appeared on Sunday
morning, Huck came groping up the hill and rapped
gently at the old Welshman's door. The inmates were asleep,
but it was a sleep that was set on a hair-trigger, on account of
the exciting episode of the night. A call came from a window:

"Who's there!"

Huck's scared voice answered in a low tone:

"Please let me in! It's only Huck Finn!"

"It's a name that can open this door night or day, lad!—and
welcome!"

These were strange words to the vagabond boy's ears, and
the pleasantest he had ever heard. He could not recollect that
the closing word had ever been applied in his case before. The
door was quickly unlocked, and he entered. Huck was given a
seat and the old man and his brace of tall sons speedily dressed
themselves.

"Now, my boy, I hope you're good and hungry, because
breakfast will be ready as soon as the sun's up, and we'll have a
piping hot one, too—make yourself easy about that! I and the
boys hoped you'd turn up and stop here last night."

"I was awful scared," said Huck, "and I run. I took out when
the pistols went off, and I didn't stop for three mile. I've come
now becuz I wanted to know about it, you know; and I come

before daylight becuz I didn't want to run across them devils, even if they was dead."

"Well, poor chap, you do look as if you'd had a hard night of it—but there's a bed here for you when you've had your breakfast. No, they ain't dead, lad—we are sorry enough for that. You see we knew right where to put our hands on them, by your description; so we crept along on tiptoe till we got within fifteen feet of them—dark as a cellar that sumach path was—and just then I found I was going to sneeze. It was the meanest kind of luck! I tried to keep it back, but no use—'twas bound to come, and it did come! I was in the lead with my pistol raised, and when the sneeze started those scoundrels a-rustling to get out of the path, I sung out, 'Fire boys!' and blazed away at the place where the rustling was. So did the boys. But they were off in a jiffy, those villains, and we after them, down through the woods. I judge we never touched them. They fired a shot apiece as they started, but their bullets whizzed by and didn't do us any harm. As soon as we lost the sound of their feet we quit chasing, and went down and stirred up the constables. They got a posse together, and went off to guard the river bank, and as soon as it is light the sheriff and a gang are going to beat up the woods. My boys will be with them presently. I wish we had some sort of description of those rascals—'twould help a good deal. But you couldn't see what they were like, in the dark, lad, I suppose?"

"Oh yes; I saw them downtown and follered them."

"Splendid! Describe them—describe them, my boy!"

"One's the old deaf and dumb Spaniard that's ben around here once or twice, and t'other's a mean-looking, ragged—"

"That's enough, lad, we know the men! Happened on them in the woods back of the widow's one day, and they slunk away. Off with you, boys, and tell the sheriff—get your breakfast tomorrow morning!"

The Welshman's sons departed at once. As they were

leaving the room Huck sprang up and exclaimed:

"Oh, please don't tell *any*body it was me that blowed on them! Oh, please!"

"All right if you say it, Huck, but you ought to have the credit of what you did."

"Oh no, no! Please don't tell!"

When the young men were gone, the old Welshman said:

"They won't tell—and I won't. But why don't you want it known?"

Huck would not explain, further than to say that he already knew too much about one of those men and would not have the man know that he knew anything against him for the whole world—he would be killed for knowing it, sure.

The old man promised secrecy once more, and said:

"How did you come to follow these fellows, lad? Were they looking suspicious?"

Huck was silent while he framed a duly cautious reply. Then he said:

"Well, you see, I'm a kind of a hard lot,—least everybody says so, and I don't see nothing agin it—and sometimes I can't sleep much, on account of thinking about it and sort of trying to strike out a new way of doing. That was the way of it last night. I couldn't sleep, and so I come along upstreet 'bout midnight, a-turning it all over, and when I got to that old shackly brick store by the Temperance Tavern, I backed up agin the wall to have another think. Well, just then along comes these two chaps slipping along close by me, with something under their arm, and I reckoned they'd stole it. One was a-smoking, and t'other one wanted a light; so they stopped right before me and the cigars lit up their faces and I see that the big one was the deaf and dumb Spaniard, by his white whiskers and the patch on his eye, and t'other one was a rusty, ragged-looking devil."

"Could you see the rags by the light of the cigars?"

This staggered Huck for a moment. Then he said:

"Well, I don't know—but somehow it seems as if I did."

"Then they went on, and you—"

"Follered 'em—yes. That was it. I wanted to see what was up—they sneaked along so. I dogged 'em to the widder's stile, and stood in the dark and heard the ragged one beg for the widder, and the Spaniard swear he'd spile her looks just as I told you and your two—"

"What! The *deaf and dumb* man said all that!"

Huck had made another terrible mistake! He was trying his best to keep the old man from getting the faintest hint of who the Spaniard might be, and yet his tongue seemed determined to get him into trouble in spite of all he could do. He made several efforts to creep out of his scrape, but the old man's eye was upon him and he made blunder after blunder. Presently the Welshman said:

"My boy, don't be afraid of me. I wouldn't hurt a hair of your head for all the world. No—I'd protect you—I'd protect you. This Spaniard is not deaf and dumb; you've let that slip without intending it; you can't cover that up now. You know something about that Spaniard that you want to keep dark. Now trust me—tell me what it is, and trust me—I won't betray you."

Huck looked into the old man's honest eyes a moment, then bent over and whispered in his ear:

"'Tain't a Spaniard—it's Injun Joe!"

The Welshman almost jumped out of his chair. In a moment he said:

"It's all plain enough, now. When you talked about notching ears and slitting noses I judged that that was your own embellishment, because white men don't take that sort of revenge. But an Injun! That's a different matter altogether."

During breakfast the talk went on, and in the course of it the old man said that the last thing which he and his sons had done, before going to bed, was to get a lantern and examine the stile and its vicinity for marks of blood. They found none, but captured a bulky bundle of—

"Of *what*?"

If the words had been lightning they could not have leaped with a more stunning suddenness from Huck's blanched lips. His eyes were staring wide, now, and his breath suspended— waiting for the answer. The Welshman started—stared in return—three seconds—five seconds—ten—then replied:

"Of burglar's tools. Why, what's the *matter* with you?"

Huck sank back, panting gently, but deeply, unutterably grateful. The Welshman eyed him gravely, curiously—and presently said:

"Yes, burglar's tools. That appears to relieve you a good deal. But what did give you that turn? What were *you* expecting we'd found?"

Huck was in a close place—the inquiring eye was upon him—he would have given anything for material for a plausible answer—nothing suggested itself—the inquiring eye was boring deeper and deeper—a senseless reply offered—there was no time to weigh it, so at a venture he uttered it—feebly:

"Sunday-school books, maybe."

Poor Huck was too distressed to smile, but the old man laughed loud and joyously, shook up the details of his anatomy from head to foot, and ended by saying that such a laugh was money in a man's pocket, because it cut down the doctor's bill like everything. Then he added:

"Poor old chap, you're white and jaded—you ain't well a bit—no wonder you're a little flighty and off your balance. But you'll come out of it. Rest and sleep will fetch you out all right, I hope."

Huck was irritated to think he had been such a goose and betrayed such a suspicious excitement, for he had dropped the idea that the parcel brought from the tavern was the treasure, as soon as he had heard the talk at the widow's stile. He had only thought it was not the treasure, however—he had not known that it wasn't—and so the suggestion of a captured bundle was too much for his self-possession. But on the whole he felt glad the little episode had happened, for now he knew beyond all question that that bundle was not *the* bundle, and so his mind was at rest and exceedingly comfortable. In fact, everything seemed to be drifting just in the right direction, now; the treasure must be still in No. 2, the men would be captured and jailed that day, and he and Tom could seize the gold that night without any trouble or any fear of interruption.

Just as breakfast was completed there was a knock at the door. Huck jumped for a hiding-place, for he had no mind to be connected even remotely with the late event. The Welshman admitted several ladies and gentlemen, among them the Widow Douglas, and noticed that groups of citizens were climbing up the hill—to stare at the stile. So the news had spread. The Welshman had to tell the story of the night to the visitors. The widow's gratitude for her preservation was outspoken.

"Don't say a word about it, madam. There's another that you're more beholden to than you are to me and my boys, maybe, but he don't allow me to tell his name. We wouldn't have been there but for him."

Of course this excited a curiosity so vast that it almost belittled the main matter—but the Welshman allowed it to eat into the vitals of his visitors, and through them be transmitted to the whole town, for he refused to part with his secret. When all else had been learned, the widow said:

"I went to sleep reading in bed and slept straight through all that noise. Why didn't you come and wake me?"

"We judged it warn't worth while. Those fellows warn't likely to come again—they hadn't any tools left to work with, and what was the use of waking you up and scaring you to death? My three negro men stood guard at your house all the rest of the night. They've just come back."

More visitors came, and the story had to be told and retold for a couple of hours more.

There was no Sabbath-school during day-school vacation, but everybody was early at church. The stirring event was well canvassed. News came that not a sign of the two villains had been yet discovered. When the sermon was finished, Judge Thatcher's wife dropped alongside of Mrs. Harper as she moved down the aisle with the crowd and said:

"Is my Becky going to sleep all day? I just expected she would be tired to death."

"Your Becky?"

"Yes," with a startled look—"didn't she stay with you last night?"

"Why, no."

Mrs. Thatcher turned pale, and sank into a pew, just as Aunt Polly, talking briskly with a friend, passed by. Aunt Polly said:

"Goodmorning, Mrs. Thatcher. Goodmorning, Mrs. Harper. I've got a boy that's turned up missing. I reckon my Tom stayed at your house last night—one of you. And now he's afraid to come to church. I've got to settle with him."

Mrs. Thatcher shook her head feebly and turned paler than ever.

"He didn't stay with us," said Mrs. Harper, beginning to look uneasy. A marked anxiety came into Aunt Polly's face.

"Joe Harper, have you seen my Tom this morning?"

"No'm".

"When did you see him last?"

Joe tried to remember, but was not sure he could say. The people had stopped moving out of church. Whispers passed along, and a boding uneasiness took possession of every countenance. Children were anxiously questioned, and young teachers. They all said they had not noticed whether Tom and Becky were on board the ferryboat on the homeward trip; it was dark; no one thought of inquiring if any one was missing. One young man finally blurted out his fear that they were still in the cave! Mrs. Thatcher swooned away. Aunt Polly fell to crying and wringing her hands.

The alarm swept from lip to lip, from group to group, from street to street, and within five minutes the bells were wildly clanging and the whole town was up! The Cardiff Hill episode sank into instant insignificance, the burglars were forgotten, horses were saddled, skiffs were manned, the ferryboat ordered out, and before the horror was half an hour old, two hundred men were pouring down highroad and river toward the cave.

All the long afternoon the village seemed empty and dead. Many women visited Aunt Polly and Mrs. Thatcher and tried to comfort them. They cried with them, too, and that was still better than words. All the tedious night the town waited for news; but when the morning dawned at last, all the word that came was, "Send more candles—and send food." Mrs. Thatcher was almost crazed; and Aunt Polly, also. Judge Thatcher sent messages of hope and encouragement from the cave, but they conveyed no real cheer.

The old Welshman came home toward daylight, spattered with candle-grease, smeared with clay, and almost worn out. He found Huck still in the bed that had been provided for him, and delirious with fever. The physicians were all at the cave, so the Widow Douglas came and took charge of the patient. She said she would do her best by him, because, whether he was good, bad, or indifferent, he was the Lord's, and nothing that was the Lord's was a thing to be neglected. The Welshman said Huck had good spots in him, and the widow said:

"You can depend on it. That's the Lord's mark. He don't leave it off. He never does. Puts it somewhere on every creature that comes from his hands."

Early in the forenoon parties of jaded men began to straggle into the village, but the strongest of the citizens continued searching. All the news that could be gained was that remotenesses of the cavern were being ransacked that had never been visited before; that every corner and crevice was going to be thoroughly searched; that wherever one wandered through the maze of passages, lights were to be seen flitting hither and thither in the distance, and shoutings and pistol-shots sent their hollow reverberations to the ear down the sombre aisles. In one place, far from the section usually traversed by tourists, the names "BECKY & TOM" had been found traced upon the rocky wall with candle-smoke, and near at hand a grease-soiled bit of ribbon. Mrs. Thatcher recognized the ribbon and cried over it. She said it was the last relic she should ever have of her child; and that no other memorial of her could ever be so precious, because this one parted latest from the living body before the awful death came. Some said that now and then, in the cave, a far-away speck of light would glimmer, and then a glorious shout would burst forth and a score of men go trooping down the echoing aisle—and then a sickening disappointment always followed; the children were not there; it was only a searcher's light.

Three dreadful days and nights dragged their tedious hours along, and the village sank into a hopeless stupor. No one had heart for anything. The accidental discovery, just made, that the proprietor of the Temperance Tavern kept liquor on his premises, scarcely fluttered the public pulse, tremendous as the fact was. In a lucid interval, Huck feebly led up to the subject of taverns, and finally asked—dimly dreading the worst—if anything had been discovered at the Temperance Tavern since he had been ill.

"Yes," said the widow.

Huck started up in bed, wildeyed:

"What? What was it?"

"Liquor!—and the place has been shut up. Lie down, child—what a turn you did give me!"

"Only tell me just one thing—only just one—please! Was it Tom Sawyer that found it?"

The widow burst into tears. "Hush, hush, child, hush! I've told you before, you must *not* talk. You are very, very sick!"

Then nothing but liquor had been found; there would have been a great powwow if it had been the gold. So the treasure was gone forever—gone forever! But what could she be crying about? Curious that she should cry.

These thoughts worked their dim way through Huck's mind, and under the weariness they gave him he fell asleep. The widow said to herself:

"There—he's asleep, poor wreck. Tom Sawyer find it! Pity but somebody could find Tom Sawyer! Ah, there ain't many left, now, that's got hope enough, or strength enough, either, to go on searching."

CHAPTER 31

An Exploring Expedition—Trouble Commences —
Lost in the Cave—Total Darkness—Found but not Saved

NOW to return to Tom and Becky's share in the picnic. They tripped along the murky aisles with the rest of the company, visiting the familiar wonders of the cave—wonders dubbed with rather over-descriptive names, such as "The Drawing-Room," "The Cathedral," "Aladdin's Palace," and so on. Presently the hide-and-seek frolicking began, and Tom and Becky engaged in it with zeal until the exertion began to grow a trifle wearisome; then they wandered down a sinuous avenue holding their candles aloft and reading the tangled webwork of names, dates, postoffice addresses, and mottoes with which the rocky walls had been frescoed (in candle-smoke). Still drifting along and talking, they scarcely noticed that they were now in a part of the cave whose walls were not frescoed. They smoked their own names under an overhanging shelf and moved on. Presently they came to a place where a little stream of water, trickling over a ledge and carrying a limestone sediment with it, had, in the slow-dragging ages, formed a laced and ruffled Niagara in gleaming and imperishable stone. Tom squeezed his small body behind it in order to illuminate it for Becky's gratification. He found that it curtained a sort of steep natural stairway which was enclosed between narrow walls, and at once the ambition to be a discoverer seized him.

Becky responded to his call, and they made a smoke-mark for future guidance, and started upon their quest. They wound this way and that, far down into the secret depths of the cave, made another mark, and branched off in search of novelties to tell the upper world about. In one place they found a spacious cavern, from whose ceiling depended a multitude of shining stalactites of the length and circumference of a man's leg; they walked all about it, wondering and admiring, and presently left it by one of the numerous passages that opened into it. This shortly brought them to a bewitching spring, whose basin was incrusted with a frostwork of glittering crystals; it was in the midst of a cavern whose walls were supported by many fantastic pillars which had been formed by the joining of great stalactites and stalagmites together, the result of the ceaseless water-drip of centuries. Under the roof vast knots of bats had packed themselves together, thousands in a bunch; the lights disturbed the creatures and they came flocking down by hundreds, squeaking and darting furiously at the candles. Tom knew their ways and the danger of this sort of conduct. He seized Becky's hand and hurried her into the first corridor that offered; and none too soon, for a bat struck Becky's light out with its wing while she was passing out of the cavern. The bats chased the children a good distance; but the fugitives plunged into every new passage that offered, and at last got rid of the perilous things. Tom found a subterranean lake, shortly, which stretched its dim length away until its shape was lost in the shadows. He wanted to explore its borders, but concluded that it would be best to sit down and rest awhile, first. Now, for the first time, the deep stillness of the place laid a clammy hand upon the spirits of the children. Becky said:

"Why, I didn't notice, but it seems ever so long since I heard any of the others."

"Come to think, Becky, we are away down below them—and I don't know how far away north, or south, or east, or whichever it is. We couldn't hear them here."

Becky grew apprehensive.

"I wonder how long we've been down here, Tom? We better start back."

"Yes, I reckon we better. P'raps we better."

"Can you find the way, Tom? It's all a mixed-up crookedness to me."

"I reckon I could find it—but then the bats. If they put our candles out it will be an awful fix. Let's try some other way, so as not to go through there."

"Well. But I hope we won't get lost. It would be so awful!" and the girl shuddered at the thought of the dreadful possibilities.

They started through a corridor, and traversed it in silence a long way, glancing at each new opening, to see if there was anything familiar about the look of it; but they were all strange. Every time Tom made an examination, Becky would watch his face for an encouraging sign, and he would say cheerily:

"Oh, it's all right. This ain't the one, but we'll come to it right away!"

But he felt less and less hopeful with each failure, and presently began to turn off into diverging avenues at sheer random, in desperate hope of finding the one that was wanted. He still said it was "all right," but there was such a leaden dread at his heart that the words had lost their ring and sounded just as if he had said, "All is lost!" Becky clung to his side in an anguish of fear, and tried hard to keep back the tears, but they would come. At last she said:

"Oh, Tom, never mind the bats, let's go back that way! We seem to get worse and worse off all the time."

"Listen!" said he.

Profound silence; silence so deep that even their breathings were conspicuous in the hush. Tom shouted. The call went echoing down the empty aisles and died out in the distance in a faint sound that resembled a ripple of mocking laughter.

"Oh, don't do it again, Tom, it is too horrid," said Becky.

"It is horrid, but I better, Becky; they *might* hear us, you know," and he shouted again.

The "might" was even a chillier horror than the ghostly laughter, it so confessed a perishing hope. The children stood still and listened; but there was no result. Tom turned upon the back track at once, and hurried his steps. It was but a little while before a certain indecision in his manner revealed another fearful fact to Becky—he could not find his way back!

"Oh, Tom, you didn't make any marks!"

"Becky, I was such a fool! Such a fool! I never thought we might want to come back! No—I can't find the way. It's all mixed up."

"Tom, Tom, we're lost! we're lost! We never can get out of this awful place! Oh, why *did* we ever leave the others!"

She sank to the ground and burst into such a frenzy of crying that Tom was appalled with the idea that she might die, or lose her reason. He sat down by her and put his arms around her; she buried her face in his bosom, she clung to him, she poured out her terrors, her unavailing regrets, and the far echoes turned them all to jeering laughter. Tom begged her to pluck up hope again, and she said she could not. He fell to blaming and abusing himself for getting her into this miserable situation; this had a better effect. She said she would try to hope again, she would get up and follow wherever he might lead if only he would not talk like that any more. For he was no more to blame than she, she said.

So they moved on again—aimlessly—simply at random—all they could do was to move, keep moving. For a little while, hope made a show of reviving—not with any reason to back it, but only because it is its nature to revive when the spring has not been taken out of it by age and familiarity with failure.

By-and-by Tom took Becky's candle and blew it out. This economy meant so much! Words were not needed. Becky understood, and her hope died again. She knew that Tom had a whole candle and three or four pieces in his pockets—yet he must economize.

By-and-by, fatigue began to assert its claims; the children tried to pay attention, for it was dreadful to think of sitting down when time was grown to be so precious, moving, in some direction, in any direction, was at least progress and might bear fruit; but to sit down was to invite death and shorten its pursuit.

At last Becky's frail limbs refused to carry her farther. She sat down. Tom rested with her, and they talked of home, and the friends there, and the comfortable beds and, above all, the light! Becky cried, and Tom tried to think of some way of comforting her, but all his encouragements were grown thread-bare with use, and sounded like sarcasms. Fatigue bore so heavily upon Becky that she drowsed off to sleep. Tom was grateful. He sat looking into her drawn face and saw it grow smooth and natural under the influence of pleasant dreams; and by-and-by a smile dawned and rested there. The peaceful face reflected somewhat of peace and healing into his own spirit, and his thoughts wandered away to bygone times and dreamy memories. While he was deep in his musings, Becky woke up with a breezy little laugh—but it was stricken dead upon her lips, and a groan followed it.

"Oh, how *could* I sleep! I wish I never, never had waked! No! No, I don't, Tom! Don't look so! I won't say it again."

"I'm glad you've slept, Becky; you'll feel rested, now, and we'll find the way out."

"We can try, Tom; but I've seen such a beautiful country in my dream. I reckon we are going there."

"Maybe not, maybe not. Cheer up, Becky, and let's go on trying."

They rose up and wandered along, hand in hand and hopeless. They tried to estimate how long they had been in the cave, but all they knew was that it seemed days and weeks, and yet it was plain that this could not be, for their candles were not gone yet. A long time after this—they could not tell how long—Tom said they must go softly and listen for dripping water—they must find a spring. They found one presently, and Tom said it was time to rest again. Both were cruelly tired, yet Becky said she thought she could go a little farther. She was surprised to hear Tom dissent. She could not understand it. They sat down, and Tom fastened his candle to the wall in front of them with some clay. Thought was soon busy; nothing was said for some time. Then Becky broke the silence:

"Tom, I am so hungry!"

Tom took something out of his pocket.

"Do you remember this?" said he.

Becky almost smiled.

"It's our wedding-cake, Tom."

"Yes—I wish it was as big as a barrel, for it's all we've got."

"I saved it from the picnic for us to dream on, Tom, the way grownup people do with wedding-cake—but it'll be our—"

She dropped the sentence where it was. Tom divided the cake and Becky ate with good appetite, while Tom nibbled at his moiety. There was abundance of cold water to finish the feast with. By-and-by Becky suggested that they move on again. Tom was silent a moment. Then he said:

"Becky, can you bear it if I tell you something?"

Becky's face paled, but she thought she could.

"Well, then, Becky, we must stay here, where there's water to drink. That little piece is our last candle!"

Becky gave loose to tears and wailings. Tom did what he could to comfort her, but with little effect. At length Becky said:

"Tom!"

"Well, Becky?"

"They'll miss us and hunt for us!"

"Yes, they will! Certainly they will!"

"Maybe they're hunting for us now, Tom."

"Why, I reckon maybe they are. I hope they are."

"When would they miss us, Tom?"

"When they get back to the boat, I reckon."

"Tom, it might be dark then—would they notice we hadn't come?"

"I don't know. But anyway, your mother would miss you as soon as they got home."

A frightened look in Becky's face brought Tom to his senses and he saw that he had made a blunder. Becky was not to have gone home that night! The children became silent and thoughtful. In a moment a new burst of grief from Becky showed Tom that the thing in his mind had struck hers also— that the Sabbath morning might be half spent before Mrs. Thatcher discovered that Becky was not at Mrs. Harper's.

The children fastened their eyes upon their bit of candle and watched it melt slowly and pitilessly away; saw the half inch of wick stand alone at last; saw the feeble flame rise and fall, climb the thin column of smoke, linger at its top a moment, and then—the horror of utter darkness reigned!

How long afterward it was that Becky came to a slow consciousness that she was crying in Tom's arms, neither could tell. All that they knew was, that after what seemed a mighty stretch of time, both awoke out of a dead stupor of sleep and resumed their miseries once more. Tom said it might be Sunday, now—maybe Monday. He tried to get Becky to talk, but her sorrows were too oppressive, all her hopes were gone. Tom said that they must have been missed long ago, and no doubt the search was going on. He would shout and maybe some one would come. He tried it; but in the darkness the distant echoes sounded so hideously that he tried it no more.

The hours wasted away, and hunger came to torment the captives again. A portion of Tom's half of the cake was left; they divided and ate it. But they seemed hungrier than before. The poor morsel of food only whetted desire.

By-and-by Tom said:

"*Sh!* Did you hear that?"

Both held their breath and listened. There was a sound like the faintest, far-off shout. Instantly Tom answered it, and leading Becky by the hand, started groping down the corridor in its direction. Presently he listened again; again the sound was heard, and apparently a little nearer.

"It's them!" said Tom; "they're coming! Come along, Becky—we're all right now!"

The joy of the prisoners was almost overwhelming. Their speed was slow, however, because pitfalls were somewhat common, and had to be guarded against. They shortly came to one and had to stop. It might be three feet deep, it might be a hundred—there was no passing it at any rate. Tom got down on his breast and reached as far down as he could. No bottom. They must stay there and wait until the searchers came. They listened; evidently the distant shoutings were growing more distant! a moment or two more and they had gone altogether. The heart-sinking misery of it! Tom whooped until he was hoarse, but it was of no use. He talked hopefully to Becky; but an age of anxious waiting passed and no sounds came again.

The children groped their way back to the spring. The weary time dragged on; they slept again, and awoke famished and woe-stricken. Tom believed it must be Tuesday by this time.

Now an idea struck him. There were some side passages near at hand. It would be better to explore some of these than bear the weight of the heavy time in idleness. He took a kite-line from his pocket, tied it to a projection, and he and Becky started, Tom in the lead, unwinding the line as he groped along. At the end of twenty steps the corridor ended in a "jumping-off place." Tom got down on his knees and felt below, and then as far around the corner as he could reach with his hands conveniently; he made an effort to stretch yet a little farther to the right, and at that moment, not twenty yards away, a human hand, holding a candle, appeared from behind a rock! Tom lifted up a glorious shout, and instantly that hand was followed by the body it belonged to—Injun Joe's! Tom was paralyzed; he could not move. He was vastly gratified the next moment, to see the "Spaniard" take to his heels and get himself out of sight. Tom wondered that Joe had not recognized his voice and come over and killed him for testifying in court. But the echoes must have disguised the voice. Without doubt, that was it, he reasoned. Tom's fright weakened every muscle in his body. He said to himself that if he had strength enough to get back to the spring he would stay there, and nothing should tempt him to run the risk of meeting Injun Joe again. He was careful to keep from Becky what it was he had seen. He told her he had only shouted "for luck."

But hunger and wretchedness rise superior to fears in the long run. Another tedious wait at the spring and another long sleep brought changes. The children awoke tortured with a raging hunger. Tom believed that it must be Wednesday or Thursday or even Friday or Saturday, now, and that the search had been given over. He proposed to explore another passage. He felt willing to risk Injun Joe and all other terrors. But Becky was very weak. She had sunk into a dreary apathy and would not be roused. She said she would wait, now, where she was, and die—it would not be long. She told Tom to go with the kite-line and explore if he chose; but she implored him to come back every little while and speak to her; and she made him promise that when the awful time came, he would stay by her and hold her hand until all was over.

Tom kissed her, with a choking sensation in his throat, and made a show of being confident of finding the searchers or an escape from the cave; then he took the kite-line in his hand and went groping down one of the passages on his hands and knees, distressed with hunger and sick with bodings of coming doom.

CHAPTER 32

Tom tells the Story of their Escape —
Tom's Enemy in Safe Quarters

TUESDAY afternoon came, and waned to the twilight. The village of St. Petersburg still mourned. The lost children had not been found. Public prayers had been offered up for them, and many and many a private prayer that had the petitioner's whole heart in it; but still no good news came from the cave. The majority of the searchers had given up the quest and gone back to their daily avocations, saying that it was plain the children could never be found. Mrs. Thatcher was very ill, and a great part of the time delirious. People said it was heartbreaking to hear her call her child, and raise her head and listen a whole minute at a time, then lay it wearily down again with a moan. Aunt Polly had drooped into a settled melancholy, and her gray hair had grown almost white. The village went to its rest on Tuesday night, sad and forlorn.

Away in the middle of the night a wild peal burst from the village bells, and in a moment the streets were swarming with frantic half-clad people, who shouted, "Turn out! turn out! they're found! they're found!" Tin pans and horns were added to the din, the population massed itself and moved toward the river, met the children coming in an open carriage drawn by shouting citizens, thronged around it, joined its homeward march, and swept magnificently up the main street roaring huzzah after huzzah!

The village was illuminated; nobody went to bed again; it

was the greatest night the little town had ever seen. During the first half-hour a procession of villagers filed through Judge Thatcher's house, seized the saved ones and kissed them, squeezed Mrs. Thatcher's hand, tried to speak but couldn't— and drifted out raining tears all over the place.

Aunt Polly's happiness was complete, and Mrs. Thatcher's nearly so. It would be complete, however, as soon as the messenger dispatched with the great news to the cave should get the word to her husband. Tom lay upon a sofa with an eager auditory about him and told the history of the wonderful adventure, putting in many striking additions to adorn it withal; and closed with a description of how he left Becky and went on an exploring expedition; how he followed two avenues as far as his kite-line would reach; how he followed a third to the fullest stretch of the kite-line, and was about to turn back when he glimpsed a far-off speck that looked like daylight; dropped the line and groped toward it, pushed his head and shoulders through a small hole, and saw the broad Mississippi rolling by!

And if it had only happened to be night he would not have seen that speck of daylight and would not have explored that passage any more! He told how he went back for Becky and broke the good news and she told him not to fret her with such stuff, for she was tired, and knew she was going to die, and wanted to. He described how he labored with her and convinced her; and how she almost died for joy when she had groped to where she actually saw the blue speck of daylight; how he pushed his way out at the hole and then helped her out; how they sat there and cried for gladness; how some men came along in a skiff and Tom hailed them and told them their situation and their famished condition; how the men didn't believe the wild tale at first, "because," said they, "you are five miles down the river below the valley the cave is in"—then took them aboard, rowed to a house, gave them supper, made them rest till two or three hours after dark and then brought them home.

Before day-dawn, Judge Thatcher and the handful of searchers with him were tracked out, in the cave, by the twine clews they had strung behind them, and informed of the great news.

Three days and nights of toil and hunger in the cave were not to be shaken off at once, as Tom and Becky soon discovered. They were bedridden all of Wednesday and Thursday, and seemed to grow more and more tired and worn, all the time. Tom got about, a little, on Thursday, was downtown Friday, and nearly as whole as ever Saturday; but Becky did not leave her room until Sunday, and then she looked as if she had passed through a wasting illness.

Tom learned of Huck's sickness and went to see him on Friday, but could not be admitted to the bedroom; neither could he on Saturday or Sunday. He was admitted daily after that, but was warned to keep still about his adventure and introduce no exciting topic. The Widow Douglas stayed by to see that he obeyed. At home Tom learned of the Cardiff Hill event; also that the "ragged man's" body had eventually been found in the river near the ferry-landing; he had been drowned while trying to escape, perhaps.

About a fortnight after Tom's rescue from the cave, he started off to visit Huck, who had grown plenty strong enough, now, to hear exciting talk, and Tom had some that would interest him, he thought. Judge Thatcher's house was on Tom's way, and he stopped to see Becky. The Judge and some friends set Tom to talking, and some one asked him ironically if he wouldn't like to go to the cave again. Tom said he thought he wouldn't mind it. The Judge said:

"Well, there are others just like you, Tom, I've not the least doubt. But we have taken care of that. Nobody will get lost in that cave any more."

"Why?"

"Because I had its big door sheathed with boiler iron two weeks ago, and triple-locked—and I've got the keys."

Tom turned as white as a sheet.

"What's the matter, boy! Here, run, somebody! Fetch a glass of water!"

The water was brought and thrown into Tom's face.

"Ah, now you're all right. What was the matter with you, Tom?"

"Oh, Judge, Injun Joe's in the cave!"

CHAPTER 33

The Fate of Injun Joe—Huck and Tom Compare Notes
—An Expedition to the Cave—Protection Against Ghosts
—"An Awful Snug Place"
—A Reception at the Widow Douglas's

WITHIN a few minutes the news had spread, and a dozen skiff-loads of men were on their way to McDougal's cave, and the ferryboat, well filled with passengers, soon followed. Tom Sawyer was in the skiff that bore Judge Thatcher.

When the cave door was unlocked, a sorrowful sight presented itself in the dim twilight of the place. Injun Joe lay stretched upon the ground, dead, with his face close to the crack of the door, as if his longing eyes had been fixed, to the latest moment, upon the light and the cheer of the free world outside. Tom was touched, for he knew by his own experience how this wretch had suffered. His pity was moved, but nevertheless he felt an abounding sense of relief and security, now, which revealed to him in a degree which he had not fully appreciated before how vast a weight of dread had been lying upon him since the day he lifted his voice against this bloody-minded outcast.

Injun Joe's bowie-knife lay close by, its blade broken in two. The great foundation-beam of the door had been chipped and hacked through, with tedious labor; useless labor, too, it was, for the native rock formed a sill outside it, and upon that stubborn material the knife had wrought no effect; the only damage done was to the knife itself. But if there had been no stony obstruction there the labor would have been useless still, for if the beam had been wholly cut away Injun Joe could not have squeezed his body under the door, and he knew it. So he had only hacked that place in order to be doing something—in order to pass the weary time—in order to employ his tortured faculties. Ordinarily one could find half a dozen bits of candle stuck around in the crevices of this vestibule, left there by tourists; but there were none now. The prisoner had searched them out and eaten them. He had also contrived to catch a few bats, and these, also, he had eaten, leaving only their claws. The poor unfortunate had starved to death. In one place, near at hand, a stalagmite had been slowly growing up from the ground for ages, builded by the water-drip from a stalactite overhead. The captive had broken off the stalagmite, and upon the stump had placed a stone, wherein he had scooped a shallow hollow to catch the precious drop that fell once in every three minutes with the dreary regularity of a clock-tick—a dessertspoonful once in four and twenty hours. That drop was falling when the Pyramids were new; when Troy fell; when the foundations of Rome were laid; when Christ was crucified; when the Conqueror created the British empire; when Columbus sailed; when the massacre at Lexington was "news."

It is falling now; it will still be falling when all these things shall have sunk down the afternoon of history, and the twilight of tradition, and been swallowed up in the thick night of oblivion. Has everything a purpose and a mission? Did this drop fall patiently during five thousand years to be ready for this flitting human insect's need? and has it another important object to accomplish ten thousand years to come? No matter. It is many and many a year since the hapless half-breed scooped out the stone to catch the priceless drops, but to this day the tourist stares longest at that pathetic stone and that slow-dropping water when he comes to see the wonders of McDougal's cave. Injun Joe's cup stands first in the list of the cavern's marvels; even "Aladdin's Palace" cannot rival it.

Injun Joe was buried near the mouth of the cave; and people flocked there in boats and wagons from the towns and from all the farms and hamlets for seven miles around; they brought their children, and all sorts of provisions, and confessed that they had had almost as satisfactory a time at the funeral as they could have had at the hanging.

This funeral stopped the further growth of one thing—the petition to the governor for Injun Joe's pardon. The petition had been largely signed; many tearful and eloquent meetings had been held, and a committee of sappy women been appointed to go in deep mourning and wail around the governor, and implore him to be a merciful ass and trample his duty under foot. Injun Joe was believed to have killed five citizens of the village, but what of that? If he had been Satan himself there would have been plenty of weaklings ready to scribble their names to a pardon-petition, and drip a tear on it from their permanently impaired and leaky water-works.

The morning after the funeral Tom took Huck to a private place to have an important talk. Huck had learned all about Tom's adventure from the Welshman and the Widow Douglas, by this time, but Tom said he reckoned there was one thing they had not told him; that thing was what he wanted to talk about now. Huck's face saddened. He said:

"I know what it is. You got into No. 2 and never found anything but whiskey. Nobody told me it was you; but I just knowed it must 'a' ben you, soon as I heard 'bout that whiskey business; and I knowed you hadn't got the money becuz you'd 'a' got at me some way or other and told me even if you was mum to everybody else. Tom, something's always told me we'd never get holt of that swag."

"Why, Huck, I never told on that tavern-keeper. *You* know his tavern was all right the Saturday I went to the picnic. Don't you remember you was to watch there that night?"

"Oh yes! Why, it seems 'bout a year ago. It was that very night that I follered Injun Joe to the widder's."

"YOU followed him?"

"Yes—but you keep mum. I reckon Injun Joe's left friends behind him, and I don't want 'em souring on me and doing me mean tricks. If it hadn't ben for me he'd be down in Texas now, all right."

Then Huck told his entire adventure in confidence to Tom, who had only heard of the Welshman's part of it before.

"Well," said Huck, presently, coming back to the main question, "whoever nipped the whiskey in No. 2, nipped the money, too, I reckon—anyways it's a goner for us, Tom."

"Huck, that money wasn't ever in No. 2!"

"What!" Huck searched his comrade's face keenly. "Tom, have you got on the track of that money again?"

"Huck, it's in the cave!"

Huck's eyes blazed.

"Say it again, Tom."

"The money's in the cave!"

"Tom—honest injun, now—is it fun, or earnest?"

"Earnest, Huck—just as earnest as ever I was in my life. Will you go in there with me and help get it out?"

"I bet I will! I will if it's where we can blaze our way to it and not get lost."

"Huck, we can do that without the least little bit of trouble in the world."

"Good as wheat! What makes you think the money's—"

"Huck, you just wait till we get in there. If we don't find it I'll agree to give you my drum and every thing I've got in the world. I will, by jings."

"All right—it's a whiz. When do you say?"

"Right now, if you say it. Are you strong enough?"

"Is it far in the cave? I ben on my pins a little, three or four days, now, but I can't walk more'n a mile, Tom—least I don't think I could."

"It's about five mile into there the way anybody but me would go, Huck, but there's a mighty short cut that they don't anybody but me know about. Huck, I'll take you right to it in a skiff. I'll float the skiff down there, and I'll pull it back again all by myself. You needn't ever turn your hand over."

"Less start right off, Tom."

"All right. We want some bread and meat, and our pipes, and a little bag or two, and two or three kite-strings, and some of these new-fangled things they call lucifer matches. I tell you, many's the time I wished I had some when I was in there before."

A trifle after noon the boys borrowed a small skiff from a citizen who was absent, and got under way at once. When they were several miles below "Cave Hollow," Tom said:

"Now you see this bluff here looks all alike all the way down from the cave hollow—no houses, no wood-yards, bushes all alike. But do you see that white place up yonder where there's been a landslide? Well, that's one of my marks. We'll get ashore, now."

They landed.

"Now, Huck, where we're a-standing you could touch that hole I got out of with a fishing-pole. See if you can find it."

Huck searched all the place about, and found nothing. Tom proudly marched into a thick clump of sumach bushes and said:

"Here you are! Look at it, Huck; it's the snuggest hole in this country. You just keep mum about it. All along I've been wanting to be a robber, but I knew I'd got to have a thing like this, and where to run across it was the bother. We've got it now, and we'll keep it quiet, only we'll let Joe Harper and Ben Rogers in—because of course there's got to be a Gang, or else there wouldn't be any style about it. Tom Sawyer's Gang—it sounds splendid, don't it, Huck?"

"Well, it just does, Tom. And who'll we rob?"

"Oh, most anybody. Waylay people—that's mostly the way."

"And kill them?"

"No, not always. Hive them in the cave till they raise a ransom."

"What's a ransom?"

"Money. You make them raise all they can, off'n their friends; and after you've kept them a year, if it ain't raised then you kill them. That's the general way. Only you don't kill the women. You shut up the women, but you don't kill them. They're always beautiful and rich, and awfully scared. You take their watches and things, but you always take your hat off and talk polite. They ain't anybody as polite as robbers—you'll see that in any book. Well, the women get to loving you, and after they've been in the cave a week or two weeks they stop crying and after that you couldn't get them to leave. If you drove them out they'd turn right around and come back. It's so in all the books."

"Why, it's real bully, Tom. I believe it's better'n to be a pirate."

"Yes, it's better in some ways, because it's close to home and circuses and all that."

By this time everything was ready and the boys entered the hole, Tom in the lead. They toiled their way to the farther end of the tunnel, then made their spliced kite-strings fast and moved on. A few steps brought them to the spring, and Tom felt a shudder quiver all through him. He showed Huck the fragment of candle-wick perched on a lump of clay against the wall, and described how he and Becky had watched the flame struggle and expire.

The boys began to quiet down to whispers, now, for the stillness and gloom of the place oppressed their spirits. They went on, and presently entered and followed Tom's other corridor until they reached the "jumping-off place." The candles revealed the fact that it was not really a precipice, but only a steep clay hill twenty or thirty feet high. Tom whispered:

"Now I'll show you something, Huck."

He held his candle aloft and said:

"Look as far around the corner as you can. Do you see that? There—on the big rock over yonder—done with candle-smoke."

"Tom, it's a *cross*!"

"*Now* where's your Number Two? '*Under the cross*,' hey? Right yonder's where I saw Injun Joe poke up his candle, Huck!"

Huck stared at the mystic sign awhile, and then said with a shaky voice:

"Tom, less git out of here!"

"What! and leave the treasure?"

"Yes—leave it. Injun Joe's ghost is round about there, certain."

"No it ain't, Huck, no it ain't. It would ha'nt the place where he died—away out at the mouth of the cave—five mile from here."

"No, Tom, it wouldn't. It would hang round the money. I know the ways of ghosts, and so do you."

Tom began to fear that Huck was right. Mis-givings gathered in his mind. But presently an idea occurred to him—

"Lookyhere, Huck, what fools we're making of ourselves! Injun Joe's ghost ain't a going to come around where there's a cross!"

The point was well taken. It had its effect.

"Tom, I didn't think of that. But that's so. It's luck for us, that cross is. I reckon we'll climb down there and have a hunt for that box."

Tom went first, cutting rude steps in the clay hill as he descended. Huck followed. Four avenues opened out of the small cavern which the great rock stood in. The boys examined three of them with no result. They found a small recess in the one nearest the base of the rock, with a pallet of blankets spread down in it; also an old suspender, some bacon rind, and the well-gnawed bones of two or three fowls. But there was no moneybox. The lads searched and researched this place, but in vain. Tom said:

"He said *under* the cross. Well, this comes nearest to being under the cross. It can't be under the rock itself, because that sets solid on the ground."

They searched everywhere once more, and then sat down discouraged. Huck could suggest nothing. By-and-by Tom said:

"Lookyhere, Huck, there's footprints and some candle-grease on the clay about one side of this rock, but not on the other sides. Now, what's that for? I bet you the money IS under the rock. I'm going to dig in the clay."

"That ain't no bad notion, Tom!" said Huck with animation.

Tom's "real Barlow" was out at once, and he had not dug four inches before he struck wood.

"Hey, Huck!—you hear that?"

Huck began to dig and scratch now. Some boards were soon uncovered and removed. They had concealed a natural chasm which led under the rock. Tom got into this and held his candle as far under the rock as he could, but said he could not see to the end of the rift. He proposed to explore. He stooped and passed under; the narrow way descended gradually. He followed its winding course, first to the right, then to the left, Huck at his heels. Tom turned a short curve, by-and-by, and exclaimed:

"My goodness, Huck, lookyhere!"

It was the treasure-box, sure enough, occupying a snug little cavern, along with an empty powder-keg, a couple of guns in leather cases, two or three pairs of old moccasins, a leather belt, and some other rubbish well soaked with the water-drip.

"Got it at last!" said Huck, ploughing among the tarnished coins with his hand. "My, but we're rich, Tom!"

"Huck, I always reckoned we'd get it. It's just too good to believe, but we *have* got it, sure! Say—let's not fool around here. Let's snake it out. Lemme see if I can lift the box."

It weighed about fifty pounds. Tom could lift it, after an awkward fashion, but could not carry it conveniently.

"I thought so," he said; "*they* carried it like it was heavy, that day at the ha'nted house. I noticed that. I reckon I was right to think of fetching the little bags along."

The money was soon in the bags and the boys took it up to the cross rock.

"Now less fetch the guns and things," said Huck.

"No, Huck—leave them there. They're just the tricks to have when we go to robbing. We'll keep them there all the time, and we'll hold our orgies there, too. It's an awful snug place for orgies."

"What orgies?"

"*I* dono. But robbers always have orgies, and of course we've got to have them, too. Come along, Huck, we've been in here a long time. It's getting late, I reckon. I'm hungry, too. We'll eat and smoke when we get to the skiff."

They presently emerged into the clump of sumach bushes, looked warily out, found the coast clear, and were soon lunching and smoking in the skiff. As the sun dipped toward the horizon they pushed out and got under way. Tom skimmed up the shore through the long twilight, chatting cheerily with Huck, and landed shortly after dark.

"Now, Huck," said Tom, "we'll hide the money in the loft of the widow's woodshed, and I'll come up in the morning and we'll count it and divide, and then we'll hunt up a place out in the woods for it where it will be safe. Just you lay quiet here and watch the stuff till I run and hook Benny Taylor's little wagon;

I won't be gone a minute."

He disappeared, and presently returned with the wagon, put the two small sacks into it, threw some old rags on top of them, and started off, dragging his cargo behind him. When the boys reached the Welshman's house, they stopped to rest. Just as they were about to move on, the Welshman stepped out and said:

"Hallo, who's that?"

"Huck and Tom Sawyer."

"Good! Come along with me, boys, you are keeping everybody waiting. Here—hurry up, trot ahead—I'll haul the wagon for you. Why, it's not as light as it might be. Got bricks in it?—or old metal?"

"Old metal," said Tom.

"I judged so; the boys in this town will take more trouble and fool away more time hunting up six bits' worth of old iron to sell to the foundry than they would to make twice the money at regular work. But that's human nature—hurry along, hurry along!"

The boys wanted to know what the hurry was about.

"Never mind; you'll see, when we get to the Widow Douglas."

Huck said with some apprehension—for he was long used to being falsely accused:

"Mr. Jones, *we* haven't been doing nothing."

The Welshman laughed.

"Well, I don't know, Huck, my boy. I don't know about that. Ain't you and the widow good friends?"

"Yes. Well, she's ben good friends to me, anyway."

"All right, then. What do you want to be afraid for?"

This question was not entirely answered in Huck's slow mind before he found himself pushed, along with Tom, into Mrs. Douglas' drawing-room. Mr. Jones left the wagon near the door and followed.

The place was grandly lighted, and everybody that was of any consequence in the village was there. The Thatchers were there, the Harpers, the Rogerses, Aunt Polly, Sid, Mary, the minister, the editor, and a great many more, and all dressed in their best. The widow received the boys as heartily as any one could well receive two such looking beings. They were covered with clay and candle-grease. Aunt Polly blushed crimson with humiliation, and frowned and shook her head at Tom. Nobody suffered half as much as the two boys did, however. Mr. Jones said:

"Tom wasn't at home, yet, so I gave him up; but I stumbled on him and Huck right at my door, and so I just brought them along in a hurry."

"And you did just right," said the widow. "Come with me, boys."

She took them to a bedchamber and said:

"Now wash and dress yourselves. Here are two new suits of clothes—shirts, socks, everything complete. They're Huck's— no, no thanks, Huck—Mr. Jones bought one and I the other. But they'll fit both of you. Get into them. We'll wait—come down when you are slicked up enough."

Then she left.

CHAPTER 34

Springing a Secret—Mr. Jones' Surprise a Failure

HUCK said: "Tom, we can slope, if we can find a rope. The window ain't high from the ground."

"Shucks! what do you want to slope for?"

"Well, I ain't used to that kind of a crowd. I can't stand it. I ain't going down there, Tom."

"Oh, bother! It ain't anything. I don't mind it a bit. I'll take care of you."

Sid appeared.

"Tom," said he, "auntie has been waiting for you all the afternoon. Mary got your Sunday clothes ready, and everybody's been fretting about you. Say—ain't this grease and clay, on your clothes?"

"Now, Mr. Siddy, you jist 'tend to your own business. What's all this blowout about, anyway?"

"It's one of the widow's parties that she's always having. This time it's for the Welshman and his sons, on account of that scrape they helped her out of the other night. And say—I can tell you something, if you want to know."

"Well, what?"

"Why, old Mr. Jones is going to try to spring something on the people here tonight, but I overheard him tell auntie today about it, as a secret, but I reckon it's not much of a secret now. Everybody knows—the widow, too, for all she tries to let on she don't. Mr. Jones was bound Huck should be here—couldn't get along with his grand secret without Huck, you know!"

"Secret about what, Sid?"

"About Huck tracking the robbers to the widow's. I reckon Mr. Jones was going to make a grand time over his surprise, but I bet you it will drop pretty flat."

Sid chuckled in a very contented and satisfied way.

"Sid, was it you that told?"

"Oh, never mind who it was. *Somebody* told—that's enough."

"Sid, there's only one person in this town mean enough to do that, and that's you. If you had been in Huck's place you'd 'a' sneaked down the hill and never told anybody on the robbers. You can't do any but mean things, and you can't bear to see anybody praised for doing good ones. There—no thanks, as the widow says"—and Tom cuffed Sid's ears and helped him to the door with several kicks. "Now go and tell auntie if you dare—and tomorrow you'll catch it!"

Some minutes later the widow's guests were at the supper-table, and a dozen children were propped up at little side-tables in the same room, after the fashion of that country and that day. At the proper time Mr. Jones made his little speech, in which he thanked the widow for the honor she was doing himself and his sons, but said that there was another person whose modesty—

And so forth and so on. He sprung his secret about Huck's share in the adventure in the finest dramatic manner he was master of, but the surprise it occasioned was largely counterfeit and not as clamorous and effusive as it might have been under happier circumstances. However, the widow made a pretty fair show of astonishment, and heaped so many compliments and so much gratitude upon Huck that he almost forgot the nearly intolerable discomfort of his new clothes in the entirely intolerable discomfort of being set up as a target for everybody's gaze and everybody's laudations.

The widow said she meant to give Huck a home under her

roof and have him educated; and that when she could spare the money she would start him in business in a modest way. Tom's chance was come. He said:

"Huck don't need it. Huck's rich."

Nothing but a heavy strain upon the good manners of the company kept back the due and proper complimentary laugh at this pleasant joke. But the silence was a little awkward. Tom broke it:

"Huck's got money. Maybe you don't believe it, but he's got lots of it. Oh, you needn't smile—I reckon I can show you. You just wait a minute."

Tom ran out of doors. The company looked at each other with a perplexed interest—and inquiringly at Huck, who was tongue-tied.

"Sid, what ails Tom?" said Aunt Polly. "He—well, there ain't ever any making of that boy out. I never—"

Tom entered, struggling with the weight of his sacks, and Aunt Polly did not finish her sentence. Tom poured the mass of yellow coin upon the table and said:

"There—what did I tell you? Half of it's Huck's and half of it's mine!"

The spectacle took the general breath away. All gazed, nobody spoke for a moment. Then there was a unanimous call for an explanation. Tom said he could furnish it, and he did. The tale was long, but brimful of interest. There was scarcely an interruption from any one to break the charm of its flow. When he had finished, Mr. Jones said:

"I thought I had fixed up a little surprise for this occasion, but it don't amount to anything now. This one makes it sing mighty small, I'm willing to allow."

The money was counted. The sum amounted to a little over twelve thousand dollars. It was more than any one present had ever seen at one time before, though several persons were there who were worth considerably more than that in property.

CHAPTER 35

A New Order of Things—Poor Huck
—New Adventures Planned

THE reader may rest satisfied that Tom's and Huck's windfall made a mighty stir in the poor little village of St. Petersburg. So vast a sum, all in actual cash, seemed next to incredible. It was talked about, gloated over, glorified, until the reason of many of the citizens tottered under the strain of the unhealthy excitement. Every "haunted" house in St. Petersburg and the neighboring villages was dissected, plank by plank, and its foundations dug up and ransacked for hidden treasure—and not by boys, but men—pretty grave, unromantic men, too, some of them. Wherever Tom and Huck appeared they were courted, admired, stared at. The boys were not able to remember that their remarks had possessed weight before; but now their sayings were treasured and repeated; everything they did seemed somehow to be regarded as remarkable; they had evidently lost the power of doing and saying commonplace things; moreover, their past history was raked up and discovered to bear marks of conspicuous originality. The village paper published biographical sketches of the boys.

The Widow Douglas put Huck's money out at six per cent., and Judge Thatcher did the same with Tom's at Aunt Polly's request. Each lad had an income, now, that was simply prodigious—a dollar for every weekday in the year and half of the Sundays. It was just what the minister got—no, it was what he was promised—he generally couldn't collect it. A dollar and a quarter a week would board, lodge, and school a boy in those old simple days—and clothe him and wash him, too, for that matter.

Judge Thatcher had conceived a great opinion of Tom. He said that no commonplace boy would ever have got his daughter out of the cave. When Becky told her father, in strict confidence, how Tom had taken her whipping at school, the Judge was visibly moved; and when she pleaded grace for the mighty lie which Tom had told in order to shift that whipping from her shoulders to his own, the Judge said with a fine outburst that it was a noble, a generous, a magnanimous lie—a lie that was worthy to hold up its head and march down through history breast to breast with George Washington's lauded Truth about the hatchet! Becky thought her father had never looked so tall and so superb as when he walked the floor and stamped his foot and said that. She went straight off and told Tom about it.

Judge Thatcher hoped to see Tom a great lawyer or a great soldier some day. He said he meant to look to it that Tom should be admitted to the National Military Academy and afterward trained in the best law school in the country, in order that he might be ready for either career or both.

Huck Finn's wealth and the fact that he was now under the Widow Douglas' protection introduced him into society—no, dragged him into it, hurled him into it—and his sufferings were almost more than he could bear. The widow's servants kept him clean and neat, combed and brushed, and they bedded him nightly in unsympathetic sheets that had not one little spot or stain which he could press to his heart and know for a friend. He had to eat with a knife and fork; he had to use napkin, cup, and plate; he had to learn his book, he had to go to church; he had to talk so properly that speech was become insipid in his mouth; whithersoever he turned, the bars and shackles of civilization shut him in and bound him hand and foot.

He bravely bore his miseries three weeks, and then one day turned up missing. For forty-eight hours the widow hunted for him everywhere in great distress. The public were profoundly concerned; they searched high and low, they dragged the river for his body. Early the third morning Tom Sawyer wisely went poking among some old empty hogsheads down behind the abandoned slaughter-house, and in one of them he found the refugee. Huck had slept there; he had just breakfasted upon some stolen odds and ends of food, and was lying off, now, in comfort, with his pipe. He was unkempt, uncombed, and clad in the same old ruin of rags that had made him picturesque in the days when he was free and happy. Tom routed him out, told him the trouble he had been causing, and urged him to go home. Huck's face lost its tranquil content, and took a melancholy cast. He said:

"Don't talk about it, Tom. I've tried it, and it don't work; it don't work, Tom. It ain't for me; I ain't used to it. The widder's good to me, and friendly; but I can't stand them ways. She makes me get up just at the same time every morning; she makes me wash, they comb me all to thunder; she won't let me sleep in the woodshed; I got to wear them blamed clothes that just smothers me, Tom; they don't seem to any air git through 'em, somehow; and they're so rotten nice that I can't set down, nor lay down, nor roll around anywher's; I hain't slid on a cellar-door for—well, it 'pears to be years; I got to go to church and sweat and sweat—I hate them ornery sermons! I can't ketch a fly in there, I can't chaw. I got to wear shoes all Sunday. The widder eats by a bell; she goes to bed by a bell; she gits up by a bell—everything's so awful reg'lar a body can't stand it."

"Well, everybody does that way, Huck."

"Tom, it don't make no difference. I ain't everybody, and I can't *stand* it. It's awful to be tied up so. And grub comes too easy—I don't take no interest in vittles, that way. I got to ask to go a-fishing; I got to ask to go in a-swimming—dern'd if I hain't got to ask to do everything. Well, I'd got to talk so nice it wasn't no comfort—I'd got to go up in the attic and rip out awhile, every day, to git a taste in my mouth, or I'd a died, Tom. The widder wouldn't let me smoke; she wouldn't let me yell, she wouldn't let me gape, nor stretch, nor scratch, before folks—" [Then with a spasm of special irritation and injury]—"And dad fetch it, she prayed all the time! I never *see* such a woman! I *had* to shove, Tom—I just had to. And besides, that school's going to open, and I'd a had to go to it—well, I wouldn't stand *that,* Tom. Looky-here, Tom, being rich ain't what it's cracked up to be. It's just worry and worry, and sweat and sweat, and a-wishing you was dead all the time. Now these clothes suits me, and this bar'l suits me, and I ain't ever going to shake 'em any more. Tom, I wouldn't ever got into all this trouble if it hadn't 'a' ben for that money; now you just take my sheer of it along with your'n, and gimme a ten-center sometimes—not many times, becuz I don't give a dern for a thing 'thout it's tollable hard to git—and you go and beg off for me with the widder."

"Oh, Huck, you know I can't do that. 'Tain't fair; and besides if you'll try this thing just a while longer you'll come to like it."

"Like it! Yes—the way I'd like a hot stove if I was to set on it long enough. No, Tom, I won't be rich, and I won't live in them cussed smothery houses. I like the woods, and the river, and hogsheads, and I'll stick to 'em, too. Blame it all! just as we'd got guns, and a cave, and all just fixed to rob, here this dern foolishness has got to come up and spile it all!"

Tom saw his opportunity—

"Lookyhere, Huck, being rich ain't going to keep me back from turning robber."

"No! Oh, good-licks; are you in real dead-wood earnest, Tom?"

"Just as dead earnest as I'm sitting here. But Huck, we can't let you into the gang if you ain't respectable, you know."

Huck's joy was quenched.

"Can't let me in, Tom? Didn't you let me go for a pirate?"

"Yes, but that's different. A robber is more high-toned than what a pirate is—as a general thing. In most countries they're awful high up in the nobility—dukes and such."

"Now, Tom, hain't you always ben friendly to me? You wouldn't shet me out, would you, Tom? You wouldn't do that, now, *would* you, Tom?"

"Huck, I wouldn't want to, and I *don't* want to—but what would people say? Why, they'd say, 'Mph! Tom Sawyer's Gang! pretty low characters in it!' They'd mean you, Huck. You wouldn't like that, and I wouldn't."

Huck was silent for some time, engaged in a mental struggle. Finally he said:

"Well, I'll go back to the widder for a month and tackle it and see if I can come to stand it, if you'll let me b'long to the gang, Tom."

"All right, Huck, it's a whiz! Come along, old chap, and I'll ask the widow to let up on you a little, Huck."

"Will you, Tom—now will you? That's good. If she'll let up on some of the roughest things, I'll smoke private and cuss private, and crowd through or bust. When you going to start the gang and turn robbers?"

"Oh, right off. We'll get the boys together and have the initiation tonight, maybe."

"Have the which?"

"Have the initiation."

"What's that?"

"It's to swear to stand by one another, and never tell the gang's secrets, even if you're chopped all to flinders, and kill anybody and all his family that hurts one of the gang."

"That's gay—that's mighty gay, Tom, I tell you."

"Well, I bet it is. And all that swearing's got to be done at midnight, in the lonesomest, awfulest place you can find—a ha'nted house is the best, but they're all ripped up now."

"Well, midnight's good, anyway, Tom."

"Yes, so it is. And you've got to swear on a coffin, and sign it with blood."

"Now, that's something *like*! Why, it's a million times bullier than pirating. I'll stick to the widder till I rot, Tom; and if I git to be a reg'lar ripper of a robber, and everybody talking 'bout it, I reckon she'll be proud she snaked me in out of the wet."

CONCLUSION

SO endeth this chronicle. It being strictly a history of a *boy*, it must stop here; the story could not go much further without becoming the history of a *man*. When one writes a novel about grown people, he knows exactly where to stop—that is, with a marriage; but when he writes of juveniles, he must stop where he best can.

Most of the characters that perform in this book still live, and are prosperous and happy. Some day it may seem worth while to take up the story of the younger ones again and see what sort of men and women they turned out to be; therefore it will be wisest not to reveal any of that part of their lives at present.

Treasure Island

Treasure Island

Robert Louis Stevenson

Trans
Atlantic
Press

This is a Transatlantic Press book
This edition published in 2012

Transatlantic Press
Sky House, Raans Road, Amersham, Bucks, HP6 6JQ, UK

A catalogue record is available for this book from the British Library

ISBN 978-1-908533-36-4

Printed and bound by CPI Group (UK) Ltd, Croydon, CR0 4YY

ROBERT LOUIS STEVENSON

Robert Louis Stevenson was born in Edinburgh in 1850, the son of an engineer who specialized in the field of lighthouse construction. He flirted briefly with the idea of following in his father's footsteps, embarking on an engineering degree in his hometown university. But he had neither the constitution —he was dogged by ill health throughout his life—nor the inclination to pursue that course and instead became a law student. His roving spirit and desire to write put the brakes on a legal career before it started. Having got into print in magazines and periodicals, Stevenson published *An Inland Voyage* (1878) and *Travels with a Donkey in the Cévennes* (1879), accounts of his travels through France and Belgium. *Treasure Island* (1883) brought him fame, and his later novels, such as *Kidnapped* (1886), its sequel *Catriona* (1893) and *The Master of Ballantrae* (1889) established his reputation in the historical adventure genre. He provided thrills of a different kind with *The Strange Case of Dr. Jekyll and Mr. Hyde*, which ranks among the best in the Gothic literature tradition. In 1888 he set sail for the South Seas with his family, settling in Samoa, where he spent his final years. He became a great advocate for the islanders, who in turn had great affection for the man they called "Tusitala"—"Teller of Tales". Stevenson died from a cerebral haemorrhage in 1894, leaving an unfinished novel, *Weir of Hermiston*, which was published posthumously.

TREASURE ISLAND

"'They got the money, you say? Well, then, Hawkins, what in fortune were they after? More money, I suppose?'
'No, sir; not money, I think,' replied I. 'In fact, sir, I believe I have the thing in my breast pocket…'"

Drunken old sea dog Billy Bones drops anchor at the Admiral Benbow, an inn run by Jim Hawkins's mother and father. When Billy's former shipmates Black Dog and Blind Pew track him down to the inn, Jim learns that they were once crewmen to notorious pirate Captain Flint. The newcomers aren't interested in talking over old times on the high seas; it's Flint's treasure map in Billy's possession they're after. The pirate gang descend on the inn to find Billy dead from a seizure, but Jim has beaten them to the map. The race is on to reach Treasure Island and unearth the booty. Jim secures the help of Squire Trelawney and Doctor Livesey and, with a crew including one-legged sea cook Long John Silver, they set off aboard the *Hispaniola* to find the place where X marks the spot. But danger and double-dealing lurk at every turn…

Robert Louis Stevenson's swashbuckling adventure has captivated readers of all ages since it first appeared in book form in 1883, setting the standard for all the pirate and buried-treasure stories that followed.

CONTENTS

PART ONE

THE OLD
BUCCANEER

CHAPTER 1

The Old Sea-dog at the "Admiral Benbow"

SQUIRE TRELAWNEY, Dr. Livesey, and the rest of these gentlemen having asked me to write down the whole particulars about Treasure Island, from the beginning to the end, keeping nothing back but the bearings of the island, and that only because there is still treasure not yet lifted, I take up my pen in the year of grace 17— and go back to the time when my father kept the "Admiral Benbow" inn and the brown old seaman with the sabre cut first took up his lodging under our roof.

I remember him as if it were yesterday, as he came plodding to the inn door, his sea-chest following behind him in a hand-barrow—a tall, strong, heavy, nut-brown man, his tarry pigtail falling over the shoulder of his soiled blue coat, his hands ragged and scarred, with black, broken nails, and the sabre cut across one cheek, a dirty, livid white. I remember him looking round the cover and whistling to himself as he did so, and then breaking out in that old sea-song that he sang so often afterwards:

"Fifteen men on the dead man's chest—
Yo-ho-ho, and a bottle of rum!"

in the high, old tottering voice that seemed to have been tuned and broken at the capstan bars. Then he rapped on the door with a bit of stick like a handspike that he carried, and when my father appeared, called roughly for a glass of rum. This, when it was brought to him, he drank slowly, like a connoisseur, lingering on the taste and still looking about him at the cliffs and up at our signboard.

"This is a handy cove," says he at length; "and a pleasant sittyated grog-shop. Much company, mate?"

My father told him no, very little company, the more was the pity.

"Well, then," said he, "this is the berth for me. Here you, matey," he cried to the man who trundled the barrow; "bring up alongside and help up my chest. I'll stay here a bit," he continued. "I'm a plain man; rum and bacon and eggs is what I want, and that head up there for to watch ships off. What you mought call me? You mought call me captain. Oh, I see what you're at—there"; and he threw down three or four gold pieces on the threshold. "You can tell me when I've worked through that," says he, looking as fierce as a commander.

And indeed bad as his clothes were and coarsely as he spoke, he had none of the appearance of a man who sailed before the mast, but seemed like a mate or skipper accustomed to be obeyed or to strike. The man who came with the barrow told us the mail had set him down the morning before at the Royal George, that he had inquired what inns there were along the coast, and hearing ours well spoken of, I suppose, and described as lonely, had chosen it from the others for his place of residence. And that was all we could learn of our guest.

He was a very silent man by custom. All day he hung round the cove or upon the cliffs with a brass telescope; all evening he sat in a corner of the parlour next the fire and drank rum and water very strong. Mostly he would not speak when spoken to, only look up sudden and fierce and blow through his nose like a fog-horn; and we and the people who came about our house soon learned to let him be. Every day when he came back from his stroll he would ask if any seafaring men had gone by along the road. At first we thought it was the want of company of his own kind that made him ask this question, but at last we began to see he was desirous to avoid them. When a seaman did put up at the "Admiral Benbow" (as now and then some did, making by the coast road for Bristol) he would look in at him through the curtained door before he entered the parlour; and he was always sure to be as silent as a mouse when any such was present. For me, at least, there was no secret about the matter, for I was, in a way, a sharer in his alarms. He had taken me aside one day and promised me a silver fourpenny on the first of every month if I would only keep my "weather-eye open for a seafaring man with one leg" and let him know the moment he appeared. Often enough when the first of the month came round and I applied to him for my wage, he would only blow through his nose at me and stare me down, but before the week was out he was sure to think better of it, bring me my four-penny piece, and repeat his orders to look out for "the seafaring man with one leg."

How that personage haunted my dreams, I need scarcely tell you. On stormy nights, when the wind shook the four corners of the house and the surf roared along the cove and up the cliffs, I would see him in a thousand forms, and with a thousand diabolical expressions. Now the leg would be cut off at the knee, now at the hip; now he was a monstrous kind of a creature who had never had but the one leg, and that in the middle of his body. To see him leap and run and pursue me over hedge and ditch was the worst of nightmares. And altogether I paid pretty dear for my monthly fourpenny piece, in the shape of these abominable fancies.

But though I was so terrified by the idea of the seafaring man with one leg, I was far less afraid of the captain himself than anybody else who knew him. There were nights when he took a deal more rum and water than his head would carry; and then he would sometimes sit and sing his wicked, old, wild sea-songs, minding nobody; but sometimes he would call for glasses round and force all the trembling company to listen to his stories or bear a chorus to his singing. Often I have heard the house shaking with "Yo-ho-ho, and a bottle of rum," all the neighbours joining in for dear life, with the fear of death upon them, and each singing louder than the other to avoid remark. For in these fits he was the most overriding companion ever known; he would slap his hand on the table for silence all round; he would fly up in a passion of anger at a question, or sometimes because none was put, and so he judged the company was not following his story. Nor would he allow anyone to leave the inn till he had drunk himself sleepy and reeled off to bed.

His stories were what frightened people worst of all. Dreadful stories they were—about hanging, and walking the plank, and storms at sea, and the Dry Tortugas, and wild deeds and places on the Spanish Main. By his own account he must have lived his life among some of the wickedest men that God ever allowed upon the sea, and the language in which he told these stories shocked our plain country people almost as much as the crimes that he described. My father was always saying the inn would be ruined, for people would soon cease coming there to be tyrannized over and put down, and sent shivering to their beds; but I really believe his presence did us good. People were frightened at the time, but on looking back they rather liked it; it was a fine excitement in a quiet country life, and there was even a party of the younger men who pretended to admire him, calling him a "true sea-dog" and a "real old salt" and such like names, and saying there was the sort of man that made England terrible at sea.

In one way, indeed, he bade fair to ruin us, for he kept on staying week after week, and at last month after month, so that all the money had been long exhausted, and still my father never plucked up the heart to insist on having more. If ever he mentioned it, the captain blew through his nose so loudly that you might say he roared, and stared my poor father out of the room. I have seen him wringing his hands after such a rebuff, and I am sure the annoyance and the terror he lived in must have greatly hastened his early and unhappy death.

All the time he lived with us the captain made no change whatever in his dress but to buy some stockings from a hawker. One of the cocks of his hat having fallen down, he let it hang from that day forth, though it was a great annoyance when it blew. I remember the appearance of his coat, which he patched himself upstairs in his room, and which, before the end, was nothing but patches. He never wrote or received a letter, and he never spoke with any but the neighbours, and with these, for the most part, only when drunk on rum. The great sea-chest none of us had ever seen open.

He was only once crossed, and that was towards the end, when my poor father was far gone in a decline that took him off. Dr. Livesey came late one afternoon to see the patient, took a bit of dinner from my mother, and went into the parlour to smoke a pipe until his horse should come down from the hamlet, for we had no stabling at the old Benbow. I followed him in, and I remember observing the contrast the neat, bright doctor, with his powder as white as snow and his bright, black eyes and pleasant manners, made with the coltish country folk, and above all, with that filthy, heavy, bleared scarecrow of a pirate of ours, sitting, far gone in rum, with his arms on the table. Suddenly he—the captain, that is—began to pipe up his eternal song:

> "Fifteen men on the dead man's chest—
>   Yo-ho-ho, and a bottle of rum!
> Drink and the devil had done for the rest—
>   Yo-ho-ho, and a bottle of rum!"

At first I had supposed "the dead man's chest" to be that identical big box of his upstairs in the front room, and the thought had been mingled in my nightmares with that of the one-legged seafaring man. But by this time we had all long ceased to pay any particular notice to the song; it was new, that night, to nobody but Dr. Livesey, and on him I observed it did not produce an agreeable effect, for he looked up for a moment quite angrily before he went on with his talk to old Taylor, the gardener, on a new cure for the rheumatics. In the meantime, the captain gradually brightened up at his own music, and at last flapped his hand upon the table before him in a way we all knew to mean silence. The voices stopped at once, all but Dr. Livesey's; he went on as before speaking clear and kind and drawing briskly at his pipe between every word or two. The captain glared at him for a while, flapped his hand again, glared still harder, and at last broke out with a villainous, low oath, "Silence, there, between decks!"

"Were you addressing me, sir?" says the doctor; and when the ruffian had told him, with another oath, that this was so, "I have only one thing to say to you, sir," replies the doctor, "that if you keep on drinking rum, the world will soon be quit of a very dirty scoundrel!"

The old fellow's fury was awful. He sprang to his feet, drew and opened a sailor's clasp-knife, and balancing it open on the palm of his hand, threatened to pin the doctor to the wall.

The doctor never so much as moved. He spoke to him as before, over his shoulder and in the same tone of voice, rather high, so that all the room might hear, but perfectly calm and steady:

"If you do not put that knife this instant in your pocket, I promise, upon my honour, you shall hang at the next assizes."

Then followed a battle of looks between them, but the captain soon knuckled under, put up his weapon, and resumed his seat, grumbling like a beaten dog.

"And now, sir," continued the doctor, "since I now know there's such a fellow in my district, you may count I'll have an eye upon you day and night. I'm not a doctor only; I'm a magistrate; and if I catch a breath of complaint against you, if it's only for a piece of incivility like tonight's, I'll take effectual means to have you hunted down and routed out of this. Let that suffice."

Soon after, Dr. Livesey's horse came to the door and he rode away, but the captain held his peace that evening, and for many evenings to come.

CHAPTER 2

Black Dog Appears and Disappears

IT was not very long after this that there occurred the first of the mysterious events that rid us at last of the captain, though not, as you will see, of his affairs. It was a bitter cold winter, with long, hard frosts and heavy gales; and it was plain from the first that my poor father was little likely to see the spring. He sank daily, and my mother and I had all the inn upon our hands, and were kept busy enough without paying much regard to our unpleasant guest.

It was one January morning, very early—a pinching, frosty morning—the cove all grey with hoar-frost, the ripple lapping softly on the stones, the sun still low and only touching the hilltops and shining far to seaward. The captain had risen earlier than usual and set out down the beach, his cutlass swinging under the broad skirts of the old blue coat, his brass telescope under his arm, his hat tilted back upon his head. I remember his breath hanging like smoke in his wake as he strode off, and the last sound I heard of him as he turned the big rock was a loud snort of indignation, as though his mind was still running upon Dr. Livesey.

Well, mother was upstairs with father and I was laying the breakfast-table against the captain's return when the parlour door opened and a man stepped in on whom I had never set my eyes before. He was a pale, tallowy creature, wanting two fingers of the left hand, and though he wore a cutlass, he did not look much like a fighter. I had always my eye open for seafaring men, with one leg or two, and I remember this one puzzled me. He was not sailorly, and yet he had a smack of the sea about him too.

I asked him what was for his service, and he said he would take rum; but as I was going out of the room to fetch it, he sat down upon a table and motioned me to draw near. I paused where I was, with my napkin in my hand.

"Come here, sonny," says he. "Come nearer here."

I took a step nearer.

"Is this here table for my mate Bill?" he asked with a kind of leer.

I told him I did not know his mate Bill, and this was for a person who stayed in our house whom we called the captain.

"Well," said he, "my mate Bill would be called the captain, as like as not. He has a cut on one cheek and a mighty pleasant way with him, particularly in drink, has my mate Bill. We'll put it, for argument like, that your captain has a cut on one cheek—and we'll put it, if you like, that that cheek's the right one. Ah, well! I told you. Now, is my mate Bill in this here house?"

I told him he was out walking.

"Which way, sonny? Which way is he gone?"

And when I had pointed out the rock and told him how the captain was likely to return, and how soon, and answered a few other questions, "Ah," said he, "this'll be as good as drink to my mate Bill."

The expression of his face as he said these words was not at all pleasant, and I had my own reasons for thinking that the stranger was mistaken, even supposing he meant what he said. But it was no affair of mine, I thought; and besides, it was difficult to know what to do. The stranger kept hanging about just inside the inn door, peering round the corner like a cat waiting for a mouse. Once I stepped out myself into the road, but he immediately called me back, and as I did not obey quick enough for his fancy, a most horrible change came over his tallowy face, and he ordered me in with an oath that made me jump. As soon as I was back again he returned to his former manner, half fawning, half sneering, patted me on the shoulder, told me I was a good boy and he had taken quite a fancy to me. "I have a son of my own," said he, "as like you as two blocks, and he's all the pride of my 'art. But the great thing for boys is discipline, sonny—discipline. Now, if you had sailed along of Bill, you wouldn't have stood there to be spoke to twice—not you. That was never Bill's way, nor the way of sich as sailed with him. And here, sure enough, is my mate Bill, with a spy-glass under his arm, bless his old 'art, to be sure. You and me'll just go back into the parlour, sonny, and get behind the door, and we'll give Bill a little surprise—bless his 'art, I say again."

So saying, the stranger backed along with me into the parlour and put me behind him in the corner so that we were both hidden by the open door. I was very uneasy and alarmed, as you may fancy, and it rather added to my fears to observe that the stranger was certainly frightened himself. He cleared the hilt of his cutlass and loosened the blade in the sheath; and all the time we were waiting there he kept swallowing as if he felt what we used to call a lump in the throat.

At last in strode the captain, slammed the door behind him, without looking to the right or left, and marched straight across the room to where his breakfast awaited him.

"Bill," said the stranger in a voice that I thought he had tried to make bold and big.

The captain spun round on his heel and fronted us; all the brown had gone out of his face, and even his nose was blue; he had the look of a man who sees a ghost, or the evil one, or something worse, if anything can be; and upon my word, I felt sorry to see him all in a moment turn so old and sick.

"Come, Bill, you know me; you know an old shipmate, Bill, surely," said the stranger.

The captain made a sort of gasp.

"Black Dog!" said he.

"And who else?" returned the other, getting more at his ease. "Black Dog as ever was, come for to see his old shipmate Billy, at the "Admiral Benbow" inn. Ah, Bill, Bill, we have seen a sight of times, us two, since I lost them two talons," holding up his mutilated hand.

"Now, look here," said the captain; "you've run me down; here I am; well, then, speak up; what is it?"

"That's you, Bill," returned Black Dog, "you're in the right of it, Billy. I'll have a glass of rum from this dear child here, as I've took such a liking to; and we'll sit down, if you please, and talk square, like old shipmates."

When I returned with the rum, they were already seated on either side of the captain's breakfast-table—Black Dog next to the door and sitting sideways so as to have one eye on his old shipmate and one, as I thought, on his retreat.

He bade me go and leave the door wide open. "None of your keyholes for me, sonny," he said; and I left them together and retired into the bar.

For a long time, though I certainly did my best to listen, I could hear nothing but a low gattling; but at last the voices began to grow higher, and I could pick up a word or two, mostly oaths, from the captain.

"No, no, no, no; and an end of it!" he cried once. And again, "If it comes to swinging, swing all, say I."

Then all of a sudden there was a tremendous explosion of oaths and other noises—the chair and table went over in a lump, a clash of steel followed, and then a cry of pain, and the next instant I saw Black Dog in full flight, and the captain hotly pursuing, both with drawn cutlasses, and the former streaming blood from the left shoulder. Just at the door the captain aimed at the fugitive one last tremendous cut, which would certainly have split him to the chine had it not been intercepted by our big signboard of "Admiral Benbow". You may see the notch on the lower side of the frame to this day.

That blow was the last of the battle. Once out upon the road, Black Dog, in spite of his wound, showed a wonderful clean pair of heels and disappeared over the edge of the hill in half a minute. The captain, for his part, stood staring at the signboard like a bewildered man. Then he passed his hand over his eyes several times and at last turned back into the house.

"Jim," says he, "rum"; and as he spoke, he reeled a little, and caught himself with one hand against the wall.

"Are you hurt?" cried I.

"Rum," he repeated. "I must get away from here. Rum! Rum!"

I ran to fetch it, but I was quite unsteadied by all that had fallen out, and I broke one glass and fouled the tap, and while I was still getting in my own way, I heard a loud fall in the parlour, and running in, beheld the captain lying full length upon the floor. At the same instant my mother, alarmed by the cries and fighting, came running downstairs to help me. Between us we raised his head. He was breathing very loud and hard, but his eyes were closed and his face a horrible colour.

"Dear, deary me," cried my mother, "what a disgrace upon the house! And your poor father sick!"

In the meantime, we had no idea what to do to help the captain, nor any other thought but that he had got his death-hurt in the scuffle with the stranger. I got the rum, to be sure, and tried to put it down his throat, but his teeth were tightly shut and his jaws as strong as iron. It was a happy relief for us when the door opened and Doctor Livesey came in, on his visit to my father.

"Oh, doctor," we cried, "what shall we do? Where is he wounded?"

"Wounded? A fiddle-stick's end!" said the doctor. "No more wounded than you or I. The man has had a stroke, as

I warned him. Now, Mrs. Hawkins, just you run upstairs to your husband and tell him, if possible, nothing about it. For my part, I must do my best to save this fellow's trebly worthless life; Jim, you get me a basin."

When I got back with the basin, the doctor had already ripped up the captain's sleeve and exposed his great sinewy arm. It was tattooed in several places. "Here's luck," "A fair wind," and "Billy Bones his fancy," were very neatly and clearly executed on the forearm; and up near the shoulder there was a sketch of a gallows and a man hanging from it—done, as I thought, with great spirit.

"Prophetic," said the doctor, touching this picture with his finger. "And now, Master Billy Bones, if that be your name, we'll have a look at the colour of your blood. Jim," he said, "are you afraid of blood?"

"No, sir," said I.

"Well, then," said he, "you hold the basin"; and with that he took his lancet and opened a vein.

A great deal of blood was taken before the captain opened his eyes and looked mistily about him. First he recognized the doctor with an unmistakable frown; then his glance fell upon me, and he looked relieved. But suddenly his colour changed, and he tried to raise himself, crying,

"Where's Black Dog?"

"There is no Black Dog here," said the doctor, "except what you have on your own back. You have been drinking rum; you have had a stroke, precisely as I told you; and I have just, very much against my own will, dragged you headforemost out of the grave. Now, Mr. Bones—"

"That's not my name," he interrupted.

"Much I care," returned the doctor. "It's the name of a buccaneer of my acquaintance; and I call you by it for the sake of shortness, and what I have to say to you is this; one glass of rum won't kill you, but if you take one you'll take another and another, and I stake my wig if you don't break off short, you'll die—do you understand that?—die, and go to your own place, like the man in the Bible. Come, now, make an effort. I'll help you to your bed for once."

Between us, with much trouble, we managed to hoist him upstairs, and laid him on his bed, where his head fell back on the pillow as if he were almost fainting.

"Now, mind you," said the doctor, "I clear my conscience—the name of rum for you is death."

And with that he went off to see my father, taking me with him by the arm.

"This is nothing," he said as soon as he had closed the door. "I have drawn blood enough to keep him quiet awhile; he should lie for a week where he is—that is the best thing for him and you; but another stroke would settle him."

CHAPTER 3

The Black Spot

ABOUT noon I stopped at the captain's door with some cooling drinks and medicines. He was lying very much as we had left him, only a little higher, and he seemed both weak and excited.

"Jim," he said, "you're the only one here that's worth anything, and you know I've been always good to you. Never a month but I've given you a silver fourpenny for yourself. And now you see, mate, I'm pretty low, and deserted by all; and Jim, you'll bring me one noggin of rum, now, won't you, matey?"

"The doctor—" I began.

But he broke in cursing the doctor, in a feeble voice but heartily. "Doctors is all swabs," he said; "and that doctor there, why, what do he know about seafaring men? I been in places hot as pitch, and mates dropping round with Yellow Jack, and the blessed land a-heaving like the sea with earthquakes— what to the doctor know of lands like that?—and I lived on rum, I tell you. It's been meat and drink, and man and wife, to me; and if I'm not to have my rum now I'm a poor old hulk on a lee shore, my blood'll be on you, Jim, and that doctor swab"; and he ran on again for a while with curses. "Look, Jim, how my fingers fidges," he continued in the pleading tone. "I can't keep 'em still, not I. I haven't had a drop this blessed day. That doctor's a fool, I tell you. If I don't have a drain o' rum, Jim, I'll have the horrors; I seen some on 'em already. I seen old Flint in the corner there, behind you; as plain as print, I seen him;

and if I get the horrors, I'm a man that has lived rough, and I'll raise Cain. Your doctor hisself said one glass wouldn't hurt me. I'll give you a golden guinea for a noggin, Jim."

He was growing more and more excited, and this alarmed me for my father, who was very low that day and needed quiet; besides, I was reassured by the doctor's words, now quoted to me, and rather offended by the offer of a bribe.

"I want none of your money," said I, "but what you owe my father. I'll get you one glass, and no more."

When I brought it to him, he seized it greedily and drank it out.

"Aye, aye," said he, "that's some better, sure enough. And now, matey, did that doctor say how long I was to lie here in this old berth?"

"A week at least," said I.

"Thunder!" he cried. "A week! I can't do that; they'd have the black spot on me by then. The lubbers is going about to get the wind of me this blessed moment; lubbers as couldn't keep what they got, and want to nail what is another's. Is that seamanly behaviour, now, I want to know? But I'm a saving soul. I never wasted good money of mine, nor lost it neither; and I'll trick 'em again. I'm not afraid on 'em. I'll shake out another reef, matey, and daddle 'em again."

As he was thus speaking, he had risen from bed with great difficulty, holding to my shoulder with a grip that almost made me cry out, and moving his legs like so much dead weight. His words, spirited as they were in meaning, contrasted sadly with the weakness of the voice in which they were uttered. He paused when he had got into a sitting position on the edge.

"That doctor's done me," he murmured. "My ears is singing. Lay me back."

Before I could do much to help him he had fallen back again to his former place, where he lay for a while silent.

"Jim," he said at length, "you saw that seafaring man today?"

"Black Dog?" I asked.

"Ah! Black Dog," says he. "*He's* a bad un; but there's worse that put him on. Now, if I can't get away nohow, and they tip me the black spot, mind you, it's my old sea-chest they're after; you get on a horse—you can, can't you? Well, then, you get on a horse, and go to—well, yes, I will!—to that eternal doctor swab, and tell him to pipe all hands—magistrates and sich— and he'll lay 'em aboard at the "Admiral Benbow"—all old Flint's crew, man and boy, all on 'em that's left. I was first mate, I was, old Flint's first mate, and I'm the on'y one as knows the place. He gave it me at Savannah, when he lay a-dying, like as if I was to now, you see. But you won't peach unless they get the black spot on me, or unless you see that Black Dog again or a seafaring man with one leg, Jim—him above all."

"But what is the black spot, captain?" I asked.

"That's a summons, mate. I'll tell you if they get that. But you keep your weather-eye open, Jim, and I'll share with you equals, upon my honour."

He wandered a little longer, his voice growing weaker; but soon after I had given him his medicine, which he took like a child, with the remark, "If ever a seaman wanted drugs, it's me," he fell at last into a heavy, swoon-like sleep, in which I left him. What I should have done had all gone well I do not know. Probably I should have told the whole story to the doctor, for I was in mortal fear lest the captain should repent of his confessions and make an end of me. But as things fell out, my poor father died quite suddenly that evening, which put all other matters on one side. Our natural distress, the visits of the neighbours, the arranging of the funeral, and all the work of the inn to be carried on in the meanwhile kept me so busy that I had scarcely time to think of the captain, far less to be afraid of him.

He got downstairs next morning, to be sure, and had his meals as usual, though he ate little and had more, I am afraid, than his usual supply of rum, for he helped himself out of the bar, scowling and blowing through his nose, and no one dared to cross him. On the night before the funeral he was as drunk as ever; and it was shocking, in that house of mourning, to hear him singing away at his ugly old sea-song; but weak as he was, we were all in the fear of death for him, and the doctor was suddenly taken up with a case many miles away and was never near the house after my father's death. I have said the captain was weak, and indeed he seemed rather to grow weaker than regain his strength. He clambered up and down stairs, and went from the parlour to the bar and back again, and sometimes put his nose out of doors to smell the sea, holding on to the walls as he went for support and breathing hard and fast like a man on a steep mountain. He never particularly addressed me, and it is my belief he had as good as forgotten his confidences; but his temper was more flighty, and allowing for his bodily weakness, more violent than ever. He had an alarming way now when he was drunk of drawing his cutlass and laying it bare before him on the table. But with all that, he minded people less and seemed shut up in his own thoughts and rather wandering. Once, for instance, to our extreme wonder, he piped up to a different air, a kind of country love-song that he must have learned in his youth before he had begun to follow the sea.

So things passed until, the day after the funeral, and about three o'clock of a bitter, foggy, frosty afternoon, I was standing at the door for a moment, full of sad thoughts about my father, when I saw someone drawing slowly near along the road. He was plainly blind, for he tapped before him with a stick and wore a great green shade over his eyes and nose; and he was hunched, as if with age or weakness, and wore a huge old tattered sea-cloak with a hood that made him appear positively deformed. I never saw in my life a more dreadful-looking figure. He stopped a little from the inn, and raising his voice in an odd sing-song, addressed the air in front of him,

"Will any kind friend inform a poor blind man, who has lost the precious sight of his eyes in the gracious defence of his native country, England—and God bless King George!—where or in what part of this country he may now be?"

"You are at the "Admiral Benbow", Black Hill Cove, my good man," said I.

"I hear a voice," said he, "a young voice. Will you give me your hand, my kind young friend, and lead me in?"

I held out my hand, and the horrible, soft-spoken, eyeless creature gripped it in a moment like a vise. I was so much startled that I struggled to withdraw, but the blind man pulled me close up to him with a single action of his arm.

"Now, boy," he said, "take me in to the captain."

"Sir," said I, "upon my word I dare not."

"Oh," he sneered, "that's it! Take me in straight or I'll break your arm."

And he gave it, as he spoke, a wrench that made me cry out.

"Sir," said I, "it is for yourself I mean. The captain is not what he used to be. He sits with a drawn cutlass. Another gentleman—"

"Come, now, march," interrupted he; and I never heard a voice so cruel, and cold, and ugly as that blind man's. It cowed me more than the pain, and I began to obey him at once, walking straight in at the door and towards the parlour, where our sick old buccaneer was sitting, dazed with rum. The blind man clung close to me, holding me in one iron fist and leaning almost more of his weight on me than I could carry. "Lead me straight up to him, and when I'm in view, cry out, 'Here's a friend for you, Bill.' If you don't, I'll do this," and with that he gave me a twitch that I thought would have made me faint. Between this and that, I was so utterly terrified of the blind beggar that I forgot my terror of the captain, and as I opened the parlour door, cried out the words he had ordered in a trembling voice.

The poor captain raised his eyes, and at one look the rum went out of him and left him staring sober. The expression of his face was not so much of terror as of mortal sickness. He made a movement to rise, but I do not believe he had enough force left in his body.

"Now, Bill, sit where you are," said the beggar. "If I can't see, I can hear a finger stirring. Business is business. Hold out your left hand. Boy, take his left hand by the wrist and bring it near to my right."

We both obeyed him to the letter, and I saw him pass something from the hollow of the hand that held his stick into the palm of the captain's, which closed upon it instantly.

"And now that's done," said the blind man; and at the words he suddenly left hold of me, and with incredible accuracy and nimbleness, skipped out of the parlour and into the road, where, as I still stood motionless, I could hear his stick go tap-tap-tapping into the distance.

It was some time before either I or the captain seemed to gather our senses, but at length, and about at the same moment, I released his wrist, which I was still holding, and he drew in his hand and looked sharply into the palm.

"Ten o'clock!" he cried. "Six hours. We'll do them yet," and he sprang to his feet.

Even as he did so, he reeled, put his hand to his throat, stood swaying for a moment, and then, with a peculiar sound, fell from his whole height face foremost to the floor.

I ran to him at once, calling to my mother. But haste was all in vain. The captain had been struck dead by thundering apoplexy. It is a curious thing to understand, for I had certainly never liked the man, though of late I had begun to pity him, but as soon as I saw that he was dead, I burst into a flood of tears. It was the second death I had known, and the sorrow of the first was still fresh in my heart.

CHAPTER 4

The Sea-chest

I LOST no time, of course, in telling my mother all that I knew, and perhaps should have told her long before, and we saw ourselves at once in a difficult and dangerous position. Some of the man's money—if he had any—was certainly due to us, but it was not likely that our captain's shipmates, above all the two specimens seen by me, Black Dog and the blind beggar, would be inclined to give up their booty in payment of the dead man's debts. The captain's order to mount at once and ride for Doctor Livesey would have left my mother alone and unprotected, which was not to be thought of. Indeed, it seemed impossible for either of us to remain much longer in the house; the fall of coals in the kitchen grate, the very ticking of the clock, filled us with alarms. The neighbourhood, to our ears, seemed haunted by approaching footsteps; and what between the dead body of the captain on the parlour floor and the thought of that detestable blind beggar hovering near at hand and ready to return, there were moments when, as the saying goes, I jumped in my skin for terror. Something must speedily be resolved upon, and it occurred to us at last to go forth together and seek help in the neighbouring hamlet. No sooner said than done. Bare-headed as we were, we ran out at once in the gathering evening and the frosty fog.

The hamlet lay not many hundred yards away, though out of view, on the other side of the next cove; and what greatly encouraged me, it was in an opposite direction from that whence the blind man had made his appearance and whither he had presumably returned. We were not many minutes on the road, though we sometimes stopped to lay hold of each other and hearken. But there was no unusual sound—nothing but the low wash of the ripple and the croaking of the inmates of the wood.

It was already candle-light when we reached the hamlet, and I shall never forget how much I was cheered to see the yellow shine in doors and windows; but that, as it proved, was the best of the help we were likely to get in that quarter. For—you would have thought men would have been ashamed of themselves—no soul would consent to return with us to the "Admiral Benbow" The more we told of our troubles, the more—man, woman, and child—they clung to the shelter of their houses. The name of Captain Flint, though it was strange to me, was well enough known to some there and carried a great weight of terror. Some of the men who had been to field-work on the far side of the "Admiral Benbow" remembered, besides, to have seen several strangers on the road, and taking them to be smugglers, to have bolted away; and one at least had seen a little lugger in what we called Kitt's Hole. For that matter, anyone who was a comrade of the captain's was enough to frighten them to death. And the short and the long of the matter was, that while we could get several who were willing enough to ride to Dr. Livesey's, which lay in another direction, not one would help us to defend the inn.

They say cowardice is infectious; but then argument is, on the other hand, a great emboldener; and so when each had said his say, my mother made them a speech. She would not, she declared, lose money that belonged to her fatherless boy; "If none of the rest of you dare," she said, "Jim and I dare. Back we will go, the way we came, and small thanks to you big, hulking, chicken-hearted men. We'll have that chest open, if we die for it. And I'll thank you for that bag, Mrs. Crossley, to bring back our lawful money in."

Of course I said I would go with my mother, and of course they all cried out at our foolhardiness, but even then not a man would go along with us. All they would do was to give me a loaded pistol lest we were attacked, and to promise to have horses ready saddled in case we were pursued on our return, while one lad was to ride forward to the doctor's in search of armed assistance.

My heart was beating finely when we two set forth in the cold night upon this dangerous venture. A full moon was beginning to rise and peered redly through the upper edges of the fog, and this increased our haste, for it was plain, before we came forth again, that all would be as bright as day, and our departure exposed to the eyes of any watchers. We slipped along the hedges, noiseless and swift, nor did we see or hear anything to increase our terrors, till, to our relief, the door of the "Admiral Benbow" had closed behind us.

I slipped the bolt at once, and we stood and panted for a moment in the dark, alone in the house with the dead captain's body. Then my mother got a candle in the bar, and holding each other's hands, we advanced into the parlour. He lay as we had left him, on his back, with his eyes open and one arm stretched out.

"Draw down the blind, Jim," whispered my mother; "they might come and watch outside. And now," said she when I had done so, "we have to get the key off *that*; and who's to touch it, I should like to know!" and she gave a kind of sob as she said the words.

I went down on my knees at once. On the floor close to his hand there was a little round of paper, blackened on the one side. I could not doubt that this was the *black spot*; and taking it up, I found written on the other side, in a very good, clear hand, this short message: "You have till ten tonight."

"He had till ten, Mother," said I; and just as I said it, our old clock began striking. This sudden noise startled us shockingly; but the news was good, for it was only six.

"Now, Jim," she said, "that key."

I felt in his pockets, one after another. A few small coins, a thimble, and some thread and big needles, a piece of pigtail tobacco bitten away at the end, his gully with the crooked handle, a pocket compass, and a tinder box were all that they contained, and I began to despair.

"Perhaps it's round his neck," suggested my mother.

Overcoming a strong repugnance, I tore open his shirt at the neck, and there, sure enough, hanging to a bit of tarry string, which I cut with his own gully, we found the key. At this triumph we were filled with hope and hurried upstairs without delay to the little room where he had slept so long and where his box had stood since the day of his arrival.

It was like any other seaman's chest on the outside, the initial "B" burned on the top of it with a hot iron, and the corners somewhat smashed and broken as by long, rough usage.

"Give me the key," said my mother; and though the lock was very stiff, she had turned it and thrown back the lid in a twinkling.

A strong smell of tobacco and tar rose from the interior, but nothing was to be seen on the top except a suit of very good clothes, carefully brushed and folded. They had never been worn, my mother said. Under that, the miscellany began—a quadrant, a tin canikin, several sticks of tobacco, two brace of very handsome pistols, a piece of bar silver, an old Spanish watch and some other trinkets of little value and mostly of foreign make, a pair of compasses mounted with brass, and five or six curious West Indian shells. I have often wondered since why he should have carried about these shells with him in his wandering, guilty, and hunted life.

In the meantime, we had found nothing of any value but

the silver and the trinkets, and neither of these were in our way. Underneath there was an old boat-cloak, whitened with sea-salt on many a harbour-bar. My mother pulled it up with impatience, and there lay before us, the last things in the chest, a bundle tied up in oilcloth, and looking like papers, and a canvas bag that gave forth, at a touch, the jingle of gold.

"I'll show these rogues that I'm an honest woman," said my mother. "I'll have my dues, and not a farthing over. Hold Mrs. Crossley's bag." And she began to count over the amount of the captain's score from the sailor's bag into the one that I was holding.

It was a long, difficult business, for the coins were of all countries and sizes—doubloons, and louis d'ors, and guineas, and pieces of eight, and I know not what besides, all shaken together at random. The guineas, too, were about the scarcest, and it was with these only that my mother knew how to make her count.

When we were about half-way through, I suddenly put my hand upon her arm, for I had heard in the silent frosty air a sound that brought my heart into my mouth—the tap-tapping of the blind man's stick upon the frozen road. It drew nearer and nearer, while we sat holding our breath. Then it struck sharp on the inn door, and then we could hear the handle being turned and the bolt rattling as the wretched being tried to enter; and then there was a long time of silence both within and without. At last the tapping recommenced, and, to our indescribable joy and gratitude, died slowly away again until it ceased to be heard.

"Mother," said I, "take the whole and let's be going," for I was sure the bolted door must have seemed suspicious and would bring the whole hornet's nest about our ears, though how thankful I was that I had bolted it, none could tell who had never met that terrible blind man.

But my mother, frightened as she was, would not consent

to take a fraction more than was due to her and was obstinately unwilling to be content with less. It was not yet seven, she said, by a long way; she knew her rights and she would have them; and she was still arguing with me when a little low whistle sounded a good way off upon the hill. That was enough, and more than enough, for both of us.

"I'll take what I have," she said, jumping to her feet.

"And I'll take this to square the count," said I, picking up the oilskin packet.

Next moment we were both groping downstairs, leaving the candle by the empty chest; and the next we had opened the door and were in full retreat. We had not started a moment too soon. The fog was rapidly dispersing; already the moon shone quite clear on the high ground on either side; and it was only in the exact bottom of the dell and round the tavern door that a thin veil still hung unbroken to conceal the first steps of our escape. Far less than half-way to the hamlet, very little beyond the bottom of the hill, we must come forth into the moonlight. Nor was this all, for the sound of several footsteps running came already to our ears, and as we looked back in their direction, a light tossing to and fro and still rapidly advancing showed that one of the newcomers carried a lantern.

"My dear," said my mother suddenly, "take the money and run on. I am going to faint."

This was certainly the end for both of us, I thought. How I cursed the cowardice of the neighbours; how I blamed my poor mother for her honesty and her greed, for her past foolhardiness and present weakness! We were just at the little bridge, by good fortune; and I helped her, tottering as she was, to the edge of the bank, where, sure enough, she gave a sigh and fell on my shoulder. I do not know how I found the strength to do it at all, and I am afraid it was roughly done, but I managed to drag her down the bank and a little way under the arch. Farther I could not move her, for the bridge was too low to let me do more than crawl below it. So there we had to stay—my mother almost entirely exposed and both of us within earshot of the inn.

CHAPTER 5

The Last of the Blind Man

MY curiosity, in a sense, was stronger than my fear, for I could not remain where I was, but crept back to the bank again, whence, sheltering my head behind a bush of broom, I might command the road before our door. I was scarcely in position ere my enemies began to arrive, seven or eight of them, running hard, their feet beating out of time along the road and the man with the lantern some paces in front. Three men ran together, hand in hand; and I made out, even through the mist, that the middle man of this trio was the blind beggar. The next moment his voice showed me that I was right.

"Down with the door!" he cried.

"Aye, aye, sir!" answered two or three; and a rush was made upon the "Admiral Benbow", the lantern-bearer following; and then I could see them pause, and hear speeches passed in a lower key, as if they were surprised to find the door open. But the pause was brief, for the blind man again issued his commands. His voice sounded louder and higher, as if he were afire with eagerness and rage.

"In, in, in!" he shouted, and cursed them for their delay.

Four or five of them obeyed at once, two remaining on the road with the formidable beggar. There was a pause, then a cry of surprise, and then a voice shouting from the house,

"Bill's dead."

But the blind man swore at them again for their delay.

"Search him, some of you shirking lubbers, and the rest of

you aloft and get the chest," he cried.

I could hear their feet rattling up our old stairs, so that the house must have shook with it. Promptly afterwards, fresh sounds of astonishment arose; the window of the captain's room was thrown open with a slam and a jingle of broken glass, and a man leaned out into the moonlight, head and shoulders, and addressed the blind beggar on the road below him.

"Pew," he cried, "they've been before us. Someone's turned the chest out alow and aloft."

"Is it there?" roared Pew.

"The money's there."

The blind man cursed the money.

"Flint's fist, I mean," he cried.

"We don't see it here nohow," returned the man.

"Here, you below there, is it on Bill?" cried the blind man again.

At that another fellow, probably him who had remained below to search the captain's body, came to the door of the inn. "Bill's been overhauled a'ready," said he; "nothin' left."

"It's these people of the inn—it's that boy. I wish I had put his eyes out!" cried the blind man, Pew. "There were no time ago—they had the door bolted when I tried it. Scatter, lads, and find 'em."

"Sure enough, they left their glim here," said the fellow from the window.

"Scatter and find 'em! Rout the house out!" reiterated Pew, striking with his stick upon the road.

Then there followed a great to-do through all our old inn, heavy feet pounding to and fro, furniture thrown over, doors kicked in, until the very rocks re-echoed and the men came out again, one after another, on the road and declared that we were nowhere to be found. And just the same whistle that had alarmed my mother and myself over the dead captain's money was once more clearly audible through the night, but this time twice repeated. I had thought it to be the blind man's trumpet, so to speak, summoning his crew to the assault, but I now found that it was a signal from the hillside towards the hamlet, and from its effect upon the buccaneers, a signal to warn them of approaching danger.

"There's Dirk again," said one. "Twice! We'll have to budge, mates."

"Budge, you skulk!" cried Pew. "Dirk was a fool and a coward from the first—you wouldn't mind him. They must be close by; they can't be far; you have your hands on it. Scatter and look for them, dogs! Oh, shiver my soul," he cried, "if I had eyes!"

This appeal seemed to produce some effect, for two of the fellows began to look here and there among the lumber, but half-heartedly, I thought, and with half an eye to their own danger all the time, while the rest stood irresolute on the road.

"You have your hands on thousands, you fools, and you hang a leg! You'd be as rich as kings if you could find it, and you know it's here, and you stand there skulking. There wasn't one of you dared face Bill, and I did it—a blind man! And I'm to lose my chance for you! I'm to be a poor, crawling beggar, sponging for rum, when I might be rolling in a coach! If you had the pluck of a weevil in a biscuit you would catch them still."

"Hang it, Pew, we've got the doubloons!" grumbled one.

"They might have hid the blessed thing," said another. "Take the Georges, Pew, and don't stand here squalling."

Squalling was the word for it; Pew's anger rose so high at these objections till at last, his passion completely taking the upper hand, he struck at them right and left in his blindness and his stick sounded heavily on more than one.

These, in their turn, cursed back at the blind miscreant, threatened him in horrid terms, and tried in vain to catch the stick and wrest it from his grasp.

This quarrel was the saving of us, for while it was still raging, another sound came from the top of the hill on the side of the hamlet—the tramp of horses galloping. Almost at the same time a pistol-shot, flash and report, came from the hedge side. And that was plainly the last signal of danger, for the buccaneers turned at once and ran, separating in every direction, one seaward along the cove, one slant across the hill, and so on, so that in half a minute not a sign of them remained but Pew. Him they had deserted, whether in sheer panic or out of revenge for his ill words and blows I know not; but there he remained behind, tapping up and down the road in a frenzy, and groping and calling for his comrades. Finally he took a wrong turn and ran a few steps past me, towards the hamlet, crying,

"Johnny, Black Dog, Dirk," and other names, "you won't leave old Pew, mates—not old Pew!"

Just then the noise of horses topped the rise, and four or five riders came in sight in the moonlight and swept at full gallop down the slope.

At this Pew saw his error, turned with a scream, and ran straight for the ditch, into which he rolled. But he was on his feet again in a second and made another dash, now utterly bewildered, right under the nearest of the coming horses.

The rider tried to save him, but in vain. Down went Pew with a cry that rang high into the night; and the four hoofs trampled and spurned him and passed by. He fell on his side, then gently collapsed upon his face and moved no more.

I leaped to my feet and hailed the riders. They were pulling up, at any rate, horrified at the accident; and I soon saw what they were. One, tailing out behind the rest, was a lad that had gone from the hamlet to Dr. Livesey's; the rest were revenue officers, whom he had met by the way, and with whom he had had the intelligence to return at once. Some news of the lugger in Kitt's Hole had found its way to Supervisor Dance and set him forth that night in our direction, and to that circumstance my mother and I owed our preservation from death.

Pew was dead, stone dead. As for my mother, when we had carried her up to the hamlet, a little cold water and salts and that soon brought her back again, and she was none the worse for her terror, though she still continued to deplore the balance of the money. In the meantime the supervisor rode on, as fast as he could, to Kitt's Hole; but his men had to dismount and grope down the dingle, leading, and sometimes supporting, their horses, and in continual fear of ambushes; so it was no great matter for surprise that when they got down to the Hole the lugger was already under way, though still close in. He hailed her. A voice replied, telling him to keep out of the moonlight or he would get some lead in him, and at the same time a bullet whistled close by his arm. Soon after, the lugger doubled the point and disappeared. Mr. Dance stood there, as he said, "like a fish out of water," and all he could do was to dispatch a man to B—— to warn the cutter. "And that," said he, "is just about as good as nothing. They've got off clean, and there's an end. Only," he added, "I'm glad I trod on Master Pew's corns," for by this time he had heard my story.

I went back with him to the "Admiral Benbow", and you cannot imagine a house in such a state of smash; the very clock had been thrown down by these fellows in their furious hunt after my mother and myself; and though nothing had actually been taken away except the captain's money-bag and a little silver from the till, I could see at once that we were ruined. Mr. Dance could make nothing of the scene.

"They got the money, you say? Well, then, Hawkins, what in fortune were they after? More money, I suppose?"

"No, sir; not money, I think," replied I. "In fact, sir, I believe I have the thing in my breast pocket; and to tell you the truth, I should like to get it put in safety."

"To be sure, boy; quite right," said he. "I'll take it, if you like."

"I thought perhaps Dr. Livesey—" I began.

"Perfectly right," he interrupted very cheerily, "perfectly right—a gentleman and a magistrate. And, now I come to think of it, I might as well ride round there myself and report to him or squire. Master Pew's dead, when all's done; not that I regret it, but he's dead, you see, and people will make it out against an officer of his Majesty's revenue, if make it out they can. Now, I'll tell you, Hawkins, if you like, I'll take you along."

I thanked him heartily for the offer, and we walked back to the hamlet where the horses were. By the time I had told mother of my purpose they were all in the saddle.

"Dogger," said Mr. Dance, "you have a good horse; take up this lad behind you."

As soon as I was mounted, holding on to Dogger's belt, the supervisor gave the word, and the party struck out at a bouncing trot on the road to Dr. Livesey's house.

CHAPTER 6

The Captain's Papers

WE rode hard all the way till we drew up before Dr. Livesey's door. The house was all dark to the front.

Mr. Dance told me to jump down and knock, and Dogger gave me a stirrup to descend by. The door was opened almost at once by the maid.

"Is Dr. Livesey in?" I asked.

No, she said, he had come home in the afternoon but had gone up to the hall to dine and pass the evening with the squire.

"So there we go, boys," said Mr. Dance.

This time, as the distance was short, I did not mount, but ran with Dogger's stirrup-leather to the lodge gates and up the long, leafless, moonlit avenue to where the white line of the hall buildings looked on either hand on great old gardens. Here Mr. Dance dismounted, and taking me along with him, was admitted at a word into the house.

The servant led us down a matted passage and showed us at the end into a great library, all lined with bookcases and busts upon the top of them, where the squire and Dr. Livesey sat, pipe in hand, on either side of a bright fire.

I had never seen the squire so near at hand. He was a tall man, over six feet high, and broad in proportion, and he had a bluff, rough-and-ready face, all roughened and reddened and lined in his long travels. His eyebrows were very black, and moved readily, and this gave him a look of some temper, not bad, you would say, but quick and high.

"Come in, Mr. Dance," says he, very stately and condescending.

"Good evening, Dance," says the doctor with a nod. "And good evening to you, friend Jim. What good wind brings you here?"

The supervisor stood up straight and stiff and told his story like a lesson; and you should have seen how the two gentlemen leaned forward and looked at each other, and forgot to smoke in their surprise and interest. When they heard how my mother went back to the inn, Dr. Livesey fairly slapped his thigh, and the squire cried "Bravo!" and broke his long pipe against the grate. Long before it was done, Mr. Trelawney (that, you will remember, was the squire's name) had got up from his seat and was striding about the room, and the doctor, as if to hear the better, had taken off his powdered wig and sat there looking very strange indeed with his own close-cropped black poll.

At last Mr. Dance finished the story.

"Mr. Dance," said the squire, "you are a very noble fellow. And as for riding down that black, atrocious miscreant, I regard it as an act of virtue, sir, like stamping on a cockroach. This lad Hawkins is a trump, I perceive. Hawkins, will you ring that bell? Mr. Dance must have some ale."

"And so, Jim," said the doctor, "you have the thing that they were after, have you?"

"Here it is, sir," said I, and gave him the oilskin packet.

The doctor looked it all over, as if his fingers were itching to open it; but instead of doing that, he put it quietly in the pocket of his coat.

"Squire," said he, "when Dance has had his ale he must, of course, be off on his Majesty's service; but I mean to keep Jim Hawkins here to sleep at my house, and with your permission, I propose we should have up the cold pie and let him sup."

"As you will, Livesey," said the squire; "Hawkins has earned better than cold pie."

So a big pigeon pie was brought in and put on a sidetable, and I made a hearty supper, for I was as hungry as a hawk, while Mr. Dance was further complimented and at last dismissed.

"And now, squire," said the doctor.

"And now, Livesey," said the squire in the same breath.

"One at a time, one at a time," laughed Dr. Livesey. "You have heard of this Flint, I suppose?"

"Heard of him!" cried the squire. "Heard of him, you say! He was the bloodthirstiest buccaneer that sailed. Blackbeard was a child to Flint. The Spaniards were so prodigiously afraid of him that, I tell you, sir, I was sometimes proud he was an Englishman. I've seen his top-sails with these eyes, off Trinidad, and the cowardly son of a rum-puncheon that I sailed with put back—put back, sir, into Port of Spain."

"Well, I've heard of him myself, in England," said the doctor. "But the point is, had he money?"

"Money!" cried the squire. "Have you heard the story? What were these villains after but money? What do they care for but money? For what would they risk their rascal carcasses but money?"

"That we shall soon know," replied the doctor. "But you are so confoundedly hot-headed and exclamatory that I cannot get a word in. What I want to know is this: Supposing that I have here in my pocket some clue to where Flint buried his treasure, will that treasure amount to much?"

"Amount, sir!" cried the squire. "It will amount to this: If we have the clue you talk about, I fit out a ship in Bristol dock, and take you and Hawkins here along, and I'll have that treasure if I search a year."

"Very well," said the doctor. "Now, then, if Jim is agreeable, we'll open the packet"; and he laid it before him on the table.

The bundle was sewn together, and the doctor had to get out his instrument case and cut the stitches with his medical scissors. It contained two things—a book and a sealed paper.

"First of all we'll try the book," observed the doctor.

The squire and I were both peering over his shoulder as he opened it, for Dr. Livesey had kindly motioned me to come round from the side-table, where I had been eating, to enjoy the sport of the search. On the first page there were only some scraps of writing, such as a man with a pen in his hand might make for idleness or practice. One was the same as the tattoo mark, "Billy Bones his fancy"; then there was "Mr. W. Bones, mate," "No more rum," "Off Palm Key he got itt," and some other snatches, mostly single words and unintelligible. I could not help wondering who it was that had "got itt," and what "itt" was that he got. A knife in his back as like as not.

"Not much instruction there," said Dr. Livesey as he passed on.

The next ten or twelve pages were filled with a curious series of entries. There was a date at one end of the line and at the other a sum of money, as in common account-books, but instead of explanatory writing, only a varying number of crosses between the two. On the 12th of June, 1745, for instance, a sum of seventy pounds had plainly become due to someone, and there was nothing but six crosses to explain the cause. In a few cases, to be sure, the name of a place would be added, as "Offe Caraccas," or a mere entry of latitude and longitude, as "62° 17' 20", 19° 2' 40".

The record lasted over nearly twenty years, the amount of the separate entries growing larger as time went on, and at the end a grand total had been made out after five or six wrong additions, and these words appended, "Bones, his pile."

"I can't make head or tail of this," said Dr. Livesey.

"The thing is as clear as noonday," cried the squire. "This is the black-hearted hound's account-book. These crosses stand for the names of ships or towns that they sank or plundered. The sums are the scoundrel's share, and where he feared an ambiguity, you see he added something clearer. 'Offe Caraccas,' now; you see, here was some unhappy vessel boarded off that coast. God help the poor souls that manned her—coral long ago."

"Right!" said the doctor. "See what it is to be a traveller. Right! And the amounts increase, you see, as he rose in rank."

There was little else in the volume but a few bearings of places noted in the blank leaves towards the end and a table for reducing French, English, and Spanish moneys to a common value.

"Thrifty man!" cried the doctor. "He wasn't the one to be cheated."

"And now," said the squire, "for the other."

The paper had been sealed in several places with a thimble by way of seal; the very thimble, perhaps, that I had found in the captain's pocket. The doctor opened the seals with great care, and there fell out the map of an island, with latitude and longitude, soundings, names of hills and bays and inlets, and every particular that would be needed to bring a ship to a safe anchorage upon its shores. It was about nine miles long and five across, shaped, you might say, like a fat dragon standing up, and had two fine land-locked harbours, and a hill in the centre part marked "The Spy-glass." There were several additions of a later date, but above all, three crosses of red ink—two on the north part of the island, one in the southwest—and beside this last, in the same red ink, and in a small, neat hand, very different from the captain's tottery characters, these words: "Bulk of treasure here."

Over on the back the same hand had written this further information:

'Tall tree, Spy-glass shoulder, bearing a point to the N. of N.N.E.

'Skeleton Island E.S.E. and by E.

'Ten feet.

'The bar silver is in the north cache; you can find it by the trend of the east hummock, ten fathoms south of the black crag with the face on it.

'The arms are easy found, in the sand-hill, N. point of north inlet cape, bearing E. and a quarter N.

'J.F.'

That was all; but brief as it was, and to me incomprehensible, it filled the squire and Dr. Livesey with delight.

"Livesey," said the squire, "you will give up this wretched practice at once. Tomorrow I start for Bristol. In three weeks' time—three weeks!—two weeks—ten days—we'll have the best ship, sir, and the choicest crew in England. Hawkins shall come as cabin-boy. You'll make a famous cabin-boy, Hawkins. You, Livesey, are ship's doctor; I am admiral. We'll take Redruth, Joyce, and Hunter. We'll have favourable winds, a quick passage, and not the least difficulty in finding the spot, and money to eat, to roll in, to play duck and drake with ever after."

"Trelawney," said the doctor, "I'll go with you; and I'll go bail for it, so will Jim, and be a credit to the undertaking. There's only one man I'm afraid of."

"And who's that?" cried the squire. "Name the dog, sir!"

"You," replied the doctor; "for you cannot hold your tongue. We are not the only men who know of this paper. These fellows who attacked the inn tonight—bold, desperate blades, for sure—and the rest who stayed aboard that lugger, and more, I dare say, not far off, are, one and all, through thick and thin, bound that they'll get that money. We must none of us go alone till we get to sea. Jim and I shall stick together in the meanwhile; you'll take Joyce and Hunter when you ride to Bristol, and from first to last, not one of us must breathe a word of what we've found."

"Livesey," returned the squire, "you are always in the right of it. I'll be as silent as the grave."

PART TWO

II SEASIDE

PART TWO

THE SEA-COOK

CHAPTER 7

I Go to Bristol

IT was longer than the squire imagined ere we were ready for the sea, and none of our first plans—not even Dr. Livesey's, of keeping me beside him—could be carried out as we intended. The doctor had to go to London for a physician to take charge of his practice; the squire was hard at work at Bristol; and I lived on at the hall under the charge of old Redruth, the gamekeeper, almost a prisoner, but full of sea-dreams and the most charming anticipations of strange islands and adventures. I brooded by the hour together over the map, all the details of which I well remembered. Sitting by the fire in the housekeeper's room, I approached that island in my fancy from every possible direction; I explored every acre of its surface; I climbed a thousand times to that tall hill they call the Spy-glass, and from the top enjoyed the most wonderful and changing prospects. Sometimes the isle was thick with savages, with whom we fought, sometimes full of dangerous animals that hunted us, but in all my fancies nothing occurred to me so strange and tragic as our actual adventures.

So the weeks passed on, till one fine day there came a letter addressed to Dr. Livesey, with this addition, "To be opened, in the case of his absence, by Tom Redruth or young Hawkins." Obeying this order, we found, or rather I found—for the gamekeeper was a poor hand at reading anything but print—the following important news:

'*Old Anchor Inn, Bristol, March 1, 17—*

'*Dear Livesey—As I do not know whether you are at the hall or still in London, I send this in double to both places.*

'*The ship is bought and fitted. She lies at anchor, ready for sea. You never imagined a sweeter schooner—a child might sail her—two hundred tons; name, Hispaniola.*

'*I got her through my old friend, Blandly, who has proved himself throughout the most surprising trump. The admirable fellow literally slaved in my interest, and so, I may say, did everyone in Bristol, as soon as they got wind of the port we sailed for—treasure, I mean.*'

"Redruth," said I, interrupting the letter, "Dr. Livesey will not like that. The squire has been talking, after all."

"Well, who's a better right?" growled the gamekeeper. "A pretty rum go if squire ain't to talk for Dr. Livesey, I should think."

At that I gave up all attempts at commentary and read straight on:

'*Blandly himself found the Hispaniola, and by the most admirable management got her for the merest trifle. There is a class of men in Bristol monstrously prejudiced against Blandly. They go the length of declaring that this honest creature would do anything for money, that the Hispaniola belonged to him, and that he sold it me absurdly high—the most transparent calumnies. None of them dare, however, to deny the merits of the ship.*

'*So far there was not a hitch. The workpeople, to be sure—riggers and what not—were most annoyingly slow; but time cured that. It was the crew that troubled me.*

'*I wished a round score of men—in case of natives, buccaneers, or the odious French—and I had the worry of the deuce itself to find so much as half a dozen, till the most remarkable stroke of fortune brought me the very man that I required.*

'I was standing on the dock, when, by the merest accident, I fell in talk with him. I found he was an old sailor, kept a public-house, knew all the seafaring men in Bristol, had lost his health ashore, and wanted a good berth as cook to get to sea again. He had hobbled down there that morning, he said, to get a smell of the salt.

'I was monstrously touched—so would you have been— and, out of pure pity, I engaged him on the spot to be the ship's cook. Long John Silver, he is called, and has lost a leg; but that I regarded as a recommendation, since he lost it in his country's service, under the immortal Hawke. He has no pension, Livesey. Imagine the abominable age we live in!

'Well, sir, I thought I had only found a cook, but it was a crew I had discovered. Between Silver and myself we got together in a few days a company of the toughest old salts imaginable— not pretty to look at, but fellows, by their faces, of the most indomitable spirit. I declare we could fight a frigate.

'Long John even got rid of two out of the six or seven I had already engaged. He showed me in a moment that they were just the sort of fresh-water swabs we had to fear in an adventure of importance.

'I am in the most magnificent health and spirits, eating like a bull, sleeping like a tree, yet I shall not enjoy a moment till I hear my old tarpaulins tramping round the capstan. Seaward, ho! Hang the treasure! It's the glory of the sea that has turned my head. So now, Livesey, come post; do not lose an hour, if you respect me.

'Let young Hawkins go at once to see his mother, with Redruth for a guard; and then both come full speed to Bristol.

'John Trelawney

'Postscript—I did not tell you that Blandly, who, by the way, is to send a consort after us if we don't turn up by the end of

August, had found an admirable fellow for sailing master—a stiff man, which I regret, but in all other respects a treasure. Long John Silver unearthed a very competent man for a mate, a man named Arrow. I have a boatswain who pipes, Livesey; so things shall go man-o'-war fashion on board the good ship Hispaniola.

'I forgot to tell you that Silver is a man of substance; I know of my own knowledge that he has a banker's account, which has never been overdrawn. He leaves his wife to manage the inn; and as she is a woman of colour, a pair of old bachelors like you and I may be excused for guessing that it is the wife, quite as much as the health, that sends him back to roving.

'J. T.

'P.P.S.—Hawkins may stay one night with his mother.
' J. T.'

You can fancy the excitement into which that letter put me. I was half beside myself with glee; and if ever I despised a man, it was old Tom Redruth, who could do nothing but grumble and lament. Any of the under-gamekeepers would gladly have changed places with him; but such was not the squire's pleasure, and the squire's pleasure was like law among them all. Nobody but old Redruth would have dared so much as even to grumble.

The next morning he and I set out on foot for the "Admiral Benbow", and there I found my mother in good health and spirits. The captain, who had so long been a cause of so much discomfort, was gone where the wicked cease from troubling. The squire had had everything repaired, and the public rooms and the sign repainted, and had added some furniture—above all a beautiful armchair for mother in the bar. He had found her a boy as an apprentice also so that she should not want help while I was gone.

It was on seeing that boy that I understood, for the first

time, my situation. I had thought up to that moment of the adventures before me, not at all of the home that I was leaving; and now, at sight of this clumsy stranger, who was to stay here in my place beside my mother, I had my first attack of tears. I am afraid I led that boy a dog's life, for as he was new to the work, I had a hundred opportunities of setting him right and putting him down, and I was not slow to profit by them.

The night passed, and the next day, after dinner, Redruth and I were afoot again and on the road. I said good-bye to Mother and the cove where I had lived since I was born, and the dear old "Admiral Benbow"—since he was repainted, no longer quite so dear. One of my last thoughts was of the captain, who had so often strode along the beach with his cocked hat, his sabre-cut cheek, and his old brass telescope. Next moment we had turned the corner and my home was out of sight.

The mail picked us up about dusk at the Royal George on the heath. I was wedged in between Redruth and a stout old gentleman, and in spite of the swift motion and the cold night air, I must have dozed a great deal from the very first, and then slept like a log up hill and down dale through stage after stage, for when I was awakened at last it was by a punch in the ribs, and I opened my eyes to find that we were standing still before a large building in a city street and that the day had already broken a long time.

"Where are we?" I asked.

"Bristol," said Tom. "Get down."

Mr. Trelawney had taken up his residence at an inn far down the docks to superintend the work upon the schooner. Thither we had now to walk, and our way, to my great delight, lay along the quays and beside the great multitude of ships of all sizes and rigs and nations. In one, sailors were singing at their work, in another there were men aloft, high over my head, hanging to threads that seemed no thicker than a spider's. Though I had lived by the shore all my life, I seemed never to have been near the sea till then. The smell of tar and salt was something new. I saw the most wonderful figureheads, that had all been far over the ocean. I saw, besides, many old sailors, with rings in their ears, and whiskers curled in ringlets, and tarry pigtails, and their swaggering, clumsy sea-walk; and if I had seen as many kings or archbishops I could not have been more delighted.

And I was going to sea myself, to sea in a schooner, with a piping boatswain and pig-tailed singing seamen, to sea, bound for an unknown island, and to seek for buried treasures!

While I was still in this delightful dream, we came suddenly in front of a large inn and met Squire Trelawney, all dressed out like a sea-officer, in stout blue cloth, coming out of the door with a smile on his face and a capital imitation of a sailor's walk.

"Here you are," he cried, "and the doctor came last night from London. Bravo! The ship's company complete!"

"Oh, sir," cried I, "when do we sail?"

"Sail!" says he. "We sail tomorrow!"

CHAPTER 8

At the Sign of the Spy-glass

WHEN I had done breakfasting the squire gave me a note addressed to John Silver, at the sign of the Spy-glass, and told me I should easily find the place by following the line of the docks and keeping a bright lookout for a little tavern with a large brass telescope for sign. I set off, overjoyed at this opportunity to see some more of the ships and seamen, and picked my way among a great crowd of people and carts and bales, for the dock was now at its busiest, until I found the tavern in question.

It was a bright enough little place of entertainment. The sign was newly painted; the windows had neat red curtains; the floor was cleanly sanded. There was a street on each side and an open door on both, which made the large, low room pretty clear to see in, in spite of clouds of tobacco smoke.

The customers were mostly seafaring men, and they talked so loudly that I hung at the door, almost afraid to enter.

As I was waiting, a man came out of a side room, and at a glance I was sure he must be Long John. His left leg was cut off close by the hip, and under the left shoulder he carried a crutch, which he managed with wonderful dexterity, hopping about upon it like a bird. He was very tall and strong, with a face as big as a ham—plain and pale, but intelligent and smiling. Indeed, he seemed in the most cheerful spirits, whistling as he moved about among the tables, with a merry word or a slap on the shoulder for the more favoured of his guests.

Now, to tell you the truth, from the very first mention of Long John in Squire Trelawney's letter I had taken a fear in my mind that he might prove to be the very one-legged sailor whom I had watched for so long at the old Benbow. But one look at the man before me was enough. I had seen the captain, and Black Dog, and the blind man, Pew, and I thought I knew what a buccaneer was like—a very different creature, according to me, from this clean and pleasant-tempered landlord.

I plucked up courage at once, crossed the threshold, and walked right up to the man where he stood, propped on his crutch, talking to a customer.

"Mr. Silver, sir?" I asked, holding out the note.

"Yes, my lad," said he; "such is my name, to be sure. And who may you be?" And then as he saw the squire's letter, he seemed to me to give something almost like a start.

"Oh!" said he, quite loud, and offering his hand. "I see. You are our new cabin-boy; pleased I am to see you."

And he took my hand in his large firm grasp.

Just then one of the customers at the far side rose suddenly and made for the door. It was close by him, and he was out in the street in a moment. But his hurry had attracted my notice, and I recognized him at glance. It was the tallow-faced man, wanting two fingers, who had come first to the "Admiral Benbow".

"Oh," I cried, "stop him! It's Black Dog!"

"I don't care two coppers who he is," cried Silver. "But he hasn't paid his score. Harry, run and catch him."

One of the others who was nearest the door leaped up and started in pursuit.

"If he were Admiral Hawke he shall pay his score," cried Silver; and then, relinquishing my hand, "Who did you say he was?" he asked. "Black what?"

"Dog, sir," said I. "Has Mr. Trelawney not told you of the buccaneers? He was one of them."

"So?" cried Silver. "In my house! Ben, run and help Harry. One of those swabs, was he? Was that you drinking with him, Morgan? Step up here."

The man whom he called Morgan—an old, grey-haired, mahogany-faced sailor—came forward pretty sheepishly, rolling his quid.

"Now, Morgan," said Long John very sternly, "you never clapped your eyes on that Black—Black Dog before, did you, now?"

"Not I, sir," said Morgan with a salute.

"You didn't know his name, did you?"

"No, sir."

"By the powers, Tom Morgan, it's as good for you!" exclaimed the landlord. "If you had been mixed up with the like of that, you would never have put another foot in my house, you may lay to that. And what was he saying to you?"

"I don't rightly know, sir," answered Morgan.

"Do you call that a head on your shoulders, or a blessed dead-eye?" cried Long John. "Don't rightly know, don't you! Perhaps you don't happen to rightly know who you was speaking to, perhaps? Come, now, what was he jawing— v'yages, cap'ns, ships? Pipe up! What was it?"

"We was a-talkin' of keel-hauling," answered Morgan.

"Keel-hauling, was you? And a mighty suitable thing, too, and you may lay to that. Get back to your place for a lubber, Tom."

And then, as Morgan rolled back to his seat, Silver added to me in a confidential whisper that was very flattering, as I thought, "He's quite an honest man, Tom Morgan, on'y stupid. And now," he ran on again, aloud, "let's see—Black Dog? No, I don't know the name, not I. Yet I kind of think I've—yes, I've seen the swab. He used to come here with a blind beggar, he used."

"That he did, you may be sure," said I. "I knew that blind

man too. His name was Pew."

"It was!" cried Silver, now quite excited. "Pew! That were his name for certain. Ah, he looked a shark, he did! If we run down this Black Dog, now, there'll be news for Cap'n Trelawney! Ben's a good runner; few seamen run better than Ben. He should run him down, hand over hand, by the powers! He talked o' keel-hauling, did he? I'LL keel-haul him!"

All the time he was jerking out these phrases he was stumping up and down the tavern on his crutch, slapping tables with his hand, and giving such a show of excitement as would have convinced an Old Bailey judge or a Bow Street runner. My suspicions had been thoroughly reawakened on finding Black Dog at the Spy-glass, and I watched the cook narrowly. But he was too deep, and too ready, and too clever for me, and by the time the two men had come back out of breath and confessed that they had lost the track in a crowd, and been scolded like thieves, I would have gone bail for the innocence of Long John Silver.

"See here, now, Hawkins," said he, "here's a blessed hard thing on a man like me, now, ain't it? There's Cap'n Trelawney— what's he to think? Here I have this confounded son of a Dutchman sitting in my own house drinking of my own rum! Here you comes and tells me of it plain; and here I let him give us all the slip before my blessed deadlights! Now, Hawkins, you do me justice with the cap'n. You're a lad, you are, but you're as smart as paint. I see that when you first come in. Now, here it is: What could I do, with this old timber I hobble on? When I was an A B master mariner I'd have come up alongside of him, hand over hand, and broached him to in a brace of old shakes, I would; but now—"

And then, all of a sudden, he stopped, and his jaw dropped as though he had remembered something.

"The score!" he burst out. "Three goes o' rum! Why, shiver my timbers, if I hadn't forgotten my score!"

And falling on a bench, he laughed until the tears ran down his cheeks. I could not help joining, and we laughed together, peal after peal, until the tavern rang again.

"Why, what a precious old sea-calf I am!" he said at last, wiping his cheeks. "You and me should get on well, Hawkins, for I'll take my davy I should be rated ship's boy. But come now, stand by to go about. This won't do. Dooty is dooty, messmates. I'll put on my old cockerel hat, and step along of you to Cap'n Trelawney, and report this here affair. For mind you, it's serious, young Hawkins; and neither you nor me's come out of it with what I should make so bold as to call credit. Nor you neither, says you; not smart—none of the pair of us smart. But dash my buttons! That was a good un about my score."

And he began to laugh again, and that so heartily, that though I did not see the joke as he did, I was again obliged to join him in his mirth.

On our little walk along the quays, he made himself the most interesting companion, telling me about the different ships that we passed by, their rig, tonnage, and nationality, explaining the work that was going forward—how one was discharging, another taking in cargo, and a third making ready for sea—and every now and then telling me some little anecdote of ships or seamen or repeating a nautical phrase till I had learned it perfectly. I began to see that here was one of the best of possible shipmates.

When we got to the inn, the squire and Dr. Livesey were seated together, finishing a quart of ale with a toast in it, before they should go aboard the schooner on a visit of inspection.

Long John told the story from first to last, with a great deal of spirit and the most perfect truth. "That was how it were, now, weren't it, Hawkins?" he would say, now and again, and I could always bear him entirely out.

The two gentlemen regretted that Black Dog had got away, but we all agreed there was nothing to be done, and after he had been complimented, Long John took up his crutch and departed.

"All hands aboard by four this afternoon," shouted the squire after him.

"Aye, aye, sir," cried the cook, in the passage.

"Well, squire," said Dr. Livesey, "I don't put much faith in your discoveries, as a general thing; but I will say this, John Silver suits me."

"The man's a perfect trump," declared the squire.

"And now," added the doctor, "Jim may come on board with us, may he not?"

"To be sure he may," says squire. "Take your hat, Hawkins, and we'll see the ship."

CHAPTER 9

Powder and Arms

THE *Hispaniola* lay some way out, and we went under the figureheads and round the sterns of many other ships, and their cables sometimes grated underneath our keel, and sometimes swung above us. At last, however, we got alongside, and were met and saluted as we stepped aboard by the mate, Mr. Arrow, a brown old sailor with earrings in his ears and a squint. He and the squire were very thick and friendly, but I soon observed that things were not the same between Mr. Trelawney and the captain.

This last was a sharp-looking man who seemed angry with everything on board and was soon to tell us why, for we had hardly got down into the cabin when a sailor followed us.

"Captain Smollett, sir, axing to speak with you," said he.

"I am always at the captain's orders. Show him in," said the squire.

The captain, who was close behind his messenger, entered at once and shut the door behind him.

"Well, Captain Smollett, what have you to say? All well, I hope; all shipshape and seaworthy?"

"Well, sir," said the captain, "better speak plain, I believe, even at the risk of offence. I don't like this cruise; I don't like the men; and I don't like my officer. That's short and sweet."

"Perhaps, sir, you don't like the ship?" inquired the squire, very angry, as I could see.

"I can't speak as to that, sir, not having seen her tried," said the captain. "She seems a clever craft; more I can't say."

"Possibly, sir, you may not like your employer, either?" says the squire.

But here Dr. Livesey cut in.

"Stay a bit," said he, "stay a bit. No use of such questions as that but to produce ill feeling. The captain has said too much or he has said too little, and I'm bound to say that I require an explanation of his words. You don't, you say, like this cruise. Now, why?"

"I was engaged, sir, on what we call sealed orders, to sail this ship for that gentleman where he should bid me," said the captain. "So far so good. But now I find that every man before the mast knows more than I do. I don't call that fair, now, do you?"

"No," said Dr. Livesey, "I don't."

"Next," said the captain, "I learn we are going after treasure—hear it from my own hands, mind you. Now, treasure is ticklish work; I don't like treasure voyages on any account, and I don't like them, above all, when they are secret and when (begging your pardon, Mr. Trelawney) the secret has been told to the parrot."

"Silver's parrot?" asked the squire.

"It's a way of speaking," said the captain. "Blabbed, I mean. It's my belief neither of you gentlemen know what you are about, but I'll tell you my way of it—life or death, and a close run."

"That is all clear, and, I dare say, true enough," replied Dr. Livesey. "We take the risk, but we are not so ignorant as you believe us. Next, you say you don't like the crew. Are they not good seamen?"

"I don't like them, sir," returned Captain Smollett. "And I think I should have had the choosing of my own hands, if you go to that."

"Perhaps you should," replied the doctor. "My friend

should, perhaps, have taken you along with him; but the slight, if there be one, was unintentional. And you don't like Mr. Arrow?"

"I don't, sir. I believe he's a good seaman, but he's too free with the crew to be a good officer. A mate should keep himself to himself—shouldn't drink with the men before the mast!"

"Do you mean he drinks?" cried the squire.

"No, sir," replied the captain, "only that he's too familiar."

"Well, now, and the short and long of it, captain?" asked the doctor. "Tell us what you want."

"Well, gentlemen, are you determined to go on this cruise?"

"Like iron," answered the squire.

"Very good," said the captain. "Then, as you've heard me very patiently, saying things that I could not prove, hear me a few words more. They are putting the powder and the arms in the fore hold. Now, you have a good place under the cabin; why not put them there?—first point. Then, you are bringing four of your own people with you, and they tell me some of them are to be berthed forward. Why not give them the berths here beside the cabin?—second point."

"Any more?" asked Mr. Trelawney.

"One more," said the captain. "There's been too much blabbing already."

"Far too much," agreed the doctor.

"I'll tell you what I've heard myself," continued Captain Smollett: "that you have a map of an island, that there's crosses on the map to show where treasure is, and that the island lies—" And then he named the latitude and longitude exactly.

"I never told that," cried the squire, "to a soul!"

"The hands know it, sir," returned the captain.

"Livesey, that must have been you or Hawkins," cried the squire.

"It doesn't much matter who it was," replied the doctor. And I could see that neither he nor the captain paid much regard to

Mr. Trelawney's protestations. Neither did I, to be sure, he was so loose a talker; yet in this case I believe he was really right and that nobody had told the situation of the island.

"Well, gentlemen," continued the captain, "I don't know who has this map; but I make it a point, it shall be kept secret even from me and Mr. Arrow. Otherwise I would ask you to let me resign."

"I see," said the doctor. "You wish us to keep this matter dark and to make a garrison of the stern part of the ship, manned with my friend's own people, and provided with all the arms and powder on board. In other words, you fear a mutiny."

"Sir," said Captain Smollett, "with no intention to take offence, I deny your right to put words into my mouth. No captain, sir, would be justified in going to sea at all if he had ground enough to say that. As for Mr. Arrow, I believe him thoroughly honest; some of the men are the same; all may be for what I know. But I am responsible for the ship's safety and the life of every man Jack aboard of her. I see things going, as I think, not quite right. And I ask you to take certain precautions or let me resign my berth. And that's all."

"Captain Smollett," began the doctor with a smile, "did ever you hear the fable of the mountain and the mouse? You'll excuse me, I dare say, but you remind me of that fable. When you came in here, I'll stake my wig, you meant more than this."

"Doctor," said the captain, "you are smart. When I came in here I meant to get discharged. I had no thought that Mr. Trelawney would hear a word."

"No more I would," cried the squire. "Had Livesey not been here I should have seen you to the deuce. As it is, I have heard you. I will do as you desire, but I think the worse of you."

"That's as you please, sir," said the captain. "You'll find I do my duty."

And with that he took his leave.

"Trelawney," said the doctor, "contrary to all my notions,

I believed you have managed to get two honest men on board with you—that man and John Silver."

"Silver, if you like," cried the squire; "but as for that intolerable humbug, I declare I think his conduct unmanly, unsailorly, and downright un-English."

"Well," says the doctor, "we shall see."

When we came on deck, the men had begun already to take out the arms and powder, yo-ho-ing at their work, while the captain and Mr. Arrow stood by superintending.

The new arrangement was quite to my liking. The whole schooner had been overhauled; six berths had been made astern out of what had been the after-part of the main hold; and this set of cabins was only joined to the galley and forecastle by a sparred passage on the port side. It had been originally meant that the captain, Mr. Arrow, Hunter, Joyce, the doctor, and the squire were to occupy these six berths. Now Redruth and I were to get two of them and Mr. Arrow and the captain were to sleep on deck in the companion, which had been enlarged on each side till you might almost have called it a round-house. Very low it was still, of course; but there was room to swing two hammocks, and even the mate seemed pleased with the arrangement. Even he, perhaps, had been doubtful as to the crew, but that is only guess, for as you shall hear, we had not long the benefit of his opinion.

We were all hard at work, changing the powder and the berths, when the last man or two, and Long John along with them, came off in a shore-boat.

The cook came up the side like a monkey for cleverness, and as soon as he saw what was doing, "So ho, mates!" says he. "What's this?"

"We're a-changing of the powder, Jack," answers one.

"Why, by the powers," cried Long John, "if we do, we'll miss the morning tide!"

"My orders!" said the captain shortly. "You may go below,

my man. Hands will want supper."

"Aye, aye, sir," answered the cook, and touching his forelock, he disappeared at once in the direction of his galley.

"That's a good man, captain," said the doctor.

"Very likely, sir," replied Captain Smollett. "Easy with that, men—easy," he ran on, to the fellows who were shifting the powder; and then suddenly observing me examining the swivel we carried amidships, a long brass nine, "Here you, ship's boy," he cried, "out o' that! Off with you to the cook and get some work."

And then as I was hurrying off I heard him say, quite loudly, to the doctor,

"I'll have no favourites on my ship."

I assure you I was quite of the squire's way of thinking, and hated the captain deeply.

CHAPTER 10

The Voyage

ALL that night we were in a great bustle getting things stowed in their place, and boatfuls of the squire's friends, Mr. Blandly and the like, coming off to wish him a good voyage and a safe return. We never had a night at the "Admiral Benbow" when I had half the work; and I was dog-tired when, a little before dawn, the boatswain sounded his pipe and the crew began to man the capstan-bars. I might have been twice as weary, yet I would not have left the deck, all was so new and interesting to me—the brief commands, the shrill note of the whistle, the men bustling to their places in the glimmer of the ship's lanterns.

"Now, Barbecue, tip us a stave," cried one voice.

"The old one," cried another.

"Aye, aye, mates," said Long John, who was standing by, with his crutch under his arm, and at once broke out in the air and words I knew so well:

> "Fifteen men on the dead man's chest—"

And then the whole crew bore chorus:—

> "Yo-ho-ho, and a bottle of rum!"

And at the third "Ho!" drove the bars before them with a will.

Even at that exciting moment it carried me back to the old "Admiral Benbow" in a second, and I seemed to hear the voice of the captain piping in the chorus. But soon the anchor was short up; soon it was hanging dripping at the bows; soon the sails began to draw, and the land and shipping to flit by on either side; and before I could lie down to snatch an hour of slumber the *Hispaniola* had begun her voyage to the Isle of Treasure.

I am not going to relate that voyage in detail. It was fairly prosperous. The ship proved to be a good ship, the crew were capable seamen, and the captain thoroughly understood his business. But before we came the length of Treasure Island, two or three things had happened which require to be known.

Mr. Arrow, first of all, turned out even worse than the captain had feared. He had no command among the men, and people did what they pleased with him. But that was by no means the worst of it, for after a day or two at sea he began to appear on deck with hazy eye, red cheeks, stuttering tongue, and other marks of drunkenness. Time after time he was ordered below in disgrace. Sometimes he fell and cut himself; sometimes he lay all day long in his little bunk at one side of the companion; sometimes for a day or two he would be almost sober and attend to his work at least passably.

In the meantime, we could never make out where he got the drink. That was the ship's mystery. Watch him as we pleased, we could do nothing to solve it; and when we asked him to his face, he would only laugh if he were drunk, and if he were sober deny solemnly that he ever tasted anything but water.

He was not only useless as an officer and a bad influence amongst the men, but it was plain that at this rate he must soon kill himself outright, so nobody was much surprised, nor very sorry, when one dark night, with a head sea, he disappeared entirely and was seen no more.

"Overboard!" said the captain. "Well, gentlemen, that saves

the trouble of putting him in irons."

But there we were, without a mate; and it was necessary, of course, to advance one of the men. The boatswain, Job Anderson, was the likeliest man aboard, and though he kept his old title, he served in a way as mate. Mr. Trelawney had followed the sea, and his knowledge made him very useful, for he often took a watch himself in easy weather. And the coxswain, Israel Hands, was a careful, wily, old, experienced seaman who could be trusted at a pinch with almost anything.

He was a great confidant of Long John Silver, and so the mention of his name leads me on to speak of our ship's cook, Barbecue, as the men called him.

Aboard ship he carried his crutch by a lanyard round his neck, to have both hands as free as possible. It was something to see him wedge the foot of the crutch against a bulkhead, and propped against it, yielding to every movement of the ship, get on with his cooking like someone safe ashore. Still more strange was it to see him in the heaviest of weather cross the deck. He had a line or two rigged up to help him across the widest spaces—Long John's earrings, they were called; and he would hand himself from one place to another, now using the crutch, now trailing it alongside by the lanyard, as quickly as another man could walk. Yet some of the men who had sailed with him before expressed their pity to see him so reduced.

"He's no common man, Barbecue," said the coxswain to me. "He had good schooling in his young days and can speak like a book when so minded; and brave—a lion's nothing alongside of Long John! I seen him grapple four and knock their heads together—him unarmed."

All the crew respected and even obeyed him. He had a way of talking to each and doing everybody some particular service. To me he was unweariedly kind, and always glad to see me in the galley, which he kept as clean as a new pin, the dishes hanging up burnished and his parrot in a cage in one corner.

"Come away, Hawkins," he would say; "come and have a yarn with John. Nobody more welcome than yourself, my son. Sit you down and hear the news. Here's Cap'n Flint—I calls my parrot Cap'n Flint, after the famous buccaneer—here's Cap'n Flint predicting success to our v'yage. Wasn't you, cap'n?"

And the parrot would say, with great rapidity, "Pieces of eight! Pieces of eight! Pieces of eight!" till you wondered that it was not out of breath, or till John threw his handkerchief over the cage.

"Now, that bird," he would say, "is, maybe, two hundred years old, Hawkins—they live forever mostly; and if anybody's seen more wickedness, it must be the devil himself. She's sailed with England, the great Cap'n England, the pirate. She's been at Madagascar, and at Malabar, and Surinam, and Providence, and Portobello. She was at the fishing up of the wrecked plate ships. It's there she learned 'Pieces of eight,' and little wonder; three hundred and fifty thousand of 'em, Hawkins! She was at the boarding of the Viceroy of the Indies out of Goa, she was; and to look at her you would think she was a babby. But you smelt powder—didn't you, cap'n?"

"Stand by to go about," the parrot would scream.

"Ah, she's a handsome craft, she is," the cook would say, and give her sugar from his pocket, and then the bird would peck at the bars and swear straight on, passing belief for wickedness. "There," John would add, "you can't touch pitch and not be mucked, lad. Here's this poor old innocent bird o' mine swearing blue fire, and none the wiser, you may lay to that. She would swear the same, in a manner of speaking, before chaplain." And John would touch his forelock with a solemn way he had that made me think he was the best of men.

In the meantime, the squire and Captain Smollett were still on pretty distant terms with one another. The squire made no bones about the matter; he despised the captain. The captain, on his part, never spoke but when he was spoken to, and then sharp and short and dry, and not a word wasted. He owned, when driven into a corner, that he seemed to have been wrong about the crew, that some of them were as brisk as he wanted to see and all had behaved fairly well. As for the ship, he had taken a downright fancy to her. "She'll lie a point nearer the wind than a man has a right to expect of his own married wife, sir. But," he would add, "all I say is, we're not home again, and I don't like the cruise."

The squire, at this, would turn away and march up and down the deck, chin in air.

"A trifle more of that man," he would say, "and I shall explode."

We had some heavy weather, which only proved the qualities of the *Hispaniola*. Every man on board seemed well content, and they must have been hard to please if they had been otherwise, for it is my belief there was never a ship's company so spoiled since Noah put to sea. Double grog was going on the least excuse; there was duff on odd days, as, for instance, if the squire heard it was any man's birthday, and always a barrel of apples standing broached in the waist for anyone to help himself that had a fancy.

"Never knew good come of it yet," the captain said to Dr. Livesey. "Spoil forecastle hands, make devils. That's my belief."

But good did come of the apple barrel, as you shall hear, for if it had not been for that, we should have had no note of warning and might all have perished by the hand of treachery.

This was how it came about.

We had run up the trades to get the wind of the island we were after—I am not allowed to be more plain—and now we were running down for it with a bright lookout day and night. It was about the last day of our outward voyage by the largest computation; some time that night, or at latest before noon of the morrow, we should sight the Treasure Island. We were heading S.S.W. and had a steady breeze abeam and a quiet sea.

The *Hispaniola* rolled steadily, dipping her bowsprit now and then with a whiff of spray. All was drawing alow and aloft; everyone was in the bravest spirits because we were now so near an end of the first part of our adventure.

Now, just after sundown, when all my work was over and I was on my way to my berth, it occurred to me that I should like an apple. I ran on deck. The watch was all forward looking out for the island. The man at the helm was watching the luff of the sail and whistling away gently to himself, and that was the only sound excepting the swish of the sea against the bows and around the sides of the ship.

In I got bodily into the apple barrel, and found there was scarce an apple left; but sitting down there in the dark, what with the sound of the waters and the rocking movement of the ship, I had either fallen asleep or was on the point of doing so when a heavy man sat down with rather a clash close by. The barrel shook as he leaned his shoulders against it, and I was just about to jump up when the man began to speak. It was Silver's voice, and before I had heard a dozen words, I would not have shown myself for all the world, but lay there, trembling and listening, in the extreme of fear and curiosity, for from these dozen words I understood that the lives of all the honest men aboard depended upon me alone.

CHAPTER 11

What I Heard in the Apple Barrel

"NO, not I," said Silver. "Flint was cap'n; I was quartermaster, along of my timber leg. The same broadside I lost my leg, old Pew lost his deadlights. It was a master surgeon, him that ampytated me—out of college and all—Latin by the bucket, and what not; but he was hanged like a dog, and sun-dried like the rest, at Corso Castle. That was Roberts' men, that was, and comed of changing names to their ships—*Royal Fortune* and so on. Now, what a ship was christened, so let her stay, I says. So it was with the Cassandra, as brought us all safe home from Malabar, after England took the viceroy of the Indies; so it was with the old *Walrus*, Flint's old ship, as I've seen amuck with the red blood and fit to sink with gold."

"Ah!" cried another voice, that of the youngest hand on board, and evidently full of admiration. "He was the flower of the flock, was Flint!"

"Davis was a man too, by all accounts," said Silver. "I never sailed along of him; first with England, then with Flint, that's my story; and now here on my own account, in a manner of speaking. I laid by nine hundred safe, from England, and two thousand after Flint. That ain't bad for a man before the mast—all safe in bank. 'Tain't earning now, it's saving does it, you may lay to that. Where's all England's men now? I dunno. Where's Flint's? Why, most on 'em aboard here, and glad to get the duff—been begging before that, some on 'em. Old Pew, as had lost his sight, and might have thought shame, spends twelve hundred pound in a year, like a lord in Parliament. Where is he now? Well, he's dead now and under hatches; but for two year before that, shiver my timbers, the man was starving! He begged, and he stole, and he cut throats, and starved at that, by the powers!"

"Well, it ain't much use, after all," said the young seaman.

"'Tain't much use for fools, you may lay to it—that, nor nothing," cried Silver. "But now, you look here: you're young, you are, but you're as smart as paint. I see that when I set my eyes on you, and I'll talk to you like a man."

You may imagine how I felt when I heard this abominable old rogue addressing another in the very same words of flattery as he had used to myself. I think, if I had been able, that I would have killed him through the barrel. Meantime, he ran on, little supposing he was overheard.

"Here it is about gentlemen of fortune. They lives rough, and they risk swinging, but they eat and drink like fighting-cocks, and when a cruise is done, why, it's hundreds of pounds instead of hundreds of farthings in their pockets. Now, the most goes for rum and a good fling, and to sea again in their shirts. But that's not the course I lay. I puts it all away, some here, some there, and none too much anywheres, by reason of suspicion. I'm fifty, mark you; once back from this cruise, I set up gentleman in earnest. Time enough too, says you. Ah, but I've lived easy in the meantime, never denied myself o' nothing heart desires, and slep' soft and ate dainty all my days but when at sea. And how did I begin? Before the mast, like you!"

"Well," said the other, "but all the other money's gone now, ain't it? You daren't show face in Bristol after this."

"Why, where might you suppose it was?" asked Silver derisively.

"At Bristol, in banks and places," answered his companion.

"It were," said the cook; "it were when we weighed anchor.

But my old missis has it all by now. And the Spy-glass is sold, lease and goodwill and rigging; and the old girl's off to meet me. I would tell you where, for I trust you, but it'd make jealousy among the mates."

"And can you trust your missis?" asked the other.

"Gentlemen of fortune," returned the cook, "usually trusts little among themselves, and right they are, you may lay to it. But I have a way with me, I have. When a mate brings a slip on his cable—one as knows me, I mean—it won't be in the same world with old John. There was some that was feared of Pew, and some that was feared of Flint; but Flint his own self was feared of me. Feared he was, and proud. They was the roughest crew afloat, was Flint's; the devil himself would have been feared to go to sea with them. Well now, I tell you, I'm not a boasting man, and you seen yourself how easy I keep company, but when I was quartermaster, *lambs* wasn't the word for Flint's old buccaneers. Ah, you may be sure of yourself in old John's ship."

"Well, I tell you now," replied the lad, "I didn't half a quarter like the job till I had this talk with you, John; but there's my hand on it now."

"And a brave lad you were, and smart too," answered Silver, shaking hands so heartily that all the barrel shook, "and a finer figurehead for a gentleman of fortune I never clapped my eyes on."

By this time I had begun to understand the meaning of their terms. By a "gentleman of fortune" they plainly meant neither more nor less than a common pirate, and the little scene that I had overheard was the last act in the corruption of one of the honest hands—perhaps of the last one left aboard. But on this point I was soon to be relieved, for Silver giving a little whistle, a third man strolled up and sat down by the party.

"Dick's square," said Silver.

"Oh, I know'd Dick was square," returned the voice of the coxswain, Israel Hands. "He's no fool, is Dick." And he turned his quid and spat. "But look here," he went on, "here's what I want to know, Barbecue: how long are we a-going to stand off and on like a blessed bumboat? I've had a'most enough o' Cap'n Smollett; he's hazed me long enough, by thunder! I want to go into that cabin, I do. I want their pickles and wines, and that."

"Israel," said Silver, "your head ain't much account, nor ever was. But you're able to hear, I reckon; leastways, your ears is big enough. Now, here's what I say: you'll berth forward, and you'll live hard, and you'll speak soft, and you'll keep sober till I give the word; and you may lay to that, my son."

"Well, I don't say no, do I?" growled the coxswain. "What I say is, when? That's what I say."

"When! By the powers!" cried Silver. "Well now, if you want to know, I'll tell you when. The last moment I can manage, and that's when. Here's a first-rate seaman, Cap'n Smollett, sails the blessed ship for us. Here's this squire and doctor with a map and such—I don't know where it is, do I? No more do you, says you. Well then, I mean this squire and doctor shall find the stuff, and help us to get it aboard, by the powers. Then we'll see. If I was sure of you all, sons of double Dutchmen, I'd have Cap'n Smollett navigate us half-way back again before I struck."

"Why, we're all seamen aboard here, I should think," said the lad Dick.

"We're all foc's'le hands, you mean," snapped Silver. "We can steer a course, but who's to set one? That's what all you gentlemen split on, first and last. If I had my way, I'd have Cap'n Smollett work us back into the trades at least; then we'd have no blessed miscalculations and a spoonful of water a day. But I know the sort you are. I'll finish with 'em at the island, as soon's the blunt's on board, and a pity it is. But you're never happy till you're drunk. Split my sides, I've a sick heart to sail with the likes of you!"

"Easy all, Long John," cried Israel. "Who's a-crossin' of you?"

"Why, how many tall ships, think ye, now, have I seen laid aboard? And how many brisk lads drying in the sun at Execution Dock?" cried Silver. "And all for this same hurry and hurry and hurry. You hear me? I seen a thing or two at sea, I have. If you would on'y lay your course, and a p'int to windward, you would ride in carriages, you would. But not you! I know you. You'll have your mouthful of rum tomorrow, and go hang."

"Everybody knowed you was a kind of a chapling, John; but there's others as could hand and steer as well as you," said Israel. "They liked a bit o' fun, they did. They wasn't so high and dry, nohow, but took their fling, like jolly companions every one."

"So?" says Silver. "Well, and where are they now? Pew was that sort, and he died a beggar-man. Flint was, and he died of rum at Savannah. Ah, they was a sweet crew, they was! On'y, where are they?"

"But," asked Dick, "when we do lay 'em athwart, what are we to do with 'em, anyhow?"

"There's the man for me!" cried the cook admiringly. "That's what I call business. Well, what would you think? Put 'em ashore like maroons? That would have been England's way. Or cut 'em down like that much pork? That would have been Flint's, or Billy Bones's."

"Billy was the man for that," said Israel. "'Dead men don't bite,' says he. Well, he's dead now hisself; he knows the long and short on it now; and if ever a rough hand come to port, it was Billy."

"Right you are," said Silver; "rough and ready. But mark you here, I'm an easy man—I'm quite the gentleman, says you; but this time it's serious. Dooty is dooty, mates. I give my

vote—death. When I'm in Parlyment and riding in my coach,
I don't want none of these sea-lawyers in the cabin a-coming
home, unlooked for, like the devil at prayers. Wait is what I say;
but when the time comes, why, let her rip!"

"John," cries the coxswain, "you're a man!"

"You'll say so, Israel when you see," said Silver. "Only one
thing I claim—I claim Trelawney. I'll wring his calf's head off
his body with these hands, Dick!" he added, breaking off. "You
just jump up, like a sweet lad, and get me an apple, to wet my
pipe like."

You may fancy the terror I was in! I should have leaped
out and run for it if I had found the strength, but my limbs
and heart alike misgave me. I heard Dick begin to rise, and
then someone seemingly stopped him, and the voice of Hands
exclaimed,

"Oh, stow that! Don't you get sucking of that bilge, John.
Let's have a go of the rum."

"Dick," said Silver, "I trust you. I've a gauge on the keg,
mind. There's the key; you fill a pannikin and bring it up."

Terrified as I was, I could not help thinking to myself that
this must have been how Mr. Arrow got the strong waters that
destroyed him.

Dick was gone but a little while, and during his absence
Israel spoke straight on in the cook's ear. It was but a word or
two that I could catch, and yet I gathered some important news,
for besides other scraps that tended to the same purpose, this
whole clause was audible: "Not another man of them'll jine."
Hence there were still faithful men on board.

When Dick returned, one after another of the trio took the
pannikin and drank—one "To luck," another with a "Here's to
old Flint," and Silver himself saying, in a kind of song, "Here's
to ourselves, and hold your luff, plenty of prizes and plenty of
duff."

Just then a sort of brightness fell upon me in the barrel,

and looking up, I found the moon had risen and was silvering
the mizzen-top and shining white on the luff of the fore-sail;
and almost at the same time the voice of the lookout shouted,
"Land ho!"

CHAPTER 12

Council of War

THERE was a great rush of feet across the deck. I could hear people tumbling up from the cabin and the forecastle, and slipping in an instant outside my barrel, I dived behind the fore-sail, made a double towards the stern, and came out upon the open deck in time to join Hunter and Dr. Livesey in the rush for the weather bow.

There all hands were already congregated. A belt of fog had lifted almost simultaneously with the appearance of the moon. Away to the south-west of us we saw two low hills, about a couple of miles apart, and rising behind one of them a third and higher hill, whose peak was still buried in the fog. All three seemed sharp and conical in figure.

So much I saw, almost in a dream, for I had not yet recovered from my horrid fear of a minute or two before. And then I heard the voice of Captain Smollett issuing orders. The *Hispaniola* was laid a couple of points nearer the wind and now sailed a course that would just clear the island on the east.

"And now, men," said the captain, when all was sheeted home, "has any one of you ever seen that land ahead?"

"I have, sir," said Silver. "I've watered there with a trader I was cook in."

"The anchorage is on the south, behind an islet, I fancy?" asked the captain.

"Yes, sir; Skeleton Island they calls it. It were a main place for pirates once, and a hand we had on board knowed all their names for it. That hill to the nor'ard they calls the Fore-mast Hill; there are three hills in a row running south'ard—fore, main, and mizzen, sir. But the main—that's the big un, with the cloud on it—they usually calls the Spy-glass, by reason of a lookout they kept when they was in the anchorage cleaning, for it's there they cleaned their ships, sir, asking your pardon."

"I have a chart here," says Captain Smollett. "See if that's the place."

Long John's eyes burned in his head as he took the chart, but by the fresh look of the paper I knew he was doomed to disappointment. This was not the map we found in Billy Bones's chest, but an accurate copy, complete in all things—names and heights and soundings—with the single exception of the red crosses and the written notes. Sharp as must have been his annoyance, Silver had the strength of mind to hide it.

"Yes, sir," said he, "this is the spot, to be sure, and very prettily drawn out. Who might have done that, I wonder? The pirates were too ignorant, I reckon. Aye, here it is: 'Capt. Kidd's Anchorage'—just the name my shipmate called it. There's a strong current runs along the south, and then away nor'ard up the west coast. Right you was, sir," says he, "to haul your wind and keep the weather of the island. Leastways, if such was your intention as to enter and careen, and there ain't no better place for that in these waters."

"Thank you, my man," says Captain Smollett. "I'll ask you later on to give us a help. You may go."

I was surprised at the coolness with which John avowed his knowledge of the island, and I own I was half-frightened when I saw him drawing nearer to myself. He did not know, to be sure, that I had overheard his council from the apple barrel, and yet I had by this time taken such a horror of his cruelty, duplicity, and power that I could scarce conceal a shudder when he laid his hand upon my arm.

"Ah," says he, "this here is a sweet spot, this island—a sweet spot for a lad to get ashore on. You'll bathe, and you'll climb trees, and you'll hunt goats, you will; and you'll get aloft on them hills like a goat yourself. Why, it makes me young again. I was going to forget my timber leg, I was. It's a pleasant thing to be young and have ten toes, and you may lay to that. When you want to go a bit of exploring, you just ask old John, and he'll put up a snack for you to take along."

And clapping me in the friendliest way upon the shoulder, he hobbled off forward and went below.

Captain Smollett, the squire, and Dr. Livesey were talking together on the quarter-deck, and anxious as I was to tell them my story, I durst not interrupt them openly. While I was still casting about in my thoughts to find some probable excuse, Dr. Livesey called me to his side. He had left his pipe below, and being a slave to tobacco, had meant that I should fetch it; but as soon as I was near enough to speak and not to be overheard, I broke immediately, "Doctor, let me speak. Get the captain and squire down to the cabin, and then make some pretence to send for me. I have terrible news."

The doctor changed countenance a little, but next moment he was master of himself.

"Thank you, Jim," said he quite loudly, "that was all I wanted to know," as if he had asked me a question.

And with that he turned on his heel and rejoined the other two. They spoke together for a little, and though none of them started, or raised his voice, or so much as whistled, it was plain enough that Dr. Livesey had communicated my request, for the next thing that I heard was the captain giving an order to Job Anderson, and all hands were piped on deck.

"My lads," said Captain Smollett, "I've a word to say to you. This land that we have sighted is the place we have been sailing for. Mr. Trelawney, being a very open-handed gentleman, as we all know, has just asked me a word or two, and as I was able to tell him that every man on board had done his duty, alow and aloft, as I never ask to see it done better, why, he and I and the doctor are going below to the cabin to drink YOUR health and luck, and you'll have grog served out for you to drink *our* health and luck. I'll tell you what I think of this: I think it handsome. And if you think as I do, you'll give a good sea-cheer for the gentleman that does it."

The cheer followed—that was a matter of course; but it rang out so full and hearty that I confess I could hardly believe these same men were plotting for our blood.

"One more cheer for Cap'n Smollett," cried Long John when the first had subsided.

And this also was given with a will.

On the top of that the three gentlemen went below, and not long after, word was sent forward that Jim Hawkins was wanted in the cabin.

I found them all three seated round the table, a bottle of Spanish wine and some raisins before them, and the doctor smoking away, with his wig on his lap, and that, I knew, was a sign that he was agitated. The stern window was open, for it was a warm night, and you could see the moon shining behind on the ship's wake.

"Now, Hawkins," said the squire, "you have something to say. Speak up."

I did as I was bid, and as short as I could make it, told the whole details of Silver's conversation. Nobody interrupted me till I was done, nor did any one of the three of them make so much as a movement, but they kept their eyes upon my face from first to last.

"Jim," said Dr. Livesey, "take a seat."

And they made me sit down at table beside them, poured me out a glass of wine, filled my hands with raisins, and all three, one after the other, and each with a bow, drank my good health, and their service to me, for my luck and courage.

"Now, captain," said the squire, "you were right, and I was

wrong. I own myself an ass, and I await your orders."

"No more an ass than I, sir," returned the captain. "I never heard of a crew that meant to mutiny but what showed signs before, for any man that had an eye in his head to see the mischief and take steps according. But this crew," he added, "beats me."

"Captain," said the doctor, "with your permission, that's Silver. A very remarkable man."

"He'd look remarkably well from a yard-arm, sir," returned the captain. "But this is talk; this don't lead to anything. I see three or four points, and with Mr. Trelawney's permission, I'll name them."

"You, sir, are the captain. It is for you to speak," says Mr. Trelawney grandly.

"First point," began Mr. Smollett. "We must go on, because we can't turn back. If I gave the word to go about, they would rise at once. Second point, we have time before us—at least until this treasure's found. Third point, there are faithful hands. Now, sir, it's got to come to blows sooner or later, and what I propose is to take time by the forelock, as the saying is, and come to blows some fine day when they least expect it. We can count, I take it, on your own home servants, Mr. Trelawney?"

"As upon myself," declared the squire.

"Three," reckoned the captain; "ourselves make seven, counting Hawkins here. Now, about the honest hands?"

"Most likely Trelawney's own men," said the doctor; "those he had picked up for himself before he lit on Silver."

"Nay," replied the squire. "Hands was one of mine."

"I did think I could have trusted Hands," added the captain.

"And to think that they're all Englishmen!" broke out the squire. "Sir, I could find it in my heart to blow the ship up."

"Well, gentlemen," said the captain, "the best that I can say is not much. We must lay to, if you please, and keep a bright lookout. It's trying on a man, I know. It would be pleasanter to come to blows. But there's no help for it till we know our men. Lay to, and whistle for a wind, that's my view."

"Jim here," said the doctor, "can help us more than anyone. The men are not shy with him, and Jim is a noticing lad."

"Hawkins, I put prodigious faith in you," added the squire.

I began to feel pretty desperate at this, for I felt altogether helpless; and yet, by an odd train of circumstances, it was indeed through me that safety came. In the meantime, talk as we pleased, there were only seven out of the twenty-six on whom we knew we could rely; and out of these seven one was a boy, so that the grown men on our side were six to their nineteen.

PART THREE

---◆◆◆◆◆---

MY SHORE
ADVENTURE

CHAPTER 13

How My Shore Adventure Began

THE appearance of the island when I came on deck next morning was altogether changed. Although the breeze had now utterly ceased, we had made a great deal of way during the night and were now lying becalmed about half a mile to the south-east of the low eastern coast. Grey-coloured woods covered a large part of the surface. This even tint was indeed broken up by streaks of yellow sand-break in the lower lands, and by many tall trees of the pine family, out-topping the others—some singly, some in clumps; but the general colouring was uniform and sad. The hills ran up clear above the vegetation in spires of naked rock. All were strangely shaped, and the Spy-glass, which was by three or four hundred feet the tallest on the island, was likewise the strangest in configuration, running up sheer from almost every side and then suddenly cut off at the top like a pedestal to put a statue on.

The *Hispaniola* was rolling scuppers under in the ocean swell. The booms were tearing at the blocks, the rudder was banging to and fro, and the whole ship creaking, groaning, and jumping like a manufactory. I had to cling tight to the backstay, and the world turned giddily before my eyes, for though I was a good enough sailor when there was way on, this standing still and being rolled about like a bottle was a thing I never learned to stand without a qualm or so, above all in the morning, on an empty stomach.

Perhaps it was this—perhaps it was the look of the island, with its grey, melancholy woods, and wild stone spires, and the surf that we could both see and hear foaming and thundering on the steep beach—at least, although the sun shone bright and hot, and the shore birds were fishing and crying all around us, and you would have thought anyone would have been glad to get to land after being so long at sea, my heart sank, as the saying is, into my boots; and from the first look onward, I hated the very thought of Treasure Island.

We had a dreary morning's work before us, for there was no sign of any wind, and the boats had to be got out and manned, and the ship warped three or four miles round the corner of the island and up the narrow passage to the haven behind Skeleton Island. I volunteered for one of the boats, where I had, of course, no business. The heat was sweltering, and the men grumbled fiercely over their work. Anderson was in command of my boat, and instead of keeping the crew in order, he grumbled as loud as the worst.

"Well," he said with an oath, "it's not forever."

I thought this was a very bad sign, for up to that day the men had gone briskly and willingly about their business; but the very sight of the island had relaxed the cords of discipline.

All the way in, Long John stood by the steersman and conned the ship. He knew the passage like the palm of his hand, and though the man in the chains got everywhere more water than was down in the chart, John never hesitated once.

"There's a strong scour with the ebb," he said, "and this here passage has been dug out, in a manner of speaking, with a spade."

We brought up just where the anchor was in the chart, about a third of a mile from each shore, the mainland on one side and Skeleton Island on the other. The bottom was clean sand. The plunge of our anchor sent up clouds of birds wheeling and crying over the woods, but in less than a minute they were down again and all was once more silent.

The place was entirely land-locked, buried in woods, the trees coming right down to high-water mark, the shores mostly flat, and the hilltops standing round at a distance in a sort of amphitheatre, one here, one there. Two little rivers, or rather two swamps, emptied out into this pond, as you might call it; and the foliage round that part of the shore had a kind of poisonous brightness. From the ship we could see nothing of the house or stockade, for they were quite buried among trees; and if it had not been for the chart on the companion, we might have been the first that had ever anchored there since the island arose out of the seas.

There was not a breath of air moving, nor a sound but that of the surf booming half a mile away along the beaches and against the rocks outside. A peculiar stagnant smell hung over the anchorage—a smell of sodden leaves and rotting tree trunks. I observed the doctor sniffing and sniffing, like someone tasting a bad egg.

"I don't know about treasure," he said, "but I'll stake my wig there's fever here."

If the conduct of the men had been alarming in the boat, it became truly threatening when they had come aboard. They lay about the deck growling together in talk. The slightest order was received with a black look and grudgingly and carelessly obeyed. Even the honest hands must have caught the infection, for there was not one man aboard to mend another. Mutiny, it was plain, hung over us like a thunder-cloud.

And it was not only we of the cabin party who perceived the danger. Long John was hard at work going from group to group, spending himself in good advice, and as for example no man could have shown a better. He fairly outstripped himself in willingness and civility; he was all smiles to everyone. If an order were given, John would be on his crutch in an instant, with the cheeriest "Aye, aye, sir!" in the world; and when there was nothing else to do, he kept up one song after another, as if to conceal the discontent of the rest.

Of all the gloomy features of that gloomy afternoon, this obvious anxiety on the part of Long John appeared the worst.

We held a council in the cabin.

"Sir," said the captain, "if I risk another order, the whole ship'll come about our ears by the run. You see, sir, here it is. I get a rough answer, do I not? Well, if I speak back, pikes will be going in two shakes; if I don't, Silver will see there's something under that, and the game's up. Now, we've only one man to rely on."

"And who is that?" asked the squire.

"Silver, sir," returned the captain; "he's as anxious as you and I to smother things up. This is a tiff; he'd soon talk 'em out of it if he had the chance, and what I propose to do is to give him the chance. Let's allow the men an afternoon ashore. If they all go, why we'll fight the ship. If they none of them go, well then, we hold the cabin, and God defend the right. If some go, you mark my words, sir, Silver'll bring 'em aboard again as mild as lambs."

It was so decided; loaded pistols were served out to all the sure men; Hunter, Joyce, and Redruth were taken into our confidence and received the news with less surprise and a better spirit than we had looked for, and then the captain went on deck and addressed the crew.

"My lads," said he, "we've had a hot day and are all tired and out of sorts. A turn ashore'll hurt nobody—the boats are still in the water; you can take the gigs, and as many as please may go ashore for the afternoon. I'll fire a gun half an hour before sundown."

I believe the silly fellows must have thought they would break their shins over treasure as soon as they were landed, for they all came out of their sulks in a moment and gave a cheer that started the echo in a faraway hill and sent the birds once more flying and squalling round the anchorage.

The captain was too bright to be in the way. He whipped out of sight in a moment, leaving Silver to arrange the party, and I fancy it was as well he did so. Had he been on deck, he could no longer so much as have pretended not to understand the situation. It was as plain as day. Silver was the captain, and a mighty rebellious crew he had of it. The honest hands—and I was soon to see it proved that there were such on board—must have been very stupid fellows. Or rather, I suppose the truth was this, that all hands were disaffected by the example of the ringleaders—only some more, some less; and a few, being good fellows in the main, could neither be led nor driven any further. It is one thing to be idle and skulk and quite another to take a ship and murder a number of innocent men.

At last, however, the party was made up. Six fellows were to stay on board, and the remaining thirteen, including Silver, began to embark.

Then it was that there came into my head the first of the mad notions that contributed so much to save our lives. If six men were left by Silver, it was plain our party could not take and fight the ship; and since only six were left, it was equally plain that the cabin party had no present need of my assistance. It occurred to me at once to go ashore. In a jiffy I had slipped over the side and curled up in the fore-sheets of the nearest boat, and almost at the same moment she shoved off.

No one took notice of me, only the bow oar saying, "Is that you, Jim? Keep your head down." But Silver, from the other boat, looked sharply over and called out to know if that were me; and from that moment I began to regret what I had done.

The crews raced for the beach, but the boat I was in, having some start and being at once the lighter and the better manned, shot far ahead of her consort, and the bow had struck among the shore-side trees and I had caught a branch and swung myself out and plunged into the nearest thicket while Silver and the rest were still a hundred yards behind.

"Jim, Jim!" I heard him shouting.

But you may suppose I paid no heed; jumping, ducking, and breaking through, I ran straight before my nose till I could run no longer.

CHAPTER 14

The First Blow

I WAS so pleased at having given the slip to Long John that I began to enjoy myself and look around me with some interest on the strange land that I was in.

I had crossed a marshy tract full of willows, bulrushes, and odd, outlandish, swampy trees; and I had now come out upon the skirts of an open piece of undulating, sandy country, about a mile long, dotted with a few pines and a great number of contorted trees, not unlike the oak in growth, but pale in the foliage, like willows. On the far side of the open stood one of the hills, with two quaint, craggy peaks shining vividly in the sun.

I now felt for the first time the joy of exploration. The isle was uninhabited; my shipmates I had left behind, and nothing lived in front of me but dumb brutes and fowls. I turned hither and thither among the trees. Here and there were flowering plants, unknown to me; here and there I saw snakes, and one raised his head from a ledge of rock and hissed at me with a noise not unlike the spinning of a top. Little did I suppose that he was a deadly enemy and that the noise was the famous rattle.

Then I came to a long thicket of these oaklike trees—live, or evergreen, oaks, I heard afterwards they should be called—which grew low along the sand like brambles, the boughs curiously twisted, the foliage compact, like thatch. The thicket stretched down from the top of one of the sandy knolls, spreading and growing taller as it went, until it reached the margin of the broad, reedy fen, through which the nearest of the little rivers soaked its way into the anchorage. The marsh was steaming in the strong sun, and the outline of the Spyglass trembled through the haze.

All at once there began to go a sort of bustle among the bulrushes; a wild duck flew up with a quack, another followed, and soon over the whole surface of the marsh a great cloud of birds hung screaming and circling in the air. I judged at once that some of my shipmates must be drawing near along the borders of the fen. Nor was I deceived, for soon I heard the very distant and low tones of a human voice, which, as I continued to give ear, grew steadily louder and nearer.

This put me in a great fear, and I crawled under cover of the nearest live-oak and squatted there, hearkening, as silent as a mouse.

Another voice answered, and then the first voice, which I now recognized to be Silver's, once more took up the story and ran on for a long while in a stream, only now and again interrupted by the other. By the sound they must have been talking earnestly, and almost fiercely; but no distinct word came to my hearing.

At last the speakers seemed to have paused and perhaps to have sat down, for not only did they cease to draw any nearer, but the birds themselves began to grow more quiet and to settle again to their places in the swamp.

And now I began to feel that I was neglecting my business, that since I had been so foolhardy as to come ashore with these desperadoes, the least I could do was to overhear them at their councils, and that my plain and obvious duty was to draw as close as I could manage, under the favourable ambush of the crouching trees.

I could tell the direction of the speakers pretty exactly, not only by the sound of their voices but by the behaviour of the few birds that still hung in alarm above the heads of the intruders.

Crawling on all fours, I made steadily but slowly towards them, till at last, raising my head to an aperture among the leaves, I could see clear down into a little green dell beside the marsh, and closely set about with trees, where Long John Silver and another of the crew stood face to face in conversation.

The sun beat full upon them. Silver had thrown his hat beside him on the ground, and his great, smooth, blond face, all shining with heat, was lifted to the other man's in a kind of appeal.

"Mate," he was saying, "it's because I thinks gold dust of you—gold dust, and you may lay to that! If I hadn't took to you like pitch, do you think I'd have been here a-warning of you? All's up—you can't make nor mend; it's to save your neck that I'm a-speaking, and if one of the wild uns knew it, where'd I be, Tom—now, tell me, where'd I be?"

"Silver," said the other man—and I observed he was not only red in the face, but spoke as hoarse as a crow, and his voice shook too, like a taut rope—"Silver," says he, "you're old, and you're honest, or has the name for it; and you've money too, which lots of poor sailors hasn't; and you're brave, or I'm mistook. And will you tell me you'll let yourself be led away with that kind of a mess of swabs? Not you! As sure as God sees me, I'd sooner lose my hand. If I turn agin my dooty—"

And then all of a sudden he was interrupted by a noise. I had found one of the honest hands—well, here, at that same moment, came news of another. Far away out in the marsh there arose, all of a sudden, a sound like the cry of anger, then another on the back of it; and then one horrid, long-drawn scream. The rocks of the Spy-glass re-echoed it a score of times; the whole troop of marsh-birds rose again, darkening heaven, with a simultaneous whirr; and long after that death yell was still ringing in my brain, silence had re-established its empire, and only the rustle of the redescending birds and the boom of the distant surges disturbed the languor of the afternoon.

Tom had leaped at the sound, like a horse at the spur, but Silver had not winked an eye. He stood where he was, resting lightly on his crutch, watching his companion like a snake about to spring.

"John!" said the sailor, stretching out his hand.

"Hands off!" cried Silver, leaping back a yard, as it seemed to me, with the speed and security of a trained gymnast.

"Hands off, if you like, John Silver," said the other. "It's a black conscience that can make you feared of me. But in heaven's name, tell me, what was that?"

"That?" returned Silver, smiling away, but warier than ever, his eye a mere pin-point in his big face, but gleaming like a crumb of glass. "That? Oh, I reckon that'll be Alan."

And at this point Tom flashed out like a hero.

"Alan!" he cried. "Then rest his soul for a true seaman! And as for you, John Silver, long you've been a mate of mine, but you're mate of mine no more. If I die like a dog, I'll die in my dooty. You've killed Alan, have you? Kill me too, if you can. But I defies you."

And with that, this brave fellow turned his back directly on the cook and set off walking for the beach. But he was not destined to go far. With a cry John seized the branch of a tree, whipped the crutch out of his armpit, and sent that uncouth missile hurtling through the air. It struck poor Tom, point foremost, and with stunning violence, right between the shoulders in the middle of his back. His hands flew up, he gave a sort of gasp, and fell.

Whether he were injured much or little, none could ever tell. Like enough, to judge from the sound, his back was broken on the spot. But he had no time given him to recover. Silver, agile as a monkey even without leg or crutch, was on the top of him next moment and had twice buried his knife up to the hilt in that defenceless body. From my place of ambush, I could hear him pant aloud as he struck the blows.

I do not know what it rightly is to faint, but I do know that for the next little while the whole world swam away from before me in a whirling mist; Silver and the birds, and the tall Spy-glass hilltop, going round and round and topsy-turvy before my eyes, and all manner of bells ringing and distant voices shouting in my ear.

When I came again to myself the monster had pulled himself together, his crutch under his arm, his hat upon his head. Just before him Tom lay motionless upon the sward; but the murderer minded him not a whit, cleansing his blood-stained knife the while upon a wisp of grass. Everything else was unchanged, the sun still shining mercilessly on the steaming marsh and the tall pinnacle of the mountain, and I could scarce persuade myself that murder had been actually done and a human life cruelly cut short a moment since before my eyes.

But now John put his hand into his pocket, brought out a whistle, and blew upon it several modulated blasts that rang far across the heated air. I could not tell, of course, the meaning of the signal, but it instantly awoke my fears. More men would be coming. I might be discovered. They had already slain two of the honest people; after Tom and Alan, might not I come next?

Instantly I began to extricate myself and crawl back again, with what speed and silence I could manage, to the more open portion of the wood. As I did so, I could hear hails coming and going between the old buccaneer and his comrades, and this sound of danger lent me wings. As soon as I was clear of the thicket, I ran as I never ran before, scarce minding the direction of my flight, so long as it led me from the murderers; and as I ran, fear grew and grew upon me until it turned into a kind of frenzy.

Indeed, could anyone be more entirely lost than I? When the gun fired, how should I dare to go down to the boats among those fiends, still smoking from their crime? Would not the first of them who saw me wring my neck like a snipe's? Would not my absence itself be an evidence to them of my alarm, and therefore of my fatal knowledge? It was all over, I thought. Good-bye to the *Hispaniola*; good-bye to the squire, the doctor, and the captain! There was nothing left for me but death by starvation or death by the hands of the mutineers.

All this while, as I say, I was still running, and without taking any notice, I had drawn near to the foot of the little hill with the two peaks and had got into a part of the island where the live-oaks grew more widely apart and seemed more like forest trees in their bearing and dimensions. Mingled with these were a few scattered pines, some fifty, some nearer seventy, feet high. The air too smelt more freshly than down beside the marsh.

And here a fresh alarm brought me to a standstill with a thumping heart.

CHAPTER 15

The Man of the Island

FROM the side of the hill, which was here steep and stony, a spout of gravel was dislodged and fell rattling and bounding through the trees. My eyes turned instinctively in that direction, and I saw a figure leap with great rapidity behind the trunk of a pine. What it was, whether bear or man or monkey, I could in no wise tell. It seemed dark and shaggy; more I knew not. But the terror of this new apparition brought me to a stand.

I was now, it seemed, cut off upon both sides; behind me the murderers, before me this lurking nondescript. And immediately I began to prefer the dangers that I knew to those I knew not. Silver himself appeared less terrible in contrast with this creature of the woods, and I turned on my heel, and looking sharply behind me over my shoulder, began to retrace my steps in the direction of the boats.

Instantly the figure reappeared, and making a wide circuit, began to head me off. I was tired, at any rate; but had I been as fresh as when I rose, I could see it was in vain for me to contend in speed with such an adversary. From trunk to trunk the creature flitted like a deer, running manlike on two legs, but unlike any man that I had ever seen, stooping almost double as it ran. Yet a man it was, I could no longer be in doubt about that.

I began to recall what I had heard of cannibals. I was within an ace of calling for help. But the mere fact that he was a man, however wild, had somewhat reassured me, and my fear of Silver began to revive in proportion. I stood still, therefore, and cast about for some method of escape; and as I was so thinking, the recollection of my pistol flashed into my mind. As soon as I remembered I was not defenceless, courage glowed again in my heart and I set my face resolutely for this man of the island and walked briskly towards him.

He was concealed by this time behind another tree trunk; but he must have been watching me closely, for as soon as I began to move in his direction he reappeared and took a step to meet me. Then he hesitated, drew back, came forward again, and at last, to my wonder and confusion, threw himself on his knees and held out his clasped hands in supplication.

At that I once more stopped.

"Who are you?" I asked.

"Ben Gunn," he answered, and his voice sounded hoarse and awkward, like a rusty lock. "I'm poor Ben Gunn, I am; and I haven't spoke with a Christian these three years."

I could now see that he was a white man like myself and that his features were even pleasing. His skin, wherever it was exposed, was burnt by the sun; even his lips were black, and his fair eyes looked quite startling in so dark a face. Of all the beggar-men that I had seen or fancied, he was the chief for raggedness. He was clothed with tatters of old ship's canvas and old sea-cloth, and this extraordinary patchwork was all held together by a system of the most various and incongruous fastenings, brass buttons, bits of stick, and loops of tarry gaskin. About his waist he wore an old brass-buckled leather belt, which was the one thing solid in his whole accoutrement.

"Three years!" I cried. "Were you shipwrecked?"

"Nay, mate," said he; "marooned."

I had heard the word, and I knew it stood for a horrible kind of punishment common enough among the buccaneers, in which the offender is put ashore with a little powder and shot and left behind on some desolate and distant island.

"Marooned three years agone," he continued, "and lived on goats since then, and berries, and oysters. Wherever a man is, says I, a man can do for himself. But, mate, my heart is sore for Christian diet. You mightn't happen to have a piece of cheese about you, now? No? Well, many's the long night I've dreamed of cheese—toasted, mostly—and woke up again, and here I were."

"If ever I can get aboard again," said I, "you shall have cheese by the stone."

All this time he had been feeling the stuff of my jacket, smoothing my hands, looking at my boots, and generally, in the intervals of his speech, showing a childish pleasure in the presence of a fellow creature. But at my last words he perked up into a kind of startled slyness.

"If ever you can get aboard again, says you?" he repeated. "Why, now, who's to hinder you?"

"Not you, I know," was my reply.

"And right you was," he cried. "Now you—what do you call yourself, mate?"

"Jim," I told him.

"Jim, Jim," says he, quite pleased apparently. "Well, now, Jim, I've lived that rough as you'd be ashamed to hear of. Now, for instance, you wouldn't think I had had a pious mother—to look at me?" he asked.

"Why, no, not in particular," I answered.

"Ah, well," said he, "but I had—remarkable pious. And I was a civil, pious boy, and could rattle off my catechism that fast, as you couldn't tell one word from another. And here's what it come to, Jim, and it begun with chuck-farthen on the blessed grave-stones! That's what it begun with, but it went further'n that; and so my mother told me, and predicked the whole, she did, the pious woman! But it were Providence that put me here. I've thought it all out in this here lonely island, and I'm back on piety. You don't catch me tasting rum so much, but just a thimbleful for luck, of course, the first chance I have. I'm bound I'll be good, and I see the way to. And, Jim"—looking all round him and lowering his voice to a whisper—"I'm rich."

I now felt sure that the poor fellow had gone crazy in his solitude, and I suppose I must have shown the feeling in my face, for he repeated the statement hotly:

"Rich! Rich! I says. And I'll tell you what: I'll make a man of you, Jim. Ah, Jim, you'll bless your stars, you will, you was the first that found me!"

And at this there came suddenly a lowering shadow over his face, and he tightened his grasp upon my hand and raised a forefinger threateningly before my eyes.

"Now, Jim, you tell me true: that ain't Flint's ship?" he asked.

At this I had a happy inspiration. I began to believe that I had found an ally, and I answered him at once.

"It's not Flint's ship, and Flint is dead; but I'll tell you true, as you ask me—there are some of Flint's hands aboard; worse luck for the rest of us."

"Not a man—with one—leg?" he gasped.

"Silver?" I asked.

"Ah, Silver!" says he. "That were his name."

"He's the cook, and the ringleader too."

He was still holding me by the wrist, and at that he give it quite a wring.

"If you was sent by Long John," he said, "I'm as good as pork, and I know it. But where was you, do you suppose?"

I had made my mind up in a moment, and by way of answer told him the whole story of our voyage and the predicament in which we found ourselves. He heard me with the keenest interest, and when I had done he patted me on the head.

"You're a good lad, Jim," he said; "and you're all in a clove hitch, ain't you? Well, you just put your trust in Ben Gunn— Ben Gunn's the man to do it. Would you think it likely, now, that your squire would prove a liberal-minded one in case of help—him being in a clove hitch, as you remark?"

I told him the squire was the most liberal of men.

"Aye, but you see," returned Ben Gunn, "I didn't mean giving me a gate to keep, and a suit of livery clothes, and such; that's not my mark, Jim. What I mean is, would he be likely to come down to the toon of, say one thousand pounds out of money that's as good as a man's own already?"

"I am sure he would," said I. "As it was, all hands were to share."

"*And* a passage home?" he added with a look of great shrewdness.

"Why," I cried, "the squire's a gentleman. And besides, if we got rid of the others, we should want you to help work the vessel home."

"Ah," said he, "so you would." And he seemed very much relieved.

"Now, I'll tell you what," he went on. "So much I'll tell you, and no more. I were in Flint's ship when he buried the treasure; he and six along—six strong seamen. They was ashore nigh on a week, and us standing off and on in the old WALRUS. One fine day up went the signal, and here come Flint by himself in a little boat, and his head done up in a blue scarf. The sun was getting up, and mortal white he looked about the cutwater. But, there he was, you mind, and the six all dead—dead and buried. How he done it, not a man aboard us could make out. It was battle, murder, and sudden death, leastways—him against six. Billy Bones was the mate; Long John, he was quartermaster; and they asked him where the treasure was. 'Ah,' says he, 'you can go ashore, if you like, and stay,' he says; 'but as for the ship, she'll beat up for more, by thunder!' That's what he said.

"Well, I was in another ship three years back, and we sighted this island. 'Boys,' said I, 'here's Flint's treasure; let's land and find it.' The cap'n was displeased at that, but my messmates were all of a mind and landed. Twelve days they looked for it, and every day they had the worse word for me, until one fine morning all hands went aboard. 'As for you, Benjamin Gunn,' says they, 'here's a musket,' they says, 'and a spade, and pick-axe. You can stay here and find Flint's money for yourself,' they says.

"Well, Jim, three years have I been here, and not a bite of Christian diet from that day to this. But now, you look here; look at me. Do I look like a man before the mast? No, says you. Nor I weren't, neither, I says."

And with that he winked and pinched me hard.

"Just you mention them words to your squire, Jim," he went on. "Nor he weren't, neither—that's the words. Three years he were the man of this island, light and dark, fair and rain; and sometimes he would maybe think upon a prayer (says you), and sometimes he would maybe think of his old mother, so be as she's alive (you'll say); but the most part of Gunn's time (this is what you'll say)—the most part of his time was took up with another matter. And then you'll give him a nip, like I do."

And he pinched me again in the most confidential manner.

"Then," he continued, "then you'll up, and you'll say this: Gunn is a good man (you'll say), and he puts a precious sight more confidence—a precious sight, mind that—in a gen'leman born than in these gen'leman of fortune, having been one hisself."

"Well," I said, "I don't understand one word that you've been saying. But that's neither here nor there; for how am I to get on board?"

"Ah," said he, "that's the hitch, for sure. Well, there's my boat, that I made with my two hands. I keep her under the white rock. If the worst come to the worst, we might try that after dark. Hi!" he broke out. "What's that?"

For just then, although the sun had still an hour or two to run, all the echoes of the island awoke and bellowed to the thunder of a cannon.

"They have begun to fight!" I cried. "Follow me."

And I began to run towards the anchorage, my terrors all forgotten, while close at my side the marooned man in his goatskins trotted easily and lightly.

"Left, left," says he; "keep to your left hand, mate Jim! Under the trees with you! Theer's where I killed my first goat. They don't come down here now; they're all mastheaded on them mountings for the fear of Benjamin Gunn. Ah! And there's the cetemery"—cemetery, he must have meant. "You see the mounds? I come here and prayed, nows and thens, when I thought maybe a Sunday would be about doo. It weren't quite a chapel, but it seemed more solemn like; and then, says you, Ben Gunn was short-handed—no chapling, nor so much as a Bible and a flag, you says."

So he kept talking as I ran, neither expecting nor receiving any answer.

The cannon-shot was followed after a considerable interval by a volley of small arms.

Another pause, and then, not a quarter of a mile in front of me, I beheld the Union Jack flutter in the air above a wood.

PART FOUR

THE STOCKADE

CHAPTER 16

Narrative Continued by the Doctor:
How the Ship Was Abandoned

IT was about half past one—three bells in the sea phrase—that the two boats went ashore from the *Hispaniola*. The captain, the squire, and I were talking matters over in the cabin. Had there been a breath of wind, we should have fallen on the six mutineers who were left aboard with us, slipped our cable, and away to sea. But the wind was wanting; and to complete our helplessness, down came Hunter with the news that Jim Hawkins had slipped into a boat and was gone ashore with the rest.

It never occurred to us to doubt Jim Hawkins, but we were alarmed for his safety. With the men in the temper they were in, it seemed an even chance if we should see the lad again. We ran on deck. The pitch was bubbling in the seams; the nasty stench of the place turned me sick; if ever a man smelt fever and dysentery, it was in that abominable anchorage. The six scoundrels were sitting grumbling under a sail in the forecastle; ashore we could see the gigs made fast and a man sitting in each, hard by where the river runs in. One of them was whistling "Lillibullero."

Waiting was a strain, and it was decided that Hunter and I should go ashore with the jolly-boat in quest of information.

The gigs had leaned to their right, but Hunter and I pulled straight in, in the direction of the stockade upon the chart. The two who were left guarding their boats seemed in a bustle at our appearance; "Lillibullero" stopped off, and I could see the pair discussing what they ought to do. Had they gone and told Silver, all might have turned out differently; but they had their orders, I suppose, and decided to sit quietly where they were and hark back again to "Lillibullero."

There was a slight bend in the coast, and I steered so as to put it between us; even before we landed we had thus lost sight of the gigs. I jumped out and came as near running as I durst, with a big silk handkerchief under my hat for coolness' sake and a brace of pistols ready primed for safety.

I had not gone a hundred yards when I reached the stockade.

This was how it was: a spring of clear water rose almost at the top of a knoll. Well, on the knoll, and enclosing the spring, they had clapped a stout loghouse fit to hold two score of people on a pinch and loopholed for musketry on either side. All round this they had cleared a wide space, and then the thing was completed by a paling six feet high, without door or opening, too strong to pull down without time and labour and too open to shelter the besiegers. The people in the log-house had them in every way; they stood quiet in shelter and shot the others like partridges. All they wanted was a good watch and food; for, short of a complete surprise, they might have held the place against a regiment.

What particularly took my fancy was the spring. For though we had a good enough place of it in the cabin of the *Hispaniola*, with plenty of arms and ammunition, and things to eat, and excellent wines, there had been one thing overlooked—we had no water. I was thinking this over when there came ringing over the island the cry of a man at the point of death. I was not new to violent death—I have served his Royal Highness the Duke of Cumberland, and got a wound myself at Fontenoy—but I know my pulse went dot and carry one. "Jim Hawkins is gone," was my first thought.

It is something to have been an old soldier, but more still to have been a doctor. There is no time to dilly-dally in our work. And so now I made up my mind instantly, and with no time lost returned to the shore and jumped on board the jolly-boat.

By good fortune Hunter pulled a good oar. We made the water fly, and the boat was soon alongside and I aboard the schooner.

I found them all shaken, as was natural. The squire was sitting down, as white as a sheet, thinking of the harm he had led us to, the good soul! And one of the six forecastle hands was little better.

"There's a man," says Captain Smollett, nodding towards him, "new to this work. He came nigh-hand fainting, doctor, when he heard the cry. Another touch of the rudder and that man would join us."

I told my plan to the captain, and between us we settled on the details of its accomplishment.

We put old Redruth in the gallery between the cabin and the forecastle, with three or four loaded muskets and a mattress for protection. Hunter brought the boat round under the stern-port, and Joyce and I set to work loading her with powder tins, muskets, bags of biscuits, kegs of pork, a cask of cognac, and my invaluable medicine chest.

In the meantime, the squire and the captain stayed on deck, and the latter hailed the coxswain, who was the principal man aboard.

"Mr. Hands," he said, "here are two of us with a brace of pistols each. If any one of you six make a signal of any description, that man's dead."

They were a good deal taken aback, and after a little consultation one and all tumbled down the fore companion, thinking no doubt to take us on the rear. But when they saw Redruth waiting for them in the sparred galley, they went about ship at once, and a head popped out again on deck.

"Down, dog!" cries the captain.

And the head popped back again; and we heard no more, for the time, of these six very faint-hearted seamen.

By this time, tumbling things in as they came, we had the jolly-boat loaded as much as we dared. Joyce and I got out through the stern-port, and we made for shore again as fast as oars could take us.

This second trip fairly aroused the watchers along shore. "Lillibullero" was dropped again; and just before we lost sight of them behind the little point, one of them whipped ashore and disappeared. I had half a mind to change my plan and destroy their boats, but I feared that Silver and the others might be close at hand, and all might very well be lost by trying for too much.

We had soon touched land in the same place as before and set to provision the block house. All three made the first journey, heavily laden, and tossed our stores over the palisade. Then, leaving Joyce to guard them—one man, to be sure, but with half a dozen muskets—Hunter and I returned to the jolly-boat and loaded ourselves once more. So we proceeded without pausing to take breath, till the whole cargo was bestowed, when the two servants took up their position in the block house, and I, with all my power, sculled back to the *Hispaniola*.

That we should have risked a second boat load seems more daring than it really was. They had the advantage of numbers, of course, but we had the advantage of arms. Not one of the men ashore had a musket, and before they could get within range for pistol shooting, we flattered ourselves we should be able to give a good account of a half-dozen at least.

The squire was waiting for me at the stern window, all his faintness gone from him. He caught the painter and made it fast, and we fell to loading the boat for our very lives. Pork, powder, and biscuit was the cargo, with only a musket and a cutlass apiece for the squire and me and Redruth and the captain. The rest of the arms and powder we dropped overboard in two fathoms and a half of water, so that we could see the bright steel shining far below us in the sun, on the clean, sandy bottom.

By this time the tide was beginning to ebb, and the ship was swinging round to her anchor. Voices were heard faintly halloaing in the direction of the two gigs; and though this reassured us for Joyce and Hunter, who were well to the eastward, it warned our party to be off.

Redruth retreated from his place in the gallery and dropped into the boat, which we then brought round to the ship's counter, to be handier for Captain Smollett.

"Now, men," said he, "do you hear me?"

There was no answer from the forecastle.

"It's to you, Abraham Gray—it's to you I am speaking."

Still no reply.

"Gray," resumed Mr. Smollett, a little louder, "I am leaving this ship, and I order you to follow your captain. I know you are a good man at bottom, and I dare say not one of the lot of you's as bad as he makes out. I have my watch here in my hand; I give you thirty seconds to join me in."

There was a pause.

"Come, my fine fellow," continued the captain; "don't hang so long in stays. I'm risking my life and the lives of these good gentlemen every second."

There was a sudden scuffle, a sound of blows, and out burst Abraham Gray with a knife cut on the side of the cheek, and came running to the captain like a dog to the whistle.

"I'm with you, sir," said he.

And the next moment he and the captain had dropped aboard of us, and we had shoved off and given way.

We were clear out of the ship, but not yet ashore in our stockade.

CHAPTER 17

Narrative Continued by the Doctor:
The Jolly-boat's Last Trip

THIS fifth trip was quite different from any of the others. In the first place, the little gallipot of a boat that we were in was gravely overloaded. Five grown men, and three of them—Trelawney, Redruth, and the captain—over six feet high, was already more than she was meant to carry. Add to that the powder, pork, and bread-bags. The gunwale was lipping astern. Several times we shipped a little water, and my breeches and the tails of my coat were all soaking wet before we had gone a hundred yards.

The captain made us trim the boat, and we got her to lie a little more evenly. All the same, we were afraid to breathe.

In the second place, the ebb was now making—a strong rippling current running westward through the basin, and then south'ard and seaward down the straits by which we had entered in the morning. Even the ripples were a danger to our overloaded craft, but the worst of it was that we were swept out of our true course and away from our proper landing-place behind the point. If we let the current have its way we should come ashore beside the gigs, where the pirates might appear at any moment.

"I cannot keep her head for the stockade, sir," said I to the captain. I was steering, while he and Redruth, two fresh men, were at the oars. "The tide keeps washing her down. Could you pull a little stronger?"

"Not without swamping the boat," said he. "You must bear up, sir, if you please—bear up until you see you're gaining."

I tried and found by experiment that the tide kept sweeping us westward until I had laid her head due east, or just about right angles to the way we ought to go.

"We'll never get ashore at this rate," said I.

"If it's the only course that we can lie, sir, we must even lie it," returned the captain. "We must keep upstream. You see, sir," he went on, "if once we dropped to leeward of the landing-place, it's hard to say where we should get ashore, besides the chance of being boarded by the gigs; whereas, the way we go the current must slacken, and then we can dodge back along the shore."

"The current's less a'ready, sir," said the man Gray, who was sitting in the fore-sheets; "you can ease her off a bit."

"Thank you, my man," said I, quite as if nothing had happened, for we had all quietly made up our minds to treat him like one of ourselves.

Suddenly the captain spoke up again, and I thought his voice was a little changed.

"The gun!" said he.

"I have thought of that," said I, for I made sure he was thinking of a bombardment of the fort. "They could never get the gun ashore, and if they did, they could never haul it through the woods."

"Look astern, doctor," replied the captain.

We had entirely forgotten the long nine; and there, to our horror, were the five rogues busy about her, getting off her jacket, as they called the stout tarpaulin cover under which she sailed. Not only that, but it flashed into my mind at the same moment that the round-shot and the powder for the gun had been left behind, and a stroke with an axe would put it all into the possession of the evil ones abroad.

"Israel was Flint's gunner," said Gray hoarsely.

At any risk, we put the boat's head direct for the landing-place. By this time we had got so far out of the run of the current that we kept steerage way even at our necessarily gentle rate of rowing, and I could keep her steady for the goal. But the worst of it was that with the course I now held we turned our broadside instead of our stern to the *Hispaniola* and offered a target like a barn door.

I could hear as well as see that brandy-faced rascal Israel Hands plumping down a round-shot on the deck.

"Who's the best shot?" asked the captain.

"Mr. Trelawney, out and away," said I.

"Mr. Trelawney, will you please pick me off one of these men, sir? Hands, if possible," said the captain.

Trelawney was as cool as steel. He looked to the priming of his gun.

"Now," cried the captain, "easy with that gun, sir, or you'll swamp the boat. All hands stand by to trim her when he aims."

The squire raised his gun, the rowing ceased, and we leaned over to the other side to keep the balance, and all was so nicely contrived that we did not ship a drop.

They had the gun, by this time, slewed round upon the swivel, and Hands, who was at the muzzle with the rammer, was in consequence the most exposed. However, we had no luck, for just as Trelawney fired, down he stooped, the ball whistled over him, and it was one of the other four who fell.

The cry he gave was echoed not only by his companions on board but by a great number of voices from the shore, and looking in that direction I saw the other pirates trooping out from among the trees and tumbling into their places in the boats.

"Here come the gigs, sir," said I.

"Give way, then," cried the captain. "We mustn't mind if we swamp her now. If we can't get ashore, all's up."

"Only one of the gigs is being manned, sir," I added; "the

crew of the other most likely going round by shore to cut us off."

"They'll have a hot run, sir," returned the captain. "Jack ashore, you know. It's not them I mind; it's the round-shot. Carpet bowls! My lady's maid couldn't miss. Tell us, squire, when you see the match, and we'll hold water."

In the meanwhile we had been making headway at a good pace for a boat so overloaded, and we had shipped but little water in the process. We were now close in; thirty or forty strokes and we should beach her, for the ebb had already disclosed a narrow belt of sand below the clustering trees. The gig was no longer to be feared; the little point had already concealed it from our eyes. The ebb-tide, which had so cruelly delayed us, was now making reparation and delaying our assailants. The one source of danger was the gun.

"If I durst," said the captain, "I'd stop and pick off another man."

But it was plain that they meant nothing should delay their shot. They had never so much as looked at their fallen comrade, though he was not dead, and I could see him trying to crawl away.

"Ready!" cried the squire.

"Hold!" cried the captain, quick as an echo.

And he and Redruth backed with a great heave that sent her stern bodily under water. The report fell in at the same instant of time. This was the first that Jim heard, the sound of the squire's shot not having reached him. Where the ball passed, not one of us precisely knew, but I fancy it must have been over our heads and that the wind of it may have contributed to our disaster.

At any rate, the boat sank by the stern, quite gently, in three feet of water, leaving the captain and myself, facing each other, on our feet. The other three took complete headers, and came up again drenched and bubbling.

So far there was no great harm. No lives were lost, and we could wade ashore in safety. But there were all our stores at the bottom, and to make things worse, only two guns out of five remained in a state for service. Mine I had snatched from my knees and held over my head, by a sort of instinct. As for the captain, he had carried his over his shoulder by a bandoleer, and like a wise man, lock uppermost. The other three had gone down with the boat.

To add to our concern, we heard voices already drawing near us in the woods along shore, and we had not only the danger of being cut off from the stockade in our half-crippled state but the fear before us whether, if Hunter and Joyce were attacked by half a dozen, they would have the sense and conduct to stand firm. Hunter was steady, that we knew; Joyce was a doubtful case—a pleasant, polite man for a valet and to brush one's clothes, but not entirely fitted for a man of war.

With all this in our minds, we waded ashore as fast as we could, leaving behind us the poor jolly-boat and a good half of all our powder and provisions.

CHAPTER 18

Narrative Continued by the Doctor:
End of the First Day's Fighting

WE made our best speed across the strip of wood that now divided us from the stockade, and at every step we took the voices of the buccaneers rang nearer. Soon we could hear their footfalls as they ran and the cracking of the branches as they breasted across a bit of thicket.

I began to see we should have a brush for it in earnest and looked to my priming.

"Captain," said I, "Trelawney is the dead shot. Give him your gun; his own is useless."

They exchanged guns, and Trelawney, silent and cool as he had been since the beginning of the bustle, hung a moment on his heel to see that all was fit for service. At the same time, observing Gray to be unarmed, I handed him my cutlass. It did all our hearts good to see him spit in his hand, knit his brows, and make the blade sing through the air. It was plain from every line of his body that our new hand was worth his salt.

Forty paces farther we came to the edge of the wood and saw the stockade in front of us. We struck the enclosure about the middle of the south side, and almost at the same time, seven mutineers—Job Anderson, the boatswain, at their head—appeared in full cry at the southwestern corner.

They paused as if taken aback, and before they recovered, not only the squire and I, but Hunter and Joyce from the block house, had time to fire. The four shots came in rather a scattering volley, but they did the business: one of the enemy actually fell, and the rest, without hesitation, turned and plunged into the trees.

After reloading, we walked down the outside of the palisade to see to the fallen enemy. He was stone dead—shot through the heart.

We began to rejoice over our good success when just at that moment a pistol cracked in the bush, a ball whistled close past my ear, and poor Tom Redruth stumbled and fell his length on the ground. Both the squire and I returned the shot, but as we had nothing to aim at, it is probable we only wasted powder. Then we reloaded and turned our attention to poor Tom.

The captain and Gray were already examining him, and I saw with half an eye that all was over.

I believe the readiness of our return volley had scattered the mutineers once more, for we were suffered without further molestation to get the poor old gamekeeper hoisted over the stockade and carried, groaning and bleeding, into the log-house.

Poor old fellow, he had not uttered one word of surprise, complaint, fear, or even acquiescence from the very beginning of our troubles till now, when we had laid him down in the log-house to die. He had lain like a Trojan behind his mattress in the gallery; he had followed every order silently, doggedly, and well; he was the oldest of our party by a score of years; and now, sullen, old, serviceable servant, it was he that was to die.

The squire dropped down beside him on his knees and kissed his hand, crying like a child.

"Be I going, doctor?" he asked.

"Tom, my man," said I, "you're going home."

"I wish I had had a lick at them with the gun first," he replied.

"Tom," said the squire, "say you forgive me, won't you?"

"Would that be respectful like, from me to you, squire?"

was the answer. "Howsoever, so be it, amen!"

After a little while of silence, he said he thought somebody might read a prayer. "It's the custom, sir," he added apologetically. And not long after, without another word, he passed away.

In the meantime the captain, whom I had observed to be wonderfully swollen about the chest and pockets, had turned out a great many various stores—the British colours, a Bible, a coil of stoutish rope, pen, ink, the log-book, and pounds of tobacco. He had found a longish fir-tree lying felled and trimmed in the enclosure, and with the help of Hunter he had set it up at the corner of the log-house where the trunks crossed and made an angle. Then, climbing on the roof, he had with his own hand bent and run up the colours.

This seemed mightily to relieve him. He re-entered the log-house and set about counting up the stores as if nothing else existed. But he had an eye on Tom's passage for all that, and as soon as all was over, came forward with another flag and reverently spread it on the body.

"Don't you take on, sir," he said, shaking the squire's hand. "All's well with him; no fear for a hand that's been shot down in his duty to captain and owner. It mayn't be good divinity, but it's a fact."

Then he pulled me aside.

"Dr. Livesey," he said, "in how many weeks do you and squire expect the consort?"

I told him it was a question not of weeks but of months, that if we were not back by the end of August Blandly was to send to find us, but neither sooner nor later. "You can calculate for yourself," I said.

"Why, yes," returned the captain, scratching his head; "and making a large allowance, sir, for all the gifts of Providence, I should say we were pretty close hauled."

"How do you mean?" I asked.

"It's a pity, sir, we lost that second load. That's what I mean," replied the captain. "As for powder and shot, we'll do. But the rations are short, very short—so short, Dr. Livesey, that we're perhaps as well without that extra mouth."

And he pointed to the dead body under the flag.

Just then, with a roar and a whistle, a round-shot passed high above the roof of the log-house and plumped far beyond us in the wood.

"Oho!" said the captain. "Blaze away! You've little enough powder already, my lads."

At the second trial, the aim was better, and the ball descended inside the stockade, scattering a cloud of sand but doing no further damage.

"Captain," said the squire, "the house is quite invisible from the ship. It must be the flag they are aiming at. Would it not be wiser to take it in?"

"Strike my colours!" cried the captain. "No, sir, not I"; and as soon as he had said the words, I think we all agreed with him. For it was not only a piece of stout, seamanly, good feeling; it was good policy besides and showed our enemies that we despised their cannonade.

All through the evening they kept thundering away. Ball after ball flew over or fell short or kicked up the sand in the enclosure, but they had to fire so high that the shot fell dead and buried itself in the soft sand. We had no ricochet to fear, and though one popped in through the roof of the log-house and out again through the floor, we soon got used to that sort of horse-play and minded it no more than cricket.

"There is one good thing about all this," observed the captain; "the wood in front of us is likely clear. The ebb has made a good while; our stores should be uncovered. Volunteers to go and bring in pork."

Gray and Hunter were the first to come forward. Well armed, they stole out of the stockade, but it proved a useless mission. The mutineers were bolder than we fancied or they put more trust in Israel's gunnery. For four or five of them were busy carrying off our stores and wading out with them to one of the gigs that lay close by, pulling an oar or so to hold her steady against the current. Silver was in the stern-sheets in command; and every man of them was now provided with a musket from some secret magazine of their own.

The captain sat down to his log, and here is the beginning of the entry:

"Alexander Smollett, master; David Livesey, ship's doctor; Abraham Gray, carpenter's mate; John Trelawney, owner; John Hunter and Richard Joyce, owner's servants, landsmen—being all that is left faithful of the ship's company—with stores for ten days at short rations, came ashore this day and flew British colours on the log-house in Treasure Island. Thomas Redruth, owner's servant, landsman, shot by the mutineers; James Hawkins, cabin-boy—"

And at the same time, I was wondering over poor Jim Hawkins' fate.

A hail on the land side.

"Somebody hailing us," said Hunter, who was on guard.

"Doctor! Squire! Captain! Hullo, Hunter, is that you?" came the cries.

And I ran to the door in time to see Jim Hawkins, safe and sound, come climbing over the stockade.

CHAPTER 19

Narrative Resumed by Jim Hawkins:
The Garrison in the Stockade

AS soon as Ben Gunn saw the colours he came to a halt, stopped me by the arm, and sat down.

"Now," said he, "there's your friends, sure enough."

"Far more likely it's the mutineers," I answered.

"That!" he cried. "Why, in a place like this, where nobody puts in but gen'lemen of fortune, Silver would fly the Jolly Roger, you don't make no doubt of that. No, that's your friends. There's been blows too, and I reckon your friends has had the best of it; and here they are ashore in the old stockade, as was made years and years ago by Flint. Ah, he was the man to have a headpiece, was Flint! Barring rum, his match were never seen. He were afraid of none, not he; on'y Silver—Silver was that genteel."

"Well," said I, "that may be so, and so be it; all the more reason that I should hurry on and join my friends."

"Nay, mate," returned Ben, "not you. You're a good boy, or I'm mistook; but you're on'y a boy, all told. Now, Ben Gunn is fly. Rum wouldn't bring me there, where you're going—not rum wouldn't, till I see your born gen'leman and gets it on his word of honour. And you won't forget my words; 'A precious sight (that's what you'll say), a precious sight more confidence'—and then nips him."

And he pinched me the third time with the same air of cleverness.

"And when Ben Gunn is wanted, you know where to find him, Jim. Just wheer you found him today. And him that comes is to have a white thing in his hand, and he's to come alone. Oh! And you'll say this: 'Ben Gunn,' says you, 'has reasons of his own.'"

"Well," said I, "I believe I understand. You have something to propose, and you wish to see the squire or the doctor, and you're to be found where I found you. Is that all?"

"And when? says you," he added. "Why, from about noon observation to about six bells."

"Good," said I, "and now may I go?"

"You won't forget?" he inquired anxiously. "Precious sight, and reasons of his own, says you. Reasons of his own; that's the mainstay; as between man and man. Well, then"—still holding me—"I reckon you can go, Jim. And, Jim, if you was to see Silver, you wouldn't go for to sell Ben Gunn? Wild horses wouldn't draw it from you? No, says you. And if them pirates camp ashore, Jim, what would you say but there'd be widders in the morning?"

Here he was interrupted by a loud report, and a cannonball came tearing through the trees and pitched in the sand not a hundred yards from where we two were talking. The next moment each of us had taken to his heels in a different direction.

For a good hour to come frequent reports shook the island, and balls kept crashing through the woods. I moved from hiding-place to hiding-place, always pursued, or so it seemed to me, by these terrifying missiles. But towards the end of the bombardment, though still I durst not venture in the direction of the stockade, where the balls fell oftenest, I had begun, in a manner, to pluck up my heart again, and after a long detour to the east, crept down among the shore-side trees.

The sun had just set, the sea breeze was rustling and tumbling in the woods and ruffling the grey surface of the anchorage; the tide, too, was far out, and great tracts of sand lay uncovered; the air, after the heat of the day, chilled me through my jacket.

The *Hispaniola* still lay where she had anchored; but, sure enough, there was the Jolly Roger—the black flag of piracy—flying from her peak. Even as I looked, there came another red flash and another report that sent the echoes clattering, and one more round-shot whistled through the air. It was the last of the cannonade.

I lay for some time watching the bustle which succeeded the attack. Men were demolishing something with axes on the beach near the stockade—the poor jolly-boat, I afterwards discovered. Away, near the mouth of the river, a great fire was glowing among the trees, and between that point and the ship one of the gigs kept coming and going, the men, whom I had seen so gloomy, shouting at the oars like children. But there was a sound in their voices which suggested rum.

At length I thought I might return towards the stockade. I was pretty far down on the low, sandy spit that encloses the anchorage to the east, and is joined at half-water to Skeleton Island; and now, as I rose to my feet, I saw, some distance further down the spit and rising from among low bushes, an isolated rock, pretty high, and peculiarly white in colour. It occurred to me that this might be the white rock of which Ben Gunn had spoken and that some day or other a boat might be wanted and I should know where to look for one.

Then I skirted among the woods until I had regained the rear, or shoreward side, of the stockade, and was soon warmly welcomed by the faithful party.

I had soon told my story and began to look about me. The log-house was made of unsquared trunks of pine—roof, walls, and floor. The latter stood in several places as much as a foot or a foot and a half above the surface of the sand. There was a porch at the door, and under this porch the little spring welled up into an artificial basin of a rather odd kind—no other than a great ship's kettle of iron, with the bottom knocked out, and sunk "to her bearings," as the captain said, among the sand.

Little had been left besides the framework of the house, but in one corner there was a stone slab laid down by way of hearth and an old rusty iron basket to contain the fire.

The slopes of the knoll and all the inside of the stockade had been cleared of timber to build the house, and we could see by the stumps what a fine and lofty grove had been destroyed. Most of the soil had been washed away or buried in drift after the removal of the trees; only where the streamlet ran down from the kettle a thick bed of moss and some ferns and little creeping bushes were still green among the sand. Very close around the stockade—too close for defence, they said—the wood still flourished high and dense, all of fir on the land side, but towards the sea with a large admixture of live-oaks.

The cold evening breeze, of which I have spoken, whistled through every chink of the rude building and sprinkled the floor with a continual rain of fine sand. There was sand in our eyes, sand in our teeth, sand in our suppers, sand dancing in the spring at the bottom of the kettle, for all the world like porridge beginning to boil. Our chimney was a square hole in the roof; it was but a little part of the smoke that found its way out, and the rest eddied about the house and kept us coughing and piping the eye.

Add to this that Gray, the new man, had his face tied up in a bandage for a cut he had got in breaking away from the mutineers and that poor old Tom Redruth, still unburied, lay along the wall, stiff and stark, under the Union Jack.

If we had been allowed to sit idle, we should all have fallen in the blues, but Captain Smollett was never the man for that. All hands were called up before him, and he divided us into watches. The doctor and Gray and I for one; the squire, Hunter, and Joyce upon the other. Tired though we all were, two were sent out for firewood; two more were set to dig a grave for Redruth; the doctor was named cook; I was put sentry at the door; and the captain himself went from one to another, keeping up our spirits and lending a hand wherever it was wanted.

From time to time the doctor came to the door for a little air and to rest his eyes, which were almost smoked out of his head, and whenever he did so, he had a word for me.

"That man Smollett," he said once, "is a better man than I am. And when I say that it means a deal, Jim."

Another time he came and was silent for a while. Then he put his head on one side, and looked at me.

"Is this Ben Gunn a man?" he asked.

"I do not know, sir," said I. "I am not very sure whether he's sane."

"If there's any doubt about the matter, he is," returned the doctor. "A man who has been three years biting his nails on a desert island, Jim, can't expect to appear as sane as you or me. It doesn't lie in human nature. Was it cheese you said he had a fancy for?"

"Yes, sir, cheese," I answered.

"Well, Jim," says he, "just see the good that comes of being dainty in your food. You've seen my snuff-box, haven't you? And you never saw me take snuff, the reason being that in my snuff-box I carry a piece of Parmesan cheese—a cheese made in Italy, very nutritious. Well, that's for Ben Gunn!"

Before supper was eaten we buried old Tom in the sand and stood round him for a while bare-headed in the breeze. A good deal of firewood had been got in, but not enough for the captain's fancy, and he shook his head over it and told us we "must get back to this tomorrow rather livelier." Then, when we had eaten our pork and each had a good stiff glass of brandy grog, the three chiefs got together in a corner to discuss our prospects.

It appears they were at their wits' end what to do, the stores being so low that we must have been starved into surrender long before help came. But our best hope, it was decided, was to kill off the buccaneers until they either hauled down their flag or ran away with the *Hispaniola*. From nineteen they were already reduced to fifteen, two others were wounded, and one at least—the man shot beside the gun—severely wounded, if he were not dead. Every time we had a crack at them, we were to take it, saving our own lives, with the extremest care. And besides that, we had two able allies—rum and the climate.

As for the first, though we were about half a mile away, we could hear them roaring and singing late into the night; and as for the second, the doctor staked his wig that, camped where they were in the marsh and unprovided with remedies, the half of them would be on their backs before a week.

"So," he added, "if we are not all shot down first they'll be glad to be packing in the schooner. It's always a ship, and they can get to buccaneering again, I suppose."

"First ship that ever I lost," said Captain Smollett.

I was dead tired, as you may fancy; and when I got to sleep, which was not till after a great deal of tossing, I slept like a log of wood.

The rest had long been up and had already breakfasted and increased the pile of firewood by about half as much again when I was wakened by a bustle and the sound of voices.

"Flag of truce!" I heard someone say; and then, immediately after, with a cry of surprise, "Silver himself!"

And at that, up I jumped, and rubbing my eyes, ran to a loophole in the wall.

CHAPTER 20

Silver's Embassy

SURE enough, there were two men just outside the stockade, one of them waving a white cloth, the other, no less a person than Silver himself, standing placidly by.

It was still quite early, and the coldest morning that I think I ever was abroad in—a chill that pierced into the marrow. The sky was bright and cloudless overhead, and the tops of the trees shone rosily in the sun. But where Silver stood with his lieutenant, all was still in shadow, and they waded knee-deep in a low white vapour that had crawled during the night out of the morass. The chill and the vapour taken together told a poor tale of the island. It was plainly a damp, feverish, unhealthy spot.

"Keep indoors, men," said the captain. "Ten to one this is a trick."

Then he hailed the buccaneer.

"Who goes? Stand, or we fire."

"Flag of truce," cried Silver.

The captain was in the porch, keeping himself carefully out of the way of a treacherous shot, should any be intended. He turned and spoke to us,

"Doctor's watch on the lookout. Dr. Livesey take the north side, if you please; Jim, the east; Gray, west. The watch below, all hands to load muskets. Lively, men, and careful."

And then he turned again to the mutineers.

"And what do you want with your flag of truce?" he cried.

This time it was the other man who replied.

"Cap'n Silver, sir, to come on board and make terms," he shouted.

"Cap'n Silver! Don't know him. Who's he?" cried the captain. And we could hear him adding to himself, "Cap'n, is it? My heart, and here's promotion!"

Long John answered for himself. "Me, sir. These poor lads have chosen me cap'n, after your desertion, sir"—laying a particular emphasis upon the word "desertion." "We're willing to submit, if we can come to terms, and no bones about it. All I ask is your word, Cap'n Smollett, to let me safe and sound out of this here stockade, and one minute to get out o' shot before a gun is fired."

"My man," said Captain Smollett, "I have not the slightest desire to talk to you. If you wish to talk to me, you can come, that's all. If there's any treachery, it'll be on your side, and the Lord help you."

"That's enough, cap'n," shouted Long John cheerily. "A word from you's enough. I know a gentleman, and you may lay to that."

We could see the man who carried the flag of truce attempting to hold Silver back. Nor was that wonderful, seeing how cavalier had been the captain's answer. But Silver laughed at him aloud and slapped him on the back as if the idea of alarm had been absurd. Then he advanced to the stockade, threw over his crutch, got a leg up, and with great vigour and skill succeeded in surmounting the fence and dropping safely to the other side.

I will confess that I was far too much taken up with what was going on to be of the slightest use as sentry; indeed, I had already deserted my eastern loophole and crept up behind the captain, who had now seated himself on the threshold, with his elbows on his knees, his head in his hands, and his eyes fixed on the water as it bubbled out of the old iron kettle in the sand.

He was whistling "Come, Lasses and Lads."

Silver had terrible hard work getting up the knoll. What with the steepness of the incline, the thick tree stumps, and the soft sand, he and his crutch were as helpless as a ship in stays. But he stuck to it like a man in silence, and at last arrived before the captain, whom he saluted in the handsomest style. He was tricked out in his best; an immense blue coat, thick with brass buttons, hung as low as to his knees, and a fine laced hat was set on the back of his head.

"Here you are, my man," said the captain, raising his head. "You had better sit down."

"You ain't a-going to let me inside, cap'n?" complained Long John. "It's a main cold morning, to be sure, sir, to sit outside upon the sand."

"Why, Silver," said the captain, "if you had pleased to be an honest man, you might have been sitting in your galley. It's your own doing. You're either my ship's cook—and then you were treated handsome—or Cap'n Silver, a common mutineer and pirate, and then you can go hang!"

"Well, well, cap'n," returned the sea-cook, sitting down as he was bidden on the sand, "you'll have to give me a hand up again, that's all. A sweet pretty place you have of it here. Ah, there's Jim! The top of the morning to you, Jim. Doctor, here's my service. Why, there you all are together like a happy family, in a manner of speaking."

"If you have anything to say, my man, better say it," said the captain.

"Right you were, Cap'n Smollett," replied Silver. "Dooty is dooty, to be sure. Well now, you look here, that was a good lay of yours last night. I don't deny it was a good lay. Some of you pretty handy with a handspike-end. And I'll not deny neither but what some of my people was shook—maybe all was shook; maybe I was shook myself; maybe that's why I'm here for terms. But you mark me, cap'n, it won't do twice, by thunder! We'll have to do sentry-go and ease off a point or so on the rum. Maybe you think we were all a sheet in the wind's eye. But I'll tell you I was sober; I was on'y dog tired; and if I'd awoke a second sooner, I'd 'a caught you at the act, I would. He wasn't dead when I got round to him, not he."

"Well?" says Captain Smollett as cool as can be.

All that Silver said was a riddle to him, but you would never have guessed it from his tone. As for me, I began to have an inkling. Ben Gunn's last words came back to my mind. I began to suppose that he had paid the buccaneers a visit while they all lay drunk together round their fire, and I reckoned up with glee that we had only fourteen enemies to deal with.

"Well, here it is," said Silver. "We want that treasure, and we'll have it—that's our point! You would just as soon save your lives, I reckon; and that's yours. You have a chart, haven't you?"

"That's as may be," replied the captain.

"Oh, well, you have, I know that," returned Long John. "You needn't be so husky with a man; there ain't a particle of service in that, and you may lay to it. What I mean is, we want your chart. Now, I never meant you no harm, myself."

"That won't do with me, my man," interrupted the captain. "We know exactly what you meant to do, and we don't care, for now, you see, you can't do it."

And the captain looked at him calmly and proceeded to fill a pipe.

"If Abe Gray—" Silver broke out.

"Avast there!" cried Mr. Smollett. "Gray told me nothing, and I asked him nothing; and what's more, I would see you and him and this whole island blown clean out of the water into blazes first. So there's my mind for you, my man, on that."

This little whiff of temper seemed to cool Silver down. He had been growing nettled before, but now he pulled himself together.

"Like enough," said he. "I would set no limits to what gentlemen might consider shipshape, or might not, as the case were. And seein' as how you are about to take a pipe, cap'n, I'll make so free as do likewise."

And he filled a pipe and lighted it; and the two men sat silently smoking for quite a while, now looking each other in the face, now stopping their tobacco, now leaning forward to spit. It was as good as the play to see them.

"Now," resumed Silver, "here it is. You give us the chart to get the treasure by, and drop shooting poor seamen and stoving of their heads in while asleep. You do that, and we'll offer you a choice. Either you come aboard along of us, once the treasure shipped, and then I'll give you my affy-davy, upon my word of honour, to clap you somewhere safe ashore. Or if that ain't to your fancy, some of my hands being rough and having old scores on account of hazing, then you can stay here, you can. We'll divide stores with you, man for man; and I'll give my affy-davy, as before to speak the first ship I sight, and send 'em here to pick you up. Now, you'll own that's talking. Handsomer you couldn't look to get, now you. And I hope"—raising his voice—"that all hands in this here block house will overhaul my words, for what is spoke to one is spoke to all."

Captain Smollett rose from his seat and knocked out the ashes of his pipe in the palm of his left hand.

"Is that all?" he asked.

"Every last word, by thunder!" answered John. "Refuse that, and you've seen the last of me but musket-balls."

"Very good," said the captain. "Now you'll hear me. If you'll come up one by one, unarmed, I'll engage to clap you all in irons and take you home to a fair trial in England. If you won't, my name is Alexander Smollett, I've flown my sovereign's colours, and I'll see you all to Davy Jones. You can't find the treasure. You can't sail the ship—there's not a man among you fit to sail the ship. You can't fight us—Gray, there, got away from five of you. Your ship's in irons, Master Silver; you're on a lee shore, and so you'll find. I stand here and tell you so; and they're the last good words you'll get from me, for in the name of heaven, I'll put a bullet in your back when next I meet you. Tramp, my lad. Bundle out of this, please, hand over hand, and double quick."

Silver's face was a picture; his eyes started in his head with wrath. He shook the fire out of his pipe.

"Give me a hand up!" he cried.

"Not I," returned the captain.

"Who'll give me a hand up?" he roared.

Not a man among us moved. Growling the foulest imprecations, he crawled along the sand till he got hold of the porch and could hoist himself again upon his crutch. Then he spat into the spring.

"There!" he cried. "That's what I think of ye. Before an hour's out, I'll stove in your old block house like a rum puncheon. Laugh, by thunder, laugh! Before an hour's out, ye'll laugh upon the other side. Them that die'll be the lucky ones."

And with a dreadful oath he stumbled off, ploughed down the sand, was helped across the stockade, after four or five failures, by the man with the flag of truce, and disappeared in an instant afterwards among the trees.

CHAPTER 21

The Attack

AS soon as Silver disappeared, the captain, who had been closely watching him, turned towards the interior of the house and found not a man of us at his post but Gray. It was the first time we had ever seen him angry.

"Quarters!" he roared. And then, as we all slunk back to our places, "Gray," he said, "I'll put your name in the log; you've stood by your duty like a seaman. Mr. Trelawney, I'm surprised at you, sir. Doctor, I thought you had worn the king's coat! If that was how you served at Fontenoy, sir, you'd have been better in your berth."

The doctor's watch were all back at their loopholes, the rest were busy loading the spare muskets, and everyone with a red face, you may be certain, and a flea in his ear, as the saying is.

The captain looked on for a while in silence. Then he spoke.

"My lads," said he, "I've given Silver a broadside. I pitched it in red-hot on purpose; and before the hour's out, as he said, we shall be boarded. We're outnumbered, I needn't tell you that, but we fight in shelter; and a minute ago I should have said we fought with discipline. I've no manner of doubt that we can drub them, if you choose."

Then he went the rounds and saw, as he said, that all was clear.

On the two short sides of the house, east and west, there were only two loopholes; on the south side where the porch was, two again; and on the north side, five. There was a round score of muskets for the seven of us; the firewood had been built into four piles—tables, you might say—one about the middle of each side, and on each of these tables some ammunition and four loaded muskets were laid ready to the hand of the defenders. In the middle, the cutlasses lay ranged.

"Toss out the fire," said the captain; "the chill is past, and we mustn't have smoke in our eyes."

The iron fire-basket was carried bodily out by Mr. Trelawney, and the embers smothered among sand.

"Hawkins hasn't had his breakfast. Hawkins, help yourself, and back to your post to eat it," continued Captain Smollett. "Lively, now, my lad; you'll want it before you've done. Hunter, serve out a round of brandy to all hands."

And while this was going on, the captain completed, in his own mind, the plan of the defence.

"Doctor, you will take the door," he resumed. "See, and don't expose yourself; keep within, and fire through the porch. Hunter, take the east side, there. Joyce, you stand by the west, my man. Mr. Trelawney, you are the best shot—you and Gray will take this long north side, with the five loopholes; it's there the danger is. If they can get up to it and fire in upon us through our own ports, things would begin to look dirty. Hawkins, neither you nor I are much account at the shooting; we'll stand by to load and bear a hand."

As the captain had said, the chill was past. As soon as the sun had climbed above our girdle of trees, it fell with all its force upon the clearing and drank up the vapours at a draught. Soon the sand was baking and the resin melting in the logs of the block house. Jackets and coats were flung aside, shirts thrown open at the neck and rolled up to the shoulders; and we stood there, each at his post, in a fever of heat and anxiety.

An hour passed away.

"Hang them!" said the captain. "This is as dull as the doldrums. Gray, whistle for a wind."

And just at that moment came the first news of the attack.

"If you please, sir," said Joyce, "if I see anyone, am I to fire?"

"I told you so!" cried the captain.

"Thank you, sir," returned Joyce with the same quiet civility.

Nothing followed for a time, but the remark had set us all on the alert, straining ears and eyes—the musketeers with their pieces balanced in their hands, the captain out in the middle of the block house with his mouth very tight and a frown on his face.

So some seconds passed, till suddenly Joyce whipped up his musket and fired. The report had scarcely died away ere it was repeated and repeated from without in a scattering volley, shot behind shot, like a string of geese, from every side of the enclosure. Several bullets struck the log-house, but not one entered; and as the smoke cleared away and vanished, the stockade and the woods around it looked as quiet and empty as before. Not a bough waved, not the gleam of a musket-barrel betrayed the presence of our foes.

"Did you hit your man?" asked the captain.

"No, sir," replied Joyce. "I believe not, sir."

"Next best thing to tell the truth," muttered Captain Smollett. "Load his gun, Hawkins. How many should say there were on your side, doctor?"

"I know precisely," said Dr. Livesey. "Three shots were fired on this side. I saw the three flashes—two close together—one farther to the west."

"Three!" repeated the captain. "And how many on yours, Mr. Trelawney?"

But this was not so easily answered. There had come many from the north—seven by the squire's computation, eight or nine according to Gray. From the east and west only a single shot had been fired. It was plain, therefore, that the attack would be developed from the north and that on the other three sides we were only to be annoyed by a show of hostilities. But

Captain Smollett made no change in his arrangements. If the mutineers succeeded in crossing the stockade, he argued, they would take possession of any unprotected loophole and shoot us down like rats in our own stronghold.

Nor had we much time left to us for thought. Suddenly, with a loud huzza, a little cloud of pirates leaped from the woods on the north side and ran straight on the stockade. At the same moment, the fire was once more opened from the woods, and a rifle ball sang through the doorway and knocked the doctor's musket into bits.

The boarders swarmed over the fence like monkeys. Squire and Gray fired again and yet again; three men fell, one forwards into the enclosure, two back on the outside. But of these, one was evidently more frightened than hurt, for he was on his feet again in a crack and instantly disappeared among the trees.

Two had bit the dust, one had fled, four had made good their footing inside our defences, while from the shelter of the woods seven or eight men, each evidently supplied with several muskets, kept up a hot though useless fire on the log-house.

The four who had boarded made straight before them for the building, shouting as they ran, and the men among the trees shouted back to encourage them. Several shots were fired, but such was the hurry of the marksmen that not one appears to have taken effect. In a moment, the four pirates had swarmed up the mound and were upon us.

The head of Job Anderson, the boatswain, appeared at the middle loophole.

"At 'em, all hands—all hands!" he roared in a voice of thunder.

At the same moment, another pirate grasped Hunter's musket by the muzzle, wrenched it from his hands, plucked it through the loophole, and with one stunning blow, laid the poor fellow senseless on the floor. Meanwhile a third, running unharmed all around the house, appeared suddenly in the doorway and fell with his cutlass on the doctor.

Our position was utterly reversed. A moment since we were firing, under cover, at an exposed enemy; now it was we who lay uncovered and could not return a blow.

The log-house was full of smoke, to which we owed our comparative safety. Cries and confusion, the flashes and reports of pistol-shots, and one loud groan rang in my ears.

"Out, lads, out, and fight 'em in the open! Cutlasses!" cried the captain.

I snatched a cutlass from the pile, and someone, at the same time snatching another, gave me a cut across the knuckles which I hardly felt. I dashed out of the door into the clear sunlight. Someone was close behind, I knew not whom. Right in front, the doctor was pursuing his assailant down the hill, and just as my eyes fell upon him, beat down his guard and sent him sprawling on his back with a great slash across the face.

"Round the house, lads! Round the house!" cried the captain; and even in the hurly-burly, I perceived a change in his voice.

Mechanically, I obeyed, turned eastwards, and with my cutlass raised, ran round the corner of the house. Next moment I was face to face with Anderson. He roared aloud, and his hanger went up above his head, flashing in the sunlight. I had not time to be afraid, but as the blow still hung impending, leaped in a trice upon one side, and missing my foot in the soft sand, rolled headlong down the slope.

When I had first sallied from the door, the other mutineers had been already swarming up the palisade to make an end of us. One man, in a red night-cap, with his cutlass in his mouth, had even got upon the top and thrown a leg across. Well, so short had been the interval that when I found my feet again all was in the same posture, the fellow with the red night-cap still half-way over, another still just showing his head above the top of the stockade. And yet, in this breath of time, the fight was over and the victory was ours.

Gray, following close behind me, had cut down the big boatswain ere he had time to recover from his last blow. Another had been shot at a loophole in the very act of firing into the house and now lay in agony, the pistol still smoking in his hand. A third, as I had seen, the doctor had disposed of at a blow. Of the four who had scaled the palisade, one only remained unaccounted for, and he, having left his cutlass on the field, was now clambering out again with the fear of death upon him.

"Fire—fire from the house!" cried the doctor. "And you, lads, back into cover."

But his words were unheeded, no shot was fired, and the last boarder made good his escape and disappeared with the rest into the wood. In three seconds nothing remained of the attacking party but the five who had fallen, four on the inside and one on the outside of the palisade.

The doctor and Gray and I ran full speed for shelter. The survivors would soon be back where they had left their muskets, and at any moment the fire might recommence.

The house was by this time somewhat cleared of smoke, and we saw at a glance the price we had paid for victory. Hunter lay beside his loophole, stunned; Joyce by his, shot through the head, never to move again; while right in the centre, the squire was supporting the captain, one as pale as the other.

"The captain's wounded," said Mr. Trelawney.

"Have they run?" asked Mr. Smollett.

"All that could, you may be bound," returned the doctor; "but there's five of them will never run again."

"Five!" cried the captain. "Come, that's better. Five against three leaves us four to nine. That's better odds than we had at starting. We were seven to nineteen then, or thought we were, and that's as bad to bear."*

*The mutineers were soon only eight in number, for the man shot by Mr. Trelawney on board the schooner died that same evening of his wound. But this was, of course, not known till after by the faithful party.

PART FIVE

MY SEA
ADVENTURE

CHAPTER 22

How My Sea Adventure Began

THERE was no return of the mutineers—not so much as another shot out of the woods. They had "got their rations for that day," as the captain put it, and we had the place to ourselves and a quiet time to overhaul the wounded and get dinner. Squire and I cooked outside in spite of the danger, and even outside we could hardly tell what we were at, for horror of the loud groans that reached us from the doctor's patients.

Out of the eight men who had fallen in the action, only three still breathed—that one of the pirates who had been shot at the loophole, Hunter, and Captain Smollett; and of these, the first two were as good as dead; the mutineer indeed died under the doctor's knife, and Hunter, do what we could, never recovered consciousness in this world. He lingered all day, breathing loudly like the old buccaneer at home in his apoplectic fit, but the bones of his chest had been crushed by the blow and his skull fractured in falling, and some time in the following night, without sign or sound, he went to his Maker.

As for the captain, his wounds were grievous indeed, but not dangerous. No organ was fatally injured. Anderson's ball—for it was Job that shot him first—had broken his shoulder-blade and touched the lung, not badly; the second had only torn and displaced some muscles in the calf. He was sure to recover, the doctor said, but in the meantime, and for weeks to come, he must not walk nor move his arm, nor so much as speak when he could help it.

My own accidental cut across the knuckles was a flea-bite.
Doctor Livesey patched it up with plaster and pulled my ears
for me into the bargain.

After dinner the squire and the doctor sat by the captain's
side awhile in consultation; and when they had talked to their
hearts' content, it being then a little past noon, the doctor
took up his hat and pistols, girt on a cutlass, put the chart in
his pocket, and with a musket over his shoulder crossed the
palisade on the north side and set off briskly through the trees.

Gray and I were sitting together at the far end of the block
house, to be out of earshot of our officers consulting; and Gray
took his pipe out of his mouth and fairly forgot to put it back
again, so thunder-struck he was at this occurrence.

"Why, in the name of Davy Jones," said he, "is Dr. Livesey
mad?"

"Why no," says I. "He's about the last of this crew for that,
I take it."

"Well, shipmate," said Gray, "mad he may not be; but if *he's*
not, you mark my words, I am."

"I take it," replied I, "the doctor has his idea; and if I am
right, he's going now to see Ben Gunn."

I was right, as appeared later; but in the meantime, the
house being stifling hot and the little patch of sand inside
the palisade ablaze with midday sun, I began to get another
thought into my head, which was not by any means so right.
What I began to do was to envy the doctor walking in the cool
shadow of the woods with the birds about him and the pleasant
smell of the pines, while I sat grilling, with my clothes stuck to
the hot resin, and so much blood about me and so many poor
dead bodies lying all around that I took a disgust of the place
that was almost as strong as fear.

All the time I was washing out the block house, and then
washing up the things from dinner, this disgust and envy kept
growing stronger and stronger, till at last, being near a bread-

bag, and no one then observing me, I took the first step towards my escapade and filled both pockets of my coat with biscuit.

I was a fool, if you like, and certainly I was going to do a foolish, over-bold act; but I was determined to do it with all the precautions in my power. These biscuits, should anything befall me, would keep me, at least, from starving till far on in the next day.

The next thing I laid hold of was a brace of pistols, and as I already had a powder-horn and bullets, I felt myself well supplied with arms.

As for the scheme I had in my head, it was not a bad one in itself. I was to go down the sandy spit that divides the anchorage on the east from the open sea, find the white rock I had observed last evening, and ascertain whether it was there or not that Ben Gunn had hidden his boat, a thing quite worth doing, as I still believe. But as I was certain I should not be allowed to leave the enclosure, my only plan was to take French leave and slip out when nobody was watching, and that was so bad a way of doing it as made the thing itself wrong. But I was only a boy, and I had made my mind up.

Well, as things at last fell out, I found an admirable opportunity. The squire and Gray were busy helping the captain with his bandages, the coast was clear, I made a bolt for it over the stockade and into the thickest of the trees, and before my absence was observed I was out of cry of my companions.

This was my second folly, far worse than the first, as I left but two sound men to guard the house; but like the first, it was a help towards saving all of us.

I took my way straight for the east coast of the island, for I was determined to go down the sea side of the spit to avoid all chance of observation from the anchorage. It was already late in the afternoon, although still warm and sunny. As I continued to thread the tall woods, I could hear from far before me not only the continuous thunder of the surf, but a certain tossing of foliage and grinding of boughs which showed me the sea breeze had set in higher than usual. Soon cool draughts of air began to reach me, and a few steps farther I came forth into the open borders of the grove, and saw the sea lying blue and sunny to the horizon and the surf tumbling and tossing its foam along the beach.

I have never seen the sea quiet round Treasure Island. The sun might blaze overhead, the air be without a breath, the surface smooth and blue, but still these great rollers would be running along all the external coast, thundering and thundering by day and night; and I scarce believe there is one spot in the island where a man would be out of earshot of their noise.

I walked along beside the surf with great enjoyment, till, thinking I was now got far enough to the south, I took the cover of some thick bushes and crept warily up to the ridge of the spit.

Behind me was the sea, in front the anchorage. The sea breeze, as though it had the sooner blown itself out by its unusual violence, was already at an end; it had been succeeded by light, variable airs from the south and south-east, carrying great banks of fog; and the anchorage, under lee of Skeleton Island, lay still and leaden as when first we entered it. The *Hispaniola*, in that unbroken mirror, was exactly portrayed from the truck to the waterline, the Jolly Roger hanging from her peak.

Alongside lay one of the gigs, Silver in the stern-sheets—him I could always recognize—while a couple of men were leaning over the stern bulwarks, one of them with a red cap—the very rogue that I had seen some hours before stride-legs upon the palisade. Apparently they were talking and laughing, though at that distance—upwards of a mile—I could, of course, hear no word of what was said. All at once there began the most horrid, unearthly screaming, which at first startled me badly, though I had soon remembered the voice of Captain Flint and even thought I could make out the bird by her bright plumage as she sat perched upon her master's wrist.

Soon after, the jolly-boat shoved off and pulled for shore, and the man with the red cap and his comrade went below by the cabin companion.

Just about the same time, the sun had gone down behind the Spy-glass, and as the fog was collecting rapidly, it began to grow dark in earnest. I saw I must lose no time if I were to find the boat that evening.

The white rock, visible enough above the brush, was still some eighth of a mile further down the spit, and it took me a goodish while to get up with it, crawling, often on all fours, among the scrub. Night had almost come when I laid my hand on its rough sides. Right below it there was an exceedingly small hollow of green turf, hidden by banks and a thick underwood about knee-deep, that grew there very plentifully; and in the centre of the dell, sure enough, a little tent of goat-skins, like what the gipsies carry about with them in England.

I dropped into the hollow, lifted the side of the tent, and there was Ben Gunn's boat—home-made if ever anything was home-made; a rude, lop-sided framework of tough wood, and stretched upon that a covering of goat-skin, with the hair inside. The thing was extremely small, even for me, and I can hardly imagine that it could have floated with a full-sized man. There was one thwart set as low as possible, a kind of stretcher in the bows, and a double paddle for propulsion.

I had not then seen a coracle, such as the ancient Britons made, but I have seen one since, and I can give you no fairer idea of Ben Gunn's boat than by saying it was like the first and the worst coracle ever made by man. But the great advantage of the coracle it certainly possessed, for it was exceedingly light and portable.

Well, now that I had found the boat, you would have thought

I had had enough of truantry for once, but in the meantime I had taken another notion and become so obstinately fond of it that I would have carried it out, I believe, in the teeth of Captain Smollett himself. This was to slip out under cover of the night, cut the *Hispaniola* adrift, and let her go ashore where she fancied. I had quite made up my mind that the mutineers, after their repulse of the morning, had nothing nearer their hearts than to up anchor and away to sea; this, I thought, it would be a fine thing to prevent, and now that I had seen how they left their watchmen unprovided with a boat, I thought it might be done with little risk.

Down I sat to wait for darkness, and made a hearty meal of biscuit. It was a night out of ten thousand for my purpose. The fog had now buried all heaven. As the last rays of daylight dwindled and disappeared, absolute blackness settled down on Treasure Island. And when, at last, I shouldered the coracle and groped my way stumblingly out of the hollow where I had supped, there were but two points visible on the whole anchorage.

One was the great fire on shore, by which the defeated pirates lay carousing in the swamp. The other, a mere blur of light upon the darkness, indicated the position of the anchored ship. She had swung round to the ebb—her bow was now towards me—the only lights on board were in the cabin, and what I saw was merely a reflection on the fog of the strong rays that flowed from the stern window.

The ebb had already run some time, and I had to wade through a long belt of swampy sand, where I sank several times above the ankle, before I came to the edge of the retreating water, and wading a little way in, with some strength and dexterity, set my coracle, keel downwards, on the surface.

CHAPTER 23

The Ebb-tide Runs

THE coracle—as I had ample reason to know before I was done with her—was a very safe boat for a person of my height and weight, both buoyant and clever in a seaway; but she was the most cross-grained, lop-sided craft to manage. Do as you pleased, she always made more leeway than anything else, and turning round and round was the manoeuvre she was best at. Even Ben Gunn himself has admitted that she was "queer to handle till you knew her way."

Certainly I did not know her way. She turned in every direction but the one I was bound to go; the most part of the time we were broadside on, and I am very sure I never should have made the ship at all but for the tide. By good fortune, paddle as I pleased, the tide was still sweeping me down; and there lay the *Hispaniola* right in the fairway, hardly to be missed.

First she loomed before me like a blot of something yet blacker than darkness, then her spars and hull began to take shape, and the next moment, as it seemed (for, the farther I went, the brisker grew the current of the ebb), I was alongside of her hawser and had laid hold.

The hawser was as taut as a bowstring, and the current so strong she pulled upon her anchor. All round the hull, in the blackness, the rippling current bubbled and chattered like a little mountain stream. One cut with my sea-gully and the *Hispaniola* would go humming down the tide.

So far so good, but it next occurred to my recollection that a taut hawser, suddenly cut, is a thing as dangerous as a kicking horse. Ten to one, if I were so foolhardy as to cut the *Hispaniola* from her anchor, I and the coracle would be knocked clean out of the water.

This brought me to a full stop, and if fortune had not again particularly favoured me, I should have had to abandon my design. But the light airs which had begun blowing from the south-east and south had hauled round after nightfall into the south-west. Just while I was meditating, a puff came, caught the *Hispaniola*, and forced her up into the current; and to my great joy, I felt the hawser slacken in my grasp, and the hand by which I held it dip for a second under water.

With that I made my mind up, took out my gully, opened it with my teeth, and cut one strand after another, till the vessel swung only by two. Then I lay quiet, waiting to sever these last when the strain should be once more lightened by a breath of wind.

All this time I had heard the sound of loud voices from the cabin, but to say truth, my mind had been so entirely taken up with other thoughts that I had scarcely given ear. Now, however, when I had nothing else to do, I began to pay more heed.

One I recognized for the coxswain's, Israel Hands, that had been Flint's gunner in former days. The other was, of course, my friend of the red night-cap. Both men were plainly the worse of drink, and they were still drinking, for even while I was listening, one of them, with a drunken cry, opened the stern window and threw out something, which I divined to be an empty bottle. But they were not only tipsy; it was plain that they were furiously angry. Oaths flew like hailstones, and every now and then there came forth such an explosion as I thought was sure to end in blows. But each time the quarrel passed off and the voices grumbled lower for a while, until the next crisis came and in its turn passed away without result.

On shore, I could see the glow of the great camp-fire burning warmly through the shore-side trees. Someone was singing, a dull, old, droning sailor's song, with a droop and a quaver at the end of every verse, and seemingly no end to it at all but the patience of the singer. I had heard it on the voyage more than once and remembered these words:

> "But one man of her crew alive,
> What put to sea with seventy-five."

And I thought it was a ditty rather too dolefully appropriate for a company that had met such cruel losses in the morning. But, indeed, from what I saw, all these buccaneers were as callous as the sea they sailed on.

At last the breeze came; the schooner sidled and drew nearer in the dark; I felt the hawser slacken once more, and with a good, tough effort, cut the last fibres through.

The breeze had but little action on the coracle, and I was almost instantly swept against the bows of the *Hispaniola*. At the same time, the schooner began to turn upon her heel, spinning slowly, end for end, across the current.

I wrought like a fiend, for I expected every moment to be swamped; and since I found I could not push the coracle directly off, I now shoved straight astern. At length I was clear of my dangerous neighbour, and just as I gave the last impulsion, my hands came across a light cord that was trailing overboard across the stern bulwarks. Instantly I grasped it.

Why I should have done so I can hardly say. It was at first mere instinct, but once I had it in my hands and found it fast, curiosity began to get the upper hand, and I determined I should have one look through the cabin window.

I pulled in hand over hand on the cord, and when I judged myself near enough, rose at infinite risk to about half my height and thus commanded the roof and a slice of the interior of the cabin.

By this time the schooner and her little consort were gliding pretty swiftly through the water; indeed, we had already fetched up level with the camp-fire. The ship was talking, as sailors say, loudly, treading the innumerable ripples with an incessant weltering splash; and until I got my eye above the window-sill I could not comprehend why the watchmen had taken no alarm. One glance, however, was sufficient; and it was only one glance that I durst take from that unsteady skiff. It showed me Hands and his companion locked together in deadly wrestle, each with a hand upon the other's throat.

I dropped upon the thwart again, none too soon, for I was near overboard. I could see nothing for the moment but these two furious, encrimsoned faces swaying together under the smoky lamp, and I shut my eyes to let them grow once more familiar with the darkness.

The endless ballad had come to an end at last, and the whole diminished company about the camp-fire had broken into the chorus I had heard so often:

"Fifteen men on the dead man's chest—
Yo-ho-ho, and a bottle of rum!
Drink and the devil had done for the rest—
Yo-ho-ho, and a bottle of rum!"

I was just thinking how busy drink and the devil were at that very moment in the cabin of the *Hispaniola*, when I was surprised by a sudden lurch of the coracle. At the same moment, she yawed sharply and seemed to change her course. The speed in the meantime had strangely increased.

I opened my eyes at once. All round me were little ripples, combing over with a sharp, bristling sound and slightly phosphorescent. The *Hispaniola* herself, a few yards in whose wake I was still being whirled along, seemed to stagger in her course, and I saw her spars toss a little against the blackness of the night; nay, as I looked longer, I made sure she also was wheeling to the southward.

I glanced over my shoulder, and my heart jumped against my ribs. There, right behind me, was the glow of the camp-fire. The current had turned at right angles, sweeping round along with it the tall schooner and the little dancing coracle; ever quickening, ever bubbling higher, ever muttering louder, it went spinning through the narrows for the open sea.

Suddenly the schooner in front of me gave a violent yaw, turning, perhaps, through twenty degrees; and almost at the same moment one shout followed another from on board; I could hear feet pounding on the companion ladder and I knew that the two drunkards had at last been interrupted in their quarrel and awakened to a sense of their disaster.

I lay down flat in the bottom of that wretched skiff and devoutly recommended my spirit to its Maker. At the end of the straits, I made sure we must fall into some bar of raging breakers, where all my troubles would be ended speedily; and though I could, perhaps, bear to die, I could not bear to look upon my fate as it approached.

So I must have lain for hours, continually beaten to and fro upon the billows, now and again wetted with flying sprays, and never ceasing to expect death at the next plunge. Gradually weariness grew upon me; a numbness, an occasional stupor, fell upon my mind even in the midst of my terrors, until sleep at last supervened and in my sea-tossed coracle I lay and dreamed of home and the old "Admiral Benbow".

CHAPTER 24

The Cruise of the Coracle

IT was broad day when I awoke and found myself tossing at the south-west end of Treasure Island. The sun was up but was still hid from me behind the great bulk of the Spy-glass, which on this side descended almost to the sea in formidable cliffs.

Haulbowline Head and Mizzen-mast Hill were at my elbow, the hill bare and dark, the head bound with cliffs forty or fifty feet high and fringed with great masses of fallen rock. I was scarce a quarter of a mile to seaward, and it was my first thought to paddle in and land.

That notion was soon given over. Among the fallen rocks the breakers spouted and bellowed; loud reverberations, heavy sprays flying and falling, succeeded one another from second to second; and I saw myself, if I ventured nearer, dashed to death upon the rough shore or spending my strength in vain to scale the beetling crags.

Nor was that all, for crawling together on flat tables of rock or letting themselves drop into the sea with loud reports I beheld huge slimy monsters—soft snails, as it were, of incredible bigness—two or three score of them together, making the rocks to echo with their barkings.

I have understood since that they were sea lions, and entirely harmless. But the look of them, added to the difficulty of the shore and the high running of the surf, was more than enough to disgust me of that landing-place. I felt willing rather to starve at sea than to confront such perils.

In the meantime I had a better chance, as I supposed, before me. North of Haulbowline Head, the land runs in a long way, leaving at low tide a long stretch of yellow sand. To the north of that, again, there comes another cape—Cape of the Woods, as it was marked upon the chart—buried in tall green pines, which descended to the margin of the sea.

I remembered what Silver had said about the current that sets northward along the whole west coast of Treasure Island, and seeing from my position that I was already under its influence, I preferred to leave Haulbowline Head behind me and reserve my strength for an attempt to land upon the kindlier-looking Cape of the Woods.

There was a great, smooth swell upon the sea. The wind blowing steady and gentle from the south, there was no contrariety between that and the current, and the billows rose and fell unbroken.

Had it been otherwise, I must long ago have perished; but as it was, it is surprising how easily and securely my little and light boat could ride. Often, as I still lay at the bottom and kept no more than an eye above the gunwale, I would see a big blue summit heaving close above me; yet the coracle would but bounce a little, dance as if on springs, and subside on the other side into the trough as lightly as a bird.

I began after a little to grow very bold and sat up to try my skill at paddling. But even a small change in the disposition of the weight will produce violent changes in the behaviour of a coracle. And I had hardly moved before the boat, giving up at once her gentle dancing movement, ran straight down a slope of water so steep that it made me giddy, and struck her nose, with a spout of spray, deep into the side of the next wave.

I was drenched and terrified, and fell instantly back into my old position, whereupon the coracle seemed to find her head again and led me as softly as before among the billows.

It was plain she was not to be interfered with, and at that rate, since I could in no way influence her course, what hope had I left of reaching land?

I began to be horribly frightened, but I kept my head, for all that. First, moving with all care, I gradually baled out the coracle with my sea-cap; then, getting my eye once more above the gunwale, I set myself to study how it was she managed to slip so quietly through the rollers.

I found each wave, instead of the big, smooth glossy mountain it looks from shore or from a vessel's deck, was for all the world like any range of hills on dry land, full of peaks and smooth places and valleys. The coracle, left to herself, turning from side to side, threaded, so to speak, her way through these lower parts and avoided the steep slopes and higher, toppling summits of the wave.

"Well, now," thought I to myself, "it is plain I must lie where I am and not disturb the balance; but it is plain also that I can put the paddle over the side and from time to time, in smooth places, give her a shove or two towards land." No sooner thought upon than done. There I lay on my elbows in the most trying attitude, and every now and again gave a weak stroke or two to turn her head to shore.

It was very tiring and slow work, yet I did visibly gain ground; and as we drew near the Cape of the Woods, though I saw I must infallibly miss that point, I had still made some hundred yards of easting. I was, indeed, close in. I could see the cool green tree-tops swaying together in the breeze, and I felt sure I should make the next promontory without fail.

It was high time, for I now began to be tortured with thirst. The glow of the sun from above, its thousandfold reflection from the waves, the sea-water that fell and dried upon me, caking my very lips with salt, combined to make my throat burn and my brain ache. The sight of the trees so near at hand had almost made me sick with longing, but the current had soon carried me past the point, and as the next reach of sea opened out, I beheld a sight that changed the nature of my thoughts.

Right in front of me, not half a mile away, I beheld the *Hispaniola* under sail. I made sure, of course, that I should be taken; but I was so distressed for want of water that I scarce knew whether to be glad or sorry at the thought, and long before I had come to a conclusion, surprise had taken entire possession of my mind and I could do nothing but stare and wonder.

The *Hispaniola* was under her main-sail and two jibs, and the beautiful white canvas shone in the sun like snow or silver. When I first sighted her, all her sails were drawing; she was lying a course about north-west, and I presumed the men on board were going round the island on their way back to the anchorage. Presently she began to fetch more and more to the westward, so that I thought they had sighted me and were going about in chase. At last, however, she fell right into the wind's eye, was taken dead aback, and stood there awhile helpless, with her sails shivering.

"Clumsy fellows," said I; "they must still be drunk as owls." And I thought how Captain Smollett would have set them skipping.

Meanwhile the schooner gradually fell off and filled again upon another tack, sailed swiftly for a minute or so, and brought up once more dead in the wind's eye. Again and again was this repeated. To and fro, up and down, north, south, east, and west, the *Hispaniola* sailed by swoops and dashes, and at each repetition ended as she had begun, with idly flapping canvas. It became plain to me that nobody was steering. And if so, where were the men? Either they were dead drunk or had deserted her, I thought, and perhaps if I could get on board I might return the vessel to her captain.

The current was bearing coracle and schooner southward

at an equal rate. As for the latter's sailing, it was so wild and intermittent, and she hung each time so long in irons, that she certainly gained nothing, if she did not even lose. If only I dared to sit up and paddle, I made sure that I could overhaul her. The scheme had an air of adventure that inspired me, and the thought of the water breaker beside the fore companion doubled my growing courage.

Up I got, was welcomed almost instantly by another cloud of spray, but this time stuck to my purpose and set myself, with all my strength and caution, to paddle after the unsteered *Hispaniola*. Once I shipped a sea so heavy that I had to stop and bail, with my heart fluttering like a bird, but gradually I got into the way of the thing and guided my coracle among the waves, with only now and then a blow upon her bows and a dash of foam in my face.

I was now gaining rapidly on the schooner; I could see the brass glisten on the tiller as it banged about, and still no soul appeared upon her decks. I could not choose but suppose she was deserted. If not, the men were lying drunk below, where I might batten them down, perhaps, and do what I chose with the ship.

For some time she had been doing the worse thing possible for me—standing still. She headed nearly due south, yawing, of course, all the time. Each time she fell off, her sails partly filled, and these brought her in a moment right to the wind again. I have said this was the worst thing possible for me, for helpless as she looked in this situation, with the canvas cracking like cannon and the blocks trundling and banging on the deck, she still continued to run away from me, not only with the speed of the current, but by the whole amount of her leeway, which was naturally great.

But now, at last, I had my chance. The breeze fell for some seconds, very low, and the current gradually turning her, the *Hispaniola* revolved slowly round her centre and at last presented me her stern, with the cabin window still gaping open and the lamp over the table still burning on into the day. The main-sail hung drooped like a banner. She was stock-still but for the current.

For the last little while I had even lost, but now redoubling my efforts, I began once more to overhaul the chase.

I was not a hundred yards from her when the wind came again in a clap; she filled on the port tack and was off again, stooping and skimming like a swallow.

My first impulse was one of despair, but my second was towards joy. Round she came, till she was broadside on to me—round still till she had covered a half and then two thirds and then three quarters of the distance that separated us. I could see the waves boiling white under her forefoot. Immensely tall she looked to me from my low station in the coracle.

And then, of a sudden, I began to comprehend. I had scarce time to think—scarce time to act and save myself. I was on the summit of one swell when the schooner came stooping over the next. The bowsprit was over my head. I sprang to my feet and leaped, stamping the coracle under water. With one hand I caught the jib-boom, while my foot was lodged between the stay and the brace; and as I still clung there panting, a dull blow told me that the schooner had charged down upon and struck the coracle and that I was left without retreat on the *Hispaniola*.

CHAPTER 25

I Strike the Jolly Roger

I HAD scarce gained a position on the bowsprit when the flying jib flapped and filled upon the other tack, with a report like a gun. The schooner trembled to her keel under the reverse, but next moment, the other sails still drawing, the jib flapped back again and hung idle.

This had nearly tossed me off into the sea; and now I lost no time, crawled back along the bowsprit, and tumbled head foremost on the deck.

I was on the lee side of the forecastle, and the mainsail, which was still drawing, concealed from me a certain portion of the after-deck. Not a soul was to be seen. The planks, which had not been swabbed since the mutiny, bore the print of many feet, and an empty bottle, broken by the neck, tumbled to and fro like a live thing in the scuppers.

Suddenly the *Hispaniola* came right into the wind. The jibs behind me cracked aloud, the rudder slammed to, the whole ship gave a sickening heave and shudder, and at the same moment the main-boom swung inboard, the sheet groaning in the blocks, and showed me the lee after-deck.

There were the two watchmen, sure enough: red-cap on his back, as stiff as a handspike, with his arms stretched out like those of a crucifix and his teeth showing through his open lips; Israel Hands propped against the bulwarks, his chin on his chest, his hands lying open before him on the deck, his face as white, under its tan, as a tallow candle.

For a while the ship kept bucking and sidling like a vicious horse, the sails filling, now on one tack, now on another, and the boom swinging to and fro till the mast groaned aloud under the strain. Now and again too there would come a cloud of light sprays over the bulwark and a heavy blow of the ship's bows against the swell; so much heavier weather was made of it by this great rigged ship than by my home-made, lop-sided coracle, now gone to the bottom of the sea.

At every jump of the schooner, red-cap slipped to and fro, but—what was ghastly to behold—neither his attitude nor his fixed teeth-disclosing grin was anyway disturbed by this rough usage. At every jump too, Hands appeared still more to sink into himself and settle down upon the deck, his feet sliding ever the farther out, and the whole body canting towards the stern, so that his face became, little by little, hid from me; and at last I could see nothing beyond his ear and the frayed ringlet of one whisker.

At the same time, I observed, around both of them, splashes of dark blood upon the planks and began to feel sure that they had killed each other in their drunken wrath.

While I was thus looking and wondering, in a calm moment, when the ship was still, Israel Hands turned partly round and with a low moan writhed himself back to the position in which I had seen him first. The moan, which told of pain and deadly weakness, and the way in which his jaw hung open went right to my heart. But when I remembered the talk I had overheard from the apple barrel, all pity left me.

I walked aft until I reached the main-mast.

"Come aboard, Mr. Hands," I said ironically.

He rolled his eyes round heavily, but he was too far gone to express surprise. All he could do was to utter one word, "Brandy."

It occurred to me there was no time to lose, and dodging the boom as it once more lurched across the deck, I slipped aft and down the companion stairs into the cabin.

It was such a scene of confusion as you can hardly fancy. All the lockfast places had been broken open in quest of the chart. The floor was thick with mud where ruffians had sat down to drink or consult after wading in the marshes round their camp. The bulkheads, all painted in clear white and beaded round with gilt, bore a pattern of dirty hands. Dozens of empty bottles clinked together in corners to the rolling of the ship. One of the doctor's medical books lay open on the table, half of the leaves gutted out, I suppose, for pipelights. In the midst of all this the lamp still cast a smoky glow, obscure and brown as umber.

I went into the cellar; all the barrels were gone, and of the bottles a most surprising number had been drunk out and thrown away. Certainly, since the mutiny began, not a man of them could ever have been sober.

Foraging about, I found a bottle with some brandy left, for Hands; and for myself I routed out some biscuit, some pickled fruits, a great bunch of raisins, and a piece of cheese. With these I came on deck, put down my own stock behind the rudder head and well out of the coxswain's reach, went forward to the water-breaker, and had a good deep drink of water, and then, and not till then, gave Hands the brandy.

He must have drunk a gill before he took the bottle from his mouth.

"Aye," said he, "by thunder, but I wanted some o' that!"

I had sat down already in my own corner and begun to eat. "Much hurt?" I asked him.

He grunted, or rather, I might say, he barked.

"If that doctor was aboard," he said, "I'd be right enough in a couple of turns, but I don't have no manner of luck, you see, and that's what's the matter with me. As for that swab, he's good and dead, he is," he added, indicating the man with the red cap. "He warn't no seaman anyhow. And where mought you have come from?"

"Well," said I, "I've come aboard to take possession of this ship, Mr. Hands; and you'll please regard me as your captain until further notice."

He looked at me sourly enough but said nothing. Some of the colour had come back into his cheeks, though he still looked very sick and still continued to slip out and settle down as the ship banged about.

"By the by," I continued, "I can't have these colours, Mr. Hands; and by your leave, I'll strike 'em. Better none than these."

And again dodging the boom, I ran to the colour lines, handed down their cursed black flag, and chucked it overboard.

"God save the king!" said I, waving my cap. "And there's an end to Captain Silver!"

He watched me keenly and slyly, his chin all the while on his breast.

"I reckon," he said at last, "I reckon, Cap'n Hawkins, you'll kind of want to get ashore now. S'pose we talks."

"Why, yes," says I, "with all my heart, Mr. Hands. Say on." And I went back to my meal with a good appetite.

"This man," he began, nodding feebly at the corpse "—O'Brien were his name, a rank Irelander—this man and me got the canvas on her, meaning for to sail her back. Well, *he's* dead now, he is—as dead as bilge; and who's to sail this ship, I don't see. Without I gives you a hint, you ain't that man, as far's I can tell. Now, look here, you gives me food and drink and a old scarf or ankecher to tie my wound up, you do, and I'll tell you how to sail her, and that's about square all round, I take it."

"I'll tell you one thing," says I: "I'm not going back to Captain Kidd's anchorage. I mean to get into North Inlet and beach her quietly there."

"To be sure you did," he cried. "Why, I ain't sich an infernal lubber after all. I can see, can't I? I've tried my fling, I have, and

I've lost, and it's you has the wind of me. North Inlet? Why, I haven't no ch'ice, not I! I'd help you sail her up to Execution Dock, by thunder! So I would."

Well, as it seemed to me, there was some sense in this. We struck our bargain on the spot. In three minutes I had the *Hispaniola* sailing easily before the wind along the coast of Treasure Island, with good hopes of turning the northern point ere noon and beating down again as far as North Inlet before high water, when we might beach her safely and wait till the subsiding tide permitted us to land.

Then I lashed the tiller and went below to my own chest, where I got a soft silk handkerchief of my mother's. With this, and with my aid, Hands bound up the great bleeding stab he had received in the thigh, and after he had eaten a little and had a swallow or two more of the brandy, he began to pick up visibly, sat straighter up, spoke louder and clearer, and looked in every way another man.

The breeze served us admirably. We skimmed before it like a bird, the coast of the island flashing by and the view changing every minute. Soon we were past the high lands and bowling beside low, sandy country, sparsely dotted with dwarf pines, and soon we were beyond that again and had turned the corner of the rocky hill that ends the island on the north.

I was greatly elated with my new command, and pleased with the bright, sunshiny weather and these different prospects of the coast. I had now plenty of water and good things to eat, and my conscience, which had smitten me hard for my desertion, was quieted by the great conquest I had made. I should, I think, have had nothing left me to desire but for the eyes of the coxswain as they followed me derisively about the deck and the odd smile that appeared continually on his face. It was a smile that had in it something both of pain and weakness—a haggard old man's smile; but there was, besides that, a grain of derision, a shadow of treachery, in his expression as he craftily watched, and watched, and watched me at my work.

CHAPTER 26

Israel Hands

THE wind, serving us to a desire, now hauled into the west. We could run so much the easier from the north-east corner of the island to the mouth of the North Inlet. Only, as we had no power to anchor and dared not beach her till the tide had flowed a good deal farther, time hung on our hands. The coxswain told me how to lay the ship to; after a good many trials I succeeded, and we both sat in silence over another meal.

"Cap'n," said he at length with that same uncomfortable smile, "here's my old shipmate, O'Brien; s'pose you was to heave him overboard. I ain't partic'lar as a rule, and I don't take no blame for settling his hash, but I don't reckon him ornamental now, do you?"

"I'm not strong enough, and I don't like the job; and there he lies, for me," said I.

"This here's an unlucky ship, this *Hispaniola*, Jim," he went on, blinking. "There's a power of men been killed in this *Hispaniola*—a sight o' poor seamen dead and gone since you and me took ship to Bristol. I never seen sich dirty luck, not I. There was this here O'Brien now—he's dead, ain't he? Well now, I'm no scholar, and you're a lad as can read and figure, and to put it straight, do you take it as a dead man is dead for good, or do he come alive again?"

"You can kill the body, Mr. Hands, but not the spirit; you must know that already," I replied. "O'Brien there is in another world, and may be watching us."

"Ah!" says he. "Well, that's unfort'nate—appears as if killing parties was a waste of time. Howsomever, sperrits don't reckon for much, by what I've seen. I'll chance it with the sperrits, Jim. And now, you've spoke up free, and I'll take it kind if you'd step down into that there cabin and get me a—well, a—shiver my timbers! I can't hit the name on 't; well, you get me a bottle of wine, Jim—this here brandy's too strong for my head."

Now, the coxswain's hesitation seemed to be unnatural, and as for the notion of his preferring wine to brandy, I entirely disbelieved it. The whole story was a pretext. He wanted me to leave the deck—so much was plain; but with what purpose I could in no way imagine. His eyes never met mine; they kept wandering to and fro, up and down, now with a look to the sky, now with a flitting glance upon the dead O'Brien. All the time he kept smiling and putting his tongue out in the most guilty, embarrassed manner, so that a child could have told that he was bent on some deception. I was prompt with my answer, however, for I saw where my advantage lay and that with a fellow so densely stupid I could easily conceal my suspicions to the end.

"Some wine?" I said. "Far better. Will you have white or red?"

"Well, I reckon it's about the blessed same to me, shipmate," he replied; "so it's strong, and plenty of it, what's the odds?"

"All right," I answered. "I'll bring you port, Mr. Hands. But I'll have to dig for it."

With that I scuttled down the companion with all the noise I could, slipped off my shoes, ran quietly along the sparred gallery, mounted the forecastle ladder, and popped my head out of the fore companion. I knew he would not expect to see me there, yet I took every precaution possible, and certainly the worst of my suspicions proved too true.

He had risen from his position to his hands and knees, and though his leg obviously hurt him pretty sharply when he moved—for I could hear him stifle a groan—yet it was at a good, rattling rate that he trailed himself across the deck. In half a minute he had reached the port scuppers and picked, out of a coil of rope, a long knife, or rather a short dirk, discoloured to the hilt with blood. He looked upon it for a moment, thrusting forth his under jaw, tried the point upon his hand, and then, hastily concealing it in the bosom of his jacket, trundled back again into his old place against the bulwark.

This was all that I required to know. Israel could move about, he was now armed, and if he had been at so much trouble to get rid of me, it was plain that I was meant to be the victim. What he would do afterwards—whether he would try to crawl right across the island from North Inlet to the camp among the swamps or whether he would fire Long Tom, trusting that his own comrades might come first to help him— was, of course, more than I could say.

Yet I felt sure that I could trust him in one point, since in that our interests jumped together, and that was in the disposition of the schooner. We both desired to have her stranded safe enough, in a sheltered place, and so that, when the time came, she could be got off again with as little labour and danger as might be; and until that was done I considered that my life would certainly be spared.

While I was thus turning the business over in my mind, I had not been idle with my body. I had stolen back to the cabin, slipped once more into my shoes, and laid my hand at random on a bottle of wine, and now, with this for an excuse, I made my reappearance on the deck.

Hands lay as I had left him, all fallen together in a bundle and with his eyelids lowered as though he were too weak to bear the light. He looked up, however, at my coming, knocked the neck off the bottle like a man who had done the same thing often, and took a good swig, with his favourite toast of "Here's luck!" Then he lay quiet for a little, and then, pulling out a stick of tobacco, begged me to cut him a quid.

"Cut me a junk o' that," says he, "for I haven't no knife and hardly strength enough, so be as I had. Ah, Jim, Jim, I reckon I've missed stays! Cut me a quid, as'll likely be the last, lad, for I'm for my long home, and no mistake."

"Well," said I, "I'll cut you some tobacco, but if I was you and thought myself so badly, I would go to my prayers like a Christian man."

"Why?" said he. "Now, you tell me why."

"Why?" I cried. "You were asking me just now about the dead. You've broken your trust; you've lived in sin and lies and blood; there's a man you killed lying at your feet this moment, and you ask me why! For God's mercy, Mr. Hands, that's why."

I spoke with a little heat, thinking of the bloody dirk he had hidden in his pocket and designed, in his ill thoughts, to end me with. He, for his part, took a great draught of the wine and spoke with the most unusual solemnity.

"For thirty years," he said, "I've sailed the seas and seen good and bad, better and worse, fair weather and foul, provisions running out, knives going, and what not. Well, now I tell you, I never seen good come o' goodness yet. Him as strikes first is my fancy; dead men don't bite; them's my views—amen, so be it. And now, you look here," he added, suddenly changing his tone, "we've had about enough of this foolery. The tide's made good enough by now. You just take my orders, Cap'n Hawkins, and we'll sail slap in and be done with it."

All told, we had scarce two miles to run; but the navigation was delicate, the entrance to this northern anchorage was not only narrow and shoal, but lay east and west, so that the schooner must be nicely handled to be got in. I think I was a good, prompt subaltern, and I am very sure that Hands was an excellent pilot, for we went about and about and dodged in, shaving the banks, with a certainty and a neatness that were a pleasure to behold.

Scarcely had we passed the heads before the land closed around us. The shores of North Inlet were as thickly wooded as those of the southern anchorage, but the space was longer and narrower and more like, what in truth it was, the estuary of a river. Right before us, at the southern end, we saw the wreck of a ship in the last stages of dilapidation. It had been a great vessel of three masts but had lain so long exposed to the injuries of the weather that it was hung about with great webs of dripping seaweed, and on the deck of it shore bushes had taken root and now flourished thick with flowers. It was a sad sight, but it showed us that the anchorage was calm.

"Now," said Hands, "look there; there's a pet bit for to beach a ship in. Fine flat sand, never a cat's paw, trees all around of it, and flowers a-blowing like a garding on that old ship."

"And once beached," I inquired, "how shall we get her off again?"

"Why, so," he replied: "you take a line ashore there on the other side at low water, take a turn about one of them big pines; bring it back, take a turn around the capstan, and lie to for the tide. Come high water, all hands take a pull upon the line, and off she comes as sweet as natur'. And now, boy, you stand by. We're near the bit now, and she's too much way on her. Starboard a little—so—steady—starboard—larboard a little—steady—steady!"

So he issued his commands, which I breathlessly obeyed, till, all of a sudden, he cried, "Now, my hearty, luff!" And I put the helm hard up, and the *Hispaniola* swung round rapidly and ran stem on for the low, wooded shore.

The excitement of these last manoeuvres had somewhat interfered with the watch I had kept hitherto, sharply enough, upon the coxswain. Even then I was still so much interested, waiting for the ship to touch, that I had quite forgot the peril that hung over my head and stood craning over the starboard bulwarks and watching the ripples spreading wide before the bows. I might have fallen without a struggle for my life had not a sudden disquietude seized upon me and made me turn my head. Perhaps I had heard a creak or seen his shadow moving with the tail of my eye; perhaps it was an instinct like a cat's; but, sure enough, when I looked round, there was Hands, already half-way towards me, with the dirk in his right hand.

We must both have cried out aloud when our eyes met, but while mine was the shrill cry of terror, his was a roar of fury like a charging bully's. At the same instant, he threw himself forward and I leapt sideways towards the bows. As I did so, I let go of the tiller, which sprang sharp to leeward, and I think this saved my life, for it struck Hands across the chest and stopped him, for the moment, dead.

Before he could recover, I was safe out of the corner where he had me trapped, with all the deck to dodge about. Just forward of the main-mast I stopped, drew a pistol from my pocket, took a cool aim, though he had already turned and was once more coming directly after me, and drew the trigger. The hammer fell, but there followed neither flash nor sound; the priming was useless with sea-water. I cursed myself for my neglect. Why had not I, long before, reprimed and reloaded my only weapons? Then I should not have been as now, a mere fleeing sheep before this butcher.

Wounded as he was, it was wonderful how fast he could move, his grizzled hair tumbling over his face, and his face itself as red as a red ensign with his haste and fury. I had no time to try my other pistol, nor indeed much inclination, for I was sure it would be useless. One thing I saw plainly: I must not simply retreat before him, or he would speedily hold me boxed into the bows, as a moment since he had so nearly boxed me in the stern. Once so caught, and nine or ten inches of the blood-stained dirk would be my last experience on this side of eternity. I placed my palms against the main-mast, which was of a goodish bigness, and waited, every nerve upon the stretch.

Seeing that I meant to dodge, he also paused; and a moment or two passed in feints on his part and corresponding movements upon mine. It was such a game as I had often played at home about the rocks of Black Hill Cove, but never before, you may be sure, with such a wildly beating heart as now. Still, as I say, it was a boy's game, and I thought I could hold my own at it against an elderly seaman with a wounded thigh. Indeed my courage had begun to rise so high that I allowed myself a few darting thoughts on what would be the end of the affair, and while I saw certainly that I could spin it out for long, I saw no hope of any ultimate escape.

Well, while things stood thus, suddenly the *Hispaniola* struck, staggered, ground for an instant in the sand, and then, swift as a blow, canted over to the port side till the deck stood at an angle of forty-five degrees and about a puncheon of water splashed into the scupper holes and lay, in a pool, between the deck and bulwark.

We were both of us capsized in a second, and both of us rolled, almost together, into the scuppers, the dead red-cap, with his arms still spread out, tumbling stiffly after us. So near were we, indeed, that my head came against the coxswain's foot with a crack that made my teeth rattle. Blow and all, I was the first afoot again, for Hands had got involved with the dead body. The sudden canting of the ship had made the deck no place for running on; I had to find some new way of escape, and that upon the instant, for my foe was almost touching me. Quick as thought, I sprang into the mizzen shrouds, rattled up hand over hand, and did not draw a breath till I was seated on the cross-trees.

I had been saved by being prompt; the dirk had struck not half a foot below me as I pursued my upward flight; and there stood Israel Hands with his mouth open and his face upturned to mine, a perfect statue of surprise and disappointment.

Now that I had a moment to myself, I lost no time in

changing the priming of my pistol, and then, having one ready for service, and to make assurance doubly sure, I proceeded to draw the load of the other and recharge it afresh from the beginning.

My new employment struck Hands all of a heap; he began to see the dice going against him, and after an obvious hesitation, he also hauled himself heavily into the shrouds, and with the dirk in his teeth, began slowly and painfully to mount. It cost him no end of time and groans to haul his wounded leg behind him, and I had quietly finished my arrangements before he was much more than a third of the way up. Then, with a pistol in either hand, I addressed him.

"One more step, Mr. Hands," said I, "and I'll blow your brains out! Dead men don't bite, you know," I added with a chuckle.

He stopped instantly. I could see by the working of his face that he was trying to think, and the process was so slow and laborious that, in my new-found security, I laughed aloud. At last, with a swallow or two, he spoke, his face still wearing the same expression of extreme perplexity. In order to speak he had to take the dagger from his mouth, but in all else he remained unmoved.

"Jim," says he, "I reckon we're fouled, you and me, and we'll have to sign articles. I'd have had you but for that there lurch, but I don't have no luck, not I; and I reckon I'll have to strike, which comes hard, you see, for a master mariner to a ship's younker like you, Jim."

I was drinking in his words and smiling away, as conceited as a cock upon a wall, when, all in a breath, back went his right hand over his shoulder. Something sang like an arrow through the air; I felt a blow and then a sharp pang, and there I was pinned by the shoulder to the mast. In the horrid pain and surprise of the moment—I scarce can say it was by my own volition, and I am sure it was without a conscious aim—both my pistols went off, and both escaped out of my hands. They did not fall alone; with a choked cry, the coxswain loosed his grasp upon the shrouds and plunged head first into the water.

CHAPTER 27

"Pieces of Eight"

OWING to the cant of the vessel, the masts hung far out over the water, and from my perch on the cross-trees I had nothing below me but the surface of the bay. Hands, who was not so far up, was in consequence nearer to the ship and fell between me and the bulwarks. He rose once to the surface in a lather of foam and blood and then sank again for good. As the water settled, I could see him lying huddled together on the clean, bright sand in the shadow of the vessel's sides. A fish or two whipped past his body. Sometimes, by the quivering of the water, he appeared to move a little, as if he were trying to rise. But he was dead enough, for all that, being both shot and drowned, and was food for fish in the very place where he had designed my slaughter.

I was no sooner certain of this than I began to feel sick, faint, and terrified. The hot blood was running over my back and chest. The dirk, where it had pinned my shoulder to the mast, seemed to burn like a hot iron; yet it was not so much these real sufferings that distressed me, for these, it seemed to me, I could bear without a murmur; it was the horror I had upon my mind of falling from the cross-trees into that still green water, beside the body of the coxswain.

I clung with both hands till my nails ached, and I shut my eyes as if to cover up the peril. Gradually my mind came back again, my pulses quieted down to a more natural time, and I was once more in possession of myself.

It was my first thought to pluck forth the dirk, but either it stuck too hard or my nerve failed me, and I desisted with a violent shudder. Oddly enough, that very shudder did the business. The knife, in fact, had come the nearest in the world to missing me altogether; it held me by a mere pinch of skin, and this the shudder tore away. The blood ran down the faster, to be sure, but I was my own master again and only tacked to the mast by my coat and shirt.

These last I broke through with a sudden jerk, and then regained the deck by the starboard shrouds. For nothing in the world would I have again ventured, shaken as I was, upon the overhanging port shrouds from which Israel had so lately fallen.

I went below and did what I could for my wound; it pained me a good deal and still bled freely, but it was neither deep nor dangerous, nor did it greatly gall me when I used my arm. Then I looked around me, and as the ship was now, in a sense, my own, I began to think of clearing it from its last passenger—the dead man, O'Brien.

He had pitched, as I have said, against the bulwarks, where he lay like some horrible, ungainly sort of puppet, life-size, indeed, but how different from life's colour or life's comeliness! In that position I could easily have my way with him, and as the habit of tragical adventures had worn off almost all my terror for the dead, I took him by the waist as if he had been a sack of bran and with one good heave, tumbled him overboard. He went in with a sounding plunge; the red cap came off and remained floating on the surface; and as soon as the splash subsided, I could see him and Israel lying side by side, both wavering with the tremulous movement of the water. O'Brien, though still quite a young man, was very bald. There he lay, with that bald head across the knees of the man who had killed him and the quick fishes steering to and fro over both.

I was now alone upon the ship; the tide had just turned.

The sun was within so few degrees of setting that already the shadow of the pines upon the western shore began to reach right across the anchorage and fall in patterns on the deck. The evening breeze had sprung up, and though it was well warded off by the hill with the two peaks upon the east, the cordage had begun to sing a little softly to itself and the idle sails to rattle to and fro.

I began to see a danger to the ship. The jibs I speedily doused and brought tumbling to the deck, but the main-sail was a harder matter. Of course, when the schooner canted over, the boom had swung out-board, and the cap of it and a foot or two of sail hung even under water. I thought this made it still more dangerous; yet the strain was so heavy that I half feared to meddle. At last I got my knife and cut the halyards. The peak dropped instantly, a great belly of loose canvas floated broad upon the water, and since, pull as I liked, I could not budge the downhall, that was the extent of what I could accomplish. For the rest, the *Hispaniola* must trust to luck, like myself.

By this time the whole anchorage had fallen into shadow—the last rays, I remember, falling through a glade of the wood and shining bright as jewels on the flowery mantle of the wreck. It began to be chill; the tide was rapidly fleeting seaward, the schooner settling more and more on her beam-ends.

I scrambled forward and looked over. It seemed shallow enough, and holding the cut hawser in both hands for a last security, I let myself drop softly overboard. The water scarcely reached my waist; the sand was firm and covered with ripple marks, and I waded ashore in great spirits, leaving the *Hispaniola* on her side, with her main-sail trailing wide upon the surface of the bay. About the same time, the sun went fairly down and the breeze whistled low in the dusk among the tossing pines.

At least, and at last, I was off the sea, nor had I returned thence empty-handed. There lay the schooner, clear at last from buccaneers and ready for our own men to board and get to sea again. I had nothing nearer my fancy than to get home to the stockade and boast of my achievements. Possibly I might be blamed a bit for my truantry, but the recapture of the *Hispaniola* was a clenching answer, and I hoped that even Captain Smollett would confess I had not lost my time.

So thinking, and in famous spirits, I began to set my face homeward for the block house and my companions. I remembered that the most easterly of the rivers which drain into Captain Kidd's anchorage ran from the two-peaked hill upon my left, and I bent my course in that direction that I might pass the stream while it was small. The wood was pretty open, and keeping along the lower spurs, I had soon turned the corner of that hill, and not long after waded to the mid-calf across the watercourse.

This brought me near to where I had encountered Ben Gunn, the maroon; and I walked more circumspectly, keeping an eye on every side. The dusk had come nigh hand completely, and as I opened out the cleft between the two peaks, I became aware of a wavering glow against the sky, where, as I judged, the man of the island was cooking his supper before a roaring fire. And yet I wondered, in my heart, that he should show himself so careless. For if I could see this radiance, might it not reach the eyes of Silver himself where he camped upon the shore among the marshes?

Gradually the night fell blacker; it was all I could do to guide myself even roughly towards my destination; the double hill behind me and the Spy-glass on my right hand loomed faint and fainter; the stars were few and pale; and in the low ground where I wandered I kept tripping among bushes and rolling into sandy pits.

Suddenly a kind of brightness fell about me. I looked up; a pale glimmer of moonbeams had alighted on the summit of the Spy-glass, and soon after I saw something broad and silvery moving low down behind the trees, and knew the moon had risen.

With this to help me, I passed rapidly over what remained to me of my journey, and sometimes walking, sometimes running, impatiently drew near to the stockade. Yet, as I began to thread the grove that lies before it, I was not so thoughtless but that I slacked my pace and went a trifle warily. It would have been a poor end of my adventures to get shot down by my own party in mistake.

The moon was climbing higher and higher, its light began to fall here and there in masses through the more open districts of the wood, and right in front of me a glow of a different colour appeared among the trees. It was red and hot, and now and again it was a little darkened—as it were, the embers of a bonfire smouldering.

For the life of me I could not think what it might be.

At last I came right down upon the borders of the clearing. The western end was already steeped in moonshine; the rest, and the block house itself, still lay in a black shadow chequered with long silvery streaks of light. On the other side of the house an immense fire had burned itself into clear embers and shed a steady, red reverberation, contrasted strongly with the mellow paleness of the moon. There was not a soul stirring nor a sound beside the noises of the breeze.

I stopped, with much wonder in my heart, and perhaps a little terror also. It had not been our way to build great fires; we were, indeed, by the captain's orders, somewhat niggardly of firewood, and I began to fear that something had gone wrong while I was absent.

I stole round by the eastern end, keeping close in shadow, and at a convenient place, where the darkness was thickest, crossed the palisade.

To make assurance surer, I got upon my hands and knees and crawled, without a sound, towards the corner of the house.

As I drew nearer, my heart was suddenly and greatly lightened. It is not a pleasant noise in itself, and I have often complained of it at other times, but just then it was like music to hear my friends snoring together so loud and peaceful in their sleep. The sea-cry of the watch, that beautiful "All's well," never fell more reassuringly on my ear.

In the meantime, there was no doubt of one thing; they kept an infamous bad watch. If it had been Silver and his lads that were now creeping in on them, not a soul would have seen daybreak. That was what it was, thought I, to have the captain wounded; and again I blamed myself sharply for leaving them in that danger with so few to mount guard.

By this time I had got to the door and stood up. All was dark within, so that I could distinguish nothing by the eye. As for sounds, there was the steady drone of the snorers and a small occasional noise, a flickering or pecking that I could in no way account for.

With my arms before me I walked steadily in. I should lie down in my own place (I thought with a silent chuckle) and enjoy their faces when they found me in the morning.

My foot struck something yielding—it was a sleeper's leg; and he turned and groaned, but without awaking.

And then, all of a sudden, a shrill voice broke forth out of the darkness:

"Pieces of eight! Pieces of eight! Pieces of eight! Pieces of eight! Pieces of eight!" and so forth, without pause or change, like the clacking of a tiny mill.

Silver's green parrot, Captain Flint! It was she whom I had heard pecking at a piece of bark; it was she, keeping better watch than any human being, who thus announced my arrival with her wearisome refrain.

I had no time left me to recover. At the sharp, clipping tone of the parrot, the sleepers awoke and sprang up; and with a mighty oath, the voice of Silver cried, "Who goes?"

I turned to run, struck violently against one person, recoiled, and ran full into the arms of a second, who for his part closed upon and held me tight.

"Bring a torch, Dick," said Silver when my capture was thus assured.

And one of the men left the log-house and presently returned with a lighted brand.

PART SIX

·····•◦●◉●◦•·····

CAPTAIN
SILVER

CHAPTER 28

In the Enemy's Camp

THE red glare of the torch, lighting up the interior of the block house, showed me the worst of my apprehensions realized. The pirates were in possession of the house and stores: there was the cask of cognac, there were the pork and bread, as before, and what tenfold increased my horror, not a sign of any prisoner. I could only judge that all had perished, and my heart smote me sorely that I had not been there to perish with them.

There were six of the buccaneers, all told; not another man was left alive. Five of them were on their feet, flushed and swollen, suddenly called out of the first sleep of drunkenness. The sixth had only risen upon his elbow; he was deadly pale, and the blood-stained bandage round his head told that he had recently been wounded, and still more recently dressed. I remembered the man who had been shot and had run back among the woods in the great attack, and doubted not that this was he.

The parrot sat, preening her plumage, on Long John's shoulder. He himself, I thought, looked somewhat paler and more stern than I was used to. He still wore the fine broadcloth suit in which he had fulfilled his mission, but it was bitterly the worse for wear, daubed with clay and torn with the sharp briers of the wood.

"So," said he, "here's Jim Hawkins, shiver my timbers! Dropped in, like, eh? Well, come, I take that friendly."

And thereupon he sat down across the brandy cask and

began to fill a pipe.

"Give me a loan of the link, Dick," said he; and then, when he had a good light, "That'll do, lad," he added; "stick the glim in the wood heap; and you, gentlemen, bring yourselves to! You needn't stand up for Mr. Hawkins; HE'LL excuse you, you may lay to that. And so, Jim"—stopping the tobacco—"here you were, and quite a pleasant surprise for poor old John. I see you were smart when first I set my eyes on you, but this here gets away from me clean, it do."

To all this, as may be well supposed, I made no answer. They had set me with my back against the wall, and I stood there, looking Silver in the face, pluckily enough, I hope, to all outward appearance, but with black despair in my heart.

Silver took a whiff or two of his pipe with great composure and then ran on again.

"Now, you see, Jim, so be as you *are* here," says he, "I'll give you a piece of my mind. I've always liked you, I have, for a lad of spirit, and the picter of my own self when I was young and handsome. I always wanted you to jine and take your share, and die a gentleman, and now, my cock, you've got to. Cap'n Smollett's a fine seaman, as I'll own up to any day, but stiff on discipline. 'Dooty is dooty,' says he, and right he is. Just you keep clear of the cap'n. The doctor himself is gone dead again you—'ungrateful scamp' was what he said; and the short and the long of the whole story is about here: you can't go back to your own lot, for they won't have you; and without you start a third ship's company all by yourself, which might be lonely, you'll have to jine with Cap'n Silver."

So far so good. My friends, then, were still alive, and though I partly believed the truth of Silver's statement, that the cabin party were incensed at me for my desertion, I was more relieved than distressed by what I heard.

"I don't say nothing as to your being in our hands," continued Silver, "though there you are, and you may lay to it.

I'm all for argyment; I never seen good come out o' threatening. If you like the service, well, you'll jine; and if you don't, Jim, why, you're free to answer no—free and welcome, shipmate; and if fairer can be said by mortal seaman, shiver my sides!"

"Am I to answer, then?" I asked with a very tremulous voice. Through all this sneering talk, I was made to feel the threat of death that overhung me, and my cheeks burned and my heart beat painfully in my breast.

"Lad," said Silver, "no one's a-pressing of you. Take your bearings. None of us won't hurry you, mate; time goes so pleasant in your company, you see."

"Well," says I, growing a bit bolder, "if I'm to choose, I declare I have a right to know what's what, and why you're here, and where my friends are."

"Wot's wot?" repeated one of the buccaneers in a deep growl. "Ah, he'd be a lucky one as knowed that!"

"You'll perhaps batten down your hatches till you're spoke to, my friend," cried Silver truculently to this speaker. And then, in his first gracious tones, he replied to me, "Yesterday morning, Mr. Hawkins," said he, "in the dog-watch, down came Doctor Livesey with a flag of truce. Says he, 'Cap'n Silver, you're sold out. Ship's gone.' Well, maybe we'd been taking a glass, and a song to help it round. I won't say no. Leastways, none of us had looked out. We looked out, and by thunder, the old ship was gone! I never seen a pack o' fools look fishier; and you may lay to that, if I tells you that looked the fishiest. 'Well,' says the doctor, 'let's bargain.' We bargained, him and I, and here we are: stores, brandy, block house, the firewood you was thoughtful enough to cut, and in a manner of speaking, the whole blessed boat, from cross-trees to kelson. As for them, they've tramped; I don't know where's they are."

He drew again quietly at his pipe.

"And lest you should take it into that head of yours," he went on, "that you was included in the treaty, here's the last

word that was said: 'How many are you,' says I, 'to leave?' 'Four,'
says he; 'four, and one of us wounded. As for that boy, I don't
know where he is, confound him,' says he, 'nor I don't much
care. We're about sick of him.' These was his words.

"Is that all?" I asked.

"Well, it's all that you're to hear, my son," returned Silver.

"And now I am to choose?"

"And now you are to choose, and you may lay to that," said
Silver.

"Well," said I, "I am not such a fool but I know pretty well
what I have to look for. Let the worst come to the worst, it's
little I care. I've seen too many die since I fell in with you. But
there's a thing or two I have to tell you," I said, and by this time
I was quite excited; "and the first is this: here you are, in a bad
way—ship lost, treasure lost, men lost, your whole business
gone to wreck; and if you want to know who did it—it was I! I
was in the apple barrel the night we sighted land, and I heard
you, John, and you, Dick Johnson, and Hands, who is now at
the bottom of the sea, and told every word you said before the
hour was out. And as for the schooner, it was I who cut her
cable, and it was I that killed the men you had aboard of her,
and it was I who brought her where you'll never see her more,
not one of you. The laugh's on my side; I've had the top of this
business from the first; I no more fear you than I fear a fly. Kill
me, if you please, or spare me. But one thing I'll say, and no
more; if you spare me, bygones are bygones, and when you
fellows are in court for piracy, I'll save you all I can. It is for you
to choose. Kill another and do yourselves no good, or spare me
and keep a witness to save you from the gallows."

I stopped, for, I tell you, I was out of breath, and to my
wonder, not a man of them moved, but all sat staring at me like
as many sheep. And while they were still staring, I broke out
again, "And now, Mr. Silver," I said, "I believe you're the best
man here, and if things go to the worst, I'll take it kind of you

to let the doctor know the way I took it."

"I'll bear it in mind," said Silver with an accent so curious that I could not, for the life of me, decide whether he were laughing at my request or had been favourably affected by my courage.

"I'll put one to that," cried the old mahogany-faced seaman—Morgan by name—whom I had seen in Long John's public-house upon the quays of Bristol. "It was him that knowed Black Dog."

"Well, and see here," added the sea-cook. "I'll put another again to that, by thunder! For it was this same boy that faked the chart from Billy Bones. First and last, we've split upon Jim Hawkins!"

"Then here goes!" said Morgan with an oath.

And he sprang up, drawing his knife as if he had been twenty.

"Avast, there!" cried Silver. "Who are you, Tom Morgan? Maybe you thought you was cap'n here, perhaps. By the powers, but I'll teach you better! Cross me, and you'll go where many a good man's gone before you, first and last, these thirty year back—some to the yard-arm, shiver my timbers, and some by the board, and all to feed the fishes. There's never a man looked me between the eyes and seen a good day a'terwards, Tom Morgan, you may lay to that."

Morgan paused, but a hoarse murmur rose from the others.

"Tom's right," said one.

"I stood hazing long enough from one," added another. "I'll be hanged if I'll be hazed by you, John Silver."

"Did any of you gentlemen want to have it out with *me*?" roared Silver, bending far forward from his position on the keg, with his pipe still glowing in his right hand. "Put a name on what you're at; you ain't dumb, I reckon. Him that wants shall get it. Have I lived this many years, and a son of a rum puncheon cock his hat athwart my hawse at the latter end of it? You know the way; you're all gentlemen o' fortune, by your account. Well, I'm ready. Take a cutlass, him that dares, and I'll see the colour of his inside, crutch and all, before that pipe's empty."

Not a man stirred; not a man answered.

"That's your sort, is it?" he added, returning his pipe to his mouth. "Well, you're a gay lot to look at, anyway. Not much worth to fight, you ain't. P'r'aps you can understand King George's English. I'm cap'n here by 'lection. I'm cap'n here because I'm the best man by a long sea-mile. You won't fight, as gentlemen o' fortune should; then, by thunder, you'll obey, and you may lay to it! I like that boy, now; I never seen a better boy than that. He's more a man than any pair of rats of you in this here house, and what I say is this: let me see him that'll lay a hand on him—that's what I say, and you may lay to it."

There was a long pause after this. I stood straight up against the wall, my heart still going like a sledge-hammer, but with a ray of hope now shining in my bosom. Silver leant back against the wall, his arms crossed, his pipe in the corner of his mouth, as calm as though he had been in church; yet his eye kept wandering furtively, and he kept the tail of it on his unruly followers. They, on their part, drew gradually together towards the far end of the block house, and the low hiss of their whispering sounded in my ear continuously, like a stream. One after another, they would look up, and the red light of the torch would fall for a second on their nervous faces; but it was not towards me, it was towards Silver that they turned their eyes.

"You seem to have a lot to say," remarked Silver, spitting far into the air. "Pipe up and let me hear it, or lay to."

"Ax your pardon, sir," returned one of the men; "you're pretty free with some of the rules; maybe you'll kindly keep an eye upon the rest. This crew's dissatisfied; this crew don't vally bullying a marlin-spike; this crew has its rights like other crews, I'll make so free as that; and by your own rules, I take

it we can talk together. I ax your pardon, sir, acknowledging
you for to be captaing at this present; but I claim my right, and
steps outside for a council."

And with an elaborate sea-salute, this fellow, a long, ill-
looking, yellow-eyed man of five and thirty, stepped coolly
towards the door and disappeared out of the house. One after
another the rest followed his example, each making a salute
as he passed, each adding some apology. "According to rules,"
said one. "Forecastle council," said Morgan. And so with one
remark or another all marched out and left Silver and me alone
with the torch.

The sea-cook instantly removed his pipe.

"Now, look you here, Jim Hawkins," he said in a steady
whisper that was no more than audible, "you're within half
a plank of death, and what's a long sight worse, of torture.
They're going to throw me off. But, you mark, I stand by you
through thick and thin. I didn't mean to; no, not till you spoke
up. I was about desperate to lose that much blunt, and be
hanged into the bargain. But I see you was the right sort. I says
to myself, you stand by Hawkins, John, and Hawkins'll stand
by you. You're his last card, and by the living thunder, John,
he's yours! Back to back, says I. You save your witness, and he'll
save your neck!"

I began dimly to understand.

"You mean all's lost?" I asked.

"Aye, by gum, I do!" he answered. "Ship gone, neck gone—
that's the size of it. Once I looked into that bay, Jim Hawkins,
and seen no schooner—well, I'm tough, but I gave out. As for
that lot and their council, mark me, they're outright fools and
cowards. I'll save your life—if so be as I can—from them. But,
see here, Jim—tit for tat—you save Long John from swinging."

I was bewildered; it seemed a thing so hopeless he was
asking—he, the old buccaneer, the ringleader throughout.

"What I can do, that I'll do," I said.

"It's a bargain!" cried Long John. "You speak up plucky, and by thunder, I've a chance!"

He hobbled to the torch, where it stood propped among the firewood, and took a fresh light to his pipe.

"Understand me, Jim," he said, returning. "I've a head on my shoulders, I have. I'm on squire's side now. I know you've got that ship safe somewheres. How you done it, I don't know, but safe it is. I guess Hands and O'Brien turned soft. I never much believed in neither of *them*. Now you mark me. I ask no questions, nor I won't let others. I know when a game's up, I do; and I know a lad that's staunch. Ah, you that's young—you and me might have done a power of good together!"

He drew some cognac from the cask into a tin cannikin.

"Will you taste, messmate?" he asked; and when I had refused: "Well, I'll take a drain myself, Jim," said he. "I need a caulker, for there's trouble on hand. And talking o' trouble, why did that doctor give me the chart, Jim?"

My face expressed a wonder so unaffected that he saw the needlessness of further questions.

"Ah, well, he did, though," said he. "And there's something under that, no doubt—something, surely, under that, Jim—bad or good."

And he took another swallow of the brandy, shaking his great fair head like a man who looks forward to the worst.

CHAPTER 29

The Black Spot Again

THE council of buccaneers had lasted some time, when one of them re-entered the house, and with a repetition of the same salute, which had in my eyes an ironical air, begged for a moment's loan of the torch. Silver briefly agreed, and this emissary retired again, leaving us together in the dark.

"There's a breeze coming, Jim," said Silver, who had by this time adopted quite a friendly and familiar tone.

I turned to the loophole nearest me and looked out. The embers of the great fire had so far burned themselves out and now glowed so low and duskily that I understood why these conspirators desired a torch. About half-way down the slope to the stockade, they were collected in a group; one held the light, another was on his knees in their midst, and I saw the blade of an open knife shine in his hand with varying colours in the moon and torchlight. The rest were all somewhat stooping, as though watching the manoeuvres of this last. I could just make out that he had a book as well as a knife in his hand, and was still wondering how anything so incongruous had come in their possession when the kneeling figure rose once more to his feet and the whole party began to move together towards the house.

"Here they come," said I; and I returned to my former position, for it seemed beneath my dignity that they should find me watching them.

"Well, let 'em come, lad—let 'em come," said Silver cheerily.

"I've still a shot in my locker."

The door opened, and the five men, standing huddled together just inside, pushed one of their number forward. In any other circumstances it would have been comical to see his slow advance, hesitating as he set down each foot, but holding his closed right hand in front of him.

"Step up, lad," cried Silver. "I won't eat you. Hand it over, lubber. I know the rules, I do; I won't hurt a depytation."

Thus encouraged, the buccaneer stepped forth more briskly, and having passed something to Silver, from hand to hand, slipped yet more smartly back again to his companions.

The sea-cook looked at what had been given him.

"The black spot! I thought so," he observed. "Where might you have got the paper? Why, hillo! Look here, now; this ain't lucky! You've gone and cut this out of a Bible. What fool's cut a Bible?"

"Ah, there!" said Morgan. "There! Wot did I say? No good'll come o' that, I said."

"Well, you've about fixed it now, among you," continued Silver. "You'll all swing now, I reckon. What soft-headed lubber had a Bible?"

"It was Dick," said one.

"Dick, was it? Then Dick can get to prayers," said Silver. "He's seen his slice of luck, has Dick, and you may lay to that."

But here the long man with the yellow eyes struck in.

"Belay that talk, John Silver," he said. "This crew has tipped you the black spot in full council, as in dooty bound; just you turn it over, as in dooty bound, and see what's wrote there. Then you can talk."

"Thanky, George," replied the sea-cook. "You always was brisk for business, and has the rules by heart, George, as I'm pleased to see. Well, what is it, anyway? Ah! 'Deposed'—that's it, is it? Very pretty wrote, to be sure; like print, I swear. Your hand o' write, George? Why, you was gettin' quite a leadin' man in this here crew. You'll be cap'n next, I shouldn't wonder. Just oblige me with that torch again, will you? This pipe don't draw."

"Come, now," said George, "you don't fool this crew no more. You're a funny man, by your account; but you're over now, and you'll maybe step down off that barrel and help vote."

"I thought you said you knowed the rules," returned Silver contemptuously. "Leastways, if you don't, I do; and I wait here—and I'm still your cap'n, mind—till you outs with your grievances and I reply; in the meantime, your black spot ain't worth a biscuit. After that, we'll see."

"Oh," replied George, "you don't be under no kind of apprehension; we're all square, we are. First, you've made a hash of this cruise—you'll be a bold man to say no to that. Second, you let the enemy out o' this here trap for nothing. Why did they want out? I dunno, but it's pretty plain they wanted it. Third, you wouldn't let us go at them upon the march. Oh, we see through you, John Silver; you want to play booty, that's what's wrong with you. And then, fourth, there's this here boy."

"Is that all?" asked Silver quietly.

"Enough, too," retorted George. "We'll all swing and sundry for your bungling."

"Well now, look here, I'll answer these four p'ints; one after another I'll answer 'em. I made a hash o' this cruise, did I? Well now, you all know what I wanted, and you all know if that had been done that we'd 'a been aboard the *Hispaniola* this night as ever was, every man of us alive, and fit, and full of good plum-duff, and the treasure in the hold of her, by thunder! Well, who crossed me? Who forced my hand, as was the lawful cap'n? Who tipped me the black spot the day we landed and began this dance? Ah, it's a fine dance—I'm with you there— and looks mighty like a hornpipe in a rope's end at Execution Dock by London town, it does. But who done it? Why, it was Anderson, and Hands, and you, George Merry! And you're the last above board of that same meddling crew; and you have the

Davy Jones's insolence to up and stand for cap'n over me—you, that sank the lot of us! By the powers! But this tops the stiffest yarn to nothing."

Silver paused, and I could see by the faces of George and his late comrades that these words had not been said in vain.

"That's for number one," cried the accused, wiping the sweat from his brow, for he had been talking with a vehemence that shook the house. "Why, I give you my word, I'm sick to speak to you. You've neither sense nor memory, and I leave it to fancy where your mothers was that let you come to sea. Sea! Gentlemen o' fortune! I reckon tailors is your trade."

"Go on, John," said Morgan. "Speak up to the others."

"Ah, the others!" returned John. "They're a nice lot, ain't they? You say this cruise is bungled. Ah! By gum, if you could understand how bad it's bungled, you would see! We're that near the gibbet that my neck's stiff with thinking on it. You've seen 'em, maybe, hanged in chains, birds about 'em, seamen p'inting 'em out as they go down with the tide. 'Who's that?' says one. 'That! Why, that's John Silver. I knowed him well,' says another. And you can hear the chains a-jangle as you go about and reach for the other buoy. Now, that's about where we are, every mother's son of us, thanks to him, and Hands, and Anderson, and other ruination fools of you. And if you want to know about number four, and that boy, why, shiver my timbers, isn't he a hostage? Are we a-going to waste a hostage? No, not us; he might be our last chance, and I shouldn't wonder. Kill that boy? Not me, mates! And number three? Ah, well, there's a deal to say to number three. Maybe you don't count it nothing to have a real college doctor to see you every day—you, John, with your head broke—or you, George Merry, that had the ague shakes upon you not six hours agone, and has your eyes the colour of lemon peel to this same moment on the clock? And maybe, perhaps, you didn't know there was a consort coming either? But there is, and not so long till then; and we'll see who'll be glad to have a hostage when it comes to that. And as for number two, and why I made a bargain—well, you came crawling on your knees to me to make it—on your knees you came, you was that downhearted—and you'd have starved too if I hadn't—but that's a trifle! You look there—that's why!"

And he cast down upon the floor a paper that I instantly recognized—none other than the chart on yellow paper, with the three red crosses, that I had found in the oilcloth at the bottom of the captain's chest. Why the doctor had given it to him was more than I could fancy.

But if it were inexplicable to me, the appearance of the chart was incredible to the surviving mutineers. They leaped upon it like cats upon a mouse. It went from hand to hand, one tearing it from another; and by the oaths and the cries and the childish laughter with which they accompanied their examination, you would have thought, not only they were fingering the very gold, but were at sea with it, besides, in safety.

"Yes," said one, "that's Flint, sure enough. J. F., and a score below, with a clove hitch to it; so he done ever."

"Mighty pretty," said George. "But how are we to get away with it, and us no ship."

Silver suddenly sprang up, and supporting himself with a hand against the wall: "Now I give you warning, George," he cried. "One more word of your sauce, and I'll call you down and fight you. How? Why, how do I know? You had ought to tell me that—you and the rest, that lost me my schooner, with your interference, burn you! But not you, you can't; you hain't got the invention of a cockroach. But civil you can speak, and shall, George Merry, you may lay to that."

"That's fair enow," said the old man Morgan.

"Fair! I reckon so," said the sea-cook. "You lost the ship; I found the treasure. Who's the better man at that? And now I resign, by thunder! Elect whom you please to be your cap'n now; I'm done with it."

"Silver!" they cried. "Barbecue forever! Barbecue for cap'n!"

"So that's the toon, is it?" cried the cook. "George, I reckon you'll have to wait another turn, friend; and lucky for you as I'm not a revengeful man. But that was never my way. And now, shipmates, this black spot? 'Tain't much good now, is it? Dick's crossed his luck and spoiled his Bible, and that's about all."

"It'll do to kiss the book on still, won't it?" growled Dick, who was evidently uneasy at the curse he had brought upon himself.

"A Bible with a bit cut out!" returned Silver derisively. "Not it. It don't bind no more'n a ballad-book."

"Don't it, though?" cried Dick with a sort of joy. "Well, I reckon that's worth having too."

"Here, Jim—here's a cur'osity for you," said Silver, and he tossed me the paper.

It was around about the size of a crown piece. One side was blank, for it had been the last leaf; the other contained a verse or two of Revelation—these words among the rest, which struck sharply home upon my mind: "Without are dogs and murderers." The printed side had been blackened with wood ash, which already began to come off and soil my fingers; on the blank side had been written with the same material the one word "Depposed." I have that curiosity beside me at this moment, but not a trace of writing now remains beyond a single scratch, such as a man might make with his thumb-nail.

That was the end of the night's business. Soon after, with a drink all round, we lay down to sleep, and the outside of Silver's vengeance was to put George Merry up for sentinel and threaten him with death if he should prove unfaithful.

It was long ere I could close an eye, and heaven knows I had matter enough for thought in the man whom I had slain that afternoon, in my own most perilous position, and above all, in the remarkable game that I saw Silver now engaged upon—

keeping the mutineers together with one hand and grasping with the other after every means, possible and impossible, to make his peace and save his miserable life. He himself slept peacefully and snored aloud, yet my heart was sore for him, wicked as he was, to think on the dark perils that environed and the shameful gibbet that awaited him.

CHAPTER 30

On Parole

I WAS wakened—indeed, we were all wakened, for I could see even the sentinel shake himself together from where he had fallen against the door-post—by a clear, hearty voice hailing us from the margin of the wood:

"Block house, ahoy!" it cried. "Here's the doctor."

And the doctor it was. Although I was glad to hear the sound, yet my gladness was not without admixture. I remembered with confusion my insubordinate and stealthy conduct, and when I saw where it had brought me—among what companions and surrounded by what dangers—I felt ashamed to look him in the face.

He must have risen in the dark, for the day had hardly come; and when I ran to a loophole and looked out, I saw him standing, like Silver once before, up to the mid-leg in creeping vapour.

"You, doctor! Top o' the morning to you, sir!" cried Silver, broad awake and beaming with good nature in a moment. "Bright and early, to be sure; and it's the early bird, as the saying goes, that gets the rations. George, shake up your timbers, son, and help Dr. Livesey over the ship's side. All a-doin' well, your patients was—all well and merry."

So he pattered on, standing on the hilltop with his crutch under his elbow and one hand upon the side of the log-house—quite the old John in voice, manner, and expression.

"We've quite a surprise for you too, sir," he continued. "We've a little stranger here—he! he! A noo boarder and lodger, sir, and looking fit and taut as a fiddle; slep' like a supercargo, he did, right alongside of John—stem to stem we was, all night."

Dr. Livesey was by this time across the stockade and pretty near the cook, and I could hear the alteration in his voice as he said,

"Not Jim?"

"The very same Jim as ever was," says Silver.

The doctor stopped outright, although he did not speak, and it was some seconds before he seemed able to move on.

"Well, well," he said at last, "duty first and pleasure afterwards, as you might have said yourself, Silver. Let us overhaul these patients of yours."

A moment afterwards he had entered the block house and with one grim nod to me proceeded with his work among the sick. He seemed under no apprehension, though he must have known that his life, among these treacherous demons, depended on a hair; and he rattled on to his patients as if he were paying an ordinary professional visit in a quiet English family. His manner, I suppose, reacted on the men, for they behaved to him as if nothing had occurred, as if he were still ship's doctor and they still faithful hands before the mast.

"You're doing well, my friend," he said to the fellow with the bandaged head, "and if ever any person had a close shave, it was you; your head must be as hard as iron. Well, George, how goes it? You're a pretty colour, certainly; why, your liver, man, is upside down. Did you take that medicine? Did he take that medicine, men?"

"Aye, aye, sir, he took it, sure enough," returned Morgan.

"Because, you see, since I am mutineers' doctor, or prison doctor as I prefer to call it," says Doctor Livesey in his pleasantest way, "I make it a point of honour not to lose a man for King George (God bless him!) and the gallows."

The rogues looked at each other but swallowed the home-thrust in silence.

"Dick don't feel well, sir," said one.

"Don't he?" replied the doctor. "Well, step up here, Dick, and let me see your tongue. No, I should be surprised if he did! The man's tongue is fit to frighten the French. Another fever."

"Ah, there," said Morgan, "that comed of sp'iling Bibles."

"That comes—as you call it—of being arrant asses," retorted the doctor, "and not having sense enough to know honest air from poison, and the dry land from a vile, pestiferous slough. I think it most probable—though of course it's only an opinion—that you'll all have the deuce to pay before you get that malaria out of your systems. Camp in a bog, would you? Silver, I'm surprised at you. You're less of a fool than many, take you all round; but you don't appear to me to have the rudiments of a notion of the rules of health.

"Well," he added after he had dosed them round and they had taken his prescriptions, with really laughable humility, more like charity schoolchildren than blood-guilty mutineers and pirates—"well, that's done for today. And now I should wish to have a talk with that boy, please."

And he nodded his head in my direction carelessly.

George Merry was at the door, spitting and spluttering over some bad-tasted medicine; but at the first word of the doctor's proposal he swung round with a deep flush and cried "No!" and swore.

Silver struck the barrel with his open hand.

"Si-lence!" he roared and looked about him positively like a lion. "Doctor," he went on in his usual tones, "I was a-thinking of that, knowing as how you had a fancy for the boy. We're all humbly grateful for your kindness, and as you see, puts faith in you and takes the drugs down like that much grog. And I take it I've found a way as'll suit all. Hawkins, will you give me your word of honour as a young gentleman—for a young gentleman you are, although poor born—your word of honour not to slip your cable?"

I readily gave the pledge required.

"Then, doctor," said Silver, "you just step outside o' that stockade, and once you're there I'll bring the boy down on the inside, and I reckon you can yarn through the spars. Good day to you, sir, and all our dooties to the squire and Cap'n Smollett."

The explosion of disapproval, which nothing but Silver's black looks had restrained, broke out immediately the doctor had left the house. Silver was roundly accused of playing double—of trying to make a separate peace for himself, of sacrificing the interests of his accomplices and victims, and, in one word, of the identical, exact thing that he was doing. It seemed to me so obvious, in this case, that I could not imagine how he was to turn their anger. But he was twice the man the rest were, and his last night's victory had given him a huge preponderance on their minds. He called them all the fools and dolts you can imagine, said it was necessary I should talk to the doctor, fluttered the chart in their faces, asked them if they could afford to break the treaty the very day they were bound a-treasure-hunting.

"No, by thunder!" he cried. "It's us must break the treaty when the time comes; and till then I'll gammon that doctor, if I have to ile his boots with brandy."

And then he bade them get the fire lit, and stalked out upon his crutch, with his hand on my shoulder, leaving them in a disarray, and silenced by his volubility rather than convinced.

"Slow, lad, slow," he said. "They might round upon us in a twinkle of an eye if we was seen to hurry."

Very deliberately, then, did we advance across the sand to where the doctor awaited us on the other side of the stockade, and as soon as we were within easy speaking distance Silver stopped.

"You'll make a note of this here also, doctor," says he, "and the boy'll tell you how I saved his life, and were deposed for it too, and you may lay to that. Doctor, when a man's steering as near the wind as me—playing chuck-farthing with the last breath in his body, like—you wouldn't think it too much, mayhap, to give him one good word? You'll please bear in mind it's not my life only now—it's that boy's into the bargain; and you'll speak me fair, doctor, and give me a bit o' hope to go on, for the sake of mercy."

Silver was a changed man once he was out there and had his back to his friends and the block house; his cheeks seemed to have fallen in, his voice trembled; never was a soul more dead in earnest.

"Why, John, you're not afraid?" asked Dr. Livesey.

"Doctor, I'm no coward; no, not I—not SO much!" and he snapped his fingers. "If I was I wouldn't say it. But I'll own up fairly, I've the shakes upon me for the gallows. You're a good man and a true; I never seen a better man! And you'll not forget what I done good, not any more than you'll forget the bad, I know. And I step aside—see here—and leave you and Jim alone. And you'll put that down for me too, for it's a long stretch, is that!"

So saying, he stepped back a little way, till he was out of earshot, and there sat down upon a tree-stump and began to whistle, spinning round now and again upon his seat so as to command a sight, sometimes of me and the doctor and sometimes of his unruly ruffians as they went to and fro in the sand between the fire—which they were busy rekindling—and the house, from which they brought forth pork and bread to make the breakfast.

"So, Jim," said the doctor sadly, "here you are. As you have brewed, so shall you drink, my boy. Heaven knows, I cannot find it in my heart to blame you, but this much I will say, be it kind or unkind: when Captain Smollett was well, you dared not have gone off; and when he was ill and couldn't help it, by George, it was downright cowardly!"

I will own that I here began to weep. "Doctor," I said, "you might spare me. I have blamed myself enough; my life's forfeit anyway, and I should have been dead by now if Silver hadn't stood for me; and doctor, believe this, I can die—and I dare say I deserve it—but what I fear is torture. If they come to torture me—"

"Jim," the doctor interrupted, and his voice was quite changed, "Jim, I can't have this. Whip over, and we'll run for it."

"Doctor," said I, "I passed my word."

"I know, I know," he cried. "We can't help that, Jim, now. I'll take it on my shoulders, holus bolus, blame and shame, my boy; but stay here, I cannot let you. Jump! One jump, and you're out, and we'll run for it like antelopes."

"No," I replied; "you know right well you wouldn't do the thing yourself—neither you nor squire nor captain; and no more will I. Silver trusted me; I passed my word, and back I go. But, doctor, you did not let me finish. If they come to torture me, I might let slip a word of where the ship is, for I got the ship, part by luck and part by risking, and she lies in North Inlet, on the southern beach, and just below high water. At half tide she must be high and dry."

"The ship!" exclaimed the doctor.

Rapidly I described to him my adventures, and he heard me out in silence.

"There is a kind of fate in this," he observed when I had done. "Every step, it's you that saves our lives; and do you suppose by any chance that we are going to let you lose yours? That would be a poor return, my boy. You found out the plot; you found Ben Gunn—the best deed that ever you did, or will do, though you live to ninety. Oh, by Jupiter, and talking of Ben Gunn! Why, this is the mischief in person. Silver!" he cried. "Silver! I'll give you a piece of advice," he continued as the cook drew near again; "don't you be in any great hurry after that treasure."

"Why, sir, I do my possible, which that ain't," said Silver. "I can only, asking your pardon, save my life and the boy's by seeking for that treasure; and you may lay to that."

"Well, Silver," replied the doctor, "if that is so, I'll go one step further: look out for squalls when you find it."

"Sir," said Silver, "as between man and man, that's too much and too little. What you're after, why you left the block house, why you given me that there chart, I don't know, now, do I? And yet I done your bidding with my eyes shut and never a word of hope! But no, this here's too much. If you won't tell me what you mean plain out, just say so and I'll leave the helm."

"No," said the doctor musingly; "I've no right to say more; it's not my secret, you see, Silver, or, I give you my word, I'd tell it you. But I'll go as far with you as I dare go, and a step beyond, for I'll have my wig sorted by the captain or I'm mistaken! And first, I'll give you a bit of hope; Silver, if we both get alive out of this wolf-trap, I'll do my best to save you, short of perjury."

Silver's face was radiant. "You couldn't say more, I'm sure, sir, not if you was my mother," he cried.

"Well, that's my first concession," added the doctor. "My second is a piece of advice: keep the boy close beside you, and when you need help, halloo. I'm off to seek it for you, and that itself will show you if I speak at random. Good-bye, Jim."

And Dr. Livesey shook hands with me through the stockade, nodded to Silver, and set off at a brisk pace into the wood.

CHAPTER 31

The Treasure-hunt—Flint's Pointer

"JIM," said Silver when we were alone, "if I saved your life, you saved mine; and I'll not forget it. I seen the doctor waving you to run for it—with the tail of my eye, I did; and I seen you say no, as plain as hearing. Jim, that's one to you. This is the first glint of hope I had since the attack failed, and I owe it you. And now, Jim, we're to go in for this here treasure-hunting, with sealed orders too, and I don't like it; and you and me must stick close, back to back like, and we'll save our necks in spite o' fate and fortune."

Just then a man hailed us from the fire that breakfast was ready, and we were soon seated here and there about the sand over biscuit and fried junk. They had lit a fire fit to roast an ox, and it was now grown so hot that they could only approach it from the windward, and even there not without precaution. In the same wasteful spirit, they had cooked, I suppose, three times more than we could eat; and one of them, with an empty laugh, threw what was left into the fire, which blazed and roared again over this unusual fuel. I never in my life saw men so careless of the morrow; hand to mouth is the only word that can describe their way of doing; and what with wasted food and sleeping sentries, though they were bold enough for a brush and be done with it, I could see their entire unfitness for anything like a prolonged campaign.

Even Silver, eating away, with Captain Flint upon his shoulder, had not a word of blame for their recklessness. And this the more surprised me, for I thought he had never shown himself so cunning as he did then.

"Aye, mates," said he, "it's lucky you have Barbecue to think for you with this here head. I got what I wanted, I did. Sure enough, they have the ship. Where they have it, I don't know yet; but once we hit the treasure, we'll have to jump about and find out. And then, mates, us that has the boats, I reckon, has the upper hand."

Thus he kept running on, with his mouth full of the hot bacon; thus he restored their hope and confidence, and, I more than suspect, repaired his own at the same time.

"As for hostage," he continued, "that's his last talk, I guess, with them he loves so dear. I've got my piece o' news, and thanky to him for that; but it's over and done. I'll take him in a line when we go treasure-hunting, for we'll keep him like so much gold, in case of accidents, you mark, and in the meantime. Once we got the ship and treasure both and off to sea like jolly companions, why then we'll talk Mr. Hawkins over, we will, and we'll give him his share, to be sure, for all his kindness."

It was no wonder the men were in a good humour now. For my part, I was horribly cast down. Should the scheme he had now sketched prove feasible, Silver, already doubly a traitor, would not hesitate to adopt it. He had still a foot in either camp, and there was no doubt he would prefer wealth and freedom with the pirates to a bare escape from hanging, which was the best he had to hope on our side.

Nay, and even if things so fell out that he was forced to keep his faith with Dr. Livesey, even then what danger lay before us! What a moment that would be when the suspicions of his followers turned to certainty and he and I should have to fight for dear life—he a cripple and I a boy—against five strong and active seamen!

Add to this double apprehension the mystery that still

hung over the behaviour of my friends, their unexplained desertion of the stockade, their inexplicable cession of the chart, or harder still to understand, the doctor's last warning to Silver, "Look out for squalls when you find it," and you will readily believe how little taste I found in my breakfast and with how uneasy a heart I set forth behind my captors on the quest for treasure.

We made a curious figure, had anyone been there to see us—all in soiled sailor clothes and all but me armed to the teeth. Silver had two guns slung about him—one before and one behind—besides the great cutlass at his waist and a pistol in each pocket of his square-tailed coat. To complete his strange appearance, Captain Flint sat perched upon his shoulder and gabbling odds and ends of purposeless sea-talk. I had a line about my waist and followed obediently after the sea-cook, who held the loose end of the rope, now in his free hand, now between his powerful teeth. For all the world, I was led like a dancing bear.

The other men were variously burthened, some carrying picks and shovels—for that had been the very first necessary they brought ashore from the *Hispaniola*—others laden with pork, bread, and brandy for the midday meal. All the stores, I observed, came from our stock, and I could see the truth of Silver's words the night before. Had he not struck a bargain with the doctor, he and his mutineers, deserted by the ship, must have been driven to subsist on clear water and the proceeds of their hunting. Water would have been little to their taste; a sailor is not usually a good shot; and besides all that, when they were so short of eatables, it was not likely they would be very flush of powder.

Well, thus equipped, we all set out—even the fellow with the broken head, who should certainly have kept in shadow— and straggled, one after another, to the beach, where the two gigs awaited us. Even these bore trace of the drunken folly of the pirates, one in a broken thwart, and both in their muddy and unbailed condition. Both were to be carried along with us for the sake of safety; and so, with our numbers divided between them, we set forth upon the bosom of the anchorage.

As we pulled over, there was some discussion on the chart. The red cross was, of course, far too large to be a guide; and the terms of the note on the back, as you will hear, admitted of some ambiguity. They ran, the reader may remember, thus:

'Tall tree, Spy-glass shoulder, bearing a point to the N. of N.N.E.
'Skeleton Island E.S.E. and by E.
'Ten feet.'

A tall tree was thus the principal mark. Now, right before us the anchorage was bounded by a plateau from two to three hundred feet high, adjoining on the north the sloping southern shoulder of the Spy-glass and rising again towards the south into the rough, cliffy eminence called the Mizzen-mast Hill. The top of the plateau was dotted thickly with pine-trees of varying height. Every here and there, one of a different species rose forty or fifty feet clear above its neighbours, and which of these was the particular "tall tree" of Captain Flint could only be decided on the spot, and by the readings of the compass.

Yet, although that was the case, every man on board the boats had picked a favourite of his own ere we were half-way over, Long John alone shrugging his shoulders and bidding them wait till they were there.

We pulled easily, by Silver's directions, not to weary the hands prematurely, and after quite a long passage, landed at the mouth of the second river—that which runs down a woody cleft of the Spy-glass. Thence, bending to our left, we began to ascend the slope towards the plateau.

At the first outset, heavy, miry ground and a matted, marish vegetation greatly delayed our progress; but by little and little the hill began to steepen and become stony under foot, and the wood to change its character and to grow in a more open order. It was, indeed, a most pleasant portion of the island that we were now approaching. A heavy-scented broom and many flowering shrubs had almost taken the place of grass. Thickets of green nutmeg-trees were dotted here and there with the red columns and the broad shadow of the pines; and the first mingled their spice with the aroma of the others. The air, besides, was fresh and stirring, and this, under the sheer sunbeams, was a wonderful refreshment to our senses.

The party spread itself abroad, in a fan shape, shouting and leaping to and fro. About the centre, and a good way behind the rest, Silver and I followed—I tethered by my rope, he ploughing, with deep pants, among the sliding gravel. From time to time, indeed, I had to lend him a hand, or he must have missed his footing and fallen backward down the hill.

We had thus proceeded for about half a mile and were approaching the brow of the plateau when the man upon the farthest left began to cry aloud, as if in terror. Shout after shout came from him, and the others began to run in his direction.

"He can't 'a found the treasure," said old Morgan, hurrying past us from the right, "for that's clean a-top."

Indeed, as we found when we also reached the spot, it was something very different. At the foot of a pretty big pine and involved in a green creeper, which had even partly lifted some of the smaller bones, a human skeleton lay, with a few shreds of clothing, on the ground. I believe a chill struck for a moment to every heart.

"He was a seaman," said George Merry, who, bolder than the rest, had gone up close and was examining the rags of clothing. "Leastways, this is good sea-cloth."

"Aye, aye," said Silver; "like enough; you wouldn't look to find a bishop here, I reckon. But what sort of a way is that for bones to lie? 'Tain't in natur.'"

Indeed, on a second glance, it seemed impossible to fancy that the body was in a natural position. But for some disarray (the work, perhaps, of the birds that had fed upon him or of the slow-growing creeper that had gradually enveloped his remains) the man lay perfectly straight—his feet pointing in one direction, his hands, raised above his head like a diver's, pointing directly in the opposite.

"I've taken a notion into my old numbskull," observed Silver. "Here's the compass; there's the tip-top p'int o' Skeleton Island, stickin' out like a tooth. Just take a bearing, will you, along the line of them bones."

It was done. The body pointed straight in the direction of the island, and the compass read duly E.S.E. and by E.

"I thought so," cried the cook; "this here is a p'inter. Right up there is our line for the Pole Star and the jolly dollars. But, by thunder! If it don't make me cold inside to think of Flint. This is one of *his* jokes, and no mistake. Him and these six was alone here; he killed 'em, every man; and this one he hauled here and laid down by compass, shiver my timbers! They're long bones, and the hair's been yellow. Aye, that would be Allardyce. You mind Allardyce, Tom Morgan?"

"Aye, aye," returned Morgan; "I mind him; he owed me money, he did, and took my knife ashore with him."

"Speaking of knives," said another, "why don't we find his'n lying round? Flint warn't the man to pick a seaman's pocket; and the birds, I guess, would leave it be."

"By the powers, and that's true!" cried Silver.

"There ain't a thing left here," said Merry, still feeling round among the bones; "not a copper doit nor a baccy box. It don't look nat'ral to me."

"No, by gum, it don't," agreed Silver; "not nat'ral, nor not nice, says you. Great guns! Messmates, but if Flint was living, this would be a hot spot for you and me. Six they were, and six are we; and bones is what they are now."

"I saw him dead with these here deadlights," said Morgan. "Billy took me in. There he laid, with penny-pieces on his eyes."

"Dead—aye, sure enough he's dead and gone below," said the fellow with the bandage; "but if ever sperrit walked, it would be Flint's. Dear heart, but he died bad, did Flint!"

"Aye, that he did," observed another; "now he raged, and now he hollered for the rum, and now he sang. 'Fifteen Men' were his only song, mates; and I tell you true, I never rightly liked to hear it since. It was main hot, and the windy was open, and I hear that old song comin' out as clear as clear—and the death-haul on the man already."

"Come, come," said Silver; "stow this talk. He's dead, and he don't walk, that I know; leastways, he won't walk by day, and you may lay to that. Care killed a cat. Fetch ahead for the doubloons."

We started, certainly; but in spite of the hot sun and the staring daylight, the pirates no longer ran separate and shouting through the wood, but kept side by side and spoke with bated breath. The terror of the dead buccaneer had fallen on their spirits.

CHAPTER 32

The Treasure-hunt—The Voice Among the Trees

PARTLY from the damping influence of this alarm, partly to rest Silver and the sick folk, the whole party sat down as soon as they had gained the brow of the ascent.

The plateau being somewhat tilted towards the west, this spot on which we had paused commanded a wide prospect on either hand. Before us, over the tree-tops, we beheld the Cape of the Woods fringed with surf; behind, we not only looked down upon the anchorage and Skeleton Island, but saw—clear across the spit and the eastern lowlands—a great field of open sea upon the east. Sheer above us rose the Spyglass, here dotted with single pines, there black with precipices. There was no sound but that of the distant breakers, mounting from all round, and the chirp of countless insects in the brush. Not a man, not a sail, upon the sea; the very largeness of the view increased the sense of solitude.

Silver, as he sat, took certain bearings with his compass.

"There are three 'tall trees'" said he, "about in the right line from Skeleton Island. 'Spy-glass shoulder,' I take it, means that lower p'int there. It's child's play to find the stuff now. I've half a mind to dine first."

"I don't feel sharp," growled Morgan. "Thinkin' o' Flint—I think it were—as done me."

"Ah, well, my son, you praise your stars he's dead," said Silver.

"He were an ugly devil," cried a third pirate with a shudder; "that blue in the face too!"

"That was how the rum took him," added Merry. "Blue! Well, I reckon he was blue. That's a true word."

Ever since they had found the skeleton and got upon this train of thought, they had spoken lower and lower, and they had almost got to whispering by now, so that the sound of their talk hardly interrupted the silence of the wood. All of a sudden, out of the middle of the trees in front of us, a thin, high, trembling voice struck up the well-known air and words:

"Fifteen men on the dead man's chest—
Yo-ho-ho, and a bottle of rum!"

I never have seen men more dreadfully affected than the pirates. The colour went from their six faces like enchantment; some leaped to their feet, some clawed hold of others; Morgan grovelled on the ground.

"It's Flint, by—!" cried Merry.

The song had stopped as suddenly as it began—broken off, you would have said, in the middle of a note, as though someone had laid his hand upon the singer's mouth. Coming through the clear, sunny atmosphere among the green tree-tops, I thought it had sounded airily and sweetly; and the effect on my companions was the stranger.

"Come," said Silver, struggling with his ashen lips to get the word out; "this won't do. Stand by to go about. This is a rum start, and I can't name the voice, but it's someone skylarking—someone that's flesh and blood, and you may lay to that."

His courage had come back as he spoke, and some of the colour to his face along with it. Already the others had begun to lend an ear to this encouragement and were coming a little to themselves, when the same voice broke out again—not this time singing, but in a faint distant hail that echoed yet fainter among the clefts of the Spy-glass.

"Darby M'Graw," it wailed—for that is the word that best

describes the sound—"Darby M'Graw! Darby M'Graw!" again and again and again; and then rising a little higher, and with an oath that I leave out: "Fetch aft the rum, Darby!"

The buccaneers remained rooted to the ground, their eyes starting from their heads. Long after the voice had died away they still stared in silence, dreadfully, before them.

"That fixes it!" gasped one. "Let's go."

"They was his last words," moaned Morgan, "his last words above board."

Dick had his Bible out and was praying volubly. He had been well brought up, had Dick, before he came to sea and fell among bad companions.

Still Silver was unconquered. I could hear his teeth rattle in his head, but he had not yet surrendered.

"Nobody in this here island ever heard of Darby," he muttered; "not one but us that's here." And then, making a great effort: "Shipmates," he cried, "I'm here to get that stuff, and I'll not be beat by man or devil. I never was feared of Flint in his life, and, by the powers, I'll face him dead. There's seven hundred thousand pound not a quarter of a mile from here. When did ever a gentleman o' fortune show his stern to that much dollars for a boozy old seaman with a blue mug—and him dead too?"

But there was no sign of reawakening courage in his followers, rather, indeed, of growing terror at the irreverence of his words.

"Belay there, John!" said Merry. "Don't you cross a sperrit."

And the rest were all too terrified to reply. They would have run away severally had they dared; but fear kept them together, and kept them close by John, as if his daring helped them. He, on his part, had pretty well fought his weakness down.

"Sperrit? Well, maybe," he said. "But there's one thing not clear to me. There was an echo. Now, no man ever seen a sperrit with a shadow; well then, what's he doing with an echo to him,

I should like to know? That ain't in natur', surely?"

This argument seemed weak enough to me. But you can never tell what will affect the superstitious, and to my wonder, George Merry was greatly relieved.

"Well, that's so," he said. "You've a head upon your shoulders, John, and no mistake. 'Bout ship, mates! This here crew is on a wrong tack, I do believe. And come to think on it, it was like Flint's voice, I grant you, but not just so clear-away like it, after all. It was liker somebody else's voice now—it was liker—"

"By the powers, Ben Gunn!" roared Silver.

"Aye, and so it were," cried Morgan, springing on his knees. "Ben Gunn it were!"

"It don't make much odds, do it, now?" asked Dick. "Ben Gunn's not here in the body any more'n Flint."

But the older hands greeted this remark with scorn.

"Why, nobody minds Ben Gunn," cried Merry; "dead or alive, nobody minds him."

It was extraordinary how their spirits had returned and how the natural colour had revived in their faces. Soon they were chatting together, with intervals of listening; and not long after, hearing no further sound, they shouldered the tools and set forth again, Merry walking first with Silver's compass to keep them on the right line with Skeleton Island. He had said the truth: dead or alive, nobody minded Ben Gunn.

Dick alone still held his Bible, and looked around him as he went, with fearful glances; but he found no sympathy, and Silver even joked him on his precautions.

"I told you," said he—"I told you you had sp'iled your Bible. If it ain't no good to swear by, what do you suppose a sperrit would give for it? Not that!" and he snapped his big fingers, halting a moment on his crutch.

But Dick was not to be comforted; indeed, it was soon plain to me that the lad was falling sick; hastened by heat, exhaustion, and the shock of his alarm, the fever, predicted by Dr. Livesey, was evidently growing swiftly higher.

It was fine open walking here, upon the summit; our way lay a little downhill, for, as I have said, the plateau tilted towards the west. The pines, great and small, grew wide apart; and even between the clumps of nutmeg and azalea, wide open spaces baked in the hot sunshine. Striking, as we did, pretty near north-west across the island, we drew, on the one hand, ever nearer under the shoulders of the Spy-glass, and on the other, looked ever wider over that western bay where I had once tossed and trembled in the oracle.

The first of the tall trees was reached, and by the bearings proved the wrong one. So with the second. The third rose nearly two hundred feet into the air above a clump of underwood—a giant of a vegetable, with a red column as big as a cottage, and a wide shadow around in which a company could have manoeuvred. It was conspicuous far to sea both on the east and west and might have been entered as a sailing mark upon the chart.

But it was not its size that now impressed my companions; it was the knowledge that seven hundred thousand pounds in gold lay somewhere buried below its spreading shadow. The thought of the money, as they drew nearer, swallowed up their previous terrors. Their eyes burned in their heads; their feet grew speedier and lighter; their whole soul was found up in that fortune, that whole lifetime of extravagance and pleasure, that lay waiting there for each of them.

Silver hobbled, grunting, on his crutch; his nostrils stood out and quivered; he cursed like a madman when the flies settled on his hot and shiny countenance; he plucked furiously at the line that held me to him and from time to time turned his eyes upon me with a deadly look. Certainly he took no pains to hide his thoughts, and certainly I read them like print. In the immediate nearness of the gold, all else had been forgotten: his promise and the doctor's warning were both things of the past, and I could not doubt that he hoped to seize upon the treasure, find and board the *Hispaniola* under cover of night, cut every honest throat about that island, and sail away as he had at first intended, laden with crimes and riches.

Shaken as I was with these alarms, it was hard for me to keep up with the rapid pace of the treasure-hunters. Now and again I stumbled, and it was then that Silver plucked so roughly at the rope and launched at me his murderous glances. Dick, who had dropped behind us and now brought up the rear, was babbling to himself both prayers and curses as his fever kept rising. This also added to my wretchedness, and to crown all, I was haunted by the thought of the tragedy that had once been acted on that plateau, when that ungodly buccaneer with the blue face—he who died at Savannah, singing and shouting for drink—had there, with his own hand, cut down his six accomplices. This grove that was now so peaceful must then have rung with cries, I thought; and even with the thought I could believe I heard it ringing still.

We were now at the margin of the thicket.

"Huzza, mates, all together!" shouted Merry; and the foremost broke into a run.

And suddenly, not ten yards further, we beheld them stop. A low cry arose. Silver doubled his pace, digging away with the foot of his crutch like one possessed; and next moment he and I had come also to a dead halt.

Before us was a great excavation, not very recent, for the sides had fallen in and grass had sprouted on the bottom. In this were the shaft of a pick broken in two and the boards of several packing-cases strewn around. On one of these boards I saw, branded with a hot iron, the name *Walrus*—the name of Flint's ship.

All was clear to probation. The *Cache* had been found and rifled; the seven hundred thousand pounds were gone!

CHAPTER 33

The Fall of a Chieftain

THERE never was such an overturn in this world. Each of these six men was as though he had been struck. But with Silver the blow passed almost instantly. Every thought of his soul had been set full-stretch, like a racer, on that money; well, he was brought up, in a single second, dead; and he kept his head, found his temper, and changed his plan before the others had had time to realize the disappointment.

"Jim," he whispered, "take that, and stand by for trouble."

And he passed me a double-barrelled pistol.

At the same time, he began quietly moving northward, and in a few steps had put the hollow between us two and the other five. Then he looked at me and nodded, as much as to say, "Here is a narrow corner," as, indeed, I thought it was. His looks were not quite friendly, and I was so revolted at these constant changes that I could not forbear whispering, "So you've changed sides again."

There was no time left for him to answer in. The buccaneers, with oaths and cries, began to leap, one after another, into the pit and to dig with their fingers, throwing the boards aside as they did so. Morgan found a piece of gold. He held it up with a perfect spout of oaths. It was a two-guinea piece, and it went from hand to hand among them for a quarter of a minute.

"Two guineas!" roared Merry, shaking it at Silver. "That's your seven hundred thousand pounds, is it? You're the man for bargains, ain't you? You're him that never bungled nothing, you wooden-headed lubber!"

"Dig away, boys," said Silver with the coolest insolence; "you'll find some pig-nuts and I shouldn't wonder."

"Pig-nuts!" repeated Merry, in a scream. "Mates, do you hear that? I tell you now, that man there knew it all along. Look in the face of him and you'll see it wrote there."

"Ah, Merry," remarked Silver, "standing for cap'n again? You're a pushing lad, to be sure."

But this time everyone was entirely in Merry's favour. They began to scramble out of the excavation, darting furious glances behind them. One thing I observed, which looked well for us: they all got out upon the opposite side from Silver.

Well, there we stood, two on one side, five on the other, the pit between us, and nobody screwed up high enough to offer the first blow. Silver never moved; he watched them, very upright on his crutch, and looked as cool as ever I saw him. He was brave, and no mistake.

At last Merry seemed to think a speech might help matters.

"Mates," says he, "there's two of them alone there; one's the old cripple that brought us all here and blundered us down to this; the other's that cub that I mean to have the heart of. Now, mates—"

He was raising his arm and his voice, and plainly meant to lead a charge. But just then—crack! crack! crack!—three musket-shots flashed out of the thicket. Merry tumbled head foremost into the excavation; the man with the bandage spun round like a teetotum and fell all his length upon his side, where he lay dead, but still twitching; and the other three turned and ran for it with all their might.

Before you could wink, Long John had fired two barrels of a pistol into the struggling Merry, and as the man rolled up his eyes at him in the last agony, "George," said he, "I reckon I settled you."

At the same moment, the doctor, Gray, and Ben Gunn

joined us, with smoking muskets, from among the nutmeg-trees.

"Forward!" cried the doctor. "Double quick, my lads. We must head 'em off the boats."

And we set off at a great pace, sometimes plunging through the bushes to the chest.

I tell you, but Silver was anxious to keep up with us. The work that man went through, leaping on his crutch till the muscles of his chest were fit to burst, was work no sound man ever equalled; and so thinks the doctor. As it was, he was already thirty yards behind us and on the verge of strangling when we reached the brow of the slope.

"Doctor," he hailed, "see there! No hurry!"

Sure enough there was no hurry. In a more open part of the plateau, we could see the three survivors still running in the same direction as they had started, right for Mizzenmast Hill. We were already between them and the boats; and so we four sat down to breathe, while Long John, mopping his face, came slowly up with us.

"Thank ye kindly, doctor," says he. "You came in in about the nick, I guess, for me and Hawkins. And so it's you, Ben Gunn!" he added. "Well, you're a nice one, to be sure."

"I'm Ben Gunn, I am," replied the maroon, wriggling like an eel in his embarrassment. "And," he added, after a long pause, "how do, Mr. Silver? Pretty well, I thank ye, says you."

"Ben, Ben," murmured Silver, "to think as you've done me!"

The doctor sent back Gray for one of the pick-axes deserted, in their flight, by the mutineers, and then as we proceeded leisurely downhill to where the boats were lying, related in a few words what had taken place. It was a story that profoundly interested Silver; and Ben Gunn, the half-idiot maroon, was the hero from beginning to end.

Ben, in his long, lonely wanderings about the island, had found the skeleton—it was he that had rifled it; he had found the treasure; he had dug it up (it was the haft of his pick-axe that lay broken in the excavation); he had carried it on his back, in many weary journeys, from the foot of the tall pine to a cave he had on the two-pointed hill at the north-east angle of the island, and there it had lain stored in safety since two months before the arrival of the *Hispaniola*.

When the doctor had wormed this secret from him on the afternoon of the attack, and when next morning he saw the anchorage deserted, he had gone to Silver, given him the chart, which was now useless—given him the stores, for Ben Gunn's cave was well supplied with goats' meat salted by himself—given anything and everything to get a chance of moving in safety from the stockade to the two-pointed hill, there to be clear of malaria and keep a guard upon the money.

"As for you, Jim," he said, "it went against my heart, but I did what I thought best for those who had stood by their duty; and if you were not one of these, whose fault was it?"

That morning, finding that I was to be involved in the horrid disappointment he had prepared for the mutineers, he had run all the way to the cave, and leaving the squire to guard the captain, had taken Gray and the maroon and started, making the diagonal across the island to be at hand beside the pine. Soon, however, he saw that our party had the start of him; and Ben Gunn, being fleet of foot, had been dispatched in front to do his best alone. Then it had occurred to him to work upon the superstitions of his former shipmates, and he was so far successful that Gray and the doctor had come up and were already ambushed before the arrival of the treasure-hunters.

"Ah," said Silver, "it were fortunate for me that I had Hawkins here. You would have let old John be cut to bits, and never given it a thought, doctor."

"Not a thought," replied Dr. Livesey cheerily.

And by this time we had reached the gigs. The doctor, with the pick-axe, demolished one of them, and then we all got aboard the other and set out to go round by sea for North Inlet.

This was a run of eight or nine miles. Silver, though he was almost killed already with fatigue, was set to an oar, like the rest of us, and we were soon skimming swiftly over a smooth sea. Soon we passed out of the straits and doubled the southeast corner of the island, round which, four days ago, we had towed the *Hispaniola*.

As we passed the two-pointed hill, we could see the black mouth of Ben Gunn's cave and a figure standing by it, leaning on a musket. It was the squire, and we waved a handkerchief and gave him three cheers, in which the voice of Silver joined as heartily as any.

Three miles farther, just inside the mouth of North Inlet, what should we meet but the *Hispaniola*, cruising by herself? The last flood had lifted her, and had there been much wind or a strong tide current, as in the southern anchorage, we should never have found her more, or found her stranded beyond help. As it was, there was little amiss beyond the wreck of the main-sail. Another anchor was got ready and dropped in a fathom and a half of water. We all pulled round again to Rum Cove, the nearest point for Ben Gunn's treasure-house; and then Gray, single-handed, returned with the gig to the *Hispaniola*, where he was to pass the night on guard.

A gentle slope ran up from the beach to the entrance of the cave. At the top, the squire met us. To me he was cordial and kind, saying nothing of my escapade either in the way of blame or praise. At Silver's polite salute he somewhat flushed.

"John Silver," he said, "you're a prodigious villain and imposter—a monstrous imposter, sir. I am told I am not to prosecute you. Well, then, I will not. But the dead men, sir, hang about your neck like mill-stones."

"Thank you kindly, sir," replied Long John, again saluting.

"I dare you to thank me!" cried the squire. "It is a gross dereliction of my duty. Stand back."

And thereupon we all entered the cave. It was a large, airy place, with a little spring and a pool of clear water, overhung with ferns. The floor was sand. Before a big fire lay Captain Smollett; and in a far corner, only duskily flickered over by the blaze, I beheld great heaps of coin and quadrilaterals built of bars of gold. That was Flint's treasure that we had come so far to seek and that had cost already the lives of seventeen men from the *Hispaniola*. How many it had cost in the amassing, what blood and sorrow, what good ships scuttled on the deep, what brave men walking the plank blindfold, what shot of cannon, what shame and lies and cruelty, perhaps no man alive could tell. Yet there were still three upon that island—Silver, and old Morgan, and Ben Gunn—who had each taken his share in these crimes, as each had hoped in vain to share in the reward.

"Come in, Jim," said the captain. "You're a good boy in your line, Jim, but I don't think you and me'll go to sea again. You're too much of the born favourite for me. Is that you, John Silver? What brings you here, man?"

"Come back to my dooty, sir," returned Silver.

"Ah!" said the captain, and that was all he said.

What a supper I had of it that night, with all my friends around me; and what a meal it was, with Ben Gunn's salted goat and some delicacies and a bottle of old wine from the *Hispaniola*. Never, I am sure, were people gayer or happier. And there was Silver, sitting back almost out of the firelight, but eating heartily, prompt to spring forward when anything was wanted, even joining quietly in our laughter—the same bland, polite, obsequious seaman of the voyage out.

CHAPTER 34

And Last

THE next morning we fell early to work, for the transportation of this great mass of gold near a mile by land to the beach, and thence three miles by boat to the *Hispaniola*, was a considerable task for so small a number of workmen. The three fellows still abroad upon the island did not greatly trouble us; a single sentry on the shoulder of the hill was sufficient to ensure us against any sudden onslaught, and we thought, besides, they had had more than enough of fighting.

Therefore the work was pushed on briskly. Gray and Ben Gunn came and went with the boat, while the rest during their absences piled treasure on the beach. Two of the bars, slung in a rope's end, made a good load for a grown man—one that he was glad to walk slowly with. For my part, as I was not much use at carrying, I was kept busy all day in the cave packing the minted money into bread-bags.

It was a strange collection, like Billy Bones's hoard for the diversity of coinage, but so much larger and so much more varied that I think I never had more pleasure than in sorting them. English, French, Spanish, Portuguese, Georges, and Louises, doubloons and double guineas and moidores and sequins, the pictures of all the kings of Europe for the last hundred years, strange Oriental pieces stamped with what looked like wisps of string or bits of spider's web, round pieces and square pieces, and pieces bored through the middle, as if to wear them round your neck—nearly every variety of money in the world must, I think, have found a place in that collection; and for number, I am sure they were like autumn leaves, so that my back ached with stooping and my fingers with sorting them out.

Day after day this work went on; by every evening a fortune had been stowed aboard, but there was another fortune waiting for the morrow; and all this time we heard nothing of the three surviving mutineers.

At last—I think it was on the third night—the doctor and I were strolling on the shoulder of the hill where it overlooks the lowlands of the isle, when, from out the thick darkness below, the wind brought us a noise between shrieking and singing. It was only a snatch that reached our ears, followed by the former silence.

"Heaven forgive them," said the doctor; "'tis the mutineers!"

"All drunk, sir," struck in the voice of Silver from behind us.

Silver, I should say, was allowed his entire liberty, and in spite of daily rebuffs, seemed to regard himself once more as quite a privileged and friendly dependent. Indeed, it was remarkable how well he bore these slights and with what unwearying politeness he kept on trying to ingratiate himself with all. Yet, I think, none treated him better than a dog, unless it was Ben Gunn, who was still terribly afraid of his old quartermaster, or myself, who had really something to thank him for; although for that matter, I suppose, I had reason to think even worse of him than anybody else, for I had seen him meditating a fresh treachery upon the plateau. Accordingly, it was pretty gruffly that the doctor answered him.

"Drunk or raving," said he.

"Right you were, sir," replied Silver; "and precious little odds which, to you and me."

"I suppose you would hardly ask me to call you a humane man," returned the doctor with a sneer, "and so my feelings may surprise you, Master Silver. But if I were sure they were raving—as I am morally certain one, at least, of them is down with fever—I should leave this camp, and at whatever risk to my own carcass, take them the assistance of my skill."

"Ask your pardon, sir, you would be very wrong," quoth Silver. "You would lose your precious life, and you may lay to that. I'm on your side now, hand and glove; and I shouldn't wish for to see the party weakened, let alone yourself, seeing as I know what I owes you. But these men down there, they couldn't keep their word—no, not supposing they wished to; and what's more, they couldn't believe as you could."

"No," said the doctor. "You're the man to keep your word, we know that."

Well, that was about the last news we had of the three pirates. Only once we heard a gunshot a great way off and supposed them to be hunting. A council was held, and it was decided that we must desert them on the island—to the huge glee, I must say, of Ben Gunn, and with the strong approval of Gray. We left a good stock of powder and shot, the bulk of the salt goat, a few medicines, and some other necessaries, tools, clothing, a spare sail, a fathom or two of rope, and by the particular desire of the doctor, a handsome present of tobacco.

That was about our last doing on the island. Before that, we had got the treasure stowed and had shipped enough water and the remainder of the goat meat in case of any distress; and at last, one fine morning, we weighed anchor, which was about all that we could manage, and stood out of North Inlet, the same colours flying that the captain had flown and fought under at the palisade.

The three fellows must have been watching us closer than we thought for, as we soon had proved. For coming through the narrows, we had to lie very near the southern point, and there we saw all three of them kneeling together on a spit of sand, with their arms raised in supplication. It went to all our hearts, I think, to leave them in that wretched state; but we could not risk another mutiny; and to take them home for the gibbet would have been a cruel sort of kindness. The doctor hailed them and told them of the stores we had left, and where they were to find them. But they continued to call us by name and appeal to us, for God's sake, to be merciful and not leave them to die in such a place.

At last, seeing the ship still bore on her course and was now swiftly drawing out of earshot, one of them—I know not which it was—leapt to his feet with a hoarse cry, whipped his musket to his shoulder, and sent a shot whistling over Silver's head and through the main-sail.

After that, we kept under cover of the bulwarks, and when next I looked out they had disappeared from the spit, and the spit itself had almost melted out of sight in the growing distance. That was, at least, the end of that; and before noon, to my inexpressible joy, the highest rock of Treasure Island had sunk into the blue round of sea.

We were so short of men that everyone on board had to bear a hand—only the captain lying on a mattress in the stern and giving his orders, for though greatly recovered he was still in want of quiet. We laid her head for the nearest port in Spanish America, for we could not risk the voyage home without fresh hands; and as it was, what with baffling winds and a couple of fresh gales, we were all worn out before we reached it.

It was just at sundown when we cast anchor in a most beautiful land-locked gulf, and were immediately surrounded by shore boats full of Negroes and Mexican Indians and half-bloods selling fruits and vegetables and offering to dive for bits of money. The sight of so many good-humoured faces (especially the blacks), the taste of the tropical fruits, and above all the lights that began to shine in the town made a most charming contrast to our dark and bloody sojourn on the island; and the doctor and the squire, taking me along with them, went ashore to pass the early part of the night. Here they met the captain of an English man-of-war, fell in talk with him, went on board his ship, and, in short, had so agreeable a time that day was breaking when we came alongside the *Hispaniola*.

Ben Gunn was on deck alone, and as soon as we came on board he began, with wonderful contortions, to make us a confession. Silver was gone. The maroon had connived at his escape in a shore boat some hours ago, and he now assured us he had only done so to preserve our lives, which would certainly have been forfeit if "that man with the one leg had stayed aboard." But this was not all. The sea-cook had not gone empty-handed. He had cut through a bulkhead unobserved and had removed one of the sacks of coin, worth perhaps three or four hundred guineas, to help him on his further wanderings.

I think we were all pleased to be so cheaply quit of him.

Well, to make a long story short, we got a few hands on board, made a good cruise home, and the Hispaniola reached Bristol just as Mr. Blandly was beginning to think of fitting out her consort. Five men only of those who had sailed returned with her. "Drink and the devil had done for the rest," with a vengeance, although, to be sure, we were not quite in so bad a case as that other ship they sang about:

> With one man of her crew alive,
> What put to sea with seventy-five.

All of us had an ample share of the treasure and used it wisely or foolishly, according to our natures. Captain Smollett is now retired from the sea. Gray not only saved his money, but being suddenly smit with the desire to rise, also studied his profession, and he is now mate and part owner of a fine full-rigged ship, married besides, and the father of a family. As for Ben Gunn, he got a thousand pounds, which he spent or lost in three weeks, or to be more exact, in nineteen days, for he was back begging on the twentieth. Then he was given a lodge to keep, exactly as he had feared upon the island; and he still lives, a great favourite, though something of a butt, with the country boys, and a notable singer in church on Sundays and saints' days.

Of Silver we have heard no more. That formidable seafaring man with one leg has at last gone clean out of my life; but I dare say he met his old Negress, and perhaps still lives in comfort with her and Captain Flint. It is to be hoped so, I suppose, for his chances of comfort in another world are very small.

The bar silver and the arms still lie, for all that I know, where Flint buried them; and certainly they shall lie there for me. Oxen and wain-ropes would not bring me back again to that accursed island; and the worst dreams that ever I have are when I hear the surf booming about its coasts or start upright in bed with the sharp voice of Captain Flint still ringing in my ears: "Pieces of eight! Pieces of eight!"